LE CARRÉ JOHN LE CARRÉ JOHN LE CARRÉ JOHN

10/79
oc

John le Carré

The Spy Who Came in from the Cold

Call for the Dead

A Murder of Quality

The Looking-Glass War

A Small Town in Germany

John le Carré

Heinemann/Octopus

The Spy Who Came in from the Cold was first published in Great Britain by
Victor Gollancz Ltd in 1963; in the United States by Coward, McCann Inc in 1964.
Call for the Dead was first published in Great Britain by
Victor Gollancz Ltd in 1961; in the United States by Walker and Company in 1962.
A Murder of Quality was first published in Great Britain by
Victor Gollancz Ltd in 1962; in the United States by Walker and Company in 1963.
The Looking-Glass War was first published in Great Britain by
William Heinemann Ltd in 1965; in the United States by Coward, McCann Inc in 1965.
A Small Town in Germany was first published in Great Britain by
William Heinemann Ltd in 1968; in the United States by Coward, McCann Inc in 1968.

This edition first published in the United States of America
in 1979 jointly by

William Heinemann Inc
450 Park Avenue, New York, NY 10022

and

Octopus Books Inc
The Olympic Towers, 645 Fifth Avenue,
New York, NY 10022

This edition first published in Great Britain
in 1979 jointly by

William Heinemann Ltd
10 Upper Grosvenor Street,
London W1X 9PA

Martin Secker & Warburg Ltd
54 Poland Street,
London W1V 3DF

and

Octopus Books Ltd
59 Grosvenor Street,
London W1X 9DA

ISBN 0 905712 31 5

The Spy Who Came in from the Cold © 1963 Victor Gollancz Ltd
Call for the Dead © 1961 Victor Gollancz Ltd
A Murder of Quality © 1962 Victor Gollancz Ltd
The Looking-Glass War © 1965 D J M Cornwell
A Small Town in Germany © 1968 le Carré Productions Ltd

Printed in the United States of America
by R. R. Donnelley and Sons Company.

Contents

John le Carré

The Spy
Who Came in
from the Cold

John le Carré

Chapter One

Checkpoint

The American handed Leamas another cup of coffee and said, 'Why don't you go back and sleep? We can ring you if he shows up.'

Leamas said nothing, just stared through the window of the checkpoint, along the empty street.

'You can't wait for ever, sir. Maybe he'll come some other time. We can have the polizei contact the Agency: you can be back here in twenty minutes.'

'No,' said Leamas, 'it's nearly dark now.'

'But you can't wait for ever; he's nine hours over schedule.'

'If you want to go, go. You've been very good,' Leamas added. 'I'll tell Kramer you've been damn' good.'

'But how long will you wait?'

'Until he comes.' Leamas walked to the observation window and stood between the two motionless policemen. Their binoculars were trained on the Eastern checkpoint.

'He's waiting for the dark,' Leamas muttered. 'I know he is.'

'This morning you said he'd come across with the workmen.'

Leamas turned on him.

'Agents aren't aeroplanes. They don't have schedules. He's blown, he's on the run, he's frightened. Mundt's after him, now, at this moment. He's only got one chance. Let him choose his time.'

The younger man hesitated, wanting to go and not finding the moment.

A bell rang inside the hut. They waited, suddenly alert. A policeman said in German, 'Black Opel Rekord, Federal registration.'

'He can't see that far in the dusk, he's guessing,' the American whispered and then he added: 'How did Mundt know?'

'Shut up,' said Leamas from the window. One of the policemen left the hut and walked to the sandbag emplacement two feet short of the white demarcation which lay across the road like the base line of a tennis court. The other waited until his companion was crouched behind the telescope in the emplacement, then put down his binoculars, took his black helmet from the peg by the door and carefully adjusted it on his head. Somewhere high above the checkpoint the arclights sprang to life, casting theatrical beams on to the road in front of them.

The policeman began his commentary. Leamas knew it by heart.

'Car halts at the first control. Only one occupant, a woman. Escorted to the Vopo hut for document check.' They waited in silence.

'What's he saying?' said the American. Leamas didn't reply. Picking up a spare pair of binoculars, he gazed fixedly towards the East German controls.

'Document check completed. Admitted to the second control.'

'Mr Leamas, is this your man?' the American persisted. 'I ought to ring the Agency.'

'Wait.'

'Where's the car now? What's it doing?'

'Currency check, Customs,' Leamas snapped.

Leamas watched the car. There were two Vopos at the driver's door, one doing the talking, the other standing off, waiting. A third was sauntering round the car. He stopped at the boot, then walked back to the driver. He wanted the key. He opened the boot, looked inside, closed it, returned the key and walked thirty yards up the road to where, midway between the two opposing checkpoints, a solitary East German sentry was standing, a squat silhouette in boots and baggy trousers. The two stood together talking, self-conscious in the glare of the arclight.

With a perfunctory gesture they waved the car on. It reached the two sentries in the middle of the road and stopped again. They walked round the car, stood off and talked again; finally, almost unwillingly, they let it continue across the line to the Western sector.

'It is a man you're waiting for, Mr Leamas?' asked the American.

'Yes, it's a man.'

Pushing up the collar of his jacket, Leamas stepped outside into the icy October wind. He remembered the crowd then. It was something you forgot inside the hut, this group of puzzled faces. The people changed but the expressions were the same. It was like the helpless crowd that gathers round a traffic accident, no one knowing how it happened, whether you should move the body. Smoke or dust rose through the beam of the arclamps, a constant shifting pall between the margins of light.

Leamas walked over to the car, and said to the woman, 'Where is he?'

'They came for him and he ran. He took the bicycle. They can't have known about me.'

'Where did he go?'

'We had a room near Brandenburg, over a pub. He kept a few things there, money, papers. I think he'll have gone there. Then he'll come over.'

'Tonight?'

'He said he would come tonight. The others have all been caught–Paul, Viereck, Ländser, Salomon. He hasn't got long.'

Leamas stared at her for a moment in silence.

'Ländser too?'

'Last night.'

A policeman was standing at Leamas' side.

'You'll have to move away from here,' he said. 'It's forbidden to obstruct the crossing point.'

Leamas half turned.

'Go to hell,' he snapped. The German stiffened, but the woman said:

'Get in. We'll drive down to the corner.'

He got in beside her and they moved slowly down the road to a side turning.

'I didn't know you had a car,' he said.

'It's my husband's,' she replied indifferently. 'Karl never told you I was married, did he?' Leamas was silent. 'My husband and I work for an optical firm. They let us over to do business. Karl only told you my maiden name. He didn't want me to be mixed up with . . . you.'

Leamas took a key from his pocket.

'You'll want somewhere to stay,' he said. His voice sounded flat. 'There's an apartment in the Albrecht-Dürer-Strasse, next to the Museum. Number 28A. You'll find everything you want. I'll telephone you when he comes.'

'I'll stay here with you.'

'I'm not staying here. Go to the flat. I'll ring you. There's no point in waiting here now.'

'But he's coming to this crossing point.'

Leamas looked at her in surprise.

'He told you that?'

'Yes. He knows one of the Vopos there, the son of his landlord. It may help. That's why he chose this route.'

'And he told *you* that?'

'He trusts me. He told me everything.'

'Christ.'

He gave her the key and went back to the checkpoint hut, out of the cold. The policemen were muttering to each other as he entered; the larger one ostentatiously turned his back.

'I'm sorry,' said Leamas. 'I'm sorry I bawled you out.' He opened a tattered briefcase and rummaged in it until he found what he was looking for: a half bottle of whisky. With a nod the elder man accepted it, half filled each coffee mug and topped them up with black coffee.

'Where's the American gone?' asked Leamas.

'Who?'

'The CIA boy. The one who was with me.'

'Bed time,' said the elder man and they all laughed.

Leamas put down his mug and said:

'What are your rules for shooting to protect a man coming over? A man on the run.'

'We can only give covering fire if the Vopos shoot into our sector.'

'That means you can't shoot until a man's over the boundary?'

The older man said, 'We can't give covering fire, Mr . . .'

'Thomas,' Leamas replied, 'Thomas.' They shook hands, the two policemen pronouncing their own names as they did so.

'We can't give covering fire. That's the truth. They tell us there'd be war if we did.'

'It's nonsense,' said the younger policeman, emboldened by the whisky. 'If the allies weren't here the Wall would be gone by now.'

'So would Berlin,' muttered the elder man.

'I've got a man coming over tonight,' said Leamas abruptly.

'Here? At this crossing point?'

'It's worth a lot to get him out. Mundt's men are looking for him.'

'There are still places where you can climb,' said the younger policeman.

'He's not that kind. He'll bluff his way through; he's got papers, if the papers are still good. He's got a bicycle.'

There was only one light in the checkpoint, a reading lamp with a green shade, but the glow of the arclights, like artificial moonlight, filled the cabin. Darkness had fallen, and with it silence. They spoke as if they were afraid of being overheard. Leamas went to the window and waited, in front of him the road and to either side the Wall, a dirty, ugly thing of breeze blocks and strands of barbed wire, lit with cheap yellow light, like the backdrop for a concentration camp. East and west of the Wall lay the unrestored part of Berlin, a half-world of ruin, drawn in two dimensions, crags of war.

That damned woman, thought Leamas, and that fool Karl who'd lied about her. Lied by omission, as they all do, agents the world over. You teach them to cheat, to cover their tracks, and they cheat you as well. He'd only produced her once, after that dinner in the Schürzstrasse last year. Karl had just had his big scoop and Control had wanted to meet him. Control always came in on success. They'd had dinner together–Leamas, Control and Karl. Karl loved that kind of thing. He turned up looking like a Sunday School boy, scrubbed and shining, doffing his hat and all respectful. Control had shaken his hand for five minutes and said: 'I want you to know how pleased we are, Karl, damn' pleased.' Leamas had watched and thought, 'That'll cost us another couple of hundred a year.' When they'd finished dinner Control pumped their hands again, nodded significantly and implying that he had to go off and risk his life somewhere else, got back into his chauffeur-driven car. Then Karl had laughed, and Leamas had laughed with him, and they'd finished the champagne, still laughing about Control. Afterwards they'd gone to the 'Alter Fass', Karl had insisted on it and there Elvira was waiting for them, a forty-year-old blonde, tough as nails.

'This is my best kept secret, Alec,' Karl had said, and Leamas was furious. Afterwards they'd had a row.

'How much does she know? Who is she? How did you meet her?' Karl sulked and refused to say. After that things went badly. Leamas tried to alter the routine, change the meeting places and the catch words, but Karl didn't like it. He knew what lay behind it and he didn't like it.

'If you don't trust her it's too late anyway,' he'd said, and Leamas took the hint and shut up. But he went carefully after that, told Karl much less, used more of the hocus-pocus of espionage technique. And there she was, out there in her car, knowing everything, the whole network, the safe house, everything; and Leamas swore, not for the first time, never to trust an agent again.

He went to the telephone and dialled the number of his flat. Frau Martha answered.

'We've got guests at the Dürer-Strasse,' said Leamas, 'a man and a woman.'

'Married?' asked Martha.

'Near enough,' said Leamas, and she laughed that frightful laugh. As he put down the receiver one of the policemen turned to him.

'Herr Thomas! Quick!' Leamas stepped to the observation window.

'A man, Herr Thomas,' the younger policeman whispered, 'with a bicycle.' Leamas picked up the binoculars.

It was Karl, the figure was unmistakable even at that distance, shrouded in an old Wehrmacht macintosh, pushing his bicycle. He's made it, thought Leamas, he must have made it, he's through the document check, only currency and customs to go. Leamas watched Karl lean his bicycle against the railing, walk casually to the Customs hut. Don't overdo it, he thought. At last Karl came out, waved cheerfully to the man on the barrier, and the red and white pole swung slowly upwards. He was through, he was coming towards them, he had made it. Only the Vopo in the middle of the road, the line and safety.

At that moment Karl seemed to hear some sound, sense danger; he glanced over his shoulder, began to pedal furiously, bending low over the handlebars. There was still the lonely sentry on the bridge, and he had turned and was watching Karl. Then, totally unexpected, the searchlights went on, white and brilliant, catching Karl and holding him in their beam like a rabbit in the headlights of a car. There came the see-saw wail of a siren, the sound of orders wildly shouted. In front of Leamas the two policemen dropped to their knees, peering through the sandbagged slits, deftly flicking the rapid load on their automatic rifles.

The East German sentry fired, quite carefully, away from them, into his own sector. The first shot seemed to thrust Karl forward, the second to pull him back. Somehow he was still moving, still on the bicycle, passing the sentry, and the sentry was still shooting at him. Then he sagged, rolled to the ground, and they heard quite clearly the clatter of the bike as it fell. Leamas hoped to God he was dead.

Chapter Two

The Circus

He watched the Templehof runway sink beneath him.

Leamas was not a reflective man and not a particularly philosophical one. He knew he was written off–it was a fact of life which he would henceforth live with, as a man must live with cancer or imprisonment. He knew there was no kind of preparation which could have bridged the gap between then and now. He met failure as one day he would probably meet death, with cynical resentment and the courage of a solitary. He'd lasted longer than most; now he was beaten. It is said a dog lives as long as its teeth; metaphorically, Leamas' teeth had been drawn; and it was Mundt who had drawn them.

Ten years ago he could have taken the other path–there were desk jobs in that anonymous government building in Cambridge Circus which Leamas could have taken and kept till he was God knows how old; but Leamas wasn't made that way. You might as well have asked a jockey to become a totalisator clerk as expect Leamas to abandon operational life for the tendentious theorising and clandestine self-interest of Whitehall. He had stayed on in Berlin, conscious that Personnel had marked his file for review at the end of every year–stubborn, wilful, contemptuous of instruction, telling himself that something would turn up. Intelligence work has one moral law–it is justified by results. Even the sophistry of Whitehall paid court to that law, and Leamas got results. Until Mundt came.

It was odd how soon Leamas had realised that Mundt was the writing on the wall.

Hans-Dieter Mundt, born forty-two years ago in Leipzig. Leamas knew his dossier, knew the photograph on the inside of the cover; the blank, hard face beneath the flaxen hair; knew by heart the story of Mundt's rise to power as second man in the Abteilung and effective head of operations. Mundt was hated even within his own department. Leamas knew that from the evidence of defectors, and from Riemeck, who as a member of the SED Praesidium sat on security committees with Mundt, and dreaded him. Rightly as it turned out, for Mundt had killed him.

Until 1959 Mundt had been a minor functionary of the Abteilung, operating in London under the cover of the East German Steel Mission. He returned to Germany in a hurry after murdering two of his own agents to save his skin and was not heard of for more than a year. Quite suddenly he reappeared at the Abteilung's headquarters in Leipzig as head of the Ways and Means Department, responsible for allocating currency, equipment and personnel for special tasks. At the end of that year came the big struggle for power within the Abteilung. The number and influence of Soviet liaison officers were drastically reduced, several of the old guard were dismissed on ideological grounds and three men emerged: Fiedler as head of counter intelligence, Jahn took over from Mundt as head of facilities, and Mundt himself got the plum—deputy director of operations—at the age of forty-one. Then the new style began. The first agent Leamas lost was a girl. She was only a small link in the network; she was used for courier jobs. They shot her dead in the street as she left a West Berlin cinema. The police never found the murderer and Leamas was at first inclined to write the incident off as unconnected with her work. A month later a railway porter in Dresden, a discarded agent from Peter Guillam's network, was found dead and mutilated beside a railway track. Leamas knew it wasn't coincidence any longer. Soon after that two members of another network under Leamas' control were arrested and summarily sentenced to death. So it went on: remorseless and unnerving.

And now they had Karl, and Leamas was leaving Berlin as he had come—without a single agent worth a farthing. Mundt had won.

Leamas was a short man with close, iron-grey hair, and the physique of a swimmer. He was very strong. This strength was discernible in his back and shoulders, in his neck, and in the stubby formation of his hands and fingers.

He had a utilitarian approach to clothes, as he did to most other things and even the spectacles he occasionally wore had steel rims. Most of his suits were of artificial fibre, none of them had waistcoats. He favoured shirts of the American kind with buttons on the points of the collars, and suede shoes with rubber soles.

He had an attractive face, muscular, and a stubborn line to his thin mouth. His eyes were brown and small; Irish, some said. It was hard to place Leamas. If he were to walk into a London club the porter would certainly not mistake him for a member; in a Berlin night club they usually gave him the best table. He looked like a man who could make trouble, a man who looked after his money, a man who was not quite a gentleman.

The air hostess thought he was interesting. She guessed he was North Country, which he might have been, and rich, which he was not. She put his age at fifty, which was about right. She guessed he was single, which was half true. Somewhere long ago there had been a divorce; somewhere there were children, now in their teens, who received their allowance from a rather odd private bank in the City.

'If you want another whisky,' said the air hostess, 'you'd better hurry. We shall be at London airport in twenty minutes.'

'No more.' He didn't look at her; he was looking out of the window at the grey-green fields of Kent.

Fawley met him at the airport and drove him to London. 'Control's pretty cross about Karl,' he said, looking sideways at Leamas. Leamas nodded.

'How did it happen?' asked Fawley.

'He was shot. Mundt got him.'

'Dead?'

'I should think so, by now. He'd better be. He nearly made it. He should never have hurried, they couldn't have been sure. The Abteilung got to the checkpoint just after he'd been let through. They started the siren and a Vopo shot him twenty yards short of the line. He moved on the ground for a moment, then lay still.'

'Poor bastard.'

'Precisely,' said Leamas.

Fawley didn't like Leamas, and if Leamas knew he didn't care. Fawley was a man who belonged to Clubs and wore representative ties, pontificated on the skills of sportsmen and assumed a service rank in office correspondence. He thought Leamas suspect, and Leamas thought him a fool.

'What section are you in?' asked Leamas.

'Personnel.'

'Like it?'

'Fascinating.'

'Where do I go now? On ice?'

'Better let Control tell you, old boy.'

'Do you know?'

'Of course.'

'Then why the hell don't you tell me?'

'Sorry, old man,' Fawley replied, and Leamas suddenly very nearly lost his temper. Then he reflected that Fawley was probably lying anyway.

'Well, tell me one thing, do you mind? Have I got to look for a bloody flat in London?'

Fawley scratched at his ear: 'I don't think so, old man, no.'

'No? Thank God for that.'

They parked near Cambridge Circus, at a parking meter, and went together into the hall.

'You haven't got a pass, have you? You'd better fill in a slip, old man.'

'Since when have we had passes? McCall knows me as well as his own mother.'

'Just a new routine. Circus is growing, you know.'

Leamas said nothing, nodded at McCall and got into the lift without a pass.

Control shook his hand rather carefully, like a doctor feeling the bones.

'You must be awfully tired,' he said apologetically, 'do sit down.' That same dreary voice, the donnish bray.

Leamas sat down in a chair facing an olive green electric fire with a bowl of water balanced on the top of it.

'Do you find it cold?' Control asked. He was stooping over the fire rubbing his hands together. He wore a cardigan under his black jacket, a shabby brown one. Leamas remembered Control's wife, a stupid little woman called Mandy who seemed to think her husband was in the Coal Board. He supposed she had knitted it.

'It's so dry, that's the trouble,' Control continued. 'Beat the cold and you parch the atmosphere. Just as dangerous.' He went to the desk and pressed a button. 'We'll try and get some coffee,' he said, 'Ginnie's on leave, that's the trouble. They've given me some new girl. It really is too bad.'

He was shorter than Leamas remembered him; otherwise, just the same. The same affected detachment, the same donnish conceits; the same horror of draughts; courteous according to a formula miles removed from Leamas' experience. The same milk-and-water smile, the same elaborate diffidence, the same apologetic adherence to a code of behaviour which he pretended to find ridiculous. The same banality.

He brought a packet of cigarettes from the desk and gave one to Leamas.

'You're going to find these more expensive,' he said, and Leamas nodded dutifully. Slipping the cigarettes into his pocket, Control sat down. There was a pause; finally Leamas said:

'Riemeck's dead.'

'Yes, indeed,' Control declared, as if Leamas had made a good point. 'It is very unfortunate. Most . . . I suppose that girl blew him–Elvira?'

'I suppose so.' Leamas wasn't going to ask him how he knew about Elvira.

'And Mundt had him shot,' Control added.

'Yes.'

Control got up and drifted round the room looking for an ash-tray. He found one and put it awkwardly on the floor between their two chairs.

'How did you feel? When Riemeck was shot, I mean? You saw it, didn't you?'

Leamas shrugged. 'I was bloody annoyed,' he said.

Control put his head on one side and half closed his eyes. 'Surely you felt more than that? Surely you were upset? That would be more natural.'

'I was upset. Who wouldn't be?'

'Did you like Riemeck–as a man?'

'I suppose so,' said Leamas helplessly. 'There doesn't seem much point in going into it,' he added.

'How did you spend the night, what was left of it, after Riemeck had been shot?'

'Look, what is this?' Leamas asked hotly; 'what are you getting at?'

'Riemeck was the last,' Control reflected, 'the last of a series of deaths. If my memory is right it began with the girl, the one they shot in Wedding, outside the cinema. Then there was the Dresden man, and the arrests at Jena. Like the ten little niggers. Now Paul, Viereck and Làndser–all dead. And finally Riemeck.' He smiled deprecatingly; 'that is quite a heavy rate of expenditure. I wondered if you'd had enough.'

'What do you mean–enough?'

'I wondered whether you were tired. Burnt out.' There was a long silence.

'That's up to you,' Leamas said at last.

'We have to live without sympathy, don't we? That's impossible of course. We act it to one another, all this hardness; but we aren't like that really, I mean . . . one can't be out in the cold all the time; one has to come in from the cold . . . d'you see what I mean?'

Leamas saw. He saw the long road outside Rotterdam, the long straight road beside the dunes, and the stream of refugees moving along it; saw the little aeroplane miles away, the procession stop and look towards it; and the plane coming in, nearly over the dunes; saw the chaos, the meaningless hell, as the bombs hit the road.

'I can't talk like this, Control,' Leamas said at last. 'What do you want me to do?'

'I want you to stay out in the cold a little longer.' Leamas said nothing, so Control went on: 'The ethic of our work, as I understand it, is based on a single assumption. That is, we are never going to be aggressors. Do you think that's fair?'

Leamas nodded. Anything to avoid talking.

'Thus we do disagreeable things, but we are *defensive*. That, I think, is still fair. We do disagreeable things so that ordinary people here and elsewhere can sleep safely in their beds at night. Is that too romantic? Of course, we occasionally do very wicked things'; he grinned like a schoolboy. 'And in weighing up the moralities, we rather go in for dishonest comparisons; after all, you can't compare the ideals of one side with the methods of the other, can you, now?'

Leamas was lost. He'd heard the man talked a lot of drivel before getting the knife in, but he'd never heard anything like this before.

'I mean you've got to compare method with method, and ideal with ideal. I would say that since the war, our methods—ours and those of the opposition—have become much the same. I mean you can't be less ruthless than the opposition simply because your government's *policy* is benevolent, can you now?' He laughed quietly to himself: 'That would *never* do,' he said.

For God's sake, thought Leamas, it's like working for a bloody clergyman. What *is* he up to?

'That is why,' Control continued, 'I think we ought to try and get rid of Mundt. . . . Oh really,' he said, turning irritably towards the door, 'Where is that damned coffee?'

Control crossed to the door, opened it and talked to some unseen girl in the outer room. As he returned he said: 'I really think we *ought* to get rid of him if we can manage it.'

'Why? We've got nothing left in East Germany, nothing at all. You just said so—Riemeck was the last. We've nothing left to protect.'

Control sat down and looked at his hands for a while.

'That is not altogether true,' he said finally; 'but I don't think I need to bore you with the details.'

Leamas shrugged.

'Tell me,' Control continued, 'are you tired of spying? Forgive me if I repeat the question. I mean that is a phenomenon we understand here, you know. Like aircraft designers . . . metal fatigue, I think the term is. Do say if you are.'

Leamas remembered the flight home that morning and wondered.

'If you were,' Control added, 'we would have to find some other way of taking care of Mundt. What I have in mind is a little out of the ordinary.'

The girl came in with the coffee. She put the tray on the desk and poured out two cups. Control waited till she had left the room.

'Such a *silly* girl,' he said, almost to himself. 'It seems extraordinary they can't find good ones any more. I do wish Ginnie wouldn't go on holiday at times like this.' He stirred his coffee disconsolately for a while.

'We really must discredit Mundt,' he said. 'Tell me, do you drink a lot? Whisky and that kind of thing?'

Leamas had thought he was used to Control.

'I drink a bit. More than most I suppose.'

Control nodded understandingly. 'What do you know about Mundt?'

'He's a killer. He was here a year or two back with the East German Steel Mission. We had an Adviser here then: Maston.'

'Quite so.'

'Mundt was running an agent, the wife of an F.O. man. He killed her.'

'He tried to kill George Smiley. And of course he shot the woman's husband. He is a very distasteful man. Ex Hitler-Youth and all that kind of thing. Not at all the intellectual kind of Communist. A practitioner of the cold war.'

'Like us,' Leamas observed drily. Control didn't smile.

'George Smiley knew the case well. He isn't with us any more, but I think you ought to ferret him out. He's doing things on seventeenth-century Germany. He lives in Chelsea, just behind Sloane Square. Bywater Street, do you know it?'

'Yes.'

'And Guillam was on the case as well. He's in Satellites Four, on the first floor. I'm afraid everything's changed since your day.'

'Yes.'

'Spend a day or two with them. They know what I have in mind. Then I wondered if you'd care to stay with me for the weekend. My wife,' he added hastily, 'is looking after her mother, I'm afraid. It will be just you and I.'

'Thanks. I'd like to.'

'We can talk about things in comfort then. It would be very nice. I think you might make a lot of money out of it. You can have whatever you make.'

'Thanks.'

'That is, of course, if you're *sure you want* to . . . no metal fatigue or anything?'

'If it's a question of killing Mundt, I'm game.'

'Do you really feel that?' Control enquired politely. And then, having looked at Leamas thoughtfully for a moment he observed: 'Yes, I really think you do. But you mustn't feel you *have* to say it. I mean in our world we pass so quickly out of the register of hate or love—like certain sounds a dog can't hear. All that's left in the end is a kind of nausea; you never want to cause suffering again. Forgive me, but isn't that rather what you felt when Karl Riemeck was shot? Not hate for Mundt, nor love for Karl, but a sickening jolt like a blow on a numb body. . . . They tell me you walked all night—just walked

through the streets of Berlin. Is that right?'
'It's right that I went for a walk.'
'All night?'
'Yes.'
'What happened to Elvira?'
'God knows . . . I'd like to take a swing at Mundt,' he said.
'Good . . . good. Incidentally, if you should meet any old friends in the meantime, I don't think there's any point in discussing this with them. In fact,' Control added after a moment, 'I should be rather short with them. Let them think we've treated you badly. It's as well to begin as one intends to continue, isn't it?'

Chapter Three

Decline

It surprised no one very much when they put Leamas on the shelf. In the main, they said, Berlin had been a failure for years, and someone had to take the rap. Besides, he was old for operational work, where your reflexes often had to be as quick as those of a professional tennis player. Leamas had done good work in the war, everyone knew that. In Norway and Holland he had somehow remained demonstrably alive, and at the end of it they gave him a medal and let him go. Later, of course, they got him to come back. It was bad luck about his pension, decidedly bad luck. Accounts Section had let it out, in the person of Elsie. Elsie said in the canteen that poor Alec Leamas would only have £400 a year to live on because of his interrupted service. Elsie felt it was a rule they really ought to change; after all, Mr Leamas had *done* the service, hadn't he? But there they were with Treasury on their backs, not a bit like the old days, and what could they do? Even in the bad days of Maston they'd managed things better.

Leamas, the new men were told, was the old school; blood, guts and cricket and School Cert. French. In Leamas' case this happened to be unfair, since he was bilingual in German and English and his Dutch was admirable; he also disliked cricket. But it was true that he had no degree.

Leamas' contract had a few months to run, and they put him in Banking to do his time. Banking Section was different from Accounts; it dealt with overseas payments, financing agents and operations. Most of the jobs in Banking could have been done by an office boy were it not for the high degree of secrecy involved, and thus Banking was one of several Sections of the Service which were regarded as laying-out places for officers shortly to be buried.

Leamas went to seed.

The process of going to seed is generally considered to be a protracted one, but in Leamas this was not the case. In the full view of his colleagues he was transformed from a man honourably put aside to a resentful, drunken wreck–and all within a few months. There is a kind of stupidity among drunks, particularly when they are sober, a kind of disconnection which the unobservant interpret as vagueness and which Leamas seemed to acquire with unnatural speed. He developed small dishonesties, borrowed insignificant sums from secretaries and neglected to return them, arrived late or left early under some mumbled pretext. At first his colleagues treated him with indulgence; perhaps his decline scared them in the same way as we are scared by cripples, beggars and invalids because we fear we could ourselves become them; but in the end his neglect, his brutal, unreasoning malice isolated him.

Rather to people's surprise, Leamas didn't seem to mind being put on the shelf. His will seemed suddenly to have collapsed. The débutante secretaries, reluctant to believe that Intelligence Services are peopled by ordinary mortals, were alarmed to notice that Leamas had become definitely seedy. He took less care of his appearance and less notice of his surroundings, he lunched in the canteen which was normally the preserve of junior staff, and it was rumoured that he was drinking. He became a solitary, belonging to that tragic class of active men prematurely deprived of activity; swimmers barred from the water or actors banished from the stage.

Some said he had make a mistake in Berlin, and that was why his network had been rolled up; no one quite knew. All agreed that he had been treated with unusual harshness, even by a personnel department not famed for its philanthropy. They would point to him covertly as he went by, as men will point to an athlete of the past, and say: 'That's Leamas. He put up a black in Berlin. Pathetic the way he's let himself go.'

And then one day he had vanished. He said good-bye to no one, not even, apparently, Control. In itself that was not surprising. The nature of the Service precluded elaborate farewells and the presentation of gold watches, but even by these standards Leamas' departure seemed abrupt. So far as could be judged, his departure occurred before the statutory termination of his contract. Elsie, of Accounts Section, offered one or two crumbs of information: Leamas had drawn the balance of his pay in cash, which, if Elsie knew anything, meant he was having trouble with his bank. His gratuity was to be paid at the turn of the month, she couldn't say how much but it wasn't four figures, poor lamb. His National Insurance card had been sent on. Personnel had an address for him, Elsie added with a sniff, but of course they weren't revealing it, not Personnel.

Then there was the story about the money. It leaked out—no one, as usual knew where from—that Leamas' sudden departure was connected with irregularities in the accounts of Banking Section. A largish sum was missing (not three figures but four, according to a lady with blue hair who worked in the telephone room) and they'd got it back, nearly all of it, and they'd stuck a lien on his pension. Others said they didn't believe it—if Alec had wanted to rob the till, they said, he'd know better ways of doing it than fiddling with H.Q. accounts. Not that he wasn't capable of it—he'd just have done it better. But those less impressed by Leamas' criminal potential pointed at his large consumption of alcohol, at the expense of maintaining a separate household, at the fatal disparity between pay at home and allowances abroad and above all at the temptations put in the way of a man handling large sums of hot money when he knew that his days in the Service were numbered. All agreed that if Alec had dipped his hands in the honey pot he was finished for all time—the Resettlement people wouldn't look at him and Personnel would give him no reference—or one so icy cold that the most enthusiastic employer would shiver at the sight of it. Peculation was the one sin Personnel would never let you forget—and they never forgot it themselves. If it was true that Alec had robbed the Circus, he would take the wrath of Personnel with him to the grave—and Personnel would not so much as pay for the shroud.

For a week or two after his departure, a few people wondered what had become of him. But his former friends had already learnt to keep clear of him. He had become a resentful bore, constantly attacking the Service and its administration, and what he called the 'Cavalry boys' who, he said, managed its affairs as if it were a regimental club. He never missed an opportunity of railing against the Americans and their intelligence agencies. He seemed to hate them more than the Abteilung, to which he seldom, if ever, referred. He would hint that it was they who had compromised his network; this seemed to be an obsession with him, and it was poor reward for attempts to console him, it made him bad company, so that those who had known and even tacitly liked him, wrote him off. Leamas' departure caused only a ripple on the water; with other winds and the changing of the seasons it was soon forgotten.

His flat was small and squalid, done in brown paint with photographs of Clovelly. It looked directly on to the grey backs of three stone warehouses, the windows of which were drawn, for aesthetic reasons, in creosote. Above the warehouse there lived an Italian family, quarrelling at night and beating carpets in the morning. Leamas had few possessions with which to brighten his rooms. He bought some shades to cover the light bulbs, and two pairs of sheets to replace the hessian squares provided by the landlord. The rest Leamas tolerated: the flower pattern curtains, not lined or hemmed, the fraying brown carpets and the clumsy darkwood furniture, like something from a seamen's hostel. From a yellow, crumbling geyser he obtained hot water for a shilling.

He needed a job. He had no money, none at all. So perhaps the stories of embezzlement were true. The offers of resettlement which the Service made had seemed to Leamas lukewarm and peculiarly unsuitable. He tried first to get a job in commerce. A firm of industrial adhesive manufacturers showed interest in his application for the post of assistant manager and personnel officer. Unconcerned by the inadequate reference with which the Service provided him, they demanded no qualifications, and offered him six hundred a year. He stayed for a week, by which time the foul stench of decaying fish oil had permeated his clothes and hair, lingering in his nostrils like the smell of death. No amount of washing would remove it, so that in the end Leamas had his hair cut short to the scalp and threw away two of his best suits. He spent another week trying to sell encyclopaedias to suburban housewives, but he was not a man that housewives liked or understood; they did not want Leamas, let alone his encyclopaedias. Night after night he returned wearily to his flat, his ridiculous sample under his arm. At the end of a week he telephoned the company and told them he had sold nothing. Expressing no surprise, they reminded him of his obligation to return the sample if he discontinued acting on their behalf, and rang off. Leamas stalked out of the telephone booth in a fury, leaving the sample behind him, went to a pub and got very drunk at a cost of twenty-five shillings, which he could not afford. They threw him out for shouting at a woman who tried to pick him up. They told him never to come back, but they'd forgotten all about it a week later. They were beginning to know Leamas there.

They were beginning to know him elsewhere too, the grey, shambling figure from the Mansions. Not a wasted word did he speak, not a friend, neither man, woman nor beast did he have. They guessed he was in trouble, run away from his wife like as not. He never knew the price of anything, never remembered it when he was told. He patted all his pockets whenever he looked for change, he never remembered to bring a basket, always buying carrier bags. They didn't like him in the Street, but they were almost sorry for him. They thought he was dirty too, the way he didn't shave weekends, and his shirts all grubby. A Mrs McCaird from Sudbury Avenue cleaned for him for a week, but having never received a civil word from him withdrew her labour. She was an important source of information in the Street, where tradesmen told one another that they needed to know in case he asked for credit. Mrs McCaird's advice was against credit. Leamas never had a letter, she said, and they agreed that that was serious. He'd no pictures and only a few books; she thought one of the books was dirty but couldn't be sure because it was in foreign writing. It was her opinion he had a bit to live on, and that that bit was running out. She knew he drew Benefit on Thursdays. Bayswater was warned, and needed no second warning. They heard from Mrs McCaird that he drank like a fish: this was confirmed by the publican. Publicans and charwomen are not in the way of accommodating their clients with credit; but their information is treasured by those who are.

Chapter Four

Liz

Finally he took the job in the library. The Labour Exchange had put him on to it each Thursday morning as he drew his unemployment benefit, and he'd always turned it down.

'It's not really your cup of tea,' Mr Pitt said, 'but the pay's fair and the work's easy for an educated man.'

'What sort of library?' Leamas asked.

'It's the Bayswater Library for Psychic Research. It's an endowment. They've got thousands of volumes, all sorts, and they've been left a whole lot more. They want another helper.'

He took his dole and the slip of paper. 'They're an odd lot,' Mr Pitt added, 'but then you're not a stayer anyway, are you? I think it's time you gave them a try, don't you?'

It was odd about Pitt. Leamas was certain he'd seen him before somewhere. At the Circus, during the war.

The library was like a church hall, and very cold. The black oil stoves at either end made it smell of paraffin. In the middle of the room was a cubicle like a witness-box and inside it sat Miss Crail, the librarian.

It had never occurred to Leamas that he might have to work for a woman. No one at the Labour Exchange had said anything about that.

'I'm the new help,' he said; 'my name's Leamas.'

Miss Crail looked up sharply from her card index, as if she had heard a rude word. 'Help? What do you mean, help?'

'Assistant. From the Labour Exchange. Mr Pitt.' He pushed across the counter a roneoed form with his particulars entered in a sloping hand. She picked it up and studied it.

'You are Mr Leamas.' This was not a question, but the first stage of a laborious fact-finding investigation.

'And you are from the Labour Exchange.'

'No. I was sent by the Exchange. They told me you needed an assistant.'

'I see.' A wooden smile.

At that moment the telephone rang: she lifted the receiver and began arguing with somebody, fiercely. Leamas guessed they argued all the time; there were no preliminaries. Her voice just rose a key and she began arguing about some tickets for a concert. He listened for a minute or two and then drifted towards the bookshelves. He noticed a girl in one of the alcoves standing on a ladder sorting large volumes.

'I'm the new man,' he said, 'my name's Leamas.'

She came down from the ladder and shook his hand a little formally.

'I'm Liz Gold. How d'you do. Have you met Miss Crail?'

'Yes, but she's on the phone at the moment.'

'Arguing with her mother I expect. What are you going to do?'

'I don't know. Work.'

'We're marking at the moment; Miss Crail's started a new index.'

She was a tall girl, ungainly, with a long waist and long legs. She wore flat, ballet type shoes to reduce her height. Her face, like her body, had large components which seemed to hesitate between plainness and beauty. Leamas guessed she was twenty-two or three, and Jewish.

'It's just a question of checking that all the books are in the shelves. This is the reference bit, you see. When you've checked you pencil in the new reference and mark it off on the index.'

'What happens then?'

'Only Miss Crail's allowed to ink in the reference. It's the rule.'

'Whose rule?'

'Miss. Crail's. Why don't you start on the archaeology?'

Leamas nodded and together they walked to the next alcove where a shoe-box full of cards lay on the floor.

'Have you done this kind of thing before?' she asked.

'No.' He stooped and picked up a handful of cards and shuffled through them. 'Mr Pitt sent me. From the Exchange.' He put the cards back.

'Is Miss Crail the only person who can ink the cards, too?' Leamas enquired.

'Yes.'

She left him there, and after a moment's hesitation he took out a book and looked at the fly-leaf. It was called *Archaeological Discoveries in Asia Minor*, Volume four. They only seemed to have volume four.

It was one o'clock and Leamas was very hungry, so he walked over to where Liz Gold was sorting and said:

'What happens about lunch?'

'Oh, I bring sandwiches.' She looked a little embarrassed. 'You can have some of mine if that would help. There's no café for miles.'

Leamas shook his head.

'I'll go out, thanks. Got some shopping to do.' She watched him push his way through the swing doors.

It was half past two when he came back. He smelt of whisky. He had one carrier bag full of vegetables and another containing groceries. He put them down in a corner of the alcove and wearily began again on the archaeology books. He'd been marking for about ten minutes when he became aware that Miss Crail was watching him.

'*Mister* Leamas.' He was half-way up the ladder, so he looked down over his shoulder and said:

'Yes?'

'Do you know where these carrier bags come from?'

'They're mine.'

'I see. They are yours.' Leamas waited. 'I regret,' she continued at last, 'that we do not allow it, bringing shopping in to the library.'

'Where else can I put it? There's nowhere else I *can* put it.'

'Not in the library,' she replied. Leamas ignored her, and returned his attention to the archaeology section.

'If you only took the normal lunch break,' Miss Crail continued, 'you would not have time to go shopping. Neither of *us* does, Miss Gold or myself; *we* do not have time to shop.'

'Why don't you take an extra half-hour?' Leamas asked, 'you'd have time then. If you're pushed you can work another half-hour in the evening. If you're pressed.'

She stayed for some moments, just watching him and obviously thinking of something to say. Finally she announced:

'I shall discuss it with Mr Ironside,' and went away.

At exactly half past five Miss Crail put on her coat and, with a pointed: 'Good night, Miss Gold', left. Leamas guessed she had been brooding on the carrier bags all afternoon. He went in to the next alcove where Liz Gold was sitting on the bottom rung of her ladder reading what looked like a tract. When she saw Leamas she dropped it guiltily into her handbag and stood up.

'Who's Mr Ironside?' Leamas asked.

'I don't think he exists,' she replied. 'He's her big gun when she's stuck for an answer. I asked her once who he was. She went all shifty and mysterious and said "never mind". I don't think he exists.'

'I'm not sure Miss Crail does,' said Leamas and Liz Gold smiled.

At six o'clock she locked up and gave the keys to the curator, a very old man with first war shellshock who, said Liz, sat awake all night in case the Germans made a counterattack. It was bitterly cold outside.

'Got far to go?' asked Leamas.

'Twenty minutes' walk. I always walk it. Have you?'

'Not far,' said Leamas. 'Good night.'

He walked slowly back to the flat. He let himself in and turned the light switch. Nothing happened. He tried the light in the tiny kitchen and finally the electric fire that plugged in by his bed. On the door mat was a letter. He picked it up and took it out into the pale, yellow light of the staircase. It was the electricity company, regretting that the area manager had no alternative but to cut off the electricity until the outstanding account of nine pounds four shillings and eightpence had been settled.

He had become an enemy of Miss Crail, and enemies were what Miss Crail liked. Either she scowled at him or she ignored him, and when he came close, she began to tremble, looking to left and right, either for something with which to defend herself, or perhaps for a line of escape. Occasionally she would take immense umbrage, such as when he hung his macintosh on *her* peg, and she stood in front of it shaking for fully five minutes, until Liz spotted her and called Leamas. Leamas went over to her and said:

'What's troubling you, Miss Crail?'

'Nothing,' she replied in a breathy, clipped way, 'nothing at all.'

'Something wrong with my coat?'

'Nothing at all.'

'Fine,' he replied, and went back to his alcove. She quivered all that day, and conducted a telephone call in a stage whisper for half the morning.

'She's telling her mother,' said Liz. 'She always tells her mother. She tells her about me too.'

Miss Crail developed such an intense hatred for Leamas that she found it impossible to communicate with him. On pay days he would come back from lunch and find an envelope on the third rung of his ladder with his name misspelt on the outside. The first time it happened he took the money over to her with the envelope and said, 'It's L-E-A, Miss Crail, and only one S,' whereupon she was seized with a veritable palsy, rolling her eyes and fumbling erratically with her pencil until Leamas went away. She conspired into the telephone for hours after that.

About three weeks after Leamas began work at the library Liz asked him to supper. She pretended it was an idea that had come to her quite suddenly, at five o'clock that evening; she seemed to realise that if she were to ask him for tomorrow or the next day he would forget or just not come, so she asked him at five o'clock. Leamas seemed reluctant to accept, but in the end he did.

They walked to her flat through the rain and they might have been anywhere–Berlin, London, any town where paving stones turn to lakes of light in the evening rain, and the traffic shuffles despondently through wet streets.

It was the first of many meals which Leamas had at her flat. He came when she asked him, and she asked him often. He never spoke much. When she discovered he would come, she took to laying the table in the morning before leaving for the library. She even prepared the vegetables beforehand and had the candles on the table, for she loved candlelight. She always knew that there was something deeply wrong with Leamas, and that one day, for some reason she could not understand, he might break and she would never see him again. She tried to tell him she knew; she said to him one evening:

'You must go when you want. I'll never follow you, Alec,' and his brown eyes rested on her for a moment: 'I'll tell you when,' he replied.

Her flat was just a bed-sitting room and a kitchen. In the sitting-room were two armchairs, a divan bed, and a bookcase full of paper-back books, mainly classics which she had never read.

After supper she would talk to him, and he would lie on the divan, smoking. She never knew how much he heard, she didn't care. She would kneel by the bed holding his hand against her cheek, talking.

Then one evening she said to him:

'Alec, what do you believe in? Don't laugh–tell me.' She waited and at last he said:

'I believe an eleven bus will take me to Hammersmith. I don't believe it's driven by Father Christmas.'

She seemed to consider this and at last she asked again:

'But what do you believe in?'

Leamas shrugged.

'You must believe in something,' she persisted: 'something like God–I know you do, Alec; you've got that look sometimes, as if you'd got something special to do, like a priest. Alec, don't smile, it's true.'

He shook his head.

'Sorry, Liz, you've got it wrong. I don't like Americans and public schools. I don't like military parades and people who play soldiers.' Without smiling he added, 'And I don't like conversations about Life.'

'But, Alec, you might as well say—'

'I should have added,' Leamas interrupted, 'that I don't like people who tell me what I ought to think.' She knew he was getting angry but she couldn't stop herself any more.

'That's because you don't *want* to think, you don't dare! There's some poison in your mind, some hate. You're a fanatic, Alec, I know you are, but I don't know what about. You're a fanatic who doesn't want to convert people, and that's a dangerous thing. You're like a

man who's . . . sworn vengeance or something.' The brown eyes
rested on her. When he spoke she was frightened by the menace in
his voice.

'If I were you,' he said roughly, 'I'd mind my own business.'

And then he smiled, a roguish Irish smile. He hadn't smiled like
that before and Liz knew he was putting on the charm.

'What does Liz believe in?' he asked, and she replied:

'I can't be had that easy, Alec.'

Later that night they talked about it again. Leamas brought it
up—he asked her whether she was religious.

'You've got me wrong,' she said, 'all wrong. I don't believe in
God.'

'Then what do you believe in?'

'History.'

He looked at her in astonishment for a moment, then laughed.

'Oh, Liz . . . oh *no*. You're not a bloody Communist?' She nodded,
blushing like a small girl at his laughter, angry and relieved that he
didn't care.

She made him stay that night and they became lovers. He left at
five in the morning. She couldn't understand it; she was so proud
and he seemed ashamed.

He left her flat and turned down the empty street towards the park. It
was foggy. Some way down the road—not far, twenty yards, perhaps
a bit more—stood the figure of a man in a raincoat, short and rather
plump. He was leaning against the railings of the park, silhouetted in
the shifting mist. As Leamas approached, the mist seemed to
thicken, closing in around the figure at the railings, and when it
parted the man was gone.

Chapter Five

Credit

Then one day about a week later, he didn't come to the library. Miss
Crail was delighted; by half past eleven she had told her mother, and
on returning from lunch she stood in front of the archaeology shelves
where he had been working since he came. She stared with theatrical
concentration at the rows of books and Liz knew she was pretending
to work out whether Leamas had stolen anything.

Liz entirely ignored her for the rest of that day, failed to reply when she addressed her and worked with assiduous application. When the evening came she walked home and cried herself to sleep.

The next morning she arrived early at the library. She somehow felt that the sooner she got there, the sooner Leamas might come; but as the morning dragged on her hopes faded, and she knew he would never come. She had forgotten to make sandwiches for herself that day so she decided to take a bus to the Bayswater Road and go to the A.B.C. She felt sick and empty, but not hungry. Should she go and find him? She had promised never to follow him, but he had promised to tell her; should she go and find him?

She hailed a taxi and gave his address.

She made her way up the dingy staircase and pressed the bell of his door. The bell seemed to be broken; she heard nothing. There were three bottles of milk on the mat and a letter from the electricity company. She hesitated a moment, then banged on the door, and she heard the faint groan of a man. She rushed downstairs to the flat below, hammered and rang at the door. There was no reply so she ran down another flight and found herself in the back room of a grocer's shop. An old woman sat in a corner, rocking back and forth in her chair.

'The top flat,' Liz almost shouted, 'somebody's very ill. Who's got a key?'

The old woman looked at her for a moment, then called towards the front room, where the shop was.

'Arthur, come in here, Arthur, there's a girl here!'

A man in a brown overall and grey trilby hat looked round the door and said:

'Girl?'

'There's someone seriously ill in the top flat,' said Liz, 'he can't get to the front door to open it. Have you got a key?'

'No,' replied the grocer, 'but I've got a hammer,' and they hurried up the stairs together, the grocer, still in his trilby, carrying a heavy screwdriver and a hammer. He knocked on the door sharply, and they waited breathless for an answer. There was none.

'I heard a groan before, I promise I did,' Liz whispered.

'Will you pay for this door if I bust it?'

'Yes.'

The hammer made a terrible noise. With three blows he had wrenched out a piece of the frame and the lock came with it. Liz went in first and the grocer followed. It was bitterly cold in the room and dark, but on the bed in the corner they could make out the figure of a man.

'Oh God,' thought Liz, 'if he's dead I don't think I can touch him,' but she went to him and he was alive. Drawing the curtains, she knelt beside the bed.

'I'll call you if I need you, thank you,' she said without looking back, and the grocer nodded and went downstairs.

'Alec, what is it, what's making you ill? What is it, Alec?'

Leamas moved his head on the pillow. His sunken eyes were closed. The dark beard stood out against the pallor of his face.

'Alec, you must tell me, please, Alec.' She was holding one of his hands in hers. The tears were running down her cheeks. Desperately she wondered what to do; then, getting up, she ran to the tiny kitchen and put on a kettle. She wasn't quite clear what she would make, but it comforted her to do something. Leaving the kettle on the gas she picked up her handbag, took Leamas' key from the bedside table and ran downstairs, down the four flights into the street, and crossed the road to Mr Sleaman, the Chemist. She bought some calvesfoot jelly, some essence of beef and a bottle of aspirin. She got to the door, then went back and bought a packet of rusks. Altogether it cost her sixteen shillings, which left four shillings in her handbag and eleven pounds in her post office book, but she couldn't draw any of that till tomorrow. By the time she returned to his flat the kettle was just boiling.

She made the beef tea like her mother used to, in a glass with a teaspoon in to stop it cracking, and all the time she glanced towards him, as if she were afraid he was dead.

She had to prop him up to make him drink the tea. He only had one pillow and there were no cushions in the room, so taking his overcoat down from the back of the door she made a bundle of it and arranged it behind the pillow. It frightened her to touch him, he was drenched in sweat, so that his short grey hair was damp and slippery. Putting the cup beside the bed she held his head with one hand, and fed him the tea with the other. After he had taken a few spoonfuls, she crushed two aspirin and gave them to him in the spoon. She talked to him as if he were a child, sitting on the edge of the bed looking at him, sometimes letting her fingers run over his head and face, whispering his name over and over again, 'Alec, Alec.'

Gradually his breathing became more regular, his body more relaxed as he drifted from the taut pain of fever to the calm of sleep; Liz, watching him, sensed that the worst was over. Suddenly she realised it was almost dark.

Then she felt ashamed, because she knew she should have cleaned and tidied. Jumping up, she fetched the carpet sweeper, and a duster from the kitchen and set to work with feverish energy. She found a clean teacloth and spread it neatly on the bedside table and she washed up the odd cups and saucers which lay around the kitchen. When everything was done she looked at her watch and it was half past eight. She put the kettle on and went back to the bed. Leamas was looking at her.

'Alec, don't be cross, please don't,' she said. 'I'll go, I promise I will, but let me make you a proper meal. You're ill, you can't go on like this, you're . . . oh, Alec,' and she broke down and wept, holding both hands over her face, the tears running between her fingers like the tears of a child. He let her cry, watching her with his brown eyes, his hands holding the sheet.

She helped him wash and shave and she found some clean bed-clothes. She gave him some calvesfoot jelly, and some breast of chicken from the jar she'd bought at Mr Sleaman's. Sitting on the bed she watched him eat, and she thought she had never been so happy before.

Soon he fell asleep, and she drew the blanket over his shoulders and went to the window. Parting the threadbare curtains, she raised the sash and looked out. Two other windows in the courtyard were lit. In one she could see the flickering blue shadow of a television screen, the figures round it held motionless in its spell; in the other a woman, quite young, was arranging curlers in her hair. Liz wanted to weep at the crabbed delusion of their dreams.

She fell asleep in the armchair and did not wake until it was nearly light, feeling stiff and cold. She went to the bed: Leamas stirred as she looked at him and she touched his lips with the tip of her finger. He did not open his eyes but gently took her arm and drew her down on to the bed and suddenly she wanted him terribly, and nothing mattered, and she kissed him again and again and when she looked at him he seemed to be smiling.

She came every day for six days. He never spoke to her much and once, when she asked him if he loved her, he said he didn't believe in fairy tales. She would lie on the bed, her head against his chest, and sometimes he would put his thick fingers in her hair, holding it quite tight, and Liz laughed and said it hurt. On the Friday evening she found him dressed but not shaved and she wondered why he hadn't shaved. For some imperceptible reason she was alarmed. Little things were missing from the room—his clock and the cheap portable wireless that had been on the table. She wanted to ask and did not dare. She had bought some eggs and ham and she cooked them for their supper while Leamas sat on the bed and smoked one cigarette after another. When it was ready he went to the kitchen and came back with a bottle of red wine.

He hardly spoke at supper, and she watched him, her fear growing until she could bear it no more and she cried out suddenly:'
'Alec . . . oh, Alec . . . what is it? Is it good-bye?'
He got up from the table, took her hands, and kissed her in a way he'd never done before and spoke to her softly for a long time, told her things she only dimly understood, only half heard because all the

time she knew it was the end and nothing mattered any more.

'Good-bye, Liz,' he said. 'Good-bye,' and then: 'Don't follow me. Not again.'

Liz nodded and muttered: 'Like we said.' She was thankful for the biting cold of the street and for the dark which hid her tears.

It was the next morning, the Saturday, that Leamas asked at the grocer's for credit. He did it without much artistry, in a way not calculated to ensure him success. He ordered half a dozen items—they didn't come to more than a pound—and when they had been wrapped and put into the carrier bag he said:

'You'd better send me that account.'

The grocer smiled a difficult smile and said:

'I'm afraid I can't do that'; the 'Sir' was definitely missing.

'Why the hell not?' asked Leamas, and the queue behind him stirred uneasily.

'Don't know you,' replied the grocer.

'Don't be bloody silly,' said Leamas, 'I've been coming here for four months.' The grocer coloured.

'We always ask for a banker's reference before giving credit,' he said, and Leamas lost his temper.

'Don't talk bloody cock,' he shouted; 'Half your customers have never seen the inside of a bank and never bloody well will.' This was heresy beyond bearing, since it was true.

'I don't know you,' the grocer repeated thickly, 'and I don't like you. Now get out of my shop.' And he tried to recover the parcel which unfortunately Leamas was already holding. Opinions later differed as to what happened next. Some said the grocer, in trying to recover the bag, pushed Leamas; others say he did not. Whether he did or not, Leamas hit him, most people think twice, without disengaging his right hand, which still held the carrier bag. He seemed to deliver the blow not with the fist but with the side of the left hand, and then, as part of the same phenomenally rapid movement, with the left elbow; and the grocer fell straight over and lay as still as a rock. It was said in court later, and not contested by the defence, that the grocer had two injuries—a fractured cheek bone from the first blow and a dislocated jaw from the second. The coverage in the daily press was adequate, but not over-elaborate.

Chapter Six

Contact

At night he lay on his bunk listening to the sounds of the prisoners. There was a boy who sobbed and an old lag who sang 'On Ilkley Moor bar t'at' beating out the time on his food tin. There was a warder who shouted, 'Shut up, George, you miserable sod', after each verse, but no one took any notice. There was an Irishman who sang songs about the IRA, though the others said he was in for rape.

Leamas took as much exercise as he could during the day in the hope that he would sleep at night; but it was no good. At night you knew you were in prison: at night there was nothing, no trick of vision or self-delusion which saved you from the nauseating enclosure of the cell. You could not keep out the taste of prison, the smell of prison uniform, the stench of prison sanitation heavily disinfected, the noises of captive men. It was then, at night, that the indignity of captivity became urgently insufferable, it was then that Leamas longed to walk in the friendly sunshine of a London park. It was then that he hated the grotesque steel cage that held him, had to force back the urge to fall upon the bars with his bare fists, to split the skulls of his gaolers and burst into the free, free space of London. Sometimes he thought of Liz. He would direct his mind towards her briefly like the shutter of a camera, recall for a moment the soft-hard touch of her long body, then put her from his memory. Leamas was not a man accustomed to living on dreams.

He was contemptuous of his cell mates, and they hated him. They hated him because he succeeded in being what each in his heart longed to be: a mystery. He preserved from collectivisation some discernible part of his personality; he could not be drawn at moments of sentiment to talk of his girl, his family or his children. They knew nothing of Leamas; they waited, but he did not come to them. New prisoners are largely of two kinds—there are those who for shame, fear or shock wait in fascinated horror to be initiated into the lore of prison life, and there are those who trade on their wretched novelty in order to endear themselves to the community. Leamas did neither of these things. He seemed pleased to despise them all, and they hated him because, like the world outside, he did not need them. After about ten days they had had enough. The great had had no homage, the small had had no comfort, so they crowded him in the dinner queue. Crowding is a prison ritual akin to the eighteenth-century practice of jostling. It has the virtue of an apparent accident, in which the prisoner's mess tin is upturned, and its contents spilt on his uniform. Leamas was barged from one side, while from the other an obliging hand descended on his forearm, and the thing was done. Leamas said nothing, looking thoughtfully at the two men on either side of him, and accepted in silence the filthy rebuke of a warder who knew quite well what had happened.

Four days later, while working with a hoe on the prison flower-bed, he seemed to stumble. He was holding the hoe with both hands across his body, the end of the handle protruding about six inches from his right fist. As he strove to recover his balance the prisoner to his right doubled up with a grunt of agony, his arms across his stomach. There was no more crowding after that.

Perhaps the strangest thing of all about prison was the brown paper parcel when he left. In a ridiculous way it reminded him of the marriage service—with this ring I thee wed, with this paper parcel I return thee to society. They handed it to him and made him sign for it, and it contained all he had in the world. There was nothing else. Leamas felt it the most dehumanising moment of the three months, and he determined to throw the parcel away as soon as he got outside.

He seemed a quiet prisoner. There had been no complaints against him. The Governor, who was vaguely interested in his case, secretly put the whole thing down to the Irish blood he swore he could detect in Leamas.

'What are you going to do,' he asked, 'when you leave here?' Leamas replied, without a ghost of a smile, that he thought he would make a new start, and the Governor said that was an excellent thing to do.

'What about your family?' he asked. 'Couldn't you make it up with your wife?'

'I'll try,' Leamas had replied indifferently; 'but she's remarried.'

The probation officer wanted Leamas to become a male nurse at a mental home in Buckinghamshire and Leamas agreed to apply. He even took down the address and noted the train times from Marylebone.

'The rail's electrified as far as Great Missenden, now,' the probation officer added, and Leamas said that would be a help. So they gave him the parcel and he left. He took a bus to Marble Arch and walked. He had a bit of money in his pocket and he intended to give himself a decent meal. He thought he would walk through Hyde Park to Piccadilly, then through Green Park and St James's Park to Parliament Square, then wander down Whitehall to the Strand where he could go to the big café near Charing Cross station and get a reasonable steak for six shillings.

London was beautiful that day. Spring was late and the parks were filled with crocuses and daffodils. A cool, cleaning wind was blowing from the south; he could have walked all day. But he still had the parcel and he had to get rid of it. The litter baskets were too small; he'd look absurd trying to push his parcel into one of those. He supposed there were one or two things he ought to take out–his wretched pieces of paper–insurance card, driving licence and his E.93 (whatever that was) in a buff OHMS envelope, but suddenly he couldn't be bothered. He sat down on a bench and put the parcel beside him, not too close, and moved a little away from it. After a couple of minutes he walked back towards the footpath, leaving the parcel where it lay. He had just reached the footpath when he heard a shout; he turned, a little sharply perhaps, and saw a man in an army macintosh beckoning to him, holding the brown paper parcel in the other hand.

Leamas had his hands in his pockets and he left them there, and stood, looking back over his shoulder at the man in the macintosh. The man hesitated, evidently expecting Leamas to come to him or give some sign of interest, but Leamas gave none. Instead, he shrugged and continued along the footpath. He heard another shout and ignored it, and he knew the man was coming after him. He heard the footsteps on the gravel, half running, approaching rapidly, and then a voice, a little breathless, a little aggrieved:

'Here, you–I say!' and then he had drawn level, so that Leamas stopped, turned and looked at him.

'Yes?'

'This is your parcel, isn't it? You left it on the seat. Why didn't you stop when I called you?'

Tall, with rather curly brown hair; orange tie and pale green shirt; a little bit petulant, a little bit of a pansy, thought Leamas. Could be a schoolmaster, ex L.S.E. and runs a suburban drama club. Weak-eyed.

'You can put it back,' said Leamas. 'I don't want it.'

The man coloured:

'You can't just leave it there,' he said, 'it's litter.'

'I bloody well can,' Leamas replied. 'Somebody will find a use for it.' He was going to move on, but the stranger was still standing in front of him, holding the parcel in both arms as if it were a baby. 'Get out of the light,' said Leamas. 'Do you mind?'

'Look here,' said the stranger, and his voice had risen a key, 'I was trying to do you a favour; why do you have to be so damned rude?'

'If you're so anxious to do me a favour,' Leamas replied, 'why have you been following me for the last half-hour?'

He's pretty good, thought Leamas. He hasn't flinched, but he must be shaken rigid.

'I thought you were somebody I once knew in Berlin, if you must know.'

'So you followed me for half an hour?'

Leamas' voice was heavy with sarcasm, his brown eyes never left the other's face.

'Nothing like half an hour. I caught sight of you in Marble Arch and I thought you were Alec Leamas, a man I borrowed some money from. I used to be in the B.B.C. in Berlin and there was this man I borrowed some money from. I've had a conscience about it ever since and that's why I followed you. I wanted to be sure.'

Leamas went on looking at him, not speaking, and thought he wasn't all that good but he was good enough. His story was scarcely plausible–that didn't matter. The point was that he'd produced a new one and stuck to it after Leamas had wrecked what promised to be a classic approach.

'I'm Leamas,' he said at last, 'who the hell are you?'

He said his name was Ashe, with an 'E' he added quickly, and Leamas knew he was lying. He pretended not to be quite sure that Leamas really was Leamas, so over lunch they opened the parcel and looked at the National Insurance card like, thought Leamas, a couple of cissies looking at a dirty post card. Ashe ordered lunch with just a fraction too little regard for expense, and they drank some Frankenwein to remind them of the old days. Leamas began by insisting he couldn't remember Ashe, and Ashe said he was surprised. He said it in the sort of tone that suggested he was hurt. They met at a party, he said, which Derek Williams gave in his flat off the Kudamm (he got that right) and all the press boys had been there; surely Alec remembered that? No, Leamas did not. Well, surely he remembered Derek Williams from the *Observer*, that *nice* man who gave such lovely pizza parties? Leamas had a lousy memory for names, after all they were talking about fifty-four; a lot of water had flowed under the bridge since then. . . . Ashe remembered (his christian name was William, by the by, most people called him Bill). Ashe remembered *vividly*. They'd been drinking stingers, brandy and crême de menthe, and were all rather tiddly, and Derek had provided some really gorgeous girls, half the cabaret from the Malkasten, *surely* Alec remembered now? Leamas thought it was probably coming back to him, if Bill would go on a bit.

Bill did go on, *ad lib.* no doubt, but he did it well, playing up the sex side a little, how they'd finished up in a night club with three of these girls; Alec, a chap from the political adviser's office and Bill, and Bill had been so embarrassed because he hadn't any money on him and Alec had paid, and Bill had wanted to take a girl home and

Alec had lent him another tenner. . . .

'Christ,' said Leamas, 'I remember now, of course I do.'

'I *knew* you would,' said Ashe happily, nodding at Leamas over his glass, 'look, do let's have the other half, this is *such* fun.'

Ashe was typical of that strata of mankind which conducts its human relationships according to a principle of challenge and response. Where there was softness, he would advance; where he found resistance, retreat. Having himself no particular opinions or tastes he relied upon whatever conformed with those of his companion. He was as ready to drink tea at Fortnum's as beer at the Prospect of Whitby; he would listen to military music in St James's Park or jazz in a Compton Street cellar; his voice would tremble with sympathy when he spoke of Sharpeville, or with indignation at the growth of Britain's coloured population. To Leamas this observably passive role was repellent; it brought out the bully in him, so that he would lead the other gently into a position where he was committed, and then himself withdraw, so that Ashe was constantly scampering back from some cul-de-sac into which Leamas had enticed him. There were moments that afternoon when Leamas was so brazenly perverse that Ashe would have been justified in terminating their conversation—not least since he was paying for it; but he did not. The little sad man with spectacles who sat alone at the neighbouring table, deep in a book on the manufacture of ball bearings, might have deduced, had he been listening, that Leamas was indulging a sadistic nature—or perhaps (if he had been a man of particular subtlety) that Leamas was proving to his own satisfaction that only a man with a strong ulterior motive would put up with that kind of treatment.

It was nearly four o'clock before they ordered the bill and Leamas tried to insist on paying his half. Ashe wouldn't hear of it, paid the bill and took out his cheque book in order to settle his debt to Leamas.

'Twenty of the best,' he said, and filled in the date on the cheque form.

Then he looked up at Leamas, all wide-eyed and accommodating.

'I say, a cheque is all right by you, isn't it?'

Colouring a little, Leamas replied:

'I haven't got a bank at the moment—only just back from abroad, something I've got to fix up. Better give me a cheque and I'll cash it at your bank.'

'My dear chap, I wouldn't *dream* of it! You'd have to go to Rotherhithe to cash this one!' Leamas shrugged and Ashe laughed, and they agreed to meet at the same place on the following day, at one o'clock, when Ashe would have the money in cash.

Ashe took a cab at the corner of Compton Street, and Leamas waved at it until it was out of sight. When it was gone, he looked at his watch. It was four o'clock. He guessed he was still being followed, so he walked down to Fleet Street and had a cup of coffee in the Black and White. He looked at bookshops, read the evening papers displayed in the show windows of newspaper offices, and then quite suddenly, as if the thought had occurred to him at the last minute, he jumped on a bus. The bus went to Ludgate Hill, where it was held up in a traffic jam near a tube station; he dismounted and caught a tube. He bought a sixpenny ticket, stood in the end carriage and alighted at the next station. He caught another train to Euston, trekked back to Charing Cross. It was nine o'clock when he reached the station and it had turned rather cold. There was a van waiting in the forecourt; the driver was fast asleep. Leamas glanced at the number, went over and called through the window:

'Are you from Clements?' The driver woke up with a start and asked:

'Mr Thomas?'

'No,' replied Leamas. 'Thomas couldn't come. I'm Amies from Hounslow.'

'Hop in, Mr Amies,' the driver replied, and opened the door. They drove west, towards the King's Road. The driver knew the way.

Control opened the door.

'George Smiley's out,' he said. 'I've borrowed his house. Come in.' Not until Leamas was inside and the front door closed, did Control put on the hall light.

'I was followed till lunch time,' Leamas said. They went into the little drawing-room. There were books everywhere. It was a pretty room; tall, with eighteenth-century mouldings, long windows and a good fireplace.

'They picked me up this morning. A man called Ashe.' He lit a cigarette. 'A pansy. We're meeting again tomorrow.'

Control listened carefully to Leamas' story, stage by stage, from the day he hit Ford, the grocer, to his encounter that morning with Ashe.

'How did you find prison?' Control enquired. He might have been asking whether Leamas had enjoyed his holiday. 'I am sorry we couldn't improve conditions for you, provide little extra comforts, but that would never have done.'

'Of course not.'

'One must be consistent. At every turn one must be consistent. Besides, it would be wrong to break the spell. I understand you were ill. I am sorry. What was the trouble?'

'Just fever.'

'How long were you in bed?'

'About ten days.'

'How very distressing; and nobody to look after you, of course.'

There was a very long silence.

'You know she's in the Party, don't you?' Control asked quietly.

'Yes,' Leamas replied. Another silence. 'I don't want her brought into this.'

'Why should she be?' Control asked sharply and for a moment, just for a moment, Leamas thought he had penetrated the veneer of academic detachment. 'Who suggested she should be?'

'No one,' Leamas replied, 'I'm just making the point. I know how these things go—all offensive operations. They have by-products, take sudden turns in unexpected directions. You think you've caught one fish and you find you've caught another. I want her kept clear of it.'

'Oh, quite, quite.'

'Who's that man in the Labour Exchange—Pitt? Wasn't he in the Circus during the war?'

'I know no one of that name. Pitt, did you say?'

'Yes.'

'No, not a name to me. In the Labour Exchange?'

'Oh, for God's sake,' Leamas muttered audibly.

'I'm sorry,' said Control, getting up, 'I'm neglecting my duties as deputy host. Would you care for a drink?'

'No. I want to get away tonight, Control. Go down to the country and get some exercise. Is the House open?'

'I've arranged a car,' he said. 'What time do you see Ashe tomorrow—one o'clock?'

'Yes.'

'I'll ring Haldane and tell him you want some squash. You'd better see a doctor, too. About that fever.'

'I don't need a doctor.'

'Just as you like.'

Control gave himself a whisky and began looking idly at the books in Smiley's shelf.

'Why isn't Smiley here?' Leamas asked.

'He doesn't like the operation,' Control replied indifferently. 'He finds it distasteful. He sees the necessity but he wants no part in it. His fever,' Control added with a whimsical smile, 'is recurrent.'

'He didn't exactly receive me with open arms.'

'Quite. He wants no part in it. But he told you about Mundt; gave you the background?'

'Yes.'

'Mundt is a very *hard* man,' Control reflected. 'We should never forget that. And a good intelligence officer.'

'Does Smiley know the reason for the operation. The special interest?'

Control nodded and took a sip of whisky.

'And he still doesn't like it?'

'It isn't a question of moralities. He is like the surgeon who has grown tired of blood. He is content that others should operate.'

'Tell me,' Leamas continued, 'how are you so certain this will get us where we want? How do you know the East Germans are on to it—not the Czechs or the Russians?'

'Rest assured,' Control said a little pompously, 'that that has been taken care of.'

As they got to the door, Control put his hand lightly on Leamas' shoulder.

'This is your last job,' he said. 'Then you can come in from the cold. About that girl—do you want anything done about her, money or anything?'

'When it's over. I'll take care of it myself then.'

'Quite. It would be very insecure to do anything now.'

'I just want her left alone,' Leamas repeated with emphasis. 'I just don't want her to be messed about. I don't want her to have a file or anything. I want her forgotten.'

He nodded to Control and slipped out into the night air. Into the cold.

Chapter Seven

Kiever

On the following day Leamas arrived twenty minutes late for his lunch with Ashe, and smelt of whisky. Ashe's pleasure on catching sight of Leamas was, however, undiminished. He claimed that he had himself only that moment arrived, he'd been a little late getting to the bank. He handed Leamas an envelope.

'Singles,' said Ashe. 'I hope that's all right.'

'Thanks,' Leamas replied, 'let's have a drink.' He hadn't shaved and his collar was filthy. He called the waiter and ordered drinks, a large whisky for himself and a pink gin for Ashe. When the drinks came Leamas' hand trembled as he poured the soda into the glass, almost slopping it over the side.

They lunched well, with a lot of drink, and Ashe made most of the running. As Leamas had expected he first talked about himself, an old trick but not a bad one.

'To be quite frank, I've got on to rather a good thing recently,' said Ashe; 'free-lancing English features for the foreign press. After Berlin I made rather a mess of things at first—the Corporation wouldn't renew the contract and I took a job running a dreary toffee-shop weekly about hobbies for the over-sixties. Can you *imagine* anything more frightful? That went under in the first printing strike–I can't tell you how relieved I was. Then I went to live with my mama in Cheltenham for a time, she runs an antique shop, does very nicely thank you, as a matter of fact. Then I got a letter from an old friend, Sam Kiever his name is actually, who was starting up a new agency for small features on English life specially slanted for foreign papers. You know the sort of thing–six hundred words on Morris dancing. Sam had a new gimmick, though; he sold the stuff already translated and do you know, it makes a hell of a difference. One always imagines anyone can pay a translator or do it themselves, but if you're looking for a half column in-fill for your foreign features you don't *want* to waste time and money on translation. Sam's gambit was to get in touch with the editors direct–he traipsed round Europe like a gypsy, poor thing, but it's paid hands *down.*'

Ashe paused, waiting for Leamas to accept the invitation to speak about himself, but Leamas ignored it. He just nodded dully and said: 'Bloody good.' Ashe had wanted to order wine, but Leamas said he'd stick to whisky and by the time the coffee came he'd had four large ones. He seemed to be in bad shape; he had the drunkard's habit of ducking his mouth towards the rim of his glass just before he drank, as if his hand might fail him and the drink escape.

Ashe fell silent for a moment.

'You don't know Sam, do you?' he asked.

'Sam?'

A note of irritation entered Ashe's voice.

'Sam Kiever, my boss. The chap I was telling you about.'

'Was he in Berlin too?'

'No. He knows Germany well, but he's never lived in Berlin. He did a bit of devilling in Bonn, free-lance stuff. You might have met him. He's a dear.'

'Don't think so.' A pause.

'What do you do these days, old chap?' asked Ashe.

Leamas shrugged.

'I'm on the shelf,' he replied, and grinned a little stupidly. 'Out of the bag and on the shelf.'

'I forget what were you doing in Berlin? Weren't you one of the mysterious cold warriors?' My God, thought Leamas, you're stepping things up a bit.

Leamas hesitated, then coloured and said savagely, 'Office boy for the bloody Yanks, like the rest of us.'

'You know,' said Ashe, as if he had been turning the idea over for some time, 'you ought to meet Sam. You'd like him,' and then, all of a bother, 'I say Alec–I don't even know where to get hold of you!'

'You can't,' Leamas replied listlessly.

'I don't get you, old chap. Where are you staying?'

'Around the place. Roughing it a bit. I haven't got a job. Bastards wouldn't give me a proper pension.'

Ashe looked horrified.

'But, Alec, that's awful; why didn't you *tell* me? Look, why not come and stay at my place? It's only tiny but there's room for one more if you don't mind a camp bed. You can't just live in the trees, my dear chap!'

'I'm all right for a bit,' Leamas replied, tapping at the pocket which contained the envelope. 'I'm going to get a job,' he nodded with determination; 'get one in a week or so. Then I'll be all right.'

'What sort of job?'

'Oh, I don't know. Anything.'

'But you can't just throw yourself away. Alec! You speak German like a native, I remember you do. There must be all sorts of things you can do!'

'I've done all sorts of things. Selling encyclopaedias for some bloody American firm, sorting books in a psychic library, punching work tickets in a stinking glue factory. What the hell *can* I do?' He wasn't looking at Ashe but at the table before him, his agitated lips moving quickly. Ashe responded to his animation, leaning forward across the table, speaking with emphasis, almost triumph.

'But Alec, you need *contacts*, don't you see? I know what it's like, I've been on the breadline myself. That's when you need to *know* people. I don't know what you were doing in Berlin, I don't want to know, but it wasn't the sort of job where you could meet people who matter, was it? If I hadn't met Sam at Poznan five years ago, I'd *still* be on the breadline. Look, Alec, come and stay with me for a week or so. We'll ask Sam round and perhaps one or two of the old press boys from Berlin if any of them are in town.'

'But I can't write,' said Leamas. 'I couldn't write a bloody thing.' Ashe had his hand on Leamas' arm: 'Now don't fuss,' he said soothingly; 'let's just take things one at a time. Where are your bits and pieces?'

'My what?'

'Your things: clothes, baggage and what not?'

'I haven't got any. I've sold what I had—except the parcel.'

'What parcel?'

'The brown paper parcel you picked up in the park. The one I was trying to throw away.'

Ashe had a flat in Dolphin Square. It was just what Leamas had expected—small and anonymous with a few hastily assembled curios from Germany: beer mugs, a peasant's pipe and a few pieces of second-rate Nymphenburg.

'I spend the weekends with my mother in Cheltenham,' he said. 'I just use this place mid week. It's pretty handy,' he added deprecatingly. They fixed the camp bed up in the tiny drawing-room. It was about four-thirty.

'How long have you been here?' asked Leamas.

'Oh—about a year or more.'

'Find it easily?'

'They come and go, you know, these flats. You put your name down and one day they ring you up and tell you you've made it.'

Ashe made tea and they drank it, Leamas sullen, like a man not used to comfort. Even Ashe seemed a little piano. After tea Ashe said: 'I'll go out and do a spot of shopping before the shops close, then we'll decide what to do about everything. I might give Sam a tinkle later this evening—I think the sooner you two get together the better. Why don't you get some sleep—you look all in.'

Leamas nodded. 'It's bloody good of you—' he made an awkward gesture with his hand, '—all this.' Ashe gave him a pat on the shoulder, picked up his army macintosh and left.

As soon as Leamas reckoned Ashe was safely out of the building, he put the front door of the flat carefully on the latch and made his way downstairs to the centre hall where there were two telephone cabins. He dialled a Maida Vale number and asked for Mr Thomas' secretary. Immediately a girl's voice said, 'Mr Thomas' secretary speaking.'

'I'm ringing on behalf of Mr Sam Kiever,' Leamas said, 'he has accepted the invitation and hopes to contact Mr Thomas personally this evening.'

'I'll pass that on to Mr Thomas. Does he know where to get in touch with you?'

'Dolphin Square,' Leamas replied, and gave the address. 'Goodbye.'

After making some enquiries at the reception desk he returned to Ashe's flat, and sat on the camp bed looking at his clasped hands. After a while he lay down. He decided to accept Ashe's advice and get some rest. As he closed his eyes he remembered Liz lying beside him in the flat in Bayswater, and he wondered vaguely what had become of her.

He was woken up by Ashe, accompanied by a small, rather plump man with long, greying hair swept back and a double breasted suit. He spoke with a slight central European accent; German perhaps, it was hard to tell. He said his name was Kiever—Sam Kiever.

They had a gin and tonic, Ashe doing most of the talking. It was just like old times, he said, in Berlin: the boys together and the night their oyster. Kiever said he didn't want to be too late; he had to work tomorrow. They agreed to eat at a Chinese restaurant that Ashe knew of—it was opposite Limehouse police station and you brought your own wine. Oddly enough Ashe had some Burgundy in the kitchen, and they took that with them in the taxi.

Dinner was very good and they drank both bottles of wine. Kiever opened up a little on the second: he'd just come back from a tour of West Germany and France. France was in a hell of a mess, de Gaulle was on the way out and God alone knew what would happen then. With a hundred thousand demoralised *colons* returning from Algeria he reckoned Fascism was on the cards.

'What about Germany?' asked Alec, prompting him.

'It's just a question of whether the Yanks can hold them.' Kiever looked invitingly at Leamas.

'What do you mean?' asked Leamas.

'What I say. Dulles gave them a foreign policy with one hand, Kennedy takes it away with the other. They're getting waspish.'

Leamas nodded abruptly and said, 'Bloody typical Yank.'

'Alec doesn't seem to like our American cousins,' said Ashe, stepping in heavily, and Kiever, with complete disinterest, murmured, 'Oh, really?' Kiever played it, Leamas reflected, very long. Like someone used to horses, he let you come to him. He conveyed to perfection a man who suspected that he was about to be asked a favour, and was not easily won.

After dinner Ashe said, 'I know a place in Wardour Street—you've been there, Sam. They do you all right there. Why don't we summon a barouche and go along?'

'Just a minute,' said Leamas, and there was something in his voice which made Ashe look at him quickly; 'just tell me something will you? Who's paying for this jolly?'

'I am,' said Ashe quickly, 'Sam and I.'

'Have you discussed it?'

'Well—no.'

'Because I haven't got any bloody money; you know that, don't you? None to throw about anyway.'

'Of course, Alec. I've looked after you up till now, haven't I?'

'Yes,' Leamas replied; 'yes, you have.'

He seemed to be going to say something else, and then to change his mind. Ashe looked worried, not offended, and Kiever as inscrutable as before.

Leamas refused to speak in the taxi. Ashe attempted some conciliatory remark and he just shrugged irritably. They arrived at Wardour Street and dismounted, neither Leamas nor Kiever making any attempt to pay for the cab. Ashe led them past a shop window full of 'girlie' magazines, down a narrow alley, at the far end of which shone a tawdry neon sign: 'Pussywillow Club. Members Only.' On either side of the door were photographs of girls, and pinned across each was a thin, hand-printed strip of paper which read, 'Nature Study. Members only.'

Ashe pressed the bell. The door was at once opened by a very large man in a white shirt and black trousers.

'I'm a member,' Ashe said. 'These two gentlemen are with me.'

'See your card?'

Ashe took a buff card from his wallet and handed it over.

'Your guests pay a quid a head temporary membership. Your recommendation, right?' He held out the card and as he did so, Leamas stretched past Ashe and took it. He looked at it for a moment, then handed it back to Ashe.

Taking two pounds from his hip pocket Leamas put them into the waiting hand of the man at the door.

'Two quid,' said Leamas, 'for the guests,' and ignoring the astonished protests of Ashe he guided them through the curtained doorway into the dim hallway of the club. He turned to the doorman.

'Find us a table,' said Leamas, 'and a bottle of Scotch. And see we're left alone.' The doorman hesitated for a moment, decided not to argue, and escorted them downstairs. As they descended they heard the subdued moan of unintelligible music.

They got a table on their own at the back of the room. A two-piece band was playing and girls sat around in twos and threes. Two got up as they came in but the big doorman shook his head.

Ashe glanced at Leamas uneasily while they waited for the whisky. Kiever seemed slightly bored. The waiter brought a bottle and three tumblers and they watched in silence as he poured a little whisky into each glass. Leamas took the bottle from the waiter and added as much again to each. This done, he leant across the table and said to Ashe, 'Now perhaps you'll tell me what the bloody hell's going on?'

'What do you mean?' Ashe sounded uncertain. 'What *do* you mean, Alec?'

'You followed me from prison the day I was released,' he began quietly, 'with some bloody silly story of meeting me in Berlin. You gave me money you didn't owe me. You've bought me expensive meals and you're putting me up in your flat.'

Ashe coloured and said, 'If that's the . . .'

'Don't interrupt,' said Leamas fiercely. 'Just damn' well wait till I've finished, do you mind? Your membership card for this place is made out for someone called Murphy. Is that your name?'

'No, it is not.'

'I suppose a friend called Murphy lent you his membership cárd?'

'No he didn't as a matter of fact. If you must know I come here occasionally to find a girl. I used a phoney name to join the club.'

'Then why,' Leamas persisted ruthlessly, 'is Murphy registered as the tenant of your flat?'

It was Kiever who finally spoke.

'You run along home,' he said to Ashe. 'I'll look after this.'

A girl performed a striptease, a young, drab girl with a dark bruise on her thigh. She had that pitiful, spindly nakedness which is embarrassing because it is not erotic; because it is artless and undesiring. She turned slowly, jerking sporadically with her arms or legs as if she only heard the music in snatches, and all the time she looked at them with the precocious interest of a child in adult company. The tempo of the music increased abruptly, and the girl responded like a dog to the whistle, scampering back and forth. Removing her brassière on the last note, she held it above her head, displaying her meagre body with its three tawdry patches of tinsel hanging from it like old Christmas decorations.

They watched in silence, Leamas and Kiever.

'I suppose you're going to tell me that we've seen better in Berlin,' Leamas suggested at last, and Kiever saw that he was still very angry.

'I expect *you* have,' Kiever replied pleasantly. 'I have often been to Berlin, but I am afraid I dislike night clubs.'

Leamas said nothing.

'I'm no prude, mind, just rational. If I want a woman I know cheaper ways of finding one; if I want to dance I know better places to do it.' Leamas might not have been listening.

'Perhaps you'll tell me why that cissy picked me up,' he suggested. Kiever nodded.

'By all means. I told him to.'

'Why?'

'I am interested in you. I want to make you a proposition, a journalistic proposition.'

There was a pause.

'Journalistic,' Leamas repeated, 'I see.'

'I run an agency, an international feature service. It pays well—very well—for interesting material.'

'Who publishes the material?'

'It pays so well, in fact, that a man with your kind of experience of . . . the international scene, a man with your background, you understand, who provided convincing, factual material, could free himself in a comparatively short time from further financial worry.'

'Who publishes the material, Kiever?' There was a threatening edge to Leamas' voice, and for a moment, just for a moment, a look of apprehension seemed to pass across Kiever's smooth face.

'International clients. I have a correspondent in Paris who disposes of a good deal of my stuff. Often I don't even know who *does* publish. I confess,' he added with a disarming smile, 'that I don't awfully care. They pay and they ask for more. They're the kind of people, you see, Leamas, who don't fuss about awkward details; they pay promptly, and they're happy to pay into foreign banks, for instance, where no one bothers about things like tax.'

Leamas said nothing. He was holding his glass with both hands, staring into it.

Christ, they're rushing their fences. Leamas thought; it's indecent. He remembered some silly musical hall joke–'This is an offer no respectable girl could accept–and besides, I don't know what it's worth.' Tactically, he reflected, they're right to rush it. I'm on my uppers, prison experience still fresh, social resentment strong. I'm an old horse, I don't need breaking in; I don't have to pretend they've offended my honour as an English gentleman. On the other hand they would expect *practical* objections. They would expect him to be afraid; for his Service pursued traitors as the eye of God followed Cain across the desert.

And finally, they would know it was a gamble. They would know that inconsistency in human decision can make nonsense of the best-planned espionage approach; that cheats, liars and criminals may resist every blandishment while respectable gentlemen have been moved to appalling treasons by watery cabbage in a Departmental canteen.

'They'd have to pay a hell of a lot,' Leamas muttered at last. Kiever gave him some more whisky.

'They are offering a down-payment of fifteen thousand pounds. The money is already lodged at the Banque Cantonale in Bern. On production of a suitable identification, with which my clients will provide you, you can draw the money. My clients reserve the right to put questions to you over the period of one year on payment of another five thousand pounds. They will assist you with any . . . resettlement problems that may arise.'

'How soon do you want an answer?'

'Now. You are not expected to commit all your reminiscences to paper. You will meet my client and he will arrange to have the material . . . ghost written.'

'Where am I supposed to meet him?'

'We felt for everybody's sake it would be simplest to meet outside the United Kingdom. My client suggested Holland.'

'I haven't got my passport,' Leamas said dully.

'I took the liberty of obtaining one for you,' Kiever replied suavely; nothing in his voice or his manner indicated that he had done other than negotiate an adequate business arrangement. 'We're flying to the Hague tomorrow morning at nine forty-five. Shall we go back to my flat and discuss any other details?'

Kiever paid and they took a taxi to a rather good address not far from St James's Park.

Kiever's flat was luxurious and expensive, but its contents somehow gave the impression of having been hastily assembled. It is said there are shops in London which will sell you bound books by the yard, and interior decorators who will harmonise the colour scheme of the walls with that of a painting. Leamas, who was not particularly receptive to such subtleties, found it hard to remember that he was in a private flat and not an hotel. As Kiever showed him to his room (which looked on to a dingy inner courtyard and not on to the street) Leamas asked him:

'How long have you been here?'

'Oh, not long,' Kiever replied lightly, 'a few months, not more.'

'Must cost a packet. Still, I suppose you're worth it.'

'Thanks.'

There was a bottle of Scotch in his room and a syphon of soda on a silver-plated tray. A curtained doorway at the further end of the room led to a bathroom and lavatory.

'Quite a little love nest. All paid for by the great Worker State?'

'Shut up,' said Kiever savagely, and added, 'If you want me, there's an internal telephone to my room. I shall be awake.'

'I think I can manage my buttons now,' Leamas retorted.

'Then good night,' said Kiever shortly, and left the room. He's on edge, too, thought Leamas.

Leamas was woken by the telephone at his bedside. It was Kiever.

'It's six o'clock,' he said, 'breakfast at half past.'

'All right,' Leamas replied, and rang off. He had a headache.

Kiever must have telephoned for a taxi, because at seven o'clock the door bell rang and Kiever asked, 'Got everything?'

'I've no luggage,' Leamas replied, 'except a toothbrush and a razor.'

'That is taken care of. Are you ready otherwise?'

Leamas shrugged. 'I suppose so. Have you got any cigarettes?'

'No,' Kiever replied, 'but you can get some on the plane. You'd better look through this,' he added, and handed Leamas a British passport. It was made out in his name with his own photograph mounted in it, embossed by the deep press Foreign Office seal running across the corner. It was neither old nor new; it described Leamas as a clerk, and gave his status as single. Holding it in his hand for the first time, Leamas was a little nervous. It was like getting married: whatever happened, things would never be the same again.

'What about money?' Leamas asked.

'You won't need any. It's on the firm.'

Chapter Eight

Le Mirage

It was cold that morning; the light mist was damp and grey, pricking the skin. The airport reminded Leamas of the war: machines, half hidden in the fog, waiting patiently for their masters; the resonant voices and their echoes, the sudden shout and the incongruous clip of a girl's heels on a stone floor; the roar of an engine that might have been at your elbow. Everywhere that air of conspiracy which generates among people who have been up since dawn–of superiority almost, derived from the common experience of having seen the night disappear and the morning come. The staff had that look which is informed by the mystery of dawn and animated by the cold, and they treated the passengers and their baggage with the remoteness of men returned from the front: ordinary mortals had nothing for them that morning.

Kiever had provided Leamas with luggage. It was a nice detail: Leamas admired it. Passengers without luggage attracted attention, and it was not part of Kiever's plan to do that. They checked in at the airline desk and followed the signs to passport control. There was a ludicrous moment when they lost the way and Kiever was rude to a porter. Leamas supposed Kiever was worried about the passport–he needn't be, thought Leamas, there's nothing wrong with it.

The passport officer was a youngish, little man with an Intelligence Corps tie and some mysterious badge in his lapel. He had a ginger moustache, and a North Country accent which was his life's enemy.

'Going to be away for a long time, Sir?' he asked Leamas.

'A couple of weeks,' Leamas replied.

'You'll want to watch it, Sir. Your passport's due for renewal on the 31st.'

'I know,' said Leamas.

They walked side by side into the passengers' waiting room. On the way Leamas said: 'You're a suspicious sod, aren't you, Kiever,' and the other laughed quietly.

'Can't have you on the loose, can we? Not part of the contract,' he replied.

They still had twenty minutes to wait. They sat down at a table and ordered coffee. 'And take these things away,' Kiever added to the waiter, indicating the used cups, saucers and ash-trays, on the table. 'There's a trolley coming round,' the waiter replied.

'Take them,' Kiever repeated, angry again. 'It's disgusting, leaving dirty crockery there like that.'

The waiter just turned and walked away. He didn't go near the service counter and he didn't order their coffee. Kiever was white, ill with anger. 'For Christ's sake,' Leamas muttered, 'let it go. Life's too short.'

'Cheeky bastard, that's what he is,' said Kiever.

'All right, all right, make a scene; you've chosen a good moment. They'll never forget us here.'

The formalities at the airport at The Hague provided no problem. Kiever seemed to have recovered from his anxieties. He became jaunty and talkative as they walked the short distance between the plane and the Customs sheds. The young Dutch officer gave a perfunctory glance at their luggage and passports and announced in awkward throaty English: 'I hope you have a pleasant stay in the Netherlands.'

'Thanks,' said Kiever, almost too gratefully, 'thanks very much.'

They walked from the Customs shed along the corridor to the reception hall on the other side of the airport buildings. Kiever led the way to the main exit, between the little groups of travellers staring vaguely at kiosk displays of scent, cameras and fruit. As they pushed their way through the revolving glass door, Leamas looked back. Standing at the newspaper kiosk, deep in a copy of the *Continental Daily Mail*, stood a small, frog-like figure in glasses, an earnest, worried little man. He looked like a civil servant. Something like that.

A car was waiting for them in the car park, a Volkswagen with a Dutch registration, driven by a woman who ignored them. She drove slowly, always stopping if the lights were amber, and Leamas guessed she had been briefed to drive that way and that they were being followed by another car. He watched the off-side wing mirror, trying to recognise the car but without success. Once he saw a black Peugeot with a CD number, but when they turned the corner there was only a furniture van behind them. He knew The Hague quite well from the war, and he tried to work out where they were heading. He guessed they were travelling north-west towards Scheveningen. Soon they had left the suburbs behind them and were approaching a colony of villas bordering the dunes along the sea front.

Here they stopped. The woman got out, leaving them in the car, and rang the front door bell of a small cream coloured bungalow which stood at the near end of the row. A wrought iron sign hung on the porch with the words 'Le Mirage' in pale blue Gothic script. There was a notice in the window which proclaimed that all the rooms were taken.

The door was opened by a kindly, plump woman who looked past the driver towards the car. Her eyes still on the car, she came down the drive towards them, smiling with pleasure. She reminded Leamas of an old aunt he once had who beat him for wasting string.

'How nice that you have come,' she declared; 'we are so *pleased* that you have come!' They followed her into the bungalow, Kiever leading the way. The driver got back into the car. Leamas glanced down the road which they had just travelled; three hundred yards away a black car, a Fiat perhaps, or a Peugeot, had parked. A man in a raincoat was getting out.

Once in the hall the woman shook Leamas warmly by the hand. 'Welcome, welcome to Le Mirage. Did you have a good journey?'

'Fine,' Leamas replied.

'Did you fly or come by sea?'

'We flew,' Kiever said; 'a very smooth flight.' He might have owned the airline.

'I'll make your lunch,' she declared; 'a special lunch. I'll make you something specially good. What shall I bring you?'

'Oh, for God's sake,' said Leamas under his breath, and the door bell rang. The woman went quickly into the kitchen; Kiever opened the front door.

He was wearing a macintosh with leather buttons. He was about Leamas' height, but older. Leamas put him at about fifty-five. His face had a hard, grey hue and sharp furrows; he might have been a soldier. He held out his hand.

'My name is Peters,' he said. The fingers were slim and polished. 'Did you have a good journey?'

'Yes,' said Kiever quickly, 'quite uneventful.'

'Mr Leamas and I have a lot to discuss; I do not think we need to keep you, Sam. You could take the Volkswagen back to town.'

Kiever smiled. Leamas saw the relief in his smile.

'Good-bye, Leamas,' said Kiever, his voice jocular; 'good luck, old man.'

Leamas nodded, ignoring Kiever's hand.

'Good-bye,' Kiever repeated and let himself quietly out of the front door.

Leamas followed Peters into a back room. Heavy lace curtains hung on the window, ornately fringed and draped. The window-sill was covered with potted plants; great cacti, tobacco plant and some curious tree with wide, rubbery leaves. The furniture was heavy, pseudo-antique. In the centre of the room was a table with two carved chairs. The table was covered with a rust-coloured counter-pane more like a carpet; on it before each chair was a pad of paper and a pencil. On a sideboard there was whisky and soda. Peters went over to it and mixed them both a drink.

'Look,' said Leamas suddenly, 'from now on I can do without the goodwill; do you follow me? We both know what we're about; both professionals. You've got a paid defector—good luck to you. For Christ's sake don't pretend you've fallen in love with me.' He sounded on edge, uncertain of himself.

Peters nodded, 'Kiever told me you were a proud man,' he observed dispassionately. Then he added without smiling, 'After all, why else does a man attack tradesmen?'

Leamas guessed he was Russian, but he wasn't sure. His English was nearly perfect, he had the ease and habits of a man long used to civilised comforts.

They sat at the table.

'Kiever told you what I am going to pay you?' Peters enquired.

'Yes. Fifteen thousand pounds to be drawn on a Bern bank.'

'Yes.'

'He said you might have follow-up questions during the next year,' said Leamas, 'you would pay another five thousand if I kept myself available.'

Peters nodded.

'I don't accept that condition,' Leamas continued. 'You know as well as I do it wouldn't work. I want to draw the fifteen thousand and get clear. Your people have a rough way with defected agents; so have mine. I'm not going to sit on my fanny in St Moritz while you roll up every network I've given you. They're not fools; they'd know who to look for. For all you and I know they're on to us now.'

Peters nodded: 'You could, of course, come somewhere . . . safer, couldn't you?'

'Behind the Curtain?'

'Yes.'

Leamas just shook his head and continued: 'I reckon you'll need about three days for a preliminary interrogation. Then you'll want to refer back for a detailed brief.'

'Not necessarily,' Peters replied.

Leamas looked at him with interest:

'I see,' he said, 'they've sent the expert. Or isn't Moscow Centre in on this?'

Peters was silent; he was just looking at Leamas, taking him in. At last he picked up the pencil in front of him and said:

'Shall we begin with your war service?'

Leamas shrugged:

'It's up to you.'
'That's right. We'll begin with your war service. Just talk.'

'I enlisted in the Engineers in 1939. I was finishing my training when a notice came round inviting linguists to apply for specialist service abroad. I had Dutch and German and a good deal of French and I was fed up with soldiering, so I applied. I knew Holland well; my father had a machine tool agency at Leiden; I'd lived there for nine years. I had the usual interviews and went off to a school near Oxford where they taught me the usual monkey tricks.'
'Who was running that set-up?'
'I didn't know till later. Then I met Steed-Asprey, and an Oxford don called Fielding. They were running it. In forty-one they dropped me into Holland and I stayed there nearly two years. We lost agents quicker than we could find them in those days—it was bloody murder. Holland's a wicked country for that kind of work—it's got no real rough country, nowhere out of the way you can keep a headquarters or a radio set. Always on the move, always running away. It made it a very dirty game. I got out in forty-three and had a couple of months in England, then I had a go at Norway—that was a picnic by comparison. In forty-five they paid me off and I came over here again, to Holland, to try and catch up on my father's old business. That was no good, so I joined up with an old friend who was running a travel agency business in Bristol. That lasted eighteen months then we were sold up. Then out of the blue I got a letter from the Department: would I like to go back? But I'd had enough of all that, I thought, so I said I'd think about it and rented a cottage on Lundy Island. I stayed there a year contemplating my stomach, then I got fed up again so I wrote to them. By late forty-nine I was back on the payroll. Broken service of course—reduction of pension rights and the usual crabbing. Am I going too fast?'
'Not for the moment,' Peters replied, pouring him some more whisky; 'we'll discuss it again of course, with names and dates.'
There was a knock at the door and the woman came in with lunch, an enormous meal of cold meats and bread and soup. Peters pushed his notes aside and they ate in silence. The interrogation had begun.

Lunch was cleared away. 'So you went back to the Circus,' said Peters.
'Yes. For a while they gave me a desk job, processing reports, making assessments of military strengths in Iron Curtain countries, tracing units and that kind of thing.'
'Which section?'
'Satellites Four. I was there from February fifty to May fifty-one.'
'Who were your colleagues?'
'Peter Guillam, Brian de Grey and George Smiley. Smiley left us

in early fifty-one and went over to Counter Intelligence. In May
fifty-one I was posted to Berlin as DCA–Deputy-Controller of Area.
That meant all the operational work.'

'Who did you have under you?' Peters was writing swiftly. Leamas
guessed he had some home-made shorthand.

'Hackett, Sarrow and de Jong. De Jong was killed in a traffic
accident in fifty-nine. We thought he was murdered but we could
never prove it. They all ran networks and I was in charge. Do you
want details?' he asked drily.

'Of course, but later. Go on.'

'It was late fifty-four when we landed our first big fish in Berlin:
Fritz Feger, second man in the DDR Defence Ministry. Up till then
it had been heavy going–but in November fifty-four we got on to
Fritz. He lasted almost exactly two years then one day we never heard
any more. I hear he died in prison. It was another three years before
we found anyone to touch him. Then, in 1959, Karl Riemeck turned
up. Karl was on the Praesidium of the East German Communist
Party. He was the best agent I ever knew.'

'He is now dead,' Peters observed.

A look of something like shame passed across Leamas' face:

'I was there when he was shot,' he muttered. 'He had a mistress
who came over just before he died. He'd told her everything–she
knew the whole damned network. No wonder he was blown.'

'We'll return to Berlin later. Tell me this. When Karl died you
flew back to London. Did you remain in London for the rest of your
service?'

'What there was of it, yes.'

'What job did you have in London?'

'Banking Section; supervision of agents' salaries, overseas payments for clandestine purposes. A child could have managed it. We
got our orders and we signed the drafts. Occasionally there was a
security headache.'

'Did you deal with agents direct?'

'How could we? The Resident in a particular country would make
a requisition. Authority would put a hoofmark on it and pass it to us
to make the payment. In most cases we had the money transferred to
a convenient foreign bank where the Resident could draw it himself
and hand it to the agent.'

'How were agents described? By cover names?'

'By figures. The Circus calls them combinations. Every network
was given a combination; every agent was described by a suffix
attached to the combination. Karl's combination was eight A stroke
one.'

Leamas was sweating. Peters watched him coolly, appraising him
like a professional gambler across the table. What was Leamas
worth? What would break him, what attract or frighten him? What

did he hate, above all, what did he know? Would he keep his best card to the end and sell it dear? Peters didn't think so; Leamas was too much off balance to monkey about. He was a man at odds with himself, a man who knew one life, one confession, and had betrayed them. Peters had seen it before. He had seen it, even in men who had undergone a complete ideological reversal, who in the secret hours of the night had found a new creed, and alone, compelled by the internal power of their convictions, had betrayed their calling, their families, their countries. Even they, filled as they were with new zeal and new hope, had had to struggle against the stigma of treachery; even they wrestled with the almost physical anguish of saying that which they had been trained never, never to reveal. Like apostates who feared to burn the Cross, they hesitated between the instinctive and the material; and Peters, caught in the same polarity, must give them comfort and destroy their pride. It was a situation of which they were both aware; thus Leamas had fiercely rejected a human relationship with Peters, for his pride precluded it. Peters knew that for those reasons, Leamas would lie; lie perhaps only by omission, but lie all the same, for pride, from defiance or through the sheer perversity of his profession; and he, Peters, would have to nail the lies. He knew, too, that the very fact that Leamas was a professional could militate against his interests, for Leamas would select where Peters wanted no selection; Leamas would anticipate the type of intelligence which Peters required—and in doing so might pass by some casual scrap which could be of vital interest to the evaluators. To all that, Peters added the capricious vanity of an alcoholic wreck.

'I think,' he said, 'we will now take your Berlin service in some detail. That would be from May 1951 to March 1961. Have another drink.'

Leamas watched him take a cigarette from the box on the table, and light it. He noticed two things: that Peters was left handed, and that once again he had put the cigarette in his mouth with the maker's name away from him, so that it burnt first. It was a gesture Leamas liked: it indicated that Peters, like himself, had been on the run.

Peters had an odd face, expressionless and grey. The colour must have left it long ago—perhaps in some prison in the early days of the Revolution—and now his features were formed and Peters would look like that till he died. Only the stiff, grey hair might turn to white, but his face would not change. Leamas wondered vaguely what Peters' real name was, whether he was married. There was something very orthodox about him which Leamas liked. It was the orthodoxy of strength, of confidence. If Peters lied there would be a reason. The lie would be a calculated, necessary lie, far removed from the fumbling dishonesty of Ashe.

Ashe, Kiever, Peters; that was a progression in quality, in authority, which to Leamas was axiomatic of the hierarchy of an intelligence network. It was also, he suspected, a progression in ideology. Ashe, the mercenary, Kiever the fellow traveller, and now Peters, for whom the end and the means were identical.

Leamas began to talk about Berlin. Peters seldom interrupted, seldom asked a question or made a comment, but when he did, he displayed a technical curiosity and expertise which entirely accorded with Leamas' own temperament. Leamas even seeemed to respond to the dispassionate professionalism of his interrogator—it was something they had in common.

It had taken a long time to build a decent East Zone network from Berlin, Leamas explained. In the earlier days the city had been thronging with second-rate agents: intelligence was discredited and so much a part of the daily life of Berlin that you could recruit a man at a cocktail party, brief him over dinner and he would be blown by breakfast. For a professional it was a nightmare: dozens of agencies, half of them penetrated by the opposition, thousands of loose ends; too many leads, too few sources, too little space to operate. They had their break with Feger in 1954, true enough. But by '56 when every Service department was screaming for high-grade intelligence, they were becalmed. Feger had spoilt them for second-rate stuff that was only one jump ahead of the news. They needed the real thing—and they had to wait another three years before they got it.

Then one day de Jong went for a picnic in the woods on the edge of East Berlin. He had a British military number plate on his car, which he parked, locked, in an unmade road beside the canal. After the picnic his children ran on ahead, carrying the basket. When they reached the car they stopped, hesitated, dropped the basket and ran back. Somebody had forced the car door—the handle was broken and the door was slightly open. De Jong swore, remembering that he had left his camera in the glove compartment. He went and examined the car. The handle had been forced; de Jong reckoned it had been done with a piece of steel tubing, the kind of thing you can carry in your sleeve. But the camera was still there, so was his coat, so were some parcels belonging to his wife. On the driving seat was a tobacco tin, and in the tin was a small nickel cartridge. De Jong knew exactly what it contained: it was the film cartridge of a sub-miniature camera, probably a Minox.

De Jong drove home and developed the film. It contained the minutes of the last meeting of the Praesidium of the East German Communist Party, the SED. By an odd coincidence there was collateral from another source; the photographs were genuine.

Leamas took the case over then. He was badly in need of a success. He'd produced virtually nothing since arriving in Berlin, and he was getting past the usual age limit for full time operational work.

Exactly a week later he took de Jong's car to the same place and went for a walk.

It was a desolate spot that de Jong had chosen for his picnic: a strip of canal with a couple of shell-torn pill-boxes, some parched, sandy fields and on the Eastern side a sparse pine wood, lying about two hundred yards from the gravel road which bordered the canal. But it had the virtue of solitude—something that was hard to find in Berlin—and surveillance was impossible. Leamas walked in the woods. He made no attempt to watch the car because he did not know from which direction the approach might be made. If he was seen watching the car from the woods, the chances of retaining his informant's confidence were ruined. He need not have worried.

When he returned there was nothing in the car so he drove back to West Berlin, kicking himself for being a damned fool; the Praesidium was not due to meet for another fortnight. Three weeks later he borrowed de Jong's car and took a thousand dollars in twenties in a picnic case. He left the car unlocked for two hours and when he returned there was a tobacco tin in the glove compartment. The picnic case had gone.

The films were packed with first grade documentary stuff. In the next six weeks he did it twice more, and the same thing happened.

Leamas knew he had hit a gold mine. He gave the source the cover name of 'Mayfair' and sent a pessimistic letter to London. Leamas knew that if he gave London half an opening they would control the case direct, which he was desperately anxious to avoid. This was probably the only kind of operation which could save him from superannuation, and it was just the kind of thing that was big enough for London to want to take over for itself. Even if he kept them at arm's length there was still the danger that the Circus would have theories, make suggestions, urge caution, demand action. They would want him to give only new dollar bills in the hope of tracing them, they would want the film cartridges sent home for examination, they would plan clumsy tailing operations and tell the Departments. Most of all they would want to tell the Departments; and that, said Leamas, would blow the thing sky-high. He worked like a madman for three weeks. He combed the personality files of each member of the Praesidium. He drew up a list of all the clerical staff who might have had access to the minutes. From the distribution list on the last page of the facsimiles he extended the total of possible informants to thirty-one, including clerks and secretarial staff.

Confronted with the almost impossible task of identifying an informant from the incomplete records of thirty-one candidates, Leamas returned to the original material, which, he said, was something he should have done earlier. It puzzled him that in none of the photostat minutes he had so far received were the pages numbered, that none was stamped with a security classification, and that in the second and fourth copy words were crossed out in pencil or crayon. He came finally to an important conclusion: that the photo copies related not to the minutes themselves, but to the *draft* minutes. This placed the source in the Secretariat and the Secretariat was very small. The draft minutes had been well and carefully photographed: that suggested that the photographer had had time and a room to himself.

Leamas returned to the personality index. There was a man called Karl Riemeck in the Secretariat, a former corporal in the Medical Corps, who had served three years as a prisoner of war in England. His sister had been living in Pomerania when the Russians overran it, and he had never heard of her since. He was married and had one daughter named Carla.

Leamas decided to take a chance. He found out from London Riemeck's prisoner of war number, which was 29012, and the date of his release which was November 10th, 1945. He bought an East German children's book of science fiction and wrote in the fly leaf in German in an adolescent hand: 'This book belongs to Carla Riemeck, born December 10th, 1945, in Bideford, North Devon. Signed Moonspacewoman 29012', and underneath, he added, 'Applicants wishing to make space flights should present themselves for instruction to C. Riemeck in person. An application form is enclosed. Long live the People's Republic of Democratic Space!'

He ruled some lines on a sheet of writing paper, made columns for name, address and age, and wrote at the bottom of the page:

'Each candidate will be interviewed personally. Write to the usual address stating when and where you wish to be met. Applications will be considered in seven days. C.R.'

He put the sheet of paper inside the book. Leamas drove to the usual place, still in de Jong's car, and left the book on the passenger seat with five used one hundred dollar bills inside the cover. When Leamas returned the book had gone, and there was a tobacco tin on the seat instead. It contained three rolls of film. Leamas developed them that night: one film contained as usual the minutes of the Praesidium's last meeting; the second showed a draft revision of the East Germans' relationship to COMECON and the third a breakdown of the East German Intelligence Service, complete with functions of departments and details of personalities.

Peters interrupted: 'Just a minute,' he said. 'Do you mean to say all this intelligence came from Riemeck?'

'Why not? You know how much he saw.'

'It's scarcely possible,' Peters observed, almost to himself; 'he must have had help.'

'He did have later on; I'm coming to that.'

'I know what you are going to tell me. But did you never have the feeling he got assistance from *above* as well as from the agents he afterwards acquired?'

'No. No, I never did. It never occurred to me.'

'Looking back on it now, does it seem likely?'

'Not particularly.'

'When you sent all this material back to the Circus, they never suggested that even for a man in Riemeck's position, the intelligence was phenomenally comprehensive?'

'No.'

'Did they ever ask where Riemeck got his camera from, who instructed him in document photography?'

Leamas hesitated.

'No . . . I'm sure they never asked.'

'Remarkable,' Peters observed drily. 'I'm sorry—do go on. I did not mean to anticipate you.'

Exactly a week later, Leamas continued, he drove to the canal and this time he felt nervous. As he turned into the unmade road he saw three bicycles lying in the grass and two hundred yards down the canal, three men fishing. He got out of the car as usual and began walking towards the line of trees on the other side of the field. He had gone about twenty yards when he heard a shout. He looked round and caught sight of one of the men beckoning to him. The other two had turned and were looking at him too. Leamas was wearing an old macintosh; he had his hands in the pockets, and it was too late to take them out. He knew that the men on either side were covering the man in the middle and that if he took his hands out of his pockets they would probably shoot him; they would think he was holding a revolver in his pocket. Leamas stopped ten yards from the centre man.

'You want something?' Leamas asked.

'Are you Leamas?' He was a small, plump man, very steady. He spoke English.

'Yes.'

'What is your British national identity number?'

'PRT stroke L 58003 stroke one.'

'Where did you spend VJ night?'

'At Leiden in Holland in my father's workshop, with some Dutch friends.'

'Let's go for a walk, Mr Leamas. You won't need your macintosh. Take it off and leave it on the ground where you are standing. My friends will look after it.'

Leamas hesitated, shrugged and took off his macintosh. Then they walked together briskly towards the wood.

'You know as well as I do who he was,' said Leamas wearily, 'third man in the Ministry of the Interior, Secretary to the SED Praesidium, head of the Co-ordinating Committee for the Protection of the People. I suppose that was how he knew about de Jong and me: he'd seen our counter intelligence files in the Abteilung. He had three strings to his bow: the Praesidium, straightforward internal political and economic reporting and access to the files of the East German Security Service.'

'But only *limited* access. They'd never give an outsider the run of all their files,' Peters insisted.

Leamas shrugged.

'They did,' he said.

'What did he do with his money?'

'After that afternoon I didn't give him any. The Circus took that over straight away. It was paid into a West German bank. He even gave me back what I'd given him. London banked it for him.'

'How much did you tell London?'

'Everything after that. I had to; then the Circus told the Departments. After that,' Leamas added venomously, 'it was only a matter of time before it packed up. With the Departments at their backs, London got greedy. They began pressing us for more, wanted to give him more money. Finally we had to suggest to Karl that he recruited other sources and we took them on to form a network. It was bloody stupid, it put a strain on Karl, endangered him, undermined his confidence in us. It was the beginning of the end.'

'How much did you get out of him?'

Leamas hesitated.

'How much? Christ, I don't know. It lasted an unnaturally long time. I think he was blown long before he was caught. The standard dropped in the last few months; think they'd begun to suspect him by then and kept him away from the good stuff.'

'Altogether, what did he give you?' Peters persisted.

Piece by piece, Leamas recounted the full extent of all Karl Riemeck's work. His memory was, Peters noted approvingly, remarkably precise considering the amount he drank. He could give dates and names, he could remember the reaction from London, the nature of corroboration where it existed. He could remember sums of money demanded and paid, the dates of the conscription of other agents in the network.

'I'm sorry,' said Peters at last, 'but I do not believe that one man, however well placed, however careful, however industrious, could have acquired such a range of detailed knowledge. For that matter, even if he had he would never have been able to photograph it.'

'He *was* able,' Leamas persisted, suddenly angry, 'he bloody well did and that's all there is to it.'

'And the Circus never told you to go into it with him, exactly how and when he saw all this stuff.'

'No,' snapped Leamas, 'Riemeck was touchy about that, and

London was content to let it go.'

'Well, well,' Peters mused.

After a moment Peters said: 'You heard about that woman, incidentally?'

'What woman?' Leamas asked sharply.

'Karl Riemeck's mistress, the one who came over to West Berlin the night Riemeck was shot.'

'Well?'

'She was found dead a week ago. Murdered. She was shot from a car as she left her flat.'

'It used to be my flat,' said Leamas mechanically.

'Perhaps,' Peters suggested, 'she knew more about Riemeck's network than you did.'

'What the hell do you mean?' Leamas demanded.

Peters shrugged.

'It's all very strange,' he observed. 'I wonder who killed her.'

When they had exhausted the case of Karl Riemeck, Leamas went on to talk of other less spectacular agents, then of the procedure of his Berlin office, its communications, its staff, its secret ramifications—flats, transport, recording and photographic equipment. They talked long into the night and throughout the next day and when at last Leamas stumbled into bed the following night he knew he had betrayed all that he knew of Allied Intelligence in Berlin, and drunk two bottles of whisky in two days.

One thing puzzled him: Peters' insistence that Karl Riemeck must have had help—must have had a high-level collaborator. Control had asked him the same question—he remembered now—Control had asked about Riemeck's access. How could they both be so sure Karl hadn't managed alone? He'd had helpers, of course; like the guards by the canal the day Leamas met him. But they were small beer—Karl had told him about them. But Peters—and Peters, after all, would know precisely how much Karl had been able to get his hands on—Peters had refused to believe Karl had managed alone. On this point, Peters and Control were evidently agreed.

Perhaps it was true. Perhaps there was somebody else. Perhaps this was the Special Interest whom Control was so anxious to protect from Mundt. That would mean that Karl Riemeck had collaborated with this special interest and provided what both of them had together obtained. Perhaps that was what Control had spoken to Karl about, alone, that evening in Leamas' flat in Berlin.

Anyway, tomorrow would tell. Tomorrow he would play his hand.

He wondered who had killed Elvira. And he wondered *why* they had killed her. Of course—here was a point, here was a possible explanation—Elvira, knowing the identity of Riemeck's special collaborator, had been murdered *by* that collaborator. . . . No, that was too far-fetched. It overlooked the difficulty of crossing from East to

West: Elvira had after all been murdered in West Berlin.

He wondered why Control had never told him Elvira had been murdered. So that he would react suitably when Peters told him? It was useless speculating. Control had his reasons; they were usually so bloody tortuous it took you a week to work them out.

As he fell asleep he muttered, 'Karl was a damn' fool. That woman did for him, I'm sure she did.' Elvira was dead now, and serve her right. He remembered Liz.

Chapter Nine

The Second Day

Peters arrived at eight o'clock the next morning, and without ceremony they sat down at the table and began.

'So you came back to London. What did you do there?'

'They put me on the shelf. I knew I was finished when that ass in Personnel met me at the airport. I had to go straight to Control and report about Karl. He was dead—what else was there to say?'

'What did they do with you?'

'They said at first I could hang around in London and wait till I was qualified for a proper pension. They were so bloody decent about it I got angry—I told them that if they were so keen to chuck money at me why didn't they do the obvious thing and count in all my time instead of bleating about broken service. Then they got cross when I told them that. They put me in Banking with a lot of women. I can't remember much about that part—I began hitting the bottle a bit. Had rather a bad patch.'

He lit a cigarette. Peters nodded.

'That was why they gave me the push, really. They didn't like me drinking.'

'Tell me what you *do* remember about Banking Section,' Peters suggested.

'It was a dreary set-up. I never was cut out for desk work, I knew that. That's why I hung on in Berlin. I knew when they recalled me I'd be put on the shelf, but, Christ . . . !'

'What did you do?'

Leamas shrugged.

'Sat on my behind in the same room as a couple of women. Thursby and Larrett. I called them Thursday and Friday.' He grinned rather stupidly. Peters looked uncomprehending.

'We just pushed paper. A letter came down from Finance: "the payment of seven hundred dollars to so and so is authorised with effect from so and so. Kindly get on with it"—that was the gist of it. Thursday and Friday would kick it about a bit, file it, stamp it and I'd sign a cheque or get the bank to make a transfer.'

'What bank?'

'Blatt and Rodney, a chichi little bank in the City. There's a sort of theory in the Circus that Etonians are discreet.'

'In fact, then, you knew the names of agents all over the world?'

'Not necessarily. That was the cunning thing. I'd sign the cheque, you see, or the order to the bank, but we'd leave a space for the name of the payee. The covering letter or what have you was all signed and then the file would go *back* to Special Despatch.'

'Who are they?'

'They're the general holders of agents' particulars. They put in the names and posted the order. Bloody clever, I must say.'

Peters looked disappointed.

'You mean you had no way of knowing the names of the payees?'

'Not usually, no.'

'But occasionally?'

'We got pretty near the knuckle now and again. All the fiddling about between Banking, Finance and Special Despatch led to cock-ups, of course. Too elaborate. Then occasionally we came in on special stuff which brightened one's life a bit.'

Leamas got up. 'I've made a list,' he said, 'of all the payments I can remember. It's in my room. I'll get it.'

He walked out of the room, the rather shuffling walk he had affected since arriving in Holland. When he returned he held in his hand a couple of sheets of lined paper torn from a cheap notebook.

'I wrote these down last night,' he said; 'I thought it would save time.'

Peters took the notes and read them slowly and carefully. He seemed impressed.

'Good,' he said, 'very good.'

'Then I remember best a thing called Rolling Stone. I get a couple of trips out of it. One to Copenhagen and one to Helsinki. Just dumping money at banks.'

'How much?'

'Ten thousand dollars in Copenhagen, forty thousand D-Marks in Helsinki.'

Peters put down his pencil.

'Who for?' he asked.

'God knows. We worked Rolling Stone on a system of deposit accounts. The Service gave me a phoney British passport; I went to the Royal Scandinavian Bank in Copenhagen and the National Bank of Finland in Helsinki, deposited the money and drew a pass book on a joint account–for me in my alias and for someone else–the agent, I suppose, in his alias. I gave the banks a sample of the co-holder's signature. I'd got that from Head Office. Later the agent was given the pass book and a false passport which he showed at the bank when he drew the money. All I knew was the alias.' He heard himself talking and it all sounded so ludicrously improbable.

'Was this procedure common?'

'No. It was a special payment. It had a subscription list.'

'What's that?'

'It had a code name known to very few people.'

'What was the code name?'

'I told you–Rolling Stone. The operation covered irregular payments of ten thousand dollars in different currencies and in different capitals.'

'Always in capital towns?'

'Far as I know. I remember reading in the file that there had been other Rolling Stone payments before I came to the section, but in those cases Banking Section got the local Resident to do it.'

'These other payments that took place before you came: where were they made?'

'One in Oslo. I can't remember where the other was.'

'Was the alias of the agent always the same?'

'No. That was an added security precaution. I heard later we pinched the whole technique from the Russians. It was the most elaborate payment scheme I'd met. In the same way I used a different alias and of course a different passport for each trip.' That would please him; help him to fill in the gaps.

'These faked passports the agent was given so that he could draw the money: did you know anything about them: how they were made out and despatched?'

'No. Oh, except that they had to have visas in them for the country where the money was deposited. And entry stamps.'

'*Entry stamps?*'

'Yes. I assumed the passports were never used at the border–only presented at the bank for identification purposes. The agent must have travelled on his own passport, quite legally entered the country where the bank was situated, then used the faked passport at the bank. That was my guess.'

'Do you know of a reason why earlier payments were made by the Residents, and later payments by someone travelling out from London?'

'I know the reason. I asked the women in Banking Section, Thursday and Friday. Control was anxious that—'

'*Control?* Do you mean to say Control himself was running the case?'

'Yes, he was running it. He was afraid the Resident might be recognised at the bank. So he used a postman: me.'

'When did you make your journeys?'

'Copenhagen on the fifteenth of June. I flew back the same night. Helsinki at the end of September. I stayed two nights there, flew back around the twenty-eighth. I had a bit of fun in Helsinki.' He grinned but Peters took no notice.

'And the other payments—when were they made?'

'I can't remember. Sorry.'

'But one was definitely in Oslo?'

'Yes, in Oslo.'

'How much time separated the first two payments, the payments made by the Residents?'

'I don't know. Not long, I think. Maybe a month. A bit more perhaps.'

'Was it your impression that the agent had been operating for some time before the first payment was made? Did the file show that?'

'No idea. The file simply covered actual payments. First payments early '59. There was no other data on it. That is the principle that operates where you have a limited subscription. Different files handle different bits of a single case. Only someone with the master file would be able to put it all together.'

Peters was writing all the time now. Leamas assumed there was a tape recorder hidden somewhere in the room but the subsequent transcription would take time. What Peters wrote down now would provide the background for this evening's telegram to Moscow, while in the Soviet Embassy in The Hague the girls would sit up all night telegraphing the verbatim transcript on hourly schedules.

'Tell me,' said Peters; 'these are large sums of money. The arrangements for paying them were elaborate and very expensive. What did you make of it yourself?'

Leamas shrugged.

'What could I make of it? I thought Control must have a bloody good source, but I never saw the material so I don't know. I didn't like the way it was done—it was too high-powered, too complicated, too clever. Why couldn't they just meet him and give him the money in cash? Did they really let him cross borders on his own passport with a forged one in his pocket? I doubt it,' said Leamas. It was time he clouded the issue, let him chase a hare.

'What do you mean?'

'I mean, that for all I know the money was never drawn from the bank. Supposing he was a highly placed agent behind the Curtain—the money would be on deposit for him when he could get at it. That was what I reckoned anyway. I didn't think about it all that much. Why should I? It's part of our work only to know pieces of the whole set-up. You know that. If you're curious, God help you.'

'If the money wasn't collected, as you suggest, why all the trouble with passports?'

'When I was in Berlin we made an arrangement for Karl Riemeck in case he ever needed to run and couldn't get hold of us. We kept a bogus West German passport for him at an address in Düsseldorf. He could collect it any time by following a pre-arranged procedure. It never expired—Special Travel renewed the passport and the visas as they expired. Control might have followed the same technique with this man. I don't know—it's only a guess.'

'How do you know for certain that passports were issued?'

'There were minutes on the file between Banking Section and Special Travel. Special Travel is the section which arranged false identity papers and visas.'

'I see.' Peters thought for a moment and then he asked: 'What names did you use in Copenhagen and Helsinki?'

'Robert Lang, electrical engineer from Derby. That was in Copenhagen.'

'When exactly were you in Copenhagen?' Peters asked.

'I told you, June the fifteenth. I got there in the morning at about eleven-thirty.'

'Which bank did you use?'

'Oh, for Christ's sake, Peters,' said Leamas, suddenly angry, 'the Royal Scandinavian. You've got it written down.'

'I just wanted to be sure,' the other replied evenly, and continued writing. 'And for Helsinki, what name?'

'Stephen Bennett, marine engineer for Plymouth. I was there,' he added sarcastically, 'at the end of September.'

'You visited the bank on the day you arrived?'

'Yes. It was the 24th or 25th, I can't be sure, as I told you.'

'Did you take the money with you from England?'

'Of course not. We just transferred it to the Resident's account in each case. The Resident drew it, met me at the airport with the money in a suitcase and I took it to the bank.'

'Who's the Resident in Copenhagen?'

'Peter Jensen, a bookseller in the University bookshop.'

'And what were the names which would be used by the agent?'

'Horst Karlsdorf in Copenhagen. I think that was it, yes it was, I remember. Karlsdorf. I kept on wanting to say Karlshorst.'

'Description?'

'Manager, from Klagenfurt in Austria.'

'And the other? The Helsinki name?'

'Fechtmann. Adolf Fechtmann from St Gallen, Switzerland. He had a title—yes, that's right: Doctor Fechtmann, archivist.'

'I see; both German-speaking?'

'Yes, I noticed that. But it can't be a German.'

'Why not?'

'I was head of the Berlin set-up, wasn't I? I'd have been in on it. A high-level agent in East Germany would have to be run from Berlin. I'd have known.' Leamas got up, went to the sideboard and poured himself some whisky. He didn't bother about Peters.

'You said yourself there were special precautions, special procedures in this case. Perhaps they didn't think you needed to know.'

'Don't be bloody silly,' Leamas rejoined shortly; 'of course I'd have known.' This was the point he would stick to through thick and thin; it made them feel they knew better, gave credence to the rest of his information. 'They will want to deduce *in spite of you*,' Control had said. 'We must give them the material and remain sceptical to their conclusions. Rely on their intelligence and conceit, on their suspicion of one another—that's what we must do.'

Peters nodded as if he were confirming a melancholy truth. 'You are a very proud man, Leamas,' he observed once more.

Peters left soon after that. He wished Leamas good day and walked down the road along the sea front. It was lunch time.

Chapter Ten

The Third Day

Peters didn't appear that afternoon, nor the next morning. Leamas stayed in, waiting with growing irritation for some message, but none came. He asked the housekeeper but she just smiled and shrugged her heavy shoulders. At about eleven o'clock the next morning he decided to go out for a walk along the front, bought some cigarettes and stared dully at the sea.

There was a girl standing on the beach throwing bread to the seagulls. Her back was turned to him. The sea wind played with her long black hair and pulled at her coat, making an arc of her body, like a bow strung towards the sea. He knew what it was then that Liz had given him; the thing that he would have to go back and find if ever he got home to England: it was the caring about little things—the faith in ordinary life; that simplicity that made you break up a bit of bread into a paper bag, walk down to the beach and throw it to the gulls. It was this respect for triviality which he had never been allowed to possess; whether it was bread for the seagulls or love, whatever it was he would go back and find it; he would make Liz find it for him. A week, two weeks perhaps, and he would be home. Control had said he could keep whatever they paid—and that would be enough. With fifteen thousand pounds, a gratuity and a pension from the Circus, a man—as Control would say—can afford to come in from the cold.

He made a detour and returned to the bungalow at a quarter to twelve. The woman let him in without a word, but when he had gone into the back room he heard her lift the receiver and dial a telephone number. She only spoke for a few seconds. At half past twelve she brought him lunch, and, to his pleasure, some English newspapers, which he read contentedly until three o'clock. Leamas who normally read nothing, read newspapers slowly and with concentration. He remembered details, like the names and addresses of people who were the subject of small news items. He did it almost unconsciously as a kind of private pelmanism, and it absorbed him entirely.

At three o'clock Peters arrived, and as soon as Leamas saw him he knew that something was up. They did not sit at the table; Peters did not take off his macintosh.

'I've got bad news for you,' he said, 'they're looking for you in England. I heard this morning. They're watching the ports.'

Leamas replied impassively: 'On what charge?'

'Nominally for failing to report to a police station within the statutory period after release from prison.'

'And in fact?'

'The word is going around that you're wanted for an offence under the Official Secrets Act. Your photograph's in all the London evening papers. The captions are very vague.'

Leamas was standing very still.

Control had done it. Control had started the hue and cry. There was no other explanation. If Ashe or Kiever had been pulled in, if they had talked—even then, the responsibility for the hue and cry was still Control's. 'A couple of weeks,' he'd said; 'I expect they'll take you off somewhere for the interrogation—it may even be abroad. A couple of weeks should see you through, though. After that, the thing should run itself. You'll have to lie low over here while the chemistry works itself out; but you won't mind that I'm sure. I've agreed to keep you on operational subsistence until Mundt is eliminated: that seemed the fairest way.'

And now this.

This wasn't part of the bargain; this was different. What the hell was he supposed to do? By pulling out now, by refusing to go along with Peters, he was wrecking the operation. It was just possible that Peters was lying, that this was the test—all the more reason that he should agree to go. But if he went, if he agreed to go east, to Poland, Czechoslovakia or God knows where, there was no good reason why they should ever let him out—there was no good reason (since he was notionally a wanted man in the West) why he should *want* to be let out.

Control had done it—he was sure. The terms had been too generous, he'd known that all along. They didn't throw money about like that for nothing—not unless they thought they might lose you. Money like that was a *douceur* for discomfort and dangers Control would not openly admit to. Money like that was a warning; Leamas had not heeded the warning.

'Now how the devil,' he asked quietly, 'could they get on to that?' A thought seemed to cross his mind and he said, 'Your friend Ashe could have told them, of course, or Kiever. . . .'

'It's possible,' Peters replied. 'You know as well as I do that such things are always possible. There is no certainty in our job. The fact is,' he added with something like impatience, 'that by now every country in Western Europe will be looking for you.'

Leamas might not have heard what Peters was saying. 'You've got me on the hook now, haven't you, Peters?' he said. 'Your people must be laughing themselves sick. Or did they give the tip off themselves?'

'You overrate your own importance,' Peters said sourly.

'Then why do you have me followed, tell me that? I went for a walk this morning. Two little men in brown suits, one twenty yards behind the other, trailed me along the sea front. When I came back the housekeeper rang you up.'

'Let us stick to what we know,' Peters suggested. 'How your own authorities have got on to you does not at the moment acutely concern us. The fact is, they have.'

'Have you brought the London evening papers with you?'

'Of course not. They are not available here. We received a telegram from London.'

'That's a lie. You know perfectly well your apparatus is only allowed to communicate with Centre.'

'In this case a direct link between two outstations was permitted,' Peters retorted angrily.

'Well, well,' said Leamas with a wry smile, 'you must be quite a big wheel. Or'—a thought seemed to strike him—'isn't Centre in on this?'

Peters ignored the question.

'You know the alternative. You let us take care of you, let us arrange your safe passage, or you fend for yourself—with the certainty of eventual capture. You've no false papers, no money, nothing. Your British passport will have expired in ten days.'

'There's a third possibility. Give me a Swiss passport and some money and let me run. I can look after myself.'

'I am afraid that is not considered desirable.'

'You mean you haven't finished the interrogation. Until you have I am not expendable?'

'That is roughly the position.'

'When you have completed the interrogation, what will you do with me?'

Peters shrugged. 'What do you suggest?'

'A new identity. Scandinavian passport perhaps. Money.'

'It's very academic,' Peters replied, 'but I will suggest it to my superiors. Are you coming with me?' Leamas hesitated then he smiled a little uncertainly and asked:

'If I didn't, what would you do? After all I've quite a story to tell, haven't I?'

'Stories of that kind are hard to substantiate. I shall be gone tonight. Ashe and Kiever . . .' he shrugged, 'what do they add up to?'

Leamas went to the window. A storm was gathering over the grey North Sea. He watched the gulls wheeling against the dark clouds. The girl had gone.

'All right,' he said at last, 'fix it up.'

'There's no plane East until tomorrow. There's a flight to Berlin in an hour. We shall take that. It's going to be very close.'

Leamas' passive role that evening enabled him once again to admire the unadorned efficiency of Peters' arrangements. The passport had been put together long ago–Centre must have thought of that. It was made out in the name of Alexander Thwaite, travel agent, and filled with visas and frontier stamps–the old, well-fingered passport of the professional traveller. The Dutch frontier guard at the airport just nodded and stamped it for form's sake–Peters was three or four behind him in the queue and took no interest in the formalities.

As they entered the 'passengers only' enclosure Leamas caught sight of a bookstall. A selection of international newspapers was on show: *Figaro, Monde, Neue Zürcher Zeitung, die Welt* and half a dozen British dailies and weeklies. As he watched, the girl came round to the front of the kiosk and pushed an *Evening Standard* into the rack. Leamas hurried across to the bookstall and took the paper from the rack.

'How much?' he asked. Thrusting his hand into his trouser pocket he suddenly realised that he had no Dutch currency.

'Thirty cents,' the girl replied. She was rather pretty; dark and jolly.

'I've only got two English shillings. That's a guilder. Will you take them?'

'Yes, please,' she replied, and Leamas gave her the florin. He looked back; Peters was still at the passport desk, his back turned to Leamas. Without hesitation he made straight for the men's lavatory. There he glanced rapidly but thoroughly at each page, then shoved the paper in the litter basket and re-emerged. It was true: there was his photograph with the vague little passage underneath. He wondered if Liz had seen it. He made his way thoughtfully to the passengers' lounge. Ten minutes later they boarded the plane for Hamburg and Berlin. For the first time since it all began, Leamas was frightened.

Chapter Eleven

Friends of Alec

The men called on Liz the same evening.

Liz Gold's room was at the northern end of Bayswater. It had two single beds in it, and a gas fire, rather a pretty one in charcoal grey, which made a modern hiss instead of an old fashioned bubble. She used to gaze into it sometimès when Leamas was there, when the gas fire shed the only light in the room. He would lie on the bed, hers, the one furthest from the door, and she would sit beside him and kiss him, or watch the gas fire with her face pressed against his. She was afraid to think of him too much now because then she forgot what he looked like, so she let her mind think of him for brief moments like running her eyes across a faint horizon, and then she would remember some small thing he had said or done, some way he had looked at her, or, more often, ignored her. That was the terrible thing, when her mind dwelled on it: she had nothing to remember him by—no photograph, no souvenir, nothing. Not even a mutual friend—only Miss Crail in the library, whose hatred of him had been vindicated by his spectacular departure. Liz had been round to his room once and seen the landlord. She didn't know why she did it quite, but she plucked up courage and went. The landlord was very kind about Alec; Mr Leamas had paid his rent like a gentleman, right till the end, then there'd been a week or two owing and a chum of Mr Leamas had dropped in and paid up handsome, no queries or nothing. He'd always said it of Mr Leamas, always would, he was a gent. Not public school, mind, nothing arsy-tarsy but a real gent. He liked to scowl a bit occasionally, and of course he drank a drop more than was good for him, though he never acted tight when he came home. But this little bloke who come round, funny little shy chap with specs, *he* said Mr Leamas had particularly requested, quite particularly, that the rent owing should be settled up. And if that wasn't gentlemanly the landlord was damned if he knew what was. Where he got the money from Heaven knows, but that Mr Leamas was a deep one and no mistake. He only did to Ford the grocer what a good many had been wanting to do ever since the war. The room?

Yes, the room had been taken—a gentleman from Korea, two days after they took Mr Leamas away.

That was probably why she went on working at the library—because there, at least, he still existed; the ladders, shelves, the books, the card index, were things he had known and touched, and one day he might come back to them. He had said he would never come back, but she didn't believe it. It was like saying you would never get better, to believe a thing like that. Miss Crail thought he would come back: she had discovered she owed him some money—wages underpaid—and it infuriated her that her monster had been so unmonstrous as not to collect it. After Leamas had gone, Liz had never given up asking herself the same question; why had he hit Mr Ford? She knew he had a terrible temper, but that was different. He had intended to do it right from the start as soon as he had got rid of his fever. Why else had he said good-bye to her the night before? He knew that he would hit Mr Ford on the following day. She refused to accept the only other possible interpretation: that he had grown tired of her and said good-bye, and the next day, still under the emotional strain of their parting, had lost his temper with Mr Ford and struck him. She knew, she had always known, that there was something Alec had got to do. He'd even told her that himself. What it was she could only guess.

First, she thought he had a quarrel with Mr Ford, some deep-rooted hatred going back for years. Something to do with a girl, or Alec's family perhaps. But you only had to look at Mr Ford and it seemed ridiculous. He was the archetypal *petit-bourgeois*, cautious, complacent, mean. And anyway, if Alec had a vendetta on with Mr Ford, why did he go for him in the shop on a Saturday, in the middle of the weekend shopping rush, when everyone could see?

They'd talked about it in the meeting of her party branch. George Hanby, the branch treasurer, had actually been passing Ford the grocer's as it happened, he hadn't seen much because of the crowd, but he'd talked to a bloke who'd seen the whole thing. Hanby had been so impressed that he'd rung the *Worker*, and they'd sent a man to the trial—that was why the *Worker* had given it a middle page spread as a matter of fact. It was just a straight case of protest—of sudden social awareness and hatred against the boss class, as the *Worker* said. This bloke that Hanby spoke to (he was just a little ordinary chap with specs, white collar type) said it had been so sudden—spontaneous was what he meant—and it just proved to Hanby once again how incendiary was the fabric of the capitalist system. Liz had kept very quiet while Hanby talked: none of them knew, of course, about her and Leamas. She realised then that she hated George Hanby; he was a pompous, dirty-minded little man, always leering at her and trying to touch her.

Then the men called.

She thought they were a little too smart for policemen: they came in a small black car with an aerial on it. One was short and rather plump. He had glasses and wore odd, expensive clothes; he was a kindly, worried little man and Liz trusted him somehow without knowing why. The other was smoother, but not glossy—rather a boyish figure, although she guessed he wasn't less than forty. They said they came from Special Branch, and they had printed cards with photographs in cellophane cases. The plump one did most of the talking.

'I believe you were friendly with Alec Leamas,' he began. She was prepared to be angry, but the plump man was so earnest that it seemed silly.

'Yes,' Liz answered. 'How did you know?'

'We found out quite by chance the other day. When you go to . . . prison, you have to give next of kin. Leamas said he hadn't any. That was a lie as a matter of fact. They asked him whom they should inform if anything happened to him in prison. He said you.'

'I see.'

'Does anyone else know you were friendly with him?'

'No.'

'Did you go to the trial?'

'No.'

'No press men called, creditors, no one at all?'

'No, I've told you. No one else knew. Not even my parents, no one. We worked together in the library, of course—the Psychical Research Library—but only Miss Crail, the librarian, would know that. I don't think it occurred to her that there was anything between us. She's queer,' Liz added simply.

The little man peered very seriously at her for a moment, then he asked:

'Did it surprise you when Leamas beat up Mr Ford?'

'Yes, of course.'

'Why did you think he did it?'

'I don't know. Because Ford wouldn't give him credit, I suppose. But I think he always meant to.' She wondered if she was saying too much, but she longed to talk to somebody about it, she was so alone and there didn't seem any harm.

'But that night, the night before it happened, we talked together. We had supper, a sort of special one; Alec said we should and I knew that it was our last night. He'd got a bottle of red wine from somewhere; I didn't like it much. Alec drank most of it. And then I asked him, "Is this good-bye?"—whether it was all over.'

'What did he say?'

'He said there was a job he'd got to do. I didn't really understand it all, not really.'

There was a very long silence and the little man looked more worried than ever. Finally he asked her:

'Do you believe that?'

'I don't know.' She was suddenly terrified for Alec, and she didn't know why. The man asked:

'Leamas has got two children by his marriage, did he tell you?' Liz said nothing. 'In spite of that he gave your name as next of kin. Why do you think he did that?' The little man seemed embarrassed by his own question. He was looking at his hands, which were pudgy and clasped together on his lap. Liz blushed.

'I was in love with him,' she replied.

'Was he in love with you?'

'Perhaps. I don't know.'

'Are you still in love with him?'

'Yes.'

'Did he ever say he would come back?' asked the younger man.

'No.'

'But he did say good-bye to you?' the other asked quickly.

'Did he say good-bye to you?' The little man repeated his question slowly, kindly. 'Nothing more can happen to him, I promise you. But we want to help him, and if you have any idea of why he hit Ford, if you have the slightest notion from something he said, perhaps casually, or something he did, then tell us for Alec's sake.'

Liz shook her head.

'Please go,' she said, 'please don't ask any more questions. Please go now.'

As he got to the door, the elder man hesitated, then took a card from his wallet and put it on the table, gingerly, as if it might make a noise. Liz thought he was a very shy little man.

'If you ever want any help—if anything happens about Leamas or . . . ring me up,' he said. 'Do you understand?'

'Who are you?'

'I'm a friend of Alec Leamas.' He hesitated. 'Another thing,' he added, 'one last question. Did Alec know you were . . . did Alec know about the Party?'

'Yes,' she replied, hopelessly, 'I told him.'

'Does the Party know about you and Alec?'

'I've told you. No one knew.' Then, white-faced, she cried out suddenly, 'Where is he; tell me where he is. Why won't you tell me where he is? I can help him, don't you see; I'll look after him . . . even if he's gone mad, I don't care, I swear I don't . . . I wrote to him in prison; I shouldn't have done, I know. I just said he could come back any time. I'd wait for him always. . . .' She couldn't speak any more, just sobbed and sobbed, standing there in the middle of the room, her broken face buried in her hands; the little man watching her.

'He's gone abroad,' he said gently. 'We don't quite know where he is. He isn't mad, but he shouldn't have said all that to you. It was a pity.'

The younger man said:

'We'll see you're looked after. For money and that kind of thing.'

'Who are you?' Liz asked again.

'Friends of Alec,' the young man repeated; 'good friends.'

She heard them go quietly down the stairs and into the street. From her window she watched them get into a small black car and drive away in the direction of the park.

Then she remembered the card. Going to the table she picked it up and held it to the light. It was expensively done, more than a policeman could afford, she thought. Engraved. No rank in front of the name, no police station or anything. Just the name with 'Mister'—and whoever heard of a policeman living in Chelsea?

'Mr George Smiley. 9 Bywater Street, Chelsea.' Then the telephone number underneath.

It was very strange.

Chapter Twelve

East

Leamas unfastened his seat-belt.

It is said that men condemned to death are subject to sudden moments of elation; as if, like moths in the fire, their destruction were coincidental with attainment. Following directly upon his decision, Leamas was aware of a comparable sensation; relief, short-lived but consoling, sustained him for a time. It was followed by fear and hunger.

He was slowing down. Control was right.

He'd noticed it first during the Riemeck case, early last year. Karl had sent a message: he'd got something special for him and was making one of his rare visits to Western Germany; some legal conference at Karlsruhe. Leamas had managed to get an air passage to Cologne, and picked up a car at the airport. It was still quite early in the morning and he'd hoped to miss most of the autobahn traffic to Karlsruhe but the heavy lorries were already on the move. He drove seventy kilometres in half an hour, weaving between the traffic, taking risks to beat the clock, when a small car, a Fiat probably, nosed its way out into the fast lane forty yards ahead of him. Leamas stamped on the brake, turning his headlights full on and sounding his horn, and by the grace of God he missed it; missed it by a fraction of a second. As he passed the car he saw out of the corner of his eye four children in the back, waving and laughing, and the stupid frightened face of their father at the wheel. He drove on, cursing, and suddenly it happened; suddenly his hands were shaking feverishly, his face was burning hot, his heart palpitating wildly. He managed to pull off the road into a lay-by, scrambled out of the car and stood breathing heavily, staring at the hurtling stream of giant lorries. He had a vision of the little car caught among them, pounded and smashed, until there was nothing left, nothing but the frenetic whine of klaxons and the blue lights flashing; and the bodies of the children, torn, like the murdered refugees on the road across the dunes.

He drove very slowly the rest of the way and missed his meeting with Karl.

He never drove again without some corner of his memory recalling the tousled children waving to him from the back of that car, and their father grasping the wheel like a farmer at the shafts of a hand plough.

Control would call it fever.

He sat dully in his seat over the wing. There was an American woman next to him wearing high-heeled shoes in polythene wrappers. He had a momentary notion of passing her some note for the people in Berlin, but he discarded it at once. She'd think he was making a pass at her, Peters would see it. Besides, what was the point? Control knew what had happened; Control had made it happen. There was nothing to say.

He wondered what would become of him. Control hadn't talked about that–only about the technique:

'Don't give it to them all at once, make them work for it. Confuse them with detail, leave things out, go back on your tracks. Be testy, be cussed, be difficult. Drink like a fish; don't give way on the ideology, they won't trust that. They want to deal with a man they've bought; they want the clash of opposites, Alec, not some half-cock convert. Above all, they want to *deduce*. The ground's prepared; we did it long ago, little things, difficult clues. You're the last stage in the treasure hunt.'

He'd had to agree to do it: you can't back out of the big fight when all the preliminary ones have been fought for you.

'One thing I can promise you: it's worth it. It's worth it for our special interest, Alec. Keep alive and we've won a great victory.'

He didn't think he could stand torture. He remembered a book by Koestler where the old revolutionary had conditioned himself for torture by holding lighted matches to his fingers. He hadn't read much but he'd read that and he remembered it.

It was nearly dark as they landed at Templehof. Leamas watched the lights of Berlin rise to meet them, felt the thud as the plane touched down, saw the Customs and immigration officials move forward out of the half light.

For a moment Leamas was anxious lest some former acquaintance should chance to recognise him at the airport. As they walked side by side, Peters and he, along the interminable corridors, through the cursory Customs and immigration check, and still no familiar face turned to greet him, he realised that his anxiety had in reality been hope; hope that somehow his tacit decision to go on would be revoked by circumstance.

It interested him that Peters no longer bothered to disown him; it was as if Peters regarded West Berlin as safe ground, where vigilance and security could be relaxed; a mere technical staging post to the East.

They were walking through the big reception hall to the main entrance when Peters suddenly seemed to alter his mind, abruptly changed direction and led Leamas to a smaller side entrance which gave on to a car park and taxi rank. There Peters hesitated a second, standing beneath the light over the door, then put his suitcase on the ground beside him, deliberately removed his newspapers from beneath his arm, folded it, pushed it into the left pocket of his raincoat and picked up his suitcase again. Immediately, from the direction of the car park, a pair of headlights sprang to life, were dipped and then extinguished.

'Come on,' said Peters and started to walk briskly across the tarmac, Leamas following more slowly. As they reached the first row of cars the rear door of a black Mercedes was opened from the inside, and the courtesy light went on. Peters, ten yards ahead of Leamas, went quickly to the car, spoke softly to the driver, then called to Leamas.

'Here's the car. Be quick.'

It was an old Mercedes 180 and he got in without a word. Peters sat beside him in the back. As they pulled out they overtook a small DKW with two men sitting in the front. Twenty yards down the road there was a telephone kiosk. A man was talking into the telephone, and he watched them go by, talking all the time. Leamas looked out of the back window and saw the DKW following them. Quite a reception, he thought.

They drove quite slowly. Leamas sat with his hands on his knees, looking straight in front of him. He didn't want to see Berlin that night. This was his last chance, he knew that. The way he was sitting now he could drive the side of his right hand into Peter's throat, smashing the promontory of the thyrax. He could get out and run, weaving to avoid the bullets from the car behind. He would be free—there were people in Berlin who would take care of him—he could get away.

He did nothing.

It was so easy crossing the sector border. Leamas had never expected it to be quite that easy. For about ten minutes they dawdled, and Leamas guessed that they had to cross at a pre-arranged time. As they approached the West German checkpoint, the DKW pulled out and overtook them with the ostentatious roar of a laboured engine, and stopped at the police hut. The Mercedes waited thirty yards behind. Two minutes later the red and white pole lifted to let through the DKW and as it did so both cars drove over together, the Mercedes engine screaming in second gear, the driver pressing himself back against his seat, holding the wheel at arms' length.

As they crossed the fifty yards which separated the two check-points, Leamas was dimly aware of the new fortifications on the Eastern side of the wall—dragon's teeth, observation towers and double aprons of barbed wire. Things had tightened up.

The Mercedes didn't stop at the second checkpoint; the booms were already lifted and they drove straight through, the Vopos just watching them through binoculars. The DKW had disappeared, and when Leamas sighted it ten minutes later it was behind them again. They were driving fast now—Leamas had thought they would stop in East Berlin, change cars perhaps, and congratulate one another on a successful operation, but they drove on eastwards through the city.

'Where are we going?' he asked Peters.

'We are there. The German Democratic Republic. They have arranged accommodation for you.'

'I thought we'd be going further east.'

'We are. We are spending a day or two here first. We thought the Germans ought to have a talk with you.'

'I see.'

'After all, most of your work has been on the German side. I sent them details from your statement.'

'And they asked to see me?'

'They've never had anything quite like you, nothing quite so . . . near the source. My people agreed that they should have the chance to meet you.'

'And from there? Where do we go from Germany?'

'East again.'

'Who will I see on the German side?'

'Does it matter?'

'Not particularly. I know most of the Abteilung people by name, that's all. I just wondered.'

'Who would you expect to meet?'

'Fiedler,' Leamas replied promptly, 'deputy head of security. Mundt's man. He does all the big interrogations. He's a bastard.'

'Why?'

'A savage little bastard. I've heard about him. He caught an agent of Peter Guillam's and bloody nearly killed him.'

'Espionage is not a cricket game,' Peters observed sourly and after that they sat in silence. So it is Fiedler, Leamas thought.

Leamas knew Fiedler all right. He knew him from the photographs on the file and the accounts of his former subordinates. A slim, neat man, quite young, smooth faced. Dark hair, bright brown eyes; intelligent and savage, as Leamas had said. A lithe, quick body containing a patient, retentive mind; a man seemingly without ambition for himself but remorseless in the destruction of others. Fiedler was a rarity in the Abteilung—he took no part in its intrigues, seemed content to live in Mundt's shadow without prospect of promotion. He could not be labelled as a member of this or that clique; even those who had worked close to him in the Abteilung could not say where he stood in its power complex. Fiedler was a solitary; feared, disliked and mistrusted. Whatever motives he had were concealed beneath a cloak of destructive sarcasm.

'Fiedler is our best bet,' Control had explained. They'd been sitting together over dinner—Leamas, Control and Peter Guillam— in the dreary little seven-dwarfs house in Surrey where Control lived with his beady wife, surrounded by carved Indian tables with brass tops. 'Fiedler is the acolyte who one day will stab the high priest in the back. He's the only man who's a match for Mundt'—here Guillam had nodded—'and he hates his guts. Fiedler's a Jew of course, and Mundt is quite the other thing. Not at all a good mixture. It has been our job,' he declared, indicating Guillam and himself, 'to give Fiedler the weapon with which to destroy Mundt. It will be yours, my dear Leamas, to encourage him to use it. Indirectly, of course, because you'll never meet him. At least I certainly hope you won't.'

They'd all laughed then, Guillam too. It had seemed a good joke at the time; good by Control's standards anyway.

It must have been after midnight.

For some time they had been travelling an unmade road, partly through a wood and partly across open country. Now they stopped and a moment later the DKW drew up beside them. As he and Peters got out Leamas noticed that there were now three people in the second car. Two were already getting out. The third was sitting in the back seat looking at some papers by the light from the car roof, a slight figure half in shadow.

They had parked by some disused stables; the building lay thirty yards back. In the headlights of the car Leamas had glimpsed a low farmhouse with walls of timber and whitewashed brick. They got out. The moon was up, and shone so brightly that the wooded hills behind were sharply defined against the pale night sky. They walked to the house, Peters and Leamas leading and the two men behind.

The other man in the second car had still made no attempt to move; he remained there, reading.

As they reached the door Peters stopped, waiting for the other two to catch them up. One of them carried a bunch of keys in his left hand, and while he fiddled with them the other stood off, his hands in his pockets, covering him.

'They're taking no chances,' Leamas observed to Peters, 'what do they think I am?'

'They are not paid to think,' Peters replied, and turning to one of them he asked in German:

'Is he coming?'

The German shrugged and looked back towards the car.

'He'll come,' he said; 'he likes to come alone.'

They went into the house, the man leading the way. It was got up like a hunting lodge, part old, part new. It was badly lit with pale overhead lights. The place had a neglected, musty air as if it had been opened for the occasion. There were little touches of officialdom here and there—a notice of what to do in case of fire, institutional green paint on the door and heavy spring-cartridge locks; and in the drawing-room, which was quite comfortably done, dark, heavy furniture, badly scratched, and the inevitable photographs of Soviet leaders. To Leamas these lapses from anonymity signified the involuntary identification of the Abteilung with bureaucracy. That was something he was familiar with in the Circus.

Peters sat down, and Leamas did the same. For ten minutes, perhaps longer, they waited, then Peters spoke to one of the two men standing awkwardly at the other end of the room.

'Go and tell him we're waiting. And find us some food, we're hungry.' As the man moved towards the door Peters called, 'And whisky—tell them to bring whisky and some glasses.' The man gave an unco-operative shrug of his heavy shoulders and went out, leaving the door open behind him.

'Have you been here before?' asked Leamas.

'Yes,' Peters replied, 'several times.'

'What for?'

'This kind of thing. Not the same, but our kind of work.'

'With Fiedler?'

'Yes.'

'Is he good?'

Peters shrugged. 'For a Jew, he's not bad,' he replied, and Leamas, hearing a sound from the other end of the room, turned and saw Fiedler standing in the doorway. In one hand he held a bottle of whisky, and in the other, glasses and some mineral water. He couldn't have been more than five foot six. He wore a dark blue single-breasted suit; the jacket was cut too long. He was sleek and slightly animal; his eyes were brown and bright. He was not looking at them but at the guard beside the door.

'Go away,' he said. He had a slight Saxonian twang; 'Go away and tell the other one to bring us food.'

'I've told him,' Peters called; 'they know already. But they've brought nothing.'

'They are great snobs,' Fiedler observed drily in English. 'They think we should have servants for the food.'

Fiedler had spent the war in Canada. Leamas remembered that, now that he detected the accent. His parents had been German Jewish refugees, Marxists, and it was not until 1946 that the family returned home, anxious to take part, whatever the personal cost, in the construction of Stalin's Germany.

'Hello,' he added to Leamas, almost by the way, 'glad to see you.'

'Hello, Fiedler.'

'You've reached the end of the road.'

'What the hell d'you mean?' asked Leamas quickly.

'I mean that contrary to anything Peters told you, you are not going further east. Sorry.' He sounded amused.

Leamas turned to Peters.

'Is this true?' His voice was shaking with rage. 'Is it true? Tell me!'

Peters nodded: 'Yes. I am the go-between. We had to do it that way. I'm sorry,' he added.

'Why?'

'*Force majeure*,' Fiedler put in. 'Your initial interrogation took place in the West, where only an embassy could provide the kind of link we needed. The German Democratic Republic has no embassies in the West. Not yet. Our liaison section therefore arranged for us to enjoy facilities and communications and immunities which are at present denied to us.'

'You bastard,' hissed Leamas, 'you lousy bastard! You knew I wouldn't trust myself to your rotten Service; that was the reason, wasn't it? That was why you used a Russian.'

'We used the Soviet Embassy at The Hague. What else could we do? Up till then it was our operation. That's perfectly reasonable. Neither we nor anyone else could have known that your own people in England would get on to you so quickly.'

'No? Not even when you put them on to me yourselves? Isn't that what happened, Fiedler? Well, isn't it?' Always remember to dislike them, Control had said. Then they will treasure what they get out of you.

'That is an absurd suggestion,' Fiedler replied shortly. Glancing towards Peters he added something in Russian. Peters nodded and stood up.

'Good-bye,' he said to Leamas. 'Good luck.'

He smiled wearily, nodded to Fiedler, then walked to the door.

He put his hand on the door handle, then turned and called to Leamas again:

'Good luck.' He seemed to want Leamas to say something, but Leamas might not have heard. He had turned very pale, he held his hands loosely across his body, the thumbs upwards as if he were going to fight. Peters remained standing at the door.

'I should have known,' said Leamas, and his voice had the odd, faulty note of a very angry man, 'I should have guessed you'd never have the guts to do your own dirty work, Fiedler. It's typical of your rotten little half-country and your squalid little Service that you get big uncle to do your pimping for you. You're not a country at all, you're not a government, you're a fifth-rate dictatorship of politicial neurotics.' Jabbing his finger in Fiedler's direction, he shouted:

'I know you, you sadistic bastard; it's typical of you. You were in Canada in the war, weren't you; a bloody good place to be then, wasn't it? I'll bet you stuck your fat head into Mummy's apron any time an aeroplane flew over. What are you now? A creeping little acolyte to Mundt and twenty-two Russian divisions sitting on your mother's doorstep. Well, I pity you, Fiedler, the day you wake up and find them gone. There'll be a killing then, and not Mummy or big uncle will save you from getting what you deserve.'

Fiedler shrugged.

'Regard it as a visit to the dentist, Leamas. The sooner it's all done, the sooner you can go home. Have some food and go to bed.'

'You know perfectly well I can't go home,' Leamas retorted. 'You've seen to that. You blew me sky high in England, you had to, both of you. You knew damn' well I'd never come here unless I had to.'

Fiedler looked at his thin, strong fingers.

'This is hardly the time to philosophise,' he said, 'but you can't really complain, you know. All our work—yours and mine—is rooted in the theory that the whole is more important than the individual. That is why a Communist sees his secret service as the natural extension of his arm, and that is why in your own country, intelligence is shrouded in a kind of *pudeur anglaise*. The exploitation of individuals can only be justified by the collective need, can't it? I find it slightly ridiculous that you should be so indignant. We are not here to observe the ethical laws of English country life. After all,' he added silkily, 'your own behaviour has not, from the purist's point of view, been irreproachable.'

Leamas was watching Fiedler with an expression of disgust.

'I know your set-up. You're Mundt's poodle, aren't you? They say you want his job. I suppose you'll get it now. It's time the Mundt dynasty ended; perhaps this is it.'

'I don't understand,' Fiedler replied.

'I'm your big success, aren't I?' Leamas sneered. Fiedler seemed to reflect for a moment, then he shrugged and said, 'The operation was successful. Whether you were worth it is questionable. We shall see. But it was a good operation. It satisfied the only requirement of our profession: it worked.'

'I suppose you take the credit?' Leamas persisted, with a glance in the direction of Peters.

'There is no question of credit,' Fiedler replied crisply, 'none at all.' He sat down on the arm of the sofa, looked at Leamas thoughtfully for a moment and then said:

'Nevertheless you are right to be indignant about one thing. Who told your people we had picked you up? We didn't. You may not believe me, but it happens to be true. We didn't tell them. We didn't even want them to know. We had ideas then of getting you to work for us later—ideas which I now realise to be ridiculous. So who told them? You were lost, drifting around, you had no address, no ties, no friends. Then how the devil did they know you'd gone? Someone told them—scarcely Ashe or Kiever, since they are both now under arrest.'

'Under arrest?'

'So it appears. Not specifically for their work on your case, but there were other things. . . .'

'Well, well.'

'It is true, what I said just now. We would have been content with Peters' report from Holland. You could have had your money and gone. But you hadn't told us everything; and I want to know everything. After all, your presence here provides us with problems too, you know.'

'Well, you've boobed. I know damn' all—and you're welcome to it.'

There was a silence, during which Peters, with an abrupt and by no means friendly nod in Fiedler's direction, quietly let himself out of the room.

Fiedler picked up the bottle of whisky and poured a little into each glass.

'We have no soda, I'm afraid,' he said. 'Do you like water? I ordered soda, but they brought some wretched lemonade.'

'Oh, go to hell,' said Leamas. He suddenly felt very tired.

Fiedler shook his head.

'You are a very proud man,' he observed, 'but never mind. Eat your supper and go to bed.'

One of the guards came in with a tray of food—black bread, sausage and cold, green salad.

'It is a little crude,' said Fiedler, 'but quite satisfying. No potato, I'm afraid. There is a temporary shortage of potato.'

They began eating in silence, Fiedler very carefully, like a man who counted his calories.

The guards showed Leamas to his bedroom. They let him carry his own luggage–the same luggage that Kiever had given him before he left England–and he walked between them along the wide central corridor which led through the house from the front door. They came to a large double door, painted dark green, and one of the guards unlocked it; they beckoned to Leamas to go first. He pushed open the door and found himself in a small barrack bedroom with two bunk beds, a chair and a rudimentary desk. It was like something in a prison camp. There were pictures of girls on the walls and the windows were shuttered. At the far end of the room was another door. They signalled him forward again. Putting down his baggage he went and opened the door. The second room was identical to the first, but there was one bed and the walls were bare.

'You bring those cases,' he said; 'I'm tired.' He lay on the bed, fully dressed, and within a few minutes he was fast asleep.

A sentry woke him with breakfast: black bread and *ersatz* coffee. He got out of bed and went to the window.

The house stood on a high hill. The ground fell steeply away from beneath his window, the crowns of pine trees visible above the crest. Beyond them, spectacular in their symmetry, unending hills, heavy with trees, stretched into the distance. Here and there a timber gully or fire-break formed a thin brown divide between the pines, seeming like Aaron's rod miraculously to hold apart massive seas of encroaching forest. There was no sign of man; not a house or church, not even the ruin of some previous habitation–only the road, the yellow unmade road, a crayon line across the basin of the valley. There was no sound. It seemed incredible that anything so vast could be so still. The day was cold but clear. It must have rained in the night; the ground was moist, and the whole landscape so sharply defined against the white sky that Leamas could distinguish even single trees on the furthest hills.

He dressed slowly, drinking the sour coffee meanwhile. He had nearly finished dressing and was about to start eating the bread when Fiedler came into the room.

'Good morning,' he said cheerfully. 'Don't let me keep you from your breakfast.' He sat down on the bed. Leamas had to hand it to Fiedler; he had guts. Not that there was anything brave about coming to see him–the sentries, Leamas supposed, were still in the adjoining room. But there was an endurance, a defined purpose in his manner which Leamas could sense and admire.

'You have presented us with an intriguing problem,' he observed.

'I've told you all I know.'

'Oh no.' He smiled. 'Oh no, you haven't. You have told us all you are *conscious* of knowing.'

'Bloody clever,' Leamas muttered pushing his food aside and

lighting a cigarette—his last.

'Let me ask *you* a question,' Fiedler suggested with the exaggerated bonhomie of a man proposing a party game. 'As an experienced intelligence officer, what would *you* do with the information you have given us?'

'What information?'

'My dear Leamas, you have only given us one piece of intelligence. You have told us about Riemeck: we knew about Riemeck. You have told us about the dispositions of your Berlin organisation, about its personalities and its agents. That, if I may say so, is old hat. Accurate—yes. Good background, fascinating reading, here and there good collateral, here and there a little fish which we shall take out of the pool. But not—if I may be crude—not fifteen thousand pounds' worth of intelligence. Not,' he smiled again, 'at current rates.'

'Listen,' said Leamas, 'I didn't propose this deal—you did. You, Kiever and Peters. I didn't come crawling to your cissy friends, peddling old intelligence. You people made the running, Fiedler; you named the price and took the risk. Apart from that, I haven't had a bloody penny. So don't blame me if the operation's a flop.' Make them come to you, Leamas thought.

'It isn't a flop,' Fiedler replied, 'it isn't finished. It can't be. You haven't told us what you *know*. I said you had given us one piece of intelligence. I'm talking about Rolling Stone. Let me ask you again—what would *you* do if I, if Peters or someone like us, had told *you* a similar story?'

Leamas shrugged:

'I'd feel uneasy,' he said; 'it's happened before. You get an indication, several perhaps, that there's a spy in some department or at a certain level. So what? You can't arrest the whole government service. You can't lay traps for a whole department. You just sit tight and hope for more. You bear it in mind. In Rolling Stone you can't even tell what country he's working in.'

'You are an operator, Leamas,' Fiedler observed with a laugh, 'not an evaluator. That is clear. Let me ask you some elementary questions.'

Leamas said nothing.

'The file—the actual file on operation Rolling Stone. What colour was it?'

'Grey with a red cross on it—that means limited subscription.'

'Was anything attached to the outside?'

'Yes, the Caveat. That's the subscription label. With a legend saying that any unauthorised person not named on this label finding the file in his possession must at once return it unopened to Banking Section.'

'Who was on the subscription list?'

'For Rolling Stone?'

'Yes.'

'P.A. to Control, Control, Control's Secretary; Banking Section, Miss Bream of Special Registry and Satellites Four. That's all, I think. And Special Despatch, I suppose–I'm not sure about them.'

'Satellites Four? What do they do?'

'Iron Curtain countries excluding the Soviet Union and China. The Zone.'

'You mean the GDR?'

'I mean the Zone.'

'Isn't it unusual for a whole section to be on a subscription list?'

'Yes, it probably is. I wouldn't know–I've never handled limited subscription stuff before. Except in Berlin, of course; it was all different there.'

'Who was in Satellites Four at that time?'

'Oh, God. Guillam, Haverlake, de Jong, I think. De Jong was just back from Berlin.'

'Were they *all* allowed to see this file?'

'I don't know, Fiedler,' Leamas retorted irritably; 'and if I were you . . .'

'Then isn't it odd that a whole section was on the subscription list while all the rest of the subscribers are individuals?'

'I tell you I don't know–how could I know? I was just a clerk in all this.'

'Who carried the file from one subscriber to another?'

'Secretaries, I suppose–I can't remember. It's bloody months since . . .'

'Then why weren't the secretaries on the list? Control's Secretary was.' There was a moment's silence.

'No, you're right; I remember now,' Leamas said, a note of surprise in his voice; 'we passed it by hand.'

'Who else in Banking dealt with that file?'

'No one. It was my pigeon when I joined the section. One of the women had done it before, but when I came I took it over and they were taken off the list.'

'Then you alone passed the file by hand to the next reader?'

'Yes . . . yes, I suppose I did.'

'To whom did you pass it?'

'I . . . I can't remember.'

'*Think!*' Fiedler had not raised his voice, but it contained a sudden urgency which took Leamas by surprise.

'To Control's P.A., I think, to show what action we had taken or recommended.'

'Who brought the file?'

'What do you mean?' Leamas sounded off balance.

'Who brought you the file to read? Somebody on the list must have brought it to you.'

'Leamas' fingers touched his cheek for a moment in an involuntary nervous gesture.

'Yes, they must. It's difficult, you see, Fiedler; I was putting back a lot of drink in those days'; his tone was oddly conciliatory. 'You don't realise how hard it is to . . .'

'I ask you again. Think. Who brought you the file?'

Leamas sat down at the table and shook his head.

'I can't remember. It may come back to me. At the moment I just can't remember, really I can't. It's no good chasing it.'

'It can't have been Control's girl, can it? You always handed the file *back* to Control's P.A. You said so. So those on the list must all have seen it *before* Control.'

'Yes, that's it, I suppose.'

'Then there is Special Registry, Miss Bream.'

'She was just the woman who ran the strong room for subscription list files. That's where the file was kept when it wasn't in action.'

'Then,' said Fiedler silkily, 'it must have been Satellites Four who brought it, mustn't it?'

'Yes, I suppose it must,' said Leamas helplessly, as if he were not quite up to Fiedler's brilliance.

'Which floor did Satellites Four work on?'

'The second.'

'And Banking?'

'The fourth. Next to Special Registry.'

'Do you remember *who* brought it up? Or do you remember, for instance, going downstairs ever to collect the file from them?'

In despair, Leamas shook his head; then suddenly he turned to Fiedler and cried:

'Yes, yes I do! Of course I do! I got it from Peter!' Leamas seemed to have woken up: his face was flushed, excited. 'That's it: I once collected the file from Peter in his room. We chatted together about Norway. We'd served there together, you see.'

'Peter Guillam?'

'Yes, Peter–I'd forgotten about him. He'd come back from Ankara a few months before. He was on the list! Peter was–of course! That's it. It was Satellites Four and PG in brackets, Peter's initials. Someone else had done it before and Special Registry had glued a bit of white paper over the old name and put Peter's initials.'

'What territory did Guillam cover?'

'The Zone. East Germany. Economic stuff; ran a small section, sort of backwater. He was the chap. He brought the file up to me once too, I remember that now. He didn't run agents though: I don't quite know how he came into it–Peter and a couple of others were doing some research job on food shortages. Evaluation really.'

'Did you not discuss it with him?'

'No, that's taboo. It isn't done with subscription files. I got a homily from the woman in Special Registry about it–Bream–no discussion, no questions.'

'But taking into account the elaborate security precautions surrounding Rolling Stone, it is possible, is it not, that Guillam's so-called research job might have involved the partial running of this agent, Rolling Stone?'

'I've told Peters,' Leamas almost shouted, banging his fist on the desk, 'it's just bloody silly to imagine that any operation could have been run against East Germany without my knowledge–without the knowledge of the Berlin organisation. I would have known, d'you see? How many times do I have to say that? I would have known!'

'Quite so,' said Fiedler softly, 'of course you would.' He stood up and went to the window.

'You should see it in the Autumn,' he said, looking out; 'it's magnificent when the beeches are on the turn.'

Chapter Thirteen

Pins or Paper Clips

Fiedler loved to ask questions. Sometimes, because he was a lawyer, he asked them for his own pleasure alone, to demonstrate the discrepancy between evidence and perfective truth. He possessed, however, that persistent inquisitiveness which for journalists and lawyers is an end in itself.

They went for a walk that afternoon, following the gravel road down into the valley, then branching into the forest along a broad, pitted track lined with felled timber. All the time, Fiedler probed, giving nothing. About the building in Cambridge Circus, and the people who worked there. What social class did they come from, what parts of London did they inhabit, did husbands and wives work in the same Department? He asked about the pay, the leave, the morale, the canteen; he asked about their love-life, their gossip, their philosophy. Most of all he asked about their philosophy.

To Leamas that was the most difficult question of all.

'What do you mean, a philosophy?' he replied; 'we're not Marxists, we're nothing. Just people.'

'Are you Christians, then?'

'Not many, I shouldn't think. I don't know many.'

'What makes them do it, then?' Fiedler persisted; 'they must have a philosophy.'

'Why must they? Perhaps they don't know; don't even care. Not everyone has a philosophy,' Leamas answered, a little helplessly.

'Then tell me what is your philosophy?'

'Oh for Christ's sake,' Leamas snapped, and they walked on in silence for a while. But Fiedler was not to be put off.

'If they do not know what they want, how can they be so certain they are right?'

'Who the hell said they were?' Leamas replied irritably.

'But what is the justification then? What is it? For us it is easy, as I said to you last night. The Abteilung and organisations like it are the natural extension of the Party's arm. They are in the vanguard of the fight for Peace and Progress. They are to the party what the party is to socialism: they *are* the vanguard. Stalin said so'–he smiled drily, 'it is not fashionable to quote Stalin–but he said once "half a million liquidated is a statistic, and one man killed in a traffic accident is a national tragedy." He was laughing, you see, at the bourgeois sensitivities of the mass. He was a great cynic. But what he meant is still true: a movement which protects itself against counter-revolution can hardly stop at the exploitation–or the elimination, Leamas–of a few individuals. It is all one, we have never pretended to be wholly just in the process of rationalising society. Some Roman said it, didn't he, in the Christian Bible–it is expedient that one man should die for the benefit of many.'

'I expect so,' Leamas replied wearily.

'Then what do you think? What is your philosophy?'

'I just think the whole lot of you are bastards,' said Leamas savagely.

Fiedler nodded, 'That is a viewpoint I understand. It is primitive, negative and very stupid–but it is a viewpoint, it exists. But what about the rest of the Circus?'

'I don't know. How should I know?'

'Have you never discussed philosophy with them?'

'No. We're not Germans.' He hesitated, then added vaguely: 'I suppose they don't like Communism.'

'And that justifies, for instance, the taking of human life? That justifies the bomb in the crowded restaurant; that justifies your write-off rate of agents–all that?'

Leamas shrugged. 'I suppose so.'

'You see, for us it does,' Fiedler continued, 'I myself would have put a bomb in a restaurant if it brought us further along the road. Afterwards I would draw the balance–so many women, so many children; and so far along the road. But Christians–and yours is a Christian society–Christians may not draw the balance.'

'Why not. They've got to defend themselves, haven't they?'

'But they believe in the sanctity of human life. They believe every man has a soul which can be saved. They believe in sacrifice.'

'I don't know. I don't much care,' Leamas added. 'Stalin didn't either, did he?'

Fiedler smiled; 'I like the English,' he said, almost to himself; 'my father did too. He was very fond of the English.'

'That gives me a nice, warm feeling,' Leamas retorted, and relapsed into silence.

They stopped while Fiedler gave Leamas a cigarette and lit it for him.

They were climbing steeply now. Leamas liked the exercise, walking ahead with long strides, his shoulders thrust forward. Fiedler followed, slight and agile, like a terrier behind his master. They must have been walking for an hour, perhaps more, when suddenly the trees broke above them and the sky appeared. They had reached the top of a small hill, and could look down on the solid mass of pine broken only here and there by grey clusters of beech. Across the valley Leamas could glimpse the hunting lodge, perched below the crest of the opposite hill, low and dark against the trees. In the middle of the clearing was a rough bench beside a pile of logs and the damp remnants of a charcoal fire.

'We'll sit down for a moment,' said Fiedler, 'then we must go back.' He paused. 'Tell me: this money, these large sums in foreign banks—what did you think they were for?'

'What do you mean? I've told you, they were payments to an agent.'

'An agent from behind the Iron Curtain?'

'Yes, I thought so,' Leamas replied wearily.

'Why did you think so?'

'First, it was a hell of a lot of money. Then the complications of paying him; the special security. And of course, Control being mixed up in it.'

'What did you think the agent did with the money?'

'Look, I've told you—I don't know. I don't even know if he collected it. I didn't know anything—I was just the bloody office boy.'

'What did you do with the pass books for the accounts?'

'I handed them in as soon as I got back to London—together with my phoney passport.'

'Did the Copenhagen or Helsinki banks ever write to you in London—to your alias, I mean?'

'I don't know. I suppose any letters would have been passed straight to Control anyway.'

'The false signatures you used to open the accounts—Control had a sample of them?'

'Yes. I practised them a lot and they had samples.'

'More than one?'

'Yes. Whole pages.'

'I see. Then letters could have gone to the banks after you had opened the accounts. You need not have known. The signatures could have been forged and the letters sent without your knowledge.'

'Yes. That's right. I suppose that's what happened. I signed a lot of blank sheets too. I always assumed someone else took care of the correspondence.'

'But you never did actually *know* of such correspondence?'

Leamas shook his head: 'You've got it all wrong,' he said; 'you've got it all out of proportion. There was a lot of paper going around–this was just part of the day's work. It wasn't something I gave much thought to. Why should I? It was hush-hush, but I've been in on things all my life where you only know a little and someone else knows the rest. Besides, paper bores me stiff. I didn't lose any sleep on it. I liked the trips of course–I drew operational subsistence which helped. But I didn't sit at my desk all day, wondering about Rolling Stone. Besides,' he added a little shame-facedly, 'I was hitting the bottle a bit.'

'So you said,' Fiedler commented, 'and of course, I believe you.'

'I don't give a damn' whether you believe me or not,' Leamas rejoined hotly.

Fiedler smiled.

'I am glad. That is your virtue,' he said, 'that is your great virtue. It is the virtue of indifference. A little resentment here, a little pride there, but that is nothing: the distortions of a tape recorder. You are objective. It occurred to me,' Fiedler continued after a slight pause, 'that you could still help us to establish whether any of that money was ever drawn. There is nothing to stop you writing to each bank and asking for a current statement. We could say you were staying in Switzerland; use an accommodation address. Do you see any objection to that?'

'It might work. It depends on whether Control has been corresponding with the bank independently, over my forged signature. It might not fit in.'

'I do not see that we have much to lose.'

'What have you got to win?'

'If the money has been drawn, which I agree is doubtful, we shall know where the agent was on a certain day. That seems to be a useful thing to know.'

'You're dreaming. You'll never find him, Fiedler, not on that kind of information. Once he's in the West he can go to any Consulate, even in a small town and get a visa for another country. How are you any the wiser? You don't even know whether the man is East German. What are you after?'

Fiedler did not answer at once. He was gazing distractedly across the valley.

'You said you are accustomed to knowing only a little, and I cannot answer your question without telling you what you should not know.' He hesitated, 'but Rolling Stone was an operation against us, I can assure you.'

'Us?'

'The GDR.' He smiled, 'the Zone if you prefer. I am not really so sensitive.'

He was watching Fiedler now, his brown eyes resting on him reflectively.

'But what about me?' Leamas asked. 'Suppose I don't write the letters?' His voice was rising. 'Isn't it time to talk about me, Fiedler?'

Fiedler nodded.

'Why not?' he replied, agreeably. There was a moment's silence, then Leamas said:

'I've done my bit, Fiedler. You and Peters between you have got all I know. I never agreed to write letters to banks—it could be bloody dangerous, a thing like that. That doesn't worry you, I know. As far as you're concerned I'm expendable.'

'Now let me be frank,' Fiedler replied. 'There are, as you know, two stages in the interrogation of a defector. The first stage in your case is nearly complete: you have told us all we can reasonably record. You have not told us whether your Service favours pins or paper clips because we haven't asked you, and because you did not consider the answer worth volunteering. There is a process on both sides of unconscious selection. Now it is always possible—and this is the worrying thing, Leamas—it is always entirely possible that in a month or two we shall unexpectedly and quite desperately need to know about the pins and paper clips. That is normally accounted for in the second stage—that part of the bargain which you refused to accept in Holland.'

'You mean you're going to keep me on ice?'

'The profession of defector,' Fiedler observed with a smile, 'demands great patience. Very few are suitably qualified.'

'How long?' Leamas insisted.

Fiedler was silent.

'Well?'

Fiedler spoke with sudden urgency. 'I give you my word that as soon as I possibly can, I will tell you the answer to your question. Look—I could lie to you, couldn't I? I could say one month or less, just to keep you sweet. But I am telling you I don't know because that is the truth. You have given us some indications: until we have run them to earth I cannot listen to talk of letting you go. But afterwards if things are as I think they are, you will need a friend and that friend will be me. I give you my word as a German.'

Leamas was so taken aback that for a moment he was silent.

'All right,' he said finally, 'I'll play, Fiedler, but if you are stringing me along, somehow I'll break your neck.'

'That may not be necessary,' Fiedler replied evenly.

A man who lives a part, not to others but alone, is exposed to obvious psychological dangers. In itself, the practice of deception is not particularly exacting; it is a matter of experience, of professional expertise, it is a facility most of us can acquire. But while a confidence trickster, a play-actor or a gambler can return from his performance to the ranks of his admirers, the secret agent enjoys no such relief. For him, deception is first a matter of self-defence. He must protect himself not only from without but from within, and against the most natural of impulses; though he earn a fortune, his role may forbid him the purchase of a razor, though he be erudite, it can befall him to mumble nothing but banalities; though he be an affectionate husband and father, he must under all circumstances withhold himself from those in whom he should naturally confide.

Aware of the overwhelming temptations which assail a man permanently isolated in his deceit, Leamas resorted to the course which armed him best; even when he was alone, he compelled himself to live with the personality he had assumed. It is said that Balzac on his deathbed enquired anxiously after the health and prosperity of characters he had created. Similarly Leamas, without relinquishing the power of invention, identified himself with what he had invented. The qualities he exhibited to Fiedler, the restless uncertainty, the protective arrogance concealing shame, were not approximations but extensions of qualities he actually possessed; hence also the slight dragging of the feet, the aspect of personal neglect, the indifference to food, and an increasing reliance on alcohol and tobacco. When alone, he remained faithful to these habits. He would even exaggerate them a little, mumbling to himself about the iniquities of his Service.

Only very rarely, as now, going to bed that evening, did he allow himself the dangerous luxury of admitting the great lie he lived.

Control had been phenomenally right. Fiedler was walking like a man led in his sleep, into the net which Control had spread for him. It was uncanny to observe the growing identity of interest between Fiedler and Control: it was as if they had agreed on the same plan, and Leamas had been despatched to fulfil it.

Perhaps that was the answer. Perhaps Fiedler was the special interest Control was fighting so desperately to preserve. Leamas didn't dwell on that possibility. He did not want to know. In matters of that kind he was wholly uninquisitive: he knew that no conceivable good could come of his deductions. Nevertheless, he hoped to God it was true. It was possible, just possible in that case, that he would get home.

Chapter Fourteen

Letter to a Client

Leamas was still in bed the next morning when Fiedler brought him the letters to sign. One was on the thin, blue writing paper of the Seiler Hotel Alpenblick, Lake Spiez, Switzerland, the other from the Palace Hotel, Gstaad.
Leamas read the first letter:

To the Manager,
The Royal Scandinavian Bank Ltd.,
Copenhagen.

Dear Sir,
  I have been travelling for some weeks and have not received any mail from England. Accordingly I have not had your reply to my letter of March 3rd requesting a current statement of the deposit account of which I am a joint signatory with Herr Karlsdorf. To avoid further delay, would you be good enough to forward a duplicate statement to me at the following address, where I shall be staying for two weeks beginning April 21st:

> c/o Madame Y. de Sanglot,
> 13 Avenue des Colombes,
> Paris XII,
> France.

  I apologise for this confusion,

Yours faithfully,

(Robert Lang)

'What's all this about a letter of March 3rd?' he asked. 'I didn't write them any letter.'
'No, you didn't. As far as we know, no one did. That will worry the bank. If there is any inconsistency between the letter we are sending them now and letters they have had from Control, they will assume the solution is to be found in the *missing* letter of March 3rd. Their reaction will be to send you the statement as you ask, with a covering note regretting that they have not received your letter of the third.'

The second letter was the same as the first; only the names were different. The address in Paris was the same. Leamas took a blank piece of paper and his fountain pen and wrote half a dozen times in a fluent hand 'Robert Lang', then signed the first letter. Sloping his pen backwards he practised the second signature until he was satisfied with it, then wrote 'Stephen Bennett' under the second letter.

'Admirable,' Fiedler observed, 'quite admirable.'

'What do we do now?'

'They will be posted in Switzerland tomorrow, in Interlaken and Gstaad. Our people in Paris will telegraph the replies to me as soon as they arrive. We shall have the answer in a week.'

'And until then?'

'We shall be constantly in one another's company. I know that is distasteful to you, and I apologise. I thought we could go for walks, drive round in the hills a bit, kill time. I want you to relax and talk; talk about London, about Cambridge Circus and working in the Department; tell me the gossip, talk about the pay, the leave, the rooms, the paper and the people. The pins and the paper clips. I want to know all the little things that don't matter. Incidentally . . .' A change of tone.

'Yes?'

'We have facilities here for people, who . . . for people who are spending some time with us. Facilities for diversion and so on.'

'Are you offering me a woman?' he asked.

'Yes.'

'No, thank you. Unlike you, I haven't reached the stage where I need a pimp.'

Fiedler seemed indifferent to his reply. He went on quickly.

'But you had a woman in England, didn't you—the girl in the library?'

Leamas turned on him, his hands open at his sides.

'One thing!' he shouted. 'Just that one thing—don't ever mention that again, not as a joke, not as a threat, not even to turn the screws, Fiedler, because it won't work, not ever; I'd dry up, d'you see, you'd never get another bloody word from me as long as I lived. Tell that to them, Fiedler, to Mundt and Stammberger or whichever little alley-cat told you to say it—tell them what I said.'

'I'll tell them,' Fiedler replied; 'I'll tell them. It may be too late.'

In the afternoon they went walking again. The sky was dark and heavy, and the air warm.

'I've only been to England once,' Fiedler observed casually, 'that was on my way to Canada, with my parents before the war. I was a child then of course. We were there for two days.'

Leamas nodded.

'I can tell you this now,' Fiedler continued. 'I nearly went there a few years back. I was going to replace Mundt on the Steel Mission–did you know he was once in London?'

'I knew,' Leamas replied cryptically.

'I always wondered what it would have been like, that job.'

'Usual game of mixing with the other Bloc Missions I suppose. Certain amount of contact with British business–not much of that.' Leamas sounded bored.

'But Mundt got about all right: he found it quite easy.'

'So I hear,' said Leamas; 'he even managed to kill a couple of people.'

'So you heard about that too?'

'From Peter Guillam. He was in on it with George Smiley. Mundt bloody nearly killed George as well.'

'The Fennan case,' Fiedler mused. 'It was amazing that Mundt managed to escape at all, wasn't it?'

'I suppose it was.'

'You wouldn't think that a man whose photograph and personal particulars were filed at the Foreign Office as a member of a Foreign Mission would have a chance against the whole of British Security.'

'From what I hear,' Leamas said, 'they weren't too keen to catch him anyway.'

Fiedler stopped abruptly.

'What did you say?'

'Peter Guillam told me he didn't reckon they wanted to catch Mundt, that's all I said. We had a different set-up then–an Adviser instead of an Operational Control–a man called Maston. Maston had made a bloody awful mess of the Fennan case from the start, that's what Guillam said. Peter reckoned that if they'd caught Mundt it would have made a hell of a stink–they'd have tried him and probably hanged him. The dirt that came out in the process would have finished Maston's career. Peter never knew quite what happened, but he was bloody sure there was no full-scale search for Mundt.'

'You are sure of that, you are sure Guillam told you that in as many words? No full-scale search?'

'Of course I am sure.'

'Guillam never suggested any other reason why they might have let Mundt go?'

'What do you mean?'

Fiedler shook his head and they walked on along the path.

'The Steel Mission was closed down after the Fennan case,' Fiedler observed a moment later, 'that's why I didn't go.'

'Mundt must have been mad. You may be able to get away with assassination in the Balkans–or here–but not London.'

'He did get away with it though, didn't he?' Fiedler put in

quickly. 'And he did good work.'

'Like recruiting Kiever and Ashe? God help him.'

'They ran the Fennan woman for long enough.'

Leamas shrugged.

'Tell me something else about Karl Riemeck,' Fiedler began again. 'He met Control once, didn't he?'

'Yes, in Berlin about a year ago, maybe a bit more.'

'Where did they meet?'

'We all met together in my flat.'

'Why?'

'Control loved to come in on success. We'd got a hell of a lot of good stuff from Karl–I suppose it had gone down well with London. He came out on a short trip to Berlin and asked me to fix up for them to meet.'

'Did you mind?'

'Why should I?'

'He was your agent. You might not have liked him to meet other operators.'

'Control isn't an operator; he's head of Department. Karl knew that and it tickled his vanity.'

'Were you all three together, all the time?'

'Yes. Well, not quite. I left them alone for a quarter of an hour or so–not more. Control wanted that–he wanted a few minutes alone with Karl, God knows why, so I left the flat on some excuse, I forget what. Oh–I know, I pretended we'd run out of Scotch. I actually went and collected a bottle from de Jong in fact.'

'Do you know what passed between them while you were out?'

'How could I? I wasn't that interested, anyway.'

'Didn't Karl tell you afterwards?'

'I didn't ask him. Karl was a cheeky sod in some ways, always pretending he had something over me. I didn't like the way he sniggered about Control. Mind you, he had every right to snigger–it was a pretty ridiculous performance. We laughed about it together a bit, as a matter of fact. There wouldn't have been any point in pricking Karl's vanity; the whole meeting was supposed to give him a shot in the arm.'

'Was Karl depressed then?'

'No, far from it. He was spoilt already. He was paid too much, loved too much, trusted too much. It was partly my fault, partly London's. If we hadn't spoilt him he wouldn't have told that bloody woman of his about his network.'

'Elvira?'

'Yes.' They walked on in silence for a while, until Fiedler interrupted his own reverie to observe:

'I'm beginning to like you. But there's one thing that puzzles me. It's odd–it didn't worry me before I met you.'

'What's that?'

'Why you ever came. Why you defected.' Leamas was going to say something when Fiedler laughed. 'I'm afraid that wasn't very tactful, was it?' he said.

They spent that week walking in the hills. In the evenings they would return to the lodge, eat a bad meal washed down with a bottle of rank white wine, sit endlessly over their Steinhäger in front of the fire. The fire seemed to be Fiedler's idea–they didn't have it to begin with, then one day Leamas overhead him telling a guard to bring logs. Leamas didn't mind the evenings then; after the fresh air all day, the fire and the rough spirit, he would talk unprompted, rambling on about his service. Leamas supposed it was recorded. He didn't care.

As each day passed in this way Leamas was aware of an increasing tension in his companion. Once they went out in the DKW–it was late in the evening–and stopped at a call-box. Fiedler left him in the car with the keys and made a long phone call. When he came back Leamas said:

'Why didn't you ring from the house?' but Fiedler just shook his head.

'We must take care,' he replied; 'you too, you must take care.'

'Why? What's going on?'

'The money you paid into the Copenhagen bank–we wrote, you remember?'

'Of course I remember.'

Fiedler wouldn't say any more, but drove on in silence into the hills. There they stopped. Beneath them, half screened by the ghostly patchwork of tall pine trees, lay the meeting point of two great valleys. The steep wooded hills on either side gradually yielded their colours to the gathering dusk until they stood grey and lifeless in the twilight.

'Whatever happens,' Fiedler said, 'don't worry. It will be all right, do you understand?' His voice was heavy with emphasis, his slim hand rested on Leamas' arm. 'You may have to look after yourself a little, but it won't last long, do you understand?' he asked again.

'No. And since you won't tell me I shall have to wait and see. Don't worry too much for my skin, Fiedler.' He moved his arm, but Fiedler's hand still held him. Leamas hated being touched.

'Do you know Mundt?' asked Fiedler, 'do you know about him?'

'We've talked about Mundt.'

'Yes,' Fiedler repeated, 'we've talked about him. He shoots first and asks questions afterwards. The deterrent principle. It's an odd system in a profession where the questions are always supposed to be more important than the shooting.' Leamas knew what Fiedler wanted to tell him. 'It's an odd system unless you're frightened of the answers,' Fiedler continued under his breath.

Leamas waited. After a moment Fiedler said:

'He's never taken on an interrogation before. He's left it to me before, always. He used to say to me—"You interrogate them, Jens, no one can do it like you. I'll catch them and you make them sing." He used to say that people who do counter-espionage are like painters—they need a man with a hammer standing behind them to strike when they have finished their work, otherwise they forget what they're trying to achieve. "I'll be your hammer," he used to say to me. It was a joke between us, at first, then it began to matter; when he began to kill, kill them before they sang, just as you said: one here, another there, shot or murdered. I asked him, I begged him, "Why not arrest them? Why not let me have them for a month or two? What good to you are they when they are dead?" He just shook his head at me and said there was a law that thistles must be cut down before they flower. I had the feeling that he'd prepared the answer before I ever asked the question. He's a good operator, very good. He's done wonders with the Abteilung—you know that. He's got theories about it; I've talked to him late at night. Coffee he drinks—nothing else—just coffee all the time. He says Germans are too introspective to make good agents, and it comes out in counter-intelligence. He says counter-intelligence people are live wolves chewing dry bones—you have to take away the bones and make them find new quarry—I see all that, I know what he means. But he's gone too far. Why did he kill Viereck? Why did he take him away from me? Viereck was fresh quarry, we hadn't even taken the meat from the bone, you see. So why did he take him? Why, Leamas, why?' The hand on Leamas' arm was clasping it tightly; in the total darkness of the car Leamas was aware of the frightening intensity of Fiedler's emotion.

'I've thought about it night and day. Ever since Viereck was shot, I've asked for a reason. At first it seemed fantastic. I told myself I was jealous, that the work was going to my head, that I was seeing treachery behind every tree, we get like that, people in our world. But I couldn't help myself, Leamas, I had to work it out. There'd been other things before. He was afraid—he was afraid that we would catch one who would talk too much!'

'What are you saying? You're out of your mind,' said Leamas, and his voice held the trace of fear.

'It all held together, you see. Mundt escaped so easily from England; you told me yourself he did. And what did Guillam say to you? He said they didn't *want* to catch him? Why not? I'll tell you why—he was their man; they turned him, they caught him, don't you see and that was the price of his freedom—that and the money he was paid.'

'I tell you you're out of your mind!' Leamas hissed. 'He'll kill you if he ever thinks you make up this kind of stuff. It's sugar candy,

Fiedler. Shut up and drive us home.' At last the hot grip on Leamas' arm relaxed.

'That's where you're wrong. You provided the answer, you yourself, Leamas. That's why we need one another.'

'It's not true!' Leamas shouted. 'I've told you again and again, they couldn't have done it. The Circus couldn't have run him against the Zone without my knowing! It just wasn't an administrative possibility. You're trying to tell me Control was personally directing the deputy head of the Abteilung without the knowledge of the Berlin station. You're mad, Fiedler, you're just bloody well off your head!' Suddenly he began to laugh quietly. 'You may want his job, you poor bastard; that's not unheard of, you know. But this kind of thing went out with bustles.' For a moment neither spoke.

'That money,' Fiedler said, 'in Copenhagen. The bank replied to your letter. The manager is very worried lest there has been a mistake. The money was drawn by your co-signatory exactly one week after you paid it in. The date it was drawn coincides with a two-day visit which Mundt paid to Denmark in February. He went there under an alias to meet an American agent we have who was attending a world scientists' conference.' Fiedler hesitated, then added, 'I suppose you ought to write to the bank and tell them everything is quite in order?'

Chapter Fifteen

Come to the Ball

Liz looked at the letter from Party Centre and wondered what it was about. She found it a little puzzling. She had to admit she was pleased, but why hadn't they consulted her first? Had the District Committee put up her name, or was it Centre's own choice? But no one in Centre knew her, so far as she was aware. She'd met odd speakers of course, and at District Congress she'd shaken hands with the Party Organiser. Perhaps that man from Cultural Relations had remembered her—that fair, rather effeminate man who was so ingratiating. Ashe, that was his name. He'd taken a bit of interest in her and she supposed he might have handed her name on, or remembered her when the Scholarship came up. An odd man, he was; took her to the Black and White for coffee after the meeting and asked her about her boy-friends. He hadn't been amorous or anything—she'd thought he was a bit queer to be honest—but he asked her masses of questions about herself. How long had she been in the Party, did she get homesick living away from her parents? Had she lots of boy-friends or was there a special one she carried a torch for? She hadn't cared for him much but his talk had gone down quite well–the worker-state in the German Democratic Republic, the concept of the worker-poet and all that stuff. He certainly knew all about Eastern Europe, he must have travelled a lot. She'd guessed he was a schoolmaster, he had that rather didactic, fluent way with him. They'd had a collection for the Fighting Fund afterwards, and Ashe had put a pound in; she'd been absolutely amazed. That was it, she was sure now: it was Ashe, who's remembered her. He'd told someone at London District, and District had told Centre or something like that. It still seemed a funny way to go about things, but then the Party always was secretive–it was part of being a revolutionary party, she supposed. It didn't appeal to Liz much, the secrecy, it seemed dishonest. But she supposed it was necessary, and Heaven knows, there were plenty who got a kick out of it.

She read the letter again. It was on Centre's writing paper, with the thick red print at the top and it began 'Dear Comrade', it sounded so military to Liz, and she hated that; she'd never quite got used to 'Comrade'.

Dear Comrade,
    We have recently had discussions with our Comrades in the Socialist Unity Party of the German Democratic Republic on the possibility of effecting exchanges between party members over here and our comrades in democratic Germany. The idea is to create a basis of exchange at the rank and file level between our parties. The S.U.P. is aware that the existing discriminatory measures by the British Home Office make it unlikely that their own delegates will be able to come to the United Kingdom in the immediate future, but they feel that an exchange of experiences is all the more important for this reason. They have generously invited us to select five Branch Secretaries with good experience and a good record of stimulating mass action at street level. Each selected comrade will spend three weeks attending Branch discussions, studying progress in industry and social welfare and seeing at first hand the evidence of fascist provocation by the West. This is a grand opportunity for our comrades to profit from the experience of a young socialist system.
    We therefore asked District to put forward the names of young Cadre workers from your areas who might get the biggest advantage from the trip, and your name has been put forward. We want you to go if you possibly can, and carry out the second part of the scheme–which is to establish contact with a Party Branch in the GDR whose members are from similar industrial backgrounds and have the same kind of problems as your own. The Bayswater South Branch has been paired with Neuenhagen, a suburb of Leipzig. Freda Lüman, Secretary of the Neuenhagen branch, is preparing a big welcome. We are sure you are

just the Comrade for the job, and that it will be a terrific success. All
expenses will be paid by the GDR Cultural Office.

We are sure you realise what a big honour this is, and are confident
you will not allow personal considerations to prevent you from accept-
ing. The visits are due to take place at the end of next month, about the
23rd, but the selected Comrades will travel separately as their invitations are not all concurrent. Will you please let us know as soon as
possible whether you can accept, and we will let you know further
details.

The more she read it, the odder it seemed. Such short notice for a
start–how could they know she could get away from the Library?
Then to her surprise she recalled that Ashe had asked her what she
did for her holidays, whether she had taken her leave this year, and
whether she had to give a lot of notice if she wanted to claim free
time. Why hadn't they told her who the other nominees were? There
was no particular reason why they should, perhaps, but it somehow
looked odd when they didn't. It was such a *long* letter, too. They
were so hard up for secretarial help at Centre they usually kept their
letters short, or asked Comrades to ring up. This was so efficient, so
well typed it might not have been done at Centre at all. But it *was*
signed by the Cultural Organiser; it was his signature all right, no
doubt about that. She'd seen it at the bottom of roneoed notices
masses of times. And the letter had that awkward, semi-
bureaucratic, semi-Messianic style she had grown accustomed to
without ever liking. It was stupid to say she had a good record of
stimulating mass action at street level. She hadn't. As a matter of fact
she hated that side of party work–the loudspeakers at the factory
gates, selling the *Daily Worker* at the street corner, going from door
to door at the local elections. Peace Work she didn't mind so much, it
meant something to her, it made sense. You could look at the kids in
the street as you went by, at the mothers pushing their prams and the
old people standing in doorways, and you could say, 'I'm doing it for
them.' That really *was* fighting for peace.

But she never quite saw the fighting for votes and the fighting for
sales in the same way. Perhaps that was because it cut them down to
size, she thought. It was easy when there were a dozen or so together
at a Branch meeting to rebuild the world, march at the vanguard of
socialism and talk of the inevitability of history. But afterwards she'd
go out into the street with an armful of *Daily Workers*, often waiting
an hour, two hours, to sell a copy. Sometimes she'd cheat, as the
others cheated, and pay for a dozen herself just to get out of it and go
home. At the next meeting they'd boast about it–forgetting they'd
bought them themselves–'Comrade Gold sold eighteen copies on
Saturday night–eighteen!' It would go in the Minutes then, and the
Branch bulletin as well. District would rub their hands, and perhaps
she'd get a mention in that little panel on the front page about the

Fighting Fund. It was such a little world, and she wished they could be more honest. But she lied to herself about it all, too. Perhaps they all did. Or perhaps the others understood more *why* you had to lie so much. It seemed so odd they'd made her Branch Secretary. It was Mulligan who'd proposed it–'Our young, vigorous *and* attractive comrade . . .' He'd thought she'd sleep with him if he got her made secretary. The others had voted for her because they liked her, and because she could type. Because she'd do the work and not try and make them go canvassing at weekends. Not too often anyway. They'd voted for her because they wanted a decent little club, nice and revolutionary and no fuss. It was all such a fraud. Alec had seemed to understand that; he just hadn't taken it seriously. 'Some people keep canaries, some people join the Party,' he'd said once, and it was true. In Bayswater South it was true anyway, and District knew that perfectly well. That's why it was so peculiar that she had been nominated; that was why she was extremely reluctant to believe that District had even had a hand in it. The explanation, she was sure, was Ashe. Perhaps he had a crush on her; perhaps he wasn't queer but just looked it.

Liz made a rather exaggerated shrug, the kind of over-stressed gesture people do make when they are excited and alone. It was abroad anyway, it was free and it sounded interesting. She had never been abroad, and she certainly couldn't afford the fare herself. It would be rather fun. She had reservations about Germans, that was true. She knew, she had been told, that West Germany was militarist and revanchist, and that East Germany was democratic and peace loving. But she doubted whether all the good Germans were on one side and all the bad ones on the other. And it was the bad ones who had killed her father. Perhaps that was why the Party had chosen her–as a generous act of reconciliation. Perhaps that was what Ashe had had in mind when he asked her all those questions. Of course–that was the explanation. She was suddenly filled with a feeling of warmth and gratitude towards the Party. They really were decent people and she was proud and thankful to belong. She went to the desk and opened the drawer where, in an old school satchel, she kept the Branch stationery and the dues stamps. Putting a sheet of paper into her old Underwood typewriter–they'd sent it down from District when they heard she could type; it jumped a bit but otherwise was fine–she typed a neat, grateful letter of acceptance. Centre was such a wonderful thing–stern, benevolent, impersonal, perpetual. They were good, good people. People who fought for peace. As she closed the drawer she caught sight of Smiley's card.

She remembered that little man with the earnest, puckered face, standing at the doorway of her room and saying: 'Did the Party know about you and Alec?' How silly she was. Well, this would take her mind off it.

Chapter Sixteen

Arrest

Fiedler and Leamas drove back the rest of the way in silence. In the dusk the hills were black and cavernous, the pinpoint lights struggling against the gathering darkness like the lights of distant ships at sea.

Fiedler parked the car in a shed at the side of the house and they walked together to the front door. They were about to enter the lodge when they heard a shout from the direction of the trees, followed by someone calling Fiedler's name. They turned, and Leamas distinguished in the twilight twenty yards away three men standing, apparently waiting for Fiedler to come.

'What do you want?' Fiedler called.

'We want to talk to you. We're from Berlin.'

Fiedler hesitated. 'Where's that damn' guard?' he asked Leamas; 'there should be a guard on the front door.'

Leamas shrugged.

'Why aren't the lights on in the hall?' he asked again: then, still unconvinced, he began walking slowly towards the men.

Leamas waited a moment, then, hearing nothing, made his way through the unlit house to the annexe behind it. This was a shoddy barrack hut attached to the back of the building and hidden from all sides by close plantations of young pine trees. The hut was divided into three adjoining bedrooms; there was no corridor. The centre room had been given to Leamas, and the room nearest to the main building was occupied by two guards. Leamas never knew who occupied the third. He had once tried to open the connecting door between it and his own room, but it was locked. He had only discovered it was a bedroom by peering through a narrow gap in the lace curtains early one morning as he went for a walk. The two guards, who followed him everywhere at fifty yards' distance, had not rounded the corner of the hut, and he looked in at the window. The room contained a single bed, made, and a small writing-desk with papers on it. He supposed that someone, with what passes for German thoroughness, watched him from that bedroom. But

Leamas was too old a dog to allow himself to be bothered by surveillance. In Berlin it had been a fact of life–if you couldn't spot it so much the worse: it only meant they were taking greater care, or you were losing your grip. Usually, because he was good at that kind of thing, because he was observant and had an accurate memory–because, in short, he was good at his job–he spotted them anyway. He knew the formations favoured by a shadowing team, he knew the tricks, the weaknesses, the momentary lapses that could give them away. It meant nothing to Leamas that he was watched, but as he walked through the improvised doorway from the lodge to the hut, and stood in the guards' bedroom, he had the distinct feeling that something was wrong.

The lights in the annexe were controlled from some central point. They were put on and off by an unseen hand. In the mornings he was often woken by the sudden blaze of the single overhead light in his room. At night he would be hastened to bed by perfunctory darkness. It was only nine o'clock as he entered the annexe, and the lights were already out. Usually they stayed on till eleven, but now they were out and the shutters had been lowered. He had left the connecting door from the house open, so that the pale twilight from the hallway reached, but scarcely penetrated, the guards' bedroom, and by it he could just see the two empty beds. As he stood there peering into the room, surprised to find it empty, the door behind him closed. Perhaps by itself, but Leamas made no attempt to open it. It was pitch dark. No sound accompanied the closing of the door, no click nor footstep. To Leamas, his instinct suddenly alert, it was as if the sound-track had stopped. Then he smelt the cigar smoke. It must have been hanging in the air but he had not noticed it till now. Like a blind man, his senses of touch and smell were sharpened by the darkness.

There were matches in his pocket but he did not use them. He took one pace sideways, pressed his back against the wall and remained motionless. To Leamas there could only be one explanation–they were waiting for him to pass from the guards' room to his own and therefore he determined to remain where he was. Then from the direction of the main building whence he had come he heard clearly the sound of a footstep. The door which had just closed was tested, the lock turned and made fast. Still Leamas did not move. Not yet. There was no pretence: he was a prisoner in the hut. Very slowly, Leamas now lowered himself into a crouch, putting his hand in the side pocket of his jacket as he did so. He was quite calm, almost relieved at the prospect of action, but memories were racing through his mind. 'You've nearly always got a weapon: an ash-tray, a couple of coins, a fountain-pen–anything that will gouge or cut.' It was the favourite dictum of the mild little Welsh sergeant at that house near Oxford in the war; 'Never use both hands at once, not with a knife, a stick or a pistol; keep your left arm free, and hold it across the belly. If you can't find anything to hit with, keep the hands open and the thumbs stiff.' Taking the box of matches in his right hand he clasped it longways, and deliberately crushed it, so that the small jagged edges of boxwood protruded from between his fingers. This done, he edged his way along the wall until he came to a chair which he knew was in the corner of the room. Indifferent now to the noise he made, he shoved the chair into the centre of the floor. Counting his footsteps as he moved back from the chair, he positioned himself in the angle of the two walls. As he did so, he heard the door of his own bedroom flung open. Vainly he tried to discern the figure who must be standing in the doorway, but there was no light from his own room either. The darkness was impenetrable. He dared not move forward to attack, for the chair was now in the middle of the room; it was his tactical advantage, for he knew where it was, and they did not. They must come for him, they must; he could not let them wait until their helper outside had reached the master switch and put on the lights.

'Come on, you windy bastards,' he hissed in German; 'I'm here, in the corner. Come and get me, can't you?' Not a move, not a sound.

'I'm here, can't you see me? What's the matter then? What's the matter, children, come on, can't you?' And then he heard one stepping forward, and another following; and then the oath of a man as he stumbled on the chair, and that was the sign that Leamas was waiting for. Tossing away the box of matches he slowly, cautiously crept forward, pace by pace, his left arm extended in the attitude of a man warding off twigs in a wood until, quite gently, he had touched an arm and felt the warm prickly cloth of a military uniform. Still with his left hand Leamas deliberately tapped the arm twice–two distinct taps–and heard a frightened voice whisper close to his ear in German:

'Hans, is it you?'

'Shut up, you fool,' Leamas whispered in reply, and in that same moment reached out and grasped the man's hair, pulling his head forward and down, then in a terrible cutting blow drove the side of his right hand on to the nape of the neck, pulled him up again by the arm, hit him in the throat with an upward thrust of his open fist, then released him to fall where the force of gravity took him. As the man's body hit the ground, the lights went on.

In the doorway stood a young captain of the Peoples' Police smoking a cigar, and behind him two men. One was in civilian clothes, quite young. He held a pistol in his hand. Leamas thought it was the Czech kind with a loading lever on the spine of the butt. They were all looking at the man on the floor. Somebody unlocked the outer door and Leamas turned to see who it was. As he turned, there was a shout–Leamas thought it was the captain–telling him to stand still. Slowly he turned back and faced the three men.

His hands were still at his side as the blow came. It seemed to crush his skull. As he fell, drifting warmly into unconsciousness, he wondered whether he had been hit with a revolver, the old kind with a swivel on the butt where you fastened the lanyard.

He was woken by the lag singing and the warder yelling at him to shut up. He opened his eyes and like a brilliant light the pain burst upon his brain. He lay quite still, refusing to close them, watching the sharp, coloured fragments racing across his vision. He tried to take stock of himself: his feet were icy cold and he was aware of the sour stench of prison denims. The singing had stopped and suddenly Leamas longed for it to start again, although he knew it never would. He tried to raise his hand and touch the blood that was caked on his cheek, but his hands were behind him, locked together. His feet too must be bound: the blood had left them, that was why they were cold. Painfully he looked about him, trying to lift his head an inch or two from the floor. To his surprise he saw his own knees in front of him. Instinctively he tried to stretch his legs and as he did so his whole body was seized with a pain so sudden and terrible that he screamed out a sobbing agonised cry of self-pity, like the last cry of a man upon the rack. He lay there panting, attempting to master the pain, then through the sheer perversity of his nature, he tried again, quite slowly, to straighten his legs. At once the agony returned, but Leamas had found the cause: his hands and feet were chained together behind his back. As soon as he attempted to stretch his legs the chain tightened, forcing his shoulders down and his damaged head on to the stone floor. They must have beaten him up while he was unconscious, his whole body was stiff and bruised and his groin ached. He wondered if he'd killed the guard. He hoped so.

Above him shone the light, large, clinical and fierce. No furniture, just whitewashed walls, quite close all round, and the grey steel door, a smart charcoal grey, the colour you see on clever London houses. There was nothing else. Nothing at all. Nothing to think about, just the savage pain.

He must have lain there hours before they came. It grew hot from the light, he was thirsty but he refused to call out. At last the door opened and Mundt stood there. He knew it was Mundt from the eyes. Smiley had told him about them.

Chapter Seventeen

Mundt

They untied him and let him try to stand. For a moment he almost succeeded, then, as the circulation returned to his hands and feet, and as the joints of his body were released from the contraction to which they had been subject, he fell. They let him lie there, watching him with the detachment of children looking at an insect. One of the guards pushed past Mundt and yelled at Leamas to get up. Leamas crawled to the wall and put the palms of his throbbing hands against the white brick. He was half-way up when the guard kicked him and he fell again. He tried once more and this time the guard let him stand with his back against the wall. He saw the guard move his weight on to his left leg and he knew he would kick him again. With all his remaining strength Leamas thrust forward, driving his lowered head into the guard's face. They fell together, Leamas on top. The guard got up and Leamas lay there waiting for the pay-off. But Mundt said something to the guard and Leamas felt himself being picked up by the shoulders and feet and heard the door of his cell close as they carried him down the corridor. He was terribly thirsty.

They took him to a small comfortable room, decently furnished with a desk and armchairs. Swedish blinds half covered the barred windows. Mundt sat at the desk and Leamas in an armchair, his eyes half closed. The guards stood at the door.

'Give me a drink,' said Leamas.

'Whisky?'

'Water.'

Mundt filled a carafe from a basin in the corner, and put it on the table beside him with a glass.

'Bring him something to eat,' he ordered, and one of the guards left the room, returning with a mug of soup and some sliced sausage. He drank and ate, and they watched him in silence.

'Where's Fiedler?' Leamas asked finally.

'Under arrest,' Mundt replied curtly.

'What for?'

'Conspiring to sabotage the security of the people.'

Leamas nodded slowly. 'So you won,' he said. 'When did you arrest him?'

'Last night.'

Leamas waited a moment, trying to focus again on Mundt.

'What about me?' he asked.

'You're a material witness. You will of course stand trial yourself later.'

'So I'm part of a put-up job by London to frame Mundt, am I?'

Mundt nodded, lit a cigarette and gave it to one of the sentries to pass to Leamas. 'That's right,' he said. The sentry came over, and with a gesture of grudging solicitude, put the cigarette between Leamas' lips.

'A pretty elaborate operation,' Leamas observed, and added stupidly, 'clever chaps these Chinese.'

Mundt said nothing. Leamas became used to his silences as the interview progressed. Mundt had rather a pleasant voice, that was something Leamas hadn't expected, but he seldom spoke. It was part of Mundt's extraordinary self-confidence perhaps, that he did not speak unless he specifically wished to, that he was prepared to allow long silences to intervene rather than exchange pointless words. In this he differed from professional interrogators who set store by initiative, by the evocation of atmosphere and the exploitation of that psychological dependency of a prisoner upon his inquisitor. Mundt despised technique: he was a man of fact and action. Leamas preferred that.

Mundt's appearance was fully consistent with his temperament. He looked an athlete. His fair hair was cut short. It lay mat and neat. His young face had a hard, clean line, and a frightening directness; it was barren of humour or fantasy. He looked young but not youthful; older men would take him seriously. He was well built. His clothes fitted him because he was an easy man to fit. Leamas found no difficulty in recalling that Mundt was a killer. There was a coldness about him, a rigorous self-sufficiency which perfectly equipped him for the business of murder. Mundt was a very hard man.

'The other charge on which you will stand trial, if necessary,' Mundt added quietly, 'is murder.'

'So the sentry died, did he?' Leamas replied.

A wave of intense pain passed through his head.

Mundt nodded: 'That being so,' he said, 'your trial for espionage is somewhat academic. I propose that the case against Fiedler should be publicly heard. That is also the wish of the Praesidium.'

'And you want my confession?'

'Yes.'

'In other words you haven't any proof.'

'We shall have proof. We shall have your confession.' There was no menace in Mundt's voice. There was no style, no theatrical twist.

'On the other hand, there could be mitigation in your case. You were blackmailed by British Intelligence; they accused you of stealing money and then coerced you into preparing a revanchist trap against myself. The court would have sympathy for such a plea.'

Leamas seemed to be taken off his guard.

'How did you know they accused me of stealing money?' But Mundt made no reply.

'Fiedler has been very stupid,' Mundt observed. 'As soon as I read the report of our friend Peters I knew why you had been sent, and I knew that Fiedler would fall into the trap. Fiedler hates me so much.' Mundt nodded, as if to emphasise the truth of his observation. 'Your people knew that of course. It was a very clever operation. Who prepared it, tell me. Was it Smiley? Did he do it?' Leamas said nothing.

'I wanted to see Fiedler's report of his own interrogation of you, you see. I told him to send it to me. He procrastinated and I knew I was right. Then yesterday he circulated it among the Praesidium, and did not send me a copy. Someone in London has been very clever.'

Leamas said nothing.

'When did you last see Smiley?' Mundt asked casually. Leamas hesitated, uncertain of himself. His head was aching terribly.

'When did you last see him?' Mundt repeated.

'I don't remember,' Leamas said at last; 'he wasn't really in the outfit any more. He'd drop in from time to time.'

'He is a great friend of Peter Guillam is he not?'

'I think so, yes.'

'Guillam, you thought, studied the economic situation in the GDR. Some odd little section in your Service; you weren't quite sure what it did.'

'Yes.' Sound and sight were becoming confused in the mad throbbing of his brain. His eyes were hot and painful. He felt sick.

'Well, when did you last see Smiley?'

'I don't remember . . . I don't remember''

Mundt shook his head.

'You have a very good memory–for anything that incriminates me. We can all remember when we *last* saw somebody. Did you for instance see him after you returned from Berlin?'

'Yes, I think so. I bumped into him . . . in the Circus once, in London.' Leamas had closed his eyes and he was sweating. 'I can't go on, Mundt . . . not much longer, Mundt; I'm sick,' he said.

'After Ashe had picked you up, after he had walked into the trap that had been set for him, you had lunch together, didn't you?'

'Yes. Lunch together.'

'Lunch ended at about four o'clock. Where did you go then?'

'I went down to the City, I think. I don't remember for sure . . . for Christ's sake, Mundt,' he said holding his head with his hand, 'I can't go on. My bloody head's . . .'

'And after that where did you go? Why did you shake off your followers, why were you so keen to shake them off?'

Leamas said nothing: he was breathing in sharp gasps, his head buried in his hands.

'Answer this one question, then you can go. You shall have a bed. You can sleep if you want. Otherwise you must go back to your cell, do you understand? You will be tied up again and fed on the floor like an animal, do you understand? Tell me where you went.'

The wild pulsation of his brain suddenly increased, the room was dancing; he heard voices around him and the sound of footsteps; spectral shapes passed and re-passed, detached from sound and gravity; someone was shouting, but not at him; the door was open, he was sure someone had opened the door. The room was full of people, all shouting now, and then they were going, some of them had gone, he heard them marching away, the stamping of their feet was like the throbbing of his head; the echo died and there was silence. Then like the touch of mercy itself, a cool cloth was laid across his forehead, and kindly hands carried him away.

He woke on a hospital bed, and standing at the foot of it was Fiedler, smoking a cigarette.

Chapter Eighteen

Fiedler

Leamas took stock. A bed with sheets. A single ward with no bars in the windows, just curtains and frosted glass. Pale green walls, dark green linoleum; and Fiedler watching him, smoking.

A nurse brought him food: an egg, some thin soup and fruit. He felt like death, but he supposed he'd better eat it. So he did and Fiedler watched.

'How do you feel?' he asked.

'Bloody awful,' Leamas replied.

'But better?'

'I suppose so.' He hesitated. 'Those sods beat me up.'

'You killed a sentry, you know that?'

'I guessed I had. . . . What do they expect if they mount such a damn' stupid operation. Why didn't they pull us both in at once?

Why put all the lights out? If anything was over-organised, that was.'

'I am afraid that as a nation we tend to over-organise. Abroad that passes for efficiency.'

Again there was a pause.

'What happened to you?' Leamas asked.

'Oh, I too was softened for interrogation.'

'By Mundt's men?'

'By Mundt's men *and* Mundt. It was a very peculiar sensation!'

'That's one way of putting it.'

'No, no; not physically. Physically it was a nightmare, but you see Mundt had a special interest in beating me up. Apart from the confession.'

'Because you dreamed up that story about—'

'Because I am a Jew.'

'Oh, Christ,' said Leamas softly.

'That is why I got special treatment. All the time he whispered to me. It was very strange.'

'What did he say?'

Fiedler didn't reply. At last he muttered:

'That's all over.'

'Why? What's happened?'

'The day we were arrested I had applied to the Praesidium for a civil warrant to arrest Mundt as an enemy of the people.'

'But you're mad—I told you, you're raving mad, Fiedler! He'll never—'

'There was other evidence against him apart from yours. Evidence I have been accumulating over the last three years, piece by piece. Yours provided the proof we need; that's all. As soon as that was clear I prepared a report and sent it to every member of the Praesidium except Mundt. They received it on the same day that I made my application for a warrant.'

'The day we were pulled in.'

'Yes. I knew Mundt would fight. I knew he had friends on the Praesidium, or yes-men at least, people who were sufficiently frightened to go running to him as soon as they got my report. And in the end, I knew he would lose. The Praesidium had the weapon it needed to destroy him; they had the report, and for those few days while you and I were being questioned they read it and re-read it until they knew it was true and each knew the others knew. In the end they acted. Herded together by their common fear, their common weakness and their common knowledge they turned against him and ordered a Tribunal.'

'Tribunal?'

'A secret one, of course. It meets tomorrow. Mundt is under arrest.'

'What is this other evidence? The evidence you've collected?'

'Wait and see,' Fiedler replied with a smile. 'Tomorrow you will see.'

Fiedler was silent for a time, watching Leamas eat.

'This Tribunal,' Leamas asked, 'how is it conducted?'

'That is up to the President. It is not a People's Court—it is important to remember that. It is more in the nature of an enquiry—a committee of enquiry, that's it, appointed by the Praesidium to investigate and report upon a certain . . . subject. Its report contains a recommendation. In a case like this the recommendation is tantamount to a verdict, but remains secret, as a part of the proceedings of the Praesidium.'

'How does it work? Are there counsel and judges?'

'There are three judges,' Fiedler said; 'and in effect, there are counsel. Tomorrow I myself shall put the case against Mundt. Karden will defend him.'

'Who's Karden?'

Fiedler hesitated.

'A very tough man,' he said. 'Looks like a country doctor, small and benevolent. He was at Buchenwald.'

'Why can't Mundt defend himself?'

'It was Mundt's wish. It is said that Karden will call a witness.'

Leamas shrugged.

'That's your affair,' he said. Again there was silence. At last Fiedler said reflectively:

'I wouldn't have minded—I don't think I would have minded, not so much anyway—if he had hurt me for myself, for hate or jealousy. Do you understand that? That long, long pain and all the time you say to yourself, "Either I shall faint or I shall grow to bear the pain, nature will see to that" and the pain just increases like a violinist going up the E string. You think it can't get any higher and it does—the pain's like that, it rises and rises, and all that nature does is bring you on from note to note like a deaf child being taught to hear. And all the time he was whispering Jew . . . Jew. I could understand, I'm sure I could, if he had done it for the idea, for the Party, if you like, or if he had hated *me*. But it wasn't that; he hated—'

'All right,' said Leamas shortly, 'you should know. He's a bastard.'

'Yes,' said Fiedler, 'he is a bastard.' He seemed excited; he wants to boast to somebody, thought Leamas.

'I thought a lot about you,' Fiedler added. 'I thought about that talk we had—you remember—about the motor.'

'What motor?'

Fiedler smiled. 'I'm sorry that is a direction translation. I mean *'Motor'*, the engine, spirit, urge; whatever Christians call it.'

'I'm not a Christian.'

Fiedler shrugged. 'You know what I mean.' He smiled again, 'the

thing that embarrasses you. . . . I'll put it another way. Suppose
Mundt is right. He asked me to confess, you know; I was to confess
that I was in league with British spies who were plotting to murder
him. You see the argument—that the whole operation was mounted
by British Intelligence in order to entice us—me, if you like—into
liquidating the best man in the Abteilung. To turn our own weapon
against us.'

'He tried that on me,' said Leamas indifferently. And he added,
'As if I'd cooked up the whole bloody story.'

'But what I mean is this: suppose you had done that, suppose it
were true—I am taking an example, you understand, a hypothesis,
would you kill a man, an innocent man—'

'Mundt's a killer himself.'

'Suppose he wasn't. Suppose it were me they wanted to kill: would
London do it?'

'It depends . . . it depends on the need. . . .'

'Ah,' said Fiedler contentedly, 'it depends on the need. Like
Stalin, in fact. The traffic accident and the statistics. That is a great
relief.'

'Why?'

'You must get some sleep,' said Fiedler. 'Order what food you
want. They will bring you whatever you want. Tomorrow you can
talk.' As he reached the door he looked back and said, 'We're all the
same, you know, that's the joke.'

Soon Leamas was asleep, content in the knowledge that Fiedler
was his ally and that they would shortly send Mundt to his death.
That was something which he had looked forward to for a very long
time.

Chapter Nineteen

Branch Meeting

Liz was happy in Leipzig. Austerity pleased her—it gave her the
comfort of sacrifice. The little house she stayed in was dark and
meagre, the food was poor and most of it had to go to the children.
They talked politics at every meal, she and Frau Ebert, Branch
Secretary for the Ward Branch of Leipzig-Hohengrün, a small, grey
woman whose husband managed a gravel quarry on the outskirts of
the city. It was like living in a religious community, Liz thought; a
convent or a kibbutz or something. You felt the world was better for

your empty stomach. Liz had some German which she had learnt
from her aunt, and she was surprised how quickly she was able to use
it. She tried it on the children first and they grinned and helped her.
The children treated her oddly to begin with, as if she were a person
of great quality or rarity value, and on the third day one of them
plucked up courage and asked her if she had brought any chocolate
from 'drüben'–from 'over there'. She'd never thought of that and
she felt ashamed. After that they seemed to forget about her.

In the evenings there was Party Work. They distributed literature,
visited Branch members who had defaulted on their dues or lagged
behind in their attendance at meetings, called in at District for a
discussion on 'Problems connected with the centralised distribution
of agricultural produce' at which all local Branch Secretaries were
present, and attended a meeting of the Workers' Consultative
Council of a machine tool factory on the outskirts of the town.

At last, on the fourth day, the Thursday, came their own Branch
Meeting. This was to be, for Liz at least, the most exhilarating
experience of all; it would be an example of all that her own Branch in
Bayswater could one day be. They had chosen a wonderful title for
the evening's discussions–'Coexistence after two wars'–and they
expected a record attendance. The whole ward had been circularised,
they had taken care to see that there was no rival meeting in the
neighbourhood that evening; it was not a late shopping day.

Seven people came.

Seven people and Liz and the Branch Secretary and the man from
District. Liz put a brave face on it but she was terribly upset. She
could scarcely concentrate on the speaker, and when she tried he
used long German compounds that she couldn't work out anyway. It
was like the meetings in Bayswater, it was like mid-week evensong
when she used to go to church–the same dutiful, little group of lost
faces, the same fussy self-consciousness, the same feeling of a great
idea in the hands of little people. She always felt the same thing–it
was awful, really, but she did–she wished no one would turn up,
because that was absolute and it suggested persecution,
humiliation–it was something you could react to.

But seven people were nothing: they were worse than nothing,
because they were evidence of the inertia of the uncapturable mass.
They broke your heart.

The room was better than the schoolroom in Bayswater, but even
that was no comfort. In Bayswater it had been fun trying to *find* a
room. In the early days they had pretended they were something
else, not the Party at all. They'd taken back rooms in pubs, a
committee room at the Ardena Café, or met secretly in one another's
houses. Then Bill Hazel had joined from the Secondary School and
they'd used his classroom. Even that was a risk–the headmaster
thought Bill ran a drama group, so theoretically at least they might

still be chucked out. Somehow that fitted better than this Peace Hall in pre-cast concrete with the cracks in the corners and the picture of Lenin. Why did they have that silly frame thing all round the picture? Bundles of organ pipes sprouting from the corners and the bunting all dusty. It looked like something from a fascist funeral. Sometimes she thought Alec was right—you believed in these things because you needed to; what you believed in had no value of its own, no function. What did he say: 'A dog scratches where it itches. Different dogs itch in different places.' No, it was wrong, Alec was wrong—it was a wicked thing to say. Peace and freedom and equality—they were facts, of course they were. And what about history—all those laws the Party proved. No, Alec was wrong: truth existed outside people, it was demonstrated in history, individuals must bow to it, be crushed by it if necessary. The Party was the vanguard of history, the spearpoint in the fight for Peace . . . she went over the rubric a little uncertainly. She wished more people had come. Seven was so few. They looked so cross; cross and hungry.

The meeting over, Liz waited for Frau Ebert to collect the unsold literature from the heavy table by the door, fill in her attendance book and put on her coat, for it was cold that evening. The speaker had left—rather rudely, Liz thought—before the general discussion. Frau Ebert was standing at the door with her hand on the light switch when a man appeared out of the darkness, framed in the doorway. Just for a moment Liz thought it was Ashe. He was tall and fair and wore one of those raincoats with leather buttons.

'Comrade Ebert?' he enquired.

'Yes?'

'I am looking for an English Comrade, Gold. She is staying with you?'

'I'm Elizabeth Gold,' Liz put in, and the man came into the hall, closing the door behind him, so that the light shone full upon his face.

'I am Holten from District.' He showed some paper to Frau Ebert who was still standing at the door, and she nodded and glanced a little anxiously towards Liz.

'I have been asked to give a message to Comrade Gold from the Praesidium,' he said. 'It concerns an alteration in your programme; an invitation to attend a special meeting.'

'Oh,' said Liz rather stupidly. It seemed fantastic that the Praesidium should even have heard of her.

'It is a gesture,' Holten said. 'A gesture of goodwill.'

'But I—but Frau Ebert . . .' Liz began helplessly.

'Comrade Ebert, I am sure will forgive you under the circumstances.'

'Of course,' said Frau Ebert quickly.

'Where is the meeting to be held?'

'It will necessitate your leaving tonight,' Holten replied. 'We have a long way to go. Nearly to Görlitz.'

'To Görlitz. . . . Where's that?'

'East,' said Frau Ebert quickly. 'On the Polish border.'

'We can drive you home now. You can collect your things and we will continue the journey at once.'

'Tonight? Now?'

'Yes.' Holten didn't seem to consider Liz had much choice.

A large black car was waiting for them. There was a driver in the front and a flagpost on the bonnet. It looked rather a military car.

Chapter Twenty

Tribunal

The court was no larger than a schoolroom. At one end, on the mere five or six benches which were provided, sat guards and warders and here and there among them spectators—members of the Praesidium and selected officials. At the other end of the room sat the three members of the Tribunal on tall-backed chairs at an unpolished oak table. Above them, suspended from the ceiling by three loops of wire, was a large red star made of plywood. The walls of the courtroom were white like the walls of Leamas' cell.

On either side, their chairs a little forward of the table, and turned inwards to face one another, sat two men; one was middle-aged, sixty perhaps, in a black suit and a grey tie, the kind of suit they wear in church in German country districts. The other was Fiedler.

Leamas sat at the back, a guard on either side of him. Between the heads of the spectators he could see Mundt, himself surrounded by police, his fair hair cut very short, his broad shoulders covered in the familiar grey of prison uniform. It seemed to Leamas a curious commentary on the mood of the court—or the influence of Fiedler—that he himself should be wearing his own clothes, while Mundt was in prison uniform.

Leamas had not long been in his place when the president of the Tribunal, sitting at the centre of the table, rang the bell. The sound directed his attention towards it, and a shiver passed over him as he realised that the president was a woman. He could scarcely be blamed for not noting it before. She was fiftyish, small-eyed and dark. Her hair was cut short like a man's, and she wore the kind of functional dark tunic favoured by Soviet wives. She looked sharply round the room, nodded to a sentry to close the door, and began at once without ceremony to address the court.

'You all know why we are here. The proceedings are secret, remember that. This is a Tribunal convened expressly by the Praesidium. It is to the Praesidium alone that we are responsible. We shall hear evidence as we think fit.' She pointed perfunctorily towards Fiedler. 'Comrade Fiedler, you had better begin.'

Fiedler stood up. Nodding briefly towards the table he drew from the briefcase beside him a sheaf of papers held together in one corner by a piece of black cord.

He talked quietly and easily, with a diffidence which Leamas had never seen in him before. Leamas considered it a good performance, well adjusted to the role of a man regretfully hanging his superior.

'You should know first, if you do not know already,' Fiedler began, 'that on the day that the Praesidium received my report on the activities of Comrade Mundt I was arrested, together with the defector Leamas. Both of us were imprisoned and both of us . . . invited, under extreme duress, to confess that this whole terrible charge was a fascist plot against a loyal comrade.

'You can see from the report I have already given you how it was that Leamas came to our notice: we ourselves sought him out, induced him to defect and finally brought him to Democratic Germany. Nothing could more clearly demonstrate the impartiality of Leamas than this: that he still refuses, for reasons I will explain, to believe that Mundt was a British agent. It is therefore grotesque to suggest that Leamas is a plant: the initiative was ours, and the fragmentary but vital evidence of Leamas provides only the final proof in a long chain of indications reaching back over the last three years.

'You have before you the written record of this case. I need do no more than interpret for you facts of which you are already aware.

'The charge against Comrade Mundt is that he is the agent of an imperialist power. I could have made other charges—that he passed information to the British Secret Service, that he turned his Department into the unconscious lackey of a bourgeois state, that he deliberately shielded revanchist anti-Party groups and accepted sums of foreign currency in reward. These other charges would derive from the first; that Hans-Dieter Mundt is the agent of an imperialist power. The penalty for this crime is death. There is no crime more serious in our penal code, none which exposes our state to greater danger, nor demands more vigilance of our Party organs.' Here he put the papers down.

'Comrade Mundt is forty-two years old. He is deputy head of the Department for the Protection of the People. He is unmarried. He has always been regarded as a man of exceptional capabilities, tireless in serving the Party's interests, ruthless in protecting them.

'Let me tell you some details of his career. He was recruited into the Department at the age of twenty-eight and underwent the customary instruction. Having completed his probationary period he undertook special tasks in Scandinavian countries–notably Norway, Sweden and Finland–where he succeeded in establishing an intelligence network which carried the battle against fascist agitators into the enemy's camp. He performed this task well, and there is no reason to suppose that at that time he was other than a diligent member of his Department. But, Comrades, you should not forget this early connection with Scandinavia. The networks established by Comrade Mundt soon after the war provided the excuse, many years later, for him to travel to Finland and Norway, where his commitments became a cover enabling him to draw thousands of dollars from foreign banks in return for his treacherous conduct. Make no mistake: Comrade Mundt has not fallen victim to those who try to disprove the arguments of history. First cowardice, then weakness, then greed were his motives; the acquirement of great wealth his dream. Ironically, it was the elaborate system by which his lust for money was satisfied that brought the forces of justice on his trail.'

Fiedler paused, and looked round the room, his eyes suddenly alight with fervour. Leamas watched, fascinated.

'Let that be a lesson,' Fiedler shouted, 'to those other enemies of the state, whose crime is so foul that they must plot in the secret hours of the night!' A dutiful murmur rose from the tiny group of spectators at the back of the room.

'They will not escape the vigilance of the people whose blood they seek to sell!' Fiedler might have been addressing a large crowd rather than the handful of officials and guards assembled in the tiny, white-walled room.

Leamas realised at this moment that Fiedler was taking no chances: the deportment of the Tribunal, prosecutors and witnesses must be politically impeccable. Fiedler, knowing no doubt that the danger of a subsequent counter-charge was inherent in such cases, was protecting his own back: the polemic would go down in the record and it would be a brave man who set himself to refute it.

Fiedler now opened the file that lay on the desk before him.

'At the end of 1956 Mundt was posted to London as a member of the East German Steel Mission. He had the additional special task of undertaking counter-subversionary measures against *emigré* groups. In the course of his work he exposed himself to great dangers–of that there is no doubt–and he obtained valuable results.'

Leamas' attention was again drawn to the three figures at the centre table. To the President's left a youngish man, dark. His eyes seemed to be half closed. He had lank, unruly hair and the grey, meagre complexion of an ascetic. His hands were slim, restlessly toying with the corner of a bundle of papers which lay before him. Leamas guessed he was Mundt's man; he found it hard to say why. On the other side of the table sat a slightly older man, balding, with an open agreeable face. Leamas thought he looked rather an ass. He guessed that if Mundt's fate hung in the balance the young man would defend him and the woman condemn. He thought the second man would be embarrassed by the difference of opinion and side with the President.

Fiedler was speaking again.

'It was at the end of his service in London that recruitment took place. I have said that he exposed himself to great dangers; in doing so he fell foul of the British secret police, and they issued a warrant for his arrest. Mundt, who had no diplomatic immunity (NATO Britain does not recognise our sovereignty), went into hiding. Ports were watched, his photograph and description were distributed throughout the British Isles. Yet, after two days in hiding, Comrade Mundt took a taxi to London Airport and flew to Berlin. "Brilliant," you will say, and so it was. With the whole of Britain's police force alerted, her road, railways, shipping and air routes under constant surveillance, Comrade Mundt takes a plane from London Airport. Brilliant indeed. Or perhaps you may feel, Comrades, with the advantage of hindsight, that Mundt's escape from England was a little *too* brilliant, a little *too* easy, that without the connivance of the British authorities it would never have been possible at all!' Another murmur, more spontaneous than the first, rose from the back of the room.

'The truth is this: Mundt *was* taken prisoner by the British; in a short historic interview they offered him the classic alternative. Was it to be years in an imperialist prison, the end of a brilliant career, or was Mundt to make a dramatic return to his home country, against all expectation, and fulfil the promise he had shown? The British, of course, made it a condition of his return that he should provide them with information, and they would pay him large sums of money. With the carrot in front and the stick behind, Mundt was recruited.

'It was now in the British interest to promote Mundt's career. We cannot yet prove that Mundt's success in liquidating minor Western intelligence agents was the work of his imperialist masters betraying their own collaborators—those who were expendable—in order that Mundt's prestige should be enhanced. We cannot prove it, but it is an assumption which the evidence permits.

'Ever since 1960—the year Comrade Mundt became Head of the Counter Espionage section of the Abteilung—indications have reached us from all over the world that there was a highly-placed spy in our ranks. You all know Karl Riemeck was a spy; we thought when he was eliminated that the evil had been stamped out. But the rumours persisted.

'In late 1960 a former collaborator of ours approached an Englishman in the Lebanon known to be in contact with their Intelligence Service. He offered him—we found out soon afterwards—a complete breakdown of the two sections of the Abteilung for which he had formerly worked. His offer, after it had been transmitted to London, was rejected. That was a very curious thing. It could only mean that the British already possessed the intelligence they were being offered, *and that it was up to date.*

'From mid-1960 onwards we were losing collaborators abroad at an alarming rate. Often they were arrested within a few weeks of their despatch. Sometimes the enemy attempted to turn our own agents back on us, but not often. It was as if they could scarcely be bothered.

'And then—it was early 1961 if my memory is correct—we had a stroke of luck. We obtained by means I will not describe, a summary of the information which British Intelligence held about the Abteilung. It was complete, it was accurate, and it was astonishingly up to date. I showed it to Mundt, of course—he was my superior. He told me it came as no surprise to him: he had certain enquiries in hand and I should take no action for fear of prejudicing them. And I confess that at that moment the thought crossed my mind, remote and fantastic as it was, that Mundt himself could have provided the information. There were other indications too. . . .

'I need hardly tell you that the last, the very last person to be suspected of espionage is the head of the Counter Espionage section. The notion is so appalling, so melodramatic that few would entertain it, let alone give expression to it! I confess that I myself have been guilty of excessive reluctance in reaching such a seemingly fantastic deduction. That was erroneous.

'But, Comrades, the final evidence has been delivered into our hands. I propose to call that evidence now.' He turned, glancing towards the back of the room. 'Bring Leamas forward.'

The guards on either side of him stood up and Leamas edged his way along the row to the rough gangway which ran not more than two feet wide, down the middle of the room. A guard indicated to him that he should stand facing the table. Fiedler stood a bare six feet away from him. First the President addressed him.

'Witness, what is your name?' she asked.

'Alec Leamas.'

'What is your age?'

'Fifty.'

'Are you married?'

'No.'

'But you were.'

'I'm not married now.'

'What is your profession?'

'Assistant librarian.'

Fiedler angrily intervened. 'You were formerly employed by British Intelligence, were you not?' he snapped.

'That's right. Till a year ago.'

'The Tribunal has read the reports of your interrogation,' Fiedler continued. 'I want you to tell them again about the conversation you had with Peter Guillam some time in May last year.'

'You mean when we talked about Mundt?'

'Yes.'

'I've told you. I was at the Circus, the office in London, our headquarters in Cambridge Circus. I bumped into Peter in the corridor. I knew he was mixed up with the Fennan case and I asked him what had become of George Smiley. Then we got talking about Dieter Frey, who died, and Mundt, who was mixed up in the thing. Peter said he thought that Maston—Maston was effectively in charge of the case then—had not wanted Mundt to be caught.'

'How did you interpret that?' asked Fiedler.

'I knew Maston had made a mess of the Fennan case. I supposed he didn't want any mud raked up by Mundt appearing at the Old Bailey.'

'If Mundt had been caught, would he have been legally charged?' the President put in.

'It depends who caught him. If the police got him they'd report it to the Home Office. After that no power on earth could stop him being charged.'

'And what if your Service had caught him?' Fiedler enquired.

'Oh, that's a different matter. I suppose they would either have interrogated him and then tried to exchange him for one of our own people in prison over here; or else they'd have given him a ticket.'

'What does that mean?'

'Get rid of him.'

'Liquidated him?' Fiedler was asking all the questions now, and the members of the Tribunal were writing diligently in the files before them.

'I don't know what they do. I've never been mixed up in that game.'

'Might they not have tried to recruit him as their agent?'

'Yes, but they didn't succeed.'

'How do you know that?'

'Oh, for God's sake, I've told you over and over again. I'm not a bloody performing seal. . . . I was head of the Berlin Command for four years. If Mundt had been one of our people, I would have known. I couldn't help knowing.'

'Quite.'

Fiedler seemed content with that answer, confident perhaps that the remainder of the Tribunal was not. He now turned his attention to Operation 'Rolling Stone', took Leamas once again through the special security complexities governing the circulation of the file, the letters to the Copenhagen and Helsinki banks and the one reply which Leamas had received. Addressing himself to the Tribunal, Fiedler commented:

'We had no reply from Helsinki. I do not know why. But let me recapitulate for you. Leamas deposited money at Copenhagen on June 15th. Among the papers before you there is the facsimile of a letter from the Royal Scandinavian Bank addressed to Robert Lang. Robert Lang was the name Leamas used to open the Copenhagen deposit account. From that letter (it is the twelfth serial in your files) you will see that the entire sum—ten thousand dollars—was drawn by the co-signatory to the account one week later. I imagine,' Fiedler continued, indicating with his head the motionless figure of Mundt in the front row, 'that it is not disputed by the Defendant that he was in Copenhagen on June 21st, nominally engaged on secret work on behalf of the Abteilung.' He paused and then continued:

'Leamas' visit to Helsinki—the second visit he made to deposit money—took place on about September 24th.' Raising his voice he turned and looked directly at Mundt. 'On the third of October Comrade Mundt made a clandestine journey to Finland—once more allegedly in the interests of the Abteilung.' There was silence. Fiedler turned slowly and addressed himself once more to the Tribunal. In a voice at once subdued and threatening he asked:

'Are you complaining that the evidence is circumstantial? Let me remind you of something more.' He turned to Leamas.

'Witness, during your activities in Berlin you became associated with Karl Riemeck, formerly Secretary to the Praesidium of the Socialist Unity Party. What was the nature of that association?'

'He was my agent, until he was shot by Mundt's men.'

'Quite so. He was shot by Mundt's men. One of several spies who were summarily liquidated by Comrade Mundt before they could be questioned. But before he was shot by Mundt's men he was an agent of the British Secret Service?'

Leamas nodded.

'Will you describe Riemeck's meeting with the man you call Control.'

'Control came over to Berlin from London to see Karl. Karl was one of the most productive agents we had, I think, and Control wanted to meet him.'

Fiedler put in: 'He was also one of the most trusted?'

'Yes, oh yes. London loved Karl; he could do no wrong. When Control came out I fixed up for Karl to come to my flat and the three of us dined together. I didn't like Karl coming there really, but I couldn't tell Control that. It's hard to explain but they get ideas in

London, they're so cut off from it and I was frightened stiff they'd find some excuse for taking over Karl themselves–they're quite capable of it.'

'So you arranged for the three of you to meet,' Fiedler put in curtly, 'what happened?'

'Control asked me beforehand to see that he had a quarter of an hour alone with Karl, so during the evening I pretended to have run out of Scotch. I left the flat and went over to de Jong's place. I had a couple of drinks there, borrowed a bottle and came back.'

'How did you find them?'

'What do you mean?'

'Were Control and Riemeck talking still? If so, what were they talking about?'

'They weren't talking at all when I came back.'

'Thank you. You may sit down.'

Leamas returned to his seat at the back of the room. Fiedler turned to the three members of the Tribunal and began:

'I want to talk first about the spy Riemeck, who was shot: Karl Riemeck. You have before you a list of all the information which Riemeck passed to Alec Leamas in Berlin, so far as Leamas can recall it. It is a formidable record of treachery. Let me summarise it for you. Riemeck gave to his masters a detailed breakdown of the work and personalities of the whole Abteilung. He was able, if Leamas is to be believed, to describe the workings of our most secret sessions. As secretary to the Praesidium he gave minutes of its most secret proceedings.

'That was easy for him; he himself compiled the record of every meeting. But Riemeck's *access* to the secret affairs of the Abteilung is a different matter. Who at the end of 1959 co-opted Riemeck on to the Committee for the Protection of the People, that vital sub-committee of the Praesidium which co-ordinates and discusses the affairs of our security organs? Who proposed that Riemeck should have the privilege of access to the files of the Abteilung? Who at every stage in Riemeck's career *since* 1959 (the year Mundt returned from England, you remember) singled him out for posts of exceptional responsibility? I will tell you,' Fiedler proclaimed. 'The same man who was uniquely placed to shield him in his espionage activities: Hans-Dieter Mundt. Let us recall how Riemeck contacted the Western Intelligence Agencies in Berlin–how he sought out de Jong's car on a picnic and put the film inside it. Are you not amazed at Riemeck's foreknowledge? How could he have known where to find that car, and on that very day? Riemeck had no car himself, he could not have followed de Jong from his house in West Berlin. There was only one way he could have known–through the agency of our own Security police, who reported de Jong's presence as a matter of routine as soon as the car passed the Inter Sector checkpoint. That knowledge was available to Mundt, and Mundt made it available to Riemeck. *That* is the case against Hans-Dieter Mundt—I tell you, Riemeck was his creature, the link between Mundt and his imperialist masters!'

Fiedler paused, then added quietly:

'Mundt—Riemeck—Leamas: that was the chain of command, and it is axiomatic of intelligence technique the whole world over that each link of the chain be kept, as far as possible, in ignorance of the others. Thus it is *right* that Leamas should maintain he knows nothing to the detriment of Mundt: that is no more than the proof of good security by his masters in London.

'You have also been told how the whole case known as 'Rolling Stone' was conducted under conditions of special secrecy, how Leamas knew in vague terms of an intelligence section under Peter Guillam which was supposedly concerned with economic conditions in our Republic—a section which surprisingly was on the distribution list of 'Rolling Stone'. Let me remind you that that same Peter Guillam was one of several British security officers who were involved in the investigation of Mundt's activities while he was in England.'

The youngish man at the table lifted his pencil, and looking at Fiedler with his hard, cold eyes wide open he asked:

'Then why did Mundt liquidate Riemeck, if Riemeck was his agent?'

'He had no alternative. Riemeck was under suspicion. His mistress had betrayed him by boastful indiscretion. Mundt gave the order that he be shot on sight, got word to Riemeck to run, and the danger of betrayal was eliminated. Later, Mundt assassinated the woman.

'I want to speculate for a moment on Mundt's technique. After his return to Germany in 1959 British Intelligence played a waiting game. Mundt's willingness to co-operate with them had yet to be demonstrated, so they gave him instructions and waited, content to pay their money and hope for the best. At that time Mundt was not a senior functionary of our Service—nor of our party—but he saw a good deal, and what he saw he began to report. He was, of course, communicating with his masters unaided. We must suppose that he was met in West Berlin, that on his short journeys abroad to Scandinavia and elsewhere he was contacted and interrogated. The British must have been wary to begin with—who would not be?—they weighed what he gave them with painful care against what they already knew, they feared that he would play a double game. But gradually they realised they had hit a gold mine. Mundt took to his treacherous work with the systematic efficiency for which he is renowned. At first—this is my guess, but it is based, Comrades, on long experience of this work and on the evidence of Leamas—for the first few months they did not dare to establish any kind of network which included Mundt. They let him be a lone wolf, they serviced him, paid and instructed him independently of their Berlin organisation. They established in London, under Guillam (for it was he who recruited Mundt in England), a tiny undercover section whose function was not known even within the Service save to a select circle. They paid Mundt by a special system which they called Rolling Stone, and no doubt they treated the information he gave them with prodigious caution. Thus, you see, it is consistent with Leamas' protestations that the existence of Mundt was unknown to him although—as you will see—he not only paid him, but in the end *actually received from Riemeck and passed to London the intelligence which Mundt obtained.*

'Towards the end of 1959 Mundt informed his London masters that he had found within the Praesidium a man who would act as intermediary between them and Mundt. That man was Karl Riemeck.

'How did Mundt find Riemeck? How did he dare to establish Riemeck's willingness to co-operate? You must remember Mundt's exceptional position: he had access to all security files, could tap telephones, open letters, employ watchers; he could interrogate anyone with undisputed right, and had before him the most detailed picture of their private life. Above all he could silence suspicion in a moment by turning against the people the very weapon'—Fiedler's voice was trembling with fury—'which was designed for their protection.' Returning effortlessly to his former rational style, he continued:

'You can see now what London did. Still keeping Mundt's identity a close secret, they connived at Riemeck's enlistment and enabled indirect contact to be established between Mundt and the Berlin command. That is the significance of Riemeck's contact with de Jong and Leamas. *That* is how you should interpret Leamas' evidence, *that* is how you should measure Mundt's treachery.' He turned and, looking Mundt full in the face, he shouted:

'There is your saboteur, terrorist! There is the man who has sold the people's right!

'I have nearly finished. Only one more thing needs to be said. Mundt gained a reputation as a loyal and astute protector of the people, and he silenced for ever those tongues that could betray his secret. Thus he killed in the name of the people to protect his fascist treachery and advanced his own career within our Service. It is not possible to imagine a crime more terrible than this. That is why—in the end—having done what he could to protect Karl Riemeck from the suspicion which was gradually surrounding him he gave the order that Riemeck be shot on sight. That is why he arranged for the assassination of Riemeck's mistress. When you come to give your judgement to the Praesidium, do not shrink from recognising the full bestiality of this man's crime. For Hans-Dieter Mundt, death is a judgement of mercy.'

Chapter Twenty-one

The Witness

The President turned to the little man in the black suit sitting directly opposite Fiedler.

'Comrade Karden, you are speaking for Comrade Mundt. Do you wish to examine the witness Leamas?'

'Yes, yes, I should like to in one moment,' he replied, getting laboriously to his feet and pulling the end of his gold-rimmed spectacles over his ears. He was a benign figure, a little rustic, and his hair was white.

'The contention of Comrade Mundt,' he began—his mild voice was rather pleasantly modulated—'is that Leamas is lying; that Comrade Fiedler either by design or ill chance has been drawn into a plot to disrupt the Abteilung, and thus bring into disrepute the organs for the defence of our socialist state. We do not dispute that Karl Riemeck was a British spy—there is evidence for that. But we dispute that Mundt was in league with him, or accepted money for betraying our Party. We say there is no objective evidence for this charge, that Comrade Fiedler is intoxicated by dreams of power and blinded to rational thought. We maintain that from the moment Leamas returned from Berlin to London he lived a part; that he simulated a swift decline into degeneracy, drunkenness and debt, that he assaulted a tradesman in full public view and affected anti-American sentiment—all solely in order to attract the attention of the Abteilung. We believe that British Intelligence has deliberately spun around Comrade Mundt a mesh of circumstantial evidence—the payment of money to foreign banks, its withdrawal to coincide with Mundt's presence in this or that country, the casual hearsay evidence from Peter Guillam, the secret meeting between Control and Riemeck at which matters were discussed that Leamas could not hear: these all provided a spurious chain of evidence and Comrade Fiedler, on whose ambitions the British so accurately counted, accepted it; and thus he became party to a monstrous plot to destroy—to murder in fact, for Mundt now stands to lose his life—one of the most vigilant defenders of our Republic.

'Is it not consistent with their record of sabotage, subversion and human trafficking that the British should devise this desperate plot? What other course lies open to them now that the rampart has been built across Berlin and the flow of Western spies has been checked? We have fallen victim to their plot; at best Comrade Fiedler is guilty of a most serious error; at worst of conniving with imperialist spies to undermine the security of the worker state, and shed innocent blood.

'We also have a witness.' He nodded benignly at the court. 'Yes. We too have a witness. For do you really suppose that all this time Comrade Mundt has been in ignorance of Fiedler's fevered plotting? Do you really suppose that? For months he has been aware of the sickness in Fiedler's mind. It was Comrade Mundt himself who authorised the approach that was made to Leamas in England: do you think he would have taken such an insane risk if he were himself to be implicated?

'And when the reports of Leamas' first interrogation in The Hague reached the Praesidium, do you suppose Comrade Mundt threw his away unread? And when, after Leamas had arrived in our country and Fiedler embarked on his own interrogation, no further reports were forthcoming, do you suppose Comrade Mundt was then so obtuse that he did not know what Fiedler was hatching? When the first reports came in from Peters in The Hague, Mundt had only to look at the dates of Leamas' visits to Copenhagen and Helsinki to realise that the whole thing was a plant—a plant to discredit Mundt himself. Those dates did indeed coincide with Mundt's visits to Denmark and Finland: they were chosen by London for that very reason. Mundt had known of those 'earlier indications' as well as Fiedler—remember that. Mundt too was looking for a spy within the ranks of the Abteilung. . . .

'And so by the time Leamas arrived in Democratic Germany, Mundt was watching with fascination how Leamas nourished Fiedler's suspicions with hints and oblique indications—never over-done, you understand, never emphasised, but dropped here and there with perfidious subtlety. And by then the ground had been prepared . . . the man in the Lebanon, the miraculous scoop to which Fiedler referred, both seeming to confirm the presence of a highly placed spy within the Abteilung. . . .

'It was wonderfully well done. It could have turned—it could still turn—the defeat which the British suffered through the loss of Karl Riemeck into a remarkable victory.

'Comrade Mundt took one precaution while the British, with Fiedler's aid, planned his murder.

'He caused scrupulous enquiries to be made in London. He examined every tiny detail of that double life which Leamas led in Bayswater. He was looking, you see, for some human error in a scheme of almost superhuman subtlety. Somewhere, he thought, in

Leamas' long sojourn in the wilderness, he would have to break faith with his oath of poverty, drunkenness, degeneracy, above all of solitude. He would need a companion, a mistress perhaps; he would long for the warmth of human contact, long to reveal a part of the other soul within his breast. Comrade Mundt was right you see. Leamas, that skilled, experienced operator, made a mistake so elementary, so human that . . .' He smiled. 'You shall hear the witness, but not yet. The witness is here; procured by Comrade Mundt. It was an admirable precaution. Later I shall call–that witness.' He looked a trifle arch, as if to say he must be allowed his little joke. 'Meanwhile I should like, if I may, to put one or two questions to this reluctant incriminator, Mr Alec Leamas.'

'Tell me,' he began, 'are you a man of means?'

'Don't be bloody silly,' said Leamas shortly; 'you know how I was picked up.'

'Yes, indeed,' Karden declared, 'it was masterly. I may take it, then, that you have no money at all?'

'You may.'

'Have you friends who would lend you money, give it to you perhaps? Pay your debts?'

'If I had I wouldn't be here now.'

'You have none? You cannot imagine that some kindly benefactor, someone perhaps you have almost forgotten about, would ever concern himself with putting you on your feet . . . settling with creditors and that kind of thing?'

'No.'

'Thank you. Another question: do you know George Smiley?'

'Of course I do. He was in the Circus.'

'He has now left British Intelligence?'

'He packed it up after the Fennan case.'

'Ah yes–the case in which Mundt was involved. Have you ever seen him since?'

'Once or twice.'

'Have you seen him since you left the Circus?'

Leamas hesitated.

'No,' he said.

'He didn't visit you in prison?'

'No. No one did.'

'And before you went to prison?'

'No.'

'After you left prison–the day of your release in fact–you were picked up, weren't you, by a man called Ashe?'

'Yes.'

'You had lunch with him in Soho. After the two of you had parted, where did you go?'

'I don't remember. Probably I went to a pub. No idea.'

'Let me help you. You went to Fleet Street eventually and caught a bus. From there you seem to have zigzagged by bus, tube and private car, rather inexpertly for a man of your experience, to Chelsea. Do you remember that? I can show you the report if you like, I have it here.'

'You're probably right. So what?'

'George Smiley lives in Bywater Street, just off the King's Road, that is my point. Your car turned into Bywater Street and our agent reported that you were dropped at number nine. That happens to be Smiley's house.'

'That's drivel,' Leamas declared. 'I should think I went to the Eight Bells; it's a favourite pub of mine.'

'By private car?'

'That's nonsense too. I went by taxi, I expect. If I have money I spent it.'

'But why all the running about beforehand?'

'That's just cock. They were probably following the wrong man. That would be bloody typical.'

'Going back to my original question, you cannot imagine that Smiley would have taken any interest in you after you left the Circus?'

'God, no.'

'Nor in your welfare after you went to prison, nor spent money on your dependants, nor wanted to see you after you had met Ashe?'

'No. I haven't the least idea what you're trying to say, Karden, but the answer's no. If you'd ever met Smiley you wouldn't ask. We're about as different as we could be.'

Karden seemed rather pleased with this, smiling and nodding to himself as he adjusted his spectacles and referred elaborately to his file.

'Oh yes,' he said, as if he had forgotten something; 'when you asked the grocer for credit, how much money had you?'

'Nothing,' said Leamas carelessly. 'I'd been broke for a week. Longer, I should think.'

'What had you lived on?'

'Bits and pieces. I'd been ill; some fever. I'd hardly eaten anything for a week. I suppose that made me nervous too—tipped the scales.'

'You were, of course, still owed money at the library, weren't you?'

'How did you know that?' asked Leamas sharply. 'Have you been—'

'Why didn't you go and collect it? Then you wouldn't have had to ask for credit, would you, Leamas?'

He shrugged.

'I forget. Probably because the library was closed on Saturday mornings.'

'I see. Are you sure it was closed on Saturday mornings?'
'No, it's just a guess.'
'Quite. Thank you, that is all I have to ask.' Leamas was sitting down as the door opened, and a woman came in. She was large and ugly, wearing a grey overall with chevrons on one sleeve. Behind her stood Liz.

Chapter Twenty-two

The President

She entered the court slowly, looking around her, wide-eyed, like a half-woken child entering a brightly-lit room. Leamas had forgotten how young she was. When she saw him sitting between two guards she stopped.
'Alec.'
The guard beside her put his hand on her arm and guided her forward to the spot where Leamas had stood. It was very quiet in the courtroom.
'What is your name, child?' the President asked abruptly. Liz's long hands hung at her sides, the fingers straight.
'What is your name?' she repeated, loudly this time.
'Elizabeth Gold.'
'You are a member of the British Communist Party?'
'Yes.'
'And you have been staying in Leipzig?'
'Yes.'
'When did you join the Party?'
'1955. No—fifty-four, I think it was—'
She was interrupted by the sound of movement; the screech of furniture forced aside, and Leamas' voice, hoarse, high-pitched, ugly, filling the room.
'You bastards! Leave her alone!'
Liz turned in terror and saw him standing, his white face bleeding and his clothes awry, saw a guard hit him with his fist, so that he half fell; then they were both upon him, had lifted him up, thrusting his arms high behind his back. His head fell forward on his chest, then jerked sideways in pain.
'If he moves again, take him out,' the President ordered, and she nodded to Leamas in warning, adding: 'You can speak again later if you want. Wait.' Turning to Liz she said sharply, 'Surely you know

when you joined the Party?'

Liz said nothing, and after waiting a moment the President shrugged. Then leaning forward and staring at Liz intently she asked:

'Elizabeth, have you ever been told in your Party about the need for secrecy?'

Liz nodded.

'And you have been told never, never to ask questions of another Comrade on the organisation and dispositions of the Party?'

Liz nodded again. 'Yes,' she said, 'of course.'

'Today you will be severely tested in that rule. It is better for you, far better, that you should know nothing. Nothing,' she added with sudden emphasis. 'Let this be enough: we three at this table hold very high rank in the Party. We are acting with the knowledge of our Praesidium, in the interests of Party security. We have to ask you some questions, and your answers are of the greatest importance. By replying truthfully, and bravely you will help the cause of Socialism.'

'But *who*,' she whispered, '*who* is on trial? What's Alec done?'

The President looked past her at Mundt and said, 'Perhaps no one is on trial. This is the point. Perhaps only the accusers. It can make no difference *who* is accused,' she added, 'it is a guarantee of your impartiality that you cannot know.'

Silence descended for a moment on the little room; and then, in a voice so quiet that the President instinctively turned her head to catch her words, she asked:

'Is it Alec? Is it Leamas?'

'I tell you,' the President insisted, 'it is better for you–far better–you should not know. You must tell the truth and go. That is the wisest thing you can do.'

Liz must have made some sign or whispered some words the others could not catch, for the President again leant forward and said, with great intensity:

'Listen, child, do you want to go home? Do as I tell you and you shall. But if you . . .' She broke off, indicated Karden with her hand and added cryptically, 'this Comrade wants to ask you some questions, not many. Then you shall go. Tell the truth.'

Karden stood again, and smiled his kindly, churchwarden smile.

'Elizabeth,' he enquired, 'Alec Leamas was your lover, wasn't he?'

She nodded.

'You met at the library in Bayswater, where you work.'

'Yes.'

'You had not met him before?'

She shook her head: 'We met at the library,' she said.

'Have you had many lovers, Elizabeth?'

Whatever she said was lost as Leamas shouted again: 'Karden, you swine,' but as she heard him she turned and said, quite loud:

'Alec, don't. They'll take you away.'

'Yes,' observed the President drily; 'they will.'

'Tell me,' Karden resumed smoothly, 'was Alec a Communist?'

'No.'

'Did he know you were a Communist?'

'Yes. I told him.'

'What did he say when you told him then, Elizabeth?'

She didn't know whether to lie, that was the terrible thing. The questions came so quickly she had no chance to think. All the time they were listening, watching, waiting for a word, a gesture, perhaps, that could do terrible harm to Alec. She couldn't lie unless she knew what was at stake; she would fumble on and Alec would die—for there was no doubt in her mind that Leamas was in danger.

'What did he say then?' Karden repeated.

'He laughed. He was above all that kind of thing.'

'Do you believe he was above it?'

'Of course.'

The young man at the Judges' table spoke for the second time. His eyes were half closed:

'Do you regard that as a valid judgement of a human being? That he is *above* the course of history and the compulsion of dialectic?'

'I don't know. It's what I believed, that's all.'

'Never mind,' said Karden; 'tell me, was he a *happy* person, always laughing and that kind of thing?'

'No. He didn't often laugh.'

'But he laughed when you told him you were in the Party. Do you know why?'

'I think he despised the Party.'

'Do you think he *hated* it?' Karden asked casually.

'I don't know,' Liz replied pathetically.

'Was he a man of strong likes and dislikes?'

'No . . . no; he wasn't.'

'But he assaulted a grocer. Now why did he do that?'

Liz suddenly didn't trust Karden any more. She didn't trust the caressing voice and the good-fairy face.

'I don't know.'

'But you thought about it?'

'Yes.'

'Well, what conclusion did you come to?'

'None,' said Liz flatly.

Karden looked at her thoughtfully, a little disappointed perhaps, as if she had forgotten her catechism.

'Did you,' he asked—it might have been the most obvious of questions—'did you *know* that Leamas was going to hit the grocer?'

'No,' Liz replied, perhaps too quickly, so that in the pause that followed Karden's smile gave way to a look of amused curiosity.

'Until now, until today,' he asked finally, 'when had you last seen Leamas?'

'I didn't see him again after he went to prison,' Liz replied.

'When did you see him last, then?'–the voice was kind but persistent. Liz hated having her back to the court; she wished she could turn and see Leamas, see his face perhaps; read in it some guidance, some sign telling how to answer. She was becoming frightened for herself; these questions which proceeded from charges and suspicions of which she knew nothing. They must know she wanted to help Alec, that she was afraid, but no one helped her– why would no one help her?

'Elizabeth, when was your last meeting with Leamas until today?' Oh that voice, how she hated it, that silken voice.

'The night before it happened,' she replied, 'the night before he had the fight with Mr Ford.'

'The fight? It wasn't a fight, Elizabeth. The grocer never hit back, did he–he never had a chance. Very unsporting!' Karden laughed, and it was all the more terrible because no one laughed with him.

'Tell me, where did you meet Leamas that last night?'

'At his flat. He'd been ill, not working. He'd been in bed and I'd been coming in and cooking for him.'

'And buying the food? Shopping for him?'

'Yes.'

'How kind. It must have cost you a lot of money,' Karden observed sympathetically: 'could you afford to keep him?'

'I didn't keep him. I got it from Alec. He . . .'

'Oh,' said Karden sharply, 'so he *did* have some money?'

Oh God, thought Liz, oh God, oh dear God, what have I said?

'Not much,' she said quickly, 'not much, I know. A pound, two pounds, not more. He didn't have more than that. He couldn't pay his bills–his electric light and his rent–they were all paid afterwards, you see, after he'd gone, by a friend. A friend had to pay, not Alec.'

'Of course,' said Karden quietly, 'a friend paid. Came specially and paid all his bills. Some old friend of Leamas, someone he knew before he came to Bayswater perhaps. Did you ever meet this friend, Elizabeth?'

She shook her head.

'I see. What other bills did this good friend pay, do you know?'

'No . . . no.'

'Why do you hesitate?'

'I said I don't know,' Liz retorted fiercely.

'But you hesitated,' Karden explained, 'I wondered if you had second thoughts.'

'No.'

'Did Leamas ever speak of this friend? A friend with money who knew where Leamas lived?'

'He never mentioned a friend at all. I didn't think he had any friends.'

'Ah.'

There was a terrible silence in the courtroom, more terrible to Liz because like a blind child among the seeing she was cut off from all those around her; they could measure her answers against some secret standard, and she could not know from the dreadful silence what they had found.

'How much money do you earn, Elizabeth?'

'Six pounds a week.'

'Have you any savings?'

'A little. A few pounds.'

'How much is the rent of your flat?'

'Fifty shillings a week.'

'That's quite a lot, isn't it, Elizabeth? Have you paid your rent recently?'

She shook her head helplessly.

'Why not,' Karden continued. 'Have you no money?'

In a whisper she replied: 'I've got a lease. Someone bought the lease and sent it to me.'

'Who?'

'I don't know.' Tears were running down her face, 'I don't know. . . . Please don't ask any more questions. I don't know who it was . . . six weeks ago they sent it, a bank in the City . . . some Charity had done it . . . a thousand pounds. I swear I don't know who . . . a gift from a Charity they said. You know everything–you tell me who . . .'

Burying her face in her hands she wept, her back still turned to the court, her shoulders moving as the sobs shook her body. No one moved, and at length she lowered her hands but did not look up.

'Why didn't you enquire?' Karden asked simply, 'or are you used to receiving anonymous gifts of a thousand pounds?'

She said nothing and Karden continued: 'You didn't enquire because you guessed. Isn't that right?'

Raising her hand to her face again, she nodded.

'You guessed it came from Leamas, or from Leamas' friend, didn't you?'

'Yes,' she managed to say, 'I heard in the street that the grocer had got some money, a lot of money from somewhere after the trial. There was a lot of talk about it, and I knew it must be Alec's friend. . . .'

'How very strange,' said Karden almost to himself. 'How odd.' And then: 'Tell me, Elizabeth, did anyone get in touch with you after Leamas went to prison?'

'No,' she lied. She knew now, she was sure they wanted to prove something against Alec, something about the money or his friends; something about the grocer.

'Are you sure?' Karden asked, his eyebrows raised above the gold rims of his spectacles.

'Yes.'

'But your neighbour, Elizabeth,' Karden objected, patiently, 'says that men called—two men—quite soon after Leamas had been sentenced; or were they just lovers, Elizabeth? Casual lovers, like Leamas, who gave you money?'

'Alec *wasn't* a casual lover,' she cried, 'how can you . . .'

'But he gave you money. Did the men give you money, too?'

'Oh God,' she sobbed, 'don't ask . . .'

'Who were they?' She did not reply, then Karden shouted, quite suddenly; it was the first time he had raised his voice.

'*Who?*'

'I don't know. They came in a car. Friends of Alec.'

'*More* friends? What did they want?'

'I don't know. They kept asking me what he had told me . . . they told me to get in touch with them if . . .'

'*How? How* get in touch with them?'

At last she replied:

'He lived in Chelsea . . . his name was Smiley . . . George Smiley . . . I was to ring him.'

'And did you?'

'No!'

Karden had put down his file. A deathly silence had descended on the court. Pointing towards Leamas Karden said, in a voice more impressive because it was perfectly under control:

'Smiley wanted to know whether Leamas had told her too much, Leamas had done the one thing British Intelligence had never expected him to do: he had taken a girl and wept on her shoulder.' Then Karden laughed quietly, as if it were all such a neat joke:

'Just as Karl Riemeck did. He's made the same mistake.'

'Did Leamas ever talk about himself?' Karden continued.

'No.'

'You know nothing about his past?'

'No. I knew he'd done something in Berlin. Something for the government.'

'Then he did talk about his past, didn't he? Did he tell you he had been married?'

There was a long silence. Liz nodded.

'Why didn't you see him after he went to prison? You could have visited him.'

'I didn't think he'd want me to.'

'I see. Did you write to him?'

'No. Yes, once . . . just to tell him I'd wait. I didn't think he'd mind.'

'You didn't think he would want that either?'

'No.'

'And when he had served his time in prison, you didn't try and get in touch with him?'

'No.'

'Did he have anywhere to go, did he have a job waiting for him—friends who would take him in?'

'I don't know . . . I don't know.'

'In fact you were finished with him, were you?' Karden asked with a sneer. 'Had you found another lover?'

'No! I waited for him . . . I'll always wait for him.' She checked herself. 'I wanted him to come back.'

'Then why had you not written? Why didn't you try and find out where he was?'

'He didn't want me to, don't you see! He made me promise . . . never to follow him . . . never to . . .'

'*So he expected to go to prison, did he?*' Karden demanded triumphantly.

'No . . . I don't know. How can I tell you what I don't know. . . .'

'And on that last evening,' Karden persisted, his voice harsh and bullying, on the evening before he hit the grocer, did he make you renew your promise? . . . Well, did he?'

With infinite weariness, she nodded in a pathetic gesture of capitulation. 'Yes.'

'And you said good-bye?'

'We said good-bye.'

'After supper, of course. It was quite late. Or did you spend the night with him?'

'After supper. I went home . . . not straight home. . . . I went for a walk first, I don't know where. Just walking.'

'What reason did he give for breaking off your relationship?'

'He didn't break it off,' she said. 'Never. He just said there was something he had to do; someone he had to get even with, whatever it cost, and afterwards, one day perhaps, when it was all over . . . he would . . . come back, if I was still there and . . .'

'And you said,' Karden suggested with irony, 'that you would always wait for him, no doubt? That you would always love him?'

'Yes,' Liz replied simply.

'Did he say he would send you money?'

'He said . . . he said things weren't as bad as they seemed . . . that I would be . . . looked after.'

'And that was why you didn't enquire, wasn't it, afterwards, when some charity in the City casually gave you a thousand pounds?'

'Yes! Yes, that's right! Now you know everything—you knew it all already. . . . Why did you send for me if you knew?'

Imperturbably Karden waited for her sobbing to stop.

'That,' he observed finally to the Tribunal before him, 'is the evidence of the defence. I am sorry that a girl whose perception is clouded by sentiment and whose alertness is blunted by money, should be considered by our British comrades a suitable person for Party office.'

Looking first at Leamas and then at Fiedler he added brutally:

'She is a fool. It is fortunate, nevertheless, that Leamas met her. This is not the first time that a revanchist plot has been uncovered through the decadence of its architects.'

With a little precise bow towards the Tribunal, Karden sat down.

As he did so, Leamas rose to his feet, and this time the guards let him alone.

London must have gone raving mad. He'd told them—that was the joke—he'd told them to leave her alone. And now it was clear that from the moment, the very moment he left England—before that, even, as soon as he went to prison—some bloody fool had gone round tidying up—paying the bills, settling the grocer, the landlord; above all, Liz. It was insane, fantastic. What were they trying to do—kill Fiedler, kill their agent? Sabotage their own operation? Was it just Smiley—had his wretched little conscience driven him to this? There was only one thing to do—get Liz and Fiedler out of it and carry the can. He was probably written off anyway. If he could save Fiedler's skin—if he could do that—perhaps there was a chance that Liz would get away.

How the hell did they know so much? He was sure, he was absolutely sure, he hadn't been followed to Smiley's house that afternoon. And the money—how did they pick up the story about him stealing money from the Circus? That was designed for internal consumption only . . . then how? For God's sake, how?

Bewildered, angry and bitterly ashamed he walked slowly up the gangway, stiffly, like a man going to the scaffold.

Chapter Twenty-three

Confession

'All right, Karden,' his face was white and hard as stone, his head tilted back, a little to one side, in the attitude of a man listening to some distant sound. There was a frightful stillness about him, not of resignation but of self-control, so that his whole body seemed to be in the iron grip of his will.

'All right, Karden, let her go.'

Liz was staring at him, her face crumpled and ugly, her dark eyes filled with tears.

'No, Alec . . . no,' she said. There was no one else in the room—just Leamas tall and straight like a soldier.

'Don't tell them,' she said, her voice rising, 'whatever it is, don't tell them just because of me. . . . I don't mind any more, Alec; I promise I don't.'

'Shut up, Liz,' said Leamas awkwardly. 'It's too late now.' His eyes turned to the President.

'She knows nothing. Nothing at all. Get her out of here and send her home. I'll tell you the rest.'

The President glanced briefly at the men on either side of her. She deliberated, then said:

'She can leave the court; but she cannot go home until the hearing is finished. Then we shall see.'

'She knows nothing, I tell you,' Leamas shouted. 'Karden's right, don't you see? It was an operation, a planned operation. How could she know that? She's just a frustrated little girl from a crackpot library—she's no good to you!'

'She is a witness,' replied the President shortly. 'Fiedler may want to question her.' It wasn't Comrade Fiedler any more.

At the mention of his name, Fiedler seemed to wake from the reverie into which he had sunk, and Liz looked at him consciously for the first time. His deep brown eyes rested on her for a moment, and he smiled very slightly, as if in recognition of her race. He was a small, forlorn figure, oddly relaxed she thought.

'She knows nothing,' Fiedler said. 'Leamas is right, let her go.' His voice was tired.

'You realise what you are saying?' the President asked. 'You realise what this means? Have *you* no questions to put to her?'

'She has said what she had to say.' Fiedler's hands were folded on his knees and he was studying them as if they interested him more than the proceedings of the court. 'It was all most cleverly done.' He nodded. 'Let her go. She cannot tell us what she does not know.' With a certain mock formality he added, 'I have no questions for the witness.'

A guard unlocked the door and called into the passage outside. In the total silence of the court they heard a woman's answering voice, and her ponderous footsteps slowly approaching. Fiedler abruptly stood up and taking Liz by the arm, he guided her to the door. As she reached the door she turned and looked back towards Leamas, but he was staring away from her like a man who cannot bear the sight of blood.

'Go back to England,' Fiedler said to her. 'You go back to England.' Suddenly Liz began to sob uncontrollably. The wardress put an arm round her shoulder, more for support than comfort, and led her from the room. The guard closed the door. The sound of her crying faded gradually to nothing.

'There isn't much to say,' Leamas began. 'Karden's right. It was a put-up job. When we lost Karl Riemeck we lost our only decent agent in the Zone. All the rest had gone already. We couldn't understand it—Mundt seemed to pick them up almost before we'd recruited them. I came back to London and saw Control. Peter Guillam was there and George Smiley. George was in retirement really, doing something clever. Philology or something.

'Anyway, they'd dreamed up this idea. Set a man to trap himself, that's what Control said. Go through the motions and see if they bite. Then we worked it out—backwards so to speak. "Inductive" Smiley called it. If Mundt *were* our agent how would we have paid him, how would the files look, and so on. Peter remembered that some Arab had tried to sell us a breakdown of the Abteilung a year or two back and we'd sent him packing. Afterwards we found out we'd made a mistake. Peter had the idea of fitting that in—as if we'd turned it down because we already knew. That was clever.

'You can imagine the rest. The pretence of going to pieces; drink, money troubles, the rumours that Leamas had robbed the till. It all hung together. We got Elsie in Accounts to help with the gossip, and one or two others. They did it bloody well,' he added with a touch of pride. 'Then I chose a morning—a Saturday morning, lots of people about—and broke out. It made the local press—it even made the *Worker* I think—and by that time you people had picked it up. From then on,' he added with contempt, 'you dug your own graves.'

'Your grave,' said Mundt quietly. He was looking thoughtfully at Leamas with his pale, pale eyes. 'And perhaps Comrade Fiedler's.'

'You can hardly blame Fiedler,' said Leamas indifferently, 'he happened to be the man on the spot; he's not the only man in the Abteilung who'd willingly hang you, Mundt.'

'We shall hang you, anyway,' said Mundt reassuringly. 'You murdered a guard. You tried to murder me.'

Leamas smiled drily.

'All cats are alike in the dark, Mundt. . . . Smiley always said it could go wrong. He said it might start a reaction we couldn't stop. His nerve's gone—you know that. He's never been the same since the Fennan case—since the Mundt affair in London. They say something happened to him then—that's why he left the Circus. That's what I can't make out, why they paid off the bills, the girl and all that. It must have been Smiley wrecking the operation on purpose, it must have been. He must have had a crisis of conscience, thought it was wrong to kill or something. It was mad after all that preparation, all that work, to mess up an operation that way.

'But Smiley hated you, Mundt. We all did, I think, although we didn't say it. We planned the thing as if it was all a bit of a game . . . it's hard to explain now. We knew we had our backs to the wall: we'd failed against Mundt and now we were going to try and kill him. But it was still a game.' Turning to the Tribunal he said: 'You're wrong about Fiedler; he's not ours. Why would London take this kind of risk with a man in Fiedler's position? They counted on him, I admit. They knew he hated Mundt—why shouldn't he? Fiedler's a Jew, isn't he? You know, you must know, all of you, what Mundt's reputation is, what he thinks about Jews.

'I'll tell you something, no one else will, so I'll tell you: Mundt had Fiedler beaten up, and all the time, while it was going on, Mundt baited him and jeered at him for being a Jew. You all know what kind of man Mundt is, and you put up with him because he's good at his job. But . . .' he faltered for a second, then continued: 'But for God's sake . . . enough people have got mixed up in all this without Fiedler's head going into the basket. Fiedler's all right, I tell you . . . ideologically sound, that's the expression, isn't it?'

He looked at the Tribunal. They watched him impassively, curiously almost, their eyes steady and cold. Fiedler, who had returned to his chair and was listening with rather studied detachment, looked at Leamas blandly for a moment:

'And you messed it all up, Leamas, is that it?' he asked. 'An old dog like Leamas, engaged in the crowning operation of his career, falls for a . . . what did you call her? . . . a frustrated little girl in a crackpot library? London must have known; Smiley couldn't have done it alone.' Fiedler turned to Mundt: 'Here's an odd thing, Mundt; they must have known you'd check up on every part of his

story. That was why Leamas lived the life. Yet afterwards they sent
money to the grocer, paid up the rent; and they bought the lease for
the girl. Of all the extraordinary things for them to do . . . people of
their experience . . . to pay a thousand pounds, to a girl–*to a member
of the Party*–who was supposed to believe he was broke. Don't tell
me Smiley's conscience goes that far. London must have done it.
What a risk?'

Leamas shrugged.

'Smiley was right. We couldn't stop the reaction. We never
expected you to bring me here–Holland yes–but not here.' He fell
silent for a moment, then continued. 'And I never thought you'd
bring the girl. I've been a bloody fool.'

'But Mundt hasn't,' Fiedler put in quickly. 'Mundt knew what to
look for–he even knew the girl would provide the proof–very clever
of Mundt I must say. He even knew about that lease–amazing really.
I mean, how *could* he have found out; she didn't tell anyone. I know
that girl; I understand her . . . she wouldn't tell anyone at all.' He
glanced towards Mundt. 'Perhaps Mundt can tell us how he knew?'

Mundt hesitated, a second too long, Leamas thought.

'It was her subscription,' he said, 'a month ago she increased her
Party contribution by ten shillings a month. I heard about it. And so
I tried to establish how she could afford it. I succeeded.'

'A masterly explanation,' Fiedler replied coolly.

There was silence.

'I think,' said the President, glancing at her two colleagues, 'that
the Tribunal is now in a position to make its report to the Praesidium. That is,' she added, turning her small, cruel eyes on Fiedler,
'unless you have anything more to say.'

Fiedler shook his head. Something still seemed to amuse him.

'In that case,' the President continued, 'my colleagues are
agreed that Comrade Fiedler should be relieved of his duties until
the disciplinary committee of the Praesidium has considered his
position.

'Leamas is already under arrest. I would remind you all that the
Tribunal has no executive powers. The peoples' prosecutor, in
collaboration with Comrade Mundt, will no doubt consider what
action is to be taken against a British *agent provocateur* and murderer.'

She glanced past Leamas at Mundt. But Mundt was looking at
Fiedler with the dispassionate regard of a hangman measuring his
subject for the rope.

And suddenly, with the terrible clarity of a man too long deceived,
Leamas understood the whole ghastly trick.

Chapter Twenty-four

The Commissar

Liz stood at the window, her back to the wardress, and stared blankly into the tiny yard outside. She supposed the prisoners took their exercise there. She was in somebody's office; there was food on the desk beside the telephones but she couldn't touch it. She felt sick and terribly tired; physically tired. Her legs ached, her face felt stiff and raw from weeping. She felt dirty and longed for a bath.

'Why don't you eat?' the woman asked again. 'It's all over now.' She said this without compassion, as if the girl were a fool not to eat when the food was there.

'I'm not hungry.'

The wardress shrugged: 'You may have a long journey,' she observed, 'and not much the other end.'

'What do you mean?'

'The workers are starving in England,' she declared complacently. 'The capitalists let them starve.'

Liz thought of saying something but there seemed no point. Besides, she wanted to know; she had to know, and this woman could tell her.

'What is this place?'

'Don't you know?' the wardress laughed. 'You should ask them over there,' she nodded towards the window. 'They can tell you what it is.'

'Who are they?'

'Prisoners.'

'What kind of prisoners?'

'Enemies of the state,' she replied promptly. 'Spies, agitators.'

'How do you know they are spies?'

'The Party knows. The Party knows more about people than they know themselves. Haven't you been told that?' The wardress looked at her, shook her head and observed, 'The English! The rich have eaten your future and your poor have given them the food—that's what's happened to the English.'

'Who told you that?'

The woman smiled and said nothing. She seemed pleased with herself.

'And this is a prison for spies?' Liz persisted.

'It is a prison for those who fail to recognise Socialist reality; for those who think they have the right to err; for those who slow down the march. Traitors,' she concluded briefly.

'But what have they done?'

'We cannot build Communism without doing away with individualism. You cannot plan a great building if some swine builds his sty on your site.'

Liz looked at her in astonishment.

'Who told you all this?'

'I am Commissar here,' she said proudly, 'I work in the prison.'

'You are very clever,' Liz observed, approaching her.

'I am a worker,' the woman replied acidly. 'The concept of brain workers as a higher category must be destroyed. There are no categories, only workers; no antithesis between physical and mental labour. Haven't you read Lenin?'

'Then the people in this prison are intellectuals?'

The woman smiled. 'Yes,' she said, 'they are reactionaries who call themselves progressive: they defend the individual against the state. Do you know what Khruschev said about the counter-revolution in Hungary?'

Liz shook her head. She must show interest, she must make the woman talk.

'He said it would never have happened if a couple of writers had been shot in time.'

'Who will they shoot now?' Liz asked quickly. 'After the trial?'

'Leamas,' she replied indifferently, 'and the Jew, Fiedler.' Liz thought for a moment she was going to fall but her hand found the back of a chair and she managed to sit down.

'What has Leamas done?' she whispered. The woman looked at her with her small, cunning eyes. She was very large, her hair was scant, stretched over her head to a bun at the nape of her thick neck. Her face was heavy, her complexion flaccid and watery.

'He killed a guard,' she said.

'Why?'

The woman shrugged.

'As for the Jew,' she continued, 'he made an accusation against a loyal comrade.'

'Will they shoot Fiedler for that?' asked Liz incredulously.

'Jews are all the same,' the woman commented. 'Comrade Mundt knows what to do with Jews. We don't need their kind here. If they join the Party they think it belongs to them. If they stay out, they think it is conspiring against them. It is said that Leamas and Fiedler plotted together against Mundt. Are you going to eat that?' she enquired, indicating the food on the desk. Liz shook her head. 'Then I must,' she declared, with a grotesque attempt at reluctance. 'They have given you potato. You must have a lover in the kitchen.' The humour of this observation sustained her until she had finished the last of Liz's meal.

Liz went back to the window.

In the confusion of Liz's mind, in the turmoil of shame and grief and fear there predominated the appalling memory of Leamas, as she had last seen him in the courtroom, sitting stiffly in his chair, his eyes averted from her own. She had failed him and he dared not look at her before he died; would not let her see the contempt, the fear perhaps, that was written on his face.

But how could she have done otherwise? If Leamas had only told her what he had to do—even now it wasn't clear to her—she would have lied and cheated for him, anything, if he had only told her? Surely he understood that; surely he knew her well enough to realise that in the end she would do whatever he said, that she would take on his form and being, his will, life, his image, his pain, if she could; that she prayed for nothing more than the chance to do so? But how could she have known, if she was not told, how to answer those veiled, insidious questions? There seemed no end to the destruction she had caused. She remembered, in the fevered condition of her mind, how, as a child, she had been horrified to learn that with every step she made, thousands of minute creatures were destroyed beneath her foot; and now, whether she had lied or told the truth—or even, she was sure, had kept silent—she had been forced to destroy a human being; perhaps two, for was there not also the Jew, Fiedler, who had been gentle with her, taken her arm and told her to go back to England? They would shoot Fiedler; that's what the woman said. Why did it have to be Fiedler—why not the old man who asked the questions, or the fair one in the front row between the soldiers, the one who smiled all the time; whenever she turned round she had caught sight of his smooth, blond head and his smooth, cruel face smiling as if it were all a great joke. It comforted her that Leamas and Fiedler were on the same side. She turned to the woman again and asked:

'Why are we waiting here?'

The wardress pushed the plate aside and stood up.

'For instructions,' she replied. 'They are deciding whether you must stay.'

'Stay?' repeated Liz blankly.

'It is a question of evidence. Fiedler may be tried. I told you: they suspect conspiracy between Fiedler and Leamas.'

'But who against? How could he conspire in England? How did he come here? He's not in the Party.'

The woman shook her head.

'It is secret,' she replied. 'It concerns only the Praesidium. Perhaps the Jew brought him here.'

'But *you* know,' Liz insisted, a note of blandishment in her voice, 'you are Commissar at the prison. Surely they told *you?*'

'Perhaps,' the woman replied, complacently. 'It is very secret,' she repeated.

The telephone rang. The woman lifted the receiver and listened. After a moment she glanced at Liz.

'Yes, Comrade. At once,' she said, and put down the receiver.

'You are to stay,' she said shortly. 'The Praesidium will consider the case of Fiedler. In the meantime you will stay here. That is the wish of Comrade Mundt.'

'Who is Mundt?'

The woman looked cunning.

'It is the wish of the Praesidium,' she said.

'I don't want to stay,' Liz cried. 'I want . . .'

'The Party knows more about us than we know ourselves,' the woman replied. 'You must stay here. It is the Party's wish.'

'Who is Mundt?' Liz asked again, but still she did not reply.

Slowly Liz followed her along endless corridors, through grilles manned by sentries, past iron doors from which no sound came, down endless stairs, across whole courtyards far beneath the ground, until she thought she had descended to the bowels of hell itself, and no one would even tell her when Leamas was dead.

She had no idea what time it was when she heard the footstep in the corridor outside her cell. It could have been five in the evening–it could have been midnight. She had been awake, staring blankly into the pitch darkness, longing for a sound. She had never imagined that silence could be so terrible. Once she had cried out, and there had been no echo, nothing. Just the memory of her own voice. She had visualised the sound breaking against the solid darkness like a fist against a rock. She had moved her hands about her as she sat on the bed, and it seemed to her that the darkness made them heavy, as if she were groping in the water. She knew the cell was small; that it contained the bed on which she sat, a handbasin without taps and a crude table: she had seen them when she first entered. Then the light had gone out, and she had run wildly to where she knew the bed had stood, and struck it with her shins, and had remained there, shivering with fright. Until she heard the footsteps, and the door of her cell was opened abruptly.

She recognised him at once, although she could only discern his silhouette against the pale blue light in the corridor. The trim, agile figure, the clear line of the cheek and the short fair hair just touched by the light behind him.

'It's Mundt,' he said. 'Come with me, at once.' His voice was contemptuous yet subdued, as if he were not anxious to be overheard.

Liz was suddenly terrified. She remembered the wardress: 'Mundt knows what to do with Jews.' She stood by the bed, staring at him, not knowing what to do.

'Hurry, you fool.' Mundt had stepped forward and seized her wrist. 'Hurry.' She let herself be drawn into the corridor. Bewildered, she watched Mundt quietly relock the door of her cell. Roughly he took her arm and forced her quickly along the first corridor, half running, half walking. She could hear the distant whirr of air conditioners; and now and then the sound of other footsteps from passages branching from their own. She noticed that Mundt hesitated, drew back even, when they came upon other corridors, would go ahead and confirm that no one was coming, then signal her forward. He seemed to assume that she would follow, that she knew the reason. It was almost as if he was treating her as an accomplice.

And suddenly he had stopped, was thrusting a key into the keyhole of a dingy metal door. She waited, panic-stricken. He pushed the door savagely outwards and the sweet, cold air of a winter's evening blew against her face. He beckoned to her again, still with the same urgency, and she followed him down two steps on to a gravel path which led through a rough kitchen garden.

They followed the path to an elaborate Gothic gateway which gave on to the road beyond. Parked in the gateway was a car. Standing beside it was Alec Leamas.

'Keep your distance,' Mundt warned her as she started to move forward:

'Wait here.'

Mundt went forward alone and for what seemed an age she watched the two men standing together, talking quietly between themselves. Her heart was beating madly, her whole body shivering with cold and fear. Finally Mundt returned.

'Come with me,' he said, and led her to where Leamas stood. The two men looked at one another for a moment.

'Good-bye,' said Mundt indifferently. 'You're a fool, Leamas,' he added. 'She's trash, like Fiedler.' And he turned without another word and walked quickly away into the twilight.

She put her hand out and touched him, and he half turned from her, brushing her hand away as he opened the car door. He nodded to her to get in, but she hesitated.

'Alec,' she whispered. 'Alec, what are you doing? Why is he letting you go?'

'Shut up!' Leamas hissed. 'Don't even think about it, d'you hear? Get in.'

'What was it he said about Fiedler? Alec, why is he letting us go?'

'He's letting us go because we've done our job. Get into the car, quick!' Under the compulsion of his extraordinary will she got into the car and closed the door. Leamas got in beside her.

'What bargain have you struck with him?' she persisted, suspicion and fear rising in her voice. 'They said you had tried to conspire against him, you and Fiedler. Then why is he letting you go?'

Leamas had started the car and was soon driving fast along the narrow road. On either side, bare fields; in the distance, dark monotonous hills were mingling with the gathering darkness. Leamas looked at his watch.

'We're five hours from Berlin,' he said. 'We've got to make Köpenick by quarter to one. We should do it easily.'

For a time Liz said nothing; she stared through the windscreen down the empty road, confused and lost in a labyrinth of half formed thoughts. A full moon had risen and the frost hovered in long shrouds across the fields. They turned on to an autobahn.

'Was I on your conscience, Alec?' she said at last. 'Is that why you made Mundt let me go?'

Leamas said nothing.

'You and Mundt are enemies, aren't you?'

Still he said nothing. He was driving fast now, the needle showed a hundred and twenty kilometres; the autobahn was pitted and bumpy. He had his headlights on full, she noticed, and didn't bother to dip for oncoming traffic on the other lane. He drove roughly, leaning forward, his elbows almost on the wheel.

'What will happen to Fiedler?' Liz asked suddenly and this time Leamas answered.

'He'll be shot.'

'Then why didn't they shoot you?' Liz continued quickly. 'You conspired with Fiedler against Mundt, that's what they said. You killed a guard. Why has Mundt let you go?'

'All right!' Leamas shouted suddenly. 'I'll tell you. I'll tell you what you were never, never to know, neither you nor I. Listen: Mundt is London's man, their agent; they bought him when he was in England. We are witnessing the lousy end to a filthy, lousy operation to save Mundt's skin. To save him from a clever little Jew in this own department who had begun to suspect the truth. They made us kill him, d'you see, kill the Jew. Now you know, and God help us both.'

Chapter Twenty-five

The Wall

'If that is so, Alec,' she said at last, 'what was my part in all this?' Her voice was quite calm, almost matter-of-fact.

'I can only guess, Liz, from what I know and what Mundt told me before we left. Fiedler suspected Mundt; had suspected him ever since Mundt came back from England; he thought Mundt was playing a double game. He hated him, of course—why shouldn't he—but he was right too: Mundt was London's man. Fiedler was too powerful for Mundt to eliminate alone, so London decided to do it for him. I can see them working it out, they're so damned academic; I can see them sitting round a fire in one of their smart bloody clubs. They knew it was no good just eliminating Fiedler—he might have told friends, published accusations: they had to eliminate *suspicion*. Public rehabilitation, that's what they organised for Mundt.'

He swung into the left-hand lane to overtake a lorry and trailer. As he did so the lorry unexpectedly pulled out in front of him, so that he had to brake violently on the pitted road to avoid being forced into the crash-fence on his left.

'They told me to frame Mundt,' he said simply; 'they said he had to be killed, and I was game. It was going to be my last job. So I went to seed, and punched the grocer . . . you know all that.'

'And made love?' she asked quietly. Leamas shook his head. 'But this is the point, you see,' he continued, 'Mundt knew it all; he knew the plan; he had me picked up, he and Fiedler. Then he let Fiedler take over, because he knew in the end Fiedler would hang himself. My job was to let them think what in fact was the truth: that Mundt was a British spy.' He hesitated. 'Your job was to discredit me. Fiedler was shot and Mundt was saved, mercifully delivered from a fascist plot. It's the old principle of love on the rebound.'

'But how could they know about me; how could they know we would come together?' Liz cried. 'Heavens above, Alec, can they even tell when people will fall in love?'

'It didn't matter—it didn't depend on that. They chose you because you were young and pretty and in the Party, because they knew you would come to Germany if they rigged an invitation. That man in the Labour Exchange, Pitt, he sent me up there; they knew I'd work at the Library. Pitt was in the Service during the war and they squared him, I suppose. They only had to put you and me in contact, even for a day, it didn't matter; then afterwards they could call on you, send you the money, make it look like an affair even if it wasn't, don't you see? Make it look like an infatuation, perhaps. The only material point was that after bringing us together they should send you money as if it came at my request. As it was, we made it very easy for them. . . .'

'Yes, we did.' And then she added, 'I feel dirty, Alec, as if I'd been put out to stud.'

Leamas said nothing.

'Did it ease your Department's conscience at all? Exploiting . . . somebody in the Party, rather than just anybody?' Liz continued.

Leamas said, 'Perhaps. They don't really think in those terms. It was an operational convenience.'

'I might have stayed in that prison, mightn't I? That's what Mundt wanted, wasn't it? He saw no point in taking the risk—I might have heard too much, guessed too much. After all, Fiedler was innocent, wasn't he? But then he's a Jew,' she added excitedly. 'So that doesn't matter so much, does it?'

'Oh, for God's sake,' Leamas exclaimed.

'It seems odd that Mundt let me go, all the same—even as part of the bargain with you,' she mused. 'I'm a risk now, aren't I? When we get back to England, I mean: a Party member knowing all this. . . . It doesn't seem logical that he should let me go.'

'I expect,' Leamas replied, 'he is going to use our escape to demonstrate to the Praesidium that there are other Fiedlers in his department who must be hunted down.'

'And other Jews?'

'It gives him a chance to secure his position,' Leamas replied curtly.

'By killing more innocent people? It doesn't seem to worry you much.'

'Of course it worries me. It makes me sick with shame and anger and . . . But I've been brought up differently, Liz; I can't see it in black and white. People who play this game take risks. Fiedler lost and Mundt won. London won—that's the point. It was a foul, foul operation. But it's paid off, and that's the only rule.' As he spoke his voice rose, until finally he was nearly shouting.

'You're trying to convince yourself,' Liz cried. 'They've done a wicked thing. How can you kill Fiedler—he was good, Alec; I know he was. And Mundt . . .'

'What the hell are you complaining about,' Leamas demanded roughly. 'Your Party's always at war, isn't it? Sacrificing the individual to the mass. That's what it says. Socialist reality: fighting night and day–that relentless battle–that's what they say, isn't it? At least you've survived. I never heard that Communists preached the sanctity of human life–perhaps I've got it wrong,' he added sarcastically. 'I agree, yes, I agree, you might have been destroyed. That was on the cards. Mundt's a vicious swine; he saw no point in letting you survive. His promise–I suppose he gave a promise to do his best by you–isn't worth a great deal. So you might have died–today, next year or twenty years on–in a prison in the worker's paradise. And so might I. But I seem to remember the Party is aiming at the destruction of a whole class. Or have I got it wrong?' Extracting a packet of cigarettes from his jacket he handed her two, together with a box of matches. Her fingers trembled as she lit them and passed one back to Leamas.

'You've thought it all out, haven't you?' she asked.

'We happened to fit the mould,' Leamas persisted, 'and I'm sorry. I'm sorry for the others too–the others who fit the mould. But don't complain about the terms, Liz; they're party terms. A small price for a big return. One sacrificed for many. It's not pretty, I know, choosing who it'll be–turning the plan into people.'

She listened in the darkness, for a moment scarcely conscious of anything except the vanishing road before them, and the numb horror in her mind.

'But they let me love you,' she said at last. 'And you let me believe in you and love you.'

'They used us,' Leamas replied pitilessly. 'They cheated us both because it was necessary. It was the only way. Fiedler was bloody nearly home already, don't you see? Mundt would have been caught; can't you understand that?'

'How can you turn the world upside down?' Liz shouted suddenly. 'Fiedler was kind and decent; he was only doing his job, and now you've killed him. Mundt is a spy and a traitor and you protect him. Mundt is a Nazi, do you know that? He hates Jews . . . what side are you on? How can you . . . ?'

'There's only one law in this game,' Leamas retorted. 'Mundt is their man; he gives them what they need. That's easy enough to understand, isn't it? Leninism–the expediency of temporary alliances. What do you think spies are: priests, saints and martyrs? They're a squalid procession of vain fools, traitors too, yes; pansies, sadists and drunkards, people who play cowboys and Indians to brighten their rotten lives. Do you think they sit like monks in London balancing the rights and wrongs? I'd have killed Mundt if I could, I hate his guts; but not now. It so happens that they need him. They need him so that the great moronic mass that you admire can sleep soundly in their beds at night. They need him for the safety of ordinary, crummy people like you and me.'

'But what about Fiedler—don't you feel anything for him?'

'This is a war,' Leamas replied. 'It's graphic and unpleasant because it's fought on a tiny scale, at close range; fought with a wastage of innocent life sometimes, I admit. But it's nothing, nothing at all beside other wars—the last or the next.'

'Oh God,' said Liz softly. 'You don't understand. You don't want to. You're trying to persuade yourself. It's far more terrible, what they are doing; to find the humanity in people, in me and whoever else they use, to turn it like a weapon in their hands, and use it to hurt and kill. . . .'

'Christ Almighty!' Leamas cried. 'What else have men done since the world began? I don't believe in anything, don't you see—not even destruction or anarchy. I'm sick, sick of killing but I don't see what else they can do. They don't proselytise; they don't stand in pulpits or on party platforms and tell us to fight for Peace or for God or whatever it is. They're the poor sods who try to keep the preachers from blowing each other sky high.'

'You're wrong,' Liz declared hopelessly; 'they're more wicked than all of us.'

'Because I made love to you when you thought I was a tramp?' Leamas asked savagely.

'Because of their contempt,' Liz replied; 'contempt for what is real and good; contempt for love, contempt for . . .'

'Yes,' Leamas agreed, suddenly weary. 'That is the price they pay; to despise God and Karl Marx in the same sentence. If that is what you mean.'

'It makes you the same,' Liz continued; 'the same as Mundt and all the rest. . . . I should know, I was the one who was kicked about, wasn't I? By them, by you because you don't care. Only Fiedler didn't. . . . But the rest of you . . . you all treated me as if I was . . . nothing . . . just currency to pay with. . . . You're all the same, Alec.'

'Oh, Liz,' he said desperately, 'for God's sake believe me. I hate it, I hate it all; I'm tired. But it's the world, it's mankind that's gone mad. We're a tiny price to pay . . . but everywhere's the same, people cheated and misled, whole lives thrown away, people shot and in prison, whole groups and classes of men written off for nothing. And you, your party—God knows it was built on the bodies of ordinary people. You've never seen men die as I have, Liz. . . .'

As he spoke Liz remembered the drab prison courtyard, and the wardress saying: 'It is a prison for those who slow down the march . . . for those who think they have the right to err.'

Leamas was suddenly tense, peering forward through the windscreen. In the headlights of the car Liz discerned a figure standing in the road. In his hand was a tiny light which he turned on and off as the car approached. 'That's him,' Leamas muttered; switched off the headlights and engine, and coasted silently forward. As they drew up, Leamas leant back and opened the rear door.

Liz did not turn round to look at him as he got in. She was staring stiffly forward, down the street at the falling rain.

'Drive at thirty kilometres,' the man said. His voice was taut, frightened. 'I'll tell you the way. When we reach the place you must get out and run to the wall. The searchlight will be shining at the point where you must climb. Stand in the beam of the searchlight. When the beam moves away begin to climb. You will have ninety seconds to get over. You go first,' he said to Leamas; 'and the girl follows. There are iron rungs in the lower part–after that you must pull yourself up as best you can. You'll have to sit on top and pull the girl up. Do you understand?'

'We understand,' said Leamas. 'How long have we got?'

'If you drive at thirty kilometres we shall be there in about nine minutes. The searchlight will be on the wall at five past one exactly. They can give you ninety seconds. Not more.'

'What happens after ninety seconds?' Leamas asked.

'They can only give you ninety seconds,' the man repeated; 'otherwise it is too dangerous. Only one detachment has been briefed. They think you are being infiltrated into West Berlin. They've been told not to make it too easy. Ninety seconds are enough.'

'I bloody well hope so,' said Leamas drily. 'What time do you make it?'

'I checked my watch with the sergeant in charge of the detachment,' the man replied. A light went on and off briefly in the back of the car. 'It is twelve forty-eight. We must leave at five to one. Seven minutes to wait.'

They sat in total silence save for the rain pattering on the roof. The cobble road reached out straight before them, staged by dingy street lights every hundred metres. There was no one about. Above them the sky was lit with the unnatural glow of arclights. Occasionally the beam of a searchlight flickered overhead, and disappeared. Far to the left Leamas caught sight of a fluctuating light just above the sky-line, constantly altering in strength, like the reflection of a fire.

'What's that?' he asked, pointing towards it.

'Information Service,' the man replied. 'A scaffolding of lights. It flashes news headlines into East Berlin.'

'Of course,' Leamas muttered. They were very near the end of the road.

'There is no turning back,' the man continued; 'he told you that? There is no second chance.'

'I know,' Leamas replied.

'If something goes wrong–if you fall or get hurt–don't turn back. They shoot on sight within the area of the wall. You *must* get over.'

'We know,' Leamas repeated; 'he told me.'

'From the moment you get out of the car you are in the area.'

'We know. Now shut up,' Leamas retorted. And then he added: 'are you taking the car back?'

'As soon as you get out of the car I shall drive it away. It is a danger for me, too,' the man replied.

'Too bad,' said Leamas drily.

Again there was silence; then Leamas asked: 'Have you got a gun?'

'Yes,' said the man; 'but I can't give it to you; he said I shouldn't give it to you . . . that you were sure to ask for it.'

Leamas laughed quietly. 'He would,' he said.

Leamas pulled the starter. With a noise that seemed to fill the street the car moved slowly forward.

They had gone about three hundred yards when the man whispered excitedly, 'Go right here, then left.' They swung into a narrow side street. There were empty market stalls on either side so that the car barely passed between them.

'Left here, now!'

They turned again, fast, this time between two tall buildings into what looked like a cul-de-sac. There was washing across the street, and Liz wondered whether they would pass under it. As they approached what seemed to be the dead end the man said: 'Left again—follow the path.' Leamas mounted the curb, crossed the pavement, and they followed a broad footpath bordered by a broken fence to their left, and a tall, windowless building to their right. They heard a shout from somewhere above them, a woman's voice, and Leamas muttered: 'Oh, shut up,' as he steered clumsily round a right-angle bend in the path and came almost immediately upon a major road.

'Which way?' he demanded.

'Straight across—past the chemist—between the chemist and the post office—there!' The man was leaning so far forward that his face was almost level with theirs. He pointed now, reaching past Leamas, the tip of his fingers pressed against the windscreen.

'Get back,' Leamas hissed. 'Get your hand away. How the hell can I see if you wave your hand around like that?' Slamming the car into first gear he drove fast across the wide road. Glancing to his left he was astonished to glimpse the plump silhouette of the Brandenburg Gate three hundred yards away, and the sinister grouping of military vehicles at the foot of it.

'Where are we going?' asked Leamas suddenly.

'We're nearly there. Go slowly now . . . left, left, go left!' he cried, and Leamas jerked the wheel in the nick of time; they passed under a narrow archway into a courtyard. Half the windows were missing or boarded up; the empty doorways gaped sightlessly at them. At the other end of the yard was an open gateway. 'Through there,' came the whispered command, urgent in the darkness; 'then hard right. You'll see a street lamp on your right. The one beyond it is broken. When you reach the second lamp switch off the engine and coast until you see a fire hydrant. That's the place.'

'Why the hell didn't you drive yourself?'

'He said you should drive; he said it was safer.'

They passed through the gate and turned sharply to the right. They were in a narrow street, pitch dark.

'Lights out!'

Leamas switched off the car lights, drove slowly forwards towards the first street lamp. Ahead, they could just see the second. It was unlit. Switching off the engine they coasted silently past it, until twenty yards ahead of them they discerned the dim outline of the fire hydrant. Leamas braked; the car rolled to a standstill.

'Where are we?' Leamas whispered. 'We crossed the Lenin-allee, didn't we?'

'Greifswalder Strasse. Then we turned north. We're north of Bernauerstrasse.'

'Pankow?'

'Just about. Look,' the man pointed down a side street to the left. At the far end they saw a brief stretch of wall, grey-brown in the weary arclight. Along the top ran a triple strand of barbed wire.

'How will the girl get over the wire?'

'It is already cut where you climb. There is a small gap. You have one minute to reach the wall. Good-bye.'

They got out of the car, all three of them. Leamas took Liz by the arm, and she started from him as if he had hurt her.

'Good-bye,' said the German.

Leamas just whispered: 'Don't start that car till we're over.'

Liz looked at the German for a moment in the pale light. She had a brief impression of a young, anxious face; the face of a boy trying to be brave.

'Good-bye,' said Liz. She disengaged her arm and followed Leamas across the road and into the narrow street that led towards the wall.

As they entered the street they heard the car start up behind them, turn and move quickly away in the direction they had come.

'Pull up the ladder, you bastard,' Leamas muttered, glancing back at the retreating car.

Liz hardly heard him.

Chapter Twenty-six

In from the Cold

They walked quickly, Leamas glancing over his shoulder from time to time to make sure she was following. As he reached the end of the alley, he stopped, drew into the shadow of a doorway and looked at his watch.

'Two minutes,' he whispered.

She said nothing. She was staring straight ahead towards the wall, and the black ruins rising behind it.

'Two minutes,' Leamas repeated.

Before them was a strip of thirty yards. It followed the wall in both directions. Perhaps seventy yards to their right was a watch tower; the beam of its searchlight played along the strip. The thin rain hung in the air, so that the light from the arclamps was sallow and chalky, screening the world beyond. There was no one to be seen; not a sound. An empty stage.

The watch tower's searchlight began feeling its way along the wall towards them, hesitant; each time it rested they could see the separate bricks and the careless lines of mortar hastily put on. As they watched the beam stopped immediately in front of them. Leamas looked at his watch.

'Ready?' he asked.

She nodded.

Taking her arm he began walking deliberately across the strip. Liz wanted to run, but he held her so tightly that she could not. They were half-way towards the wall now, the brilliant semi-circle of light drawing them forward, the beam directly above them. Leamas was determined to keep Liz very close to him, as if he were afraid that Mundt would not keep his word and somehow snatch her away at the last moment.

They were almost at the wall when the beam darted to the North leaving them momentarily in total darkness. Still holding Liz's arm, Leamas guided her forward blindly, his left hand reaching ahead of him until suddenly he felt the coarse, sharp contact of the cinder brick. Now he could discern the wall and, looking upwards, the triple strand of wire and the cruel hooks which held it. Metal wedges, like climbers' pitons, had been driven into the brick. Seizing the highest one, Leamas pulled himself quickly upwards until he had reached the top of the wall. He tugged sharply at the lower strand of wire and it came towards him, already cut.

'Come on,' he whispered urgently, 'start climbing.'

Laying himself flat he reached down, grasped her upstretched hand and began drawing her slowly upwards as her foot found the first metal rung.

Suddenly the whole world seemed to break into flame; from everywhere, from above and beside them, massive lights converged, bursting upon them with savage accuracy.

Leamas was blinded, he turned his head away, wrenching wildly at Liz's arm. Now she was swinging free; he thought she had slipped and he called frantically, still drawing her upwards. He could see nothing—only a mad confusion of colour dancing in his eyes.

Then came the hysterical wail of sirens, orders frantically shouted. Half kneeling astride the wall he grasped both her arms in his, and began dragging her to him inch by inch, himself on the verge of falling.

Then they fired—single rounds, three or four and he felt her shudder. Her thin arms slipped from his hands. He heard a voice in English from the Western side of the wall:

'Jump, Alec! Jump, man!'

Now everyone was shouting, English, French and German mixed; he heard Smiley's voice from quite close:

'The girl, where's the girl?'

Shielding his eyes he looked down at the foot of the wall and at last he managed to see her, lying still. For a moment he hesitated, then quite slowly he climbed back down the same rungs, until he was standing beside her. She was dead; her face was turned away, her black hair drawn across her cheek as if to protect her from the rain.

They seemed to hesitate before firing again; someone shouted an order, and still no one fired. Finally they shot him, two or three shots. He stood glaring round him like a blinded bull in the arena. As he fell, Leamas saw a small car smashed between great lorries, and the children waving cheerfully through the window.

Call for
the Dead

John le Carré

Chapter One

A Brief History of George Smiley

When Lady Ann Sercomb married George Smiley towards the end of the war she described him to her astonished Mayfair friends as breathtakingly ordinary. When she left him two years later in favour of a Cuban motor racing driver, she announced enigmatically that if she hadn't left him then, she never could have done; and Viscount Sawley made a special journey to his club to observe that the cat was out of the bag.

This remark, which enjoyed a brief season as a *mot*, can only be understood by those who knew Smiley. Short, fat, and of a quiet disposition, he appeared to spend a lot of money on really bad clothes, which hung about his squat frame like skin on a shrunken toad. Sawley, in fact, declared at the wedding that 'Sercomb was mated to a bullfrog in a sou'wester'. And Smiley, unaware of this description, had waddled down the aisle in search of the kiss that would turn him into a Prince.

Was he rich or poor, peasant or priest? Where had she got him from? The incongruity of the match was emphasized by Lady Ann's undoubted beauty, its mystery stimulated by the disproportion between the man and his bride. But gossip must see its characters in black and white, equip them with sins and motives easily conveyed in the shorthand of conversation. And so Smiley, without school, parents, regiment or trade, without wealth or poverty, travelled without labels in the guard's van of the social express, and soon became lost luggage, destined, when the divorce had come and gone, to remain unclaimed on the dusty shelf of yesterday's news.

When Lady Ann followed her star to Cuba, she gave some thought to Smiley. With grudging admiration she admitted to herself that if there were an only man in her life, Smiley would be he. She was gratified in retrospect that she had demonstrated this by holy matrimony.

The effect of Lady Ann's departure upon her former husband did not interest society—which indeed is unconcerned with the aftermath of sensation. Yet it would be interesting to know what Sawley and his flock might have made of Smiley's reaction; of that fleshy, bespectacled face puckered in energetic concentration as he read so deeply among the lesser German poets, the chubby wet hands clenched beneath the tumbling sleeves. But Sawley profited by the occasion with the merest of shrugs by remarking *partir c'est courir un peu*, and he appeared to be unaware that though Lady Ann just ran away, a little of George Smiley had indeed died.

That part of Smiley which survived was as incongruous to his appearance as love, or a taste for unrecognized poets: it was his profession, which was that of intelligence officer. It was a profession he enjoyed, and which mercifully provided him with colleagues equally obscure in character and origin. It also provided him with what he had once loved best in life: academic excursions into the mystery of human behaviour, disciplined by the practical application of his own deductions.

Some time in the twenties when Smiley had emerged from his unimpressive school and lumbered blinking into the murky cloisters of his unimpressive Oxford College, he had dreamed of Fellowships and a life devoted to the literary obscurities of seventeenth-century Germany. But his own tutor, who knew Smiley better, guided him wisely away from the honours that would undoubtedly have been his. On a sweet July morning in 1928, a puzzled and rather pink Smiley had sat before an interviewing board of the Overseas Committee for Academic Research, an organization of which he had unaccountably never heard. Jebedee (his tutor) had been oddly vague about the introduction: 'Give these people a try, Smiley, they might have you and they pay badly enough to guarantee you decent company.' But Smiley was annoyed and said so. It worried him that Jebedee, usually so precise, was so evasive. In a slight huff he agreed to postpone his reply to All Souls until he had seen Jebedee's 'mysterious people'.

He wasn't introduced to the Board, but he knew half of its members by sight. There was Fielding, the French medievalist from Cambridge, Sparke from the School of Oriental Languages, and Steed-Asprey who had been dining at High Table the night Smiley had been Jebedee's guest. He had to admit he was impressed. For Fielding to leave his rooms, let alone Cambridge, was in itself a miracle. Afterwards Smiley always thought of that interview as a fan dance; a calculated progression of disclosures, each revealing different parts of a mysterious entity. Finally Steed-Asprey, who seemed to be Chairman, removed the last veil, and the truth stood before him in all its dazzling nakedness. He was being offered a post in what, for want of a better name, Steed-Asprey blushingly described as the Secret Service.

Smiley had asked for time to think. They gave him a week. No one mentioned pay.

That night he stayed in London at somewhere rather good and

took himself to the theatre. He felt strangely light-headed and this worried him. He knew very well that he would accept, that he could have done so at the interview. It was only an instinctive caution, and perhaps a pardonable desire to play the coquette with Fielding, which prevented him from doing so.

Following his affirmation came training; anonymous country houses, anonymous instructors, a good deal of travel and, looming ever larger, the fantastic prospect of working completely alone.

His first operational posting was relatively pleasant: a two-year appointment as *englischer Dozent* at a provincial German University: lectures on Keats and vacations in Bavarian hunting lodges with groups of earnest and solemnly promiscuous German students. Towards the end of each long vacation he brought some of them back to England, having already earmarked the likely ones and conveyed his recommendations by clandestine means to an address in Bonn; during the entire two years he had no idea of whether his recommendations had been accepted or ignored. He had no means of knowing even whether his candidates were approached. Indeed he had no means of knowing whether his messages ever reached their destination; and he had no contact with the Department while in England.

His emotions in performing this work were mixed, and irreconcilable. It intrigued him to evaluate from a detached position what he had learnt to describe as 'the agent potential' of a human being; to devise minuscule tests of character and behaviour which could inform him of the qualities of a candidate. This part of him was bloodless and inhuman—Smiley in this role was the international mercenary of his trade, amoral and without motive beyond that of personal gratification.

Conversely it saddened him to witness in himself the gradual death of natural pleasure. Always withdrawn, he now found himself shrinking from the temptations of friendship and human loyalty; he guarded himself warily from spontaneous reaction. By the strength of his intellect, he forced himself to observe humanity with clinical objectivity, and because he was neither immortal nor infallible he hated and feared the falseness of his life.

But Smiley was a sentimental man and the long exile strengthened his deep love of England. He fed hungrily on memories of Oxford; its beauty, its rational ease, and the mature slowness of its judgements. He dreamt of windswept autumn holidays at Hartland Quay, of long trudges over the Cornish cliffs, his face smooth and hot against the sea wind. This was his other secret life, and he grew to hate the bawdy intrusion of the new Germany, the stamping and shouting of uniformed students, the scarred, arrogant faces and their cheapjack answers. He resented, too, the way in which the Faculty had tampered with his subject—*his* beloved German literature. And there

had been a night, a terrible night in the winter of 1937, when Smiley
had stood at his window and watched a great bonfire in the university
court: round it stood hundreds of students, their faces exultant and
glistening in the dancing light. And into the pagan fire they threw
books in their hundreds. He knew whose books they were: Thomas
Mann, Heine, Lessing and a host of others. And Smiley, his damp
hand cupped round the end of his cigarette, watching and hating,
triumphed that he knew his enemy.

Nineteen thirty-nine saw him in Sweden, the accredited agent of a
well-known Swiss small-arms manufacturer, his association with the
firm conveniently backdated. Conveniently, too, his appearance had
somehow altered, for Smiley had discovered in himself a talent for
the part which went beyond the rudimentary change to his hair and
the addition of a small moustache. For four years he had played the
part, travelling back and forth between Switzerland, Germany and
Sweden. He had never guessed it was possible to be frightened for so
long. He developed a nervous irritation in his left eye which
remained with him fifteen years later; the strain etched lines on his
fleshy cheeks and brow. He learnt what it was never to sleep, never to
relax, to feel at any time of day or night the restless beating of his own
heart, to know the extremes of solitude and self-pity, the sudden
unreasoning desire for a woman, for drink, for exercise, for any drug
to take away the tension of his life.

Against this background he conducted his authentic commerce
and his work as a spy. With the progress of time the network grew,
and other countries repaired their lack of foresight and preparation.
In 1943 he was recalled. Within six weeks he was yearning to return,
but they never let him go.

'You're finished,' Steed-Asprey said: 'train new men, take time
off. Get married or something. Unwind.'

Smiley proposed to Steed-Asprey's secretary, the Lady Ann
Sercomb.

The war was over. They paid him off, and he took his beautiful
wife to Oxford to devote himself to the obscurities of seventeenth-
century Germany. But two years later Lady Ann was in Cuba, and
the revelations of a young Russian cypher-clerk in Ottawa had
created a new demand for men of Smiley's experience.

The job was new, the threat elusive and at first he enjoyed it. But
younger men were coming in, perhaps with fresher minds. Smiley
was no material for promotion and it dawned on him gradually that
he had entered middle age without ever being young, and that he
was—in the nicest possible way—on the shelf.

Things changed. Steed-Asprey was gone, fled from the new world
to India, in search of another civilization. Jebedee was dead. He had
boarded a train at Lille in 1941 with his radio operator, a young
Belgian, and neither had been heard of again. Fielding was wedded

to a new thesis on Roland–only Maston remained, Maston the career man, the war-time recruit, the Ministers' Adviser on Intelligence; 'the first man,' Jebedee had said, 'to play power tennis at Wimbledon.' The NATO alliance, and the desperate measures contemplated by the Americans, altered the whole nature of Smiley's Service. Gone for ever were the days of Steed-Asprey, when as like as not you took your orders over a glass of port in his rooms at Magdalen; the inspired amateurism of a handful of highly qualified, under-paid men had given way to the efficiency, bureaucracy, and intrigue of a large Government department–effectively at the mercy of Maston, with his expensive clothes and his knighthood, his distinguished grey hair and silver coloured ties; Maston, who even remembered his secretary's birthday, whose manners were a byword among the ladies of the registry; Maston, apologetically extending his empire and regretfully moving to even larger offices; Maston, holding smart house-parties at Henley and feeding on the success of his subordinates.

They had brought him in during the war, the professional civil servant from an orthodox department, a man to handle paper and integrate the brilliance of his staff with the cumbersome machine of bureaucracy. It comforted the Great to deal with a man they knew, a man who could reduce any colour to grey, who knew his masters and could walk among them. And he did it so well. They liked his diffidence when he apologized for the company he kept, his insincerity when he defended the vagaries of his subordinates, his flexibility when formulating new commitments. Nor did he let go the advantages of a cloak and dagger man *malgré lui*, wearing the cloak for his masters and preserving the dagger for his servants. Ostensibly, his position was an odd one. He was not the nominal Head of Service, but the Ministers' Adviser on Intelligence, and Steed-Asprey had described him for all time as the Head Eunuch.

This was a new world for Smiley: the brilliantly lit corridors, the smart young men. He felt pedestrian and old-fashioned, homesick for the dilapidated terrace house in Knightsbridge where it had all begun. His appearance seemed to reflect this discomfort in a kind of physical recession which made him more hunched and frog-like than ever. He blinked more, and acquired the nickname of 'Mole'. But his débutante secretary adored him, and referred to him invariably as 'My darling teddy-bear'.

Smiley was now too old to go abroad. Maston had made that clear: 'Anyway, my dear fellow, as like as not you're blown after all the ferreting about in the war. Better stick at home, old man, and keep the home fires burning.'

Which goes some way to explaining why George Smiley sat in the back of a London taxi at two o'clock on the morning of Wednesday, 4 January, on his way to Cambridge Circus.

Chapter Two

We Never Closed

He felt safe in the taxi. Safe and warm. The warmth was contraband, smuggled from his bed and hoarded against the wet January night. Safe because unreal: it was his ghost that ranged the London streets and took note of their unhappy pleasure-seekers, scuttling under commissionaires' umbrellas; and of the tarts, gift-wrapped in poly-thene. It was his ghost, he decided, which had climbed from the well of sleep and stopped the telephone shrieking on the bedside table . . . Oxford Street . . . why was London the only capital in the world that lost its personality at night? Smiley, as he pulled his coat more closely about him, could think of nowhere, from Los Angeles to Berne, which so readily gave up its daily struggle for identity.

The cab turned into Cambridge Circus, and Smiley sat up with a jolt. He remembered why the Duty Officer had rung, and the memory woke him brutally from his dreams. The conversation came back to him word for word—a feat of recollection long ago achieved.

'Duty Officer speaking, Smiley. I have the Adviser on the line . . .'

'Smiley; Maston speaking. You interviewed Samuel Arthur Fen-nan at the Foreign Office on Monday, am I right?'

'Yes . . . yes I did.'

'What was the case?'

'Anonymous letter alleging Party membership at Oxford. Routine interview, authorized by the Director of Security.'

(Fennan *can't* have complained, thought Smiley; he knew I'd clear him. There was nothing irregular, nothing.)

'Did you go for him at all? Was it hostile, Smiley, tell me that?'

(Lord, he does sound frightened. Fennan must have put the whole Cabinet on to us.)

'No. It was a particularly friendly interview; we liked one another, I think. As a matter of fact I exceeded my brief in a way.'

'How, Smiley, how?'

'Well, I more or less told him not to worry.'

'You *what?*'

'I told him not to worry; he was obviously in a bit of a state, and so I told him.'

'*What* did you tell him?'

'I said I had no powers and nor had the Service; but I could see no reason why we should bother him further.'

'Is that all?'

Smiley paused for a second; he had never known Maston like this, never known him so dependent.

'Yes, that's all. Absolutely all.' (He'll never forgive me for this. So much for the studied calm, the cream shirts and silver ties, the smart luncheons with ministers.)

'He says you cast doubts on his loyalty, that his career in the FO is ruined, that he is the victim of paid informers.'

'He said *what*? He must have gone stark mad. He knows he's cleared. What else does he want?'

'Nothing. He's dead. Killed himself at 10.30 this evening. Left a letter to the Foreign Secretary. The police rang one of his secretaries and got permission to open the letter. Then they told us. There's going to be an inquiry. Smiley, you're sure, aren't you?'

'Sure of what?'

'. . . never mind. Get round as soon as you can.'

It had taken him hours to get a taxi. He rang three cab ranks and got no reply. At last the Sloan Square rank replied, and Smiley waited at his bedroom window wrapped in his overcoat until he saw the cab draw up at the door. It reminded him of the air raids in Germany, this unreal anxiety in the dead of night.

At Cambridge Circus he stopped the cab a hundred yards from the office, partly from habit and partly to clear his head in anticipation of Maston's febrile questioning.

He showed his pass to the constable on duty and made his way slowly to the lift.

The Duty Officer greeted him with relief as he emerged, and they walked together down the bright cream corridor.

'Maston's gone to see Sparrow at Scotland Yard. There's a squabble going on about which police department handles the case. Sparrow says Special Branch, Evelyn says CID and the Surrey police don't know what's hit them. Bad as a will. Come and have coffee in the DO's glory hole. It's out of a bottle but it does.'

Smiley was grateful it was Peter Guillam's duty that night. A polished and thoughtful man who had specialized in Satellite espionage, the kind of friendly spirit who always has a timetable and a penknife.

'Special branch rang at twelve five. Fennan's wife went to the theatre and didn't find him till she got back alone at quarter to eleven. She eventually rang the poice.'

'He lived down in Surrey somewhere.'

'Walliston, off the Kingston by-pass. Only just outside the Metro-politan area. When the police arrived they found a letter to the Foreign Secretary on the floor beside the body. The Superintendent rang the Chief Constable, who rang the Duty Officer at the Home Office, who rang the Resident Clerk at the Foreign Office, and eventually they got permission to open the letter. Then the fun started.'

'Go on.'

'The Director of Personnel at the Foreign Office rang us. He wanted the Adviser's home number. Said this was the last time Security tampered with his staff, that Fennan had been a loyal and talented officer, bla . . . bla . . . bla . . .'

'So he was. So he was.'

'Said the whole affair demonstrated conclusively that Security had got out of hand—Gestapo methods which were not even mitigated by a genuine threat . . . bla . . .

'I gave him the Adviser's number and dialled it on the other phone while he went on raving. By a stroke of genius I got the FO off one line and Maston on the other and gave him the news. That was at 12.20. Maston was here by one o'clock in a state of advanced pregnancy—he'll have to report to the Minister tomorrow morning.'

They were silent for a moment, while Guillam poured coffee essence into the cups and added boiling water from the electric kettle.

'What was he like?' he asked.

'Who? Fennan? Well, until tonight I could have told you. Now he doesn't make sense. To look at, obviously a Jew. Orthodox family, but dropped all that at Oxford and turned Marxist. Perceptive, cultured . . . a reasonable man. Soft spoken, good listener. Still educated; you know, facts galore. Whoever denounced him was right of course: he *was* in the Party.'

'How old?'

'Forty-four. Looks older really.' Smiley went on talking as his eyes wandered round the room. '. . . sensitive face—mop of straight dark hair undergraduate fashion, profile of a twenty-year-old, fine dry skin, rather chalky. Very lined too—lines going all ways, cutting the skin into squares. Very thin fingers . . . compact sort of chap; self-contained unit. Takes his pleasures alone. Suffered alone too, I suppose.'

They got up as Maston came in.

'Ah, Smiley. Come in.' He opened the door and put out his left arm to guide Smiley through first. Maston's room contained not a single piece of government property. He had once bought a collec-tion of nineteenth-century water-colours, and some of these were hanging on the walls. The rest was off the peg, Smiley decided. Maston was off the peg too, for that matter. His suit was just too light for respectability; the string of his monocle cut across the invariable cream shirt. He wore a light grey woollen tie. A German would call him *flott* thought Smiley; chic, that's what he is–a barmaid's dream of a real gentleman.

'I've seen Sparrow. It's a clear case of suicide. The body has been removed and beyond the usual formalities the Chief Constable is taking no action. There'll be an inquest within a day or two. It has been agreed–I can't emphasize this too strongly, Smiley–that no word of our former interest in Fennan is to be passed to the Press.'

'I see.' (You're dangerous, Maston. You're weak and frightened. Anyone's neck before yours, I know. You're looking at me that way–measuring me for the rope.)

'Don't think I'm criticizing, Smiley; after all if the Director of Security authorized the interview you have nothing to worry about.'

'Except Fennan.'

'Quite so. Unfortunately the Director of Security omitted to sign off your minute suggesting an interview. He authorized it verbally, no doubt?'

'Yes. I'm sure he'll confirm that.'

Maston looked at Smiley again, sharp, calculating; something was beginning to stick in Smiley's throat. He knew he was being uncompromising, that Maston wanted him nearer, wanted him to conspire.

'You know Fennan's office has been in touch with me?'

'Yes.'

'There will have to be an inquiry. It may not even be possible to keep the Press out. I shall certainly have to see the Home Secretary first thing tomorrow.' (Frighten me and try again . . . I'm getting on . . . pension to consider . . . unemployable, too . . . but I won't share your lie, Maston.) 'I must have all the facts, Smiley. I must do my duty. If there's anything you feel you should tell me about that interview, anything you haven't recorded, perhaps, tell me now and let me be the judge of its significance.'

'There's nothing to add, really, to what's already on the file, and what I told you earlier tonight. It might help you to know' (the 'you' was a trifle strong, perhaps)–'it might help you to know that I conducted the interview in an atmosphere of exceptional informality. The allegation against Fennan was pretty thin–university membership in the thirties and vague talk of current sympathy. Half the Cabinet were in the party in the thirties.' Maston frowned. 'When I got to his room in the Foreign Office it turned out to be rather public–people trotting in and out the whole time, so I suggested we should go out for a walk in the park.'

'Go on.'

'Well, we did. It was a sunny, cold day and rather pleasant. We watched the ducks.' Maston made a gesture of impatience. 'We spent about half an hour in the park–he did all the talking. He was an intelligent man, fluent and interesting. But nervous, too, not unnaturally. These people love talking about themselves, and I think he was pleased to get it off his chest. He told me the whole story–seemed quite happy to mention names–and then we went to an espresso café he knew near Millbank.'

'A *what*?'

'An espresso bar. They sell a special kind of coffee for a shilling a cup. We had some.'

'I see. It was under these . . . convivial circumstances that you told him the Department would recommend no action.'

'Yes. We often do that, but we don't normally record it.' Maston nodded. That was the kind of thing he understood, thought Smiley; goodness me, he really is rather contemptible. It was exciting to find Maston being as unpleasant as he expected.

'And I may take it therefore that his suicide–and his letter, of course–come as a complete surprise to you? You find no explanation?'

'It would be remarkable if I did.'

'You have no idea who denounced him?'

'No.'

'He was married, you know.'

'Yes.'

'I wonder . . . it seems conceivable that his wife might be able to fill in some of the gaps. I hesitate to suggest it, but perhaps someone from the Department ought to see her and, so far as good feeling allows, question her on all this.'

'Now?' Smiley looked at him, expressionless.

Maston was standing at his big flat desk, toying with the businessman's cutlery–paper knife, cigarette box, lighter–the whole chemistry set of official hospitality. He's showing a full inch of cream cuff, thought Smiley, and admiring his white hands.

Maston looked up, his face composed in an expression of sympathy.

'Smiley, I know how you feel, but despite this tragedy you must try to understand the position. The Minister and the Home Secretary will want the fullest possible account of this affair and it is my specific task to provide one. Particularly any information which points to Fennan's state of mind immediately after his interview with . . . with us. Perhaps he spoke to his wife about it. He's not supposed to have done but we must be realistic.'

'You want *me* to go down there?'

'Someone must. There's a question of the inquest. The Home Secretary will have to decide about that of course, but at present we just haven't the facts. Time is short and you know the case, you made the background inquiries. There's no time for anyone else to brief himself. If anyone goes it will have to be you, Smiley.'

'When do you want me to go?'

'Apparently Mrs Fennan is a somewhat unusual woman. Foreign. Jewish, too, I gather, suffered badly in the war, which adds to the embarrassment. She is a strong-minded woman and relatively un-moved by her husband's death. Only superficially, no doubt. But sensible and communicative. I gather from Sparrow that she is proving cooperative and would probably see you as soon as you can get there. Surrey police can warn her you're coming and you can see her first thing in the morning. I shall telephone you there later in the day.'

Smiley turned to go.

'Oh–and Smiley . . .' He felt Maston's hand on his arm and turned to look at him. Maston wore the smile normally reserved for the older ladies of the Service. 'Smiley, you can count on me, you know; you can count on my support.'

My God, thought Smiley; you really do work round the clock. A twenty-four-hour cabaret, you are–'We Never Closed.' He walked out into the street.

Chapter Three

Elsa Fennan

Merridale Lane is one of those corners of Surrey where the in-habitants wage a relentless battle against the stigma of suburbia. Trees, fertilized and cajoled into being in every front garden, half obscure the poky 'Character dwellings' which crouch behind them. The rusticity of the environment is enhanced by the wooden owls that keep guard over the names of houses, and by crumbling dwarfs indefatigably poised over goldfish ponds. The inhabitants of Mer-ridale Lane do not paint their dwarfs, suspecting this to be a suburban vice, nor, for the same reason, do they varnish the owls; but wait patiently for the years to endow these treasures with an appearance of weathered antiquity, until one day even the beams on the garage may boast of beetle and woodworm.

The lane is not exactly a cul-de-sac although estate agents insist that it is; the further end from the Kingston by-pass dwindles nervously into a gravel path, which in turn degenerates into a sad little mud track across Merries Field–leading to another lane in-distinguishable from Merridale. Until about 1920 this path had led to the parish church, but the church now stands on what is virtually a traffic island adjoining the London road, and the path which once led the faithful to worship provides a superfluous link between the inhabitants of Merridale Lane and Cadogan Road. The strip of open land called Merries Field has already achieved an eminence far beyond its own aspirations; it has driven a wedge deep into the District Council, between the developers and the preservers, and so effectively that on one occasion the entire machinery of local government in Walliston was brought to a standstill. A kind of natural compromise has now established itself: Merries Field is neither developed nor preserved by the three steel pylons, placed at regular intervals across it. At the centre is a cannibal hut with a thatched roof called 'The War Memorial Shelter', erected in 1951 in grateful memory to the fallen of two wars, as a haven for the weary and old. No one seems to have asked what business the weary and old would have in Merries Field, but the spiders have at least found a haven in the roof, and as a sitting-out place for pylon-builders the hut was unusually comfortable.

Smiley arrived there on foot just after eight o'clock that morning, having parked his car at the police station, which was ten minutes' walk away.

It was raining heavily, driving cold rain, so cold it felt hard upon the face.

Surrey police had no further interest in the case, but Sparrow had sent down independently a Special Branch officer to remain at the police station and act if necessary as liaison between Security and the police. There was no doubt about the manner of Fennan's death. He had been shot through the temple at point blank range by a small French pistol manufactured in Lille in 1957. The pistol was found beneath the body. All the circumstances were consistent with suicide.

Number fifteen Merridale Lane was a low, Tudor-style house with the bedrooms built into the gables, and a half-timbered garage. It had an air of neglect, even disuse. It might have been occupied by artists, thought Smiley. Fennan didn't seem to fit here. Fennan was Hampstead and au-pair foreign girls.

He unlatched the gate and walked slowly up the drive to the front door, trying vainly to discern some sign of life through the leaded windows. It was very cold. He rang the bell.

Elsa Fennan opened the door.

'They rang and asked me if I minded. I didn't know what to say. Please come in.' A trace of a German accent.

She must have been older than Fennan. A slight, fierce woman in her fifties with hair cut very short and dyed to the colour of nicotine. Although frail, she conveyed an impression of endurance and courage, and the brown eyes that shone from her crooked little face were of an astonishing intensity. It was a worn face, racked and ravaged long ago, the face of a child grown old on starving and exhaustion, the eternal refugee face, the prison-camp face, thought Smiley.

She was holding out her hand to him—it was scrubbed and pink, bony to touch. He told her his name.

'You're the man who interviewed my husband,' she said; 'about loyalty.' She led him into the low, dark drawing-room. There was no fire. Smiley felt suddenly sick and cheap. Loyalty to whom, to what. She didn't sound resentful. He was an oppressor, but she accepted oppression.

'I liked your husband very much. He would have been cleared.'

'Cleared? Cleared of what?'

'There was a prima facie case for investigation—an anonymous letter—I was given the job.' He paused and looked at her with real concern. 'You have had a terrible loss, Mrs Fennan . . . you must be exhausted. You can't have slept all night . . .'

She did not respond to his sympathy: 'Thank you, but I can scarcely hope to sleep today. Sleep is not a luxury I enjoy.' She looked down wryly at her own tiny body; 'My body and I must put up with one another twenty hours a day. We have lived longer than most people already.

'As for the terrible loss. Yes, I suppose so. But you know, Mr Smiley, for so long I owned nothing but a toothbrush, so I'm not really used to possession, even after eight years of marriage. Besides, I have the experience to suffer with discretion.'

She bobbed her head at him, indicating that he might sit, and with an oddly old-fashioned gesture she swept her skirt beneath her and sat opposite him. It was very cold in that room. Smiley wondered whether he ought to speak; he dared not look at her, but peered vaguely before him, trying desperately in his mind to penetrate the worn, travelled face of Elsa Fennan. It seemed a long time before she spoke again.

'You said you liked him. You didn't give him that impression, apparently.'

'I haven't seen your husband's letter, but I have heard of its contents.' Smiley's earnest, pouchy face was turned towards her now: 'It simply doesn't make sense. I as good as told him he was . . . that we would recommend that the matter be taken no further.'

She was motionless, waiting to hear. What could he say: 'I'm sorry I killed your husband, Mrs Fennan, but I was only doing my duty.' (Duty to *whom* for God's sake?) 'He was in the Communist Party at Oxford twenty-four years ago; his recent promotion gave him access to highly secret information. Some busybody wrote us an anonymous letter and we had no option but to follow it up. The investigation induced a state of melancholia in your husband, and drove him to suicide.' He said nothing.

'It was a game,' she said suddenly, 'a silly balancing trick of ideas; it had nothing to do with him or any real person. Why do you bother yourself with us? Go back to Whitehall and look for more spies on your drawing boards.' She paused, showing no sign of emotion beyond the burning of her dark eyes. 'It's an old illness you suffer from, Mr Smiley,' she continued, taking a cigarette from the box; 'and I have seen many victims of it. The mind becomes separated from the body; it thinks without reality, rules a paper kingdom and devises without emotion the ruin of its paper victims. But sometimes the division between your world and ours is incomplete; the files grow heads and arms and legs, and that's a terrible moment, isn't it? The names have families as well as records, and human motives to explain the sad little dossiers and their makebelieve sins. When that happens I am sorry for you.' She paused for a moment, then continued:

'It's like the State and the People. The State is a dream too, a symbol of nothing at all, an emptiness, a mind without a body, a game played with clouds in the sky. But States make war, don't they, and imprison people? To dream in doctrines—how tidy! My husband and I have both been tidied now, haven't we?' She was looking at him steadily. Her accent was more noticeable now.

'You call yourself the State, Mr Smiley; you have no place among real people. You dropped a bomb from the sky: don't come down here and look at the blood or hear the scream.'

She had not raised her voice, she looked above him now, and beyond.

'You seem shocked. I should be weeping, I suppose, but I've no more tears, Mr Smiley—I'm barren; the children of my grief are dead. Thank you for coming, Mr Smiley; you can go back, now—there's nothing you can do here.'

He sat forward in his chair, his podgy hands nursing one another on his knees. He looked worried and sanctimonious, like a grocer reading the lesson. The skin of his face was white and glistened at the temples and on the upper lip. Only under his eyes was there any colour: mauve half-moons bisected by the heavy frame of his spectacles.

'Look, Mrs Fennan; that interview was almost a formality. I think your husband enjoyed it, I think it even made him happy to get it over.'

'How *can* you say that, how can you, now this . . .'

'But I tell you it's true: why, we didn't even hold the thing in a Government office—when I got there I found Fennan's office was a sort of right of way between two other rooms, so we walked out into the park and finished up at a café—scarcely an inquisition, you see. I even told him not to worry—I told him that. I just don't understand the letter–it doesn't . . .'

'It's not the letter, Mr Smiley, that I'm thinking of. It's what he said to me.'

'How do you mean?'

'He was deeply upset by the interview, he told me so. When he came back on Monday night he was desperate, almost incoherent. He collapsed in a chair and I persuaded him to go to bed. I gave him a sedative which lasted him half the night. He was still talking about it the next morning. It occupied his whole mind until his death.'

The telephone was ringing upstairs. Smiley got up.

'Excuse me–that will be my office. Do you mind?'

'It's in the front bedroom, directly above us.'

Smiley walked slowly upstairs in a state of complete bewilderment. What on earth should he say to Maston now?

He lifted the receiver, glancing mechanically at the number on the apparatus.

'Walliston 2944.'

'Exchange here. Good morning. Your eight-thirty call.'

'Oh–Oh yes, thank you very much.'

He rang off, grateful for the temporary respite. He glanced briefly round the bedroom. It was the Fennan's own bedroom, austere but comfortable. There were two armchairs in front of the gas fire. Smiley remembered now that Elsa Fennan had been bedridden for three years after the war. It was probably a survival from those years that they still sat in the bedroom in the evenings. The alcoves on either side of the fireplace were full of books. In the furthest corner, a typewriter on a desk. There was something intimate and touching about the arrangement, and perhaps for the first time Smiley was filled with an immediate sense of the tragedy of Fennan's death. He returned to the drawing-room.

'It was for you. Your eight-thirty call from the exchange.'

He was aware of a pause and glanced incuriously towards her. But she had turned away from him and was standing looking out of the window, her slender back very straight and still, her stiff, short hair dark against the morning light.

Suddenly he stared at her. Something had occurred to him which he should have realized upstairs in the bedroom, something so improbable that for a moment his brain was unable to grasp it. Mechanically he went on talking; he must get out of there, get away from the telephone and Maston's hysterical questions, get away from Elsa Fennan and her dark, restless house. Get away and think.

'I have intruded too much already, Mrs Fennan, and I must now take your advice and return to Whitehall.'

Again the cold, frail hand, the mumbled expressions of sympathy. He collected his coat from the hall and stepped out into the early sunlight. The winter sun had just appeared for a moment after the rain, and it repainted in pale, wet colours the trees and houses of Merridale Lane. They sky was still dark grey, and the world beneath it strangely luminous, giving back the sunlight it had stolen from nowhere.

He walked slowly down the gravel path, fearful of being called back.

He returned to the police station, full of disturbing thoughts. To begin with it was not Elsa Fennan who had asked the exchange for an eight-thirty call that morning.

Chapter Four

Coffee at the Fountain

The CID superintendent at Walliston was a large, genial soul who measured professional competence in years of service and saw no fault in the habit. Sparrow's Inspector Mendel on the other hand was a thin, weasel-faced gentleman who spoke very rapidly out of the corner of his mouth. Smiley secretly likened him to a gamekeeper—a man who knew his territory and disliked intruders.

'I have a message from your Department, sir. You're to ring the Adviser at once.' The Superintendent indicated his telephone with an enormous hand and walked out through the open door of his office. Mendel remained. Smiley looked at him owlishly for a moment, guessing his man.

'Shut the door.' Mendel moved to the door and pulled it quietly to.

'I want to make an inquiry of the Walliston telephone exchange. Who's the most likely contact?'

'Assistant Supervisor normally. Supervisor's always in the clouds; Assistant Supervisor does the work.'

'Someone at 15 Merridale Lane asked to be called by the exchange at eight-thirty this morning. I want to know what time the request was made and who by. I want to know whether there's a standing request for a morning call, and if so let's have the details.'

'Know the number?'

'Walliston 2944. Subscriber Samuel Fennan, I should think.'

Mendel moved to the telephone and dialled o. While he waited for a reply he said to Smiley: 'You don't want anyone to know about this, do you?'

'No one. Not even you. There's probably nothing in it. If we start bleating about murder we'll . . .'

Mendel was through to the exchange, asking for the Assistant Supervisor.

'Walliston CID here, Superintendent's office. We have an inquiry . . . yes, of course . . . ring me back then . . . CID outside line, Walliston 2421.'

He replaced the receiver and waited for the exchange to ring him. 'Sensible girl,' he muttered, without looking at Smiley. The telephone rang and he began speaking at once.

'We're investigating a burglary in Merridale Lane. Number 18. Just possible they used No. 15 as an observation point for a job on the opposite house. Have you got any way of finding out whether calls were originated or received on Walliston 2944 in the last twenty-four hours?'

There was a pause. Mendel put his hand over the mouthpiece and turned to Smiley with a very slight grin. Smiley suddenly liked him a good deal.

'She's asking the girls,' said Mendel; 'and she'll look at the dockets.' He turned back to the telephone and began jotting down figures on the Superintendent's pad. He stiffened abruptly and leaned forward on the desk.

'Oh yes.' His voice was casual, in contrast to his attitude; 'I wonder when she asked for that?' Another pause . . . '19.55 hours . . . a man, eh? The girl's sure of that, is she? . . . Oh, I see, oh, well, that fixes that. Thanks very much indeed all the same. Well, at least we know where we stand . . . not at all, you've been very helpful . . . just a theory, that's all . . . have to think again, won't we? Well, thanks very much. Very kind, keep it under your hat . . . Cheerio.' He rang off, tore the page from the pad, and put it in his pocket.

Smiley spoke quickly: 'There's a beastly café down the road. I need some breakfast. Come and have a cup of coffee.' The telephone was ringing; Smiley could almost feel Maston the other end. Mendel looked at him for a moment and seemed to understand. They left it ringing and walked quickly out of the police station towards the High Street.

The Fountain Café (Proprietor Miss Gloria Adam) was all Tudor and horse brasses and local honey at sixpence more than anywhere else. Miss Adam herself dispensed the nastiest coffee south of Manchester and spoke of her customers as 'My Friends'. Miss Adam did not do business with friends, but simply robbed them, which somehow added to the illusion of genteel amateurism which Miss Adam was so anxious to preserve. Her origin was obscure, but she often spoke of her late father as 'The Colonel'. It was rumoured among those of Miss Adam's friends who had paid particularly dearly for their friendship that the colonelcy in question had been granted by the Salvation Army.

Mendel and Smiley sat at a corner table near the fire, waiting for their order. Mendel looked at Smiley oddly: 'The girl remembers the call clearly; it came right at the end of her shift—five to eight last night. A request for an 8.30 call this morning. It was made by Fennan himself—the girl is positive of that.'

'How?'

'Apparently this Fennan had rung the exchange on Christmas Day and the same girl was on duty. Wanted to wish them all a Happy Christmas. She was rather bucked. They had quite a chat. She's sure it was the same voice yesterday, asking for the call. "Very cultured gentleman", she said.'

'But it doesn't make sense. He wrote a suicide letter at 10.30. What happened between 8 and 10.30?'

Mendel picked up a battered old briefcase. It had no lock—more like a music case, thought Smiley. He took from it a plain buff folder and handed it to Smiley. 'Facsimile of the letter. Super said to give you a copy. They're sending the original to the FO and another copy straight to Marlene Dietrich.'

'Who the devil's she?'

'Sorry, sir. What we call your Adviser, sir. Pretty general in the Branch, sir. Very sorry, sir.'

How beautiful, thought Smiley, how absolutely beautiful. He opened the folder and looked at the facsimile. Mendel went on talking: 'First suicide letter I've ever seen that was typed. First one I've seen with the time on it, for that matter. Signature looks OK though. Checked it at the station against a receipt he once signed for lost property. Right as rain.'

The letter was typed, probably a portable. Like the anonymous denunciation; that was a portable too. This one was signed with Fennan's neat, legible signature. Beneath the printed address at the head of the page was typed the date, and beneath that the time: 10.30 p.m.:

> Dear Sir David,
>   After some hesitation I have decided to take my life. I cannot spend my remaining years under a cloud of disloyalty and suspicion. I realize that my career is ruined, that I am the victim of paid informers.
>   Yours sincerely,
>   Samuel Fennan

Smiley read it through several times, his mouth pursed in concentration, his eyebrows raised a little as if in surprise. Mendel was asking him something:

'How d'you get on to it?'

'On to what?'

'This early call business.'

'Oh, I took the call. Thought it was for me. It wasn't—it was the exchange with this thing. Even then the penny didn't drop. I assumed it was for her, you see. Went down and told her.'

'Down?'

'Yes. They keep the telephone in the bedroom. It's a sort of bed-sitter, really . . . she used to be an invalid, you know, and they've left the room as it was then, I suppose. It's like a study, one end; books, typewriter, desk and so forth.'

'Typewriter?'

'Yes. A portable. I imagine he did this letter on it. But you see when I took that call I'd forgotten it couldn't possibly be Mrs Fennan who'd asked for it.'

'Why not?'

'She's an insomniac—she told me. Made a sort of joke of it. I told her to get some rest and she just said: "My body and I must put up with one another twenty hours a day. We have lived longer than most people already." There was more of it—something about not enjoying the luxury of sleep. So why should she want a call at 8.30?'

'Why should her husband—why should anyone? It's damn nearly lunch time. God help the Civil Service.'

'Exactly. That puzzles me too. The Foreign Office admittedly starts late—ten o'clock, I think. But even then Fennan would be pushed to dress, shave, breakfast and catch the train on time if he didn't wake till 8.30. Besides, his wife could call him.'

'She might have been shooting a line about not sleeping,' said Mendel. 'Women do, about insomnia and migraine and stuff. Makes people think they're nervous and temperamental. Cock, most of it.'

Smiley shook his head: 'No, she couldn't have made the call, could she? She wasn't home till 10.45. But even supposing she made a mistake about the time she got back, she couldn't have gone to the telephone without seeing her husband's body first. And you're not going to tell me that her reaction on finding her husband dead was to go upstairs and ask for an early call?'

They drank their coffee in silence for a while.

'Another thing,' said Mendel.

'Yes?'

'His wife got back from the theatre at quarter to eleven, right?'

'That's what she says.'

'Did she go alone?'

'No idea.'

'Bet she didn't. I'll bet she *had* to tell the truth there, and timed the letter to give herself an alibi.'

Smiley's mind went back to Elsa Fennan, her anger, her submission. It seemed ridiculous to talk about her in this way. No: not Elsa Fennan. No.

'Where was the body found?' Smiley asked.

'Bottom of the stairs.'

'Bottom of the stairs?'

'True. Sprawled across the hall floor. Revolver underneath him.'

'And the note. Where was that?'

'Beside him on the floor.'

'Anything else?'

'Yes. A mug of cocoa in the drawing-room.'

'I see. Fennan decides to commit suicide. He asks the exchange to ring him at 8.30. He makes himself some cocoa and puts it in the drawing-room. He goes upstairs and types his last letter. He comes down again to shoot himself, leaving the cocoa undrunk. It all hangs together nicely.'

'Yes, doesn't it. Incidentally, hadn't you better ring your office?'

He looked at Mendel equivocally. 'That's the end of a beautiful friendship,' he said. As he walked towards the coin box beside a door marked 'Private' he heard Mendel saying: 'I bet you say that to all the boys.' He was actually smiling as he asked for Maston's number.

Maston wanted to see him at once.

He went back to their table. Mendel was stirring another cup of coffee as if it required all his concentration. He was eating a very large bun.

Smiley stood beside him. 'I've got to go back to London.'

'Well, this will put the cat among the pigeons.' The weasel face turned abruptly towards him; 'or will it?' He spoke with the front of his mouth while the back of it continued to deal with the bun.

'If Fennan was murdered, no power on earth can prevent the Press from getting hold of the story,' and to himself added: 'I don't think Maston would like that. He'd prefer suicide.'

'Still, we've got to face that, haven't we?'

Smiley paused, frowning earnestly. Already he could hear Maston deriding his suspicions, laughing them impatiently away. 'I don't know,' he said, 'I really don't know.'

Back to London, he thought, back to Maston's Ideal Home, back to the rat-race of blame. And back to the unreality of containing a human tragedy in a three-page report.

It was raining again, a warm incessant rain now, and in the short distance between the Fountain Café and the police station he got very wet. He took off his coat and threw it into the back of the car. It was a relief to be leaving Walliston—even for London. As he turned on to the main road he saw out of the corner of his eye the figure of Mendel stoically trudging along the pavement towards the station, his grey trilby shapeless and blackened by the rain. It hadn't occurred to Smiley that he might want a lift to London, and he felt ungracious. Mendel, untroubled by the niceties of the situation, opened the passenger door and got in.

'Bit of luck,' he observed. 'Hate trains. Cambridge Circus you going to? You can drop me Westminster way, can't you?'

They set off and Mendel produced a shabby green tobacco tin and rolled himself a cigarette. He directed it towards his mouth, changed his mind and offered it to Smiley, lighting it for him with an extraordinary lighter that threw a two-inch blue flame. 'You look worried sick,' said Mendel.

'I am.'

There was a pause. Mendel said: 'It's the devil you don't know that gets you.'

They had driven another four or five miles when Smiley drew the car in to the side of the road. He turned to Mendel.

'Would you mind awfully if we drove back to Walliston?'

'Good idea. Go and ask her.'

He turned the car and drove slowly back to Walliston, back to Merridale Lane. He left Mendel in the car and walked down the familiar gravel path.

She opened the door and showing him into the drawing-room without a word. She was wearing the same dress, and Smiley wondered how she had passed the time since he had left her that morning.

Had she been walking about the house or sitting motionless in the drawing-room? Or upstairs in the bedroom with the leather chairs? How did she see herself in her new widowhood? Could she take it seriously yet, was she still in that secretly elevated state which immediately follows bereavement? Still looking at herself in mirrors, trying to discern the change, the horror in her own face, and weeping when she could not?

Neither of them sat down–both instinctively avoided a repetition of that morning's meeting.

'There was one thing I felt I must ask you, Mrs Fennan. I'm very sorry to have to bother you again.'

'About the call, I expect; the early morning call from the exchange.'

'Yes.'

'I thought that might puzzle you. An insomniac asks for an early morning call.' She was trying to speak brightly.

'Yes. It did seem odd. Do you often go to the theatre?'

'Yes. Once a fortnight. I'm a member of the Weybridge Repertory Club you know. I try and go to everything they do. I have a seat reserved for me automatically on the first Tuesday of each run. My husband worked late on Tuesdays. He never came; he'd only go to classical theatre.'

'But he liked Brecht didn't he? He seemed very thrilled with the Berliner Ensemble performances in London.'

She looked at him for a moment, and then smiled suddenly–the first time he had seen her do so. It was an enchanting smile; her whole face lit up like a child's.

Smiley had a fleeting vision of Elsa Fennan as a child–a spindly, agile tomboy like George Sand's 'Petite Fadette'–half woman, half glib, lying girl. He saw her as a wheedling *Backfisch*, fighting like a cat for herself alone, and he saw her too, starved and shrunken in prison camp, ruthless in her fight for self-preservation. It was pathetic to witness in that smile the light of her early innocence, and a steeled weapon in her fight for survival.

'I'm afraid the explanation of that call is very silly,' she said. 'I suffer from a terrible memory–really awful. Go shopping and forget what I've come to buy, make an appointment on the telephone and forget it the moment I replace the receiver. I ask people to stay the week-end and we are out when they arrive. Occasionally, when there is something I simply have to remember, I ring the exchange and ask for a call a few minutes before the appointed time. It's like a knot in one's handkerchief, but a knot can't ring a bell at you, can it?'

Smiley peered at her. His throat felt rather dry, and he had to swallow before he spoke.

'And what was the call for this time, Mrs Fennan?'

Again the enchanting smile: 'There you are. I completely forget.'

Chapter Five

Maston and Candelight

As he drove slowly back towards London Smiley ceased to be conscious of Mendel's presence.

There had been a time when the mere business of driving a car was a relief to him; when he had found in the unreality of a long, solitary journey a palliative to his troubled brain, when the fatigue of several hours' driving had allowed him to forget more sombre cares.

It was one of the subtler landmarks of middle age, perhaps, that he could no longer thus subdue his mind. It needed sterner measures now: he even tried on occasion to plan in his head a walk through a European city–to record the shops and buildings he would pass, for instance, in Berne on a walk from the Münster to the University. But despite such energetic mental exercise, the ghosts of time present would intrude and drive his dreams away. It was Ann who had robbed him of his peace, Ann who had once made the present so important and taught him the habit of reality, and when she went there was nothing.

He could not believe that Elsa Fennan had killed her husband. Her instinct was to defend, to hoard the treasures of her life, to build about herself the symbols of normal existence. There was no aggression in her, no will but the will to preserve.

But who could tell? What did Hesse write? 'Strange to wander in the mist, each is alone. No tree knows his neighbour. Each is alone.' We know nothing of one another, nothing, Smiley mused. However closely we live together, at whatever time of day or night we sound the deepest thoughts in one another, we know nothing. How am I judging Elsa Fennan? I think I understand her suffering and her frightened lies, but what do I know of her? Nothing.

Mendel was pointing at a sign-post.

'. . . That's where I live. Mitcham. Not a bad spot really. Got sick of bachelor quarters. Bought a decent little semi-detached down here. For my retirement.'

'Retirement? That's a long way off.'

'Yes. Three days. That's why I got this job. Nothing to it; no complications. Give it to old Mendel, he'll muck it up.'

'Well, well. I expect we shall both be out of a job by Monday.'

He drove Mendel to Scotland Yard and went on to Cambridge Circus.

He realized as he walked into the building that everyone knew. It was the way they looked; some shade of difference in their glance, their attitude. He made straight for Maston's room. Maston's secretary was at her desk and she looked up quickly as he entered.

'Adviser in?'

'Yes. He's expecting you. He's alone. I should knock and go in.' But Maston had opened the door and was already calling him. He was wearing a black coat and pin-stripe trousers. Here goes the cabaret, thought Smiley.

'I've been trying to get in touch with you. Did you not receive my message?' said Maston.

'I did, but I couldn't possibly have spoken to you.'

'I don't quite follow?'

'Well, I don't believe Fennan committed suicide–I think he was murdered. I couldn't say that on the telephone.'

Maston took off his spectacles and looked at Smiley in blank astonishment.

'Murdered? Why?'

'Well, Fennan wrote his letter at 10.30 last night, if we are to accept the time on his letter as correct.'

'Well?'

'Well, at 7.55 he rang up the exchange and asked to be called at 8.30 the next morning.'

'How on earth do you know that?'

'I was there this morning when the exchange rang. I took the call thinking it might be from the Department.'

'How can you possibly say that it was Fennan who ordered the call?'

'I had inquiries made. The girl at the exchange knew Fennan's voice well; she was sure it was he, and that he rang at five to eight last night.'

'Fennan and the girl knew each other, did they?'

'Good heavens no. They just exchanged pleasantries occasionally.'

'And how do you conclude from this that he was murdered?'

'Well I asked his wife about this call . . .'

'And?'

'She lied. Said she ordered it herself. She claimed to be frightfully absent-minded—she gets the exchange to ring her occasionally, like tying a knot in a handkerchief, when she has an important appointment. And another thing—just before shooting himself he made some cocoa. He never drank it.'

Maston listened in silence. At last he smiled and got up.

'We seem to be at cross-purposes,' he said. 'I send you down to discover why Fennan shot himself. You come back and say he didn't. We're not policemen, Smiley.'

'No. I sometimes wonder what we are.'

'Did you hear anything that affects our position here—anything that explains his action at all? Anything to substantiate the suicide letter?'

Smiley hesitated before replying. He had seen it coming.

'Yes. I understood from Mrs Fennan that her husband was very upset after the interview.' He might as well hear the whole story. 'It obsessed him, he couldn't sleep after it. She had to give him a sedative. Her account of Fennan's reaction to my interview entirely substantiates the letter.' He was silent for a minute, blinking rather stupidly before him. 'What I am trying to say is that I don't believe her. I don't believe Fennan wrote that letter, or that he had any intention of dying.' He turned to Maston. 'We simply cannot dismiss the inconsistencies. Another thing,' he plunged on, 'I haven't had an expert comparison made but there's a similarity between the anonymous letter and Fennan's suicide note. The type looks identical. Its' ridiculous I know but there it is. We must bring the police in—give them the facts.'

'Facts?' said Maston. 'What facts? Suppose she did lie—she's an odd woman by all accounts, foreign, Jewish. Heaven knows the tributaries of her mind. I'm told she suffered in the war, persecuted and so forth. She may see in you the oppressor, the inquisitor. She spots you're on to something, panics and tells you the first lie that comes into her head. Does that make her a murderess?'

'Then why did Fennan make the call? Why make himself a nightcap?'

'Who can tell?' Maston's voice was richer now, more persuasive.

'If you or I, Smiley, were ever driven to that dreadful point where we were determined to destroy ourselves, who can tell what our last thoughts on earth would be? And what of Fennan? He sees his career in ruins, his life has no meaning. Is it not conceivable that he should wish, in a moment of weakness or irresolution, to hear another human voice, feel again the warmth of human contact before he dies? Fanciful, sentimental, perhaps; but not improbable in a man so overwrought, so obsessed that he takes his own life.'

Smiley had to give him credit—it was a good performance and he was no match for Maston when it came to this. Abruptly he felt inside himself the rising panic of frustration beyond endurance. With panic came an uncontrollable fury with this posturing syco-phant, this obscene cissy with his greying hair and his reasonable smile. Panic and fury welled up in a sudden tide, flooding his breast, suffusing his whole body. His face felt hot and red, his spectacles blurred, and tears sprang to his eyes, adding to his humiliation.

Maston went on, mercifully unaware: 'You cannot expect me to suggest to the Home Secretary on this evidence that the police have reached a false conclusion; you know how tenuous our police liaison is. On the one hand we have your suspicions: that in short Fennan's behaviour last night was not consistent with the intent to die. His wife has apparently lied to you. Against that we have the opinion of trained detectives, who found nothing disturbing in the circum-stances of death, and we have Mrs Fennan's statement that her husband was upset by his interview. I'm sorry, Smiley, but there it is.'

There was complete silence. Smiley was slowly recovering him-self, and the process left him dull and inarticulate. He peered myopically before him, his pouchy, lined face still pink, his mouth slack and stupid. Maston was waiting for him to speak, but he was tired and suddenly utterly disinterested. Without a glance at Maston he got up and walked out.

He reached his own room and sat down at the desk. Mechanically he looked through his work. His in-tray contained little—some office circulars and a personal letter addressed to G. Smiley Esq., Ministry of Defence. The handwriting was unfamiliar; he opened the en-velope and read the letter.

Dear Smiley,
It is essential that I should lunch with you tomorrow at the Compleat Angler at Marlow. Please do your best to meet me there at one o'clock. There is something I have to tell you.
Yours,
Samuel Fennan

The letter was handwritten and dated the previous day, Tuesday, 3 January. It had been postmarked in Whitehall at 6.0 p.m.

He looked at it stodgily for several minutes, holding it stiffly before him and inclining his head to the left. Then he put the letter down, opened a drawer of the desk and took out a single clean sheet of paper. He wrote a brief letter of resignation to Maston, and attached Fennan's invitation with a pin. He pressed the bell for a secretary, left the letter in his out-tray and made for the lift. As usual it was stuck in the basement with the registry's tea trolley, and after a short wait he began walking downstairs. Half-way down he remembered that he had left his mackintosh and a few bits and pieces in his room. Never mind, he thought, they'll send them on.

He sat in his car in the car park, staring through the drenched windscreen.

He didn't care, he just damn well didn't care. He was surprised certainly. Surprised that he had so nearly lost control. Interviews had played a great part in Smiley's life, and he had long ago come to consider himself proof against them all: disciplinary, scholastic, medical, and religious. His secretive nature detested the purpose of all interviews, their oppressive intimacy, their inescapable reality. He remembered one deliriously happy dinner with Ann at Quaglino's when he had described to her the Chameleon-Armadillo system for beating the interviewer.

They had dined by candlelight; white skin and pearls—they were drinking brandy—Ann's eyes wide and moist, only for him; Smiley playing the lover and doing it wonderfully well; Ann loving him and thrilled by their harmony.

'. . . and so I learned first to be a chameleon.'

'You mean you sat there burping, you rude toad?'

'No, it's a matter of colour. Chameleons change colour.'

'Of course they change colour. They sit on green leaves and go green. Did you go green, toad?'

His fingers ran lightly over the tips of hers. 'Listen, minx, while I explain the Smiley Chameleon-Armadillo technique for the impertinent interviewer.' Her face was very close to his and she adored him with her eyes.

'The technique is based on the theory that the interviewer, loving no one as well as himself, will be attracted by his own image. You therefore assume the exact social, temperamental, political and intellectual colour of your inquisitor.'

'Pompous toad. But intelligent lover.'

'Silence. Sometimes this method founders against the idiocy or ill-disposition of the inquisitor. If so, become an armadillo.'

'And wear linear belts, toad?'

'No, place him in a position so incongruous that you are superior to him. I was prepared for confirmation by a retired bishop. I was his whole flock, and received on one half holiday sufficient guidance for a diocese. But by contemplating the bishop's face, and imagining that under my gaze it became covered in thick fur, I maintained the ascendancy. From then on the skill grew. I could turn him into an ape, get him stuck in sash windows, send him naked to Masonic banquets, condemn him, like the serpent, to go about on his belly . . .'

'*Wicked* lover-toad.'

And so it had been. But in his recent interviews with Maston the power of detachment had left him; he was getting too involved. When Maston made the first moves, Smiley had been too tired and disgusted to compete. He supposed Elsa Fennan had killed her husband, that she had some good reason and it just did not bother him any more. The problem no longer existed; suspicion, experience, perception, common sense—for Maston these were not the organs of fact. Paper was fact, Ministers were fact, Home Secretaries were hard fact. The Department did not concern itself with the vague impressions of a single officer when they conflicted with policy.

Smiley was tired, deeply, heavily tired. He drove slowly homewards. Dinner out tonight. Something rather special. It was only lunchtime now—he would spend the afternoon pursuing Olearius across the Russian continent on his Hansa voyage. Then dinner at Quaglino's, and a solitary toast to the successful murderer, to Elsa perhaps, in gratitude for ending the career of George Smiley with the life of Sam Fennan.

He remembered to collect his laundry in Sloane Street, and finally turned into Bywater Street, finding a parking space about three houses from his own. He got out carrying the brown paper parcel of laundry, locked the car laboriously, and walked all round it from habit, testing the handles. A thin rain was still falling. It annoyed him that someone had parked outside his house again. Thank goodness Mrs Chapel had closed his bedroom window, otherwise the rain would have . . .

He was suddenly alert. Something had moved in the drawing-room. A light, a shadow, a human form; something, he was certain. Was it sight or instinct? Was it the latent skill of his own tradecraft which informed him? Some fine sense or nerve, some remote faculty of perception warned him now and he heeded the warning.

Without a moment's thought he dropped his keys back into his overcoat pocket, walked up the steps to his own front door and rang the bell.

It echoed shrilly through the house. There was a moment's silence, then came to Smiley's ears the distinct sound of footsteps approaching the door, firm and confident. A scratch of the chain, a click of the Ingersoll latch and the door was opened, swiftly, cleanly.

Smiley had never seen him before. Tall, fair, handsome, thirty-five odd. A light grey suit, white shirt and silver tie—*habillé en diplomate.* German or Swede. His left hand remained nonchalantly in his jacket pocket.

Smiley peered at him apologetically:

'Good afternoon. Is Mr Smiley in, please?'

The door was opened to its fullest extent. A tiny pause.

'Yes. Won't you come in?'

For a fraction of a second he hesitated. 'No thanks. Would you please give him this?' He handed him the parcel of laundry, walked down the steps again, to his car. He knew he was still being watched. He started the car, turned and drove into Sloane Square without a glance in the direction of his house. He found a parking space in Sloane Street, pulled in and rapidly wrote in his diary seven sets of numbers. They belonged to the seven cars parked along Bywater Street.

What should he do? Stop a policeman? Whoever he was, he was probably gone by now. Besides there were other considerations. He locked the car again and crossed the road to a telephone kiosk. He rang Scotland Yard, got through to Special Branch and asked for Inspector Mendel. But it appeared that the Inspector, having reported back to the Superintendent, had discreetly anticipated the pleasures of retirement and left for Mitcham. Smiley got his address after a good deal of prevarication, and set off once more in his car, covering three sides of the square and emerging at Albert Bridge. He had a sandwich and a large whisky at a new pub overlooking the river and a quarter of an hour later was crossing the bridge on the way to Mitcham, the rain still beating down on his inconspicuous little car. He was worried, very worried indeed.

Chapter Six

Tea and Sympathy

It was still raining as he arrived. Mendel was in his garden wearing the most extraordinary hat Smiley had ever seen. It had begun life as an Anzac hat but its enormous brim hung low all the way round, so that he resembled nothing so much as a very tall mushroom. He was brooding over a tree stump, a wicked looking pick-axe poised obediently in his sinewy right hand.

He looked at Smiley sharply for a moment, then a grin slowly crossed his thin face as he extended his hand.

'Trouble,' said Mendel.

'Trouble.'

Smiley followed him up the path and into the house. Suburban and comfortable.

'There's no fire in the living-room—only just got back. How about a cup of tea in the kitchen?'

They went into the kitchen. Smiley was amused to notice the extreme tidiness, the almost feminine neatness of everything about him. Only the police calendar on the wall spoilt the illusion. While Mendel put a kettle on and busied himself with cups and saucers, Smiley related dispassionately what had happened in Bywater Street. When he had finished Mendel looked at him for a long time in silence.

'But why did he ask you in?'

Smiley blinked and coloured a little. 'That's what I wondered. It put me off my balance for a moment. It was lucky I had the parcel.'

He took a drink of tea. 'Though I don't believe he was taken in by the parcel. He may have been, but I doubt it. I doubt it very much.'

'Not taken in?'

'Well, I wouldn't have been. Little man in a Ford delivering parcels of linen. Who could I have been? Besides, I asked for Smiley and then didn't want to see him—he must have thought that was pretty queer.'

'But what was he after? What would he have done with you? Who did he think you were?'

'That's just the point, that's just it, you see. I think it was me he was waiting for, but of course he didn't expect me to ring the bell. I put him off balance. I think he wanted to kill me. That's why he asked me in: he recognized me but only just, probably from a photograph.'

Mendel looked at him in silence for a while.

'Christ,' he said.

'Suppose I'm right,' Smiley continued, 'all the way. Suppose Fennan *was* murdered last night and I *did* nearly follow him this morning. Well, unlike your trade, mine doesn't normally run to a murder a day.'

'Meaning what?'

'I don't know. I just don't know. Perhaps before we go much further you'd check on these cars for me. They were parked in Bywater Street this morning.'

'Why not do it yourself?'

Smiley looked at him, puzzled for a second. Then it dawned on him that he hadn't mentioned his resignation.

'Sorry. I didn't tell you, did I? I resigned this morning. Just managed to get it in before I was sacked. So I'm free as air. And about as employable.'

Mendel took the list of numbers from him and went into the hall to telephone. He returned a couple of minutes later.

'They'll ring back in an hour,' he said. 'Come on. I'll show you round the estate. Know anything about bees, do you?'

'Well, a very little, yes. I got bitten with the natural history bug at Oxford.' He was going to tell Mendel how he had wrestled with Goethe's metamorphoses of plants and animals in the hope of discovering, like Faust, 'what sustains the world at its inmost point.' He wanted to explain why it was impossible to understand nineteenth-century Europe without a working knowledge of the naturalistic sciences, he felt earnest and full of important thoughts, and knew secretly that this was because his brain was wrestling with the day's events, that he was in a state of nervous excitement. The palms of his hands were moist.

Mendel led him out of the back door: three neat beehives stood against the low brick wall which ran along the end of the garden. Mendel spoke as they stood in the fine rain.

'Always wanted to keep them, see what it's all about. Been reading it all up—frightens me stiff, I can tell you. Odd little beggars.' He nodded a couple of times in support of this statement, and Smiley looked at him again with interest. His face was thin but muscular, its expression entirely uncommunicative; his iron grey hair was cut very short and spiky. He seemed quite indifferent to the weather, and the weather to him. Smiley knew exactly the life that lay behind Mendel, had seen in policemen all over the world the same leathern skin, the same reserves of patience, bitterness, and anger. He could guess the long, fruitless hours of surveillance in every kind of weather, waiting for someone who might never come . . . or come and go too quickly. And he knew how much Mendel and the rest of them were at the mercy of personalities—capricious and bullying, nervous and changeful, occasionally wise and sympathetic. He knew how intelligent men could be broken by the stupidity of their superiors, how weeks of patient work night and day could be cast aside by such a man.

Mendel led him up the precarious path laid with broken stone to the beehives and, still oblivious of the rain, began taking one to pieces, demonstrating and explaining. He spoke in jerks, with quite long pauses between phrases, indicating precisely and slowly with his slim fingers.

At last they went indoors again, and Mendel showed him the two downstairs rooms. The drawing-room was all flowers: flowered curtains and carpet, flowered covers on the furniture. In a small cabinet in one corner were some Toby jugs and a pair of very handsome pistols beside a cup for target shooting.

Smiley followed him upstairs. There was a smell of paraffin from the stove on the landing, and a surly bubbling from the cistern in the lavatory.

Mendel showed him his own bedroom.

'Bridal chamber. Bought the bed at a sale for a quid. Box spring mattress. Amazing what you can pick up. Carpets are ex-Queen Elizabeth. They change them every year. Bought them at a store in Watford.'

Smiley stood in the doorway, somehow rather embarrassed. Mendel turned back and passed him to open the other bedroom door.

'And that's your room. If you want it.' He turned to Smiley. 'I wouldn't stay at your place tonight if I were you. You never know, do you? Besides, you'll sleep better here. Air's better.'

Smiley began to protest.

'Up to you. You do what you like.' Mendel grew surly and embarrassed. 'Don't understand your job, to be honest, any more than you know police work. You do what you like. From what I've seen of you, you can look after yourself.'

They went downstairs again. Mendel had lit the gas fire in the drawing-room.

'Well, at least you must let me give you dinner tonight,' said Smiley.

The telephone rang in the hall. It was Mendel's secretary about the car numbers.

Mendel came back. He handed Smiley a list of seven names and addresses. Four of the seven could be discounted; the registered addresses were in Bywater Street. Three remained: a hired car from the firm of Adam Scarr and Sons of Battersea, a trade van belonging to the Severn Tile Company, Eastbourne; and the third was listed specially as the property of the Panamanian Ambassador.

'I've got a man on the Panamanian job now. There'll be no difficulty there–they've only got three cars on the Embassy strength.

'Battersea's not far,' Mendel continued. 'We could pop over there together. In your car.'

'By all means, by all means,' Smiley said quickly; 'and we can go in to Kensington for dinner. I'll book a table at the Entrechat.'

It was four o'clock. They sat for a while talking in a rather desultory way about bees and house-keeping. Mendel quite at ease and Smiley still bothered and awkward, trying to find a way of talking, trying not to be clever. He could guess what Ann would have said about Mendel. She would have loved him, made a person of him, had a special voice and face for imitating him, would have made a story of him until he fitted into their lives and wasn't a mystery any more: 'Darling, who'd have thought he could be so *cosy*! The last man I'd ever thought would tell me where to buy cheap fish. And what a darling little house–*no bother*–he must know Toby jugs are hell and he just doesn't care. I think he's a pet. Toad, do ask him to dinner. You must. Not to giggle at but to *like*.' He wouldn't have asked him, of course, but Ann would be content—she'd found a way to like him. And having done so, forgotten him.

That was what Smiley wanted, really—a way to like Mendel. He was not as quick as Ann at finding one. But Ann was Ann—she practically murdered an Etonian nephew once for drinking claret with fish, but if Mendel had lit a pipe over her *crêpe suzette*, she probably would not have noticed.

Mendel made more tea and they drank it. At about a quarter past five they set off for Battersea in Smiley's car. On the way Mendel bought an evening paper. He read it with difficulty, catching the light from the street lamps. After a few minutes he spoke with sudden venom:

'Krauts. *Bloody* Krauts. God, I hate them!'

'Krauts?'

'Krauts. Huns. Jerries. Bloody Germans. Wouldn't give you sixpence for the lot of them. Carnivorous ruddy sheep. Kicking Jews about again. Us all over. Knock 'em down, set 'em up. Forgive and forget. *Why* bloody well forget, I'd like to know? Why forget theft, ·murder, and rape just because millions committed it? Christ, one poor little sod of a bank clerk pinches ten bob and the whole of the Metropolitan's on to him. But Krupp and all that mob—oh no. Christ, if I was a Jew in Germany I'd . . .'

Smiley was suddenly wide awake: 'What would you do? What would you do, Mendel?'

'Oh, I suppose I'd sit down under it. It's statistics now, politics. It isn't sense to give them H-bombs so its politics. And there's the Yanks—millions of ruddy Jews in America. What do they do? Damn all: give the Krauts more bombs. All chums together—blow each other up.'

Mendel was trembling with rage, and Smiley was silent for a while, thinking of Elsa Fennan.

'What's the answer?' he asked, just for something to say.

'Christ knows,' said Mendel savagely.

They turned into Battersea Bridge Road and drew up beside a constable standing on the pavement. Mendel showed his police card.

'Scarr's garage? Well it isn't hardly a garage, sir, just a yard. Scrap metal he handles mostly, and secondhand cars. If they won't do for one they'll do for the other, that's what Adam says. You want to go down Prince of Wales Drive till you come to the hospital. It's tucked in there between a couple of pre-fabs. Bomb site it is really. Old Adam straightened it out with some cinders and no one's ever moved him.'

'You seem to know a lot about him,' said Mendel.

'I should do, I've run him in a few times. There's not much in the book that Adam hasn't been up to. He's one of our hardy perennials, Scarr is.'

'Well, well. Anything on him at present?'

'Couldn't say, sir. But you can have him any time for illegal betting. And Adam's practically under the Act already.'

They drove towards Battersea Hospital. The park on their right looked black and hostile behind the street lamps.

'What's under the Act?' asked Smiley.

'Oh, he's only joking. It means your record's so long you're eligible for Preventive Detention—years of it. He sounds like my type,' Mendel continued. 'Leave him to me.'

They found the yard as the constable had described, between two dilapidated pre-fabs in an uncertain row of hutments erected on the bomb site. Rubble, clinker, and refuse lay everywhere. Bits of asbestos, timber, and old iron, presumably acquired by Mr Scarr for resale or adaptation, were piled in a corner, dimly lit by the pale glow which came from the farther pre-fab. The two men looked round them in silence for a moment. Then Mendel shrugged, put two fingers in his mouth and whistled shrilly.

'Scarr!' he called. Silence. The outside light on the far pre-fab went on, and three or four pre-war cars in various stages of dilapidation became dimly discernible.

The door opened slowly and a girl of about twelve stood on the threshold.

'Your dad in, dear?' asked Mendel.

'Nope. Gone to the Prod, I 'spect.'

'Righto, dear. Thanks.'

They walked back to the road.

'What on earth's the Prod, or daren't I ask?' said Smiley.

'Prodigal's Calf. Pub round the corner. We can walk it—only a hundred yards. Leave the car here.'

It was only just after opening time. The public bar was empty, and as they waited for the landlord to appear the door swung open and a very fat man in a black suit came in. He walked straight to the bar and hammered on it with a half-crown.

'Wilf,' he shouted. 'Take your finger out, you got customers, you lucky boy.' He turned to Smiley; 'Good evening, friend.'

From the rear of the pub a voice replied: 'Tell 'em to leave their money on the counter and come back later.'

The fat man looked at Mendel and Smiley blankly for a moment, then suddenly let out a peal of laughter: 'Not them, Wilf—they're busies!' The joke appealed to him so much that he was finally compelled to sit on the bench that ran along the side of the room, with his hands on his knees, his huge shoulders heaving with laughter, the tears running down his cheeks. Occasionally he said 'Oh dear, Oh dear,' as he caught his breath before another outburst.

Smiley looked at him with interest. He wore a very dirty stiff white collar with rounded edges, a flowered red tie carefully pinned outside

the black waistcoat, army boots and a shiny black suit, very threadbare and without a vestige of a crease in the trousers. His shirt cuffs
were black with sweat, grime, and motor oil and held in place by
paper-clips twisted into a knot.

The landlord appeared and took their orders. The stranger bought
a large whisky and ginger wine and took it at once to the saloon bar,
where there was a coal fire. The landlord watched with disapproval.

'That's him all over, mean sod. Won't pay saloon prices, but likes
the fire.'

'Who is he?' asked Mendel.

'Him? Scarr his name is. Adam Scarr. Christ knows why Adam.
See him in the Garden of Eden: bloody grotesque, that's what it is.
They say round here that if Eve gave him an apple he'd eat the ruddy
core.' The landlord sucked his teeth and shook his head. Then he
shouted to Scarr: 'Still, you're good for business, aren't you, Adam?
They come bloody miles to see you, don't they? Teenage monster
from outer space, that's what you are. Come and see Adam Scarr:
one look and you'll sign the pledge.'

More hilarious laughter. Mendel leant over to Smiley. 'You go and
wait in the car—you're better out of this. Got a fiver?'

Smiley gave him five pounds from his wallet, nodded his agree-
ment and walked out. He could imagine nothing more frightful than
dealing with Scarr.

'You Scarr?' said Mendel.

'Friend, you are correct.'

'TRX 0891. That your car?'

Mr Scarr frowned at his whisky and ginger. The question seemed
to sadden him.

'Well?' said Mendel.

'She was, squire, she was.'

'What the hell do you mean?'

Scarr raised his right hand a few inches then let it gently fall. 'Dark
waters, squire, murky waters.'

'Listen, I've got bigger fish to fry than ever you dreamed of. I'm
not made of glass, see? I couldn't care bloody less about your racket.
Where's that car?'

Scarr appeared to consider this speech on its merits. 'I see the
light, friend. You wish for information.'

'Of course I bloody well do.'

'These are hard times, squire. The cost of living, dear boy, is a
rising star. Information is an item, a saleable item, is it not?'

'You tell me who hired that car and you won't starve.'

'I don't starve now, friend. I want to eat better.'

'A fiver.'

Scarr finished his drink and replaced his glass noisily on the table.

Mendel got up and bought him another.

'It was pinched,' said Scarr. 'I had it a few years for self-drive, see. For the deepo.'

'The *what?*'

'The deepo–the deposit. Bloke wants a car for a day. You take twenty quid deposit in notes, right? When he comes back he owes you forty bob, see? You give him a cheque for thirty-eight quid, show it on your books as a loss and the job's worth a tenner. Got it?'

Mendel nodded.

'Well, three weeks ago a bloke come in. Tall Scotsman. Well-to-do, he was. Carried a stick. He paid the deepo, took the car, and I never see him nor the car again. Robbery.'

'Why not report it to the police?'

Scarr paused and drank from his glass. He looked at Mendel sadly.

'Many factors would argue against, squire.'

'Meaning you'd pinched it yourself?'

Scarr looked shocked. 'I have since heard distressing rumours about the party from which I obtained the vehicle. I will say no more,' he added piously.

'When you rented him the car he filled in forms, didn't he? Insurance, receipt, and so on? Where are they?'

'False, all false. He gave me an address in Ealing. I went there and it didn't exist. I have no doubt the name was also fictitious.'

Mendel screwed the money into a roll in his pocket, and handed it across the table to Scarr. Scarr unfolded it and, quite unselfconscious, counted it in full view of anyone who cared to look.

'I know where to find you,' said Mendel; 'and I know a few things about you. If that's a load of cock you've sold me I'll break your bloody neck.'

It was raining again and Smiley wished he had brought a hat. He crossed the road, entered the side street which accommodated Mr Scarr's establishment, and walked towards the car. There was no one in the street, and it was oddly quiet. Two hundred yards down the road Battersea General Hospital, small and neat, shed multiple beams of light from its uncurtained windows. The pavement was very wet and the echo of his own footsteps was crisp and startling.

He drew level with the first of the two pre-fabs which bordered Scarr's yard. A car was parked in the yard with its sidelights on. Curious, Smiley turned off the street and walked towards it. It was an old MG saloon, green probably, or that brown they went in for before the war. The number-plate was barely lit, and caked in mud. He stooped to read it, tracing the letters with his forefinger: TRX 0891. Of course–that was one of the numbers he had written down this morning.

He heard a footstep behind him and stood up, half turning. He had begun to raise his arm as the blow fell.

It was a terrible blow—it seemed to split his skull in two. As he fell he could feel the warm blood running freely over his left ear. 'Not again, oh Christ, not again,' thought Smiley. But he hardly felt the rest—just a vision of his own body, far away, being slowly broken like rock; cracked and split into fragments, then nothing. Nothing but the warmth of his own blood as it ran over his face into the cinders, and far away the beating of the stonebreakers. But not here. Far away.

Chapter Seven

Mr Scarr's Story

Mendel looked at him and wondered whether he was dead. He emptied the pockets of his own overcoat and laid it gently over Smiley's shoulders, then he ran, ran like a madman towards the hospital, crashed through the swingdoors of the out-patients' department into the bright, twenty-four-hour interior of the hospital. A young coloured doctor was on duty. Mendel showed him his card, shouted something to him, took him by the arm, tried to lead him down the road. The doctor smiled patiently, shook his head and telephoned for an ambulance.

Mendel ran back down the road and waited. A few minutes later the ambulance arrived and skilful men gathered Smiley up and took him away.

'Bury him,' thought Mendel; 'I'll make the bastard pay.'

He stood there for a moment, staring down at the wet patch of mud and cinders where Smiley had fallen; the red glow of the car's rear lights showed him nothing. The ground had been hopelessly churned by the feet of the ambulance men and a few inhabitants from the pre-fabs who had come and gone like shadowy vultures. Trouble was about. They didn't like trouble.

'Bastard,' Mendel hissed, and walked slowly back towards the pub.

The saloon bar was filling up. Scarr was ordering another drink. Mendel took him by the arm. Scarr turned and said:

'Hello, friend, back again. Have a little of what killed Auntie.'

'Shut up,' said Mendel; 'I want another word with you. Come outside.'

Mr Scarr shook his head and sucked his teeth sympathetically.

'Can't be done, friend, can't be done. Company.' He indicated with his head an eighteen-year-old blonde with off-white lipstick and an improbable bosom, who sat quite motionless at a corner table. Her painted eyes had a permanently startled look.

'Listen,' whispered Mendel; 'in just two seconds I'll tear your bloody ears off, you lying sod.'

Scarr consigned his drinks to the care of the landlord and made a slow, dignified exit. He didn't look at the girl.

Mendel led him across the street towards the pre-fabs. The sidelights of Smiley's car shone towards them eighty yards down the road.

They turned into the yard. The MG was still there. Mendel had Scarr firmly by the arm, ready if necessary to force the forearm back and upwards, breaking or dislocating the shoulder joint.

'Well, well,' cried Scarr with apparent delight: 'She's returned to the bosom of her ancestors.'

'Stolen, was it?' said Mendel. 'Stolen by a tall Scotsman with a walking stick and an address in Ealing. Decent of him to bring it back, wasn't it. Friendly gesture, after all this time. You've mistaken your bloody market, Scarr.' Mendel was shaking with anger. 'And why are the sidelights on? Open the door.'

Scarr turned to Mendel in the dark, his free hand slapping his pockets in search of keys. He extracted a bunch of three or four, felt through them and finally unlocked the car door. Mendel got in, found the passenger light in the roof and switched it on. He began methodically to search the inside of the car. Scarr stood outside and waited.

He searched quickly but thoroughly. Glove tray, seats, floor, rear window-ledge: nothing. He slipped his hand inside the map pocket on the passenger door, and drew out a map and an envelope. The envelope was long and flat, a grey-blue in colour with a linen finish. Continental, thought Mendel. There was no writing on it. He tore it open. There were ten used five-pound notes inside and a piece of plain postcard. Mendel held it to the light and read the message printed on it with a ball-point pen:

FINISHED NOW. SELL IT.

There was no signature.

He got out of the car, and seized Scarr by the elbows. Scarr stepped back quickly. 'What's your problem, friend?' he asked.

Mendel spoke softly. 'It's not my problem, Scarr, it's yours. The biggest bloody problem you ever had. Conspiracy to murder, attempted murder, offences under the Official Secrets Act. And you can add to that contravention of the Road Traffic Act, conspiracy to defraud the Inland Revenue, and about fifteen other charges that will occur to me while you nurse your problem on a cell bed.'

'Just a minute, copper, let's not go over the moon. What's the story? Who the hell's talking about murder?'

'Listen, Scarr, you're a little man, come in on the fringe of the big spenders, aren't you. Well now you're the big spender. I reckon it'll cost you fifteen years.'

'Look, shut up, will you.'

'No, I won't, little man. You're caught between two big ones, see, and you're the mug. And what will I do? I'll bloody well laugh myself sick while you rot in the Scrubs and contemplate your fat belly. See that hospital, do you? There's a bloke dying there, murdered by your tall Scotsman. They found him half an hour ago bleeding like a pig in your yard. There's another one dead in Surrey, and for all I know there's one in every bloody home county. So it's your problem, you poor sod, not mine. Another thing–you're the only one who knows who he is, aren't you? He might want to tidy that up a bit, mightn't he?'

Scarr walked slowly round to the other side of the car.

Mendel sat in the driving seat and unlocked the passenger door from the inside. Scarr sat himself beside him. They didn't put the light on.

'I'm in a nice way of business round here,' said Scarr quietly, 'and the pickings is small but regular. Or was till this bloke come along.'

'What bloke?'

'Bit by bit, copper, don't rush me. That was four years ago. I didn't believe in Father Christmas till I met him. Dutch, he said he was, in the diamond business. I'm not pretending I thought he was straight, see, because you're not barmy and nor am I. I never asked what he done and he never told me, but I guessed it was smuggling. Money to burn he had, came off him like leaves in autumn. "Scarr," he said; "you're a man of business. I don't like publicity, never did, and I hears we're birds of a feather. I want a car. Not to keep, but to borrow." He didn't put it quite like that because of the lingo, but that's the sense of it. "What's your proposition?" I says. "Let's have a proposition."

'"Well," he says; "I'm shy. I want a car that no one can ever get on to, supposing I had an accident. Buy a car for me, Scarr, a nice old car with something under the bonnet. Buy it in your own name," he says, "and keep it wrapped up for me. There's five hundred quid for a start, and twenty quid a month for garaging. And there's a bonus, Scarr, for every day I take it out. But I'm shy, see, and you don't know me. That's what the money's for," he says. "It's for not knowing me."

'I'll never forget that day. Raining cats and dogs it was, and me bent over an old taxi I'd got off a bloke in Wandsworth. I owed a bookie forty quid, and the coppers were sensitive about a car I'd bought on the never never and flogged in Clapham.'

Mr Scarr drew breath, and let it out again with an air of comic resignation.

'And there he was, standing over me like my own conscience, showering old singles on me like used tote tickets.'

'What did he look like?' asked Mendel.

'Quite young he was. Tall, fair chap. But cool–cool as charity. I never saw him after that day. He sent me letters posted in London and typed on plain paper. Just "Be ready Monday night", "Be ready Thursday night", and so on. We had it all arranged. I left the car out in the yard, full of petrol and teed up. He never said when he'd be back. Just ran it in about closing time or later, leaving the lights on and the doors locked. He'd put a couple of quid in the map pocket for each day he's been away.'

'What happened if anything went wrong, if you got pinched for something else?'

'We had a telephone number. He told me to ring and ask for a name.'

'What name?'

'He told me to choose one. I chose Blondie. He didn't think that was very funny but we stuck to it. Primrose 0098.'

'Did you ever use it?'

'Yes, a couple of years ago I took a bint to Margate for ten days. I thought I'd better let him know. A girl answered the phone–Dutch too, by the sound of her. She said Blondie was in Holland, and she'd take a message. But after that I didn't bother.'

'Why not?'

'I began to notice, see. He came regular once a fortnight, the first and third Tuesdays except January and February. This was the first January he come. He brought the car back Thursday usually. Odd him coming back tonight. But this is the end of him, isn't it?' Scarr held in his enormous hand the piece of postcard he had taken from Mendel.

'Did he miss at all? Away long periods?'

'Winters he kept away more. January he never come, nor February. Like I said.'

Mendel still had the £50 in his hand. He tossed them into Scarr's lap.

'Don't think you're lucky. I wouldn't be in your shoes for ten times that lot. I'll be back.'

Mr Scarr seemed worried.

'I wouldn't have peached,' he said; 'but I don't want to be mixed up in nothing, see. Not if the old country's going to suffer, eh, squire?'

'Oh, shut up,' said Mendel. He was tired. He took the postcard back, got out of the car and walked away towards the hospital.

There was no news at the hospital. Smiley was still unconscious. The CID had been informed. Mendel would do better to leave his name and address and go home. The hospital would telephone as soon as they had any news. After a good deal of argument Mendel obtained from the sister the key to Smiley's car.

Mitcham, he decided, was a lousy place to live.

Chapter Eight

Reflections in a Hospital Ward

He hated the bed as a drowning man hates the sea. He hated the sheets that imprisoned him so that he could move neither hand nor foot.

And he hated the room because it frightened him. There was a trolley by the door with instruments on it, scissors, bandages, and bottles, strange objects that carried the terror of the unknown, swathed in white linen for the last Communion. There were jugs, tall ones half covered with napkins, standing like white eagles waiting to tear at his entrails, little glass ones with rubber tubing coiled inside them like snakes. He hated everything, and he was afraid. He was hot and the sweat ran off him, he was cold and the sweat held him, trickling over his ribs like cold blood. Night and day alternated without recognition from Smiley. He fought a relentless battle against sleep, for when he closed his eyes they seemed to turn inwards on the chaos of his brain; and when sometimes by sheer weight his eyelids drew themselves together he would summon all his strength to tear them apart and stare again at the pale light wavering somewhere above him.

Then came a blessed day when someone must have drawn the blinds and let in the grey winter light. He heard the sound of traffic outside and knew at last that he would live.

So the problem of dying once more became an academic one–a debt he would postpone until he was rich and could pay in his own way. It was a luxurious feeling, almost of purity. His mind was wonderfully lucid, ranging like Prometheus over his whole world; where had he heard that: 'the mind becomes separated from the body, rules a paper kingdom . . . ?' He was bored by the light above him, and wished there was more to look at. He was bored by the grapes, the smell of honeycomb and flowers, the chocolates. He wanted books, and literary journals; how could he keep up with his reading if they gave him no books? There was so little research done on his period as it was, so little creative criticism on the seventeenth century.

It was three weeks before Mendel was allowed to see him. He walked in holding a new hat and carrying a book about bees. He put his hat on the end of the bed and the book on the bedside table. He was grinning.

'I bought you a book,' he said; 'about bees. They're clever little beggars. Might interest you.'

He sat on the edge of the bed. 'I got a new hat. Daft really. Celebrate my retirement.'

'Oh yes, I forgot. You're on the shelf too.' They both laughed, and were silent again.

Smiley blinked. 'I'm afraid you're not very distinct at the moment. I'm not allowed to wear my old glasses. They're getting me some new ones.' He paused. 'You don't know who did this to me, do you?'

'May do. Depends. Got a lead, I think. I don't know enough, that's the trouble. About your job, I mean. Does the East German Steel Mission mean anything to you?'

'Yes, I think so. It came here four years ago to try and get a foot in the Board of Trade.'

Mendel gave an account of his transactions with Mr Scarr. '. . . Said he was Dutch. The only way Scarr had of getting in touch with him was by ringing a Primrose telephone number. I checked the subscriber. Listed as the East German Steel Mission, in Belsize Park. I sent a bloke to sniff round. They've cleared out. Nothing there at all, no furniture, nothing. Just the telephone, and that's been ripped out of its socket.'

'When did they go?'

'The third of January. Same day as Fennan was murdered.' He looked at Smiley quizzically. Smiley thought for a minute and said:

'Get hold of Peter Guillam at the Ministry of Defence and bring him here tomorrow. By the scruff of the neck.'

Mendel picked up his hat and walked to the door.

'Good-bye,' said Smiley; 'thank you for the book.'

'See you tomorrow,' said Mendel, and left.

Smiley lay back in bed. His head was aching. Damn, he thought, I never thanked him for the honey. It had come from Fortnum's, too.

Why the early morning call? That was what puzzled him more than anything. It was silly, really, Smiley supposed, but of all the unaccountables in the case, that worried him most.

Elsa Fennan's explanation had been so stupid, so noticeably unlikely. Ann, yes; she would make the exchange stand on its head if she'd felt like it, but not Elsa Fennan. There was nothing in that alert, intelligent little face, nothing in her total independence to support the ludicrous claim to absent-mindedness. She could have said the exchange had made a mistake, had called the wrong day, anything. Fennan, yes; he had been absent-minded. It was one of the odd inconsistencies about Fennan's character which had emerged in the inquiries before the interview. A voracious reader of Westerns and a passionate chess player, a musician and a spare-time philosopher, a deep thinking man–but absent-minded. There had been a frightful row once about him taking some secret papers out of the Foreign Office, and it turned out that he had put them in his despatch case with his *Times* and the evening paper before going home to Walliston.

Had Elsa Fennan, in her panic, taken upon herself the mantle of her husband? Or the *motive* of her husband? Had Fennan asked for the call to remind *him* of something, and had Elsa borrowed the motive? Then what did Fennan need to be reminded of–and what did his wife so strenuously wish to conceal?

Samuel Fennan. The new world and the old met in him. The eternal Jew, cultured, cosmopolitan, self-determinate, industrious and perceptive: to Smiley, immensely attractive. The child of his century; persecuted, like Elsa, and driven from his adopted Germany to University in England. By the sheer weight of his ability he had pushed aside disadvantage and prejudice, finally to enter the Foreign Office. It had been a remarkable achievement, owed to nothing but his own brilliance. And if he was a little conceited, a little disinclined to bide the decision of minds more pedestrian than his own, who could blame him? There had been some embarrassment when Fennan pronounced himself in favour of a divided Germany, but it had all blown over, he had been transferred to an Asian desk, and the affair was forgotten. For the rest, he had been generous to a fault, and popular both in Whitehall and in Surrey, where he devoted several hours each week-end to charity work. His great love was skiing. Every year he took all his leave at once and spent six weeks in Switzerland or Austria. He had visited Germany only once, Smiley remembered–with his wife about four years ago.

It had been natural enough that Fennan should join the Left at Oxford. It was the great honeymoon period of University Communism, and its causes, heaven knows, lay close enough to his heart. The rise of Fascism in Germany and Italy, the Japanese invasion of Manchuria, the Franco rebellion in Spain, the slump in America, and above all the wave of anti-Semitism that was sweeping across Europe: it was inevitable that Fennan should seek an outlet for his anger and revulsion. Besides, the Party was respectable then; the failure of the Labour Party and the Coalition Government had convinced many intellectuals that the Communists alone could provide an effective alternative to Capitalism and Fascism. There was the excitement, an air of conspiracy and comradeship which must have appealed to the flamboyance in Fennan's character and given him comfort in his loneliness. There was talk of going to Spain; some *had* gone, like Cornford from Cambridge, never to return.

Smiley could imagine Fennan in those days—volatile and earnest, no doubt bringing to his companions the experience of real suffering, a veteran among cadets. His parents had died—his father had been a banker with the foresight to keep a small account in Switzerland. There had not been much, but enough to see him through Oxford, and protect him from the cold wind of poverty.

Smiley remembered so well that interview with Fennan; one among many, yet different. Different because of the language. Fennan was so articulate, so quick, so sure. 'Their greatest day,' he had said, 'was when the miners came. They came from the Rhondda, you know, and to the comrades it seemed the spirit of Freedom had come down with them from the hills. It was a hunger march. It never seemed to occur to the Group that the marchers might actually *be* hungry, but it occurred to me. We hired a truck and the girls made stew—tons of it. We got the meat cheap from a sympathetic butcher in the market. We drove the truck out to meet them. They ate the stew and marched on. They didn't like us really you know, didn't trust us.' He laughed. 'They were so small—that's what I remember best—small and dark like elves. We hoped they'd sing and they did. But not for us—for themselves. That was the first time I had met Welshmen.

'It made me understand my own race better, I think—I'm a Jew, you know.'

Smiley had nodded.

'They didn't know what to do when the Welshmen had gone. What do you do when a dream has come true? They realized then why the Party didn't much care about intellectuals. I think they felt cheap, mostly, and ashamed. Ashamed of their beds and their rooms, their full bellies and their clever essays. Ashamed of their talents and their humour. They were always saying how Keir Hardie taught himself shorthand with a piece of chalk on the coal face, you know. They were ashamed of having pencils and paper. But it's no good just throwing them away, is it? That's what I learnt in the end. That's why I left the Party, I suppose.'

Smiley wanted to ask him how Fennan himself had felt, but Fennan was talking again. He had shared nothing with them, he had come to realize that. They were not men, but children, who dreamed of freedom-fires, gipsy music, and one world tomorrow, who rode on white horses across the Bay of Biscay or with a child's pleasure bought beer for starving elves from Wales; children who had no power to resist the Eastern sun, and obediently turned their tousled heads towards it. They loved each other and believed they loved mankind, they fought each other and believed they fought the world.

Soon he found them comic and touching. To him, they might as well have knitted socks for soldiers. The disproportion between the dream and reality drove him to a close examination of both; he put all his energy into philosophical and historical reading, and found, to his surprise, comfort and peace in the intellectual purity of Marxism. He feasted on its intellectual ruthlessness, was thrilled by its fearlessness, its academic reversal of traditional values. In the end it was this and not the Party that gave him strength in his solitude, a philosophy which exacted total sacrifice to an unassailable formula, which humiliated and inspired him; and when he finally found success, prosperity, and integration, he turned his back sadly upon it as a treasure he had outgrown and must leave at Oxford with the days of his youth.

This was how Fennan had described it and Smiley had understood. It was scarcely the story of anger and resentment that Smiley had come to expect in such interviews, but (perhaps because of that) it seemed more real. There was another thing about that interview: Smiley's conviction that Fennan had left something important unsaid.

Was there any *factual* connection between the incident in Bywater Street and Fennan's death? Smiley reproached himself for being carried away. Seen in perspective, there was nothing but the sequence of events to suggest that Fennan and Smiley were part of a single problem.

The sequence of events, that is, and the weight of Smiley's intuition, experience or what you will—the extra sense that had told him to ring the bell and not use his key, the sense that did not, however, warn him that a murderer stood in the night with a piece of lead piping.

The interview had been informal, that was true. The walk in the park reminded him more of Oxford than of Whitehall. The walk in the park, the café in Millbank—yes, there had been a procedural difference too, but what did it amount to? An official of the Foreign Office walking in the park, talking earnestly with an anonymous little man . . . Unless the little man was *not* anonymous!

Smiley took a paper-back book and began to write in pencil on the fly-leaf:

'Let us assume what is by no means proven: that the murder of Fennan and the attempted murder of Smiley *are* related. What circumstances connected Smiley with Fennan *before* Fennan's death?

1. Before the interview on Monday, 2 January, I had never met Fennan. I read his file at the Department and I had certain preliminary inquiries made.

2. On 2 January I went alone to the Foreign Office by taxi. The FO arranged the interview, but did not, repeat not, know in advance who would conduct it. Fennan therefore had no prior knowledge of my identity, nor had anyone else outside the Department.

3. The interview fell into two parts; the first at the FO, when people wandered through the room and took no notice of us at all, the second outside when anyone could have seen us.'

What followed? Nothing, unless . . .

Yes, that was the only possible conclusion: unless whoever saw them together recognized not only Fennan but Smiley as well, and was violently opposed to their association.

Why? In what way was Smiley dangerous? His eyes suddenly opened very wide. Of course–in one way, in one way only–*as a security officer.*

He put down his pencil.

And so whoever killed Sam Fennan was anxious that he should not talk to a security officer. Someone in the Foreign Office, perhaps. But essentially someone who knew Smiley too. Someone Fennan had known at Oxford, known as a communist, someone who feared exposure, who thought that Fennan would talk, had talked already, perhaps? And if he had talked already then of course Smiley would have to be killed–killed quickly before he could put in his report.

That would explain the murder of Fennan and the assault on Smiley. It made some sense, but not much. He had built a card-house as high as it would go, and he still had cards in his hand. What about Elsa, her lies, her complicity, her fear? What about the car and the 8.30 call? What about the anonymous letter? If the murderer was frightened of contact between Smiley and Fennan, he would scarcely call attention to Fennan by denouncing him. Who then? Who?

He lay back and closed his eyes. His head was throbbing again. Perhaps Peter Guillam could help. He was the only hope. His head was going round. It hurt terribly.

Chapter Nine

Tidying Up

Mendel showed Peter Guillam into the ward, grinning hugely.

'Got him,' he said.

The conversation was awkward; strained for Guillam at least, by the recollection of Smiley's abrupt resignation and the incongruity of meeting in a hospital ward. Smiley was wearing a blue bedjacket, his hair was spiky and untidy above the bandages and he still had the trace of a heavy bruise on his left temple.

After a particularly awkward pause, Smiley said: 'Look, Peter,

Mendel's told you what happened to me. You're the expert—what do we know about the East German Steel Mission?'

'Pure as the driven snow, dear boy, except for their sudden departure. Only about three men and a dog in the thing. They hung out in Hampstead somewhere. No one quite knew why they were here when they first came but they've done quite a decent job in the last four years.'

'What are their terms of reference?'

'God knows. I think they thought when they arrived that they were going to persuade the Board of Trade to break the European steel rings, but they got the cold shoulder. Then they went in for consular stuff with the accent on machine tools and finished products, exchange of industrial and technical information and so on. Nothing to do with what they came for but rather more acceptable, I gather.'

'Who were they?'

'Oh—couple of technicians—Professor Doktor someone and Doktor someone else—couple of girls and a general dogsbody.'

'Who was the dogsbody?'

'Don't know. Some young diplomat to iron out the wrinkles. We have them recorded at the Department. I can send you details, I suppose.'

'If you don't mind.'

'No, of course not.'

There was another awkward pause. Smiley said: 'Photographs would be a help, Peter. Could you manage that?'

'Yes, yes, of course.' Guillam looked away from Smiley in some embarrassment. 'We don't know much about the East Germans really, you know. We get odd bits here and there, but on the whole they're something of a mystery. If they operate at all they don't do it under Trade or Diplomatic cover—that's why, if you're right about this chap, it's so odd him coming from the Steel Mission.'

'Oh,' said Smiley flatly.

'How do they operate?' asked Mendel.

'It's hard to generalize from the very isolated cases we do know of. My impression is that they run their agents direct from Germany with no contact between controller and agent in the operational zone.'

'But that must limit them terribly,' cried Smiley. 'You may have to wait months before your agent can travel to a meeting place outside his own country. He may not have the necessary cover to make the journey at all.'

'Well, obviously it does limit him, but their targets seem to be so insignificant. They prefer to run foreign nationals—Swedes, expatriate Poles and what not, on short-term missions, where the limitations of their technique don't matter. In exceptional cases where they have an agent resident in the target country, they work on a courier system, which corresponds to the Soviet pattern.'

Smiley was listening now.

'As a matter of fact,' Guillam went on, 'the Americans intercepted a courier quite recently, which is where we learnt the little we do know about GDR technique.'

'Such as what?'

'Oh well, never waiting at a rendezvous, never meeting at the stated time but twenty minutes before; recognition signals—all the usual conjuring tricks that give a gloss to low-grade information. They muck about with names, too. A courier may have to contact three or four agents—a controller may run as many as fifteen. They never invent cover names for themselves.'

'What do you mean? Surely they must.'

'They get the agent to do it for them. The agent chooses a name, any name he likes, and the controller adopts it. A gimmick really—' he stopped, looking at Mendel in surprise.

Mendel had leapt to his feet.

Guillam sat back in his chair and wondered if he were allowed to smoke. He decided reluctantly that he wasn't. He could have done with a cigarette.

'Well?' said Smiley. Mendel had described to Guillam his interview with Mr Scarr.

'It fits,' said Guillam. 'Obviously it fits with what we know. But then we don't know all that much. If Blondie was a courier, it is exceptional—in my experience at least—that he should use a trade delegation as a staging post.'

'You said the Mission had been here four years,' said Mendel. 'Blondie first came to Scarr four years ago.'

No one spoke for a moment. Then Smiley said earnestly: 'Peter, it is possible, isn't it? I mean they might under certain operational conditions need to have a station over here as well as couriers.'

'Well, of course, if they were on to something really big they might.'

'Meaning if they had a highly placed resident agent in play?'

'Yes, roughly.'

'And assuming they had such an agent, a Maclean or Fuchs, it is conceivable that they would establish a station here under trade cover with no operational function except to hold the agent's hand?'

'Yes, it's conceivable. But it's a tall order, George. What you're suggesting is that the agent is run from abroad, serviced by courier and the courier is serviced by the Mission, which is also the agent's personal guardian angel. He'd have to be some agent.'

'I'm not suggesting quite that—but near enough. And I accept that the system demands a high-grade agent. Don't forget we only have

Blondie's word for it that he came from abroad.'

Mendel chipped in: 'This agent—would he be in touch with the Mission direct?'

'Good lord, no,' said Guillam. 'He'd probably have an emergency procedure for getting in touch with them—a telephone code or something of the sort.'

'How does that work?' asked Mendel.

'Varies. Might be on the wrong number system. You dial the number from a call box and ask to speak to George Brown. You're told George Brown doesn't live there so you apologize and ring off. The time and the rendezvous are prearranged—the emergency signal is contained in the name you ask for. Someone will be there.'

'What else would the Mission do?' asked Smiley.

'Hard to say. Pay him probably. Arrange a collecting place for reports. The controller would make all those arrangements for the agent, of course, and tell him his part of it by courier. They work on the Soviet principle a good deal, as I told you—even the smallest details are arranged by control. The people in the field are allowed very little independence.'

There was another silence. Smiley looked at Guillam and then at Mendel, then blinked and said:

'Blondie didn't come to Scarr in January and February, did he?'

'No,' said Mendel; 'this was the first year.'

'Fennan always went skiing in January and February. This was the first time in four years he'd missed.'

'I wonder,' said Smiley, 'whether I ought to go and see Maston again.'

Guillam stretched luxuriously and smiled: 'You can always try. He'll be thrilled to hear you've been brained. I've a sneaking feeling he'll think Battersea's on the coast, but not to worry. Tell him you were attacked while wandering about in someone's private yard—he'll understand. Tell him about your assailant, too, George. You've never seen him, mind, and you don't know his name, but he's a courier of the East German Intelligence Service. Maston will back you up; he always does. Specially when he's got to report to the Minister.'

Smiley looked at Guillam and said nothing.

'After your bang on the head, too,' Guillam added; 'he'll understand.'

'But, Peter—'

'I know, George, I know.'

'Well, let me tell you another thing. Blondie collected his car on the first Tuesday of each month.'

'So?'

'Those were the nights Elsa Fennan went to the Weybridge Rep.

Fennan worked late on Tuesday, she said.'

Guillam got up. 'Let me dig about, George. Cheerio Mendel, I'll probably give you a ring tonight. I don't see what we can do now, anyway, but it would be nice to know, wouldn't it?' He reached the door. 'Incidentally, where are Fennan's possessions—wallet, diary, and so forth? Stuff they found on the body?'

'Probably still at the Station,' said Mendel; 'until after the inquest.'

Guillam stood looking at Smiley for a moment, wondering what to say.

'Anything you want, George?'

'No thanks—oh, there is one thing.'

'Yes?'

'Could you get the CID off my back? They've visited me three times now and of course they've got nowhere locally. Could you make this an Intelligence matter for the time being? Be mysterious and soothing?'

'Yes, I should think so.'

'I know it's difficult, Peter, because I'm not—'

'Oh, another thing just to cheer you up. I had that comparison made between Fennan's suicide note and the anonymous letter. They were done by different people on the same machine. Different pressures and spacing but identical typeface. So long, old dear. Tuck into the grapes.'

Guillam closed the door behind him. They heard his footsteps echoing crisply down the bare corridor.

Mendel rolled himself a cigarette.

'Lord,' said Smiley; 'does nothing frighten you? Haven't you seen the Sister here?'

Mendel grinned and shook his head.

'You can only die once,' he said, putting the cigarette between his thin lips. Smiley watched him light it. He produced his lighter, took the hood off it and rotated the wheel with his stained thumb, swiftly cupping both hands around it and nursing the flame towards the cigarette. There might have been a hurricane blowing.

'Well, you're the crime expert,' said Smiley. 'How are we doing?'

'Messy,' said Mendel. 'Untidy.'

'Why?'

'Loose ends everywhere. No police work. Nothing checked. Like algebra.'

'What's algebra got to do with it?'

'You've got to prove what *can* be proved, first. Find the constants. Did she really go to the theatre? Was she alone? Did the neighbours hear her come back? If so, what time? Was Fennan really late Tuesdays? Did his Missus go to the theatre regularly *every* fortnight like she said?'

'And the 8.30 call. Can you tidy that for me?'

'You've got that call on the brain, haven't you?'

'Yes. Of all the loose ends, that's the loosest. I brood over it, you know, and there just isn't any sense in it. I've been through his train timetable. He was a punctual man—often got to the FO before anyone else, unlocked his own cupboard. He would have caught the 8.54, the 9.8, or at worst the 9.14. The 8.54 got him in at 9.38—he liked to be at his office by a quarter to ten. He couldn't possibly want to be woken at 8.30.'

'Perhaps he just liked bells,' said Mendel, getting up.

'And the letters,' Smiley continued. 'Different typists but the same machine. Discounting the murderer two people had access to that machine: Fennan and his wife. If we accept that Fennan typed the suicide note—and he certainly signed it—we must accept that it was Elsa who typed the denunciation. Why did she do that?'

Smiley was tired out, relieved that Mendel was going.

'Off to tidy up. Find the constants.'

'You'll need money,' said Smiley, and offered him some from the wallet beside his bed. Mendel took it without ceremony, and left.

Smiley lay back. His head was throbbing madly, burning hot. He thought of calling the nurse and cowardice prevented him. Gradually the throbbing eased. He heard from outside the ringing of an ambulance bell as it turned off Prince of Wales Drive into the hospital yard. 'Perhaps he just liked bells,' he muttered, and fell asleep.

He was woken by the sound of argument in the corridor—he heard the Sister's voice raised in protest; he heard footsteps and Mendel's voice, urgent in contradiction. The door opened suddenly and someone put the light on. He blinked and sat up, glancing at his watch. It was a quarter to six. Mendel was talking to him, almost shouting. What was he trying to say? Something about Battersea Bridge . . . the river police . . . missing since yesterday . . . He was wide awake. Adam Scarr was dead.

Chapter Ten

The Virgin's Story

Mendel drove very well, with a kind of schoolma'amish pedantry that Smiley would have found comic. The Weybridge road was packed with traffic as usual. Mendel hated motorists. Give a man a car of his own and he leaves humility and common sense behind him in the garage. He didn't care who it was–he'd seen bishops in purple doing seventy in a built-up area, frightening pedestrians out of their wits. He liked Smiley's car. He liked the fussy way it had been maintained, the sensible extras, wing mirrors and reversing light. It was a decent little car.

He liked people who looked after things, who finished what they began. He liked thoroughness and precision. No skimping. Like this murderer. What had Scarr said? 'Young, mind, but cool. Cool as charity.' He knew that look, and Scarr had known it too . . . the look of complete negation that reposes in the eyes of a young killer. Not the look of a wild beast, not the grinning savagery of a maniac, but the look born of supreme efficiency, tried and proven. It was a stage beyond the experience of war. The witnessing of death in war brings a sophistication of its own; but beyond that, far beyond, is the conviction of supremacy in the heart of the professional killer. Yes, Mendel had seen it before: the one that stood apart from the gang, pale eyed, expressionless, the one the girls went after, spoke of without smiling. Yes, he was a cool one all right.

Scarr's death had frightened Mendel. He made Smiley promise not to go back to Bywater Street when he was released from hospital. With any luck they'd think he was dead, anyway. Scarr's death proved one thing, of course: the murderer was still in England, still anxious to tidy up. 'When I get up,' Smiley had said last night, 'we must get him out of his hole again. Put out bits of cheese.' Mendel knew who the cheese would be: Smiley. Of course if they were right about the motive there would be other cheese too: Fennan's wife. In fact, Mendel thought grimly, it doesn't say much for her that she hasn't been murdered. He felt ashamed of himself and turned his mind to other things. Such as Smiley again.

Odd little beggar, Smiley was. Reminded Mendel of a fat boy he'd played football with at school. Couldn't run, couldn't kick, blind as a bat but played like hell, never satisfied till he'd got himself torn to bits. Used to box, too. Came in wide open swinging his arms about: got himself half killed before the referee stopped it. Clever bloke, too.

Mendel stopped at a roadside café for a cup of tea and a bun, then drove into Weybridge. The Repertory Theatre was in a one-way street leading off the High Street where parking was impossible. Finally he left the car at the railway station and walked back into the town.

The front doors of the theatre were locked. Mendel walked round to the side of the building under a brick archway. A green door was propped open. It had push bars on the inside and the words 'stage door' scribbled in chalk. There was no bell; a faint smell of coffee issued from the dark green corridor within. Mendel stepped through the doorway and walked down the corridor, at the end of which he found a stone staircase with a metal handrail leading upwards to another green door. The smell of coffee was stronger, and he heard the sound of voices.

'Oh rot, darling, frankly. If the culture vultures of blissful Surrey want Barrie three months running let them have it, say I. It's either Barrie or *A Cuckoo in the Nest* for the third year running and for me Barrie gets it by a short head'–this from a middle-aged female voice.

A querulous male replied: 'Well, Ludo can always do Peter Pan, can't you, Ludo?'

'Bitchie, bitchie,' said a third voice, also male, and Mendel opened the door.

He was standing in the wings of the stage. On his left was a piece of thick hardboard with about a dozen switches mounted on a wooden panel. An absurd rococo chair in gilt and embroidery stood beneath it for the prompter and factotum.

In the middle of the stage two men and a woman sat on barrels smoking and drinking coffee. The décor represented the deck of a ship. A mast with rigging and rope ladders occupied the centre of the stage, and a large cardboard cannon pointed disconsolately towards a backcloth of sea and sky.

The conversation stopped abruptly as Mendel appeared on the stage. Someone murmured: 'My dear, the ghost at the feast,' and they all looked at him and giggled.

The woman spoke first: 'Are you looking for someone, dear?'

'Sorry to butt in. Wanted to talk about becoming a subscriber to the theatre. Join the club.'

'Why yes, of course. How nice,' she said, getting up and walking over to him. 'How *very* nice.' She took his left hand in both of her own and squeezed it, stepping back at the same time and extending her arms to their full length. It was her chatelaine gesture–Lady Macbeth receives Duncan. She put her head on one side and smiled girlishly, retained his hand and led him across the stage to the opposite wing. A door led into a tiny office littered with old programmes and posters, greasepaint, false hair and tawdry pieces of nautical costume.

'Have you seen our panto this year? *Treasure Island*. Such a *gratifying* success. And so much more *social content*, don't you think, than those vulgar nursery tales?'

Mendel said: 'Yes, wasn't it,' without the least idea of what she was talking about, when his eye caught a pile of bills rather neatly assembled and held together by a bull-dog clip. The top one was made out to Mrs Ludo Oriel and was four months overdue.

She was looking at him shrewdly through her glasses. She was small and dark, with lines on her neck and a great deal of make-up.

The lines under her eyes had been levelled off with greasepaint but the effect had not lasted. She was wearing slacks and a chunky pullover liberally splashed with distemper. She smoked incessantly. Her mouth was very long, and she held her cigarette in the middle of it in a direct line beneath her nose, her lips formed an exaggerated convex curve, distorting the lower half of her face and giving her an ill-tempered and impatient look. Mendel thought she would probably be difficult and clever. It was a relief to think she couldn't pay her bills.

'You *do* want to join the club, don't you?'

'No.'

She suddenly flew into a rage: 'If you're another bloody tradesman you can get out. I've said I'll pay and I will, just don't pester me. If you let people think I'm finished I *will* be and you'll be the losers, not me.'

'I'm not a creditor, Mrs Oriel. I've come to offer you money.'

She was waiting.

'I'm a divorce agent. Rich client. Like to ask you a few questions. We're prepared to pay for your time.'

'Christ,' she said with relief. 'Why didn't you say so in the first place?' They both laughed. Mendel put five pounds on top of the bills, counting them down.

'Now,' said Mendel; 'how do you keep your club subscription list? What are the benefits of joining?'

'Well, we have watery coffee on stage every morning at eleven sharp. Members of the club can mix with the cast during the break between rehearsals from 11.0 to 11.45. They pay for whatever they have, of course, but entry is strictly limited to club members.'

'Quite.'

'That's probably the part that interests you. We seem to get nothing but pansies and nymphos in the morning.'

'It may be. What else goes on?'

'We put on a different show each fortnight. Members can reserve seats for a particular day of each run–the second Wednesday of each run, and so on. We always begin a run on the first and third Mondays of the month. The show begins at 7.30 and we hold the club reservations until 7.20. The girl at the box office has the seating plan and strikes off each seat as it's sold. Club reservations are marked in red and aren't sold off till last.'

'I see. So if one of your members doesn't take his usual seat, it will be marked off on the seating plan.'

'Only if it's sold.'

'Of course.'

'We're not often full after the first week. We're trying to do a show a week, you see, but it's not easy to get the–er–facilities. There isn't the support for two-week runs really.'

'No, no, quite. Do you keep old seating plans?'

'Sometimes, for the accounts.'

'How about Tuesday the third of January?'

She opened a cupboard and took out a sheaf of printed seating plans. 'This is the second fortnight of our pantomime, of course. Tradition.'

'Quite,' said Mendel.

'Now who is it you're so interested in?' asked Mrs Oriel, picking up a ledger from the desk.

'Small blonde party, aged about forty-two or three. Name of Fennan, Elsa Fennan.'

Mrs Oriel opened her ledger. Mendel quite shamelessly looked over her shoulder. The names of club members were entered neatly in the left-hand column. A red tick on the extreme left of the page indicated that the member had paid his subscription. On the right-hand side of the page were notes of standing reservations made for the year. There were about eighty members.

'Name doesn't ring a bell. Where does she sit?'

'No idea.'

'Oh, yes, here we are. Merridale Lane, Walliston. Merridale!—I *ask* you. Let's look. A rear stall at the end of a row. Very odd choice, don't you think? Seat number R2. But God knows whether she took it on the third of January. I shouldn't think we've got the plan any more, though I've never thrown anything away in my life. Things just evaporate, don't they?' She looked at him out of the corner of her eye, wondering whether she'd earned her five pounds. 'Tell you what, we'll ask the Virgin.' She got up and walked to the door; 'Fennan . . . Fennan . . .' she said. 'Half a sec, that does ring a bell. I wonder why. Well I'm damned—of course—the music case.' She opened the door. 'Where's the Virgin?' she said, talking to someone on the stage.

'God knows.'

'Helpful pig,' said Mrs Oriel, and closed the door again. She turned to Mendel: 'The Virgin's our white hope. English rose, local solicitor's stage-struck daughter, all lisle stockings and get-me-if-you-can. We loathe her. She gets a part occasionally because her father pays tuition fees. She does seating in the evenings sometimes when there's a rush—she and Mrs Torr, the cleaner, who does cloaks. When things are quiet, Mrs Torr does the whole thing and the Virgin mopes about in the wings hoping the female lead will drop dead.' She paused. 'I'm damned sure I remember "Fennan". Damn sure I do. I wonder where that cow *is*.' She disappeared for a couple of minutes and returned with a tall and rather pretty girl with fuzzy blonde hair and pink cheeks—good at tennis and swimming.

'This is Elizabeth Pidgeon. She may be able to help. Darling, we want to find out a Mrs Fennan, a club member. Didn't you tell me something about her?'

'Oh, *yes*, Ludo.' She must have thought she sounded sweet. She smiled vapidly at Mendel, put her head on one side and twined her fingers together. Mendel jerked his head towards her.

'Do you know her?' asked Mrs Oriel.

'Oh *yes*, Ludo. She's madly musical; at least I think she must be because she always brings her music. She's madly thin and odd. She's foreign, isn't she, Ludo?'

'Why odd?' asked Mendel.

'Oh, well, last time she came she got in a frightful pet about the seat next to her. It was a club reservation you see and simply hours after twenty past. We'd just started the panto season and there were millions of people wanting seats so I let it go. She kept on saying she was sure the person would come because he always did.'

'Did he?' asked Mendel.

'No. I let the seat go. She must have been in an awful pet because she left after the second act, and forgot to collect her music case.'

'This person she was sure would turn up,' said Mendel, 'is he friendly with Mrs Fennan?'

Ludo Oriel gave Mendel a suggestive wink.

'Well, gosh, I should think *so*, he's her husband, isn't he?'

Mendel looked at her for a minute and then smiled: 'Couldn't we find a chair for Elizabeth?' he said.

'Gosh, thanks,' said the Virgin, and sat on the edge of an old gilt chair like the prompter's chair in the wings. She put her red, fat hands on her knees and leaned forward, smiling all the time, thrilled to be the centre of so much interest. Mrs Oriel looked at her venomously.

'What makes you think he was her husband, Elizabeth?' There was an edge to his voice which had not been there before.

'Well, I know they arrive separately, but I thought that as they had seats apart from the rest of the club reservations, they must be husband and wife. And of course he always brings a music case too.'

'I see. What else can you remember about that evening, Elizabeth?'

'Oh, well, lots really because you see I felt awful about her leaving in such a pet and then later that night she rang up. Mrs Fennan did, I mean. She said her name and said she'd left early and forgotten her music case. She'd lost the ticket for it, too, and was in a frightful state. It sounded as if she was crying. I heard someone's voice in the background, and then she said someone would drop in and get it if that would be all right without the ticket. I said of course, and half an hour later the man came. He's rather super. Tall and fair.'

'I see,' said Mendel; 'thank you very much, Elizabeth, you've been very helpful.'

'Gosh, that's O.K.' She got up.

'Incidentally,' said Mendel. 'This man who collected her music case—he wasn't by any chance the same man who sits beside her in the theatre, was he?'

'Rather. Gosh, sorry. I should have said that.'

'Did you talk to him?'

'Well, just to say here you are, sort of thing.'

'What kind of voice had he?'

'Oh, foreign, like Mrs Fennan's—she *is* foreign, isn't she? That's what I put it down to—all her fuss and state—foreign temperament.'

She smiled at Mendel, waited a moment, then walked out like Alice.

'Cow,' said Mrs Oriel, looking at the closed door. Her eyes turned to Mendel. 'Well, I hope you've got your five quids' worth.'

'I think so,' said Mendel.

Chapter Eleven

The Unrespectable Club

Mendel found Smiley sitting in an armchair fully dressed. Peter Guillam was stretched luxuriously on the bed, a pale green folder held casually in his hand. Outside, the sky was black and menacing.

'Enter the third murderer,' said Guillam as Mendel walked in. Mendel sat down at the end of the bed and nodded happily to Smiley, who looked pale and depressed.

'Congratulations. Nice to see you on your feet.'

'Thank you. I'm afraid if you did see me on my feet you wouldn't congratulate me. I feel as weak as a kitten.'

'When are they letting you go?'

'I don't know when they expect me to go—'

'Haven't you asked?'

'No.'

'Well, you'd better. I've got news for you. I don't know what it means but it means something.'

'Well, well,' said Guillam; 'everyone's got news for everyone else. Isn't that exciting. George has been looking at my family snaps'—he raised the green folder a fraction of an inch—'and recognizes all his old chums.'

Mendel felt baffled and rather left out of things. Smiley intervened: 'I'll tell you all about it over dinner tomorrow evening. I'm getting out of here in the morning, whatever they say. I think we've found the murderer and a lot more besides. Now let's have your news.' There was no triumph in his eyes. Only anxiety.

Membership of the club to which Smiley belonged is not quoted among the respectable acquisitions of those who adorn the pages of *Who's Who*. It was formed by a young renegade of the Junior Carlton named Steed-Asprey, who had been warned off by the Secretary for blaspheming within the hearing of a South African bishop. He persuaded his former Oxford landlady to leave her quiet house in Holywell and take over two rooms and a cellar in Manchester Square which a monied relative put at his disposal. It had once had forty members who each paid fifty guineas a year. There were thirty-one left. There were no women and no rules, no secretary and no bishops. You could take sandwiches and buy a bottle of beer, you could take sandwiches and buy nothing at all. As long as you were reasonably sober and minded your own business, no one gave twopence what you wore, did, or said, or whom you brought with you. Mrs Sturgeon no longer devilled at the bar, or brought you your chop in front of the fire in the cellar, but presided in genial comfort over the ministrations of two retired sergeants from a small border regiment.

Naturally enough, most of the members were approximate contemporaries of Smiley at Oxford. It had always been agreed that the club was to serve one generation only, that it would grow old and die with its members. The war had taken its toll of Jebedee and others, but no one had ever suggested they should elect new members. Besides, the premises were now their own, Mrs Sturgeon's future had been taken care of, and the club was solvent.

It was a Saturday evening and only half a dozen people where there. Smiley had ordered their meal, and a table was set for them in the cellar, where a bright coal fire burned in a brick hearth. They were alone, there was sirloin and claret; outside the rain fell continuously. For all three of them the world seemed an untroubled and decent place that night, despite the strange business that brought them together.

'To make sense of what I have to tell you,' began Smiley at last, addressing himself principally to Mendel, 'I shall have to talk at length about myself. I'm an intelligence officer by trade as you know—I've been in the Service since the Flood, long before we were mixed up in power politics with Whitehall. In those days we were understaffed and underpaid. After the usual training and probation in South America and Central Europe, I took a job lecturing at a German University, talent spotting for young Germans with an agent potential.' He paused, smiled at Mendel and said: 'Forgive the jargon.' Mendel nodded solemnly and Smiley went on. He knew he was being pompous, and didn't know how to prevent himself.

'It was shortly before the last war, a terrible time in Germany then, intolerance run mad. I would have been a lunatic to approach anyone myself. My only chance was to be as nondescript as I could, politically and socially colourless, and to put forward candidates for recruitment by someone else. I tried to bring some back to England for short periods on students' tours. I made a point of having no contact at all with the Department when I came over because we hadn't any idea in those days of the efficiency of German Counter Intelligence. I never knew who was approached, and of course it was much better that way. In case I was blown, I mean.

'My story really begins in 1938. I was alone in my rooms one summer evening. It had been a beautiful day, warm and peaceful. Fascism might never have been heard of. I was working in my shirt sleeves at a desk by my window, not working very hard because it was such a wonderful evening.'

He paused, embarrassed for some reason, and fussed a little with the port. Two pink spots appeared high on his cheeks. He felt slightly drunk though he had had very little wine.

'To resume,' he said, and felt an ass. 'I'm sorry, I feel a little inarticulate . . . Anyway, as I sat there, there was a knock on the door and a young student came in. He was nineteen, in fact, but he looked younger. His name was Dieter Frey. He was a pupil of mine, an intelligent boy and remarkable to look at.' Smiley paused again, staring before him. Perhaps it was his illness, his weakness, which brought the memory so vividly before him.

'Dieter was a very handsome boy, with a high forehead and a lot of unruly black hair. The lower part of his body was deformed, I think by infantile paralysis. He carried a stick and leaned heavily upon it when he walked. Naturally he cut a rather romantic figure at a small university; they thought him Byronic and so on. In fact I could never find him romantic myself. The Germans have a passion for discovering young genius, you know, from Herder to Stefan George—somebody lionized them practically from the cradle. But you couldn't lionize Dieter. There was a fierce independence, a ruthlessness about him which scared off the most determined patron. This defensiveness in Dieter derived not only from his deformity, but his race, which was Jewish. How on earth he kept his place at University I could never understand. It was possible that they didn't know he was a Jew—his beauty might have been southern, I suppose, Italian, but I don't really see how. To me he was obviously Jewish.

'Dieter was a socialist. He made no secret of his views even in those days. I once considered him for recruitment, but it seemed futile to take on anyone who was so obviously earmarked for concentration camp. Besides he was too volatile, too swift to react, too brightly painted, too vain. He led all the societies at the University—debating, political, poetry and so on. In all the athletic guilds he held honorary positions. He had the nerve not to drink in a University where you proved your manhood by being drunk most of your first year.

'That was Dieter, then: a tall, handsome, commanding cripple, the idol of his generation; a Jew. And that was the man who came to see me that hot summer evening.

'I sat him down and offered him a drink, which he refused. I made some coffee, I think, on a gas ring. We spoke in a desultory way about my last lecture on Keats. I had complained about the application of German critical methods to English poetry, and this had led to some discussion—as usual—on the Nazi interpretation of "decadence" in art. Dieter dragged it all up again and became more and more outspoken in his condemnation of modern Germany and finally of Nazism itself. Naturally, I was guarded—I think I was less of a fool in those days than I am now. In the end he asked me point blank what I thought of the Nazis. I replied rather pointedly that I was disinclined to criticize my hosts, and that anyway I didn't think politics were much fun. I shall never forget his reply. He was furious, struggled to his feet and shouted at me: "*Von Freude ist nicht die Rede!*"—"We're not talking about fun!"' Smiley broke off and looked across the table to Guillam: 'I'm sorry Peter, I'm being rather long-winded.'

'Nonsense, old dear. You tell the story in your own way.' Mendel grunted his approval; he was sitting rather stiffly with both hands on the table before him. There was no light in the room now except the bright glow of the fire, which threw tall shadows on the roughcast wall behind them. The port decanter was three parts empty; Smiley gave himself a little and passed it on.

'He raved at me. He simply did not understand how I could apply an independent standard of criticism to art and remain so insensitive to politics, how I could bleat about artistic freedom when a third of Europe was in chains. Did it mean nothing to me that contemporary civilization was being bled to death? What was so sacred about the eighteenth century that I could throw the twentieth away? He had come to me because he enjoyed my seminars and thought me an enlightened man, but he now realized that I was worse than all of them.

'I let him go. What else could I do? On paper he was suspect anyway—a rebellious Jew with a University place still mysteriously free. But I watched him. The term was nearly over and the long vacation soon to begin. In the closing debate of the term three days later he was dreadfully outspoken. He really frightened people, you know, and they grew silent and apprehensive. The end of the term came and Dieter departed without a word of farewell to me. I never expected to see him again.

'It was about six months before I did. I had been visiting friends near Dresden, Dieter's home town, and I arrived half an hour early at the station. Rather than hang around on the platform I decided to go for a stroll. A couple of hundred metres from the station was a tall, rather grim seventeenth-century house. There was a small courtyard in front of it with tall iron railings and a wrought-iron gate. It had apparently been converted into a temporary prison: a group of shaven prisoners, men and women, were being exercised in the yard, walking round the perimeter. Two guards stood in the centre with tommy guns. As I watched I caught sight of a familiar figure, taller than the rest, limping, struggling to keep up with them. It was Dieter. They had taken his stick away.

'When I thought about it afterwards, of course, I realized that the Gestapo would scarcely arrest the most popular member of the University while he was still up. I forgot about my train, went back into the town and looked for his parents in the telephone book. I knew his father had been a doctor so it wasn't difficult. I went to the address and only his mother was there. The father had died already in a concentration camp. She wasn't inclined to talk about Dieter, but it appeared that he had not gone to a Jewish prison but to a general one, and ostensibly for "a period of correction" only. She expected him back in about three months. I left him a message to say I still had some books of his and would be pleased to return them if he would call on me.

'I'm afraid the events of 1939 must have got the better of me, because I don't believe I gave Dieter another thought that year. Soon after I returned from Dresden my Department ordered me back to England. I packed and left within forty-eight hours, to find London in a turmoil. I was given a new assignment which required intensive preparation, briefing, and training. I was to go back to Europe at once and activate almost untried agents in Germany who had been recruited against such an emergency. I began to memorize the dozen odd names and addresses. You can imagine my reaction when I discovered Dieter Frey among them.

'When I read his file I found he had more or less recruited himself by bursting in on the consulate in Dresden and demanding to know why no one lifted a finger to stop the persecution of the Jews.' Smiley paused and laughed to himself; 'Dieter was a great one for getting people to do things.' He glanced quickly at Mendel and Guillam. Both had their eyes fixed on him.

'I suppose my first reaction was pique. The boy had been right under my nose and I hadn't considered him suitable–what was some ass in Dresden up to? And then I was alarmed to have this firebrand on my hands, whose impulsive temperament could cost me and others our lives. Despite the slight changes in my appearance and the new cover under which I was operating, I should obviously have to declare myself to Dieter as plain George Smiley from the University, so he could blow me sky high. It seemed a most unfortunate beginning, and I was half resolved to set up my network without

Dieter. In the event I was wrong. He was a magnificent agent.

'He didn't curb his flamboyance, but used it skilfully as a kind of double bluff. His deformity kept him out of the Services and he found himself a clerical job on the railways. In no time he worked his way to a position of real responsibility and the quantity of information he obtained was fantastic. Details of troop and ammunition transports, their destination and date of transit. Later he reported on the effectiveness of our bombing, pinpointed key targets. He was a brilliant organizer and I think that was what saved him. He did a wonderful job on the railways, made himself indispensable, worked all hours of the night and day; became almost inviolate. They even gave him a civilian decoration for exceptional merit and I suppose the Gestapo conveniently lost his file.

'Dieter had a theory that was pure Faust. Thought alone was valueless. You must act for thought to become effective. He used to say that the greatest mistake man ever made was to distinguish between the mind and the body: an order does not exist if it is not obeyed. He used to quote Kleist a great deal: "if all eyes were made of green glass, and if all that seems white was really green, who would be the wiser?" Something like that.

'As I say, Dieter was a magnificent agent. He even went so far as to arrange for certain freights to be transported on good flying nights for the convenience of our bombers. He had tricks all his own–a natural genius for the nuts and bolts of espionage. It seemed absurd to suppose it could last, but the effect of our bombing was often so widespread that it would have been childish to attribute it to one person's betrayal–let alone a man so notoriously outspoken as Dieter.

'Where he was concerned my job was easy. Dieter put in a lot of travelling as it was–he had a special pass to get him around. Communication was child's play by comparison with some agents. Occasionally we would actually meet and talk in a café, or he would pick me up in a Ministry car and drive me sixty or seventy miles along a main road, as if he were giving me a lift. But more often we would take a journey in the same train and swap briefcases in the corridor or go to the theatre with parcels and exchange cloakroom tickets. He seldom gave me actual reports but just carbon copies of transit orders. He got his secretary to do a lot–he made her keep a special float which he "destroyed" every three months by emptying it into his briefcase in the lunch hour.

'Well, in 1943 I was recalled. My trade cover was rather thin by then I think, and I was getting a bit shop-soiled.' He stopped and took a cigarette from Guillam's case.

'But don't let's get Dieter out of perspective,' he said: 'He was my best agent, but he wasn't my only one. I had a lot of headaches of my own–running him was a picnic by comparison with some. When the

war was over I tried to find out from my successor what had become
of Dieter and the rest of them. Some were resettled in Australia and
Canada, some just drifted away to what was left of their home towns.
Dieter hesitated, I gather. The Russians were in Dresden, of course,
and he may have had doubts. In the end he went—he had to really,
because of his mother. He hated the Americans, anyway. And of
course he was a socialist.

'I heard later that he had made his career there. The administrative experience he had picked up during the war got him some
Government job in the new republic. I suppose that his reputation as
a rebel and the suffering of his family cleared the way for him. He
must have done pretty well for himself.'

'Why?' asked Mendel.

'He was over here until a month ago running the Steel Mission.'

'That's not all,' said Guillam quickly. 'In case you think your cup
is full, Mendel, I spared you another visit to Weybridge this morning
and called on Elizabeth Pidgeon. It was George's idea.' He turned to
Smiley: 'She's a sort of Moby Dick isn't she—big white man-eating
whale.'

'Well?' said Mendel.

'I showed her a picture of that young diplomat by the name of
Mundt they kept in tow there to pick up the bits. Elizabeth
recognized him at once as the nice man who collected Elsa Fennan's
music case. Isn't that jolly?'

'But—'

'I know what you're going to ask, you clever youth. You want to
know whether George recognized him too. Well, George did. It's the
same nasty fellow who tried to lure him into his house in Bywater
Street. Doesn't he get around?'

Mendel drove to Mitcham. Smiley was dead tired. It was raining
again and cold. Smiley hugged his greatcoat round him and, despite
his tiredness, watched with quiet pleasure the busy London night go
by. He had always loved travelling. Even now, if he had the choice,
he would cross France by train rather than fly. He could still respond
to the magic noises of a night journey across Europe, the oddly
cacophonous chimes and the French voices suddenly waking him
from English dreams. Ann had loved it too and they had twice
travelled overland to share the dubious joys of that uncomfortable
journey.

When they got back Smiley went straight to bed while Mendel
made some tea. They drank it in Smiley's bedroom.

'What do we do now?' asked Mendel.

'I thought I might go to Walliston tomorrow.'

'You ought to spend the day in bed. What do you want to do
there?'

'See Elsa Fennan.'

'You're not safe on your own. You'd better let me come. I'll sit in the car while you do the talking. She's a Yid, isn't she?'

Smiley nodded.

'My dad was Yid. He never made such a bloody fuss about it.'

Chapter Twelve

Dream for Sale

She opened the door and stood looking at him for a moment in silence.

'You could have let me know you were coming,' she said.

'I thought it safer not to.'

She was silent again. Finally she said: 'I don't know what you mean.' It seemed to cost her a good deal.

'May I come in?' said Smiley. 'We haven't much time.'

She looked old and tired, less resilient perhaps. She led him into the drawing-room and with something like resignation indicated a chair.

Smiley offered her a cigarette and took one himself. She was standing by the window. As he looked at her, watched her quick breathing, her feverish eyes, he realized that she had almost lost the power of self-defence.

When he spoke, his voice was gentle, concessive. To Elsa Fennan it must have seemed like a voice she had longed for, irresistible, offering all strength, comfort, compassion and safety. She gradually moved away from the window and her right hand, which had been pressed against the sill, trailed wistfully along it, then fell to her side in a gesture of submission. She sat opposite him, her eyes upon him in complete dependence, like the eyes of a lover.

'You must have been terribly lonely,' he said. 'No one can stand it for ever. It takes courage, too, and it's hard to be brave alone. They never understand that, do they? They never know what it costs—the sordid tricks of lying and deceiving, the isolation from ordinary people. They think you can run on their kind of fuel—the flag waving and the music. But you need a different kind of fuel, don't you, when you're alone? You've got to hate, and it needs strength to hate all the time. And what you must love is so remote, so vague when you're not part of it.' He paused. Soon, he thought, soon you'll break. He prayed desperately that she would accept him, accept his comfort. He looked at her. Soon she would break.

'I said we hadn't much time. Do you know what I mean?'

She had folded her hands on her lap and was looking down at them. He saw the dark roots of her yellow hair and wondered why on earth she dyed it. She showed no sign of having heard his question.

'When I left you that morning a month ago I drove to my home in London. A man tried to kill me. That night he nearly succeeded–he hit me on the head three or four times. I've just come out of hospital. As it happens I was lucky. Then there was the garage man he hired the car from. The river police recovered his body from the Thames not long ago. There were no signs of violence–he was just full of whisky. They can't understand it–he hadn't been near the river for years. But then we're dealing with a competent man, aren't we? A trained killer. It seems he's trying to remove anyone who can connect him with Samuel Fennan. Or his wife, of course. Then there's that young blonde girl at the Repertory Theatre . . .'

'What are you saying?' she whispered. 'What are you trying to tell me?'

Smiley suddenly wanted to hurt her, to break the last of her will, to remove her utterly as an enemy. For so long she had haunted him as he had lain helpless, had been a mystery and a power.

'What games did you think you were playing, you two? Do you think you can flirt with power like theirs, give a little and not give all? Do you think that *you* can stop the dance–control the strength you give them? What dreams did you cherish, Mrs Fennan, that had so little of the world in them?'

She buried her face in her hands and he watched the tears run between her fingers. Her body shook with great sobs and her words came slowly, wrung from her.

'No, no dreams. I had no dream but him. He had one dream, yes . . . one great dream.' She went on crying, helpless, and Smiley, half in triumph, half in shame, waited for her to speak again. Suddenly she raised her head and looked at him, the tears still running down her cheeks. 'Look at me,' she said. 'What dream did they leave me? I dreamed of long golden hair and they shaved my head, I dreamed of a beautiful body and they broke it with hunger. I have seen what human beings are, how could I believe in a formula for human beings? I said to him, oh I said to him a thousand times; "only make no laws, no fine theories, no judgements, and the people may love, but give them one theory, let them invent one slogan, and the game begins again." I told him that. We talked whole nights away. But no, that little boy must have his dream, and if a new world was to be built, Samuel Fennan must build it. I said to him, "Listen," I said. "They have given you all you have, a home, money, and trust. Why do you do it to them?" And he said to me: "I do it *for* them. I am the surgeon and one day they will understand." He was a child, Mr Smiley, they led him like a child.'

He dared not speak, dared put nothing to the test.

'Five years ago he met that Dieter. In a ski hut near Garmisch. Freitag told us later that Dieter had planned it that way–Dieter couldn't ski anyway because of his legs. Nothing seemed real then; Freitag wasn't a real name. Fennan christened him Freitag like Man Friday in Robinson Crusoe. Dieter found that so funny and afterwards we never talked of Dieter but always of Mr Robinson and Freitag.' She broke off now and looked at him with a very faint smile: 'I'm sorry,' she said; 'I'm not very coherent.'

'I understand,' said Smiley.

'That girl–what did you say about that girl?'

'She's alive. Don't worry. Go on.'

'Fennan liked you, you know. Freitag tried to kill you . . . why?'

'Because I came back, I suppose, and asked you about the 8.30 call. You told Freitag that, didn't you?'

'Oh, God,' she said, her fingers at her mouth.

'You rang him up, didn't you? As soon as I'd gone?'

'Yes, yes. I was frightened. I wanted to warn him to go, him and Dieter, to go away and never come back, because I knew you'd find out. If not today then one day, but I knew you'd find out in the end. Why would they never leave me alone? They were frightened of me because they knew I had no dreams, that I only wanted Samuel, wanted him safe to love and care for. They relied on that.'

Smiley felt his head throbbing erratically. 'So you rang him straight away,' he said. 'You tried the Primrose number first and couldn't get through.'

'Yes,' she said vaguely. 'Yes, that's right. But they're both Primrose numbers.'

'So you rang the *other* number, the alternative . . .'

She drifted back to the window, suddenly exhausted and limp; she seemed happier now–the storm had left her reflective and, in a way, content.

'Yes. Freitag was a great one for alternative plans.'

'What was the other number?' Smiley insisted. He watched her anxiously as she stared out of the window into the dark garden.

'Why do you want to know?'

He came and stood beside her at the window, watching her profile. His voice was suddenly harsh and energetic.

'I said the girl was all right. You and I are alive, too. But don't think that's going to last.'

She turned to him with fear in her eyes, looked at him for a moment, then nodded. Smiley took her by the arm and guided her to a chair. He ought to make her a hot drink or something. She sat down quite mechanically, almost with the detachment of incipient madness.

'The other number was 9747.'

'Any address—did you have an address?'

'No, no address. Only the telephone. Tricks on the telephone. No address,' she repeated, with unnatural emphasis, so that Smiley looked at her and wondered. A thought suddenly struck him—a memory of Dieter's skill in communication.

'Freitag didn't meet you the night Fennan died, did he? He didn't come to the theatre?'

'No.'

'That was the first time he had missed, wasn't it? You panicked and left early.'

'No . . . yes, yes, I panicked.'

'No you didn't! You left early because you had to, it was the arrangement. *Why* did you leave early? Why?'

Her hands hid her face.

'Are you still mad?' Smiley shouted. 'Do you still think you can control what you have made? Freitag will kill you, kill the girl, kill, kill, kill. Who are you trying to protect, a girl or a murderer?'

She wept and said nothing. Smiley crouched beside her, still shouting.

'I'll tell you why you left early, shall I? I'll tell you what I think. It was to catch the last post that night from Weybridge. He hadn't come, you hadn't exchanged cloakroom tickets, had you, so you obeyed the instructions, you posted your ticket to him and you *have* got an address, not written down but remembered, remembered for ever: "if there is a crisis, if I do not come, this is the address": is that what he said? An address never to be used or spoken of, an address forgotten and remembered for ever? Is that right? Tell me!'

She stood up, her head turned away, went to the desk and found a piece of paper and a pencil. The tears still ran freely over her face. With agonizing slowness she wrote the address, her hand faltering and almost stopping between the words.

He took the paper from her, folded it carefully across the middle and put it in his wallet.

Now he would make her some tea.

She looked like a child rescued from the sea. She sat on the edge of the sofa holding the cup tightly in her frail hands, nursing it against her body. Her thin shoulders were hunched forward, her feet and ankles pressed tightly together. Smiley, looking at her, felt he had broken something he should never have touched because it was so fragile. He felt an obscene, coarse bully, his offerings of tea a futile recompense for his clumsiness.

He could think of nothing to say. After a while, she said: 'He liked you, you know. He really liked you . . . he said you were a clever little man. It was quite a surprise when Samuel called anyone clever.' She shook her head slowly. Perhaps it was the reaction that made her smile: 'He used to say there were two forces in the world, the positive and the negative. "What shall I do then?" he would ask me. "Let them ruin their harvest because they give me bread? Creation, progress, power, the whole future of mankind waits at their door; shall I not let them in?" And I said to him: "But Samuel, maybe the people are happy without these things?" But you know he didn't think of people like that.

'But I couldn't stop him. You know the strangest thing about Fennan? For all that thinking and talking, he had made up his mind long ago what he would do. All the rest was poetry. He wasn't coordinated, that's what I used to tell him . . .'

'. . . and yet you helped him,' said Smiley.

'Yes, I helped him. He wanted help so I gave it him. He was my life.'

'I see.'

'That was a mistake. He was a little boy, you know. He forgot things just like a child. And so vain. He had made up his mind to do it and he did it so badly. He didn't think of it as you do, or I do. He simply didn't think of it like that. It was his work and that was all.

'It began so simply. He brought home a draft telegram one night and showed it to me. He said: "I think Dieter ought to see that"—that was all. I couldn't believe it to begin with—that he was a spy, I mean. Because he was, wasn't he? And gradually, I realized. They began to ask for special things. The music case I got back from Freitag began to contain orders, and sometimes money. I said to him: "Look at what they are sending you—do you want this?" We didn't know what to do with the money. In the end we gave it away mostly, I don't know why. Dieter was very angry that winter, when I told him.'

'What winter was that?' asked Smiley.

'The second winter with Dieter—1956 in Mürren. We met him first in January 1955. That was when it began. And shall I tell you something? Hungary made no difference to Samuel, not a tiny bit of difference. Dieter was frightened about him then, I know, because Freitag told me. When Fennan gave me the things to take to Weybridge that November I nearly went mad. I shouted at him: "Can't you see it's the same? The same guns, the same children dying in the streets? Only the dream has changed, the blood is the same colour. Is that what you want?" I asked him: "Would you do this for Germans, too? It's me who lies in the gutter, will you let them do it to *me*?" But he just said: "No Elsa, this is different." And I went on taking the music case. Do you understand?'

'I don't know. I just don't know. I think perhaps I do.'

'He was all I had. He was my life. I protected myself, I suppose. And gradually I became a part of it, and then it was too late to stop . . . And then you know,' she said, in a whisper; 'there were times when I was glad, times when the world seemed to applaud what Samuel was doing. It was not a pretty sight for us, the new Germany. Old names had come back, names that had frightened us as children. The dreadful, plump pride returned, you could see it even in the photographs in the papers, they marched with the old rhythm. Fennan felt that too, but then thank God he hadn't seen what I saw.

'We were in a camp outside Dresden, where we used to live. My father was paralysed. He missed tobacco more than anything and I used to roll cigarettes from any rubbish I could find in the camp—just to pretend with. One day a guard saw him smoking and began laughing. Some others came and they laughed too. My father was holding the cigarette in his paralysed hand and it was burning his fingers. He didn't know, you see.

'Yes, when they gave guns to the Germans again, gave them money and uniforms, then sometimes—just for a little while—I was pleased with what Samuel had done. We are Jews, you know, and so . . .'

'Yes, I know, I understand,' said Smiley. 'I saw it too, a little of it.'

'Dieter said you had.'

'Dieter said that?'

'Yes. To Freitag. He told Freitag you were a very clever man. You once deceived Dieter before the war, and it was only long afterwards that he found out, that's what Freitag said. He said you were the best he'd ever met.'

'When did Freitag tell you that?'

She looked at him for a long time. He had never seen in any face such hopeless misery. He remembered how she had said to him before: 'The children of my grief are dead.' He understood that now, and heard it in her voice when at last she spoke:

'Why, isn't it obvious? The night he murdered Samuel.

'That's the great joke, Mr Smiley. At the very moment when Samuel could have done so much for them—not just a piece here and a piece there, but all the time—so many music cases—at that moment their own fear destroyed them, turned them into animals and made them kill what they had made.

'Samuel always said: "They will win because they *know* and the others will perish because they do not: men who work for a dream will work for ever"—that's what he said. But I knew their dream, I knew it would destroy us. What has not destroyed? Even the dream of Christ.'

'It was Dieter then, who saw me in the park with Fennan?'

'Yes.'

'And thought—'

'Yes. Thought that Samuel had betrayed him. Told Freitag to kill Samuel.'

'And the anonymous letter?'

'I don't know. I don't now who wrote it. Someone who knew

Samuel I suppose, someone from the office who watched him and knew. Or from Oxford, from the Party. I don't know. Samuel didn't know either.'

'But the suicide letter—'

She looked at him, and her face crumpled. She was almost weeping again. She bowed her head:

'I wrote it. Freitag brought the paper, and I wrote it. The signature was already there. Samuel's signature.'

Smiley went over to her, sat beside her on the sofa and took her hand. She turned on him in a fury and began screaming at him:

'Take your hands off me! Do you think I'm yours because I don't belong to them? Go away! Go away and kill Freitag and Dieter, keep the game alive, Mr Smiley. But don't think I'm on *your* side, d'you hear? Because I'm the wandering Jewess, the no-man's land, the battlefield for your toy soldiers. You can kick me and trample on me, see, but never, never touch me, never tell me you're sorry, d'you hear? Now get out! Go away and kill.'

She sat there, shivering as if from cold. As he reached the door he looked back. There were no tears in her eyes.

Mendel was waiting for him in the car.

Chapter Thirteen

The Inefficiency of Samuel Fennan

They arrived at Mitcham at lunch time. Peter Guillam was waiting for them patiently in his car.

'Well, children; what's the news?'

Smiley handed him the piece of paper from his wallet. 'There was an emergency number, too–Primrose 9747. You'd better check it but I'm not hopeful of that either.'

Peter disappeared into the hall and began telephoning. Mendel busied himself in the kitchen and returned ten minutes later with beer, bread, and cheese on a tray. Guillam came back and sat down without saying anything. He looked worried. 'Well,' he said at last, 'what did she say, George?'

Mendel cleared away as Smiley finished the account of his interview that morning.

'I see,' said Guillam. 'How very worrying. Well, that's it, George, I shall have to put this on paper today, and I'll have to go to Maston at once. Catching dead spies is a poor game really—and causes a lot of unhappiness.'

'What access did he have at the FO?' asked Smiley.

'Recently a lot. That's why they felt he should be interviewed, as you know.'

'What kind of stuff, mainly?'

'I don't know yet. He was on an Asian desk until a few months ago but his new job was different.'

'American, I seem to remember,' said Smiley. 'Peter?'

'Yes.'

'Peter, have you thought at all *why* they wanted to kill Fennan so much. I mean, supposing he *had* betrayed them, as they thought, why kill him? They had nothing to gain.'

'No; no, I suppose they hadn't. That does need some explaining, come to think of it . . . or does it? Suppose Fuchs or Maclean had betrayed them, I wonder what would have happened. Suppose they had reason to fear a chain reaction—not just here but in America—all over the world? Wouldn't they kill him to prevent that? There's so much we shall just never know.'

'Like the 8.30 call?' said Smiley.

'Cheerio. Hang on here till I ring you, will you? Maston's bound to want to see you. They'll be running down the corridors when I tell them the glad news. I shall have to wear the special grin I reserve for bearing really disastrous tidings.'

Mendel saw him out and then returned to the drawing-room. 'Best thing you can do is put your feet up,' he said. 'You look a ruddy mess, you do.'

'Either Mundt's here or he's not,' thought Smiley as he lay on the bed in his waistcoat, his hands linked under his head. 'If he's not, we're finished. It will be for Maston to decide what to do with Elsa Fennan, and my guess is he'll do nothing.

'If Mundt *is* here, it's for one of three reasons: A, because Dieter told him to stay and watch the dust settle; B, because he's in bad odour and afraid to go back; C, because he has unfinished business.

'A is improbable because it's not like Dieter to take needless risks. Anyway, it's a woolly idea.

'B is unlikely because, while Mundt may be afraid of Dieter he must also, presumably, be frightened of a murder charge here. His wisest plan would be to go to another country.

'C is more likely. If I was in Dieter's shoes I'd be worried sick about Elsa Fennan. The Pidgeon girl is immaterial—without Elsa to fill in the gaps she presents no serious danger. She was not a conspirator and there is no reason why she should particularly remember Elsa's friend at the theatre. No, Elsa constitutes the real danger.'

There was, of course, a final possibility, which Smiley was quite unable to judge: the possibility that Dieter had other agents to control here through Mundt. On the whole he was inclined to discount this, but the thought had no doubt crossed Peter's mind.

'No . . . it still didn't make sense—it wasn't tidy. He decided to begin again.

What do we know? He sat up to look for pencil and paper and at once his head began throbbing. Obstinately he got off the bed and took a pencil from the inside pocket of his jacket. There was a writing pad in his suitcase. He returned to the bed, shaped the pillows to his satisfaction, took four aspirin from the bottle on the table and propped himself against the pillows, his short legs stretched before him. He began writing. First he wrote the heading in a neat, scholarly hand, and underlined it.

'What do we know?'

Then he began, stage by stage, to recount as dispassionately as possible the sequence of events hitherto:

'On Monday, 2 January, Dieter Frey saw me in the park talking to his agent and concluded . . .' Yes, what *did* Dieter conclude? That Fennan had confessed, was going to confess? That Fennan was *my* agent? '. . . and concluded that Fennan was dangerous, for reasons still unknown. The following evening, the first Tuesday in the month, Elsa Fennan took her husband's reports in a music case to the Weybridge Repertory Theatre, in the agreed way, and left the case in the cloakroom in exchange for a ticket. Mundt was to bring his own music case and do the same thing. Elsa and Mundt would then exchange tickets during the performance. Mundt did not appear. Accordingly she followed the emergency procedure and posted the ticket to a prearranged address, having left the theatre early to catch the last post from Weybridge. She then drove home to be met by Mundt, who had, by then, murdered Fennan, probably on Dieter's orders. He had shot him at point blank range as soon as he met him in the hall. Knowing Dieter, I suspect that he had long ago taken the precaution of keeping in London a few sheets of blank writing paper signed with samples, forged or authentic, of Sam Fennan's signature, in case it was ever necessary to compromise or blackmail him. Assuming this to be so, Mundt brought a sheet with him in order to type the suicide letter over the signature on Fennan's own typewriter. In the ghastly scene which must have followed Elsa's arrival, Mundt realized that Dieter had wrongly interpreted Fennan's encounter with Smiley, but relied on Elsa to preserve her dead husband's reputation—not to mention her own complicity. Mundt was therefore reasonably safe. Mundt made Elsa type the letter, perhaps because he did not trust his English. (Note: But who the devil typed the *first* letter, the denunciation?)

'Mundt then, presumably, demanded the music case he had failed to collect, and Elsa told him that she had obeyed standing instructions and posted the cloakroom ticket to the Hampstead address, leaving the music case at the theatre. Mundt reacted significantly: he forced her to telephone the theatre and to arrange for him to collect the case that night on his way back to London. Therefore either the address to which the ticket was posted was no longer valid, or Mundt intended at that stage to return home early the next morning without having time to collect the ticket and the case.

'Smiley visits Walliston early on the morning of Wednesday, 4 January, and during the *first* interview takes an 8.30 call from the exchange which (beyond reasonable doubt) Fennan requested at 7.55 the previous evening. WHY?

'Later that morning S. returns to Elsa Fennan to ask about the 8.30 call–which she knew (on her own admission) would "worry me" (no doubt Mundt's flattering description of my powers had had its effect). Having told S. a futile story about her bad memory she panics and rings Mundt.

'Mundt, presumably equipped with a photograph or a description from Dieter, decides to liquidate S. (on Dieter's authority?) and later that day nearly succeeds. (Note: Mundt did not return the car to Scarr's garage till the night of the 4th. This does not necessarily prove that Mundt had no plans for flying earlier in the day. If he had originally meant to fly in the morning he might well have left the car at Scarr's earlier and gone to the airport by bus.)

'It does seem pretty likely that Mundt changed his plans after Elsa's telephone call. It is not clear that he changed them *because* of her call.' Would Mundt really be panicked by Elsa? Panicked into staying, panicked into murdering Adam Scarr, he wondered.

The telephone was ringing in the hall . . .

'George, it's Peter. No joy with the address or the telephone number. Dead end.'

'What do you mean?'

'The telephone number and the address both led to the same place–furnished apartment in Highgate village.'

'Well?'

'Rented by a pilot in Lufteuropa. He paid his two months' rent on the fifth of January and hasn't come back since.'

'Damn.'

'The landlady remembers Mundt quite well. The pilot's friend. A nice polite gentleman he was, for a German, very open-handed. He used to sleep on the sofa quite often.'

'Oh God.'

'I went through the room with a toothcomb. There was a desk in the corner. All the drawers were empty except one, which contained a cloakroom ticket. I wonder where that came from . . . Well, if you want a laugh, come round to the Circus. The whole of Olympus is seething with activity. Oh, incidentally—'

'Yes?'

'I dug around at Dieter's flat. Another lemon. He left on the fourth of January. Didn't tell the milkman.'

'What about his mail?'

'He never received any, apart from bills. I also had a look at Comrade Mundt's little nest: couple of rooms over the Steel Mission. The furniture went out with the rest of the stuff. Sorry.'

'I see.'

'I'll tell you an odd thing though, George. You remember I thought I might get on to Fennan's personal possessions—wallet, note-book, and so on? From the police.'

'Yes.'

'Well, I did. His diary's got Dieter's full name entered in the address section with the Mission telephone number against it. Bloody cheek.'

'It's more than that. It's lunacy. Good Lord.'

'Then for the fourth of January the entry is "Smiley C.A. Ring 8.30". That was corroborated by an entry for the third which ran "request call for Wed. morning." There's your mysterious call.'

'Still unexplained.' A pause.

'George, I sent Felix Taverner round to the FO to do some ferreting. It's worse than we feared in one way, but better in another.'

'Why?'

'Well, Taverner got his hands on the registry schedules for the last two years. He was able to work out what files have been marked to Fennan's section. Where a file was particularly requested by that section they still have a requisition form.'

'I'm listening.'

'Felix found that three or four files were usually marked in to Fennan on a Friday afternoon and marked out again on Monday morning; the inference is that he took the stuff home at week-ends.'

'Oh my Lord!'

'But the odd thing is, George, that during the last six months, since his posting in fact, he tended to take home *unclassified* stuff which wouldn't have been of interest to anyone.'

'But it was during the last months that he began dealing mainly with secret files,' said Smiley. 'He could take home anything he wanted.'

'I know, but he didn't. In fact you'd almost say it was deliberate. He took home very low-grade stuff barely related to his daily work. His colleagues can't understand it now they think about it—he even took back some files handling subjects outside the scope of his section.'

'And unclassified.'

'Yes—of no conceivable intelligence value.'

'How about earlier, before he came into his new job? What kind of stuff went home then?'

'Much more what you'd expect—files he'd used during the day, policy and so on.'

'Secret?'

'Some were, some weren't. As they came.'

'But nothing unexpected—no particularly delicate stuff that didn't concern him?'

'No. Nothing. He had opportunity galore quite frankly and didn't use it. Windy, I suppose.'

'So he ought to be if he puts his controller's name in his diary.'

'And make what you like of this: he'd arranged at the FO to take a day off on the fourth—the day after he died. Rather an event apparently—he was a glutton for work, they say.'

'What's Maston doing about all this?' asked Smiley, after a pause.

'Going through the files at the moment and rushing in to see me with bloody fool questions every two minutes. I think he gets lonely in there with hard facts.'

'Oh, he'll beat them down, Peter, don't worry.'

'He's already saying that the whole case against Fennan rests on the evidence of a neurotic woman.'

'Thanks for ringing, Peter.'

'Be seeing you, dear boy. Keep your head down.'

Smiley replaced the receiver and wondered where Mendel was. There was an evening paper on the hall table, and he glanced vaguely at the headline 'Lynching: World Jewry Protests' and beneath it the account of the lynching of a Jewish shopkeeper in Düsseldorf. He opened the drawing-room door—Mendel was not there. Then he caught sight of him through the window wearing his gardening hat, hacking savagely with a pick-axe at a tree stump in the front garden. Smiley watched him for a moment, then went upstairs again to rest. As he reached the top of the stairs the telephone began ringing again.

'George—sorry to bother you again. It's about Mundt.'

'Yes?'

'Flew to Berlin last night by BEA. Travelled under another name but was easily identified by the air hostess. That seems to be that. Hard luck, chum.'

Smiley pressed down the cradle with his hand for a moment, then dialled Walliston 2944. He heard the number ringing the other end. Suddenly the dialling tone stopped and instead he heard Elsa Fennan's voice:

'Hullo . . . Hullo . . . *Hullo?*'

Slowly he replaced the receiver. She was alive.

Why on earth *now*? Why should Mundt go home *now*, five weeks after murdering Fennan, three weeks after murdering Scarr; why had he eliminated the lesser danger–Scarr–and left Elsa Fennan unharmed, neurotic and embittered, liable at any moment to throw aside her own safety and tell the whole story? What effect might that terrible night not have had upon her? How could Dieter trust a woman now so lightly bound to him? Her husband's good name could no longer be preserved; might she not, in God knows what mood of vengeance or repentance, blurt out the whole truth? Obviously, a little time must elapse between the murder of Fennan and the murder of his wife, but what event, what information, what danger, had decided Mundt to return last night? A ruthless and elaborate plan to preserve the secrecy of Fennan's treason had now apparently been thrown aside unfinished. What had happened yesterday that Mundt could know of? Or was the timing of his departure a coincidence? Smiley refused to believe it was. If Mundt had remained in England after the two murders and the assault on Smiley, he had done so unwillingly, waiting upon some opportunity or event that would release him. He would not stay a moment longer than he need. Yet what had he done since Scarr's death? Hidden in some lonely room, locked away from light and news. Then why did he now fly home so suddenly?

And Fennan–what spy was this who selected innocuous information for his masters when he had such gems at his fingertips? A change of heart, perhaps? A weakening of purpose? Then why did he not tell his wife, for whom his crime was a constant nightmare, who would have rejoiced at his conversion? It seemed now that Fennan had never shown any preference for secret papers–he had simply taken home whatever files currently might occupy him. But certainly a weakening of purpose would explain the strange summons to Marlow and Dieter's conviction that Fennan was betraying him. And who wrote the anonymous letter?

Nothing made sense, nothing. Fennan himself–brilliant, fluent, and attractive–had deceived so naturally, so expertly. Smiley had really liked him. Why then had this practised deceiver made the incredible blunder of putting Dieter's name in his diary–and shown so little judgement or interest in the selection of intelligence?

Smiley went upstairs to pack the few possessions which Mendel had collected for him from Bywater Street. It was all over.

Chapter Fourteen

The Dresden Group

He stood on the doorstep and put down his suitcase, fumbling for his latchkey. As he opened the door he recalled how Mundt had stood there looking at him, those very pale blue eyes calculating and steady. It was odd to think of Mundt as Dieter's pupil. Mundt had proceeded with the inflexibility of a trained mercenary—efficient, purposeful, narrow. There had been nothing original in his technique: in everything he had been a shadow of his master. It was as if Dieter's brilliant and imaginative tricks had been compressed into a manual which Mundt had learnt by heart, adding only the salt of his own brutality.

Smiley had deliberately left no forwarding address and a heap of mail lay on the door mat. He picked it up, put it on the hall table and began opening doors and peering about him, a puzzled, lost expression on his face. The house was strange to him, cold and musty. As he moved slowly from one room to another he began for the first time to realize how empty his life had become.

He looked for matches to light the gas fire, but there were none. He sat in an armchair in the living-room and his eyes wandered over the bookshelves and the odds and ends he had collected on his travels. When Ann had left him he had begun by rigorously excluding all trace of her. He had even got rid of her books. But gradually he had allowed the few remaining symbols that linked his life with hers to reassert themselves: wedding presents from close friends which had meant too much to be given away. There was a Watteau sketch from Peter Guillam, a Dresden group from Steed-Asprey.

He got up from his chair and went over to the corner cupboard where the group stood. He loved to admire the beauty of those figures, the tiny rococo courtesan in shepherd's costume, her hands outstretched to one adoring lover, her little face bestowing glances on another. He felt inadequate before that fragile perfection, as he had felt before Ann when he first began the conquest which had amazed society. Somehow those little figures comforted him: it was as useless to expect fidelity of Ann as of this tiny shepherdess in her glass case. Steed-Asprey had bought the group in Dresden before the war, it had been the prize of his collection and he had given it to them. Perhaps he had guessed that one day Smiley might have need of the simple philosophy it propounded.

Dresden: of all German cities, Smiley's favourite. He had loved its architecture, its odd jumble of medieval and classical buildings, sometimes reminiscent of Oxford, its cupolas, towers, and spires, its copper-green roofs shimmering under a hot sun. Its name meant 'town of the forest-dwellers' and it was there that Wenceslas of Bohemia had favoured the minstrel poets with gifts and privilege. Smiley remembered the last time he had been there, visiting a University acquaintance, a Professor of Philology he had met in England. It was on that visit that he had caught sight of Dieter Frey, struggling round the prison courtyard. He could see him still, tall and angry, monstrously altered by his shaven head, somehow too big for that little prison. Dresden, he remembered, had been Elsa's birthplace. He remembered glancing through her personal particulars at the ministry: Elsa *née* Freimann, born 1917 in Dresden, Germany, of German parents; educated Dresden: imprisoned 1938–45. He tried to place her against the background of her home, the patrician Jewish family living out its life amid insult and persecution. 'I dreamed of long golden hair and they shaved my head.' He realized with sickening accuracy why she dyed her hair. She might have been like this shepherdess, round-bosomed and pretty. But the body had been broken with hunger so that it was frail and ugly, like the carcass of a tiny bird.

He could picture her on the terrible night when she found her husband's murderer standing by his body: hear her breathless, sobbing explanation of why Fennan had been in the park with Smiley: and Mundt unmoved, explaining and reasoning, compelling her finally to conspire once more against her will in this most dreadful and needless of crimes, dragging her to the telephone and forcing her to ring the theatre, leaving her finally tortured and exhausted to cope with the enquiries that were bound to follow, even to type that futile suicide letter over Fennan's signature. It was inhuman beyond belief and, he added to himself, for Mundt a fantastic risk.

She had, of course, proved herself a reliable enough accomplice in the past, cool-headed and, ironically, more skilful than Fennan in the techniques of espionage. And, heaven knows, for a woman who had been through such a night as that, her performance at their first meeting had been a marvel.

As he stood gazing at the little shepherdess, poised eternally between her two admirers, he realized dispassionately that there was another quite different solution to the case of Samuel Fennan, a solution which matched every detail of circumstance, reconciled the

nagging inconsistencies apparent in Fennan's character. The realiza-
tion began as an academic exercise without reference to personalities; Smiley manoeuvred the characters like pieces in a puzzle,
twisting them this way and that to fit the complex framework of
established facts–and then, in a moment, the pattern had suddenly
re-formed with such assurance that it was a game no more.

His heart beat faster, as with growing astonishment Smiley retold
to himself the whole story, reconstructed scenes and incidents in the
light of his discovery. Now he knew why Mundt had left England
that day, why Fennan chose so little that was of value to Dieter, had
asked for the 8.30 call, and why his wife had escaped the systematic
savagery of Mundt. Now at last he knew who had written the
anonymous letter. He saw how he had been the fool of his own
sentiment, had played false with the power of his mind.

He went to the telephone and dialled Mendel's number. As soon as
he had finished speaking to him he rang Peter Guillam. Then he put
on his hat and coat and walked round the corner to Sloane Square. At
a small newsagent's beside Peter Jones he bought a picture postcard
of Westminster Abbey. He made his way to the underground station
and travelled north to Highgate, where he got out. At the main post
office he bought a stamp and addressed the postcard in stiff,
continental capitals to Elsa Fennan. In the panel for correspondence
he wrote in spiky longhand: 'Wish you were here.' He posted the
card and noted the time, after which he returned to Sloane Square.
There was nothing more he could do.

He slept soundly that night, rose early the following morning, a
Saturday, and walked round the corner to buy croissants and coffee
beans. He made a lot of coffee and sat in the kitchen reading *The Times*
and eating his breakfast. He felt curiously calm and when the
telephone rang at last he folded his paper carefully together before
going upstairs to answer it.

'George, it's Peter'–the voice was urgent, almost triumphant:
'George, she's bitten. I swear she has!'

'What happened?'

'The post arrived at exactly 8.35. By 9.30 she was walking briskly
down the drive, booted and spurred. She made straight for the
railway station and caught the 9.52 to Victoria. I put Mendel on the
train and hared up by car, but I was too late to meet the train this
end.'

'How will you make contact with Mendel again?'

'I gave him the number of the Grosvenor Hotel and I'm there now.
He's going to ring me as soon as he gets a chance and I'll join him
wherever he is.'

'Peter, you're taking this gently, aren't you?'

'Gentle as the wind, dear boy. I think she's losing her head.

Moving like a greyhound.'

Smiley rang off. He picked up his *Times* and began studying the theatre column. He must be right . . . he must be.

After that the morning passed with agonizing slowness. Sometimes he would stand at the window, his hands in his pockets, watching leggy Kensington girls going shopping with beautiful young men in pale blue pullovers, or the car-cleaning brigade toiling happily in front of their houses, then drifting away to talk motoring shop and finally setting off purposefully down the road for the first pint of the week-end.

At last, after what seemed an interminable delay, the front-door bell rang and Mendel and Guillam came in, grinning cheerfully, ravenously hungry.

'Hook, line, and sinker,' said Guillam. 'But let Mendel tell you–he did most of the dirty work. I just got in for the kill.'

Mendel recounted his story precisely and accurately, looking at the ground a few feet in front of him, his thin head slightly on one side.

'She caught the 9.52 to Victoria. I kept well clear of her on the train and picked her up as she went through the barrier. Then she took a taxi to Hammersmith.'

'A taxi?' Smiley interjected. 'She must be out of her mind.'

'She's rattled. She walks fast for a woman anyway, mind, but she damn nearly ran going down the platform. Got out at the Broadway and walked to the Sheridan Theatre. Tried the doors to the box office but they were locked. She hesitated a moment then turned back and went to a café a hundred yards down the road. Ordered coffee and paid for it at once. About forty minutes later she went back to the Sheridan. The box office was open and I ducked in behind her and joined the queue. She bought two rear stalls for next Thursday, Row T, 27 and 28. When she got outside the theatre she put one ticket in an envelope and sealed it up. Then she posted it. I couldn't see the address but there was a sixpenny stamp on the envelope.'

Smiley sat very still. 'I wonder,' he said; 'I wonder if he'll come.'

'I caught up with Mendel at the Sheridan,' said Guillam. 'He saw her into the café and then rang me. After that he went in after her.'

'Felt like a coffee myself,' Mendel went on. 'Mr Guillam joined me. I left him there when I joined the ticket queue, and he drifted out of the café a bit later. It was a decent job and no worries. She's rattled, I'm sure. But not suspicious.'

'What did she do after that?' asked Smiley.

'Went straight back to Victoria. We left her to it.'

They were silent for a moment, then Mendel said:

'What do we do now?'

Smiley blinked and gazed earnestly into Mendel's grey face.

'Book tickets for Thursday's performance at the Sheridan.'

They were gone and he was alone again. He still had not begun to cope with the quantity of mail which had accumulated in his absence. Circulars, catalogues from Blackwells, bills and the usual collection of soap vouchers, frozen pea coupons, football pool forms and a few private letters still lay unopened on the hall table. He took them into the drawing-room, settled in an armchair and began opening the personal letters first. There was one from Maston, and he read it with something approaching embarrassment.

> My dear George,
>   I was so sorry to hear from Guillam about your accident, and I do hope that by now you have made a full recovery.
>   You may recall that in the heat of the moment you wrote me a letter of resignation before your misfortune, and I just wanted to let you know that I am not, of course, taking this seriously. Sometimes when events crowd in upon us our sense of perspective suffers. But old campaigners like ourselves, George, are not so easily put off the scent. I look forward to seeing you with us again as soon as you are strong enough, and in the meantime we continue to regard you as an old and loyal member of the staff

Smiley put this on one side and turned to the next letter. Just for a moment he did not recognize the handwriting; just for a moment he looked bleakly at the Swiss stamp and the expensive hotel writing paper. Suddenly he felt slightly sick, his vision blurred and there was scarcely strength enough in his fingers to tear open the envelope. What did she want? If money, she could have all he possessed. The money was his own, to spend as he wished; if it gave him pleasure to squander it on Ann, he would do so. There was nothing else he had to give her—she had taken it long ago. Taken his courage, his love, his compassion, carried them jauntily away in her little jewel case to fondle occasionally on odd afternoons when the time hung heavy in the Cuban sun, to dangle them perhaps before the eys of her newest lover, to compare them even with similar trinkets which others before or since had brought her.

> My darling George,
>   I want to make you an offer which no gentleman could accept. I want to come back to you.
>   I'm staying at the Baur-au-Lac at Zurich till the end of the month. Let me know.
>   Ann

Smiley picked up the envelope and looked at the back of it: 'Madame Juan Alvida.' No, no gentleman could accept that offer. No dream could survive the daylight of Ann's departure with her saccharine Latin and his orange-peel grin. Smiley had once seen a news film of Alvida winning some race in Monte Carlo. The most repellent thing about him, he remembered, had been the hair on his arms. With his goggles and the motor oil and that ludicrous laurel-wreath he had looked exactly like an anthropoid ape fallen from a tree. He was wearing a white tennis shirt with short sleeves, which had somehow remained spotlessly clean throughout the race, setting off those black monkey arms with repulsive clarity.

That was Ann: Let me know. Redeem your life, see whether it can be lived again and let me know. I have wearied my lover, my lover has wearied me, let me shatter your world again: my own bores me. I want to come back to you . . . I want, I want . . .

Smiley got up, the letter still in his hand and stood again before the porcelain group. He remained there several minutes, gazing at the little shepherdess. She was so beautiful.

Chapter Fifteen

The Last Act

The Sheridan's three-act production of *Edward II* was playing to a full house. Guillam and Mendel sat in adjacent seats at the extreme end of the circle, which formed a wide U facing the stage. The left-hand end of the circle afforded a view of the rear stalls, which were otherwise concealed. An empty seat separated Guillam from a party of young students buzzing with anticipation.

They looked down thoughtfully on a restless sea of bobbing heads and fluttering programmes, stirring in sudden waves as later arrivals took their places. The scene reminded Guillam of an Oriental dance, where the tiny gestures of hand and foot animate a motionless body. Occasionally he would glance towards the rear stalls, but there was still no sign of Elsa Fennan or her guest.

Just as the recorded overture was ending he looked again briefly towards the two empty stalls in the back row and his heart gave a sudden leap as he saw the slight figure of Elsa Fennan sitting straight and motionless, staring fixedly down the auditorium like a child learning deportment. The seat on her right, nearest the gangway, was still empty.

Outside in the street taxis were drawing up hastily at the theatre entrance and an agreeable selection of the established and the disestablished hurriedly over-tipped their cabmen and spent five minutes looking for their tickets. Smiley's taxi took him past the theatre and deposited him at the Clarendon Hotel, where he went straight downstairs to the dining-room and bar.

'I'm expecting a call any moment,' he said. 'My name's Savage. You'll let me know, won't you?'

The barman turned to the telephone behind him and spoke to the receptionist.

'And a small whisky and soda, please; will you have one yourself?'

'Thank you sir, I never touch it.'

The curtain rose on a dimly lit stage and Guillam, peering towards the back of the auditorium, tried at first without success to penetrate the sudden darkness. Gradually his eyes accustomed themselves to the faint glow cast by the emergency lamps, until he could just discern Elsa in the half light; and still the empty seat beside her.

Only a low partition separated the rear stalls from the gangway which ran along the back of the auditorium, and behind it were several doors leading to the foyer, bar, and cloakrooms. For a brief moment one of these opened and an oblique shaft of light was cast as if by design upon Elsa Fennan, illuminating with a thin line one side of her face, making its hollows black by contrast. She inclined her head slightly, as if listening to something behind her, half rose in her seat, then sat down again, deceived, and resumed her former attitude.

Guillam felt Mendel's hand on his arm, turned, and saw his lean face thrust forward, looking past him. Following Mendel's gaze, he peered down into the well of the theatre, where a tall figure was slowly making his way towards the back of the stalls; he was an impressive sight, erect and handsome, a lock of black hair tumbling over his brow. It was he whom Mendel watched with such fascination, this elegant giant limping up the gangway. There was something different about him, something arresting and disturbing. Through his glasses Guillam watched his slow and deliberate progress, admired the grace and measure of his uneven walk. He was a man apart, a man you remember, a man who strikes a chord deep in your experience, a man with the gift of universal familiarity: to Guillam he was a living component of all our romantic dreams, he stood at the mast with Conrad, sought the lost Greece with Byron, and with Goethe visited the shades of classical and medieval hells.

As he walked, thrusting his good leg forward, there was a defiance, a command, that could not go unheeded. Guillam noticed how heads turned in the audience, and eyes followed him obediently.

Pushing past Mendel, Guillam stepped quickly through the emergency exit into the corridor behind. He followed the corridor down some steps and arrived at last at the foyer. The box office had closed down, but the girl was still poring hopelessly over a page of laboriously compiled figures, covered with alterations and erasures.

'Excuse me,' said Guillam; 'but I must use your telephone—it's urgent, do you mind?'

'Ssh!' She waved her pencil at him impatiently, without looking up. Her hair was mousy, her oily skin glistened from the fatigue of late nights and a diet of chipped potatoes. Guillam waited a moment, wondering how long it would be before she found a solution to that tangle of spidery numerals which would match the pile of notes and silver in the open cash box beside her.

'Listen,' he urged; 'I'm a police officer—there's a couple of heroes upstairs who are after your cash. Now will you let me use that telephone?'

'Oh Lord,' she said in a tired voice, and looked at him for the first time. She wore glasses and was very plain. She was neither alarmed nor impressed. 'I wish they'd perishing well take the money. It sends me up the wall.' Pushing her accounts to one side she opened a door beside the little kiosk and Guillam squeezed in.

'Hardly decent, is it?' the girl said with a grin. Her voice was nearly cultured—probably a London undergraduate earning pin-money, thought Guillam. He rang the Clarendon and asked for Mr Savage. Almost immediately he heard Smiley's voice.

'He's here,' said Guillam, 'been here all the time. Must have bought an extra ticket; he was sitting in the front stalls. Mendel suddenly spotted him limping up the aisle.'

'Limping?'

'Yes, it's not Mundt. It's the other one, Dieter.'

Smiley did not reply and after a moment Guillam said: 'George—are you there?'

'We've had it I'm afraid, Peter. We've got nothing against Frey. Call the men off, they won't find Mundt tonight. Is the first act over yet?'

'Must be just coming up for the interval.'

'I'll be round in twenty minutes. Hang on to Elsa like grim death—if they leave and separate Mendel's to stick to Dieter. You stay in the foyer for the last act in case they leave early.'

Guillam replaced the receiver and turned to the girl. 'Thanks,' he said, and put four pennies on her desk. She hastily gathered them together and pressed them firmly into his hand.

'For God's sake,' she said, 'don't add to my troubles.'

He went outside into the street and spoke to a plain clothes man loitering on the pavement. Then he hurried back and rejoined Mendel as the curtain fell on the first act.

Elsa and Dieter were sitting side by side. They were talking happily together, Dieter laughing, Elsa animated and articulate like a puppet brought to life by her master. Mendel watched them in fascination. She laughed at someting Dieter said, leant forward and put her hand on his arm. He saw her thin fingers against his dinner jacket, saw Dieter incline his head and whisper something to her, so that she laughed again. As Mendel watched, the theatre lights dimmed and the noise of conversation subsided as the audience quickly prepared for the second act.

Smiley left the Clarendon and walked slowly along the pavement towards the theatre. Thinking about it now, he realized that it was logical enough that Dieter should come, that it would have been madness to send Mundt. He wondered how long it could be before Elsa and Dieter discovered that it was not Dieter who had summoned her, not Dieter who had sent the postcard by a trusted courier. That, he reflected, should be an interesting moment. All he prayed for now was the opportunity of one more interview with Elsa Fennan.

A few minutes later he slipped quietly into the empty seat beside Guillam. It was a long time since he had seen Dieter.

He had not changed. He was the same improbable romantic with the magic of a charlatan; the same unforgettable figure which had struggled over the ruins of Germany, implacable of purpose, satanic in fulfilment, dark and swift like the Gods of the North. Smiley had lied to them that night in his club; Dieter *was* out of proportion, his cunning, his conceit, his strength and his dream—all were larger than life, undiminished by the moderating influence of experience. He was a man who thought and acted in absolute terms, without patience or compromise.

Memories returned to Smiley that night as he sat in the dark theatre and watched Dieter across a mass of motionless faces, memories of dangers shared, of mutual trust when each had held in his hand the life of the other . . . Just for a second Smiley wondered whether Dieter had seen him, had the feeling that Dieter's eyes were upon him, watching him in the dim half light.

Smiley got up as the second half drew to a close; as the curtain fell he made quickly for the side exit and waited discreetly in the corridor until the bell rang for the last act. Mendel joined him shortly before the end of the interval, and Guillam slipped past them to take up his post in the foyer.

'There's trouble,' Mendel said. 'They're arguing. She looks frightened. She keeps on saying something and he just shakes his head. She's panicking I think, and Dieter looks worried. He's started looking round the theatre as if he was trapped, getting the measure of the place, making plans. He glanced up to where you'd been sitting.'

'He won't let her leave alone,' said Smiley. 'He'll wait and get out with the crowd. They won't leave before the end. He probably reckons he's surrounded: he'll bargain on flustering us by parting from her suddenly in the middle of a crowd—just losing her.'

'What's our game? Why can't we go down there and get them?'

'We just wait; I don't know what for. We've no proof. No proof of murder and none of espionage until Maston decides to do something. But remember this: Dieter doesn't know that. If Elsa's jumpy and Dieter's worried, they'll do *something*—that's certain. So long as *they* think the game is up, we've a chance. Let them bolt, panic, anything. So long as they do something. . . .'

It was dark in the theatre again, but out of the corner of his eye Smiley saw Dieter leaning over Elsa whispering to her. His left hand held her arm, his whole attitude was one of urgent persuasion and reassurance.

The play dragged on, the shouts of soldiers and the screams of the demented king filled the theatre, until the dreadful climax of his foul death, when an audible sigh rose from the stalls beneath them. Dieter had his arm round Elsa's shoulders now, he had gathered the folds of her thin wrap about her neck and protected her as if she were a sleeping child. They remained like this until the final curtain. Neither applauded, Dieter looked about for Elsa's handbag, said something reassuring to her and put it on her lap. She nodded very slightly. A warning roll of the drums brought the audience to its feet for the national anthem—Smiley rose instinctively and noticed to his surprise that Mendel had vanished. Dieter slowly stood up and as he did so Smiley realized that something had happened. Elsa was still sitting and though Dieter gently prevailed on her to rise, she made no answering sign. There was something oddly dislocated in the way she sat, in the way her head lolled forward on her shoulders . . .

The last line of the anthem was beginning as Smiley rushed to the door, ran down the corridor, down the stone stairs to the foyer. He was just too late—he was met by the first crowd of anxious theatre-goers hastening towards the street in search of taxis. He looked wildly among the crowd for Dieter and knew it was hopeless—that Dieter had done what he himself would have done, had chosen one of the dozen emergency exits which led to the street and safety. He pushed his bulky frame gradually through the middle of the crowd towards the entrance to the stalls. As he twisted this way and that, forcing himself between oncoming bodies, he caught sight of Guillam at the edge of the stream searching hopelessly for Dieter and Elsa. He shouted to him, and Guillam turned quickly.

Struggling on, Smiley at last found himself against the low partition and he could see Elsa Fennan sitting motionless as all around her men stood up and women felt for their coats and handbags. Then he heard the scream. It was sudden, short and utterly expressive of horror and disgust. A girl was standing in the gangway looking at Elsa. She was young and very pretty, the fingers of her right hand were raised to her mouth, her face was deathly white. Her father, a tall cadaverous man, stood behind her. He grasped her shoulders quickly and drew her back as he caught sight of the dreadful thing before him.

Elsa's wrap had slipped from her shoulders and her head was lolling on to her chest.

Smiley had been right. 'Let them bolt, panic, anything . . . so long as they do *something* . . .' And this was what they had done: this broken, wretched body was witness to their panic.

'You'd better get the police, Peter. I'm going home. Keep me out of it, if you can. You know where to find me.' He nodded, as if to himself; 'I'm going home.'

It was foggy, and a fine rain was falling as Mendel quickly darted across the Fulham Palace Road in pursuit of Dieter. The headlights of cars came suddenly out of the wet mist twenty yards from him; the noise of traffic was high-pitched and nervous as it groped its uncertain way.

He had no choice but to keep close on Dieter's heels, never more than a dozen paces behind him. The pubs and cinemas had closed but the coffee bars and dance halls still attracted noisy groups crowding the pavements. As Dieter limped ahead of him Mendel staged his progression by the street lamps, watching his silhouette suddenly clarify each time it entered the next cone of light.

Dieter was walking swiftly despite his limp. As his stride lengthened his limp became more pronounced, so that he seemed to swing his left leg forward by a sudden effort of his broad shoulders.

There was a curious expression on Mendel's face, not of hatred or iron purpose but of frank distaste. To Mendel, the frills of Dieter's profession meant nothing. He saw in his quarry only the squalor of a criminal, the cowardice of a man who paid others to do his killing. When Dieter had gently disengaged himself from the audience and moved towards the side exit, Mendel saw what he had been waiting for: the stealthy act of a common criminal. It was something he expected and understood. To Mendel there was only one criminal class, from pickpocket and sneak-thief to the big operator tampering with company law; they were outside the law and it was his distasteful but necessary vocation to remove them to safe keeping. This one happened to be German.

The fog grew thick and yellow. Neither of them wore a coat. Mendel wondered what Mrs Fennan would do now. Guillam would take care of her. She hadn't even looked at Dieter when he slinked off. She was an odd one that, all skin and bones and good works by the look of her. Lived on dry toast and Bovril.

Dieter turned abruptly down a side street to the right then another to the left. They had been walking for nearly an hour and he showed no sign of slowing down. The street seemed empty: certainly Mendel could hear no other footsteps but their own, crisp and short, the echo corrupted by the fog. They were in a narrow street of Victorian houses with hastily contrived Regency-style façades, heavy porches and sash windows. Mendel guessed they were somewhere near Fulham Broadway, perhaps beyond it, nearer the King's Road. Still Dieter's pace did not flag, still the crooked shadow thrust forward into the fog, confident of its path, urgent in its purpose.

As they approached a main road Mendel heard again the plaintive whine of traffic, brought almost to a standstill by the fog. Then from somewhere above them a yellow street light shed a pale glow, its outline clearly drawn like the aura of a winter sun. Dieter hesitated a moment on the kerb, then chancing the ghostly traffic that nosed its way past them from nowhere, he crossed the road and plunged at once into one of the innumerable side streets that led, Mendel was certain, towards the river.

Mendel's clothes were soaking wet, and the thin rain ran over his face. They must be near the river now; he thought he could detect the smell of tar and coke, feel the insidious cold of the black water. Just for a moment he thought Dieter had vanished. He moved forward quickly, nearly tripped on a kerb, went forward again and saw the railings of the embankment in front of him. Steps led upwards to an iron gate in the railings and this was slightly open. He stood at the gate and peered beyond, down into the water. There was a stout wooden gangway and Mendel heard the uneven echo as Dieter, hidden by the fog, followed his strange course to the water's edge. Mendel waited, then, wary and silent, he made his way down the gangway. It was a permanent affair with heavy pine handrails on either side. Mendel reckoned it had been there some time. The low end of the gangway was joined to a long raft made of duckboard and oil-drums. Three dilapidated houseboats loomed in the fog, rocking gently on their moorings.

Noiselessly Mendel crept on to the raft, examining each of the houseboats in turn. Two were close together, connected by a plank. The third was moored some fifteen feet away, and a light was burning in her forward cabin. Mendel returned to the embankment, closing the iron gate carefully behind him.

He walked slowly down the road, still uncertain of his bearings. After about five minutes the pavement took him suddenly to the right and the ground rose gradually. He guessed he was on a bridge. He lit his cigarette lighter, and its long flame cast a glow over the stone wall on his right. He moved the lighter back and forth, and finally came upon a wet and dirty metal plate bearing the words 'Battersea Bridge.' He made his way back to the iron gate and stood for a moment, orientating himself in the light of his knowledge.

Somewhere above him and to his right the four massive chimneys of Fulham Power Station stood hidden in the fog. To his left was

Cheyne Walk with its row of smart little boats reaching to Battersea Bridge. The place where he now stood marked the dividing line between the smart and the squalid, where Cheyne Walk meets Lots Road, one of the ugliest streets in London. The southern side of this road consists of vast warehouses, wharves, and mills, and the northern side presents an unbroken line of dingy houses typical of the side streets of Fulham.

It was in the shadow of the four chimneys, perhaps sixty feet from the Cheyne Walk mooring, that Dieter Frey had found a sanctuary. Yes, Mendel knew the spot well. It was only a couple of hundred yards up river from where the earthly remains of Mr Adam Scarr had been recovered from the unyielding arms of the Thames.

Chapter Sixteen

Echoes in the Fog

It was long after midnight when Smiley's telephone rang. He got up from the armchair in front of the gas fire and plodded upstairs to his bedroom, his right hand gripping the banisters tightly as he went. It was Peter, no doubt, or the police, and he would have to make a statement. Or even the Press. The murder had taken place just in time to catch today's papers and mercifully too late for last night's news broadcast. What would this be? 'Maniac killer in theatre'? 'Death-lock murder—woman named'? He hated the Press as he hated advertising and television, he hated mass-media, the relentless persuasion of the twentieth century. Everything he admired or loved had been the product of intense individualism. That was why he hated Dieter now, hated what he stood for more strongly than ever before: it was the fabulous impertinence of renouncing the individual in favour of the mass. When had mass philosophies ever brought benefit or wisdom? Dieter cared nothing for human life: dreamed only of armies of faceless men bound by their lowest common denominators; he wanted to shape the world as if it were a tree, cutting off what did not fit the regular image; for this he fashioned blank, soulless automatons like Mundt. Mundt was faceless like Dieter's army, a trained killer born of the finest killer breed.

He picked up the telephone and gave his number. It was Mendel.

'Where are you?'

'Near Chelsea Embankment. Pub called the Balloon, in Lots Road. Landlord's a chum of mine. I knocked him up . . . Listen,

Elsa's boy friend is lying up in a houseboat by Chelsea flour mill. Bloody miracle in the fog, he is. Must have found his way by Braille.'

'*Who?*'

'Her boy friend, her escort at the theatre. Wake up, Mr Smiley; what's eating you?'

'You followed Dieter?'

'Of course I did. That was what you told Mr Guillam, wasn't it? He was to stick to the woman and me the man . . . How did Mr Guillam get on by the way? Where did Elsa get to?'

'She didn't get anywhere. She was dead when Dieter left. Mendel, are you there? Look, for God's sake, how do I find you? Where is this place, will the police know it?'

'They'll know. Tell them he's in a converted landing craft called "Sunset Haven". She's lying against the eastern side of Sennen Wharf, between the flour mills and Fulham Power Station. They'll know . . . but the fog's thick, mind, very thick.'

'Where can I meet you?'

'Cut straight down to the river. I'll meet you where Battersea Bridge joins the north bank.'

'I'll come at once, as soon as I've rung Guillam.'

He had a gun somewhere, and for a moment he thought of looking for it. Then, somehow, it seemed pointless. Besides, he reflected grimly, there'd be the most frightful row if he used it. He rang Guillam at his flat and gave him Mendel's message: 'And Peter, they must cover all ports and airfields; order a special watch on river traffic and seabound craft. They'll know the form.'

He put on an old mackintosh and a pair of thick leather gloves and slipped quickly out into the fog.

Mendel was waiting for him by the bridge. They nodded to one another and Mendel led him quickly along the embankment, keeping close to the river wall to avoid the trees that grew along the road. Suddenly Mendel stopped, seizing Smiley by the arm in warning. They stood motionless, listening. Then Smiley heard it too, the hollow ring of footsteps on a wooden floor, irregular like the footsteps of a limping man. They heard the creak of an iron gate, the clang as it was closed, then the footsteps again, firm now upon the pavement, growing louder, coming towards them. Neither moved. Louder, nearer, then they faltered, stopped. Smiley held his breath, trying desperately at the same time to see an extra yard into the fog, to glimpse at the waiting figure he knew was there.

Then suddenly he came, rushing like a massive wild beast, bursting through them, knocking them apart like children and running on, lost again, the uneven echo fading in the distance. They turned and chased after him, Mendel in front and Smiley following as best he could, the image vivid in his mind of Dieter, gun in hand, bursting on them out of the night fog. Ahead, the shadow of Mendel turned abruptly to the right, and Smiley followed blindly. Then suddenly the rhythm had changed to the scuffle of fighting. Smiley ran forward, heard the unmistakable sound of a heavy weapon striking a human skull, and then he was upon them: saw Mendel on the ground, and Dieter stooping over him, raising his arm to hit him again with the heavy butt of an automatic pistol.

Smiley was out of breath. His chest was burning from the bitter, rank fog, his mouth hot and dry, filled with a taste like blood. Somehow he summoned breath, and he shouted desperately:

'Dieter!'

Frey looked at him, nodded and said:

'*Servus*, George,' and hit Mendel a hard, brutal blow with the pistol. He got up slowly, holding the pistol downwards and using both hands to cock it.

Smiley ran at him blindly, forgetting what little skill he had ever possessed, swinging with his short arms, striking with his open hands. His head was against Dieter's chest and he pushed forward, punching Dieter's back and sides. He was mad and, discovering in himself the energy of madness, pressed Dieter back still further towards the railing of the bridge while Dieter, off balance and hindered by his weak leg, gave way. Smiley knew Dieter was hitting him, but the decisive blow never came. He was shouting at Dieter; 'Swine, swine!' and as Dieter receded still further Smiley found his arms free and once more struck at his face with clumsy, childish blows. Dieter was leaning back and Smiley saw the clean curve of his throat and chin, as with all this strength he thrust his open hand upwards. His fingers closed over Dieter's jaw and mouth and he pushed further and further. Dieter's hands were at Smiley's throat, then suddenly they were clutching at his collar to save himself as he sank slowly backwards. Smiley beat frantically at his arms, and then he was held no more and Dieter was falling, falling into the swirling fog beneath the bridge, and there was silence. No shout, no splash. He was gone; offered like a human sacrifice to the London fog and the foul black river lying beneath it.

Smiley leant over the bridge, his head throbbing wildly, blood pouring from his nose, the fingers of his right hand feeling broken and useless. His gloves were gone. He looked down into the fog and could see nothing.

'Dieter!' he cried in anguish; 'Dieter!'

He shouted again, but his voice choked and tears sprang to his eyes. 'Oh dear God what have I done, Oh Christ, Dieter, why didn't you stop me, why didn't you hit me with the gun, why didn't you shoot?' He pressed his clenched hands to his face, tasting the salt blood in the palms mixed with the salt of his tears. He leant against the parapet and cried like a child. Somewhere beneath him a cripple dragged himself through the filthy water, lost and exhausted, yielding at last to the stenching blackness till it held him and drew him down.

He woke to find Peter Guillam sitting on the end of his bed pouring out tea.

'Ah, George. Welcome home. It's two in the afternoon.'

'And this morning—'

'This morning, dear boy, you were carolling on Battersea Bridge with Comrade Mendel.'

'How is he . . . Mendel, I mean?'

'Suitably ashamed of himself. Recovering fast.'

'And Dieter—'

'Dead.'

Guillam handed him a cup of tea and some ratafia biscuits from Fortnum's.

'How long have you been here, Peter?'

'Well, we came here in a series of tactical bounds, as it were. The first was to Chelsea Hospital where they licked your wounds and gave you a fairly substantial tranquillizer. Then we came back here and I put you to bed. That was disgusting. Then I did a spot of telephoning and, so to speak, went round with a pointed stick tidying up the mess. I looked in on you now and again. Cupid and Psyche. You were either snoring like a saddleback or reciting Webster.'

'God.'

'Duchess of Malfi, I think it was. "I bade thee, when I was distracted of my wits, go kill my dearest friend, and thou hast done it!" Dreadful nonsense, George, I'm afraid.'

'How did the police find us—Mendel and me?'

'George, you may not know it but you were bellowing pejoratives at Dieter as if—'

'Yes, of course. You heard.'

'We heard.'

'What about Maston? What does Maston say about all this?'

'I think he wants to see you. I have a message from him asking you to drop in as soon as you feel well enough. I don't know what he thinks about it. Nothing at all, I should imagine.'

'What do you mean?'

Guillam poured out more tea.

'Use your loaf, George. All three principals in this little fairy tale have now been eaten by bears. No secret information has been compromised for the last six months. Do you really think Maston wants to dwell on the details? Do you really think he is bursting to tell the Foreign Office the good tidings—and admit that we only catch spies when we trip over their dead bodies?'

The front-door bell rang and Guillam went downstairs to answer it. In some alarm Smiley heard him admit the visitor to the hall, then the subdued sound of voices, footsteps coming up the stairs. There was a knock on the door and Maston came in. He was carrying an absurdly large bunch of flowers and looked as though he had just been to a garden party. Smiley remembered it was Friday: no doubt he was going to Henley this week-end. He was grinning. He must have been grinning all the way up the stairs.

'Well, George, in the wars again!'

'Yes, I'm afraid so. Another accident.'

He sat on the edge of the bed, leaning across it, one arm supporting him the other side of Smiley's legs.

There was a pause and then he said:

'You got my note, George?'

'Yes.'

Another pause.

'There has been talk of a new section in the Department, George. We (your Department, that is) feel we should devote more energy to technique research, with particular application to satellite espionage. That is also the Home Office view, I'm pleased to say. Guillam has agreed to advise on terms of reference. I wondered if you'd take it on for us. Running it. I mean, with the necessary promotion of course and the option of extending your service after the statutory retirement age. Our personnel people are right behind me on this.'

'Thank you . . . perhaps I could think about it, may I?'

'Of course . . . of course,' Maston looked slightly put out. 'When will you let me know? It may be necessary to take on some new men and the question of space arises . . . Have the week-end to think about it will you and let me know on Monday. The Secretary was quite willing for you to—'

'Yes, I'll let you know. It's very good of you.'

'Not at all. Besides I am only the Adviser you know, George. This is really an internal decision. I'm just the bringer of good news. George; my usual function of errand boy.'

Maston looked at Smiley hard for a moment, hesitated and then said: 'I've put the Ministers in the picture . . . as far as is necessary. We discussed what action should be taken. The Home Secretary was also present.'

'When was this?'

'This morning. Some very grave issues were raised. We considered a protest to the East Germans and an extradition order for this man Mundt.'

'But we don't recognize East Germany.'

'Precisely. That was the difficulty. It is however possible to lodge a protest with an intermediary.'

'Such as Russia?'

'Such as Russia. In the event, however, certain factors militated against this. It was felt that publicity, whatever form it took, would ultimately rebound against the nation's interests. There is already considerable popular hostility in this country to the rearmament of Western Germany. It was felt that any evidence of German intrigue in Britain—whether inspired by the Russians or not—might encourage this hostility. There is, you see, no positive evidence that Frey was operating for the Russians. It might well be represented to the public that he was operating on his own account or on behalf of a united Germany.'

'I see.'

'So far very few people indeed are aware of the facts at all. That is most fortunate. On behalf of the police the Home Secretary has tentatively agreed that they will do their part in playing the affair down as far as possible . . . Now this man Mendel, what's he like? Is he trustworthy?'

Smiley hated Maston for that.

'Yes,' he said.

Maston got up. 'Good,' he said, 'good. Well, I must get along. Anything you want at all, anything I can do?'

'No, thank you. Guillam is looking after me admirably.'

Maston reached the door. 'Well good luck, George. Take the job if you can.' He said this quickly in a subdued voice with a pretty, sidelong smile as if it meant rather a lot to him.

'Thank you for the flowers,' said Smiley.

Dieter was dead, and he had killed him. The broken fingers of his right hand, the stiffness of his body and the sickening headache, the nausea of guilt, all testified to this. And Dieter had let him do it, had not fired the gun, had remembered their friendship when Smiley had not. They had fought in a cloud, in the rising stream of the river, in a clearing in a timeless forest: they had met, two friends rejoined, and fought like beasts. Dieter had remembered and Smiley had not. They had come from different hemispheres of the night, from different worlds of thought and conduct. Dieter, mercurial, absolute, had fought to build a civilization. Smiley, rationalistic, protective, had fought to prevent him. 'Oh God,' said Smiley aloud, 'who was then the gentleman . . . ?'

Laboriously he got out of bed and began to dress. He felt better standing up.

Chapter Seventeen

Dear Adviser

Dear Adviser,

I am at last able to reply to Personnel's offer of a higher appointment in the Department. I am sorry that I have taken so long to do this, but as you know, I have not been well recently, and have also had to contend with a number of personal problems outside the scope of the Department.

As I am not entirely free of my indisposition, I feel it would be unwise for me to accept their offer. Kindly convey this decision to Personnel.

I am sure you will understand.

> Yours
> George Smiley

Dear Peter,

I enclose a note on the Fennan Case. This is the only copy. Please pass it to Maston when you have read it. I thought it would be valuable to record the events—even if they did not take place.

> Ever,
> George

The Fennan Case

On Monday, 2 January, I interviewed Samuel Arthur Fennan, a senior member of the Foreign Office, in order to clarify certain allegations made against him in an anonymous letter. The interview was arranged in accordance with the customary procedure, that is to say with the consent of the FO. We knew of nothing adverse to Fennan beyond communist sympathy while at Oxford in the thirties, to which little significance was attached. The interview was therefore in a sense a strictly routine affair.

Fennan's room at the Foreign Office was found to be unsuitable and we agreed to continue our discussion in St James's Park, availing ourselves of the good weather.

It has subsequently transpired that we were recognized and observed in this by an agent of the East German Intelligence Service, who had cooperated with me during the war. It is not certain whether he had placed Fennan under some kind of surveillance, or whether his presence in the park was coincidental.

On the night of 3 January it was reported by Surrey police that Fennan had committed suicide. A typewritten suicide note signed by Fennan claimed that he had been victimized by the security authorities.

The following facts, however, emerged during investigation, and suggested foul play:

1. At 7.55 p.m. on the night of his death Fennan had asked the Walliston exchange to call him at 8.30 the following morning.

2. Fennan had made himself a cup of cocoa shortly before his death, and had not drunk it.

3. He had supposedly shot himself in the hall, at the bottom of the stairs. The note was beside the body.

4. It seemed inconsistent that he should type his last letter, as he seldom used a typewriter, and even more remarkable that he should come downstairs to the hall to shoot himself.

5. On the day of his death he posted a letter inviting me in urgent terms to lunch with him at Marlow the following day.

6. Later it also transpired that Fennan had requested a day's leave for Wednesday, 4 January. He did not apparently mention this to his wife.

7. It was also noted that the suicide letter had been typed on Fennan's own machine—and that it contained certain peculiarities in the typescript similar to those in the anonymous letter. The laboratory report concluded, however, that the two letters had not been typed by the same hand, though originating from the same machine.

Mrs Fennan, who had been to the theatre on the night her husband died, was invited to explain the 8.30 call from the exchange and falsely claimed to have requested it herself. The exchange was positive that this was not the case. Mrs Fennan claimed that her husband had been nervous and depressed since his security interview, which corroborated the evidence of his final letter.

On the afternoon of 4 January, having left Mrs Fennan earlier in the day, I returned to my house in Kensington. Briefly observing somebody at the window, I rang the front-door bell. A man opened the door who has since been identified as a member of the East German Intelligence Service. He invited me into the house but I declined his offer and returned to my car, noting at the same time the numbers of cars parked nearby.

That evening I visited a small garage in Battersea to inquire into the origin of one of these cars which was registered in the name of the proprietor of the garage. I was attacked by an unknown assailant and beaten senseless. Three weeks later the proprietor himself, Adam Scarr, was found dead in the Thames near Battersea Bridge. He had been drunk at the time of drowning. There were no signs of violence and he was known as a heavy drinker.

It is relevant that Scarr had for the last four years provided an anonymous foreigner with the use of a car, and had received generous rewards for doing so. Their arrangements were designed to conceal the identity of the borrower even from Scarr himself, who only knew his client by the nickname 'Blondie' and could only reach him through a telephone number. The telephone number is of importance: it was that of the East German Steel Mission.

Meanwhile, Mrs Fennan's alibi for the evening of the murder had been investigated and significant information came to light:

1. Mrs Fennan attend the Weybridge Repertory Theatre twice a month, on the first and third Tuesdays. (N.B. Adam Scarr's client had collected his car on the first and third Tuesdays of each month.)

2. She always brought a music case and left it in the cloakroom.

3. When visiting the theatre she was always joined by a man whose description corresponded with that of my assailant and Scarr's client. It was even mistakenly assumed by a member of the theatre staff that this man was Mrs Fennan's husband. He too brought a music case and left it in the cloakroom.

4. On the evening of the murder Mrs Fennan had left the theatre early after her friend had failed to arrive and had forgotten to reclaim her music case. Late that night she telephoned the theatre to ask if the case could be called for at once. She had lost her cloakroom ticket. The case was collected–by Mrs Fennan's usual friend.

At this point the stranger was identified as an employee of the East German Steel Mission named Mundt. The principal of the Mission was Herr Dieter Frey, a war-time collaborator of our Service, with extensive operational experience. After the war he had entered Government service in the Soviet zone of Germany. I should mention that Frey had operated with me during the war in enemy territory and had shown himself to be a brilliant and resourceful agent.

I now decided to conduct a third interview with Mrs Fennan. She broke down and confessed to having acted as an intelligence courier for her husband, who had been recruited by Frey on a skiing holiday five years ago. She herself had cooperated unwillingly, partly in loyalty to her husband and partly to protect him from his own carelessness in performing his espionage role. Frey had seen Fennan talking to me in the park. Assuming I was still operationally employed, he had concluded that Fennan was either under suspicion or a double agent. He instructed Mundt to liquidate Fennan, and his wife had been compelled into silence by her own complicity. She had even typed the text of the suicide letter on Fennan's typewriter over a specimen of her husband's signature.

The means whereby she passed to Mundt the intelligence pro-cured by her husband is relevant. She placed notes and copied documents in a music case, which she took to the theatre. Mundt brought a similar case containing money and instructions and, like Mrs Fennan, left it in the cloakroom. They had only to exchange cloakroom tickets. When Mundt failed to appear at the theatre on the night in question, Mrs Fennan obeyed standing instructions and posted the ticket to an address in Highgate. She left the theatre in order to catch the last post from Weybridge. When later that night Mundt demanded the music case she told him what she had done. Mundt insisted on collecting the case that night, for he did not wish to make another journey to Weybridge.

When I interviewed Mrs Fennan the following morning, one of my questions (about the 8.30 call) alarmed her so much that she telephoned Mundt. This accounts for the assault upon me later that day.

Mrs Fennan provided me with the address and telephone number she used when contacting Mundt–whom she knew by the cover name of Freitag. Both led to the apartment of a 'Lufteuropa' pilot who often entertained Mundt and provided accommodation for him when he required it. The pilot (presumably a courier of the East German Intelligence Service) has not returned to this country since 5 January.

This, then, was the sum of Mrs Fennan's revelations, and in a sense they led nowhere. The spy was dead, his murderers had vanished. It only remained to assess the extent of the damage. An official approach was now made to the Foreign Office and Mr Felix Taverner was instructed to calculate from Foreign Office schedules what information had been compromised. This involved listing all files to which Fennan had had access since his recruitment by Frey. Remarkably, this revealed no systematic acquisition of secret files. Fennan had drawn no secret files except those which directly concerned him in his duties. During the last six months, when his access to sensitive papers was substantially increased, he had actually taken home *no* files of secret classification. The files he took home over this period were of universally low grade, and some treated subjects actually outside the scope of his section. This was not consistent with Fennan's role as a spy. It was, however, possible that he had lost heart for his work, and that his luncheon invitation to me was a first step to confession. With this in mind he might also have written the anonymous letter which could have been designed to put him in touch with the Department.

Two further facts should be mentioned at this point. Under an assumed name and with a fake passport, Mundt left the country by air on the day after Mrs Fennan made her confession. He evaded the notice of the airport authorities, but was retrospectively identified by the air hostess. Secondly, Fennan's diary contained the full name and official telephone number of Dieter Frey–a flagrant breach of the most elementary rule of espionage.

It was hard to understand why Mundt had waited three weeks in England after murdering Scarr, and even harder to reconcile Fennan's activities as described by his wife with the obviously unplanned and unproductive selection of files. Re-examination of the facts led repeatedly to this conclusion: the only evidence that Fennan was a spy came from his wife. If the facts were as she described them, why had she been allowed to survive the determination of Mundt and Frey to eliminate those in possession of dangerous knowledge?

On the other hand, might she not herself be the spy?

This would explain the date of Mundt's departure: he left as soon as he had been reassured by Mrs Fennan that I had accepted her ingenious confession. It would explain the entry in Fennan's diary: Frey was a chance skiing acquaintance and an occasional visitor to Walliston. It would make sense of Fennan's choice of files—if Fennan deliberately chose unclassified papers at a time when his work was mainly secret there could be only one explanation: he had come to suspect his wife. Hence the invitation to Marlow, following naturally upon our encounter the previous day. Fennan had decided to tell me of his apprehensions and had taken a day's leave to do so—a fact of which his wife was not apparently aware. This would also explain why Fennan denounced himself in an anonymous letter: he wished to put himself in touch with us *as a preliminary to denouncing his wife*.

Continuing the supposition it was remarkable that in matters of tradecraft Mrs Fennan alone was efficient and conscientious. The technique used by herself and Mundt recalled that of Frey during the war. The secondary arrangement to post the cloakroom ticket if no meeting took place was typical of his scrupulous planning. Mrs Fennan, it seemed, had acted with a precision scarcely compatible with her claim to be an unwilling party to her husband's treachery.

While logically Mrs Fennan now came under suspicion as a spy, there was no reason to believe that her account of what happened on the night of Fennan's murder was necessarily untrue. Had she known of Mundt's intention to murder her husband she would not have taken the music case to the theatre, and would not have posted the cloakroom ticket.

There seemed no way of proving the case against her unless it was possible to reactivate the relationship between Mrs Fennan and her controller. During the war Frey had devised an ingenious code for emergency communication by the use of snapshots and picture postcards. The actual subject of the photograph contained the message. A religious subject such as a painting of a Madonna or a church conveyed a request for an early meeting. The recipient would send in reply an entirely unrelated letter, making sure to date it. A meeting would take place at a prearranged time and place exactly five days after the date on the letter.

It was just possible that Frey, whose tradecraft had evidently altered so little since the war, might have clung to this system—which, after all, would only seldom be needed. Relying on this I therefore posted to Elsa Fennan a picture postcard depicting a church. The card was posted from Highgate. I hoped somewhat forlornly that she would assume it had come to her through the agency of Frey. She reacted at once by sending to an unknown address abroad a ticket for a London theatre performance five days ahead. Mrs Fennan's communication reached Frey, who accepted it as an *urgent summons*. Knowing that Mundt had been compromised by Mrs Fennan's 'confession' he decided to come himself.

They therefore met at the Sheridan Theatre, Hammersmith, on Tuesday, 15 February.

At first each assumed that the other had initiated the meeting, but when Frey realized they had been brought together by a deception he took drastic action. It may be that he suspected Mrs Fennan of luring him into a trap, that he realized he was under surveillance. We shall never know. In any event, he murdered her. His method of doing this is best described in the coroner's report at the inquest: 'a single degree of pressure had been applied on the larynx, in particular to the horns of the thyroid cartilage, causing almost immediate death. It would appear that Mrs Fennan's assailant was no layman in these matters.'

Frey was pursued to a houseboat moored near Cheyne Walk, and while violently resisting arrest he fell into the river, from which his body has now been recovered.

Chapter Eighteen

Between Two Worlds

Smiley's unrespectable club was usually empty on Sundays, but Mrs Sturgeon left the door unlocked in case any of her gentlemen chose to call in. She adopted the same stern, possessive attitude towards her gentlemen as she had done in her landlady days at Oxford, when she had commanded from her fortunate boarders more respect than the entire assembly of dons and proctors. She forgave everything, but somehow managed to suggest on each occasion that her forgiveness was unique, and would never, never happen again. She had once made Steed-Asprey put ten shillings in the poor box for bringing seven guests without warning, and afterwards provided the dinner of a lifetime.

They sat at the same table as before. Mendel looked a shade sallower, a shade older. He scarcely spoke during the meal, handling his knife and fork with the same careful precision which he applied to any task. Guillam supplied most of the conversation, for Smiley, too, was less talkative than usual. They were at ease in their companionship and no one felt unduly the need to speak.

'Why did she do it?' Mendel asked suddenly.

Smiley shook his head slowly: 'I think I know, but we can only guess. I think she dreamed of a world without conflict, ordered and preserved by the new doctrine. I once angered her, you see, and she shouted at me: "I'm the wandering Jewess," she said; "the no-man's land, the battlefield of your toy soldiers." As she saw the new Germany rebuilt in the image of the old, saw the plump pride return, as she put it, I think it was just too much for her; I think she looked at the futility of her suffering and the prosperity of her persecutors and rebelled. Five years ago, she told me, they met Dieter on a skiing holiday in Germany. By that time the re-establishment of Germany as a prominent western power was well under way.'

'Was she a communist?'

'I don't think she liked labels. I think she wanted to help build one society which could live without conflict. Peace is a dirty word now, isn't it? I think she wanted peace.'

'And Dieter?' asked Guillam.

'God knows what Dieter wanted. Honour, I think, and a socialist world.' Smiley shrugged. 'They dreamed of peace and freedom. Now they're murderers and spies.'

'Christ Almighty,' said Mendel.

Smiley was silent again, looking into his glass. At last he said: 'I can't expect you to understand. You only saw the end of Dieter. I saw the beginning. He went the full circle. I don't think he ever got over being a traitor in the war. He had to put it right. He was one of those world-builders who seem to do nothing but destroy: that's all.'

Guillam gracefully intervened: 'What about the 8.30 call?'

'I think it's pretty obvious. Fennan wanted to see me at Marlow and he'd taken a day's leave. He can't have told Elsa he was having a day off or she'd have tried to explain it away to me. He staged a phone call to give himself an excuse for going to Marlow. That's my guess, anyway.'

The fire crackled in the wide hearth.

He caught the midnight plane to Zurich. It was a beautiful night, and through the small window beside him he watched the grey wing, motionless against the starlit sky, a glimpse of eternity between two worlds. The vision soothed him, calmed his fears and his doubts, made him fatalistic towards the inscrutable purpose of the universe. It all seemed to matter to little—the pathetic quest for love, or the return to solitude.

Soon the lights of the French coast came in sight. As he watched, he began to sense vicariously the static life beneath him; the rank smell of Gauloises Bleues, garlic and good food, the raised voices in the bistro. Maston was a million miles off, locked away with his arid paper and his shiny politicians.

Smiley presented an odd figure to his fellow passengers—a little fat man, rather gloomy, suddenly smiling, ordering a drink. The young, fair-haired man beside him examined him closely out of the corner of his eye. He knew the type well—the tired executive out for a bit of fun. He found it rather disgusting.

A Murder
of Quality

John le Carré

A Murder of Quality

To Ann

There are probably a dozen great schools of
whom it will be confidently asserted that Carne is
their deliberate image. But he who looks among
their common rooms for the D'Arcys, Fieldings
and Hechts will search in vain.

JOHN LE CARRÉ

Chapter One

Black Candles

The greatness of Carne School has been ascribed by common consent to Edward VI, whose educational zeal is ascribed by history to the Duke of Somerset. But Carne prefers the respectability of the monarch to the questionable politics of his adviser, drawing strength from the conviction that Great Schools, like Tudor Kings, were ordained in Heaven.

And indeed its greatness is little short of miraculous. Founded by obscure monks, endowed by a sickly boy king, and dragged from oblivion by a Victorian bully, Carne had straightened its collar, scrubbed its rustic hands and face and presented itself shining to the courts of the twentieth century. And in the twinkling of an eye, the Dorset bumpkin was London's darling: Dick Whittington had arrived. Carne had parchments in Latin, seals in wax and Lammas Land behind the abbey. Carne had property, cloisters and wood-worm, a whipping block and a line in the Domesday Book—then what more did it need to instruct the sons of the rich?

And they came; each Half they came (for terms are not elegant things), so that throughout a whole afternoon the trains would unload sad groups of black-coated boys on to the station platform. They came in great cars that shone with mournful purity. They came to bury poor King Edward, trundling hardcarts over the cobbled streets or carrying tuck boxes like little coffins. Some wore gowns, and when they walked they looked like crows, or black angels come for the burying. Some followed singly like undertakers' mutes, and you could hear the clip of their boots as they went. They were always in mourning at Carne; the small boys because they must stay and the big boys because they must leave, the masters because mourning was respectable and the wives because respectability was underpaid; and now, as the Lent Half (as the Easter term was called) drew to its end, the cloud of gloom was as firmly settled as ever over the grey towers of Carne.

Gloom and the cold. The cold was crisp and sharp as flint. It cut the

faces of the boys as they moved slowly from the deserted playing
fields after the school match. It pierced their black topcoats and
turned their stiff, pointed collars into icy rings round their necks.
Frozen, they plodded from the field to the long walled road which led
to the main tuck shop and the town, the line gradually dwindling into
groups, and the groups into pairs. Two boys who looked even colder
than the rest crossed the road and made their way along a narrow
path which led towards a distant but less populated tuck shop.

'I think I shall die if ever I have to watch one of those beastly
rugger games again. The noise is fantastic,' said one. He was tall with
fair hair, and his name was Caley.

'People only shout because the dons are watching from the
pavilion,' the other rejoined; 'that's why each house has to stand
together. So that the house dons can swank about how loud their
houses shout.'

'What about Rode?' asked Caley. 'Why does he stand with us and
make us shout, then? He's not a house don, just a bloody usher.'

'He's sucking up to house dons all the time. You can see him in the
quad between lessons buzzing round the big men. All the junior
masters do.' Caley's companion was a cynical red-haired boy called
Perkins, Captain of Fielding's house.

'I've been to tea with Rode,' said Caley.

'Rode's hell. He wears brown boots. What was tea like?'

'Bleak. Funny how tea gives them away. Mrs Rode's quite decent,
though—homely in a plebby sort of way: doyleys and china birds.
Food's good: Women's Institute, but good.'

'Rode's doing Corps next Half. That'll put the lid on it. He's so
keen, bouncing about all the time. You can tell he's not a gentleman.
You know where he went to school?'

'No.'

'Branxome Grammar. Fielding told my Mama, when she came
over from Singapore last Half.'

'God. Where's Branxome?'

'On the coast. Near Bournemouth. I haven't been to tea with
anyone except Fielding,' Perkins added after a slight pause. 'You get
roast chestnuts and crumpets. You're never allowed to thank him,
you know. He says emotionalism is only for the lower classes. That's
typical of Fielding. He's not like a don at all. I think boys bore him.
The whole house goes to tea with him once a half, he has us in turn,
four at a time, and that's about the only time he talks to most men.'

They walked on in silence for a while until Perkins said:

'Fielding's giving another dinner party tonight.'

'He's pushing the boat out these days,' Caley replied, with
disapproval. 'Suppose the food in your house is worse than ever?'

'It's his last Half before he retires. He's entertaining every don and
all the wives separately by the end of the Half. Black candles every

evening. For mourning. Hells extravagant.'

'Yes. I suppose it's a sort of gesture.'

'My Pater says he's a queer.'

They crossed the road and disappeared into the tuck shop, where they continued to discuss the weighty affairs of Mr Terence Fielding, until Perkins drew their meeting reluctantly to a close. Being a poor hand at science, he was unfortunately obliged to take extra tuition in the subject.

The dinner party to which Perkins had alluded that afternoon was now drawing to a close. Mr Terence Fielding, senior housemaster of Carne, gave himself some more port and pushed the decanter wearily to his left. It was his port, the best he had. There was enough of the best to last the Half—and after that, be damned. He felt a little tired after watching the match, and a little drunk, and a little bored with Shane Hecht and her husband. Shane was so hideous. Massive and enveloping, like a faded Valkyrie. All that black hair. He should have asked someone else. The Snows for instance, but he was too clever. Or Felix D'Arcy, but D'Arcy interrupted. Ah well, a little later he would annoy Charles Hecht, and Hecht would get in a pet and leave early.

Hecht was fidgeting, wanting to light his pipe, but Fielding damn well wouldn't have it. Hecht could have a cigar if he wanted to smoke. But his pipe could stay in his dinner-jacket pocket, where it belonged, or didn't belong, and his athletic profile could remain unadorned.

'Cigar, Hecht?'

'No thanks, Fielding. I say, do you mind if I. . . .'

'I can recommend the cigars. Young Havelake sent them from Havana. His father's ambassador there, you know.'

'Yes, dear,' said Shane tolerantly; 'Vivian Havelake was in Charles' troop when Charles was commandant of the Cadets.'

'Good boy, Havelake,' Hecht observed, and pressed his lips together to show he was a strict judge.

'It's amusing how things have changed.' Shane Hecht said this rapidly with a rather wooden smile, as if it weren't really amusing. 'Such a grey world we live in, now.

'I remember before the war when Charles inspected the Corps on a white horse. We don't do that kind of thing now, do we? I've got nothing against Mr Iredale as commandant, nothing at all. What *was* his regiment, Terence, do you know? I'm sure he does it very nicely, whatever they do now in the Corps—he gets on so well with the boys, doesn't he? His wife's such a nice person. . . . I wonder why they can never keep their servants. I hear Mr Rode will be helping out with the Corps next Half.'

'Poor little Rode,' said Fielding slowly; 'running about like a puppy, trying to earn his biscuits. He tries so hard; have you seen him cheering at school matches? He'd never seen a game of rugger before he came here, you know. They don't play rugger at grammar schools—it's all soccer. Do you remember when he first came, Charles? It was fascinating. He lay very low at first, drinking us in: the games, the vocabulary, the manners. Then, one day it was as if he had been given the power of speech, and he spoke in our language. It was amazing, like plastic surgery. It was Felix D'Arcy's work of course—I've never seen anything quite like it before.'

'Dear Mrs Rode,' said Shane Hecht in that voice of abstract vagueness which she reserved for her most venomous pronouncements: 'So sweet . . . and such simple taste, don't you think? I mean, whoever would have dreamed of putting those china ducks on the wall? Big ones at the front and little ones at the back. Charming, don't you think? Like one of those teashops. I wonder where she bought them. I must ask her. I'm told her father lives near Bournemouth. It must be so lonely for him, don't you think? Such a vulgar place; no one to talk to.'

Fielding sat back and surveyed his own table. The silver was good. The best in Carne, he had heard it said, and he inclined to agree. This Half he had nothing but black candles. It was the sort of thing people remembered when you'd gone: 'Dear old Terence—marvellous host. He dined every member of the staff during his last Half, you know, wives too. Black candles, rather touching. It broke his heart giving up his house.' But he must annoy Charles Hecht. Shane would like that. Shane would egg him on because she hated Charles, because within her great ugly body she was as cunning as a snake.

Fielding looked at Hecht and then at Hecht's wife, and she smiled back at him, the slow rotten smile of a whore. For a moment Fielding thought of Hecht pasturing in that thick body: it was a scene redolent of Lautrec . . . yes, that was it! Charles pompous and top-hatted, seated stiffly upon the plush coverlet; she massive, pendulous and bored. The image pleased him: so perverse to consign that fool Hecht from the Spartan cleanliness of Carne to the brothels of nineteenth-century Paris. . . .

Fielding began talking, pontificating rather, with an air of friendly objectivity which he knew Hecht would resent.

'When I look back on my thirty years at Carne, I realise I have achieved rather less than a road sweeper.' They were watching him now—'I used to regard a road sweeper as a person inferior to myself. Now, I rather doubt it. Something is dirty, he makes it clean, and the state of the world is advanced. But I—what have *I* done. Entrenched a ruling class which is distinguished by neither talent, culture nor wit; kept alive for one more generation the distinctions of a dead age.'

Charles Hecht, who had never perfected the art of not listening to Fielding, grew red and fussed at the other end of the table.

'Don't we teach them, Fielding? What about our successes, our scholarships?'

'I have never taught a boy in my life, Charles. Usually the boy wasn't clever enough; occasionally, I wasn't. In most boys you see, perception dies with puberty. In a few it persists, though where we find it we take good care at Carne to kill it. If it survives our efforts the boy wins a scholarship. . . . Bear with me, Shane; it's my last Half.'

'Last Half or not, you're talking through your hat, Fielding,' said Hecht, angrily.

'That is traditional at Carne. These successes, as you call them, are the failures, the rare boys who have not learned the lessons of Carne. They have ignored the cult of mediocrity. We can do nothing for them. But for the rest, for the puzzled little clerics and the blind little soldiers, for them the truth of Carne is written on the wall, and they hate us.'

Hecht laughed rather heavily.

'Why do so many come back, then, if they hate us so much? Why do they remember us and come and see us?'

'Because we, dear Charles, are the writing on the wall! The one lesson of Carne they never forget. They come back to read *us*, don't you see? It was from us they learnt the secret of life: that we grow old without growing wise. They realised that nothing happened when we grew up: no blinding light on the road to Damascus, no sudden feeling of maturity.' Fielding put his head back and gazed at the clumsy Victorian moulding on the ceiling, and the halo of dirt round the light rose.

'We just got a little older. We made the same jokes, thought the same thoughts, wanted the same things. Year in, year out, Hecht, we were the same people, not wiser, not better; we haven't had an original thought between us for the last fifty years of our lives. They saw what a trick it all was, Carne and us; our academic dress, our schoolroom jokes, our wise little offerings of guidance. And that's why they come back year after year of their puzzled barren lives to gaze fascinated at you and me, Hecht, like children at a grave, searching for the secret of life and death. Oh yes, they have learned *that* from us.'

Hecht looked at Fielding in silence for a moment.

'Decanter, Hecht?' said Fielding, in a slightly conciliatory way, but Hecht's eyes were still upon him.

'If that's a joke . . .' he began, and his wife observed with satisfaction that he was very angry indeed.

'I wish I knew, Charles,' Fielding replied with apparent earnestness. 'I really wish I knew. I used to think it was clever to confuse comedy with tragedy. Now I wish I could distinguish them.' He rather liked that.

They had coffee in the drawing-room, where Fielding resorted to gossip, but Hecht was not to be drawn. Fielding rather wished he had let him light his pipe. Then he recalled his vision of the Hechts in Paris, and it restored him. He had been rather good this evening. There were moments when he convinced himself.

While Shane fetched her coat, the two men stood together in the hall, but neither spoke. Shane returned, an ermine stole, yellow with age, draped over her great white shoulders. She inclined her head to the right, smiled and held out her hand to Fielding, the fingers down.

'Terence, darling,' she said, as Fielding kissed her fat knuckles, 'so kind. And in your last Half. You must dine with us before you go. So sad. So few of us left.' She smiled again, half closing her eyes to indicate emotional disturbance, then followed her husband into the street. It was still bitterly cold and snow was in the air.

Fielding closed and carefully bolted the door behind them—perhaps a fraction earlier than courtesy required—and returned to the dining-room. Hecht's port glass was still about half full. Fielding picked it up and carefully poured the contents back into the decanter. He hoped Hecht wasn't too upset; he hated people to dislike him. He snuffed the black candles and damped their wicks between his forefinger and thumb. Switching on the light, he took from the sideboard a sixpenny notebook, and opened it. It contained his list of dining guests for the remainder of the Half. With his fountain pen he placed a neat tick against the name Hecht. They were done. On Wednesday he would have the Rodes. The husband was quite good value, but she, of course, was hell. . . . It was not always the way with married couples. The wives as a rule were so much more sympathetic.

He opened the sideboard and took from it a bottle of brandy and a tumbler. Holding them both in the same hand, he shuffled wearily back to the drawing-room, resting his other hand on the wall as he went. God! He felt old, suddenly; that thin line of pain across the chest, that heaviness in the legs and feet. Such an effort being with people—on stage all the time. He hated to be alone, but people bored him. Being alone was like being tired, but unable to sleep. Some German poet had said that; he'd quoted it once, 'You may sleep but I must dance.' Something like that.

'That's how I am,' thought Fielding. 'That's how Carne is, too; an old satyr dancing to the music.' The music grew faster and their bodies older, but they must dance on—there were young men waiting in the wings. It had been funny once dancing the old dances in a new world. He poured himself some more brandy. He'd be pleased to leave in a way, even though he'd have to go on teaching somewhere else.

But it had its beauty, Carne. . . . The Abbey Close in spring . . . the flamingo figures of boys waiting for the ritual of worship . . . the ebb and flow of children, like the seasons of the year, and the old man dying among them. He wished he could paint; he would paint the pageant of Carne in the fallow browns of autumn. . . . What a shame, thought Fielding, that a mind so perceptive of beauty had no talent for creation.

He looked at his watch. Quarter to twelve. Nearly time to go out . . . to dance, and not to sleep.

Chapter Two

The Thursday Feeling

It was Thursday evening and the *Christian Voice* had just been put to bed. This was scarcely an historic event in Fleet Street. The pimply boy from Despatch who took away the ragged pile of page-proofs showed no more ceremony than was strictly demanded by the eventual prospect of his Christmas bonus. And even in this respect he had learned that the secular journals of Unipress were more provident of material charity than the *Christian Voice*; charity being in strict relation to circulation.

Miss Brimley, the journal's editor, adjusted her air cushion beneath her and lit a cigarette. Her secretary and sub-editor–the appointment carried both responsibilities–yawned, dropped the aspirin bottle into her handbag, combed out her ginger hair and bade Miss Brimley good night, leaving behind her as usual the smell of strongly scented powder and an empty paper-tissue box. Miss Brimley listened contentedly to the clipping echo of her footsteps as it faded down the corridor. It pleased her to be alone at last, tasting the anticlimax. She never failed to wonder at herself, how every Thursday morning brought the same slight uneasiness as she entered the vast Unipress building and stood a little absurdly on one escalator after the other, like a drab parcel on a luxury liner. Heaven knows, she had run the *Voice* for fourteen years, and there were those who said its layout was the best thing Unipress did. Yet the Thursday feeling never left her, the wakeful anxiety that one day, perhaps today, they wouldn't be ready when the despatch boy came. She often wondered what would happen then. She had heard of failures elsewhere in that vast combine, of features disapproved and staff rebuked. It was a mystery to her why they kept the *Voice* at all, with its expensive room on the seventh floor and a circulation which, if Miss Brimley knew anything, hardly paid for the paper-clips.

The *Voice* had been founded at the turn of the century by old Lord Landsbury, together with a Nonconformist daily newspaper and the *Temperance Gazette*. But the *Gazette* and the daily were long since dead, and Landsbury's son had woken one morning not long ago to find his whole business and every man and woman of it, every stick of furniture, ink, paperclips, and galley-pins, bought by the hidden gold of Unipress.

That was three years ago and every day she had waited for her dismissal. But it never came; no directive, no question, no word. And so, being a sensible woman, she continued exactly as before and ceased to wonder.

And she was glad. It was easy to sneer at the *Voice*. Every week it offered humbly and without fanfares evidence of the Lord's intervention in the world's affairs, retold in simple and somewhat unscientific terms the early history of the Jews, and provided over a fictitious signature motherly advice to whomever should write and ask for it. The *Voice* scarcely concerned itself with the fifty-odd millions of the population who had never heard of it. It was a family affair, and rather than abuse those who were not members, it did its best for those who were. For them it was kind, optimistic, and informative. If a million children were dying of the plague in India, you may be sure that the weekly editorial described the miraculous escape from fire of a Methodist family in Kent. The *Voice* did not advise you how to disguise the encroaching wrinkles round your eyes, or control your spreading figure; did not dismay you, if you were old, by its own eternal youth. It was itself middle-aged and middle class, counselled caution to girls and charity to all. Nonconformity is the most conservative of habits and families which took the *Voice* in 1903 continued to take it in 1960.

Miss Brimley was not quite the image of her journal. The fortunes of war and the caprice of Intelligence work had thrown her into partnership with the younger Lord Landsbury, and for the six years of war they had worked together efficiently and inconspicuously in an unnamed building in Knightsbridge. The fortunes of peace rendered both unemployed, but Landsbury had the good sense, as well as the generosity, to offer Miss Brimley a job. The *Voice* had ceased publication during the war, and no one seemed anxious to renew it. At first Miss Brimley had felt a little ashamed at reviving and editing a journal which in no way expressed her own vague deism, but quite soon, as the touching letters came in and the circulation recovered, she developed an affection for her job—and for her readers—which outweighed her earlier misgivings. The *Voice* was her life, and its readers her preoccupation. She struggled to answer their odd, troubled questions, sought advice of others where she could not provide it herself, and in time, under a handful of pseudonyms, became if not their philosopher, their guide, friend and universal aunt.

Miss Brimley put out her cigarette, absently tidied the pins, paper-clips, scissors and paste into the top right-hand drawer of her desk, and gathered together the afternoon mail from her in-tray which, because it was Thursday, she had left untouched. There were several letters addressed to Barbara Fellowship, under which name the *Voice* had, since its foundation, answered both privately and through its published columns the many problems of its correspondents. They could wait until tomorrow. She rather enjoyed the 'problem post', but Friday morning was when she read it. She opened the little filing cabinet at her elbow and dropped the letters into a box file at the front of the compartment. As she did so, one of them fell on its back and she noticed with surprise that the sealed flap was embossed with an elegant blue dolphin. She picked the envelope out of the cabinet and looked at it curiously, turning it over several times. It was of pale grey paper, very faintly lined. Expensive— perhaps hand-made. Beneath the dolphin was a tiny scroll on which she could just discern the legend, *Regem defendere diem videre*. The postmark was Carne, Dorset. That must be the school crest. But why was Carne familiar to her? Miss Brimley was proud of her memory, which was excellent, and she was vexed when it failed her. As a last resort she opened the envelope with her faded ivory paper knife and read the letter.

Dear Miss Fellowship,

I don't know if you are a real person but it doesn't matter, because you always give such good, kind answers. It was me who wrote last June about the pastry mix. I am not mad and I know my husband is trying to kill me. Could I please come and see you as soon as it's convenient? I'm sure you'll believe me, and understand that I am normal. Could it be *as soon as possible* please, I am so afraid of the long nights. I don't know who else to turn to. I could try Mr Cardew at the Tabernacle but he wouldn't believe me and Dad's too sensible. I might as well be dead. There's something not quite right about him. At night when he thinks I'm asleep he just lies watching the darkness. I know it's wrong to think such wicked things and have fear in our hearts, but I can't help it.

I hope you don't get many letters like this.

Yours faithfully,

Stella Rode (Mrs)

née Glaston

She sat quite still at her desk for a moment, looking at the address in handsome blue engraving at the top of the page: 'North Fields, Carne School, Dorset.' In that moment of shock and astonishment one phrase forced itself upon her mind. 'The value of intelligence depends on its breeding.' That was John Landsbury's favourite dictum. Until you know the pedigree of the information you cannot evaluate a report. Yes, that was what he used to say: 'We are not democratic. We close the door on intelligence without parentage.' And she used to reply: 'Yes, John, but even the best families had to begin somewhere.'

But Stella Rode *had* parentage. It all came back to her now. She was the Glaston girl. The girl whose marriage was reported in the editorial, the girl who won the summer competition; Samuel Glaston's daughter from Branxome. She had a card in Miss Brimley's index.

Abruptly she stood up, the letter still in her hand, and walked to the uncurtained window. Just in front of her was a contemporary window-box of woven white metal. It was odd, she reflected, how she could never get anything to grow in that window-box. She looked down into the street, a slight sensible figure leaning forward a little and framed by the incandescent fog outside; fog made yellow from the stolen light of London's streets. She could just distinguish the street lamps far below, pale and sullen. She suddenly felt the need for fresh air, and on an impulse quite alien to her usual calm, she opened the window wide. The quick cold and the angry surge of noise burst in on her, and the insidious fog followed. The sound of traffic was constant, so that for a moment she thought it was the turning of some great machine. Then above its steady growl she heard the newsboys. Their cries were like the cries of gulls against a gathering storm. She could see them now, sentinels among the hastening shadows.

It might be true. That had always been the difficulty. Right through the war it was the same restless search. It might be true. It was no use relating reports to probability when there was no quantum of knowledge from which to start. She remembered the first intelligence from France on flying bombs, wild talk of concrete runways in the depths of the forest. You had to resist the dramatic, you had to hold out against it. Yet it might be true. Tomorrow, the day after, those newsboys down there might be shouting it, and Stella Rode *née* Glaston might be dead. And if that was so, if there was the remotest chance that this man was plotting to kill this woman, then she, Ailsa Brimley, must do what she could to prevent it. Besides, Stella Glaston had a claim on her assistance if anyone did: both her father and her grandfather had taken the *Voice*, and when Stella married five years ago Miss Brimley had put a couple of lines about it in the editorial. The Glastons sent her a Christmas card every year. They were one of the original families to subscribe. . . .

It was cold at the window, but she remained there, still fascinated by the half hidden shadows joining and parting beneath her, and the useless street lights burning painfully among them. She began to imagine him as one of those shadows, pressing and jostling, his murderer's eyes turned to sockets of dark. And suddenly she was frightened and needed help.

But not the police, not yet. If Stella Rode had wanted that she would have gone herself. Why hadn't she? For love? For fear of looking a fool? Because instinct was not evidence? They wanted fact. But the fact of murder was death. Must they wait for that?

Who would help? She thought at once of Landsbury, but he was farming in Rhodesia. Who else had been with them in the war? Fielding and Jebedee were dead, Steed, Asprey vanished. Smiley—where was he? George Smiley, the cleverest and perhaps the oddest of them all. Of course, Miss Brimley remembered now. He made that improbable marriage and went back to research at Oxford. But he hadn't stayed there. . . . The marriage had broken up. . . . What *had* he done after that?

She returned to her desk and picked up the S–Z directory. Ten minutes later she was sitting in a taxi, heading for Sloane Square. In her neatly gloved hand she held a cardboard folder containing Stella Rode's card from the index and the correspondence which had passed between them at the time of the Summer Competition. She was nearly at Piccadilly when she remembered she'd left the office window open. It didn't seem to matter much.

'With other people it's Persian cats or golf. With me it's the *Voice* and my readers. I'm a ridiculous spinster, I know, but there it is. I won't go to the police until I've tried *something*, George.'

'And you thought you'd try me?'

'Yes.'

She was sitting in the study of George Smiley's house in Bywater Street; the only light came from the complicated lamp on his desk, a black spider of a thing shining brightly on to the manuscript notes which covered the desk.

'So you've left the Service?' she said.

'Yes, yes, I have.' He nodded his round head vigorously, as if reassuring himself that a distasteful experience was really over, and mixed Miss Brimley a whisky and soda. 'I had another spell there after . . . Oxford. It's all very different in peacetime, you know,' he continued.

Miss Brimley nodded.

'I can imagine it. More time to be bitchy.' Smiley said nothing, just lit a cigarette and sat down opposite her.

'And the people have changed. Fielding, Steed, Jebedee. All gone.' She said this in a matter-of-fact way as she took from her large sensible handbag Stella Rode's letter. 'This is the letter, George.'

When he had read it, he held it briefly towards the lamp, his round face caught by the light in a moment of almost comic earnestness. Watching him, Miss Brimley wondered what impression he made on those who did not know him well. She used to think of him as the most forgettable man she had ever met; short and plump, with heavy spectacles and thinning hair, he was at first sight the very prototype of an unsuccessful middle-aged bachelor in a sedentary occupation. His natural diffidence in most practical matters was reflected in his clothes, which were costly and unsuitable, for he was clay in the hands of his tailor, who robbed him.

He had put down the letter on the small marquetry table beside him, and was looking at her owlishly.

'This other letter she sent you, Brim. Where is it?'

She handed him the folder. He opened it and after a moment read aloud Stella Rode's other letter:

> Dear Miss Fellowship,
>
> I would like to submit the following suggestion for your 'Kitchen Hints' competition.
>
> Make your basic batch of cake mixture once a month. Cream equal quantities of fat and sugar and add one egg for every six ounces of the mixture. For puddings and cakes, add flour to the required quantity of basic mixture.
>
> This will keep well for a month.
>
> I enclose stamped addressed envelope.
>
> > Yours sincerely,
> > Stella Rode (*née* Glaston)
>
> P.S.–Incidentally, you can prevent wire wool from rusting by keeping it in a jar of soapy water. Are we allowed two suggestions? If so, please can this be my second?

'She won the competition,' Miss Brimley observed, 'but that's not the point. This is what I want to tell you George. She's a Glaston, and the Glastons have been reading the *Voice* since it started. Stella's grandfather was old Rufus Glaston, a Lancashire pottery king; he and John Landsbury's father built chapels and tabernacles in practically every village in the Midlands. When Rufus died the *Voice* put out a memorial edition and old Landsbury himself wrote the obituary. Samuel Glaston took on his father's business, but had to move south because of his health. He ended up near Bournemouth, a widower with one daughter, Stella. She's the last of all that family. The whole lot are as down to earth as you could wish, Stella included, I should think. I don't think any of them is likely to be suffering from delusions of persecution.'

Smiley was looking at her in astonishment.

'My dear Brim, I can't possibly take that in. How on earth do you know all this?'

Miss Brimley smiled apologetically.

'The Glastons are easy–they're almost part of the magazine. They send us Christmas cards, and boxes of chocolates on the anniversary of our foundation. We've got about five hundred families who form what I call our Establishment. They were in on the *Voice* from the start and they've kept up ever since. They write to us, George; if they're worried they write and say so; if they're getting married, moving house, retiring from work, if they're ill, depressed, or angry, they write. Not often, Heaven knows; but enough.'

'How do you remember it all?'

'I don't. I keep a card index. I always write back you see . . . only . . .'

'Yes?'

Miss Brimley looked at him earnestly.

'This is the first time anyone has written because she's frightened.'

'What do you want me to do?'

'I've only had one bright idea so far. I seem to remember Adrian Fielding had a brother who taught at Carne. . . .'

'He's a housemaster there, if he hasn't retired.'

'No, he retires this Half–it was in *The Times* some weeks ago, in that little bit on the Court page where Carne always announces itself. It said: "Carne School reassembles today for the Lent Half. Mr T.R. Fielding will retire at the end of the Half, having completed his statutory fifteen years as a housemaster."'

Smiley laughed.

'Really, Brim, your memory is absurd!'

'It was the mention of Fielding . . . Anyway, I thought you could ring him up. You must know him.'

'Yes, yes. I know him. At least, I met him once at Magdalen High Table. But–' Smiley coloured a little.

'But what, George?'

'Well he's not quite the man his brother was, you know.'

'How could he be?' Miss Brimley rejoined a little sharply. 'But he can tell you something about Stella Rode. And her husband.'

'I don't think I could do that on the telephone. I think I'd rather go and see him. But what's to stop you ringing up Stella Rode?'

'Well, I can't tonight, can I? Her husband will be in. I thought I'd put a letter in the post to her tonight telling her she can come to see me any time. But,' she continued, making a slight, impatient movement with her foot, 'I want to do something *now*, George.'

Smiley nodded and went to the telephone. He rang directory enquiries and asked for Terence Fielding's number. After a long delay he was told to ring Carne School central exchange, who would connect him with whomever he required. Miss Brimley, watching him, wished she knew a little more about George Smiley, how much of that diffidence was assumed, how vulnerable he was.

'The best,' Adrian had said. 'The strongest and the best.'

But so many men learnt strength during the war, learnt terrible things, and put aside their knowledge with a shudder when it ended.

The number was ringing now. She heard the dialling tone and for a moment was filled with apprehension. For the first time she was afraid of making a fool of herself, afraid of becoming involved in unlikely explanations with angular, suspicious people.

'Mr Terence Fielding, please. . . .' A pause.

'Fielding, good evening. My name is George Smiley; I knew your brother well in the war. We have in fact met. . . . Yes, yes, quite right—Magdalen, was it not, the summer before last? Look, I wonder if I might come and see you on a personal matter . . . it's a little difficult to discuss on the telephone. A friend of mine has received a rather disturbing letter from the wife of a Carne master. . . . Well, I—Rode, Stella Rode; her husband . . .'

He suddenly stiffened, and Miss Brimley, her eyes fixed upon him, saw with alarm how his chubby face broke into an expression of pain and disgust. She no longer heard what he was saying. She could only watch the dreadful transformation of his face, the whitening knuckles of his hand clutching the receiver. He was looking at her now, saying something . . . it was too late. Stella Rode was dead. She had been murdered late on Wednesday night. They'd actually been dining with Fielding the night it happened.

Chapter Three

The Night of the Murder

The seven-five from Waterloo to Yeovil is not a popular train, though it provides an excellent breakfast. Smiley had no difficulty in finding a first-class compartment to himself. It was a bitterly cold day, dark and the sky heavy with snow. He sat huddled in a voluminous travelling coat of Continental origin, holding in his gloved hands a bundle of the day's papers. Because he was a precise man and did not care to be hurried, he had arrived thirty minutes before the train was due to depart. Still tired after the stresses of the previous night, when he had sat up talking with Ailsa Brimley until Heaven knew what hour, he was disinclined to read. Looking out of the window on to an almost empty station, he caught sight, to his great surprise, of Miss Brimley herself making her way along the platform, peering in at the windows, a carrier bag in her hand. He lowered the window and called to her.

'My dear Brim, what are you doing here at this dreadful hour? You should be in bed.'

She sat down opposite him and began unpacking her bag and handing him its contents: thermos, sandwiches and chocolate.

'I didn't know whether there was a breakfast car,' she explained; 'and besides, I wanted to come and see you off. You're such a dear, George, and I wish I could come with you, but Unipress would go mad if I did. The only time they notice you is when you're not there.'

'Have you seen the papers?' he asked.

'Just briefly, on the way here. They seem to think it wasn't him, but some madman. . . .'

'I know, Brim. That's what Fielding said, wasn't it?' There was a moment's awkward silence.

'George, am I being an awful ass, letting you go off like this? I was so sure last night, but now I wonder . . .'

'After you left I rang Ben Sparrow of Special Branch. You remember him, don't you? He was with us in the war. I told him the whole story.'

'George! At three in the morning?'

'Yes. He's ringing the Divisional Superintendent at Carne. He'll tell him about the letter, and that I'm coming down. Ben had an idea that a man named Rigby would be handling the case. Rigby and Ben were at police college together.' He looked at her kindly for a moment. 'Besides, I'm a man of leisure, Brim. I shall enjoy the change.'

'Bless you, George,' said Miss Brimley, woman enough to believe him. She got up to go, and Smiley said to her:

'Brim, if you should need any more help or anything and can't get hold of me, there's a man called Mendel who lives in Mitcham, a retired police inspector. He's in the book. If you get hold of him and mention me, he'll do what he can for you. I've booked a room at the Sawley Arms.'

Alone again, Smiley surveyed uneasily the assortment of food and drink which Miss Brimley had provided. He had promised himself the luxury of breakfast in the restaurant car. He would keep the sandwiches and coffee for later, that would be the best thing; for lunch, perhaps. And he would breakfast properly.

In the restaurant car Smiley read first the less sensational reports on the death of Stella Rode. It appeared that on Wednesday evening Mr and Mrs Rode had been guests at dinner of Mr Terence Fielding, the senior housemaster at Carne and brother of the late Adrian Fielding, the celebrated French scholar who had vanished during the war while specially employed by the War Office. They had left Mr

Fielding's house together at about ten to eleven and walked the half mile from the centre of Carne to their house, which stood alone at the edge of the famous Carne playing fields. As they reached their house Mr Rode remembered that he had left at Mr Fielding's house some examination papers which urgently required correction that night. (At this point Smiley remembered that he had failed to pack his dinner jacket, and that Fielding would almost certainly ask him to dine.) Rode determined to walk back to Fielding's house and collect the papers, therefore, starting back at about five past eleven. It appears that Mrs Rode made herself a cup of tea and sat down in the drawing-room to await his return.

Adjoining the back of the house is a conservatory, the inner door of which leads to the drawing-room. It was there that Rode eventually found his wife when he returned. There were signs of a struggle, and certain inexpensive articles of jewellery were missing from the body. The confusion in the conservatory was terrible. Fortunately there had been a fresh fall of snow on Wednesday afternoon, and detectives from Dorchester were examining the footprints and other traces early on Thursday morning. Mr Rode had been treated for shock at Dorchester Central Hospital. The police wished to interview a woman from the adjacent village of Pylle who was locally known as 'Mad Janie' on account of her eccentric and solitary habits. Mrs Rode who was well known in Carne for her energetic work on behalf of the International Refugee Year, had apparently shown a charitable interest in her welfare, and she had vanished without trace since the night of the murder. The police were currently of the opinion that the murderer had caught sight of Mrs Rode through the drawing-room window (she had not drawn the curtains) and that Mrs Rode had admitted the murderer at the front door in the belief that it was her husband returning from Mr Fielding's house. The Home Office pathologist had been asked to conduct a post-mortem examination.

The other reports were not so restrained: 'Murder most foul has desecrated the hallowed playing fields of Carne' one article began, and another, 'Science teacher discovers murdered wife in blood-spattered conservatory'. A third screamed, 'Mad woman sought in Carne murder'. With an expression of distaste, Smiley screwed up all the newspapers except the *Guardian* and *The Times* and tossed them on to the luggage rack.

He changed at Yeovil for a local line to Sturminster, Okeford and Carne. It was something after eleven o'clock when he finally arrived at Carne station.

He telephoned the hotel from the station and sent his luggage ahead by taxi. The Sawley Arms was only full at Commemoration and on St Andrew's Day. Most of the year it was empty; sitting like a prim

Victorian lady, its slate roof in the mauve of half mourning, on ill tended lawns midway between the station and Carne Abbey.

Snow still lay on the ground, but the day was fine and dry, and Smiley decided to walk into the town and arrange to meet the police officer conducting the investigation of the murder. He left the station, with its foretaste of Victorian austerity, and walked along the avenue of bare trees which led towards the great Abbey tower, flat and black against the colourless winter sky. He crossed the Abbey Close, a serene and beautiful square of mediaeval houses, the roofs snow-covered, the white lawns shaded with pin strokes of grass. As he passed the west door of the Abbey, the soft snow creaking where he trod, the clock high above him struck the half-hour, and two knights on horseback rode out from their little castle over the door, and slowly raised their lances to each other in salute. Then, as if it were all part of the same clockwork mechanism, other doors all round the Close opened too, releasing swarms of black-coated boys who stampeded across the snow towards the Abbey. One boy passed so close that his gown brushed against Smiley's sleeve. Smiley called to him as he ran past:

'What's going on?'

'Sext,' shouted the boy in reply, and was gone.

He passed the main entrance to the school and came at once upon the municipal part of the town, a lugubrious nineteenth-century fairyland in local stone, stitched together by a complexity of Gothic chimneys and crenel windows. Here was the town hall, and beside it, with the flag of St George floating at its masthead, the Carne Constabulary Headquarters, built ninety years ago to withstand the onslaughts of archery and battering rams.

He gave his name to the Duty Sergeant, and asked to see the officer investigating the death of Mrs Rode. The Sergeant, an elderly, inscrutable man, addressed himself to the telephone with a certain formality, as if he were about to perform a difficult conjuring trick. To Smiley's surprise, he was told that Inspector Rigby would be pleased to see him at once, and a police cadet was summoned to show him the way. He was led at a spanking pace up the wide staircase in the centre of the hall, and in a matter of moments found himself before the Inspector.

He was a very short man, and very broad. He could have been a Celt from the tin-mines of Cornwall or the collieries of Wales. His dark grey hair was cut very close; it came to a point in the centre of his brow like a devil's cap. His hands were large and powerful, he had the trunk and stance of a wrestler, but he spoke slowly, with a Dorset burr to his soft voice. Smiley quickly noticed that he had one quality rare among small men: the quality of openness. Though his eyes were dark and bright and the movements of his body swift, he imparted a feeling of honesty and straight dealing.

'Ben Sparrow rang me this morning, sir. I'm very pleased you've come. I believe you've got a letter for me.'

Rigby looked at Smiley thoughtfully over his desk, and decided that he liked what he saw. He had got around in the war and had heard a little, just a very little, of the work of George Smiley's service. If Ben said Smiley was all right, that was good enough for him—or almost. But Ben had said more than that.

'Looks like a frog, dresses like a bookie, and has a brain I'd give my eyes for. Had a very nasty war. Very nasty indeed.'

Well, he looked like a frog, right enough. Short and stubby, round spectacles with thick lenses that made his eyes big. And his clothes *were* odd. Expensive, mind, you could see that. But his jacket seemed to drape where there wasn't any room for drape. What did surprise Rigby was his shyness. Rigby had expected someone a little brash, a little too smooth for Carne, whereas Smiley had an earnest formality of manner which appealed to Rigby's conservative taste.

Smiley took the letter from his wallet and put it on the desk, while Rigby extracted an old pair of gold-rimmed spectacles from a battered metal case and adjusted the ends carefully over his ears.

'I don't know if Ben explained,' said Smiley, 'but this letter was sent to the correspondence section of a small Nonconformist journal to which Mrs Rode subscribed.'

'And Miss Fellowship is the lady who brought you the letter?'

'No; her name is Brimley. She is the editor of the magazine. Fellowship is just a pen-name for the correspondence column.'

The brown eyes rested on him for a moment.

'When did she receive this letter?'

'Yesterday, the seventeenth. Thursday's the day they go to press, their busy day. The afternoon mail doesn't get opened till the evening, usually. This was opened about six o'clock, I suppose.'

'And she brought it straight to you?'

'Yes.'

'Why?'

'She worked for me during the war, in my department. She was reluctant to go straight to the police—I was the only person she could think of who wasn't a policeman,' he added stupidly. 'Who could help, I mean.'

'May I ask what you yourself, sir, do for a living?'

'Nothing much. A little private research on seventeenth-century Germany.' It seemed a very silly answer.

Rigby didn't seem bothered.

'What's this earlier letter she talks about?'

Smiley offered him the second envelope, and again the big, square hand received it.

'It appears she won this competition,' Smiley explained. 'That was her winning entry. I gather she comes from a family which has subscribed to the magazine since its foundation. That's why Miss Brimley was less inclined to regard the letter as nonsense. Not that it follows.'

'Not that what follows?'

'I meant that the fact that her family had subscribed to a journal for fifty years does not logically affect the possibility that she was unbalanced.'

Rigby nodded, as if he saw the point, but Smiley had an uncomfortable feeling that he did not.

'Ah,' said Rigby, with a slow smile. 'Women, eh?'

Smiley, completely bewildered, gave a little laugh. Rigby was looking at him thoughtfully.

'Know any of the staff, here, do you, sir?'

'Only Mr Terence Fielding. We met at an Oxford dinner some time ago. I thought I'd call round and see him. I knew his brother pretty well.'

Rigby appeared to stiffen slightly at the mention of Fielding, but he said nothing, and Smiley went on:

'It was Fielding I rang when Miss Brimley brought me the letter. He told me the news. That was last night.'

'I see.'

They looked at one another again in silence. Smiley discomfited and slightly comic. Rigby appraising him, wondering how much to say.

'How long are you staying?' he said at last.

'I don't know,' Smiley replied. 'Miss Brimley wanted to come herself, but she has her paper to run. She attached great importance, you see, to doing all she could for Mrs Rode, even though she was dead. Because she was a subscriber, I mean. I promised to see that the letter arrived quickly in the right hands. I don't imagine there's much else I can do. I shall probably stay on for a day or two just to have a word with Fielding . . . go to the funeral, I suppose. I've booked in at the Sawley Arms.'

'Fine hotel, that.'

Rigby put his spectacles carefully back into their case and dropped the case into a drawer.

'Funny place, Carne. There's a big gap between the Town and Gown, as we say; neither side knows nor likes the other. It's fear that does it, fear and ignorance. It makes it hard in a case like this. Oh, I can call on Mr Fielding and Mr D'Arcy and they say, "Good day, Sergeant," and give me a cup of tea in the kitchen, but I can't get among them. They've got their own community, see, and no one outside it can get in. No gossip in the pubs, no contacts, nothing . . . just cups of tea and bits of seed cake, and being called Sergeant.'

Rigby laughed suddenly, and Smiley laughed with him in relief.

'There's a lot I'd like to ask them, a lot of things; who liked the Rodes and who didn't, whether Mr Rode's a good teacher and whether his wife fitted in with the others. I've got all the facts I want, but I've got no clothes to hang on them.' He looked at Smiley expectantly. There was a very long silence.

'If you want me to help, I'd be delighted,' said Smiley at last. 'But give me the facts first.'

'Stella Rode was murdered between about ten past eleven and quarter to twelve on the night of Wednesday the sixteenth. She must have been struck fifteen to twenty times with a cosh or bit of piping or something. It was a terrible murder . . . terrible. There are marks all over her body. At a guess I would say she came from the drawing-room to the front door to answer the bell or something, when she opened the door she was struck down and dragged to the conservatory. The conservatory door was unlocked, see?'

'I see. . . . It's odd that he should have known that, isn't it?'

'The murderer may have been hiding there already: we can't tell from the prints just there. He was wearing boots—wellington boots, size 10½. We would guess from the spacing of the footprints in the garden that he was about six foot tall. When he had got her to the conservatory he must have hit her again and again—mainly on the head. There's a lot of what we call travelled blood in the conservatory, that's to say, blood spurted from an open artery. There's no sign of that anywhere else.'

'And no sign of it on her husband?'

'I'll come to that later, but the short answer is, no.' He paused a moment and continued:

'Now, I said there were footprints, and so there were. The murderer came through the back garden. Where he came from and went to, Heaven alone knows. You see, there are no tracks leading away—not wellingtons. None at all. Of course, it's possible the outgoing tracks followed the path to the front gate and got lost in all the to-ing and fro-ing later that night. But I don't think we'd have lost them even then.' He glanced at Smiley, then went on:

'He left one thing behind him in the conservatory—an old cloth belt, navy blue, from a cheap overcoat by the look of it. We're working on that now.'

'Was she . . . robbed or anything?'

'No sign of interference. She was wearing a string of green beads round her neck, and they've gone, and it looks as though he tried to get the rings off her finger, but they were too tight.' He paused.

'I need hardly tell you that we've had reports from every corner of the country about tall men in blue overcoats and gumboots. But none of them had wings as far as I know. Or seven-league boots for jumping from the conservatory to the road.'

They paused, while a police cadet brought in tea on a tray. He put it on the desk, looked at Smiley out of the corner of his eye and decided to let the Inspector pour out. He guided the teapot round so that the handle was towards Rigby and withdrew. Smiley was amused by the immaculate condition of the tray cloth, by the matching china and the tea-strainer, laid before them by the enormous hands of the cadet. Rigby poured out the tea and they drank for a moment in silence. There was, Smiley reflected, something devastatingly competent about Rigby. The very ordinariness of the man and his room identified him with the society he protected. The nondescript furniture, the wooden filing cupboards, the bare walls, the archaic telephone with its separate earpiece, the brown frieze round the wall and the brown paint on the door, the glistening linoleum and the faint smell of carbolic, the burbling gas-fire and the calendar from the Prudential—these were the evidence of rectitude and moderation; their austerity gave comfort and reassurance. Rigby continued:

'Rode went back to Fielding's house for the examination papers. Fielding confirms that, of course. He arrived at Fielding's house at about 11.35, near as Fielding can say. He hardly spent any time there at all—just collected his papers at the door—they were in a small writing-case he used for carrying exercise books. He doesn't remember whether he saw anyone on the road. He thinks a bicycle overtook him, but he can't be sure. If we take Rode's word for it, he walked straight home. When he got there he rang the bell. He was wearing a dinner jacket and so he hadn't got his key with him. His wife was expecting him to ring the bell, you see. That's the devil of it. It was a moonlit night, mind, and snow on the ground, so you could see a mighty long way. He called her, but she didn't answer. Then he saw the footprints going round to the side of the house. Not just footprints, but blood marks and the snow all churned up where the body had been dragged to the conservatory. But he didn't know it was blood in the moonlight, it just showed up dark, and Rode said afterwards he thought it was the dirty water from the gutters running over on to the path.

'He followed the prints round until he came to the conservatory. It was darker in there and he fumbled for the light switch, but it didn't work.'

'Did he light a match?'

'No, he didn't have any. He's a non-smoker. His wife didn't approve of smoking. He moved forward from the door. The conservatory walls are mainly glass except for the bottom three feet, but the roof is tiled. The moon was high that night, and not much light got in at all, except through the partition window between the drawing-room and the conservatory—but she'd only had the little table light on in the drawing-room. So he groped his way forward, talking all the time, calling Stella, his wife. As he went, he tripped over something and nearly fell. He knelt down and felt with his hands, up and down her body. He realised that his hands were covered in blood. He doesn't remember much after that, but there's a senior master living a hundred yards up the road–Mr D'Arcy his name is, lives with his sister, and he heard him screaming on the road. D'Arcy went out to him. Rode had blood all over his hands and face and seemed to be out of his mind. D'Arcy rang for the police and I got there at about one o'clock that morning. I've seen some nasty things in my time, but this is the worst. Blood everywhere. Whoever killed her must have been covered in it. There's an outside tap against the conservatory wall. The tap had been turned on, probably by the murderer to rinse his hands. The boffins have found traces of blood in the snow underneath it. The tap was lagged recently by Rode I gather. . . .'

'And fingerprints?' Smiley asked. 'What about them?'

'Mr Rode's were everywhere. On the floor, the walls and windows, on the body itself. But there were other prints; smudges of blood, little more, made with a gloved hand probably.'

'And they were the murderer's?'

'They had been made *before* Rode made his. In some cases Rode's prints were partly superimposed on the glove prints.'

Smiley was silent for a moment.

'These examination papers he went back for. Were they as important as all that?'

'Yes. I gather they were. Up to a point anyway? The marks had to be handed in to Mr D'Arcy by midday on Friday.'

'But why did he take them to Fielding's in the first place?'

'He didn't. He'd been invigilating exams all afternoon and the papers were handed in to him at six o'clock. He put them in his little case and had them taken to Fielding's by a boy–head boy in Mr Fielding's house, name of Perkins. Rode was on Chapel duty last week, so he didn't have time to return home before dinner.'

'Where did he change then?'

'In the Tutors' Robing Room, next to the Common Room. There are facilities there, mainly for games tutors who live some distance from Carne.'

'The boy who brought this case to Fielding's house–who was he?'

'I can't tell you much more than I've said. His name is Perkins; he's head of Mr Fielding's house. Fielding has spoken to him and confirmed Rode's statement. . . . House tutors are very possessive about their boys, you know . . . don't like them to be spoken to by rough policemen.' Rigby seemed to be slightly upset.

'I see,' Smiley said at last, helplessly, and then: 'But how do you explain the letter?'

'It isn't only the letter we've got to explain.'

Smiley looked at him sharply.

'What do you mean?'

'I mean,' said Rigby slowly, 'that Mrs Rode did several pretty queer things in the last few weeks.'

Chapter Four

Town and Gown

'Mrs Rode was Chapel, of course,' Rigby continued, 'and we've quite a community in Carne. Truth to tell,' he added with a slow smile, 'my wife belongs to it.

'A couple of weeks ago our Minister called round to see me. It was in the evening, about half past six, I suppose. I was just thinking of going home, see. He walked in here and sat himself down where you're sitting now. He's a big fellow, the Minister, a fine man; comes from up North, where Mrs Rode came from. Cardew, his name is.'

'The Mr Cardew in the letter?'

'That's him. He knew all about Mrs Rode's family before the Rodes ever came here. Glaston's quite a name up North, and Mr Cardew was pleased when he heard that Stella Rode was Mr Glaston's daughter; very pleased indeed. Mrs Rode came to the Tabernacle regular as clockwork—you can imagine, and they like to see that round here. My wife was pleased as Punch, I can tell you. It was the first time, I suppose, that anyone from the School had done that. Most of the Chapel people here are tradespeople—what we call the locals.' Rigby smiled again. 'It isn't often that town and gown come together so to speak. Not here.'

'How about her husband? Was he Chapel too?'

'Well, he had been, so she told Mr Cardew. Mr Rode was born and bred in Branxome, and all his family were Chapel people. That's how Mr and Mrs Rode first met, I gather—at Branxome Tabernacle. Ever been there, have you? A fine church Branxome, right up on the hill there, overlooking the sea.'

Smiley shook his head and Rigby's wide brown eyes rested on him thoughtfully for a moment.

'You should,' he said, 'you should go and see that. It seems,' he continued, 'that Mr Rode turned Church of England when he came to Carne. Even tried to persuade his wife to do the same. They're very strong at the School. I heard that from my wife, as a matter of fact. I never let her gossip as a rule, being a policeman's wife and that, but Mr Cardew told her that himself.'

'I see,' said Smiley.

'Well now, Cardew came and saw me. He was all worried and bothered with himself. He didn't know what he should make of it, but he wanted to talk to me as a friend and not as a policeman.' Rigby looked sour, 'When people say that to me, I always know that they want to talk to me as a policeman. Then he told me his story. Mrs Rode had called to see him that afternoon. He'd been out visiting a farmer's wife over in Okeford and didn't come home until half past five or thereabouts, so Mrs Cardew had had to talk to her and hold the fort until the Minister came home. Mrs Rode was white as a sheet, sitting very still by the fire. As soon as the Minister arrived, Mrs Cardew left them alone and Stella Rode started talking about her husband.'

He paused. 'She said Mr Rode was going to kill her. In the long nights. She seemed to have a kind of fixation about being murdered in the long nights. Cardew didn't take it too seriously at first, but thinking about it afterwards, he decided to let me know.'

Smiley looked at him sharply.

'He couldn't make out what she meant. He thought she was out of her mind. He's a down-to-earth man, see, although he's a Minister. I think he was probably a bit too firm with her. He asked her what put this dreadful thought into her head, and she began to weep. Not hysterical, apparently, but just crying quietly to herself. He tried to calm her down, promised to help her any way he could, and asked her again what had given her this idea. She just shook her head, then got up, walked over to the door, still shaking her head in despair. She turned to him, and he thought she was going to say something, but she didn't. She just left.'

'How very curious,' said Smiley, 'that she lied about that in her letter. She went out of her way to say she *hadn't* told Cardew.'

Rigby shrugged his great shoulders.

'If you'll pardon me,' he said, 'I'm in a darned awkward position. The Chief Constable would sooner cut his throat than call in Scotland Yard. He wants an arrest and he wants one quick. We've got enough clues to cover a Christmas tree; footprints, time of the murder, indication of murderer's clothing and even the weapon itself.'

Smiley looked at him in surprise.

'You've *found* the weapon, then?'

Rigby hesitated. 'Yes, we've found it. There's hardly a soul knows this, sir, and I'll trouble you to remember that. We found it the morning after the murder, four miles north of Carne on the Okeford road, tossed into a ditch. Eighteen inches of what they call coaxial cable. Know what that is, do you? It comes in all sizes, but this piece is about two inches in diameter. It has a copper rod running down the middle and plastic insulation between the rod and the outer cover. There was blood on it: Stella Rode's blood group, and hairs from her head, stuck to the blood. We're keeping that very dark indeed. By the Grace of God, it was found by one of our own men. It pinpoints the time of the murderer's departure.'

'There's no doubt, I suppose, that it *is* the weapon?' Smiley asked lamely.

'We found particles of copper in the wounds on the body.'

'It's odd, isn't it,' Smiley suggested reflectively, 'that the murderer should have carried the weapon so far before getting rid of it? Specially if he was walking. You'd think he'd want to get rid of it as soon as he could.'

'It is odd. Very odd. The Okeford road runs beside the canal for half of those four miles; he could have pitched the cable into the canal anywhere along there. We'd never have been the wiser.'

'Was the cable old?'

'Not particularly. Just standard type. It could have come from almost anywhere.' Rigby hesitated a minute, then burst out:

'Look, sir, this is what I am trying to say. The circumstances of this case demand a certain type of investigation: wide-scale search, detailed laboratory work, mass enquiry. That's what the Chief wants, and he's right. We've no case against the husband at all, and to be frank he's precious little use to us. He seems a bit lost, a bit vague, contradicting himself on little things that don't matter, like the date of his marriage or the name of his doctor. It's a shock, of course, I've seen it before. I know all about your letter, sir, and it's damned odd, but if you can tell me how he could have produced wellington boots out of a hat and got rid of them afterwards, battered his wife to death without leaving more than a few smudges of blood on himself, and got the weapon four miles from the scene of the crime, all within ten minutes of being at Fielding's house, I'll be grateful to you. We're looking for a stranger, six foot tall, wearing newish Dunlop wellington boots size 10½, leather gloves and an old blue overcoat stained with blood. A man who travels on foot who was in the area of North Fields between 11.10 and 11.45 on the night of the murder, who left in the direction of Okeford, taking with him one and a half feet of coaxial cable, a string of green beads and an imitation diamond clip, valued at twenty-three and six. We're looking for a maniac, a man who kills for pleasure or the price of a meal.' Rigby paused, smiled wistfully and added, 'Who can fly fifty feet through the air. But with information like this how else should we spend our time? What else can we look for? I can't put men on to chasing shadows when there's work like that to be done.'

'I understand that.'

'But I'm an old policeman, Mr Smiley, and I like to know what I'm about. I don't like looking for people I can't believe in, and I don't like being cut off from witnesses. I like to meet people and talk to them, nose about here and there, get to know the country. But I can't do that, not at the school. Do you follow me? So we've got to rely on laboratories, tracker dogs and nation-wide searches, but somehow in my bones I don't think it's altogether one of those cases.'

'I read in the paper about a woman, a Mad Janie . . .'

'I'm coming to that. Mrs Rode was a kindly woman, easy to talk to. I always found her so, anyway. Some of the women at Chapel took against her, but you know what women are. It seems she got friendly with this Janie creature. Janie came begging, selling herbs and charms at the back door; you know the kind of thing. She's queer, talks to birds and all that. She lives in a disused Norman chapel over to Pylle. Stella Rode used to give her food and clothes–the poor soul was often as not half-starved. Now Janie's disappeared. She was seen early Wednesday night on the lane towards North Fields and hasn't been seen since. That don't mean a thing. These people come and go in their own way. They'll be all over the neighbourhood for years, then one day they're gone like snow in the fire. They've died in a ditch, maybe, or they've took ill and crept away like a cat. Janie's not the only queer one round here. There's a lot of excitement because we found a spare set of footprints running along the fringe of trees at the far end of the garden. They were a woman's prints by the look of them, and at one point they come quite close to the conservatory. Could be a gypsy or a beggar woman. Could be anything, but I expect it's Janie right enough. I hope to Heaven it was, sir; we could do with an eye-witness, even a mad one.'

Smiley stood up. As they shook hands, Rigby said, 'Goodbye, sir. Ring me any time, any time at all.' He scribbled a telephone number on the pad in front of him, tore off the sheet and gave it to Smiley. 'That's my home number.' He showed Smiley to the door, seemed to hesitate, then he said, 'You're not a Carnian yourself by any chance, are you, sir?'

'Good heavens, no.'

Again Rigby hesitated. 'Our Chief's a Carnian. Ex-Indian Army. Brigadier Havelock. This is his last year. He's very interested in this case. Doesn't like me messing around the school. Won't have it.'

'I see.'

'He wants an arrest quickly.'

'And outside Carne, I suppose?'

'Goodbye, Mr Smiley. Don't forget to ring me. Oh, another thing I should have mentioned. That bit of cable . . .'

'Yes?'

'Mr Rode used a length of the same stuff in a demonstration lecture on elementary electronics. Mislaid it about three weeks ago.'

Smiley walked slowly back to his hotel.

My Dear Brim,

As soon as I arrived I handed your letter over to the C.I.D. man in charge of the case–it was Rigby, as Ben had supposed: he looks like a mixture of Humpty-Dumpty and a Cornish elf–very short and broad–and I don't think he's anyone's fool.'

To begin at the middle–our letter didn't have quite the effect we expected; Stella Rode evidently told Cardew, the local Baptist Minister, two weeks ago, that her husband was trying to kill her in the long nights, whatever they are. As for the circumstances of the murder–the account in the *Guardian* is substantially correct.

In fact, the more Rigby told me, the less likely it became that she was killed by her husband. Almost everything pointed away from him. Quite apart from motive, there is the location of the weapon, the footprints in the snow (which indicate a tall man in wellingtons), the presence of unidentified glove-prints in the conservatory. Add to that the strongest argument of all: whoever killed her must have been covered in blood–the conservatory was a dreadful sight, Rigby tells me. Of course, there *was* blood on Rode when he was picked up by his colleague in the lane, but only smears which could have resulted from stumbling over the body in the dark. Incidentally, the footprints only go into the garden and not out.

As things stand at the moment, there is, as Rigby points out, only one interpretation–the murderer was a stranger, a tramp, a madman perhaps, who killed her for pleasure or for her jewellery (which was worthless) and made off along the Okeford road, throwing the weapon into a ditch. (But why carry it four miles–and why not throw it into the canal the other side of the ditch? The Okeford road crosses Okemoor, which is all cross-dyked to prevent flooding.) If this interpretation is correct, then I suppose we attribute Stella's letter and her interview with Cardew to a persecuted mind, or the premonition of death, depending on whether we're superstitious. If that is so, it is the most monstrous coincidence I have ever head of. Which brings me to my final point.

I rather gathered from what Rigby *didn't* say that his Chief Constable was treading on his tail, urging him to scour the country for tramps in bloodstained blue overcoats (you remember the belt). Rigby, of course, has no alternative but to follow the signs and do as his Chief expects–but he is clearly uneasy about something–either something he hasn't told me, or something he just feels in his bones. I think he was sincere when he asked me to tell him anything I found out about the *School* end–the Rodes themselves, the way they fitted in, and so on. Carne's monastery walls are still pretty high, he feels. . . .

So I'll just sniff around a bit, I think, and see what goes on. I rang Fielding when I got back from the police station and he's asked me to supper tonight. I'll write again as soon as I have anything to tell you.

George

Having carefully sealed the envelope, pressing down the corners with his thumbs, Smiley locked his door and made his way down the wide marble staircase, treading carefully on the meagre coconut matting that ran down the centre. There was a red wooden letter box in the hall for the use of residents, but Smiley, being a cautious man, avoided it. He walked to the pillar box at the corner of the road, posted his letter and wondered what to do about lunch. There were, of course, the sandwiches and coffee provided by Miss Brimley. Reluctantly he returned to the hotel. It was full of journalists, and Smiley hated journalists. It was also cold, and he hated the cold. And there was something very familiar about sandwiches in a hotel bedroom.

Chapter Five

Cat and Dog

It was just after seven o'clock that evening when George Smiley climbed the steps which led up to the front door of Mr Terence Fielding's house. He rang, and was admitted to the hall by a little plump woman in her middle fifties. To his right a log fire burned warmly on a pile of wood ash and above him he was vaguely aware of a minstrel gallery and a mahogany staircase, which rose in a spiral to the top of the house. Most of the light seemed to come from the fire, and Smiley could see that the walls around him were hung with a great number of paintings of various styles and periods, and the chimney-piece was laden with all manner of *objets d'art*. With an involuntary shudder, he noticed that neither the fire nor the pictures quite succeeded in banishing the faint smell of school—of polish bought wholesale, of cocoa and community cooking. Corridors led from the hall, and Smiley observed that the lower part of each wall was painted a dark brown or green according to the inflexible rule of school decorators. From one of these corridors the enormous figure of Mr Terence Fielding emerged.

He advanced on Smiley, massive and genial, with his splendid mane of grey hair falling anyhow across his forehead, and his gown billowing behind him.

'Smiley? Ah! You've met True, have you—Miss Truebody, my housekeeper? Marvellous this snow, isn't it? Pure Breughel! Seen the boys skating by the Eyot? Marvellous sight! Black suits, coloured scarves, pale sun; all there, isn't it, all there! Breughel to the life. Marvellous!' He took Smiley's coat and flung it on to a decrepit deal chair with a rush seat which stood in the corner of the hall.

'You like that chair—you recognise it?'

'I don't think I do,' Smiley replied in some confusion.

'Ah, you should, you know, you should! Had it made in Provence before the war. Little carpenter I knew. Place it now? Facsimile of Van Gogh's yellow chair; some people recognise it.' He led the way down a corridor and into a large comfortable study adorned with Dutch tiles, small pieces of Renaissance sculpture, mysterious bronzes, china dogs and unglazed vases; and Fielding himself towering magnificent among them.

As senior housemaster of Carne, Fielding wore, in place of the customary academic dress, a wonderful confection of heavy black skirts and legal bib, like a monk in evening dress. All this imparted a suggestion of clerical austerity in noted contrast to the studied flamboyance of his personality. Evidently conscious of this, he sought to punctuate the solemnity of his uniform and gave to it a little of his own temperament, by adorning it with flowers carefully chosen from his garden. He had scandalised the tailors of Carne, whose frosted windows carried the insignia of royal households, by having buttonholes let into his gown. These he would fill according to his mood with anything from hibernia to bluebells. This evening he wore a rose, and from its freshness Smiley deduced that he had this minute put it into place, having ordered it specially.

'Sherry wine or Madeira?'

'Thank you; a glass of sherry.'

'Tart's drink, Madeira,' Fielding called, as he poured from a decanter, 'but boys like it. Perhaps that's why. They're frightful flirts.' He handed Smiley a glass and added, with a dramatic modification of his voice:

'We're all rather subdued at the moment by this dreadful business. We've never had anything quite like it, you know. Have you seen the evening papers?'

'No, I'm afraid I haven't. But the Sawley Arms is packed with journalists of course.'

'They've really gone to town. They've got the Army out in Hampshire, playing about with mine-detectors. God knows what they expect to find.'

'How have the boys taken it?'

'They adore it! My own house has been particularly fortunate, of course, because the Rodes were dining here that night. Some oaf from the police even wanted to question one of my boys.'

'Indeed,' said Smiley innocently. 'What on earth about?'

'Oh, God knows,' Fielding replied abruptly, and then, changing the subject, he asked, 'You knew my brother well, didn't you? He talked about you, you know.'

'Yes, I knew Adrian very well. We were close friends.'

'In the war, too?'

'Yes.'

'Were you in his crowd, then?'

'What crowd?'

'Steed-Asprey, Jebedee. All those people.'

'Yes.'

'I never really heard how he died. Did you?'

'No.'

'We didn't see much of one another in later years, Adrian and I. Being a fraud, I can't afford to be seen beside the genuine article,' Fielding declared, with something of his earlier panache. Smiley was spared the embarrassment of a reply by a quiet knock at the door, and a tall red-haired boy came timidly into the room.

'I've called the Adsum, sir, if you're ready, sir.'

'Damn,' said Fielding, emptying his glass. 'Prayers.' He turned to Smiley.

'Meet Perkins, my head prefect. Musical genius, but a problem in the schoolroom. That right, Tim? Stay here or come as you like. It only lasts ten minutes.'

'Rather less tonight, sir,' said Perkins. 'It's the Nunc Dimittis.'

'Thank God for small mercies,' Fielding declared, tugging briefly at his bib, as he led Smiley at a spanking pace out into the corridor and across the hall, with Perkins stalking along behind them. Fielding was speaking all the time without bothering to turn his head:

'I'm glad you've chosen this evening to come. I never entertain on Saturdays as a rule because everyone else does, though none of us quite knows what to do about entertaining at the moment. Felix D'Arcy will be coming tonight, but that's hardly entertaining. D'Arcy's a professional. Incidentally, we normally dress in the evening, but it doesn't matter.'

Smiley's heart sank. They turned a corner and entered another corridor.

'We have prayers at all hours here. The Master's revived the seven Day Hours for the Offices: Prime, Terce, Sext and so on. A surfeit during the Half, abstinence during the holidays, that's the system, like games. Useful in the house for roll-calls, too.' He led the way down yet another corridor, flung open a double door at the end of it and marched straight into the dining-room, his gown filling gracefully behind him. The boys were waiting for him.

'More sherry? What did you think of prayers? They sing quite nicely, don't they? One or two good tenors. We tried some plainsong last Half; quite good, really quite good. D'Arcy will be here soon. He's a frightful toad. Looks like a Sickert model fifty years after—all trousers and collar. However, you're lucky his sister isn't accompanying him. She's worse!'

'What's his subject?' They were back in Fielding's study.

'Subject! I'm afraid we don't have subjects here. None of us has read a word on any subject since we left University.' He lowered his voice and added darkly, 'That's if we *went* to University. D'Arcy teaches French. D'Arcy is senior tutor by election, bachelor by profession, sublimated pansy by inclination . . .' he was standing quite still now, his head thrown back and his right hand stretched out towards Smiley, '. . . and his subject is other people's shortcomings. He is principally, however, self-appointed majordomo of Carne protocol. If you wear a gown on a bicycle, reply incorrectly to an invitation, make a fault in the *placement* of your dinner guests or speak of a colleague as 'Mister', D'Arcy will find you out and admonish you.'

'What are the duties of Senior Tutor, then?' Smiley asked, just for something to say.

'He's the referee between the classics and the scientists; arranges the timetable and vets the exam. results. But principally, poor man, he must reconcile the Arts with the Sciences.' He shook his head sagely. 'And it takes a better man than D'Arcy to do that. Not, mind you,' he added wearily, 'that it makes the least difference who wins the extra hour on Friday evenings. Who cares? Not the boys, poor dears, that's certain.'

Fielding talked on, at random and always in superlatives, sometimes groping in the air with his hand as if to catch the more elusive metaphors; now of his colleagues with caustic derision, now of boys with compassion if not with understanding; now of the Arts with fervour—and the studied bewilderment of a lonely disciple.

'Carne isn't a school. It's a sanatorium for intellectual lepers. The symptoms began when we came down from University; a gradual putrefication of our intellectual extremities. From day to day our minds die, our spirits atrophy and rot. We watch the process in one another, hoping to forget it in ourselves.' He paused, and looked reflectively at his hands.

'In me the process is complete. You see before you a dead soul, and Carne is the body I live in.' Much pleased by this confession, Fielding held out his great arms so that the sleeves of his gown resembled the wings of a giant bat, 'the Vampire of Carne', he declared, bowing deeply. 'Alcoholique et poète!' A bellow of laughter followed this display.

Smiley was fascinated by Fielding, by his size, his voice, the wanton inconstancy of his temperament, by his whole big-screen style; he found himself attracted and repelled by this succession of contradictory poses; he wondered whether he was supposed to take part in the performance, but Fielding seemed so dazzled by the footlights that he was indifferent to the audience behind them. The more Smiley watched, the more elusive seemed the character he was trying to comprehend: changeful but sterile, daring but fugitive;

colourful, unbounded, ingenuous, yet deceitful and perverse. Smiley began to wish he could acquire the material facts of Fielding–his means, his ambitions and disappointments.

His reverie was interrupted by Miss Truebody. Felix D'Arcy had arrived.

No candles, and a cold supper admirably done by Miss Truebody. Not claret, but hock, passed round like port. And at last, at long last, Fielding mentioned Stella Rode.

They had been talking rather dutifully of the Arts and the Sciences. This would have been dull (for it was uninformed) had not D'Arcy constantly been goaded by Fielding, who seemed anxious to exhibit D'Arcy in his worst light. D'Arcy's judgements of people and problems were largely coloured by what he considered 'seemly' (a favourite word) and by an effeminate malice towards his colleagues. After a while Fielding asked who was replacing Rode during his absence, to which D'Arcy said, 'No one,' and added unctuously:

'It was a terrible shock to the community, this affair.'

'Nonsense,' Fielding retorted. 'Boys love disaster. The further we are from death the more attractive it seems. They find the whole affair most exhilarating.'

'The publicity has been most unseemly,' said D'Arcy, 'most. I think that has been prominent in the minds of many of us in the Common Room.' He turned to Smiley:

'The press, you know, is a constant worry here. In the past it could never have happened. Formerly our great families and institutions were not subjected to this intrusion. No, indeed not. But today all that is changed. Many of us are compelled to subscribe to the cheaper newspapers for this very reason. One Sunday newspaper mentioned no fewer than four of Hecht's old boys in one edition. All of them in an unseemly context, I may say. And of course such papers never fail to mention that the boy is a Carnian. You know, I suppose, that we have the young prince here. (I myself have the honour to supervise his French studies.) The young Sawley is also at Carne. The activity of the press during his parents' divorce suit was deplorable. Quite deplorable. The Master wrote to the Press Council, you know. I drafted the letter myself. But on this tragic occasion they have excelled themselves. We even had the press at Compline last night, you know, waiting for the Special Prayer. They occupied the whole of the two rear pews on the west side. Hecht was doing Chapel Duty and tried to have them removed.' He paused, raised his eyebrows in gentle reproach and smiled. 'He had no business to, of course, but that never stopped the good Hecht.' He turned to Smiley, 'One of our *athletic* brethren,' he explained.

'Stella was too common for you, Felix, wasn't she?'

'Not at all,' said D'Arcy quickly. 'I would not have you say that of me, Terence. I am by no means discriminatory in the matter of class; merely of manners. I grant you, in that particular field, I found her wanting.'

'In many ways she was just what we needed,' Fielding continued, addressing Smiley and ignoring D'Arcy. 'She was everything we're forced to ignore–she was red-brick, council estates, new towns, the very antithesis of Carne!' He turned suddenly to D'Arcy and said, 'But to you, Felix, she was just bad form.'

'Not at all; merely unsuitable.'

Fielding turned to Smiley in despair.

'Look,' he said. 'We talk academic here, you know, wear academic dress and hold high table dinners in the Common Room; we have long graces in Latin that none of us can translate. We go to the Abbey and the wives sit in the hencoop in their awful hats. But it's a charade. It means nothing.'

D'Arcy smiled wanly.

'I cannot believe, my dear Terence, that anyone who keeps such an excellent table as yourself can have so low an opinion of the refinements of social conduct.' He looked to Smiley for support and Smiley dutifully echoed the compliment. 'Besides, we know Terence of old at Carne. I am afraid we are accustomed to his roar.'

'I know why you disliked that woman, Felix. She was honest, and Carne has no defence against that kind of honesty.'

D'Arcy suddenly became very angry indeed.

'Terence, I will not have you say this. I simply will not have it. I feel I have a certain duty at Carne, as indeed we all have, to restore and maintain those standards of behaviour which suffered so sadly in the war. I am sensible that this determination has made me on more than one occasion unpopular. But such comment or advice as I offer is never–I beg you to notice this–is *never* directed against personalities, only against behaviour, against unseemly lapses in conduct. I will acknowledge that more than once I was compelled to address Rode on the subject of his wife's conduct. That is a matter quite divorced from personalities, Terence. I will not have it said that I disliked Mrs Rode. Such a suggestion would be disagreeable at all times, but under the present tragic circumstances it is deplorable. Mrs Rode's own . . . background and education did not naturally prepare her for our ways; that is quite a different matter. It does, however, illustrate the point that I wish to emphasise, Terence: it was a question of enlightenment, not of criticism. Do I make myself clear?'

'Abundantly,' Fielding answered dryly.

'Did the other wives like her?' Smiley ventured.

'Not entirely,' D'Arcy replied crisply.

'The wives! My God!' Fielding groaned, putting his hand to his brow. There was a pause.

'Her clothes, I believe, were a source of distress to some of them. She also frequented the public laundry. This, too, would not make a favourable impression. I should add that she did not attend our church. . . .'

'Did she have any close friends among the wives?' Smiley persisted.

'I believe young Mrs Snow took to her.'

'And you say she was dining here the night she was murdered?'

'Yes,' said Fielding quietly, 'Wednesday. And it was Felix and his sister who took in poor Rode afterwards. . . .' He glanced at D'Arcy.

'Yes, indeed,' said D'Arcy abruptly. His eyes were on Fielding, and it seemed to Smiley that something had passed between them. 'We shall never forget, never. . . . Terence, if I may talk shop for just one moment, Perkins' construe is abysmal; I declare I have never seen work like it. Is he unwell? His mother is a most cultured woman, a cousin of the Samfords, I am told.'

Smiley looked at him and wondered. His dinner jacket was faded, green with age. Smiley could almost hear him saying it had belonged to his grandfather. The skin of his face was so unlined that he somehow suggested fatness without being fat. His voice was pitched on one insinuating note, and he smiled all the time, whether he was speaking or not. The smile never left his smooth face, it was worked into the malleable fabric of his flesh, stretching his lips across his perfect teeth and opening the corners of his red mouth, so that it seemed to be held in place by the invisible fingers of his dentist. Yet D'Arcy's face was far from unexpressive; every mark showed. The smallest movement of his mouth or nose, the quickest glance or frown, were there to read and interpret. And he wanted to change the subject. Not away from Stella Rode (for he returned to discussing her himself a moment later), but away from the particular evening on which she died, away from the precise narration of events. And what was more, there was not a doubt in Smiley's mind that Fielding had seen it too, that in that look which passed between them was a pact of fear, a warning perhaps, so that from that moment Fielding's manner changed, he grew sullen and preoccupied, in a way that puzzled Smiley long afterwards.

D'Arcy turned to Smiley and addressed him with cloying intimacy.

'*Do* forgive my deplorable descent into Carne gossip. You find us a little cut off here, do you not? We are often held to be cut off, I know. Carne is a 'Snob School', that is the cry. You may read it every day in the gutter press. And yet, despite the claims of the *avant-garde*,' he said, glancing slyly at Fielding, 'I may say that *no one* could be less of a snob than Felix D'Arcy.' Smiley noticed his hair. It was very fine and ginger, growing from the top and leaving his pink neck bare.

'Take poor Rode, for instance. I certainly don't hold Rode's background against him in any way, poor fellow. The Grammar Schools do a splendid job, I am sure. Besides, he settled down here very well. I told the Master so. I said to him that Rode had settled down well; he does Chapel duty quite admirably–that was the very point I made. I hope I have played my part, what is more, in helping him to fit in. With careful instruction, such people can, as I said to the Master, learn our customs and even our manners; and the Master agreed.'

Smiley's glass was empty and D'Arcy without consulting Fielding, filled it for him from the decanter. His hands were polished and hairless, like the hands of a girl.

'But,' he continued, 'I must be honest. Mrs Rode did not adapt herself so willingly to our ways.' Still smiling, he sipped delicately from his glass. He wants to put the record straight, thought Smiley.

'She would never really have fitted in at Carne; that is my opinion–though I am sure I never voiced it while she was alive. Her background was against her. The fault was not hers–it was her background which, as I say, was unfortunate. Indeed, if we may speak frankly and in confidence, I have reason to believe it was her past that brought about her death.'

'Why do you say that?' asked Smiley quickly, and D'Arcy replied with a glance at Fielding, 'It appears she was expecting to be attacked.'

'My sister is devoted to dogs,' D'Arcy continued. 'You may know that already perhaps. King Charles spaniels are her *forte*. She took a first at the North Dorset last year and was commended at Cruft's shortly afterwards for her 'Queen of Carne'. She sells to America, you know. I dare say there are few people in the country with Dorothy's knowledge of the breed. The Master's wife found occasion to say the very same thing a week ago. Well, the Rodes were our neighbours, as you know, and Dorothy is not a person to neglect her neighbourly duties. Where duty is concerned, you will not find her discriminatory, I assure you. The Rodes also had a dog, a large mongrel, quite an intelligent animal, which they brought with them. (I have little idea where they came from, but that is another matter.) They appeared quite devoted to the dog, and I have no doubt they were. Rode took it with him to watch the football until I had occasion to advise him against it. The practice was giving rise to unseemly humour among the boys. I have found the same thing myself when exercising Dorothy's spaniels.

'I shall come to the point presently. Dorothy uses a vet called Harriman, a superior type of person who lives over toward Sturminster. A fortnight ago she sent for him. 'Queen of Carne' was coughing badly and Dorothy asked Harriman to come over. A bitch of her quality is not to be taken lightly, I assure you.'

Fielding groaned, and D'Arcy continued, oblivious:

'I happened to be at home, and Harriman stayed for a cup of coffee. He is, as I say, a superior type of person. Harriman made some reference to the Rodes' dog and then the truth came out; Mrs Rode had had the dog destroyed the previous day. She said it had bitten the postman. Some long and confused story; the Post Office would sue, the police had been round and I don't know what else. And, anyway, she said, the dog couldn't really protect, it could only warn. She had said so to Harriman, "It wouldn't do any good."'

'Wasn't she upset about losing the dog?' asked Smiley.

'Oh, indeed, yes. Harriman said she was in tears when she arrived. Mrs Harriman had to give her a cup of tea. They suggested she should give the dog another chance, put it in kennels for a while, but she was adamant, quite adamant. Harriman was most perplexed. So was his wife. When they discussed it afterwards they agreed that Mrs Rode's behaviour had not been quite normal. Not normal at all, in fact. Another curious fact was the condition of dog: it had been maltreated, seriously so. Its back was marked as if from beatings.'

'Did Harriman follow up this remark she made? About not doing any good? What did Harriman make of it?' Smiley was watching D'Arcy intently.

'She repeated it to Mrs Harriman, but she wouldn't explain it. However, I think the explanation is obvious enough.'

'Oh?' said Fielding.

D'Arcy put his head on one side and plucked coyly at the lobe of his ear.

'We all have a little of the detective in us,' he said. 'Dorothy and I talked it over after the—death. We decided that Stella Rode had formed some unsavoury association before coming to Carne, which had recently been revived . . . possibly against her will. Some violent ruffian—an old admirer—who would resent the improvement in her station.'

'How badly was the postman bitten by the dog?' Smiley asked.

D'Arcy turned to him again.

'That is the extraordinary thing. That is the very crux of the story, my dear fellow: the postman hadn't been bitten at all. Dorothy enquired. Her whole story was an absolute string of lies from beginning to end.'

They rose from the table and made their way to Fielding's study, where Miss Truebody had put the coffee. The conversation continued to wander back and forth over Wednesday's tragedy. D'Arcy was obsessed with the indelicacy of it all—the persistence of journalists, the insensitivity of the police, the uncertainty of Mrs Rode's origin, the misfortune of her husband. Fielding was still oddly silent, sunk in his own thoughts, from which he occasionally emerged to glance at D'Arcy with a look of hostility. At exactly a quarter to eleven D'Arcy pronounced himself tired, and the three of them went into the great hall, where Miss Truebody produced a coat for Smiley and a coat and muffler and cap for D'Arcy. Fielding accepted D'Arcy's thanks with a sullen nod. He turned to Smiley:

'That business you rang me about. What was it exactly?'

'Oh—a letter from Mrs Rode just before she was murdered,' said Smiley vaguely, 'the police are handling it now, but they do not regard it as . . . significant. Not significant at all. She seems to have had a sort of'—he gave an embarrassed grin—'persecution complex. Is that the expression? However, we might discuss it some time. You must dine with me at the Sawley before I go back. Do you come to London at all? We might meet in London perhaps, at the end of the Half.'

D'Arcy was standing in the doorway, looking at the new fall of snow which lay white and perfect on the pavement before him.

'Ah,' he said, with a little knowing laugh, 'the long nights, eh, Terence, the long nights.'

Chapter Six

Holly for the Devil

'What are the long nights?' Smiley asked, as he and D'Arcy walked briskly away from Fielding's house through the new snow towards the Abbey close.

'We have a proverb that it always snows at Carne in the long nights. That is the traditional term here for the nights of Lent,' D'Arcy replied. 'Before the Reformation the monks of the Abbey kept a vigil during Lent between the Offices of Compline and Lauds. You may know that already perhaps. As there is no longer a religious order attached to the Abbey, the custom has fallen into disuse. We continue to observe it, however, by the saying of Compline during Lent. Compline was the last of the Canonical Day Hours and was said before retiring for the night. The Master, who has a great respect for traditions of this kind, has reintroduced the old words for our devotions. Prime was the dawn Office, as you are no doubt aware. Terce was at the third hour of daylight—that is to say at 9.0 a.m. Thus we no longer refer to Morning Prayer, but to Terce. I find it delightful. Similarly, during Advent and Lent we say Sext at midday in the Abbey.'

'Are all these services compulsory?'

'Of course. Otherwise it would be necessary to make arrangements for those boys who did not attend. That is not desirable. Besides, you forget that Carne is a religious foundation.'

It was a beautiful night. As they crossed the Close, Smiley looked up at the tower. It seemed smaller and more peaceful in the moonlight. The whiteness of the new snow lit the very sky itself; the whole Abbey was so sharply visible against it that even the mutilated images of saints were clear in every sad detail of their defacement, wretched figures, their purpose lost, with no eyes to see the changing world.

They reached the cross-roads to the south of the Abbey.

'The parting of the ways, I fear,' said D'Arcy, extending his hand.

'It's a beautiful night,' Smiley replied quickly, 'Let me come with you as far as your house.'

'Gladly,' said D'Arcy dryly.

They turned down North Fields Lane. A high stone wall ran along one side; and on the other the great expanse of playing fields, twenty or more rugby pitches, bordered the road for over half a mile. They walked this distance in silence, until D'Arcy stopped and pointed with his stick past Smiley towards a small house on the edge of the playing fields.

'That's North Fields, the Rodes' house. It used to belong to the head groundsman, but the school added a wing a few years ago, and now it's a staff house. My own house is rather larger, and lies further up the road. Happily, I am fond of walking.'

'Was it along here that you found Stanley Rode that night?'

There was a pause, then D'Arcy said: 'It was nearer to my house, about a quarter of a mile further on. He was in a terrible condition, poor fellow, terrible. I am myself unable to bear the sight of blood. If I had known how he would look when I brought him into the house, I do not think I could have done it. Mercifully, my sister Dorothy is a most competent woman.'

They walked on in silence, until Smiley said: 'From what you were saying at dinner, the Rodes were a very ill-assorted couple.'

'Precisely. If her death had happened any other way, I would describe it as providential: a blessed release for Rode. She was a thoroughly mischievous woman, Smiley, who made it her business to hold her husband up to ridicule. I believe it was intentional. Others do not. I do, and I have my reasons. She took pleasure in deriding her husband.'

'And Carne too, no doubt.'

'Just so. This is a critical moment in Carne's development. Many Public Schools have conceded to the vulgar clamour for change—change at any price. Carne, I am pleased to say, has not joined these Gadarene swine. That makes it more important than

ever that we protect ourselves from within as well as from without.'
He spoke with surprising vehemence.

'But was she really such a problem? Surely her husband could
have spoken to her?'

'I never encouraged him to do so, I assure you. It is not my
practice to interfere between man and wife.'

They reached D'Arcy's house. A high laurel hedge entirely
concealed the house from the road, except for two multiple chimney-
stacks which were visible over the top of it, confirming Smiley's
impression that the house was large and Victorian.

'I am not ashamed of the Victorian taste,' said D'Arcy as he slowly
opened the gate; 'but then, I am afraid we are not close to the modern
idiom at Carne. This house used to be the rectory for North Fields
Church, but the church is now served by a priest-in-charge from the
Abbey. The vicarage is still within the school's gift, and I was
fortunate enough to receive it. Good night. You must come for
sherry before you go. Do you stay long?'

'I doubt it,' Smiley replied, 'but I am sure you have enough
worries at the moment.'

'What do you mean?' D'Arcy said sharply.

'The press, the police and all the attendant fuss.'

'Ah yes, just so. Quite so. Nevertheless, our community life must
continue. We always have a small party in the middle of the Half, and
I feel it is particularly important that we should do so on this
occasion. I will send a note to the Sawley tomorrow. My sister would
be charmed. Good night.' He clanged the gate to, and the sound was
greeted by the frantic barking of dogs from somewhere behind the
house. A window opened and a harsh female voice called:

'Is that you, Felix?'

'Yes, Dorothy.'

'Why do you have to make such a bloody noise? You've woken
those dogs again.' The window closed with a significant thud, and
D'Arcy, without so much as a glance in Smiley's direction, disappeared quickly into the shadow of the house.

Smiley set off along the road again, back towards the town. After
walking for about ten minutes he stopped and looked again towards
the Rodes' house a hundred yards across the playing fields. It lay in
the shadow of a small coppice of fir trees, dark and secret against the
white fields. A narrow lane led towards the house; there was a brick
pillar-box on one corner and a small oak sign-post, quite new,
pointed along the lane, which must, he decided, lead to the village of
Pylle. The legend upon the sign was obscured by a film of snow, and
Smiley brushed it away with his hand, so that he could read the
words 'North Fields', done in a contrived Gothic script which must
have caused D'Arcy considerable discomfort. The snow in the lane

was untrodden; obviously more had fallen recently. There could not be much traffic between Pylle and Carne. Glancing quickly up and down the main road he began making his way long the lane. The hedge rose high on either side, and soon Smiley could see nothing but the pale sky above him, and the straggling willow wands reaching towards it. Once he thought he heard the sound of a footstep close behind him, but when he stopped he heard nothing but the furtive rustle of the laden hedges. He grew more conscious of the cold: it seemed to hang in the still damp of the sunken road, to clutch and hold him like the chill air of an empty house. Soon the hedge on his left gave way to a sparse line of trees, which Smiley judged to belong to the coppice he had seen from the road. The snow beneath the trees was patchy, and the bare ground looked suddenly ugly and torn. The lane took him in a gradual curve to the left and, quite suddenly the house stood before him, gaunt and craggy in the moonlight. The walls were brick and flint, half obscured by the mass of ivy which grew in profusion across them, tumbling over the porch in a tangled mane.

He glanced towards the garden. The coppice which bordered the lane encroached almost as far as the corner of the house, and extended to the far end of the lawn, screening the house from the playing fields. The murderer had reached the house by a path which led across the lawn and through the trees to the lane at the farthest end of the garden. Looking carefully at the snow on the lawn, he was able to discern the course of the path. The white glazed door to the left of the house must lead to the conservatory . . . And suddenly he knew he was afraid—afraid of the house, afraid of the sprawling dark garden. The knowledge came to him like an awareness of pain. The ivy walls seemed to reach forward and hold him, like an old woman cosseting an unwilling child. The house was large, yet dingy, holding to itself unearthly shapes, black and oily in the sudden contrasts of moonlight. Fascinated despite his fear, he moved towards it. The shadows broke and reformed, darting swiftly and becoming still, hiding the abundant ivy, or merging with the black windows.

He observed in alarm the first involuntary movement of panic. He was afraid, then suddenly the senses joined in one concerted cry of terror, where sight and sound and touch could no longer be distinguished in the frenzy of his brain. He turned round and ran back to the gate. As he did so, he looked over his shoulder towards the house.

A woman was standing in the path, looking at him, and behind her the conservatory door swung slowly on its hinges.

For a second she stood quite still, then turned and ran back towards the conservatory. Forgetting his fear, Smiley followed. As he reached the corner of the house he saw to his astonishment that she was standing at the door, rocking it gently back and forth in a thoughtful, leisurely way, like a child. She had her back to Smiley, until suddenly she turned to him and spoke, with a soft Dorset drawl, and the childish lilt of a simpleton:

'I thought you was the Devil, Mister, but you'm got no wings.'

Smiley hesitated. If he moved forward, she might take fright again and run. He looked at her across the snow, trying to make her out. She seemed to be wearing a bonnet or shawl over her head, and a dark cape over her shoulders. In her hand she held a sprig of leaves, and these she gently waved back and forth as she spoke to him.

'But you'm carn't do nothin', Mister, 'cos I got the holly fer to hold yer. So you do bide there, Mister, for little Jane can hold yer.' She shook the leaves vehemently towards him and began laughing softly. She still had one hand upon the door, and as she spoke her head lolled to one side.

'You bide away from little Jane, Mister, however pretty she'm do be.'

'Yes, Jane,' said Smiley softly, 'you're a very pretty girl I can see that; and that's a pretty cape you're wearing, Jane.'

Evidently pleased with this, she clutched the lapels of her cape and turned slowly round, in a child's parody of a fine lady.

As she turned, Smiley saw the two empty sleeves of an overcoat swinging at her sides.

'There's some do laugh at Janie,' she said, a note of petulance in her voice, 'but there's not many seen the Devil fly, Mister. But Janie seed 'im, Janie seed 'im. Silver wings like fishes, 'e done 'ad, Janie saw.'

'Where did you find that coat, Janie?'

She put her hands together and shook her head slowly from side to side.

'He'm a bad one. Ooh, he'm a bad one, Mister,' and she laughed softly. 'I seed 'im flying, riding on the wind,' she laughed again, 'and the moon be'ind 'im, lightin' up the way! They'm close as sisters, moon and Devil.'

On an impulse Smiley seized a handful of ivy from the side of the house and held it out to her, moving slowly forward as he did so.

'Do you like flowers, Janie? Here are flowers for Janie; pretty flowers for pretty Janie.' He had nearly reached her when with remarkable speed she ran across the lawn, disappeared into the trees and ran off down the lane. Smiley let her go. He was drenched in sweat.

As soon as he reached the hotel he telephoned Detective Inspector Rigby.

Chapter Seven

King Arthur's Church

The coffee lounge of the Sawley Arms resembles nothing so much as the Tropical Plants Pavilion at Kew Gardens. Built in an age when cactus was the most fashionable of plants and bamboo its indispensable companion, the lounge was conceived as the architectural image of a jungle clearing. Steel pillars, fashioned in segments like the trunk of a palm tree, supported a high glass roof whose regal dome replaced the African sky. Enormous urns of bronze or green-glazed earthenware contained all that was elegant and prolific in the cactus world, and between them very old residents could relax on sofas of spindly bamboo, sipping warm coffee and re-living the discomforts of safari.

Smiley's efforts to obtain a bottle of whisky and a syphon of soda at half past eleven at night were not immediately rewarded. It seemed that, like carrion from the carcase, the journalists had gone. The only sign of life in the hotel was the night porter, who treated his request with remote disapproval and advised him to go to bed. Smiley, by no means naturally persistent, discovered a half-crown in his overcoat pocket and thrust it a little irritably into the old man's hand. The result, though not magical, was effective, and by the time Rigby had made his way to the hotel, Smiley was seated in front of a bright gas fire in the coffee lounge with glasses and a whisky bottle before him.

Smiley retold his experiences of the evening with careful accuracy.

'It was the coat that caught my eye. It was a heavy overcoat like a man's,' he concluded. 'I remembered the blue belt and . . .' He left the sentence unfinished. Rigby nodded, got up and walked briskly across the lounge and through the swing doors to the porter's desk. Ten minutes later, he returned.

'I think we'd better go and pull her in,' he said simply. 'I've sent for a car.'

'We?' asked Smiley.

'Yes, if you wouldn't mind. What's the matter? Are you frightened?'

'Yes,' he replied, 'Yes, I am.'

The village of Pylle lies to the south of North Fields, upon a high spur which rises steeply from the flat, damp pastures of the Carne valley. It consists of a handful of stone cottages and a small inn where you may drink beer in the landlord's parlour. Seen from Carne playing fields, the village could easily be mistaken for an outcrop of rock upon a tor, for the hill on which it stands appears conical from the northern side. Local historians claim that Pylle is the oldest settlement in Dorset, that its name is Anglo-Saxon for harbour, and that it served the Romans as a port when all the lowlands around were covered by the sea. They will tell you, too, that King Arthur rested there after seven months at sea, and paid homage to Saint Andrew, the patron saint of sailors, on the site of Pylle Church, where he burned a candle for each month he had spent afloat; and that in the church, built to commemorate his visit and standing to this day lonely and untended on the hillside, there is a bronze coin as witness to his visit—the very one King Arthur gave to the verger before he set sail again for the Isle of Avalon.

Inspector William Rigby, himself a keen local historian, gave Smiley a somewhat terse précis of Pylle's legendary past as he drove cautiously along the snow-covered lanes.

'These small, out-of-the-way villages are pretty strange places,' he concluded. 'Often only three or four families, all so inbred you can no more sort them out than a barnful of cats. That's where your village idiots come from. They call it the Devil's Mark; I call it incest. They hate to have them in the village, you know—they'll drive them away at any price, like trying to wash away their shame, if you follow me.'

'I follow you.'

'This Jane's the religious sort. There's one or two of them turn that way. The villagers at Pylle are all Chapel now, see, so there's been no use for King Arthur's Church since Wesley. It's empty, falling to bits. There's a few from the valley go up to see it, for its history, like, but no one cares for it, or didn't not till Janie moved in.'

'Moved in?'

'Yes. She's taken to cleaning the church out night and day, bringing in wild flowers and such. That's why they say she's a witch.'

They passed Rode's house in silence and after turning a sharp bend began climbing the long steep hill that led to Pylle village. The snow in the lane was untouched and apart from occasional skidding they progressed without difficulty. The lower slopes of the hill were wooded, and the lane dark, until suddenly they emerged to find themselves on a smooth plateau, where a savage wind blew the fine snow like smoke across the fields, whipping it against the car. The snow had risen in drifts to one side of the lane, and the going became increasingly difficult.

Finally Rigby stopped the car and said:

'We'll walk from here, sir, if you don't mind.'

'How far is it?'

'Short and sour, I'd say. That's the village straight ahead.'

Through the windscreen, Smiley could discern behind the drifting veils of blown snow two low buildings about a quarter of a mile away. As he looked, a tall, muffled figure advanced towards them along the lane.

'That's Ted Mundy,' said Rigby with satisfaction, 'I told him to be here. He's the sergeant from Okeford.' He leaned out of the car window and called merrily:

'Hullo, Ted there, you old buzzard, how be?' Rigby opened the back door of the car and the sergeant climbed in. Smiley and Mundy were briefly introduced.

'There's a light in the church,' said Mundy, 'but I don't know whether Janie's there. I can't ask no one in the village, see, or I'd have the whole lot round me. They thought she'd gone for good.'

'Does she sleep there then, Ted? She got a bed there or something?' Rigby asked, and Smiley noticed with pleasure that his Dorset accent was more pronounced when he spoke to Mundy.

'So they say, Bill. I couldn't find no bed when I looked in there Saturday. But I tell you an odd thing, Bill. It seems Mrs Rode used to come up here sometimes, to the chapel, to see Janie.'

'I heard about that,' said Rigby shortly. 'Now which way's the church, Ted?'

'Over the hill,' said Mundy. 'Outside the village, in a paddock.' He turned to Smiley. 'That's quite common round here, sir, as I expect you know.' Mundy spoke very slowly, choosing his words. 'You see, when they had the plague they left their dead in the villages and moved away; not far though, on account of their land and the church. Terrible it was, terrible.' Somehow Mundy managed to imply that the Black Death was a fairly recent disaster in those parts, if not actually within living memory.

They got out of the car, forcing the doors against the strong wind, and made their way towards the village, Mundy leading and Smiley in third place. The driven snow, fine and hard, stung their faces. It was an unearthly walk, high on that white hill on such a night. The curve of the bleak hill's crest and the moaning of the wind, the snow cloud which sped across the moon, the dismal, unlit cottages so cautiously passed, belonged to another corner of the world.

Mundy led them sharply to the left, and Smiley guessed that by avoiding the centre of the village he hoped to escape the notice of its inhabitants. After about twenty minutes' walking, often through deep snow, they found themselves following a low hedge between two fields. In the furthest corner of the right hand field they saw a pale light glimmering across the snow, so pale that at first Smiley had to look away from it, then run his eyes back along the line of that distant hedge to make sure he was not deceived. Rigby stopped, beckoning to the others.

'I'll take over now,' he said. He turned to Smiley. 'I'd be obliged, sir, if you'd stand off a little. If there's any trouble we don't want you mixed up in it, do we?'

'Of course.'

'Ted Mundy, you come up by me.'

They followed the hedge until they came to a stile. Through the gap in the hedge they saw the church clearly now, a low building more like a tithe barn than a church. At one end a pale glow, like the uncertain light of a candle, shone dimly through the leaded windows.

'She's there,' said Mundy, under his breath, as he and Rigby moved forward. Smiley following some distance behind.

They were crossing the field now, Rigby leading, and the church drawing ever closer. New sounds disturbed the moaning of the storm; the parched creak of a door, the mutter of a crumbling roof, the incessant sigh of wind upon a dying house. The two men in front of Smiley had stopped, almost in the shadow of the church wall, and were whispering together. Then Mundy walked quietly away, disappearing round the corner of the church. Rigby waited a moment, then approached the narrow entrance in the rear wall, and pushed the door.

It opened slowly, creaking painfully on its hinges. Then he disappeared into the church. Smiley was waiting outside when suddenly above all the sounds of night he heard a scream, so taut and shrill and clear that it seemed to have no source, but to ride everywhere upon the wind, to mount the ravaged sky on wings; and Smiley had a vision of Mad Janie as he had seen her earlier that night, and he heard again in her demented cry the dreadful note of madness. For a moment he waited. The echo died. Then slowly, terrified, he walked through the snow to the open doorway.

Two candles and an oil lamp on the bare altar shed a dim light over the tiny chapel. In front of the altar, on the sanctuary step, sat Jane, looking vaguely towards them. Her vacuous face was daubed with stains of green and blue, her filthy clothes were threaded with sprigs of evergreen and all about her on the floor were the bodies of small animals and birds.

The pews were similarly decorated with dead creatures of all kinds; and on the altar, broken twigs and little heaps of holly leaves. Between the candles stood a crudely-fashioned cross. Stepping forward past Rigby, Smiley walked quickly down the aisle, past the lolling figure of Jane, until he stood before the altar. For a moment he hesitated, then turned and called softly to Rigby.

On the cross, draped over its three ends like a crude diadem, was a string of green beads.

Chapter Eight

Flowers for Stella

He woke with the echo of her scream in his ears. He had meant to sleep late, but his watch said half-past seven. He put on his bedside lamp, for it was still half-dark, and peered owlishly round the room. There were his trousers, flung over the chair, the legs still sodden from the snow. There were his shoes; he'd have to buy another pair. And there beside him were the notes he had made early that morning before going to sleep, transcriptions from memory of some of Mad Janie's monologue on the journey back to Carne, a journey he would never forget. Mundy had sat with her in the back. She spoke to herself as a child does, asking questions and then in the patient tones of an adult for whom the reply is self-evident, providing the answer.

One obsession seemed to fill her mind: she had seen the devil. She had seen him flying on the wind, his silver wings stretched out behind him. Sometimes the recollection amused her, sometimes inflated her with a sense of her own importance or beauty, and sometimes it terrified her, so that she moaned and wept and begged him to go away. Then Mundy would speak kindly to her, and try to calm her. Smiley wondered whether policemen grew accustomed to the squalor of such things, to clothes that were no more than stinking rags wound round wretched limbs, to puling imbeciles who clutched and screamed and wept. She must have been living on the run for nights on end, finding her food in the fields and dustbins since the night of the murder. . . . What had she done that night? What had she seen? Had she killed Stella Rode? Had she seen the murderer, and fancied *him* to be the devil flying on the wind? Why should she think that? If Janie did not kill Stella Rode, what had she seen that so frightened her that for three long winter nights she prowled in terror like an animal in the forest? Had the devil within taken hold of Janie and given power to her arm as she struck down Stella? Was that the devil who rode upon the wind?

But the beads and the coat and the footprints which were not hers—what of them? He lay there thinking, and achieving nothing. At last it was time to get up: it was the morning of the funeral.

As he was getting out of bed the telephone rang. It was Rigby. His voice sounded strained and urgent. 'I want to see you,' he said. 'Can you call round?'

'Before or after the funeral?'

'Before, if possible. What about now?'

'I'll be there in ten minutes.'

Rigby looked, for the first time since Smiley had met him, tired and worried.

'It's Mad Janie,' he said. 'The Chief thinks we should charge her.'

'What for?'

'Murder,' Rigby replied crisply, pushing a thin file across the table. 'The old fool's made a statement . . . a sort of confession.'

They sat in silence while Smiley read the extraordinary statement. It was signed with Mad Janie's mark–J. L.–drawn in a childish hand in letters an inch high. The constable who had taken it down had begun by trying to condense and simplify her account, but by the end of the first page he had obviously despaired. At last Smiley came to the description of the murder:

> 'So I tells my darling, I tells her: "You are a naughty creature to go with the devil," but her did not hearken, see, and I took angry with her, but she paid no call. I can't abide them as go with devils in the night, and I told her. She ought to have had holly, mister, there's the truth. I told her, mister, but she never would hearken, and that's all Janie's saying, but she drove the devil off, Janie did, and there's one will thank me, that's my darling and I took her jewels for the saints I did, to pretty out the church, and a coat for to keep me warm.'

Rigby watched him as he slowly replaced the statement on the desk.

'Well, what do you think of it?'

Smiley hesitated; 'It's pretty good nonsense as it stands,' he replied at last.

'Of course it is,' said Rigby, with something like contempt. 'She saw something, Lord knows what, when she was out on the prowl; stealing, I shouldn't wonder. She may have robbed the body, or else she picked up the beads where the murderer dropped them. We've traced the coat. Belonged to a Mr Jardine, a baker in Carne East. Mrs Jardine gave it to Stella Rode last Wednesday morning for the refugees. Janie must have pinched it from the conservatory. That's what she meant by 'a coat for to keep me warm'. But she no more killed Stella Rode than you or I did. What about the footprints, the glovemarks in the conservatory? Besides, she's not strong enough, Janie isn't, to heave that poor woman forty feet through the snow. This is a man's work, as anyone can see.'

'Then what exactly . . . ?'

'We've called off the search, and I'm to prepare a case against one Jane Lyn of the village of Pylle for the wilful murder of Stella Rode. I wanted to tell you myself before you read it all over the papers. So that you'd know how it was.'

'Thanks.'

'In the meantime, if there's any help I can give you, we're still willing.' He hesitated, seemed about to say something, then to change his mind.

As he made his way down the wide staircase Smiley felt useless and very angry, which was scarcely the right frame of mind in which to attend a funeral.

It was an admirably conducted affair. Neither the flowers nor the congregation exceeded what was fitting to the occasion. She was not buried at the Abbey, out of deference perhaps to her simplicity of taste, but in the parish churchyard not far from Northfields. The Master was detained that day, as he was on most days, and had sent instead his wife, a small, very vague woman who had spent a long time in India. D'Arcy was much in evidence, fluttering here and there before the ceremony like an anxious beadle; and Mr Cardew had come to guide poor Stella through the unfamiliarities of High Anglican procedure. The Hechts were there, Charles all in black, scrubbed and shining, and Shane in dramatic weeds, and a hat with a very broad brim.

Smiley, who, like the others, had arrived early in anticipation of the unwholesome public interest which the ceremony might arouse, found himself a seat near the entrance of the church. He watched each new arrival with interest, waiting for his first sight of Stanley Rode.

Several tradesmen arrived, pressed into bulging serge and black ties, and formed a small group south of the aisle, away from the staff and their wives. Soon they were joined by other members of the town community, women who had known Mrs Rode at the Tabernacle; and then by Rigby, who looked straight at Smiley and gave no sign. Then on the stroke of three a tall old man walked slowly through the doorway, looking straight before him, neither knowing nor seeing anyone. Beside him was Stanley Rode.

It was a face which at first sight meant nothing to Smiley, seeming to have neither the imprint of temperament nor the components of character; it was a shallow, ordinary face, inclining to plumpness, and lacking quality. It matched his short, ordinary body and his black, ordinary hair; it was suitably compressed into an expression of sorrow. As Smiley watched him turn into the centre aisle and take his place among the principal mourners, it occurred to him that Rode's very walk and bearing successfully conveyed something entirely alien to Carne. If it is vulgar to wear a pen in the breast pocket of your jacket, to favour Fair Isle pullovers and brown ties, to bob a little and turn your feet out as you walk, then Rode beyond a shadow of doubt was vulgar, for though he did not now commit these sins, his manner implied them all.

They followed the coffin into the churchyard and gathered round the open grave. D'Arcy and Fielding were standing together, seemingly intent upon the service. The tall, elderly figure who had entered the church with Rode was now visibly moved, and Smiley guessed that he was Stella's father, Samuel Glaston. As the service ended, the old man walked quickly away from the crowd, nodding briefly to Rode, and disappeared into the church. He seemed to struggle as he went, like a man walking against a strong wind.

The little group moved slowly away from the graveside, until only Rode remained, an oddly stiff figure, taut and constrained, his eyes wide but somehow sightless, his mouth set in a strict, pedagogic line. Then, as Smiley watched, Rode seemed to wake from a dream; his body suddenly relaxed and he too walked slowly but quite confidently away from the grave towards the small group which by now had reassembled at the churchyard gate. As he did so, Fielding, at the edge of the group, caught sight of him approaching and, to Smiley's astonishment, walked deliberately and quite quickly away with an expression of strong distaste. It was not the calculated act of a man wishing to insult another, for it attracted the notice neither of Rode nor of anyone else standing by. Terence Fielding, for once, appeared to be in the grip of a genuine emotion, and indifferent to the impression he created.

Reluctantly Smiley approached the group. Rode was rather to one side, The D'Arcys were there, and three or four members of the staff. No one was talking much.

'Mr Rode?' he enquired.

'That's right, yes.' He spoke slowly, a trace of an accent carefully avoided.

'I'm representing Miss Brimley of the *Christian Voice*.'

'Oh, yes.'

'She was most anxious that the journal should be represented. I thought you would like to know that.'

'I saw your wreath; very kind, I am sure.'

'Your wife was one of our most loyal supporters,' Smiley continued. 'We regarded her almost as one of the family.'

'Yes, she was very keen on the *Voice*.' Smiley wondered whether Rode was always as impassive as this, or whether bereavement had made him listless.

'When did you come?' Rode asked suddenly.

'On Friday.'

'Making a week-end of it, eh?'

Smiley was so astonished that for a moment he could think of nothing to say. Rode was still looking at him, waiting for an answer.

'I have one or two friends here . . . Mr Fielding. . . .'

'Oh, Terence.' Smiley was convinced that Rode was not on Christian-name terms with Fielding.

'I would like, if I may,' Smiley ventured, 'to write a small obituary for Miss Brimley. Would you have any objection?'

'Stella would have liked that.'

'If you are not too upset, perhaps I could call round tomorrow for one or two details?'

'Certainly.'

'Eleven o'clock?'

'It will be a pleasure,' Rode replied, almost pertly, and they walked together to the churchyard gate.

Chapter Nine

The Mourners

It was a cheap trick to play on a man who had suddenly lost his wife. Smiley knew that. As he gently unlatched the gate and entered the drive, where two nights ago he had conducted his strange conversation with Jane Lyn, he acknowledged that in calling on Rode under any pretext at such a time he was committing a thoroughly unprincipled act. It was a peculiarity of Smiley's character that throughout the whole of his clandestine work he had never managed to reconcile the means to the end. A stringent critic of his own motives, he had discovered after long observation that he tended to be less a creature of intellect than his tastes and habits might suggest; once in the war he had been described by his superiors as possessing the cunning of Satan and the conscience of a virgin, which seemed to him not wholly unjust.

He pressed the bell and waited.

Stanley Rode opened the door. He was very neatly dressed, very scrubbed.

'Oh hullo,' he said, as if they were old friends. 'I say, you haven't got a car, have you?'

'I'm afraid I left it in London.'

'Never mind.' Rode sounded disappointed. 'Thought we might have gone out for a drive, had a chat as we went. I get a bit fed-up, kicking around here on my own. Miss D'Arcy asked me to stay over at their place. Very good people they are, very good indeed; but somehow I didn't wish it, not yet.'

'I understand.'

'Do you?' They were in the hall now, Smiley was getting out of his overcoat, Rode waiting to receive it. 'I don't think many do—the loneliness I mean. Do you know what they've done, the Master and Mr D'Arcy? They meant it well, I know. They've farmed out all my correcting—my exam. correcting, you understand. What am I supposed to do here, all on my own? I've no teaching, nothing; they've all taken a hand. You'd think they wanted to get rid of me.'

Smiley nodded vaguely. They moved towards the drawing-room, Rode leading the way.

'I know they did it for the best, as I said. But after all, I've got to spend the time somehow. Simon Snow got some of my division to correct. Have you met him by any chance? Sixty-one per cent. he gave one boy—sixty-one. The boy's an absolute fool; I told Fielding at the beginning of the Half that he wouldn't possibly get his Remove. Perkins his name is, a nice enough boy; head of Fielding's house. He'd have been lucky to get thirty per cent. . . . sixty-one, Snow gave him. I haven't seen the papers yet, of course, but it's impossible, quite impossible.'

They sat down.

'Not that I don't want the boy to get on. He's a nice enough boy, nothing special, but well-mannered. Mrs Rode and I meant to have him to tea this Half. We would have done, in fact, if it hadn't been for . . .' There was a moment's silence. Smiley was going to speak when Rode stood up and said:

'I've a kettle on the stove, Mr . . .'

'Smiley.'

'I've a kettle on the stove, Mr Smiley. May I make you a cup of coffee?' That little stiff voice with the corners carefully defined, like a hired morning suit, thought Smiley.

Rode returned a few minutes later with a tray and measured their coffee in precise quantities, according to their taste.

Smiley found himself continually irritated by Rode's social assumptions, and his constant struggle to conceal his origin. You could tell all the time, from every word and gesture, what he was; from the angle of his elbow as he drank his coffee, from the swift, expert pluck at the knee of his trouser leg as he sat down.

'I wonder,' Smiley began, 'whether perhaps I might now . . .'

'Go ahead, Mr Smiley.'

'We are, of course, largely interested in Mrs Rode's association with . . . our Church.'

'Quite.'

'You were married at Branxome, I believe.'

'Branxome Hill Tabernacle; fine church.' D'Arcy wouldn't have liked the way he said that; cocksure lad on a motor-bike. Pencils in the outside pocket.

'When was that?'

'September, fifty-one.'

'Did Mrs Rode engage in charitable work in Branxome? I know she was very active here.'

'No, not at Branxome, but a lot here. She had to look after her father at Branxome, you see. It was refugee relief she was keen on here. That didn't get going much until late 1956–the Hungarians began it, and then this last year . . .'

Smiley peered thoughtfully at Rode from behind his spectacles, forgot himself, blinked, and looked away.

'Did she take a large part in the social activities of Carne? Does the staff have its own Women's Institute and so on?' he asked innocently.

'She did a bit, yes. But, being Chapel, she kept mainly with the Chapel people from the town . . . you should ask Mr Cardew about that; he's the Minister.'

'But may I say, Mr Rode, that she took an active part in school affairs as well?'

Rode hesitated.

'Yes, of course,' he said.

'Thank you.'

There was a moment's silence, then Smiley continued: 'Our readers will, of course, remember Mrs Rode as the winner of our Kitchen Hints competition. Was she a good cook, Mr Rode?'

'Very good, for plain things, not fancy.'

'Is there any little fact that you would specially like us to include, anything she herself would like to be remembered by?'

Rode looked at him with expressionless eyes. Then he shrugged.

'No, not really. I can't think of anything. Oh, you could say her father was a magistrate up North. She was proud of that.'

Smiley finished his coffee and stood up.

'You've been very patient with me, Mr Rode. We're most grateful, I assure you. I'll take care to send you an advance copy of our notice. . . .'

'Thanks. I did it for her, you see. She liked the *Voice*; always did. Grew up with it.'

They shook hands.

'By the way, do you know where I can find old Mr Glaston? Is he staying in Carne or has he returned to Branxome?'

'He was up here yesterday. He's going back to Branxome this afternoon. The police wanted to see him before he left.'

'I see.'

'He's staying at the Sawley.'

'Thank you. I might try and see him before I go.'

'When do you leave, then?'

'Quite soon, I expect. Goodbye, then, Mr Rode. Incidentally–' Smiley began.

'Yes?'

'If ever you're in London and at a loose end, if ever you want a chat . . . and a cup of tea, we're always pleased to see you at the *Voice*, you know. Always.'

'Thanks. Thanks very much Mr–'

'Smiley.'

'Thanks, that's very decent. No one's said that to me for a long time. I'll take you up on that one day. Very good of you.'

'Goodbye.' Again they shook hands; Rode's was dry and cool. Smooth.

He returned to the Sawley Arms, sat himself at a desk in the empty residents' lounge and wrote a note to Mr Glaston:

> Dear Mr Glaston,
> I am here on behalf of Miss Brimley of the *Christian Voice*. I have some letters from Stella which I think you would like to see. Forgive me for bothering you at this sad moment; I understand you are leaving Carne this afternoon and wondered if I might see you before you left.

He carefully sealed the envelope and took it to the reception desk. There was no one there, so he rang the bell and waited. At last a porter came, an old turnkey with a grey, bristly face, and after examining the envelope critically for a long time, he agreed, against an excessive fee, to convey it to Mr Glaston's room. Smiley stayed at the desk, waiting for his answer.

Smiley himself was one of those solitaries who seem to have come into the world fully educated at the age of eighteen. Obscurity was his nature, as well as his profession. The byways of espionage are not populated by the brash and colourful adventurers of fiction. A man who, like Smiley, has lived and worked for years among his country's enemies learns only one prayer: that he may never, never be noticed. Assimilation is his highest aim, he learns to love the crowds who pass him in the street without a glance; he clings to them for his anonymity and his safety. His fear makes him servile–he could embrace the shoppers who jostle him in their impatience, and force him from the pavement. He could adore the officials, the police, the bus conductors, for the terse indifference of their attitudes.

But this fear, this servility, this dependence, had developed in Smiley a perception for the colour of human beings: a swift, feminine sensitivity to their characters and motives. He knew mankind as a huntsman knows his cover, as a fox the wood. For a spy must hunt while he is hunted, and the crowd is his estate. He could collect their gestures and their words, record the interplay of glance and move-ment, as a huntsman can record the twisted bracken and the broken twig, or as a fox detects the signs of danger.

Thus, while he waited patiently for Glaston's reply and recalled the crowded events of the last forty-eight hours, he was able to order and assess them with detachment. What was the cause of D'Arcy's attitude to Fielding, as if they were unwilling partners to a shabby secret? Staring across the neglected hotel gardens towards Carne Abbey, he was able to glimpse behind the lead roof of the Abbey the familiar battlements of the school: keeping the new world out and the old world secure. In his mind's eye he saw the Great Court now, as the boys came out of Chapel: The black-coated groups in the leisured attitudes of eighteenth-century England. And he remembered the other school beside the police station: Carne High School; a little tawdry place like a porter's lodge in an empty graveyard, as detached from the tones of Carne as its brick and flint from the saffron battlements of School Hall.

Yes, he reflected, Stanley Rode had made a long, long journey from the Grammar School at Branxome. And if he killed his wife, then the motive, Smiley was sure, and even the means, were to be found in that hard road to Carne.

'It was kind of you to come,' said Glaston; 'kind of Miss Brimley to send you. They're good people at the *Voice*; always were.' He said this as if 'good' were an absolute quality with which he was familiar.

'You'd better read the letters, Mr Glaston. The second one will shock you, I'm afraid, but I'm sure you'll agree that it would be wrong of me not to show it to you.' They were sitting in the lounge, the mammoth plants like sentinels beside them.

He handed Glaston the two letters, and the old man took them firmly and read them. He held them a good way from him to read, thrusting his strong head back, his eyes half closed, the crisp line of his mouth turned down at the corners. At last he said:

'You were with Miss Brimley in the war, were you?'

'I worked with John Landsbury, yes.'

'I see. That's why she came to you?'

'Yes.'

'Are you Chapel?'

'No.'

He was silent for a while, his hands folded on his lap, the letters before him on the table.

'Stanley was Chapel when they married. Then he went over. Did you know that?'

'Yes.'

'Where I come from in the North, we don't do that. Chapel was something we'd stood up for and won. Almost like the vote.'

'I know.'

His back was as straight as a soldier's. He looked stern rather than sad. Quite suddenly, his eyes turned towards Smiley, and he looked at him long and carefully.

'Are you a schoolmaster?' he asked, and it occurred to Smiley that in his day Samuel Glaston had been a very shrewd man of business.

'No. . . . I'm more or less retired.'

'Married?'

'I was.'

Again the old man fell silent, and Smiley wished he had left him alone.

'She was a great one for chatter,' he said at last.

Smiley said nothing.

'Have you told the police?'

'Yes, but they knew already. That is, they knew that Stella thought her husband was going to murder her. She'd tried to tell Mr Cardew. . . .'

'The Minister?'

'Yes. He thought she was overwrought and . . . deluded.'

'Do you think she wasn't?'

'I don't know. I just don't know. But from what I have heard of your daughter I don't believe she was unbalanced. *Something* roused her suspicions, something frightened her very much. I don't believe we can just disregard that. I don't believe it was a coincidence that she was frightened before she died. And therefore I don't believe that the beggar-woman murdered her.'

Samuel Glaston nodded slowly. It seemed to Smiley that the old man was trying to show interest, partly to be polite, and partly because if he did not it would be a confession that he had lost interest in life itself.

Then, after a long silence, he carefully folded up the letters and gave them back. Smiley waited for him to speak, but he said nothing.

After a few moments Smiley got up and walked quietly from the room.

Chapter Ten

Little Women

Shane Hecht smiled, and drank some more sherry. 'You must be dreadfully important,' she said to Smiley, 'for D'Arcy to serve decent sherry. What are you, *Almanach de Gotha*?'

'I'm afraid not. D'Arcy and I were both dining at Terence Fielding's on Saturday night and D'Arcy asked me for a sherry.'

'Terence is *wicked*, isn't he? Charles loathes him. I'm afraid they see Sparta in quite different ways. . . . Poor Terence. It's his last Half, you know.'

'I know.'

'So sweet of you to come to the funeral yesterday. I hate funerals, don't you? Black is so insanitary. I always remember King George V's funeral. Lord Sawley was at Court in those days, and gave Charles two tickets. So kind. I always think it's *spoilt* us for ordinary funerals in a way. Although I'm never quite *sure* about funerals, are you? I have a suspicion that they are largely a lower-class recreation; cherry brandy and seed cake in the parlour. I think the tendency of people like ourselves is for a *quiet* funeral these days; no flowers, just a short obituary and a memorial service later.' Her small eyes were bright with pleasure. She finished her sherry and held out her empty glass to Smiley.

'Would you mind, dear. I hate sherry, but Felix is so mean.'

Smiley filled her glass from the decanter on the table.

'Dreadful about the murder, wasn't it? That beggar-woman must be mad. Stella Rode was such a nice person, I always thought . . . and so *unusual*. She did such clever things with the same dress. . . . But she had such curious friends. All for Hans the woodcutter and Pedro the fisherman, if you know what I mean.'

'Was she popular at Carne?'

Shane Hecht laughed gently: 'No one is popular at Carne . . . but she wasn't easy to like. . . . She would wear black crêpe on Sundays. . . . Forgive me, but do the lower classes always do that? The townspeople liked her, I believe. They adore anyone who betrays Carne. But then she was a Christian Scientist or something.'

'Baptist, I understand,' said Smiley unthinkingly.

She looked at him for a moment with unfeigned curiosity. 'How sweet,' she murmured. 'Tell me, what *are* you?'

Smiley made some facetious reply about being unemployed, and realised that it was only by a hair's-breadth that he had avoided explaining himself to Shane Hecht like a small boy. Her very ugliness, her size, and voice, coupled with the sophisticated malice of her conversation, gave her the dangerous quality of command. Smiley was tempted to compare here with Fielding, but for Fielding other people scarcely existed. For Shane Hecht they did exist: they were there to be found wanting in the minute tests of social behaviour, to be ridiculed, cut off and destroyed.

'I read in the paper that her father was quite well off. From the North. Second generation. Remarkable really how *unspoilt* she was . . . so natural. . . . You wouldn't think she *needed* to go to the launderette or to make friends with beggars. . . . Though, of course, the Midlands are different, aren't they? Only about three good families between Ipswich and Newcastle. Where did you say you came from, dear?'

'London.'

'How nice. I went to tea with Stella once. Milk in first and Indian. So different,' and she looked at Smiley suddenly and said 'I'll tell you something. She almost aroused an admiration in me, I found her so insufferable. She was one of those tiresome little snobs who think that only the humble are virtuous.' Then she smiled and added, 'I even agreed with Charles about Stella Rode, and that's saying something. If you're a student of mankind, do go and have a look at him, the contrast is riveting.' But at the moment they were joined by D'Arcy's sister, a bony, virile woman with untidy grey hair and an arrogant, hunting mouth.

'Dorothy darling,' Shane murmured; 'such a lovely party. So *kind*. And so *exciting* to meet somebody from London, don't you think? We were talking about poor Mrs Rode's funeral.'

'Stella Rode may have been damn' bad form, Shane, but she did a lot for my refugees.'

'Refugees?' asked Smiley innocently.

'Hungarians. Collecting for them. Clothes, furniture, money. One of the few wives who *did* anything.' She looked sharply at Shane Hecht, who was smiling benignly past her towards her husband: 'Busy little creature, she was, didn't mind rolling her sleeves up, going from door to door. Got her little women on to it at the Baptist chapel and brought in a mass of stuff. You've got to hand it to them, you know. They've got *spirit*. Felix, more sherry!'

There were about twenty in the two rooms, but Smiley, who had arrived a little late, found himself attached to a group of about eight who stood nearest the door: D'Arcy and his sister; Charles and

Shane Hecht; a young mathematician called Snow and his wife; a curate from the Abbey and Smiley himself, bewildered and mole-like behind his spectacles. Smiley looked quickly round the room, but could see no sign of Fielding.

'. . . Yes,' Dorothy D'Arcy continued, 'she was a good little worker, very . . . right to the end. I went over there on Friday with that parson man from the tin tabernacle–Cardew–to see if there was any refugee stuff to tidy up. There wasn't a thing out of place–every bit of clothing she had was all packed up and addressed; we just had to send it off. She was a damn' good little worker, I will say. Did a splendid job at the bazaar, you know.'

'Yes, darling,' said Shane Hecht sweetly. 'I remember it well. It was the day I presented her to Lady Sawley. She wore such a *nice* little hat–the one she wore on Sundays, you know. And *so* respectful. She called her "my lady".' She turned to Smiley and breathed: 'Rather feudal, don't you think, dear? I always liked that: so few of us left.'

The mathematician and his wife were talking to Charles Hecht in a corner and a few minutes later Smiley managed to extricate himself from the group and join them.

Anne Snow was a pretty girl with a rather square face and a turned-up nose. Her husband was tall and thin, with an agreeable stoop. He held his sherry glass between straight, slender fingers as if it were a chemical retort and when he spoke he seemed to address the sherry rather than his listener; Smiley remembered them from the funeral. Hecht was looking pink and rather cross, sucking at his pipe. They talked in a desultory way, their conversation dwarfed by the exchanges of the adjoining group. Hecht eventually drifted away from them, still frowning and withdrawn, and stood ostentatiously alone near the door.

'Poor Stella,' said Ann Snow after a moment's silence. 'Sorry,' she added. 'I can't get her out of my mind yet. It seems mad, just mad. I mean why should she *do* it, that Janie woman?'

'Did you like Stella?' Smiley asked.

'Of course we did. She was sweet. We've been here four Halves now, but she was the only person here who's ever been *kind* to us.' Her husband said nothing, just nodded at his sherry. 'Simon wasn't a boy at Carne, you see–most of the staff were–so we didn't know anyone and no one was really interested. They all pretended to be terribly pleased with us, of course, but it was Stella who really . . .'

Dorothy D'Arcy was descending on them. 'Mrs Snow,' she said crisply, 'I've been meaning to talk to you. I want you to take over Stella Rode's job on the refugees.' She cast an appraising look in Simon's direction: 'The Master's very keen on refugees.'

'Oh, my goodness!' Ann Snow replied, aghast. 'I couldn't

possibly, Miss D'Arcy, I . . .'

'Couldn't? Why couldn't you? You helped Mrs Rode with her stall at the bazaar, didn't you?'

'So that's where she got her clothes from,' breathed Shane Hecht behind them. Ann was fumbling on:

'But . . . well I haven't quite got Stella's nerve, if you understand what I mean; and besides, she was a Baptist: all the locals helped her and gave her things, and they all liked her. With me it would be different.'

'Lot of damn' nonsense,' declared Miss D'Arcy, who spoke to all her juniors as if they were grooms or erring children; and Shane Hecht beside her said: 'Baptists are the people who don't like private pews, aren't they? I do so agree—one feels that if one's paid one simply has to go.'

The curate who had been talking cricket in a corner, was startled into mild protest: 'Oh, come, Mrs Hecht, the private pew had many advantages . . . ' and embarked on a diffuse apologia for ancient custom, to which Shane listened with every sign of the most assiduous interest. When at last he finished she said: 'Thank you, William dear, so sweet,' turned her back on him and added to Smiley in a stage whisper: 'William Trumper—one of Charles' old pupils—such a triumph when he passed his Certificate.'

Smiley, anxious to dissociate himself from Shane Hecht's vengeance on the curate, turned to Ann Snow, but she was still at the mercy of Miss D'Arcy's charitable intentions, and Shane was still talking to him:

'The only Smiley I ever heard of married Lady Ann Sercombe at the end of the war. She left him soon afterwards, of course. A very curious match. I understand he was quite unsuitable. She was Lord Sawley's cousin, you know. The Sawleys have been connected with Carne for four hundred years. The present heir is a pupil of Charles; we often dine at the Castle. I never did hear what became of Ann Sercombe . . . she went to Africa, you know . . . or was it India? No it was America. So tragic. One doesn't talk about it at the Castle.' For a moment the noise in the room stopped. For a moment, no more, he could discern nothing but the steady gaze of Shane Hecht upon him, and knew she was waiting for an answer. And then she released him as if to say: 'I could crush you, you see. But I won't, I'll let you live,' and she turned and walked away.

He contrived to take his leave at the same time as Ann and Simon Snow. They had an old car and insisted on running Smiley back to his hotel. On the way there, he said:

'If you have nothing better to do, I would be happy to give you both dinner at my hotel. I imagine the food is dreadful.'

The Snows protested and accepted, and a quarter of an hour later they were all three seated in a corner of the enormous dining-room of the Sawley Arms, to the great despondency of three waiters and a dozen generations of Lord Sawley's forbears, puffy men in crumbling pigment.

'We really got to know her our second Half,' Ann Snow ran on. 'Stella didn't do much mixing with the other wives—she'd learnt her lesson by then. She didn't go to coffee parties and things, so it was really luck that we did meet. When we first came there wasn't a staff house available for us: we had to spend the first Half in a hotel. We moved in to a little house in Bread Street at the end of our second Half. Moving was chaos—Simon was examining for the scholarships and we were terribly broke, so we had to do everything we possibly could for ourselves. It was a wet Thursday morning when we moved. The rain was simply teeming down; but none of our good pieces would get in through the front door, and in the end Mulligan's just dumped me on the doorstep and let me sort it out.' She laughed, and Smiley thought what an agreeable child she was. 'They were absolutely foul. They would have just driven off, I think, but they wanted a cheque as soon as they'd done the delivery, and the bill was pounds more than the estimate. I hadn't got the cheque-book of course, Simon had gone off with it. Mulligan's even threatened to take all the stuff away again. It was monstrous. I think I was nearly in tears.' She nearly is now, thought Smiley. 'Then out of the blue Stella turned up. I can't think how she even knew we were moving—I'm sure no one else did. She'd brought an overall and an old pair of shoes and she'd come to help. When she saw what was going on she didn't bother with the men at all, just went to a phone and rang Mr Mulligan himself. I don't know what she said to him, but she made the foreman talk to him afterwards and there was no more trouble after that. She was terribly happy—happy to *help*. She was that sort of person. They took the door right out and managed to get everything in. She was marvellous at helping without managing. The rest of the wives,' she added bitterly, 'are awfully good at managing, but don't help at all.'

Smiley nodded, and discreetly filled their glasses.

'Simon's leaving,' Ann said, suddenly confidential. 'He's got a grant and we're going back to Oxford. He's going to do a D.Phil. and get a University job.'

They drank to his success, and the conversation turned to other things until Smiley asked: 'What's Rode himself like to work with?'

'He's a good schoolmaster,' said Simon, slowly, 'but tiring as a colleague.'

'Oh, he was *quite* different from Stella,' said Ann; 'Terribly Carne-minded. D'Arcy adopted him and he got the bug. Simon says all the grammar school people go that way—it's the fury of the convert. It's sickening. He even changed his religion when he got to Carne. Stella didn't, though; she wouldn't dream of it.'

'The Established Church has much to offer at Carne,' Simon observed, and Smiley enjoyed the dry precision of his delivery.

'Stella can't exactly have hit it off with Shane Hecht,' Smiley probed gently.

'Of *course* she didn't!' Ann declared angrily. 'Shane was horrid to her, always sneering at her because she was honest and simple about the things she liked. Shane hated Stella—I think it was because Stella didn't *want* to be a lady of quality. She was quite happy to be herself. That's what really worried Shane. Shane likes people to compete so that she can make fools of them.'

'So does Carne,' said Simon, quietly.

'She was awfully good at helping out with the refugees. That was how she got into real trouble.' Ann Snow's slim hands gently rocked her brandy glass.

'Trouble?'

'Just before she died. Hasn't anyone told you? About her frightful row with D'Arcy's sister?'

'No.'

'Of course, they wouldn't have done. Stella never gossiped.'

'Let me tell you,' said Simon. 'It's a good story. When the Refugee Year business started, Dorothy D'Arcy was fired with charitable enthusiasm. So was the Master. Dorothy's enthusiasms always seem to correspond with his. She started collecting clothes and money and packing them off to London. All very laudable, but there was a perfectly good town appeal going, launched by the Mayor. That wasn't good enough for Dorothy, though: the school must have its own appeal; you can't mix your charity. I think Felix was largely behind it. Anyway, after the thing had been going for a few months the refugee centre in London apparently wrote to Dorothy and asked whether anyone would be prepared to accommodate a refugee couple. Instead of publicising the letter, Dorothy wrote straight back and said she would put them up herself. So far so good. The couple turned up, Dorothy and Felix pointed a proud finger at them and the local press wrote it all up as an example of British humanity.

'About six weeks later, one afternoon, these two turned up on Stella's doorstep. The Rodes and the D'Arcys are neighbours, you see, and anyway Stella had tried to take an interest in Dorothy's refugees. The woman was in floods of tears and the husband was shouting blue murder, but that didn't worry Stella. She had them straight into the drawing-room and gave them a cup of tea. Finally, they managed to explain in basic English that they had run away from the D'Arcys because of the treatment they received. The girl was expected to work from morning till night in the kitchen, and the husband was acting as unpaid kennel-boy for those beastly spaniels that Dorothy breeds. The ones without noses.'

'King Charles,' Anne prompted.

'It was about as awful as it could be. The girl was pregnant and he was a fully qualified engineer, so neither of them were exactly suited to domestic service. They told Stella that Dorothy was away till the evening–she'd gone to a dog show. Stella advised them to stay with her for the time being, and that evening she went round and told Dorothy what had happened. She had quite a nerve, you see. Although it wasn't nerve really. She just did the simple thing. Dorothy was furious, and demanded that Stella should return "her refugees" immediately. Stella replied that she was sure that they wouldn't come, and went home. When Stella got home she rang up the refugee people in London and asked their advice. They sent a woman down to see Dorothy and the couple, and the result was that they returned to London the following day. . . . You can imagine what Shane Hecht would have made of that story.'

'Didn't she ever find out?'

'Stella never told anyone except us, and we didn't pass it on. Dorothy just let it be known that the refugees had gone to some job in London, and that was that.'

'How long ago did this happen?'

'They left exactly three weeks ago,' said Ann to her husband. 'Stella told me about it when she came to supper the night you were in Oxford for your interview. That was three weeks ago tonight.' She turned to Smiley:

'Poor Simon's been having an awful time. Felix D'Arcy unloaded all Rode's exam. correcting on to him. It's bad enough doing one person's correction–two is frantic.'

'Yes,' replied Simon reflectively. 'It's been a bad week. And rather humiliating in a way. Several of the boys who were up to me for science last Half are now in Rode's forms. I'd regarded one or two of them as practically unteachable, but Rode seems to have brought them on marvellously. I corrected one boy's paper–Perkins–sixty-one per cent for elementary science. Last Half he got fifteen per cent in a much easier paper. He only got his Remove because Fielding raised hell. He was in Fielding's house.'

'Oh I know–a red-haired boy, a prefect.'

'Good Lord,' cried Simon. 'Don't say you know him?'

'Oh, Fielding introduced us,' said Smiley vaguely. 'Incidentally–no one else ever mentioned that incident to you about Miss D'Arcy's refugees, did they? Confirmed it, as it were?'

Ann Snow looked at him oddly. 'No. Stella told us about it, but of course Dorothy D'Arcy never referred to it at all. She must have *hated* Stella, though.'

He saw them to their car, and waited despite their protests while

Simon cranked it. At last they drove off, the car bellowing down the silent street. Smiley stood for a moment on the pavement, an odd, lonely figure peering down the empty road.

Chapter Eleven

A Coat to Keep Her Warm

A dog that had not bitten the postman; a devil that rode upon the wind; a woman who knew that she would die; a little, worried man in an overcoat standing in the snow outside his hotel and the laborious chime of the Abbey clock telling him to go to bed.

Smiley hesitated, then with a shrug crossed the road to the hotel entrance, mounted the step and entered the cheap, yellow light of the residents' hall. He walked slowly up the stairs.

He detested the Sawley Arms. That muted light in the hall was typical: inefficient, antiquated and smug. Like the waiters in the dining-room and the lowered voices in the residents' lounge, like his own hateful bedroom with its blue and gilt urns, and the framed tapestry of a Buckinghamshire garden.

His room was bitterly cold; the maid must have opened the window. He put a shilling in the meter and lit the gas. The fire bubbled grumpily and went out. Muttering, Smiley looked around for some paper to write on, and discovered some, much to his surprise, in the drawer of the writing desk. He changed into his pyjamas and dressing gown and crawled miserably into bed. After sitting there uncomfortably for some minutes he got up, fetched his overcoat and spread it over the eiderdown. A coat for to keep her warm. . . .

How did her statement read? 'There's one will thank me, that's my darling and I took her jewels for the saints I did, and a coat for to keep me warm. . . .' The coat had been given to Stella last Wednesday for the refugees. It seemed reasonable to assume from the way the statement read that Janie had taken the coat from the outhouse at the same time as she took the beads from Stella's body. But Dorothy D'Arcy had been round there on Friday morning—of course she had, with Mr Cardew—she was talking about it at her party that very evening: 'There wasn't a thing out of place—every bit of clothing she had was all packed up and addressed—a damn' good little worker, I will say. . . .' Then why hadn't Stella packed the overcoat? If she packed everything else, why not the overcoat too?

Or had Janie stolen the coat earlier in the day, before Stella made her parcel? If that was so, it went some way to weakening the case against her. But it was not so. It was not so because it was utterly improbable that Janie should steal a coat in the afternoon and return to the house the same evening.

'Start at the beginning,' Smiley muttered, a little sententiously to the crested paper on his lap. 'Janie stole the coat at the same time as she stole the beads—that is, after Stella was dead. Therefore either the coat was not packed with the other clothes, or . . .'

Or what? *Or somebody else, somebody who was not Stella Rode, packed up the clothes after Stella had died and before Dorothy D'Arcy and Mr Cardew went round to North Fields on Friday morning. And why the devil, thought Smiley, should anyone do that?*

It had been one of Smiley's cardinal principles in research, whether among the incunabula of an obscure poet or the laboriously gathered fragments of intelligence, not to proceed beyond the evidence. A fact, once logically arrived at, should not be extended beyond its natural significance. Accordingly he did not speculate with the remarkable discovery he had made, but turned his mind to the most obscure problem of all: motive for murder.

He began writing:

'Dorothy D'Arcy—resentment after refugee fiasco. As a motive for murder—definitely thin.' Yet why did she seem to go out of her way to sing Stella's praises?

'Felix D'Arcy—resented Stella Rode for not observing Carne's standards. As a motive for murder—ludicrous.

'Shane Hecht—hatred.

'Terence Fielding—in a sane world, no conceivable motive.'

Yet was it a sane world? Year in year out they must share the same life, say the same things to the same people, sing the same hymns. They had no money, no hope. The world changed, fashion changed; the woman saw it second-hand in the glossy papers, took in their dresses and pinned up their hair, and hated their husbands a little more. Shane Hecht—did she kill Stella Rode? Did she conceal in the sterile omniscience of her huge body not only hatred and jealousy, but the courage to kill? Was she frightened for her stupid husband, frightened of Rode's promotion, of his cleverness? Was she really so angry when Stella refused to take part in the rat race of gentility?

Rigby was right—it was impossible to know. You had to be ill, you had to be sick to understand, you had to be there in the sanatorium, not for weeks, but for years, had to be one in the line of white beds, to know the smell of their food and the greed in their eyes. You had to hear it and see it, to be part of it, to know their rules and recognise their transgressions. The world was compressed into a mould of anomalous conventions: blind, pharasaical but real.

Yet some things were written plain enough; the curious bond which tied Felix D'Arcy and Terence Fielding despite their mutual dislike; D'Arcy's reluctance to discuss the night of the murder; Fielding's evident preference for Stella Rode rather than her husband; Shane Hecht's contempt for everyone.

He could not get Shane out of his mind. If Carne were a rational place, and somebody had to die, then Shane Hecht should clearly be the one. She was a depository of other people's secrets, she had an infallible sense for weakness. Had she not found even Smiley out? She had taunted him with his wretched marriage, she had played with him for her own pleasure. Yes, she was an admirable candidate for murder.

But why on earth should Stella die? Why and how? Who tied up the parcel after her death? and why?

He tried to sleep, but could not. Finally, as the Abbey clock chimed three, he put the light on again and sat up. The room was much warmer and at first Smiley wondered if someone had switched on the central heating in the middle of the night, after it had been off all day. Then he became aware of the sound of rain outside; he went to the window and parted the curtains. A steady rain was falling; by tomorrow the snow would be washed away. Two policemen walked slowly down the road; he could hear the squelch of their boots as they trod in the melting snow. Their wet capes glistened in the arc of the street lamp.

And suddenly he seemed to hear Rigby's voice: 'Blood everywhere. Whoever killed her must have been covered in it.' And then Mad Janie calling to him across the moonlit snow: 'Janie seed 'im . . . silver wings like fishes . . . flying on the wind . . . there's not many seen the devil fly. . . .' Of course: the parcel! He remained a long time at the window, watching the rain. Finally, content at last, he climbed back into bed and fell asleep.

He tried to telephone Miss Brimley throughout the morning. Each time she was out and he left no message. Eventually, at about midday, he spoke to her:

'George, I'm terribly sorry—some missionary is in London—I had to go for an interview and I've got a Baptist Conference this afternoon. They've both got to be in this week. Will first thing tomorrow do?'

'Yes,' said Smiley. 'I'm sure it will.' There was no particular hurry. There were one or two ends he wanted to tie up that afternoon, anyway.

Chapter Twelve

Uncomfortable Words

He enjoyed the bus. The conductor was a very surly man with a great deal to say about the bus company, and why it lost money. Gently encouraged by Smiley, he expanded wonderfully so that by the time they arrived at Sturminster he had transformed the Directors of the Dorset and General Traction Company into a herd of Gadarene swine charging into the abyss of voluntary bankruptcy. The conductor directed Smiley to the Sturminster Kennels, and when he alighted in the tiny village he set out confidently towards a group of cottages which stood about a quarter of a mile beyond the church, on the Okeford road.

He had a nasty feeling he wasn't going to like Mr Harriman. The very fact that D'Arcy had described him as a superior type of person inclined Smiley against him. Smiley was not opposed to social distinctions but he liked to make his own.

A notice stood at the gate: '*Sturminster Kennels, proprietor, C.J.Reid-Harriman, Veterinary Surgeon. Breeder of Alsatian and Labrador Dogs. Boarding.*'

A narrow path led to what seemed to be a back-yard. There was washing everywhere, shirts, underclothes and sheets, most of it khaki. There was a rich smell of dog. There was a rusted hand-pump with a dozen or so dog leads draped over it, and there was a small girl. She watched him sadly as he picked his way through the thick mud towards the door. He pulled on the bell-rope and waited. He tried again, and the child said:

'It doesn't work. It's bust. It's been bust for years.'

'Is anyone at home?' Smiley asked.

'I'll see,' she replied coolly, and after another long look at him she walked round the side of the house and disappeared from view. Then Smiley heard from inside the house the sound of someone approaching, and a moment later the door opened.

'Good day to you.' He had sandy hair and a moustache. He wore a khaki shirt and a khaki tie of a lighter shade; old Service dress trousers and a tweed jacket with leather buttons.

'Mr Harriman?'

'Major,' he replied lightly. 'Not that it matters, old boy. What can we do for you?'

'I'm thinking of buying an Alsatian,' Smiley replied, 'as a guard dog.'

'Surely. Come in, won't you. Lady wife's out. Ignore the child: she's from next door. Just hangs around; likes the dogs.' He followed Harriman into the living-room and they sat down. There was no fire.

'Where are you from?' Harriman asked.

'I'm staying at Carne at the moment; my father lives over at Dorchester. He's getting on and he's nervous, and he wants me to find him a good dog. There's a gardener to look after it in the daytime, feed it and exercise it and so on. The gardener doesn't live in at night, of course, and it's at night that the old man gets so worried. I've been meaning to get him a dog for some time—this recent business at Carne rather brought it home to me.' Harriman ignored the hint.

'Gardener good chap?'

'Yes, very.'

'You don't want anything brilliant,' said Harriman. 'You want a good, steady type. I'd take a bitch if I were you.' His hands were dark brown, his wrists too. His handkerchief was tucked into his cuff. Smiley noticed that his wrist-watch faced inwards, conforming with the obscure rites of the military *demi-monde* from which he seemed to come.

'What will it do, a dog like that? Will it attack, or what?'

'Depends how she's trained, old boy; depends how she's trained. She'll warn, though; that's the main thing. Frighten the fellers away. Shove a notice up, "Fierce Dog", let her sniff at the tradesmen a bit and the word will get around. You won't get a burglar within a mile of the place.'

They walked out into the garden again, and Harriman led the way to an enclosure with half a dozen Alsatian puppies yapping furiously at them through the wire.

'They're good little beasts, all of them,' he shouted. 'Game as hell.' He unlocked the door and finally emerged with a plump bitch puppy chewing fiercely at his jacket.

'This little lady might do you,' he said. 'We can't show her—she's too dark.'

Smiley pretended to hesitate, allowed Harriman to persuade him and finally agreed. They went back into the house.

'I'd like to pay a deposit,' said Smiley, 'and collect her in about ten days. Would that be all right?' He gave Harriman a cheque for five pounds and again they sat down, Harriman foraging in his desk for inoculation certificates and pedigrees. Then Smiley said:

'It's a pity Mrs Rode didn't have a dog, isn't it? I mean, it might have saved her life.'

'Oh, she *had* a dog, but she had it put down just before she was killed,' said Harriman. 'Damned odd story between ourselves. She was devoted to the beast. Odd little mongrel, a bit of everything, but she loved it. Brought it here one day with some tale about it biting the postman, got me to put it down—said it was dangerous. It wasn't anything of the sort. Some friends of mine in Carne made enquiries. No complaints anywhere. Postman liked the brute. Damned silly sort of lie to tell in a small community. Bound to be found out.'

'Why on earth did she tell it then?'

Harriman made a gesture which particularly irritated Smiley. He ran his forefinger down the length of his nose, then flicked either side of his absurd moustache very quickly. There was something shame-faced about the whole movement, as if he were assuming the ways of senior officers, and fearful of rebuke.

'She was trouble,' he said crisply. 'I can spot 'em. I've had a few in the regiment, wives who are trouble. Little simpering types. Butter-wouldn't-melt, holier-than-thou. Arrange the flowers in the church and all that—pious as you please. I'd say she was the hysterical kind, self-dramatising, weeping all over the house for days on end. Anything for a bit of drama.'

'Was she popular?' Smiley offered him a cigarette.

'Shouldn't think so. Thanks. She wore black on Sundays, I gather. Typical. We used to call them 'crows' out East, the ones who wore black—Sunday virgins. They were O.D. mostly—other denomi-nations. Not C. of E.—some were Romans, mind. . . . I hope I'm not . . .'

Not at all.'

'You never know, do you? Can't stand 'em myself; no prejudice, but I don't like Romans—that's what my old father used to say.'

'Did you know her husband?'

'Not so well, poor devil, not so well.'

Harriman, Smiley reflected, seemed to have a great deal more sympathy for the living than the dead. Perhaps soldiers were like that. He wouldn't know.

'He's terribly cut up, I hear. Dreadful shock—fortunes of war, eh?' he added and Smiley nodded. 'He's the other type. Humble origin, good officer qualities, credit to the mess. Those are the ones that cut up most, the ones women get at.'

They walked along the path to the gate. Smiley said goodbye, and promised to return in a week or so to collect the puppy. As he walked away Harriman called to him:

'Oh—incidentally . . .'

Smiley stopped and turned round.

'I'll pay that cheque in, shall I, and credit you with the amount?'

'Of course,' said Smiley. 'That will do very well,' and he made his way to the bus stop pondering on the strange byways of the military mind.

The same bus took him back to Carne, the same conductor railed against his employers, the same driver drove the entire distance in second gear. He got out at the station and made his way to the red-brick Tabernacle. Gently opening the Gothic door, made of thickly-varnished ochre pine, he stepped inside. An elderly woman in an apron was polishing the heavy brass chandelier which hung over the centre aisle. He waited a moment, then tiptoed up to her and asked for the Minister. She pointed towards the vestry door. Obeying her mimed directions, he crossed to it, knocked and waited. A tall man in a clerical collar opened the door.

'I'm from the *Christian Voice*,' said Smiley quietly. 'Can I have a word with you?'

Mr Cardew led him through the side entrance and into a small vegetable garden, carefully tilled, with bright yellow paths running between the empty beds. The sun shone through the crisp air. It was a cold, beautiful day. They crossed the garden and entered a paddock. The ground was hard despite last night's rain, and the grass short. They strolled side by side, talking as they went.

'This is Lammas Land, belonging to the School. We hold our fêtes here in the summer. It's very practical.'

Cardew seemed a little out of character. Smiley, who had a rather childish distrust of clergymen, had expected a Wesleyan hammer, a wordy, forbidding man with a taste for imagery.

'Miss Brimley, our editor, sent me,' Smiley began. 'Mrs Rode subscribed to our journal; her family has taken it since it began. She was almost a part of the family. We wanted to write an obituary about her work for the Church.'

'I see.'

'I managed to have a word with her husband; we wanted to be sure to strike the right note.'

'What did he say?'

'He said I should speak to you about her work—her refugee work particularly.'

They walked on in silence for a while, then Cardew said, 'She came from up North, near Derby. Her father used to be a man of substance in the North—though money never altered him.'

'I know.'

'I've known the family for years, off and on. I saw her old father before the funeral.'

'What may I say about her work for the Church, her influence on the Chapel community here? May I say she was universally loved?'

'I'm afraid,' said Cardew, after a slight pause, 'that I don't hold much with that kind of writing, Mr Smiley. People are never universally loved, even when they're dead.' His North Country accent was strong.

'Then what may I say?' Smiley persisted.

'I don't know,' Cardew replied evenly. 'And when I don't know, I usually keep quiet. But since you're good enough to ask me, I've never met an angel, and Stella Rode was no exception.'

'But was she not a leading figure in refugee work?'

'Yes. Yes, she was.'

'And did she not encourage others to make similar efforts?'

'Of course. She was a good worker.'

They walked on together in silence. The path across the field led downwards, then turned and followed a stream which was almost hidden by the tangled gorse and hawthorn on either side. Beyond the stream was a row of stark elm trees, and behind them the familiar outline of Carne.

'Is that all you wanted to ask me?' said Cardew suddenly.

'No,' replied Smiley. 'Our editor was very worried by a letter she received from Mrs Rode just before her death. It was a kind of . . . accusation. We put the matter before the police. Miss Brimley reproaches herself in some way for not having been able to help her. It's illogical, perhaps, but there it is. I would like to be able to assure her that there was no connection between Stella Rode's death and this letter. That is another reason for my visit. . . .'

'Whom did the letter accuse?'

'Her husband.'

'I should tell your Miss Brimley,' said Cardew slowly, and with some emphasis, 'that she has nothing whatever for which to reproach herself.'

Chapter Thirteen

The Journey Home

It was Monday evening. At about the time that Smiley returned to his hotel after his interview with Mr Cardew, Tim Perkins, the Head of Fielding's house, was taking his leave of Mrs Harlowe, who taught him the 'cello. She was a kindly woman, if neurotic, and it distressed her to see him so worried. He was quite the best pupil that Carne had sent her, and she liked him.

'You played foully today, Tim,' she said as she wished him

goodbye at the door, 'quite foully. You needn't tell me—you've only got one more Half and you still haven't got three passes in A level and you've got to get your remove, and you're in a tizz. We won't practise next Monday if you don't want—just come and have buns and we'll play some records.'

'Yes, Mrs Harlowe.' He strapped his music-case on to the carrier of his bicycle.

'Lights working, Tim?'

'Yes, Mrs Harlowe.'

'Well, don't try and beat the record tonight, Tim. You've plenty of time till Boys' Tea. Remember the lane's still quite slippery from the snow.'

Perkins said nothing. He pushed the bicycle on to the gravel path and started towards the gate.

'Haven't you forgotten something, Tim?'

'Sorry, Mrs Harlowe.'

He turned back and shook hands with her in the doorway. She always insisted on that.

'Look, Tim, what *is* the matter? Have you done something silly? You can tell me, can't you? I'm not Staff, you know.'

Perkins hesitated, then said:

'It's just exams., Mrs Harlowe.'

'Are your parents all right? No trouble at home?'

'No, Mrs Harlowe; they're fine.' Again he hesitated, then: 'Good night, Mrs Harlowe.'

'Good night.'

She watched him close the gate behind him and cycle off down the narrow lane. He would be in Carne in quarter of an hour; it was downhill practically all the way.

Usually he loved the ride home. It was the best moment of the week. But tonight he hardly noticed it. He rode fast, as he always did; the hedge raced against the dark sky and the rabbits scuttled from the beam of his lamp, but tonight he hardly noticed them.

He would have to tell somebody. He should have told Mrs Harlowe; he wished he had. She'd know what to do. Mr Snow would have been all right, but he wasn't up to him for science any longer, he was up to Rode. That was half the trouble. That and Fielding.

He could tell True—yes, that's who he'd tell, he'd tell True. He'd go to Miss Truebody tonight after evening surgery and he'd tell her the truth. His father would never get over it, of course, because it meant failure and perhaps disgrace. It meant not going to Sandhurst at the end of next Half, it meant more money they couldn't afford. . . .

He was coming to the steepest part of the hill. The hedge stopped on one side and instead there was a marvellous view of Sawley Castle

against the night sky, like a backcloth for *Macbeth*. He loved acting—
he wished the Master let them act at Carne.

He leant forward over the handlebars and allowed himself to
gather speed to go through the shallow ford at the bottom of the hill.
The cold air bit into his face, and for a moment he almost forgot. . . .
Suddenly he braked; felt the bike skid wildly beneath him.

Something was wrong; there was a light ahead, a flashing light, and
a familiar voice calling to him urgently across the darkness.

Chapter Fourteen

The Quality of Mercy

The Public Schools Committee for Refugee Relief (Patroness:
Sarah, Countess of Sawley) has an office in Belgrave Square. It is not
at all clear whether this luxurious situation is designed to entice the
wealthy or encourage the dispossessed—or, as some irreverent voices
in Society whispered, to provide the Countess of Sawley with an
inexpensive *pied-à-terre* in the West End of London. The business of
assisting refugees has been suitably relegated to the south of the
river, to one of those untended squares in Kennington which are part
of London's architectural schizophrenia. York Gardens, as the
square is called, will one day be discovered by the world, and its
charm lost, but go there now, and you may see real children playing
hopscotch in the road, and their mothers, shod in bedroom slippers,
abusing them from doorways.

Miss Brimley, despatched on her way by Smiley's telephone call
the previous morning, had the rare gift of speaking to children as if
they were human beings, and thus discovered without difficulty the
dilapidated, unnamed house which served the Committee as a
collecting centre. With the assistance of seven small boys, she pulled
on the bell and waited patiently. At last she heard the clatter of feet
descending un uncarpeted staircase, and the door was opened by a
very beautiful girl. They looked at one another with approval for a
moment.

'I'm sorry to be a nuisance,' Miss Brimley began, 'but a friend of
mine in the country has asked me to make some enquiries about a
parcel of clothes that was sent up a day or two ago. She's made rather
a stupid mistake.'

'Oh goodness, how awful,' said the girl pleasantly. 'Would you like
to come in? Everything's frightfully chaotic, I'm afraid, and there's

nothing to sit on, but we can give you powdered coffee in a mug.'

Miss Brimley followed her in, closing the door firmly on the seven children, who were edging gently forward in her wake. She was in the hall, and everywhere she looked there were parcels of every kind, some wrapped in jute with smart labels, some in brown paper, torn and clumsy, some in crates and laundry baskets, old suitcases and even an antiquated cabin trunk with a faded yellow label on it which read: 'Not wanted on voyage.'

The girl led the way upstairs to what was evidently the office, a large room containing a deal table littered with correspondence, and a kitchen chair. An oil stove sputtered in one corner, and an electric kettle was steaming in a melancholy way beside it.

'I'm sorry,' said the girl as they entered the room, 'but there just isn't anywhere to talk downstairs. I mean, one can't talk on one leg like Incas. Or isn't it Incas? Perhaps it's Afghans. However did you find us?'

'I went to your West End office first,' Miss Brimley replied, 'and they told me I should come and see you. I think they were rather cross. After that I relied on children. They always know the way. You are Miss Dawney, aren't you?'

'Lord, no. I'm the sort of daily help. Jill Dawney's gone to see the Customs people at Rotherhithe–she'll be back at tea time if you want to see her.'

'Gracious, my dear, I'm sure I shan't keep you two minutes. A friend of mine who lives in Carne–('Goodness! How grand,' said the girl) she's a sort of cousin really, but it's simpler to call her a friend, isn't it?–gave an old grey dress to the refugee people last Thursday and now she's convinced she left her brooch pinned to the bodice. I'm sure she hasn't done anything of the sort, mind you–she's a scatter-brain creature–but she rang me up yesterday morning in a dreadful state and made me promise to come round at once and ask. I couldn't come yesterday, unfortunately–tied to my little paper from dawn till dusk. But I gather you're a bit behind, so it won't be too late?'

'Gosh, no! We're miles behind. That's all the stuff downstairs, waiting to be unpacked and sorted. It comes from the voluntary reps. at each school–sometimes boys and sometimes Staff–and they put all the clothes together and send them up in big parcels, either by train or ordinary mail, usually by train. We sort them here before sending abroad.'

'That's what I gathered from Jane. As soon as she realised she'd made this mistake she got hold of the woman doing the collecting and sending, but of course it was too late. The parcel had gone.'

'How frantic. . . . Do you know when the parcel was sent off?'

'Yes. On Friday morning.'

'From Carne? Train or post?'

Miss Brimley had been dreading this question, but she made a guess:

'Post, I believe.'

Darting past Miss Brimley, the girl foraged among the pile of papers on her desk and finally produced a stiff-backed exercise book with a label on it marked 'Ledger'. Opening it at random, she whisked quickly back and forth through the pages, licking the tip of one finger now and then in a harassed sort of way.

'Wouldn't have arrived till yesterday at the earliest,' she said. 'We certainly won't have opened it yet. Honestly, I don't know how we shall *ever* cope, and with Easter coming up we shall just get worse and worse. On top of that, half our stuff is rotting in the Customs sheds—hullo, here we are!' She pushed the ledger over to Miss Brimley, her slim finger pointing to a pencilled entry in the central column: 'Carne, parcel post, 27 lb.'

'I wonder,' said Miss Brimley, 'whether you would mind awfully if we had a quick look inside?'

They went downstairs to the hall.

'It's not quite as hideous as it looks,' the girl called over her shoulder. 'All the Monday lot will be nearest the door.'

'How do you know where they come from if you can't read the postmark?' asked Miss Brimley as the girl began to forage among the parcels.

'We issue the volunteer reps. with our printed labels. The labels have an originator's number on. In other cases we just ask them to write the name of the school in capitals on the outside. You see, we simply can't allow covering letters; it would be *too* desperate. When we get a parcel all we have to do is send off a printed card acknowledging with thanks receipt of a parcel of such and such a date weighing so and so much. People who aren't reps. won't send parcels to this address, you see—they'll send to the advertised address in Belgrave Square.'

'Does the system work?'

'No,' replied the girl, 'it doesn't. The reps. either forget to use our labels or they run out and can't be bothered to tell us. Ten days later they ring up in a rage because they haven't had an acknowledgement. Reps. change, too, without letting us know, and the packing and labelling instructions don't get passed on. Sometimes the boys will suddenly decide to do it themselves, and no one tells them the way to go about it. Lady Sarah gets as mad as a snake if parcels turn up at Head Office—they all have to be carted over here for repacking and inventories.'

'I see.' Miss Brimley watched anxiously as the girl foraged among the parcels, still talking.

'Did you say your friend actually *taught* at Carne? She must be terribly grand. I wonder what the Prince is like: he looks rather soft in his photographs. My cousin went to Carne–he's an utter wet. Do you know what he told me? During Ascot week they all . . . Hello! Here we are!' The girl stood up, a large square parcel in her arms, and carried it to a table which stood in the shadow of the staircase. Miss Brimley, standing beside her as she began carefully to untie the stout twine, looked curiously at the printed label. In its top left-hand corner was stamped the symbol which the Committee had evidently allocated to Carne: C4. After the four the letter B had been written in with ballpoint pen.

'What does the B mean?' asked Miss Brimley.

'Oh, that's a local arrangement at Carne. Miss D'Arcy's the rep. there, but they've done so well recently that she co-opted a friend to help with despatch. When we acknowledge we always mention whether it was A or B. B must be terribly keen, whoever she is.'

Miss Brimley forebore from enquiring what proportion of the parcels from Carne had originated from Miss D'Arcy, and what proportion from her anonymous assistant.

The girl removed the string and turned the parcel upside down in order to liberate the overlap of wrapping paper. As she did so Miss Brimley caught sight of a faint brown smudge, no more, about the size of a shilling, near the join. It was consistent with her essential rationalism that she should search for any explanation other than that which so loudly presented itself. The girl continued the work of unwrapping, saying suddenly: 'I say, Carne was where they had that dreadful murder, wasn't it–that master's wife who got killed by the gypsy? It really *is* awful isn't it, how much of that kind of thing goes on? Hm! Thought as much,' she remarked, suddenly interrupting herself. She had removed the outer paper, and was about to unwrap the bundle inside when her attention was evidently arrested by the appearance of the inner parcel.

'What?' Miss Brimley said quickly.

The girl laughed. 'Oh, only the packing,' she said; 'The C4Bs are usually so neat–quite the best we get. This is quite different. Not the same person at all. Must be a stand-in. I thought so from the outside.'

'How can you be so sure?'

'Oh, it's like handwriting. We can tell.' She laughed again, and without more ado removed the last wrapping. 'Grey dress, you said, didn't you? Let's see.' With both hands she began picking clothes from the top of the pile and laying them to either side. She was nearly half way through when she exclaimed 'Well, *honestly*! They must be having a brain-storm,' and drew from the bundle of partworn clothes a transparent plastic mackintosh, a very old pair of leather gloves, and a pair of rubber overshoes.

Miss Brimley was holding the edge of the table very tightly. The palms of her hands were throbbing.

'Here's a cape. Damp, too,' the girl added in disgust, and tossed the offending articles on to the floor beside the table. Miss Brimley could only think of Smiley's letter: 'Whoever killed her must have been covered in blood.' Yes, and whoever killed her wore a plastic cape and a hood, rubber overshoes and those old leather gloves with the terra-cotta stains. Whoever killed Stella Rode had not chanced upon her in the night, but had plotted long ahead, had waited. 'Yes,' thought Miss Brimley, 'had waited for the long nights.'

The girl was talking to her again: 'I'm afraid it really isn't here.'

'No, my dear,' Miss Brimley replied, 'I see that. Thank you. You've been very sweet.' Her voice faltered for a moment, then she managed to say: 'I think, my dear, you should leave the parcel exactly as it is now, the wrapping and everything in it. Something very dreadful has happened, and the police will want to . . . know about it and see the parcel. . . . You must trust me, my dear—things aren't quite what they seem. . . .' And somehow she escaped to the comforting freedom of York Gardens and the large-eyed wonder of its waiting children.

She went to a telephone box. She got through to the Sawley Arms and asked a very bored receptionist for Mr Smiley. Total silence descended on the line until the Trunks operator asked her to put in another three and sixpence. Miss Brimley replied sharply that all she had so far had for her money was a three-minute vacuum; this was followed by the unmistakable sound of the operator sucking her teeth, and then, quite suddenly, by George Smiley's voice:

'George, it's Brim. A plastic mackintosh, a cape, rubber overshoes and some leather gloves that look as though they're stained with blood. Smudges on some of the wrapping paper too by the look of it.'

A pause.

'Handwriting on the outside of the parcel?'

'None. The Charity organisers issue printed labels.'

'Where is the stuff now? Have you got it?'

'No. I've told the girl to leave everything exactly as it is. It'll be all right for an hour or two. George, are you there?'

'Yes.'

'Who did it? Was it the husband?'

'I don't know. I just don't know.'

'Do you want me to do anything—about the clothes, I mean? Phone Sparrow or anything?'

'No. I'll see Rigby at once. Goodbye, Brim. Thanks for ringing.'

She put back the receiver. He sounded strange, she thought. He seemed to lose touch sometimes. As if he'd switched off.

She walked north-west towards the Embankment. It was long after ten o'clock—the first time she'd been late for Heaven knows how long. She had better take a taxi. Being a frugal women, however, she took a bus.

Ailsa Brimley did not believe in emergencies, for she enjoyed a discipline of mind uncommon in men and even rarer in women. The greater the emergency, the greater her calm. John Landsbury had remarked upon it: 'You have sales resistance to the dramatic, Brim; the rare gift of contempt for what is urgent. I know of a dozen people who would pay you five thousand a year for telling them every day that what is important is seldom urgent. Urgent equals ephemeral, and ephemeral equals unimportant.'

She got out of the bus, carefully putting the ticket in the rubbish compartment. As she stood in the warm sunlight of the street she caught sight of the hoardings advertising the first edition of the evening papers. If it hadn't been for the sun, she might never have looked; but the sun dazzled her and made her glance downwards. And so she did see; she read it in the plump black of the wet newsprint, in the prepacked hysteria of Fleet Street: 'All-night search for missing Carne boy.'

Chapter Fifteen

The Road to Fielding

Smiley put down the receiver and walked quickly past the reception desk towards the front door. He must see Rigby at once. Just as he was leaving the hotel he heard his name called. Turning, he saw his old enemy, the night porter, braving the light of day, beckoning to him like Charon with his grey hand.

'They've been on to you from the police station,' he observed with undisguised pleasure; 'Mr Rigby wants you, the Inspector. You're to go there at once. At once, see?'

'I'm on my way there now,' Smiley replied irritably, and as he pushed his way through the swing doors he heard the old man repeat; 'At once, mind; they're waiting for you.'

Making his way through the Carne streets, he reflected for the hundredth time on the obscurity of motive in human action: there is no true thing on earth. There is no constant, no dependable point, not even in the purest logic or the most obscure mysticism; least of all in the motives of men when they are moved to act violently.

Had the murderer, now so near discovery, found contentment in the meticulous administration of his plans? For now it was clear beyond a doubt; this was a murder devised to the last detail, even to the weapon inexplicably far from the place of its use; a murder with clues cast to mislead, a murder planned to look unplanned, a murder for a string of beads. Now the mystery of the footprints was solved: having put the overshoes into the parcel, the murderer had walked down the path to the gate, and his own prints had been obscured by the subsequent traffic of feet.

Rigby looked tired.

'You've heard the news, sir, I suppose?'

'What news?'

'About the boy, the boy in Fielding's house, missing all night?'

'No.' Smiley felt suddenly sick. 'No, I've heard nothing.'

'Good Lord, I thought you knew! Half-past eight last night Fielding rang us here. Perkins, his head boy, hadn't come back from a music lesson with Mrs Harlowe, who lives over to Longemede. We put out an alert and started looking for him. They sent a patrol car along the road he should have come back on–he was cycling, you see. The first time they didn't see anything, but on the way back the driver stopped the car at the bottom of Longemede Hill, just where the water-splash is. It occurred to him the lad might have taken a long run at the water-splash from the top of the hill, and come to grief in the dip. They found him half in the ditch, his bike beside him. Dead.'

'Oh, my dear God.'

'We didn't let on to the press at first. The boy's parents are in Singapore. The father's an Army officer. Fielding sent them a telegram. We've got on to the War Office, too.'

They were silent for a moment, then Smiley asked. 'How did it happen?'

'We've closed the road and we've been trying to reconstruct the accident. I've got a detective over there now, just having a look. Trouble is, we couldn't do much till the morning. Besides, the men trampled everywhere; you can't blame them. It looks as though he must have fallen near the bottom of the hill and hit his head on a stone: his right temple.'

'How did Fielding take it?'

'He was very shaken. Very shaken indeed. I wouldn't have believed it, to be quite honest. He just seemed to . . . give up. There was a lot that had to be done–telegraph the parents, get in touch with the boy's uncle at Windsor, and so on. But he just left all that to Miss Truebody, his housekeeper. If it hadn't been for her, I don't know how he'd have managed. I was with him for about half an hour, then he just broke down, completely, and asked to be left alone.'

'How do you mean, broke down?' Smiley asked quickly.

'He cried. Wept like a child,' said Rigby evenly. 'I'd never have thought it.'

Smiley offered Rigby a cigarette and took one himself.

'I suppose,' he ventured, 'it was an accident?'

'I suppose so.' Rigby replied woodenly.

'Perhaps,' said Smiley, 'before we go any further, I'd better give you my news. I was on my way to see you when you rang. I've just heard from Miss Brimley.' And in his precise, rather formal way, he related all that Ailsa Brimley had told him, and how he had become curious about the contents of the parcel.

Smiley waited while Rigby telephoned to London. Almost mechanically, Rigby described what he wanted done: the parcel and its contents were to be collected and arrangements made to subject them immediately to forensic examination; the surfaces should be tested for finger-prints. He would be coming up to London himself with some samples of a boy's handwriting and an examination paper; he would want the opinion of a handwriting expert. No, he would be coming by train on the 4.25 from Carne, arriving at Waterloo at 8.05. Could a car be sent to the station to collect him? There was silence, then Rigby said testily, 'All right, I'll take a ruddy taxi,' and rang off rather abruptly. He looked at Smiley angrily for a moment, then grinned, plucked at his ear and said:

'Sorry, sir; getting a bit edgy.' He indicated the far wall with his head and added, 'Fighting on too many fronts, I suppose. I shall have to tell the Chief about that parcel, but he's out shooting at the moment–only pigeon, with a couple of friends, he won't be long–but I haven't mentioned your presence here in Carne, as a matter of fact, and if you don't mind I'll . . .'

'Of course,' Smiley cut in quickly. 'It's much simpler if you keep me out of it.'

'I shall tell him it was just a routine enquiry. We shall have to mention Miss Brimley later . . . but there's no point in making things worse, is there?'

'No.'

'I shall have to let Janie go, I suppose. . . . She was right, wasn't she? Silver wings in the moonlight.'

'I wouldn't–no, I wouldn't let her go, Rigby,' said Smiley with unaccustomed vehemence. 'Keep her with you as long as you can possibly manage. No more accidents, for heaven's sake. We've had enough.'

'Then you don't believe Perkins' death was an accident?'

'Good Lord, no,' cried Smiley suddenly, 'and nor do you, do you?'

'I've put a detective on to it,' Rigby replied coolly. 'I can't take the case myself. I shall be needed on the Rode murder. The Chief will have to call the Yard in now; there'll be hell to pay I can tell you. He thought it was all over bar the shouting.'

'And in the meantime?'

'In the meantime, sir, I'm going to do my damnedest to find out who killed Stella Rode.'

'If,' said Smiley slowly, 'if you find fingerprints on that mackintosh, which I doubt, will you have anything . . . local . . . to compare them with?'

'We've got Rode's, of course, and Janie's.'

'But not Fielding's?'

Rigby hesitated.

'As a matter of fact, we have,' he said at last. 'From long ago. But nothing to do with this kind of thing.'

'It was during the war,' said Smiley. 'His brother told me. Up in the North. It was hushed up, wasn't it?'

Rigby nodded. 'So far as I heard, only the D'Arcys knew; and the Master, of course. It happened in the holidays–some Air Force boy. The Chief was very helpful. . . .'

Smiley shook hands with Rigby and made his way down the familiar pine staircase. He noticed again the vaguely institutional smell of floor polish and carbolic soap, like the smell at Fielding's house.

He walked slowly back towards the Sawley Arms. At the point where he should have turned left to his hotel, however, he hesitated, then seemed to change his mind. Slowly, almost reluctantly, he crossed the road to the Abbey Close, and walked along the southern edge towards Fielding's house. He looked worried, almost frightened.

Chapter Sixteen

A Taste for Music

Miss Truebody opened the door. The rims of her eyes were pink, as though she had been weeping.

'I wonder if I might see Mr Fielding? To say goodbye.'

She hesitated: 'Mr Fielding's very upset. I doubt whether he'll want to see anyone.' He followed her into the hall and watched her go to the study door. She knocked, inclined her head, then gently turned the handle and let herself in. It was a long time before she returned. 'He'll be out shortly,' she said, without looking at him. 'Will you take off your coat?' She waited while he struggled out of his overcoat, then took it from him and hung it beside the Van Gogh chair. They stood together in silence, both looking towards the study door.

Then, quite suddenly, Fielding was standing in the half-open doorway, unshaven and in his shirt-sleeves. 'For Christ's sake,' he said thickly. 'What do you want?'

'I just wanted to say goodbye, Fielding, and to offer you my condolences.'

Fielding looked at him hard for a moment; he was leaning heavily against the door; 'Well, goodbye. Thank you for calling.' He waved one hand vaguely in the air. 'You needn't have bothered really, need you?' he added rudely. 'You could have sent me a card, couldn't you?'

'I could have done, yes; it just seemed so very tragic, when he was so near success.'

'What do you mean? What the devil do you mean?'

'I mean in his work . . . the improvement. Simon Snow was telling me all about it. Amazing really, the way Rode brought him on.'

A long silence, then Fielding spoke: 'Goodbye, Smiley. Thanks for coming.' He was turning back into the study as Smiley called:

'Not at all . . . not at all. I suppose poor Rode must have been bucked with those exam. results, too. I mean it was more or less a matter of life and death for Perkins, passing that exam., wasn't it? He wouldn't have got his remove next Half if he'd failed in science. They might have superannuated him, I suppose, even though he was head of the house; then he couldn't have sat for the Army. Poor Perkins, he had a lot to thank Rode for, didn't he? And you, too, Fielding, I'm sure. You must have helped him wonderfully . . . both of you did, you and Rode; Rode and Fielding. His parents ought to know that. They're rather hard up, I gather; the father's in the Army, isn't he, in Singapore? It must have been a great effort keeping the boy at Carne. It will comfort them to know how much was done for him, won't it, Fielding?'

Smiley was very pale. 'You've heard the latest. I suppose,' he continued. 'About that wretched gypsy woman who killed Stella Rode? They've decided she's fit to plead. I suppose they'll hang her. That'll be the third death, won't it? You know, I'll tell you an odd thing—just between ourselves, Fielding. I don't believe she did it. Do you? I don't believe she did it at all.'

He was not looking at Fielding. He had clasped his little hands tightly behind his back, and he stood with his shoulders bowed and his head inclined to one side, as though listening for an answer.

Fielding seemed to feel Smiley's words like a physical pain. Slowly he shook his head:

'No,' he said; 'No. Carne killed them; it was Carne. It could only happen here. It's the game we play: the exclusion game. Divide and rule!' He looked Smiley full in the face, and shouted: 'Now for God's sake go! You've got what you want, haven't you? You can pin me on your little board, can't you?' And then, to Smiley's distress, he began sobbing in great uncontrollable gulps, holding his hand across his brow. He appeared suddenly grotesque, stemming the childish tears with his chalky hand, his cumbersome feet turned inwards. Gently, Smiley coaxed him back into the study, gently sat him before the dead fire. Then he began talking to him softly and with compassion.

'If what I think is true, there isn't much time,' he began. 'I want you to tell me about Tim Perkins—about the exam.'

Fielding, his face buried in his hands, nodded.

'He would have failed, wouldn't he? He would have failed and not got his remove; he'd have had to leave.' Fielding was silent. 'After the exam. that day, Rode gave him the writing case to bring here, the case that contained the papers; Rode was doing chapel duty that week and wouldn't be going home before dinner, but he wanted to correct the papers that night, after his dinner with you.'

Fielding took his hands from his face and leant back in his chair, his great head tilted back, his eyes closed. Smiley continued:

'Perkins came home, and that evening he brought the case to you, as Rode told him to, for safe keeping. Perkins, after all, was head of your house, a responsible boy. . . . He gave you the case and you asked him how he'd done in the exam.'

'He wept,' said Fielding suddenly. 'He wept as only a child can.'

'And after breaking down he told you he had cheated? That he had looked up the answers and copied them on to his paper. Is that right? And after the murder of Stella Rode he remembered what else he had seen in the suitcase?'

Fielding was standing up. 'No! Don't you see? Tim wouldn't have cheated to save his life! That's the whole point, the whole bloody irony of it,' he shouted. 'He never cheated at all. *I* cheated for him.'

'But you couldn't! You couldn't copy his handwriting!'

'He wrote with a ball-pen. It was only formulae and diagrams. When he'd gone, and left me along with the case, I looked at his paper. It was hopeless—he'd only done two out of seven questions. So I cheated for him. I just cribbed them from the science book, and wrote them with blue ball-point, the kind we all use. Abbots' sell them. I copied his hand as best I could. It only needed about three lines of figures. The rest was diagrams.'

'Then it was you who opened the case? You who saw . . .'

'Yes. It was me, I tell you, not Tim! He couldn't cheat to save his life! But Tim paid for it, don't you see? When the marks were published Tim must have known something was wrong with them. After all, he'd only attempted two questions out of seven and yet he'd got sixty-one per cent. But he knew *nothing* else, *nothing*!'

For a long time neither spoke. Fielding was standing over Smiley, exultant with the relief of sharing his secret, and Smiley was looking vaguely past him, his face drawn in deep concentration.

'And of course,' he said finally, 'when Stella was murdered, you knew who had done it.'

'Yes,' replied Fielding. 'I knew that Rode had killed her.'

Fielding poured himself a brandy and gave one to Smiley. He seemed to have recovered his self-control. He sat down and looked at Smiley thoughtfully for a time.

'I've got no money,' he said at last. 'None. Nobody knows that except the Master. Oh, they know I'm more or less broke, but they don't know *how* broke. Long ago I made an ass of myself. I got into trouble. It was in the war, when staff was impossible. I had a boys' house and was practically running the school–D'Arcy and I. We were running it together, and the Master running us. Then I made an ass of myself. It was during the holidays. I was up North at the time, giving a course of talks at an R.A.F. educational place. And I stepped out of line. Badly. They pulled me in. And along came D'Arcy wearing his country overcoat and bringing the Master's terms: Come back to Carne, my dear fellow, and we'll say no more about it; go on running your house, my dear fellow, and giving of your wisdom. There's been no publicity. We know it will never happen again, my dear fellow, and we're dreadfully hard up for staff. Come back as a temporary. So I did, and I've been one ever since, going cap in hand to darling D'Arcy every December asking for my contract to be renewed. And, of course–no pension. I shall have to teach at a crammer's. There's a place in Somerset where they'll take me. I'm seeing their Headmaster in London on Thursday. It's a sort of breaker's yard for old dons. The Master had to know, because he gave me a reference.'

'That was why you couldn't tell anyone? Because of Perkins?'

'In a way, yes. I mean they'd want to know all sorts of things. I did it for Tim, you see. The Governors wouldn't have liked that much ... inordinate affection.... It looks bad, doesn't it? But it wasn't that kind of affection, Smiley, not any more. You never heard him play the 'cello. He wasn't marvellous, but just sometimes he would play so beautifully, with a kind of studious simplicity, that was indescribably good. He was an awkward boy, and when he played well it was such a surprise. You should have heard him play.

'You didn't want to drag him into it. If you told the police what you had seen it would ruin Tim too?'

Fielding nodded. 'In the whole of Carne, he was the one thing I loved.'

'Loved?' asked Smiley.

'For God's sake,' said Fielding in an exhausted voice, 'why not?'

'His parents wanted him to go to Sandhurst; I didn't, I'm afraid. I thought that if I could keep him here another Half or two I might be able to get him a music scholarship. That's why I made him Head of House: I wanted his parents to keep him on because he was doing so well.' Fielding paused; 'He was a rotten Head of House,' he added.

'And what exactly was in the writing-case,' Smiley asked, 'when you opened it that evening to look at Tim's exam. paper?'

'A sheet of transparent plastic . . . it may have been one of those pack-away cape things—an old pair of gloves, and a pair of home-made galoshes.'

'Home-made?'

'Yes. Hacked from a pair of wellington boots, I should think.'

'That's all?'

'No. There was a length of heavy cable, I presumed for demon-strating something in his science lessons. It seemed natural enough in winter to carry waterproofs about. Then, after the murder, I realised how he had done it.'

'Did you know,' asked Smiley, '*why* he had done it?'

Fielding seemed to hesitate: 'Rode's a guinea-pig,' he began, 'the first man we've had from a grammar school. Most of us are old Carnians ourselves, in fact. Focused when we start. Rode wasn't, and Carne thrilled him. The very name Carne means quality, and Rode loved quality. His wife wasn't like that. She had her standards and they were different, but just as good. I used to watch Rode in the Abbey sometimes on Sunday mornings. Tutors sit at the end of pews, right by the aisle, you know. I used to watch his face as the choir processed past him in white and scarlet, and the Master in his doctor's robes and the Governors and Guardians behind him. Rode was drunk—drunk with the pride of Carne. We're heady wine for the grammar school men, you know. It must have hurt him terribly that Stella wouldn't share any of that. You could see it did. The night they came to dinner with me, the night she died, they argued. I never told anyone, but they did. The Master had preached a sermon at Compline that evening: "Hold fast to that which is good." Rode talked about it at dinner; he couldn't take much drink, you know, he wasn't used to it. He was full of this sermon and of the eloquence of the Master. She never came to the Abbey—she went to that drab tabernacle by the station. He went on and on about the beauty of the Abbey service, the dignity, the reverence. She kept quiet till he'd finished, then laughed, and said: "Poor old Stan. You'll always be Stan to me." I've never seen anyone so angry as he was then. He went quite pale.'

Fielding swept his grey hair from his eyes and went on, with something like the old panache: 'I've watched her, too, at meals. Not just here, but at dinner parties elsewhere, when we've both been invited. I've watched her do the simplest things—like eating an apple.

She'd peel it in one piece, round and round till the whole peel fell off. Then she'd cut the apple and dice the quarters, getting it all ready before she ate it. She might have been a miner's wife preparing it for her husband. She must have *seen* how people do things here, but it never occurred to her that she ought to copy them. I admire that. So do you, I expect. But Carne doesn't–and Rode didn't; above all, Rode didn't. He'd watch her, and I think he grew to hate her for not conforming. He came to see her as the bar to his success, the one factor which would deprive him of a great career. Once he'd reached that conclusion, what could he do? He couldn't divorce her–that would do him more harm than remaining married to her. Rode knew what Carne would think of divorce; we're a Church foundation, remember. So he killed her. He plotted a squalid murder, and with his little scientist's mind he gave them all the clues they wanted. Fabricated clues. Clues that would point to a murderer who didn't exist. But something went wrong; Tim Perkins got sixty-one per cent. He'd got an impossible mark–he must have cheated. He'd had the opportunity–he'd had the papers in the case. Rode put his little mind to it and decided what had happened: Tim had opened the case and he'd seen the cape and the boots and the gloves. And the cable. So Rode killed him too.'

With surprising energy, Fielding got up and gave himself more brandy. His face was flushed, almost exultant.

Smiley stood up. 'When did you say you'll be coming to London? Thursday, wasn't it?'

'Yes. I had arranged to lunch with my crammer man at one of those dreadful clubs in Pall Mall. I always go into the wrong one, don't you? But I'm afraid there's not much point in my seeing him now, is there, if all this is going to come out? Not even a crammer's will take me then.'

Smiley hesitated.

'Come and dine with me that evening. Spend the night if you want. I'll ask one or two other people. We'll have a party. You'll feel better by then. We can talk a bit. I might be able to help you . . . for Adrian's sake.'

'Thank you. I should like to. Interview apart, I've got some odds and ends to clear up in London, anyway.'

'Good. Quarter to eight. Bywater Street, Chelsea, number 9A.' Fielding wrote it down in his diary. His hand was quite steady.

'Black tie?' asked Fielding, his pen poised, and some imp made Smiley reply:

'I usually do, but it doesn't matter.' There was a moment's silence.

'I suppose,' Fielding began tentatively, 'that all this *will* come out in the trial, about Tim and me? I'll be ruined if it does, you know, ruined.'

'I don't see how they can prevent it.'

'I feel much better now, anyway,' said Fielding; 'much.'

With a cursory goodbye, Smiley left him alone. He walked quickly back to the police station, reasonably confident that Terence Fielding was the most accomplished liar he had met for a long time.

Chapter Seventeen

Rabbit Run

He knocked on Rigby's door and walked straight in.

'I'm awfully afraid you'll have to arrest Stanley Rode,' he began, and recounted his interview with Fielding.

'I shall have to tell the Chief,' said Rigby, doubtfully. 'Would you like to repeat all that in front of him? If we're going to pull in a Carne master, I think the Chief had better know first. He's just come back. Hang on a minute.' He picked up the telephone on his desk and asked for the Chief Constable. A few minutes later they were walking in silence down a carpeted corridor. On either wall hung photographs of rugby and cricket teams, some yellow and faded from the Indian sun, others done in a sepia tint much favoured by Carne photographers in the early part of the century. At intervals along the corridor stood empty buckets of brilliant red, with FIRE printed carefully in white on the outside. At the far end of the corridor was a dark oak door. Rigby knocked and waited. There was silence. He knocked again and was answered with a cry of 'Come!'

Two very large spaniels watched them come in. Behind the spaniels, at an enormous desk, Brigadier Havelock, O.B.E., Chief Constable of Carne, sat like a water rat on a raft.

The few strands of white hair which ran laterally across his otherwise bald head were painstakingly adjusted to cover the maximum area. This gave him an oddly wet look, as if he had just emerged from the river. His moustache, which lavishly compensated for the scarcity of other hair, was yellow and appeared quite solid. He was a very small man, and he wore a brown suit and a stiff white collar with rounded corners.

'Sir,' Rigby began, 'may I introduce Mr Smiley from London?'

He came out from behind his desk as if he were giving himself up, unconvinced but resigned. Then he pushed out a little, knobbly hand and said, 'From London, eh? How d'you do, sir,' all at once, as if he'd learnt it by heart.

'Mr Smiley's here on a private visit, sir,' Rigby continued. 'He is an acquaintance of Mr Fielding.'

'Quite a card, Fielding, quite a card,' the Chief Constable snapped.

'Yes, indeed, sir,' said Rigby, and went on:

'Mr Smiley called on Mr Fielding just now, sir, to take his leave before returning to London.' Havelock shot a beady glance at Smiley, as if wondering whether he were fit to make the journey.

'Mr Fielding made a kind of statement, which he substantiated with new evidence of his own. About the murder, sir.'

'Well, Rigby?' he said challengingly. Smiley intervened:

'He said that the husband had done it; Stanley Rode. Fielding said that when his head boy brought him Rode's writing-case containing the examination papers . . .'

'What examination papers?'

'Rode was invigilating that afternoon, you remember. He was also doing chapel duty before going on to dinner at Fielding's house. As an expediency, he gave the papers to Perkins to take . . .'

'The boy who had the accident?' Havelock asked.

'Yes.'

'You know a lot about it,' said Havelock darkly.

'Fielding said that when Perkins brought him the case, Fielding opened it. He wanted to see how Perkins had done in the science paper. It was vital to the boy's future that he should get his remove,' Smiley went on.

'Oh, work's the only thing now,' said Havelock bitterly. 'Wasn't the way when I was a boy here, I assure you.'

'When Fielding opened the case, the papers were inside. So was a plastic cape, an old pair of leather gloves and a pair of rubber overshoes, cut from wellingtons.'

A pause.

'Good God! Good God! Hear that, Rigby? That's what they found in the parcel in London. Good God!'

'Finally, there was a length of cable, heavy cable, in the case as well. It was this writing-case that Rode went back for, you remember, on the night of the murder,' Smiley concluded. It was like feeding a child—you couldn't overload the spoon.

There was a very long silence indeed. Then Rigby, who seemed to know his man, said:

'Motive was self-advancement in the profession, sir. Mrs Rode showed no desire to improve her station, dressed in a slovenly manner and took no part in the religious life of the school.'

'Just a minute,' said Havelock. 'Rode planned the murder from the start, correct?'

'Yes, sir.'

'He wanted to make it look like robbery with violence.'

'Yes, sir.'

'Having collected the writing-case, he walked back to North Fields. Then what does he do?'

'He puts on the plastic cape and hood, overshoes and gloves. He arms himself with the weapon, sir. He lets himself in by the garden gate, crosses the back garden, goes to the front door and rings the bell, sir. His wife comes to the door. He knocks her down, drags her to the conservatory and murders her. He rinses the clothes under the tap and puts them in the parcel. Having sealed the parcel, he walks down the drive this time to the front gate, following the path, sir, knowing that his own footprints will soon be obscured by other people's. Having got to the road, where the snow was hard and showed no prints, he turned round and re-entered the house, playing the part of the distressed husband, taking care, when he discovers the body, sir, to put his own fingerprints over the glove-marks. There was one article that was too dangerous to send, sir. The weapon.'

'All right, Rigby. Pull him in. Mr Borrow will give you a warrant if you want one; otherwise I'll ring Lord Sawley.'

'Yes sir. And I'll send Sergeant Low to take a full statement from Mr Fielding, sir?'

'Why the devil didn't he speak up earlier, Rigby?'

'Have to ask him that, sir,' said Rigby woodenly, and left the room.

'You a Carnian?' Havelock asked, pushing a silver cigarette-box across the desk.

'No. No, I'm afraid not,' Smiley replied.

'How d'you know Fielding?'

'We met at Oxford after the war.'

'Queer card, Fielding, very queer. Say your name was Smiley?'

'There was a fellow called Smiley married Anne Sercombe, Lord Sawley's cousin. Damned pretty girl, Ann was, and went and married this fellow. Some funny little beggar in the Civil Service with an O.B.E. and a gold watch. Sawley was damned annoyed.' Smiley said nothing. 'Sawley got a son at Carne. Know that?'

'I read it in the press, I think.'

'Tell me—this fellow Rode. He's a grammar-school chap, isn't he?'

'I believe so, yes.'

'Damned odd business. Experiments never pay, do they. You can't experiment with tradition.'

'No. No, indeed.'

'That's the trouble today. Like Africa. Nobody seems to understand you can't build society overnight. It takes centuries to make a gentleman.' Havelock frowned to himself and fiddled with the paper-knife on his desk.

'Wonder how he got his cable into that ditch, the thing he killed her with. He wasn't out of our sight for forty-eight hours after the murder.'

'That,' said Smiley, 'is what puzzles me. So does Jane Lyn.'

'What d'you mean?'

'I don't believe Rode would have had the nerve to walk back to the house after killing his wife knowing that Jane Lyn had seen him do it. Assuming, of course, that he *did* know, which seems likely. It's too cool . . . too cool altogether.'

'Odd, damned odd,' muttered Havelock. He looked at his watch, pushing his left elbow outwards to do so, in a swift equestrian movement which Smiley found comic, and a little sad. The minutes ticked by. Smiley wondered if he should leave, but he had a vague feeling that Havelock wanted his company.

'There'll be a hell of a fuss,' said Havelock. 'It isn't every day you arrest a Carne tutor for murder.' He put down the paper-knife sharply on the desk.

'Those bloody journalists ought to be horsewhipped!' he declared. 'Look at the stuff they print about the Royal Family. Wicked, wicked!' he got up, crossed the room and sat himself in a leather armchair by the fire. One of the spaniels went and sat at his feet.

'What made him do it, I wonder. What the devil made him do it? His own wife, I mean; a fellow like that.' Havelock said this simply, appealing for enlightenment.

'I don't believe,' said Smiley slowly, 'that we can ever entirely know what makes anyone do anything.'

'My God, you're dead right. . . . What do you do for a living, Smiley?'

'After the war I was at Oxford for a bit. Teaching and research. I'm in London now.'

'One of those clever coves, eh?'

Smiley wondered when Rigby would return.

'Know anything about this fellow's family? Has he got people, or anything?'

'I think they're both dead,' Smiley answered, and the telephone on Havelock's desk rang sharply. It was Rigby. Stanley Rode had disappeared.

Chapter Eighteen

After the Ball

He caught the 1.30 train to London. He just made it after an argument at his hotel about the bill. He left a note for Rigby giving his address and telephone number in London and asking him to telephone that night when the laboratory tests were completed. There was nothing else for him to do in Carne.

As the train pulled slowly out of Carne and one by one the familiar landmarks disappeared into the cold February mist, George Smiley was filled with a feeling of relief. He hadn't wanted to come, he knew that. He'd been afraid of the place where his wife had spent her childhood, afraid to see the fields where she had lived. But he had found nothing, not the faintest memory, neither in the lifeless outlines of Sawley Castle, nor in the surrounding countryside, to remind him of her. Only the gossip remained, as it would while the Hechts and the Havelocks survived to parade their acquaintance with the first family in Carne.

He took a taxi to Chelsea, carried his suitcase upstairs and unpacked with the care of a man accustomed to living alone. He thought of having a bath, but decided to ring Ailsa Brimley first. The telephone was by his bed. He sat on the edge of the bed and dialled the number. A tinny model-voice sang: 'Unipress, good afternoon,' and he asked for Miss Brimley. There was a long silence, then, 'Ah'm afraid Miss Brimley is in conference. Can someone else answer your query?'

Query, thought Smiley. Good God! Why on earth query—why not question or enquiry?

'No,' he replied. 'Just tell her Mr Smiley rang.' He put back the receiver and went into the bathroom and turned on the hot tap. He was fiddling with his cuff-links when the telephone rang. It was Ailsa Brimley:

'George? I think you'd better come round at once. We've got a visitor. Mr Rode from Carne. He wants to talk to us.' Pulling on his jacket, he ran out into the street and hailed a taxi.

Chapter Nineteen

Disposal of a Legend

The descending escalator was packed with the staff of Unipress, homebound and heavy-eyed. To them, the sight of a fat, middle-aged gentleman bounding up the adjoining staircase provided unexpected entertainment, so that Smiley was hastened on his way by the jeers of office-boys and the laughter of typists. On the first floor he paused to study an enormous board carrying the titles of a quarter of the national dailies. Finally, under the heading of 'Technical and Miscellaneous', he spotted the *Christian Voice*, Room 619. The lift seemed to go up very slowly. Formless music issued from behind its plush, while a boy in a monkey jacket flicked his hips in the heavier beats. The golden doors parted with a sigh, the boy said 'Six', and Smiley stepped quickly into the corridor. A moment or two later he was knocking on the door of Room 619. It was opened by Ailsa Brimley.

'George, how nice,' she said brightly. 'Mr Rode will be dreadfully pleased to see you.' And without any further introduction she led him into her office. In an armchair near the window sat Stanley Rode, tutor of Carne, in a neat black overcoat. As Smiley entered he stood up and held out his hand. 'Good of you to come, sir,' he said woodenly. 'Very.' The same flat manner, the same cautious voice.

'How can I help you?' asked Smiley.

They all sat down. Smiley offered Miss Brimley a cigarette and lit it for her.

'It's about this article you're writing about Stella,' he began. 'I feel awful about it really, because you've been so good to her, and her memory, if you see what I mean. I know you wish well, but I don't want you to write it.'

Smiley said nothing, and Ailsa was wise enough to keep quiet. From now on it was Smiley's interview. The silence didn't worry him, but it seemed to worry Rode.

'It wouldn't be right; it wouldn't do at all. Mr Glaston agreed; I spoke to him yesterday before he left and he agreed. I just couldn't let you write that stuff.'

'Why not?'

'Too many people know, you see. Poor Mr Cardew, I asked him. He knows a lot; and a lot about Stella, so I asked him. He understands why I gave up Chapel too; I couldn't bear to see her going there every Sunday and going down on her knees.' He shook his head. 'It was all wrong. It just made a fool of your faith.'

'What did Mr Cardew say?'

'He said we should not be the judges. We should let God judge. But I said to him it wouldn't be right, those people knowing what she'd done, and then reading all that stuff in the *Voice*. They'd think it was crazy. He didn't seem to see that, he just said to leave it to God. But I can't, Mr Smiley.'

Again no one spoke for a time. Rode sat quite still, save for a very slight rocking movement of his head. Then he began to talk again:

'I didn't believe old Mr Glaston at first. He said she was bad, but I didn't believe it. They lived upon the hill then, Gorse Hill, only a step from the Tabernacle; Stella and her father. They never seemed to keep servants for long, so she did most of the work. I used to call in Sunday mornings sometimes after church. Stella looked after her father, cooked for him and everything, and I always wondered how I'd ever have the nerve to ask Mr Glaston for her. The Glastons were big people in Branxome. I was teaching at Grammar School in those days. They let me teach part-time while I read for my degree, and I made up my mind that if I passed the exam. I'd ask her to marry me.

'The Sunday after the results came out I went round to the house after morning service. Mr Glaston opened the door himself. He took me straight into the study. You could see half the potteries in Poole from the window, and the sea beyond. He sat me down and he said: "I know what you're here for, Stanley. You want to marry Stella. But you don't know her," he said, "you don't know her." "I've been visiting two years, Mr Glaston," I said, "and I think I know my mind." Then he started talking about her. I never thought to hear a human being talk like that of his own child. He said she was bad—bad in her heart. That she was full of malice. That was why no servants would stay at the Hill. He told me how she'd lead people on, all kind and warm, till they'd told her everything, then she'd hurt them, saying wicked things, half true, half lies. He told me a lot more besides, and I didn't believe it, not a word. I think I lost my head; I called him a jealous old man who wanted his child to wait on him till he died. I said it was him who was bad, not Stella, and I shouted at him liar, liar. He didn't seem to hear, just shook his head, and I ran out into the hall and called Stella. She'd been in the kitchen, I think, and she came to me and put her arms round me and kissed me.

'We were married a month later, and the old man gave her away. He shook my hand at the wedding and called me a fine man, and I thought what an old hypocrite he was. He gave us money–to me, not her–two thousand pounds. I thought perhaps he was trying to make up for the dreadful things he'd said, and later I wrote to him and said I forgave him. He never answered and I didn't see him often after that.

'For a year or more we were happy enough at Branxome. She was just what I thought she'd be, neat and simple. She liked to go for walks and kiss at the stiles; she liked to be a bit grand sometimes, going to the Dolphin for dinner all dressed up. It meant a lot to me then, I don't mind admitting, going to the right places with Mr Glaston's daughter. He was Rotary and on the Council and quite a figure in Branxome. She used to tease me about it–in front of other people too, which got me a bit. I remember one time we went to the Dolphin, one of the waiters there was a bloke called Johnnie Raglan. We'd been to school together. Johnnie was a bit of a tear-about and hadn't done anything much since he'd left school except run after girls and get into trouble. Stella knew him, I don't know how, and she waved to him as soon as we'd sat down. Johnnie came over and Stella made him bring another chair and sit with us. The Manager looked daggers, but he didn't dare to do anything because she was Samuel Glaston's daughter. Johnnie stayed there all the meal and Stella talked to him about school and what I was like. Johnnie was pleased as punch and got cheeky, saying I'd been a swot and a good boy and all the rest, and how Johnnie had knocked me about–lies most of it, and she egged him on. I went for her afterwards and said I didn't pay good money at the Dolphin to hear Johnnie Raglan tell a lot of tall stories, and she turned on me fast like a cat. It was her money, she said, and Johnnie was as good as me any day. Then she was sorry and kissed me and I pretended to forgive her.'

Sweat was forming on his face; he was talking fast, the words tripping over each other. It was like a man recalling a nightmare, as if the memory were still there, the fear only half gone. He paused and looked sharply at Smiley as if expecting him to speak, but Smiley seemed to be looking past him, his face impassive, its soft contours grown hard.

'Then we went to Carne. I'd just started reading *The Times* and I saw the advert. They wanted a science tutor and I applied. Mr D'Arcy interviewed me and I got the job. It wasn't till we got to Carne that I knew that what her father had said was true. She hadn't been very keen on Chapel before, but as soon as she got here she went in for it in a big way. She knew it would look wrong, that it would hurt me. Branxome's a fine big church, you see; there was nothing funny about going to Branxome Tabernacle. But at Carne it was different; Carne Tabernacle's a little out-of-the-way place with a tin roof. She wanted to be different, to spite the school and me, by playing the humble one. I wouldn't have minded if she'd been sincere, but she wasn't, Mr Cardew knew that. He got to know Stella, Mr Cardew did. I think her father told him; anyway, Mr Cardew was up North before, and he knew the family well. For all I know he wrote to Mr Glaston, or went and saw him or something.

'She began there well enough. The townspeople were all pleased enough to see her–a wife from the School coming to the Tabernacle, that had never happened before. Then she took to running the appeal for the refugees–to collecting clothes and all that. Miss D'Arcy was running it for the school, Mr D'Arcy's sister, and Stella wanted to beat her at her own game–to get more from the Chapel people than Miss D'Arcy got from the School. But I knew what she was doing, and so did Mr Cardew, and so did the townspeople in the end. She listened. Every drop of gossip and dirt, she hoarded it away. She'd come home of an evening sometimes–Wednesdays and Fridays she did her Chapel work–and she'd throw off her coat and laugh till I thought she'd gone mad.

'"I've got them! I've got them all," she'd say. "I know all their little secrets and I've got them in the hollow of my hand, Stan." That's what she'd say. And those that realised grew to be frightened of her. They all gossiped, Heaven knows, but not to profit from it, not like Stella. Stella was cunning; anything decent, anything good, she'd drag it down and spoil it. There were a dozen she'd got the measure of. There was Mulligan the furniture man; he's got a daughter with a kid near Leamington. Somehow she found out the girl wasn't married–they'd sent her to an aunt to have her baby and begin again up there. She rang up Mulligan once, something to do with a bill for moving Simon Snow's furniture, and she said 'Greetings from Leamington Spa, Mr Mulligan. We need a little co-operation.' She told me that–she came home laughing her head off and told me. But they got her in the end, didn't they? They got their own back!'

Smiley nodded slowly, his eyes now turned fully upon Rode.

'Yes,' he said at last, 'they got their own back.'

'They thought Mad Janie did it, but I didn't. Janie'd as soon have killed her own sister as Stella. They were as close as moon and stars, that's what Stella said. They'd talk together for hours in the evenings when I was out late on Societies or Extra Tuition. Stella cooked food for her, gave her clothes and money. It gave her a feeling of power to help a creature like Janie, and have her fawning round. Not because she was kind, but because she was cruel.

'She'd brought a little dog with her from Branxome, a mongrel. One day a few months ago I came home and found it lying in the garage whimpering, terrified. It was limping and had blood on its back. She'd beaten it. She must have gone mad. I knew she'd beaten it before, but never like that; never. Then something happened–I shouted at her and she laughed and then I hit her. Not hard, but hard enough. In the face. I gave her twenty-four hours to have the dog destroyed or I'd tell the police. She screamed at me—it was her dog and she'd damn' well do what she liked with it—but next day she put on her little black hat and took the dog to the vet. I suppose she told him some tale. She could spin a good tale about anything, Stella could. She kind of stepped into a part and played it right through. Like the tale she told the Hungarians. Miss D'Arcy had some refugees to stay from London once and Stella told them such a tale they ran away and had to be taken back to London. Miss D'Arcy paid for their fares and everything, even had the welfare officer down to see them and try and put things right. I don't think Miss D'Arcy ever knew who'd got at them, but I did—Stella told me. She laughed, always the same laugh: "There's your fine lady, Stan. Look at her charity now."

'After the dog, she took to pretending I was violent, cringing away whenever I came near, holding her arm up as though I was going to hit her again. She even made out I was plotting to murder her: she went and told Mr Cardew I was. She didn't believe it herself; she'd laugh about it sometimes. She said to me: "It's no good killing me now, Stan; they'll all know who's done it." But other times she'd whine and stroke me, begging me not to kill her. "You'll kill me in the long nights!" She'd scream it out—it was the words that got her, the long nights, she liked the sound of them the way an actor does, and she'd build a whole story round them. "Oh, Stan," she'd say, "keep me safe in the long nights." You know how it is when you never meant to do anything anyway, and someone goes on begging you not to do it? You think you might do it after all, you begin to consider the possibility.'

Miss Brimley drew in her breath rather quickly. Smiley stood up and walked over to Rode.

'Why don't we go back to my house for food?' he said. 'We can talk this over quietly. Among friends.'

They took a taxi to Bywater Street. Rode sat beside Ailsa Brimley, more relaxed now, and Smiley, opposite him on a drop-seat, watched him and wondered. And it occurred to him that the most important thing about Rode was that he had no friends. Smiley was reminded of Büchner's fairy tale of the child left alone in an empty world who, finding no one to talk to, went to the moon because it smiled at him, but the moon was made of rotten wood. And when the sun and moon and stars had all turned to nothing, he tried to go back to the earth, but it had gone.

Perhaps because Smiley was tired, or perhaps because he was getting a little old, he felt a movement of sudden compassion towards Rode, such as children feel for the poor and parents for their children. Rode had tried so hard—he had used Carne's language, bought the right clothes, and thought as best he could the right thoughts, yet remained hopelessly apart, hopelessly alone.

He lit the gas-fire in the drawing-room while Ailsa Brimley went to the delicatessen in the King's Road for soup and eggs. He poured out whisky and soda and gave one to Rode, who drank it in short sips, without speaking.

'I had to tell somebody,' he said at last. 'I thought you'd be a good person. I didn't want you to print that article, though. Too many knew, you see.'

'How many really knew?'

'Only those she'd gone for, I think. I suppose about a dozen townspeople. And Mr Cardew, of course. She was terribly cunning, you see. She didn't often pass on gossip. She knew to a hair how far she could go. Those who knew were the ones she'd got on the hook. Oh, and D'Arcy, Felix D'Arcy, he knew. She had something special there, something she never told me about. There were nights when she'd put on her shawl and slip out, all excited as if she was going to a party. Quite late sometimes, eleven or twelve. I'd never ask her where she was going because it only bucked her, but sometimes she'd nod at me all cunning and say, "You don't know, Stan, but D'Arcy does. D'Arcy knows and he can't tell," and then she'd laugh again and try and look mysterious, and off she'd go.'

Smiley was silent for a long time, watching Rode and thinking. Then he asked suddenly: 'What was Stella's blood group, do you know?'

'Mine's B. I know that. I was a donor at Branxome. Hers was different.'

'How do you know that?'

'She had a test before we were married. She used to suffer from anaemia. I remember hers being different, that's all. Probably A. I can't remember for sure. Why?'

'Where were you registered as a donor?'

'North Poole Transfusion Centre.'

'Will they know you there still? Are you still recorded there?'

'I suppose so.'

The front door bell rang. It was Ailsa Brimley, back from her shopping.

Ailsa installed herself in the kitchen, while Rode and Smiley sat in the warm comfort of the drawing-room.

'Tell me something else,' said Smiley, 'about the night of the murder. Why did you leave the writing-case behind? Was it absent-mindedness?'

'No, not really. I was on Chapel duty that night, so Stella and I arrived separately at Fielding's house. She got there before I did and

I think Fielding gave the case to her—right at the start of the evening so that it wouldn't get forgotten. He said something about it later that evening. She'd put the case beside her coat in the hall. It was only a little thing about eighteen inches by twelve. I could have sworn she was carrying it as we stood in the hall saying goodbye, but I must have been mistaken. It wasn't till we got to the house that she asked me what I'd done with it.'

'*She* asked *you* what you'd done with it?'

'Yes. Then she threw a temper and said I expected her to remember everything. I didn't particularly want to go back, I could have rung Fielding and arranged to collect it first thing next morning, but Stella wouldn't hear of it. She made me go. I didn't like to tell the police all this stuff about us quarrelling, it didn't seem right.'

Smiley nodded. 'When you got back to Fielding's you rang the bell?'

'Yes. There's the front door, then a glass door inside, a sort of french window to keep out draughts. The front door was still open, and light was on in the hall. I rang the bell and collected the case from Fielding.'

They had finished supper when the telephone rang.

'Rigby here, Mr Smiley. I've got the laboratory results. They're rather puzzling.'

'The exam. paper first: it doesn't tally?'

'No, it doesn't. The boffins here say all the figures and writing were done with the same ball point pen. They can't be sure about the diagrams but they say the legend on all the diagrams corresponds to the rest of the script on the sheet.'

'All done by the boy after all in fact?'

'Yes. I brought up some other samples of his hand-writing for comparison. They match the exam. paper right the way through. Fielding couldn't have tinkered with it.'

'Good. And the clothing? Nothing there either?'

'Traces of blood, that's all. No prints on the plastic.'

'What was her blood group, by the way?'

'Group A.'

Smiley sat down on the edge of the bed. Pressing the receiver to this ear, he began talking quietly. Ten minutes later he was walking slowly downstairs. He had come to the end of the chase, and was already sickened by the kill.

It was nearly an hour before Rigby arrived.

Chapter Twenty

The Dross of the River

Albert Bridge was as preposterous as ever; bony steel, rising to Wagnerian pinnacles, against the patient London sky; the Thames crawling beneath it with resignation, edging its filth into the wharves of Battersea, then sliding towards the mist down river.

The mist was thick. Smiley watched the driftwood, as it touched it, turning first to white dust, then seeming to lift, dissolve and vanish.

This was how it would end, on a foul morning like this when they dragged the murderer whimpering from his cell and put the hempen rope round his neck. Would Smiley have the courage to recall this two months from now, as the dawn broke outside his window and the clock rang out the time? When they broke a man's neck on the scaffold and put him away like the dross of the river.

He made his way along Beaumont Street towards the King's Road. The milkman chugged past him in his electric van. He would breakfast out this morning, then take a cab to Curzon Street and order the wine for dinner. He would choose something good. Fielding would like that.

Fielding closed his eyes and drank, his left hand held lightly across his chest.

'Divine,' he said 'divine!' And Ailsa Brimley, opposite him, smiled gently.

'How are you going to spend your retirement, Mr Fielding,' she asked. 'Drinking Frankenwein?'

His glass still held before his lips he looked into the candles. The silver was good, better than his own. He wondered why they were only dining three. 'In peace,' he replied at last. 'I have recently made a discovery.'

'What's that?'

'That I have been playing to an empty house. But now I'm comforted to think that no one remembers how I forgot my words or missed an entry. So many of us wait patiently for our audience to die.

At Carne no one will remember for more than a Half or two what a mess I've made of life. I was too vain to realise that until recently.' He put the glass down in front of him and smiled suddenly at Ailsa Brimley. 'That is the peace I mean. Not to exist in anyone's mind, but my own; to be a secular monk, safe and forgotten.'

Smiley gave him more wine: 'Miss Brimley knew your brother Adrian well in the war. We were all in the same department,' he said. 'She was Adrian's secretary for a while. Weren't you, Brim?'

'It's depressing how the bad live on,' Fielding declared. 'Rather embarrassing. For the bad, I mean.' He gave a little gastronomic sigh. 'The moment of truth in a good meal! *Übergansperiode* between *entrement* and dessert,' and they all laughed, and then were silent. Smiley put down his glass, and said:

'The story you told me on Thursday, when I came and saw you . . .'

'Well?' Fielding was irritated.

'About cheating for Tim Perkins . . . how you took the paper from the case and altered it . . .'

'Yes?'

'It isn't true.' He might have been talking about the weather. 'They've examined it and it isn't true. The writing was all one person's . . . the boy's. If anyone cheated, it must have been the boy.'

There was a long silence. Fielding shrugged.

'My dear fellow, you can't expect me to believe that. These people are practically moronic.'

'Of course, it doesn't necessarily signify anything. I mean you could be protecting the boy, couldn't you? By lying for him, for his honour so to speak. Is that the explanation?'

'I've told you the truth,' he replied shortly. 'Make what you want of it.'

'I mean, I can see a situation where there might have been collusion, where you were moved by the boy's distress when he brought you the papers; and on the spur of the moment you opened the case and took out his paper and told him what to write.'

'Look here,' said Fielding hotly, 'why don't you keep off this? What's it got to do with you?' And Smiley replied with sudden fervour:

'I'm trying to help, Fielding. I beg you to believe me, I'm trying to help. For Adrian's sake. I don't want there to be . . . more trouble than there need, more pain. I want to get it straight before Rigby comes. They've dropped the charge against Janie. You know that, don't you? They seem to think it's Rode, but they haven't pulled him in. They could have done, but they haven't. They just took more statements from him. So you see, it matters terribly about the writing-case. Everything hangs by whether you really saw inside it; and whether Perkins did. Don't you see that? If it was Perkins who cheated after all, if it was only the boy who opened the case and not you, then they'll want to know the answer to a very important question: *they'll want to know how you knew what was inside it.*'

'What are you trying to say?'

'They're not really moronic, you know. Let's start from the other end for a moment. Suppose it was you who killed Stella Rode, suppose you had a reason, a terribly good reason, and they knew what that reason might be; suppose you went ahead of Rode after giving him the case that night—by bicycle, for instance, like Janie said, riding on the wind. If that were really so, none of those things you saw would have been in the case at all. You could have made it up. And when later the exam. results came out and you realised that Perkins had cheated, then you guessed he had seen inside the case, had seen that it contained nothing, *nothing but exam. papers.* I mean that would explain why you had to kill the boy.' He stopped and glanced towards Fielding. 'And in a way,' he added almost reluctantly, 'it makes better sense, doesn't it?'

'And what, may I ask, was the reason you speak of?'

'Perhaps she blackmailed you. She certainly knew about your conviction in the war from when she was up North. Her father was a magistrate, wasn't he? I understand they've looked up the files. The police, I mean. It was her father who heard the case. She knew you're broke and need another job and she kept you on a hook. It seems D'Arcy knew too. She told him. She'd nothing to lose; he was in on the story from the start, he'd never allow the papers to get hold of it; she knew that, she knew her man. Did *you* tell D'Arcy as well, Fielding? I think you may have done. When she came to you and told you she knew, jeered and laughed at you, you went to D'Arcy and told him. You asked him what to do. And he said—what would he say?—perhaps he said find out what she wants. But she wanted nothing; not money at least, but something more pleasing, more gratifying to her twisted little mind: she wanted to command and own you. She loved to conspire, she summoned you to meetings at absurd times and places; in woods, in disused churches, and above all at night. And she wanted nothing from you but your will, she made you listen to her boasts and her mad intrigues, made you fawn and cringe, then let you run away till the next time.' He looked up again. 'They might think along those lines, you see. That's why we need to know who saw inside the case. And who cheated in the exam.' They were both looking at him, Ailsa in horror, Fielding motionless, impassive.

'If they think that,' asked Fielding at last, 'how do they suppose I knew Rode would come back for the case that night?'

'Oh, they knew she was expecting you to meet her that night, after the dinner at your house.' Smiley threw this off as if it were a tedious detail, 'It was part of the game she liked to play.'

'How do they know that?'

'From what Rode says,' Smiley continued, 'Stella was carrying the case in the hall, actually had it in her hand. When they arrived at North Fields she was without it; she flew into a rage and accused him of forgetting it. She made him go back for it. You see the inference?'

'Oh, clearly,' said Fielding, and Smiley heard Ailsa Brimley whisper his name in horror.

'In other words, when Stella devised this trick to gratify her twisted will, you saw it as an opportunity to kill her, putting the blame on a non-existent tramp, or failing that, on Rode, as a second line of defence. Let us suppose you had been meaning to kill her. You had meant, I expect, to ride out there one night when Rode was teaching late. You had your boots and your cape, even the cable stolen from Rode's room, and you meant to lay a false trail. But what a golden opportunity when Perkins turned up with the hand-case! Stella wanted her meeting—the forgotten hand-case was agreed upon as the means of achieving it. That, I fear, is the way their minds may work. And you see, they *know* it wasn't Rode.'

'How do they know? How *can* they know? He's got no alibi.' Smiley didn't seem to hear. He was looking towards the window, and the heavy velvet curtains stirring uneasily.

'What's that? What are you looking at?' Fielding asked with sudden urgency, but Smiley did not answer.

'You know, Fielding,' he said at last, 'we just don't know what people are like, we can never tell; there isn't any truth about human beings, no formula that meets each one of us. And there are some of us—aren't there?—who are nothing, who are so labile that we astound ourselves; we're the chameleons. I read a story once about a poet who bathed himself in cold fountains so that he could recognise his own existence in the contrast. He had to reassure himself, you see, like a child being hateful to its parents. You might say he had to make the sun shine on him so that he could see his shadow and feel alive.'

Fielding made an impatient movement with his hand. 'How do you know it wasn't Rode?'

'The people who are like that—there really are some, Fielding—do you know their secret? They can't feel anything inside them, no pleasure or pain, no love or hate; they're ashamed and frightened that they can't feel. And their shame, this shame, Fielding, drives them to extravagance and colour; they must make themselves feel that cold water, and without that they're nothing. The world sees them as showmen, fantasists, liars, as sensualists perhaps, not for what they are: the living dead.'

'How do you know? How do you know it wasn't Rode?' Fielding cried with anger in his voice, and Smiley replied:

'I'll tell you.'

'If Rode murdered his wife, he had planned to do so long ago. The plastic cape, the boots, the weapons, the intricate timing, the use of Perkins to carry the case to your house–these are evidence of long premeditation. Of course one could ask: it that'so, why did he bother with Perkins at all–why didn't he keep the case with him all the time? But never mind. Let's see how he does it. He walks home with his wife after dinner, having deliberately forgotten the writing-case. Having left Stella at home, he returns to your house to collect it. It was a risky business, incidentally, leaving that case behind. Quite apart from the fact that one would expect him to have locked it, his wife might have noticed he hadn't got it as they left–or you might have noticed, or Miss Truebody–but luckily no one did. He collects the case, hurries back, kills her, fabricating the clues which mislead the police. He thrusts the cape, boots and gloves into the refugees' parcel, ties it up and prepares to make good his escape. He is alarmed by Mad Janie, perhaps, but reaches the lane and re-enters the house as Stanley Rode. Five minutes later he is with the D'Arcy's. From then on for the next forty-eight hours he is under constant supervision. Perhaps you didn't know this, Fielding, but the police found the murder weapon four miles down the road in a ditch. They found it within ten hours of the murder being discovered, long before Rode had a chance to throw it there.

'This is the point, though, Fielding. This is what they can't get over. I suppose it would be possible to make a phoney murder weapon. Rode could have taken hairs from Stella's comb, stuck them with human blood to a length of coaxial cable and planted the thing in a ditch *before* he committed the murder. But the only blood he could use was his own–which belongs to a different blood group. The blood on the weapon they found belonged to Stella's blood group. He didn't do it. There's a rather more concrete piece of evidence, to do with the parcel. Rigby had a word with Miss Truebody yesterday. It seems she telephoned Stella Rode on the morning of the day she was murdered. Telephoned at your request, Fielding, to say a boy would be bringing some old clothes up to North Fields on Thursday morning–would she be sure to keep the parcel open till then? . . . What did Stella threaten to do, Fielding? Write an anonymous letter to your next school?'

Then Smiley put his hand on Fielding's arm and said: 'Go now, in God's name go now. There's very little time, for Adrian's sake go now,' and Ailsa Brimley whispered something he could not hear.

Fielding seemed not to hear. His great head was thrown back, his eyes half closed, his wine glass still held between his thick fingers.

And the front-door bell rang out, like the scream of a woman in an empty house.

Smiley never knew what made the noise, whether it was Fielding's hands on the table as he stood up, or his chair, falling backwards. Perhaps it was not a noise at all, but simply the shock of violent movement when it was least expected; the sight of Fielding, who a moment before had sat lethargic in his chair, springing forward across the room. Then Rigby was holding him, had taken Fielding's right arm and done something to it so that Fielding cried out in pain and fear, swinging round to face them under the compulsion of Rigby's grip. Then Rigby was saying the words, and Fielding's terrified gaze fell upon Smiley.

'Stop him, stop him, Smiley, for God's sake! They'll hang me.' And he shouted the last two words again and again: 'Hang me, hang me,' until the detectives came in from the street, and shoved him without ceremony into a waiting car.

Smiley watched the car go. It didn't hurry, just picked its way down the wet street and disappeared. He remained there long after it had gone, looking towards the end of the road, so that passers-by stared oddly at him, or tried to follow his gaze. But there was nothing to see. Only the half-lit street, and the shadows moving along it.

The Looking-Glass War

John le Carré

The Looking-Glass War

To James Kennaway

I wouldn't mind being a Pawn,
if only I might join
—Alice

FOREWORD

None of the characters, clubs, institutions nor
intelligence organizations I have described here or
elsewhere exists, or has existed to my knowledge in
real life. I wish to make that very clear.

My thanks are due to the Radio Society of Great
Britain and to Mr R. E. Molland, to the editors and
staff of *Aviation Week and Space Technology* and to
Mr Ronald Coles, all of whom provided me with
valuable technical advice; and to Miss Elizabeth
Tollinton for her secretarial help.

I must thank above all my wife for her untiring
co-operation.

John le Carré,
Agíos Nikolaos,
Crete

May, 1964

'The carrying of a very heavy weight such as a large suitcase or trunk, immediately before sending practice, renders the muscles of the forearm, wrist and fingers too insensitive to produce good Morse.'

F. Tait's *Complete Morse Instructor*, Pitman

TAYLOR'S RUN

A fool lies here who tried to hustle the East.
KIPLING

Chapter One

Snow covered the airfield.

It had come from the north, in the mist, driven by the night wind, smelling of the sea. There it would stay all Winter, threadbare on the grey earth, an icy, sharp dust; not thawing and freezing, but static like a year without seasons. The changing mist, like the smoke of war, would hang over it, swallow up now a hangar, now the radar hut, now the machines; release them piece by piece, drained of colour, black carrion on a white desert.

It was a scene of no depth, no recession and no shadows. The land was one with the sky; figures and buildings locked in the cold like bodies in an icefloe.

Beyond the airfield there was nothing; no house, no hill, no road; not even a fence, a tree; only the sky pressing on the dunes, the running fog that lifted on the muddy Baltic shore. Somewhere inland were the mountains.

A group of children in school caps had gathered at the long observation window, chattering in German. Some wore ski clothes. Taylor gazed dully past them, holding a glass in his gloved hand. A boy turned round and stared at him, blushed and whispered to the other children. They fell silent.

He looked at his watch, making a wide arc with his arm, partly to free the sleeve of his overcoat and partly because it was his style; a military man, he wished you to say, decent regiment, decent club, knocked around in the war.

Ten to four. The plane was an hour late. They would have to announce the reason soon over the loudspeaker. He wondered what they would say: delayed by fog, perhaps; delayed take-off. They probably didn't even know—and they certainly would not admit—that she was two hundred miles off course, and south of Rostock. He finished his drink, turned to get rid of the empty glass. He had to admit that some of these foreign hooches, drunk in their own country, weren't at all bad. On the spot, with a couple of hours to kill and ten degrees of frost the other side of the window, you could do a lot worse than Steinhäger. He'd make them order it at the Alias Club when he got back. Cause quite a stir.

The loudspeaker was humming; it blared suddenly, faded out and began again, properly tuned. The children stared expectantly at it. First, the announcement in Finnish, then in Swedish, now in English. Northern Air Services regretted the delay to their charter flight two-nine-zero from Düsseldorf. No hint of how long, no hint of why. They probably didn't know themselves.

But Taylor knew. He wondered what would happen if he sauntered over to that pert little hostess in the glass box and told her: two-nine-zero will be a bit of time yet, my dear, she's been blown off course by heavy northerly gales over the Baltic, bearing all to Hades. The girl wouldn't believe him, of course, she'd think he was a crank. Later she'd know better. She'd realize he was something rather unusual, something rather special.

Outside it was already growing dark. Now the ground was lighter than the sky; the swept runways stood out against the snow like dykes, stained with the amber glow of marking lights. In the nearest hangars neon tubes shed a weary pallor over men and aeroplanes; the foreground beneath him sprang briefly to life as a beam from the control tower flicked across it. A fire engine had pulled away from the workshops on the left and joined the three ambulances already parked short of the centre runway. Simultaneously they switched on their blue rotating lights, and stood in line patiently flashing out their warning. The children pointed at them, chattering excitedly.

The girl's voice began again on the loudspeaker, it could only have been a few minutes since the last announcement. Once more the children stopped talking and listened. The arrival of flight two-nine-zero would be delayed at least another hour. Further information would be given as soon as it became available. There was something in the girl's voice, midway between surprise and anxiety, which seemed to communicate itself to the half-dozen people sitting at the other end of the waiting-room. An old woman said something to her husband, stood up, took her handbag and joined the group of children. For a time she peered stupidly into the twilight. Finding no comfort there, she turned to Taylor and said in English, 'What is become of the Düsseldorf plane?' Her voice had the throaty, indignant lilt of a Dutchwoman. Taylor shook his head. 'Probably the snow,' he replied. He was a brisk man; it went with his military way.

Pushing open the swing door, Taylor made his way downstairs to the reception hall. Near to the main entrance he recognized the yellow pennant of Northern Air Services. The girl at the desk was very pretty.

'What's happened to the Düsseldorf flight?' His style was confiding; they said he had a knack with little girls. She smiled and shrugged her shoulders.

'I expect it is the snow. We are often having delays in Autumn.'

'Why don't you ask the boss?' he suggested, indicating with a nod the telephone in front of her.

'They will tell it on the loudspeaker,' she said, 'as soon as they know.'

'Who's the skipper, dear?'

'Please?'

'Who's the skipper, the captain?'

'Captain Lansen.'

'Is he any good?'

The girl was shocked. 'Captain Lansen is a very experienced pilot.'

Taylor looked her over, grinned and said, 'He's a very *lucky* pilot anyway, my dear.' They said he knew a thing or two, old Taylor did. They said it at the Alias on Friday nights.

Lansen. It was odd to hear a name spoken out like that. In the outfit they simply never did it. They favoured circumlocution, cover names, anything but the original: Archie boy, our flying friend, our friend up north, the chappie who takes the snapshots; they would even use the tortuous collection of figures and letters by which he was known on paper; but never in any circumstances the name.

Lansen. Leclerc had shown him a photograph in London: a boyish thirty-five, fair and goodlooking. He'd bet those hostesses went mad about him; that's all they were, anyway, cannon-fodder for the pilots. No one else got a look in. Taylor ran his right hand quickly over the outside of his overcoat pocket just to make sure the envelope was still there. He'd never carried this sort of money before. Five thousand dollars for one flight; seventeen hundred pounds, tax free, to lose your way over the Baltic. Mind you, Lansen didn't do that every day. This was special, Leclerc had said so. He wondered what she would do if he leant across the counter and told her who he was; showed her the money in that envelope. He'd never had a girl like that, a real girl, tall and young.

He went upstairs again to the bar. The barman was getting to know him. Taylor pointed to the bottle of Steinhäger on the centre shelf and said, 'Give me another of those, d'you mind? That's it, the fellow just behind you; some of your local poison.'

'It's German,' the barman said.

He opened his wallet and took out a banknote. In the cellophane compartment there was a photograph of a girl, perhaps nine years old, wearing glasses and holding a doll. 'My daughter,' he explained to the barman, and the barman gave a watery smile.

His voice varied a lot, like the voice of a commercial traveller. His phoney drawl was more extravagant when he addressed his own class, when it was a matter of emphasizing a distinction which did not exist; or as now, when he was nervous.

He had to admit: he was windy. It was an eerie situation for a man of his experience and age, going over from routine courier work to operational stuff. This was a job for those swine in the Circus, not for his outfit at all. A different kettle of fish altogether, this was, from the ordinary run-of-the-mill stuff he was used to; stuck out on a limb, miles from nowhere. It beat him how they ever came to put an airport in a place like this. He quite liked the foreign trips as a rule: a visit to old Jimmy Gorton in Hamburg, for instance, or a night on the tiles in Madrid. It did him good to get away from Joanie. He'd done the Turkish run a couple of times, though he didn't care for wogs. But even that was a piece of cake compared to this: first-class travel and the bags on the seat beside him, a Nato pass in his pocket; a man had status, doing a job like that; good as the diplomatic boys, or nearly. But this was different, and he didn't like it.

Leclerc had said it was big, and Taylor believed him. They had got him a passport with another name. Malherbe. Pronounced Mallaby, they said. Christ alone knew who'd chosen it. Taylor couldn't even spell it; made a botch of the hotel register when he signed in that morning. The subsistence was fantastic, of course: fifteen quid a day operational expenses, no vouchers asked for. He'd heard the Circus gave seventeen. He could make a good bit on that, buy something for Joanie. She'd probably rather have the money.

He'd told her, of course: he wasn't supposed to, but Leclerc didn't know Joanie. He lit a cigarette, drew from it and held it in the palm of his hand like a sentry smoking on duty. How the hell was he supposed to push off to Scandinavia without telling his wife?

He wondered what those kids were doing, glued to the window all this time. Amazing the way they managed the foreign language. He looked at his watch again, scarcely noticing the time, touched the envelope in his pocket. Better not have another drink; he must keep a clear head. He tried to guess what Joanie was doing now. Probably having a sit-down with a gin and something. A pity she had to work all day.

He suddenly realized that everything had gone silent. The barman was standing still, listening. The old people at the table were listening too, their silly faces turned towards the observation window. Then he heard it quite distinctly, the sound of an aircraft, still far away, but approaching the airfield. He made quickly for the window, was half-way there when the loudspeaker began; after the first few words of German the children, like a flock of pigeons, fluttered away to the reception lounge. The party at the table had stood up; the women were reaching for their gloves, the men for their coats and briefcases. At last the announcer gave the English. Lansen was coming in to land.

Taylor stared into the night. There was no sign of the plane. He waited, his anxiety mounting. It's like the end of the world, he thought, the end of the bloody world out there. Supposing Lansen crashed; supposing they found the cameras. He wished someone else were handling it. Woodford, why hadn't Woodford taken it over, or sent that clever college boy Avery? The wind was stronger; he could swear it was far stronger; he could tell from the way it stirred the snow, flinging it over the runway; the way it tore at the flares; the way it made white columns on the horizon, dashing them vehemently away like a hated creation. A gust struck suddenly at the windows in front of him, making him recoil, and there followed the rattle of ice grains and the short grunt of the wooden frame. Again he looked at his watch; it had become a habit with Taylor. It seemed to help, knowing the time.

Lansen will never make it in this, never.

His heart stood still. Softly at first, then rising swiftly to a wail, he heard the klaxons, all four together, moaning out over that godforsaken airfield like the howl of starving animals. Fire . . . the plane must be on fire. He's on fire and he's going to try and land . . . he turned frantically, looking for someone who could tell him.

The barman was standing beside him, polishing a glass, looking through the window.

'What's going on?' Taylor shouted. 'Why are the sirens going?'

'They always make the sirens in bad weather,' he replied. 'It is the law.'

'Why are they letting him land?' Taylor insisted. 'Why don't they route him farther south? It's too small, this place; why don't they send him somewhere bigger?'

The barman shook his head indifferently. 'It's not so bad,' he said indicating the airfield. 'Besides, he is very late. Maybe he has no petrol.'

They saw the plane low over the airfield, her lights alternating above the flares; her spotlights scanned the runway. She was down, safely down, and they heard the roar of her throttle as she began the long taxi to the reception point.

The bar had emptied. He was alone. Taylor ordered a drink. He knew his drill: stay put in the bar, Leclerc had said, Lansen will meet you in the bar. He'll take a bit of time; got to cope with his flight documents, clear his cameras. Taylor heard the children singing downstairs, and a woman leading them. Why the hell did he have to be surrounded by kids and women? He was doing a man's job, wasn't he, with five thousand dollars in his pocket and a phoney passport?

'There are no more flights today,' the barman said. 'They have forbidden all flying now.'

Taylor nodded. 'I know. It's bloody shocking out there, shocking.' The barman was putting away bottles. 'There was no danger,' he added soothingly. 'Captain Lansen is a very good pilot.' He hesitated, not knowing whether to put away the Steinhäger.

'Of course there wasn't any danger,' Taylor snapped. 'Who said anything about danger?'

'Another drink?' the barman said.

'No, but you have one. Go on, have one yourself.'

The barman reluctantly gave himself a drink, locked the bottle away.

'All the same, how do they do it?' Taylor asked. His voice was conciliatory, putting it right with the barman. 'They can't see a thing in weather like this, not a damn thing.' He smiled knowingly. 'You sit there in the nose and you might just as well have your eyes shut for all the good they do. I've seen it,' Taylor added, his hands loosely cupped in front of him as though he were at the controls. 'I know what I'm talking about . . . and they're the first to catch it, those boys, if something *does* go wrong.' He shook his head. 'They can keep it,' he declared. 'They're entitled to every penny they earn. Specially in a kite that size. They're held together with string, those things; string.'

The barman nodded distantly, finished his drink, washed up the empty glass, dried it and put it on the shelf under the counter. He unbuttoned his white jacket.

Taylor made no move.

'Well,' said the barman with a mirthless smile, 'we have to go home now.'

'What do you mean, *we?*' Taylor asked, opening his eyes wide and tilting back his head. 'What do you mean?' He'd take on anyone now; Lansen had landed.

'I have to close the bar.'

'Go home indeed. Give us another drink, come on. You can go home if you like. I happen to live in London.' His tone was challenging, half playful, half resentful, gathering volume. 'And since your aircraft companies are unable to *get* me to London, or any other damn place until tomorrow morning, it's a bit silly of you to tell me to go there, isn't it, old boy?' He was still smiling, but it was the short, angry smile of a nervous man losing his temper. 'And next time you accept a drink from me, chum, I'll trouble you to have the courtesy . . .'

The door opened and Lansen came in.

This wasn't the way it was supposed to happen; this wasn't the way they'd described it at all. Stay in the bar, Leclerc had said, sit at the corner table, have a drink, put your hat and coat on the other chair as if you're waiting for someone. Lansen always has a beer when he clocks in. He likes the public lounge, it's Lansen's style. There'll be people milling about, Leclerc said. It's a small place but there's always something going on at these airports. He'll look around for somewhere to sit—quite open and above board—then he'll come over and ask you if anyone's using the chair. You'll say you kept it free for a friend but the friend hadn't turned up: Lansen will ask if he can sit there. He'll order a beer, then say, 'Boy friend or girl friend?' You'll tell him not to be indelicate, and you'll both laugh a bit and get talking. Ask the two questions: height and airspeed. Research Section must know the height and airspeed. Leave the money in your overcoat pocket. He'll pick up your coat, hang his own beside it and help himself quietly, without any fuss, taking the envelope and dropping the film into your coat pocket. You finish your drinks, shake hands, and Bob's your uncle. In the morning you fly home. Leclerc had made it sound so simple.

Lansen strode across the empty room towards them, a tall, strong figure in a blue mackintosh and cap. He looked briefly at Taylor and spoke past him to the barman: 'Jens, give me a beer.' Turning to Taylor he said, 'What's yours?'

Taylor smiled thinly. 'Some of your local stuff.'

'Give him whatever he wants. A double.'

The barman briskly buttoned up his jacket, unlocked the cupboard and poured out a large Steinhäger. He gave Lansen a beer from the cooler.

'Are you from Leclerc?' Lansen inquired shortly. Anyone could have heard.

'Yes.' He added tamely, far too late, 'Leclerc and Company, London.'

Lansen picked up his beer and took it to the nearest table. His hand was shaking. They sat down.

'Then you tell me,' he said fiercely, 'which damn fool gave me those instructions?'

'I don't know.' Taylor was taken aback. 'I don't even know what your instructions were. It's not my fault. I was sent to collect the film, that's all. It's not even my job, this kind of thing. I'm on the overt side—courier.'

Lansen leant forward, his hand on Taylor's arm. Taylor could feel him trembling. 'I was on the overt side too. Until today. There were kids on that plane. Twenty-five German schoolchildren on Winter holidays. A whole load of kids.'

'Yes.' Taylor forced a smile. 'Yes, we had the reception committee in the waiting-room.'

Lansen burst out, 'What were we *looking* for, that's what I don't understand. What's so exciting about Rostock?'

'I tell you I'm nothing to do with it.' He added inconsistently: 'Leclerc said it wasn't Rostock but the area south.'

'The triangle south: Kalkstadt, Langdorn, Wolken. You don't have to tell me the area.'

Taylor looked anxiously towards the barman.

'I don't think we should talk so loud,' he said. 'That fellow's a bit anti.' He drank some Steinhäger.

Lansen made a gesture with his hand as if he were brushing something from in front of his face. 'It's finished,' he said. 'I don't want any more. It's finished. It was OK when we just stayed on course photographing whatever there was; but this is too damn much, see? Just too damn, damn much altogether.' His accent was thick and clumsy, like an impediment.

'Did you get any pictures?' Taylor asked. He must get the film and go.

Lansen shrugged, put his hand in his raincoat pocket and, to Taylor's horror, extracted a zinc container for thirty-five-millimetre film, handing it to him across the table.

'What was it?' Lansen asked again. 'What were they after in such a place? I went under the cloud, circled the whole area. I didn't see any atom bombs.'

'Something important, that's all they told me. Something big. It's got to be done, don't you see? You can't make illegal flights over an area like that.' Taylor was repeating what someone had said. 'It has to be an airline, a registered airline, or nothing. There's no other way.'

'Listen. They picked us up as soon as we got into the place. Two MIGs. Where did they come from, that's what I want to know? As soon as I saw them I turned into cloud; they followed me. I put out a signal, asking for bearings. When we came out of the cloud, there they were again. I thought they'd force me down, order me to land. I tried to jettison the camera but it was stuck. The kids were all crowding the windows, waving at the MIGs. They flew alongside for a time, then peeled off. They came close, very close. It was bloody dangerous for the kids.' He hadn't touched his beer. 'What the hell did they want?' he asked. 'Why didn't they order me down?'

'I told you: it's not my fault. This isn't my kind of work. But whatever London are looking for, they know what they're doing.' He seemed to be convincing himself; he needed to believe in London. 'They don't waste their time. Or yours, old boy. They know what they're up to.' He frowned, to indicate conviction, but Lansen might not have heard.

'They don't believe in unnecessary risks either,' Taylor said. 'You've done a good job, Lansen. We all have to do our bit . . . take risks. We all do. I did in the war, you know. You're too young to remember the war. This is the same job; we're fighting for the same thing.' He suddenly remembered the two questions. 'What height were you doing when you took the pictures?'

'It varied. We were down to six thousand feet over Kalkstadt.'

'It was Kalkstadt they wanted most,' Taylor said with appreciation. 'That's first-class, Lansen, first-class. What was your airspeed?'

'Two hundred. . .two forty. Something like this. There was nothing there, I'm telling you, nothing.' He lit a cigarette.

'It's the end now,' Lansen repeated. 'However big the target is.' He stood up. Taylor got up too; he put his right hand in his overcoat pocket. Suddenly his throat went dry: the money, where was the money?

'Try the other pocket,' Lansen suggested.

Taylor handed him the envelope. 'Will there be trouble about this? About the MIGs, I mean?'

Lansen shrugged. 'I doubt it, it hasn't happened to me before. They'll believe me once; they'll believe it was the weather. I went off course about half-way. There could have been a fault in the ground control. In the hand-over.'

'What about the navigator? What about the rest of the crew? What do they think?'

'That's my business,' said Lansen sourly. 'You can tell London it's the end.'

Taylor looked at him anxiously. 'You're just upset,' he said, 'after the tension.'

'Go to hell,' said Lansen softly. 'Go to bloody hell.' He turned away, put a coin on the counter and strode out of the bar, stuffing carelessly into his raincoat pocket the long buff envelope which contained the money.

After a moment Taylor followed him. The barman watched him push his way through the door and disappear down the stairs. A very distasteful man, he reflected; but then he never had liked the English.

Taylor thought at first that he would not take a taxi to the hotel. He could walk it in ten minutes and save a bit of subsistence. The airline girl nodded to him as he passed her on his way to the main entrance. The reception hall was done in teak; blasts of warm air rose from the floor. Taylor stepped outside. Like the thrust of a sword the cold cut through his clothes; like the numbness of an encroaching poison it spread swiftly over his naked face, feeling its way into his neck and shoulders. Changing his mind, he looked round hastily for a taxi. He was drunk. He suddenly realized: the fresh air had made him drunk. The rank was empty. An old Citroën was parked fifty yards up the road, its engine running. He's got the heater on, lucky devil, thought Taylor and hurried back through the swing doors.

'I want a cab,' he said to the girl. 'Where can I get one, d'you know?' He hoped to God he looked all right. He was mad to have drunk so much. He shouldn't have accepted that drink from Lansen.

She shook her head. 'They have taken the children,' she said. 'Six in each car. That was the last flight today. We don't have many taxis in Winter.' She smiled. 'It's a very *little* airport.'

'What's that up the road, that old car? Not a cab, is it?' His voice was indistinct.

She went to the doorway and looked out. She had a careful balancing walk, artless and provocative.

'I don't see any car,' she said.

Taylor looked past her. 'There was an old Citroën. Lights on. Must have gone. I just wondered.' Christ, it went past and he'd never heard it.

'The taxis are all Volvos,' the girl remarked. 'Perhaps one will come back after he has dropped the children. Why don't you go and have a drink?'

'Bar's closed,' Taylor snapped. 'Barman's gone home.'

'Are you staying at the airport hotel?'

'The Regina, yes. I'm in a hurry, as a matter of fact.' It was easier now. 'I'm expecting a phone call from London.'

She looked doubtfully at his coat; it was of rainproof material in a pebble weave. 'You could walk,' she suggested. 'It is ten minutes, straight down the road. They can send your luggage later.'

Taylor looked at his watch, the same wide gesture. 'Luggage is already at the hotel. I arrived this morning.'

He had that kind of crumpled, worried face which is only a hair's breadth from the music halls and yet is infinitely sad; a face in which the eyes are paler than their environment, and the contours converge upon the nostrils. Aware of this, perhaps, Taylor had grown a trivial moustache, like a scrawl on a photograph, which made a muddle of his face without concealing its shortcoming. The effect was to inspire disbelief, not because he was a rogue but because he had no talent for deception. Similarly he had tricks of movement crudely copied from some lost original, such as an irritating habit which soldiers have of arching his back suddenly, as if he had discovered himself in an unseemly posture, or he would affect an agitation about the knees and elbows which feebly caricatured an association with horses. Yet the whole was dignified by pain, as if he were holding his little body stiff against a cruel wind.

'If you walk quickly,' she said, 'it takes less than ten minutes.'

Taylor hated waiting. He had a notion that people who waited were people of no substance: it was an affront to be seen waiting. He pursed his lips, shook his head, and with an ill-tempered 'Goodnight, lady,' stepped abruptly into the freezing air.

Taylor had never seen such a sky. Limitless, it curved downward to the snowbound fields, its destiny broken here and there by films of mist which frosted the clustered stars and drew a line round the yellow half moon. Taylor was frightened, like a landsman frightened by the sea. He hastened his uncertain step, swaying as he went.

He had been walking about five minutes when the car caught him up. There was no footpath. He became aware of its headlights first, because the sound of its engine was deadened by the snow, and he only noticed a light ahead of him, not realizing where it came from. It traced its way languidly over the snowfields and for a time he thought it was the beacon from the airport. Then he saw his own shadow shortening on the road, the light became suddenly brighter, and he knew it must be a car. He was walking on the right, stepping briskly along the edge of the icy rubble that lined the road. He observed that the light was unusually yellow and he guessed the headlamps were masked according to the French rule. He was rather pleased with this little piece of deduction; the old brain was pretty clear after all.

He didn't look over his shoulder because he was a shy man in his way and did not want to give the impression of asking for a lift. But it did occur to him, a little late perhaps, that on the Continent they actually drove on the right, and that therefore strictly speaking he was walking on the wrong side of the road, and ought to do something about it.

The car hit him from behind, breaking his spine. For one dreadful moment Taylor described a classic posture of anguish, his head and shoulders flung violently backwards, fingers extended. He made no cry. It was as if his entire body and soul were concentrated in this final attitude of pain, more articulate in death than any sound the living man had made. It is quite possible that the driver was unaware of what he had done; that the impact of the body on the car was not to be distinguished from a thud of loose snow against the axle.

The car carried him for a yard or two then threw him aside, dead on the empty road, a stiff, wrecked figure at the fringe of the wilderness. His trilby hat lay beside him. A sudden blast seized it, carrying it across the snow. The shreds of his pebble-weave coat fluttered in the wind, reaching vainly for the zinc capsule as it rolled gently with the camber to lodge for a moment against the frozen bank, then to continue wearily down the slope.

AVERY'S RUN

'There are some things that no one has a right to ask
of any white man.'
Mr Standfast, JOHN BUCHAN

Chapter Two
PRELUDE

It was three in the morning.

Avery put down the telephone, woke Sarah and said, 'Taylor's dead.' He shouldn't have told her, of course.

'Who's Taylor?'

A bore, he thought; he only remembered him vaguely. A dreary English bore, straight off Brighton pier.

'A man in courier section,' he said. 'He was with them in the war. He was rather good.'

'That's what you always say. They're all good. How did he die, then? How did he die?' She had sat up in bed.

'Leclerc's waiting to hear.' He wished she wouldn't watch him while he dressed.

'And he wants you to help him wait?'

'He wants me to go to the office. He wants me. You don't expect me to turn over and go back to sleep, do you?'

'I was only asking,' Sarah said. 'You're always so considerate to Leclerc.'

'Taylor was an old hand. Leclerc's very worried.' He could still hear the triumph in Leclerc's voice: 'Come at once, get a taxi; we'll go through the files again.'

'Does this often happen? Do people often die?' There was indignation in her voice, as if no one ever told her anything; as if she alone thought it dreadful that Taylor had died.

'You're not to tell anyone,' said Avery. It was a way of keeping her from him. 'You're not even to say I've gone out in the middle of the night. Taylor was travelling under another name.' He added, 'Someone will have to tell his wife.' He was looking for his glasses.

She got out of bed and put on a dressing-gown. 'For God's sake stop talking like a cowboy. The secretaries know; why can't the wives? Or are they only told when their husbands die?' She went to the door.

She was of medium height and wore her hair long, a style at odds with the discipline of her face. There was a tension in her expression, an anxiety, an incipient discontent, as if tomorrow would only be worse. They had met at Oxford; she had taken a better degree than Avery. But somehow marriage had made her childish; dependence had become an attitude, as if she had given him something irredeemable, and were always asking for it back. Her son was less her projection than her excuse; a wall against the world and not a channel to it.

'Where are you going?' Avery asked. She sometimes did things to spite him, like tearing up a ticket for a concert. She said, 'We've got a child, remember?' He noticed Anthony crying. They must have woken him.

'I'll ring from the Office.'

He went to the front door. As she reached the nursery she looked back and Avery knew she was thinking they hadn't kissed.

'You should have stuck to publishing,' she said.

'You didn't like that any better.'

'Why don't they send a car?' she asked. 'You said they had masses of cars.'

'It's waiting at the corner.'

'Why, for God's sake?'

'More secure,' he replied.

'Secure against what?'

'Have you got any money? I seem to have run out.'

'What for?'

'Just money, that's all! I can't run around without a penny in my pocket.' She gave him ten shillings from her bag. Closing the door quickly behind him he went down the stairs into Prince of Wales Drive.

He passed the ground-floor window and knew without looking that Mrs Yates was watching him from behind her curtain, as she watched everybody night and day, holding her cat for comfort.

It was terribly cold. The wind seemed to come from the river, across the park. He looked up and down the road. It was empty. He should have telephoned the rank at Clapham but he wanted to get out of the flat. Besides, he had told Sarah the car was coming. He walked a hundred yards or so towards the Power Station, changed his mind and turned back. He was sleepy. It was a curious illusion that even in the street he still heard the telephone ringing. There was a cab that hung round Albert Bridge at all hours; that was the best bet. So he passed the entrance to his part of the Mansions, glanced up at the nursery window, and there was Sarah looking out. She must have been wondering where the car was. She had Anthony in her arms and he knew she was crying because he hadn't kissed her. He took half an hour to find a taxi to Blackfriars Road.

Avery watched the lamps come up the street. He was quite young, belonging to that intermediate class of contemporary Englishman which must reconcile an Arts degree with an uncertain provenance. He was tall and bookish in appearance, slow-eyed behind his spectacles, with a gently self-effacing manner which endeared him to his elders. The motion of the taxi comforted him, as rocking consoles a child.

He reached St George's Circus, passed the Eye Hospital and entered Blackfriars Road. Suddenly he was upon the house, but told the driver to drop him at the next corner because Leclerc had said be careful.

'Just here,' he called. 'This will do fine.'

The Department was housed in a crabbed, sooty villa of a place with a fire extinguisher on the balcony. It was like a house eternally for sale. No one knew why the Ministry put a wall round it; perhaps to protect it from the gaze of the people, like the wall round a cemetery; or the people from the gaze of the dead. Certainly not for the garden's sake, because nothing grew in it but grass which had worn away in patches like the coat of an old mongrel. The front door was painted dark green; it was never opened. By day anonymous vans of the same colour occasionally passed down the shabby drive, but they transacted their business in the back yard. The neighbours, if they referred to the place at all, spoke of the Ministry House, which was not accurate, for the Department was a separate entity, and the Ministry its master. The building had that unmistakable air of controlled dilapidation which characterizes government hirings all over the world. For those who worked in it, its mystery was like the mystery of motherhood, its survival like the mystery of England. It shrouded and contained them, cradled them and, with sweet anachronism, gave them the illusion of nourishment.

Avery could remember it when the fog lingered contentedly against its stucco walls, or in the Summer, when the sunlight would briefly peer through the mesh curtains of his room, leaving no warmth, revealing no secrets. And he would remember it on that Winter dawn, its façade stained black, the street lights catching the raindrops on the grimy windows. But however he remembered it, it was not as a place where he worked, but where he lived.

Following the path to the back, he rang the bell and waited for Pine to open the door. A light shone in Leclerc's window.

He showed Pine his pass. Perhaps both were reminded of the war: for Avery a vicarious pleasure, while Pine could look back on experience.

'A lovely moon, sir,' said Pine.

'Yes.' Avery stepped inside. Pine followed him in, locking up behind him.

'Time was, the boys would curse a moon like this.'

'Yes, indeed,' Avery laughed.

'Heard about the Melbourne test, sir? Bradley's out for three.'

'Oh dear,' said Avery pleasantly. He disliked cricket.

A blue lamp glowed from the hall ceiling like the night light in a Victorian hospital. Avery climbed the staircase; he felt cold and uneasy. Somewhere a bell rang. It was odd how Sarah had not heard the telephone.

Leclerc was waiting for him: 'We need a man,' he said. He spoke involuntarily, like someone waking. A light shone on the file before him.

He was sleek, small and very bland; a precise cat of a man, clean shaven and groomed. His stiff collars were cut away; he favoured ties of one colour, knowing perhaps that a weak claim was worse than none. His eyes were dark and quick; he smiled as he spoke, yet conveyed no pleasure. His jackets had twin vents, he kept his handkerchief in his sleeve. On Fridays he wore suède shoes, and they said he was going to the country. No one seemed to know where he lived. The room was in half darkness.

'We can't do another overflight. This was the last; they warned me at the Ministry. We'll have to put a man in. I've been going through the old cards, John. There's one called Leiser, a Pole. He would do.'

'What happened to Taylor? Who killed him?'

Avery went to the door and switched on the main light. They looked at one another awkwardly. 'Sorry. I'm still half asleep,' Avery said. They began again, finding the thread.

Leclerc spoke up. 'You took a time, John. Something go wrong at home?' He was not born to authority.

'I couldn't get a cab. I phoned the rank at Clapham but they didn't reply. Nor Albert Bridge; nothing there either.' He hated to disappoint Leclerc.

'You can charge for it,' Leclerc said distantly, 'and the phone calls, you realize. Your wife all right?'

'I told you: there was no reply. She's fine.'

'She didn't mind?'

'Of course not.'

They never talked about Sarah. It was as if they shared a single relationship to Avery's wife, like children who are able to share a toy they no longer care for. Leclerc said, 'Well, she's got that son of yours to keep her company.'

'Yes, rather.'

Leclerc was proud of knowing it was a son and not a daughter.

He took a cigarette from the silver box on his desk. He had told

Avery once: the box was a gift, a gift from the war. The man who gave it to him was dead, the occasion for giving it was past; there was no inscription on the lid. Even now, he would say, he was not entirely certain whose side the man had been on, and Avery would laugh to make him happy.

Taking the file from his desk, Leclerc now held it directly under the light as if there were something in it which he must study very closely.

'John.'

Avery went to him, trying not to touch his shoulder.

'What do you make of a face like that?'

'I don't know. It's hard to tell from photographs.'

It was the head of a boy, round and blank, with long, fair hair swept back.

'Leiser. He *looks* all right, doesn't he? That was twenty years ago, of course,' Leclerc said. 'We gave him a very high rating.' Reluctantly he put it down, struck his lighter and held it to the cigarette. 'Well,' he said briskly, 'we seem to be up against something. I've no idea what happened to Taylor. We have a routine consular report, that's all. A car accident apparently. A few details, nothing informative. The sort of thing that goes out to next of kin. The Foreign Office sent us the teleprint as it came over the wire. They knew it was one of our passports.' He pushed a sheet of flimsy paper across the desk. He loved to make you read things while he waited. Avery glanced at it:

'Malherbe? Was that Taylor's cover name?'

'Yes. I'll have to get a couple of cars from the Ministry pool,' Leclerc said. 'Quite absurd not having our own cars. The Circus has a whole fleet.' And then, 'Perhaps the Ministry will believe me now. Perhaps they'll finally accept we're still an operational department.'

'Did Taylor collect the film?' Avery asked. 'Do we know whether he got it?'

'*I've* no inventory of his possessions,' Leclerc replied indignantly. 'At the moment, all his effects are impounded by the Finnish police. Perhaps the film is among them. It's a small place and I imagine they like to stick to the letter of the law.' And casually, so that Avery knew it mattered, 'The Foreign Office is afraid there may be a muddle.'

'Oh dear,' said Avery automatically. It was their practice in the Department: antique and understated.

Leclerc looked directly at him now, taking interest. 'The Resident Clerk at the Foreign Office spoke to the Assistant half an hour ago. They refuse to involve themselves. They say we're a clandestine service and must do it our own way. Somebody's got to go out there as next of kin; that is the course they favour. To claim the body and effects and get them back here. I want you to go.'

Avery was suddenly aware of the pictures round the room, of the boys who had fought in the war. They hung in two rows of six, either side of the model of a Wellington bomber, rather a dusty one, painted black with no insignia. Most of the photographs had been taken out of doors. Avery could see the hangars behind, and between the young, smiling faces the half-hidden fuselages of parked aircraft.

Beneath each photograph were signatures, already brown and faded, some fluent and racy, others—they must have been the other-ranks—self-conscious and elaborate, as if the writers had come unnaturally to fame. There were no surnames, but sobriquets from children's magazines: Jacko, Shorty, Pip and Lucky Joe. Only the Mae West was uniform, the long hair and the sunny, boyish smile. They seemed to like having their photographs taken, as if being together were an occasion for laughter which might not be repeated. The men in front were crouching comfortably, like men used to crouching in gun turrets, and those behind had put their arms carelessly over one another's shoulders. There was no affectation but a spontaneous goodwill which does not seem to survive war on photographs.

One face was common to every picture, right to the end; the face of a slim, bright-eyed man in a duffle coat and corduroy trousers. He wore no life jacket and stood a little apart from the men as if he were somehow extra. He was smaller than the rest, older. His features were formed; he had a purpose about him which the others lacked. He might have been their schoolmaster. Avery had once looked for his signature to see if it had altered in the nineteen years, but Leclerc had not signed his name. He was still very like his photographs: a shade more set around the jaw perhaps, a shade less hair.

'But that would be an operational job,' said Avery uncertainly.

'Of course. We're an operational department, you know.' A little buck of the head. 'You are entitled to operational subsistence. All you have to do is collect Taylor's stuff. You're to bring back everything except the film, which you deliver to an address in Helsinki. You'll be instructed about that separately. You come back and you can help me with Leiser—'

'Couldn't the Circus take it on? I mean, couldn't they do it more simply?'

This smile came slowly. 'I'm afraid that wouldn't answer at all. It's our show, John: the commitment is within our competence. A military target. I would be shirking our responsibility if I gave it to the Circus. Their charter is political, exclusively political.'

His small hand ran over his hair, a short, concise movement, tense and controlled. 'So it's our problem. Thus far, the Ministry approves my reading'—a favourite expression—'I can send someone else if you prefer—Woodford or one of the older men. I thought you'd enjoy it. It's an important job, you know; something new for you to tackle.'

'Of course. I'd like to go . . . if you trust me.'

Leclerc enjoyed that. Now he pushed a piece of blue draft paper into Avery's hand. It was covered with Leclerc's own writing, boyish and rounded. He had written 'Ephemeral' at the top and underlined it. In the left-hand margin were his initials, all four, and beneath them the word *Unclassified*. Once more Avery began reading.

'If you follow it carefully,' he said, 'you'll see that we don't specifically state that you *are* next of kin; we just quote from Taylor's application form. That's as far as the Foreign Office people are prepared to go. They've agreed to send this to the local consulate via Helsinki.'

Avery read: 'Following from Consular Department. Your Teleprint re Malherbe. John Somerton Avery, holder of British passport no—, half-brother of deceased, is named in Malherbe's passport application as next of kin. Avery informed and proposes fly out today take over body and effects. NAS flight 201 via Hamburg, ETA 1820 local time. Please provide usual facilities and assistance.'

'I didn't know your passport number,' Leclerc said. 'The plane leaves at three this afternoon. It's only a small place; I imagine the Consul will meet you at the airport. There's a flight from Hamburg every other day. If you don't have to go to Helsinki you can take the same plane back.'

'Couldn't I be his brother?' Avery asked lamely. 'Half-brother looks fishy.'

'There's no time to rig the passport. The Foreign Office are being very sticky about passports. We had a lot of trouble about Taylor's.' He had returned to the file. 'A *lot* of trouble. It would mean calling *you* Malherbe as well, you see. I don't think they'd like that.' He spoke without attention, paying out rope.

The room was very cold.

Avery said, 'What about our Scandinavian friend. . . ?' Leclerc looked uncomprehending. 'Lansen. Shouldn't someone contact him?'

'I'm attending to that.' Leclerc, hating questions, replied cautiously as if he might be quoted.

'And Taylor's wife?' It seemed pedantic to say widow. 'Are you attending to her?'

'I thought we'd go round first thing in the morning. She's not on the telephone. Telegrams are so cryptic.'

'We?' said Avery. 'Do we both need to go?'

'You're my aide, aren't you?'

It was too quiet. Avery longed for the sound of traffic and the buzz of telephones. By day they had people about them, the tramp of messengers, the drone of Registry trolleys. He had the feeling, when alone with Leclerc, that the third person was missing. No one else made him so conscious of behaviour, no one else had such a disintegrating effect on conversation. He wished Leclerc would give him something else to read.

'Have you heard anything about Taylor's wife?' Leclerc asked. 'Is she a secure sort of person?'

Seeing that Avery did not understand, he continued:

'She could make it awkward for us, you know. If she decided to. We shall have to tread carefully.'

'What will you say to her?'

'We shall play it by ear. The way we did in the war. She won't know, you see. She won't even know he was abroad.'

'He might have told her.'

'Not Taylor. Taylor's an old hand. He had his instructions and knew the rules. She must have a pension, that's most important. Active service.' He made another brisk, finite gesture with his hand.

'And the staff; what will you tell them?'

I shall hold a meeting this morning for Heads of Sections. As for the rest of the Department, we shall say it was an accident.'

'Perhaps it was,' Avery suggested.

Leclerc was smiling again; an iron bar of a smile, like an affliction.

'In which case we shall have told the truth; and have more chance of getting that film.'

There was still no traffic in the street outside. Avery felt hungry. Leclerc glanced at his watch.

'You were looking at Gorton's report,' Avery said.

He shook his head, wistfully touched a file, revisiting a favourite album. 'There's nothing there. I've read it over and over again. I've had the other photographs blown up to every conceivable size. Haldane's people have been on them night and day. We just can't get any farther.'

Sarah was right: to help him wait.

Leclerc said—it seemed suddenly the point of their meeting—'I've arranged for you to have a short talk with George Smiley at the Circus after this morning's conference. You've heard of him?'

'No,' Avery lied. This was delicate ground.

'He used to be one of their best men. Typical of the Circus in some ways, of the better kind. He resigns, you know, and comes back. His conscience. One never knows whether he's there or not. He's a bit past it now. They say he drinks a good deal. Smiley has the North European desk. He can brief you about dropping the film. Our own courier service is disbanded, so there's no other way: the FO don't want to know us; after Taylor's death I can't allow you to run around with the thing in your pocket. How much do you know about the Circus?' He might have been asking about women, wary, an older man without experience.

'A bit,' said Avery. 'The usual gossip.'

Leclerc stood up and went to the window. 'They're a curious

crowd. Some good, of course. Smiley was good. But they're cheats,' he broke out suddenly. 'That's an odd word, I know, to use about a sister service, John. Lying's second nature to them. Half of them don't know any longer when they're telling the truth.' He was inclining his head studiously this way and that to catch sight of whatever moved in the waking street below. 'What wretched weather. There was a lot of rivalry during the war, you know.'

'I heard.'

'That's all over now. I don't grudge them their work. They've more money and more staff than we have. They do a bigger job. However, I doubt whether they do a better one. Nothing can touch our Research Section, for example. Nothing.' Avery suddenly had the feeling that Leclerc had revealed something intimate, a failed marriage or a discreditable act, and that now it was all right.

'When you see Smiley, he may ask you about the operation. I don't want you to tell him *anything*, do you see, except that you are going to Finland and you may be handling a film for urgent dispatch to London. If he presses you, suggest it is a training matter. That's all you're authorized to say. The background, Gorton's report, future operations; none of that concerns them in the least. A training matter.'

'I realize that. But he'll know about Taylor, won't he, if the FO knows?'

'Leave that to me. And don't be misled into believing the Circus has a monopoly of agent running. We have the same right. We just don't use it unnecessarily.' He had restated his text.

Avery watched Leclerc's slim back against the lightening sky outside; a man excluded, a man without a card, he thought.

'Could we light the fire?' he asked, and went into the corridor where Pine had a cupboard for mops and brushes. There was kindling wood and some old newspaper. He came back and knelt in front of the fireplace, keeping the best pieces of cinder and coaxing the ash through the grate, just as he would in the flat at Christmas. 'I wonder if it was really wise to let them meet at the airport,' he asked.

'It was urgent. After Jimmy Gorton's report, it was very urgent. It still is. We haven't a moment to lose.'

Avery held a match to the newspaper and watched it burn. As the wood caught, the smoke began to roll gently into his face, causing his eyes to water behind his glasses. 'How could they know Lansen's destination?'

'It was a scheduled flight. He had to get clearance in advance.'

Tossing more coal on the fire, Avery got up and rinsed his hands at the basin in the corner, drying them on his handkerchief.

'I keep asking Pine to put me out a towel,' said Leclerc. 'They haven't enough to do, that's half the trouble.'

'Never mind.' Avery put the wet handkerchief in his pocket. It felt cold against his thigh. 'Perhaps they will have now,' he added without irony.

'I thought I'd get Pine to make me up a bed here. A sort of ops room.' Leclerc spoke cautiously, as if Avery might deprive him of the pleasure. 'You can ring me here tonight from Finland. If you've got the film, just say the deal's come off.'

'And if not?'

'Say the deal's off.'

'It sounds rather alike,' Avery objected. 'If the line's bad, I mean. "Off" and "Come off".'

'Then say they're not interested. Say something negative. You know what I mean.'

Avery picked up the empty scuttle. 'I'll give this to Pine.'

He passed the duty-room. An Air Force clerk was half asleep beside the telephones. He made his way down the wooden staircase to the front door.

'The Boss wants some coal, Pine.' The porter stood up, as he always did when anyone spoke to him, at attention by his bed in a barrack-room.

'I'm sorry, sir. Can't leave the door.'

'For God's sake, I'll look after the door. We're freezing up there.'

Pine took the scuttle, buttoned his tunic and disappeared down the passage. He didn't whistle these days.

'And a bed made up in his room,' he continued when Pine returned. 'Perhaps you'd tell the duty clerk when he wakes up. Oh, and a towel. He must have a towel by his basin.'

'Yes, sir. Wonderful to see the old Department on the march again.'

'Where can we get breakfast round here? Is there anywhere near by?'

'There's the Cadena,' Pine replied doubtfully, 'but I don't know whether it would do for the Boss, sir.' A grin. 'We had the canteen in the old days. Slinger and wadge.'

It was quarter to seven. 'When does the Cadena open?'

'Couldn't say, sir.'

'Tell me, do you know Mr Taylor at all?' He nearly said 'did'.

'Oh yes, sir.'

'Have you met his wife?'

'No, sir.'

'What's she like? Have you any idea? Heard anything?'

'Couldn't say, I'm sure, sir. Very sad business indeed, sir.'

Avery looked at him in astonishment. Leclerc must have told him, he thought, and went upstairs. Sooner or later he would have to telephone Sarah.

Chapter Three

They breakfasted somewhere. Leclerc refused to go into the Cadena and they walked interminably until they found another café, worse than the Cadena and more expensive.

'I can't remember him,' Leclerc said. 'That's the absurd thing. He's a trained radio operator apparently. Or was in those days.'

Avery thought he was talking about Taylor. 'How old did you say he was?'

'Forty, something over. That's a good age. A Danzig Pole. They speak German, you know. Not as mad as the pure Slav. After the war he drifted for a couple of years, pulled himself together and bought a garage. He must have made a nice bit.'

'Then I don't suppose he'll . . .'

'Nonsense. He'll be grateful, or should be.'

Leclerc paid the bill and kept it. As they left the restaurant he said something about subsistence, and putting in a bill to Accounts. 'You can claim for night duty as well, you know. Or time in lieu.' They walked down the road. 'Your air ticket is booked. Carol did it from her flat. We'd better make you an advance for expenses. There'll be the business of having his body sent and that kind of thing. I understand it can be very costly. You'd better have him flown. We'll do a post-mortem privately over here.'

'I've never seen a dead man before,' Avery said.

They were standing on a street corner in Kennington, looking for a taxi; a gas works on one side of the road, nothing on the other: the sort of place they could wait all day.

'John, you've to keep very quiet about that side of it; about putting a man in. No one's to know, not even in the Department, no one at all. I thought we'd call him Mayfly. Leiser, I mean. We'll call him Mayfly.'

'All right.'

'It's very delicate; a question of timing. I've no doubt there'll be opposition, within the Department as well as outside.'

'What about my cover and that kind of thing?' Avery asked. 'I'm not quite—' A taxi with its flag up passed them without stopping.

'Bloody man,' Leclerc snapped. 'Why didn't he pick us up?'

'He lives out here, I expect. He's making for the West End. About cover,' he prompted.

'You're travelling under your own name. I don't see that there's any problem. You can use your own address. Call yourself a publisher. After all you *were* one. The Consul will show you the ropes. What are you worried about?'

'Well—just the details.'

Leclerc, coming out of his reverie, smiled. 'I'll tell you something about cover; something you'll learn for yourself. Never volunteer information. People don't *expect* you to explain yourself. After all, what is there to explain? The ground's prepared; the Consul will have our teleprint. Show your passport and play the rest by ear.'

'I'll try,' said Avery.

'You'll succeed,' Leclerc rejoined with feeling, and they both grinned shyly.

'How far is it to the town?' Avery asked. 'From the airport?'

'About three miles. It feeds the main ski resorts. Heaven knows what the Consul does all day.'

'And to Helsinki?'

'I told you. A hundred miles. Perhaps more.'

Avery proposed they took a bus but Leclerc wouldn't queue, so they remained standing at the corner. He began talking about official cars again. 'It's utterly absurd,' he said. 'In the old days we had a pool of our own, now we have two vans and the Treasury won't let us pay the driver overtime. How can I run a Department under those conditions?'

In the end they walked. Leclerc had the address in his head; he made a point of remembering such things. It was awkward for Avery to walk beside him for long, because Leclerc adjusted his pace to that of the taller man. Avery tried to keep himself in check, but sometimes he forgot and Leclerc would stretch uncomfortably beside him thrusting upwards with each stride. A fine rain was falling. It was still very cold.

There were times when Avery felt for Leclerc a deep, protective love. Leclerc had that indefinable quality of arousing guilt, as if his companion but poorly replaced a departed friend. Somebody had been there, and gone; perhaps a whole world, a generation; somebody had made him and disowned him, so that while at one moment Avery could hate him for his transparent manipulation, detest his prinking gestures as a child detests the affectations of a parent, at the next he ran to protect him, responsible and deeply caring. Beyond all the vicissitudes of their relationship, he was somehow grateful that Leclerc had engendered him; and thus they created that strong love which only exists between the weak; each became the stage to which the other related his actions.

'It would be a good thing,' Leclerc said suddenly, 'if you shared the handling of Mayfly.'

'I'd like to.'

'When you get back.'

They had found the address on the map. Thirty-four Roxburgh Gardens; it was off Kennington High Street. The road soon became dingier, the houses more crowded. Gas lights burned yellow and flat like paper moons.

'In the war they gave us a hostel for the staff.'

'Perhaps they will again,' Avery suggested.

'It's twenty years since I did an errand like this.'

'Did you go alone then?' Avery asked, and wished at once that he had not. It was so easy to inflict pain on Leclerc.

'It was simpler in those days. We could say they'd died for their country. We didn't have to tell them the details; they didn't expect that.' So it *was* we, thought Avery. Some other boy, one of those laughing faces on the wall.

'They died every day then, the pilots. We did reconnaissance, you know, as well as special operations . . . I'm ashamed sometimes: I can't even remember their names. They were so young, some of them.'

There passed across Avery's mind a tragic procession of horror-struck faces; mothers and fathers, girl friends and wives, and he tried to visualize Leclerc standing among them, naïve yet footsure, like a politician at the scene of a disaster.

They stood at the top of a rise. It was a wretched place. The road led downward into a line of dingy, eyeless houses; above them rose a single block of flats: Roxburgh Gardens. A string of lights shone on to the glazed tiles, dividing and re-dividing the whole structure into cells. It was a large building, very ugly in its way, the beginning of a new world, and at its feet lay the black rubble of the old: crumbling, oily houses, haunted by sad faces which moved through the rain like driftwood in a forgotten harbour.

Leclerc's frail fists were clenched; he stood very still.

'There?' he said. 'Taylor lived there?'

'What's wrong? It's part of a scheme, redevelopment . . .' Then Avery understood. Leclerc was ashamed. Taylor had disgracefully deceived him. This was not the society they protected, these slums with their Babel's Tower: they had no place in Leclerc's scheme of things. To think that a member of Leclerc's staff should daily trudge from the breath and stink of such a place to the sanctuary of the Department: had he no money, no pension? Had he not a little bit beside, as we all have, just a hundred or two, to buy himself out of this squalor?

'It's no worse than Blackfriars Road,' Avery said involuntarily; it was meant to comfort him.

'Everyone knows we used to be in Baker Street,' Leclerc retorted.

They made their way quickly to the base of the block, past shop windows filled with old clothes and rusted electric fires, all the sad muddle of useless things which only the poor will buy. There was a chandler; his candles were yellow and dusty like fragments of a tomb.

'What number?' Leclerc asked.

'You said thirty-four.'

They passed between heavy pillars crudely ornamented with mosaics, followed plastic arrows marked with pink numbers; they squeezed between lines of aged, empty cars, until finally they came to a concrete entrance with cartons of milk on the step. There was no door, but a flight of rubberized steps which squeaked as they trod. The air smelt of food and that liquid soap they give in railway lavatories. On the heavy stucco wall a hand-painted notice discouraged noise. Somewhere a wireless played. They continued up two flights, and stopped before a green door, half-glazed. Mounted on it in letters of white bakelite was the number thirty-four. Leclerc took off his hat and wiped the sweat from his temples. He might have been entering church. It had been raining more than they realized; their coats were quite wet. He pressed the bell. Avery was suddenly very frightened; he glanced at Leclerc and thought: this is your show; you tell her.

The music seemed louder. They strained their ears to catch some other sound, but there was none.

'Why did you call him Malherbe?' Avery asked suddenly.

Leclerc pressed the bell again; and then they heard it, both of them, a whimper midway between the sob of a child and the whine of a cat, a throttled, metallic sigh. While Leclerc stepped back, Avery seized the bronze knocker on the letter box and banged it violently. The echo died away and they heard from inside the flat a light, reluctant tread; a bolt was slid from its housing, a spring lock disengaged. Then they heard again, much louder and more distinctly, the same plaintive monotone. The door opened a few inches and Avery saw a child, a frail, pallid rag of a girl not above ten years old. She wore steel-rimmed spectacles, the kind Anthony wore. In her arms, its pink limbs splayed stupidly about it, its painted eyes staring from between fringes of ragged cotton, was a doll. Its daubed mouth was lolling open, its head hung sideways as if it were broken or dead. It is called a talking doll, but no living thing uttered such a sound.

'Where is your mother?' asked Leclerc. His voice was aggressive, frightened.

The child shook her head. 'Gone to work.'

'Who looks after you, then?'

She spoke slowly as if she were thinking of something else. 'Mum comes back tea-times. I'm not to open the door.'

'Where is she? Where does she go?'

'Work.'

'Who gives you lunch?' Leclerc insisted.

'What?'

'Who gives you dinner?' Avery said quickly.

'Mrs Bradley. After school.'

Then Avery asked, 'Where's your father?' and she smiled and put a finger to her lips.

'He's gone on an aeroplane,' she said. 'To get money. But I'm not to say. It's a secret.'

Neither of them spoke. 'He's bringing me a present,' she added.

'Where from?' said Avery.

'From the North Pole, but it's a secret.' She still had her hand on the doorknob. 'Where Father Christmas comes from.'

'Tell your mother some men were here,' Avery said. 'From your Dad's office. We'll come again tea-time.'

'It's important,' said Leclerc.

She seemed to relax when she heard they knew her father.

'He's on an aeroplane,' she repeated. Avery felt in his pocket and gave her two half-crowns, the change from Sarah's ten shillings. She closed the door, leaving them on that damned staircase with the wireless playing dreamy music.

Chapter Four

They stood in the street not looking at one another. Leclerc said, 'Why did you ask that question, the question about her father?'

When Avery did not reply he added incongruously, 'It isn't a matter of liking people.'

Sometimes Leclerc seemed neither to hear nor to feel; he drifted away, listening for a sound, like a man who having learnt the steps had been deprived of the music; this mood read like a deep sadness, like the bewilderment of a man betrayed.

'I'm afraid I shan't be able to come back here with you this afternoon,' Avery said gently. 'Perhaps Bruce Woodford would be prepared—'

'Bruce is no good.' He added: 'You'll be at the meeting; at ten forty-five?'

'I may have to leave before the end to get to the Circus and collect my things. Sarah hasn't been well. I'll stay at the office as long as I can. I'm sorry I asked that question, I really am.'

'I don't want anyone to know. I must speak to her mother first. There may be some explanation. Taylor's an old hand. He knew the rules.'

'I shan't mention it, I promise I shan't. Nor Mayfly.'

'I must tell Haldane about Mayfly. He'll object, of course. Yes, that's what we'll call it . . . the whole operation. We'll call it Mayfly.' The thought consoled him.

They hurried to the office, not to work but for refuge; for anonymity, a quality they had come to need.

His room was one along from Leclerc's. It had a label on the door saying, 'Director's Aide'. Two years ago Leclerc had been invited to America, and the expression dated from his return. Within the Department, staff were referred to by the function they fulfilled. Hence Avery was known simply as Private Office; though Leclerc might alter the title every week, he could not alter the vernacular.

At a quarter to eleven Woodford came into his room. Avery guessed he would: a little chat before the meeting began, a quiet word about some matter not strictly on the agenda.

'What's it all about, John?' He lit his pipe, tilted back his large head and extinguished the match with long, swinging movements of his hand. He had once been a schoolmaster; an athletic man.

'You tell me.'

'Poor Taylor.'

'Precisely.'

'I don't want to jump the gun,' he said, and settled himself on the edge of the desk, still absorbed in his pipe.

'I don't want to jump the gun, John,' he repeated. 'But there's another matter we ought to look at, tragic as Taylor's death is.' He stowed the tobacco tin in the pocket of his green suit and said, 'Registry.'

'That's Haldane's parish. Research.'

'I've got nothing against old Adrian. He's a good scout. We've been working together for over twenty years.' And therefore you're a good scout too, thought Avery.

Woodford had a way of coming close when he spoke; riding his heavy shoulder against you like a horse rubbing itself against a gate. He leaned forward and looked at Avery earnestly: a plain man perplexed, he was saying, a decent man choosing between friendship and duty. His suit was hairy, too thick to crease, forming rolls like a blanket; rough-cut buttons of brown bone.

'John, Registry's all to the devil; we both know that. Papers aren't being entered, files aren't brought up on the right dates.' He shook his head in despair. 'We've been missing a policy file on marine freight since mid-October. Just vanished into thin air.'

'Adrian Haldane put out a search notice,' Avery said. 'We were all involved, not just Adrian. Files do get lost—this is the first since April, Bruce. I don't think that's bad, considering the amount we handle. I thought Registry was one of our best things. The files are immaculate. I understand our Research index is unique. That's all

Adrian's doing, isn't it? Still, if you're worried why not speak to Adrian about it?'

'No, no. It's not *that* important.'

Carol came in with the tea. Woodford had his in a pottery jumbo-cup, with his initials drawn large, embossed like icing. As Carol put it down, she remarked, 'Wilf Taylor's dead.'

'I've been here since one,' Avery lied, 'coping with it. We've been working all night.'

'The Director's very upset,' she said.

'What was his wife like, Carol?' She was a well-dressed girl, a little taller than Sarah.

'Nobody's met her.'

She left the room, Woodford watching her. He took his pipe from his mouth and grinned. Avery knew he was going to say something about sleeping with Carol and suddenly he'd had enough.

'Did your wife make that cup, Bruce?' he asked quickly. 'I hear she's quite a potter.'

'Made the saucer as well,' he said. He began talking about the classes she went to, the amusing way it had caught on in Wimbledon, how his wife was tickled to death.

It was nearly eleven; they could hear the others gathering in the corridor.

'I'd better go next door,' Avery said, 'and see if he's ready. He's taken quite a beating in the last eight hours.'

Woodford picked up his mug and took a sip of tea. 'If you get a chance, mention that Registry business to the Boss, John. I don't want to drag it up in front of everyone else. Adrian's getting a bit past it.'

'The Director's very tied up at the moment, Bruce.'

'Oh, quite.'

'He hates to interfere with Haldane, you know that.' As they reached the door of his room he turned to Woodford and asked, 'Do you remember a man called Malherbe in the Department?'

Woodford stopped dead. 'God, yes. A young chap, like you. In the war. Good Lord.' And earnestly, but quite unlike his usual manner: 'Don't mention that name to the Boss. He was very cut up about young Malherbe. One of the special fliers. The two of them were quite close in a way.'

Leclerc's room by daylight was not so much drab as of an impermanent appearance. You would think its occupant had re-quisitioned it hastily, under conditions of emergency, and had not known how long he would be staying. Maps lay sprawled over the trestle table, not in threes or fours but dozens, some of a scale large enough to show streets and buildings. Teletape, pasted in strips on pink paper, hung in batches on the notice board, fastened with a heavy bulldog clip like galley proofs awaiting correction. A bed had been put in one corner with a counterpane over it. A clean towel hung beside the basin. The desk was new, of grey steel, government issue. The walls were filthy. Here and there the cream paint had peeled, showing dark green beneath. It was a small, square room with Ministry of Works curtains. There had been a row about the curtains, a question of equating Leclerc's rank to the Civil Service scale. It was the one occasion, so far as Avery knew, when Leclerc had made any effort to improve the disorder of the room. The fire was nearly out. Sometimes when it was very windy the fire would not burn at all, and all through the day Avery could hear from next door the soot falling in the chimney.

Avery watched them come in; Woodford first, then Sandford, Dennison and McCulloch. They all heard about Taylor. It was easy to imagine the news going round the Department, not as headlines, but as a small and gratifying sensation, passed from room to room, lending a briskness to the day's activity, as it had to these men; giving them a moment's optimism, like a rise in pay. They would watch Leclerc, watch him as prisoners watch a warder. They knew his routine by instinct, and they waited for him to break it. There would not be a man or woman in the Department but knew they had been called in the middle of the night, and that Leclerc was sleeping in the office.

They settled themselves at the table, putting their cups in front of them noisily like children at a meal, Leclerc at the head, the others on either side, an empty chair at the farther end. Haldane came in, and Avery knew as soon as he saw him that it would be Leclerc versus Haldane.

Looking at the empty chair, he said, 'I see I'm to take the draughtiest place.'

Avery rose, but Haldane had sat down. 'Don't bother, Avery, I'm a sick man already.' He coughed, just as he coughed all year. Not even the Summer could help him, apparently; he coughed in all seasons.

The others fidgeted uncomfortably; Woodford helped himself to a biscuit. Haldane glanced at the fire. 'Is that the best the Ministry of Works can manage?' he asked.

'It's the rain,' Avery said. 'The rain disagrees with it. Pine's had a go but he made no difference.

'Ah.'

Haldane was a lean man with long, restless fingers; a man locked in himself, slow in his movements, agile in his features, balding, spare, querulous and dry; a man seemingly contemptuous of everything, keeping his own hours and his own counsel; addicted to crossword puzzles and nineteenth-century water colours.

Carol came in with files and maps, putting them on Leclerc's desk, which in contrast to the remainder of his room was very tidy. They waited awkwardly until she had gone. The door securely closed,

Leclerc passed his hand cautiously over his dark hair as if he were not quite familiar with it.

'Taylor's been killed. You've all heard it by now. He was killed last night in Finland, travelling under another name.' Avery noticed he never mentioned Malherbe. 'We don't know the details. He appears to have been run over. I've told Carol to put it about that it was an accident. Is that clear?'

Yes, they said, it was quite clear.

'He went to collect a film from . . . a contact, a Scandinavian contact. You know whom I mean. We don't normally use the routine couriers for operational work, but this was different; something very special indeed. I think Adrian will back me up there.' He made a little upward gesture with his open hands, freeing the wrists from his white cuffs, laying the palms and fingers vertically together; praying for Haldane's support.

'Special?' Haldane repeated slowly. His voice was thin and sharp like the man himself, cultivated, without emphasis and without affectation; an enviable voice. 'It was different, yes. Not least because Taylor died. We should never have used him, never,' he observed flatly. 'We broke a first principle of intelligence. We used a man on the overt side for a clandestine job. Not that we have a clandestine side any more.'

'Shall we let our masters be the judges of that?' Leclerc suggested demurely. 'At least you'll agree the Ministry is pressing us daily for results.' He turned to those on either side of him, now to the left, now to the right, bringing them in like shareholders. 'It is time you all knew the details. We are dealing with something of exceptional security classification, you understand. I propose to limit to Heads of Sections. So far, only Adrian Haldane and one or two of his staff in Research have been initiated. And John Avery as my aide. I wish to emphasize that our sister service knows nothing whatever about it. Now about our own arrangements. The operation has the codeword Mayfly.' He was speaking in his clipped, effective voice. 'There is one action file, which will be returned to me personally, or to Carol if I am out, at the end of each day; and there is a library copy. That is the system we used in the war for operational files and I think you are all familiar with it. It's the system we shall use henceforth. I shall add Carol's name to the subscription list.'

Woodford pointed at Avery with his pipe, shaking his head. Not young John there; John was not familiar with the system. Sandford, sitting beside Avery, explained. The library copy was kept in the cypher-room. It was against regulations to take it away. All new serials were to be entered on it as soon as they were made; the subscription list was the list of persons authorized to read it. No pins were allowed; all the papers had to be fast. The others looked on complacently.

Sandford was Administration; he was a fatherly man in gold-rimmed spectacles and came to the office on a motorbike. Leclerc had objected once, on no particular grounds, and now he parked it down the road opposite the hospital.

'Now, about the operation,' Leclerc said. The thin line of his joined hands bisected his bright face. Only Haldane was not watching him; his eyes were turned away towards the window. Outside, the rain was falling gently against the buildings like Spring rain in a dark valley.

Abruptly Leclerc rose and went to a map of Europe on the wall. There were small flags pinned to it. Stretching upwards with his arm, riding on his toes to reach the Northern Hemisphere, he said, 'We're having a spot of trouble with the Germans.' A little laugh went up. 'In the area south of Rostock; a place called Kalkstadt, just here.' His finger traced the Baltic coastline of Schleswig-Holstein, moved east and stopped an inch or two south of Rostock.

'To put it in a nutshell, we have three indicators which suggest–I cannot say prove–that something big is going on there in the way of military installations.'

He swung round to face them. He would remain at the map and say it all from there, to show he had the facts in his memory and didn't need the papers on the table.

'The first indicator came exactly a month ago when we received a report from our representative in Hamburg, Jimmy Gorton.'

Woodford smiled: Good God, was old Jimmy still going?

'An East German refugee crossed the border mear Lübeck, swam the river; a railwayman from Kalkstadt. He went to our Consulate and offered to sell them information about a new rocket site near Rostock. I need hardly tell you the Consulate threw him out. Since the Foreign Office will not even give us the facilities of its bag service it is unlikely'–a thin smile–'that they will assist us by buying military information.' A nice murmur greeted this joke. 'However, by a stroke of luck Gorton got to hear of the man and went to Flensburg to see him.'

Woodford would not let this pass. Flensburg? Was not that the place where they had located German submarines in 'forty-one? Flensburg had been a hell of a show.

Leclerc nodded at Woodford indulgently, as if he too had been amused by the recollection. 'The wretched man had been to every Allied office in North Germany, but no one would look at him. Jimmy Gorton had a chat with him.' Implicit in Leclerc's way of describing things was an assumption that Gorton was the only intelligent man among a lot of fools. He crossed to his desk, took a cigarette from the silver box, lit it, picked up a file with a heavy red cross on the cover and laid it noiselessly on the table in front of them. 'This is Jimmy's report,' he said. 'It's a first-class bit of work by any standard.' The cigarette looked very long between his fingers. 'The defector's name,' he added inconsequentially, 'was Fritsche.'

'Defector?' Haldane put in quickly. 'The man's a low-grade refugee, a railwayman. We don't usually talk about men like that *defecting*.'

Leclerc replied defensively, 'The man's not only a railwayman. He's a bit of a mechanic and a bit of a photographer.'

McCulloch opened the file and began methodically turning over the serials, Sandford watched him through his gold-rimmed spectacles.

'On the first or second of September—we don't know which because he can't remember—he happened to be doing a double shift in the dumping sheds at Kalkstadt. One of his comrades was sick. He was to work from six till twelve in the morning, and four till ten at night. When he arrived to report for work there were a dozen Vopos, East German people's police, at the station entrance. All passenger traffic was forbidden. They checked his identity papers against a list and told him to keep away from the sheds on the eastern side of the station. They said,' Leclerc added deliberately, 'that if he approached the eastern sheds he was liable to be shot.'

This impressed them. Woodford said it was typical of the Germans.

'It's the Russians we're fighting,' Haldane put in.

'He's an odd fish, our man. He seems to have argued with them. He told them he was as reliable as they were, a good German and a Party member. He showed them his union card, photographs of his wife and Heaven knows what. It didn't do any good, of course, because they just told him to obey orders and keep away from the sheds. But he must have caught their fancy because when they brewed up some soup at ten o'clock they called him over and offered him a cup. Over the soup he asked them what was going on. They were cagey, but he could see they were excited. Then something happened. Something very important,' he continued. 'One of the younger ones blurted out that whatever they had in the sheds could blow the Americans out of West Germany in a couple of hours. At this point an officer came along and told them to get back to work.'

Haldane coughed a deep, hopeless cough, like an echo in an old vault.

What sort of officer, someone asked, was he German or Russian?

'German. That is most relevant. There were no Russians in evidence at all.'

Haldane interrupted sharply. 'The refugee saw none. That's all we know. Let us be accurate.' He coughed again. It was very irritating.

'As you wish. He went home and had lunch. He was disgruntled at being ordered around in his own station by a lot of young fellows playing soldiers. He had a couple of glasses of schnapps and sat there

brooding about the dumping shed. Adrian, if your cough is troubling
you . . . ?' Haldane shook his head. 'He remembered that on the
northern side it abutted with an old storage hut, and that there was a
shutter-type ventilator let into the party wall. He formed the notion
of looking through the ventilator to see what was in the shed. As a
way of getting his own back on the soldiers.'

Woodford laughed.

'Then he decided to go one further and photograph whatever was
there.'

'He must have been mad,' Haldane commented. 'I find this part
impossible to accept.'

'Mad or not, that's what he decided to do. He was cross because
they wouldn't trust him. He felt he had a right to know what was in
the shed.' Leclerc missed a beat then took refuge in technique. 'He
had an Exa-two camera, single lens reflex. East German manufacture. It's cheap housing but takes all the Exakta range lenses; far
fewer speeds than the Exakta, of course.' He looked inquiringly at
the technicians, Dennison and McCulloch. 'Am I right, gentlemen?'
he asked. 'You must correct me.' They smiled sheepishly because
there was nothing to correct. 'He had a good wide-angle lens. The
difficulty was the light. His next shift didn't begin till four, by which
time dusk would be falling and there would be even less light inside
the shed. He had one fast Agfa film which he'd been keeping for a
special occasion; it had a DIN speed of twenty-seven. He decided to
use that.' He paused, more for effect than for questions.

'Why didn't he wait till next morning?' Haldane asked.

'In the report,' Leclerc continued blandly, 'you'll find a very full
account by Gorton of how the man got into the hut, stood on an oil
drum and took his photographs through the ventilator. I'm not going
to repeat all that now. He used the maximum aperture of two point
eight, speeds ranging from a quarter of a second to two seconds. A
fortunate piece of German thoroughness.' No one laughed. 'The
speeds were guesswork, of course. He was bracketing an estimated
exposure time of one second. Only the last three frames show
anything. Here they are.'

Leclerc unlocked the steel drawer of his desk and extracted a set of
high-gloss photographs twelve inches by nine. He was smiling a
little, like a man looking at his own reflection. They gathered round,
all but Haldane and Avery, who had seen them before.

Something was there.

You could see it if you looked quickly; something hid in the
disintegrating shadows; but keep looking and the dark closed in and
the shape was gone. Yet something was there; the muffled form of a
gun barrel, but pointed and too long for its carriage, the suspicion of
a transporter, a vague glint of what might have been a platform.

'They would put protective covers over them, of course,' Leclerc commented, studying their faces hopefully, waiting for their optimism.

Avery looked at his watch. It was twenty past eleven. 'I shall have to go soon, Director,' he said. He still hadn't rung Sarah.'I have to see the accountant about my air ticket.'

'Stay another ten minutes,' Leclerc pleaded, and Haldane asked, 'Where's he going?'

Leclerc replied, 'To take care of Taylor. He has a date at the Circus first.'

'What do you mean, take care of him? Taylor's dead.'

There was an uncomfortable silence.

'You know very well that Taylor was travelling under an alias. Somebody has to collect his effects; recover the film. Avery is going out as next of kin. The Ministry has already given its approval; I wasn't aware that I needed yours.'

'To claim the body?'

'To get the film,' Leclerc repeated hotly.

'That's an operational job; Avery's not trained.'

'They were younger than he in the war. He can look after himself.'

'Taylor couldn't. What will he do when he's got it; bring it back in his sponge bag?'

'Shall we discuss that afterwards?' Leclerc suggested, and addressed himself once more to the others, smiling patiently as if to say old Adrian must be humoured.

'That was all we had to go on till ten days ago. Then came the second indicator. The area round Kalkstadt has been declared a prohibited area.' There was an excited murmur of interest. 'For a radius of—as far as we can establish—thirty kilometres. Sealed off; closed to all traffic. They brought in frontier guards.' He glanced round the table. 'I then informed the Minister. I cannot tell even you all the implications. But let me name one.' He said the last sentence quickly, at the same time flicking upwards the little horns of greying hair that grew above his ears.

Haldane was forgotten.

'What puzzled us in the beginning'—he nodded at Haldane, a conciliatory gesture at a moment of victory, but Haldane ignored it—'was the absence of Soviet troops. They have units in Rostock, Witmar, Schwerin.' His fingers darted among the flags. 'But none—this is confirmed by other agencies—none in the immediate area of Kalkstadt. If there *are* weapons there, weapons of high destructive capacity, why are there no Soviet troops?'

McCulloch made a suggestion: might there not be technicians, Soviet technicians in civilian dress?

'I regard that as unlikely.' A demure smile. 'In comparable cases where tactical weapons were being transported we have always identified at least one Soviet unit. On the other hand, five weeks ago a few Russian troops *were* seen at Gustweiler, farther south.' He was back to the map. 'They billeted for one night at a pub. Some wore artillery flashes; others had no shoulder-boards at all. They moved away southwards early next morning. One might conclude they had brought something, left it and gone away again.'

Woodford was becoming restless. What did it all add up to, he wanted to know, what did they make of it over at the Ministry? Woodford had no patience with riddles.

Leclerc adopted his academic tone. It had a bullying quality as if facts were facts and could not be disputed. 'Research Section have done a magnificent job. The overall length of the object in these photographs—they can compute it pretty exactly—is equal to the length of a Soviet middle-range rocket. On present information'—he lightly tapped the map with his knuckles so that it swung sideways on its hook—'the Ministry believes it is *conceivable* we are dealing with Soviet missiles under East German control. Research,' he added quickly, 'are not prepared to go so far. Now if the Ministry view prevails, if they are right, that is, we would have on our hands'—this was his moment—'a sort of Cuba situation all over again, only'—he tried to sound apologetic, to make it a throw-away line—'more dangerous.'

He had them.

'It was at this point,' Leclerc explained, 'that the Ministry felt entitled to authorize an overflight. As you know, for the last four years the Department has been limited to aerial photographs along orthodox civilian or military air routes. Even these required Foreign Office approval.' He drifted away. 'It really was too bad.' His eyes seemed to be searching for something not in the room. The others watched him anxiously, waiting for him to continue.

'For once the Ministry agreed to waive the ruling, and I am pleased to say the task of mounting the operation was given to this Department. We selected the best pilot we could find on our books: Lansen.' Someone looked up in surprise; agents' names were never used that way. 'Lansen undertook, for a price, to go off course on a charter flight from Düsseldorf to Finland. Taylor was dispatched to collect the film; he died at the landing field. A road accident, apparently.'

Outside they could hear the sound of cars moving through the rain like the rustling of paper in the wind. The fire had gone out; only the smoke remained, hanging like a shroud over the table.

Sandford had raised his hand. What kind of missile was this supposed to be?

'A Sandal, Medium Range. I am told by Research that is was first shown in Red Square in November 'sixty-two. It has achieved a certain notoriety since then. It was the Sandal which the Russians installed in Cuba. The Sandal is also'—a glance at Woodford—'the linear descendant of the wartime German V2.'

He fetched other photographs from the desk and laid them on the table.

'Here is a Research Section photograph of the Sandal missile. They tell me it is distinguished by what is called a flared skirt'–he pointed to the formation at the base–'and by small fins. It is about forty foot long from base to cone. If you look carefully you will see tucks near the clamp–just here–which hold the protective cloth cover in position. There is, ironically, no extant picture of the Sandal in protective covers. Possibly the Americans have one, but I don't feel able to approach them at this stage.'

Woodford reacted quickly. 'Of course not,' he said.

'The Minister was anxious that we shouldn't alarm them prematurely. One only has to *suggest* rockets to the Americans to get the most drastic reaction. Before we know where we are they'll be flying U2s over Rostock.' Encouraged by their laughter, Leclerc continued: 'The Minister made another point which I think I might pass on to you. The country which comes under maximum threat from these rockets–they have a range of around eight hundred miles–might well be our own. It is certainly not the United States. Politically, this would be a bad moment to go hiding our faces in the Americans' skirts. After all, as the Minister put it, we still *have* one or two teeth of our own.'

Haldane said sarcastically, 'That is a charming notion,' and Avery turned on him with all the anger he had fought away.

'I think you might do better than that,' he said. He nearly added: have a little mercy.

Haldane's cold gaze held Avery for a moment, then released him, his case not forgiven but suspended.

Someone asked what they would do next: suppose Avery did not find Taylor's film? Suppose it just wasn't there? Could they mount another overflight?

'No,' Leclerc replied. 'Another overflight is out of the question. Far too dangerous. We shall have to try something else.' He seemed disinclined to go further, but Haldane said, 'What, for instance?'

'We may have to put a man in. It seems to be the only way.'

'This Department?' Haldane asked incredulously. 'Put a man in? The Ministry would never tolerate such a thing. You mean, surely, you'll ask the Circus to do it?'

'I have already told you the position. Heaven knows, Adrian, you're not going to tell me we can't do it?' He looked appealingly round the table. 'Every one of us here except young Avery has been in the business twenty years or more. You yourself have forgotten more about agents than half those people in the Circus ever knew.'

'Hear, hear!' Woodford cried.

'Look at your own section, Adrian; look at Research. There must have been half a dozen occasions in the last five years when the Circus actually came to you, asked you for advice, used your facilities and skills. The time may come when they do the same with agents! The Ministry granted us an overflight. Why not an agent too?'

'You mentioned a third indicator. I don't follow you. What was that?'

'Taylor's death,' said Leclerc.

Avery got up, nodded goodbye and tiptoed to the door. Haldane watched him go.

Chapter Five

There was a note on his desk from Carol: 'Your wife rang.'

He walked into her office and found her sitting at her typewriter but not typing. 'You wouldn't talk about poor Wilf Taylor like that,' she said, 'if you'd known him better.'

'Like what? I haven't talked about him at all.'

He thought he should comfort her, because sometimes they touched one another; he thought she might expect that now.

He bent forward, advancing until the sharp ends of her hair touched his cheek. Inclining his head inwards so that their temples met, he felt her skin travel slightly across the flat bone of her skull. For a moment they remained thus, Carol sitting upright, looking straight ahead of her, her hands either side of the typewriter, Avery awkwardly stooping. He thought of putting his hand beneath her arm and touching her breast, but did not; both gently recoiling, they separated and were alone again. Avery stood up.

'Your wife telephoned,' she said. 'I told her you were at the meeting. She wants to talk to you urgently.'

'Thanks. I'm on my way.'

'John, what *is* going on? What's all this about the Circus? What's Leclerc up to?'

'I thought you knew. He said he'd put you on the list.'

'I don't mean that. Why's he lying to them again? He's dictated a memorandum to Control about some training scheme and you going abroad. Pine took it round by hand. He's gone mad about her pension; Mrs Taylor's; looking up precedents and Heaven knows what. Even the application is Top Secret. He's building one of his card houses, John, I know he is. Who's Leiser, for instance?'

'You're not supposed to know. He's an agent; a Pole.'

'Does he work for the Circus?' She changed her tack.

'Well, why are *you* going? That's another thing I don't understand. For that matter, why did Taylor have to go? If the Circus has couriers in Finland, why couldn't we have used them in the first place? Why send poor Taylor? Even now the FO could iron it out. I'm sure they could. He just won't give them a chance: he *wants* to send you.'

'You don't understand,' Avery said shortly.

'Another thing,' she demanded as he was going, 'why does Adrian Haldane hate you so?'

He visited the accountant then took a taxi to the Circus. Leclerc had said he could claim for it. He was cross that Sarah had tried to reach him at such a moment. He had told her never to ring him at the Department. Leclerc said it was insecure.

'What did you read at Oxford? It was Oxford, wasn't it?' Smiley asked, and gave him a cigarette, rather a muddled one from a packet of ten.

'Languages.' Avery patted his pockets for a match. 'German and Italian.' When Smiley said nothing he added, 'German principally.'

Smiley was a small, distracted man with plump fingers and a shadowy, blinking way with him which suggested discomfort. Whatever Avery had expected, it was not this.

'Well, well.' Smiley nodded to himself, a very private comment. 'It's a question of a courier, I believe, in Helsinki. You want to give him a film. A training scheme.'

'Yes.'

'It's a most unusual request. You're sure . . . do you know the *size* of the film?'

'No.'

A long pause.

'You should try to find out that kind of thing,' Smiley said kindly. 'I mean, the courier may want to conceal it, you see.'

'I'm sorry.'

'Oh, it doesn't matter.'

Avery was reminded of Oxford, and reading essays to his tutor.

'Perhaps,' said Smiley thoughtfully, 'I might say one thing. I'm sure Leclerc has already had it from Control. We want to give you all the help we can—*all* the help. There used to be a time,' he mused, with that curious air of indirection which seemed to characterize all his utterances, 'when our departments *competed*. I always found that very painful. But I wondered whether you could tell me a *little*, just a little . . . Control was so anxious to help. We should hate to do the wrong thing out of ignorance.'

'It's a training exercise. Full dress. I don't know much about it myself.'

'We want to help,' Smiley repeated simply. 'What is your target country, your *putative* target?'

'I don't know. I'm only playing a small part. It's training.'

'But if it's training, why so much secrecy?'

'Well, Germany,' Avery said.

'Thank you.'

Smiley seemed embarrassed. He looked at his hands folded lightly on the desk before him. He asked Avery whether it was still raining. Avery said he was afraid so.

'I'm sorry to hear about Taylor,' he said. Avery said yes he was a good man.

'Do you know what time you'll have your film? Tonight? Tomorrow? Leclerc rather thought tonight, I gather.'

'I don't know. It depends how it goes. I just can't tell at the moment.'

'No.' There followed a long, unexplained silence. He's like an old man, thought Avery, he forgets he's not alone. 'No, there are so many imponderables. Have you done this kind of thing before?'

'Once or twice.' Again Smiley said nothing and did not seem to notice the gap.

'How *is* everyone in Blackfriars Road? Do you know Haldane at all?' Smiley asked. He didn't care about the reply.

'He's Research now.'

'Of course. A good brain. Your Research people enjoy quite a reputation, you know. We have consulted them ourselves more than once. Haldane and I were contemporaries at Oxford. Then in the war we worked together for a while. A Greats man. We'd have taken him here after the war; I think the medical people were worried about his chest.'

'I hadn't heard.'

'Hadn't you?' The eyebrows rose comically. 'There's a hotel in Helsinki called the Prince of Denmark. Opposite the main station. Do you know it by any chance?'

'No. I've never been to Helsinki.'

'Haven't you, now?' Smiley peered at him anxiously. 'It's a very *strange* story. This Taylor: was he training too?'

'I don't know. But I'll find the hotel,' Avery said with a touch of impatience.

'They sell magazines and postcards just inside the door. There's only the one entrance.' He might have been talking about the house next door. 'And flowers. I think the best arrangement would be for you to go there once you have the film. Ask the people at the flower stall to send a dozen red roses to Mrs Avery at the Imperial Hotel at Torquay. Or half a dozen would be enough, we don't want to waste money, do we? Flowers are so expensive up there. Are you travelling under your own name?'

'Yes.'

'Any particular reason? I don't mean to be curious,' he added hastily, 'but one has such a short life anyway . . . I mean before one's blown.'

'I gather it takes a bit of time to get a fake passport. The Foreign Office . . .' He shouldn't have answered. He should have told him to mind his own business.

'I'm sorry,' said Smiley, and frowned as if he had made an error of tact. 'You can always come to us, you know. For passports, I mean.' It was meant as a kindness. 'Just send the flowers. As you leave the hotel, check your watch by the hall clock. Half an hour later return to the main entrance. A taxi driver will recognize you and open the door of his car. Get in, drive around, give him the film. Oh, and pay him please. Just the ordinary fare. It's so easy to forget the *little* things. What *kind* of training precisely?'

'What if I don't get the film?'

'In that case do nothing. Don't go near the hotel. Don't go to Helsinki. Forget about it.' It occurred to Avery that his instructions had been remarkably clear.

'When you were reading German, did you touch on the seventeenth century by any chance?' Smiley inquired hopefully as Avery rose to go. 'Gryphius, Lohenstein; those people?'

'It was a special subject. I'm afraid I didn't.'

'*Special*,' muttered Smiley. 'What a *silly* word. I suppose they mean extrinsic; it's a very impertinent notion.'

As they reached the door he said, 'Have you a briefcase or anything?'

'Yes.'

'When you have that film, put it in your pocket,' he suggested, 'and carry the briefcase in your hand. If you *are* followed, they tend to watch the briefcase. It's natural, really. If you just drop the briefcase somewhere, they may go looking for that instead. I don't think the Finns are very *sophisticated* people. It's only a training hint, of course. But don't *worry*. It's such a mistake, I always feel, to put one's trust in *technique*.' He saw Avery to the door, then made his way ponderously along the corridor to Control's room.

Avery walked upstairs to the flat, guessing how Sarah would react. He wished he had telephoned after all because he hated to find her in the kitchen, and Anthony's toys all over the drawing-room carpet. It never worked, turning up without warning. She took fright as if she expected him to have done something dreadful.

He did not carry a key; Sarah was always in. She had no friends of her own as far as he knew; she never went to coffee parties or took herself shopping. She seemed to have no talent for independent pleasure.

He pressed the bell, heard Anthony calling Mummy, Mummy, and waited to hear her step. The kitchen was at the end of the passage, but this time she came from the bedroom, softly as though she were barefooted.

She opened the door without looking at him. She was wearing a cotton nightdress and a cardigan.

'God, you took your time,' she said, turned and walked uncertainly back to the bedroom. 'Something wrong?' she asked over her shoulder. 'Someone else been murdered?'

'What's the matter, Sarah? Aren't you well?'

Anthony was running about shouting because his father had come home. Sarah climbed back into bed. 'I rang the doctor. *I* don't know what it is,' she said, as if illness were not her subject.

'Have you a temperature?'

She had put a bowl of cold water and the bathroom flannel beside her. He wrung out the flannel and laid it on her head. 'You'll have to cope,' she said. 'I'm afraid it's not as exciting as spies. Aren't you going to ask me what's wrong?'

'When's the doctor arriving?'

'He has surgery till twelve. He'll turn up after that, I suppose.'

He went to the kitchen, Anthony following. The breakfast things were still on the table. He telephoned her mother in Reigate and asked her to come straight away.

It was just before one when the doctor arrived. A fever, he said; some germ that was going the rounds.

He thought she would weep when he told her he was going abroad; she took it in, reflected for a while and then suggested he went and packed.

'Is it important?' she said suddenly.

'Of course. Terribly.'

'Who for?'

'You, me. All of us, I suppose.'

'And for Leclerc?'

'I told you. For all of us.'

He promised Anthony he would bring him something.

'Where are you going?' Anthony asked.

'In an aeroplane.'

'Where?'

He was going to tell him it was a great secret when he remembered Taylor's little girl.

He kissed her goodbye, took his suitcase to the hall and put it on the mat. There were two locks on the door for Sarah's sake and they had to be turned simultaneously. He heard her say:

'Is it dangerous too?'

'I don't know. I only know it's very big.'

'You're really sure of that, are you?'

He called almost in despair, 'Look, how far am I supposed to think? It isn't a question of politics, don't you see? It's a question of fact. Can't you believe? Can't you tell me for once in my life that I'm doing something good?' He went into the bedroom, reasoning. She held a paperback in front of her and was pretending to read. 'We all have to, you know, we all have to draw a line round our lives. It's no good asking me the whole time, "Are you sure?" It's like asking whether we should have children, whether we should have married. There's just no point.'

'Poor John,' she observed, putting down the book and analysing him. 'Loyalty without faith. It's very hard for you.' She said this with total dispassion as if she had identified a social evil. The kiss was like a betrayal of her standards.

Haldane watched the last of them leave the room: he had arrived late, he would leave late, never with the crowd.

Leclerc said, 'Why do you do that to me?' He spoke like an actor tired from the play. The maps and photographs were strewn on the table with the empty cups and ashtrays.

Haldane didn't answer.

'What are you trying to prove, Adrian?'

'What was that you said about putting a man in?'

Leclerc went to the basin and poured himself a glass of water from the tap. 'You don't care for Avery, do you?' he asked.

'He's young. I'm tired of that cult.'

'I get a sore throat, talking all the time. Have some yourself. Do your cough good.'

'How old is Gorton?' Haldane accepted the glass, drank, and handed it back.

'Fifty.'

'He's more. He's our age. He was our age in the war.'

'One forgets. Yes, he must be fifty-five or six.'

'Established?' Haldane persisted.

Leclerc shook his head. 'He's not qualified. Broken service. He went to the Control Commission after the war. When that packed up he wanted to stay in Germany. German wife, I think. He came to us and we gave him a contract. We could never afford to keep him there if he were established.' He took a sip of water, delicately, like a girl. 'Ten years ago we'd thirty men in the field. Now we've nine. We haven't even got our own couriers, not clandestine ones. They all knew it this morning; why didn't they say so?'

'How often does he put in a refugee report?'

Leclerc shrugged. 'I don't see all his stuff,' he said. 'Your people should know. The market's dwindling, I suppose, now they've closed the Berlin border.'

'They only put the better reports up to me. This must be the first

I've seen from Hamburg for a year. I always imagined he had some other function.'

Leclerc shook his head. Haldane asked, 'When does his contract come up for renewal?'

'I don't know. I just don't know.'

'I suppose he must be fairly worried. Does he get a gratuity on retirement?'

'It's just a three-year contract. There's no gratuity. No frills. He has the chance of going on after sixty, of course, if we want him. That's the advantage of being a temporary.'

'When was his contract last renewed?'

'You'd better ask Carol. It must be two years ago. Maybe longer.'

Haldane said again, 'You talked about putting a man in.'

'I'm seeing the Minister again this afternoon.'

'You've sent Avery already. You shouldn't have done that, you know.'

'Somebody had to go. Did you want me to ask the Circus?'

'Avery was very impertinent,' Haldane observed.

The rain was running in the gutters, tracing grey tracks on the dingy panes. Leclerc seemed to want Haldane to speak, but Haldane had nothing to say. 'I don't know yet what the Minister thinks about Taylor's death. He'll ask me this afternoon and I shall give him my opinion. We're all in the dark, of course.' His voice recovered its strength. 'But he may instruct me—it's on the cards, Adrian—he may *instruct* me to get a man in.'

'Well?'

'Suppose I asked you to form an operations section, make the research, prepare papers and equipment; suppose I asked you to find, train and field the agent. Would you do it?'

'Without telling the Circus?'

'Not in detail. We may need their facilities from time to time. That doesn't mean we need tell them the whole story. There's the question of security: *need to know.*'

'Then without the Circus?'

'Why not?'

Haldane shook his head. 'Because it isn't our work. We're just not equipped. Give it to the Circus and help them out with the military stuff. Give it to an old hand, someone like Smiley or Leamas . . .'

'Leamas is dead.'

'All right then, Smiley.'

'Smiley is blown.'

Haldane coloured. 'Then Guillam or one of the others. One of the pros. They've got a big enough stable these days. Go and see Control, let him have the case.'

'No,' Leclerc said firmly, putting the glass on the table. 'No, Adrian. You've been in the Department as long as I have, you know our brief. *Take all necessary steps*–that's what it says–*all necessary steps for the procurement, analysis and verification of military intelligence in those areas where the requirement cannot be met from conventional military resources.*' He beat out the words with his little fist as he spoke. 'How else do you think I got authority for the overflight?'

'All right,' Haldane conceded. 'We have our brief. But things have changed. It's a different game now. In those days we were top of the tree–rubber boats on a moonless night; a captured enemy plane; wireless and all that. You and I know; we did it together. But it's changed. It's a different war; a different kind of fighting. They know that at the Ministry perfectly well.' He added, 'And don't place too much trust in the Circus; you'll get no charity from those people.'

They looked at one another in surprise, a moment of recognition. Leclerc said, his voice scarcely above a whisper: 'It began with the networks, didn't it? Do you remember how the Circus swallowed them up one by one? The Ministry would say: "We're in danger of duplication on the Polish desks, Leclerc. I've decided Control should look after Poland." When was that? July 'forty-eight. Year after year it's gone on. Why do you think they patronize your Research Section? Not just for your beautiful files; they've got us where they want us, don't you see? Satellites! Non-operational! It's a way of putting us to sleep! You know what they call us in Whitehall these days? The Grace and Favour boys.'

There was a long silence.

Haldane said, 'I'm a collator, not an operational man.'

'You *used* to be operational, Adrian.'

'So did we all.'

'You know the target. You know the whole background. There's no one else. Take whom you want–Avery, Woodford, whoever you want.'

'We're not used to people any more. Handling them, I mean.' Haldane had become unusually diffident. 'I'm a Research man. I work with files.'

'We've had nothing else to give you until now. How long is it? Twenty years.'

'Do you know what it means, a rocket site?' Haldane demanded. 'Do you know how much mess it makes? They need launch pads, blast shields, cable troughs, control buildings; they need bunkers for storing the warheads, trailers for fuel and oxidizers. All those things come first. Rockets don't creep about in the night; they move like a travelling fair; we'd have other indicators before now; or the Circus would. As for Taylor's death—'

'For Heaven's sake, Adrian, do you think Intelligence consists of unassailable philosophical truths? Does every priest have to *prove* that Christ was born on Christmas Day?'

His little face was thrust forward as he tried to draw from Haldane something he seemed to know was there. 'You can't do it all by sums, Adrian. We're not academics, we're Civil Servants. We have to deal with things as they are. We have to deal with people, with events!'

'Very well, events then: if he swam the river, how did he preserve the film? How did he *really* take the pictures? Why isn't there any trace of camera shake? He'd been drinking, he was balancing on tiptoe; they're long enough exposures, you know, time exposures, he said.' Haldane seemed afraid, not of Leclerc, not of the operation, but of himself. 'Why did he give Gorton for nothing what he'd offered elsewhere for money? Why did he risk his life at all, taking those photographs? I sent Gorton a list of supplementaries. He's still trying to find the man, he says.'

His eyes drifted to the model aeroplane and the files on Leclerc's desk. 'You're thinking of Peenemünde, aren't you?' he continued. 'You want it to be like Peenemünde.'

'You haven't told me what you'll do if I get those instructions.'

'You never will. You never, never will.' He spoke with great finality almost triumph. 'We're dead, don't you see? You said it yourself. They want us to go to sleep, not go to war.' He stood up. 'So it doesn't matter. It's all academic, after all. Can you *really* imagine Control would help us?'

'They've agreed to help us with a courier.'

'Yes. I find that most odd.'

Haldane stopped before a photograph by the door. 'That's Malherbe, isn't it? The boy who died. Why did you choose that name?'

'I don't know. It just came into my head. One's memory plays odd tricks.'

'You shouldn't have sent Avery. We've no business to use him for a job like that.'

'I went through the cards last night. We've got a man who'd do. A man we could send, I mean.' Daring, he added, 'An agent. Trained wireless operator, German speaker, unmarried.' Haldane stood quite still.

'Age?' he asked at last.

'Forty. A bit over.'

'He must have been very young.'

'He put up a good show. They caught him in Holland and he got away.'

'How did he get caught?'

The slightest pause. 'It isn't recorded.'

'Intelligent?'

'He seems quite well qualified.'

The same long silence.

'So am I. Let's see what Avery brings back.'

'Let's see what the Ministry says.'

Leclerc waited till the sound of coughing had faded down the corridor before he put on his coat. He would go for a walk, take some fresh air and have lunch at his club; the best they had. He wondered what it would be; the place had gone off badly in the last few years. After lunch he would go round to Taylor's widow. Then to the Ministry.

Woodford, lunching with his wife at Gorringe's, said, 'Young Avery's on his first run. Clarkie sent him. He should make a good job of it.'

'Perhaps he'll get himself killed, too,' she said nastily. She was off the drink, doctor's orders. 'Then you can have a real ball. Christ, that would be a party and a half! Come to the Black Friars' Ball!' Her lower lip was quivering. 'Why are the young ones always so bloody marvellous? We were young, weren't we? . . . Christ, we still are! What's wrong with us? We can't wait to grow old, can we? We can't—'

'All right, Babs,' he said. He was afraid she might cry.

Chapter Six
TAKE-OFF

Avery sat in the aeroplane remembering the day when Haldane failed to appear. It was, by coincidence, the first of the month, July it must have been, and Haldane did not come to the office. Avery knew nothing of it until Woodford rang him on the internal telephone to tell him. Haldane was probably ill, Avery had said; some personal matter had cropped up. But Woodford was adamant. He had been to Leclerc's room, he said, and had looked at the leave roster: Haldane was not due for leave till August.

'Telephone his flat, John, telephone his flat,' he had urged. 'Speak to his wife. Find out what's become of him.' Avery was so astonished that he did not know what to say: those two had worked together for twenty years, and even he knew Haldane was a bachelor.

'Find out where he is,' Woodford had persisted. 'Go on, I order you: ring his flat.'

So he did. He might have told Woodford to do it himself, but he hadn't the heart. Haldane's sister answered. Haldane was in bed, his chest was playing him up; he had refused to tell her the Department's telephone number. As Avery's eye caught the calendar, he realized why Woodford had been so agitated: it was the beginning of a quarter. Haldane might have got a new job and left the Department without telling Woodford. A day or two later, when Haldane returned, Woodford was uncommonly warm towards him, bravely ignoring his sarcasm; he was grateful to him for coming back. For some time after that, Avery had been frightened. His faith shaken, he examined more closely its object.

He noticed that they ascribed—it was a plot in which all but Haldane compounded—legendary qualities to one another. Leclerc, for instance, would seldom introduce Avery to a member of his parent Ministry without some catchword. 'Avery is the brightest of our new stars'—or, to more senior men, 'John is my memory. You must ask John.' For the same reason they lightly forgave one another their trespasses, because they dared not think, for their own sakes, that the Department had room for fools. He recognized that it provided shelter from the complexities of modern life, a place where frontiers still existed. For its servants, the Department had a religious quality. Like monks, they endowed it with a mystical identity far away from the hesitant, sinful band which made up its ranks. While they might be cynical of the qualities of one another, contemptuous of their own hierarchial preoccupations, their faith in the Department burned in some separate chapel and they called it patriotism.

For all that, as he glanced at the darkening sea beneath him, at the cold sunlight slanting on the waves, he felt his heart thrilling with love. Woodford with his pipe and his plain way became part of that secret élite to which Avery now belonged; Haldane, Haldane above all, with his crosswords and his eccentricities, fitted into place as the uncompromising intellectual, irritable and aloof. He was sorry he had been rude to Haldane. He saw Dennison and McCulloch as the matchless technicians, quiet men, not articulate at meetings, but tireless and, in the end, right. He thanked Leclerc, thanked him warmly, for the privilege of knowing these men, for the excitement of this mission; for the opportunity to advance from the uncertainty of the past towards experience and maturity, to become a man, shoulder to shoulder with the others, tempered in the fire of war; he thanked him for the precision of command, which made order out of the anarchy of his heart. He imagined that when Anthony grew up, he too might be led into those dowdy corridors, and be presented to old Pine, who with tears in his eyes would stand up in his box and warmly grasp the child's tender hand.

It was a scene in which Sarah played no part.

Avery lightly touched a corner of the long envelope in his inside pocket. It contained his money: two hundred pounds in a blue envelope with the Government crest. He had heard of people in the war sewing such things into the lining of their clothes, and he rather wished they had done that for him. It was a childish conceit, he knew; he even smiled to discover himself given to such fancies.

He remembered Smiley that morning; in retrospect he was just a little frightened of Smiley. And he remembered the child at the door. A man must steel himself against sentiment.

'Your husband did a very good job,' Leclerc was saying, 'I cannot tell you the details. I am sure that he died very gallantly.'

Her mouth was stained and ugly. Leclerc had never seen anyone cry so much; it was like a wound that would not close.

'What do you mean, gallantly?' she blinked. 'We're not fighting a war. That's finished, all that fancy talk. He's dead,' she said stupidly, and buried her face in her crooked arm, slouching across the dining-room table like a puppet abandoned. The child was staring from a corner.

'I trust,' Leclerc said, 'that I have your permission to apply for a pension. You must leave all that to us. The sooner we take care of it the better. A pension,' he declared, as if it were the maxim of his house, 'can make a lot of difference.'

The Consul was waiting beside the Immigration Officer; he came forward without a smile, doing his duty. 'Are you Avery?' he asked. Avery had the impression of a tall man in a trilby and a dark overcoat; red-faced and severe. They shook hands.

'You're the British Consul, Mr Sutherland.'

'H.M. Consul, actually,' he replied, a little tartly. 'There's a difference you know.' He spoke with a Scottish accent. 'How did you know my name?'

They walked together towards the main entrance. It was all very simple. Avery noticed the girl at the desk; fair and rather pretty.

'It's kind of you to come all this way,' Avery said.

'It's only three miles from the town.' They got into the car.

'He was killed just up the road,' said Sutherland. 'Do you want to see the spot?'

'I might as well. To tell my mother.' He was wearing a black tie.

'Your name *is* Avery, isn't it?'

'Of course it is; you saw my passport at the desk.' Sutherland didn't like that, and Avery rather wished he hadn't said it. He started the engine. They were about to pull into the centre of the road when a Citroën swung out and overtook them.

'Damn fool,' Sutherland snapped. 'Roads are like ice. One of these pilots, I suppose. No idea of speed.' They could see a peak cap silhouetted against the windscreen as the car hurried down the long road across the dunes, throwing up a small cloud of snow behind it.

'Where do you come from?' he asked.

'London.'

Sutherland pointed straight ahead: 'That's where your brother died. Up there on the brow. The police reckon the driver must have been tight. They're very hot on drunken driving here, you know.' It sounded like a warning. Avery stared at the flat reaches of snow-bound country on either side and thought of lonely, English Taylor struggling along the road, his weak eyes streaming from the cold.

'We'll go to the police afterwards,' said Sutherland. 'They're expecting us. They'll tell you all the details. Have you booked yourself a room here?'

'No.'

As they reached the top of the rise Sutherland said with grudging deference, 'It was just here, if you want to get out.'

'It's all right.'

Sutherland accelerated a little as if he wanted to get away from the place.

'Your brother was walking to the hotel. The Regina, just here. There was no taxi.' They descended the slope on the other side; Avery caught sight of the long lights of a hotel across the valley.

'No distance at all, really,' Sutherland commented. 'He'd have done it in fifteen minutes. Less. Where does your mother live?'

The question took Avery by surprise.

'Woodbridge, in Suffolk.' There was a by-election going on there; it was the first town that came into his head, though he had no interest in politics.

'Why didn't he put her down?'

'I'm sorry, I don't understand.'

'As next of kin. Why didn't Malherbe put his mother down instead of you?'

Perhaps it was not meant as a serious question; perhaps he just wanted to keep Avery talking because he was upset; nevertheless, it was unnerving. He was still strung up from the journey, he wanted to be taken for granted, not subjected to this interrogation. He realized, too, that he had not sufficiently worked out the supposed relationship between Taylor and himself. What had Leclerc written in the teleprint; half-brother or step-brother? Hastily he tried to visualize a train of family events, death, remarriage or estrangement, which would lead him to the answer to Sutherland's question.

'There's the hotel,' the Consul said suddenly, and then, 'it's nothing to do with me, of course. He can put down whoever he wants.' Resentment had become a habit of speech with Sutherland, a philosophy. He spoke as if everything he said were the contradiction of a popular view.

'She's old,' Avery replied at last. 'It's a question of protecting her from shock. I expect that's what he had in mind when he filled in his passport application. She's been ill; a bad heart. She's had an operation.' It sounded very childish.

'Ah.'

They had reached the outskirts of the town.

'There has to be a post-mortem,' Sutherland said. 'It's the law here, I'm afraid, in the case of violent death.'

Leclerc was going to be angry about that. Sutherland continued, 'For us, it makes the formalities more complicated. The Criminal Police take over the body until the post-mortem is complete. I asked them to be quick, but one can't insist.'

'Thanks. I thought I'd have the body flown back.' As they turned off the main road into the market square, Avery asked casually, as if he had no personal interest in the outcome, 'What about his effects? I'd better take them with me, hadn't I?'

'I doubt whether the police will hand them over until they've had the go-ahead from the public prosecutor. The post-mortem report goes to him; he gives clearance. Did your brother leave a will?'

'I've no idea.'

'You'd not happen to know whether you're an executor?'

'No.'

Sutherland gave a dry, patient laugh. 'I can't help feeling you're a little premature. Next of kin is not quite the same as executor,' he said. 'It gives you no legal rights, I'm afraid, apart from the disposal of the body.' He paused, looking back over his seat while he reversed the car into a parking space. Even if the police hand your brother's effects over to me, I'm not allowed to release them until I've had instructions from the Office, and *they*,' he continued quickly, for Avery was about to interrupt him, 'won't issue such instructions to *me* until a grant of probate has been made or a Letter of Administration issued. But I can give you a death certificate,' he added consolingly, opening his door, 'if the insurance companies require it.' He looked at Avery sideways, as if wondering whether he stood to inherit anything. 'It'll cost you five shillings for the Consular registration and five shillings per certified copy. What was that you said?'

'Nothing.' Together they climbed the steps to the police station.

'We'll be seeing Inspector Peersen,' Sutherland explained. 'He's quite well disposed. You'll kindly let me handle him.'

'Of course.'

'He's been a lot of help with my DBS problems.'

'Your what?'

'Distressed British Subjects. We get one a day in Summer. They're a disgrace. Did your brother drink a lot, incidentally? There's some suggestion he was—'

'It's possible,' Avery said. 'I hardly knew him in the last few years.' They entered the building.

Leclerc himself was walking carefully up the broad steps of the Ministry. It lay between Whitehall Gardens and the river; the doorway was large and new, surrounded with that kind of Fascist statuary which is admired by local authorities. Partly modernized, the building was guarded by sergeants in red sashes and contained two escalators; the one which descended was full, for it was half past five.

'Under Secretary,' Leclerc began diffidently. 'I shall have to ask the Minister for another overflight.'

'You'll be wasting your time,' he replied with satisfaction. 'He was most apprehensive about the last one. He's made a policy decision; there'll be no more.'

'Even with a target like this?'

'Particularly with a target like this.'

The Under Secretary lightly touched the corners of his in-tray as a bank manager might touch a statement. 'You'll have to think of something else,' he said. 'Some other way. Is there no *painless* method?'

'None. I suppose we could try to stimulate a defection from the area. That's a lengthy business. Leaflets, propaganda broadcasts, financial inducements. It worked well in the war. We would have to approach a lot of people.'

'It sounds a most improbable notion.'

'Yes. Things are different now.'

'What other ways are there, then?' he insisted.

Leclerc smiled again, as if he would like to help a friend, but could not work miracles. 'An agent. A short-term operation. In and out: a week altogether perhaps.'

The Under Secretary said, 'But who could you find for a job like that? These days?'

'Who indeed? It's a very long shot.'

The Under Secretary's room was large but dark, with rows of bound books. Modernization had encroached as far as his Private Office, which was done in the contemporary style, but there the process had stopped. They could wait till he retired to do his room. A gas fire burned in the marble fireplace. On the wall hung an oil painting of a battle at sea. They could hear the sound of barges in the fog. It was an oddly maritime atmosphere.

'Kalkstadt's pretty close to the border,' Leclerc suggested. 'We wouldn't have to use a scheduled airline. We could do a training flight, lose our way. It's been done before.'

'Precisely,' said the Under Secretary, then: 'This man of yours who died.'

'Taylor?'

'I'm not concerned with names. He was murdered, was he?'

'There's no proof,' Leclerc said.

'But you assume it?'

Leclerc smiled patiently. 'I think we both know, Under Secretary, that it is very dangerous to make broad assumptions when decisions of policy are involved. I'm still asking for another overflight.'

The Under Secretary coloured.

'I told you it's out of the question. No! Does that make it clear? We were talking of alternatives.'

'There's one alternative, I suppose, which would scarcely touch on my Department. It's more a matter for yourselves and the Foreign Office.'

'Oh?'

'Drop a hint to the London newspapers. Stimulate publicity. Print the photographs.'

'And?'

'Watch them. Watch the East German and Soviet diplomacy, watch their communications. Throw a stone into the nest and see what comes out.'

'I can tell you exactly what would come out. A protest from the Americans that would ring through these corridors for another twenty years.'

'Of course. I was forgetting that.'

'Then you're lucky. You suggested putting an agent in.

'Only tentatively. We've no one in mind.'

'Look,' said the Under Secretary, with the finality of a man much tried. 'The Minister's position is very simple. You have produced a report. If it is true, it alters our entire defence position. In fact it alters everything. I detest sensation, so does the Minister. Having put up the hare, the least you can do is have a shot at it.'

Leclerc said, 'If I found a man there's the problem of resources. Money, training and equipment. Extra staff perhaps. Transport. Whereas an overflight . . .'

'Why do you raise so many difficulties? I understood you people existed for this kind of thing.'

'We have the expertise, Under Secretary. But I cut down, you know. I have cut down a lot. Some of our functions have lapsed: one must be honest. I have never tried to put the clock back. This is, after all'—a delicate smile—'a slightly *anachronistic* situation.'

The Under Secretary glanced out of the window at the lights along the river.

'It seems pretty contemporary to me. Rockets and that kind of thing. I don't think the Minister considers it anachronistic.'

'I'm not referring to the target but the method of attack: it would have to be a crash operation at the border. That has scarcely been done since the war. Althought it is a form of clandestine warfare with which my Department is traditionally at home. Or used to be.'

'What are you getting at?'

'I'm only thinking aloud, Under Secretary. I wonder whether the Circus might not be better equipped to deal with this. Perhaps you should approach Control. I can promise him the support of my armaments people.'

'You mean you don't think you can handle it?'

'Not with my existing organization. Control can. As long, that is, as the Minister doesn't mind bringing in another Department. Two, really. I didn't realize you were so worried about publicity.'

'Two?'

'Control will feel bound to inform the Foreign Office. It's his duty. Just as I inform you. And from then on, we must accept that it will be their headache.'

'If *those* people know,' the Under Secretary said with contempt, 'it'll be round every damned club by tomorrow.'

'There is that danger,' Leclerc conceded. 'More particularly, I wonder whether the Circus has the *military* skills. A rocket site is a complicated affair: launch pads, blast shields, cable troughs; all these things require proper processing and evaluation. Control and I could combine forces, I suppose—'

'That's out of the question. You people make poor bedfellows. Even if you succeeded in co-operating, it would be against policy: no monolith.'

'Ah yes. Of course.'

'Assume you do it yourself, then; assume you find a man, what would that involve?'

'A supplementary estimate. Immediate resources. Extra staff. A training establishment. Ministerial protection; special passes and authority.' The knife again: 'And *some* help from Control . . . we could obtain that under a pretext.'

A foghorn echoed mournfully across the water.

'If it's the only way . . .'

'Perhaps you'd put it to the Minister,' Leclerc suggested.

Silence. Leclerc continued, 'In practical terms we need the best part of thirty thousand pounds.'

'Accountable?'

'Partially. I understood you wanted to be spared details.'

'Except where the Treasury's concerned. I suggest that you make a minute about costs.'

'Very well. Just an outline.'

The silence returned.

'That is hardly a large sum when set against the risk,' the Under Secretary said, consoling himself.

'The potential risk. We want to clarify. I don't pretend to be convinced. Merely suspicious, heavily suspicious.' He couldn't resist adding, 'The Circus would ask twice as much. They're very free with money.'

'Thirty thousand pounds, then, and our protection?'

'And a man. But I must find him for myself.' A small laugh. The Under Secretary said abruptly: 'There are certain details the Minister will not want to know. You realize that?'

'Of course. I imagine you will do most of the talking.'

'I imagine the Minister will. You've succeeded in worrying him a good deal.'

Leclerc remarked with impish piety, 'We should never do that to our master; our common master.'

The Under Secretary did not seem to feel they had one. They stood up.

'Incidentally,' Leclerc said, 'Mrs Taylor's pension. I'm making an application to the Treasury. They feel the Minister should sign it.'

'Why, for God's sake?'

'It's a question of whether he was killed in action.'

The Under Secretary froze. 'That is most presumptuous. You're asking for Ministerial confirmation that Taylor was murdered.'

'I'm asking for a widow's pension,' Leclerc protested gravely. 'He was one of my best men.'

'Of course. They always are.'

The Minister did not look up as they came in.

But the Police Inspector rose from his chair, a short, plump man with a shaven neck. He wore plain clothes. Avery supposed him to be a detective. He shook their hands with an air of professional bereavement, sat them in modern chairs with teak arms and offered cigars out of a tin. They declined, so he lit one himself, and used it thereafter both as a prolongation of his short fingers when making gestures of emphasis, and as a drawing instrument to describe in the smoke-filled air objects of which he was speaking. He deferred frequently to Avery's grief by thrusting his chin downwards into his collar and casting from the shadow of his lowered eyebrows confiding looks of sympathy. First he related the circumstances of the accident, praised in tiresome detail the efforts of the police to track down the car, referred frequently to the personal concern of the President of Police, whose anglophilia was a byword, and stated his own conviction that the guilty man would be found out, and punished with the full severity of Finish law. He dwelt for some time on his own admiration of the British, his affection for the Queen and Sir Winston Churchill, the charms of Finnish neutrality and finally he came to the body.

The post-mortem, he was proud to say, was complete, and Mr Public Prosecutor (his own words) had declared that the circumstances of Mr Malherbe's death gave no grounds for suspicion despite the presence of a considerable amount of alcohol in the blood. The barman at the airport accounted for five glasses of Steinhäger. He returned to Sutherland.

'Does he want to see his brother?' he inquired, thinking it apparently a delicacy to refer the question to a third party.

Sutherland was embarrassed. 'That's up to Mr Avery,' he said, as if the matter were outside his competence. They both looked at Avery.

'I don't think so,' Avery said.

'There is one difficulty. About the identification,' Peersen said.

'Identification?' Avery repeated. 'Of my brother?'

'You saw his passport,' Sutherland put in, 'before you sent it up to me. What's the difficulty?'

The policeman nodded. 'Yes, yes.' Opening a drawer he took out a handful of letters, a wallet and some photographs.

'His name was Malherbe,' he said. He spoke fluent English with a heavy American accent which somehow suited the cigar. 'His passport was Malherbe. It was a *good* passport, wasn't it?' Peersen glanced at Sutherland. For a second Avery thought he detected in Sutherland's clouded face a certain honest hesitation.

'Of course.'

Peersen began to sort through the letters, putting some in a file before him and returning others to the drawer. Every now and then, as he added to the pile, he muttered: 'Ah, so,' or 'Yes, yes.' Avery could feel the sweat running down his body; it drenched his clasped hands.

'And your brother's name was Malherbe?' he asked again, when he had finished his sorting.

Avery nodded. 'Of course.'

Peersen smiled. 'Not of course,' he said, pointing his cigar and nodding in a friendly way as if he were making a debating point. 'All his possessions, his letters, his clothes, driving licence, all belong to Mr Taylor. You know anything of Taylor?'

A dreadful block was forming in Avery's mind. The envelope, what should he do with the envelope? Go to the lavatory, destroy it now before it was too late? He doubted whether it would work: the envelope was stiff and shiny. Even if he tore it, the pieces would float. He was aware of Peersen and Sutherland looking at him, waiting for him to speak and all he could think of was the envelope weighing so heavily in his inside pocket.

He managed to say, 'No, I don't. My brother and I . . .' Step-brother or half-brother? '. . . my brother and I did not have much to do with one another. He was older. We didn't really grow up together. He had a lot of different jobs, he could never quite settle down to anything. Perhaps this Taylor was a friend of his . . . who . . .' Avery shrugged, bravely trying to imply that Malherbe had been something of a mystery to him also.

'How old are you?' Peersen asked. His respect for the bereaved seemed to be dwindling.

'Thirty-two.'

'And Malherbe?' he threw out conversationally. 'He was how

many years older, please?'

Sutherland and Peersen had seen his passport and knew his age. One remembers the age of people who die. Only Avery, his brother, had no idea how old the dead man was.

'Twelve,' he hazarded. 'My brother was forty-four.' Why did he have to say so much?

Peersen raised his eyebrows. 'Only forty-four? Then the passport is wrong as well.'

Peersen turned to Sutherland, poked his cigar towards the door at the far end of the room and said happily, as if he had ended an old argument between friends, 'Now you are seeing why I have a problem about identification.'

Sutherland was looking very angry.

'It would be nice if Mr Avery looked at the body,' Peersen suggested, 'then we can be sure.'

Sutherland said, 'Inspector Peersen. The identity of Mr Malherbe has been established from his passport. The Foreign Office in London has ascertained that Mr Avery's name was quoted by Mr Malherbe as his next of kin. You tell me there is nothing suspicious about the circumstances of his death. The customary procedure is now for you to release his effects to me for custody pending the completion of formalities in the United Kingdom. Mr Avery may presumably take charge of his brother's body.'

Peersen seemed to deliberate. He extracted the remainder of Taylor's papers from the steel drawer of his desk, added them to the pile already in front of him. He telephoned somebody and spoke in Finnish. After some minutes an orderly brought in an old leather suitcase with an inventory which Sutherland signed. Throughout all this, neither Avery nor Sutherland exchanged a word with the Inspector.

Peersen accompanied them all the way to the front door. Sutherland insisted on carrying the suitcase and papers himself. They went to the car. Avery waited for Sutherland to speak, but he said nothing. They drove for about ten minutes. The town was poorly lit. Avery noticed there was chemical on the road, in two lanes. The crown and gutters were still covered with snow. He was reminded of riding in the Mall, a thing he had never done. The street lamps were neon, shedding a sickly light which seemed to shrink before the gathering darkness. Now and then Avery was aware of steep timbered roofs, the clanging of a tram or the tall white hat of a policeman.

Occasionally he stole a glance through the rear window.

Chapter Seven

Woodford stood in the corridor smoking his pipe, grinning at the staff as they left. It was his hour of magic. The mornings were different. Tradition demanded that the junior staff arrived at half past nine; officer grades at ten or quarter past. Theoretically, senior members of the Department stayed late in the evening, clearing their papers. A gentleman, Leclerc would say, never watched the clock. The custom dated from the war, when officers spent the early hours of the morning debriefing reconnaissance pilots back from a run, or the late hours of the night despatching an agent. The junior staff had worked shift in those days, but not the officers, who came and went as their work allowed. Now tradition fulfilled a different purpose. Now there were days, often weeks, when Woodford and his colleagues scarcely knew how to fill the time until five thirty; all but Haldane, who supported on his stooping shoulders the Department's reputation for research. The rest would draft projects which were never submitted, bicker gently among themselves about leave, duty rosters and the quality of their official furniture, give excessive attention to the problems of their section staff.

Berry, the cypher clerk, came into the corridor, stooped and put on his bicycle clips.

'How's the missus, Berry?' Woodford asked. A man must keep his finger on the pulse.

'Doing very nicely, thank you, sir.' He stood up, ran a comb through his hair. 'Shocking about Wilf Taylor, sir.'

'Shocking. He was a good scout.'

'Mr Haldane's locking up Registry, sir. He's working late.'

'Is he? Well, we all have our hands full now.'

Berry lowered his voice. 'And the Boss is sleeping in, sir. Quite a crisis, really. I hear he's gone to see the Minister. They sent a car for him.'

'Goodnight, Berry.' They hear too much, Woodford reflected with satisfaction, and began sauntering along the passage.

The illumination in Haldane's room came from an adjustable reading-lamp. It threw a brief, intense beam on to the file in front of him, touching the contours of his face and hands.

'Working late?' Woodford inquired.

Haldane pushed one file into his out-tray and picked up another.

'Wonder how young Avery's faring; he'll do well, that boy. I hear the Boss isn't back yet. Must be a long session.' As he spoke Woodford settled himself in the leather armchair. It was Haldane's own, he had brought it from his flat and sat in it to do his crossword after luncheon.

'Why should he do well? There is no particular precedent,' Haldane said, without looking up.

'How did Clarkie get on with Taylor's wife?' Woodford now asked. 'How'd she take it?'

Haldane sighed and put his file aside.

'He broke it to her. That's all I know.'

'You didn't hear how she took it? He didn't tell you?'

Woodford always spoke a little louder than necessary, for he was used to competing with his wife.

'I've really no idea. He went alone, I understand. Leclerc prefers to keep these things to himself.'

'I thought perhaps with you . . .'

Haldane shook his head. 'Only Avery.'

'It's a big thing, this, isn't it, Adrian . . . could be?'

'It could be. We shall see,' Haldane said gently. He was not always unkind towards Woodford.

'Anything new on the Taylor front?'

'The Air Attaché at Helsinki has located Lansen. He confirms that he handed Taylor the film. Apparently the Russians intercepted him over Kalkstadt; two MIGS. They buzzed him, then let him go.'

'God,' said Woodford stupidly. 'That clinches it.'

'It does nothing of the kind; it's consistent with what we know. If they declare the area closed why shouldn't they patrol it? They probably closed it for manoeuvres, ground–air exercises. Why didn't they force Lansen down? The whole thing is entirely inconclusive.'

Leclerc was standing in the doorway. He had put on a clean collar for the Minister and a black tie for Taylor.

'I came by car,' he said. 'They've given us one from the Ministry pool on indefinite loan. The Minister was quite distressed to hear we hadn't one. It's a Humber, chauffeur-driven like Control's. They tell me the chauffeur is a secure sort of person.' He looked at Haldane. 'I've decided to form Special Section, Adrian. I want you to take it over. I'm giving Research to Sandford for the time being. The change will do him good.' His face broke into a smile as if he could contain himself no longer. He was very excited. 'We're putting a man in. The Minister's given his consent. We go to work at once. I want to see Heads of Sections first thing tomorrow. Adrian, I'll give you Woodford and Avery. Bruce, you keep in touch with the boys; get on to the old training people. The Minister will support three-month

contracts for temporary staff. No peripheral liabilities, of course.
The usual programme: wireless, weapon training, cyphers, observation, unarmed combat and cover. Adrian, we'll need a house.
Perhaps Avery could go into that when he comes back. I'll approach
Control about documentation; the forgers all went over to him. We'll
want frontier records for the Lübeck area, refugee reports, details of
minefields and obstructions.' He glanced at his watch. 'Adrian, shall
we have a word?'

'Tell me one thing,' Haldane said. 'How much does the Circus
know about this?'

'Whatever we choose to tell them. Why?'

'They know Taylor is dead. It's all over Whitehall.'

'Possibly.'

'They know Avery's picking up a film in Finland. They may very
well have noticed the Air Safety Centre report on Lansen's plane.
They have a way of noticing things . . .'

'Well?'

'So it isn't only a question of what we tell them, is it?'

'You'll come to tomorrow's meeting?' Leclerc asked a little
pathetically.

'I think I have the meat of my instructions. If you have no
objection I would like to make one or two inquiries. This evening
and tomorrow perhaps.'

Leclerc bewildered, said, 'Excellent. Can we help you?'

'Perhaps I might have the use of your car for an hour?'

'Of course. I want us all to use it—to our common benefit.
Adrian—this is for you.'

He handed him a green card in a cellophane folder.

'The Minister signed it, personally.' He implied that, like a Papal
blessing, there were degrees of authenticity in a Ministerial signature. 'Then you'll do it, Adrian? You'll take the job?'

Haldane might not have heard. He had reopened the file and was
looking curiously at the photograph of a Polish boy who had fought
the Germans twenty years ago. It was a young, strict face; humour-
less. It seemed to be concerned not with living but with survival.

'Why, Adrian,' Leclerc cried with sudden relief, 'you've taken the
second vow!'

Reluctantly Haldane smiled, as if the phrase had called to mind
something he thought he had forgotten. 'He seems to have a talent
for survival,' he observed, finally indicating the file. 'Not an easy
man to kill.'

'As next of kin,' Sutherland began, 'you have the right to state your
wishes concerning the disposal of your brother's body.'

'Yes.'

Sutherland's house was a small building with a picture window full of potted plants. Only these distinguished it, either externally or internally, from its model in the dormitory areas of Aberdeen. As they walked down the drive, Avery caught sight of a middle-aged woman in the window. She wore an apron and was dusting something. She reminded him of Mrs Yates and her cat.

'I have an office at the back,' said Sutherland, as if to emphasize that the place was not wholly given over to luxury. 'I suggest we tie up the rest of the details now. I shan't keep you long.' He was telling Avery he needn't expect to stay to supper. 'How do you propose to get him back to England?'

They sat down either side of the desk. Behind Sutherland's head hung a water colour of mauve hills reflected in a Scottish loch.

'I should like it flown home.'

'You know that is an expensive business?'

'I should like him flown all the same.'

'For burial?'

'Of course.'

'It isn't "of course" at all,' Sutherland countered with distaste. If your brother'—he said it in inverted commas now, but he would play the game to the end—'were to be cremated, the flight regulations would be totally different.'

'I see. I'm sorry.'

'There is a firm of undertakers in the town, Barford and Company. One of the partners is English, married to a Swedish girl. There is a substantial Swedish minority here. We do our best to support the British community. In the circumstances I would prefer you to return to London as soon as you can. I suggest you empower me to use Barford.'

'All right.'

'As soon as he has taken over the body, I will provide him with your brother's passport. He will have to obtain a medical certificate regarding the cause of death. I'll put him in touch with Peersen.'

'Yes.'

'He will also require a death certificate issued by a local registrar. It is cheaper if one attends to that side of things oneself. If money matters to your people.'

Avery said nothing.

'When he has found out a suitable flight he will look after the freight warrant and bill of lading. I understand these things are usually moved at night. The freight rate is cheaper and . . .'

'That's all right.'

'I'm glad. Barford will make sure the coffin is airtight. It may be of metal or wood. He will also append his own certificate that the coffin contains nothing but the body—and the same body as that to which the passport and the death certificate refer. I mention this for when you take delivery in London. Barford will do all this very quickly. I shall see to that. He has some pull with the charter companies here. The sooner he—'

'I understand.'

'I'm not sure you do.' Sutherland raised his eyebrows, as if Avery had been impertinent. 'Peersen has been very reasonable. I don't wish to test his patience. Barford will have a correspondent firm in London—it *is* London, isn't it?'

'London, yes.'

'I imagine he will expect some payment in advance. I suggest you leave the money with me against a receipt. As regards your brother's effects, I take it that whoever sent you wished you to recover these letters?' He pushed them across the table.

Avery muttered, 'There was a film, an undeveloped film.' He put the letters in his pocket.

Deliberately Sutherland extracted a copy of the inventory which he had signed at the police station, spread it out before him and ran his finger down the left-hand column, suspiciously, as if he were checking someone else's figures.

'There is no film entered here. Was there a camera too?'

'No.'

'Ah.'

He saw Avery to the door. 'You'd better tell whoever sent you that Malherbe's passport was not valid. The Foreign Office sent out a circular about a group of numbers, twenty-odd. Your brother's was one of them. There must have been a slip-up. I was about to report it when a Foreign Office teleprint arrived empowering you to take over Malherbe's effects.' He gave a short laugh. He was very angry. 'That was nonsense, of course. The Office would never have sent that on their own. They've no authority, not unless you'd Letters of Administration, and you couldn't have got *those* in the middle of the night. Have you somewhere to stay? The Regina's quite good, near the airport. Out of town, too. I assume you can find your own way. I gather you people get excellent subsistence.'

Avery made his way quickly down the drive, carrying in his memory the indelible image of Sutherland's thin, bitter face set angrily against the Scottish hills. The wooden houses beside the road shone half white in the darkness like shadows round an operating table.

Somewhere not far from Charing Cross, in the basement of one of those surprising eighteenth-century houses between Villiers Street and the river, is a club with no name on the door. You reach it by descending a curving stone staircase. The railing, like the woodwork of the house in Blackfriars Road, is painted dark green and needs replacing.

Its members are an odd selection. Some of a military kind, some in the teaching profession, others clerical; others again from that no-man's-land of London society which lies between the bookmaker and the gentleman, presenting to those around them, and perhaps even to themselves, an image of vacuous courage; conversing in codes and phrases which a man with a sense of language can only listen to at a distance. It is a place of old faces and young bodies; of young faces and old bodies; where the tensions of war have become the tensions of peace, and voices are raised to drown the silence, and glasses to drown the loneliness; it is the place where the searchers meet, finding no one but each other and the comfort of a shared pain; where the tired watchful eyes have no horizon to observe. It is their battlefield still; if there is love, they find it here in one another, shyly like adolescents, thinking all the time of other people.

From the war, none but the dons were missing.

It is a small place, run by a thin, dry man called Major Dell; he has a moustache and a tie with blue angels on a black background. He stands the first drink, and they buy him the others. It is called the Alias Club, and Woodford was a member.

It is open in the evenings. They come at about six, detaching themselves with pleasure from the moving crowd, furtive but determined, like men from out of town visiting a disreputable theatre. You notice first the things that are not there: no silver cups behind the bar, no visitors' book nor list of membership; no insignia, crest or title. Only on the whitewashed brick walls a few photo-graphs hang, framed in passe-partout, like the photographs in Leclerc's room. The faces are indistinct, some enlarged, apparently from a passport, taken from the front with both ears showing according to the regulation; some are of women, a few of them attractive, with high square shoulders and long hair after the fashion of the war years. The men are wearing a variety of uniforms; Free French and Poles mingle with their British comrades. Some are fliers. Of the English faces one or two, grown old, still haunt the club.

When Woodford came in everyone looked round and Major Dell, much pleased, ordered his pint of beer. A florid, middle-aged man was talking about a sortie he once made over Belgium but he stopped when he lost the attention of his audience.

'Hello, Woodie,' somebody said in surprise. 'How's the lady?'

'Fit,' Woodford smiled genially. 'Fit.' He drank some beer. Cigarettes were passed round. Major Dell said, 'Woodie's jolly shifty tonight.'

'I'm looking for someone. It's all a bit top secret.'

'We know the form,' the florid man replied. Woodford glanced round the bar and asked quietly, a note of mystery in his voice, 'What did Dad do in the war?'

A bewildered silence. They had been drinking for some time.

'Kept Mum, of course,' said Major Dell uncertainly and they all laughed.

Woodford laughed with them, savouring the conspiracy, reliving the half-forgotten ritual of secret mess nights somewhere in England.

'And where did he keep her?' he demanded, still in the same confiding tone: this time two or three voices called in unison, 'Under his blooming hat!'

They were louder, happier.

'There was a man called Johnson,' Woodford continued quickly, 'Jack Johnson. I'm trying to find out what became of him. He was a trainer in wireless transmission; one of the best. He was at Bovingdon first with Haldane until they moved him up to Oxford.'

'Jack Johnson!' the florid man cried excitedly. 'The WT man? I bought a car radio from Jack two weeks ago! Johnson's Fair Deal in the Clapham Broadway, that's the fellow. Drops in here from time to time. Amateur wireless enthusiast. Little bloke, speaks out of the side of his face?'

'That's him,' someone else said. 'He knocks off twenty per cent for the old gang.'

'He didn't for me,' the florid man said.

'That's Jack; he lives at Clapham.'

The others took it up: that was the fellow and he ran this shop, at Clapham; king of ham radio, been a ham before the war even when he was a kid; yes, on the Broadway, hung out there for years; must be worth a ransom. Liked to come into the club round Christmas time. Woodford, flushed with pleasure, ordered drinks.

In the bustle that followed, Major Dell took Woodford gently by the arm and guided him to the other end of the bar.

'Woodie, is it true about Wilf Taylor? Has he really bought it?'

Woodford nodded, his face grave. 'He was on a job. We think someone's been a little bit naughty.'

Major Dell was all solicitude. 'I haven't told the boys. It would only worry them. Who's caring for the Missus?'

'The Boss is taking that up now. It looks pretty hopeful.'

'Good,' said the Major. 'Good.' He nodded, patting Woodford's arm in a gesture of consolation. 'We'll keep it from the boys, shall we?'

'Of course.'

'He had one or two bills. Nothing very big. He liked to drop in Friday nights.' The Major's accent slipped from time to time like a made-up tie.

'Send them along. We'll take care of those.'

'There was a kid, wasn't there? A little girl?' They were moving back to the bar. 'How old was she?'

'Eightish. Maybe more.'

'He talked about her a lot,' said the Major.

Somebody called, 'Hey, Bruce, when are you chaps going to take another crack at the Jerries? They're all over the bloody place. Took the wife to Italy in the Summer–full of arrogant Germans.'

Woodford smiled. 'Sooner than you think. Now let's try this one.' The conversation died. Woodford was real. He still did the job.

'There was an unarmed combat man, a staff sergeant; a Welshman. He was short too.'

'Sounds like Sandy Lowe,' the florid man suggested.

'Sandy, that's him!' They all turned to the florid man in admiration. 'He was a Taffy. Randy Sandy we called him.'

'Of course,' said Woodford contentedly. 'Now didn't he go off to some public school as a boxing instructor?' He was looking at them narrowly, holding a good deal back, playing it long because it was so secret.

'That's him, that's Sandy!'

Woodford wrote it down, taking care because he had learnt from experience that he tended to forget things which he entrusted to memory.

As he was going, the Major asked, 'How's Clarkie?'

'Busy,' Woodford said. 'Working himself to death, as always.'

'The boys talk about him a lot, you know. I wish he'd come here now and then; give them a hell of a boost, you know. Perk them up.'

'Tell me,' said Woodford. They were by the door. 'Do you remember a fellow called Leiser? Fred Leiser, a Pole? Used to be with our lot. He was in the Holland show.'

'Still alive?'

'Yes.'

'Sorry,' said the Major vaguely. 'The foreigners have stopped coming; I don't know why. I don't discuss it with the boys.'

Closing the door behind him, Woodford stepped into the London night. He looked about him, loving all he saw–the mother city in his rugged care. He walked slowly, an old athlete on an old track.

Chapter Eight

Avery, on the other hand, walked fast. He was afraid. There is no terror so consistent, so elusive to describe, as that which haunts a spy in a strange country. The glance of a taxi driver, the density of people in the street, the variety of official uniform–was he a policeman or a postman?–the obscurity of custom and language, and the very noises which comprised the world into which Avery had moved contributed to a state of constant anxiety, which, like a nervous pain, became virulent now that he was alone. In the shortest time his spirit ranged between panic and cringing love, responding with unnatural gratitude to a kind glance or word. It was part of an effeminate dependence upon those whom he deceived. Avery needed desperately to win from the uncaring faces around him the absolution of a trusting smile. It was no help that he told himself: you do them no harm, you are their protector. He moved among them like a hunted man in search of rest and food.

He took a cab to the hotel and asked for a room with a bath. They gave him the register to sign. He had actually put his pen to the page when he saw, not ten lines above, done in a laborious hand, the name Malherbe, broken in the middle as if the writer could not spell it. His eye followed the entry along the line: Address, London; Profession, Major (retired); Destination, London. His last vanity, Avery thought, a false profession, a false rank, but little English Taylor had stolen a moment's glory. Why not Colonel? Or Admiral? Why not give himself a peerage and an address in Park Lane? Even when he dreamed, Taylor had known his limits.

The concierge said, 'The valet will take your luggage.'

'I'm sorry,' said Avery, a meaningless apology, and signed his name, while the man watched him curiously.

He gave the valet a coin and it occurred to him as he did so that he had given him eight and six. He closed the bedroom door. For a while he sat on his bed. It was a carefully planned room but bleak and without sympathy. On the door was a notice in several languages warning against the perils of theft, and by the bed another which explained the financial disadvantages of failing to breakfast in the hotel. There was a magazine about travel on the writing-desk, and a Bible bound in black. There was a small bathroom, very clean, and a built-in wardrobe with one coat-hanger. He had forgotten to bring a book. He had not anticipated having to endure leisure.

He was cold and hungry. He thought he would have a bath. He ran it and undressed. He was about to get into the water when he remembered Taylor's letters in his pocket. He put on a dressing-gown, sat on the bed and looked through them. One from his bank about an overdraft, one from his mother, one from a friend which began Dear Old Wilf, the rest from a woman. He was suddenly frightened of the letters: they were evidence. They could compromise him. He determined to burn them all. There was a second basin in the bedroom. He put all the papers into it and held a match to them. He had read somewhere that was the thing to do. There was a membership card for the Alias Club made out in Taylor's name so he burnt that too, then broke up the ash with his fingers and turned on the water; it rose swiftly. The plug was a built-in metal affair operated by a lever between the taps. The sodden ash was packed beneath it. The basin was blocked.

He looked for some instrument to probe under the lip of the plug. He tried his fountain pen but it was too fat, so he fetched the nail file. After repeated attempts he persuaded the ash into the outlet. The water ran away, revealing a heavy brown stain on the enamel. He rubbed it, first with his hand then with the scrubbing brush, but it wouldn't go. Enamel didn't stain like that, there must have been some quality in the paper, tar or something. He went into the bathroom, looking vainly for a detergent.

As he re-entered his bedroom he became aware that it was filled with the smell of charred paper. He went quickly to the window and opened it. A blast of freezing wind swept over his naked limbs. He was gathering the dressing-gown more closely about him when there was a knock on the door. Paralysed with fear, he stared at the door handle, heard another knock, called, watched the handle turn. It was the man from Reception.

'Mr Avery?'

'Yes?'

'I'm sorry. We need your passport. For the police.'

'Police.'

'It's the customary procedure.'

Avery had backed against the basin. The curtains were flapping wildly beside the open window.

'May I close the window?' the man asked.

'I wasn't well. I wanted some fresh air.'

He found his passport and handed it over. As he did so, he saw the man's gaze fixed upon the basin, on the brown mark and the small flakes which still clung to the sides.

He wished as never before that he was back in England.

The row of villas which lines Western Avenue is like a row of pink graves in a field of grey; an architectural image of middle age. Their uniformity is the discipline of growing old, of dying without violence and living without success. They are houses which have got the better of their occupants, whom they change at will, and do not change themselves. Furniture vans glide respectfully among them like hearses, discreetly removing the dead and introducing the living. Now and then some tenant will raise his hand, expending pots of paint on the woodwork or labour on the garden, but his efforts no more alter the house than flowers a hospital ward, and the grass will grow its own way, like grass on a grave.

Haldane dismissed the car and turned off the road towards South Park Gardens, a crescent five minutes from the Avenue. A school, a post office, four shops and a bank. He stooped a little as he walked; a black briefcase hung from his thin hand. He made his way quietly along the pavement; the tower of a modern church rose above the houses; a clock struck seven. A grocer's on the corner, new façade, self-service. He looked at the name: Smethwick. Inside, a youngish man in a brown overall was completing a pyramid of cereal foods. Haldane rapped on the glass. The man shook his head and added a packet to the pyramid. He knocked again, sharply. The grocer came to the door.

'I'm not allowed to sell you anything,' he shouted, 'so it's no good knocking, is it?' He noticed the briefcase and asked, 'Are you a rep, then?'

Haldane put his hand in his inside pocket and held something to the window—a card in a cellophane wrapper like a season ticket. The grocer stared at it. Slowly he turned the key.

'I want a word with you in private,' Haldane said, stepping inside.

'I've never seen one of those,' the grocer observed uneasily. 'I suppose it's all right.'

'It's quite all right. A security inquiry. Someone called Leiser, a Pole. I understand he worked here long ago.'

'I'll have to call my Dad,' the grocer said. 'I was only a kid then.'

'I see,' said Haldane, as if he disliked youth.

It was nearly midnight when Avery rang Leclerc. He answered straight away. Avery could imagine him sitting up in the steel bed, the Air Force blankets thrown back, his small, alert face anxious for the news.

'It's John,' he said cautiously.

'Yes, yes, I know who you are.' He sounded cross that Avery had mentioned his name.

'The deal's off I'm afraid. They're not interested . . . negative. You'd better tell the man I saw; the little, fat man . . . tell him we shan't need the services of his friend here.'

'I see. Never mind.' He sounded utterly uninterested.

Avery didn't know what to say; he just didn't know. He needed desperately to go on talking to Leclerc. He wanted to tell him about Sutherland's contempt and the passport that wasn't right. 'The people here, the people I'm negotiating with, are rather worried about the whole deal.'

He waited.

He wanted to call him by his name but he had no name for him. They did not use 'Mister' in the Department; the elder men addressed one another by their surnames and called the juniors by their Christian names. There was no established style of addressing one's superior. So he said, 'Are you still there?' and Leclerc replied, 'Of course. Who's worried? What's gone wrong?' Avery thought: I could have called him 'Director', but that would have been insecure.

'The representative here, the man who looks after our interests . . . he's found out about the deal,' he said. 'He seems to have guessed.'

'You stressed it was highly confidential?'

'Yes, of course.' How could he ever explain about Sutherland?

'Good. We don't want any trouble with the Foreign Office just now.' In an altered tone Leclerc continued, 'Things are going very well over here, John, very well. When do you get back?'

'I've got to cope with the . . . with bringing our friend home. There are a lot of formalities. It's not as easy as you'd think.'

'When will you be finished?'

'Tomorrow.'

'I'll send a car to meet you at Heathrow. A lot's happened in the last few hours; a lot of improvements. We need you badly.' Leclerc added, throwing him a coin, 'And well done, John, well done indeed.'

'All right.'

He expected to sleep heavily that night, but after what might have been an hour he woke, alert and watchful. He looked at his watch; it was ten past one. Getting out of bed he went to the window and looked on to the snow-covered landscape, marked by the darker lines of the road which led to the airport; he thought he could discern the little rise where Taylor had died.

He was desolate and afraid. His mind was obsessed by confused visions: Taylor's dreadful face, the face he so nearly saw, drained of blood, wide-eyed as if communicating a crucial discovery; Leclerc's voice, filled with vulnerable optimism; the fat policeman, staring at him in envy, as if he were something he could not afford to buy. He realized he was a person who did not take easily to solitude. Solitude saddened him, made him sentimental. He found himself thinking, for the first time since he had left the flat that morning, of Sarah and Anthony. Tears came suddenly to his tired eyes when he recalled his boy, the steel-rimmed spectacles like tiny irons; he wanted to hear his voice, he wanted Sarah, and the familiarity of his home. Perhaps he could telephone the flat, speak to her mother, ask after her. But what if she were ill? He had suffered enough pain that day, he had given enough of his energy, fear and invention. He had lived a nightmare: he could not be expected to ring her now. He went back to bed.

Try as he might, he could not sleep. His eyelids were hot and heavy, his body deeply tired, but still he could not sleep. A wind rose, rattling the double windows; now he was too hot, now too cold. Once he dozed, only to be woken violently from his uneasy rest by the sound of crying, it might have been in the next room, it might have been Anthony, or it might have been—since he did not hear it properly, but only half knew in waking what kind of a sound it had been—the metallic sobbing of a child's doll.

And once, it was shortly before dawn, he heard a footfall outside his room, a single tread in the corridor, not imagined but real, and he lay in chill terror waiting for the handle of his door to turn or the peremptory knocking of Inspector Peersen's men. As he strained his ears he swore he detected the faintest rustle of clothing, the subdued intake of human breath, like a tiny sigh; then silence. Though he listened for minutes on end, he heard nothing more.

Putting on the light, he went to the chair, felt in his jacket for his fountain pen. It was by the basin. From his briefcase he took a leather holdall which Sarah had given him.

Settling himself at the flimsy table in front of the window, he began writing a love letter to a girl, it might have been to Carol. When at last morning came, he destroyed it, tearing it into small pieces and flushing them down the lavatory. As he did so he caught sight of something white on the floor. It was a photograph of Taylor's child carrying a doll; she was wearing glasses, the kind Anthony wore. It must have been among his papers. He thought of destroying it but somehow he couldn't. He slipped it into his pocket.

Chapter Nine
HOMECOMING

Leclerc was waiting at Heathrow as Avery knew he would be, standing on tiptoe, peering anxiously between the heads of the waiting crowd. He had squared the customs somehow, he must have got the Ministry to do it, and when he saw Avery he came forward into the hall and guided him in a managing way as if he were used to being spared formalities. This is the life we lead, Avery thought; the same airport with different names; the same hurried, guilty meetings; we live outside the walls of the town, black friars from a dark house in Lambeth. He was desperately tired. He wanted Sarah. He wanted to say sorry, make it up with her, get a new job, try again, play with Anthony more. He felt ashamed.

'I'll just make a telephone call. Sarah wasn't too well when I left.'

'Do it from the Office,' Leclerc said. 'Do you mind? I have a meeting with Haldane in an hour.' Thinking he detected a false note in Leclerc's voice, Avery looked at him suspiciously, but the other's eyes were turned away towards the black Humber standing in the privilege car park. Leclerc let the driver open the door for him; a silly muddle took place until Avery sat on his left as protocol apparently demanded. The driver seemed tired of waiting. There was no partition between him and themselves.

'This is a change,' Avery said, indicating the car.

Leclerc nodded in a familiar way as if the acquisition were no longer new. 'How are things?' he asked, his mind elsewhere.

'All right. There's nothing the matter, is there? With Sarah, I mean.'

'Why should there be?'

'Blackfriars Road?' the driver inquired, without turning his head, as a sense of respect might have indicated.

'Headquarters, yes, please.'

'There was a hell of a mess in Finland,' Avery observed brutally. 'Our friend's papers . . . Malherbe's . . . weren't in order. The Foreign Office had cancelled his passport.'

'Malherbe? Ah yes. You mean Taylor. We know all about that. It's all right now. Just the usual jealousy. Control is rather upset about it, as a matter of fact. He sent round to apologize. We've a lot of people on our side now, John, you've no idea. You're going to be very useful, John; you're the only one who's seen it on the ground.' Seen what? Avery wondered. They were together again. The same intensity, the same physical unease, the same absences. As Leclerc turned to him Avery thought for one sickening moment he was going to put a hand on his knee. 'You're tired, John, I can tell. I know how it feels. Never mind—you're back with us now. Listen, I've good news for you. The Ministry's woken up to us in a big way. We're to form a special operational unit to mount the next phase.'

'Next phase?'

'Of course. The man I mentioned to you. We can't leave things as they are. We're clarifiers, John, not simply collators. I've revived Special Section; do you know what that is?'

'Haldane ran it during the war; training . . .'

Leclerc interrupted quickly for the driver's sake: '. . . training the travelling salesmen. And he's going to run it again now. I've decided you're to work with him. You're the two best brains I've got.' A sideways glance.

Leclerc had altered. There was a new quality to his bearing, something more than optimism or hope. When Avery had seen him last he had seemed to be living against adversity; now he had a freshness about him, a purpose, which was either new or very old.

'And Haldane accepted?'

'I told you. He's working night and day. You forget, Adrian's a professional. A real technician. Old heads are the best for a job like this. With one or two young heads among them.'

Avery said, 'I want to talk to you about the whole operation . . . about Finland. I'll come to your office after I've rung Sarah.'

'Come straight away, then I can put you in the picture.'

'I'll phone Sarah first.'

Again Avery had the unreasonable feeling that Leclerc was trying to keep him from communicating with Sarah.

'She *is* all right, isn't she?'

'So far as I know. Why do you ask?' Leclerc went on, charming him: 'Glad to be back, John?'

'Yes, of course.'

He sank back into the cushions of the car. Leclerc, noticing his hostility, abandoned him for a time; Avery turned his attention to the road and the pink, healthy villas drifting past in the light rain.

Leclerc was talking again, his committee voice, 'I want you to start straight away. Tomorrow if you can. We've got your room ready. There's a lot to be done. This man: Haldane has him in play. We should hear something when we get home. From now on you're Adrian's creature. I trust that pleases you. Our masters have agreed to provide you with a special Ministry pass. The same kind of thing that they have in the Circus.'

Avery was familiar with Leclerc's habit of speech; there were times when he resorted entirely to oblique allusion, offering a raw material which the consumer, not the purveyor, must refine.

'I want to talk to you about the whole thing. When I've rung Sarah.'

'That's right,' Leclerc replied nicely. 'Come and talk to me about it. Why not come now?' He looked at Avery, offering his whole face; a thing without depth, a moon with one side. 'You've done well,' he said generously, 'I hope you'll keep it up.' They entered London. 'We're getting some help from the Circus,' he added. 'They seem to be quite willing. They don't know the whole picture of course. The Minister was very firm on that point.'

They passed down Lambeth Road, where the God of Battle presides; the Imperial War Museum one end, schools the other, hospitals in between; a cemetery wired off like a tennis court. You cannot tell who lives there. The houses are too many for the people, the schools too large for the children. The hospitals may be full, but the blinds are drawn. Dust hangs everywhere, like the dust of war. It hangs over the hollow façades, chokes the grass in the graveyard: it has driven away the people, save those who loiter in the dark places like the ghosts of soldiers, or wait sleepless behind their yellow-lighted windows. It is a road which people seem to have left often. The few who returned brought something of the living world, according to their voyages. One piece of field, another a broken Regency terrace, a warehouse or dumping yard; or a pub called the Flowers of the Forest.

It is a road filled with faithful institutions. Over one presides Our Lady of Consolation, over another, Archbishop Amigo. Whatever is not hospital, school, pub or seminary is dead, and the dust has got its body. There is a toyshop with a padlocked door. Avery looked into it every day on the way to the office; the toys were rusting on the shelves. The window looked dirtier than ever; the lower part was striped with children's fingermarks. There is a place that mends your teeth while you wait. He glimpsed them now from the car, counting them off as they drove past, wondering whether he would ever see them again as a member of the Department. There are warehouses with barbed wire across their gates, and factories which produce nothing. In one of them a bell rang but no one heard. There is a broken wall with posters on it. You are somebody today in the Regular Army. They rounded St George's Circus and entered Blackfriars Road for the home run.

As they approached the building, Avery sensed that things had changed. For a moment he imagined that the very grass on the wretched bit of lawn had thickened and revived during his brief absence; that the concrete steps leading to the front door, which even in Midsummer managed to appear moist and dirty, were now clean and inviting. Somehow he knew, before he entered the building at all, that a new spirit had infected the Department.

It had reached the most humble members of the staff. Pine, impressed no doubt by the black staff car and the sudden passage of busy people, looked spruce and alert. For once he said nothing about cricket scores. The stair case was daubed with wax polish.

In the corridor they met Woodford. He was in a hurry. He was carrying a couple of files with red caution notices on the cover.

'Hullo, John! You've landed safely, then? Good party?' He really did seemed pleased to see him. 'Sarah all right now?'

'He's done well,' said Leclerc quickly. 'He had a very difficult run.'

'Ah yes; poor Taylor. We shall need you in the new section. Your wife will have to spare you for a week or two.'

'What was that about Sarah?' Avery asked. Suddenly he was frightened. He hastened down the corridor. Leclerc was calling but he took no notice. He entered his room and stopped dead. There was a second telephone on his desk, and a steel bed like Leclerc's along the side wall. Beside the new telephone was a piece of military board with a list of emergency telephone numbers pinned to it. The numbers for use during the night were printed in red. On the back of the door hung a two-colour poster depicting in profile the head of a man. Across his skull was written, 'Keep it here', and across his mouth, 'Don't let it out here'. It took him a moment or two to realize that the poster was an exhortation to security, and not some dreadful joke about Taylor. He lifted the receiver and waited. Carol came in with a tray of papers for signature.

'How did it go?' she asked. 'The Boss seems pleased.' She was standing quite close to him.

'Go? There's no film. It wasn't among his things. I'm going to resign; I've decided. What the hell's wrong with this phone?'

'They probably don't know you're back. There's a thing from Accounts about your claim for a taxi. They've queried it.'

'Taxi?'

'From your flat to the office. The night Taylor died. They say it's too much.'

'Look, go and stir up the exchange, will you, they must be fast asleep.'

Sarah answered the telephone herself.

'Oh, thank God it's you.'

Avery said yes, he had got in an hour ago. 'Sarah, look, I've had enough, I'm going to tell Leclerc—' But before he could finish she burst out, 'John, for *God's* sake, what *have* you been doing? We had the police here, detectives; they want to talk to you about a body that's arrived at London airport; somebody called Malherbe. They say it was sent from Finland on a false passport.'

He closed his eyes. He wanted to put down the receiver, he held it away from his ear but he still heard her voice, saying John, John. 'They say he's your brother; it's addressed to *you*, John; some London undertaker was supposed to be doing it all for you . . . John, John, are you still there?'

'Listen,' he said, 'it's all right. I'll take care of it now.'

'I told them about Taylor: I had to.'

'Sarah!'

'What else could I do? They thought I was a criminal or something; they didn't believe me, John! They asked how they could get hold of you; I had to say I didn't know; I didn't even know which country or which plane; I was ill, John, I felt awful, I've got this damn 'flu and I'd forgotten to take my pills. They came in the middle of the night, two of them. John, why did they come in the night?'

'What did you tell them? For Christ's sake, Sarah, what else did you say to them?'

'Don't swear at me! I should be swearing at you and your beastly Department! I said you were doing something secret; you'd had to go abroad for the Department—John, I don't even know its *name*!—that you'd been rung in the night and you'd gone away. I said it was about a courier called Taylor.'

'You're mad,' Avery shouted, 'you're absolutely mad. I told you never to say!'

'But, John, they were *policemen*! There can't be any harm in telling them.' She was crying, he could hear the tears in her voice. 'John, *please* come back. I'm so frightened. You've got to get out of this, go back to publishing; I don't care what you do but . . .'

'I can't. It's terribly big. More important than you can possibly understand. I'm sorry, Sarah. I just can't leave the office.' He added savagely, a useful lie, 'You may have wrecked the whole thing.'

There was a very long silence.

'Sarah, I'll have to sort this out. I'll ring you later.'

When at last she answered he detected in her voice the same flat resignation with which she had sent him to pack his things. 'You took the cheque book. I've no money.'

He told her he would send it round. 'We've got a car,' he added, "specially for this thing, chauffeur driven.' As he rang off he heard her say, 'I thought you'd got lots of cars.'

He ran into Leclerc's room. Haldane was standing behind the desk; his coat still wet from the rain. They were bent over a file. The pages were faded and torn.

'Taylor's body!' he blurted out. 'It's at London Airport. You've messed the whole thing up. They've been on to Sarah! In the middle of the night!'

'Wait!' It was Haldane who spoke. 'You have no business to come running in here,' he declared furiously. 'Just wait.' He did not care for Avery.

He returned to the file, ignoring him. 'None at all,' he muttered, adding to Leclerc: 'Woodford has already had some success, I gather. Unarmed combat's all right; he's heard of a wireless operator, one of the best. I remember him. The garage is called the King of Hearts; it is clearly prosperous. We inquired at the bank; they were quite helpful if not specific. He's unmarried. He has a reputation for women; the usual Polish style. No political interests, no known hobbies, no debts, no complaints. He seems to be something of a nonentity. They say he's a good mechanic. As for character—' he shrugged. 'What do we know about anybody?'

'But what did they *say*? Good Heavens, you can't be fifteen years in a community without leaving *some* impression. There was a grocer wasn't there–Smethwick?–he lived with them after the war.'

Haldane allowed himself a smile. 'They said he was a good worker and very polite. Everyone says he's polite. They remember one thing only: he had a passion for hitting a tennis ball round their backyard.'

'Did you take a look at the garage?'

'Certainly not. I didn't go near it. I propose to call there this evening. I don't see that we have any other choice. After all, the man's been on our cards for twenty years.'

'Is there nothing more you can find out?'

'We would have to do the rest through the Circus.'

'Then let John Avery clear up the details.' Leclerc seemed to have forgotten Avery was in the room. 'As for the Circus, I'll deal with them myself.' His interest had been arrested by a new map on the wall, a town plan of Kalkstadt showing the church and railway station. Beside it hung an older map of Eastern Europe. Rocket bases whose existence had already been confirmed were here related to the putative site south of Rostock. Supply routes and chains of command, the order of battle of supporting arms, were indicated with lines of thin wool stretched between pins. A number of these led to Kalkstadt.

'It's good, isn't it? Sandford put it together last night,' Leclerc said. 'He does that kind of thing rather well.'

On his desk lay a new whitewood pointer like a giant bodkin threaded with a loop of barrister's ribbon. He had a new telephone, green, smarter than Avery's, with a notice on it saying 'Speech on this telephone is NOT secure.' For a time Haldane and Leclerc studied the map, referring now and then to a file of telegrams which Leclerc held open in both hands as a choirboy holds a psalter.

Finally Leclerc turned to Avery and said, 'Now, John.' They were waiting for him to speak.

He could feel his anger dying. He wanted to hold on to it but it was slipping away. He wanted to cry out in indignation: how dare you involve my wife? He wanted to lose control, but he could not. His eyes were on the map.

'Well?'

'The police have been round to Sarah. They woke her in the middle of the night. Two men. Her mother was there. They came about the body at the airport: Taylor's body. They knew the passport was phoney and thought she was involved. They woke her up,' he repeated lamely.

'We know all about that. It's straightened out. I wanted to tell you but you wouldn't let me. The body's been released.'

'It was wrong to drag Sarah in.'

Haldane lifted his head quickly: 'What do you mean by that?'

'We're not competent to handle this kind of thing.' It sounded very impertinent. 'We shouldn't be doing it. We ought to give it to the Circus. Smiley or someone–they're the people, not us.' He struggled on: 'I don't even believe that report. I don't believe it's true! I wouldn't be surprised if that refugee never existed; if Gorton made the whole thing up! I don't believe Taylor was murdered.'

'Is that all?' Haldane demanded. He was very angry.

'It's not something I want to go on with. The operation, I mean. It isn't right.'

He looked at the map and at Haldane, then laughed a little stupidly. 'All the time I've been chasing a dead man you've been after a live one! It's easy here, in the dream factory . . . but they're people out there, real people!'

Leclerc touched Haldane lightly on the arm as if to say he would handle this himself. He seemed undisturbed. He might almost have been gratified to recognize symptoms which he had previously diagnosed. 'Go to your room, John, you're suffering from strain.'

'But what do I tell Sarah?' He spoke with despair.

'Tell her she won't be troubled any more. Tell her it was a mistake . . . tell her whatever you like. Get some hot food and come back in an hour. These airline meals are useless. Then we'll hear the rest of your news.' Leclerc was smiling, the same neat, bland smile with which he had stood among the dead fliers. As Avery reached the door he heard his name called softly, with affection: he stopped and looked back.

Leclerc raised one hand from the desk and with a semicircular movement indicated the room in which they were standing.

'I'll tell you something, John. During the war we were in Baker Street. We had a cellar and the Ministry fixed it up as an emergency operations room. Adrian and I spent a lot of time down there. *A lot* of time.' A glance at Haldane. 'Remember how the oil lamp used to swing when the bombs fell? We had to face situations where we had one rumour, John, no more. One indicator and we'd take the risk. Send a man in, two if necessary, and maybe they wouldn't come back. Maybe there wouldn't be anything there. Rumours, a guess, a hunch one follows up; it's easy to forget what intelligence consists of: luck and speculation. Here and there a windfall, here and there a scoop. Sometimes you stumbled on a thing like this: it could be very big, it could be a shadow. It may have been from a peasant in Flensburg, or it may come from the Provost of King's, but you're left with a possibility you dare not discount. You get instructions: find a man, put him in. So we did. And many *didn't* come back. They were sent to resolve doubt, don't you see? We sent them because we didn't know. All of us have moments like this, John. Don't think it's always easy.' A reminiscent smile. 'Often we had scruples like you. We had to overcome them. We used to call that the second vow.' He leant against the desk, informally. 'The second vow,' he repeated.

'Now, John, if you want to wait until the bombs are falling, till people are dying in the street . . .' He was suddenly serious, as if revealing his faith. 'It's a great deal harder, I know, in peacetime. It requires courage. Courage of a different kind.'

Avery nodded. 'I'm sorry,' he said.

Haldane was watching him with distaste.

'What the Director means,' he said acidly, 'is that if you wish to stay in the Department and do the job, do it. If you wish to cultivate your emotions, go elsewhere and do so in peace. We are too old for your kind here.'

Avery could still hear Sarah's voice, see the rows of little houses hanging in the rain; he tried to imagine his life without the Department. He realized that it was too late, as it always had been, because he had gone to them for the little they could give him, and they had taken the little he had. Like a doubting cleric, he had felt that whatever his small heart contained was safely locked in the place of his retreat: now it was gone. He looked at Leclerc, then at Haldane. They were his colleagues. Prisoners of silence, the three of them would work side by side, breaking the arid land all four seasons of the year, strangers to each other, needing each other, in a wilderness of abandoned faith.

'Did you hear what I said?' Haldane demanded.

Avery muttered: 'Sorry.'

'You didn't fight in the war, John,' Leclerc said kindly. 'You don't understand how these things take people. You don't understand what real duty is.'

'I know,' said Avery. 'I'm sorry. I'd like to borrow the car for an hour . . . send something round to Sarah, if that's all right.'

'Of course.'

He realized he had forgotten Anthony's present. 'I'm sorry,' he said again.

'Incidentally—' Leclerc opened a drawer of the desk and took out an envelope. Indulgently he handed it to Avery. 'That's your pass, a special one from the Ministry. To identify yourself. It's in your own name. You may need it in the weeks to come.'

'Thanks.'

'Open it.'

It was a piece of thick pasteboard bound in cellophane, green, the colour washed downwards, darker at the bottom. His name was printed across it in capitals with an electric typewriter: Mr John Avery. The legend entitled the bearer to make inquiries on behalf of the Ministry. There was a signature in red ink.

'Thanks.'

'You're safe with that,' Leclerc said. 'The Minister signed it. He uses red ink, you know. It's tradition.'

He went back to his room. There were times when he confronted his own image as a man confronts an empty valley, and the vision propelled him forward again to experience, as despair compels us to extinction. Sometimes he was like a man in flight, but running towards the enemy, desperate to feel upon his vanishing body the blows that would prove his being; desperate to imprint upon his sad conformity the mark of real purpose, desperate perhaps, as Leclerc had hinted, to abdicate his conscience in order to discover God.

BOOK THREE

LEISER'S RUN

To turn as swimmers into cleanness leaping
Glad from a world grown old and cold and weary.
RUPERT BROOKE, *1914*

Chapter Ten
PRELUDE

The Humber dropped Haldane at the garage.

'You needn't wait. You have to take Mr Leclerc to the Ministry.'

He picked his way reluctantly over the tarmac, past the yellow petrol pumps and the advertisement shields rattling in the wind. It was evening; there was rain about. The garage was small but very smart; showrooms one end, workshops the other, in the middle a tower where somebody lived. Swedish timber and open plan; lights on the tower in the shape of a heart, changing colour continuously. From somewhere came the whine of a metal lathe. Haldane went into the office. It was empty. There was a smell of rubber. He rang the bell and began coughing wretchedly. Sometimes when he coughed he held his chest, and his face betrayed the submissiveness of a man familiar with pain. Calendars with showgirls hung on the wall beside a small handwritten notice, like an amateur advertisement, which read, 'St Christopher and all his angels, please protect us from road accidents. F.L.' At the window a budgerigar fluttered nervously in its cage. The first drops of rain thumped lazily against the panes. A boy came in, about eighteen, his fingers black with engine oil. He wore an overall with a red heart sewn to the breast pocket with a crown above it.

'Good evening,' said Haldane. 'Forgive me. I'm looking for an old acquaintance; a friend. We knew one another long ago. A Mr Leiser. Fred Leiser. I wondered if you had any idea . . .'

'I'll get him,' the boy said, and disappeared.

Haldane waited patiently, looking at the calendars and wondering whether it was the boy or Leiser who had hung them there. The door opened a second time. It was Leiser. Haldane recognized him from his photograph. There was really very little change. The twenty years were not drawn in forceful lines but in tiny webs beside each eye, in marks of discipline around the mouth. The light above him was diffuse and cast no shadow. It was a face which at first sight recorded nothing but loneliness. Its complexion was pale.

'What can I do for you?' Leiser asked. He stood almost at attention.

'Hullo, I wonder if you remember me?'

Leiser looked at him as if he were being asked to name a price, blank but wary.

'Sure it was me?'

'Yes.'

'It must have been a long time ago,' he said at last. 'I don't often forget a face.'

'Twenty years.' Haldane coughed apologetically.

'In the war then, was it?'

He was a short man, very straight; in build he was not unlike Leclerc. He might have been a waiter. His sleeves were rolled up a little way, there was a lot of hair on the forearms. His shirt was white and expensive; a monogram on the pocket. He looked like a man who spent a good deal on his clothes. He wore a gold ring; a golden wristband to his watch. He took great care of his appearance; Haldane could smell the lotion on his skin. His long brown hair was full, the line along the forehead straight. Bulging a little at the sides, the hair was combed backwards. He wore no parting; the effect was definitely Slav. Though very upright, he had about him a certain swagger, a looseness of the hips and shoulders, which suggested a familiarity with the sea. It was here that any comparison with Leclerc abruptly ceased. He looked, despite himself, a practical man, handy in the house or starting the car on a cold day; and he looked an innocent man, but travelled. He wore a tartan tie.

'Surely you remember me?' Haldane pleaded.

Leiser stared at the thin cheeks, touched with points of high colour, at the hanging, restless body and the gently stirring hands, and there passed across his face a look of painful recognition, as if he were identifying the remains of a friend.

'You're not Captain Hawkins, are you?'

'That's right.'

'God Christ,' said Leiser, without moving. 'You're the people who've been asking about me.'

'We're looking for someone with your experience, a man like you.'

'What do you want him for, sir?'

He still hadn't moved. It was very hard to tell what he was thinking. His eyes were fixed on Haldane.

'To do a job, one job.'

Leiser smiled, as if it all came back to him. He nodded his head towards the window. 'Over there?' He meant somewhere beyond the rain.

'Yes.'

'What about getting back?'

'The usual rules. It's up to the man in the field. The war rules.'

He pushed his hands into his pockets, discovered cigarettes and a lighter. The budgerigar was singing.

'The war rules. You smoke?' He gave himself a cigarette and lit it, his hands cupped round the flame as if there were a high wind. He dropped the match on to the floor for someone else to pick up.

'God Christ,' he repeated. 'Twenty years. I was a kid in those days, just a kid.'

Haldane said, 'You don't regret it, I trust. Shall we go and have a drink?' He handed Leiser a card. It was newly printed: Captain A. Hawkins. Written underneath was a telephone number.

Leiser read it and shrugged. 'I don't mind,' he said and fetched his coat. Another smile, incredulous this time. 'But you're wasting your time, Captain.'

'Perhaps you know someone. Someone else from the war who might take it on.'

'I don't know a lot of people,' Leiser replied. He took a jacket from the peg and a nylon raincoat of dark blue. Going ahead of Haldane to the door, he opened it elaborately as if he valued formality. His hair was laid carefully upon itself like the wings of a bird.

There was a pub on the other side of the Avenue. They reached it by crossing a footbridge. The rush hour traffic thundered beneath them; the cold, plump raindrops seemed to go with it. The bridge trembled to the drumming of the cars. The pub was Tudor with new horse brasses and a ship's bell very highly polished. Leiser asked for a White Lady. He never drank anything else, he said. 'Stick to one drink, Captain, that's my advice. Then you'll be all right. Down the hatch.'

'It's got to be someone who knows the tricks,' Haldane observed. They sat in a corner near the fire. They might have been talking about trade. 'It's a very important job. They pay far more than in the war.' He gave a gaunt smile. 'They pay a lot of money these days.'

'Still, money's not everything, is it?' A stiff phrase, borrowed from the English.

'They remembered you. People whose names you've forgotten, if you even knew them.' An unconvincing smile of reminiscence crossed his thin lips: it might have been years since he had lied. 'You left quite an impression behind you, Fred; there weren't many as good as you. Even after twenty years.'

'They remember me then, the old crowd?' He seemed grateful for that, but shy as if it were not his place to be held in memory. 'I was only a kid then,' he repeated. 'Who's there still, who's left?'

Haldane, watching him, said, 'I warned you: we play the same rules, Fred. *Need to know*, it's all the same.' It was very strict.

'God Christ,' Leiser declared. 'All the same. Big as ever, then, the outfit?'

'Bigger,' Haldane fetched another White Lady. 'Take much interest in politics?'

Leiser lifted a clean hand and let it fall.

'You know the way we are,' he said. 'In Britain, you know.' His voice carried the slightly impertinent assumption that he was as good as Haldane.

'I mean,' Haldane prompted, 'in a *broad* sense.' He coughed his dusty cough. 'After all, they took over your country, didn't they?' Leiser said nothing. 'What did you think of Cuba, for instance?'

Haldane did not smoke, but he had bought some cigarettes at the bar, the brand Leiser preferred. He removed the cellophane with his slim, ageing fingers, and offered them across the table. Without waiting for an answer, he continued, 'The point was, you see, in the Cuba thing the Americans *knew*. It was a matter of information. Then they could act. Of course *they* made overflights. One can't always do that.' He gave another little laugh. 'One wonders what they would have done without them.'

'Yes, that's right.' He nodded his head like a dummy. Haldane paid no attention.

'They might have been stuck,' Haldane suggested and sipped his whisky. 'Are you married, by the way?'

Leiser grinned, held his hand out flat, tipped it briskly to left and right, like a man talking about aeroplanes. 'So, so,' he said. His tartan tie was fastened to his shirt with a heavy gold pin the shape of a riding crop against a horse's head. It was very incongruous.

'How about you, Captain?'

Haldane shook his head.

'No,' Leiser observed thoughtfully. 'No.'

'Then there have been other occasions,' Haldane went on, 'where very serious mistakes were made because they hadn't the *right* information, or not enough. I mean not even we can have people permanently everywhere.'

'No, of course,' Leiser said politely.

The bar was filling up.

'I wonder whether you know of a different place where we might talk?' Haldane inquired. 'We could eat, chat about some of the old gang. Or have you another engagement?' The lower classes eat early.

Leiser glanced at his watch. 'I'm all right till eight,' he said. 'You want to do something about that cough, sir. It can be dangerous, a cough like that.' The watch was of gold; it had black face and compartment for indicating phases of the moon.

The Under Secretary, similarly conscious of the time, was bored to be kept so late.

'I think I mentioned to you,' Leclerc was saying, 'that the Foreign Office has been awfully sticky about providing operational passports. They've taken to consulting the Circus in every case. We have no status, you understand; it's hard for me to make myself unpleasant about these things—they have only the vaguest notion of how we work. I wondered whether the best system might not be for my Department to route passport requisitions through your Private Office. That would save the bother of going to the Circus every time.'

'What do you mean, sticky?'

'You will remember we sent poor Taylor out under another name. The Office revoked his operational passport a matter of hours before he left London. I fear the Circus made an administrative blunder. The passport which accompanied the body was therefore challenged on arrival in the United Kingdom. It gave us a lot of trouble. I had to send one of my best men to sort it out,' he lied. 'I'm sure that if the Minister insisted, Control would be quite agreeable to a new arrangement.'

The Under Secretary jabbed a pencil at the door which led to his Private Office. 'Talk to them in there. Work something out. It sounds very stupid. Who do you deal with at the Office?'

'De Lisle,' said Leclerc with satisfaction, 'in General Department. He's the Assistant. And Smiley at the Circus.'

The Under Secretary wrote it down. 'One never knows *who* to talk to in that place; they're so top-heavy.'

'Then I may have to approach the Circus for technical resources. Wireless and that kind of thing. I propose to use a cover story for security reasons: a notional training scheme is the most appropriate.'

'Cover story? Ah yes: a lie. You mentioned it.'

'It's a precaution, no more.'

'You must do as you think fit.'

'I imagined you would prefer the Circus not to know. You said yourself: no monolith. I have proceeded on that assumption.'

The Under Secretary glanced again at the clock above the door. 'He's been in rather a difficult mood: a dreary day with the Yemen. I think it's partly the Woodbridge by-election: he gets so upset about the marginals. How's this thing going, by the way? It's been very worrying for him, you know. I mean, what's he to believe?' He paused. 'It's these Germans who terrify me . . . You mentioned you'd found a fellow who fitted the bill.' They moved to the corridor.

'We're on to him now. We've got him in play. We shall know tonight.'

The Under Secretary wrinkled his nose very slightly, his hand on the Minister's door. He was a churchman and disliked irregular things.

'What makes a man take on a job like that? Not you; him, I mean.'

Leclerc shook his head in silence, as if the two of them were in close sympathy. 'Heaven knows. It's something we don't even understand ourselves.'

'What kind of person is he? What sort of class? Only generally, you appreciate.'

'Intelligent. Self-educated. Polish extraction.'

'Oh, I see.' He seemed relieved. 'We'll keep it gentle, shall we? Don't paint it too black. He loathes drama. I mean any fool can see what the *dangers* are.'

They went in.

Haldane and Leiser took their places at a corner table, like lovers in a coffee bar. It was one of those restaurants which rely on empty chainti bottles for their charm and on very little else for their custom. It would be gone tomorrow, or the next day, and scarcely anyone would notice, but while it was there and new and full of hope, it was not at all bad. Leiser had steak, it seemed to be habit, and sat primly while he ate it, his elbows firmly at his sides.

At first Haldane pretended to ignore the purpose of his visit. He talked badly about the war and the Department; about operations he had half forgotten until that afternoon, when he had refreshed his memory from the files. He spoke—no doubt it seemed desirable—mainly of those who had survived.

He referred to the courses Leiser had attended; had he kept up his interest in radio at all? Well, no, as a matter of fact. How about unarmed combat? There hadn't been the opportunity, really.

'You had one or two rough moments in the war, I remember,' Haldane prompted. 'Didn't you have some trouble in Holland?' They were back to vanity and old times' sake.

A stiff nod. 'I had a spot of trouble,' he conceded. 'I was younger then.'

'What happened exactly?'

Leiser looked at Haldane, blinking, as if the other had woken him, then began to talk. It was one of those wartime stories which have been told with variations since war began, as remote from the neat little restaurant as hunger or poverty, less credible for being articulate. He seemed to tell it at second hand. It might have been a big fight he had heard on the wireless. He had been caught, he had escaped, he had lived for days without food, he had killed, been taken into refuge and smuggled back to England. He told it well; perhaps it was what the war meant to him now, perhaps it was true, but as with a Latin widow relating the manner of her husband's death, the passion had gone out of his heart and into the telling. He seemed to speak because he had been told to; his affectations, unlike Leclerc's, were designed less to impress others than to protect himself. He seemed a very private man whose speech was exploratory; a man who had been a long time alone and had not reckoned with society; poised, not settled. His accent was good but exclusively foreign, lacking the slur and the elision which escapes even gifted imitators; a voice familiar with its environment, but not at home there.

Haldane listened courteously. When it was over he asked, 'How did they pick you up in the first place, do you know?' The space between them was very great.

'They never told me,' he said blankly, as if it were not proper to inquire.

'Of course you *are* the man we need. You've got the German background, if you understand me. You know them, don't you; you have the German experience.'

'Only from the war,' Leiser said.

They talked about the training school. 'How's that fat one? George somebody. Little sad bloke.'

'Oh . . . he's well, thank you.'

'He married a pretty girl.' He laughed obscenely, raising his right forearm in an Arab gesture of sexual prowess. 'God Christ,' he said, laughing again. 'Us little blokes! Go for anything.' It was an extraordinary lapse. It seemed to be what Haldane had been waiting for.

He watched Leiser for a long time. The silence became remarkable. Deliberately he stood up; he seemed suddenly very angry; angry at Leiser's silly grin and this whole cheap, incompetent flirtation; at these meaningless repetitive blasphemies and this squalid derision of a person of quality.

'Do you mind not saying that? George Smiley happens to be a friend of mine.'

He called the waiter and paid the bill, stalked quickly from the restaurant, leaving Leiser bewildered and alone, his White Lady held delicately in his hand, his brown eyes turned anxiously towards the doorway through which Haldane had so abruptly vanished.

Eventually he left, making his way back by the footbridge, slowly through the dark and the rain, staring down on the double alley of streetlamps and the traffic passing between them. Across the road was his garage, the line of illuminated pumps, the tower crowned with its neon heart of sixty-watt bulbs alternating green and red. He entered the brightly lit office, said something to the boy, walked slowly upstairs towards the blare of music.

Haldane waited till he had disappeared from sight, then hurried back to the restaurant to order a taxi.

She had put the gramophone on. She was listening to dance music, sitting in his chair, drinking.

'Christ, you're late,' she said. 'I'm starving.'

He kissed her.

'You've eaten,' she said. 'I can smell the food.'

'Just a snack, Bett. I had to. A man called; we had a drink.'

'Liar.'

He smiled. 'Come off it, Betty. We've got a dinner date, remember?'

'What man?'

The flat was very clean. Curtains and carpets were flowered, the polished surfaces protected with lace. Everything was protected; vases, lamps, ashtray, all were carefully guarded, as if Leiser expected nothing from nature but stark collision. He favoured a suggestion of the antique: it was reflected in the scrolled woodwork of the furniture and the wrought iron of the lamp brackets. He had a mirror framed in gold and a picture made of fretwork and plaster; a new clock with weights which turned in a glass case.

When he opened the cocktail cabinet it played a brief tune on a music box.

He mixed himself a White Lady, carefully, like a man making up medicine. She watched him, moving her hips to the record, holding her glass away to one side as if it were her partner's hand, and the partner were not Leiser.

'What man?' she repeated.

He stood at the window, straight-backed like a soldier. The flashing heart on the roof played over the houses, caught the staves of the bridge and quivered in the wet surface of the Avenue. Beyond the houses was the church, like a cinema with a spire, fluted brick with vents where the bells rang. Beyond the church was the sky. Sometimes he thought the church was all that remained, and the London sky was lit with the glow of a burning city.

'Christ, you're really gay tonight.'

The church bells were recorded, much amplified to drown the noise of traffic. He sold a lot of petrol on Sundays. The rain was running harder against the road; he could see it shading the beams of the car lights, dancing green and red on the tarmac.

'Come on, Fred, dance.'

'Just a minute, Bett.'

'Oh, for Christ's sake, what's the matter with you? Have another drink and forget it.'

He could hear her feet shuffling across the carpet to the music; the tireless jingle of her charm bracelet.

'Dance, for Christ's sake.'

She had a slurred way of talking, slackly dragging the last syllable of a sentence beyond its natural length; it was the same calculated disenchantment with which she gave herself, sullenly, as if she were giving money, as if men had all the pleasure and women the pain.

She stopped the record, careless as she pulled the arm. The needle scratched in the loudspeaker.

'Look, what the hell goes on?'

'Nothing, I tell you. I've just had a hard day, that's all. Then this man called, somebody I used to know.'

'I keep asking you: who? Some woman, wasn't it? Some tart.'

'No, Betty, it was a man.'

She came to the window, nudging him indifferently. 'What's so bloody marvellous about the view, anyway? Just a lot of rotten little houses. You always said you hated them. Well, who was it?'

'He's from one of the big companies.'

'And they want you?'

'Yes . . . they want to make me an offer.'

'Christ, who'd want a bloody Pole?'

He hardly stirred. 'They do.'

'Someone came to the bank, you know, asking about you. They all sat together in Mr Dawnay's office. You're in trouble, aren't you?'

He took her coat and helped her into it, very correct, elbows wide. She said: 'Not that new place with waiters, for Christ's sake.'

'It's nice there, isn't it? I thought you fancied it there. You can dance too; you like that. Where do you want to go then?'

'With you? For Christ's sake! Somewhere where there's a bit of life, that's all.'

He stared at her. He was holding the door open. Suddenly he smiled.

'OK, Bett. It's your night. Slip down and start the car, I'll book a table.' He gave her the key. 'I know a place, a real place.'

'What the hell's come over you now?'

'You can drive. We'll have a night out.' He went to the telephone.

It was shortly before eleven when Haldane returned to the Department. Leclerc and Avery were waiting for him. Carol was typing in the Private Office.

'I thought you'd be here earlier,' Leclerc said.

'It's no good. He said he wouldn't play. I think you'd better try the next one yourself. It's not my style any more.' He seemed undisturbed. He sat down. They stared at him incredulously.

'Did you offer money?' Leclerc asked finally. 'We have clearance for five thousand pounds.'

'Of course I offered him money. I tell you he's just not interested. He was a singularly unpleasant person.'

'I'm sorry.' He didn't say why.

They could hear the tapping of Carol's typewriter. Leclerc said, 'Where do we go from here?'

'I have no idea.' He glanced restlessly at his watch.

'There must be others, there must be.'

'Not on our cards. Not with his qualifications. There are Belgians, Swedes, Frenchmen. But Leiser was the only German speaker with technical experience. On paper, he's the only one.'

'Still young enough. Is that what you mean?'

'I suppose so. It would have to be an old hand. We haven't the time to train a new man, nor the facilities. We'd better ask the Circus. They'll have someone.'

'We can't do that,' Avery said.

'What kind of man was he?' Leclerc persisted, reluctant to abandon hope.

'Common, in a Slav way. Small. He plays the Rittmeister. It's most unattractive.' He was looking in his pockets for the bill. 'He dresses like a bookie, but I suppose they all do that. Do I give this to you or Accounts?'

'Secure?'

'I don't see why not.'

'And you spoke about the urgency? New loyalties and that kind of thing?'

'He found the old loyalties more attractive.' He put the bill on the table.

'And politics . . . some of these exiles are very . . .'

'We spoke about politics. He's not that sort of exile. He considers himself integrated, naturalized British. What do you expect him to do? Swear allegiance to the Polish royal house?' Again he looked at his watch.

'You never wanted to recruit him!' Leclerc cried, angered by Haldane's indifference. 'You're pleased, Adrian, I can see it in your face! Good God, what about the Department! Didn't that mean anything to him? You don't believe in it any more, you don't care! You're sneering at me!'

'Who of us does believe?' asked Haldane with contempt. 'You said yourself: we do the job.'

'I believe,' Avery declared.

Haldane was about to speak when the green telephone rang.

'That will be the Ministry,' Leclerc said. 'Now what do I tell them?' Haldane was watching him.

He picked up the receiver, put it to his ear then handed it across the table. 'It's the exchange. Why on earth did they come through on green? Somebody asking for Captain Hawkins. That's you, isn't it?'

Haldane listened, his thin face expressionless. Finally he said, 'I imagine so. We'll find someone. There should be no difficulty. Tomorrow at eleven. Kindly be punctual,' and rang off. The light in Leclerc's room seemed to ebb towards the thinly curtained window. The rain fell ceaselessly outside.

'That was Leiser. He's decided he'll do the job. He wants to know whether we can find someone to take care of his garage while he's away.'

Leclerc looked at him in astonishment. Pleasure spread comically over his face. 'You expected it!' he cried. He stretched out his small hand. 'I'm sorry, Adrian. I misjudged you. I congratulate you warmly.'

'Why did he accept?' Avery asked excitedly. 'What made him change his mind?'

'Why do agents ever do anything? Why do any of us?' Haldane sat down. He looked old but inviolate, like a man whose friends had already died. 'Why do they consent or refuse, why do they lie or tell the truth? Why do any of us?' He began coughing again. 'Perhaps he's under-employed. It's the Germans: he hates them. That's what he says. I place no value on that. Then he said he couldn't let us down. I assume he means himself.'

To Leclerc he added, 'The war rules: that was right, wasn't it?'

But Leclerc was dialling the Ministry.

Avery went into the Private Office. Carol was standing up.

'What's going on?' she said quickly. 'What's the excitement?'

'It's Leiser.' Avery closed the door behind him. 'He's agreed to go.' He stretched out his arms to embrace her. It would be the first time.

'Why?'

'Hatred of the Germans, he says. My guess is money.'

'Is that a good thing?'

Avery grinned knowingly. 'As long as we pay him more than the other side.'

'Shouldn't you go back to your wife?' she said sharply. 'I can't believe you need to sleep here.'

'It's operational.' Avery went to his room. She did not say goodnight.

Leiser put down the telephone. It was suddenly very quiet. The lights on the roof went out, leaving the room in darkness. He went quickly downstairs. He was frowning, as if his entire mental force were concentrated on the prospect of eating a second dinner.

Chapter Eleven

They chose Oxford as they had done in the war. The variety of nationalities and occupations, the constant coming and going of visiting academics and the resultant anonymity, the proximity of open country, all perfectly suited their needs. Besides, it was a place they could understand. The morning after Leiser had rung, Avery went ahead to find a house. The following day he telephoned Haldane to say he had taken one for a month in the north of the town, a large Victorian affair with four bedrooms and a garden. It was very expensive. It was known in the Department as the Mayfly house and carded under Live Amenities.

As soon as Haldane heard, he told Leiser. At Leiser's suggestion it was agreed that he should put it about that he was attending a course in the Midlands.

'Don't give any details,' Haldane had said. 'Have your mail sent *poste restante* to Coventry. We'll get it picked up from there.' Leiser was pleased when he heard it was Oxford.

Leclerc and Woodford had searched desperately for someone to run the garage in Leiser's absence; suddenly they thought of McCulloch. Leiser gave him power of attorney and spent a hasty morning showing him the ropes. 'We'll offer you some kind of guarantee in return,' Haldane said.

'I don't need it,' Leiser replied, explaining quite seriously, 'I'm working for English gentlemen.'

On the Friday night Leiser had telephoned his consent; by the Wednesday preparations were sufficiently advanced for Leclerc to convene a meeting of Special Section and outline his plans. Avery and Haldane were to be with Leiser in Oxford; the two of them would leave the following evening, by which time he understood that Haldane would be ready with his syllabus. Leiser would arrive in Oxford a day or two later, as soon as his own arrangements were complete. Haldane was to supervise his training, Avery to act as Haldane's assistant. Woodford would remain in London. Among his tasks was that of consulting with the Ministry (and Sandford of Research) in order to assemble instructional material on the external specifications of short- and medium-range rockets, and thus provided come himself to Oxford.

Leclerc had been tireless, now at the Ministry to report on progress, now at the Treasury to argue the case for Taylor's widow, now, with Woodford's aid, engaging former instructors in wireless transmission, photography and unarmed combat.

Such time as remained to Leclerc he devoted to Mayfly Zero: the moment at which Leiser was to be infiltrated into Eastern Germany. At first he seemed to have no firm idea of how this was to be done. He talked vaguely of a sea operation from Denmark; small fishing craft and a rubber dinghy to evade radar detection; he discussed illegal frontier crossing with Sandford and telegraphed Gorton for information on the border area round Lübeck. In veiled terms he even consulted the Circus. Control was remarkably helpful.

All this took place in that atmosphere of heightened activity and optimism which Avery had observed on his return. Even those who were kept, supposedly, in ignorance of the operation were infected by the air of crisis. The little lunch group that gathered daily at a corner table of the Cadena café was alive with rumours and speculation. It was said, for instance, that a man named Johnson, known in the war as Jack Johnson, a wireless instructor, had been taken on to the strength of the Department. Accounts had paid him subsistence and—most intriguing of all—they had been asked to draft a three-month contract for submission to the Treasury. Who ever heard, they asked, of a three-month contract? Johnson had been concerned with the French drops during the war; a senior girl remembered him. Berry, the cypher clerk, had asked Mr Woodford what Johnson was up to (Berry was always the cheeky one) and Mr Woodford had grinned and told him to mind his own business, but it was for an operation, he'd said, a very secret one they were running in Europe . . . northern Europe, as a matter of fact, and it might interest Berry to know that poor Taylor had not died in vain.

There was now a ceaseless traffic of cars and Ministry messengers in the front drive; Pine requested and received from another Government establishment a junior whom he treated with sovereign brutality. In some oblique way he had learnt that Germany was the target, and the knowledge made him diligent.

It was even rumoured among the local tradesmen that the Ministry House was changing hands; private buyers were named and great hopes placed upon their custom. Meals were sent for at all hours, lights burned day and night; the front door, hitherto permanently sealed for reasons of security, was opened, and the sight of Leclerc with bowler hat and briefcase entering his black Humber became a familiar one in Blackfriars Road.

And Avery, like an injured man who would not look at his own wound, slept within the walls of his little office, so that they became the boundary of his life. Once he sent out Carol to buy Anthony a present. She came back with a toy milk lorry with plastic bottles. You could lift the caps off and fill the bottles with water. They tried it out one evening, then sent it round to Battersea in the Humber.

When all was ready Haldane and Avery travelled to Oxford first class on a Ministry Warrant. At dinner on the train they had a table to themselves. Haldane ordered half a bottle of wine and drank it while he completed *The Times* crossword. They sat in silence, Haldane occupied, Avery too diffident to interrupt him.

Suddenly Avery noticed Haldane's tie; before he had time to think, he said, 'Good Lord, I never knew you were a cricketer.'

'Did you expect me to tell you?' Haldane snapped. 'I could hardly wear it in the Office.'

'I'm sorry.'

Haldane looked at him closely. 'You shouldn't apologize so much,' he observed. 'You both do it.' He helped himself to some coffee and ordered a brandy. Waiters noticed Haldane.

'Both?'

'You and Leiser. He does it by implication.'

'It's going to be different with Leiser, isn't it?' Avery said quickly.

'Leiser's a professional.'

'Leiser is not one of us. Never make that mistake. We touched him long ago, that's all.'

'What's he like? What sort of man is he?'

'He's an agent. He's a man to be handled, not known.'

He returned to his crossword.

'He must be loyal,' Avery said. 'Why else would he accept?'

'You heard what the Director said: the two vows. The first is often quite frivolously taken.'

'And the second?'

'Ah, that is different. We shall be there to help him take it.'

'But why did he accept the first time?'

'I mistrust reasons. I mistrust words like loyalty. And above all,' Haldane declared, 'I mistrust *motive*. We're running an agent; the arithmetic is over. You read German, didn't you? In the beginning was the deed.'

Shortly before they arrived Avery ventured one more question.

'Why *was* that passport out of date?'

Haldane had a way of inclining his head when addressed.

'The Foreign Office used to allocate a series of passport numbers to the Department for operational purposes. The arrangement ran from year to year. Six months ago the Office said they wouldn't issue any more without reference to the Circus. It seems Leclerc had been making insufficient claims on the facility and Control cut him out of the market. Taylor's passport was one of the old series. They revoked the whole lot three days before he left. There was no time to do anything about it. It might never have been noticed. The Circus has been very devious.' A pause. 'Indeed I find it hard to understand what Control *is* up to.'

They took a taxi to North Oxford and got out at the corner of their road. As they walked along the pavement Avery looked at the houses in the half darkness, glimpsed grey-haired figures moving across the lighted windows, velvet-covered chairs trimmed with lace, Chinese screens, music stands and a bridge-four sitting like bewitched courtiers in a castle. It was a world he had known about once; for a time he had almost fancied he was part of it; but that was long ago.

They spent the evening preparing the house. Haldane said Leiser should have the rear bedroom overlooking the garden, they themselves would take the rooms on the street side. He had sent some academic books in advance, a typewriter and some imposing files. These he unpacked and arranged on the dining-room table for the benefit of the landlord's housekeeper who would come each day. 'We shall call this room the study,' he said. In the drawing-room he installed a tape-recorder.

He had some tapes which he locked in a cupboard, meticulously adding the key to his key ring. Other luggage was still waiting in the hall: a projector, Air Force issue, a screen, and a suitcase of green canvas, securely fastened, with leather corners.

The house was spacious and well kept; the furniture was of mahogany, with brass inlay. The walls were filled with pictures of some unknown family: sketches in sepia, miniatures, photographs faded with age. There was a bowl of pot-pourri on the sideboard and a palm cross pinned to the mirror; chandeliers hung from the ceiling, clumsy, but inoffensive; in one corner, a bible table; in another a small cupid, very ugly, its face turned to the dark. The whole house gently asserted an air of old age; it had a quality, like incense, of courteous but inconsolable sadness.

By midnight they had finished unpacking. They sat down in the drawing-room. The marble fireplace was supported by blackamoors of ebony; the light of the gas fire played over the gilded rose-chains which linked their thick ankles. The fireplace came from an age, it might have been the seventeenth century, it might have been the nineteenth, when blackamoors had briefly replaced borzois as the decorative beasts of society; they were quite naked, as a dog might be, and chained with golden roses. Avery gave himself a whisky, then went to bed, leaving Haldane sunk in his own thoughts.

His room was large and dark; above the bed hung a light shade of blue china; there were embroidered covers on the tables and a small enamelled notice saying, 'God's blessing on this house'; beside the window a picture of a child saying its prayers while his sister ate breakfast in bed.

He lay awake, wondering about Leiser; it was like waiting for a girl. From across the passage he could hear Haldane's solitary cough, on and on. It had not ended when he fell asleep.

Leclerc thought Smiley's club a very strange place; not at all the kind of thing he had expected. Two half-basement rooms and a dozen people dining at separate tables before a large fire. Some of them were vaguely familiar. He suspected they were connected with the Circus.

'This is rather a good spot. How do you join?'

'Oh, you don't,' said Smiley apologetically, then blushed and continued, 'I mean, they don't have new members. Just one generation . . . several went in the war, you know, some have died or gone abroad. What was it you had in mind, I wonder?'

'You were good enough to help young Avery out.'

'Yes . . . yes of course. How did that go, by the way? I never heard.'

'It was just a training run. There was no film in the end.'

'I'm sorry,' Smiley spoke hastily, covering up, as if someone were dead and he had not known.

'We didn't really expect there would be. It was just a precaution. How much did Avery tell you, I wonder? We're training up one or two of the old hands . . . and some of the new boys too. It's something to do,' Leclerc explained, 'during the slack season . . . Christmas, you know. People on leave.'

'I know.'

Leclerc noticed that the claret was very good. He wished he had joined a smaller club; his own had gone off terribly. They had such difficulty with staff.

'You have probably heard,' Leclerc added, officially, as it were, 'that Control has offered me full assistance for training purposes.'

'Yes, yes of course.'

'My Minister was the moving spirit. He likes the idea of a pool of trained agents. When the plan was first mooted I went and spoke to Control myself. Later, Control called on me. You knew that, perhaps?'

'Yes. Control wondered . . .'

'He has been most helpful. Don't think I am unappreciative. It has been agreed—I think I should give you the background, your own office will confirm it—that if the training is to be effective, we must create as nearly as possible an operational atmosphere. What we used to call battle conditions.' An indulgent smile. 'We've chosen an area in Western Germany. It's bleak and unfamiliar ground, ideal for frontier crossing exercises and that kind of thing. We can ask for the Army's co-operation if we need it.'

'Yes, indeed. What a good idea.'

'For elementary reasons of security, we all accept that your office should only be briefed in the aspects of this exercise in which you are good enough to help.'

'Control told me,' said Smiley. 'He wants to do whatever he can. He didn't know you touched this kind of thing any more. He was pleased.'

'Good,' Leclerc said shortly. He moved his elbows forward a little across the polished table. 'I thought I might pick your brains . . . quite informally. Rather as you people from time to time have made use of Adrian Haldane.'

'Of course.'

'The first thing is false documents. I looked up our old forgers in the index. I see Hyde and Fellowby went over to the Circus some years ago.'

'Yes. It was the change in emphasis.'

'I've written down a personal description of a man in our employment; he is supposedly resident at Magdeburg for the purposes of the scheme. One of the men under training. Do you think they could prepare documents, Identity Card, Party Membership and that kind of thing? Whatever is necessary.'

'The man would have to sign them,' Smiley said. 'We would then stamp on top of his signature. We'd need photographs too. He'd have to be briefed on how the documents worked; perhaps Hyde could do that on the spot with your agent.'

A slight hesitation. 'No doubt. I have selected a cover name. It closely approximates his own; we find that a useful technique.'

'I might just make the point,' Smiley said, with a rather comic frown, 'since this is such an *elaborate* exercise, that forged papers are of very *limited* value. I mean, one telephone call to the Magdeburg Town Administration and the best forgery in the world is blown sky high . . .'

'I think we know about that. We want to teach them cover, submit them to interrogation . . . you know the kind of thing.'

Smiley sipped his claret. 'I just thought I'd make the point. It's so easy to get hypnotized by *technique*. I didn't mean to imply . . . How is Haldane, by the way? He read Greats, you know. We were up together.'

'Adrian is well.'

'I liked your Avery,' Smiley said politely. His heavy small face contracted in pain. 'Do you realize,' he asked impressively, 'they *still* don't include the Baroque period in the German syllabus? They call it a special subject.'

'Then there is the question of clandestine wireless. We haven't used that kind of thing much since the war. I understand it has all become a great deal more sophisticated. High-speed transmission and so on. We want to keep up with the times.'

'Yes. Yes, I believe the message is taped on a miniature recorder and sent over the air in a matter of seconds.' He sighed. 'But no one really tells us much. The technical people hold their cards very close to their chests.'

'Is that a method in which our people could profitably be trained . . . in a month, say?'

'And use under operational conditions?' Smiley asked in astonishment. 'Straight away, after a month's training?'

'Some are technically minded, you understand. People with wireless experience.'

Smiley was watching Leclerc incredulously. 'Forgive me. Would he, would they,' he inquired, 'have *other* things to learn in that month as well?'

'For some it's more a refresher course.'

'Ah.'

'What do you mean?'

'Nothing, nothing,' Smiley said vaguely and added, 'I don't *think* our technical people would be very keen to part with this kind of equipment unless . . .'

'Unless it were their own training operation?'

'Yes,' Smiley blushed. 'Yes, that's what I mean. They're very particular, you know; jealous.'

Leclerc lapsed into silence, lightly tapping the base of his wine glass on the polished surface of the table. Suddenly he smiled and said, as if he had shaken off depression, 'Oh well. We shall just have to use a conventional set. Have direction-finding methods also improved since the war? Interception, location of an illegal transmitter?'

'Oh yes. Yes, indeed.'

'We would have to incorporate that. How long can a man remain on the air before they spot him?'

'Two or three minutes, perhaps. It depends. Often it's a matter of luck how soon they hear him. They can only pin him down while he's transmitting. Much depends on the frequency. Or so they tell me.'

'In the war,' said Leclerc reflectively, 'we gave an agent several crystals. Each vibrated at a fixed frequency. Every so often he changed the crystal; that was usually a safe enough method. We could do that again.'

'Yes. Yes, I remember that. But there was the headache of returning the transmitter . . . possibly changing the coil . . . matching the aerial.'

'Suppose a man is used to a conventional set. You tell me the chances of interception are greater now than they were in the war? You say allow two or three minutes?'

'Or less,' said Smiley, watching him. 'It depends on a lot of things . . . luck, reception, amount of signal traffic, density of population . . .'

'Supposing he changed his frequency after every two and a half minutes on the air. Surely that would meet the case?'

'It could be a slow business.' His sad, unhealthy face was wrinkled in concern. 'You're quite sure this *is* only training?'

'As far as I remember,' Leclerc persisted, courting his own idea, 'these crystals are the size of a small matchbox. We could give them several. We're only aiming at a few transmissions; perhaps only three or four. Would you consider my suggestion impractical?'

'It's hardly my province.'

'What is the alternative? I asked Control; he said speak to you. He said you'd help, find me the equipment. What else can I do? Can I *talk* to your technical people?'

'I'm sorry. Control rather agreed with the technical side, that we should give all the help we can, but not compromise new equipment. *Risk* compromising it, I mean. After all, it *is* only training. I think he felt that if you hadn't full technical resources you should . . .'

'Hand over the commitment?'

'No, no,' Smiley protested, but Leclerc interrupted him. 'These people would eventually be used against military targets,' he said angrily. 'Purely military. Control accepts that.'

'Oh quite.' He seemed to have given up. 'And if you want a

conventional set, no doubt we can dig one up.'

The waiter brought a decanter of port. Leclerc watched Smiley pour a little into his glass, then slide the decanter carefully across the polished table.

'It's quite good, but I'm afraid it's nearly finished. When this is gone we shall have to break into the younger ones. I'm seeing Control first thing tomorrow. I'm sure he'll have no objection. About the documents, I mean. And crystals. We could advise you on frequencies, I'm sure. Control made a point of that.'

'Control's been very good,' Leclerc confessed. He was slightly drunk. 'It puzzles me sometimes.'

Chapter Twelve

Two days later, Leiser arrived at Oxford. They waited anxiously for him on the platform, Haldane peering among the hurrying faces in the crowd. It was Avery, curiously, who saw him first: a motionless figure in a camel-hair coat at the window of an empty compartment.

'Is that him?' Avery asked.

'He's travelling first class. He must have paid the difference.' Haldane spoke as if it were an affront.

Leiser lowered the window and handed out two pigskin cases shaped for the boot of a car, a little too orange for nature. They greeted one another briskly, shaking hands for everyone to see. Avery wanted to carry the luggage to the taxi, but Leiser preferred to take it himself, a piece in each hand, as if it were his duty. He walked a little away from them, shoulders back, staring at the people as they went by, startled by the crowd. His long hair bounced with each step.

Avery, watching him, felt suddenly disturbed.

He was a man; not a shadow. A man with force to his body and purpose to his movement, but somehow theirs to direct. There seemed to be nowhere he would not walk. He was recruited; and had assumed already the anxious, brisk manner of an enlisted man. Yet, Avery accepted, no single factor wholly accounted for Leiser's recruitment. Avery was already familiar, during his short association with the Department, with the phenomenon of organic motivation; with operations which had no discernible genesis and no conclusion, which formed part of an unending pattern of activity until they ceased to have any further identity; with that progress of fruitless courtships which, in the aggregate, passed for an active love life. But as he observed this man bobbing beside him, animate and quick, he recognized that hitherto they had courted ideas, incestuously among themselves; now they had a human being upon their hands, and this was he.

They climbed into the taxi, Leiser last because he insisted. It was mid-afternoon, a slate sky behind the plane trees. The smoke rose from the North Oxford chimneys in ponderous columns like proof of a virtuous sacrifice. The houses were of a modest stateliness; romantic hulls redecked, each according to a different legend. Here the turrets of Avalon, there the carved trellis of a pagoda; between them the monkey-puzzle trees, and the half-hidden washing like butterflies in the wrong season. The houses sat decently in their own gardens, the curtains drawn, first lace and then brocade, petticoats and skirts. It was like a bad water colour, the dark things drawn too heavy, the sky grey and soiled in the dusk, the paint too worked.

They dismissed the taxi at the corner of the street. A smell of leaf mould lingered in the air. If there were children they made no noise. The three men walked to the gate. Leiser, his eyes on the house, put down his suitcases.

'Nice place,' he said with appreciation. He turned to Avery: 'Who chose it?'

'I did.'

'That's nice.' He patted his shoulder. 'You did a good job.' Avery, pleased, smiled and opened the gate; Leiser was determined that the others should pass through first. They took him upstairs and showed him his room. He still carried his own luggage.

'I'll unpack later,' he said. 'I like to make a proper job of it.'

He walked through the house in a critical way, picking things up and looking at them; he might have come to bid for the place.

'It's a nice spot,' he repeated finally; 'I like it.'

'Good,' said Haldane, as if he didn't give a damn.

Avery went with him to his room to see if he could help.

'What's your name?' Leiser asked. He was more at ease with Avery; more vulgar.

'John.'

They shook hands again.

'Well, hullo, John; glad to meet you. How old are you?'

'Thirty-four,' he lied.

A wink. 'Christ, I wish I was thirty-four. Done this kind of thing before, have you?'

'I finished my own run last week.'

'How did it go?'

'Fine.'

'That's the boy. Where's your room?'

Avery showed him.

'Tell me, what's the set-up here?'

'What do you mean?'

'Who's in charge?'

'Captain Hawkins.'

'Anyone else?'

'Not really. I shall be around.'

'All the time?'

'Yes.'

He began unpacking. Avery watched. He had brushes backed with leather, hair lotion, a whole range of little bottles of things for men, an electric shaver of the newest kind and ties, some in tartan, others in silk, to match his costly shirts. Avery went downstairs. Haldane was waiting. He smiled as Avery came in. 'Well?'

Avery shrugged, too big a gesture. He felt elated, ill at ease. 'What do *you* make of him?' he asked.

'I hardly know him,' Haldane said drily. He had a way of terminating conversations. 'I want you to be always in his company. Walk with him, shoot with him, drink with him if you must. He's not to be alone.'

'What about his leave in between?'

'We'll see about that. Meanwhile, do as I say. You will find he enjoys your company. He's a very *lonely* man. And remember he's British: British to the core. One more thing–this is most important–do not let him think we have changed since the war. The Department has remained exactly as it was: that is an illusion you must foster even'–he did not smile–'even though you are too young to make the comparison.'

They began next morning. Breakfast over, they assembled in the drawing-room and Haldane addressed them.

The training would be divided into two periods of a fortnight each, with a short rest in between. The first was to be a refresher course; in the second, old skills, now revived, would be related to the task which lay ahead. Not until the second period would Leiser be told his operational name, his cover and the nature of his mission; even then, the information would reveal neither the target area nor the means by which he was to be infiltrated.

In communications as in all other aspects of his training he would graduate from the general to the particular. In the first period he would familiarize himself once more with the technique of cyphers, signal plans and schedules. In the second he would spend much time actually transmitting under semi-operational conditions. The instructor would arrive during that week.

Haldane explained all this with pedagogic acrimony while Leiser listened carefully, now and then briskly nodding his assent. Avery found it strange that Haldane took so little care to conceal his distaste.

'In the first period we shall see what you remember. We shall give you a lot of running about, I'm afraid. We want to get you fit.

There'll be small arms training, unarmed combat, mental exercises, tradecraft. We shall try to take you walking in the afternoons.'

'Who with? Will John come?'

'Yes. John will take you. You should regard John as your adviser on all minor matters. If there is anything you wish to discuss, any complaint or anxiety, I trust you will not hesitate to mention it to either one of us.'

'All right.'

'On the whole, I must ask you not to venture out alone. I should prefer John to accompany you if you wish to go to the cinema, do some shopping or whatever else the time allows. But I fear you may not have much chance of recreation.'

'I don't expect it,' Leiser said; 'I don't need it.' He seemed to mean he didn't want it.

'The wireless instructor when he comes, will not know your name. That is a customary precaution: please observe it. The daily woman believes we are participating in an academic conference. I cannot imagine you will have occasion to talk to her, but if you do, remember that. If you wish to make inquiries about your business, kindly consult me first. You should not telephone without my consent. Then there will be other visitors: photographers, medical people, technicians. They are what we call ancillaries and are not in the picture. Most of them believe you're here as part of a wider training scheme. Please remember this.'

'OK,' said Leiser. Haldane looked at his watch.

'Our first appointment is at ten o'clock. A car will collect us from the corner of the road. The driver is not one of us: no conversation on the journey, please. Have you no other clothes?' he asked. 'Those are scarcely suitable for the range.'

'I've got a sports coat and a pair of flannels.'

'I could wish you less conspicuous.'

As they went upstairs to change, Leiser smiled wryly at Avery. 'He's a real boy, isn't he? The old school.'

'But good,' Avery said.

Leiser stopped. 'Of course. Here, tell me something. Was this place always here? Have you used it for many people?'

'You're the first,' Avery said.

'Look, I know you can't tell me much. Is the outfit still like it was . . . people everywhere . . . the same set-up?'

'I don't think you'd find much difference. I suppose we've expanded a bit.'

'Are there many young ones like you?'

'Sorry, Fred.'

Leiser put his open hand on Avery's back. He used his hands a lot.

'You're good, too,' he said. 'Don't bother about me. Not to worry, eh, John?'

They went to Abingdon: the Ministry had made arrangements with the parachute base. The instructor was expecting them.

'Used to any particular gun, are you?'

'Browning three-eight automatic, please,' Leiser said, like a child ordering groceries.

'We call it the nine-millimetre now. You'll have had the Mark One.'

Haldane stood in the gallery at the back while Avery helped wind in the man-sized target to a distance of ten yards and paste squares of gum-strip over the old holes.

'You call me "Staff",' the instructor said and turned to Avery. 'Like to have a go as well, sir?'

Haldane put in quickly, 'Yes, they are both shooting, please, Staff.'

Leiser took first turn. Avery stood beside Haldane while Leiser, his long back towards them, waited in the empty range, facing the plywood figure of a German soldier. The target was black, framed against the crumbling whitewash of the walls; over its belly and groin a heart had been crudely described in chalk, its interior extensively repaired with fragments of paper. As they watched, he began testing the weight of the gun, raising it quickly to the level of his eye, then lowering it slowly; pushing home the empty magazine, taking it out and thrusting it in again. He glanced over his shoulder at Avery, with his left hand brushing from his forehead a strand of brown hair which threatened to impede his view. Avery smiled encouragement, then said quickly to Haldane, talking business, 'I still can't make him out.'

'Why not? He's a perfectly ordinary Pole.'

'Where does he come from? What part of Poland?'

'You've read the file. Danzig.'

'Of course.'

The instructor began. 'We'll just try it with the empty gun first, both eyes open, and look along the line of sight, feet nicely apart now, thank you, that's lovely. Relax now, be nice and comfy, it's not a drill movement, it's a firing position, oh yes, we've done *this* before! Now traverse the gun, point it but never aim. Right!' The instructor drew breath, opened a wooden box and took our four magazines. 'One in the gun and one in the left hand,' he said and handed the other two up to Avery, who watched with fascination as Leiser deftly slipped a full magazine into the butt of the automatic and advanced the safety catch with his thumb.

'Now cock the gun, pointing it at the ground three yards ahead of you. Now take up a firing position, keeping the arm straight. Pointing the gun but not aiming it, fire off one magazine, two shots at a time, remembering that we don't regard the automatic as a weapon of science but more in the order of a stopping weapon for close combat. Now slowly, very slowly . . .'

Before he could finish the range was vibrating with the sound of Leiser's shooting—he shot fast, standing very stiff, his left hand holding the spare magazine precisely at his side like a grenade. He shot angrily, a mute man finding expression. Avery could feel with rising excitement the fury and purpose of his shooting; now two shots, and another two, then three, then a long volley, while the haze gathered round him and the plywood soldier shook and Avery's nostrils filled with the sweet smell of cordite.

'Eleven out of thirteen on the target,' the instructor declared. 'Very nice, very nice indeed. Next time, stick to two shots at a time, please, and wait till I give the fire order.' To Avery, the subaltern, he said, 'Care to have a go, sir?'

Leiser had walked up to the target and was lightly tracing the bullet holes with his slim hands. The silence was suddenly oppressive. He seemed lost in meditation, feeling the plywood here and there, running a finger thoughtfully along the outline of the German helmet, until the instructor called:

'Come on. We haven't got all day.'

Avery stood on the gym mat, measuring the weight of the gun. With the instructor's help he inserted one magazine, clutching the other nervously in his left hand. Haldane and Leiser looked on.

Avery fired, the heavy gun thudding in his ears, and he felt his young heart stir as the silhouette flicked passively to his shooting.

'Good shot, John, good shot!'

'Very good,' said the instructor automatically. 'A very good first effort, sir.' He turned to Leiser: 'Do you mind not shouting like that?' He knew a foreigner when he saw one.

'How many?' Avery asked eagerly, as he and the sergeant gathered round the target, touching the blackened perforations scattered thinly over the chest and belly. 'How many, Staff?'

'You'd better come with me, John,' Leiser whispered, throwing his arm over Avery's shoulder. 'I could do with you over there.' For a moment Avery recoiled. Then, with a laugh, he put his own arm round Leiser, feeling the warm, crisp cloth of his sports jacket in the palm of his hand.

The instructor led them across the parade ground to a brick barrack like a theatre with no windows, tall at one end. There were walls half crossing one another like the entrance to a public lavatory.

'Moving targets,' Haldane said, 'and shooting in the dark.'

At lunch they played the tapes.

The tapes were to run like a theme through the first two weeks of his training. They were made from old gramophone records; there was a crack in one which recurred like a metronome. Together, they comprised a massive parlour game in which things to be remembered were not listed but mentioned, casually, obliquely, often against a distracting background of other noises, now contradicted in conversation, now corrected or contested. There were three principal voices, one female and two male. Others would interfere. It was the woman who got on their nerves.

She had that antiseptic voice which air hostesses seem to acquire. In the first tape she read from lists, quickly; first it was a shopping-list, two pounds of this, one kilo of that; without warning she was talking about coloured skittles–so many green so many ochre; then it was weapons, guns, torpedoes, ammunition of this and that calibre; then a factory with capacity, waste and production figures, annual targets and monthly achievements. In the second tape she had not abandoned these topics, but unfamiliar voices distracted her and led the dialogue into unexpected paths.

While shopping she entered into an argument with the grocer's wife about certain merchandise which did not meet with her approval; eggs that were not sound, the outrageous cost of butter. When the grocer himself attempted to mediate he was accused of favouritism; there was talk of points and ration cards, the extra allowance of sugar for jam-making; a hint of undisclosed treasures under the counter. The grocer's voice was raised in anger but he stopped when the child intervened, talking about skittles. 'Mummy, Mummy, I've knocked over the three green ones, but when I tried to put them up, seven black ones fell down; Mummy, why are there only eight black ones left?'

The scene shifted to a public house. It was the woman again. She was reciting armaments statistics; other voices joined in. Figures were disputed, new targets stated, old ones recalled; the performance of a weapon–a weapon unnamed, undescribed–was cynically questioned and heatedly defended.

Every few minutes a voice shouted 'break!'–it might have been a referee–and Haldane stopped the tape and made Leiser talk about football or the weather, or read aloud from a newspaper for five minutes by his watch (the clock on the mantelpiece was broken). The tape recorder was switched on again, and they heard a voice, vaguely familiar, trailing a little like a parson's; a young voice, deprecating and unsure, like Avery's: 'Now here are the four questions. Discounting those eggs which were not sound, how many has she bought in the last three weeks? How many skittles are there altogether? What was the annual overall output of proved and calibrated gun barrels for the years 1937 and 1938? Finally, put in telegraph form any information from which the length of the barrels might be computed.'

Leiser rushed into the study–he seemed to know the game–to write down his answers. As soon as he had left the room Avery said accusingly, 'That was you. That was your voice speaking at the end.'

'Was it?' Haldane replied. He might not have known.

There were other tapes too, and they had the smell of death; the running of feet on a wooden staircase, the slamming of a door, a click, and a girl's voice asking—she might have been offering lemon or cream—'Catch of a door, cocking of a gun?'

Leiser hesitated. 'A door,' he said. 'It was just the door.'

'It was a gun,' Haldane retorted. 'A Browning nine-millimetre automatic. The magazine was being slid into the butt.'

In the afternoon they went for their first walk, the two of them, Leiser and Avery, through Port Meadow and into the country beyond. Haldane had sent them. They walked fast, striding over the whip grass, the wind catching at Leiser's hair and throwing it wildly about his head. It was cold but there was no rain; a clear, sunless day when the sky above the flat fields was darker than the earth.

'You know your way round here, don't you?' Leiser asked. 'Were you at school here?'

'I was an undergraduate here, yes.'

'What did you study?'

'I read languages. German principally.'

They climbed a stile and emerged in a narrow lane.

'You married?' he asked.

'Yes.'

'Kids?'

'One.'

'Tell me something, John. When the Captain turned up my card . . . what happened?'

'What do you mean?'

'What does it look like, an index for so many? It must be a big thing in an outfit like ours.'

'It's in alphabetical order,' Avery said helplessly. 'Just cards. Why?'

'He said they remembererd me: the old hands. I was the best, he said. Well, *who* remembered?'

'They all did. There's a special index for the best people. Practically everyone in the Department knows Fred Leiser. Even the new ones. You can't have a record like yours and get forgotten, you know.' He smiled. 'You're part of the furniture, Fred.'

'Tell me something else, John. I don't want to rock the boat, see, but tell me this . . . Would I be any good on the inside?'

'The inside?'

'In the Office, with you people. I suppose you've got to be born to it really, like the Captain.'

'I'm afraid so, Fred.'

'What cars do you use up there, John?'

'Humbers.'

'Hawk or Snipe?'

'Hawk.'

'Only four-cylinder? The Snipe's a better job, you know.'

'I'm talking about non-operational transport,' Avery said. 'We've a whole range of stuff for the special work.'

'Like the van?'

'That's it.'

'How long before . . . how long does it take to train you? You, for instance; you just did a run. How long before they let you go?'

'Sorry, Fred. I'm not allowed . . . not even you.'

'Not to worry.'

They passed a church set back on a rise above the road, skirted a field of plough and returned, tired and radiant, to the cheerful embrace of the Mayfly house and the gas fire playing on the golden roses.

In the evening, they had the projector for visual memory: they would be in a car, passing a marshalling yard; or in a train beside an airfield; they would be taken on a walk through a town, and suddenly they would become aware that a vehicle or a face had reappeared, and they had not remembered its features. Sometimes a series of disconnected objects were flashed in rapid succession on to the screen, and there would be voices in the background, like the voices on the tape, but the conversation was not related to the film, so that the student must consult both his senses and retain what was valuable from each.

Thus the first day ended, setting the pattern for those that followed: carefree, exciting days for them both, days of honest labour and cautious but deepening attachment as the skills of boyhood became once more the weapons of war.

For the unarmed combat they had rented a small gymnasium near Headington which they had used in the war. An instructor had come by train. They called him Sergeant.

'Will he be carrying a knife at all? Not wanting to be curious,' he asked respectfully. He had a Welsh accent.

Haldane shrugged. 'It depends what he likes. We don't want to clutter him up.'

'There's a lot to be said for a knife, sir.' Leiser was still in the changing-room. 'If he knows how to use it. And the Jerries don't like them, not one bit.' He had brought some knives in a handcase, and he unpacked them in a private way, like a traveller unpacking his samples. 'They never could take cold steel,' he explained. 'Nothing too long, that's the trick of it, sir. Something flat with the two cutting edges.' He selected one and held it up. 'You can't do much better than this, as a matter of fact.' It was wide and flat like a laurel leaf, the blade unpolished, the handle waisted like an hour-glass, cross-hatched to prevent slip. Leiser was walking towards them, smoothing a comb through his hair.

'Used one of these, have you?'

Leiser examined the knife and nodded. The sergeant looked at him carefully. 'I know you, don't I? My name's Sandy Lowe. I'm a bloody Welshman.'

'You taught me in the war.'

'Christ,' said Lowe softly, 'so I did. You haven't changed much, have you?' They grinned shyly at one another, not knowing whether to shake hands. 'Come on, then, see what you remember.' They walked to the coconut matting in the centre of the floor. Lowe threw the knife at Leiser's feet and he snatched it up, grunting as he bent.

Lowe wore a jacket of torn tweed, very old. He stepped quickly back, took it off and with a single movement wrapped it round his left forearm, like a man preparing to fight a dog. Drawing his own knife he moved slowly round Leiser, keeping his weight steady but riding a little from one foot to the other. He was stooping, his bound arm held loosely in front of his stomach, fingers outstretched, palm facing the ground. He had gathered his body behind the guard, letting the blade play restlessly in front of it while Leiser kept steady, his eyes fixed upon the sergeant. For a time they feinted back and forth; once Leiser lunged and Lowe sprang back, allowing the knife to cut the cloth of the jacket on his arm. Once Lowe dropped to his kneees, as if to drive the knife upwards beneath Leiser's guard, and it was Leiser's turn to spring back, but too slowly, it seemed, for Lowe shook his head, shouted 'Halt!' and stood upright.

'Remember that?' He indicated his own belly and groin, pressing his arms and elbows in as if to reduce the width of his body. 'Keep the target small.' He made Leiser put his knife away and showed him holds, crooking his left arm round Leiser's neck and pretending to stab him in the kidneys or the stomach. Then he asked Avery to stand as a dummy, and the two of them moved round him with detachment, Lowe indicating the places with his knife and Leiser nodding, smiling occasionally when a particular trick came back to him.

'You didn't weave with the blade enough. Remember thumb on top, blade parallel to the ground, forearm stiff, wrist loose. Don't let his eye settle on it, not for a moment. And left hand in over your own target, whether you've got the knife or not. Never be generous about offering the body, that's what I say to my daughter.' They laughed dutifully, all but Haldane.

After that, Avery had a turn. Leiser seemed to want it. Removing his glasses, he held the knife as Lowe showed him, hesitant, alert, while Leiser trod crabwise, feinted and darted lightly back, the sweat running off his face, his small eyes alight with concentration. All the time Avery was conscious of the sharp grooves of the haft against the flesh of his palm, the aching in his calves and buttocks as he kept his weight forward on his toes, and Leiser's angry eyes searching his own. Then Leiser's foot had hooked round his ankle; as he lost balance he felt the knife being wrenched from his hand; he fell back, Leiser's full weight upon him, Leiser's hand clawing at the collar of his shirt.

They helped him up, all laughing, while Leiser brushed the dust from Avery's clothes. The knives were put away while they did physical training; Avery took part.

When it was over Lowe said: 'We'll just have a spot of unarmed combat and that will do nicely.'

Haldane glanced at Leiser. 'Have you had enough?'

'I'm all right.'

Lowe took Avery by an arm and stood him in the centre of the gym mat. 'You sit on the bench,' he called to Leiser, 'while I show you a couple of things.'

He put a hand on Avery's shoulder. 'We're only concerned with five marks, whether we got a knife or not. What are they?'

'Groin, kidneys, belly, heart and throat,' Leiser replied wearily.

'How do you break a man's neck?'

'You don't. You smash his windpipe at the front.'

'What about a blow on the back of the neck?'

'Not with the bare hand. Not without a weapon.' He had put his face in his hands.

'Correct.' Lowe moved his open palm in slow motion towards Avery's throat. 'Hand open, fingers straight, right?'

'Right,' Leiser said.

'What else do you remember?'

A pause. 'Tiger's Claw. An attack on the eyes.'

'Never use it,' the sergeant replied shortly. 'Not as an attacking blow. You leave yourself wide open. Now for the strangle holds. All from behind, remember? Bend the head back, so, hand on the throat, so, and *squeeze.*' Lowe looked over his shoulder: 'Look this way, please. I'm not doing this for my own benefit . . . come on, then, if you know it all, show us some throws!'

Leiser stood up, locking arms with Lowe, and for a while they struggled back and forth, each waiting for the other to offer an opening. Then Lowe gave way, Leiser toppled and Lowe's hand slapped the back of his head, thrusting it down so that Leiser fell face forward heavily on to the mat.

'You fall a treat,' said Lowe with a grin, and then Leiser was upon him, twisting Lowe's arm savagely back and throwing him very hard so that his little body hit the carpet like a bird hitting the windscreen of a car.

'You play fair!' Leiser demanded. 'Or I'll damn well hurt you.'

'Never lean on your opponent,' Lowe said shortly. 'And don't lose your temper in the gym.'

He called across to Avery. 'You have a turn now, sir; give him some exercise.'

Avery stood up, took off his jacket and waited for Leiser to approach him. He felt the strong grasp upon his arms and was suddenly conscious of the fraility of his body when matched against this adult force. He tried to seize the forearms of the older man, but his hands could not encompass them; he tried to break free, but Leiser held him; Leiser's head was against his own, filling his nostrils with the smell of hair oil. He felt the damp stubble of his cheek and the close, rank heat of his thin, straining body. Putting his hands on Leiser's chest he forced himself back, throwing all his energy into one frantic effort to escape the suffocating constriction of the man's embrace. As he drew away they caught sight of one another, it might have been for the first time, across the heaving cradle of their entangled arms; Leiser's face, contorted with exertion, softened into a smile; the grip relaxed.

Lowe walked over to Haldane. 'He's foreign, isn't he?'

'A Pole. What's he like?'

'I'd say he was quite a fighter in his day. Nasty. He's a good build. Fit too, considering.'

'I see.'

'How are you these days, sir, in yourself. All right, then?'

'Yes, thank you.'

'That's right. Twenty years. Amazing really. Kiddies all grown up.'

'I'm afraid I have none.'

'Mine, I mean.'

'Ah.'

'See any of the old crowd, then, sir? How about Mr Smiley?'

'I'm afraid I have not kept in touch. I am not a gregarious kind of person. Shall we settle up?'

Lowe stood lightly to attention while Haldane prepared to pay him; travelling money, salary and thirty-seven and six for the knife, plus twenty-two shillings for the sheath, a flat metal one with a spring to facilitate extraction. Lowe wrote him a receipt, signing it S. L. for reasons of security. 'I got the knife at cost,' he explained. 'It's a fiddle we work through the sports club.' He seemed proud of that.

Haldane gave Leiser a trenchcoat and Wellingtons and Avery took him for a walk. They went by bus as far as Headington, sitting on the top deck.

'What happened this morning?' Avery asked.

'I thought we were fooling about, that's all. Then he threw me.'

'He remembered you, didn't he?'

'Of course he did: then why did he hurt me?'

'He didn't mean to.'

'Look, it's all right, see.' He was still upset.

They got out at the terminus and began trudging through the rain.

Avery said, 'It's because he wasn't one of us; that's why you didn't like him.'

Leiser laughed, slipped his arm through Avery's. The rain drifting in slow waves across the empty street, ran down their faces and trickled into the collars of their mackintoshes. Avery pressed his arm to his side, holding Leiser's hand captive, and they continued their walk in shared contentment, forgetting the rain or playing with it, treading in the deepest parts and not caring about their clothes.

'Is the Captain pleased, John?'

'Very. He says it's going fine. We begin the wireless soon, just the elementary stuff. Jack Johnson's expected tomorrow.'

'It's coming back to me, John, the shooting and that. I hadn't forgotten.' He smiled. 'The old three-eight.'

'Nine-millimetre. You're doing fine, Fred. Just fine. The Captain said so.'

'Is that what he said, John, the Captain?'

'Of course. And he's told London. London's pleased too. We're only afraid you're a bit too . . .'

'Too what?'

'Well–too English.'

Leiser laughed. 'Not to worry, John.'

The inside of Avery's arm, where he held Leiser's hand, felt dry and warm.

They spent a morning on cyphers. Haldane acted as instructor. He had brought pieces of silk cloth imprinted with a cypher of the type Leiser would use, and a chart backed with cardboard for converting letters into numerals. He put the chart on the chimney-piece, wedging it behind the marble clock, and lectured them, rather as Leclerc would have done, but without affectation. Avery and Leiser sat at the table, pencils in hand, and under Haldane's tuition converted one passage after another into numbers according to the chart, deducted the result from figures on the silk cloth, finally re-translating into letters. It was a process which demanded application rather than concentration, and perhaps because Leiser was trying too hard he became bothered and erratic.

'We'll have a timed run over twenty groups,' Haldane said, and dictated from the sheet of paper in his hand a message of eleven words with the signature Mayfly. 'From next week you will have to manage without the chart. I shall put it in your room and you must commit it to memory. Go!'

He pressed the stopwatch and walked to the window while the two men worked feverishly at the table, muttering almost in unison while they jotted elementary calculations on the scrap paper in front of them. Avery could detect the increasing flurry of Leiser's movements, the suppressed sighs and imprecations, the angry erasures;

deliberately slowing down, he glanced over the other's arm to ascertain his progress and noticed that the stub of pencil buried in his little hand was smeared with sweat. Without a word, he silently changed his paper for Leiser's. Haldane, turning round, might not have seen.

Even in those first few days, it had become apparent that Leiser looked to Haldane as an ailing man looks to his doctor; a sinner to his priest. There was something terrible about a man who derived his strength from such a sickly body.

Haldane affected to ignore him. He adhered stubbornly to the habits of his private life. He never failed to complete his crossword. A case of burgundy was delivered from the town, half bottles, and he drank one alone at each meal while they listened to the tapes. So complete, indeed, was his withdrawal that one might have thought him revolted by the man's proximity. Yet the more elusive, the more aloof Haldane became, the more surely he drew Leiser after him. Leiser, by some obscure standards of his own, had cast him as the English gentleman, and whatever Haldane did or said only served, in the eyes of the other, to fortify him in the part.

Haldane grew in stature. In London he was a slow-walking man; he picked his way pedantically along the corridors as if he were looking for footholds; clerks and secretaries would hover impatiently behind him, lacking the courage to pass. In Oxford he betrayed an agility which would have astonished his London colleagues. His parched frame had revived, he held himself erect. Even his hostility acquired the mark of command. Only the cough remained, that racked, abandoned sob too heavy for such a narrow chest, bringing dabs of red to his thin cheeks and causing Leiser the mute concern of a pupil for his admired master.

'Is the Captain sick?' he once asked Avery, picking up an old copy of Haldane's *Times*.

'He never speaks of it.'

'I suppose that would be bad form.' His attention was suddenly arrested by the newspaper. It was unopened. Only the crossword had been done, the margins round it sparsely annotated with permutations of a nine-letter anagram. He showed it to Avery in bewilderment.

'He doesn't read it,' he said. 'He's only done the competition.'

That night, when they went to bed, Leiser took it with him, furtively as if it contained some secret which study could reveal.

So far as Avery could judge, Haldane was content with Leiser's progress. In the great variety of activities to which Leiser was now subjected, they had been able to observe him more closely; with the corrosive perception of the weak they discovered his failing and tested his power. He acquired, as they gained his trust, a disarming frankness; he loved to confide. He was their creature; he gave them everything, and they stored it away as the poor do. They saw that the Department had provided direction for his energy: like a man of uncommon sexual appetite, Leiser had found in his new employment a love which he could illustrate with his gifts. They saw that he took pleasure in their command, giving in return his strength as homage for fulfilment. They even knew perhaps that between them they constituted for Leiser the poles of absolute authority: the one by his bitter adherence to standards which Leiser could never achieve, the other by his youthful accessibility, the apparent sweetness and dependence of his nature.

He liked to talk to Avery. He talked about his women or the war. He assumed—it was irritating for Avery, but nothing more—that a man in his middle thirties, whether married or not, led an intense and varied love life. Later in the evening when the two of them had put on their coats and hurried to the pub at the end of the road, he would lean his elbows on the small table, thrust his bright face forward and relate the smallest detail of his exploits, his hand beside his chin, his slim fingertips rapidly parting and closing in unconscious imitation of his mouth. It was not vanity which made him thus but friendship. These betrayals and confessions, whether truth or fantasy, were the simple coinage of their intimacy. He never mentioned Betty.

Avery came to know Leiser's face with an accuracy no longer related to memory. He noticed how its features seemed structurally to alter shape according to his mood, how when he was tired or depressed at the end of a long day the skin on his cheekbones was drawn upwards rather than down, and the corners of his eyes and mouth rose tautly so that his expression was at once more Slav and less familiar.

He had acquired from his neighbourhood or his clients certain turns of phrase which, though wholly without meaning, impressed his foreign ear. He would speak, for instance, of 'some measure of satisfaction', using an impersonal construction for the sake of dignity. He had assimilated also a variety of clichés. Expressions like 'not to worry', 'don't rock the boat,' 'let the dog see the rabbit', came to him continually, as if he were aspiring after a way of life which he only imperfectly understood, and these were the offerings that would buy him in. Some expressions, Avery remarked, were out of date.

Once or twice Avery suspected that Haldane resented his intimacy with Leiser. At other times it seemed that Haldane was deploying emotions in Avery over which he himself no longer disposed. One evening at the beginning of the second week, while Leiser was engaged in that lengthy toilet which preceded almost any recreational engagement, Avery asked Haldane whether he did not wish to go out himself.

'What do you expect me to do? Make a pilgrimage to the shrine of my youth?'

'I thought you might have friends there; people you still know.'

'If I do, it would be insecure to visit them. I am here under another name.'

'I'm sorry. Of course.'

'Besides'—a dour smile—'we are not all so prolific in our friendships.'

'You told me to stay with him!' Avery said hotly.

'Precisely; and you have. It would be churlish of me to complain. You do it admirably.'

'Do what?'

'Obey instructions.'

At that moment the door bell rang and Avery went downstairs to answer it. By the light of the streetlamp he could see the familiar shape of a Department van parked in the road. A small, homely figure stood on the doorstep. He was wearing a brown suit and overcoat. There was a high shine on the toes of his brown shoes. He might have come to read the meter.

'Jack Johnson's my name,' he said uncertainly. 'Johnson's Fair Deal, that's me.'

'Come in,' Avery said.

'This the right place, isn't it? Captain Hawkins . . . and all that?'

He carried a soft leather bag which he laid carefully on the floor as if it contained all he possessed. Half closing his umbrella he shook it expertly to rid it of the rain, then placed it on the stand beneath his overcoat.

'I'm John.'

Johnson took his hand and squeezed it warmly.

'Very pleased to meet you. The Boss has talked a lot about you. You're quite the blue-eyed boy, I hear.'

They laughed.

He took Avery by the arm in a quick confiding gesture. 'Using your own name, are you?'

'Yes. Christian name.'

'And the Captain?'

'Hawkins.'

'What's he like, Mayfly? How's he bearing up?'

'Fine. Just fine.'

'I hear he's quite a one for the girls.'

While Johnson and Haldane talked in the drawing-room Avery slipped upstairs to Leiser.

'It's no go, Fred. Jack's come.'

'Who's Jack?'

'Jack Johnson, the wireless chap.'

'I thought we didn't start that till next week.'

'Just the elementary this week, to get your hand in. Come down and say hello.'

He was wearing a dark suit and held a nail file in one hand.

'What about going out, then?'

'I told you; we can't tonight, Fred; Jack's here.'

Leiser went downstairs and shook Johnson briefly by the hand, without formality, as if he did not care for latecomers. They talked awkwardly for quarter of an hour until Leiser, protesting tiredness, went sullenly to bed.

Johnson made his first report. 'He's slow,' he said. 'He hasn't worked a key for a long time, mind. But I daren't try him on a set till he's quicker on the key. I know it's all of twenty years, sir; you can't blame him. But he *is* slow, sir, very.' He had an attentive, nursery-rhyme way of talking as if he spent much time in the company of children. 'The Boss says I'm to play him all the time–when he starts the job, too. I understand we're all going over to Germany, sir.'

'Yes.'

'Then we shall have to get to know each other,' he insisted, 'Mayfly and me. We ought to be together a lot, sir, the moment I begin working him on the set. It's like handwriting, this game, we've got to get used to one another's handwriting. Then there's schedules, times for coming up and that; signal plans for his frequencies. Safety devices. That's a lot to learn in a fortnight.'

'Safety devices?' Avery asked.

'Deliberate mistakes, sir; like a misspelling in a particular group, an E for an A or something of that kind. If he wants to tell us he's been caught and is transmitting under control, he'll miss the safety device.' He turned to Haldane. 'You know the kind of thing, Captain.'

'There was talk in London of teaching him high-speed transmission on tape. Do you know what became of that idea?'

'The Boss did mention it to me, sir. I understand the equipment wasn't available. I can't say I know much about it, really; since my time, the transistorized stuff. The Boss said we were to stick to the old methods but change the frequency every two and a half minutes, sir; I understand the Jerries are very hot on the direction-finding these days.'

'What set did they send down? It seemed very heavy for him to carry about.'

'It's the kind Mayfly used in the war, sir, that's the beauty of it. The old B2 in the waterproof casing. If we've only got a couple of weeks there doesn't hardly seem time to go over anything else. Not that he's ready to work it yet—'

'What does it weigh?'

'About fifty pound, sir, all in. The ordinary suitcase set. It's the waterproofing that adds the weight, but he's got to have it if he's going over rough country. Specially at this time of year.' He hesitated. 'But he's slow on his Morse, sir.'

'Quite. Do you think you can bring him up to scratch in the time?'

'Can't tell yet, sir. Not till we really get cracking on the set. Not till the second period, when he's had his little bit of leave. I'm just letting him handle the buzzer at present.'

'Thank you,' said Haldane.

Chapter Thirteen

At the end of the first two weeks they gave him forty-eight hours leave of absence. He had not asked for it and when they offered it to him he seemed puzzled. In no circumstances was he to visit his own neighbourhood. He could depart for London on the Friday but he said he preferred to go on Saturday. He could return on Monday morning but he said it depended and he might come back late on Sunday. They stressed that he was to keep clear of anyone who might know him, and in some curious fashion this seemed to console him.

Avery, worried, went to Haldane.

'I don't think we should send him off into the blue. You've told him he can't go back to South Park; or visit his friends, even if he's got any; I don't see quite where he can go.'

'You think he'll be lonely?'

Avery blushed. 'I think he'll just want to come back all the time.'

'We can hardly object to that.'

They gave him subsistence money in old notes, fives and ones. He wanted to refuse it, but Haldane pressed it on him as if a principle were involved. They offered to book him a room but he declined. Haldane assumed he was going to London, so in the end he went, as if he owed it to them.

'He's got some woman,' said Johnson with satisfaction.

He left on the midday train, carrying one pigskin suitcase and wearing his camel-hair coat; it had a slightly military cut, and leather buttons, but no person of breeding could ever have mistaken it for a British warm.

He handed in his suitcase to the depository at Paddington Station and wandered out into Praed Street because he had nowhere to go. He walked about for half an hour, looking at the shop windows and reading the tarts' advertisements on the glazed notice boards. It was Saturday afternoon: a handful of old men in trilby hats and raincoats hovered between the pornography shops and the pimps on the corner. There was very little traffic: an atmosphere of hopeless recreation filled the street.

The cinema club charged a pound and gave him a predated membership card because of the law. He sat among ghost figures on a kitchen chair. The film was very old; it might have come over from Vienna when the persecutions began. Two girls, quite naked, took tea. There was no sound track and they just went on drinking tea, changing position a little as they passed their cups. They would be sixty by now, if they had survived the war. He got up to go because it was after half past five and the pubs were open. As he passed the kiosk at the doorway, the manager said: 'I know a girl who likes a gay time. Very young.'

'No, thanks.'

'Two and a half quid; she likes foreigners. She gives it foreign if you like. French.'

'Run away.'

'Don't you tell me to run away.'

'Run away.' Leiser returned to the kiosk, his small eyes suddenly alight. 'Next time you offer me a girl, make it something English, see.'

The air was warmer, the wind had dropped, the street emptied; pleasures were indoors now. The woman behind the bar said, 'Can't mix it for you now, dear, not till the rush dies down. You can see for yourself.'

'It's the only thing I drink.'

'Sorry, dear.'

He ordered gin and Italian instead and got it warm with no cherry. Walking had made him tired. He sat on the bench which ran along the wall, watching the darts four. They did not speak, but pursued their game with quiet devotion, as if they were deeply conscious of tradition. It was like the film club. One of them had a date, and they called to Leiser, 'Make a four, then?'

'I don't mind,' he said, pleased to be addressed, and stood up; but a friend came in, a man called Henry, and Henry was preferred. Leiser was going to argue but there seemed no point.

Avery too had gone out alone. To Haldane he had said he was taking a walk, to Johnson that he was going to the cinema. Avery had a way of lying which defied rational explanation. He found himself drawn to the old places he had known; his college in the Turl; the bookshops, pubs and libraries. The term was just ending. Oxford had a smell of Christmas about it, and acknowledged it with prudish ill will, dressing the shop windows with last year's tinsel.

He took the Banbury Road until he reached the street where he and Sarah had lived for the first year of marriage. The flat was in darkness. Standing before it, he tried to detect in the house, in himself, some trace of the sentiment, or affection, or love, or whatever it was that explained their marriage, but it was not to be found and he supposed it had never been. He sought desperately, wanting to find the motive of youth; but there was none. He was staring into an empty house. He hastened home to the place where Leiser lived.

'Good film?' Johnson asked.

'Fine.'

'I thought you were going for a walk,' Haldane complained, looking up from his crossword.

'I changed my mind.'

'Incidentally,' Haldane said, 'Leiser's gun. I understand he prefers the three-eight.'

'Yes. They call it the nine-millimetre now.'

'When he returns he should start to carry it with him; take it everywhere, unloaded of course.' A glance at Johnson. 'Particularly when he begins transmission exercises on any scale. He must have it on him all the time; we want him to feel lost without it. I have arranged for one to be issued; you'll find it in your room, Avery, with various holsters. Perhaps you'd explain it to him, would you?'

'Won't you tell him yourself?'

'You do it. You get on with him so nicely.'

He went upstairs to telephone Sarah. She had gone to stay with her mother. Conversation was very formal.

Leiser dialled Betty's number, but there was no reply.

Relieved, he went to a cheap jewellers, near the station, which was open on Saturday afternoon and bought a gold coach and horses for a charm bracelet. It cost eleven pounds, which was what they had given him for subsistence. He asked them to send it by registered mail to her address in South Park. He put a note in saying 'Back in two weeks. Be good', signing it, in a moment of aberration, F. Leiser, so he crossed it out and wrote 'Fred'.

He walked for a bit, thought of picking up a girl, and finally booked in at the hotel near the station. He slept badly because of the noise of traffic. In the morning he rang her number again; there was no reply. He replaced the receiver quickly; he might have waited a little longer. He had breakfast, went out and bought the Sunday papers, took them to his room and read the football reports till lunch time. In the afternoon he went for a walk, it had become a habit, right through London, he hardly knew where. He followed the river as far as Charing Cross and found himself in an empty garden filled with drifting rain. The tarmac paths were strewn with yellow leaves. An old man sat on the bandstand, quite alone. He wore a black overcoat and a rucksack of green webbing like the case of a gas mask. He was asleep, or listening to music.

He waited till evening in order not to disappoint Avery, then caught the last train home to Oxford.

Avery knew a pub behind Balliol where they let you play bar billiards on Sundays. Johnson liked a game of bar billiards. Johnson was on Guinness, Avery was on whisky. They were laughing a good deal; it had been a tough week. Johnson was winning; he went for the lower numbers, methodically, while Avery tried to cushion shots at the hundred pocket.

'I wouldn't mind a bit of what Fred's having,' Johnson said with a snigger. He played a shot; a white ball dropped dutifully into its hole. 'Poles are dead randy. Go up anything, a Pole will. Specially Fred, he's a real terror. He's got the walk.'

'Are you that way, Jack?'

'When I'm in the mood. I wouldn't mind a little bit now, as a matter of fact.'

They played a couple of shots, each lost in an alcoholic euphoria of erotic fancy.

'Still,' said Johnson gratefully, 'I'd rather be in our shoes, wouldn't you?'

'Any day.'

'You know,' Johnson said, chalking his cue, 'I shouldn't be speaking to you like this, should I? You've had college and that. You're different class, John.'

They drank to each other, both thinking of Leiser.

'For Christ's sake,' Avery said. 'We're fighting the same war, aren't we?'

'Quite right.'

Johnson poured the rest of the Guinness out of the bottle. He took great care, but a little ran over the side on to the table.

'Here's to Fred,' Avery said.

'To Fred. On the nest. And bloody good luck to him.'

'Good luck, Fred.'

'I don't know how he'll manage the B2,' Johnson murmured. 'He's got a long way to go.'

'Here's to Fred.'

'Fred. He's a lovely boy. Here: do you know this bloke Woodford, the one who picked me up?'

'Of course. He'll be coming down next week.'

'Met his wife at all; Babs? She was a girl, she was; give it to anyone. . . . Christ! Past it now, I suppose. Still, many a good tune, eh?'

'That's right.'

'To him that hath shalt be given,' Johnson declared.

They drank; that joke went astray.

'She used to go with the admin bloke, Jimmy Gorton. What happened to him then?'

'He's in Hamburg. Doing very well.'

They got home before Leiser. Haldane was in bed.

It was after midnight when Leiser hung his wet camel-hair coat in the hall, on a hanger because he was a precise man: tiptoed to the drawing-room and put on the light. His eye ran fondly over the heavy furniture, the tallboy elaborately decorated with fretwork and heavy brass handles; the escritoire and the bible table. Lovingly he revisited the handsome women at croquet, handsome men at war, disdainful boys in boaters, girls at Cheltenham; a whole long history of discomfort and not a breath of passion. The clock on the chimney-piece was like a pavilion in blue marble. The hands were of gold, so ornate, so fashioned, so flowered and spreading that you had to look twice to see where the points of them lay. They had not moved since he went away, perhaps not since he was born, and somehow that was a great achievement for an old clock.

He picked up his suitcase and went upstairs. Haldane was cough-ing but no light came from his room. He tapped on Avery's door.

'You there, John?'

After a moment he heard him sit up. 'Nice time, Fred?'

'You bet.'

'Woman all right?'

'Just the job. See you tomorrow, John.'

'See you in the morning. Night, Fred. Fred . . .'

'Yes, John?'

'Jack and I had a bit of a session. You should have been there.'

'That's right, John.'

Slowly he made his way along the corridor, content in his weariness, entered his room, took off his jacket, lit a cigarette and threw himself gratefully into the armchair. It was tall and very comfortable, with wings on the side. As he did so he caught sight of something. A chart hung on the wall for turning letters into figures, and beneath it, on the bed, lying in the middle of the eiderdown, was an old suitcase of continental pattern, dark green canvas with leather on the corners. It was open; inside were two boxes of grey steel. He got up, staring at them in mute recognition; reached out and touched them, wary as if they might be hot; turned the dials, stooped and read the legend by the switches. It could have been the set he had in Holland: transmitter and receiver in one box; power unit, key and earphones in the other. Crystals, a dozen of them, in a bag of parachute silk with a green drawstring threaded through the top. He tested the key with his finger; it seemed much smaller than he remembered.

He returned to the armchair, his eyes still fixed upon the suitcase; sat there, stiff and sleepless, like a man conducting a wake.

He was late for breakfast. Haldane said, 'You spend all day with Johnson. Morning and afternoon.'

'No walk?' Avery was busy with his egg.

'Tomorrow perhaps. From now on we're concerned with technique. I'm afraid walks take second place.'

Control quite often stayed in London on Monday nights, which he said was the only time he could get a chair at his club; Smiley suspected he wanted to get away from his wife.

'I hear the flowers are coming out in Blackfriars Road,' he said. 'Leclerc's driving around in a Rolls Royce.'

'It's a perfectly ordinary Humber,' Smiley retorted. 'From the Ministry pool.'

'Is that where it comes from?' Control asked, his eyebrows very high. 'Isn't it fun? So the black friars have won the pool.'

Chapter Fourteen

'You know the set, then?' Johnson asked.

'The B2.'

'OK. Official title, Type three, Mark two; runs on AC or a six-volt car battery, but you'll be using the mains, right? They've queried the current where you're going and it's AC. Your mains consumption with this set is fifty-seven watts on transmit and twenty-five on receive. So if you *do* end up somewhere and they've only got DC, you're going to have to borrow a battery, right?'

Leiser did not laugh.

'Your mains lead is provided with adaptors for all continental sockets.'

'I know.'

Leiser watched Johnson prepare the set for operation. First he linked the transmitter and receiver to the power pack by means of six-pin plugs, adjusting the twin claws to the terminals; having plugged in the set and turned it on, he joined the miniature Morse key to the transmitter and the earphones to the receiver.

'That's a smaller key than we had in the war,' Leiser objected. 'I tried it last night. My fingers kept slipping.'

Johnson shook his head.

'Sorry, Fred; same size.' He winked. 'Perhaps your finger's grown.'

'All right, come on.'

Now he extracted from the spares box a coil of multi-stranded wire, plastic covered, attaching one end to the aerial terminals. 'Most of your crystals will be around the three megacycle mark, so you may

not have to change your coil—get a nice stretch on your aerial and
you'll be a hundred per cent, Fred; specially at night. Now watch the
tuning. You've connected up your aerial, earth, key, headphones and
power pack. Look at your signal plan and see what frequency you're
on; fish out the corresponding crystal, right?' He held up a small
capsule of black bakelite, guided the pins into the double
socket—'Shoving the male ends into the doodahs, like so. All right so
far, Fred? Not hurrying you, am I?'

'I'm watching. Don't keep asking.'

'Now turn the crystal selector dial to "fundamental all crystals",
and adjust your wave band to match your frequency. If you're on
three and a half megs you want the wave-band knob on three to four,
like so. Now insert your plug-in coil either way round, Fred; you've
got a nice overlap there.'

Leiser's head was supported in his hand as he tried desperately to
remember the sequence of movements which once had come so
naturally to him. Johnson proceeded with the method of a man born
to his trade. His voice was soft and easy, very patient, his hands
moving instinctively from one dial to another with perfect familiarity. All the time the monologue continued:

'TRS switch on T for tune; put your anode tuning and aerial
matching on ten; now you can switch on your power pack, right?' He
pointed to the meter window. 'You should get the three hundred
reading, near enough, Fred. Now I'm ready to have a go: I shove my
meter selector on three and twiddle the PA tuning till I get maximum
meter reading; now I put her on six—'

'What's PA?'

'Power Amplifier, Fred: didn't you know that?'

'Go on.'

'Now I move the anode tuning knob till I get my minimum
value—here you are! She's a hundred with the knob on two, right?
Now push your TRS over to S–S for send, Fred— and you're ready
to tune the aerial. Here—press the key. That's right, see? You get a
bigger reading because you're putting power into the aerial, follow
it?'

Silently he performed the brief ritual of tuning the aerial until the
meter obediently dipped to the final reading.

'And Bob's your uncle!' he declared triumphantly. 'Now it's
Fred's turn. Here, your hand's sweating. You must have had a week-
end, you must. Wait a minute, Fred!' He left the room, returning
with an oversized white pepperpot, from which he carefully sprin-
kled french chalk over the black lozenge on the key lever.

'Take my advice,' Johnson said, 'just leave the girls in peace, see,
Fred? Let it grow.'

Leiser was looking at his open hand. Particles of sweat had
gathered in the grooves. 'I couldn't sleep.'

'I'll bet you couldn't.' He slapped the case affectionately. 'From now on you sleep with *her*. She's Mrs Fred, see, and no one else!' He dismantled the set and waited for Leiser to begin. With childish slowness Leiser painfully reassembled the equipment. It was all so long ago.

Day after day Leiser and Johnson sat at the small table in the bedroom tapping out their messages. Sometimes Johnson would drive away in the van leaving Leiser alone, and they would work back and forth till early morning. Or Leiser and Avery would go—Leiser was not allowed out alone—and from a borrowed house in Fairford they would pass their signals, encoding, sending and receiving *en clair* trivialities disguised as amateur transmissions. Leiser discernibly changed. He became nervy and irritable; he complained to Haldane about the complications of transmitting on a series of frequences, the difficulty of constant retuning, the shortage of time. His relationship to Johnson was always uneasy. Johnson had arrived late, and for some reason Leiser insisted on treating him as an outsider, not admitting him properly to the companionship which he fancied to exist between Avery, Haldane and himself.

There was a particularly absurd scene one breakfast. Leiser raised the lid of a jam-pot, peered inside and, turning to Avery, asked, 'Is this bee-honey?'

Johnson leant across the table, knife in one hand, bread and butter in the other.

'We don't say that, Fred. We just call it honey.'

'That's right, honey. Bee-honey.'

'Just honey,' Johnson repeated. 'In England we just call it honey.'

Leiser carefully replaced the lid, pale with anger. 'Don't you tell me what to say.'

Haldane looked up sharply from his paper. 'Be quiet, Johnson. Bee-honey is perfectly accurate.'

Leiser's courtesy had something of the servant, his quarrels with Johnson something of the backstairs.

Despite such incidents as this, like any two men engaged daily upon a single project, they came gradually to share their hopes, moods and depressions. If a lesson had gone well, the meal that followed it would be a happy affair. The two of them would exchange esoteric remarks about the state of the ionosphere, the skip distance on a given frequency, or an unnatural meter reading which had occurred during tuning. If badly, they would speak little or not at all, and everyone but Haldane would hasten through his food for want of anything to say. Occasionally Leiser would ask whether he might not take a walk with Avery, but Haldane shook his head and said there was no time. Avery, a guilty lover, made no move to help.

As the two weeks neared their end, the Mayfly house was several times visited by specialists of one kind or another from London. A

photographic instructor came, a tall, hollow-eyed man, who demonstrated a sub-miniature camera with interchangeable lenses;
there was a doctor, benign and wholly incurious, who listened to
Leiser's heart for minutes on end. The Treasury had insisted upon it;
there was the question of compensation. Leiser declared he had no
dependants, but he was examined all the same to satisfy the
Treasury.

With the increase in these activities Leiser came to derive great
comfort from his gun. Avery had given it to him after his week-end's
leave. He favoured a shoulder holster (the drape of his jackets nicely
concealed the bulge) and sometimes at the end of a long day he would
draw the gun and finger it, looking down the barrel, raising it and
lowering it as he had done on the range. 'There isn't a gun to beat it,'
he would say. 'Not for the size. You can have your continental types
any time. Women's guns, they are, like their cars. Take my advice,
John, a three-eight's best.'

'Nine-millimetre they call it now.'

His resentment of strangers reached its unexpected climax in the
visit of Hyde, a man from the Circus. The morning had gone badly.
Leiser had been making a timed run, encoding and transmitting
forty groups; his bedroom and Johnson's were now linked on an
internal circuit; they played back and forth behind closed doors.
Johnson had taught him a number of international code signs: QRJ,
your signals are too weak to read: QRW, send faster: QSD, your
keying is bad: QSM, repeat the last message: QSZ, send each word
twice: QRU, I have nothing for you. As Leiser's transmission
became increasingly uneven, Johnson's comments, thus cryptically
expressed, added to his confusion, until with a shout of irritation he
switched off his set and stalked downstairs to Avery. Johnson
followed him.

'It's no good giving up, Fred.'

'Leave me alone.'

'Look, Fred, you did it all wrong. I *told* you to send the numbers of
groups *before* you send the message. You can't remember a thing, can
you—'

'Look, leave me alone, I said!' He was about to add something
when the door bell rang. It was Hyde. He had brought an assistant, a
plump man who was sucking something against the weather.

They did not play the tapes at lunch. Their guests sat side by side,
eating glumly as if they had the same food every day because of the
calories. Hyde was a meagre, dark-faced man without a trace of
humour who reminded Avery of Sutherland. He had come to give
Leiser a new identity. He had papers for him to sign, identity
documents, a form of ration card, a driving licence, a permit to enter
the border zone along a specified area, and an old shirt in a briefcase.
After lunch he laid them all out on the drawing-room table while the

photographer put up his camera.

They dressed Leiser in the shirt and took him full face with both ears showing according to the German regulations, then led him to sign the papers. He seemed nervous.

'We're going to call you Freiser,' Hyde said, as if that were an end to the matter.

'Freiser? That's like my own name.'

'That's the idea. That's what your people wanted. For signatures and things, so that there's no slip-up. You'd better practise it a bit before you sign.'

'I'd rather have it different. Quite different.'

'We'll stick to Freiser, I think,' said Hyde. 'It's been decided at high level.' Hyde was a man who leaned heavily upon the Passive Voice.

There was an uncomfortable silence.

'I want it different. I don't like Freiser and I want it different.' He didn't like Hyde either, and in half a minute he was going to say so.

Haldane intervened. 'You're under instructions. The Department has taken the decision. There is no question of altering it now.'

Leiser was very pale.

'Then they can bloody well change the instructions. I want a different name, that's all. Christ, it's only a little thing, isn't it? That's all I'm asking for: another name, a proper one, not a half-cock imitation of my own.'

'I don't understand,' Hyde said. 'It's only training, isn't it?'

'You don't have to understand! Just change it, that's all. Who the hell d'you think you are, coming in here and ordering me about?'

'I'll telephone London,' Haldane said, and went upstairs. They waited awkwardly until he came down.

'Will you accept Hartbeck?' Haldane inquired. There was a note of sarcasm in his voice.

Leiser smiled. 'Hartbeck. That's fine.' He spread out his hands in a gesture of apology. 'Hartbeck's fine.'

Leiser spent ten minutes practising a signature then signed the papers, with a little flourish each time as if there were dust on them. Hyde gave them a lecture on the documents. It took a very long time. There were no actual ration cards in East Germany, Hyde said, but there existed a system of registration with food shops, who provided a certificate. He explained the principle of travel permits and the circumstances under which they were granted, he talked at length about the obligation on Leiser to show his identity card, unasked, when he bought a railway ticket or put up at an hotel. Leiser argued with him and Haldane attempted to terminate the meeting. Hyde paid no attention. When he had finished he nodded and went away with his photographer, folding the old shirt into his briefcase as if it were part of his equipment.

This outburst of Leiser's appeared to cause Haldane some concern. He telephoned to London and ordered his assistant, Gladstone, to go over Leiser's file for any trace of the name Freiser; he had a search made in all the indices, but without success. When Avery suggested Haldane was making too much of the incident the other shook his head. 'We're waiting for the second vow,' he said.

Following upon Hyde's visit, Leiser now received daily briefings about his cover. Stage by stage he, Avery and Haldane constructed in tireless detail the background of the man Hartbeck, establishing him in his work, his tastes and recreations, in his love life and choice of friends. Together, they entered the most obscure corners of the man's conjectured existence, gave him skills and attributes which Leiser himself barely possessed.

Woodford came with news of the Department.

'The Director's putting up a marvellous show.' From the way he spoke, Leclerc might have been fighting an illness. 'We leave for Lübeck a week today. Jimmy Gorton's been on to the German frontier people–he says they're pretty reliable. We've got a crossing point lined up and we've taken a farmhouse on the outskirts of the town. He's let it be known that we're a team of academics wanting a quiet time and a bit of fresh air.' Woodford looked confidingly at Haldane. 'The Department is working wonderfully. As one man. And what a *spirit*, Adrian! No watching the clock these days. And no *rank*. Dennison, Sandford . . . we're just a single team. You should see the way Clarkie's going for the Ministry about poor Taylor's pension. How's Mayfly bearing up?' he added in a low voice.

'All right. He's doing wireless upstairs.'

'Any more signs of nerves? Outbreaks or anything?'

'None so far as I know,' Haldane replied, as if he were unlikely to know anyway.

'Is he getting frisky? Sometimes they want a girl about now.'

Woodford had brought drawings of Soviet rockets. They had been made by Ministry draughtsmen from photographs held in Research Section, enlarged to about two foot by three, neatly mounted on showcards. Some were stamped with a security classification. Prominent features were marked with arrows; the nomenclature was curiously childish: fin, cone, fuel compartment, payload. Beside each rocket stood a gay little figure like a penguin in a flying helmet, and printed beneath him: 'size of average man'. Woodford arranged them round the room as if they were his own work; Avery and Haldane watched in silence.

'He can look at them after lunch,' Haldane said. 'Put them together till then.'

'I've brought along a film to give him some background. Launchings, transportation, a bit about destructive capacity. The Director said he should have an idea what these things can do. Give him a shot in the arm.'

'He doesn't need a shot in the arm,' Avery said.

Woodford remembered something. 'Oh–and your little Gladstone wants to talk to you. He said it was urgent–didn't know how to get hold of you. I told him you'd give him a ring when you had time. Apparently you asked him to do a job on the Mayfly area. Industry, was it, or manoeuvres? He says he's got the answer ready for you in London. He's the best type of NCO, that fellow.' He glanced at the ceiling. 'When's Fred coming down?'

Haldane said abruptly, 'I don't want you to meet him, Bruce.' It was unusual in Haldane to use a Christian name. 'I'm afraid you must take luncheon in the town. Charge it to Accounts.'

'Why on earth not?'

'Security. I see no point in his knowing more of us than is strictly necessary. The charts speak for themselves; so, presumably, does the film.'

Woodford, profoundly insulted, left. Avery knew then that Haldane was determined to preserve Leiser in the delusion that the Department housed no fools.

For the last day of the course, Haldane had planned a full-scale exercise to last from ten in the morning until eight in the evening, a combined affair including visual observation in the town, clandestine photography and listening to tapes. The information which Leiser assembled during the day was to be made into a report, encoded and communicated by wireless to Johnson in the evening. A certain hilarity infected the briefing that morning. Johnson made a joke about not photographing the Oxford Constabulary by mistake; Leiser laughed richly and even Haldane allowed himself a wan smile. It was the end of term; the boys were going home.

The exercise was a success. Johnson was pleased; Avery enthusiastic; Leiser manifestly delighted. They had made two faultless transmissions, Johnson said, Fred was steady as a rock. At eight o'clock they assembled for dinner wearing their best suits. A special menu had been arranged. Haldane had presented the rest of his burgundy; toasts were made; there was talk of an annual reunion in years to come. Leiser looked very smart in a dark blue suit and a pale tie of watered silk.

Johnson got rather drunk and insisted on bringing down Leiser's wireless set, raising his glass to it repeatedly and calling it Mrs Hartbeck. Avery and Leiser sat together: the estrangement of the last week was over.

The next day, a Saturday, Avery and Haldane returned to London. Leiser was to remain in Oxford with Johnson until the whole party left for Germany on Monday. On the Sunday, an Air Force van would call at the house to collect the suitcase. This would be independently conveyed to Gorton in Hamburg together with Johnson's own base equipment, and thence to the farmhouse near Lübeck from which Operation Mayfly would be launched. Before he left the house Avery took a last look round, partly for reasons of sentiment, and partly because he had signed the lease and was concerned about the inventory.

Haldane was ill at ease on the journey to London. He was still waiting, apparently, for some unknown crisis in Leiser.

Chapter Fifteen

It was the same evening. Sarah was in bed. Her mother had brought her to London.

'If you ever want me,' he said, 'I'll come to you, wherever you are.'

'You mean when I'm dying.' Analysing, she added, 'I'll do the same for you, John. Now can I repeat my question?'

'Monday. There's a group of us going.' It was like children: parallel playing.

'Which part of Germany?'

'Just Germany, West Germany. For a conference.'

'More bodies?'

'Oh, for God's sake, Sarah, do you think I want to keep it from you?'

'Yes, John, I do,' she said simply. 'I think if you were allowed to tell me you wouldn't care about the job. You've got a kind of licence I can't share.'

'I can only tell you it's a big thing . . . a big operation. With agents. I've been training them.'

'Who's in charge?'

'Haldane.'

'Is that the one who confides in you about his wife? I think he's utterly disgusting.'

'No, that's Woodford. This man's quite different. Haldane's odd. Donnish. Very good.'

'But they're all good, aren't they? Woodford's good too.'

Her mother came in with tea.

'When are you getting up?' he asked.

'Monday, probably. It depends on the doctor.'

'She'll need quiet,' her mother said, and went out.

'If you believe in it, do it,' Sarah said. 'But don't . . .' she broke off, shook her head, little girl now.

'You're jealous. You're jealous of my job and the secrecy. You don't *want* me to believe in my work!'

'Go on. Believe in it if you can.'

For a while they did not look at one another. 'If it weren't for Anthony I really would leave you,' Sarah declared at last.

'What for?' Avery asked hopelessly, and then, seeing the opening, 'Don't let Anthony stop you.'

'You never talk to me: any more than you talk to Anthony. He hardly knows you.'

'What is there to talk about?'

'Oh, God.'

'I can't talk about my work, you know that. I tell you more than I should as it is. That's why you're always sneering at the Department, isn't it? You can't understand it, you don't want to; you don't *like* it being secret but you despise me when I break the rules.'

'Don't go over that again.'

'I'm not coming back,' Avery said. 'I've decided.'

'This time, perhaps you'll remember Anthony's present.'

'I bought him that milk lorry.'

They sat in silence again.

'You ought to meet Leclerc,' said Avery; 'I think you ought to talk to him. He keeps suggesting it. Dinner . . . he might convince you.'

'What of?'

She found a piece of cotton hanging from the seam of her bed-jacket. Sighing, she took a pair of nail scissors from the drawer in the bedside table and cut it off.

'You should have drawn it through at the back,' Avery said. 'You ruin your clothes that way.'

'What are they like?' she asked. 'The agents? Why do they do it?'

'For loyalty, partly. Partly money, I suppose.'

'You mean you bribe them?'

'Oh shut up!'

'Are they English?'

'One of them is. Don't ask me any more, Sarah; I can't tell you.' He advanced his head towards her. 'Don't ask me, Sweet.' He took her hand; she let him.

'And they're all men?'

'Yes.'

Suddenly she said, it was a complete break, no tears, no precision, but quickly, with compassion, as if the speeches were over and this were the choice: 'John, I want to know, I've got to know, now, before you go. It's an awful, unEnglish question, but all the time you've been telling me something, ever since you took this job. You've been telling me people don't matter, that *I* don't, Anthony doesn't; that the agents don't. You've been telling me you've found a vocation. Well, who calls you, that's what I mean: what *sort* of vocation? That's the question you never answer: that's why you hide from me. Are you a martyr, John? Should I admire you for what you're doing? Are you making sacrifices?'

Flatly, avoiding her, Avery replied, 'It's nothing like that. I'm doing a job. I'm a technician; part of the machine. You want me to say double-think, don't you? You want to demonstrate the paradox.'

'No. You've said what I want you to say. You've got to draw a circle and not go outside it. That's not double-think, it's unthink. It's very humble of you. Do you really believe you're that small?'

'You've made me small. Don't sneer. You're making me small now.'

'John, I swear it, I don't mean to. When you came back last night you looked as though you'd fallen in love. The kind of love that gives you comfort. You looked free and at peace. I thought for a moment you'd found a woman. That's why I asked, really it is, whether they were all men. . . . I thought you were in love. Now you tell me you're nothing, and you seem proud of that too.'

He waited, then smiling, the smile he gave Leiser, he said, 'Sarah, I missed you terribly. When I was in Oxford I went to the house, the house in Chandos Road, remember? It was fun there, wasn't it?' He gave her hand a squeeze. 'Real fun. I thought about it, our marriage and you. And Anthony. I love you, Sarah; I love you. For everything . . . the way you bring up our baby.' A laugh. 'You're both so vulnerable, sometimes I can hardly tell you apart.'

She remained silent, so he continued, 'I thought perhaps if we lived in the country, bought a house . . . I'm established now: Leclerc would arrange a loan. Then Anthony could run about more. It's only a matter of increasing our range. Going to the theatre, like we used to at Oxford.'

She said absently, 'Did we? We can't go to the theatre in the country, can we?'

'The Department gives me something, don't you understand? It's a real job. It's important, Sarah.'

She pushed him gently away. 'My mother's asked us to Reigate for Christmas.'

'That'll be fine. Look . . . about the office. They owe me something now, after all I've done. They accept me on equal terms. As a colleague, I'm one of them.'

'Then you're not responsible, are you? Just one of the team. So there's no sacrifice.' They were back to the beginning. Avery, not realizing this, continued softly. 'I can tell him, can't I? I can tell him you'll come to dinner?'

'For pity's sake, John,' she snapped, 'don't try to run me like one of your wretched agents.'

Haldane, meanwhile, sat at his desk, going through Gladstone's report.

There had twice been manoeuvres in the Kalkstadt area; in 1952 and 1960. On the second occasion the Russians had staged an infantry attack on Rostock with heavy armoured support but no air cover. Little was known of the 1952 exercise, except that a large detachment of troops had occupied the town of Wolken. They were believed to be wearing magenta shoulder-boards. The report was unreliable. On both occasions the area had been declared closed; the restriction had been enforced as far as the northern coast. There followed a long recitation of the principal industries. There was some evidence—it came from the Circus, who refused to release the source—that a new refinery was being constructed on a plateau to the east of Wolken, and that the machinery for it had been transported from Leipzig. It was conceivable (but unlikely) that it had come by rail and been sent by way of Kalkstadt. There was no evidence of civil or industrial unrest, nor of any incident which could account for a temporary closure of the town.

A note from Registry lay in his in-tray. They had put up the files he had asked for, but some were Subscription Only; he would have to read them in the library.

He went downstairs, opened the combination lock on the steel door of General Registry, groped vainly for the light switch. Finally he made his way in the dark between the shelves to the small, windowless room at the back of the building where documents of special interest or secrecy were kept. It was pitch dark. He struck a match, put on the light. On the table were two sets of files: *Mayfly*, heavily restricted, now in its third volume, with a subscription list pasted on the cover, and Deception (*Soviet and East Germany*), an immaculately kept collection of papers and photographs in hard folders.

After glancing briefly at the Mayfly files he turned his attention to the folders, thumbing his way through the depressing miscellany of rogues, double agents and lunatics who in every conceivable corner of the earth, under every conceivable pretext, had attempted, sometimes successfully, to delude the Western intelligence agencies. There was the boring similiarity of technique; the grain of truth carefully reconstructed, culled from newspaper reports and bazaar gossip; the follow-up, less carefully done, betraying the deceiver's contempt for the deceived; and finally the flight of fancy, the stroke of artistic impertinence which wantonly terminated a relationship already under sentence.

On one report he found a flag with Gladstone's initials; written above them in his cautious, rounded hand were the words: 'Could be of interest to you.'

It was a refugee report of Soviet tank trials near Gustweiler. It was marked: 'Should not issue. Fabrication.' There followed a long justification citing passages in the report which had been abstracted almost verbatim from a 1949 Soviet military manual. The originator appeared to have enlarged every dimension by a third, and added some ingenious flavouring of his own. Attached were six photographs, very blurred, purporting to have been taken from a train with a telephoto lens. On the back of the photographs was written in McCulloch's careful hand: 'Claims to have used Exa-two camera, East German manufacture. Cheap housing. Exakta range lens. Low shutter speed. Negatives very blurred owing to camera shake from train. Fishy.' It was all very inconclusive. The same make of camera, that was all. He locked up the Registry and went home. Not his duty, Leclerc had said, to prove that Christ was born on Christmas Day; any more, Haldane reflected, than it was his business to prove that Taylor had been murdered.

Woodford's wife added a little soda to her Scotch, a splash: it was habit rather than taste.

'Sleep in the office, my foot,' she said. 'Do you get operational subsistence?'

'Yes, of course.'

'Well, it *isn't* a conference then, is it? A conference isn't operational. Not unless,' she added with a giggle, 'you're having it in the Kremlin.'

'All right, it's not a conference. It's an operation. That's why I'm getting subsistence.'

She looked at him cruelly. She was a thin, childless woman, her eyes half shut from the smoke of the cigarette in her mouth.

'There's nothing going on at all. You're making it up.' She began laughing, a hard false laugh. 'You poor sod,' she said and laughed again, derisively. 'How's little Clarkie? You're all scared of him, aren't you? Why don't you ever say anything against him? Jimmy Gorton used to: *he* saw through him.'

'Don't mention Jimmy Gorton to me!'

'Jimmy's *lovely*.'

'Babs, I warn you!'

'Poor Clarkie. Do you remember,' his wife asked reflectively, 'that nice little dinner he gave us in his club? The time he remembered it was our turn for welfare? Steak and kidney and frozen peas.' She sipped her whisky.'And warm gin.' Something struck her. 'I wonder if he's ever had a woman,' she said. 'Christ, I wonder why I never thought of that before.'

Woodford returned to safer ground.

'All right, so nothing's going on.' He got up, a silly grin on his face, collected some matches from the desk.

'You're not smoking that damn pipe in here,' she said automatically.

'So nothing's going on,' he repeated smugly, and lit his pipe, sucking noisily.

'God, I hate you.'

Woodford shook his head, still grinning. 'Never mind,' he urged, 'just never mind. You said it, my dear, I didn't. I'm not sleeping in the office so everything's fine, isn't it? So I didn't go to Oxford either; I didn't even go to the Ministry; I haven't got a car to bring me home at night.'

She leant forward, her voice suddenly urgent, dangerous. 'What's happening?' she hissed. 'I've got a right to know, haven't I? I'm your wife, aren't I? You tell those little tarts in the office, don't you? Well, tell me!'

'We're putting a man over the border,' Woodford said. It was his moment of victory. 'I'm in charge of the London end. There's a crisis. There could even be a war. It's a damn ticklish thing.' The match had gone out, but he was still swinging it up and down with long movements of his arm, watching her with triumph in her eyes.

'You bloody liar,' she said. 'Don't give me that.'

Back in Oxford, the pub at the corner was three-quarters empty. They had the saloon bar to themselves. Leiser sipped a White Lady while the wireless operator drank best bitter at the Department's expense.

'Just take it gently, that's all you got to do, Fred,' he urged kindly. 'You came up lovely on the last run through. We'll hear you, don't worry about that–you're only eighty miles from the border. It's a piece of cake as long as you remember your procedure. Take it gently on the tuning or we're all done for.'

'I'll remember. Not to worry.'

'Don't get all bothered about the Jerries picking it up; you're not sending love letters, just a handful of groups. Then a new call sign and a different frequency. They'll never home on that, not for the time you're there.'

'Perhaps they can, these days,' Leiser said. 'Maybe they got better since the war.'

'There'll be all sorts of other traffic getting in their hair; shipping, military, air control, Christ knows what. They're not supermen, Fred; they're like us. A dozy lot. Don't worry.'

'I'm not worried. They didn't get me in the war; not for long.'

'Now listen, Fred, how about this? One more drink and we'll slip home and just have a nice run through with Mrs Hartbeck. No lights, mind. In the dark: she's shy, see? Get it a hundred per cent before we turn in. Then tomorrow we'll take it easy. After all, it's Sunday tomorrow, isn't it?' he added solicitously.

'I want to sleep. Can't I sleep a little, Jack?'

'Tomorrow, Fred. Then you can have a nice rest.' He nudged Leiser's elbow. 'You're married now, Fred. Can't always go to sleep, you know. You've taken the vow, that's what we used to say.'

'All right, forget about it, will you?' Leiser sounded on edge. 'Just leave it alone, see?'

'Sorry, Fred.'

'When do we go to London?'

'Monday, Fred.'

'Will John be there?'

'We meet him at the airport. And the Captain. They wanted us to have a bit more practice . . . on the routine and that.'

Leiser nodded, drumming his second and third fingers lightly on the table as if he were tapping the key.

'Here—why don't you tell us about one of those girls you had on your week-end in London?' Johnson suggested.

Leiser shook his head.

'Come on, then, let's have the other half and you give us a nice game of billiards.'

Leiser smiled shyly, his irritation forgotten. 'I got a lot more money than you, Jack. White Lady's an expensive drink. Not to worry.'

He chalked his cue and put in the sixpence. 'I'll play you double or quits; for last night.'

'Look, Fred,' Johnson pleaded gently. 'Don't always go for the big money, see, trying to put the red into the hundred slot. Just take the twenties and fifties—they mount up, you know. Then you'll be home and dry.'

Leiser was suddenly angry. He put his cue back in the cradle and took down his camel-hair coat from its peg.

'What's the matter, Fred, what the hell's the matter now?'

'For Christ's sake let me loose! Stop behaving like a bloody gaoler. I'm going on a job, like we all did in the war. I'm not sitting in the hanging cell.'

'Don't you be daft,' Johnson said gently, taking his coat and putting it back on the peg. 'Anyway we don't say hanging, we say condemned.'

Carol put the coffee on the desk in front of Leclerc. He looked up brightly and said thank you, tired but well drilled, like a child at the end of a party.

'Adrian Haldane's gone home,' Carol observed. Leclerc went back to the map.

'I looked in his room. He might have said goodnight.'

'He never does,' Leclerc said proudly.

'Is there anything I can do?'

'I never remember how you turn yards into metres.'

'Neither do I.'

'The Circus say this gully is two hundred metres long. That's about two hundred and fifty yards, isn't it?'

'I think so. I'll get the book.'

She went to her room and took a ready-reckoner from the bookcase.

'One metre is thirty-nine point three seven inches,' she read. 'A hundred metres is a hundred and nine yards and thirteen inches.'

Leclerc wrote it down.

'I think we should make a confirmatory telegram to Gorton. Have your coffee first, then come in with your pad.'

'I don't want any coffee.'

'Routine Priority will do, we don't want to haul old Jimmy out of bed.' He ran his small hand briskly over his hair. 'One. Advance party, Haldane, Avery, Johnson and Mayfly arrive BEA flight so and so, such and such a time December nine.' He glanced up. 'Get the details from Administration. Two. All will travel under their own names and proceed by train to Lübeck. For security reasons you will not repeat not meet party at airport but you may discreetly contact Avery by telephone at Lübeck base. We can't put him on to old Adrian,' he observed with a short laugh. 'The two of them don't hit it off at all . . .' He raised his voice: 'Three. Party number two consisting of Director only arriving morning flight December ten. You will meet him at airport for short conference before he proceeds to Lübeck. Four. Your role is discreetly to provide advice and assistance at all stages in order to bring operation Mayfly to successful conclusion.'

She stood up.

'Does John Avery have to go? His poor wife hasn't seen him for weeks.'

'Fortunes of war,' Leclerc replied without looking at her. 'How long does a man take to crawl two hundred and twenty yards?' he muttered. 'Oh, Carol–put another sentence on to that telegram: Five. Good Hunting. Old Jimmy likes a bit of encouragement, stuck out there all on his own.'

He picked a file from the in-tray and looked critically at the cover, aware perhaps of Carol's eyes upon him.

'Ah.' A controlled smile. 'This must be the Hungarian report. Did you ever meet Arthur Fielden in Vienna?'

'No.'

'A nice fellow. Rather your type. One of our best chaps . . . knows his way around. Bruce tells me he's done a very good report on unit changes in Budapest. I must get Adrian to look at it. Such a *lot* going on just now.' He opened the file and began reading.

Control said: 'Did you speak to Hyde?'

'Yes.'

'Well, what did he say? What have they got down there?'

Smiley handed him a whisky and soda. They were sitting in

Smiley's house in Bywater Street. Control was in the chair he preferred, nearest the fire.

'He said they'd got first-night nerves.'

'Hyde said that? Hyde used an expression like that? How extraordinary.'

'They've taken over a house in North Oxford. There was just this one agent, a Pole of about forty, and they wanted him documented as a mechanic from Magdeburg, a name like Freiser. They wanted travel papers to Rostock.'

'Who else was there?'

'Haldane and that new man, Avery. The one who came to me about the Finnish courier. And a wireless operator, Jack Johnson. We had him in the war. No one else at all. So much for their big team of agents.'

'What *are* they up to? And whoever gave them all that money just for *training*? We lent them some equipment, didn't we?'

'Yes, a B2.'

'What on earth's that?'

'A wartime set,' Smiley replied with irritation. 'You said it was all they could have. That and the crystals. Why on earth did you bother with the crystals?'

'Just charity. A B2 was it? Oh well,' Control observed with apparent relief. 'They wouldn't get far with *that*, would they?'

'Are you going home tonight?' Smiley asked impatiently.

'I thought you might give me a bed here,' Control suggested. 'Such a *fag* always traipsing home. It's the people. . . . They seem to get worse every time.'

Leiser sat at the table, the taste of the White Ladies still in his mouth. He stared at the luminous dial of his watch, the suitcase open in front of him. It was eleven eighteen; the second hand struggled jerkily towards twelve. He began tapping, JAJ, JAJ,–you can remember that, Fred, my name's Jack Johnson, see?–he switched over to receive, and there was Johnson's reply, steady as a rock.

Take your time, Johnson had said, don't rush your fences. We'll be listening all night, there are plenty more schedules. By the beam of a small torch he counted the encoded groups. There were thirty-eight. Putting out the torch he tapped a three and an eight; numerals were easy but long. His mind was very clear. He could hear Jack's gentle repetitions all the time: You're too quick on your shorts, Fred, a dot is one third of a dash, see? That's longer than you think. Don't rush the gaps, Fred; five dots between each word, three dots between each letter. Forearm horizontal, in a straight line with the key lever; elbow just clear of the body. It's like knife fighting, he thought with a little smile, and began keying. Fingers loose, Fred, relax, wrist clear of the table. He tapped out the first two groups, slurring a little on the gaps, but not as much as he usually did. Now came the third group: put in the safety signal. He tapped an S, cancelled it and tapped the next ten groups, glancing now and then at the dial of his watch. After two and a half minutes he went off the air, groped for the small capsule which contained the crystal, discovered with the tips of his fingers the twin sockets of the housing, inserted it, then stage by stage followed the tuning procedure, moving the dials, flashing his torch on the crescent window to watch the black tongue tremble across it.

He tapped out the second call sign, PRE, PRE, switched quickly to receive and there was Johnson again, QRK 4, your signal readable. For the second time he began transmitting, his hand moving slowly but methodically as his eye followed the meaningless letters, until with a nod of satisfaction he heard Johnson's reply: Signal received. QRU: I have nothing for you.

When they had finished Leiser insisted on a short walk. It was bitterly cold. They followed Walton Street as far as the main gates of Worcester, thence by way of Banbury Road once more to the respectable sanctuary of their dark North Oxford house.

Chapter Sixteen

TAKE-OFF

It was the same wind. The wind that had tugged at Taylor's frozen body and drove the rain against the blackened walls of Blackfriars Road, the wind that flailed the grass of Port Meadow now ran headlong against the shutters of the farmhouse.

The farmhouse smelt of cats. There were no carpets. The floors were of stone: nothing would dry them. Johnson lit the tiled oven in the hall as soon as they arrived but the damp still lay on the flagstones, collecting in the dips like a tired army. They never saw a cat all the time they were there, but they smelt them in every room. Johnson left corned beef on the doorstep: it was gone in ten minutes.

It was built on one floor with a high granary roof, of brick, and lay against a small coppice beneath a vast Flemish sky, a long, rectangular building with cattle sheds on the sheltered side. It was two miles north of Lübeck. Leclerc had said they were not to enter the town.

A ladder led to the loft, and there Johnson installed his wireless, stretching the aerial between the beams, thence through a skylight to an elm tree beside the road. He wore plimsolls in the house, brown ones of military issue, and a blazer with a squadron crest. Gorton had had food delivered from the Naafi in Celle. It covered the kitchen floor in old cardboard boxes, with an invoice marked 'Mr Gorton's party'. There were two bottles of gin and three of whisky. They had two bedrooms; Gorton had sent army beds, two to each room, and reading lights with standard green shades. Haldane was very angry about the beds. 'He must have told every damned department in the area,' he complained. 'Cheap whisky, Naafi food, army beds. I suppose we shall find he requisitioned the house next. God, what a way to mount an operation.'

It was late afternoon when they arrived. Johnson, having put up his set, busied himself in the kitchen. He was a domesticated man; he cooked and washed up without complaint, treading lightly over the flagstones in his neat plimsolls. He assembled a hash of bully beef and egg, and gave them cocoa with a great deal of sugar. They ate in the hall in front of the stove. Johnson did most of the talking; Leiser, very quiet, scarcely touched his food.

'What's the matter, Fred? Not hungry, then?'

'Sorry, Jack.'

'Too many sweets on the plane, that's your trouble.' Johnson winked at Avery. 'I saw you giving that air hostess a look. You shouldn't do it, Fred, you know, you'll break her heart.' He frowned round the table in mock disapproval. 'He really looked her over, you know. A proper tip-to-toe job.'

Avery grinned dutifully. Haldane ignored him.

Leiser was concerned about the moon, so after supper they stood at the back door in a small shivering group, staring at the sky. It was strangely light; the clouds drifted like black smoke, so low that they seemed to mingle with the swaying branches of the coppice and half obscure the grey fields beyond.

'It will be darker at the border, Fred,' said Avery. 'It's higher ground; more hills.'

Haldane said they would have an early night; they drank another whisky and at quarter past ten they went to bed, Johnson and Leiser to one room. Avery and Haldane to the other. No one dictated the arrangement. Each knew, apparently, where he belonged.

It was after midnight when Johnson came into their room. Avery was woken by the squeak of his rubber shoes.

'John, are you awake?'

Haldane sat up.

'It's about Fred. He's sitting alone in the hall. I told him to try and sleep, sir; gave him a couple of tablets, the kind my mother takes; he wouldn't even get into bed at first, now he's gone along to the hall.'

Haldane said, 'Leave him alone. He's all right. None of us can sleep with this damned wind.'

Johnson went back to his room. An hour must have passed; there was still no sound from the hall. Haldane said, 'You'd better go and see what he's up to.'

Avery put on his overcoat and went along the corridor, past tapestries of Biblical quotations and an old print of Lübeck harbour. Leiser was sitting on a chair beside the tiled oven.

'Hello, Fred.'

He looked old and tired.

'It's near here, isn't it, where I cross?'

'About five kilometres. The Director will brief us in the morning. They say it's quite an easy run. He'll give you all your papers and that kind of thing. In the afternoon we'll show you the place. They've done a lot of work on it in London.'

'In London,' Leiser repeated, and suddenly: 'I did a job in Holland in the war. The Dutch were good people. We sent a lot of agents to Holland. Women. They were all picked up. You were too young.'

'I read about it.'

'The Germans caught a radio operator. Our people didn't know. They just went on sending more agents. They said there was nothing else to do.' He was talking faster. 'I was only a kid then; just a quick job they wanted, in and out. They were short of operators. They said it didn't matter me not speaking Dutch, the reception party would meet me at the drop. All I had to do was work the set. There'd be a safe house ready.' He was far away. 'We fly in and nothing moves, not a shot or a searchlight, and I'm jumping. And when I land, there they are: two men and a woman. We say the words and they take me to the road to get the bikes. There's no time to bury the parachute—we aren't bothering by then. We find the house and they give me food. After supper we go upstairs where the set is—no schedules, London listened all the time those days. They give the message: 'I'm sending a call sign—"Come in TYR, come in TYR"—then the message in front of me, twenty-one groups, four-letter.'

He stopped.

'Well?'

'They were following the message, you see; they wanted to know where the safety signal came. It was in the ninth letter; a back shift of one. They let me finish the message and then they were on me, one hitting me, men all over the house.'

'But *who*, Fred? Who's *they*?'

'You can't talk about it like that: you never know. It's never that easy.'

'But for God's sake, whose fault was it? Who did it? Fred!'

'Anyone's. You can never tell. You'll learn that.' He seemed to have given up.

'You're alone this time. Nobody has been told. Nobody's expecting you.'

'No. That's right.' His hands were clasped on his lap. He made a hunched figure, small and cold. 'In the war it was easier because, however bad it got, you thought one day we'd win. Even if you were picked up, you thought, "They'll come and get me, they'll drop some men or make a raid." You knew they never would, see, but you could think it. You just wanted to be left alone to think it. But nobody wins this one, do they?'

'It's not the same. But more important.'

'What do you do if I'm caught?'

'We'll get you back. Not to worry, eh, Fred?'

'Yes, but how?'

'We're a big outfit, Fred. A lot goes on you don't know about. Contacts here and there. You can't see the whole picture.'

'Can you?'

'Not all of it, Fred. Only the Director sees it all. Not even the Captain.'

'What's he like, the Director?'

'He's been in it a long time. You'll see him tomorrow. He's a very remarkable man.'

'Does the Captain fancy him?'

'Of course.'

'He never talks about him,' Leiser said.

'None of us talk about him.'

'There was this girl I had. She worked in the bank. I told her I was going away. If anything goes wrong I don't want anything said, see. She's just a kid.'

'What was her name?'

A moment of mistrust. 'Never mind. But if she turns up just keep it all right with her.'

'What do you mean, Fred?'

'Never mind.'

Leiser didn't talk after that. When the morning came Avery returned to his room.

'What's it all about?' Haldane asked.

'He was in some mess in the war, in Holland. He was betrayed.'

'But he's giving us a second chance. How nice. Just what they always said.' And then: 'Leclerc arrives this morning.'

His taxi came at eleven. Leclerc was getting out almost before it had pulled up. He was wearing a duffle coat, heavy brown shoes for rough country and a soft cap. He looked very well.

'Where's Mayfly?'

'With Johnson,' Haldane said.

'Got a bed for me?'

'You can have Mayfly's when he's gone.'

At eleven thirty Leclerc held a briefing; in the afternoon they were to make a tour of the border.

The briefing took place in the hall. Leiser came in last. He stood in the doorway, looking at Leclerc, who smiled at him winningly, as if he liked what he saw. They were about the same height.

Avery said, 'Director, this is Mayfly.'

His eyes still on Leiser, Leclerc replied, 'I think I'm allowed to call him Fred. Hullo.' He advanced and shook him by the hand, both formal, two weather men coming out of a box.

'Hullo,' said Leiser.

'I hope they haven't been working you too hard?'

'I'm all right, sir.'

'We're all very impressed,' Leclerc said. 'You've done a grand job.' He might have been talking to his constituents.

'I haven't started yet.'

'I always feel the training is three-quarters of the battle. Don't you, Adrian?'

'Yes.'

They sat down. Leclerc stood a little away from them. He had hung a map on the wall. By some indefinable means—it may have been his maps, it may have been the precision of his language, or it may have been his strict deportment, which so elusively combined purpose with restraint—Leclerc evoked in that hour that same nostalgic, campaigning atmosphere which had informed the briefing in Blackfriars Road a month before. He had the illusionist's gift, whether he spoke of rockets or wireless transmission, of cover or the point at which the border was to be crossed, of implying great familiarity with his subject.

'Your target is Kalkstadt'—a little grin—'hitherto famous only for a remarkably fine fourteenth-century church.' They laughed, Leiser too. It was so good, Leclerc knowing about old churches.

He had brought a diagram of the crossing point, done in different inks, with the border drawn in red. It was all very simple. On the western side, he said, there was a low, wooded hill overgrown with gorse and bracken. This ran parallel to the border until the southern end curved eastwards in a narrow arm stopping about two hundred and twenty yards short of the border, directly opposite an observation tower. The tower was set well back from the demarcation line: at its foot ran a fence of barbed wire. It had been observed that this wire was laid out in a single apron and only loosely fixed to its staves. East German guards had been seen to detach it in order to pass through and patrol the undefended strip of territory which lay between the demarcation line and the physical border. That afternoon Leclerc would indicate the precise staves. Mayfly, he said, should not be alarmed at having to pass so close to the tower; experience had shown that the attention of the guards was concentrated on the more distant parts of their area; the night was ideal; a high wind was forecast; there would be no moon. Leclerc had set the crossing time for 0235 hours; the guard changed at midnight, each watch lasted three hours. It was reasonable to suppose that the sentries would not be as alert after two and a half hours on duty as they would be at the start of their watches. The relief guard, which had to approach from a barrack some distance to the north, would not yet be under way.

Much attention had been given, Lerclerc continued, to the possibility of mines. They would see from the map—the little forefinger traced the green dotted line from the end of the rise across the border—that there was an old footpath which did indeed follow the very route which Leiser would be taking. The frontier guards had been seen to avoid this path, striking a track of their own some ten yards to the south of it. The assumption was, Leclerc said, that the path was mined, while the area to the side of it had been left clear for the benefit of patrols. Leclerc proposed that Leiser should use the track made by the frontier guards.

Wherever possible over the two hundred odd yards between the foot of the hill and the tower, Leiser should crawl, keeping his head below the level of the bracken. This eliminated the small danger that he would be sighted from the tower. He would be comforted to hear, Leclerc added with a smile, that there was no record of any patrol operating on the western side of the wire during the hours of darkness. The East German guards seemed to fear that one of their own number might slip away unseen.

Once across the border Leiser should keep clear of any path. The country was rough, partly wooded. The going would be hard but all the safer for that; he was to head south. The reason for this was simple. To the south, the border turned westward for some ten kilometres. Thus Leiser, by moving southwards, would put himself not two but fifteen kilometres from the border, and more quickly escape the zonal patrols which guarded the eastern approaches. Leclerc would advise him thus—he withdrew one hand casually from the pocket of his duffle coat and lit a cigarette, conscious all the time of their eyes upon him—march east for half an hour, then turn due south, making for the Marienhorst lake. At the eastern end of the lake was a disused boathouse. There he could lie up for an hour and give himself some food. By that time Leiser might care for a drink—relieved laughter—and he would find a little brandy in his rucksack.

Leclerc had a habit, when making a joke, of holding himself at attention and lifting his heels from the ground as if to launch his wit upon the higher air.

'I couldn't have something with gin, could I?' Leiser asked. 'White Lady's my drink.'

There was a moment's bewildered silence.

'That wouldn't do at all,' Leclerc said shortly, Leiser's master.

Having rested, he should walk to the village of Marienhorst and look around for transport to Schwerin. From then on, Leclerc added lightly, he was on his own.

'You have all the papers necessary for a journey from Magdeburg to Rostock. When you reach Schwerin, you are on the legitimate route. I don't want to say too much about cover because you have been through that with the Captain. Your name is Fred Hartbeck, you are an unmarried mechanic from Magdeburg with an offer of employment at the State Co-operative shipbuilding works at Rostock.' He smiled, undeterred. 'I am sure you have all been through every detail of this already. Your love life, your pay, medical history, war service and the rest. There is just one thing that *I* might add about cover. Never *volunteer* information. People don't *expect* you to explain yourself. If you are cornered, play it by ear. Stick as closely to the truth as you can. Cover,' he declared, stating a favourite maxim, 'should never be *fabricated* but only an extension of the truth.' Leiser laughed in a reserved way. It was as if he could have wished Leclerc a taller man.

Johnson brought coffee from the kitchen, and Leclerc said briskly, 'Thank you, Jack,' as if everything were quite as it should be.

Leclerc now addressed himself to the question of Leiser's target; he gave a résumé of the indicators, implying somehow that they only confirmed suspicions which he himself had long harboured. He employed a tone which Avery had not heard in him before. He sought to imply, as much by omission and inference as by direct allusion, that theirs was a Department of enormous skill and knowledge, enjoying in its access to money, its intercourse with other services and in the unchallenged authority of its judgements an unearthly, oracular immunity, so that Leiser might well have wondered why, if all this were so, he need bother to risk his life at all.

'The rockets are in the area now,' Leclerc said. 'The Captain has told you what signs to look for. We want to know what they look like, where they are and above all who mans them.'

'I know.'

'You must try the usual tricks. Pub gossip, tracing an old soldier friend, you know the kind of thing. When you find them, come back.'

Leiser nodded.

'At Kalkstadt there's a workers' hostel.' He unfolded a chart of the town. 'Here. Next to the church. Stay there if you can. You may run into people who have actually been engaged . . .'

'I know,' Leiser repeated. Haldane stirred, glanced at him anxiously.

'You might even hear something of a man who used to be employed at the station, Fritsche. He gave us some interesting details about the rockets, then disappeared. If you get the chance, that is. You could ask at the station, say you're a friend of his . . .'

There was a very slight pause.

'Just disappeared,' Leclerc repeated, for them, not for himself. His mind was elsewhere. Avery watched him anxiously, waiting for him to go on. At last he said, rapidly, 'I have deliberately avoided the question of communication,' indicating by his tone that they were nearly done. 'I imagine you have gone over that enough times already.'

'No worries there,' Johnson said. 'All the schedules are at night. That leaves the frequency range pretty simple. He'll have a clear hand during the day, sir. We've had some very nice dummy runs, haven't we, Fred?'

'Oh yes. Very nice.'

'As regards getting back,' Leclerc said, 'we play the war rules. There are no submarines any more, Fred; not for this kind of thing. When you return, you should report at once to the nearest British Consulate or Embassy, give your proper name and ask to be repatriated. You should represent yourself as a distressed British subject. My instinct would be to advise you to come out the way you went in. If you're in trouble, don't necessarily move west straight away. Lie up for a bit. You're taking plenty of money.'

Avery knew he would never forget that morning, how they had sat at the farmhouse table like sprawling boys at the Nissen hut desks, their strained faces fixed upon Leclerc as in the stillness of a church he read the liturgy of their devotion, moving his little hand across the map like a priest with the taper. All of them in that room—but Avery perhaps best of all—knew the fatal disproportion between the dream and reality, between motive and action. Avery had talked to Taylor's child, stammered out his half-formed lies to Peersen and the Consul: he had heard that dreadful footfall in the hotel, and returned from a nightmare journey to see his own experiences remade into the images of Leclerc's world. Yet Avery, like Haldane and Leiser, listened to Leclerc with the piety of an agnostic, feeling perhaps that this was how, in some clean and magic place, it really ought to be.

'Excuse me,' said Leiser. He was looking at the plan of Kalkstadt. He was very much the small man just then. He might have been pointing to a fault in an engine. The station, hostel and church were marked in green; an inset at the bottom left-hand corner depicted the railway warehouses and dumping sheds. At each side, the point of the compass was given adjectivally: Western Prospect, Northern Prospect.

'What's a prospect, sir?' Leiser inquired.

'A view, an outlook.'

'What's it for? What's it for on the map, please?'

Leclerc smiled patiently. 'For purpose of orientation, Fred.'

Leiser got up and examined the chart closely. 'And this is the church?'

'That's right, Fred.'

'Why does it face north? Churches go from east to west. You've got the entrance on the eastern side where the altar should be.'

Haldane leaned forward, the index finger of his right hand resting on his lip.

'It's only a sketch map,' Leclerc said. Leiser returned to his place and sat to attention, straighter than ever. 'I see. Sorry.'

When the meeting was over Leclerc took Avery on one side. 'Just one point , John, he's not to take a gun. It's quite out of the question. The Minister was adamant. Perhaps you'll mention it to him.'

'No gun?'

'I think we can allow the knife. That could be a general-purpose thing; I mean if anything went wrong we could say it was general purpose.'

After lunch they made a tour of the border—Gorton had provided a car. Leclerc brought with him a handful of notes he had made from the Circus frontier report, and these he kept on his knee, together with a folded map.

The extreme northern part of the frontier which divides the two halves of Germany is largely a thing of depressing inconsequence. Those who look eagerly for dragon's teeth and substantial fortifications will be disappointed. It crosses land of considerable variety; gullies and small hills overgrown with bracken and patches of untended forest. Often the Eastern defences are set so far behind the demarcation line as to be hidden from Western eyes—only a forward pillbox, crumbling roads, a vacated farmhouse or an occasional observation tower excite the imagination.

By way of emphasis the Western side is adorned with the grotesque statuary of political impotence: a plywood model of the Brandenburg Gate, the screws rusting in their sockets, rises absurdly from an untended field; notice boards, broken by wind and rain, display fifteen-year-old slogans across an empty valley. Only at night, when the beam of a searchlight springs from the darkness and draws its wavering finger across the cold earth, does the heart chill for the captive crouching like a hare in the plough, waiting to break cover and run in terror till he fall.

They followed an unmade road along the top of a hill, and wherever it ran close to the frontier they stopped the car and got out. Leiser was shrouded in a mackintosh and hat. The day was very cold. Leclerc wore his duffle coat and carried a shooting stick—Heaven knows where he had found it. The first time they stopped, and the second, and again at the next, Leclerc said quietly, 'Not this one.' As they got into the car for the fourth time he declared, 'The next stop is ours.' It was the kind of brave joke favoured in battle.

Avery would not have recognized the place from Leclerc's sketch map. The hill was there, certainly, turning inwards towards the frontier, then descending sharply to the plain below. But the land beyond it was hilly and partly wooded, its horizon fringed with trees against which, with the aid of glasses, they could discern the brown shape of a wooden tower. 'It's the three staves to the left,' Leclerc said. As they scanned the ground, Avery could make out here and there the worn mark of the old path.

'It's mined. The path is mined the whole way. Their territory begins at the foot of the hill.' Leclerc turned to Leiser. 'You start from here.' He pointed with his shooting stick. 'You proceed to the brow of the hill and lie up till take-off time. We'll have you here early so that your eyes grow used to the light. I think we should go now. We mustn't attract attention, you know.'

As they drove back to the farmhouse the rain came bursting against the windscreen, thundering on the roof of the car. Avery, sitting next to Leiser, was sunk in his own thoughts. He realized with what he took to be utter detachment that, while his own mission had unfolded as comedy, Leiser was to play the same part as tragedy; that he was witnessing an insane relay race in which each contestant ran faster and longer than the last, arriving nowhere but at his own destruction.

'Incidentally,' he said suddenly, addressing himself to Leiser, 'hadn't you better do something about your hair? I don't imagine they have much in the way of lotions over there. A thing like that could be insecure.'

'He needn't cut it,' Haldane observed. 'The Germans go in for long hair. Just wash it, that's all that's needed. Get the oil out. A nice point, John, I congratulate you.'

Chapter Seventeen

The rain had stopped. The night came slowly, struggling with the wind. They sat at the table in the farmhouse, waiting; Leiser was in his bedroom. Johnson made tea and attended to his equipment. No one talked. The pretending was over. Not even Leclerc, master of the public-school catchword, bothered any more. He seemed to resent being made to wait, that was all, at the tardy wedding of an unloved friend. They had relapsed into a state of somnolent fear, like men in a submarine, while the lamp over their heads rocked gently. Now and then Johnson would be sent to the door to look for the moon, and each time he announced that there was none.

'The met reports were pretty good,' Leclerc observed, and drifted away to the attic to watch Johnson check his equipment.

Avery, alone with Haldane, said quickly, 'He says the Ministry's ruled against the gun. He's not to take it.'

'And what bloody fool told him to consult the Ministry in the first place?' Haldane demanded, beside himself with anger. Then: 'You'll have to tell him. It depends on you.'

'Tell Leclerc?'

'No, you idiot; Leiser.'

They had some food and afterwards Avery and Haldane took Leiser to his bedroom.

'We must dress you up,' they said.

They made him strip, taking from him piece by piece his warm, expensive clothes: jacket and trousers of matching grey, cream silk shirt, black shoes without toecaps, socks of dark blue nylon. As he loosened the knot of his tartan tie his fingers discovered the gold pin with the horse's head. He unclipped it carefully and held it out to Haldane.

'What about this?'

Haldane had provided envelopes for valuables. Into one of these he slipped the tie-pin, sealed it, wrote on the back, tossed it on the bed.

'You washed your hair?'

'Yes.'

'We had difficulty in obtaining East German soap. I'm afraid you'll have to try and get some when you're over there. I understand it's in short supply.'

'All right.'

He sat on the bed naked except for his watch, crouched forward, his broad arms folded across his hairless thighs, his white skin mottled from the cold. Haldane opened a trunk and extracted a bundle of clothes and half a dozen pairs of shoes.

As Leiser put on each unfamiliar thing, the cheap, baggy trousers of coarse serge, broad at the foot and gathered at the waist, the grey, threadbare jacket with arched pleats, the shoes, brown with a bright unhealthy finish, he seemed to shrink before their eyes, returning to some former estate which they had only guessed at. His brown hair, free from oil, was streaked with grey and fell undisciplined upon his head. He glanced shyly at them, as if he had revealed a secret; a peasant in the company of his masters.

'How do I look?'

'Fine,' Avery said. 'You look marvellous, Fred.'

'What about a tie?'

'A tie would spoil it.'

He tried the shoes one after another, pulling them with difficulty over the coarse woollen socks.

'They're Polish,' Haldane said, giving him a second pair. 'The Poles export them to East Germany. You'd better take these as well–you don't know how much walking you'll have to do.'

Haldane fetched from his own bedroom a heavy cashbox and unlocked it.

First he took a wallet, a shabby brown one with a centre compartment of cellophane which held Leiser's identity card, fingered and stamped; it lay open behind its flat frame, so that the photograph of Leiser looked outwards, a little prison picture. Beside it was an authority to travel and a written offer of employment from the State Co-operative for shipbuilding in Rostock. Haldane emptied one pocket of the wallet and then replaced the contents paper for paper, describing each in turn.

'Food registration card–driving licence . . . Party card. How long have you been a Party member?'

'Since 'forty-nine.'

He put in a photograph of a woman and three or four grimy letters, some still in their envelopes.

'Love letters,' he explained shortly.

Next came a Union card and a cutting from a Magdeburg newspaper about production figures at a local engineering works; a photograph of the Brandenburg Gate before the war, a tattered testimonial from a former employer.

'That's the wallet, then,' Haldane said. 'Except for the money. The rest of your equipment is in the rucksack. Provisions and that kind of thing.'

He handed Leiser a bundle of banknotes from the box. Leiser stood in the compliant attitude of a man being searched, his arms raised a little from his sides and his feet slightly apart. He would accept whatever Haldane gave him, put it carefully away, then resume the same position. He signed a receipt for the money. Haldane glanced at the signature and put the paper in a black briefcase which he had put separately on a side table.

Next came the odds and ends which Hartbeck would plausibly have about him: a bunch of keys on a chain–the key to the suitcase was among them–a comb, a khaki handkerchief stained with oil and a couple of ounces of substitute coffee in a twist of newspaper; a screwdriver, a length of fine wire and fragments of metal ends newly turned–the meaningless rubble of a working man's pockets.

'I'm afraid you can't take that watch,' Haldane said.

Leiser unbuckled the gold armband and dropped the watch into Haldane's open palm. They gave him a steel one of Eastern manufacture and set it with great precision by Avery's bedside clock.

Haldane stood back. 'That will do. Now remain there and go through your pockets. Make sure things are where you would naturally keep them. Don't touch anything else in the room, do you understand?'

'I know the form,' said Leiser, glancing at his gold watch on the table. He accepted the knife and hooked the black scabbard into the waistband of his trouser.

'What about my gun?'

Haldane guided the steel clip of the briefcase into its housing and it snapped like the latch of a door.

'You don't take one,' Avery said.

'No gun?'

'It's not on, Fred. They reckon it's too dangerous.'

'Who for?'

'It could lead to a dangerous situation. Politically, I mean. Sending an armed man into East Germany. They're afraid of an incident.'

'Afraid.'

For a long time he stared at Avery, his eyes searching the young, unfurrowed face for something that was not there. He turned to Haldane.

'Is that true?'

Haldane nodded.

Suddenly he thrust out his empty hands in front of him, cupped in a terrible gesture of poverty, the fingers crooked and pressed together as if to catch the last water, his shoulders trembling in the cheap jacket, his face drawn, half in supplication, half in panic.

'The gun, John! You can't send a man without a gun! For mercy's sake, let me have the gun!'

'Sorry, Fred.'

His hands still extended, he swung round to Haldane. 'You don't know what you're doing!'

Leclerc had heard the noise and came to the doorway. Haldane's face was arid as rock; Leiser could have beaten his empty fists upon it for all the charity it held. His voice fell to a whisper. 'What are you doing? God Christ, what are you trying to do?' To both of them he cried in revelation, 'You hate me, don't you! What have I done to you? John, what have I done? We were pals, weren't we?'

Leclerc's voice, when at last he spoke, sounded very pure, as if he were deliberately emphasizing the gulf between them.

'What's the trouble?'

'He's worried about the gun,' Haldane explained.

'I'm afraid there's nothing we can do. It's out of our hands. You know how we feel about it, Fred. Surely you know that. It's an order, that's all. Have you forgotten how it used to be?' He added stiffly, a man of duty and decision, 'I can't question my orders: what do you want me to say?'

Leiser shook his head. His hands fell to his sides. The discipline had gone out of his body.

'Never mind.' He was looking at Avery.

'A knife's better in some ways, Fred,' Leclerc added consolingly, 'quieter.'

'Yes.'

Haldane picked up Leiser's spare clothes. 'I must put these into the rucksack,' he said, and with a sideways glance at Avery, walked quickly from the room, taking Leclerc with him. Leiser and Avery looked at one another in silence. Avery was embarrassed to see him so ugly. At last Leiser spoke.

'It was us three. The Captain, you and me. It was all right, then. Don't worry about the others, John. They don't matter.'

'That's right, Fred.'

Leiser smiled. 'It was the best ever, that week, John. It's funny, isn't it: we spend all our time chasing girls, and it's the men that matter; just the men.'

'You're one of us, Fred. You always were; all the time your card was there, you were one of us. We don't forget.'

'What does it look like?'

'It's two pinned together. One for then, one for now. It's in the index . . . live agents, we call it. Yours is the first name. You're the best man we've got.' He could imagine it now; the index was something they had built together. He could believe in it, like love.

'You said it was alphabetical order,' Leiser said sharply. 'You said it was a special index for the best.'

'Big cases go to the front.'

'And men all over the world?'

'Everywhere.'

Leiser frowned as if it were a private matter, a decision to be privately taken. He stared slowly round the bare room, then at the cuffs on his coarse jacket, then at Avery, interminably at Avery, until, taking him by the wrist, but lightly, more to touch than to lead, he said under his breath, 'Give us something. Give me something to take. From you. Anything.'

Avery felt in his pockets, pulling out a handkerchief, some loose change and a twist of thin cardboard, which he opened. It was the photograph of Taylor's little girl.

'Is that your kid?' Leiser looked over the other's shoulder at the small, bespectacled face; his hand closed on Avery's. 'I'd like that.' Avery nodded. Leiser put it in his wallet, then picked up his watch from the bed. It was gold with a black dial for the phases of the moon. 'You have it,' he said. 'Keep it. I've been trying to remember,' he continued, 'at home. There was this school. A big courtyard like a barracks with nothing but windows and drainpipes. We used to bang a ball round after lunch. Then a gate, and a path to the church, and the river on the other side. . . .' He was laying out the town with his hands, placing bricks. 'We went Sunday, through the side door, the kids last see?' A smile of success. 'That church was facing north,' he declared, 'not east at all.' Suddenly he asked: 'How long, how long have you been in, John?'

'In the outfit?'

'Yes.'

'Four years.'

'How old were you then?'

'Twenty-eight. It's the youngest they take you.'

'You told me you were thirty-four.'

'They're waiting for us,' Avery said.

In the hall they had the rucksack and the suitcase, green canvas with leather corners. He tried the rucksack on, adjusting the straps until it sat high on his back, like a German schoolboy's satchel. He lifted the suitcase and felt the weight of the two things together.

'Not too bad,' he muttered.

'It's the minimum,' Leclerc said. They had begun to whisper, though no one could hear. One by one they got into the car.

A hurried handshake and he walked away towards the hill. There were no fine words; not even from Leclerc. It was as if they had all taken leave of Leiser long ago. The last they saw of him was the rucksack gently bobbing as he disappeared into the darkness. There had always been a rhythm about the way he walked.

Chapter Eighteen

Leiser lay in the bracken on the spur of the hill, stared at the luminous dial of his watch. Ten minutes to wait. The key chain was swinging from his belt. He put the keys back in his pocket, and as he drew his hand away he felt the links slip between his thumb and finger like the beads of a rosary. For a moment he let them linger there; there was comfort in their touch; they were where his childhood was. St Christopher and all his angels, please preserve us from road accidents.

Ahead of him the ground descended sharply, then evened out. He had seen it; he knew. But now, as he looked down, he could make out nothing in the darkness below him. Suppose it were marshland down there? There had been rain; the water had drained into the valley. He saw himself struggling through mud to his waist, carrying the suitcase above his head, the bullets splashing round him.

He tried to discern the tower on the opposite hill, but if it was there it was lost against the blackness of the trees.

Seven minutes. Don't worry about the noise, they said, the wind will carry it south. They'll hear nothing in a wind like this. Run beside the path, on the south side, that means to the right, keep on the new trail through the bracken, it's narrow but clear. If you meet anyone, use your knife, but for the love of Heaven don't go near the path.

His rucksack was heavy. Too heavy. So was the case. He'd quarrelled about it with Jack. He didn't care for Jack. 'Better be on the safe side, Fred,' Jack had explained. 'These little sets are sensitive as virgins: all right for fifty miles, dead as mutton on sixty. Better to have the margin, Fred, then we know where we are. They're experts, real experts where this one comes from.'

One minute to go. They'd set his watch by Avery's clock.

He was frightened. Suddenly he couldn't keep his mind from it any more. Perhaps he was too old, too tired, perhaps he'd done enough. Perhaps the training had worn him out. He felt his heart pounding his chest. His body wouldn't stand any more; he hadn't the strength. He lay there, talking to Haldane: Christ, Captain, can't you see I'm past it? The old body's cracking up. That's what he'd tell them; he would stay there when the minute hand came up, he would stay there too heavy to move. 'It's my heart, it's packed in,' he'd tell them. 'I've had a heart attack, skipper, didn't tell you about my dickie heart, did I? It just came over me as I lay here in the bracken.'

He stood up. Let the dog see the rabbit.

Run down the hill, they'd said; in this wind they won't hear a thing; run down the hill, because that's where they may spot you, they'll be looking at that hillside hoping for a silhouette. Run fast through the moving bracken, keep low and you'll be safe. When you reach level ground, lie up and get your breath back, then begin the crawl.

He was running like a madman. He tripped and the rucksack brought him down, he felt his knee against his chin and the pain as he bit his tongue, then he was up again and the suitcase swung him round. He half fell into the path and waited for the flash of a bursting mine. He was running down the slope, the ground gave way beneath his heels, the suitcase rattling like an old car. Why wouldn't they let him take the gun? The pain rose in his chest like fire, spreading under the bone, burning the lungs: he counted each step, he could feel the thump of each footfall and the slowing drag of the case and rucksack. Avery had lied. Lied all the way. Better watch that cough, Captain; better see a doctor, it's like barbed wire in your guts. The ground levelled out; he fell again and lay still, panting like an animal, feeling nothing but fear and the sweat that drenched his woollen shirt.

He pressed his face to the ground. Arching his body, he slid his hand beneath his belly and tightened the belt of his rucksack.

He began crawling up the hill, dragging himself forward with his elbows and his hands, pushing the suitcase in front of him, conscious all the time of the hump on his back rising above the undergrowth. The water was seeping through his clothes; soon it ran freely over his thighs and knees. The stink of leaf mould filled his nostrils; twigs tugged at his hair. It was as if all nature conspired to hold him back. He looked up the slope and caught sight of the observation tower against the line of black trees on the horizon. There was no light on the tower.

He lay still. It was too far: he could never crawl so far. It was quarter to three by his watch. The relief guard would be coming from the north. He unbuckled his rucksack, stood up, holding it under his arm like a child. Taking the suitcase in his other hand he began walking cautiously up the rise, keeping the trodden path to his left, his eyes fixed upon the skeleton outline of the tower. Suddenly it rose before him like the dark bones of a monster.

The wind clattered over the brow of the hill. From directly above him he could hear the slats of old timber banging, and the long creak of a casement. It was not a single apron but double; when he pulled, it came away from the staves. He stepped across, reattached the wire and stared into the forest ahead. He felt even in that moment of unspeakable terror while the sweat blinded him and the throbbing of his temples drowned the rustling of the wind, a full, confiding gratitude towards Avery and Haldane, as if he knew they had deceived him for his own good.

Then he saw the sentry, like the silhouette in the range, not ten yards from him, back turned, standing on the old path, his rifle slung over his shoulder, his bulky body swaying from left to right as he stamped his feet on the sodden ground to keep them from freezing. Leiser could smell tobacco—it was past him in a second—and coffee warm like a blanket. He put down the rucksack and suitcase and move instinctively towards him; he might have been in the gymnasium at Headington. He felt the haft sharp in his hand, crosshatched to prevent slip. The sentry was quite a young boy under his greatcoat; Leiser was surprised how young. He killed him hurriedly, one blow, as a fleeing man might shoot into a crowd; shortly; not to destroy but to preserve; impatiently, for he had to get along; indifferently because it was a fixture.

'Can you see anything?' Haldane repeated.

'No.' Avery handed him the glasses. 'He just went into the dark.'

'Can you see a light from the watch-tower? They'd shine a light if they heard him.'

'No, I was looking for Leiser,' Avery answered.

'You should have called him Mayfly,' Leclerc objected from

behind. 'Johnson knows his name now.'

'I'll forget it, sir.'

'He's over, anyway,' Leclerc said and walked back to the car. They drove home in silence.

As they entered the house Avery felt a friendly touch upon the shoulder and turned, expecting to see Johnson; instead he found himself looking into the hollow face of Haldane, but so altered, so manifestly at peace, that it seemed to possess the youthful calm of a man who has survived a long illness; the last pain had gone out of him.

'I am not given to eulogies,' Haldane said.

'Do you think he's safely over?'

'You did well.' He was smiling.

'We'd have heard, wouldn't we? Heard the shots or seen the lights?'

'He's out of our care. Well done.' He yawned. 'I propose we go early to bed. There is nothing more for us to do. Until tomorrow night, of course.' At the door he stopped, and without turning his head he remarked, 'You know, it doesn't seem real. In the war, there was no question. They went or they refused. Why did he go, Avery? Jane Austen said money or love, those were the only two things in the world. Leiser didn't go for money.'

'You said one could never know. You said so the night he telephoned.'

'He told me it was hate. Hatred for the Germans; and I didn't believe him.'

'He went anyway. I thought that was all that mattered to you, you said you didn't trust motive.'

'He wouldn't do it for hatred, we know that. What is he, then? We never knew him, did we? He's near the mark, you know; he's on his deathbed. What does he think of? If he dies now, tonight, what will be in his mind?'

'You shouldn't speak like that.'

'Ah.' At last he turned and looked at Avery and the peace had not left his face. 'When we met him he was a man without love. Do you know what love is? I'll tell you; it is whatever you can still betray. We ourselves live without it in our profession. We don't force people to do things for us. We let them discover love. And, of course, Leiser did, didn't he? He married us for money, so to speak, and left us for love. He took his second vow. I wonder when.'

Avery said quickly, 'What do you mean, for money?'

'I mean whatever we gave to him. Love is what he gave to us. I see you have his watch, incidentally.'

'I'm keeping it for him.'

'Ah. Goodnight. Or good morning, I suppose.' A little laugh. 'How quickly one loses one's sense of time.' Then he commented, as if to himself: 'And the Circus helped us all the way. It's most strange. I wonder why.'

Very carefully Leiser rinsed the knife. The knife was dirty and must be washed. In the boathouse, he ate the food and drank the brandy in the flask. 'After that,' Haldane had said, 'you live off the land; you can't run around with tinned meat and French brandy.' He opened the door and stepped outside to wash his hands and face in the lake.

The water was quite still in the darkness. Its unruffled surface was like a perfect skin shrouded with floating veils of grey mist. He could see the reeds along the bank; the wind, subdued by the approach of dawn, touched them as it moved across the water. Beyond the lake hung the shadow of low hills. He felt rested and at peace. Until the memory of the boy passed over him like a shudder.

He threw the empty meat can and the brandy bottle far out, and as they hit the water a heron rose languidly from the reeds. Stooping, he picked up a stone and sent it skimming across the lake. He heard it bounce three times before it sank. He threw another but he couldn't beat three. Returning to the hut he fetched his rucksack and suitcase. His right arm was aching painfully, it must have been from the weight of the case. From somewhere came the bellow of cattle.

He began walking east, along the track which skirted the lake. He wanted to get as far as he could before morning came.

He must have walked through half a dozen villages. Each was empty of life, quieter than the open road because they gave a moment's shelter from the rising wind. There were no signposts and no new buildings, it suddenly occurred to him. That was where the peace came from, it was the peace of no innovation—it might have been fifty years ago, a hundred. There were no street lights, no gaudy signs on the pubs or shops. It was the darkness of indifference, and it comforted him. He walked into it liked a tired man breasting the sea; it cooled and revived him like the wind; until he remembered the boy. He passed a farmhouse. A long drive led to it from the road. He stopped. Half-way up the drive stood a motorbike, an old mackintosh thrown over the saddle. There was no one in sight.

The oven smoked gently.

'When did you say his first schedule was?' Avery asked. He had asked already.

'Johnson said twenty-two twenty. We start scanning an hour before.'

'I thought he was on a fixed frequency,' Leclerc muttered, but without much interest.

'He may start with the wrong crystal. It's the kind of thing that happens under strain. It's safest for base to scan with so many crystals.'

'He must be on the road by now.'

'Where's Haldane?'

'Asleep.'

'How can anyone sleep at a time like this?'

'It'll be daylight soon.'

'Can't you do something about that fire?' Leclerc asked. 'It shouldn't smoke like that, I'm sure.' He shook his head, suddenly, as if shaking off water and said, 'John, there's a most interesting report from Fielden. Troop movements in Budapest. Perhaps when you get back to London . . .' He lost the thread of his sentence and frowned.

'You mentioned it,' Avery said softly.

'Yes, well you must take a look at it.'

'I'd like to. It sounds very interesting.'

'It does, doesn't it?'

'Very.'

'You know,' he said—he seemed to be reminiscing—'they *still* won't give that wretched woman her pension.'

He sat very straight on the motorbike, elbows in as if he were at table. It made a terrible noise; it seemed to fill the dawn with sound, echoing across the frosted fields and stirring the roosting poultry. The mackintosh had leather pieces on the shoulders; as he bounced along the unmade road its skirts fluttered behind, rattling against the spokes of the rear wheel. Daylight came.

Soon he would have to eat. He couldn't understand why he was so hungry. Perhaps it was the exercise. Yes, it must be the exercise. He would eat, but not in a town, not yet. Not in a café where strangers came. Not in a café where the boy had been.

He drove on. His hunger taunted him. He could think of nothing else. His hand held down the throttle and drove his ravening body forward. He turned on to a farm track and stopped.

The house was old, falling with neglect; the drive overgrown with grass, pitted with cart tracks. The fences were broken. There was a terraced garden once partly under plough, now left as if it were beyond all use.

A light burned in the kitchen window. Leiser knocked at the door. His hand was trembling from the motorbike. No one came; he knocked again, and the sound of his knocking frightened him. He thought he saw a face, it might have been the shadow of the boy sinking across the window as he fell, or the reflection of a swaying branch.

He returned quickly to his motorbike, realizing with terror that his hunger was not hunger at all but loneliness.He must lie up somewhere and rest. He thought: I've forgotten how it takes you. He drove on until he came to the wood, where he lay down. His face was hot against the bracken.

It was evening; the fields were still light but the wood in which he lay gave itself swiftly to the darkness, so that in a moment the red pines had turned to columns of black.

He picked the leaves from his jacket and laced up his shoes. They pinched badly at the instep. He never had a chance to wear them in. He caught himself thinking, it's all right for them, and he remembered that nothing ever bridged the gulf between the man who went and the man who stayed behind, between the living and the dying.

He struggled into the harness of his rucksack and once again felt gratefully the hot, raw pain in his shoulders as the straps found the old bruises. Picking up the suitcase he walked across the field to the road where the motorbike was waiting; five kilometres to Langdorn. He guessed it lay beyond the hill: the first of the three towns. Soon he would meet the road block; soon he would have to eat.

He drove slowly, the case across his knees, peering ahead all the time along the wet road, straining his eyes for a line of red lights or a cluster of men and vehicles. He rounded a bend and saw to his left a house with a beer sign propped in the window. He entered the forecourt; the noise of the engine brought an old man to the door. Leiser lifted the bike on to its stand.

'I want a beer,' he said, 'and some sausage. Have you got that here?'

The old man showed him inside, sat him at a table in the front room from which Leiser could see his motorbike parked in the yard. He brought him a bottle of beer, some sliced sausage and a piece of black bread; then stood at the table watching him eat.

'Where are you making for?' His thin face was shaded with beard.

'North,' Leiser knew this game.

'Where are you from?'

'What's the next town?'

'Langdorn.'

'Far?'

'Five kilometres.'

'Somewhere to stay?'

The old man shrugged. It was a gesture not of indifference nor of refusal, but of negation, as if he rejected everything and everything rejected him.

'What's the road like?' Leiser asked.

'It's all right.'

'I heard there was a diversion.'

'No diversion,' the old man said, as if a diversion were hope, or comfort, or companionship; anything that might warm the damp air or lighten the corners of the room.

'You're from the east,' the man declared. 'One hears it in the voice.'

'My parents,' he said. 'Any coffee?'

The old man brought him coffee, very black and sour, tasting of nothing.

'You're from Wilmsdorf,' the old man said. 'You've got a Wilmsdorf registration.'

'Much custom?' Leiser asked, glancing at the door.

The old man shook his head.

'Not a busy road, eh?' Still the old man said nothing. 'I've got a friend near Kalkstadt. Is that far?'

'Not far. Forty kilometres. They killed a boy near Wilmsdorf.'

'He runs a café. On the northern side. The Tom Cat. Know it at all?'

'No.'

Leiser lowered his voice. 'They had trouble there. A fight. Some soldiers from the town. Russians.'

'Go away,' the old man said.

He tried to pay him but he only had a fifty-mark note.

'Go away,' the old man repeated.

Leiser picked up the suitcase and rucksack. 'You old fool,' he said roughly. 'What do you think I am?'

'You are either good or bad, and both are dangerous. Go away.'

There was no road block. Without warning he was in the centre of Langdorn; it was already dark; the only lights in the main street stole from the shuttered windows, barely reaching the wet cobbles. There was no traffic. He was alarmed by the din of his motorbike; it sounded like a trumpet blast across the market square. In the war, Leiser thought, the went to bed early to keep warm; perhaps they still did.

It was time to get rid of the motorbike. He drove through the town, found a disused church and left it by the vestry door. Walking back into the town he made for the railway station. The official wore uniform.

'Kalkstadt. Single.'

The official held out his hand. Leiser took a banknote from his wallet and gave it to him. The official shook it impatiently. For a moment Leiser's mind went blank while he looked stupidly at the flicking fingers in front of him and the suspicious, angry face behind the grille.

Suddenly the official shouted: 'Identity card!'

Leiser smiled apologetically. 'One forgets,' he said, and opened his wallet to show the card in the cellophane window.

'Take it out of the wallet,' the official said. Leiser watched him examine it under the light on his desk.

'Travel authority?'

'Yes, of course.' Leiser handed him the paper.

'Why do you want to go to Kalkstadt if you are travelling to Rostock?'

'Our co-operative in Magdeburg sent some machinery by rail to Kalkstadt. Heavy turbines and some tooling equipment. It has to be installed.'

'How did you come this far?'

'I got a lift.'

'The granting of lifts is forbidden.'

'One must do what one can these days.'

'These days?'

The man pressed his face against the glass, looking down at Leiser's hands.

'What's that you're fiddling with down there?' he demanded roughly.

'A chain; a key chain.'

'So the equipment has to be installed. Well? Go on!'

'I can do the job on the way. The people in Kalkstadt have been waiting six weeks already. The consignment was delayed.'

'So?'

'We made inquiries . . . of the railway people.'

'And?'

'They didn't reply.'

'You've got an hour's wait. It leaves at six thirty.' A pause. 'You heard the news? They've killed a boy at Wilmsdorf,' he said. 'Swine.' He handed him his change.

He had nowhere to go; he dared not deposit his luggage. There was nothing else to do. He walked for half an hour, then returned to the station. The train was late.

'You both deserve great credit,' Leclerc said, nodding gratefully at Haldane and Avery. 'You too, Johnson. From now on there's nothing any of us can do: it's up to Mayfly.' A special smile for Avery: 'How about you, John; you've been keeping very quiet? Do you think you've profited from the experience?' He added with a laugh, appealing to the other two, 'I do hope we shan't have a divorce on our hands; we must get you home to your wife.'

He was sitting at the edge of the table, his small hands folded tidily on his knee. When Avery said nothing he declared brightly. 'I had a ticking off from Carol, you know, Adrian; breaking up the young home.'

Haldane smiled as if it were an amusing notion. 'I'm sure there's no danger of that,' he said.

'He made a great hit with Smiley, too; we must see they don't poach him away!'

Chapter Nineteen

When the train reached Kalkstadt, Leiser waited until the other passengers had left the platform. An elderly guard collected the tickets. He looked a kindly man.

'I'm looking for a friend,' Leiser said. 'A man called Fritsche. He used to work here.'

The guard frowned.

'Fritsche?'

'Yes.'

'What was his first name?'

'I don't know.'

'How old then; how old about?'

He guessed: 'Forty.'

'Fritsche, here, at this station?'

'Yes. He had a small house down by the river; a single man.'

'A whole house? And worked at this station?'

'Yes.'

The guard shook his head. 'Never heard of him.' He peered at Leiser. 'Are you sure?' he said.

'That's what he told me.' Something seemed to come back to him. 'He wrote to me in November . . . he complained that Vopos had closed the station.'

'You're mad,' the guard said. 'Goodnight.'

'Goodnight,' Leiser replied; as he walked away he was conscious all the time of the man's gaze upon his back.

There was an inn in the main street called the Old Bell. He waited at the desk in the hall and nobody came. He opened a door and found himself in a big room, dark at the farther end. A girl sat at a table in front of an old gramophone. She was slumped forward, her head buried in her arms, listening to the music. A single light burned above her. When the record stopped she played it again, moving the arm of the record player without lifting her head.

'I'm looking for a room,' Leiser said. 'I've just arrived from Langdorn.'

There were stuffed birds round the room: herons, pheasants and a kingfisher. 'I'm looking for a room,' he repeated. It was dance music, very old.

'Ask at the desk.'

'There's no one there.'

'They have nothing, anyway. They're not allowed to take you. There's a hostel near the church. You have to stay there.'

'Where's the church?'

With an exaggerated sigh she stopped the record, and Leiser knew she was glad to have someone to talk to.

'It was bombed,' she declared. 'We just talk about it still. There's only the tower left.'

Finally he said, 'Surely they've got a bed here? It's a big place.' He put his rucksack in a corner and sat at the table next to her. He ran a hand through his thick dry hair.

'You look all in,' the girl said.

His blue trousers were still caked with mud from the border. 'I've been on the road all day. Takes a lot out of you.'

She stood up self-consciously and went to the end of the room where a wooden staircase led upwards towards a glimmer of light. She called out but no one came.

'Steinhäger?' she asked him from the dark.

'Yes.'

She returned with a bottle and a glass. She was wearing a mackintosh, an old brown one of military cut with epaulettes and square shoulders.

'Where are you from?' she asked.

'Magdeburg. I'm making north. Got a job in Rostock.' How many more times would he say it? 'This hostel; do I get a room to myself?'

'If you want one.'

The light was so poor that at first he could scarcely make her out. Gradually she came alive. She was about eighteen, and heavily built; quite a pretty face but bad skin. The same age as the boy; older perhaps.

'Who are you?' he asked. She said nothing. 'What do you do?'

She took his glass and drank from it, looking at him precociously over the brim as if she were a great beauty. She put it down slowly, still watching him, touched the side of her hair. She seemed to think her gestures mattered. Leiser began again:

'Been here long?'

'Two years.'

'What do you do?'

'Whatever you want.' Her voice was quite earnest.

'Much going on here?'

'It's dead. Nothing.'

'No boys?'

'Sometimes.'

'Troops?' A pause.

'Now and then. Don't you know it's forbidden to ask that?'

Leiser helped himself to more Steinhäger from the bottle.
She took his glass, fumbling with his fingers.
'What's wrong with this town?' he asked. 'I tried to come here six
weeks ago. They wouldn't let me in. Kalkstadt, Langdorn, Wolken,
all closed, they said. What was going on?'
Her fingertips played over his hand.
'What was up?' he repeated
'Nothing was closed.'
'Come off it,' Leiser laughed. 'They wouldn't let me near the
place, I tell you. Road blocks here and on the Wolken road.' He
thought: 'It's eight twenty; only two hours till the first schedule.'
'Nothing was closed.' Suddenly she added, 'So you came from the
west: you came by road. They're looking for someone like you.'
He stood up to go. 'I'd better find the hostel.' He put some money
on the table. The girl whispered. 'I've got my own room. In a new
flat behind the Friedensplatz. A workers' block. They don't mind.
I'll do whatever you want.'
Leiser shook his head. He picked up his luggage and went to the
door. She was still looking at him and he knew she suspected him.
'Goodbye,' he said.
'I won't say anything. Take me with you.'
'I had a Steinhäger,' Leiser muttered. 'We didn't even talk. You
played your record all the time.' They were both frightened.
The girl said, 'Yes. Records all the time.'
'It was never closed, you are sure of that? Langdorn, Wolken,
Kalkstadt, six weeks ago?'
'What would anyone close this place for?'
'Not even the station?'
She said quickly, 'I don't know about the station. The area was
closed for three days in November. No one knows why. Russian
troops stayed, about fifty. They were billeted in the town. Mid
November.'
'Fifty? Any equipment?'
'Lorries. There were manoeuvres farther north, that's the rumour.
Stay with me tonight. Stay with me! Let me come with you. I'll go
anywhere.'
'What colour shoulder-boards?'
'I don't remember.'
'Where did they come from?'
'They were new. Some came from Leningrad, two brothers.'
'Which way did they go?'
'North. Listen, no one will ever know. I don't talk, I'm not the
kind. I'll give it to you, anything you want.'
'Towards Rostock?'
'They said they were going to Rostock. They said not to tell. The
Party came round all the houses.'

Leiser nodded. He was sweating. 'Goodbye,' he said.

'What about tomorrow, tomorrow night? I'll do whatever you want.'

'Perhaps. Don't tell anyone, do you understand?'

She shook her head. 'I won't tell them,' she said, 'because I don't care. Ask for the Hochhaus behind the Friedensplatz. Apartment nineteen. Come any time. I'll open the door. You give two rings and they know it's for me. You needn't pay. Take care,' she said. 'There are people everywhere. They've killed a boy in Wilmsdorf.'

He walked to the market square, correct again because everything was closing in, looking for the church tower and the hostel. Huddled figures passed him in the darkness; some wore pieces of uniform; forage caps and the long coats they had in the war. Now and then he would glimpse their faces, catching them in the pale glow of a street light and he would seek in their locked, unseeing features the qualities he hated. He would say to himself, 'Hate him—he is old enough,' but it did not stir him. They were nothing. Perhaps in some other town, some other place, he would find them and hate them; but not here. These were old and nothing; poor, like him, and alone. The tower was black and empty. It reminded him suddenly of the turret on the border, and the garage after eleven, of the moment when he killed the sentry: just a kid, like himself in the war; even younger than Avery.

'He should be there by now,' Avery said.

'That's right, John. He should be there, shouldn't he? One hour to go. One more river to cross.' He began singing. No one took him up.

They looked at each other in silence.

'Know the Alias Club at all?' Johnson asked suddenly. 'Off Villiers Street? A lot of the old gang meet up there. You ought to come along one evening, when we get home.'

'Thanks,' Avery replied. 'I'd like to.'

'It gets nice Christmas time,' he said. 'That's when I go. A good crowd. There's even one or two come in uniform.'

'It sounds fine.'

'They have a mixed do at New Year. You could take your wife.'

'Grand.'

Johnson winked. 'Or your fancy-girl.'

'Sarah's the only girl for me,' Avery said.

The telephone was ringing. Leclerc rose to answer it.

Chapter Twenty
HOMECOMING

He put down the rucksack and the suitcase and looked round the walls. There was an electric point beside the window. The door had no lock so he pushed the armchair against it. He took off his shoes and lay on the bed. He thought of the girl's fingers on his hands and the nervous movement of her lips; he remembered her deceitful eyes watching him from the shadows and he wondered how long it would be before she betrayed him.

He remembered Avery: the warmth and English decency of their early companionship; he remembered his young face glistening in the rain, and his shy, dazzled glance as he dried his spectacles, and he thought: he must have said thirty-two all the time. I misheard.

He looked at the ceiling. In an hour he would put up the aerial.

The room was large and bare with a round marble basin in one corner. A single pipe ran from it to the floor and he hoped to God it would do for the earth. He ran some water and to his relief it was cold, because Jack had said a hot pipe was dicey. He drew his knife and carefully scraped the pipe clean on one side. The earth was important; Jack had said so. If you can't do anything else, he'd said, lay your earth wire zig-zag fashion under the carpet, the same length as the aerial. But there was no carpet; the pipe would have to do. No carpet, no curtains.

Opposite him stood a heavy wardrobe with bow doors. The place must once have been the main hotel. There was a smell of Turkish tobacco and rank, unscented disinfectant. The walls were of grey plaster; the damp had spread over them in dark shadows, arrested her and there by some mysterious inner property of the house which had dried a path across the ceiling. In some places the plaster had crumbled with the damp, leaving a ragged island of white mildew; in others it had contracted and the plasterer had returned to fill the cavities with paste which described white rivers along the corners of the room. Leiser's eye followed them carefully while he listened for the smallest sound outside.

There was a picture on the wall of workers in a field, leading a horse plough. On the horizon was a tractor. He heard Johnson's benign voice running on about the aerial: 'If it's indoors it's a headache, and indoors it'll be. Now listen: zig-zag fashion across the room, quarter the length of your wave and one foot below the ceiling. Space them wide as possible, Fred, and not parallel to metal girders, electric wires and that. And don't double her back on herself, Fred, or you'll muck her up properly, see?' Always the joke, the copulative innuendo to aid the memory of simple men.

Leiser thought: 'I'll take it to the picture frame, then back and forth to the far corner. I can put a nail into that soft plaster; he looked around for a nail or pin, and noticed a bronze hanger on one of the pelmets. He got up, unscrewed the handle of his razor. The thread began to the right, it was considered an ingenious detail, so that a suspicious man who gave the handle a casual twist to the left would be going against the thread. From the recess he extracted the knot of silk cloth which he smoothed carefully over his knee with his thick fingers. He found a pencil in his pocket and sharpened it, not moving from the edge of his bed because he did not want to disturb the silk cloth. Twice the point broke; the shavings collected on the floor at his feet. He began writing in the notebook, capital letters, like a prisoner writing to his wife, and every time he made a full stop he drew a ring round it the way he was taught long ago.

The message composed, he drew a line after every two letters, and beneath each compartment he entered the numerical equivalent according to the chart he had memorized: sometimes he had to resort to a mnemonic rhyme in order to recall the numbers; sometimes he remembered wrong and had to rub out and begin again. When he had finished he divided the line of numbers into groups of four and deducted each in turn from the groups on the silk cloth; finally he converted the figures into letters again and wrote out the result, redividing them into groups of four.

Fear like an old pain had again taken hold of his belly so that with every imagined sound he looked sharply towards the door, his hand arrested in the middle of writing. But he heard nothing; just the creaking of an ageing house, like the noise of wind in the rigging of a ship.

He looked at the finished message, conscious that it was too long, and that if he were better at that kind of thing, if his mind were quicker, he could reduce it, but just now he couldn't think of a way, and he knew, he had been taught, better put in a word or two too many than make it ambiguous the other end. There were forty-two groups.

He pushed the table away from the window and lifted the suitcase; with the key from his chain he unlocked it, praying all the time that nothing was broken from the journey. He opened the spares box, discovering with his trembling fingers the silk bag of crystals bound with green ribbon at the mouth. Loosening the ribbon, he shook the crystals on to the coarse blanket with covered the bed. Each was labelled in Johnson's handwriting, first the frequency and below it a single figure denoting the place where it came in the signal plan. He arranged them in line, pressing them on to the blanket so that they lay flat. The crystals were the easiest part. He tested the door against the armchair. The handle slipped in his palm. The chair provided no protection. In the war, he remembered, they had given him steel wedges. Returning to the suitcase he connected the transmitter and receiver to the power pack, plugged in the earphones and unscrewed the Morse key from the lid of the spares box. Then he saw it.

Mounted inside the suitcase lid was a piece of adhesive paper with half a dozen groups of letters and beside each its Morse equivalent; they were the international code for standard phrases, the ones he could never remember.

When he saw those letters, drawn out in Jack's neat, post-office hand, tears of gratitude started to his eyes. He never told me, he thought, he never told me he'd done it. Jack was all right, after all. Jack, the Captain and young John; what a team to work for, he thought; a man could go through life and never meet a set of blokes like that. He steadied himself, pressing his hands sharply on the table. He was trembling a little, perhaps from the cold; his damp shirt clung to his shoulder-blades; but he was happy. He glanced at the chair in front of the door and thought; when I've got the headphones on I shan't hear them coming, the way the boy didn't hear me because of the wind.

Next he attached aerial and earth to their terminals, led the earth wire to the water pipe and fastened the two strands to the cleaned surface with tabs of adhesive plaster. Standing on the bed, he stretched the aerial across the ceiling in eight lengths, zig-zag as Johnson had instructed, fixing it as best he could to the curtain rail or plaster on either side. This done, he returned to the set, and adjusted the wavebank switch to the fourth position, because he knew that all the frequencies were in the three-megacycle range. He took from the bed the first crystal in the line, plugged it into the far left-hand corner of the set, and settled down to tune the transmitter, muttering gently as he performed each movement. Adjust crystal selector to 'fundamental all crystals', plug the coil; anode tuning and aerial matching controls to ten.

He hesitated, trying to remember what happened next. A block was forming in his mind. 'PA—don't you know what PA stands for?' He set the meter switch to three to read the Power Amplifier grid current . . . TSR switch to T for tuning. It was coming back to him. Meter switch to six to ascertain total current . . . anode tuning for minimum reading.

Now he turned the TSR switch to S for send, pressed the key

briefly, took a reading, manipulated the aerial matching control so that the meter reading rose slightly; hastily readjusted the anode tuning. He repeated the procedure until to his profound relief he saw the finger dip against the white background of the kidney-shaped dial and knew that the transmitter and aerial were correctly tuned, and that he could talk to John and Jack.

He sat back with a grunt of satisfaction, lit a cigarette, wished it were an English one because if they came in now they wouldn't have to bother about the brand of cigarette he was smoking. He looked at his watch, turning the winder until it was stiff, terrified lest it run down; it was matched with Avery's and in a simple way this gave him comfort. Like divided lovers, they were looking at the same star.

He had killed that boy.

Three minutes to schedule. He unscrewed the Morse key from the spares box because he couldn't manage it properly while it was on that lid. Jack had said it was all right; he said it didn't matter. He had to hold the key base with his left hand so that it didn't slide about, but Jack said every operator had his quirks. He was sure it was smaller than the one they gave him in the war; he was sure of it. Traces of french chalk clung to the lever. He drew in his elbows and straightened his back. The third finger of his right hand crooked over the key. JAJ's my first call sign, he thought, Johnson's my name, they call me Jack, that's easy enough to remember. JA, John Avery; JJ, Jack Johnson. Then he was tapping it out. A dot and three dashes, dot dash, a dot and three dashes, and he kept thinking: it's like the house in Holland, but there's no one with me.

Say it twice, Fred, then get off the air. He switched over to receive, pushed the sheet of paper farther towards the middle of the table and suddenly realized he had nothing to write with when Jack came through.

He stood up and looked around for his notebook and pencil, the sweat breaking out on his back. They were nowhere to be seen. Dropping hastily to his hands and knees he felt in the thick dust under the bed, found the pencil, groped vainly for his notebook. As he was getting up he heard a crackle from the earphones. He ran to the table, pressed one phone to his ear, at the same time trying to hold still the sheet of paper so that he could write in a corner of it beside his own message.

'QSA3: hearing you well enough,' that's all they were saying. 'Steady, boy, steady,' he muttered. He settled into the chair, switched to transmit, looked at his own encoded message and tapped out four-two because there were forty-two groups. His hand was coated with dust and sweat, his right arm ached, perhaps from carrying the suitcase. Or struggling with the boy.

You've got all the time in the world, Johnson had said. We'll be listening: you're not passing an exam. He took his handkerchief from his pocked and wiped away the grime from his hands. He was terribly tired; the tiredness was like a physical despair, like the moment of guilt before making love. Groups of four letters, Johnson had said, think of four-letter words, eh, Fred. You don't need to do it all at once, Fred, have a little stop in the middle if you like; two and a half minutes on the first frequency, two and a half on the second, that's the way we go; Mrs Hartbeck will wait, I'm sure. With his pencil he drew a heavy line under the ninth letter because that was where the safety device came. That was something he dared think of only in passing.

He put his face in his hands, summoning the last of his concentration, then reached for the key and began tapping. Keep the hand loose, first and second fingers on top of the key, thumb beneath the edge, no putting the wrist on the table, Fred, breathe regular, Fred, you'll find it helps you to relax.

God, why were his hands so slow? Once he took his fingers from the key and stared impotently at his open palm; once he ran his left hand across his forehead to keep the sweat from his eyes, and he felt the key drifting across the table. His wrist was too stiff: the hand he killed the boy with. All the time he was saying it over to himself—dot, dot, dash, then a K, he always knew that one, a dot between two dashes—his lips were spelling out the letters, but his hand wouldn't follow, it was a kind of stammer that got worse the more he spoke, and always the boy in his mind, only the boy. Perhaps he was quicker than he thought. He lost all notion of time; the sweat was running into his eyes, he couldn't stop it any more.He kept mouthing the dots and dashes, and he knew that Johnson would be angry because he shouldn't be thinking in dots and dashes at all but musically, de-dah, dah, the way the professionals did, but Johnson had not killed the boy. The pounding of his heart outran the weary tapping of the key; his hand seemed to grow heavier and still he went on signalling because it was the only thing left to do, the only thing to hold on to while his body gave way. He was waiting for them now, wishing they'd come—take me, take it all—longing for the footsteps. Give us your hand, John; give us a hand.

When at last he had finished, he went back to the bed. Almost with detachment he caught sight of the line of crystals on the blanket, untouched, still and ready, dressed by the left and numbered; flat on their backs, like dead sentries.

Avery looked at his watch. It was quarter past ten. 'He should come on in five minutes,' he said.

Leclerc announced suddenly: 'That was Gorton on the telephone. He's received a telegram from the Ministry. They have some news for us apparently. They're sending out a courier.'

'What could that be?' Avery asked.

'I expect it's the Hungarian thing. Fielden's report. I may have to go back to London.' A satisfied smile. 'But I think you people can get along without me.'

Johnson was wearing earphones, sitting forward on a high-backed wooden chair carried up from the kitchen. The dark green receiver hummed gently from the mains transformer; the tuning dial, illuminated from within, glowed palely in the half light of the attic.

Haldane and Avery sat uncomfortably on a bench. Johnson had a pad and pencil in front of him. He lifted the phones above his ears and said to Leclerc who stood beside him, 'I shall take him straight through the routine, sir; I'll do my best to tell you what's going on. I'm recording, too, mind, for safety's sake.'

'I understand.'

They waited in silence. Suddenly–it was their moment of utter magic–Johnson had sat bolt upright, nodded sharply to them, switched on the tape recorder. He smiled, quickly turned to transmission and was tapping. 'Come in, Fred,' he said out loud. 'Hearing you nicely.'

'He's made it!' Leclerc hissed. 'He's on target now!' His eyes were bright with excitement. 'Do you hear that, John? Do you hear?'

'Shall we be quiet?' Haldane suggested.

'Here he comes,' Johnson said. His voice was level, controlled. 'Forty-two groups.'

'Forty-two!' Leclerc repeated.

Johnson's body was motionless, his head inclined a little to one side, his whole concentration given to the earphones, his face impassive in the pale light.

' 'I'd like silence now, please.'

For perhaps two minutes his careful hand moved briskly across the pad. Now and then he muttered inaudibly, whispered a letter or shook his head, until the message seemed to come more slowly, his pencil pausing while he listened, until it was tracing out each letter singly with agonizing care. He glanced at the clock.

'Come on, Fred,' he urged. 'Come on, change over, that's nearly three minutes.' But still the message was coming through, letter by letter, and Johnson's simple face assumed an expression of alarm.

'What's going on?' Leclerc demanded. 'Why hasn't he changed his frequency?'

But Johnson only said, 'Get off the air, for Christ's sake, Fred, get off the air.'

Leclerc touched him impatiently on the arm. Johnson raised one earphone.

'Why's he not changed frequency? Why's he still talking?'

'He must have forgotten! He never forgot on training. I *know* he's slow, but Christ!' He was still writing automatically. 'Five minutes,' he muttered. 'Five bloody minutes. Change the bloody crystal!'

'Can't you tell him?' Leclerc cried.

'Of course I can't. How can I? He can't receive and send at the same time!'

They sat or stood in dreadful fascination. Johnson had turned to them, his voice beseeching. 'I told him; if I told him once I told him a dozen times. It's bloody suicide, what he's doing!' He looked at his watch. 'He's been on damn near six minutes. Bloody, bloody, *bloody* fool.'

'What will they do?' said Haldane.

'If they pick up the signal? Call in another station. Take a fix, then it's simple trigonometry when he's on this long.' He banged his open hands helplessly on the table, indicated the set as if it were an affront. 'A kid could do it. Do it with a pair of compasses. Christ Almighty! Come on, Fred, for Jesus' sake, come on!' He wrote down a handful of letters then threw his pencil aside. 'It's on tape, anyway,' he said.

Leclerc turned to Haldane. 'Surely there's something we can do!'

'Be quiet,' Haldane said.

The message stopped. Johnson tapped an acknowledgement, fast, a stab of hatred. He wound back the tape recorder and began transcribing. Putting the coding sheet in front of him he worked without interruption for perhaps quarter of an hour, occasionally making simple runs on the rough paper at his elbow. No one spoke. When he had finished he stood up, a half-forgotten gesture of respect. 'Message reads: Area Kalkstadt closed three days mid November when fifty unidentified Soviet troops seen in town. No special equipment. Rumours of Soviet manoeuvres farther north. Troops believed moved to Rostock. Fritsche not repeat not known Kalkstadt railway station. No road check in Kalkstadt road.' He tossed the paper on to the desk. 'There are fifteen groups after that which I can't unbutton. I think he's muddled his coding.'

The Vopo sergeant in Rostock picked up the telephone; he was an elderly man, greying and thoughtful. He listened for a moment then began dialling on another line. 'It must be a child,' he said, still dialling. 'What frequency did you say?' He put the other telephone to his ear and spoke into it fast, repeating the frequency three times. He walked into the adjoining hut. 'Witmar will be through in a minute,' he said. 'They're taking a fix. Are you still hearing him?' The corporal nodded. The sergeant held a spare headphone to his ear.

'It couldn't be an amateur,' he muttered. 'Breaking the regulations. But what is it? No agent in his right mind would put out a signal like that. What are the neighbouring frequencies? Military or civilian?'

'It's near the military. Very near.'

'That's odd,' the sergeant said. 'That would fit, wouldn't it? That's what they did in the war.'

The corporal was staring at the tapes slowly revolving on their spindles. 'He's still transmitting. Groups of four.'

'Four?' The sergeant was searching in his memory for something that had happened long ago.

'Let me hear again. Listen, listen to the fool! He's as slow as a child.'

The sound struck some chord in his memory—the slurred gaps, the dots so short as to be little more than clicks. He could swear he knew that hand . . . from the war, in Norway but not so slow: nothing had ever been as slow as this. Not Norway . . . France. Perhaps it was only imagination. Yes, it was imagination.

'Or an old man,' the corporal said.

The telephone rang. The sergeant listened for a moment, then ran, ran as fast as he could, through the hut to the officers' mess across the tarmac path.

The Russian captain was drinking beer; his jacket was slung over the back of his chair and he looked very bored.

'You wanted something, Sergeant?' He affected the languid style.

'He's come. The man they told us about. The one who killed the boy.'

The Captain put down his beer quickly.

'You heard him?'

'We've taken a fix. With Witmar. Groups of four. A slow hand. Area Kalkstadt. Close to one of our own frequencies. Sommer recorded the transmission.'

'Christ,' he said quietly. The sergeant frowned.

'What's he looking for? Why should they send him here?' the sergeant asked.

The Captain was buttoning his jacket. 'Ask them in Leipzig. Perhaps they know that too.'

Chapter Twenty-one

It was very late.

The fire in Control's grate was burning nicely, but he poked at it with effeminate discontent. He hated working at night.

'They want you at the Ministry,' he said irritably. 'Now, of all hours. It really is too bad. Why does everyone get so *agitato* on a Thursday? It will *ruin* the week-end.' He put down the poker and returned to his desk. 'They're in a dreadful state. Some idiot talking about ripples in a pond. It's extraordinary what the night does to people. I do *detest* the telephone.' There were several in front of him.

Smiley offered him a cigarette and he took one without looking at it, as if he could not be held responsible for the actions of his limbs.

'What Ministry?' Smiley asked.

'Leclerc's. Have you *any* idea what's going on?'

Smiley said, 'Yes. Haven't you?'

'Leclerc's so *vulgar*. I admit, I find him vulgar. He thinks we compete. What on earth would *I* do with his dreadful militia? Scouring Europe for mobile laundries. He thinks I want to gobble him up.'

'Well, don't you? Why *did* we cancel that passport?'

'What a *silly* man. A silly, vulgar man. However did Haldane fall for it?'

'He had a conscience once. He's like all of us. He's learnt to live with it.'

'Oh dear. Is that a dig at me?'

'What does the Ministry want?' Smiley asked sharply.

Control held up some papers, flapping them. 'You've seen these from Berlin?'

'They came in an hour ago. The Americans have taken a fix. Groups of four; a primitive letter code. They say it comes from the Kalkstadt area.'

'Where on *earth's* that?'

'South of Rostock. The message ran six minutes on the same frequency. They said it sounded like an amateur on a first run through. One of the old wartime sets: they wanted to know if it was ours.'

'And you replied?' Control asked quickly.

'I said no.'

'So I should hope. Good Lord.'

'You don't seem very concerned,' Smiley said.

Control seemed to remember something from long ago. 'I hear Leclerc's in Lübeck. Now *there's* a pretty town. I adore Lübeck. The Ministry wants you immediately. I said you'd go. Some meeting.' He added in apparent earnest, 'You must, George. We've been the most awful fools. It's in every East German newspaper; they're screaming about peace conferences and sabotage.' He prodded at a telephone. 'So is the Ministry. God, how I loathe Civil Servants.'

Smiley watched him with scepticism. 'We could have stopped them,' he said. 'We knew enough.'

'Of course we could,' Control said blandly. 'D'you know why we didn't? Plain, idiot Christian charity. We let them have their war game. You'd better go now. And Smiley . . .'

'Yes?'

'Be gentle.' And in his silly voice: 'I do envy them Lübeck, all the same. There's that restaurant, isn't there; what do they call it? Where Thomas Mann used to eat. So interesting.'

'He never did,' Smiley said. 'The place you're thinking of was bombed.'

Smiley still did not go. 'I wonder,' he said. 'You'll never tell me, will you? I just wonder.' He was not looking at Control.

'My dear George, what *has* come over you?'

'We handed it to them. The passport that was cancelled . . . a courier service they never needed . . . a clapped-out wireless set . . . papers, frontier reports . . . who told Berlin to listen for him? Who told them what frequencies? We even gave Leclerc the crystals, didn't we? Was that just Christian charity too? Plain, idiot Christian charity?'

Control was shocked.

'What *are* you suggesting? How *very* distasteful. Who ever would do a thing like that?'

Smiley was putting on his coat.

'Goodnight, George,' Control said; and fiercely, as if he were tired of sensibility: 'Run along. And preserve the difference between us: your country needs you. It's not *my* fault they've taken so long to die.'

The dawn came and Leiser had not slept. He wanted to wash but dared not go into the corridor. He dared not move. If they were looking for him, he knew he must leave normally, not bolt from the hostel before the morning came. Never run, they used to say: walk like the crowd. He could go at six: that was late enough. He rubbed his chin against the back of his hand: it was sharp and rough, marking the brown skin.

He was hungry and no longer knew what to do, but he would not run.

He half turned on the bed, pulled the knife from inside the waistband of his trousers and held it before his eyes. He was shivering. He could feel across his brow the unnatural heat of incipient fever. He looked at the knife, and remembered the clean, friendly way they had talked: 'thumb on top, blade parallel to the ground, forearm stiff. 'Go away,' the old man had said. 'You are either good or bad and both are dangerous.' How should he hold the knife when people spoke to him like that? The way he held it for the boy?

It was six o'clock. He stood up. His legs were heavy and stiff. His shoulders still ached from carrying the rucksack. His clothes, he noticed, smelt of pine and leaf mould. He picked the half-dried mud from his trousers and put on his second pair of shoes.

He went downstairs, looking for someone to pay, the new shoes squeaking on the wooden steps. There was an old woman in a white overall sorting lentils into a bowl, talking to a cat.

'What do I owe?'

'You fill in the form,' she said sourly. 'That's the first thing you owe. You should have done it when you came.'

'I'm sorry.'

She rounded on him, muttering but not daring to raise her voice. 'Don't you know it's forbidden, staying in a town and not reporting your presence to the police?' She looked at his new shoes. 'Or are you so rich that you think you need not trouble?'

'I'm sorry,' Leiser said again. 'Give me the form and I'll sign it now. I'm not rich.'

The woman fell silent, picking studiously among the lentils.

'Where do you come from?' she asked.

'East,' said Leiser. He meant south, from Magdeburg, or west from Wilmsdorf.

'You should have reported last night. It's too late now.'

'What do I pay?'

'You can't,' the woman replied. 'Never mind. You haven't filled in the form. What will you say if they catch you?'

'I'll say I slept with a girl.'

'It's snowing outside,' the woman said. 'Mind your nice shoes.'

Grains of hard snow drifted forlornly in the wind, collecting in the cracks between the black cobbles, lingering on the stucco of the houses. A drab, useless snow, dwindling where it fell.

He crossed the Friedensplatz and saw a new, yellow building, six or seven storeys high, standing on a patch of waste land beside a new estate. There was washing hanging on the balconies, touched with snow. The staircase smelt of food and Russian petrol. The flat was on the third floor. He could hear a child crying and a wireless playing. For a moment he thought he should turn and go away, because he was dangerous for them. He pressed the bell twice, as the girl had told him. She opened the door, she was half asleep. She had put on her mackintosh over the cotton nightdress and she held it at the neck, because of the freezing cold. When she saw him she hesitated, not knowing what to do, as if he had brought bad news. He said nothing, just stood there with the suitcase swinging gently at his side. She beckoned with her head; he followed her across the corridor to her room, put the suitcase and rucksack in the corner. There were travel posters on the walls, pictures of desert, palm trees and the moon over a tropical sea. They got into bed and she covered him with her heavy body, trembling a little because she was afraid.

'I want to sleep,' he said. 'Let me sleep first.'

The Russian captain said, 'He stole a motorbike at Wilmsdorf and asked for Fritsche at the station. What will he do now?'

'He'll have another schedule. Tonight,' the sergeant replied. 'If he's got anything to say.'

'At the same time?'

'Of course not. Nor the same frequency. Nor from the same place. He may go to Witmar or Langdorn or Wolken; he may even go to Rostock. Or he may stay in town but go to another house. Or he may not send at all.'

'House? Who would harbour a spy?'

The sergeant shrugged as if to say he might himself. Stung, the Captain asked, 'How do you know he's sending from a house? Why not a wood or a field? How can you be so sure?'

'It's a very strong signal. A powerful set. He couldn't get a signal like that from a battery, not a battery you could carry around alone. He's using the mains.'

'Put a cordon round the town,' the Captain said. 'Search every house.'

'We want him alive.' The sergeant was looking at his hands. 'You want him alive.'

'Then tell me what we should do?' the Captain insisted.

'Make sure he transmits. That's the first thing. And make him stay in town. That is the second.'

'Well?'

'We would have to act quickly,' the sergeant observed.

'Well?'

'Bring some troops into the town. Anything you can find. As soon as possible. Armour, infantry, it doesn't matter. Create some movement. Make him pay attention. But be quick!'

'I'll go soon,' Leiser said. 'Don't let me stay. Give me coffee and I'll go.'

'Coffee?'

'I've got money,' Leiser said, as if it were the only thing he had. 'Here.' He climbed out of bed, fetched the wallet from his jacket and drew a hundred-mark note from the wad.

'Keep it.'

She took the wallet and with a little laugh emptied it out on the bed. She had a ponderous, kittenish way which was not quite sane; and the quick instinct of an illiterate. He watched her indifferently, running her fingers along the line of her naked shoulder. She held up a photograph of a woman; a blonde, round head.

'Who is she? What is her name?'

'She doesn't exist,' he said.

She found the letters and read one aloud, laughing at the affectionate passages. 'Who is she?' she kept taunting him. 'Who is she?'

'I tell you, she doesn't exist.'

'Then I can tear them up?' She held a letter before him with both hands, teasing him, waiting for him to protest. Leiser said nothing. She made a little tear, still watching him, then tore it completely, and a second and a third.

She found a picture of a child, a girl in spectacles, eight or nine years old perhaps, and again she asked, 'Who is it? Is it your child? Does *she* exist?'

'Nobody. Nobody's kid. Just a photograph.' She tore that too, scattering the pieces dramatically over the bed, then fell on him, kissing him on the face and neck. 'Who are you? What is your name?'

He wanted to tell her when she pushed him away.

'No!' she cried. 'No!' She lowered her voice. 'I want you with nothing. Alone from it all. You and me alone. We'll make our own names, our own rules. Nobody, no one at all, no father, no mother. We'll print our own newspapers, passes, ration cards; make our own people.' She was whispering, her eyes shining.

'You're a spy,' she said, her lips in his ear. 'A secret agent. You've got a gun.'

'A knife is quieter,' he said. She laughed, on and on, until she noticed the bruises on his shoulders. She touched them curiously, with respect, as a child might touch a dead thing.

She went out carrying a shopping basket, still clutching the mackintosh at her neck. Leiser dressed, shaving in cold water, staring at his lined face in the distorted mirror above the basin. When she returned it was nearly midday and she looked worried.

'The town's full of soldiers. And Army trucks. What do they want here?'

'Perhaps they are looking for someone.'

'They are just sitting about, drinking.'

'What kind of soldiers?'

'I don't know what kind. Russian. How can I tell?'

He went to the door. 'I'll come back in an hour.'

She said, 'You're trying to get away from me.' She held his arm, looking up at him, wanting to make a scene.

'I'll come back. Maybe not till later. Maybe this evening. But if I do . . .'

'Yes?'

'It will be dangerous. I shall have to . . . do something here. Something dangerous.'

She kissed him, a light, silly kiss. 'I like danger,' she said.

'Four hours,' Johnson said. 'If he's still alive.'

'Of course he's alive,' Avery said angrily. 'Why do you talk like that?'

Haldane interrupted. 'Don't be an ass, Avery. It's a technical term. Dead or live agents. It has nothing to do with his physical condition.'

Leclerc was drumming his fingers lightly on the table.

'He'll be all right,' he said. 'Fred's a hard man to kill. He's an old hand.' The daylight had revived him apparently. He glanced at his watch. 'What the devil's happened to that courier, I wonder.'

Leiser blinked at the soldiers like a man emerging from the dark. They filled the cafés, gazed into shop windows, looked at the girls. Trucks were parked in the square, their wheels thick with red mud, a thin surface of snow on their bonnets. He counted them and there were nine. Some had heavy couplings at the rear for pulling trailers; some a line of Cyrillic script on their battered doors, or the imprint of unit insignia and a number. He noted the emblems of the drivers' uniforms, the colour of their shoulder-boards; they came, he realized, from a variety of units.

Walking back to the main street he pushed his way into a café and ordered a drink. Half a dozen soldiers sat disconsolately at a table sharing three bottles of beer. Leiser grinned at them; it was like the encouragement of a tired whore. He lifted his fist in a Soviet salute and they watched him as if he were mad. He left his drink and made his way back to the square; a group of children had gathered round the trucks and the drivers kept telling them to go away.

He made a tour of the town, went into a dozen cafés, but no one would talk to him because he was a stranger. Everywhere the soldiers sat or stood in groups, aggrieved and bewildered, as if they had been roused to no purpose.

He ate some sausage and drank a Steinhäger, walked to the station to see if anything was going on. The same man was there, watching him, this time without suspicion, from behind his little window; and somehow Leiser knew, though it made no difference, that the man had told the police.

Returning from the station, he passed a cinema. A group of girls had gathered round the photographs and he stood with them pretending to look. Then the noise came, a metallic, irregular drone, filling the street with the piping, rattling of engines, metal and war. He drew back into the cover of the foyer, saw the girls turn and the ticket-seller stand up in her box. An old man crossed himself; he had lost one eye, and wore his hat at an angle. The tanks rolled through the town; they carried troops with rifles. The gun barrels were too long, marked white with snow. He watched them pass, then made his way across the square, quickly.

She smiled as he came in; he was out of breath.

'What are they doing?' she asked. She caught sight of his face. 'You're afraid,' she whispered, but he shook his head. 'You're afraid,' she repeated.

'I killed the boy,' he said.

He went to the basin, examined his face with the great care of a man under sentence. She followed him, clasped him round the chest, pressing herself against his back. He turned and seized her, wild, held her without skill, forced her across the room. She fought him with the rage of a daughter, calling some name, hating someone, cursing him, taking him, the world burning and only they alive; they were weeping, laughing together, falling, clumsy lovers clumsily triumphant, recognizing nothing but each himself, each for that moment completing lives half-lived, and for that moment the whole damned dark forgotten.

Johnson leant out of the window and gently drew on the aerial to make sure it was still fast, then began looking over his receiver like a racing driver before the start, needlessly touching terminals and adjusting dials. Leclerc watched him admiringly.

'Johnson, that was nobly done last time. Nobly done. We owe you a vote of thanks.' Leclerc's face was shiny, as if he had only recently shaved. He looked oddly fragile in the pale light. 'I propose to hear one more schedule and get back to London.' He laughed. 'We've work to do, you know. This isn't the season for continental holidays.'

Johnson might not have heard. He held up his hand. 'Thirty minutes,' he said. 'I shall be asking you for a little hush soon, gentlemen.' He was like a conjurer at a children's party. 'Fred's a devil for punctuality,' he observed loudly.

Leclerc addressed himself to Avery. 'You're one of those lucky people, John, who have seen action in peacetime.' He seemed anxious to talk.

'Yes. I'm very grateful.'

'You don't have to be. You've done a good job, and we recognize that. There's no question of *gratitude*. You've achieved something very rare in our work; I wonder if you know what it is?'

Avery said he did not.

'You've induced an agent to *like* you. In the ordinary way—Adrian will bear me out—the relationship between an agent and his controllers is clouded with suspicion. He resents them, that's the first thing, for not doing the job themselves. He suspects them of ulterior motives, ineptitude, duplicity. But we're not the Circus, John: that's not the way we do things.'

Avery nodded. 'No, quite.'

'You've done something else, you and Adrian. I would like to feel that if a similar need arose in the future we could use the same technique, the same facilities, the same *expertise*—that means the Avery–Haldane combination. What I'm trying to say is'—Leclerc raised one hand and with his forefinger and thumb lightly touched the bridge of his nose in an unusual gesture of English diffidence—'the experience you've made is to our mutual advantage. Thank you.'

Haldane moved to the stove and began warming his hands, rubbing them gently as if he were separating wheat.

'That Budapest thing,' Leclerc continued, raising his voice, partly in enthusiasm and partly perhaps to dispel the atmosphere of intimacy which suddenly threatened them, 'it's a complete reorganization. Nothing less. They're moving their armour to the border, d'you see. The Ministry is talking about forward strategy. They're really most interested.'

Avery said, 'More interested than in the Mayfly area?'

'No, no,' Leclerc protested lightly. 'It's all part of the same complex—they think very big over there, you know—a move here and a move there—it all has to be pieced together.'

'Of course,' Avery said gently. 'We can't see it ourselves, can we? We can't see the whole picture.' He was trying to make it better for Leclerc. 'We haven't the perspective.'

'When we get back to London,' Leclerc proposed, 'you must come and dine with me, John: you and your wife; both come. I've been meaning to suggest it for some time. We'll go to my club. They do a rather good dinner in the Ladies' Room; your wife would enjoy it.'

'You mentioned it. I asked Sarah. We'd love to. My mother-in-law's with us just now. She could baby-sit.'

'How nice. Don't forget.'

'We're looking forward to it.'

'Am I not invited?' Haldane asked coyly.

'Why, of course, Adrian. Then we shall be four. Excellent.' His voice changed. 'Incidentally, the landlords have complained about the house in Oxford. They say we left it in a poor state.'

'Poor state?' Haldane echoed angrily.

'It appears we have been overloading the electrical circuit. Parts of it are quite burnt out. I told Woodford to cope with it.'

'We should have our own place,' said Avery. 'Then we wouldn't have to worry.'

'I agree. I spoke to the Minister about it. A training centre is what we need. He was enthusiastic. He's keen on this kind of thing, now, you know. They have a new phrase for it over there. They are speaking of ICOs. Immediate Clarification Operations. He suggests we find a place and take it for six months. He proposes to speak to the Treasury about a lease.'

'That's terrific,' Avery said.

'It could be very useful. We must be sure not to abuse our trust.'

'Of course.'

There was a draught, followed by the sound of someone cautiously ascending the stairs. A figure appeared in the attic doorway. He wore an expensive overcoat of brown tweed, a little too long in the sleeve. It was Smiley.

Chapter Twenty-two

Smiley peered round the room, at Johnson, now in earphones, busy with the controls of his set, at Avery staring over Haldane's shoulder at the signal plan, at Leclerc, who stood like a soldier, who alone had noticed him, whose face, though turned to him, was empty and far away.

'What do you want here?' Leclerc said at last. 'What do you want with me?'

'I'm sorry. I was sent.'

'So were we all,' Haldane said, not moving.

A note of warning entered Leclerc's voice. 'This is my operation, Smiley. We've no room for your people here.'

There was nothing in Smiley's face but compassion, nothing in his voice but that dreadful patience with which we speak to the insane.

'It wasn't Control who sent me,' he said. 'It was the Ministry. They asked for me, you see, and Control let me go. The Ministry laid on a plane.'

'Why?' Haldane inquired. He seemed almost amused.

One by one they stirred, waking from a single dream. Johnson laid his earphones carefully on the table.

'Well?' Leclerc asked. 'Why did they send you?'

'They called me round last night.' He managed to indicate that he was as bewildered as they. 'I had to admire the operation, the way you'd conducted it; you and Haldane. All done from nothing. They showed me the files. Scrupulously kept . . . Library Copy, Operational Copy, sealed minutes: just like in the war. I congraulate you . . . I really do.'

'They showed you the files? *Our* files?' Leclerc repeated. 'That's a breach of security: interconsciousness between Departments. You've committed an offence, Smiley. They must be mad! Adrian, do you hear what Smiley has told me?'

Smiley said, 'Is there a schedule tonight, Johnson?'

'Yes, sir. Twenty-one hundred.'

'I was surprised, Adrian, that you felt that the indicators were strong enough for such a *big* operation.'

'Haldane was not responsible,' Leclerc said crisply. 'The decision was a collective one; ourselves on the one side, the Ministry on the other.' His voice changed key. 'When the schedule is finished I shall want to know, Smiley, I have a right to know, how you came to see those files.' It was his committee voice, powerful and fluent; for the first time it had the ring of dignity.

Smiley moved towards the centre of the room. 'Something's happened; something you couldn't know about. Leiser killed a man on the border. Killed him with a knife as he went over, two miles from here, at the crossing point.'

Haldane said, 'That's absurd. It needn't be Leiser. It could have been a refugee coming west. It could have been anyone.'

'They found tracks leading east. Traces of blood in the hut by the lake. It's in all the East German papers. They've been putting it over the wireless since midday yesterday . . .'

Leclerc cried, 'I don't believe it. I don't believe he did it. It's some trick of Control's.'

'No,' Smiley replied gently. 'You've got to believe me. It's true.'

'They killed Taylor,' Leclerc said. 'Have you forgotten that?'

'No, of course not. But we shall never know, shall we? How he died, I mean . . . whether he was murdered. . . .' Hurriedly he continued, 'Your Ministry informed the Foreign Office yesterday afternoon. The Germans are bound to catch him, you see; we have to assume that. His transmissions are slow . . . very slow. Every policeman, every soldier is after him. They want him alive. We think they're going to stage a show trial, extract a public confession, display the equipment. It could be very embarrassing. You don't have to be a politician to sympathize with the Minister. So there's the question of what to do.'

Leclerc said, 'Johnson, keep an eye on the clock.' Johnson put his earphones on again, but without conviction.

Smiley appeared to want someone else to speak, but no one did, so he repeated ponderously, 'It's a question of what to do. As I say, we're not politicians, but one can see the dangers. A party of Englishmen in a farmhouse two miles from where the body was found, posing as academics, stores from the Naafi and a house full of radio equipment. You see what I mean? Making your transmissions,' he went on, 'on a single frequency . . . the frequency Leiser receives on. . . . There could be a very big scandal indeed. One can imagine even the West Germans getting awfully angry.'

Haldane spoke first again: 'What are you trying to say?'

'There's a military plane waiting at Hamburg. You fly in two hours; all of you. A truck will collect the equipment. You're to leave nothing behind, not even a pin. Those are my instructions.'

Leclerc said, 'What about the target? Have they forgotten why we're here? They're asking a lot, you know, Smiley: a great lot.'

'Yes, the target,' Smiley conceded. 'We'll have a conference in London. Perhaps we could do a joint operation.'

'It's a military target. I shall want my Ministry represented. No monolith; it's a policy decision, you know.'

'Of course. And it'll be your show.'

'I suggest the product go out under our joint title: my Ministry could retain autonomy in the matter of distribution. I imagine that would meet their more obvious objections. How about your people?'

'Yes, I think Control would accept that.'

Leclerc said casually, everyone watching, 'And the schedule? Who takes care of that? We've an agent in the field, you know.' It was only a small point.

'He'll have to manage by himself.'

'The war rules.' Leclerc spoke proudly. 'We play the war rules. He knew that. He was well trained.' He seemed reconciled; the thing was dismissed.

Avery spoke for the first time. 'You can't leave him out there alone.' His voice was flat.

Leclerc intervened: 'You know Avery, my aide?' This time no one came to his rescue. Smiley, ignoring him, observed, 'The man's probably been caught already. It's only a matter of hours.'

'You're leaving him there to die!' Avery was gathering courage.

'We're disowning him. It's never a pretty process. He's as good as caught already, don't you see?'

'You can't do it,' he shouted. 'You can't just leave him there for some squalid diplomatic reason!'

Now Haldane swung round on Avery, furious. 'You of all people should not complain! You wanted a faith, didn't you? You wanted an eleventh Commandment that would match your rare soul!' He indicated Smiley and Leclerc. 'Well, here you have it: here is the law you were looking for. Congratulate yourself; you found it. We sent him because we needed to; we abandon him because we must. That is the discipline you admired.' He turned to Smiley. 'You too: I find you contemptible. You shoot us, then preach to the dying. Go away. We're technicians, not poets. Go away!'

Smiley said, 'Yes. You're a very good technician, Adrian. There's no pain in you any more. You've made technique a way of life . . . like a whore . . . technique replacing love.' He hesitated. 'Little flags . . . the old war piping in the new. There was all that, wasn't there? And then the man . . . he must have been heady wine. Comfort yourself, Adrian, you weren't fit.'

He straightened his back, making a statement. 'A British-naturalized Pole with a criminal record escapes across the border to East Germany. There is no extradition treaty. The Germans will say he is a spy and produce the equipment; we shall say they planted it and point out it's twenty-five years old. I understand he put out a cover story that he was attending a course in Coventry. That is easily disproved: there is no such course. The conclusion is that he proposed to flee the country; and we shall imply that he owed money. He was keeping some young girl, you know; she worked in a bank. That ties in quite nicely, I mean with the criminal record, since we have to make one up . . .' He nodded to himself. 'As I say, it's not an attractive process. By then we shall all be in London.'

'And he'll be transmitting,' Avery said, 'and no one will listen.'

'To the contrary,' Smiley retorted bitterly. 'They'll be listening.'

Haldane asked: 'Control too, no doubt. Isn't that right?'

'Stop!' Avery shouted suddenly. 'Stop, for God's sake! If anything matters, if anything is real, we've got to hear him now! For the sake of . . .'

'Well?' Haldane inquired with a sneer.

'Love. Yes, love! Not yours, Haldane, mine. Smiley's right! You made me do it for you, made me love him! It wasn't in you any more! I brought him to you, I kept him in your house, made him dance to the music of your bloody war! I piped for him, but there's no breath in me now. He's Peter Pan's last victim, Haldane, the last one, the last love; the last music gone.'

Haldane was looking at Smiley: 'My congratulations to Control,' he said. 'Thank him, will you? Thank him for the help, the *technical* help, Smiley; for the encouragement, thank him for the rope. For the kind words too: for lending you to bring the flowers. So nicely done.'

But Leclerc seemed impressed by the neatness of it.

'Let's not be hard on Smiley, Adrian. He's only doing his job. We must all get back to London. There's the Fielden report . . . I'd like to show you that, Smiley. Troop dispositions in Hungary: something new.'

'And I'd like to see it,' Smiley replied politely.

'He's right, you know, Avery,' Leclerc repeated. His voice was quite eager. 'Be a soldier. Fortunes of war; keep to the rules! We play the war rules in this game. Smiley, I owe you an apology. And Control too, I fear. I had thought the old rivalry was still awake. I'm wrong.' He inclined his head. 'You must dine with me in London. My club is not your mark I know, but it's quiet there; a good set. Very good. Haldane must come. Adrian, I invite you!'

Avery had buried his face in his hands.

'There's something else I want to discuss with you, Adrian–Smiley, you won't mind this I'm sure, you're practically one of the family–the question of Registry. The system of library files is really out of date. Bruce was on to me about it just before I left. Poor Miss Courtney can hardly keep pace. I fear the answer is more copies . . . top copy to the case officer, carbons for information. There's a new machine on the market, cheap photostats, threepence halfpenny a copy, that seems quite reasonable in these dog days. . . . I must speak to the people about it . . . the Ministry . . . they know a good thing when they see one. Perhaps—' he broke off. 'Johnson, I could wish you made less noise, we're still operational, you know.' He spoke like a man intent upon appearances, conscious of tradition.

Johnson had gone to the window. Leaning on the sill he reached outside and with his customary precision began winding in the aerial. He held a spool in his left hand like a bobbin. As he gathered in the wire he gently turned it as an old woman spins her thread. Avery was sobbing like a child. No one heeded him.

Chapter Twenty-three

The green van moved slowly down the road, crossed the Station Square where the empty fountain stood. On its roof the small loop aerial turned this way and that like a hand feeling for the wind. Behind it, well back, were two trucks. The snow was settling at last. They drove on sidelights, twenty yards apart, following each other's tyre marks.

The Captain sat in the back of the van with a microphone for speaking to the driver, and beside him the sergeant, lost in private memories. The corporal crouched at his receiver, his hand constantly turning the dial as he watched the line tremble in the small screen.

'The transmission's stopped,' he said suddenly.

'How many groups have you recorded?' the sergeant asked.

'A dozen. The call sign over and over again, then part of a message. I don't think he's getting any reply.'

'Five letters or four?'

'Still four.'

'Did he sign off?'

'No.'

'What frequency was he using?'

'Three six five zero.'

'Keep scanning across it. Two hundred either side.'

'There's nothing there.'

'Keep searching,' he said sharply. 'Right across the band. He's changed the crystal. He'll take a few minutes to tune up.'

The operator began spinning the large dial, slowly, watching the eye of green light in the centre of the set which opened and closed as he crossed one station after another. 'Here he is. Three eight seven zero. Different call sign but the same handwriting. Quicker than yesterday; better.'

The tape recorder wound monotonously at his elbow. 'He's working on alternating crystals,' the sergeant said. 'Like they did in the war. It's the same trick.' He was embarrassed, an elderly man confronted with his past.

The corporal slowly raised his head. 'This is it,' he said. 'Zero. We're right on top of him.'

Quietly the two men dismounted from the van. 'Wait here,' the sergeant told the corporal. 'Keep listening. If the signal breaks, even for a moment, tell the driver to flash the headlights, do you understand?'

'I'll tell him.' The corporal looked frightened.

'If it stops altogether, keep searching and let me know.'

'Pay attention,' the Captain warned as he dismounted. The sergeant was waiting impatiently; behind him, a tall building standing on waste land.

In the distance, half hidden in the falling snow, lay row after row of small houses. No sound came.

'What do they call this place?' the Captain asked.

'A block of flats; workers' flats. They haven't named it yet.'

'No, beyond.'

'Nothing. Follow me,' the sergeant said.

Pale lights shone in almost every window; six floors. Stone steps, thick with leaves, led to the cellar. The sergeant went first, shining his torch ahead of them on to the shoddy walls. The Captain nearly fell. The first room was large and airless, half of brick and half unrendered plaster. At the far end were two steel doors. On the ceiling a single bulb burned behind a wire cage. The sergeant's torch was still on; he shone it needlessly into the corners.

'What are you looking for?' the Captain asked.

The steel doors were locked.

'Find the janitor,' the sergeant ordered. 'Quickly.'

The Captain ran up the stairs and returned with an old man, unshaven, gently grumbling; he held a bunch of long keys on a chain. Some were rusty.

'The switches,' said the sergeant. 'For the building. Where are they?'

The old man sorted through the keys. He pushed one into the lock and it would not fit, he tried another and a third.

'Quick, you fool,' the Captain shouted.

'Don't fuss him,' said the sergeant.

The door opened. They pushed into the corridor, their torches playing over the whitewash. The janitor was holding up a key, grinning. 'Always the last one,' he said. The sergeant found what he was looking for, hidden on the wall behind the door; a box with a glass front. The Captain put his hand to the main lever, had half pulled it when the other struck him roughly away.

'No! Go to the top of the stairs; tell me when the driver flashes his headlights.'

'Who's in charge here?' the Captain complained.

'Do as I ask.' He had opened the box and was tugging gently at the first fuse, blinking through his gold-rimmed spectacles; a benign man.

With diligent, surgical fingers the sergeant drew out the fuse, cautiously, as if he were expecting an electric shock, then immediately replaced it, his eyes turning towards the figure at the top of the steps; then a second and still the Captain said nothing. Outside the motionless soldiers watched the windows of the block, saw how floor by floor the lights went out, then quickly on again. The sergeant tried another and a fourth and this time he heard an excited cry from above him: 'The headlights! The headlights have gone out.'

'Quiet! Go and ask the driver which floor. But *quietly*.'

'They'll never hear us in this wind,' the Captain said irritably, and a moment later: 'The driver says third floor. The third floor light went out and the transmission stopped at the same time. It's started again now.'

'Put the men round the building,' the sergeant said. 'And pick five men to come with us. He's on the third floor.'

Softly, like animals, the Vopos dismounted from the two trucks, their carbines held loosely in their hands, advancing in a ragged line, ploughing the thin snow, turning it to nothing; some to the foot of the building, some standing off, staring at the windows. A few wore helmets, and their square silhouette was redolent of the war. From here and there came a click as the first bullet was sprung gently into the breech; the sound rose to a faint hail and died away.

Leiser unhooked the aerial and wound it back on the reel, screwed the Morse key into the lid, replaced the earphones in the spares box and folded the silk cloth into the handle of the razor.

'Twenty years,' he protested, holding up the razor, 'and they still haven't found a better place.'

'Why do you do it?'

She was sitting contentedly on the bed in her nightdress, wrapped in the mackintosh as if it gave her company.

'Who do you talk to?' she asked again.

'No one. No one heard.'

'Why do you do it, then?'

He had to say something, so he said, 'For peace.'

He put on his jacket, went to the window and peered outside. Snow lay on the houses. The wind blew angrily across them. He glanced into the courtyard below, where the silhouettes were waiting.

'Whose peace?' she asked.

'The light went out, didn't it, while I was working the set?'

'Did it?'

'A short break, a second or two, like a power cut?'

'Yes.'

'Put it out again now.' He was very still. 'Put the light out.'

'Why?'

'I like to look at the snow.'

She put the light out and he drew the threadbare curtains. Outside the snow reflected a pale glow into the sky. They were in half darkness.

'You said we'd love now,' she complained.

'Listen; what's your name?'

He heard the rustle of raincoat.

'What is it?' His voice was rough.

'Anna.'

'Listen, Anna.' He went to the bed. 'I want to marry you,' he said. 'When I met you, in that inn, when I saw you sitting there, listening to the records, I fell in love with you, do you understand? I'm an engineer from Magdeburg, that's what I said. Are you listening?'

He seized her arms and shook her. His voice was urgent.

'Take me away,' she said.

'That's right! I said I'd make love to you, take you away to all the places you dreamed of, do you understand?' He pointed to the posters on the wall. 'To islands, sunny places—'

'Why?' she whispered.

'I brought you back here. You thought it was to make love, but I drew this knife and threatened you. I said if you made a sound, I'd kill you with the knife, like I—I told you I'd killed the boy and I'd kill you.'

'Why?'

'I had to use the wireless. I needed a house, see? Somewhere to work the wireless. I'd nowhere to go. So I picked you up and used you. Listen: if they ask you, that's what you must say.'

She laughed. She was afraid. She lay back uncertainly on her bed, inviting him to take her, as if that were what he wanted.

'If they ask, remember what I said.'

'Make me happy. I love you.'

She put out her arms and pulled his head towards her. Her lips were cold and damp, too thin against her sharp teeth. He drew away but she still held him. He strained his ears for any sound above the wind, but there was none.

'Let's talk a bit,' he said. 'Are you lonely, Anna? Who've you got?'

'What do you mean?'

'Parents, boy friend. Anyone.'

She shook her head in the darkness. 'Just you.'

'Listen; here, let's button your coat up. I like to talk first. I'll tell you about London. You want to hear about London, I'll bet. I went for a walk, once, it was raining and there was this man by the river, drawing on the pavement in the rain. Fancy that! Drawing with chalk in the rain, and the rain just washing it away.'

'Come now. Come.'

'Do you know what he was drawing? Just dogs, cottages and that. And the people, Anna—listen to this!—standing in the rain, watching him.'

'I want you. Hold me. I'm frightened.'

'Listen! D'you know why I went for a walk: they wanted me to make love to a girl. They sent me to London and I went for this walk instead.'

He could make her out as she watched him, judging him according to some instinct he did not understand.

'Are you alone too?'

'Yes.'

'Why did you come?'

'They're crazy people, the English! That old fellow by the river: they think the Thames is the biggest river in the world, you know that. And it's nothing! Just a little brown stream, you could nearly jump across it some places!'

'What's that noise?' she said suddenly. 'I know that noise! It was a gun; the cocking of a gun!'

He held her tightly to stop her trembling.

'It was just a door,' he said, 'the latch of a door. This place is made of paper. How could you hear anything in such a wind?'

There was a footfall in the corridor. She struck at him in terror, the raincoat swinging round her. As they came in he was standing away from her, the knife at her throat, his thumb uppermost, the blade parallel to the ground. His back was very straight and his small face was turned to her, empty, held by some private discipline, a man once more intent upon appearances, conscious of tradition.

The farmhouse lay in darkness, blind and not hearing, motionless against the swaying larches and the running sky.

They had left a shutter open and it banged slowly without rhythm, according to the strength of the storm. Snow gathered like ash and was dispersed. They had gone, leaving nothing behind them but tyre tracks in the hardening mud, a twist of wire, and the sleepless tapping of the north wind.

A Small Town in Germany

John le Carré

Prologue

The Hunter and the Hunted

Ten minutes to midnight: a pious Friday in May and a fine river mist lying in the market square. Bonn was a Balkan city, stained and secret, drawn over with tramwire. Bonn was a dark house where someone had died, a house draped in Catholic black and guarded by policemen. Their leather coats glistened in the lamplight, the black flags hung over them like birds. It was as if all but they had heard the alarm and fled. Now a car, now a pedestrian hurried past, and the silence followed like a wake. A tram sounded, but far away. In the grocer's shop, from a pyramid of tins, the handwritten notice advertised the emergency: 'Lay in your store now!' Among the crumbs, marzipan pigs like hairless mice proclaimed the forgotten Saint's Day.

Only the posters spoke. From trees and lanterns they fought their futile war, each at the same height as if that were the regulation; they were printed in radiant paint, mounted on hardboard, and draped in thin streamers of black bunting, and they rose at him vividly as he hastened past. 'Send the Foreign Workers Home!' 'Rid us of the Whore Bonn!' 'Unite Germany First, Europe Second!' And the largest was set above them, in a tall streamer right across the street: 'Open the road East, the road West has failed'. His dark eyes paid them no attention. A policeman stamped his boots and grimaced at him, making a joke of the weather; another challenged him but without conviction; and one called 'Guten Abend' but he offered no reply; for he had no mind for any but the plumper figure a hundred paces ahead of him who trotted hurriedly down the wide avenue, entering the shadow of a black flag, emerging as the tallow lamplight took him back.

The dark had made no ceremony of coming nor the grey day of leaving, but the night was crisp for once and smelt of winter. For most months, Bonn is not a place of seasons; the climate is all indoors, a climate of headaches, warm and flat like bottled water, a climate of waiting, of bitter tastes taken from the slow river, of fatigue and reluctant growth, and the air is an exhausted wind fallen on the plain, and the dusk when it comes is nothing but a darkening of the day's mist, a lighting of tube lamps in the howling streets. But on that spring night the winter had come back to visit, slipping up the Rhine valley under cover of the predatory darkness, and it quickened them as they went, hurt them with its unexpected chill. The eyes of the smaller man, straining ahead of him, shed tears of cold.

The avenue curved, taking them past the yellow walls of the University. 'Democrats! Hang the Press Baron!' 'The World belongs to the Young!' 'Let the English Lordlings beg!' 'Alex Springer to the gallows!' 'Long Live Axel Springer!' 'Protest is Freedom'. These posters were done in woodcut on a student press. Overhead the young foliage glittered in a fragmented canopy of green glass. The lights were brighter here, the police fewer. The men strode on, neither faster nor slower; the first busily, with a beadle's flurry. His stride though swift was stagy and awkward, as if he had stepped down from somewhere grander; a walk replete with a German burgher's dignity. His arms swung shortly at his sides and his back was straight. Did he know he was being followed? His head was held stiff in authority, but authority became him poorly. A man drawn forward by what he saw? Or driven by what lay behind? Was it fear that prevented him from turning? A man of substance does not move his head. The second man stepped lightly in his wake. A sprite, weightless as the dark, slipping through the shadows as if they were a net: a clown stalking a courtier.

They entered a narrow alley; the air was filled with the smells of sour food. Once more the walls cried to them, now in the tell-tale liturgy of German advertising: 'Strong Men Drink Beer!' 'Knowledge is Power, Read Molden Books!' Here for the first time the echo of their footsteps mingled in unmistakeable challenge; here for the first time the man of substance seemed to waken, sensing the danger behind. It was no more than a slur, a tiny imperfection in the determined rhythm of his portly march; but it took him to the edge of the pavement, away from the darkness of the walls, and he seemed to find comfort in the brighter places, where the lamplight and the policemen could protect him. Yet his pursuer did not relent. 'Meet us in Hanover!' the poster cried. 'Karfield speaks in Hanover!' 'Meet us in Hanover on Sunday!'

An empty tram rolled past, its windows protected with adhesive mesh. A single church bell began its monotonous chime, a dirge for Christian virtue in an empty city. They were walking again, closer together, but still the man in front did not look back. They rounded another corner; ahead of them, the great spire of the Minster was cut like thin metal against the empty sky. Reluctantly the first chimes were answered by others, until all over the town there rose a slow cacophony of uncertain peals. An Angelus? An air raid? A young policeman, standing in the doorway of a sports shop, bared his head. In the Cathedral porch, a candle burned in a bowl of red glass; to one side stood a religious bookshop. The plump man paused, leaned forward as if to examine something in the window; glanced down the road; and in that moment the light from the window shone full upon his features. The smaller man ran forward: stopped; ran forward again; and was too late.

The limousine had drawn up, an Opel Rekord driven by a pale man hidden in the smoked glass. Its back door opened and closed; ponderously it gathered speed, indifferent to the one sharp cry, a cry of fury and of accusation, of total loss and total bitterness which, drawn as if by force from the breast of him who uttered it, rang abruptly down the empty street and, as abruptly, died. The policeman spun around, shone his torch. Held in its beam, the small man did not move; he was staring after the limousine. Shaking over the cobble, skidding on the wet tramlines, disregarding the traffic lights, it had vanished westward towards the illuminated hills.

'Who are you?'

The beam rested on the coat of English tweed, too hairy for such a little man, the fine, neat shoes grey with mud, the dark, unblinking eyes.

'Who are you?' the policeman repeated; for the bells were everywhere now, and their echoes persisted eerily.

One small hand disappeared into the folds of the coat and emerged with a leather holder. The policeman accepted it gingerly, unfastened the catch while he juggled with his torch and the black pistol which he clutched inexpertly in his left hand.

'What was it?' the policeman asked, as he handed back the wallet. 'Why did you call out?'

The small man gave no answer. He had walked a few paces along the pavement.

'You never saw him before?' he asked, still looking after the car. 'You don't know who he was?' He spoke softly, as if there were children sleeping upstairs; a vulnerable voice, respectful of silence.

'No.'

The sharp, lined face broke into a conciliatory smile. 'Forgive me. I made a silly mistake. I thought I recognized him.' His accent was neither wholly English nor wholly German, but a privately elected no-man's land, picked and set between the two. And he would move it, he seemed to say, a little in either direction, if it chanced to inconvenience the listener.

'It's the season,' the small man said, determined to make conversation. 'The sudden cold, one looks at people more.' He had opened a tin of small Dutch cigars and was offering them to the policeman. The policeman declined so he lit one for himself.

'It's the riots,' the policeman answered slowly, 'The flags, the slogans. We're all nervous these days. This week Hanover, last week Frankfurt. It upsets the natural order.' He was a young man and had studied for his appointment. 'They should forbid them more,' he added, using the common dictum. 'Like the Communists.'

He saluted loosely; once more the stranger smiled, a last affecting smile, dependent, hinting at friendship, dwindling reluctantly. And was gone. Remaining where he was, the policeman listened attentively to the fading footfall. Now it stopped; to be resumed again, more quickly—was it his imagination?—with greater conviction than before. For a moment he pondered.

'In Bonn,' he said to himself with an inward sigh, recalling the stranger's weightless tread, 'even the flies are official.'

Taking out his notebook, he carefully wrote down the time and place and nature of the incident. He was not a fast-thinking man, but admired for his thoroughness. This done, he added the number of the motor-car, which for some reason had remained in his mind. Suddenly he stopped; and stared at what he had written; at the name and the car number; and he thought of the plump man and the long, marching stride, and his heart began beating very fast. He thought of the secret instruction he had read on the recreation-room notice-board, and the little muffled photograph from long ago. The notebook still in his hand, he ran off for the telephone kiosk as fast as his boots would carry him.

Way over there in a
Small town in Germany
There lived a shoemaker
Schumann was his name
Ich bin ein Musikant
Ich bin für das Vaterland
I have a big bass drum
And this is how I play!

A drinking song sung in British military messes
in Occupied Germany, with obscene variations,
to the tune of the *Marche Militaire*

Chapter One

Mr Meadowes and Mr Cork

'Why don't you get out and walk? I would if I was your age. Quicker than sitting with this scum.'

'It'll be all right,' said Cork, the albino cypher clerk, and looked anxiously at the older man in the driving seat beside him. 'We'll just have to hurry slowly,' he added in his most conciliatory tone. Cork was a cockney, bright as paint, and it worried him to see Meadowes all het up. 'We'll just have to let it happen to us, won't we, Arthur?'

'I'd like to throw the whole bloody lot of them in the Rhine.'

'You know you wouldn't really.'

It was Saturday morning, nine o'clock. The road from Friesdorf to the Embassy was packed tight with protesting cars, the pavements lined with photographs of the Movement's leader, and the banners were stretched across the road like advertisements at a rally: 'The West had deceived us; Germans can look East without shame.' 'End the Coca-Cola culture now!' At the very centre of the long column sat Cork and Meadowes, becalmed while the clamour of horns rose all round them in unceasing concert. Sometimes they sounded in series starting at the front and working slowly back, so that their roar passed overhead like an aeroplane sometimes in unison, dash dot dash, K for Karfeld our elected leader; and sometimes they just had a free for all, tuning for the symphony.

'What the hell do they want with it then? All the screaming? Bloody good haircut, that's what half of them need, a good hiding and back to school.'

'It's the farmers,' Cork said, 'I told you, they're picketing the Bundestag.'

'Farmers? This lot? They'd die if they got their feet wet, half of them. Kids. Look at that crowd there then. Disgusting, that's what I call it.'

To their right, in a red Volkswagen, sat three students, two boys and a girl. The driver wore a leather jacket and very long hair, and he was gazing intently through his windscreen at the car in front, his slim palm poised over the steering wheel, waiting for the signal to blow his horn. His two companions, intertwined, were kissing deeply.

'They're the supporting cast,' Cork said. 'It's a lark for them. You know the students' slogan: "Freedom's only real when you're fighting for it." It's not so different from what's going on at home, is it? Hear what they did in Grosvenor Square last night?' Cork asked, attempting once again to shift the ground. 'If that's education, I'll stick to ignorance.'

But Meadowes would not be distracted.

'They ought to bring in the National Service,' he declared, glaring at the Volkswagen. 'That would sort them out.'

'They've got it already. They've had it twenty years or more.' Sensing that Meadowes was preparing to relent, Cork chose the subject most likely to encourage him. 'Here, how did Myra's birthday party go, then? Good show was it? I'll bet she had a lovely time.'

But for some reason the question only cast Meadowes into even deeper gloom, and after that Cork chose silence as the wiser course. He had tried everything, and to no effect. Meadowes was a decent, churchy sort of bloke, the kind they didn't make any more, and worth a good deal of anybody's time; but there was a limit even to Cork's filial devotion. He'd tried the new Rover which Meadowes had bought for his retirement, tax free and at a ten per cent discount. He'd admired its build, its comfort and its fittings until he was blue in the face, and all he'd got for his trouble was a grunt. He'd tried the Exiles Motoring Club, of which Meadowes was a keen supporter; he'd tried the Commonwealth Children's Sports which they hoped to run that afternoon in the Embassy gardens. And now he had even tried last night's big party, which they hadn't liked to attend because of Janet's baby being so near; and as far as Cork was concerned, that was the whole menu and Meadowes could lump it. Short of a holiday, Cork decided, short of a long, sunny holiday away from Karfeld and the Brussels negotiations, and away from his daughter Myra, Arthur Meadowes was heading for the bend.

'Here,' said Cork trying one more throw, 'Dutch Shell's up another bob.'

'And Guest Keen are down three.'

Cork had resolutely invested in non-British stock, but Meadowes preferred to pay the price of patriotism.

'They'll go up again after Brussels, don't you worry.'

'Who are you kidding? The talks are as good as dead aren't they? I may not have your intelligence but I can read, you know.'

Meadowes, as Cork was the very first to concede, had every excuse for melancholy, quite apart from his investments in British steel. He'd come with hardly a break from four years in Warsaw which was enough to make anyone jumpy. He was on his last posting and facing retirement in the autumn, and in Cork's experience they got worse, not better, the nearer the day came. Not to mention having a nervous wreck for a daughter: Myra Meadowes was on the road to recovery, true enough, but if one half of what they said of her was to be believed, she'd got a long way to go yet.

Add to that the responsibilities of Chancery Registrar–of handling, that is, a political archive in the hottest crisis any of them could remember–and you had more than your work cut out. Even Cork, tucked away in Cyphers, had felt the draught a bit, what with the extra traffic, and the extra hours, and Janet's baby coming on, and the do-this-by-yesterday that you got from most of Chancery; and his own experience, as he well knew, was nothing beside what old Arthur had had to cope with. It was the coming from all directions, Cork decided, that threw you these days. You never knew where it would happen next. One minute you'd be getting off a Reply Immediate on the Bremen riots, or tomorrow's jamboree in Hanover, the next they'd be coming back at you with the gold rush, or Brussels, or raising another few hundred millions in Frankfurt and Zurich; and if it was tough in Cyphers, it was tougher still for those who had to track down the files, enter up the loose papers, mark in the new entries and get them back into circulation again . . . which reminded him, for some reason, that he must telephone his accountant. If the Krupp labour front was going on like this, he might take a little look at Swedish steel, just an in-and-outer for the baby's bank account . . .

'Hullo,' said Cork brightening. 'Going to have a scrap, are we?'

Two policemen had stepped off the kerb to remonstrate with a large agricultural man in a Mercedes Diesel. First he lowered the window and shouted at them; now he opened the door and shouted at them again. Quite suddenly, the police withdrew. Cork yawned in disappointment.

Once upon a time, Cork remembered wistfully, panics came singly. You had a scream on the Berlin corridor, Russian helicopters teasing up the border, an up-and-downer with the Four Power Steering Committee in Washington. Or there was intrigue: suspected German diplomatic initiative in Moscow that had to be nipped in the bud, a suspected fiddle on the Rhodesian embargo, hushing up a Rhine Army riot in Minden. And that was that. You bolted your food, opened shop, and stayed till the job was done; and you went home a free man. That was that; that was what life was made of; that was Bonn. Whether you were a dip like de Lisle, or a non-dip behind the green baize door, the scene was the same; a bit of drama, a lot of hot air, then tickle up the stocks and shares a bit, back to boredom and roll on your next posting.

Until Karfeld. Cork gazed disconsolately at the posters. Until Karfeld came along. Nine months, he reflected–the vast features were plump and lifeless, the expression one of flatulent sincerity—nine months since Arthur Meadowes had come bustling through the connecting door from Registry with the news of the Kiel demonstrations, the surprise nomination, the student sit-in, and the little bit of violence they had gradually learnt to expect. Who caught it that time? Some Socialist counter-demonstrators. One beaten to death, one stoned . . . it used to shock them in the old days. They were green then. Christ, he thought, it might have been ten years ago; but Cork could date it almost to the hour.

Kiel was the morning the Embassy doctor announced that Janet was expecting. From that day on, nothing had ever been the same.

The horns broke wildly into song again; the convoy jerked forward and stopped abruptly, clanging and screeching all different notes.

'Any luck with those files then?' Cork enquired, his mind lighting upon the suspected cause of Meadowes' anxiety.

'No.'

'Trolley hasn't turned up?'

'No, the trolley has *not* turned up.'

Ball-bearings, Cork thought suddenly: some nice little Swedish outfit with a get-up-and-go approach, a firm capable of moving in fast . . . two hundred quid's worth and away we all go . . .

'Come on Arthur, don't let it get you down. It's not Warsaw you know: you're in Bonn now. Look: know how many cups they're shy of in the canteen, just on the last six weeks alone? Not broken, mind, just lost: twenty-four.'

Meadowes was unimpressed.

'Now who wants to pinch an Embassy cup? No one. People are absent-minded. They're *involved*. It's the crisis, see. It's happening everywhere. It's the same with files.'

'Cups aren't secret, that's the difference.'

'Nor's file trolleys,' Cork pleaded, 'If it comes to that. Nor's the two-bar electric fire from the conference room which Admin are doing their nut about. Nor's the long-carriage typewriter from the Pool, nor—listen Arthur, *you* can't be blamed, not with so much going on; how can you? You know what dips are when they get to drafting telegrams. Look at de Lisle, look at Gaveston: dreamers. I'm not saying they aren't geniuses but they don't know where they are half the time, their heads in the clouds. You can't be blamed for that.'

'I *can* be blamed. I'm responsible.'

'All right, torture yourself,' Cork snapped, his last patience gone. 'Anyway it's Bradfield's responsibility, not yours. He's Head of Chancery; he's responsible for security.'

With this parting comment, Cork once more fell to surveying the unprepossessing scene about him. In more ways than one, he decided, Karfeld had a lot to answer for.

The prospect which presented itself to Cork would have offered little comfort to any man, whatever his preoccupation. The weather was wretched. A blank Rhineland mist, like breath upon a mirror, lay over the whole developed wilderness of bureaucratic Bonn. Giant buildings, still unfinished, rose glumly out of the untilled fields. Ahead of him the British Embassy, all its windows lit, stood on its brown heathland like a makeshift hospital in the twilight of the battle. At the front gate, the Union Jack, mysteriously at half mast, dropped sadly over a cluster of German policemen.

The very choice of Bonn as the waiting house for Berlin has long been an anomaly; it is now an abuse. Perhaps only the Germans, having elected a Chancellor, would have brought their capital city to his door. To accommodate the immigration of diplomats, politicians and government servants which attended this unlooked for honour—and also to keep them at a distance—the townspeople have built a complete suburb outside their city walls. It was through the southern end of this that the traffic was now attempting to pass: a jumble of stodgy towers and lowflung contemporary hutments which stretched along the dual carriageway almost as far as the amiable sanatorium settlement of Bad Godesberg, whose principal industry, having once been bottled water, is now diplomacy. True, some Ministries have been admitted to Bonn itself, and have added their fake masonry to the cobble courtyards; true, some Embassies are in Bad Godesberg; but the seat of Federal Government and the great majority of the ninety odd Foreign Missions accredited to it, not to mention the lobbyists, the press, the political parties, the refugee organizations, the official residences of Federal Dignitaries, the Kuratorium for Indivisible Germany, and the whole bureaucratic superstructure of West Germany's provisional capital, are to be found to either side of this one arterial carriageway between the former seat of the Bishop of Cologne and the Victorian villas of a Rhineland spa.

Of this unnatural capital village, of this island state, which lacks both political identity and social hinterland, and is permanently committed to the condition of impermanence, the British Embassy is an inseparable part. Imagine a sprawling factory block of no merit, the kind of building you see in dozens on the Western by-pass, usually with a symbol of its product set out on the roof; paint about it a sullen Rhenish sky, add an indefinable hint of Nazi architecture, just a breath, no more, and erect in the rough ground behind it two fading goalposts for the recreation of the unwashed, and you have portrayed with fair accuracy the mind and force of England in the Federal Republic. With one sprawling limb it holds down the past, with another it smoothes the present; while a third searches anxiously in the wet Rhenish earth to find what is buried for the future. Built as the Occupation drew to its premature end, it catches precisely that mood of graceless renunciation; a stone face turned towards a former foe, a grey smile offered to the present ally. To Cork's left, as they finally entered its gates, lay the headquarters of the Red Cross, to his right a Mercedes factory; behind him, across the road, the Social Democrats and a Coca-Cola depot. The Embassy is cut off from these improbable neighbours by a strip of waste land which, strewn with sorrel and bare clay, runs flatly to the neglected Rhine. This field is known as Bonn's green belt and is an object of great pride to the city's planners.

One day, perhaps, they will move to Berlin; the contingency, even in Bonn, is occasionally spoken of. One day, perhaps, the whole grey mountain will slip down the autobahn and silently take its place in the wet car parks of the gutted Reichstag; until that happens, these concrete tents will remain, discreetly temporary in deference to the dream, discreetly permanent in deference to reality; they will remain, multiply, and grow; for in Bonn, movement has replaced progress, and whatever will not grow must die.

Parking the car in his customary place behind the canteen, Meadowes walked slowly round it, as he always did after a journey, testing the handles and checking the coachwork for the marks of an errant pebble. Still deep in thought he crossed the forecourt to the front porch where two British military policemen, a sergeant and a corporal, were examining passes. Cork, still offended, followed at a distance, so that by the time he reached the front door Meadowes was already deep in conversation with the sentries.

'Who are *you* then?' the sergeant was wanting to know.

'Meadowes of Registry. He works for me.' Meadowes tried to look over the sergeant's shoulder, but the sergeant drew back the list against his tunic. 'He's been off sick you see. I wanted to enquire.'

'Then why's he under Ground Floor?'

'He has a room there. He has two functions. Two different jobs. One with me, one on the ground floor.'

'Zero,' said the sergeant, looking at the list again. A bunch of typists, their skirts as short as the Ambassadress permitted, came fluttering up the steps behind them.

Meadowes lingered, still unconvinced. 'You mean he's not come in?' he asked with the tenderness which longs for contradiction.

'That's what I do mean. Zero. He's not come in. He's not here. Right?'

They followed the girls into the lobby. Cork took his arm and drew him back into the shadow of the basement grille.

'What's going on, Arthur? What's your problem? It's not just the missing files, is it? What's eating you up?'

'Nothing's eating me.'

'Then what's all that about Leo being ill? He hasn't had a day's illness in his life.'

Meadowes did not reply.

'What's Leo been up to?' Cork demanded with deep suspicion.

'Nothing.'

'Then why did you ask about him? You can't have lost him as well! Blimey, they've been trying to lose Leo for twenty years.'

Cork felt the decent hesitation in Meadowes, the proximity of revelation and the reluctant drawing back.

'You can't be responsible for Leo. Nobody can. You can't be everyone's father, Arthur. He's probably out flogging a few petrol coupons.'

The words were barely spoken before Meadowes rounded on him, very angry indeed.

'Don't you talk like that, d'you hear? Don't you dare! Leo's not like that; it's a shocking thing to say of anyone; flogging petrol coupons. Just because he's–a temporary.'

Cork's expression, as he followed Meadowes at a safe distance up the open-tread staircase to the first floor, spoke for itself. If that was what age did for you, retirement at sixty didn't come a day too early. Cork's own retirement would be from it to a Greek island. Crete, he thought; Spetsai. I could swing it at forty if those ball-bearings come home. Well, forty-five anyway.

A step along the corridor from Registry lay the cypher room and a step beyond that, the small, bright office occupied by Peter de Lisle. Chancery means no more than political section; its young men are the elite. It is here, if anywhere, that the popular dream of the brilliant English diplomat may be realized; and in no one more nearly than Peter de Lisle. He was an elegant, willowy, almost beautiful person, whose youth had persisted obstinately into his early forties, and his manner was languid to the point of lethargy. This lethargy was not affected, but simply deceptive. De Lisle's family tree had been disastrously pruned by two wars, and further depleted by a succession of small but violent catastrophes. A brother had died in a car accident; an uncle had committed suicide; a second brother was drowned on holiday in Penzance. Thus by degrees de Lisle himself had acquired both the energies and the duties of an improbable survivor. He had much rather not been called at all, his manner implied; but since that was the way of things, he had no alternative but to wear the mantle.

As Meadowes and Cork entered their separate estates, de Lisle was on the point of gathering together the sheets of blue draft paper which lay scattered in artistic confusion on his desk. Having shuffled them casually into order, he buttoned his waistcoat, stretched, cast a wistful look at the picture of Lake Windermere, issued by the

Ministry of Works with the kind permission of the London, Midland and Scottish Railway, and drifted contentedly on to the landing to greet the new day. Lingering at the long window, he peered downward for a moment at the spines of the farmers' black cars and the small islands of blue where the police lights flashed.

'They have this *passion* for steel,' he observed to Mickie Crabbe, a ragged, leaky-eyed man permanently crippled by a hangover. Crabbe was slowly ascending the stairs, one hand reassuringly upon the banister, his thin shoulders hunched protectively. 'I'd quite forgotten. I'd remembered the blood, but forgotten the steel.'

'Rather,' Crabbe muttered, 'Rather,' and his voice trailed after him like the shreds of his own life. Only his hair had not aged; it grew dark and luxuriant on his little head, as if fertilized by alcohol.

'Sports,' Crabbe cried, making an unscheduled halt. 'Bloody marquee isn't up.'

'It'll come,' de Lisle assured him kindly. 'It's been held up by the Peasants' Revolt.'

'Back way empty as a church on the other road; bloody Huns,' Crabbe added vaguely as if it were a greeting, and continued painfully down his appointed track.

Slowly following him along the passage, de Lisle pushed open door after door, peering inside to call a name or a greeting, until he arrived by degrees at the Head of Chancery's room; and here he knocked hard, and leaned in.

'All present, Rawley,' he said. 'Ready when you are.'

'I'm ready now.'

'I say, you haven't pinched my electric fan by any chance, have you? It's absolutely vanished.'

'Fortunately I am not a kleptomaniac.'

'Ludwig Siebkron's asking for a meeting at four o'clock,' de Lisle added quietly, 'At the Ministry of the Interior. He won't say why. I pressed him and he got shirty. He just said he wanted to discuss our security arrangements.'

'Our arrangements are perfectly adequate as they stand. We discussed them with him last week; he is dining with me on Tuesday. I cannot imagine we need to do any more. The place is crawling with police as it is. I refuse to let him make a fortress of us.'

The voice was austere and self sufficient, an academic voice, yet military; a voice which held much in reserve; a voice which guarded its secrets and its sovereignty, drawled out but bitten short.

Taking a step into the room, de Lisle closed the door and dropped the latch.

'How did it go last night?'

'Adequately. You may read the minute if you wish. Meadowes is taking it to the Ambassador.'

'I imagined that was what Siebkron was ringing about.'

'I am not obliged to report to Siebkron; nor do I intend to. And I have no idea why he telephoned at this hour, nor why he should call a meeting. Your imagination is ahead of my own.'

'All the same, I accepted for you. It seemed wise.'

'At what time are we bidden?'

'Four o'clock. He's sending transport.'

Bradfield frowned in disapproval.

'He's worried about the traffic. He thinks an escort would make things easier,' de Lisle explained.

'I see. I thought for a moment he was saving us the expense.'

It was a joke they shared in silence.

Chapter Two

'I could hear their screaming on the telephone . . .'

The daily Chancery meeting in Bonn takes place in the ordinary way at ten o'clock, a time which allows everyone to open his mail, glance at his telegrams and his German newspapers and perhaps recover from the wearisome social round of the night before. As a ritual, de Lisle often likened it to morning prayers in an agnostic community: though contributing little in the way of inspiration or instruction, it set a tone for the day, served as a roll-call and imparted a sense of corporate activity. Once upon a time, Saturdays had been tweedy, voluntary, semi-retired affairs which restored one's lost detachment and one's sense of leisure. All that was gone now. Saturdays had been assumed into the general condition of alarm, and subjected to the discipline of weekdays.

They entered singly, de Lisle at their head. Those whose habit was to greet one another did so; the rest took their places silently in the half circle of chairs, either glancing through their bundles of coloured telegrams or staring blankly out of the big window at the remnants of their weekend. The morning fog was dispersing; black clouds had collected over the concrete rear wing of the Embassy; the aerials on the flat roof hung like surrealist trees against the new dark.

'Pretty ominous for the sports, I must say,' Mickie Crabbe called out, but Crabbe had no standing in Chancery and no one bothered to reply.

Facing them, alone at his steel desk, Bradfield ignored their arrival. He belonged to that school of civil servants who read with a pen; for it ran swiftly with his eye from line to line, poised at any time to correct or annotate.

'Can anyone tell me,' he enquired without lifting his head, 'How I translate *Geltungsbedürfnis?*'

'A need to assert oneself,' de Lisle suggested, and watched the pen pounce, and kill, and rise again.

'How very good. Shall we begin?'

Jenny Pargiter was the Information Officer and the only woman present. She read querulously as if she were contradicting a popular view; and she read without hope, secretly knowing that it was the lot of any woman, when imparting news, not to be believed.

'Apart from the farmers, Rawley, the main news item is yesterday's incident in Cologne, when student demonstrators, assisted by steel workers from Krupps, overturned the American Ambassador's car.'

'The American Ambassador's *empty* car. There is a difference you know.' He scribbled something in the margin of a telegram. Mickie Crabbe from his place at the door, mistakenly assuming this interruption to be humorous, laughed nervously.

'They also attacked an old man and chained him to the railings in the station square with his head shaved and a label round his neck saying "I tore down the Movement's posters". He's not supposed to be seriously hurt.'

'Supposed?'

'Considered.'

'Peter, you made a telegram during the night. We shall see a copy no doubt?'

'It sets out the principal implications.'

'Which are?'

De Lisle was equal to this. 'That the alliance between the dissident students and Karfeld's Movement is progressing fast. That the vicious circle continues: unrest creates unemployment, unemployment creates unrest. Halbach, the student leader, spent most of yesterday closeted with Karfeld in Cologne. They cooked the thing up together.'

'It was Halbach, was it not, who also led the anti-British student delegation to Brussels in January? The one that pelted Haliday-Pride with mud?'

'I have made that point in the telegram.'

'Go on, Jenny, please.'

'Most major papers carry comment.'

'Samples only.'

'*Neue Ruhrzeitung* and allied papers put their main emphasis on the youth of the demonstrators. They insist that they are not brownshirts and hooligans, but young Germans wholly disenchanted with the institutions of Bonn.'

'Who isn't?' de Lisle murmured.

'Thank you, Peter,' Bradfield said, without a trace of gratitude, and Jenny Pargiter blushed quite needlessly.

'Both *Welt* and *Frankfurter Allgemeine* draw parallels with recent events in England; they refer specifically to the anti-Vietnam protests in London, the race riots in Birmingham and the Owner Tenants Association protests on coloured housing. Both speak of the widespread alienation of voters from their elected Governments whether in England or Germany. The trouble begins with taxation, according to the *Frankfurter*; if the taxpayer doesn't think his money is being sensibly used, he argues that his vote is being wasted as well. They call it the new inertia.'

'Ah. Another slogan has been forged.'

Weary from his long vigil and the sheer familiarity of the topics, de Lisle listened at a distance, hearing the old phrases like an off-station broadcast: *increasingly worried by the anti-democratic sentiments of both left and right . . . the Federal Coalition Government should understand that only a really strong leadership, even at the expense of certain extravagant minorities, can contribute to European unity. . . . Germans must recover confidence, must think of politics as the solvent between thought and action . . .*

What was it, he wondered idly, about the jargon of German politics which, even in translation, rendered them totally unreal? Metaphysical fluff, that was the term he had introduced into his telegram last night, and he was rather pleased with it. A German had only to embark upon a political topic to be swept away in a current of ludicrous abstracts. . . . Yet was it only the abstracts that were so elusive? Even the most obvious fact was curiously implausible; even the most gruesome event, by the time it had travelled to Bonn, seemed to have lost its flavour. He tried to imagine what it would be like to be beaten up by Halbach's students; to be slapped until your cheeks bled; to be shaved and chained and kicked . . . it all seemed so far away. Yet where *was* Cologne? Seventeen miles? Seventeen thousand? He should get about more, he told himself, he should attend the meetings and see it happen on the ground. Yet how could he, when he and Bradfield between them drafted every major policy despatch? And when so many delicate and potentially embarrassing matters had to be taken care of here . . .

Jenny Pargiter was warming to her task. The *Neue Zürcher* had a speculative piece on our chances in Brussels, she was saying; she considered it vital that everyone in Chancery read it *most* closely. De Lisle sighed audibly. Would Bradfield never turn her off?

'The writer says we have *absolutely* no negotiating points left, Rawley. None. HMG is as played out as Bonn; no support with the electorate and very little with the parliamentary party. HMG sees Brussels as the magic cure for all the British ills; but ironically can only succeed by the goodwill of another failing Government.'

'Quite.'

'And even more ironically, the Common Market has virtually ceased to exist.'

'Quite.'

'The piece is called *The Beggar's Opera*. They also make the point that Karfeld is undermining our chances of effective German support for our application.'

'It all sounds very predictable to me.'

'And that Karfeld's plea for a Bonn-Moscow trade axis to exclude the French *and* the Anglo-Saxons is receiving serious attention in some circles.'

'What circles I wonder?' Bradfield murmured and the pen descended once more. 'The term Anglo-Saxon is out of court,' he added. 'I refuse to have my provenance dictated by de Gaulle.' This was a cue for the older graduates to raise a judicious intellectual laugh.

'What do the *Russians* think about the Bonn-Moscow axis?' someone ventured from the centre. It might have been Jackson, an ex-Colonial man who liked to offer commonsense as an antidote to intellectual hot air. 'I mean surely that's half the point, isn't it? Has anyone put it to them as a proposition?'

'See our last despatch,' de Lisle said.

Through the open window he fancied he could still hear the plaintive chorus of the farmers' horns. That's Bonn he thought suddenly: that road is our world: how many names did it have on those five miles between Mehlem and Bonn? Six? Seven? That's us: a verbal battle for something nobody wants. A constant, sterile cacophony of claim and protest. However new the models, however fast the traffic, however violent the collision, however high the buildings, the route is unchanged and the destination irrelevant.

'We'll keep the rest very short, shall we? Mickie?'

'I say my God yes.'

Crabbe, jerking into life, embarked upon a long and unintelligible story he had picked up from the *New York Times* correspondent at the American Club, who in turn had heard it from Karl-Heinz Saab, who in turn had heard it from someone in Siebkron's office. It was said that Karfeld was actually in Bonn last night; that after appearing with the students in Cologne yesterday, he had not, as was popularly believed, returned to Hanover to prepare for tomorrow's rally, but had driven himself by a back route to Bonn and attended a secret meeting in the town.

'They say he spoke to Ludwig Siebkron, you see, Rawley,' said Crabbe, but whatever conviction his voice might once have carried was strained thin by innumerable cocktails.

Bradfield, however, was irritated by this report, and struck back quite hard.

'They *always* say he spoke to Ludwig Siebkron. Why the devil shouldn't the two of them talk to one another? Siebkron's in charge of public order; Karfeld has a lot of enemies. Tell London,' he added wearily, making another note. 'Send them a telegram reporting the rumour. It can do no harm.' A gust of rain struck suddenly upward at the steel-framed window, and the angry rattle startled them all.

'Poor old Commonwealth Sports,' Crabbe whispered, but once again his concern received no recognition.

'Discipline,' Bradfield continued. 'Tomorrow's rally in Hanover begins at ten-thirty. It seems an extraordinary time to demonstrate but I understand they have a football match in the afternoon. They play on Sundays here. I cannot imagine it will have any effect on us, but the Ambassador is asking all staff to remain at home after Matins unless they have business in the Embassy. At Siebkron's request there will be additional German police at the front and rear gates throughout Sunday, and for some extraordinary reasons of his own, plain clothes men will be in attendance at the sports this afternoon.'

'And plainer clothes,' de Lisle breathed, recalling a private joke, 'I have *never* seen.'

'Be quiet. Security. We have received the printed Embassy passes from London and these will be distributed on Monday and shown at all times thereafter. Fire Drill. For your information there will be a practice muster at midday on Monday. Perhaps you should all make a point of being available, it sets an example for the Junior Staff. Welfare. Commonwealth Sports this afternoon in the rear gardens of the Embassy; eliminating races. Once again I suggest you all put in an appearance. With your wives of course,' he added, as if that placed an even heavier burden on them. 'Mickie, the Ghanaian Chargé will need looking after. Keep him away from the Ambassadress.'

'Can I just make a point here, Rawley?' Crabbe writhed nervously; the cords of his neck were like chicken legs, stiffeners in the declining flesh. 'The Ambassadress is presenting the prizes at four, you see. Four. Could everyone sort of gravitate to the main marquee at quarter to? Sorry,' he added. 'Quarter to four, Rawley. Sorry.' It was said that he had been one of Montgomery's aides in the war and this was all that was left.

'Noted. Jenny?'

Nothing that *they* would listen to, her shrug declared.

De Lisle addressed them all, using as his focal point that middle air which is the special territory of the British ruling class.

'May I ask whether anyone is working on the Personalities Survey? Meadowes is pestering me for it and I swear I haven't touched it for months.'

'Who's it marked out to?'

'Well me apparently.'

'In that case,' Bradfield said shortly, 'Presumably you drew it.'

'I don't think I did, that's the point. I'm perfectly happy to take the rap, but I can't imagine what I would have wanted with it.'

'Well *has* anyone got it?'

All Crabbe's statements were confessions.

'It's marked out to me, too,' he whispered, from his dark place by the door, 'You see, Rawley.'

They waited.

'Before Peter, I'm supposed to have had it, and put it back. According to Meadowes, Rawley.'

Still no one helped him.

'Two weeks, Rawley. Only I never touched it. Sorry. Arthur Meadowes went for me like a maniac. No good, you see. Didn't have it. Lot of dirt about German industrialists. Not my form. I told Meadowes: best thing is to ask Leo. He does Personalities. They're Leo's pigeon.'

He grinned weakly along the line of his colleagues until he came to the window where the empty chair was. Suddenly they were all peering in the same direction, at the empty chair; not with alarm or revelation, but curiously, noticing an absence for the first time. It was a plain chair of varnished pine, different from the others and slightly pink in colour, hinting remotely at the boudoir; and it had a small, embroidered cushion on the seat.

'Where is he?' Bradfield asked shortly. He alone had not followed Crabbe's gaze. 'Where's Harting?'

No one answered. No one looked at Bradfield. Jenny Pargiter, scarlet in the face, stared at her mannish, practical hands which rested on her broad lap.

'Stuck on that dreary ferry, I should think,' said de Lisle, coming too quickly to the rescue. 'God knows what the farmers are doing *that* side of the river.'

'Someone find out, will they?' Bradfield asked, in the most disinterested tone. 'Ring his house or something will you?'

It is a matter of record that no one who was present took this instruction as his own; and that they left the room in curious disarray, looking neither at Bradfield nor at one another, nor at Jenny Pargiter, whose confusion seemed beyond all bearing.

The last sack race was over. The strong wind, whipping over the waste land, dashed pebbles of rain against the flapping canvas. The wet rigging creaked painfully. Inside the marquee, the surviving children, mostly coloured, had rallied to the mast. The small flags of the Commonwealth, creased by storage and diminished by secession, swung unhappy in disarray. Beneath them, Mickie Crabbe, assisted by Cork the cypher clerk, was mustering the winners for the prize-giving.

'M'butu, Alistair,' Cork whispered. 'Where the hell's he got to?'

Crabbe put the megaphone to his mouth:

'Will Master Alistair M'butu please come forward. Alistair M'butu . . . Jesus,' he muttered, 'I can't even tell them apart.'

'And Kitty Delassus. She's white.'

'And Miss Kitty Delassus, please,' Crabbe added, nervously slurring the final 's'; for names, he had found by bitter experience, were a source of unholy offence.

The Ambassadress, in ragged mink, waited benignly at her trestle table behind a motley of gift-wrapped parcels from the Naafi. The wind struck again, venomously; the Ghanaian Chargé, despondent at Crabbe's side, shuddered and pulled up the fur collar of his overcoat.

'Disqualify them,' Cork urged. 'Give the prizes to the runners up.'

'I'll ring his neck,' Crabbe declared, blinking violently. 'I'll ring his bloody neck. Skulking the other side of the river. Whoopsadaisy.'

Janet Cork, heavily pregnant, had located the missing children and added them to the winners' enclosure.

'Wait till Monday,' Crabbe whispered, raising the megaphone to his lips, 'I'll tell him a thing or two.'

He wouldn't though, come to think of it. He wouldn't tell Leo anything. He'd keep bloody clear of Leo as a matter of fact; keep his head down and wait till it blew over.

'Ladies and Gentlemen, the Ambassadress will now present the prizes!'

They clapped, but not for Crabbe. The end was in sight. With a perfect *insouciance* that was as well suited to the launching of a ship as to the acceptance of a hand in marriage, the Ambassadress stepped forward to read her speech. Crabbe listened mindlessly: a family event . . . equal nations of the Commonwealth . . . if only the greater rivalries of the world could be resolved in so friendly a fashion . . . a heartfelt word of thanks to the Sports Committee, Messrs Jackson, Crabbe, Harting, Meadowes . . .

Lamentably unmoved, a plain clothes policeman, posted against the canvas wall, took a pair of gloves from the pocket of his leather coat and stared blankly at a colleague. Hazel Bradfield, wife of the Head of Chancery, caught Crabbe's eye and smiled beautifully. Such a bore, she managed to imply, but it will soon be over, and then we might even have a drink. He looked quickly away. The only thing, he told himself fervently, is to know nothing and see nothing. Doggo, that's the word. Doggo. He glanced at his watch. Just one hour till the sun was over the yardarm. In Greenwich if not in Bonn. He'd have a beer first, just to keep his eye in; and afterwards he would have a little of the hard stuff. Doggo. See nothing and slip out the back way.

'Here,' said Cork into his ear, 'Listen. You remember that tip you gave me?'

'Sorry old boy?'

'South African Diamonds. Consols. They're down six bob.'

'Hang on to them,' Crabbe urged with total insincerity, and withdrew prudently to the edge of the marquee. He had barely found the kind of dark, protective crevice which naturally appealed to his submerged nature when a hand seized his shoulder and swung him roughly round on his heel. Recovering from his astonishment he found himself face to face with a plain clothes policeman. 'What the hell—' he broke out furiously, for he was a small man and hated to be handled. 'What the hell—' But the policeman was already shaking his head and mumbling an apology. He was sorry, he said, he had mistaken the gentleman for someone else.

Urbane or not, de Lisle was meanwhile growing quite angry. The journey from the Embassy had irritated him considerably. He detested motor-bikes and he detested being escorted, and a noisy combination of the two was almost more than he could bear. And he detested deliberate rudeness, whether he or some one else was the object of it. And deliberate rudeness, he reckoned, was what they were getting. No sooner had they drawn up in the courtyard of the Ministry of the Interior than the doors of the car had been wrenched open by a team of young men in leather coats all shouting at once.

'Herr Siebkron will see you immediately! Now please! Yes! Immediately please!'

'I shall go at my own pace,' Bradfield had snapped as they were ushered into the unpainted steel lift. 'Don't you dare order me about.' And to de Lisle, 'I shall speak to Siebkron. It's like a trainload of monkeys.'

The upper floors restored them. This was the Bonn they knew; the pale, functional interiors, the pale, functional reproductions on the wall, the pale unpolished teak; the white shirts, the grey ties and faces pale as the moon. They were seven. The two who sat to either side of Siebkron had no names at all, and de Lisle wondered maliciously whether they were clerks brought in to make up the numbers. Lieff, an empty-headed parade horse from Protocol Department, sat on his left; opposite him, on Bradfield's right, an old *Polizeidirektor* from Bonn, whom de Lisle instinctively liked: a battle-scarred monument of a man, with white patches like covered bullet-holes in the leather of his skin. Cigarettes lay in packets on a plate. A stern girl offered decaffeinated coffee, and they waited until she had withdrawn.

What *does* Siebkron want? he wondered for the hundredth time since the terse summons at nine o'clock that morning.

The Conference began, like all conferences, with a résumé of what was said at a previous occasion. Lieff read the minutes in a tone of unctuous flattery, like a man awarding a medal. It was an occasion, he implied, of the greatest felicity. The *Polizeidirektor* unbuttoned his green jacket, and lit a length of Dutch cigar till it burned like a spill.

Siebkron coughed angrily but the old policeman ignored him.

'You have no objection to these minutes, Mr Bradfield?'

Siebkron usually smiled when he asked this question, and although his smile was as cold as the north wind, de Lisle could have wished for it today.

'Off the cuff, none,' Bradfield replied easily, 'But I must see them in writing before I can sign them.'

'No one is asking you to sign.'

De Lisle looked up sharply.

'You will allow me,' Siebkron declared, 'To read the following statement. Copies will be distributed.'

It was quite short.

The *doyen*, he said, had already discussed with Herr Lieff of Protocol Department, and with the American Ambassador, the question of the physical security of diplomatic premises in the event of civil unrest arising out of minority demonstrations in the Federal Republic. Siebkron regretted that additional measures were proving necessary, but it was desirable to anticipate unhappy eventualities rather than attempt to correct them when it was too late. Siebkron had received the *doyen*'s assurance that all diplomatic Heads of Mission would cooperate to the utmost with the Federal Authorities. The British Ambassador had already associated himself with this undertaking. Siebkron's voice had found a hard edge which was uncommonly close to anger. Lieff and the old policeman had turned deliberately to face Bradfield, and their expressions were frankly hostile.

'I am sure you subscribe to this opinion,' Siebkron said in English, handing a copy of the statement down the table.

Bradfield had noticed nothing. Taking his fountain pen from an inside pocket, he unscrewed the cap, fitted it carefully over the butt and ran the nib along line after line of the text.

'This is an *aide-memoire?*'

'A memorandum. You will find the German translation attached.'

'I can see nothing here that requires to be in writing at all,' Bradfield said easily. 'You know very well, Ludwig, that we always agree on such matters. Our interests are identical.'

Siebkron disregarded this pleasant appeal: 'You also understand that Doktor Karfeld is not well disposed towards the British. This places the British Embassy in a special category.'

Bradfield's smile did not flinch. 'It has not escaped our notice. We rely on you to see that Herr Karfeld's sentiments are not expressed in physical terms. We have every confidence in your ability to do so.'

'Precisely. Then you will appreciate my concern for the safety of all personnel of the British Embassy.'

Bradfield's voice came quite close to banter. 'Ludwig, what is this? A declaration of love?'

The rest came very fast, thrown down like an ultimatum: 'I must accordingly ask you that until further notice all British Embassy staff below the rank of Counsellor be confined to the area of Bonn. You will kindly instruct them that for their safety they will please be in their residences—' he was reading again from the folder before him–'Henceforth and until further notice, by eleven o'clock at night, local time.'

The white faces peered at them through the swathes of tobacco smoke like lamps through an anaesthetic. In the momentary confusion and bewilderment, only Bradfield's voice, fluent and decisive as the voice of a commander in battle, did not waver.

It was a principle of civil order which the British had learned by bitter experience in many parts of the world, he said, that unpleasant incidents were actually provoked by over-elaborate precautions.

Siebkron offered no comment.

While making every allowance for Siebkron's professional and personal concern, Bradfield felt obliged to warn him strongly against any gesture which might be misinterpreted by the outside world.

Siebkron waited.

Like Siebkron, Bradfield insisted, he himself had a responsibility to preserve Embassy morale and thus fortify the Junior Staff against strains yet to come. He could not support any measure at this stage which would look like a retreat in the face of an enemy who as yet had barely advanced . . . did Siebkron really wish it said that he could not control a handful of hooligans? . . .

Siebkron was standing up, the others with him. A terse inclination of the head replaced the obligatory handshake. The door opened and the leather coats led them briskly to the lift. They were in the wet courtyard. The roar of the motor-cycles deafened them. The Mercedes swept them into the carriageway. What on earth have we done? de Lisle wondered. What on earth have we done to deserve this? Whoever has thrown the rock through teacher's window?

'It's nothing to do with last night?' he asked Bradfield at last, as they approached the Embassy.

'There is no conceivable connection,' Bradfield retorted. He was sitting bolt upright, his expression stiff and angry.

'Whatever the reason,' he added, more as a memorandum to himself than by way of a confidence to de Lisle, 'Siebkron is the one thread I dare not cut.'

'Quite,' said de Lisle and they got out. The sports were just ending.

Behind the English Church, on a wooded hill, in a semi-rural avenue away from the centre of Bad Godesberg, the Embassy has built itself a modest piece of suburban Surrey. Comfortable stockbrokers' houses with open fireplaces and long corridors for servants they no longer have, hide behind the exiguous privet and laburnum of splendid isolation. The air trembles to the gentle music of the British Forces Network. Dogs of unmistakeably English breed ramble in the long gardens; the pavements are obstructed by the runabout cars of British Counsellors' wives. In this avenue, on each Sunday throughout the warmer months, a more agreeable ritual replaces the Chancery meeting. At a few minutes before eleven o'clock, dogs are summoned indoors, cats banished to the garden, as a dozen wives in coloured hats and matching handbags emerge from a dozen front doors, followed by their husbands in Sunday suits.

Soon a little crowd has gathered in the road; someone has made a joke; someone has laughed; they glance round anxiously for stragglers, and upwards at the nearer houses. Have the Crabbes overslept? Should someone give them a ring? No, here they come at last. Gently they begin the move downhill to the Church, the women leading, men following, their hands deep in their pockets. Reaching the Church steps they all pause, smiling invitingly at the senior wife present. She, with a little gesture of surprise, climbs the steps ahead of them and disappears through the green curtain, leaving her inferiors to follow, quite by accident, the order of succession which protocol, had they cared about such things, would exactly have demanded.

That Sunday morning, Rawley Bradfield, accompanied by Hazel, his beautiful wife, entered the Church and sat in their customary pew beside the Tills, who by the nature of things had gone ahead of them in the procession. Bradfield, though theoretically a Roman Catholic, regarded it as his iron duty to attend the Embassy Chapel; it was a matter on which he declined to consult either his Church or his conscience. They made a handsome couple. The Irish blood had come through richly in Hazel, whose auburn hair shone where the sunbeams touched it from the leaded window; and Bradfield had a way of deferring to her in public which was both gallant and commanding. Directly behind them, Meadowes the Registrar sat expressionless beside his blonde and very nervous daughter. She was a pretty girl, but the wives in particular were inclined to wonder how a man of her father's rectitude could tolerate such a quantity of make-up.

Having settled into his pew, Bradfield searched the hymnal for the advertised numbers–there were certain of them which he had proscribed on the grounds of taste–then glanced round the Church to check absentees. There being none, he was about to return to his hymnal when Mrs Vandelung, the Dutch Counsellor's wife, and currently Vice-President of the International Ladies, leaned over her pew to enquire in a breathy, somewhat hysterical undertone why there was no organist. Bradfield glanced at the little lighted alcove, at the empty stool with the embroidered cushion on the seat, and in the same instant he appeared to become aware of the embarrassed silence all round him which was accentuated by the creaking of the west door as Mickie Crabbe, whose turn it was to act as sidesman, closed it without benefit of a Voluntary. Rising quickly Bradfield walked down the aisle. From the front row of the choir, John Gaunt, the Chancery Guard, watched with veiled apprehension. Jenny Pargiter, upright as a bride, looked stiffly ahead of her, seeing nothing but the light of God. Janet Cork, wife of the cypher clerk, stood beside her, her mind upon her unborn child. Her husband was in the Embassy, serving a routine shift in the cypher room.

'Where the devil's Harting?' Bradfield asked, but one glance at Crabbe's expression told him that his question was wasted. Slipping out into the road, he hastened a short way up the hill and opened a small iron gate leading to the vestry, which he entered without knocking.

'Harting's failed to appear,' he said curtly. 'Who else plays the organ?'

The Chaplain, who found the Embassy a challenge but believed he was making headway, was a Low Church man with a wife and four children in Wales. No one knew why they would not join him.

'He's never missed before. Never.'

'Who else can play?'

'Perhaps the ferry isn't running. There's a lot of trouble about, I hear.'

'He could come the long way by the bridge. He's done it often enough. Can no one stand in for him?'

'Not that I know,' said the Chaplain, fingering the tip of his golden stole, his thoughts far away. 'But there's never been occasion to enquire, not really.'

'Then what are you going to do?'

'Perhaps someone could give a note,' the Chaplain suggested doubtfully, but his gaze had fixed on a baptismal postcard that was tucked behind a calendar. 'Maybe that would be the answer. Johnny Gaunt has a nice tenor, being Welsh.'

'Very well, the choir must lead. You'd better tell them at once.'

'Trouble *is* you see, they don't know the hymns, Mr Bradfield,' the Chaplain said. 'He wasn't at Friday's choir practice either you see. He didn't come, not really. We had to scrap it, see.'

Stepping back into the fresh air, Bradfield found himself face to face with Meadowes, who had quietly left his place beside his daughter and followed him to the back of the Church.

'He's vanished,' Meadowes said, dreadfully quietly. 'I've checked everywhere. Sick list, the doctor; I've been to his house. His car's in the garage; he's not used his milk. No one's seen or heard of him since Friday. He didn't come to Exiles. It was a special occasion for my daughter's birthday, but he didn't come to that either. He'd got engagements but he was going to look in. He'd promised her a hair-dryer as a present; it's not like him, Mr Bradfield, it's not his way at all.'

For one moment, just for one moment, Bradfield's composure seemed to desert him. He stared furiously at Meadowes, then back at the Church, as if undecided which to destroy; as if either in anger or despair he would rush down the path and burst open the doors and cry out the news to those who waited so complacently within.

'Come with me.'

Even as they entered the main gates of the Embassy and long before the police check cleared them, they could recognize the signs of crisis. Two army motor-cycles were parked on the front lawn. Cork, the cypher clerk on call, was waiting on the steps, an Everyman guide to investments still in his hand. A green German police van, its blue light flashing, had stationed itself beside the canteen, and they could hear the crackle of its radio.

'Thank the Lord you've come, sir,' said Macmullen the Head Guard, 'I sent the duty driver down; he must have passed you on the carriageway.'

All over the building bells were ringing.

'There's a message in from Hanover, sir, from the Consulate General; I didn't hear too well. The rally's gone mad, sir; all hell's broken loose. They're storming the library and they're going to march on the Consulate; I don't know what the world's coming to; worse than Grosvenor Square. I could hear their screaming on the telephone, sir.'

Meadowes followed Bradfield hastily up the stairs.

'You said a hair-dryer? He was giving your daughter a hair-dryer?'

It was a moment of deliberate inconsequence, of deliberate slowness perhaps, a nervous gesture before battle was joined. Meadowes at least construed it thus.

'He'd ordered it specially,' he said.

'Never mind,' said Bradfield, and was about to enter the cypher room when Meadowes addressed him once more.

'The file's gone,' he whispered. 'The green file for the special minutes. It's been gone since Friday.'

Chapter Three

Alan Turner

It was a day to be nearly free; a day to stay in London and dream of the country. In St James's Park, the premature summer was entering its third week. Along the lake, girls lay like cut flowers in the unnatural heat of a Sunday afternoon in May. An attendant had lit an improbable bonfire and the smell of burnt grass drifted with the echoes of the traffic. Only the pelicans, hobbling fussily round their island pavilion, seemed disposed to move; only Alan Turner, his big shoes crunching on the gravel, had anywhere to go; for once, not even the girls could distract him.

His shoes were of a heavy brown brogue and much repaired at the welts. He wore a stained tropical suit and carried a stained canvas bag. He was a big, lumbering man, fair-haired, plain-faced and pale, with the high shoulders and square fingers of an alpinist, and he walked with the thrusting slowness of a barge; a broad, aggressive, policeman's walk, wilfully without finesse. His age was hard to guess. Undergraduates would have found him old, but old for an undergraduate. He could alarm the young with age, and the aged with his youth. His colleagues had long ceased to speculate. It was known that he was a late entrant, never a good sign, and a former fellow of St Anthony's College, Oxford, which takes all kinds of people. The official Foreign Office publications were reserved. While they shed a merciless light on the origin of all their other Turners, in the matter of Alan they remained tight-lipped, as if, having considered all the facts, they felt that silence was the kindest policy.

'They've called you in too, then,' said Lambert, catching him up. 'I must say, Karfeld's really gone to town this time.'

'What the hell do they expect us to do? Man the barricades? Knit blankets?'

Lambert was a small, vigorous man and he liked it said of him that he could mix with anyone. He occupied a senior position in Western Department and ran a cricket team open to all grades.

They began the ascent of Clive Steps.

'You'll never change them,' said Lambert. 'That's my view. A nation of psychopaths. Always think they're being got at. Versailles, encirclement, stab in the back; persecution mania, that's their trouble.'

He allowed time for Turner to agree with him.

'We're bringing in the whole of the Department. Even the girls.'

'Christ, that'll really frighten them. That's calling up the reserves, that is.'

'This could put paid to Brussels you know. Bang it clean on the nose. If the German Cabinet loses its nerve on the home front, we're all up a gum-tree.' The prospect filled him with relish. 'We shall have to find a quite different solution in that case.'

'I thought there wasn't one.'

'The Secretary of State has already spoken to their Ambassador; I am told they have agreed full compensation.'

'Then there's nothing to worry about is there? We can get on with our weekend. All go back to bed.'

They had reached the top of the steps. The founder of India, one foot casually upon a plateau of vanquished bronze, stared contentedly past them into the glades of the park.

'They've kept the doors open.' Lambert's voice was tender with reverence. 'They're on the week-day schedule. My, they *are* going it. Well,' he remarked, receiving no admiring echo, 'You go your way, I go mine. Mind you,' he added shrewdly, 'It could do us a lot of good. Unite the rest of Europe behind us against the Nazi menace. Nothing like the stamp of jackboots to stiffen the old alliances.' With a final nod of undeterred goodwill he was assumed into the imperial darkness of the main entrance. For a moment, Turner stared after him, measuring his slight body against the Tuscan pillars of the great portico, and there was even something wistful in his expression, as if actually he would quite like to be a Lambert, small and neat and adept and unbothered. Rousing himself at last, he continued towards a smaller door at the side of the building. It was a scruffy door with brown hardboard nailed to the inside of the glass and a notice denying entrance to unauthorized persons. He had some difficulty getting through.

'Mister Lumley's looking for you,' said the porter. '*When* you can spare a minute, I'm sure.'

He was a young, effeminate man and preferred the other side of the building. 'He was enquiring *most* particularly, as a matter of fact. All packed for Germany, I see.'

His transistor radio was going all the time; someone was reporting direct from Hanover and there was a roar in the background like the roar of the sea.

'Well, you'll get a nice reception by the sound of it. They've already done the library, and now they're having a go at the Consulate.'

'They'd done the library by lunchtime. It was on the one o'clock. The police have cordoned off the Consulate. Three deep. There's not a hope in hell of them getting anywhere near.'

'It's got worse since then,' the porter called after him. 'They're burning books in the market place; you wait!'

'I will. That's just what I bloody well will do.' His voice was awfully quiet but it carried a long way; a Yorkshire voice, and common as a mongrel.

'He's booked your passage to Germany. You ask Travel Section! Overland route and Second Class! Mr Shawn goes First!'

Shoving open the door of his room he found Shawn lounging at the desk, his Brigade of Guards jacket draped over the back of Turner's chair. The eight buttons glinted in the stray sunbeams which, bolder than the rest, had penetrated the coloured glass. He was talking on the telephone. 'They're to put everything in one room,' he said in that soothing tone of voice which reduces the calmest of men to hysteria. He had said it several times before, apparently, but was repeating it for the benefit of simpler minds. '*With* the incendiaries *and* the shredder. That's point one. Point two, *all* locally employed staff are to go *home* and lie low; we can't pay compensation to German citizens who get hurt on our behalf. Tell them that first, then call me back. Christ Almighty!' he screamed to Turner as he rang off, 'Have you *ever* tried to deal with that man?'

'What man?'

'That bald-headed clown in E and O. The one in charge of nuts and bolts.'

'His name is Crosse.' He flung his bag into the corner. 'And he's not a clown.'

'He's mental,' Shawn muttered, losing courage, 'I swear he is.'

'Then keep quiet about it or they'll post him to Security.'

'Lumley's looking for you.'

'I'm not going,' Turner said. 'I'm bloody well not wasting my time. Hanover's a D post. They've no codes, no cyphers, nothing. What am I supposed to do out there? Rescue the bloody Crown Jewels?'

'Then why did you bring your bag?'

He picked up a sheaf of telegrams from the desk.

'They've known about that rally for months. Everyone has, from Western Department down to us. Chancery reported it in March. For once, we saw the telegram. Why didn't they evacuate staff? Why didn't they send the kids home? No money, I suppose. No third class seats available. Well sod them!'

'Lumley said immediately.'

'Sod Lumley too,' said Turner, and sat down. 'I'm not seeing him till I've read the papers.'

'It's *policy* not to send them home,' Shawn continued taking up

Turner's point. Shawn thought of himself as *attached* rather than *posted* to Security Department; as resting, as it were, between appointments, and he missed no opportunity to demonstrate his familiarity with the larger political world. 'Business as usual, that's the cry. We can't allow ourselves to be stampeded by mob rule. After all, the Movement is a minority. The British lion,' he added, making an unconfident joke, 'can't allow itself to be upset by the pinpricks of a few hooligans.'

'Oh it can *not*; my God it can't.'

Turner put aside one telegram and began another. He read fast and without effort, with the confidence of an academic, arranging the papers into separate piles according to some undisclosed criterion.

'So what's going on? What have they got to lose apart from their honour?' he demanded, still reading. 'Why the hell call *us* in? Compensation's Western Department's baby, right? Evacuation's E and O's baby, right? If they're worried about the lease, they can go and cry at the Ministry of Works. So why the hell can't they leave us in peace?'

'Because it's Germany,' Shawn suggested weakly.

'Oh roll on.'

'Sorry if it *spoilt* something,' Shawn said with an unpleasant sneer, for he suspected Turner of a more colourful sex life than his own.

The first relevant telegram was from Bradfield. It was marked Flash; it had been despatched at eleven-forty and submitted to the Resident Clerk at two twenty-eight. Skardon, Consul General in Hanover, had summoned all British staff and families to the Residence, and was making urgent representations to the police. The second telegram consisted of a Reuter newsflash timed at eleven fifty-three: demonstrators had broken into the British Library; police were unequal to the situation; the fate of Fraulein Eick [*sic*] the librarian was unknown.

Hard upon this came a second rush telegram from Bonn: 'Norddeutscher Rundfunk reports Eick repeat Eick killed by mob.' But this was in turn immediately contradicted, for Bradfield, through the good offices of Herr Siebkron of the Ministry of the Interior, ('with whom I have a close relationship') had by then succeeded in obtaining direct contact with the Hanover police. According to their latest assessment, the British Library had been sacked and its books burned before a large crowd. Printed posters had appeared with anti-British slogans such as 'The Farmers won't Pay for your Empire!' and 'Work for your own bread, don't steal ours!' Fraulein Gerda Eich [*sic*] aged fifty-one of 4 Hohenzollernweg, Hanover, had been dragged down two flights of stone steps, kicked and punched in the face and made to throw her own books into the fire. Police with horses and anti-riot equipment were being brought in from neighbouring towns.

A marginal annotation by Shawn stated that Tracing Section had turned up a record of the unfortunate Fraulein Eich. She was a retired school teacher, sometime in British Occupational employment, sometime secretary of the Hanover Branch of the Anglo-German Society, who in 1962 had been awarded a British decoration for services to international understanding.

'Another anglophile bites the dust,' Turner muttered.

There followed a long if hastily compiled summary of broadcasts and bulletins. This, too, Turner studied with close application. No one, it seemed, and least of all those who had been present, was able to say precisely what had triggered off the riot, nor what had attracted the crowd towards the library in the first place. Though demonstrations were now a commonplace of the German scene, a riot on this scale was not; Federal authorities had confessed themselves 'deeply concerned'. Herr Ludwig Siebkron of the Ministry of the Interior had broken his habitual silence to remark to a Press Conference that there was 'cause for very real anxiety'. An immediate decision had been taken to provide additional protection for all official and quasi-official British buildings and residences throughout the Federal Republic. The British Ambassador, after some initial hesitation, had agreed to impose a voluntary curfew on his staff.

Accounts of the incident by police, press and even delegates themselves were hopelessly confused. Some declared it was spontaneous; a collective gesture aggravated by the word 'British' which happened to be exhibited on the side of the library building. It was natural, they said, that as the day of decision in Brussels drew rapidly closer, the Movement's policy of opposition to the Common Market should assume a specifically anti-British form. Others swore they had seen a sign, a white handkerchief that fluttered from a window; one witness even claimed that a rocket had risen behind the town hall and emitted stars of red and gold. For some the crowd had surged with a positive impulse, for others it had 'flowed'; for others again it had trembled. 'It was led from the centre,' one senior police officer reported. 'The periphery was motionless until the centre moved.' 'Those at the centre,' Western Radio maintained, 'kept their composure. The outrage was perpetrated by a few hooligans at the front. The others were then obliged to follow.' On one point only they seemed to agree: the incident had taken place when the music was loudest. It was even suggested by a woman witness that the music itself had been the sign which started the crowd running.

The *Spiegel* correspondent, on the other hand, speaking on Northern Radio, had a circumstantial account of how a grey omnibus chartered by a mysterious Herr Meyer of Luneburg conveyed 'a bodyguard of thirty picked men' to the town centre of Hanover one hour before the demonstration began and that this bodyguard, drawn partly from students and partly from young farmers, had formed a 'protective ring' round the Speaker's podium. It was these 'picked men' who had started the rush. The entire action had therefore been inspired by Karfeld himself. 'It is an open declaration,' he insisted, 'that from now on, the Movement proposes to march to its own music.'

'This Eich,' Turner said at last. 'What's the latest?'

'She's as well as can be expected.'

'How well's that?'

'That's all they said.'

'Oh fine.'

'Fortunately neither Eich nor the Library are a British responsibility. The Library was founded during the Occupation but handed over the Germans quite soon afterwards. It's now controlled and owned exclusively by the *Land* authority. There's nothing British about it.'

'So they've burnt their own books.'

Shawn gave a startled smile.

'Well yes, actually,' he said. 'Come to think of it, they have. That's rather a useful point; we might even suggest it to Press Section.'

The telephone was ringing. Shawn lifted the receiver and listened.

'It's Lumley,' he said, putting his hand over the mouthpiece. 'The porter told him you're in.'

Turner appeared not to hear. He was studying another telegram, two paragraphs, not more; it was headed 'personal for Lumley' and marked 'immediate' and this was the second copy passed to Turner.

'He wants you, Alan.' Shawn held out the receiver.

Turner read the text once and then read it again. Rising, he went to the steel cupboard and drew out a small black notebook, unused, which he thrust into the recesses of his tropical suit.

'You stupid bugger,' he said very quietly, from the door. 'Why don't you learn to read your telegrams? All the time you've been bleating about fire extinguishers we've had a bloody defector on our hands.'

He held up the sheet of pink paper for Shawn to read.

'A planned departure, that's what they call it. Forty-three files missing, not one of them below Confidential. One green classified Maximum and Limit, gone since Friday. I'll say it was planned.'

Leaving Shawn with the telephone still in his hand, Turner thudded down the corridor in the direction of his master's room. His eyes were a swimmer's eyes, very pale, washed colourless by the sea.

Shawn stared after him. That's what happens, he decided, when you open your doors to the other ranks. They leave their wives and children, use filthy language in the corridors and play ducks and drakes with all the common courtesies. With a sigh, he replaced the receiver, raised it again and dialled News Department. This was Shawn, he said, s-h-a-w-n. He had had rather a good idea about the riots in Hanover, the way one might play it at Press Conference: it was nothing to do with *us* after all, if the Germans decided to burn their own books. . . . He thought that might go down pretty well as an example of cool English wit. Yes, Shawn, s-h-a-w-n. Not at all; they might even have lunch together some time.

Lumley had a folder open before him and his old hand rested on it like a claw.

'We know nothing about him. He's not even carded. As far as we're concerned, he doesn't exist. He hasn't even been vetted, let alone cleared. I had to scrounge his papers from Personnel.'

'And?'

'There's a smell, that's all. A foreign smell. Refugee background, emigrated in the thirties. Farm school, Pioneer Corps, Bomb Disposal. He gravitated to Germany in forty-five. Temporary sergeant; Control Commission; one of the old carpetbaggers by the sound of it. Professional expatriate. There was one in every mess in Occupied Germany in those days. Some survived, some drifted into the consulates. Quite a few of them reverted; went into the night or took up German citizenship again. A few went crooked. No childhood, most of them, that's the trouble. Sorry,' Lumley said abruptly, and almost blushed.

'Any form?'

'Nothing to set the Thames on fire. We traced the next of kin. An uncle living in Hampstead; Otto Harting. Sometime adoptive father. No other relations living. He was in the pharmaceutical business. More an alchemist by the sound of it. Patent medicines, that kind of thing. He's dead now. Dead ten years. He was a member of the Hampstead Branch of the British Communist Party from forty-one to forty-five. One conviction for little girls.'

'How little?'

'Does it matter? His nephew Leo lived with him for a bit. Something may have rubbed off. The old man might even have recruited him then I suppose. . . . Long term penetration. That would fit the mould. Or someone may have reminded him of it later on. They never let you go, mind, once you've had a taste of it. Bad as Catholics.'

Lumley hated faith.

'What's his success?'

'Obscure. His function is listed as Claims and Consular, whatever that means. He has diplomatic rank, just. A Second Secretary. You know the kind of arrangement. Unpromotable, unpostable, unpensionable. Chancery gave him living space. Not a *proper* diplomat.'

'Lucky bloke.'

Lumley let that go.

'Entertainment allowance'—Lumley glanced at the file—'A hundred and four pounds per annum, to be spread over fifty cocktail guests and thirty-four dinner guests. Accountable. Pretty small beer. He's locally employed. A temporary, of course. He's been one for twenty years.'

'That leaves me sixteen to go.'

'In fifty-six he put in an application to marry a girl called Aickman. Margaret Aickman. Someone he'd met in the Army. The application was never pursued, apparently. There's no record of whether he's married since.'

'Perhaps they've stopped asking. What are the missing files about?'

Lumley hesitated. 'Just a hotchpotch,' he said casually, 'a general hotchpotch. Bradfield's trying to put a list together now.' They could hear the porter's radio blaring again in the corridor.

Turner caught the tone and held on to it: 'What sort of hotchpotch?'

'Policy,' Lumley retorted. 'Not your field at all.'

'You mean I can't know?'

'I mean you needn't know.' He said this quite casually; Lumley's world was dying and he wished no one ill. 'He's chosen a good moment, I must say,' he continued, 'With all this going on. Perhaps he just took a handful and ran for it.'

'Discipline?'

'Nothing much. He got in a fight five years ago in Cologne. A night-club brawl. They managed to hush it up.'

'And they didn't sack him?'

'We like to give people a second chance.' Lumley was still deep in the file, but his tone was pregnant with innuendo.

He was sixty or more, coarse-spoken and grey; a grey-faced, grey-clothed owl of a man, hunched and dried out. Long ago he had been Ambassador to somewhere small, but the appointment had not endured.

'You're to cable me every day. Bradfield is arranging facilities. But don't ring me up, do you understand? That direct line is a menace.' He closed the folder. 'I've cleared it with Western Department. Bradfield's cleared it with the Ambassador. They'll let you go on one condition.'

'That's handsome of them.'

'The Germans mustn't know. Not on any account. They mustn't know he's gone; they mustn't know we're looking for him; they mustn't know there's been a leak.'

'What if he's compromised secret Nato material? That's as much their pigeon as ours.'

'Decisions of that kind are none of your concern. Your instructions are to go gently. Don't lead with your chin. Understand?'

Turner said nothing.

'You're not to disturb, annoy or offend. They're walking on a knife edge out there; *anything* could tilt the balance. Now, tomorrow, any time. There's even a danger that the Huns might think we were playing a double game with the Russians. If that idea got about it could balls everything up.'

'We seem to find it hard enough,' Turner said, borrowing from Lumley's vocabulary, 'Playing a single game with the Huns.'

'The Embassy have got one idea in their heads, and it's not Harting and it's not Karfeld and least of all is it you. It's Brussels. So just remember that. You'd better, because if you don't you'll be out on your arse.'

'Why not send Shawn? He's tactful. Charm them all, he would.'

Lumley pushed a memorandum across the desk. It contained a list of Harting's personal particulars. 'Because you'll find him and Shawn won't. Not that I admire you for that. You'd pull down the whole forest, you would, to find an acorn. What drives you? What are you looking for? Some bloody absolute. If there's one thing I really hate it's a cynic in search of God. Maybe a bit of failure is what you need.'

'There's plenty of it about.'

'Heard from your wife?'

'No.'

'You could forgive her, you know. It's been done before.'

'Jesus, you take chances,' Turner breathed. 'What the hell do you know about my marriage?'

'Nothing. That's why I'm qualified to give advice. I just wish you'd stop punishing us all for not being perfect.'

'Anything else?'

Lumley examined him like an old magistrate who had not many cases left.

'Christ, you're quick to despise,' he said at last. 'You frighten me, I'll tell you that for nothing. You're going to have to start liking people soon, or it'll be too late. You'll need us, you know, before you die. Even if we are a second best.' He thrust a file into Turner's hand. 'Go on then. Find him. But don't think you're off the leash. I should take the midnight train if I were you. Get in at lunchtime.' His hooded yellow eyes flickered towards the sunlit park. 'Bonn's a foggy bloody place.'

'I'll fly if it's all the same.'

Lumley slowly shook his head.

'You can't wait, can you. You can't wait to get your hands on him. Pawing the bloody earth, aren't you? Christ, I wish I had your enthusiasm.'

'You had once.'

'And get yourself a suit or something. Try and look as though you belong.'

'I don't though, do I?'

'All right,' said Lumley, not caring any more. 'Wear the cloth cap. Christ,' he added, 'I'd have thought your class was suffering from too much recognition already.'

'There's something you haven't told me. Which do they want most: the man or the files?'

'Ask Bradfield,' Lumley replied, avoiding his eye.

Turner went to his room and dialled his wife's number. Her sister answered.

'She's out,' she said.

'You mean they're still in bed.'

'What do you want?'

'Tell her I'm leaving the country.'

As he rang off he was again distracted by the sound of the porter's wireless. He had turned it on full and tuned it to the European network. A well-bred lady was giving a summary of the news. The Movement's next rally would be held in Bonn, she said; on Friday, five days from today.

Turner grinned. It was a little like an invitation to tea. Picking up his bag, he set off for Fulham, an area well known for boarding houses and married men in exile from their wives.

Chapter Four

Decembers of Renewal

De Lisle picked him up from the airport. He had a sports car that was a little too young for him and it rattled wildly on the wet cobble of the villages. Though it was quite a new car, the paintwork was already dulled by the chestnut gum of Godesberg's wooded avenues. The time was nine in the morning but the street lights still burned. To either side, on flat fields, farm-houses and new building estates lay upon the strips of mist like hulks left over by the sea. Drops of rain prickled on the small windscreen.

'We've booked you in at the Adler; I suppose that's all right. We didn't know quite what sort of subsistence you people get.'

'What are the posters saying?'

'Oh, we hardly read them any more. Reunification . . . alliance with

Moscow. . . . Anti-America. . . . Anti-Britain.'

'Nice to know we're still in the big league.'

'You've hit a real Bonn day I'm afraid. Sometimes the fog is a little colder,' de Lisle continued cheerfully, 'Then we call it winter. Sometimes it's warmer, and that's summer. You know what they say about Bonn: either it rains or the level crossings are down. In fact, of course, both things happen at the same time. An island cut off by fog, that's us. It's a very *metaphysical* spot; the dreams have quite replaced reality. We live somewhere between the recent future and the not so recent past. Not *personally*, if you know what I mean. Most of us feel we've been here for ever.'

'Do you always get an escort?'

The black Opel lay thirty yards behind them. It was neither gaining nor losing ground. Two pale men sat in the front and the headlights were on.

'They're protecting us. That's the theory. Perhaps you heard of our meeting with Siebkron?' They turned right and the Opel followed them. 'The Ambassador is *quite* furious. And *now*, of course, they can say it's all vindicated by Hanover: no Englishman is safe without a bodyguard. It's not our view at all. Still, perhaps after Friday we'll lose them again. How are things in London? I hear Steed-Asprey's got Lima.'

'Yes, we're all thrilled about it.'

A yellow road sign said six kilometres to Bonn.

'I think we'll go round the city if you don't mind; there's liable to be rather a hold-up getting in and out. They're checking passes and things.'

'I thought you said Karfeld didn't bother you.'

'We all say that. It's part of our local religion. We're trained to regard Karfeld as an irritant, not an epidemic. You'll have to get used to that. I have a message for you from Bradfield, by the way. He's sorry not to have collected you himself, but he's been rather under pressure.'

They swung sharply off the main road, bumped over a tramline and sped along a narrow open lane. Occasionally a poster or photograph rose before them and darted away into the mist.

'Was that the whole of Bradfield's message?'

'There was the question of who knows what. He imagined you'd like to have that clear at once. *Cover*, is that what you'd call it?'

'I might.'

'Our friend's disappearance has been noticed in a *general* way,' de Lisle continued in the same amiable tone. 'That was inevitable. But fortunately Hanover intervened, and we've been able to mend a few fences. Officially, Rawley has sent him on compassionate leave. He's published no details; merely hinted at personal problems and left it at that. The Junior Staff can think what they like: nervous

breakdown; family troubles; they can make up their own rumours.
Bradfield mentioned the matter at this morning's meeting: we're all
backing him up. As for yourself . . .'

'Well?'

'A general security check in view of the crisis? How would that
sound to you? It seemed quite convincing to us.'

'Did you know him?'

'Harting?'

'That's right. Did you know him?'

'I think perhaps,' de Lisle said, pulling up at a traffic light, 'We
ought to leave the first bite to Rawley, don't you? Tell me, what news
of our little Lords of York?'

'Who the hell are they?'

'I'm *so* sorry,' de Lisle said in genuine discomfort. 'It's our local
expression for the Cabinet. It was silly of me.'

They were approaching the Embassy. As they filtered left to cross
the carriageway, the black Opel slid slowly past like an old nanny
who had seen her children safely over the road. The lobby was in
turmoil. Despatch riders mingled with journalists and police. An
iron grille, painted a protective orange, sealed off the basement
staircase. De Lisle led him quickly to the first floor. Someone must
have telephoned from the desk because Bradfield was already
standing as they entered.

'Rawley, this is Turner,' de Lisle said, as if there were not much he
could do about it, and prudently closed the door on them.

Bradfield was a hard-built, self-denying man, thin-boned and well-
preserved, of that age and generation which can do with very little
sleep. Yet the strains of the last twenty-four hours were already
showing in the small, uncommon bruises at the corners of his eyes,
and the unnatural pallor of his complexion. He studied Turner
without comment: the canvas bag clutched in the heavy fist, the
battered fawn suit, the unyielding, classless features; and it seemed
for a moment as if an impulse of involuntary anger would threaten
his customary composure; of aesthetic objection that anything so
offensively incongruous should have been set before him at such a
time. Outside in the corridor Turner heard the hushed murmur of
busy voices, the clip of feet, the faster chatter of the typewriters, and
the phantom throb of code machines from the cypher room.

'It was good of you to come at such an awkward time. You'd better
let me have that.' He took the canvas bag and dumped it behind the
chair.

'Christ it's hot,' said Turner. Walking to the window, he rested his
elbows on the sill and gazed out. Away to his right in the far distance,
the Seven Hills of Königswinter, chalked over by fine cloud, rose like
Gothic dreams against the colourless sky. At their feet he could make

out the dull glint of water and the shadows of motionless vessels.

'He lived out that way didn't he? Königswinter?'

'We have a couple of hirings on the other bank. They are never much in demand. The ferry is a great inconvenience.'

On the trampled lawn, workmen were dismantling the marquee under the watchful eye of two German policeman.

'I imagine you have a routine in such cases,' Bradfield continued, addressing Turner's back. 'You must tell us what you want and we shall do our best to provide it.'

'Sure.'

'The cypher clerks have a dayroom where you'll be undisturbed. They are instructed to send your telegrams ' ithout reference to anyone else. I've had a desk and a telephon ·· ut in there for you. I have also asked Registry to prepare a list of the missing files. If there's anything more you want, I am sure de Lisle will do his best to provide it. And on the social side'–Bradfield hesitated–'I am to invite you to dine with us tomorrow night. We would be very pleased. It's the usual Bonn evening. De Lisle will lend you a dinner jacket, I am sure.'

'There's lots of routines,' Turner replied at last. He was leaning against the radiator, looking round the room. 'In a country like this it should be dead simple. Call in the police. Check hospitals, nursing homes, prisons, Salvation Army hostels. Circulate his photograph and personal description and square the local press. Then I'd look for him myself.'

'Look for him? Where?'

'In other people. In his background. Motive, political associations, boy friends, girl friends, contacts. Who else was involved; who knew; who half-knew; who quarter-knew; who ran him; who did he meet and where; how did he communicate; safe houses, pick-up points; how long's it been going on. Who's protected him, may be. That's what I call looking. Then I'd write a report: point the blame, make new enemies.' He continued to examine the room, and it seemed that nothing was innocent under his clear, inscrutable eye. 'That's one routine. That's for a friendly country, of course.'

'Most of what you suggest is quite unacceptable here.'

'Oh sure. I've had all that from Lumley.'

'Perhaps before we go any further, you had better have it from me as well.'

'Please yourself,' said Turner, in a manner which might have been deliberately chosen to annoy.

'I imagine that in your world, secrets are an absolute standard. They matter more than anything. Those who preserve them are your allies; those who betray them are your quarry. Here, that is simply not the case. As of now, the local political considerations far exceed those of security.'

Suddenly, Turner was grinning. 'They always do,' he said. 'It's amazing.'

'Here in Bonn we have at present one contribution to make: to maintain at all costs the trust and good will of the Federal Government. To stiffen their resolve against mounting criticism from their own electorate. The Coalition is sick; the most casual virus could kill it. Our job is to pamper the invalid. To console, encourage and occasionally threaten him, and pray to God he survives long enough to see us into the Common Market.'

'What a lovely picture.' He was looking out of the window again. 'The only ally we've got, and he's on crutches. The two sick men of Europe propping one another up.'

'Like it or not, it happens to be the truth. We are playing a poker game here. With open cards and nothing in our hand. Our credit is exhausted, our resources are nil. Yet in return for no more than a smile, our partners bid and play. That smile is all we have. The whole relationship between HMG and the Federal Coalition rests upon that smile. Our situation is as delicate as that; and as mysterious. And as critical. Our whole future with Europe could be decided in ten days from now.' He paused, apparently expecting Turner to speak. 'It is no coincidence that Karfeld has chosen next Friday for his rally in Bonn. By Friday, our friends in the German Cabinet will be forced to decide whether to bow to French pressure or honour their promises to ourselves and their partners in the Six. Karfeld detests the Market and favours an opening to the East. In the short term he inclines to Paris; in the long term, to Moscow. By marching on Bonn and increasing the tempo of his campaign, he is deliberately placing pressure on the Coalition at the most critical moment. Do you follow me?'

'I can manage the little words,' Turner said. A Kodachrome portrait of the Queen hung directly behind Bradfield's head. Her crest was everywhere: on the blue leather chairs, the silver cigarette box, even the jotting pads set out on the long conference table. It was as if the monarchy had flown here first class and left its free gifts behind.

'That is why I am asking you to move with the greatest possible circumspection. Bonn is a village,' Bradfield continued. 'It has the manners, vision and dimensions of the parish pump, and yet it is a State within a village. Nothing matters for us more than the confidence of our hosts. There are already indications that we have caused them offence. I do not even know how we have done that. Their manner, even in the last forty-eight hours, has become noticeably cool. We are under surveillance; our telephone calls are interrupted; and we have the greatest difficulty in reaching even our official ministerial contacts.'

'All right,' Turner said. He had had enough. 'I've got the message.

I'm warned off. We're on tender ground. Now what?'

'Now this,' Bradfield snapped. 'We both know what Harting may be, or may have been. God knows, there are precedents. The greater his treachery here, the greater the potential embarrassment, the greater the shock to German confidence. Let us take the worst contingency. If it were possible to prove—I am not yet saying that it is, but there are indications—if it were possible to prove that by virtue of Harting's activities in this Embassy, our inmost secrets had been betrayed to the Russians over many years—secrets which to a great extent we share with the Germans—then that shock, trivial as it may be in the long term, could sever the last thread by which our credit here hangs. Wait.' He was sitting very straight at his desk, with an expression of controlled distaste upon his handsome face. 'Hear me out. There is something here that does not exist in England. It is called the anti-Soviet alliance. The Germans take it very seriously, and we deride it at our peril: *it is still our ticket to Brussels*. For twenty years or more, we have dressed ourselves in the shining armour of the defender. We may be bankrupt, we may beg for loans, currency and trade; we may occasionally . . . reinterpret . . . our Nato commitments; when the guns sound, we may even bury our heads under the blankets; our leaders may be as futile as theirs.'

What was it Turner discerned in Bradfield's voice at that moment? Self-disgust? A ruthless sense of his own decline? He spoke like a man who had tried all remedies, and would have no more of doctors. For a moment the gap between them had closed, and Turner heard his own voice speaking through the Bonn mist.

'For all that, in terms of popular psychology, it is the one great unspoken strength we have: that when the Barbarians come from the East, the Germans may count on our support. That Rhine Army will hastily gather on the Kentish hills and the British independent nuclear deterrent will be hustled into service. Now do you see what Harting could mean in the hand of a man like Karfeld?'

Turner had taken the black notebook from his inside pocket. It crackled sharply as he opened it. 'No. I don't. Not yet. You don't want him found, you want him lost. If you had your way you wouldn't have sent for me.' He nodded his large head in reluctant admiration. 'Well, I'll say this for you: no one's ever warned me off this early. Christ. I've hardly sat down. I hardly know his full names. We've not heard of him in London, did you know that? He's not even had any access, not in our book. Not even one bloody military manual. He may have been abducted. He may have gone under a bus, run off with a bird for all *we* know. But *you*; Christ? You've really gone the bank, haven't you? He's all the spies we've ever had rolled into one. So what *has* he pinched? What do you know that I don't?' Bradfield tried to interrupt but Turner rode him down implacably. 'Or maybe I shouldn't ask? I mean I don't want to upset anyone.'

They were glaring at one another across centuries of suspicion: Turner clever, predatory and vulgar, with the hard eye of the upstart; Bradfield disadvantaged but not put down, drawn in upon himself, picking his language as if it had been made for him.

'Our most secret file has disappeared. It vanished on the same day that Harting left. It covers the whole spectrum of our most delicate conversations with the Germans, formal and informal, over the last six months. For reasons which do not concern you, its publication would ruin us in Brussels.'

He thought at first that it was the roar of the aeroplane engines still ringing in his ears, but the traffic in Bonn is as constant as the mist. Gazing out of the window he was suddenly assailed by the feeling that from now on he would neither see nor hear with clarity; that his senses were being embraced and submerged by the cloying heat and the disembodied sound.

'Listen.' He indicated his canvas bag. 'I'm the abortionist. You don't want me but you've got to have me. A neat job with no aftermath, that's what you're paying for. All right; I'll do my best. But before we all go over the wall, let's do a bit of counting on our fingers, shall we?'

The catechism began.

'He was unmarried?'

'Yes.'

'Always has been?'

'Yes.'

'Lived alone?'

'So far as I know.'

'Last seen?'

'On Friday morning, at the Chancery meeting. In here.'

'Not afterwards?'

'I happen to know the pay clerk saw him, but I'm limited in whom I can ask.'

'Anyone else missing at all?'

'No one.'

'Had a full count have you? No little long-legged bird from Registry?'

'People are constantly on leave; no one is unaccountably absent.'

'Then why didn't Harting take leave? They usually do, you know. Defect in comfort, that's my advice.'

'I have no idea.'

'You weren't close to him?'

'Certainly not.'

'What about his friends? What do they say?'

'He has no friends worth speaking of.'

'Any not worth speaking of?'

'So far as I know, he has no close friends in the community. Few of us have. We have acquaintances, but few friends. That is the way of Embassies. With such an intensive social life, one learns to value privacy.'

'How about Germans?'

'I have no idea. He was once on familiar terms with Harry Praschko.'

'Praschko?'

'We have a parliamentary opposition here: the free Democrats. Praschko is one of its more colourful members. He has been most things in his time: not least a fellow traveller. There is a note on file to say they were once friendly. They knew one another during the Occupation, I believe. We keep an index of useful contacts. I once questioned him about Praschko as a matter of routine and he told me that the relationship was discontinued. That is all I can tell you.'

'He was once engaged to be married to a girl called Margaret Aickman. This Harry Praschko was named as a character reference. In his capacity as a member of the Bundestag.'

'Well?'

'You've never heard of Aickman?'

'Not a name to me, I'm afraid.'

'Margaret.'

'So you said. I never heard of any engagement, and I never heard of the woman.'

'Hobbies? Photography? Stamps? Ham radio?'

Turner was writing all the time. He might have been filling in a form.

'He was musical. He played the organ in Chapel. I believe he also had a collection of gramophone records. You would do better to enquire among the Junior Staff; he was more at home with them.'

'You never went to his house?'

'Once. For dinner.'

'Did he come to yours?'

There was the smallest break in the rhythm of their interrogation while Bradfield considered.

'Once.'

'For dinner?'

'For drinks. He wasn't quite dinner party material. I am sorry to offend your social instincts.'

'I haven't got any.'

Bradfield did not appear surprised.

'Still, you did go to him, didn't you? I mean you gave him hope.' He rose and ambled back to the window like a great moth lured to the light. 'Got a file on him, have you?' His tone was very detached; he might have been infected by Bradfield's own forensic style.

'Only paysheets, annual reports, a character reference from the Army. It's all very standard stuff. Read it if you want.' When Turner did not reply, he added: 'We keep very little here on staff; they change so often. Harting was the exception.'

'He's been here twenty years.'

'Yes. As I say, he is the exception.'

'And never vetted.'

Bradfield said nothing.

'Twenty years in the Embassy, most of them in Chancery. And never vetted once. Name never even submitted. Amazing really.' He might have been commenting on the view.

'I suppose we all thought it had been done already. He came from the Control Commission after all; one assumes they exacted a certain standard.'

'Quite a privilege being vetted, mind. Not the kind of thing you do for anyone.'

The marquee had gone. Homeless, the two German policemen paced the grey lawn, their wet leather coats flapping lazily round their boots. It's a dream, Turner thought. A noisy unwilling dream. 'Bonn's a very metaphysical place,' de Lisle's agreeable voice reminded him. 'The dreams have quite replaced reality.'

'Shall I tell you something?'

'I can hardly stop you.'

'All right: you've warned me off. That's usual enough. But where's the rest of it?'

'I've no idea what you mean.'

'You've no theory, that's what I mean. It's not like anything I've ever met. There's no panic. No explanation. Why not? He worked for you. You knew him. Now you tell me he's a spy; he's pinched your best files. He's garbage. Is it always like that here when somebody goes? Do the gaps seal that fast?' He waited. 'Let me help you, shall I? "He's been working here for twenty years. We trusted him implicitly. We still do." How's that?'

Bradfield said nothing.

'Try again. "I always had my suspicions about him ever since that night we were discussing Karl Marx. Harting swallowed an olive without spitting out the pip." Any good?'

Still Bradfield did not reply.

'You see, it's not usual. See what I mean? He's unimportant. How you wouldn't have him to dinner. How you washed your hands of him. And what a sod he is. What he's betrayed.'

Turner watched him with his pale, hunter's eyes; watched for a movement, or a gesture, head cocked waiting for the wind. In vain. 'You don't even *bother* to explain him, not to me, not to yourself. Nothing. You're just . . . blank about him. As if you'd sentenced him to death. You don't mind my being personal, do you? Only I'm sure you've not much time: that's the next thing you're going to tell me.'

'I was not aware,' Bradfield said, ice-cold, 'that I was expected to do your job. Nor you mine.'

'Capri. How about that? He's got a bird. The Embassy's in chaos, he pinches some files, flogs them to the Czechs and bolts with her.'

'He has no girl.'

'Aickman. He's dug her up. Gone off with Praschko, two on a bird. Bride, best man and groom.'

'I told you, he has no girl.'

'Oh. So you *do* know that? I mean there are some things you *are* sure of. He's a traitor and he's got no bird.'

'So far as anyone knows, he has no woman. Does that satisfy you?'

'Perhaps he's queer.'

'I'm sure he's nothing of the sort.'

'It's broken out in him. We're all a bit mad, aren't we, round about our age? The male menopause, how about that?'

'That is an absurd suggestion.'

'Is it?'

'To the best of my knowledge, yes.' Bradfield's voice was trembling with anger; Turner's barely rose above a murmur.

'We never know though, do we? Not till it's too late. Did he handle money at all?'

'Yes. But there's none missing.'

Turner swung on him. 'Jesus,' he said, his eyes bright with triumph. 'You checked. You *have* got a dirty mind.'

'Perhaps he's just walked into the river,' Turner suggested comfortingly, his eyes still upon Bradfield. 'No sex. Nothing to live for. How's that?'

'Ridiculous, since you ask.'

'Important to a bloke like Harting, though, sex. I mean if you're alone, it's the only thing. I mean I don't know how some of these chaps manage, do you? I know I couldn't. About a couple of weeks is as long as I can go, me. It's the only reality, if you live alone. Or that's what I reckon. Apart from politics of course.'

'Politics? Harting? I shouldn't think he read a newspaper from one year to the next. He was a child in such matters. A complete innocent.'

'They often are,' said Turner. 'That's the remarkable thing.' Sitting down again, Turner folded one leg over the other and leaned back in the chair like a man about to reminisce. 'I knew a man once who sold his birthright because he couldn't get a seat on the underground. I reckon there's more of that kind go wrong than was ever converted to it by the Good Book. Perhaps that *was* his problem? Not right for dinner parties: no room on the train. After all, he was a temporary, wasn't he?'

Bradfield did not reply.

'And he'd been here a long time. Permanent staff, sort of thing. Not fashionable, that isn't, not in an Embassy. They go native if they're around too long. But then he *was* native, wasn't he? Half. Half a Hun, as de Lisle would say. He never talked politics?'

'Never.'

'You sensed it in him, a political spin?'

'No.'

'No crack-up? No tension?'

'No.'

'What about that fight in Cologne?'

'What fight?'

'Five years back. In the night club. Someone worked him over; he was in hospital for six weeks. They managed to hush it up.'

'That was before my time.'

'Did he drink a lot?'

'Not to my knowledge.'

'Speak Russian? Take lessons?'

'No.'

'What did he do with his leave?'

'He seldom claimed any. If he did, I understand he stayed at his home in Königswinter. He took a certain interest in his garden, I believe.'

For a long time Turner frankly searched Bradfield's face for something he could not find.

'He didn't screw around,' he said. 'He wasn't queer. He'd no friends, but he wasn't a recluse. He wasn't vetted and you've no record of him. He was a political innocent but he managed to get his hands on the one file that really matters to you. He never stole money, he played the organ in Chapel, took a certain interest in his garden and loved his neighbour as himself. Is that it? He wasn't any bloody thing, positive or negative. What was he then, for Christ's sake? The Embassy eunuch? Haven't you any opinion at all'–Turner persisted in mock supplication–'to help a poor bloody investigator in his lonely task?'

A watch chain hung across Bradfield's waistcoat, no more than a thread of gold, a tiny devotional token of ordered society.

'You seem deliberately to be wasting time on matters which are not at issue. I have neither the time nor the interest to play your devious games. Insignificant though Harting was, obscure though his motive may be, for the last three months he unfortunately had a considerable access to secret information. He obtained that access by stealth, and I suggest that instead of speculating on his sexual proclivities, you give some attention to what he has stolen.'

'Stolen?' Turner repeated softly. 'That's a funny word,' and he wrote it out with deliberate clumsiness in tall capital letters along the top of one page of the notebook. The Bonn climate had already made its mark upon him: dark dabs of sweat had appeared on the thin fabric of his disgraceful suit.

'All right,' he said with sudden fierceness, 'I'm wasting your bloody time. Now let's start at the beginning and find out why you love him so.'

Bradfield examined his fountain pen. You could be queer, Turner's expression said, if you didn't love honour more.

'Will you put that into English?'

'Tell me about him from your own point of view. What his work was, what he was like.'

'His sole task when I first arrived was handling German civilian claims against Rhine Army. Tank damage to crops; stray shells from the range; cattle and sheep killed on manoeuvres. Ever since the end of the war that's been quite an industry in Germany. By the time I took over Chancery two and a half years ago, he had made a corner of it.'

'You mean he was an expert.'

'As you like.'

'It's just the emotive terms, you see. They put me off. I can't help liking him when you talk that way.'

'Claims was his *métier* then, if you prefer. They got him into the Embassy in the first place; he knew the job inside out; he's done it for many years in many different capacities. First for the Control Commission, then for the Army.'

'What did he do *before* that? He came out in forty-five.'

'He came out in uniform, of course. A sergeant or something of the sort. His status was then altered to that of civilian assistant. I've no idea what his work was. I imagine the War Office could tell you.'

'They can't. I also tried the old Control Commission archive. It's mothballs for posterity. They'll take weeks to dig out his file.'

'In any event, he had chosen well. As long as British units were stationed in Germany, there would be manoeuvres; and German civilians would claim reparations. One might say that his job, though specialized, was at least secured by our military presence in Europe.'

'Christ, there's not many would give you a mortgage on *that*,' said Turner with a sudden, infectious smile, but Bradfield ignored him.

'He acquitted himself perfectly adequately. More than adequately; he was good at it. He had a smattering of law from somewhere. German as well as military. He was naturally acquisitive.'

'A thief,' Turner suggested, watching him.

'When he was in doubt, he could call upon the Legal Attaché. It wasn't everybody's cup of tea, acting as a broker between the German farmers and the British Army, smoothing their feathers, keeping things away from the press. It required a certain instinct. He possessed that,' Bradfield observed, once more with undisguised contempt. 'On his own level, he was a competent negotiator.'

'But that wasn't your level, was it?'

'It was no one's,' Bradfield replied, choosing to avoid the innuendo. 'Professionally, he was a solitary. My predecessors had found it best to leave him alone and when I took over I saw no reason to change the practice. He was attached to Chancery so that we could exert a certain disciplinary control; no more. He came to morning meetings, he was punctual, he made no trouble. He was liked up to a point but not, I suppose, trusted. His English was never perfect. He was socially energetic at a certain level; mainly in the less discriminating Embassies. They say he got on well with the South Americans.'

'Did he travel for his work?'

'Frequently and widely. All over Germany.'

'Alone?'

'Yes.'

'And he knew the Army inside out: he'd get the manoeuvre reports; he knew their dispositions, strengths, he knew the lot, right?'

'He knew far more than that; he heard the mess gossip up and down the country; many of the manoeuvres were inter-allied affairs. Some involved the experimental use of new weapons. Since they also caused damage, he was obliged to know the extent of it. There is a great deal of loose information he could have acquired.'

'Nato stuff?'

'Mainly.'

'How long's he been doing that work?'

'Since nineteen forty-eight or nine I suppose. I cannot say, without reference to the files, when the British first paid compensation.'

'Say twenty-one years, give or take a bit.'

'That is my own calculation.'

'Not a bad run for a temporary.'

'Shall I go on?'

'Do. Sure. Go on,' Turner said hospitably, and thought: if I was you I'd throw me out for that.

'That was the situation when I took over. He was a contract man; his employment was subject to annual revision. Each December his contract came up for renewal, each December renewal was recommended. That was how matters stood until eighteen months ago.'

'When Rhine Army pulled out.'

'We prefer to say here that Rhine Army has been added to our strategic reserve in the United Kingdom. You must remember the Germans are still paying support costs.'

'I'll remember.'

'In any event, only a skeleton force remained in Germany. The withdrawal occurred quite suddenly; I imagine it took us all by surprise. There had been disputes about offset agreements, there were riots in Minden. The Movement was just getting under way; the students in particular were becoming extremely noisy; the troops were becoming a provocation. The decision was taken at the highest level; the Ambassador was not even consulted. The order came; and Rhine Army had gone in a month. We had been making a great number of cuts around that time. It's all the rage in London these days. They throw things away and call it economy.' Once more Turner glimpsed that inner bitterness in Bradfield, a family shame to which no guest alluded.

'And Harting was left high and dry.'

'For some time, no doubt, he had seen which way the wind was blowing. That doesn't lessen the shock.'

'He was still a temporary?'

'Of course. Indeed his chances of establishment, if they ever seriously existed, were diminishing rapidly. The moment it became apparent that Rhine Army must withdraw, the writing was on the wall. For that reason alone, I felt that it would have been quite mistaken to make any permanent arrangement for him.'

'Yes,' said Turner, 'I see that.'

'It is easily argued that he was unjustly treated,' Bradfield retorted. 'It could equally be argued that he had a damn good run for his money.' The conviction came through like a stain, suppress it as he might.

'You said he handled official cash.' Turner thought: this is what doctors do. They probe until they can diagnose.

'Occasionally he passed on cheques for the Army. He was a postbox, that was all. A middle man. The Army drew the money, Harting handed it over and obtained a receipt. I checked his accounts regularly. The Army Auditors, as you know, are notoriously suspicious. There were no irregularities. The system was watertight.'

'Even for Harting?'

'That's not what I said. Besides, he always seemed quite comfortably off. I don't think he's an avaricious person; I don't have that impression.'

'Did he live above his means?'

'How should I know what means he has? If he lived on what he got here, I suppose he lived up to them. His house in Kònigswinter was quite large; certainly it was above his grade. I gather he maintained a certain standard there.'

'I see.'

'Last night I made a point of examining his cash drawings for the last three months preceding his departure. On Friday, after Chancery meeting, he drew seventy-one pounds and fourpence.'

'That's a bloody odd sum.'

'To the contrary, it's a very logical sum. Friday was the tenth of the month. He had drawn exactly one third of his monthly entitlement of pay and allowances, less tax, insurance, stoppages for dilapidation and personal telephone calls.' He paused. 'That is an aspect of him which perhaps I have not emphasized: he was a very self-sufficient person.'

'You mean he *is*.'

'I have never yet caught him in a lie. Having decided to leave, he seems to have taken what was owing to him and no more.'

'Some people would call that honourable.'

'Not to steal? I would call that a negative achievement. He might also know, from his knowledge of the law, that an act of theft would have justified an approach to the German police.'

'Christ,' said Turner, watching him, 'You won't even give him marks for conduct.'

Miss Peate, Bradfield's personal assistant, brought coffee. She was a middle-aged, under-decorated woman, stitched taut and full of disapproval. She seemed to know already where Turner came from, for she cast him a look of sovereign contempt. It was his shoes, he noticed to his pleasure, that she most objected to; and he thought: bloody good, that's what shoes are for.

Bradfield continued: 'Rhine Army withdrew at short notice and he was left without a job. That was the nub of it.'

'And without access to Nato military intelligence? That's what you're telling me.'

'That is my hypothesis.'

'Ah,' said Turner, affecting enlightenment, and wrote laboriously in his notebook *hypothesis* as if the very word were an addition to his vocabulary.

'On the day Rhine Army left, Harting came to see me. That was eighteen months ago, near enough.'

He fell silent, struck by his own recollection.

'He is so *trivial*,' he said at last, in a moment of quite uncharacteristic softness. 'Can't you understand that? So utterly lightweight.' It seemed to surprise him still. 'It's easy to lose sight of now: the sheer insignificance of him.'

'He never will be again,' Turner said carelessly, 'You might as well get used to it.'

'He walked in; he looked pale, that was all; otherwise quite unchanged. He sat down in that chair over there. That is his cushion, by the way.' He permitted himself a small, unloving smile 'The cushion was a territorial claim. He was the only member of the Chancery who reserved his seat.'

'And the only one who might lose it. Who embroidered it?'

'I really have no idea.'

'Did he have a housekeeper?'

'Not to my knowledge.'

'All right.'

'He didn't say anything at all about his altered situation. They were actually listening to the radio broadcast in Registry, I remember. The regiments were being piped on to the trains.'

'Quite a moment for him, that.'

'I suppose it was. I asked him what I could do for him. Well, he said, he wanted to be useful. It was all very low-key, all very delicate. He'd noticed Miles Gaveston was under strain, what with the Berlin disturbances and the Hanover students and various other pressures: might he not help out? I pointed out to him he was not qualified to handle internal matters; they were the preserve of regular members of Chancery. No, he said, that wasn't what he meant at all. He wouldn't for a minute presume to trespass upon our major effort. But he had been thinking: Gaveston had one or two little jobs; could he not take them over? He had in mind for instance the Anglo-German Society, which was pretty well dormant by then but still entailed a certain amount of low-level correspondence. Then there was Missing Persons: might he not take over a few things of that kind in order to disencumber the busier Chancery officers? It made some sense, I had to admit.'

'So you said yes.'

'I agreed to it. On a purely provisional basis, of course. An interim arrangement. I assumed we would give him notice in December when his contract ran out; until then, he could fill in his time with whatever small jobs he could find. That was the thin end of the wedge. I was no doubt foolish to listen to him.'

'I didn't say that.'

'You don't have to. I gave him an inch; he took the rest. Within a month he had gathered them all in; all the end-clippings of Chancery work, all the dross a big Embassy attracts: Missing Persons, Petitions to the Queen, Unannounced Visitors, Official Tours, the Anglo-German Society, letters of abuse, threats, all the things that should never have come to Chancery in the first place. By the same token, he spread his talents across the social field as well. Chapel, the choir, the Catering Committee, the Sports Committee. He even started up a National Savings group. At some point he asked to be allowed to use the title "Consular" and I consented. We have no Consular duties here, you understand; that all goes up to Cologne.' He shrugged. 'By December he had made himself useful. His contract was brought forward'–he had taken up his fountain pen and was again staring at the nib–'and I renewed it. I gave him another year.'

'You treated him well,' Turner said, his eyes all the time upon

Bradfield. 'You were quite kind to him really.'

'He had no standing here, no security. He was already on the doorstep and he knew it. I suppose that plays a part. We are more inclined to care for the people we can easily get rid of.'

'You were sorry for him. Why won't you admit it? It's a fair enough reason, for God's sake.'

'Yes. Yes I suppose I was. That first time, I was actually sorry for him.' He was smiling, but only at his own stupidity.

'Did he do the work well?'

'He was unorthodox, but not ineffectual. He preferred the telephone to the written word, but that was only natural; he had had no proper instruction in drafting. English was not his native language.' He shrugged. 'I gave him another year,' he said again.

'Which expired last December. Like a licence really. A licence to work; to be one of us.' He continued to watch Bradfield. 'A licence to spy. And you renewed it a second time.'

'Yes.'

'Why?'

Once more Turner was aware of that hesitation which seemed to signify concealment.

'You weren't sorry for him, were you? Not this time?'

'My feelings are irrelevant.' He put down the pen with a snap. 'The reasons for keeping him on were totally objective.'

'I didn't say they weren't. But you can still be sorry for him.'

'We were understaffed and overworked. The Inspectors had already reduced us by two against my most strenuous advice. The allowances had been halved. Not just Europe was in flux. There were no constants anywhere any more. Rhodesia, Hong Kong, Cyprus. . . . British troops were running from one to the other trying to stamp out a forest fire. We were half-way into Europe and half-way out again. There was talk of a Nordic Federation; God knows what fool gave birth to that idea!' Bradfield declared with utter contempt. 'We were putting out feelers in Warsaw, Copenhagen and Moscow. One minute we were conspiring against the French, the next we were conspiring with them. While that was going on we found the energy to scrap three-quarters of the Navy and nine-tenths of our independent deterrent. It was our worst time; our most humiliating time, and our busiest. To crown everything, Karfeld had just taken over the Movement.'

'So Harting took you through the act again.'

'Not the same act.'

'What do you mean?'

A pause.

'It had more purpose. It had more urgency. I felt it and I did nothing about it. I blame myself. I was conscious of a new mood in him and I did not pursue it.' He continued: 'At the time I put it down to the general state of intensity in which we were all living. I realize now that he was playing his biggest card.'

'Well?'

'He began by saying he still didn't feel he was pulling his weight. He had had a good year, but he felt he could do more. These were bad days; he would like to feel he was really helping to get things on an even keel. I asked him what he had in mind; I thought he'd just about swept the board by then. He said well, it *was* December–that was the nearest he ever came to referring to his contract–and he had naturally been wondering about the Personalities survey.'

'The what?'

'Biographies of prominent figures in German life. Our own confidential Who's Who. We prepare it every year, each of us takes a hand and contributes something on the German personalities with whom he deals. The Commercial people write about their commercial contacts, the Economists about the economists, the Attachés, Press, Information, they all add their bit. Much of the material is highly unflattering; some of it is derived from secret sources.'

'And Chancery edits?'

'Yes. Once again he had chosen very accurately. It was another of those chores which interfered with our proper duties. It was already overdue. De Lisle, who should have compiled it, was in Berlin; it was becoming a confounded nuisance.'

'So you gave him the job.'

'On a provisional basis, yes.'

'Until the next December, for instance?'

'For instance. It is easy now to think of reasons why he wanted that particular job. The survey provided him with a *laissez-passer* to any part of the Embassy. It runs across the board; it covers the whole range of Federal affairs: industrial, military, administrative. Once charged with the survey, he could call on whomever he liked without questions being asked. He could draw files from any other Registry: Commercial, Economic, Naval, Military, Defence–they all opened their doors to him.'

'And the question of vetting never crossed your mind?'

The self-critical note returned: 'Never.'

'Well we all have our moments,' said Turner quietly. 'And that's how he got his access?'

'There's more to it than that.'

'More? That's just about the lot, isn't it?'

'We not only have archives here; we have a Destruction programme as well. It has been running for years. The purpose is to keep Registry space available for new files and to get rid of old ones we no longer need. It sounds a somewhat academic project and in many ways it is; nevertheless, it happens to be vital. There is a clearly defined economic limit to the amount of paper Registry can handle, and to the amount of paper it will hold. The problem is akin to that of road traffic: we are constantly creating more paper than we can digest. Very naturally, it was another of those jobs we took up and put down as time allowed; it was also an absolute curse. For a while it would be forgotten; then the Office would write and ask for our latest figures.' He shrugged. 'As I say, it's very simple. We can't go on indefinitely, even in a place this size, building up more files than we destroy. Registry's bursting at the seams already.'

'So Harting proposed himself for the task.'

'Precisely.'

'And you agreed.'

'On a provisional basis. He should try his hand and see how it went. He has been working at it off and on for five months. When in doubt, I told him, he was to consult de Lisle. He never did so.'

'Where did he actually do this work? In his room?'

Bradfield barely hesitated. 'In Chancery Registry, where the most sensitive documents are kept. He had the run of the strong-room. He could draw whatever he wanted provided he didn't overplay his hand. There isn't even any record of what he did look at. There are also some letters missing; the Registrar will give you the details.'

Slowly Turner stood up, brushing his hands together as if they had sand on them.

'Of the forty-odd missing files, eighteen are drawn from the Personalities Survey and contain the most sensitive material on high-ranking German politicians. A careful reading would point clearly to our most delicate sources. The rest are Top Secret and cover Anglo-German agreements on a variety of subjects: secret treaties, secret codicils to published agreements. If he wished to embarrass us, he could hardly have chosen better. Some of the files go right back to forty-eight or nine.'

'And the one special file? "Conversations Formal and Informal"?'

'Is what we call a Green. It is subject to special procedures.'

'How many Greens are there in the Embassy?'

'This is the only one. It was in its place in Registry strong-room on Thursday morning. The Registrar noticed its absence on Thursday evening and assumed it was in operation. By Saturday morning he was deeply concerned. On Sunday he reported the loss to me.'

'Tell me,' said Turner at last. 'What happened to him during last year? What happened between the two Decembers? Apart from Karfeld.'

'Nothing specific.'

'Then why did you go off him?'

'I didn't,' Bradfield replied with contempt. 'Since I never had any feeling for him either way, the question does not arise. I merely learned during the intervening year to recognize his technique. I saw how he operated on people; how he wheedled his way in. I saw through him, that's all.'

Turner stared at him.

'And what did you see?'

Bradfield's voice was as crisp and as finite and as irreducible as a mathematical formula. 'Deceit. I'd have thought I had made that plain by now.'

Turner got up.

'I'll begin with his room.'

'The Chancery Guard has the keys. They're expecting you. Ask for Macmullen.'

'I want to see his house, his friends, his neighbours; if necessary I'll talk to his foreign contacts. I'll break whatever eggs I've got to, no more no less. If you don't like it, tell the Ambassador. Who's the Registrar?'

'Meadowes.'

'Arthur Meadowes?'

'I believe so.'

Something held him back: a reluctance, a hint of uncertainty, almost of dependence, a middle tone quite out of character with anything that had gone before.

'Meadowes was in Warsaw, wasn't he?'

'That's correct.'

Louder now: 'And Meadowes has a list of the missing files, has he?'

'And letters.'

'And Harting worked for him, of course.'

'Of course. He is expecting you to call on him.'

'I'll see his room first.' It was a resolution he seemed to have reached already.

'As you wish. You mentioned you would also visit his house—'

'Well?'

'I am afraid that at present it is not possible. It is under police protection since yesterday.'

'Is that general?'

'What?'

'The police protection?'

'Siebkron insists upon it. I cannot quarrel with him now.'

'It applies to all hirings?.

'Principally the more senior ones. I imagine they have included Harting's because it is remote.'

'You don't sound convinced.'

'I cannot think of any other reason.'

'What about Iron Curtain Embassies; did Harting hang around them at all?'

'He went to the Russians occasionally; I cannot say how often.'

'This man Praschko, the friend he had, the politician. You said he used to be a fellow traveller.'

'That was fifteen years ago.'

'And when did the assocation end?'

'It's on the file. About five years ago.'

'That's when he had the fight in Cologne. Perhaps it was with Praschko.'

'Anything is possible.'

'One more question.'

'Well?'

'That contract he had. If it had expired . . . say last Thursday?'

'Well?'

'Would you have renewed it? Again?'

'We are under great strain. Yes, I would have renewed it.'

'You must miss him.'

The door was opened from the outside by de Lisle. His gentle features were drawn and solemn.

'Ludwig Siebkron rang: the exchange had orders not to put through your calls. I spoke to him myself.'

'Well?'

'About the librarian, Eich: the wretched woman they beat up in Hanover.'

'About her?'

'I'm afraid she died an hour ago.'

Bradfield considered this intelligence in silence. 'Find out where the funeral is. The Ambassador must make a gesture; a telegram to the dependants rather than flowers. Nothing too conspicuous; just his deepest sympathy. Talk to them in Private Office, they'll know the wording. And something from the Anglo-German Society. You'd better handle that yourself. And send a cable to the Association of Assistant Librarians; they were enquiring about her. And ring Hazel will you, and tell her? She asked particularly to be kept informed.'

He was poised and perfectly in control. 'If you require anything,' he added to Turner, 'Tell de Lisle.'

Turner was watching him.

'Otherwise we shall expect you tomorrow night. About five to eight? Germans are very punctual. It is the local custom that we assemble before they arrive. And if you're going down to his room, perhaps you would take that cushion. I see no point in our having it up here.'

Albino Cork, stooped over the cypher machines while he coaxed the strips of print from the rollers, heard the thud and turned his pink eyes sharply towards the large figure in the doorway.

'That's my bag. Leave it where it is; I'll be in later.'

'Righty-ho,' said Cork and thought: a Funny. Just his luck, with the whole ruddy world blowing up in his face, and Janet's baby due any minute, and that poor woman in Hanover turning up her toes, to be landed with a Funny in the dayroom. This was not his only grudge. The German steel strike was spreading nicely; if he had only thought of it on Friday and not Saturday, that little flutter on Swedish steel would have shown a four-bob capital profit in three days; and five per cent per day, in Cork's losing battle with clerical status, was what villas in the Adriatic were made of. Top Secret, he read wearily, Personal for Bradfield and Decypher Yourself: how much longer will *that* go on? Capri . . . Crete . . . Spetsai . . . Elba . . . *Give me an island to myself*, he sang, in a high-pitched pop improvisation—for Cork had dreams of cutting his own discs as well—*Give me an Island to myself, Any Island, Any Island but Bonn.*

Chapter Five

John Gaunt

The crowd in the lobby had thinned. The Post Office clock above the sealed lift said ten thirty-five; those who dared not risk a trip to the canteen had gathered at the front desk; the Chancery Guard had made mid-morning tea, and they were drinking it and talking in subdued voices when they heard his approaching footsteps. His heels had metal quarters and they echoed against the pseudo-marble walls like shots on a valley range. The despatch riders, with that nose for authority which soldiers have, gently set down their cups and fastened the buttons of their tunics.

'Macmullen?'

He stood on the lowest step, one hand propped massively on the banister, the other clutching the embroidered cushion. To either side of him, corridors, haunted with iron riot grilles and free-standing pillars of chrome, led into the dark like ghettos from a splendid city. The silence was suddenly important, making a fool of all that had gone before.

'Macmullen's off duty, sir. Gone down to Naafi.'

'Who are you?'

'Gaunt, sir. I'm standing in for him.'

'My name's Turner. I'm checking physical security. I want to see Room Twenty-one.'

Gaunt was a small man, a devout Welshman, with a long memory of the Depression inherited from his father. He had come to Bonn from Cardiff, where he had driven motor-cars for the police. He carried the keys in his right hand, low down by his side, and his gait was square and rather solemn, so that as he preceded Turner into the dark mouth of the corridor, he resembled a miner making for the pithead.

'Shocking really, all what they've been up to,' Gaunt chanted, talking ahead of him and letting the sound carry backwards. 'Peter Aldock, he's my stringer see, he's got a brother in Hanover, used to be with the Occupation, married a German girl and opened a grocer's shop. Terrified he was for sure: well, he says, they all know my George is English. What'll happen to *him*? Worse than the Congo. Hullo there, Padre!'

The Chaplain sat at a portable typewriter in a small white cell opposite the telephone exchange, beneath a picture of his wife, his door wide open for confession. A rush cross was tucked behind the cord. 'Good morning John then,' he replied in a slightly reproving tone which recalled for both of them the granite intractability of their Welsh God; and Gaunt said, 'Hullo there' again but did not alter his pace. From all around them came the unmistakable sounds of a multi-lingual community: the lonely German drone of the Head Press Reader dictating a translation; the bark of the travel clerk shouting into the telephone; the distant whistling, tuneful and un-English, that seemed to come from everywhere, piped in from other corridors. Turner caught the smell of salami and second breakfasts, of newsprint and disinfectant and he thought: all change at Zurich, you're abroad at last.

'It's mainly the locally-employed down here,' Gaunt explained above the din, 'They aren't allowed no higher, being German.' His sympathy for foreigners was felt but controlled: a nurse's sympathy, tempered by vocation.

A door opened to their left; a shaft of white light broke suddenly upon them, catching the poor plaster of the walls and the tattered green of a bilingual noticeboard. Two girls, about to emerge from Information Registry, drew back to let them by and Turner looked them over mechanically, thinking: This was his world. Second class and foreign. One carried a thermos, the other laboured under a stack of files. Beyond them, through an outer window protected with jeweller's screens, he glimpsed the car park and heard the roar of a motor-bike as a despatch rider drove off. Gaunt had ducked away to the right, down another passage; he stopped, and they were at the door, Gaunt fumbling with the key and Turner staring over his shoulder at the notice which hung from the centre panel: 'Harting Leo, Claims and Consular', a sudden witness to the living man, or a sudden monument to the dead.

The characters of the first two words were a good two inches high,

ruled at the edges and cross-hatched in red and green crayon; the
word 'Consular' was done a good deal larger, and the letters were
outlined in ink to give them that extra substance which the title
evidently demanded. Stooping, Turner lightly touched the surface;
it was paper mounted on hardboard, and even by that poor light he
could make out the faint ruled lines of pencil dictating the upper and
lower limits of each letter; defining the borders of a modest existence
perhaps; or of a life unnaturally curtailed by deceit. 'Deceit. I'd have
thought I'd have made that plain by now.'

'Hurry,' he said.

Gaunt unlocked the door. As Turner seized the handle and shoved
it open, he heard his sister's voice on the telephone again and his own
reply as he slammed down the receiver: 'Tell her I've left the
country.' The windows were closed. The heat struck up at them
from the linoleum. There was a stink of rubber and wax. One curtain
was slightly drawn. Gaunt reached out to pull it back.

'Leave it. Keep away from the window. And stay there. If anyone
comes, tell them to get out.' He tossed the embroidered cushion on to
a chair and peered round the room.

The desk had chrome handles; it was better than Bradfield's desk.
The calendar on the wall advertised a firm of Dutch diplomatic
importers. Turner moved very lightly, for all his bulk, examining
but never touching. An old army map hung on the wall, divided into
the original zones of military occupation. The British was marked in
bright green, a fertile patch among the foreign deserts. It's like a
prison cell, he thought, maximum security; maybe it's just the bars.
What a place to break out of, and who wouldn't? The smell was
foreign but he couldn't place it.

'Well, I *am* surprised,' Gaunt was saying. 'There's a lot gone I
must say.'

Turner did not look at him.

'Such as what?'

'I don't know. Gadgets, All sorts. This is Mr Harting's room,' he
explained. 'Very gadget-minded, Mr Harting is.'

'What sort of gadgets?'

'Well he had a *tea* machine, you know the kind that wakes you up?
Made a lovely cup of tea, that did. Pity that's gone, really.'

'What else?'

'A fire. The new fan type with the two bars over. And a lamp. A
smashing one, Japanese. Go all directions, that lamp would. Turn it
half-way and it burned *soft*. Very cheap to run as well, he told me.
But I wouldn't have one, you know, not now they've cut the
allowances. Still,' he continued consolingly, 'I expect he's taken
them home, don't you, if that's where he's gone.'

'Yes. Yes, I expect he has.'

On the window-sill stood a transistor radio. Stooping until his eyes were on a level with the panel, Turner switched it on. At once they heard the mawkish tones of a British Forces announcer commenting on the Hanover riots and the prospects for a British victory in Brussels. Slowly Turner rolled the tuning needle along the lighted band, his ear cocked all the time to the changing babel of French, German and Dutch.

'I thought you said physical security.'

'I did.'

'You haven't hardly looked at the windows. Or the locks.'

'I will, I will.' He had found a Slav voice and he was listening with deep concentration. 'Know him well, did you? Come in here often for a cup?'

'Quite. Depends on how busy, really.'

Switching off the radio, Turner stood up. 'Wait outside,' he said. 'And give me the keys.'

'What's he done then?' Gaunt demanded, hesitating. 'What's gone wrong?'

'Done? Nothing. He's on compassionate leave. I want to be alone, that's all.'

'They say he's in trouble.'

'Who?'

'Talkers.'

'What sort of trouble?'

'I don't know. Car smash maybe. He wasn't at choir practice, see. Nor Chapel.'

'Does he drive badly?'

'Can't say really.'

Part defiant, part curious, Gaunt stayed by the door, watching as Turner pulled open the wooden wardrobe and peered inside. Three hair-dryers, still in their boxes, lay on the floor beside a pair of rubber overshoes.

'You're a friend of his, aren't you?'

'Not really. Only from choir, see.'

'Ah,' said Turner, staring at him now. 'You sang for him. I used to sing in choir myself.'

'Oh really now, where's that then?'

'Yorkshire,' Turner said with awful friendliness, while his pale gaze continued to fix upon Gaunt's plain face. 'I hear he's a lovely organist.'

'Not at all bad, I will say,' Gaunt agreed, rashly recognizing a common interest.

'Who's his *special* friend; someone else in the choir, was it? A lady perhaps?' Turner enquired, still not far from piety.

'He's not close to anyone, Leo.'

'Then who does he buy these for?'

The hair-dryers were of varying quality and complexity; the prices on the box ran from eighty to two hundred marks. 'Who for?' he repeated.

'All of us. Dips, non dips; it didn't signify. He runs a service see; works the diplomatic discounts. Always do you a favour Leo will. Don't matter what you fancy: radios, dishwashers, cars; he'll get you a bit off, like; you know.'

'Knows his way round, does he?'

'That's right.'

'Takes a cut too, I expect. For his trouble,' Turner suggested coaxingly. 'Quite right too.'

'I didn't say so.'

'Do you a girl as well, would he? Mister Fixit, is that it?'

'Certainly not,' said Gaunt, much shocked.

'What was in it for him?'

'Nothing. Not that I know of.'

'Just a little friend of all the world, eh? Likes to be liked. Is that it?'

'Well, we all do really, don't we?'

'Philosopher, are we?'

'Always *willing*,' Gaunt continued, very slow to follow the changes in Turner's mood. 'You ask Arthur Meadowes now, there's an example. The moment Leo's in Registry, not hardly a day after, he's down here collecting the mail. "Don't you bother," he says to Arthur. "Save your legs, you're not so young as you were and you've plenty to worry about already. I'll fetch it for you, look." That's Leo. Obliging, Saintly really, considering his disadvantages.'

'What mail?'

'Everything. Classified or Unclassified, it didn't make no difference. He'd be down here signing for it, taking it up to Arthur.'

Very still, Turner said, 'Yes, I see that. And maybe he'd drop in here on the way, would he? Check on his own room; brew up a cup of tea.'

'That's it,' said Gaunt, 'Always ready to oblige.' He opened the door. 'Well, I'll be leaving you to it.'

'You stay here,' said Turner, still watching him. 'You'll be all right. You stay and talk to me, Gaunt. I like company. Tell me about his disadvantages.'

Returning the hair-dryers to their boxes, he pulled out a linen jacket, still on its hanger. A summer jacket; the kind that barmen wear. A dead rose hung from the buttonhole.

'What disadvantages?' he asked, throwing the rose into the waste bag. 'You can tell me, Gaunt,' and he noticed the smell again, the wardrobe smell he had caught but not defined, the sweet, familiar, continental smell of male unguents and cigar.

'Only his childhood, that's all. He had an uncle.'

'Tell me about the uncle.'

'Nothing; only how he was daft. Always changing politics. He had a lovely way of narrative, Leo did. Told us how he used to sit down in the cellar in Hampstead with his uncle while the bombs were falling, making pills in a machine. Dried fruit. Squashed them all up and rolled them in sugar, then put them in the tins, see. Used to spit on them, Leo did, just to spite his uncle. My wife was very shocked when she heard that–I said don't be silly, that's deprivation. He hasn't had the love, see, not what you've had.'

Having felt the pockets, Turner cautiously detached the jacket from the hanger and held the shoulders against his own substantial frame.

'Little bloke?'

'He's a keen dresser,' said Gaunt, 'Always well turned out, Leo is.'

'Your size?'

Turner held the jacket towards him, but Gaunt drew back in distaste.

'Smaller,' he said, his eyes still on the jacket. 'More the dancer type. Butterfly. You'd think he wore pumps all the time.'

'Pansy?'

'Certainly not,' said Gaunt, very shocked again, and colouring at the notion.

'How do you know?'

'He's a decent fellow, that's why,' said Gaunt, fiercely. 'Even if he has done something wrong.'

'Pious?'

'Respectful, very. And about religion. Never cheeky or brash, although he was foreign.'

'What else did he say about his uncle?'

'Nothing.'

'What else about his politics?' He was looking at the desk, examining the locks on the drawers.

Tossing the jacket on to a chair, he held out his hand for the keys. Reluctantly Gaunt released them.

'Nothing. I don't know nothing about his politics.'

'Who says anything about him doing something wrong?'

'You. All this hunting him. Measuring him; I don't fancy it.'

'What would he have done, I wonder? To make me hunt him like this?'

'God only knows.'

'In his wisdom.' He had opened the top drawers. 'Have you got a diary like this?'

It was bound in blue rexine and stamped in gold with the Royal crest.

'No.'

'Poor Gaunt. Too humble?' He was turning the pages, working back. Once he stopped and frowned; once he wrote something in his black notebook.

'It was Counsellors and above, that's why,' Gaunt retorted. 'I wouldn't accept it.'

'He offered you one, did he? That was another of his fiddles, I suppose. What happened? He scrounged a bundle did he, from Registry, and handed them out to his old chums on the Ground Floor. "Here you are boys: the streets are paved with gold up there. Here's a keepsake from your old winger." Is that the way of it, Gaunt? And Christian virtue held you back, did it?' Closing the diary, he pulled open the lower drawers.

'What if he did? You've no call to go rifling through his desk there, have you? Not for a little thing like that! Pinching a handful of diaries; well that's hardly all the world, is it?' His Welsh accent had jumped all the hurdles and was running free.

'You're a Christian man, Gaunt. You know how the devil works better than I do. Little things lead to big things, don't they? Pinch an apple one day, you'll be hi-jacking a lorry the next. *You* know the way it goes, Gaunt. What else did he tell you about himself? Any more little childhood reminiscences?'

He had found a paper knife, a slim, silver affair with a broad, flat handle, and he was reading the engraving by the desk lamp.

'L. H. from Margaret. Now who was Margaret, I wonder?'

'I never heard of her.'

'He was engaged to be married once, did you know that?'

'No.'

'Miss Aickman. Margaret Aickman. Ring a bell?'

'No.'

'How about the Army. Did he tell you about that?'

'He loved the Army. In Berlin, he said, he used to watch the cavalry going over the jumps. He loved it.'

'He was in the infantry, was he?'

'I don't really know.'

'No.'

Turner had put the knife aside, next to the blue diary, made another note in his pocket-book and picked up a small flat tin of Dutch cigars.

'Smoker?'

'He liked a cigar. Yes. That's all he smoked, see. Always *carried* cigarettes mind. But I only ever saw him smoke those things. There was one or two in Chancery complained, so I hear. About the cigars. Didn't fancy them. But Leo could be stubborn when he had the mind, I will say.'

'How long have you been here, Gaunt?'

'Five years.'

'He was in a fight in Cologne. That in your time?'

Gaunt hesitated.

'Amazing the way things are hushed up here, I must say. You give a new meaning to the "need to know", you do. Everyone knows except the people who need to. What happened?'

'It was just a fight. They say he asked for it, that's all.'

'How?'

'I don't know. They say he deserved it, see. I heard from my predecessor: they brought him back one night, you couldn't hardly recognize him, that's what he said. Serve him right, he said; that's what they told him. Mind you, he could be pugnacious, I'm not denying it.'

'Who? Who told him?'

'I don't know. I didn't ask. That would be prying.'

'Often fighting, is he?'

'No.'

'Was there a woman involved? Margaret Aickman perhaps?'

'I don't know.'

'Then why's he pugnacious?'

'I don't know,' Gaunt said, torn once more between suspicion and a native passion for communication. 'Why are you then for that matter?' he muttered, venturing aggression, but Turner ignored him.

'That's right. Never pry. Never tell on a friend. God wouldn't like it. I admire a man who sticks to his principles.'

'I don't care what he's done,' Gaunt continued, gathering courage as he went. 'He wasn't a bad man. He was a bit sharp maybe, but so he would be, being continental, we all know that.' He pointed to the desk and the open drawers. 'But he wasn't bad like this.'

'No one is. Know that? No one's ever this bad. That's what mercy's about. We're all lovely people, really. There's a hymn about that, isn't there? One of the hymns he used to play, and you and I used to sing, Gaunt, before we grew up and got elegant. That's a lovely thing about hymns: we never forget them, do we. Like limericks. God knew a thing or two when he invented rhyme I will say. What did he learn when he was a kid, tell me that? What did Leo learn on his uncle's knee, eh?'

'He could speak Italian,' Gaunt said suddenly, as if it were a trump card he had been holding back.

'He could, could he?'

'And he learnt it in England. At the Farm School. The other kids wouldn't speak to him, see, him being German, so he used to go out on a bicycle and talk to the Italian prisoners of war. And he's never forgotten it, never. He's got a lovely memory, I tell you. Never forgets a word you say to him, I'm sure.'

'Wonderful.'

'A real brain he could have been, if he'd had your advantages.'

Turner looked at him blankly. 'Who the hell says I've got any advantages?'

He had opened another drawer; it was filled with the small junk of any private life in any office: a stapler, pencils, elastic bands, foreign coins and used railway tickets.

'How often was choir, Gaunt? Once a week, was it? You'd have a nice sing-song and a prayer and afterwards you'd slip out and have a beer down the road, and he'd tell you all about himself. Then there was outings, I suppose. Coach trips, I expect. That's what we like, isn't it, you and I? Something corporate but spiritual. Coaches, institutions, choirs. And Leo came along, did he? Got to know everyone, hear their little confidences, hold their little hands. Quite the entertainer he must have been by the sound of it.'

All the while they spoke, he continued to record items in his notebook: sewing materials, a packet of needles, pills of different colours and descriptions. Fascinated despite himself, Gaunt drew nearer.

'Well not only that, see. Only I live on the top floor, there's a flat up there: it should have been Macmullen's but he can't occupy, him having too many children, they couldn't have *them* running wild up there now, could they? We practised in the Assembly Room first, Fridays, see, that's on the other side of the lobby next to the pay office, and then he'd come on up after, for a cup of tea, like. Well, you know, I had a few cups here too for that matter; quite a joy to pay back it was, after all he done for us; things he brought for us and that. He loved a cup of tea,' said Gaunt simply. 'He loved a fire too. I always had that feeling, he loved a family, him not having one.'

'He told you that, did he? He told you he'd no family?'

'No.'

'Then how do you know?'

'It was too evident to be talked about, really. He'd no education either; dragged up really, you could tell.'

Turner had found a bottle of long yellow pills and he was shaking them into the palm of his hand, sniffing cautiously at them.

'And that's been going on for years, has it? Cosy chats after practice?'

'Oh no. He didn't hardly notice me really, not till a few months ago and I didn't like to press him at all, him being a dip, see. It's only recently he took the interest. Same as Exiles.'

'Exiles?'

'Motoring Club.'

'How recent? When did he take you up?'

'New Year,' Gaunt said, now very puzzled. 'Yes. Since January I'd say. He seems to have had a change of heart since January.'

'This January?'

'That's right,' Gaunt said, as if he were seeing it for the first time. 'Late January. Since he started with Arthur, really. Arthur's had a *great* influence on Leo. Made him more *contemplative*, you know.

More the meditating kind. A great improvement, I'd say. And my wife agrees, you know.'

'I'll bet. How else did he change?'

'That's it really. More reflective.'

'Since January when he took you up. Bang: in comes the New Year and Leo's reflective.'

'Well, steadier. Like he was ill. We did wonder, you know. I said to my wife'—Gaunt lowered his voice in reverence at the notion—'I wouldn't be surprised if the doctor hadn't warned him.'

Turner was looking at the map again, first directly and then sideways, noting the pin-holes of vanished units. In an old bookcase lay a heap of census reports, press cuttings and magazines. Kneeling, he began working through them.

'What else did you talk about?'

'Nothing serious.'

'Just politics.'

'I like serious conversation myself,' Gaunt said. 'But I didn't somehow fancy it with him, you didn't quite know where it would end.'

'Lost his temper, did he?'

The cuttings referred to the Movement. The census reports concerned the rise of public support for Karfeld.

'He was too gentle. Like a woman in that way; you could disappoint him dreadfully; just a word would do it. Vulnerable he was. *And* quiet. That's what I did never understand about Cologne, see. I said to my wife, well I don't know I'm sure, but if Leo started that fight, it was the devil got hold of him. But he had *seen* a lot, hadn't he?'

Turner had come upon a photograph of students rioting in Berlin. Two boys were holding an old man by the arms and a third was slapping him with the back of his hand. His fingers were turned upwards, and the light divided the knuckles like a sculpture. A line had been drawn round the frame in red ball point.

'I mean you never knew when you were being *personal*, like.' Gaunt continued, 'Touching him too near. I used to think sometimes, I said to my wife as a matter of fact, she was never quite at home with him herself, I said, "Well, I wouldn't like to have his dreams."'

Turner stood up. 'What dreams?'

'Just dreams. Things he's seen, I suppose. They say he saw a lot, don't they? All the atrocities.'

'Who does?'

'Talkers. One of the drivers, I think. Marcus. He's gone now. He had a turn with him up there in Hamburg in forty-six or that. Shocking.'

Turner had opened an old copy of *Stern* which lay on the

bookcase. Large photographs of the Bremen riots covered both pages. There was a picture of Karfeld speaking from a high wooden platform; young men shouted in ecstasy.

'I think that bothered him you know,' Gaunt continued, looking over his shoulder. 'He spoke a lot about Fascism off and on.'

'Did he though?' Turner asked softly, 'Tell us about that, Gaunt. I'm interested in talk like that.'

'Well, just sometimes.' Gaunt sounded nervous. 'He could get very worked up about that. It could happen again, he said, and the West would just stand by; and the bankers all put in a bit, and that would be it. He said Socialist and Conservative, it didn't have no meaning any more, not when all the decisions were made in Zurich or Washington. You could see that, he said, from recent events. Well it was true really, I had to admit.'

For a moment, the whole sound-track stopped: the traffic, the machines, the voices, and Turner heard nothing but the beating of his own heart.

'What was the remedy then?' he asked softly.

'He didn't have one.'

'Personal action for instance?'

'He didn't say so.'

'God?'

'No, he wasn't a believer. Not truly, in his heart.'

'Conscience?'

'I told you. He didn't say.'

'He never suggested you might put the balance right? You and he together?'

'He wasn't *like* that,' Gaunt said impatiently. 'He didn't fancy company. Not when it came to . . . well, to his own *matters*, see.'

'Why didn't your wife fancy him?'

Gaunt hesitated.

'She liked to keep close to me when he was around, that's all. Nothing he ever said or did, mind, but she just liked to keep close.' He smiled indulgently. 'You know how they are,' he said. 'Very *natural*.'

'Did he stay long? Did he sit and talk for hours at a time? About nothing? Ogling your wife?'

'Don't say that,' Gaunt snapped.

Abandoning the desk, Turner opened the cupboard again and noted the printed number on the soles of the rubber overshoes.

'Besides he didn't stay long. He liked to go off and work night times, didn't he? Recently I mean. In Registry and that. He said to me: "John," he said, "I like to make my contribution." And he did. He was proud of his work these last months. It was beautiful; wonderful to see, really. Work half the night sometimes, wouldn't he? All night, even.'

Turner's pale, pale eyes rested on Gaunt's dark face.

'Would he?'

He dropped the shoes back into the cupboard and they clattered absurdly in the silence.

'Well he'd a lot to do, you know; a great lot. Loaded with responsibilities, Leo is. A fine man, really. Too good for this floor; that's what I say.'

'And that's what happened every Friday night since January. After choir. He'd come up and have a nice cup of tea and a chat, hang about till the place was quiet, then slip off and work in Registry?'

'Regular as clockwork. Come in prepared, he would. Choir practice first, then up for a cup of tea till the rest had cleared out like, then down to Registry. "John," he'd say. "I can't work when there's bustle, I can't stand it, I love peace and quiet to be truthful. I'm not as young as I was and that's a fact." Had a bag with him, all ready. Thermos, maybe a sandwich. Very efficient man, he was; handy.'

'Sign the night book, did he?'

Gaunt faltered, waking at long last to the full menace in that quiet, destructive monotone. Turner slammed together the wooden doors of the cupboard. 'Or didn't you bloody well bother? Well, not right really is it? You can't come over all official, not to a guest. A dip too, at that, a dip who graced your parlour. Let him come and go as he pleased in the middle of the bloody night, didn't you? Wouldn't have been respectful to check up at all, would it? One of the family really, wasn't he? Pity to spoil it with formalities. Wouldn't be Christian, that wouldn't. No idea what time he left the building, I suppose? Two o'clock, four o'clock?'

Gaunt had to keep very still to catch the words, they were to softly spoken.

'It's nothing *bad*, is it?' he asked.

'And that bag of his,' Turner continued in the same terribly low key. 'It wouldn't have been proper to look inside, I suppose? Open the thermos, for instance. The Lord wouldn't fancy that, would he? Don't you worry, Gaunt, it's nothing bad. Nothing that a prayer and a cup of tea won't cure.' He was at the door and Gaunt had to watch him. 'You were just playing happy families, weren't you; letting him stroke your leg to make you feel good.' His voice picked up the Welsh intonation and lampooned it cruelly. "Look how virtuous we are . . . How much in love. . . . Look how grand, having the dips in. . . . Salt of the earth, we are. . . . Always something on the hod. . . . And sorry you can't have her, but that's my privilege." Well, you've bought it, Gaunt, the whole book. A guard they called you: he'd have charmed you into bed for half-a-crown.' He pushed open the door. 'He's on compassionate leave, and don't you forget it or you'll be in hotter water than you are already.'

'That may be the world you've come from,' Gaunt said suddenly, staring at him as if in revelation, 'But it isn't mine, Mr Turner, so don't come taking it out on me, see. I did my best by Leo and I would again, and I don't know what's all twisted in your mind. Poison, that's what it is: poison.'

'Go to hell.' Turner tossed him the keys, and Gaunt let them fall at his feet.

'If there's something else you know about him, some other gorgeous bit of gossip, you'd better tell me now. Fast. Well?'

Gaunt shook his head. 'Go away.'

'What else do the talkers say? A bit of fluff in the choir was there, Gaunt? You can tell me, I won't eat you.'

'I never heard.'

'What did Bradfield think of him?'

'How should I know? Ask Bradfield.'

'Did he like him?'

Gaunt's face had darkened with disapproval.

'I've no occasion to say,' he snapped. 'I don't gossip about my superiors.'

'Who's Praschko? Praschko a name to you?'

'There's nothing else. I don't know.'

Turner pointed at the small pile of Leo's possessions on the desk. 'Take those up to the cypher room. I'll need them later. And the press cuttings. Give them to the clerk and make him sign for them, understand? Whether you fancy him or not. And make a list of everything that's missing. Everything he's taken home.'

He did not go immediately to Meadowes, but went outside and stood on the grass verge beside the car park. A veil of mist hung over the barren field and the traffic stormed like an angry sea. The Red Cross building was dark with scaffolding and capped by an orange crane: an oil rig anchored to the tarmac. The policemen watched him curiously, for he remained quite still and his eyes seemed to be trained upon the horizon, though the horizon was obscure. At last—it might have been in response to a command they did not hear—he turned and walked slowly back to the front steps.

'You ought to get a proper pass,' the weasel-faced sergeant said, 'Coming in and out all day.'

Registry smelt of dust and sealing wax and printer's ink. Meadowes was waiting for him. He looked haggard and deeply tired. He did not move as Turner came towards him, pushing his way between the desks and files, but watched him dully and with contempt.

'Why did they have to send you?' he asked. 'Haven't they got anyone else? Who are you going to wreck this time?'

Chapter Six

The Memory Man

They stood in a small sanctum, a steel-lined tank which served both as a strong-room and an office. The windows were barred twice over, once with fine mesh and once with steel rods. From the adjoining room came the constant shuffle of feet and paper. Meadowes wore a black suit. The edges of the lapels were studded with pins. Steel lockers like sentinels stood along the walls, each with a stencilled number and a combination lock.

'Of all the people I swore I'd never see again—'

'Turner was at the top of the list. All right. All right, you're not the only one. Let's get it over, shall we?'

They sat down.

'She doesn't know you're here,' said Meadowes. 'I'm not going to tell her you're here.'

'All right.'

'He met her a few times; there was nothing between them.'

'I'll keep away from her.'

'Yes,' said Meadowes. He did not speak to Turner, but past him, at the lockers. 'Yes, you must.'

'Try and forget it's me,' Turner said. 'Take your time.' For a moment his expression seemed to yield, as the shadows formed upon his plain complexion, until in its way his face was as old as Meadowes', and as weary.

'I'll tell it you once,' Meadowes said, 'And that's all. I'll tell you all I know, and then you clear out.'

Turner nodded.

'It began with the Exiles Motoring Club,' Meadowes said. 'That's how I met him really. I like cars, always have done. I'd brought a Rover, Three Litre, for retirement—'

'How long have you been here?'

'A year. Yes, a year now.'

'Straight from Warsaw?'

'We did a spell in London in between. Then they sent me here. I was fifty-eight. I'd two more years to run and after Warsaw I reckoned I'd take things quietly. I wanted to look after her, get her right again—'

'All right.'

'I don't go out much as a rule but I joined this club, UK and Commonwealth it is mainly, but decent. I reckoned that would do us nicely: one evening a week, the rallies in the summer, get-togethers in the winter. I could take Myra, see; get her back into things, keep an eye on her. She wanted that herself, in the beginning. She was lost; she wanted company. I'm all she's got.'

'All right,' Turner said.

'They were a good lot when we joined, though it's like any other club, of course, it goes up and down; depends who runs it. Get a good crowd in and you have a lot of fun; get a bad crowd, there's jiving and all the rest.'

'And Harting was big there, was he?'

'You let me go at my own speed, right?' Meadowes' manner was firm and disapproving: a father corrects his son. 'No. He was not big there, not at that time. He was a member there, that's all, just a member. I shouldn't think he showed up, not once in six meetings. Well he didn't *belong* really. After all he was a diplomat, and the Exiles isn't meant for dips. Mid-November, we have the Annual General Meeting. Haven't you got your black notebook then?'

'November,' Turner said, not moving, 'The AGM. Five months ago.'

'It was a funny sort of do really. Funny atmosphere. Karfeld had been on the go about six weeks and we were all wondering what would happen next, I think. Freddie Luxton was in the chair and he was just off to Nairobi; Bill Aintree was Social Secretary and they'd warned him for Korea, and the rest of us were in a flutter trying to elect new officers, get through the agenda and fix up the winter outing. That's when Leo pipes up, and in a way that was his first step into Registry.'

Meadowes fell silent. 'I don't know what kind of fool I am,' he said. 'I just don't know.'

Turner waited.

'I tell you: we'd never *heard* of him, not really, not as somebody keen on the Exiles. And he had this reputation you see—'

'What reputation?'

'Well, they said he was a bit of a gypsy. Always on the fiddle. There was some story about Cologne. I didn't fancy what I'd heard, to be frank, and I didn't want him mixed up with Myra.'

'What story about Cologne?'

'Hearsay, that's all it is. He was in a fight. A night-club brawl.'

'No details?'

'None.'

'Who else was there?'

'I've no idea. Where was I?'

'The Exiles, AGM.'

'The winter outing. Yes. "Right," says Bill Aintree. "Any suggestions from the floor?" And Leo's on his feet straight away. He was about three chairs down from me. I said to Myra: "Here, what's *he* up to?" Well, Leo had a proposal, he said. For the winter outing. He knew an old man in Königswinter who owned a string of barges, very rich and very fond of the English, he said; quite high in the Anglo-German. And this old fellow had agreed to lend us two barges and two crews to run the whole club up to Koblenz and back. As some kind of *quid pro quo* for a favour the British had done him in the Occupation. Leo always knew people like that,' said Meadowes; and a brief smile of affection illuminated the sadness of his features. 'There'd be covered accommodation, rum and coffee on the way and a big lunch when we got to Koblenz. Leo had worked the whole thing out; he reckoned he could lay it on at twenty-one marks eighty a head including drinks and a present for his friend.' He broke off. 'I can't go any quicker, it's not my way.'

'I didn't say anything.'

'You're pressing all the time, I can feel it,' Meadowes said querulously, and sighed. 'They fell for it, we all did, Committee or not. You know what people are like: if one man knows what he wants . . .'

'And he did.'

'I suppose some reckoned he'd got an axe to grind, but no one cared. There was a few of us thought he was taking a cut to be honest, but well, maybe he deserved it. And the price was fair enough any time. Bill Aintree was getting out: *he* didn't care; he proposed it. Freddie Luxton was already packed: *he* didn't care. He seconded. The motion's carried and recorded without a word being said against, and as soon as the meeting's over, Leo comes straight across to me and Myra, smiling his head off. "She'll love that," he says, "Myra will. A nice trip on the river. Take her out of herself." Just as if he'd done it specially for her. I said yes, she would, and bought him a drink. It seemed wrong really, him doing so much and no one else paying him a blind bit of notice, whatever they say about him. I was sorry for him. *And* grateful,' he added simply. 'I still am: we had a lovely outing.'

Again he fell silent, and again Turner waited while the older man wrestled with private conflicts and private perplexities. From the barred window came the tireless throb of Bonn's iron heartbeat: the far thunder of drills and cranes, the moan of vainly galloping cars.

'I thought he was after Myra to be honest,' he said at last. 'I watched out for that, I don't mind admitting. But there wasn't a breath of it, not on either side. Goodness knows, I'm sharp enough on *that* after Warsaw.'

'I believe you.'

'I don't care whether you believe me or not. It's the truth.'

'He had a reputation for that as well, did he?'

'A bit.'

'Who with?'

'I'll go on with the story if you don't mind,' Meadowes said, looking at his hands. 'I'm not going to pass on that kind of muck. Least of all to you. There's more nonsense talked in this place than is good for any of us.'

'I'll find out,' Turner said, his face frozen like a dead man's. 'It'll take me longer, but that needn't worry you.'

'Dreadfully cold, it was,' Meadowes continued. 'Lumps of ice on the water, and beautiful, if that means anything to you. Just like Leo said: rum and coffee for the grown-ups, cocoa for the kids, and everyone happy as a cricket. We started from Königswinter and kicked off with a drink at his place before we went aboard, and from the moment we get there, Leo's looking after us. Me and Myra. He'd singled us out and that was it. We might have been the only people there for him. Myra loved it. He put a shawl round her shoulders, told her jokes. . . . I hadn't seen her laugh like it since Warsaw. She kept saying to me: "I haven't been so happy for years."'

'What sort of jokes?'

'About himself mainly . . . running on. He had a story about Berlin, him shoving a cartload of files across the parade ground in the middle of a cavalry practice, and the sergeant-major on his horse, and Leo down there with the handcart. . . . He could do all the voices, Leo could; one minute he was up on his horse, the next minute he's the Guard corporal. . . . He could even do the trumpets and that. Wonderful really; wonderful gift. Very entertaining man, Leo . . . very.'

He glanced at Turner as if he expected to be contradicted, but Turner's face was without expression. 'On the way back, he takes me aside. "Arthur, a quiet word," he says; that's him, a quiet word. You know the way he talks.'

'No.'

'Confiding. Everyone's special. "Arthur," he says, "Rawley Bradfield's just sent for me; they want me to move up to Registry and give you a hand up there, and before I tell him yes or no, I'd like to hear what *you* feel." Putting it in my hands, you see. If I didn't fancy the idea, he'd head it off; that's what he was hinting at. Well it came as a surprise, I don't mind telling you. I didn't quite know what to think; after all he was a Second Secretary . . . it didn't seem right, that was my first reaction. And to be frank I wasn't sure I believed him. So I asked him: "Have you any experience of archives?" Yes, but long ago, he said, though he'd always fancied going back to them.'

'When was that then?'

'When was what?'

'When was he dealing with archives?'

'Berlin I suppose. I never asked. You didn't ask Leo about his background really; you never knew what you might hear.'

Meadowes shook his head. 'So here he was with this suggestion. It didn't seem right, but what could I say? "It's up to Bradfield," I told him. "If he sends you, and you want to come, there's work enough." Well it worried me for a bit to be honest. I even thought of talking to Bradfield about it but I didn't. Best thing is, I thought, let it blow over; I'll probably hear no more of it. For a time that's just what happened. Myra was bad again, there was the leadership crisis at home and the gold row in Brussels. And as for Karfeld, he was going hammer and tongs all over the place. There were deputations out from England, Trade Union protests, old comrades and I don't know what. He was Social Secretary of the Exiles by then, but otherwise I hardly saw him. I mean he didn't rate. There was too much else to think of.'

'I get it.'

'The next thing I knew was, Bradfield sends for me. It was just before the holiday–about 20th December. First, he asks me how I'm getting along with the Destruction programme. I was a bit put out; we'd really been going it those last months. Destruction was about the last thing anyone had been bothering with.'

'Go carefully now: I want the fat as well as the lean.'

'I said it was hanging fire. Well, he says, how would I feel if he sent me someone to help out with it, come and work in Registry and bring it up to date? There'd been the suggestion, he said, nothing definite, and he wanted to sound me out first, there'd been the suggestion Harting might be able to lend a hand.'

'Whose suggestion?'

'He didn't say.'

It was suddenly upon them; and each in his way was mystified:

'Whoever suggested anything to Bradfield,' Meadowes asked. 'It makes no sense.'

'That's rather what I wondered,' Turner confessed, and the silence returned.

'So you said you'd have him?'

'No, I told him the truth. I said I didn't need him.'

'You didn't *need* him? You told Bradfield that?'

'Don't press me like that. Bradfield knew very well I didn't need anyone. Not for Destruction anyway. I'd been on to Library in London and spoken to them, back in November that was, once the Karfeld panic began. I'd told them I was worried about the programme, I was way behind, could I let it go till the crisis was over? Library told me to forget it.'

Turner stared at him.

'And Bradfield knew that? You're certain Bradfield knew?'

'I'd sent him a minute of the conversation. He never even referred to it. Afterwards I asked that PA of his and she was certain she'd put it up to him.'

'Where is it? Where's the minute now?'

'Gone. It was a loose minute: it was Bradfield's responsibility whether he preserved it or not. But they'll know about it in Library all right; they were quite surprised later on to find we'd bothered with Destruction at all.'

'Who did you speak to in Library?'

'Once to Maxwell, once to Cowdry.'

'Did you remind Bradfield of that?'

'I began to, but he just cut me off. Closed right down on me. "It's all arranged," he says. "Harting's joining you mid-January and he'll manage Personalities and Destruction." So lump it, in other words. "You can forget he's a diplomat," he said. "Treat him as your subordinate. Treat him how you like. But he's coming mid-January and that's a fact." You know how he throws people away. Specially Harting.'

Turner was writing in his notebook but Meadowes paid no attention.

'So that's how he came to me. That's the truth. I didn't want him, I didn't trust him, not completely anyway, and to begin with I suppose I let him know it. We were just too busy: *I* didn't want to waste time breaking in a man like Leo. What was I supposed to do with him?'

A girl brought tea. A brown woolly cosy covered the pot and the cubes of sugar were individually wrapped and stamped with the Naafi's insignia. Turner grinned at her but she ignored him. He could hear someone shouting about Hanover.

'They do say things are bad in England too,' Meadowes said. 'Violence; demonstrations; all the protests. What is it that gets into your generation? What have we *done* to you? That's what I don't understand.'

'We'll start with when he arrived,' Turner said. That's what it would be like, he thought, to have a father you believed in: values for their own sake and a gap as wide as the Atlantic.

'I said to Leo when he came, "Leo, just keep out of the way. Don't get between my feet, and don't go bothering other people." He took it like a lamb. 'Right-ho Arthur, whatever you say." I asked him whether he'd got something to get on with. Yes, he said, Personalities would keep him going for a bit.'

'It's like a dream,' Turner said softly looking up at last from his notebook. 'It's a lovely dream. First of all he takes over the Exiles. A one-man takeover, real Party tactics; I'll do the dirty work, you go back to sleep. Then he cons you, then he cons Bradfield, and within a couple of months he's got the pick of Registry. How was he? Cocky? I should think he could hardly stand up for laughing.'

'He was quiet. Not cocky at all. Subdued I'd say. Not at all what they told me he was like.'

'Who?'

'Oh . . . I don't know. There's a lot didn't like him; there's a lot more were jealous of him.'

'Jealous?'

'Well, he was a diplomat, wasn't he? Even if he was a temporary. They said he'd be running the place in a fortnight, taking ten per cent on the files. You know the way they talk. But he'd changed. They all admitted that, even young Cork and Johnny Slingo. You could almost date it, they said, from when the crisis began. It sobered him down.' Meadowes shook his head as if he hated to see a good man go wrong. 'And he was useful.'

'Don't tell me. He took you by surprise.'

'I don't know how he managed it. He knew nothing about archives, not our kind anyway; and I can't for the life of me see how he got near enough to anyone in Registry to ask; but by mid-February, that Personalities Survey was drafted, signed off and away, and the Destruction programme was back on the rails. We were working all round him: Karfeld, Brussels, the Coalition crisis and the rest of it. And there was Leo, still as a rock, working away at his own bits and pieces. No one told him anything twice, I think that was half the secret. He'd a lovely memory. He'd scrounge a bit of information, tuck it away, and bring it out weeks later when you'd forgotten all about it. I don't think he forgot a word anyone ever said to him. He could listen with his eyes, Leo could.' Meadowes shook his head at the reminiscence: 'The memory man, that's what Johnny Slingo used to call him.'

'Handy. For an archivist of course.'

'You see it all differently,' Meadowes said at last. 'You can't distinguish the good from the bad.'

'You tell me when I go wrong,' Turner replied, writing all the time. 'I'll be grateful for that. Very.'

'Destruction's a weird game,' Meadowes said, in the reflective tone of a man reviewing his own craft. 'To begin with, you'd think it was simple. You select a file, a big one, say a subject file with twenty-five volumes. I'll give you an example: *Disarmament*. There's a real rag-bag. You turn up the back numbers first to check the material, all right? So what do you find? Industrial dismantling in the Ruhr, 1946; Control Commission policy on the allocation of shotgun licences, 1949. Re-establishment of German military potential, 1950. Some of it's so old you'd laugh. You take a look at the current columns to compare, and what do you find? Warheads for the Bundeswehr. It's a million miles away. All right, you say, let's burn the back papers, they're irrelevant. There's fifteen volumes at least we can chuck out. Who's the desk officer for disarmament? Peter de Lisle: put it up to him: "Please may we destroy up to nineteen-sixty?" No objection, he says, so you're off.' Meadowes shook his head. 'Only you're not. You're not even half-way to off. You can't just carve off the back ten volumes and shove them in the fire. There's the ledger for a start: who's going to cancel all entries? There's the card index; that's got to be weeded. Were there treaties? Right: clear with legal department. Is there a military interest? Clear it with the MA. Are there duplicates in London? No. So we all sit back and wait another two months: no destruction of originals without written permission from Library. See what I mean?'

'I get the idea,' said Turner, waiting.

'Then there's all the cross references, the sister files in the same series: will *they* be affected? Should they be destroyed as well? Or should we make up residuals to be on the safe side? Before you know where you are, you're wandering all over Registry, looking in every nook and cranny; there's no end to it once you start; nothing's holy.'

'I should think it suited him down to the ground.'

'There's no *restriction*,' Meadowes observed simply, as if replying to a question. 'It may offend you, but it's the only system I can understand. Anyone can look at anything, that's my rule. Anyone sent up here, I trust them. There's no other way to run the place. I can't go sniffing round asking who's looking at what, can I?' he demanded, ignoring Turner's bewildered gaze.

'He took to it like a duck to water. I was amazed. He was happy, that was the first thing. It tickled him, working in here, and quite soon it tickled me having him. He liked the company.' He broke off. 'The only thing we ever *really* minded,' he said with an unexpected smile, 'was those ruddy cigars he smoked. Javanese Dutch I believe they were. Stank the place out. We used to tease him about them but he wouldn't budge. Still, I think I miss them now.' He continued quietly: 'He'd been out of his depth in Chancery, he's not their sort at all, and the ground floor didn't have much for him either in my opinion, but this place was just right.' He inclined his head towards the closed door. 'It's like a shop in there, sometimes: you have the customers and you have one another. Johnny Slingo, Valerie . . . well, they took to him too and that's all there is to it. They were all against him when he came, and they all took to him within a week, and that's the truth of it. He'd got a *way* with him. I know what you're thinking: it flattered my ego, I suppose you'd say. All right, it did. Everyone wants to be liked and he liked us. All right, I'm lonely; Myra's a worry, I've failed as a parent and I never had a son; there was a bit of that about it too, I suppose, although there's only ten years between us. Perhaps it's him being little that makes the difference.'

'Go for the girls, did he?' Turner asked, more to break the uncomfortable silence than because he had been preparing questions in his mind.

'Only banter.'

'Ever hear of a woman called Aickman?'

'No.'

'Margaret Aickman. They were engaged to be married, her and Leo.'

'No.'

Still they did not look at one another.

'He liked the work too,' Meadowes continued. 'In those first weeks. I don't think he'd ever realized till then how much he *knew* by comparison with the rest of us. About Germany, I mean, the *soil* of it.'

He broke off, remembering, and it might have been fifty years ago. 'He knew *that* world too,' he added. 'He knew it inside out.'

'What world?'

'Post-war Germany. The Occupation; the years they don't want to know about any more. He knew it like the back of his hand. "Arthur," he said to me once, "I've seen these towns when they were car parks. I've heard these people talk when even their language was forbidden." It used to knock him clean off course sometimes. I'd catch sight of him deep in a file, still as a mouse, just fascinated. Or he'd look away, look round the room, for someone with a moment to spare, just so he could tell them about something he'd come across: "Here," he'd say. "See that? We disbanded that firm in 1947. Look at it now!" Other times, he'd go right off into a dream, and then you'd lost him altogether; he was on his own. I think it bothered him to *know* so much. It was queer. I think he almost felt guilty sometimes. He went on quite a lot about his memory. 'You're making me destroy my childhood,' he says one time—we were breaking up some files for the machine—"You're making an old man of me." I said, "If that's what I'm doing you're the luckiest man alive." We had a good laugh about that.'

'Did he ever mention politics?'

'No.'

'What did he say about Karfeld?'

'He was concerned. Naturally. That's why he was so glad to be helping out.'

'Oh sure.'

'It was trust,' Meadowes said defiantly. 'You wouldn't understand that. And that was true, what he said: it *was* the old stuff we were trying to get rid of; it *was* his childhood; it *was* the old stuff that meant the most to him.'

'All right.'

'Listen: I'm not holding any brief for him. He's ruined my career for all I know, what there was left after you finished with it. But I'm telling you: you've got to see the *good* in him too.'

'I'm not arguing with you.'

'It did *bother* him, his memory. I remember once with the music: he got me listening to gramophone records. Mainly so that he could sell them to me, I suppose; he'd worked some deal he was very proud of, with one of the shops in town. "Look," I said. "It's no good Leo; you're wasting your time. I get to know one record so I learn another. By that time I've forgotten the first one." He comes right back at me, very fast: "Then you ought to be a politician, Arthur," he says. "That's what they do." He meant it, believe me.'

Turner grinned suddenly. 'That's quite funny.'

'It would have been,' said Meadowes, 'if he hadn't looked so darned fierce with it. Then another time we're talking about Berlin, something to do with the crisis, and I said, "Well never mind, no one thinks of Berlin any more," which is true really. Files I mean; no one draws the files or bothers with the contingencies; not like they used to, anyway. I mean *politically* it's a dead duck. "No," he says. "We've got the big memory and the small memory. The small memory's to remember the small things and the big memory's to forget the big ones." That's what he said; it touched me, that did. I mean there's a lot of us think that way, you can't help it these days.'

'He came home with you, did he, sometimes? You'd make an evening of it?'

'Now and then. When Myra was out. Sometimes I'd slip over there.'

'Why when Myra was out?' Turner pounced quite hard on that: 'You *still* didn't trust him did you?'

'There's rumours,' Meadowes said evenly. 'There was talk about him. I didn't want her connected.'

'Him and who?'

'Just girls. Girls in general. He was a bachelor and he liked his fun.'

'*Who*?'

Meadowes shook his head. 'You've got it wrong,' he said. He was playing with a couple of paper clips, trying to make them interlock.

'Did he ever talk about England in the war? About an uncle in Hampstead?'

'He told me once he arrived at Dover with a label round his neck. That wasn't usual either.'

'What wasn't—'

'Him talking about himself. Johnny Slingo said he'd known him four years before he came to Registry and he'd never got a word out of him. He was all opened up, that's what Johnny said, it must be old age setting in.'

'Go on.'

'Well that was all he had, a label: Harting Leo. They shaved his head and deloused him and sent him to a Farm School. He was allowed to choose apparently: domestic science or agriculture. He chose agriculture because he wanted to own land. It seemed daft to me, Leo wanting to be a farmer, but there it is.'

'Nothing about Communists? A left-wing group of kids in Hampstead? Nothing like that at all?'

'Nothing.'

'Would you tell me if there was something?'

'I doubt it.'

'Did he ever mention a man called Praschko? In the Bundestag.'

Meadowes hesitated. 'He said one night that Praschko had walked out on him.'

'How? Walked out *how*?'

'He wouldn't say. He said they'd emigrated to England together, and returned here together after the war; Praschko had chosen one path and Leo had chosen another.' He shrugged. 'I didn't press him. Why should I? After that night he never mentioned him again.'

'All that talk about his *memory*: what do you think he had in mind?'

'Something historical, I suppose. He thought a lot about history, Leo did. Mind you, that's a couple of months back now.'

'What difference does that make?'

'That was before he went on his track.'

'His what?'

'He went on a track,' Meadowes said simply. 'That's what I'm trying to tell you.'

'I want to hear about the missing files,' Turner said. 'I want to check the ledgers and the mail.'

'You'll wait your turn. There's some things that aren't just *facts*, and if you'll only pay attention you'll maybe hear about them. You're like Leo, you are: always wanting the answer before you've even heard the question. What I'm trying to tell you is, I knew from the day he came here that he was looking for something. We all did. You felt it with Leo. You felt he was looking for something. Well we all are in a way, but Leo was looking for something real. Something you could almost touch, it meant so much to him. That's rare in this place, believe me.'

It was a whole life which Meadowes seemed to draw upon.

'An archivist is like an historian; he has time-periods he's faddy about; places, Kings and Queens. All the files here are related, they're bound to be. Give me any file from next door; any file you want, I could trace you a path clean through the whole Registry, from Icelandic shipping rights to the latest guidance on gold prices. That's the fascination of files; there's nowhere to stop.'

Meadowes ran on. Turner studied the grey, parental face, the grey eyes clouded with concern, and he felt the dawning of excitement.

'You think you run an archive,' Meadowes said. 'You don't. It runs you. There's qualities to an archive that just get you, and there's not a thing you can do about it. Take Johnny Slingo now. You saw him as you came in, on the left there, the old fellow in the jacket. He's the intellectual type, college and all the rest. Johnny's only been at it a year, came to us from Admin as a matter of fact, but he's stuck with the nine-nine fours: Federal Germany's relations with Third Parties. He could sit where you are and recite the date and place of every single negotiation there's ever been about the Hallstein Doctrine. Or take my case, I'm mechanical. I like cars, inventions, all that world. I reckon I know more about German infringement of patent rights than any desk officer in Commercial Section.'

'What was Leo's track?'

'Wait. It's important what I'm telling. I've spent a lot of time thinking about it in the last twenty-four hours, and you're going to hear it *right*, whether you like it or not. The files get hold of you; you can't help it. They'd rule your life if you ever let them. They're wife and child to some men, I've seen it happen. And times they just *take* you, and then you're on a track and you can't get off it; and that's what they did to Leo. I don't know how it happens. A paper catches your eye, something silly: a threatened strike of sugar-workers in Surabaya, that's our favourite joke at the moment. "Hullo," you say to yourself, "Why hasn't Mr So-andSo signed that off?" You check back: Mr So-and-So never saw it. He never read the telegram at all. Well he must see it then, mustn't he? Only it all happened three years ago, and Mr So-and-So is Ambassador in Paris. So you start trying to find out what action was taken, or wasn't taken. Who was consulted? Why didn't they inform Washington? You chase the cross references, draw the original material. By then it's too late; you've lost your sense of proportion; you're away, and by the time you shake yourself out of it you're ten days older and none the wiser, but maybe you're safe again for a couple of years. Obsession, that's what it is. A private journey. It happens to all of us. It's the way we're made.'

'And it happened to Leo?'

'Yes. Yes, it happened to Leo. Only from the first day he came here, I had that feeling he was . . . well, that he was waiting. Just the way he looked, the way he handled paper . . . Always peering over the hedge. I'd glance up and catch sight of him and there was those little brown eyes looking all the time. I know you'll say I'm fanciful; I don't care. I didn't make a lot of it, why should I? We all have problems, and besides it was like a factory in here by then. But it's true all the same. I've thought about it and it's true. It was nothing much to begin with; I just noticed it. Then gradually he got on his track.'

A bell rang suddenly; a long, assertive peal up and down the corridors. They heard the slamming of doors and the sound of running feet. A girl was calling: 'Where's Valerie, where's Valerie?'

'Fire practice,' Meadowes said. 'We're running to two or three a week at present. Don't worry. Registry's exempt.'

Turner sat down. He looked even paler than before. He ran a big hand through his tufted, fair hair.

'I'm listening.' he said.

'Ever since March now he's been working on a big project: all the seven-o-sevens. That's Statutes. There's about two hundred of them or more, and mainly to do with the handover when the Occupation ended. Terms of withdrawal, residual rights, rights of evocation, phases of autonomy and God knows what. All forty-nine to fifty-five stuff, not relevant here at all. He might have started in half a dozen places on the Destruction, but the moment he saw the seven-o-sevens, they were the ones for him. "Here," he said. "That's just right for me Arthur, I can cut my milk teeth on them. I know what they're talking about; it's familiar ground." I shouldn't think anyone had looked at it for fifteen years. But *tricky*, even if it was obsolete. Full of technical talk. Surprising what Leo knew, mind. All the terms, German and English, all the legal phrases.' Meadowes shook his head in admiration. 'I saw a minute of his go to the Legal Attaché, a résumé of a file; *I* couldn't have put it together I'm sure, and I doubt whether there's anyone in Chancery could either. All about the Prussian Criminal Code and regional sovereignty of justice. And half of it in German, too.'

'He knew more than he was prepared to let on: is that what you're saying?'

'No, it's not,' said Meadowes. 'And don't you go putting words into my mouth. He was being *used*, that's what I mean; he had a lot of knowledge in him that he hadn't done anything with for a long time. All of a sudden, he could put it to work.'

Meadowes resumed: 'With the seven-o-sevens there wasn't any real question of *destruction*: more of sending it back to London and getting it stored out of the way, but it all had to be read and submitted the same as everything else, and he'd been getting very deep in it these last few weeks. I told you he was quiet up here; well he was. And once he got tucked into the Statutes he got quieter and quieter. He was on a track.'

'When did this happen?'

At the back of Turner's notebook there was a diary; he had it open before him.

'Three weeks ago. He went further and further *in*. Still jolly, mind; still bouncing up and down to get the girls a chair or help them with a parcel. But something had got hold of him, and it meant a lot to him. Still quizzy: no one will ever cure him of that: he had to know exactly what each of us was up to. But subdued. And he got worse. More and more thoughtful; more and more *serious*. Then on Monday, last Monday, he changed.'

'A week ago today,' said Turner, 'The fifth.'

'Seven days. Is that all? My God.' There was a sudden smell of hot wax from next door, and the muffled thud of a large seal being pressed on to a packet.

'That'll be the two o'clock bag they're getting ready,' he muttered inconsequentially, and glanced at his silver pocket watch. 'It's due down there at twelve thirty.'

'I'll come back after lunch if you like.'

'I'd rather be done with you before,' Meadowes said. 'If you don't mind.' He put the watch away. 'Where is he? Do *you* know? What's happened to him? He's gone to Russia, is that it?'

'Is that what you think?'

'He might have gone anywhere, you couldn't tell. He wasn't like us. He tried to be, but he wasn't. More like you, I suppose, in some ways. Perverse. Always busy but always doing things back to front. Nothing was simple, I reckon that was his trouble. Too much childhood. Or none. It comes to the same thing really. I like people to grow *slowly*.'

'Tell me about last Monday. He changed: how?'

'Changed for the better. He'd shaken himself out of it, whatever it was. The track was over. He was smiling when I came in, really happy. Johnny Slingo, Valerie, they both noticed it, same as I did. We'd all been going full tilt of course; I'd been in most of Saturday, all Sunday; the others had been coming and going.'

'What about Leo?'

'Well, he'd been busy too, there was no doubt to that, but we didn't see him around an awful lot. An hour up here, three hours down there—'

'Down where?'

'In his own room. He did that sometimes, took a few files downstairs to work on. It was quieter. "I like to keep it warm." he said. "It's my old room, Arthur, and I don't like to let it grow cold."'

'And he took his files down there, did he?' Turner asked, very quiet.

'Then there was Chapel; that took up a part of Sunday, of course. Playing the organ.'

'How long's he been doing that, by the way?'

'Oh, years and years. It was reinsurance,' Meadowes said with a little laugh. 'Just to keep himself indispensable.'

'So Monday he was happy.'

'Serene. There's no other word for it. "I like it here, Arthur," he said. "I want you to know that." Sat down and got on with his work.'

'And he stayed that way till he left?'

'More or less.'

'What do you mean, "More or less"?'

'Well, we had a bit of a row. That was Wednesday. He'd been all right Tuesday, happy as a sandboy, then Wednesday I caught him at it.' He had folded his hands before him on his lap and he was looking at them, head bowed.

'He was trying to look at the Green File. The Maximum Limit.' He touched the top of his head in a small gesture of nervousness. 'He was always quizzy, I told you. Some people are like that, they can't help it. Didn't matter what it was; I could leave a letter from my own mother on the desk: I'm damn sure that if Leo had half a chance he'd have read it. Always thought people were conspiring against him. It drove us mad to begin with; look in anything, he would. Files, cupboards, anywhere. He hadn't been here a week before he was signing for the mail. The whole lot, down in the bagroom. I didn't care for that at all at first, but he got all huffy when I told him to stop and in the end I let it go.' He opened his hands, seeking an answer. 'Then in March we had some Trade Contingency papers from London—special guidance for Econ on new alignments and forward planning, and I caught him with the whole bundle on his desk. "Here," I said. "Can't you read? They're subscription only, they're not for you." He didn't turn a hair. In fact he was really angry. "I thought I could handle anything!" he says. He'd have hit me for two pins. "Well you thought wrong," I told him. That was March. It took us both a couple of days to cool down.'

'God save us,' said Turner softly.

'Then we had this Green. A Green's rare. *I* don't know what's in it; Johnny doesn't, Valerie doesn't. It lives in its own despatch box. H.E.'s got one key, Bradfield's got the other and he shares it with de Lisle. The box has to come back here to the strong-room every night. It's signed in and signed out, and only I handle it. So anyway: lunchtime Wednesday it was. Leo was up here on his own; Johnny and me went down to the canteen.'

'Often here on his own lunchtimes, was he?'

'He liked to be, yes. He liked the quiet.'

'All right.'

'There was a big queue at the canteen and I can't stand queuing, so I said to Johnny, "You stay here, I'll go back and do a spot of work and try again in half an hour." So I came in unexpectedly. Just walked in. No Leo, and the strong-room was open. And there he was; standing there, with the Green despatch box.'

'What do you mean, *with* it?'

'Just holding it. Looking at the lock as far as I could make out. Just curious. He smiled when he saw me, cool as anything. He's sharp, I've told you that. "Arthur," he says, "you've caught me at it, you've discovered my guilty secret." I said, "What the hell are you up to?

Look what you've got there in your hands!" Like that. "You know me," he says, very disarming. "I just can't help it." He puts down the box. "I was *actually* looking for some seven-o-sevens, you don't happen to have seen them anywhere, do you? For March and February fifty-eight." Something like that.'

'So then what?'

'I read him the Riot Act. What else could I do? I said I'd report him to Bradfield, the lot. I was furious.'

'But you didn't?'

'No.'

'Why not?'

'You wouldn't understand,' Meadowes said at last. 'You think I'm soft in the head, I know. It was Myra's birthday Friday; we were having a special do at the Exiles. Leo had choir practice and a dinner party.'

'Dinner party? Where?'

'He didn't say.'

'There's nothing in his diary.'

'That's not my concern.'

'Go on.'

'He'd promised to drop in sometime during the evening and give her her present. It was going to be a hair-dryer; we'd chosen it together.' He shook his head again. 'How can I explain it? I've told you: I felt responsible for him. He was that kind of bloke. You and I could blow him over with one puff if we wanted.'

Turner gazed at him incredulously.

'And I suppose there was something else too.' He looked Turner full in the face. 'If I tell Bradfield, that's it. Leo's had it. There's nowhere for him to go, is there? See what I mean. Like now, for instance: I mean I hope he *has* gone to Moscow, because there's nowhere else going to take him.'

'You mean you suspected him?'

'I suppose so, yes. Deep down I suppose I did. Warsaw's done that for me, you know. I'd like Myra to have settled there. With her student. All right, they put him up to it; they made him seduce her. But he did say he'd marry her, didn't he? For the baby. I'd have loved that baby more than I can say. That's what you took away from me. From her as well. That's what it was all about. You shouldn't have done that you know.'

He was grateful for the traffic then, for any noise to fill that damned tank and take away the accusing echo of Meadowes' flat voice.

'And on Thursday the box disappeared?'

Meadowes shrugged it away. 'Private Office returned it Thursday midday. I signed it in myself and left it in the strong-room. Friday it wasn't there. That was that.'

He paused.

'I should have reported it at once. I should have gone running to Bradfield Friday afternoon when I noticed. I didn't. I slept on it. I brooded about it all Saturday. I chewed Cork's head off, went for Johnny Slingo, made their lives hell. It was driving me mad. I didn't want to raise a hare. We'd lost all manner of things in the crisis. People get light-fingered. Someone's pinched our trolley, I don't know who: one of the Military Attachés' clerks, that's my guess. Someone else has lifted our swivel chair. There's a long-carriage typewriter from the Pool; diaries, all sorts, cups from the Naafi even. Anyway, those were the excuses. I thought one of the users might have taken it: de Lisle, Private Office . . .'

'Did you ask Leo?'

'He'd gone by then, hadn't he?'

Once more Turner had slipped into the routine of interrogation.

'He carried a briefcase, didn't he?'

'Yes.'

'Was he allowed to bring it in here?'

'He brought in sandwiches and a thermos.'

'So he was allowed?'

'Yes.'

'Did he have the briefcase Thursday?'

'I think so. Yes, he would have done.'

'Was it big enough to hold the despatch box?'

'Yes.'

'Did he have lunch in here Thursday?'

'He went out at about twelve.'

'And came back?'

'I told you: Thursday's his special day. Conference day. It's a left-over from his old job. He goes to one of the Ministries in Bad Godesberg. Something to do with outstanding claims. Last Thursday he had a lunch date first I suppose. Then went on to the meeting.'

'Has he always been to that meeting? Every Thursday?'

'Ever since he came into Registry.'

'He had a key, didn't he?'

'What for? Key to where?'

Turner was on unsure ground. 'To let himself in and out of Registry. Or he knew the combination.'

Meadowes actually laughed.

'There's me and Head of Chancery knows how to get in and out of here, and no one else. There's three combinations and half a dozen burglar switches and there's the strong-room as well. Not Slingo, not de Lisle, *no one* knows. Just us two.'

Turner was writing fast.

'Tell me what else is missing,' he said at last.

Meadowes unlocked a drawer of his desk and drew out a list of references. His movements were brisk and surprisingly confident.

'Bradfield didn't tell you?'

'No.'

Meadowes handed him the list. 'You can keep that. There's forty-three of them. They're all box files, they've all disappeared since March.'

'Since he went on his track.'

'The security classifications vary from Confidential to Top Secret, but the majority are plain Secret. There's Organization files, Conference, Personality and two Treaty files. The subjects range from the dismantling of chemical concerns in the Ruhr in 1947 to minutes of unofficial Anglo-German exchanges at working level over the last three years. Plus the Green and that's Formal and Informal Conversations—'

'Bradfield told me.'

'They're like pieces, believe me, pieces in a puzzle . . . that's what I thought at first . . . I've moved them round in my mind. Hour after hour. I haven't slept. Now and then—' he broke off. 'Now and then I thought I had an idea, a sort of picture, a half-picture, I'd say . . .' Stubbornly he concluded:

'There's no clear pattern to it, and no reason. Some are marked out by Leo to different people; some are marked "certified for destruction" but most are just plain missing. You can't tell, you see. You just can't keep tabs, it's impossible. Until someone *asks* for the file you don't know you haven't got it.'

'*Box* files?'

'I told you. All forty-three. They weigh a couple of hundred-weights between them I should think.'

'And the letters? There are letters missing too.'

'Yes,' Meadowes said reluctantly. 'We're short of thirty-three incoming letters.'

'Never entered, were they? Just lying about for anyone to pick up? What were the subjects? You haven't put it down.'

'We don't know. That's the truth. They're letters from German Departments. We know the references because the Bag Room's written them in the log. They never reached Registry.'

'But you've checked the references?'

Very stiffly Meadowes said: 'The missing letters belong on the missing files. The references are the same. That's all we can tell. As they're from German Departments, Bradfield has ruled that we do not ask for duplicates until the Brussels decision is through: in case our curiosity alerts them to Harting's absence.'

Having returned his black notebook to his pocket, Turner rose and went to the barred window, touching the locks, testing the strength of the wire mesh.

'There was something about him. He was special. Something *made* you watch him.'

From the carriageway they heard the two-tone wail of an emergency horn approach and fade again.

'He was special,' Turner repeated. 'All the time you've been talking, I've heard it. Leo this, Leo that. You had your eye on him; you *felt* him, I know you did. Why?'

'There was nothing.'

'What were these rumours? What was it they said about him that frightened you? Was he somebody's fancy-boy, Arthur? Something for Johnny Slingo, was he, in his old age? Working the queers' circuit was he, is that what all the blushing's for?'

Meadowes shook his head. 'You've lost your sting,' he said. 'You can't frighten me any more. I know you; I know your worst. It's nothing to do with Warsaw. He wasn't that kind. I'm not a child and Johnny's not a homosexual either.'

Turner continued to stare at him. 'There's something you heard. Something you knew. You watched him, I know you did. You watched him cross a room; how he stood, how he reached for a file. He was doing the silliest bloody job in Registry and you talk about him as if he was the Ambassador. There was chaos in here, you said so yourself. Everyone except Leo chasing files, making up, entering, connecting, all standing on your heads to keep the ball rolling in a crisis. And what was Leo doing? Leo was on Destruction. He could have been making flax for all his work mattered. You said so, not me. So what *was* it about him? *Why* did you watch him?'

'You're dreaming. You're twisted and you can't see anything straight. But if by any chance you were right, I wouldn't even whisper it to you on my deathbed.'

A notice outside the cypher room said: 'Back at two fifteen. Phone 333 for emergencies.' He banged on Bradfield's door and tried the handle; it was locked. He went to the banister and looked angrily down into the lobby. At the front desk a young Chancery Guard was reading a learned book on engineering. He could see the diagrams on the right-hand page. In the glass-fronted waiting-room, the Ghanaian Chargé in a velvet collar was staring thoughtfully at a photograph of Clydeside taken from very high up.

'All at lunch, old boy,' a voice whispered from behind him.

'Not a Hun will stir till three. Daily truce. Show must go on.' A hanging, vulpine figure stood among the fire extinguishers. 'Crabbe,' he explained, 'Mickie Crabbe, you see,' as if the name itself were an excuse. 'Peter de Lisle's just back, if you don't mind. Been down at the Ministry of the Interior, saving women and children. Rawley's sent him to feed you.'

'I want to send a telegram. Where's room three double three?'

'Proles' rest room, old boy. They're having a bit of a kip after all the hoohah. Troubled times. Give it a break,' he suggested. 'If it's urgent it'll keep, if it's important it's too late, that's what I say.' Saying it, Crabbe led him along the silent corridor like a decrepit courtier lighting him to bed. Passing the lift, Turner paused and stared at it once more. It was firmly padlocked and the notice said 'Out of order.'

Jobs are separate, he told himself, why worry, for God's sake? Bonn is not Warsaw. Warsaw was a hundred years ago. Bonn is today. We do what we have to do and move on. He saw it again, the Rococo room in the Warsaw Embassy, the chandelier dark with dust, and Myra Meadowes alone on the daft sofa. 'Another time they post you to an Iron Curtain country,' Turner was shouting, 'you bloody well choose your lovers with more care!'

Tell her I'm leaving the country, he thought; I've gone to find a traitor. A full-grown, four-square, red-toothed, paid-up traitor.

Come on, Leo, we're of one blood, you and I: underground men, that's us. I'll chase you through the sewers, Leo; that's why I smell so lovely. We've got the earth's dirt on us, you and I. I'll chase you, you chase me and each of us will chase ourselves.

Chapter Seven

de Lisle

The American Club was not as heavily guarded as the Embassy. 'It's no one's gastronomic dream,' de Lisle explained, as he showed his papers to the GI at the door, 'but it does have a gorgeous swimming-pool.' He had booked a window table overlooking the Rhine. Fresh from their bathe, they drank Martinis and watched the giant brown helicopters wavering past them towards the landing-strip up river. Some were marked with red crosses, others had no markings at all. Now and then white passenger ships, sliding through the mist, bore huddled groups of tourists towards the land of the Nibelungs; the boom of their own loudspeakers followed them like small thunder. Once a crowd of schoolchildren passed, and they heard the strains of the Lorelei banged out on an accordion, and the devoted accompaniment of a heavenly, if imperfect, choir. The seven hills of Königs-winter were much nearer now, though the mist confused their outline.

With elaborate diffidence de Lisle pointed out the Petersberg, a regular wooded cone capped by a rectangular hotel. Neville Chamberlain had stayed there in the thirties, he explained; 'That was when he gave away Czechoslovakia, of course. The first time, I mean.' After the war it had been the seat of the Allied High Commission; more recently the Queen had used it for her State Visit. To the right of it was the Drachenfels, where Siegfried had slain the dragon and bathed in its magic blood.

'Where's Harting's house?'

'You can't quite see it,' de Lisle said quietly, not pointing any more. 'It's at the foot of the Petersberg. He lives, so to speak, in Chamberlain's shadow.' And with that he led the conversation into more general fields.

'I suppose the trouble with being a visiting fireman is that you so often arrive on the scene after the fire's gone out. Is that it?'

'Did he come here often?'

'The smaller Embassies hold receptions here; if their drawing-rooms aren't big enough. That was rather his mark, of course.'

Once again his tone became reticent, though the dining-room was empty. Only in the corner near the entrance, seated in their glass-walled bar, the inevitable group of foreign correspondents mimed, drank and mouthed like sea horses in solemn ritual.

'Is *all* America like this?' de Lisle enquired. 'Or worse?' He looked slowly round. 'Though it does give a sense of *dimension*, I suppose. And optimism. That's the trouble with Americans, isn't it, really? All that emphasis on the future. So dangerous. It makes them destructive of the present. Much kinder to look *back*, I always think. I see no hope at all for the future, and it gives me a *great* sense of freedom. And of caring: we're much nicer to one another in the condemned cell aren't we? Don't take me too seriously, will you?'

'If you wanted Chancery files late at night, what would you do?'

'Dig out Meadowes.'

'Or Bradfield?'

'Oh, that would be really going it. Rawley has the combinations, but only as a long stop. If Meadowes goes under a bus, Rawley can still get at the papers. You really *have* had a morning of it, haven't you,' he added solicitously. 'I can see you're still under the ether.'

'What would *you* do?'

'Oh, I'd draw the files in the afternoon.'

'Now; with all this working at night?'

'If Registry's open on a crisis schedule there's no problem. If it's closed, well, most of us have safes and strong-boxes, and they're cleared for overnight storage.'

'Harting didn't have one.'

'Shall we just say *he* from now on?'

'So where would he work? If he drew files in the evening, classified files, and worked late: what would he do?'

'He'd take them to his room I suppose, and hand in the files to the Chancery Guard when he left. If he's not working in Registry. The Guard has a safe.'

'And the Guard would sign for them?'

'Oh Lordy, yes. We're not *that* irresponsible.'

'So I could tell from the Guard's night-book?'

'You could.'

'He left without saying good-night to the Guard.'

'Oh my,' said de Lisle, clearly very puzzled. 'You mean he took them home?'

'What kind of car did he have?'

'A mini shooting-brake.'

They were both silent.

'There's nowhere else he might have worked, a special reading room, a strong-room on the ground floor?'

'Nowhere,' de Lisle said flatly. 'Now I think you'd better have another of those things, hadn't you, and cool the brain a little?'

He called the waiter.

'Well I've had a simply *ghastly* hour at the Ministry of the Interior with Ludwig Siebkron's faceless men.'

'What doing?'

'Oh, mourning the poor Miss Eich. That was gruesome. It was also very *odd*,' he confessed. 'It really was very odd indeed.' He drifted away. 'Did you know that blood plasma came in tins? The Ministry now say that they want to store some in the Embassy canteen, just in case. It's the most Orwellian thing I've ever heard; Rawley's going to be quite furious. He thinks they've gone much too far already. Apparently none of us belongs to groups any more: *uniblood.* I suppose it makes for equality.' He continued, 'Rawley's getting pretty cross about Siebkron.'

'Why?'

'The lengths he insists on going to, just for the sake of the poor English. All right, Karfeld is desperately anti-British and anti-Common Market. And Brussels is crucial, and British entry touches the nationalist nerve and maddens the Movement, and the Friday rally is alarming and everyone's very much on edge. One accepts all that wholeheartedly. And nasty things happened in Hanover. But we still don't deserve *so* much attention, we really don't. First the curfew, then the bodyguards, and now these wretched motor-cars. I think we feel he's crowding us on purpose.' Reaching past Turner, de Lisle took the enormous menu in his slender, woman's hand. 'How about oysters? Isn't that what real people eat? They have them in all seasons here. I gather they get them from Portugal or somewhere.'

'I've never tried them,' Turner said with a hint of aggression.

'Then you must have a dozen to make up,' de Lisle replied easily and drank some more Martini. 'It's so nice to meet someone from *outside*. I don't suppose you can understand that.'

A string of barges chased up river with the current.

'The unsettling thing is, I suppose, one doesn't feel that ultimately all these precautions are for our own good. The Germans seem suddenly to have their horns drawn in, as if we were being deliberately provocative; as if *we* were doing the demonstrating. They barely talk to us down there. A *total* freeze up. Yes. That's what I mean,' he concluded. 'They're treating us as if we were hostile. Which is doubly frustrating when all we ask is to be loved.'

'He had a dinner party on Friday night,' Turner said suddenly.

'Did he?'

'But it wasn't marked in his diary.'

'Silly man.' He peered round but no one came. 'Where *is* that wretched boy?'

'Where was Bradfield on Friday night?'

'Shut up,' said de Lisle crisply. 'I don't like that kind of thing. And then there's Siebkron himself,' he continued as if nothing had happened, 'Well, we all know *he's* shifty; we all know he's juggling with the Coalition and we all know he has political aspirations. We also know he has an appalling security problem to cope with next Friday, and a lot of enemies waiting to say he did it badly. Fine—' he nodded his head at the river, as if in some way it were involved in his perplexities—'So why spend six hours at the deathbed of poor Fraülein Eich? What's so fascinating about watching her die? And why go to the ridiculous lengths of putting the sentries on every tiny British hiring in the area? He's got an obsession about us, I swear he has; he's worse than Karfeld.'

'Who is Siebkron? What's his job?'

'Oh, muddy pools. Your world in a way. I'm sorry, I shouldn't have said that.' He blushed, acutely distressed. Only the timely arrival of the waiter rescued him from his embarrassment. He was quite a young boy, and de Lisle addressed him with inordinate courtesy, seeking his opinion on matters beyond his competence, deferring to his judgment in the selection of the Moselle and enquiring minutely after the quality of the meat.

'They say in Bonn,' he continued when they were alone again, 'to borrow a phrase, that if you have Ludwig Siebkron for a friend you don't need an enemy. Ludwig's very much a local species. Always someone's left arm. He keeps saying he doesn't want any of us to die. That's exactly why he's frightening: he makes it so possible. It's easy to forget,' he continued blandly, 'that Bonn may be a democracy but it's *frightfully* short of democrats.' He fell silent. 'The trouble with *dates*,' he reflected at last, 'is that they create compartments in time. Thirty-nine to forty-five. Forty-five to fifty. Bonn isn't pre-war, or war, or even post-war. It's just a small town in Germany. You can no more slice it up than you can the Rhine. It plods along, or whatever the song says. And the mist drains away the colours.'

Blushing suddenly, he unscrewed the cap of the tabasco and applied himself to the delicate task of allocating one drop to each oyster. It claimed his entire attention. 'We all apologize for Bonn. That's how you recognize the natives. I wish I collected model trains,' he continued brightly. 'I would like to place *far* greater emphasis on trivia. Do you have anything like that: a hobby, I mean?'

'I don't get the time,' said Turner.

'*Nominally* he heads something called the Ministry of the Interior Liaison Committee; I understand he chose the name himself. I asked him once: liaison with whom, Ludwig? He thought that was a great joke. He's our age of course. Front generation minus five; slightly cross at having missed the war, I suspect, and can't *wait* to grow old. He also flirts with CIA, but that's a status symbol here. His principal occupation is knowing Karfeld. When anyone wants to conspire with the Movement, Ludwig Siebkron lays it on. It *is* a bizarre life,' he conceded, catching sight of Turner's expression. 'But Ludwig revels in it. Invisible Government: that's what he likes. The fourth estate. Weimar would have suited him down to the ground. And you have to understand about the Government here: *all* divisions are very artificial.'

Compelled, apparently, by a single urge, the foreign correspondents had left their bar and were floating in a long shoal towards the centre table already prepared for them. A very large man, catching sight of de Lisle, pulled a long strand of black hair over his right eye, and extended his arm in a Nazi greeting. De Lisle lifted his glass in reply.

'That's Sam Allerton,' he explained in an aside. 'He really *is* rather a pig. Where was I? Artificial divisions. Yes. They absolutely bedevil us here. Always the same: in a grey world we reach frantically for absolutes. Anti-French, pro-French, Communist, anti-Communist. Sheer nonsense, but we do it time and again. That's why we're so wrong about Karfeld. So dreadfully wrong. We argue about *definitions* when we should be arguing about *facts*. Bonn will go to the gallows arguing about the width of the rope that hangs us. *I* don't know how you define Karfeld; who does? The German Poujade? The middle-class revolution? If that's what he is then we *are* ruined, I agree, because in Germany they're *all* middle class. Like America: reluctantly equal. They don't want to be equal, who does? They just are. Uniblood.'

The waiter had brought the wine, and de Lisle pressed Turner to taste it. 'I'm sure your palate is fresher than mine.' Turner declined, so he sampled it himself, elaborately. 'How very clever,' he said appreciatively to the waiter. 'How *good*.'

'All the smart definitions apply to him, every one, of course they do; they apply to anyone. Just like psychiatry: presume the symptoms and you can *always* find a name for them. He's isolationist, chauvinist, pacifist, revanchist. And he wants a trade alliance with Russia. He's progressive, which appeals to the German old, he's reactionary, which appeals to the German young. The young are so *puritanical* here. They want to be cleansed of prosperity; they want bows and arrows and Barbarossa.' He pointed wearily towards the Seven Hills. 'They want all that in modern dress. No wonder the old are hedonistic. But the young—' He broke off. 'The young,' he said, with deep distaste, 'have discovered the cruellest of all truths: that the most effective way of punishing their parents is to imitate them. Karfeld is the students' adopted grown-up . . . I'm sorry. This is my hobby-horse. *Do* tell me to shut up.'

Turner appeared not to have heard. He was staring at the policemen who stood at intervals along the footpath. One of them had found a dinghy tethered under the bank, and he was playing with the sheet, swinging it round and round like a skipping rope.

'They keep asking us in London: who are his supporters? Where does he get his money from? Define, define. What am I to tell them? "The man in the street," I wrote once, "traditionally the most elusive social class." They adore that kind of answer until it reaches Research Department. "The disenchanted," I said, "the orphans of a dead democracy, the casualities of coalition government." Socialists who think they've been sold out to conservatism, anti-socialists who think they've been sold out to the reds. People who are just too intelligent to vote at all. Karfeld is the one hat that covers all their heads. How do you *define* a mood? *God* they are obtuse. We get no instructions any more: just questions. I told them: "Surely you have the same kind of thing in England? It's all the rage everywhere else." And after all, no one suspected a world plot in Paris: why look for it here? Mood . . . ignorance . . . boredom.' He leaned across the table. 'Have *you* ever voted? I'm sure you have. What's it like? Did you feel altered? Was it like Mass? Did you walk away ignoring everybody?' De Lisle ate another oyster. 'I think London has been bombed. Is that the answer? And you're just a blind to cheer us up. Perhaps only Bonn is left. What a frightful thought. A world in exile. That's what we are though. Inhabited by exiles, too.'

'Why does Karfeld hate the British?' Turner asked. His mind was far away.

'That, I confess, is one of life's unsolved mysteries. We've all tried our hand at it in Chancery. We've talked about it, read about it, argued about it. No one has the answer.' He shrugged. 'Who believes in motive these days, least of all in a politician? We did *try* to define that. Something we once did to him, perhaps. Something he once did to us. It's the childhood impressions that last the longest they say.

Are you married, by the way?'

'What's that got to do with it?'

'*My*,' said de Lisle admiringly, 'you *are* prickly.'

'What does he do for money?'

'He's an industrial chemist; he runs a big plant outside Essen. There's a theory the British gave him a rough time during the Occupation, dismantled his factory and ruined his business. I don't know how true it all is. We've attempted a certain amount of research but there's very little to go on and Rawley, quite rightly, forbids us to enquire outside. God knows,' he declared with a small shudder, 'what Siebkron would think of us if we started *that* game. The press just says he hates us, as if it required no explanations. Perhaps they're right.'

'What's his record?'

'Predictable. Graduated before the war, drafted into the Engineers. Russian front as a demolitions expert; wounded at Stalingrad but managed to get out. The disillusionment of peace. The hard struggle and the slow build-up. All very romantic. The death of the spirit, the gradual revival. There are the usual boring rumours that he was Himmler's aunt or something of the sort. No one pays them much heed; it's a sign of arriving in Bonn these days, when the East Germans dig up an improbable allegation against you.'

'But there's nothing to it?'

'There's always something; there's never enough. Anyway, it doesn't impress anyone except us, so why bother? He came by degrees to politics, he says; he speaks of his years of sleep and his years of awakening. He has a rather Messianic turn of phrase, I fear, at least when he talks about himself.'

'You've never met him, have you?'

'Good God no. Just read about him. Heard him on the radio. He's very *present* in our lives in some ways.'

Turner's pale eyes had returned to the Petersberg; the sun, slanting between the hills, glinted directly upon the windows of the grey hotel. There is one hill over there that is broken like a quarry; small engines, white with dust, shuffle at its feet.

'You have to hand it to him. In six months he's changed the whole *galère*. The cadre, the organization, the jargon. They were cranks before Karfeld; gypsies, wandering preachers, Hitler's risen, all that nonsense. Now they're a patrician, graduate group. No shirt-sleeved hordes for him, thank you; none of your socialist nonsense, apart from the students, and he's very clever about tolerating them. He knows what a narrow line there is between the pacifist who attacks the policeman and the policeman who attacks the pacifist. But for most of us Barbarossa wears a clean shirt and has a doctorate in chemical engineering. *Herr Doktor Barbarossa*, that's the cry these days. Economists, historians, statisticians . . . above all, lawyers, of course. Lawyers are the great German gurus, always have been; you know how illogical lawyers are. But not *politicians*: politicians aren't a bit respectable. And for Karfeld of course, they smack far too much of representation; Karfeld doesn't want anyone representing him, thank you. Power without rule, that's the cry. The right to know better, the right not to be responsible. It's the *end*, you see, not the beginning,' he said, with a conviction quite disproportionate to his lethargy. 'Both we and the Germans have been through democracy and no one's given us credit for it. Like shaving. No one *thanks* you for shaving, no one *thanks* you for democracy. Now we've come out the other side. Democracy was only possible under a class system, that's why: it was an indulgence granted by the privileged. We haven't time for it any more: a flash of light between feudalism and automation, and now it's gone. What's left? The voters are cut off from parliament, parliament is cut off from the Government and the Government is cut off from everyone. Government by silence, that's the slogan. Government by alienation. I don't need to tell *you* about that; it's a British product.'

He paused, expecting Turner to make some further interjection but Turner was still lost in thought. At their long table, the journalists were arguing. Someone had threatened to hit someone else; a third was promising to bang their heads together.

'*I* don't know what I'm defending. Or what I'm representing; who does? "A gentleman who lies for the good of his country," they told us with a wink in London. "Willingly," I say. "But first tell me what truth I must conceal." They haven't the least idea. Outside the Office, the poor world dreams we have a book bound in gold with POLICY written on the cover. . . . God, if only they knew.' He finished his wine. 'Perhaps *you* know? I am supposed to obtain the maximum advantage with the minimum of friction. What do they mean by advantage, I wonder: power? I doubt whether power is to our advantage. Perhaps we *should* go into decline. Perhaps we need a Karfeld? A new Oswald Mosley? I'm afraid we would barely notice him. The opposite of love isn't hate; it's apathy. Apathy is our daily bread here. Hysterical apathy. Have some more Moselle.'

'Do you think it's possible,' Turner said, his gaze still upon the hill, 'that Siebkron already *knows* about Harting? Would that make them hostile? Would that account for the extra attention?'

'Later,' de Lisle said quietly. 'Not in front of the children if you don't mind.'

The sun landed upon the river, lighting it from nowhere like a great gold bird, spreading its wings over the whole valley, frisking the water's surface into the light-hearted movements of a new spring day. Ordering the boy to bring two of his *nicest* brandies to the tennis garden, de Lisle picked his way elegantly between the empty tables to the side door. At the centre of the room the journalists had fallen silent; sullen with drink, slumped in their leather chairs, they gracelessly awaited the stimulus of new political catastrophe.

'Poor old thing,' he observed as they entered the fresh air. 'What a bore I've been. Do you get this wherever you go? I suppose we all unburden our hearts to the stranger, do we? And do we all finish up like little Karfelds? Is that it? Middle-class patriotic anarchists? How awfully dreary for you.'

'I've got to see his house,' Turner said. 'I've got to find out.'

'You're out of court,' de Lisle replied evenly. 'Ludwig Siebkron's got it picketed.'

It was three o'clock; a white sun had broken through the clouds. They sat in the garden under beach umbrellas, sipping their brandy and watching the diplomatic daughters volley and laugh in the wet, red clay of the tennis courts.

'Praschko, I suspect, is a baddie,' de Lisle declared. 'We used to have him on the books long ago, but he went sour on us.' He yawned. 'He was quite dangerous in his day; a political pirate. No conspiracy was complete without him. I've met him a few times; the English still bother him. Like all converts, he does hanker for the lost loyalties. He's a Free Democrat these days; or did Rawley tell you? That's a home for lost causes if ever there was one; they've got some *very* weird creatures over there.'

'But he was a friend.'

'You are innocent,' de Lisle said drowsily, 'Like Leo. We can know people all our lives without becoming friends. We can know people five minutes and they're our friends for life. Is Praschko so important?'

'He's all I've got,' said Turner. 'He's all I've got to go on. He's the only person I've heard of who knew him outside the Embassy. He was going to be best man at his wedding.'

'*Wedding? Leo?*' de Lisle sat bolt upright, his composure gone.

'He was engaged long ago to someone called Margaret Aickman. They seem to have known one another in Leo's pre-Embassy days.'

De Lisle fell back in apparent relief.

'If you're thinking of approaching Praschko—' he said.

'I'm not, don't worry; that's one message I have got.' He drank. 'But someone tipped Leo off. *Someone* did. He went mad. He knew he was living on borrowed time and he took whatever he could get his hands on. Anything. Letters, files . . . and when he finally ran for it, he didn't even bother to apply for leave.'

'Rawley wouldn't have granted it; not in this situation.'

'Compassionate leave; he'd have got that all right, it was the first thing Bradfield thought of.'

'Did he pinch the trolley too?'

Turner did not answer.

'I suppose he helped himself to my nice electric fan. He'll need *that* in Moscow for sure.' De Lisle leaned even farther back into his chair. The sky was quite blue, the sun as hot and intense as if it came through glass. 'If *this* keeps up, I'll have to get a new one.'

'Someone tipped him off,' Turner insisted. 'It's the only explanation. He panicked. That's why I thought of Praschko, you see: he's got a left-wing past. Fellow traveller was Rawley's term. He was old chums with Leo; they'd even spent the war together in England.' He stared at the sky.

'You're going to advance a *theory*,' de Lisle murmured. 'I can hear it ticking.'

'They come back to Germany in forty-five; do some army service; then part. They go different ways: Leo stays British and covers *that* target. Praschko goes native and gets himself mixed up in German politics. They'd be a useful pair, those two, as long-term agents, I must say. Maybe they were both at the same game . . . recruited by the same person back in England when Russia was the ally. Gradually they run down their relationship. That's standard, that is. Not safe to associate any more . . . bad security to have our names linked: but they keep it up; keep it up in secret. Then one day Praschko gets word. Just a few weeks ago. Out of the blue perhaps. He hears it on the Bonn grapevine you're all so proud of: Siebkron's on the trail. Some old trace has come up; someone's talked; we're betrayed. Or maybe they're only after Leo. Pack your bags, he says, take what you can and run for it.'

'What a horrid mind you must have,' de Lisle said luxuriously. 'What a nasty, inventive mind.'

'The trouble is, it doesn't work.'

'Not really, does it? Not in *human* terms. I'm glad you recognize that. Leo wouldn't *panic*, that's not his way. He had himself much under control. And it sounds very silly, but he loved us. Modestly, he loved us. He was *our* kind of man, Alan. Not theirs. He expected dreadfully little from life. Pit pony. That's how I used to think of him in those wretched groundfloor stables. Even when he came upstairs, he seemed to bring a bit of the dark with him. People thought of him as *jolly*. The jolly extrovert . . .'

'No one I've talked to thought he was jolly.'

De Lisle turned his head and looked at Turner with real interest.

'Didn't they? What a horrifying thought. Each of us thought the other was laughing. Like clowns at the tragedy. That's very nasty,' he said.

'All right,' Turner conceded. 'He wasn't a believer. But he might have been when he was younger, mightn't he?'

'Might.'

'Then he goes to sleep . . . his conscience goes to sleep, I mean—'

'Ah.'

'Until Karfeld wakes him up again–the new Nationalism . . . the old enemy. . . . Wakes him with a bang. "Hey, what's going on?" He saw it all happening again; he told people that: history repeating itself.'

'Was it really Marx who said that: "History repeats itself, but the first time it's tragedy, and the second time it's comedy?" It seems _far_ too witty for a German. Though I will admit: Karfeld does make Communism awfully inviting.'

'What was he _like?_' Turner insisted, 'What was he really _like?_'

'Leo? God, what are any of us like?'

'You knew him. I didn't.'

'You won't interrogate me, will you?' he asked, not altogether as a joke; 'I'm damned if I'll buy you lunch for you to unmask me.'

'Did Bradfield like him?'

'Who does Bradfield like?'

'Did he keep a close eye on him?'

'On his work, no doubt, where it was relevant. Rawley's a professional.'

'He's Roman Catholic too, isn't he?'

'My goodness,' de Lisle declared with quite unexpected vehemence, 'what an awful thing to say. You really mustn't compartment people like that, it won't do. Life just isn't made up of so many cowboys and so many Red Indians. Least of all diplomatic life. If _that's_ what you think life is, you'd better defect yourself.' With this he threw back his head and closed his eyes, letting the sun restore him. 'After all,' he added, his equability quite revived, 'that's what you object to in Leo, isn't it? He's gone and attached himself to some silly faith. God is dead. You can't have it both ways, that would be _too_ medieval.' He lapsed once more into a contented silence.

'I have a particular vision of Leo,' he said at last. 'Here's something for your little notebook. What do you make of this? One gorgeous winter afternoon, I'd been to a boring German conference and it was half past four and I'd nothing much to do, so I took myself for a drive up into the hills behind Godesberg. Sun, frost, a bit of snow, a bit of wind . . . it was how I imagine ascending into Heaven. Suddenly, there was Leo. Indisputably, unquestionably, positively Leo, shrouded to the ears in Balkan black, with one of those dreadful Homburg hats they wear in the Movement. He was standing at the edge of a football field watching some kids kicking a ball and smoking one of those little cigars everyone complained about.'

'Alone?'

'All alone. I thought of stopping but I didn't. He hadn't any car that I could see and he was miles from anywhere. And suddenly I thought, no; don't stop; he's at Church. He's looking at the childhood he never had.'

'You were fond of him, weren't you?'

De Lisle might have replied, for the question did not seem to disconcert him, but he was interrupted by an unexpected intruder.

'Hullo. A new flunkey?' The voice was slurred and gritty. As its owner was standing directly in the sun, Turner had to screw up his eyes in order to make him out at all; at length he discerned the gently swaying outline and the black unkempt hair of the English journalist who had saluted them at lunch. He was pointing at Turner, but his question, to judge by the cast of his head, was addressed to de Lisle.

'What is he,' he demanded, 'pimp or spy?'

'Which do you want to be, Alan?' de Lisle asked cheerfully, but Turner declined to answer. 'Alan Turner, Sam Allerton,' he continued, quite unbothered. 'Sam represents a lot of newspapers, don't you, Sam? He's enormously powerful. Not that he cares for power of course. Journalists never do.'

Allerton continued to stare at Turner.

'Where's he come from then?'

'London Town,' said de Lisle.

'What part of London Town?'

'Ag and Fish.'

'Liar.'

'The Foreign Office, then. Hadn't you guessed?'

'How long's he here for?'

'Just visiting.'

'How long for?'

'You know what visits are.'

'I know what *his* visits are,' said Allerton. 'He's a bloodhound.' His dead, yellow eyes slowly took him in: the heavy shoes, the tropical suit, the blank face and the pale, unblinking gaze.

'Belgrade,' he said at last. 'That's where. Some bloke in the Embassy screwed a female spy and got photographed. We all had to hush it up or the Ambassador wasn't going to give us any more port. *Security* Turner, that's who you are. The Bevin boy. You did a job in Warsaw, didn't you? I remember that too. That was a balls-up, wasn't it? Some girl tried to kill herself. Someone you'd been too rough with. We had to sweep that under the carpet as well.'

'Run away, Sam,' said de Lisle.

Allerton began laughing. It was quite a terrible noise, mirthless and cancered; indeed it seemed actually to cause him pain, for as he sat down, he interrupted himself with low, blasphemous cries. His black, greasy mane shook like an ill-fitted wig; his paunch, hanging forward over his waistband, trembled uncertainly.

'Well, Peter, how was Luddi Siebkron? Going to keep us safe and sound, is he? Save the Empire?'

Without a word, Turner and de Lisle got up and made their way across the lawn towards the car park.

'Heard the news, by the way?' Allerton called after them.

'What news?'

'You chaps don't know a thing, do you? Federal Foreign Minister's just left for Moscow. Top level talks on Soviet-German trade treaty. They're joining Comecon and signing the Warsaw Pact. All to please Karfeld and bugger up Brussels. Britain out, Russia in. Non-aggressive Rappallo. What do you think of that?'

'We think you're a bloody liar,' said de Lisle.

'Well, it's nice to be fancied,' Allerton replied, with a deliberate homosexual lisp. 'But don't tell me it won't happen, lover boy, because one day it will. One day they'll do it. They'll have to. Slap Mummy in the face. Find a Daddy for the Fatherland. It isn't the West any more, is it? So who's it going to be?' He raised his voice as they continued walking. 'That's what you stupid flunkies don't understand! Karfeld's the only one in Germany who's telling the truth: the Cold War's over for everyone except the fucking diplomats!' His Parthian shot reached them as they closed the doors. 'Never mind darlings,' they heard him say. 'We can all sleep soundly now Turner's here.'

The little sports car nosed its way slowly down the sanitary arcades of the American Colony. A church bell, much amplified, was celebrating the sunlight. On the steps of the New England chapel, a bride and groom faced the flashing cameras. They entered the Koblenzerstrasse and the noise hit them like a gale. Overhead, electronic indicators flashed out theoretical speed checks. The photographs of Karfeld had multiplied. Two Mercedes with Egyptian lettering on their number plates raced past them, cut in, swung out again and were gone.

'That lift,' Turner said suddenly. 'In the Embassy. How long's it been out of action?'

'God, when was anything? Mid-April I suppose.'

'You're sure of that?'

'You're thinking of the trolley? Which also disappeared in mid-April?'

'You're not bad,' Turner said. 'You're not bad at all.'

'And you would be making a most terrible mistake if you ever thought you were a specialist,' de Lisle retorted, with that same unpredictable force which Turner had discerned in him before. 'Just don't go thinking you're in a white coat, that's all; don't go thinking we're all laboratory specimens.' He swung violently to avoid a double lorry and at once a motorized scream of fury rose from behind them. 'I'm saving your soul though you may not notice it.' He smiled. 'Sorry. I've got Siebkron on my nerves, that's all.'

'He put P. in his diary,' Turner said suddenly. 'After Christmas: meet P. Give P. dinner. Then it faded out again. It could have been Praschko.'

'It could have been.'

'What Ministries are there in Bad Godesberg?'

'Buildings, Scientific, Health. Just those three so far as I know.'

'He went to a conference every Thursday afternoon. Which one would that be?'

De Lisle pulled up at the traffic lights and Karfeld frowned down on them like a cyclops, one eye ripped off by a dissenting hand.

'I don't think he *did* go to a conference,' de Lisle said cautiously. 'Not recently anyway.'

'What do you mean?'

'Just that.'

'For Christ's sake?'

'Who told you he went?'

'Meadowes. And Meadowes got it from Leo and Leo said it was a regular weekly meeting and cleared with Bradfield. Something to do with claims.'

'Oh my God,' said de Lisle softly. He pulled away, holding the left-hand lane against the predatory flashing of a white Porsche.

'What does "Oh God" mean?'

'I don't know. Not what you think perhaps. There was no conference, not for Leo. Not in Bad Godesberg, not anywhere else; not on Thursdays, not on any other day. Until Rawley came, it's true, he attended a low-level conference at the Buildings Ministry. They discussed private contracts for repairing German houses damaged by Allied manoeuvres. Leo rubber stamped their proposals.'

'Until Bradfield came?'

'Yes.'

'Then what happened? The conference had run down, had it? Like the rest of his work.'

'More or less.'

Instead of turning right into the Embassy gateway, de Lisle filtered to the left bay and prepared to make the circuit a second time.

'What do you mean? *"More or less"*?'

'Rawley put a stop to it.'

'To the conference?'

'I told you: it was mechanical. It could be done by correspondence.'

Turner was almost in despair. 'Why are you fencing with me? What's going on? Did he stop the conference or not? What part's he playing in this?'

'Take care,' de Lisle warned him, lifting one hand from the steering-wheel. 'Don't rush in. Rawley sent me instead of him. He didn't like the Embassy to be represented by someone like Leo.'

'Someone like—'

'By a temporary. That's all! By a temporary without full status. He felt it was wrong so he got me to go along in his place. After that, Leo never spoke to me again. He thought I'd intrigued against him. Now that's enough. Don't ask me any more.' They were passing the Aral garage again, going north. The petrol attendant recognized the car and waved cheerfully to de Lisle. 'That's your mede or measure. I'm not going to discuss Bradfield with you if you bully me till you're blue in the face. He's my colleague, my superior and—'

'And your friend? Christ forgive me: who do you represent out here? Yourselves or the bloody taxpayer? I'll tell you who: the Club. *Your* Club. The bloody Foreign Office; and if you saw Rawley Bradfield standing on Westminster Bridge hawking his files for an extra pension, you'd bloody well look the other way.'

Turner was not shouting. It was rather the massive slowness of his speech which gave it urgency.

'You make me puke. All of you. The whole sodding circus. You didn't give a twopenny damn for Leo, any of you, while he was here. Common as dirt, wasn't he? No background, no childhood, no nothing. Shove him the other side of the river where he won't be noticed! Tuck him away in the catacombs with the German staff! Worth a drink but not worth dinner! What happens now? He bolts, and he takes half your secrets with him for good measure, and suddenly you've got the guilts and you're blushing like a lot virgins holding your hands over your fannies and not talking to strange men. Everybody: you, Meadowes, Bradfield. You *know* how he wormed his way in there, how he conned them all; how he stole and cheated. You know something else too: a friendship, a love affair, something that made him special for you, made him interesting. There's a whole world he lived in and none of you will put a name to it. What was it? Who was it? Where the hell did he go on Thursday afternoons if he didn't go to the Ministry? Who ran him? Who protected him? Who gave him his orders and his money and took his information off him? Who held his hand? He's a spy, for Christ's sake! He's put his hand in the till! And the moment you find out, you're all on his side!'

'No,' said de Lisle. They were pulling up at the gate; the police were converging on them, tapping on the window. He let them wait. 'You've got it wrong. You and Leo form a team of your own. You're the other side of the wire. Both of you. That's your problem. Whatever definitions, whatever labels. That's why you're beating the air.'

They entered the car park and de Lisle drove round to the canteen side where Turner had stood that morning, staring across the field.

'I've got to see his house,' Turner said. 'I've got to.' They were both looking ahead of them, through the windscreen.

'I thought you'd ask me that.'

'All right, forget it.'

'Why should I? I've no doubt you'll go anyway. Sooner or later.'

They got out and walked slowly over the tarmac. The despatch riders were lying on the lawn, their motor-bikes stacked round the flagpole. The geraniums, martially arranged, glinted like tiny guardsmen along the verges.

'He loved the Army,' de Lisle said, as they climbed the steps. 'He really loved it.'

As they paused to show their passes yet again to the weasel sergeant, Turner chanced to look back at the carriageway.

'Look!' he said suddenly. 'That's the pair that picked us up at the airport.'

A black Opel had lumbered into the filter bay; two men sat in the front; from his vantage point on the steps, Turner could make out easily the multiple reflectors of the long driving mirror glittering in the sunlight.

'Ludwig Siebkron took us to lunch,' de Lisle said with a dry smile, 'and now he's brought us home. I told you: don't go thinking you're a specialist.'

'Then where were you on Friday night?'

'In the woodshed,' de Lisle snapped, 'waiting to murder Lady Anne for her priceless diamonds.'

The cypher room was open again. Cork lay on a truckle bed, a handbook on Caribbean bungalows lay beside him on the floor. On the desk in the dayroom was a blue Embassy envelope addressed to Alan Turner Esquire. His name was typewritten; the style was stiff and rather gauche. There was a number of things, the writer said, which Mr Turner might care to know about in connection with the matter which had brought him to Bonn. If it were convenient, the writer continued, he might care to call for a glass of sherry wine at the above address at half past six o'clock. The address was in Bad Godesberg and the writer was Miss Jenny Pargiter of Press and Information Section, presently on attachment to Chancery. She had signed her name and typed it beneath the signature for reasons of clarity; the P was written rather large, Turner decided; and as he opened the blue rexine diary he permitted himself a rare if puzzled smile of anticipation. P for Praschko; P for Pargiter. And P was the initial on the diary. Come on, Leo, let's have a look at your guilty secret.

Chapter Eight

Jenny Pargiter

'I assume,' Jenny Pargiter began, in a prepared statement, 'that you are used to dealing in delicate matters.'

The sherry stood between them on the glass-topped sofa table. The flat was dark and ugly: the chairs were Victorian wicker, the drapes German and very heavy. Constable reproductions hung in the dining alcove.

'Like a doctor, you have standards of professional confidence.'

'Oh sure,' said Turner.

'It was mentioned at Chancery meeting this morning that you were investigating Leo Harting's disappearance. We were warned not to discuss it, even among ourselves.'

'You're allowed to discuss it with me,' said Turner.

'No doubt. But I naturally would wish to be told how much further any confidence might go. What, for instance, is the relationship between yourselves and Personnel Department?'

'It depends on the information.'

She had raised the sherry glass to the level of her eye and appeared to be measuring the fluid content. It was an attitude evidently designed to demonstrate her sophistication and her ease of mind.

'Supposing someone—supposing I myself had been injudicious. In a personal matter.'

'It depends who you've been injudicious *with*,' Turner replied, and Jenny Pargiter coloured suddenly.

'That's not what I mean at all.'

'Look,' said Turner, watching her, 'if you come and tell me in confidence that you've left a bundle of files in the bus, I'll have to give details to Personnel Department. If you tell me you've been going out with a boy friend now and then, I'm not going to fall over in a faint. Mainly,' he said, pushing his sherry glass across the table for her to replenish, 'Personnel Department don't want to know we exist.' His manner was very casual, as if he barely cared. He sat impassively, filling the whole chair.

'There is the question of protecting other people, third parties who cannot necessarily speak for themselves.'

Turner said, 'There's also the question of security. If you didn't think it was important, you wouldn't ask to see me in the first place. It's up to you. I can't give you any guarantees.'

She lit a cigarette with sharp, angular movements. She was not an ugly girl, but she seemed to dress either too young or too old, so that whatever Turner's age, she was not his contemporary.

'I accept that,' she said and regarded him darkly for a moment, as if assessing how much Turner could take. 'However, you have misunderstood the reason why I asked you to call here. It is this. Since you are quite certain to be told all manner of rumours about Harting and myself, I thought it best if you heard the truth from me.'

Turner put down his glass and opened his notebook.

'I arrived here just before Christmas,' Jenny Pargiter said, 'from London. Before that I was in Djakarta. I returned to London intending to be married. You may have read of my engagement?'

'I think I must have missed it,' said Turner.

'The person to whom I was engaged decided at the last minute that we were not suited. It was a very courageous decision. I was then posted to Bonn. We had known one another for many years; we had read the same subject at University and I had always assumed we had much in common. The person decided otherwise. That is what engagements are for. I am perfectly content. There is no *reason* for anyone to be sorry for me.'

'You got here at Christmas?'

'I asked particularly to be here in time for the holiday. In previous years, we had always spent Christmas together. Unless I was in Djakarta of course. The . . . separation on this occasion was certain to be painful to me. I was most anxious to mitigate the distress with a new atmosphere.'

'Quite.'

'As a single woman in an Embassy, one is very often overcome with invitations at Christmas. Almost everyone in Chancery invited me to spend the festive days with them. The Bradfields, the Crabbes, the Jacksons, the Gavestons: they all asked me. I was also invited by the Meadowes. You have met Arthur Meadowes no doubt.'

'Yes.'

'Meadowes is a widower and lives with his daughter, Myra. He is in fact a B 3, though we no longer use those grades. I found it very touching to be invited by a member of the Junior Staff.'

Her accent was very slight, provincial rather than regional, and for all her attempts at disowning it, it mocked her all the time.

'In Djakarta we always had that tradition. We *mixed* more. In a larger Embassy like Bonn, people tend to remain in their groups. I am not suggesting there should be total assimilation: I would even regard that as *bad*. The A's, for instance, tend to have different tastes as well as different intellectual interests to the B's. I am suggesting that in Bonn the distinctions are too *rigid*, and too many. The A's remain with the A's and the B's with the B's even inside the different sections: the economists, the attachés, Chancery; they all form cliques. I do not consider that right. Would you care for more sherry?'

'Thanks.'

'So I accepted Meadowes' invitation. The other guest was Harting. We spent a pleasant day, stayed there till evening, then left. Myra Meadowes was going out–she has been very ill, you know; she had a liaison in Warsaw, I understand, with a local undesirable and it very nearly ended in tragedy. Personally I am against anticipated marriages. Myra Meadowes was going to a young people's party and Meadowes himself was invited to the Corks, so there was no question of our remaining. As we were leaving, Harting suggested we went for a walk. He knew a place not far away; it would be nice to drive up there and get some fresh air after so much food and drink. I am very fond of exercise. We had our walk and then he proposed that I should go back with him for supper. He was very insistent.'

She was no longer looking at him. Her fingertips were pressed together on her lap, making a basket of her hands.

'I felt it would be wrong to refuse. It was one of those decisions which women find extremely difficult. I would have been quite glad of an early night, but I did not wish to cause offence. After all, it was Christmas Day, and his behaviour during the walk had been perfectly unobjectionable. On the other hand it must be said that I had barely seen him before that day. In the event, I agreed, but I said that I would not wish to be late home. He accepted this provision and I followed him to Königswinter in my car. To my surprise I found that he had prepared everything for my arrival. The table was laid for two. He had even persuaded the boilerman to come and light the fire. After supper, he told me that he loved me.' Picking up her cigarette she drew sharply upon it. Her tone was more factual than ever: certain things had to be said. 'He told me that in all his life he had never felt such emotion. From that first day that I had appeared at Chancery meeting, he had been going out of his mind. He pointed to the lights of the barges on the river. "I stand at my bedroom window," he said, "and I watch every one of them, right through the night. Morning after morning, I watch the dawn rise on the river." It was all due to his obsession for me. I was dumbfounded.'

'What did you say?'

'I had no chance to say anything. He wished to give me a present. Even if he never saw me again, he wished me to have this Christmas gift as a token of his love. He disappeared into the study and came back with a parcel, all wrapped up and ready, with a label, "To my love." I was naturally completely at a loss. "I can't accept this," I said. "I refuse. I can't allow you to give me things. It puts me at a disadvantage." I explained to him that though he was completely English in many ways, in this respect the English did things differently. On the Continent, it was quite customary to take women by storm, but in England courtship was a long and thoughtful matter. We would have to get to know one another, compare our views. There was the discrepancy in our ages; I had my career to consider. I didn't know what to do,' she added helplessly. The brittleness had vanished from her voice: she was helpless and a little pathetic. 'He kept saying, after all it was *Christmas*; I should think of it as just an ordinary Christmas present.'

'What was in the parcel?'

'A hair-dryer. He said he admired my hair above everything. He watched the sun shine on it in the mornings. During Chancery meeting you understand. He must have been speaking figuratively; we were having a wretched winter.' She took a short breath. 'It must have cost him twenty pounds. No one, not even my ex-fiancé during our most intimate period, has ever given me anything so valuable.'

She performed a second ritual with the cigarette box, ducking her hand forward and arresting it suddenly, selecting a cigarette as if it were a chocolate, not this one but that one, lighting it with a heavy frown. 'We sat down and he put on a gramophone record. I am afraid I am not very musical, but I thought that music might distract him. I was extremely sorry for him, and most reluctant to leave him in that condition. He just stared at me. I didn't know where to look. Finally he came over and tried to embrace me, and I said I had to go home. He saw me to the car. He was very correct. Fortunately we had two more days of holiday. I was able to decide what to do. He telephoned twice to invite me to supper and I refused. By the end of the holiday, I had made up my mind. I wrote him a letter and returned the gift. I felt no other course was open to me. I went in early and left the parcel with the Chancery Guard. I explained in my letter that I had given great thought to all he had said and I was convinced I would never be able to return his affection. It would therefore be wrong for me to encourage him, and since we were colleagues and would be seeing a lot of each other, I felt it was only prudent to tell him this immediately, before—'

'Before what?'

'The gossip started,' she said with sudden passion. 'I've never known anywhere for such gossip. You can't move without them making up some wicked story about you.'

'What story have they made up about you?'

'God knows,' she said uselessly. 'God knows.'

'Which Guard did you leave the parcel with?'

'Walter, the younger one. Macmullen's son.'

'Did he tell other people?'

'I particularly asked him to regard the matter as confidential.'

'I should think that impressed him,' Turner said.

She stared at him angrily, her face red with embarrassment.

'All right. So you gave him the bird. What did he do about it?'

'That day he appeared at Chancery meeting and wished me good morning as if nothing had happened. I smiled at him and that was that. He was pale but brave . . . sad but in command. I felt that the worst was over. . . . Fortunately he was about to begin a new job in Chancery Registry and I hoped that this would take his mind off other things. For a couple of weeks I barely spoke to him. I saw him either in the Embassy or at social functions and he seemed quite happy. He made no allusion to Christmas evening or to the hair-dryer. Occasionally at cocktail parties he would come and stand quite close to me and I knew that . . . he wished for my proximity. Sometimes I would be conscious of his eyes on me. A woman can tell these things; I knew that he had still not completely given up hope. He had a way of catching my eye that was . . . beyond all doubt. I continued to give him no encouragement. That was the decision I had taken, and whatever the short-term temptations to alleviate his distress, I knew that in the long term no purpose could be served by . . . leading him on. I was also confident that anything so sudden and . . . irrational would quickly pass.'

'And did it?'

'We continued in this way for about a fortnight. It was beginning to get on my nerves. I seemed unable to go to a single party, to accept a single invitation without seeing him. He didn't even address me any more. He just looked. Wherever I went, his eyes followed me. . . . They are very dark eyes. I would call them soulful. Dark brown, as one would expect, and they imparted a remarkable sense of dependence. . . . In the end I was almost frightened to go out. I'm afraid that at that stage, I even had an unworthy thought. I wondered whether he was reading my mail.'

'Did you now?'

'We all have our own pigeonholes in Registry. For telegrams and mail. Everyone in Registry takes a hand at sorting the incoming papers. It is of course the custom here as in England that invitations are sent unsealed. It would have been quite possible for him to look inside.'

'Why was the thought unworthy?'

'It was untrue, that's why,' she retorted. 'I taxed him with it and he assured me it was quite untrue.'

'I see.'

Her voice became even more pedagogic; the tones came very crisply, brooking no question whatever.

'He would never do such a thing. It was not in his nature, it had not crossed his mind. He assured me categorically that he was not . . .

stalking me. That was the expression I used; it was one I instantly regretted. I cannot imagine how I came on such a ridiculous metaphor. To the contrary, he said, he was merely following his usual social pattern; if it bothered me he would change it, or decline all further invitations until I instructed him otherwise. Nothing was further from his mind than to be a burden to me.'

'So after that you were friends again, were you?'

He watched her search for the wrong words, watched her balance awkwardly at the edge of truth, and awkwardly withdraw.

'Since the twenty-third of January he has not spoken to me again,' she blurted. Even in that sad light, Turner saw the tears running down her rough cheeks as her head fell forward and her hand rose quickly to cover them. 'I can't go on. I think of him all the time.'

Rising, Turner opened the door of the drinks cupboard and half filled a tumbler with whisky.

'Here,' he said gently, 'This is what you like; drink it up and stop pretending.'

'It's overwork.' She took the glass. 'Bradfield never relaxes. He doesn't like women. He hates them. He wants to drive us all into the ground.'

'Now tell me what happened on the twenty-third of January.'

She was sitting sideways in the chair, her back towards him, and her voice had risen beyond her control.

'He ignored me. He pretended to lose himself in work. I'd go into Registry to collect my papers and he wouldn't even look up. Not for me. Not any more. He might for other people, but not for me. Oh no. He had never taken much interest in work—you only had to watch him in Chancery meetings to realize that. He was idle at heart. Glib. But the moment he heard me come along, he couldn't work hard enough. He saw through me, even if I greeted him. Even if I walked straight into him in the corridor, it was the same. He didn't notice me. I didn't exist. I thought I'd go off my head. It wasn't right: after all, he's only a B you know, and a temporary; he's nothing really. He carries no weight at all, you only have to hear how they talk about him. . . . Cheap, that's what they say of him. A quick mind but quite unsound.' For a moment she was far above his grade. 'I wrote him letters. I rang his number at Königswinter.'

'They all knew did they? You made a display of it did you?'

'First of all he chases after me . . . besieges me with declarations of love . . . like a gigolo really. Of course, I mean there's part of me that sees through *that* all right, don't you worry. Running hot and cold like that: who does he think he is?'

She lay across the chair, her head buried in the crook of her elbow, her shoulders shaking to the rhythm of her sobbing.

'You've got to tell me,' Turner said. He was standing over her, his hand on her arm. 'Listen. You've got to tell me what happened at the end of January. It was something important wasn't it? Something he asked you to do for him. Something political. Something special you're afraid of. First of all he made up to you. He worked on you, took you by surprise . . . then he got what he wanted; something very simple he couldn't get for himself. And when he'd got it he didn't want you any more.'

The sobbing started.

'You told him something he needed to know; you did him a favour: a favour to help him along the line. All right, you're not unique. There's a good few others have done the same thing one way or the other, believe me. So what is it?' He knelt down beside her. 'What was it that was injudicious? What was it that involved third parties? Tell me! it was something that frightened the life out of you! *Tell me what it was!*'

'Oh God, I lent him the keys. I lent him the keys,' she said.

'Hurry.'

'The Duty Officer's. The whole lot. He came to me and begged me . . . no, not begged. No.'

She was sitting up, white in the face. Turner refilled her glass and put it back in her hand.

'I was on duty. Night Duty Officer. Thursday January the twenty-third. Leo wasn't allowed to be Duty Officer. There are things temporaries can't see: special instructions . . . contingency plans. I'd stayed in to cope with a rush of telegrams; it must have been half past seven, eight o'clock. I was leaving the cypher room . . . just going to Registry, and I saw him standing there. As if he'd been waiting. Smiling. "Jenny," he said, "What a nice surprise." I was so happy.'

The sobbing broke out again.

'I was so happy. I'd been longing for him to speak to me again. He'd been waiting for me, I knew he had; he was pretending it was an accident. And I said to him: "Leo." I'd never called him that before. Leo. We just talked, standing in the corridor. What a *lovely* surprise he kept saying. Perhaps he could give me dinner? I reminded him, in case he had forgotten, that I was on duty. That didn't bother him either. What a pity, how about tomorrow night? Then the weekend? He would ring me on Saturday morning, how would that be? That would be fine, I said, I'd like that. And we could go for a walk first, he said, up on the football field? I was so happy. I still had the telegrams in my arms, a whole bundle, so I said well, I'd better get along, post these into Arthur Meadowes. He wanted to take them for me but I said no, I could manage them, it was all right. I was just turning away. . . . I wanted to be first to go, you see, I didn't want him walking away from me. I was just going and he said, "Oh Jenny, look here, by the way . . ." You know the way he talks. "Well, a ridiculous thing has happened, the choir are all hanging around downstairs and no one can unlock the Assembly Room door. Somebody's locked it and we can't find the key and we wondered whether you had one." It seemed a bit odd really; I couldn't think why anyone should *want* to lock it in the first place. So I said, yes, I'd come down and open it; I'd just have to check in some telegrams for distribution. I mean he knew I'd got a key; the Duty Officer has a spare key for every room in the Embassy. "Don't bother to come down," he says. "Just give me the key and I'll do it for you. It won't take two minutes." And he saw me hesitate.'

She closed her eyes.

'He was so *little*,' she burst out. 'You could hurt him so easily. I'd already accused him of opening my letters. I loved him. . . . I swear I've never loved anyone . . .' Gradually her crying stopped.

'So you gave him the keys? The whole bunch? That's room keys, safe keys—'

'Keys to all desks and steel cupboards; to the front and rear doors of the building and the key to turn off the alarm in Chancery Registry.'

'Lift keys?'

'The lift wasn't bolted by then . . . the grilles weren't up. . . . They did that the next weekend.'

'How long did he have them for?'

'Five minutes. Maybe less. It's not long enough, is it?' She had seized his arm beseeching him. 'Say it's not long enough.'

'To take an impression? He could take fifty impressions if he knew what he was about.'

'He'd need wax or plasticine or something: I asked. I looked it up.'

'He'd have had it ready in his room,' Turner said indifferently. 'He lived on the ground floor. Don't worry,' he added gently. 'He may just have been letting in the choir. Don't let your imagination run away with you.'

She had stopped crying. Her voice calmed. She spoke with a sense of private recognition: 'It wasn't choir practice night. Choir practice is on Fridays. This was Thursday.'

'You found out did you? Asked the Chancery Guard?'

'I knew already! I knew when I handed him the keys! I tell myself I didn't, but I did. But I had to trust him. It was an act of giving. Don't you see? An act of giving, an act of love. How can I expect a man to understand that?'

'And after you'd given,' Turner said, getting up, 'he didn't want you any more, did he?'

'That's like all men, isn't it?'

'Did he ring you Saturday?'

'You know he didn't.' Her face was still buried in her forearm. He closed the notebook. 'Can you hear me?'

'Yes.'

'Did he ever mention a woman to you; a Margaret Aickman? He was engaged to her. She knew Harry Praschko as well.'

'No.'

'No other woman?'

'No.'

'Did he ever talk politics?'

'No.'

'Did he ever give you any cause to suppose he was a person of strong left-wing leanings?'

'No.'

'Ever see him in the company of suspicious persons?'

'No.'

'Did he talk about his childhood? His uncle? An uncle who lived in Hampstead. A communist who brought him up?'

'No.'

'Uncle Otto?'

'No.'

'Did he ever mention Praschko? Well, did he? Did he ever mention Praschko, do you hear?'

'He said Praschko was the only friend he'd ever had.' She broke down again, and again he waited.

'Did he mention Praschko's politics?'

'No.'

'Did he say they were still friends?'

She shook her head.

'Somebody had lunch with Harting last Thursday. The day before he left. At the Maternus. Was that you?'

'I told you! I swear to you!'

'Was it?'

'No!'

'He's marked it down as you. It's marked P. That's how he wrote you down other times.'

'It wasn't me!'

'Then it was Praschko, was it?'

'How should I know?'

'Because you had an affair with him! You told me half and not the rest! You were sleeping with him up to the day he left!'

'It's not true!'

'Why did Bradfield protect him? He hated Leo's guts: why did he look after him like that? Give him jobs? Keep him on the payroll?'

'Please go,' she said. 'Please go. Never come back.'

'Why!'

'She sat up.

'Get out,' she said.

'You had dinner with him Friday night. The night he left. You were sleeping with him and you won't admit it!'

'No!'

'He asked you about the Green File! He made you get the Despatch Box for him!'

'He didn't! He didn't! Get out!'

'I want a cab.'

He waited while she telephoned. '*Sofort*,' she said, '*Sofort*,' come at once and take him away.

He was at the door.

'What will you do when you find him?' she asked with that slack voice that follows passion.

'Not my business.'

'Don't you care?'

'We never will find him, so what does it matter?'

'Then why look for him?'

'Why not? That's how we spend our lives, isn't it? Looking for people we'll never find.'

He walked slowly down the stairs to the hall. From another flat came the growl of a cocktail party. A group of Arabs, very drunk, swept past him pulling off their coats and shouting. He waited on the doorstep. Across the river, the narrow lights of Chamberlain's Petersberg hung like a necklace in the warm dark. A new block stood directly before him. It seemed to have been built from the top, beginning with the crane and working downwards. He thought he had seen it before from a different angle. A railway bridge straddled the end of the avenue. As the express thundered over it, he saw the silent diners grazing at their food.

'The Embassy,' he said. 'British Embassy.'

'*Englische Botschaft?*'

'Not English. British. I'm in a hurry.'

The driver swore at him, shouting about diplomats. They drove extremely fast and once they nearly hit a tram.

'Get a bloody move on, can't you?'

He demanded a receipt. The driver kept a rubber stamp and a pad in his glove tray, and he hit the paper so hard that it crumpled. The Embassy was a ship, all its windows blazing. Black figures moved in the lobby with the slow coupling of a ballroom dance. The car park was full. He threw away the receipt. Lumley didn't countenance taxi fares. It was a new rule since the last cut. There was no one he could claim from. Except Harting, whose debts appeared to be accumulating.

Bradfield was in conference, Miss Peate said. He would probably be flying to Brussels with the Ambassador before morning. She had put away her papers and was fiddling with a blue leather *placement* tray, fitting the names round a dinner table in order of precedence, and she spoke to him as if it were her duty to frustrate him. And de Lisle was at the Bundestag, listening to the debate on Emergency Legislation.

'I want to see the Duty Officer's keys.'

'I'm afraid you can only have *them* with Mr Bradfield's consent.'

He fought with her and that was what she wanted. He overcame her and that was what she wanted too. She gave him a written authority signed by Administration Section and countersigned by the Minister (Political). He took it to the front desk where Macmullen was on duty. Macmullen was a big, steady man, sometime sergeant of Edinburgh constabulary, and whatever he had heard about Turner had given him no pleasure.

'And the night book,' Turner said. 'Show me the night book since January.'

'Please,' said Macmullen and stood over him while he looked through it in case he took it away. It was half past eight and the Embassy was emptying. 'See you in the morning,' Mickie Crabbe whispered as he passed. 'Old boy.'

There was no reference to Harting.

'Mark me in,' Turner said, pushing the book across the counter. 'I'll be in all night.'

As Leo was, he thought.

Chapter Nine

Guilty Thursday

There were about fifty keys and only half a dozen were labelled. He stood in the first floor corridor where Leo had stood, drawn back into the shadow of a pillar, staring at the cypher room door. It was about seven thirty, Leo's time, and he imagined Jenny Pargiter coming out with a bundle of papers in her arm. The corridor was very noisy now, and the steel trap on the cypher room door was rising and falling like a guillotine for the Registry girls to hand in telegrams and collect them; but that Thursday night had been a quiet time, a lull in the mounting crisis, and Leo had spoken to her *here*, where Turner stood now. He looked at his watch and then at the keys again and thought: five minutes. What *would* he have done? The noise was deafening; worse than day; not only the voices but the very pounding of the machines proclaimed a world entering emergency. But that night was calm, and Leo was a creature of silence, waiting here to draw his quarry and destroy. In five minutes.

He walked along the corridor as far as the lobby and looked down into the stair well and watched the evening shift of typists slip into the dark, survivors from a burning ship, letting the night recover them. Brisk but nonchalant would be his manner, for Jenny would watch him all the way till here; and Gaunt or Macmullen would see him descend these stairs; brisk but not triumphant.

He stood in the lobby. But *what* a risk, he thought suddenly: what a hazardous game. The crowd parted to admit two German officials. They were carrying black briefcases and they walked portentously as though they had come to perform an operation. They wore grey scarves put on before the overcoat, and folded broad and flat like Russian tunics. *What* a risk. She could revoke; she could pursue him; she would know within minutes, if she had not known already, that Leo was lying, she would know the moment she reached the lobby and heard no singing from the Assembly Room, saw no trace at all of a dozen singers entered in the night book, saw no hats and coats on those very pegs beside the door where the German officials were even now disencumbering themselves; she would know that Harting Leo, refugee, fringe-man, lover *manqué* and trader in third-rate artifices, had lied to her to get the keys.

'A gift of love, an act of love: how can I expect a *man* to understand that?'

Before entering the corridor, he stopped and examined the lift. The gold-painted door was bolted; the central panel of glass was black, boarded from the inside. Two heavy steel bars had been fastened horizontally for added security.

'How long's that been there?'

'Since Bremen, sir,' Macmullen said.

'When was Bremen?'

'January, sir. Late January. The Office advised it, sir. They sent a man out specially. He did the cellars and the lift, sir.' Macmullen gave information as if it were evidence before the bailies of Edinburgh, in a series of verbal drill movements, breathing at regulation intervals. 'He worked the whole weekend,' Macmullen added with awe; for he was a self-indulgent man and readily exhausted by work.

He made his way slowly through the gloom to Harting's room thinking: *these* doors would be closed; these lights extinguished, these rooms silent. Was there a moon to shine through the bars? Or only these blue night lights burning for a cheaper Britain, and his own footsteps echoing in the vaults?

Two girls passed him, dressed for the emergency. One wore jeans and she looked at him very straight, guessing his weight. Jesus, he thought, quite soon I'm going to grab one, and he unlocked the door to Leo's room and stood there in the dark. What *were* you up to, he wondered, you little thief?

Tins. Cigar tins would do, filled with white hardening putty; a child's plasticine from that big Woolworths in Bad Godesberg would do; a little white talc to ensure a clean imprint. Three movements of the key, this side, that side, a straight stab into the flesh, and make sure the shoulders are clearly visible. It may not be a perfect fit; that depends on the blanks and the print, but a nice soft metal will yield a little in the womb and form itself to fit the inner walls. . . . Come on Turner, the sergeant used to say, you'd find it if it had hairs round it. He had them ready, then. All fifty tins? Or just one?

Just one key. Which? Which Aladdin's cave, which secret chamber hid the secret treasures of this grumbling English house?

Harting, you thief. He began on Harting's own door, just to annoy him, to bring it home to an absent thief that *his* door can be fiddled with as well, and he worked slowly along the passage fitting the keys to the locks, and each time he found a key that matched he took it off the ring and dropped it into his pocket and thought, What good did *that* one do? Most of the doors were not even locked, so that the keys were redundant anyway: cupboards, lavatories, washrooms, rest-rooms, offices, a first-aid room that stank of alcohol and a junction box for electric cables.

A microphone job? Was that the nature of your technical interest, thief? The gimmicks, the flex, the hair-dryers, the bits and pieces: was that all a lovely cover for carting in some daft conjuring set for eavesdropping? 'Balls,' he said out loud, and with a dozen keys already tapping against his thigh, he plodded up the stairs again straight into the arms of the Ambassador's private secretary, a strutting, fussy man who had borrowed a good deal of his master's authority.

'H.E. will be leaving in a minute; I should make yourself scarce if I were you,' he said with chilling ease. 'He's not awfully keen on you people.'

In most of the corridors it was daytime. Commercial Section was celebrating Scottish week. A mauve grousemoor, draped in Camp-bell tartan, hung beside a photograph of the Queen in Highland dress. Miniatures of Scotch Whisky were mounted in a *collage* with dancers and bagpipes, and framed in plywood battens. In the Open Plan, under radiant exhortations to buy from the North, pale-faced clerks struck doggedly at machines for adding and subtracting. *Deadline Brussels!* A placard warned them, but the machines seemed un-impressed. He climbed a floor and was in Whitehall with the Service Attachés, each with his tiny Ministry and his stencilled title on the door.

'What the hell are you up to?' a sergeant clerk demanded, and Turner told him to keep a civil tongue in his head. Somewhere a military voice wrestled gallantly with dictation. In the Typing Pool, the girls sat forlornly in schoolroom lines: two juniors in green overalls gently nursed a mammoth duplicator while a third laid out the coloured telegrams as if they were fine linen for going away. Raised above them all, the Head Girl, blue haired and fully sixty, sat on a separate dais checking stencils. She alone, scenting the enemy, looked up sharply, nose towards the wind. The walls behind her were lined with Christmas cards from Head Girls in other missions. Some depicted camels, others the royal crest.

'I'm going over the locks,' he muttered, and her look said 'Go over what you like, but not my girls.'

Christ, I could do with one, I'm telling you. Surely you could spare just one for a quick drop into paradise? Harting, you thief.

It was ten o'clock. He had visited every room to which Harting had acquired access; he had gained nothing but a headache for his trouble. Whatever Harting wanted was no longer there, or else so hidden as to require weeks of searching; or so obvious as to be invisible. He felt the sickness which follows tension and his mind was racing with unco-ordinated recollections. Christ: one single day. From enthusiasm to frustration in one day. From an aeroplane to the day-room desk, all the clues and none; I've lived a whole bloody life and it's only Monday. He stared at the blank foolscap pages of the telegram form, wondering what the hell to write. Cork was asleep and the robots were silent. The keys lay in a heap before him. One by one he began threading them back on to the ring. Put together, he thought; *construct*. You will not go to bed until you are at least aware of the trail you must follow. The task of an intellectual, his fart-arsed tutor brayed, is to make order out of chaos. Define anarchy. It is a mind without a system. Please teacher, what is a system without a mind? Taking a pencil he lazily drew a chart of the days of the week and divided each day into panels of one hour. He opened the blue diary. Re-form the fragments, make of all the pieces one piece. You'll find him and Shawn won't. Harting Leo, Claims and Consular, thief and hunter, will hunt you down.

'You don't know anything about shares by any chance?' Cork enquired, waking with a start.

'No, I don't'

'My query is, you see,' he continued, rubbing his pink eyes, 'If there's a slump on Wall Street and a slump in Frankfurt and we don't make the Market on this run, how will it affect Swedish Steel?'

'If I were you,' Turner said, 'I'd put the whole lot on red and forget it.'

'Only I have this firm intention,' Cork explained. 'We've got a bit of land lined up in the Caribbean—'

'Shut up.'

Construct. Put your ideas on a blackboard and *then* see what happens to them. Come on, Turner, you're a philosopher, tell us how the world goes round. What little absolute will we put into

Harting's mouth, for instance? Facts. Construct. Did you not, after all, my dear Turner, abandon the *contemplative* life of the academic in favour of the *functional* life of the civil servant? Construct; put your theories to work and de Lisle will call you a real person.

Mondays first. Mondays are for invitations out. Buffet parties are favoured, de Lisle had told him in an aside at luncheon; they eliminate the pains of *placement*. Mondays are reserved for away matches. England plays the wogs. Away to a different kind of slavery. Harting was essentially a second division man. The minor Embassies. Embassies with small drawing rooms. The B team played away on Mondays.

'–and if it's a girl, I reckon we could get a coloured nanny, an Amah; she could do the teaching, up to O-level at least.'

'Can't you keep quiet?'

'Provided we have the funds,' Cork added. 'You can't get them for nothing, I'm sure.'

'I'm working, can't you understand?'

I'm trying, he thought and his mind drifted into other fields. He was with the little girl in the corridor, whose full unpainted lips faded so reluctantly into the feathery skin; he imagined that long appraising stare upon his nascent paunch and he heard her laughing as his own wife had laughed: Alan darling, you're supposed to take me, not fight me. It's rhythm, it's like dancing, can't you understand? And Tony's such a *beautiful* dancer, Alan darling, and I shall be a little late tonight, and I shall be away tomorrow, playing an away match with my Monday lover. Alan stop. Stop! Alan please don't hit me! I'll never touch him again, I swear. Until Tuesday.

Harting, you thief.

Tuesdays were for entertaining at home. Home is a Tuesday; home is having people in. He made a list of them and thought: it's worse than Blackheath. It's worse than her bloody mother fighting for her fragment of power; it's worse than Bournemouth and seed cake for the minister; it's worse than black Sundays in Yorkshire and weddings timed for six o'clock tea; it is a custom built, unassailable preventive detention of vacuous social exchange. The Vandelungs (Dutch) . . . the Canards (Canadian) . . . the Obutus (Ghanaian) . . . the Cortezanis (Italian) . . . the Allertons, the Crabbes, and once, sure enough, the Bradfields; this happy band was mingled with no fewer than forty-eight accountable bores defined only by their quantity: the Obutus plus six . . . the Allertons plus two . . . the Bradfields alone. You gave them your *full* attention, didn't you? 'I understand he maintains a certain standard there.' Champagne and two veg *that* night. Plover's eggs paid for by the Russian taxpayer. His wife interrupted him: darling why don't we go out tonight? The Willoughbys won't mind, they know I loathe cooking and Tony *adores* Italian food. Oh sure, sure: anything to please Tony.

'–And if it's a boy,' Cork said, 'I'll take it on myself. There must be *some* facilities for boys, even in a place like that. I mean it's a paradise, isn't it, specially for teachers.'

Wednesday was welfare. Ping pong night. Sing song night. The sergeants' mess: 'Have a little something in that gin and whisky, Mr Turner, sir, just to give it bite. The boys say one thing about you, sir, and I'm sure you won't mind me repeating it, sir, seeing it's Christmas: Mr Turner, they say–they always give you the Mister, sir, it's not something they do for everyone–Mr Turner is tough; Mr Turner is firm. But Mr Turner is *fair*. Now, sir, about my leave . . .' Exiles night. A night for worming an inch or two further into the flesh of the Embassy; come back little girl and just slip off those jeans. A night strictly for business. He studied the engagements in detail and thought: you really did work for your secrets, I will admit. You really hawked yourself, didn't you? Scottish Dancing, Skittles Club, Exiles Motoring, Sports Committee. Sooner you than me, boy: you really believed. I'll say that for you too. You really went for goal, didn't you? You kept the ball and you went through the lot of them, you thief.

Which left–since the weekends were not marked with anything but references to gardening and a couple of trips to Hanover–which left Thursdays.

Guilty Thursdays.

Draw a box round Thursday, telephone the Adler and find out what time they lock up. They don't. Draw another box round *that* box, measuring one and a half inches by half an inch and decorate the margins in between with sinuous snakes; cause their forked tongues to lick suggestively at the sweet Gothic curves of the letter T, and wait for the throbbing of a tormented head to be assumed into the waking drumbeat of the cypher machines. And the result?

Silence. Bloody silence.

The result is a Thursday shrouded in sexual mystery, tantalized by abstinence. A Thursday surrounded by meticulous entries written in a swollen, boring mayoral hand by a man with nothing to do and a lot of time to do it in. 'Remember Mary Crabbe's coffee grinder,' the worshipful mayor of Turner's home town in Yorkshire warned his fortunate biographer; remember to grind Mary Crabbe, you thief. 'Speak to Arthur about Myra's birthday,' Mr Crail the Minister, well known throughout all Yorkshire for the inanity of his sermons, whispered in a benevolent aside; 'Anglo-German Society Buffet Luncheon for Friends of the Free City of Hamburg,' 'International Ladies Subscription Luncheon, Costumes of All Nations, DM. 15.00 Incl. wine,' the Master of Ceremonies proclaimed, puffing his Mess-Night capitals over the lined pages. And make a mental note to ruin Jenny Pargiter's career. And Meadowes' retirement. And Gaunt? And Bradfield? And who else along the path?

Myra Meadowes? You wrecker, Harting.

'Can't you turn those bloody things off?'

'I wish I could,' said Cork. 'Something's up, don't ask me what. Personal for Bradfield decypher yourself. Following for Bradfield by hand of officer . . . it must be his bloody birthday.'

'Funeral more likely,' Turner growled and returned to the diary.

But on Thursdays Harting *did* have something to do, something real; and not yet realized. Something he kept quiet about. Very. Something urgent and constructive; something secret. Something that made all the other days worthwhile, something to believe in. On Thursdays, Leo Harting touched the hem; and kept his mouth shut. Not even the weekly lie was recorded. Only last Thursday carried any entry at all, and that read: '*Maternus. One o'clock. P.*' The rest were as blank, as innocent as unrevealing as the little virgins in the ground floor corridor.

Or as guilty.

All Harting's life took place that day. He had lived from Thursday to Thursday as others live from year to year. What *kind* of meeting did they have, Harting and his master? What kind of relationship after all these years of collaboration? Where did they meet? Where did he unpack those files and letters and breathlessly recite his intelligence? In the tower room of a slate-roofed villa? In a soft, linen bed with a soft silk girl and the jeans hanging on the bedpost? Under the bridge where the train went over? Or in the crumbling Embassy with a dusty chandelier, and old father Meadowes holding his little hand on the gilded sofa? In a pretty baroque bedroom of a Godesberg Hotel? In a grey block on the new housing estates? In a coy bungalow with a wrought-iron name and stained glass let into the door? He tried to imagine them. Harting and his master, furtive yet assured, the whispered jokes and the whispered laughter. Here: this is a good one the porno seller whispers; I hardly like to part with this myself. You do *like* it straight don't you? 'Well, it's nice to be fancied,' Allerton lisped. Did they sit over a bottle as they casually planned their next assault upon the citadel, while in the background the camera clicked and the assistant gently shuffled the papers? Give it me once more darling but gently, like Tony. You're not confident, dear, you haven't read the manuals and learned the parts of the rifle.

Or was it a hasty pick-up? A back-street encounter, a frantic exchange as they drove through the small alleys and prayed to God they had no accident? Or on a hilltop? By a football field, where Harting wore the Balkan hat and the grey uniform of the Movement?

Cork was on the telephone to Miss Peate, and a note of awe had entered his voice:

'Stand by for seven hundred groups from Washington. London

please pass and decypher yourself. You'd better warn him now: He's going to be in all night. Look dear, I don't care whether he's conferring with the Queen of England. This one's top priority, and it's my job to let him know so if you won't I will. *Ooh*, she is a bitch.'

'I'm glad you think that,' Turner said with one of his rare grins.

'I reckon she captains the team.'

'England versus the Rest of the World,' Turner agreed and they both laughed.

Was it with Praschko, then, that he had lunched at the *Maternus*? If so, Praschko could hardly be his regular contact, for *he* would not add the tell-tale P, that Harting, who covered his tracks so well; and would not lunch with Praschko in public either, after the trouble he had taken to sever his relationship. Was there, in that case, a middleman, a cut-out, between Praschko and Harting? Or was this the day the system failed? Hold the line Turner, hold on to reason, for unreason will be your downfall. Make order out of chaos. Was this P the sign that Praschko proposed to see him in person, to warn him perhaps that Siebkron was on his trail? To order him—here was a chance—to order him *at any risk* and *at all costs* to steal the Green File before he ran?

Thursday.

He lifted the keys and swung them gently from his finger. Thursday was the day for meeting . . . pressure day . . . the day he was warned . . . the day before he left . . . the day of the weekly briefing and de-briefing . . . the day he borrowed the keys from Pargiter.

Christ: had he really slept with Pargiter? There are certain sacrifices, General Shlobodovitch, which not even Leo Harting will make in the service of Mother Russia.

The useless keys. What did he suppose he would get from them? Entry to the coveted despatch box? Balls. He would have observed the procedure; Meadowes had even instructed him in it. He would know very well there were no spare keys to the despatch box in the Duty Officer's bunch. Entry to Registry itself then? Balls again. He would know at a glance that Registry was protected with better locks than these.

So what key did he want?

What key did he want so desperately that he imperilled his whole career as a spy in order to get a copy of it? What key did he want, that he made up to Jenny Pargiter and risked the disapproval of the Embassy—incurred it, indeed, if Meadowes and Gaunt were anything to go by. What key? The key to the lift, so that he could smuggle out his files, dump them in some hideaway on an upper floor and remove them singly and at leisure in his briefcase? Was that what the missing trolley meant?

Fantastic visions presented themselves. He saw the little figure of

Harting sprinting down the dark corridor, pushing the trolley ahead of him into the open lift, saw the pyramid of box files trembling on the upper shelf, and on the lower shelf the accidental by-product: the stationery, the seal, the diaries, the long-carriage typewriter from the pool. . . . He saw the mini van waiting at the side entrance and Harting's nameless master holding the door and he said: 'Oh bugger it,' schoolboy-style at the very moment when Miss Peate came to fetch the telegrams, and Miss Peate's sigh was a statement of sexual abstinence.

'He'll want his code books too,' Cork warned her.

'He happens to be quite aware of the decoding procedure thank you.'

'Here, what's up then, what's going on in Brussels?' Turner asked.

'Rumours.'

'What of?'

'If they wanted you to know *that*, they would hardly use the person to person procedure would they?'

'You don't know London,' said Turner.

As she left she managed even in her walk—in her loping, English touch-nothing, feel nothing, sex-is-for-the-lower-classes walk—to convey her particular contempt for Turner and all his works.

'I could murder her,' Cork said confidently, 'I could cut her nasty throat. I wouldn't have a moment's regret. Three years she's been here and the only time she smiled was when the Old Man creased his Rolls Royce.'

It was absurd. No questions; he knew it was absurd. Spies of Harting's calibre do not steal; they record, memorize, photograph; spies of Harting's calibre act by graft and calculation, not by impulse. They cover their tracks and survive to deceive again tomorrow.

Nor do they tell transparent lies.

They do not tell Jenny Pargiter that choir practice takes place on Thursdays when she can find out within five minutes that they take place on Fridays. They do not tell Meadowes that they are attending conferences in Bad Godesberg, when both Bradfield and de Lisle know that they are not; and have not done so for two years or more. They do not draw their balance of pay and allowances before they defect, as a signal to anyone who happens to be interested; they do not risk the curiosity of Gaunt in order to work late at night.

Work *where*?

He wanted privacy. He wanted to do by night things he could not do by day. What things? Use his camera in some remote room where he had concealed the files, where he could turn the lock upon himself? Where *was* the trolley? Where *was* the typewriter? Or was their disappearance, as Meadowes had assumed, really unconnected with Harting? At present there was only one answer: Harting had hidden the files in a cache during the day, he had photographed them at night in privacy, and he returned them the next morning. . . . Except that he hadn't returned them. So why steal?

A spy does not steal. Rule one. An Embassy, discovering a loss, can change its plans, re-make or revoke treaties, take a dozen prophylactic measures to anticipate and minimize the harm that has been done. The best girl is the girl you don't have. The most effective deceit is the deceit which is never discovered. Then why steal? The reason was already clear. Harting was under pressure. Calculated though his actions might be, they had all the marks of a man racing against time. What was the hurry? What was the deadline?

Slowly, Alan; gently Alan; be like Tony, Alan. Be like lovely, slow, willowy, rhythmical, anatomically conversant, friendly Tony Willoughby, well known in the best clubs and famous for his copulative technique.

'I'd rather have a boy really, first,' said Cork. 'I mean, when you've got one behind you, you can branch out. Mind you, I don't hold with large families I will say. Not unless you can solve the servant problem. Are you married by the by? Oh dear, sorry I asked.'

Suppose for a moment that that furious private journey in Registry was the result of a dormant Communist sympathy re-awakened by the events of last autumn; suppose that was what had driven him. Then to what hasty end was his fury *directed*? Merely to the deadline dictated by a greedy master? The first stage was easily deduced: Karfeld came to power in October. From then on, a popular nationalist party was a reality; even a nationalist government was not impossible. For a month, two months, Harting broods. He sees Karfeld's face on every hoarding, hears the familiar slogans, 'He really *is* an invitation to Communism,' de Lisle had said. . . . The awakening is slow and reluctant, the old associations and sympathies lie deep and are slow in coming to the surface. Then the moment of decision, the turning point. Either alone, or as a result of Praschko's persuasion, he determines to betray. Praschko approaches him: the Green File. Get the Green File and our old cause will be served. . . . Get the Green File by decision-day in Brussels. . . . The contents of the file, Bradfield had said, could effectively compromise our entire posture in Brussels. . . .

Or was he being blackmailed? Was that the nature of the race? Must he choose between satisfying a greedy master or being compromised by an unknown indiscretion? Was there something in the Cologne incident, for example, which reflected to his discredit: a woman, an involvement in some seedy racket? Had he embezzled Rhine Army funds? Was he selling off tax-free whisky and cigarettes? Had he drifted into a homosexual entanglement? Had he, in fact, succumbed to any one of the dozen classic temptations which are the staple diet of diplomatic espionage? Girl, replace those jeans immediately.

It was not in character. De Lisle was right: there was a thrust, a driving purpose to Harting's actions which went beyond self-preservation; an aggression, a ruthlessness, a fervour which was infinitely more positive than the reluctant compliance of a man under threat. In this underworld life which Turner was now investigating, Harting was not a servant but a principal. He was not deputed but appointed; he was not oppressed, but an oppressor, a hunter, a pursuer. In that, at least, there was an identity between Turner and Harting. But Turner's quarry was named. His tracks, up to a point, were clear. Beyond that point they vanished into the Rhine mist. And most confusing of all was this; though Harting hunted alone, Turner reflected, he had not wanted for patronage . . .

Was Harting blackmailing Bradfield?

Turner asked the question suddenly, sitting up quite straight. Was that the explanation of Bradfield's reluctant protection? Was that why he had found him work in Registry, allowed him to vanish without explanation on Thursday afternoons, to wander round the corridors with a briefcase?

He looked once more at the diary and thought: question fundamentals. Madam, show this tired schoolboy your fundamentals, learn the parts, read the book from scratch . . . that was your tutor's advice and who are you to ignore the advice of your tutor. Do not ask *why* Christ was born on Christmas Day, ask whether he was born at all. If God gave us our wit, my dear Turner, He gave us also the wit to see through His simplicity. So why Thursday at all? Why the afternoon? Why *regular* meetings? However desperate, why did Harting meet his contact in the daylight, in working hours, in Godesberg, when his absence from the Embassy had to be the occasion of a lie in the first place? It was absurd: Balls, Turner, such as they are. Harting could meet his contact at any time. At night in Königswinter: on the forest slopes of Chamberlain's Petersberg; in Cologne, Koblenz, in Luxembourg or over the Dutch border at weekends when no excuse, truthful or untruthful, need be offered to anyone.

He dropped his pencil and swore out loud.

'Trouble?' Cork enquired. The robots were chattering wildly and Cork was tending them like hungry children.

'Nothing that prayer won't cure,' said Turner, recalling something he had said to Gaunt that morning.

'If you want to send that telegram,' Cork warned him, unperturbed, 'You'd better hurry.' He was moving quickly from one machine to the other, tugging at papers and knobs as if his task were to keep them all at work. 'The balloon's going up in Brussels by the look of it. Threat of a complete Hun walk-out if we don't raise our ante on the Agricultural Fund. Haliday-Pride says he thinks it's a pretext. In half an hour I'll be taking bookings for June if we go on at this rate.'

'What sort of pretext?'

Cork read out aloud. 'A convenient door by which to leave Brussels until the situation in the Federal Republic returns to normal.'

Yawning, Turner pushed the telegram forms aside. 'I'll send it tomorrow.'

'It is tomorrow,' said Cork gently.

If I smoked I'd smoke one of your cigars. I could do with a bit of soma just now, he thought; if I can't have one of *those*, I'll have a cigar instead. From beginning to end, he knew the whole thesis was wrong.

Nothing worked, nothing interlocked, nothing explained the *energy*, nothing explained itself. He had constructed a chain of which no one link was capable of supporting the others. Holding his head in his hand, he let the Furies loose and watched them posture in grotesque slow motion before his tired imagination: the faceless Praschko, master spy, controlling from a position of parliamentary impregnability a network of refugee agents; Siebkron, the self-seeking custodian of public security, suspecting the Embassy of complicity in a massive betrayal to Russia, alternately guarding and persecuting those whom he believes to be responsible. Bradfield, rigorous, upper-class academic, hater and protector of spies, inscrutable for all his guilty knowledge, keeper of the keys to Registry, to the lift and the despatch box, about to vanish to Brussels after staying up all night; fornicating Jenny Pargiter, compelled into far more sinister complicity by an illusory passion which had already blackened her name all over the Embassy; Meadowes, blinded by a frustrated father's love for the little Harting, precariously loading the last of the forty files on to his trolley; de Lisle, the ethical queer, fighting for Harting's right to betray his friends. Each, magnified and distorted, looked towards him, danced, twisted and vanished in the face of Turner's own derisive objections. The very facts which only hours before had brought him to the brink of revelation now threw him back into the forests of his own doubt.

Yet how else, he told himself, as he locked away his possessions in the steel cupboard and abandoned Cork to the protesting machines; how else, the minister would ask, breaking the seed cake on the little plate with his soft, enormous hand, how else do fancies multiply, how else is wisdom forged, and a course of Christian action finally resolved upon, if not through doubt? Surely, my dear Mr Turner, doubt is Our Lord's greatest gift to those in need of faith? As he walked into the corridor feeling giddy and very sick, he asked himself once more: what secrets are kept in the magic Green File? And who the hell is going to tell me: me, Turner, a temporary?

The dew was rising out of the field and rolling on to the carriageway like steam. The roads glistened under the wet grey clouds, the wheels of the traffic crackled in the heavy damp. Back to the grey, he thought wearily. No more hunt today. No little angel to submit to this old hairless ape. No absolutes yet at the end of the trail; nothing to make a defector of me.

The night porter at the Adler looked at him kindly. 'You were entertained?' he asked, handing him the key.

'Not much.'

'One should go to Cologne. It is like Paris.'

De Lisle's dinner jacket was draped carefully over his armchair with an envelope pinned to the sleeve. A bottle of Naafi whisky stood on the table. 'If you want to take a look at that property,' Turner read, 'I'll collect you on Wednesday morning at five.' A postscript wished him a pleasant evening at the Bradfields, and requested him in a facetious aside not to pour tomato soup down the lapels as de Lisle did not wish to have his politics misread; particularly, he added, since Herr Ludwig Siebkron of the Federal Ministry of the Interior was expected to be of the company.

Turner ran a bath, took the tumbler from the basin and half filled it with whisky. Why had de Lisle relented? Out of compassion for a lost soul? Save us. And since this was the end to a night of silly questions, why was he being invited to meet Siebkron? He went to bed and half slept until afternoon, dreaming of Bournemouth and the spiky, unclimbable conifers that ran along the bare cliffs at Branksome; and he heard his wife say, as she packed the children's clothes into the suitcase, 'I'll find my road, you find yours, and let's see who gets to Heaven first.' And he heard Jenny Pargiter's crying again, on and on, a call for pity in an empty world. Don't worry, Arthur, he thought, I wouldn't go near Myra to save my life.

Chapter Ten

Kultur at the Bradfields

'You should forbid them more, Siebkron,' Herr Saab declared recklessly, his voice thick with burgundy. 'They are crazy damn fools, Siebkron. Turks.' Saab had out-talked and out-drunk them all, forcing them into embarrassed silence. Only his wife, a little blonde doll of unknown origin and a sweet, revealed bosom, continued to vouchsafe him admiring glances. Invalids, incapable of retaliation, the remaining guests sat dying under the sheer tedium of Herr Saab's diatribe. Behind them, two Hungarian servants moved like nurses along the beds, and they had been told—there was no doubt in Turner's mind—that Herr Ludwig Siebkron merited more attention than all the other patients put together. And needed it. His pale, magnified eyes were already drained of all but the last drops of life; his white hands were folded like napkins beside his plate, and his entire listless manner was that of a person waiting to be moved.

Four silver candlesticks, 1729, by Paul de Lamerie, octagonal based and, in the words of Bradfield's father, quite decently marked, joined Hazel Bradfield to her husband like a line of diamonds down the long table. Turner sat at the centre, midway between the second and third, held rigid by the iron bands of de Lisle's dinner jacket. Even the shirt was too small for him. The head porter had obtained it for him in Bad Godesberg for more money that he had ever paid for a shirt in his life, and now it was choking him and the points of the half-starched collar were stabbing the flesh of his neck.

'Already they are coming in from the villages. Twelve thousand people they will have in that damn Market Place. You know what they are building? They are building a *Schaffott*.' His English had once more defeated him. 'What the hell is *Schaffott*?' he demanded of the company at large.

Siebkron stirred as if he had been offered water. 'Scaffold,' he murmured, and the dying eyes, lifting in Turner's direction, flickered and went out.

'Siebkron's English is fantastic!' Saab cried happily. 'Siebkron dreams of Palmerston in the daytime and Bismarck in the dark. Now is evening, you see: he is in the middle!' Siebkron heard the diagnosis and it gave him no comfort at all. 'A *scaffold*. I hope they maybe hang the damn fellow on it. Siebkron, you are too kind to him.' He lifted his glass to Bradfield and proposed a long toast pregnant with unwelcome compliments.

'Karl-Heinz also has fantastic English,' the little doll said. 'You are too modest, Karl-Heinz. It is just as good as Herr Siebkron's.' Between her breasts, deep down, Turner glimpsed a tiny flash of white. A handkerchief? A letter? Frau Saab did not care for Siebkron; she cared for no man, indeed, whose virtue was extolled above her husband's. Her interjection had cut the thread: once more the conversation lay like a fallen kite, and for a moment not even her husband had the wind to lift it.

'You said forbid him.' Siebkron had picked up a silver nutmeg grater in his soft hand and was gently turning it in the candlelight, searching for tell-tale flaws. The plate before him was licked quite clean, a cat's plate on a Sunday. He was a sulky, pale man, well-scrubbed and no more than Turner's age, with something of the hotelier about him, a man used to walking on other people's carpets. His features were rounded but unyielding; his lips autonomous, parting to perform one function, closing to perform another. His words were not a help but a challenge, part of a silent interrogation which only fatigue, or the deep cold sickness of his heart, prevented him from conducting aloud.

'*Ja.* Forbid him,' Saab assented, leaning well across the table in order to reach his audience. 'Forbid the meetings, forbid the marching, forbid it all. Like the Communists, that's the only damn thing they understand. *Siebkron, Sie waren ja auch in Hanover!* Siebkron was there also: why don't he forbid it? They are wild beasts out there. They have a power, *nicht wahr Siebkron?* My God, I have also made my experiences.' Saab was an older man, a journalist who had served a number of newspapers in his time, but most of them had disappeared since the war. No one seemed in much doubt what sort of experiences Herr Saab had made. 'But I have never hated the English. Siebkron, you can confirm that. *Das Können sie ja bestätigen.* Twenty years I have written about this crazy Republic. I have been critical—sometimes damn critical—but I have never been *hard* against the English. That I never was,' he concluded, jumbling his last words in a way which at once cast doubt upon the whole assertion.

'Karl-Heinz is fantastically strong for the English,' the little doll said. 'He eats English, he drinks English.' She sighed as if the rest of his activities were rather English too. She ate a great deal, and some of it was still in her mouth as she spoke, and her tiny hands held other things that she would eat quite soon.

'We owe you a debt,' said Bradfield with heavy cheerfulness, 'Long may you keep it up, Karl-Heinz.' He had arrived back from Brussels half an hour ago, and his eye was on Siebkron all the time.

Mrs Vandelung, the wife of the Dutch Counsellor, drew her stole more snugly over her ample shoulders. 'We are going to England every year,' she said complacently, apropos of nothing at all. 'Our daughter is at school in England, our son is at school in England . . .' She ran on. Nothing she loved, cherished or possessed was not of an English character. Her husband, a shrivelled, nautical man, touched Hazel Bradfield's beautiful wrist and nodded with reflected fervour.

'Always,' he whispered, as if it were a pledge. Hazel Bradfield, waking from her reverie, smiled rather solemnly at him while her eyes regarded with detachment the grey hand that still held her. 'Why, Bernhard,' she said gently, 'what a darling you are tonight. You will make the women jealous of me.' It was not, all the same, a comfortable joke. Her voice had its ugly edge; she could be one of several daughters, Turner decided, intercepting her angry glance as Saab resumed his monologue; but she was not merciful to her plainer sisters. 'Am I sitting in Leo's place?' he wondered, 'Eating Leo's portion?' But Leo stayed at home on Tuesdays . . . and besides, Leo was not allowed here, he reminded himself, raising his glass to answer a toast from Saab, except for a drink.

Saab's subject, miraculously, was still the British, but he had enriched it with autobiographical matter on the discomforts of bombing: 'You know what they say about Hamburg? Question: what is the difference between an Englishman and a man of Hamburg? Answer: the man of Hamburg speaks German. You know in those cellars, what we were saying? *Thank God they are British bombs!* Bradfield prosit! Never again.'

'Never again indeed,' Bradfield replied, and wearily toasted him in the German style, looking at him over the brim of his glass, drinking and looking again.

'Bradfield, you are the *best piece*. Your ancestors fought at Waterloo, and your wife is as beautiful as the Queen. You are the best piece in the British Embassy and you didn't invite the damn Americans and you didn't invite the damn French. You are a good fellow. Frenchmen is bastards,' he concluded to everyone's alarm, and there was a moment's startled silence.

'Karl-Heinz, I'm sure that isn't very loyal,' said Hazel and a little laugh went up at her end of the table, originated by a pointless elderly Gräfin summoned at the last moment to partner Alan Turner. An unwelcome shaft of electric light broke upon the company. The Hungarians marched in from the kitchen like the morning shift and cleared away bottles and china with inconsiderate *panache*.

Saab leaned still further across the table and pointed a big, not very clean finger at the guest of honour. 'You see this fellow Ludwig Siebkron here is a damn odd fellow. We all admire him in the Press Corps, because we can't never damn well get hold of him, and in journalism we admire only what we cannot have. And do you know why we cannot have Siebkron?'

The question amused Saab very much. He looked happily round the table, his dark face glistening with delight. 'Because he is so damn busy with his good friend and . . . Kumpan.' He snapped his fingers in frustration. '*Kumpan*,' he repeated. '*Kumpan?*'

'*Drinking companion*,' Siebkron suggested. Saab stared at him lamely, bewildered by assistance from such an unexpected quarter. 'Drinking companion,' he muttered; 'Klaus Karfeld,' and fell silent.

'Karl-Heinz, you must remember *Kumpan*,' his wife said softly, and he nodded and smiled at her valiantly.

'You have come to join us, Mister Turner?' Siebkron enquired, addressing the nutmeg grater. Suddenly the lights were on Turner, and Siebkron, risen from his bed, was conducting the rare surgery of a private practice.

'For a few days,' Turner said. The audience was slow in gathering, so that for a moment the two men faced one another in secret communion while the others continued their separate pursuits. Bradfield had engaged in a desultory cross-talk with Vandelung; Turner caught a reference to Vietnam. Saab, suddenly returning to the field, took up the subject and made it his own.

'The Yanks would fight in Saigon,' he declared, 'but they wouldn't fight in Berlin. Seems a bit of a pity they didn't build the Berlin Wall in Saigon.' His voice was louder and more offensive, but Turner heard it out of the dark that was beyond Siebkron's unflinching gaze. 'All of a sudden the Yanks are going crazy about self-determination. Why don't they try it in East Germany a little bit? Everyone fights for the damn Negroes. Everyone fights for the damn jungle. Maybe it's a pity we don't wear no feathers.' He seemed to be challenging Vandelung, but without effect: the old Dutchman's grey skin was as smooth as a coffin, and nothing would sprout there any more. 'Maybe it's a pity we don't have no palm trees in Berlin.' They heard him pause to drink. 'Vietnam is shit. But at least this time maybe they can't say we started it,' he added with more than a trace of self-pity.

'War is terrible,' the Gräfin whickered, 'We lost everything,' but she was talking after the curtain had gone up. Herr Ludwig Siebkron proposed to speak, and had put down the silver nutmeg grater in order to signify his will.

'And where do you come from, Mister Turner?'

'Yorkshire.' There was silence. 'I spent the war in Bournemouth.'

'Herr Siebkron meant which Department,' Bradfield said crisply.

'Foreign Office,' said Turner. 'Same as everyone else,' and looked at him indifferently across the table. Siebkron's white eyes neither condemned nor admired, but waited for the moment to insert the scalpel.

'And may we ask Mr Turner which section of the Foreign Office is so fortunate as to have his services?'

'Research.'

'He's also a distinguished mountaineer,' Bradfield put in from far away, and the little doll cried out with the sharp surprise of sexual delight. '*Die Berge!*' Out of the corner of his eye Turner saw one china hand touch the halter of her dress as if she would take it clean off in her enthusiasm. 'Karl-Heinz—'

'Next year,' Saab's brown voice assured her in a whisper. 'Next year we go to the mountains,' and Siebkron smiled to Turner as if that were one joke they could surely share.

'But now Mr Turner is in the valley. You are staying in Bonn, Mr Turner?'

'Godesberg.'

'In a hotel, Mr Turner?'

'The Adler. Room Ten.'

'And what kind of research, I wonder, is conducted from the Hotel Adler, Room Ten?'

'Ludwig, my dear chap,' Bradfield interposed–his jocularity was not so very hollow–'Surely you recognize a spy when you see one. Alan's our Mata Hari. He entertains the Cabinet in his bedroom.'

Laughter, Siebkron's expression said, does not last for ever; he waited until it had subsided. 'Alan,' he repeated quietly. 'Alan Turner from Yorkshire, working in Foreign Office Research Department and staying at the Adler Hotel, a distinguished mountaineer. You must forgive my curiosity, Mr Turner. We are all on edge here in Bonn, you know. As, for my sins, I am charged with the physical protection of the British Embassy, I have naturally a certain interest in the people I protect. Your presence here is reported to Personnel Department no doubt? I must have missed the bulletin.'

'We put him down as a technician,' Bradfield said, clearly irritated now to be questioned before his own guests.

'How sensible,' said Siebkron. 'So much simpler than Research. He does research but you put him down as a technician. Your technicians on the other hand are all engaged in research. It's a perfectly simple arrangement. But your research is of a practical nature, Mr Turner? A statistician? Or you are an academic perhaps?'

'Just general.'

'General research. A very catholic responsibility. You will be here long?'

'A week. Maybe more. Depends how long the project lasts.'

'The research project? Ah. Then you have a project. I had imagined at first you were replacing someone. Ewan Waldebere for instance; he was engaged in commercial research, was he not, Bradfield? Or Peter McCreedy, on scientific development. Or Harting: you are not replacing Leo Harting for instance? Such a pity he's gone. One of your oldest and most valuable collaborators.'

'Oh Harting!' Mrs Vandelung had taken up the name, and it was already clear she had strong views. 'You know what they are saying now already? That Harting is drunk in Cologne. He goes on *fits* you know.' She was much entertained to hold their interest. 'And the week he wears angels' wings and plays the organ and sings like a Christian; but at weekends he goes to Cologne and fights the Germans. He is quite a Jekyll and Hyde I assure you!' She laughed indulgently. 'Oh he is very wicked. Rawley, you remember André de Hoog I am sure. He has heard it all from the police here: Harting made a great fight in Cologne. In a night club. It was all to do with a bad woman. Oh, he is *very* mysterious I assure you. And now we have no one to play the organ.'

Through the mist Siebkron repeated his question.

'I'm not replacing anyone,' Turner said and he heard Hazel Bradfield's voice, quite steady from his left, but vibrant for all that with anger unexpressed.

'Mrs Vandelung, you know our silly English ways. We are supposed to leave the men to their jokes.'

Reluctantly the women departed. Little Frau Saab, desolated to leave her husband, kissed his neck and made him promise to be sober. The Gräfin said that in Germany one expected a cognac after a meal: it aided the digestion. Only Frau Siebkron followed without complaint; she was a quiet, deserted beauty who had learned very early in marriage that it paid not to resist.

Bradfield was at the sideboard with decanters and silver coasters; the Hungarians had brought coffee in a Hester Bateman jug which sat in unremarked magnificence at Hazel's end of the table. Little Vandelung was lost in memories; he was standing at the French windows, staring down the sloping dark lawn at the lights of Bad Godesberg.

'Now we will get port,' Saab assured them all. 'With Bradfield that is always a fantastic experience.' He selected Turner. 'I have had ports here, I can tell you, that are older than my father. What are we getting tonight, Bradfield? A Cockburn? Maybe he will give us a Cruft's. Bradfield knows all the brands. *Ein richtiger Kenner:* Siebkron, what is *Kenner auf Englisch?*'

'Connoisseur.'

'French!' Saab was outraged. 'The English have no word for *Kenner?* They use a French word? Bradfield! Telegram! Tonight! *Sofort an Ihre Majestät!* Personal recommendation top secret to the damn Queen. All Connoisseurs are forbidden. Only Kenner permitted! You are married, Mister Turner?'

Bradfield, having sat himself in Hazel's chair, now passed the port to his left. The coaster was a double one, joined elaborately with silver cords.

'No,' said Turner, and it was a word thrown down hard for anyone to pick up who wanted it. Saab, however, heard no music but his own.

'Crazy! The English should breed! Many babies. Make a culture. England, Germany and Scandinavia! To hell with the French, to hell with the Americans, to hell with the Africans. *Klein-Europa,* do you understand me, Turner?' He held up his clenched fist, stiff from the elbow. 'Tough and good. What can speak and think. I am not so damn crazy. *Kultur.* You know what that means, *Kultur?*' He drank 'Fantastic!' he cried. 'The best ever! Number one.' He held up his glass to the candle. 'The best damn port I ever had. You can see the blood in the heart. Bradfield, what is it? A Cockburn for sure, but he always contradicts me.'

Bradfield hesitated, caught in a genuine dilemma. His eye turned first to Saab's glass, then to the decanters, then to his glass again.

'I'm delighted you enjoyed it. Karl-Heinz,' he said. 'I rather think, as a matter of fact, that what you are drinking is Madeira.'

Vandelung, from the French windows, began laughing. It was a cracked, vengeful laugh and it went on for a long time, while his whole little body shook to the tune of it, rising and falling with the bellows of his old lungs.

'Well now, Saab,' he said at last, walking slowly back to the table, 'maybe you will bring a little of your culture to the Netherlands as well.'

He began laughing again like a schoolboy, holding his knobbly hand to his mouth in order to conceal the gaps, and Turner was sorry for Saab just then, and did not care for Vandelung at all.

Siebkron had taken no port.

'You went to Brussels today. I hope very much that you had a successful journey, Bradfield? I hear there are renewed difficulties. I am sorry. My colleagues tell me New Zealand presents a serious problem.'

'Sheep!' Saab ᴄried. 'Who will eat the sheep? The English have made a damn farm out there and now no one won't eat the sheep.'

Bradfield's voice was all the more deliberate. 'No new problem has been raised at Brussels. The questions of New Zealand and the Agricultural Fund have both been on the table for years. They present no problems that cannot be ironed out between friends.'

'Between good friends. Let us hope you are right. Let us hope the friendship is good enough and the difficulties small enough. Let us hope so.' Siebkron's gaze was on Turner again. 'So Harting is gone,' he remarked, laying his hands flatly together in prayer. 'Such a loss to our community. Particularly for the Church.' And looking directly at Turner he added: 'My colleagues tell me you know Mr Sam Allerton, the distinguished British journalist. You spoke with him today, I believe.'

Vandelung had given himself a glass of Madeira and was sampling it ostentatiously. Saab, sullen and dark faced, stared from one of them to the other, comprehending little.

'Ludwig, what an extraordinary idea. What do you mean, "Harting is gone"? He's on leave. I cannot imagine how all these silly rumours have got about. Poor fellow, his only crime was not to tell the Chaplain.' Bradfield's laughter was wholly artificial, but it was an act of courage in itself. 'Compassionate leave. It is not like you, Ludwig, to get your information wrong.'

'You see, Mr Turner, I have great difficulties here. For my sins, I am responsible for civil order during the demonstrations. Responsible to my Minister, you understand; and only in a modest capacity. But responsible all the same.'

His modesty was saintly. Put a ruff on him and a surplice and he could sing in Harting's choir any time. 'We are expecting a little demonstration on Friday. I am afraid that among certain minority groups the English are at present not very popular. You will appreciate that I don't want anybody to get hurt; anybody at all. Naturally therefore I like to know where everybody is. So that I can protect them. But poor Mister Bradfield is often so overworked he does not tell me.' He broke off and glanced once at Bradfield, and then no more. 'Now I am not *blaming* Bradfield that he does not tell me. Why should he?' The white hands parted in concession. 'There are many little things and there are even one or two big things which Bradfield does not tell me. Why should he? That would not be consistent with his vocation as a diplomat. I am correct, Mister Turner?'

'It's not my problem.'

'But it is mine. Let me explain what happens. My colleagues are observant people. They look around, count heads, and notice that somebody is missing. They make enquiries, question servants and friends perhaps, and they are told that he has disappeared. Immediately I am worried for him. So are my colleagues. My colleagues are compassionate people. They don't like anyone to go astray. What could be more human? They are boys, some of them. Just boys. Harting has gone to England?'

The last question was spoken directly to Turner, but Bradfield took it on himself and Turner blessed him.

'He has family problems. Clearly we cannot advertise them. I don't propose to put a man's private life upon the table in order to satisfy your files.'

'That is a very excellent principle. And one we must all follow. Do you hear that, Mr Turner?' His voice was remarkably emphatic. 'What is the point of a paper chase? What *is* the point?'

'Why on earth are you so bothered about Harting?' Bradfield demanded, as if it were a joke of which he had tired. 'I'm astonished you even know of his existence. Let's go and get some coffee, shall we?'

He stood up; but Siebkron remained where he was.

'But of *course* we know of his existence,' he declared. 'We admire his work. We admire it very much indeed. In a department such as mine, Mr Harting's ingenuity finds many admirers. My colleagues speak of him constantly.'

'What are you talking about?' Bradfield had coloured in anger. 'What *is* all this? What work?'

'He used to be with the Russians, you know,' Siebkron explained to Turner. 'In Berlin. That was a long time ago, of course, but I am sure that he learnt a great deal from them, don't you think so, Mr Turner? A little technique, a little ideology perhaps? And *grip*. The

Russians *never* let go.'

Bradfield had put the two decanters on a tray and was standing at the doorway waiting for them to go ahead of him.

'What work was that?' Turner asked gruffly, as Siebkron reluctantly rose from his chair.

'Research. Just general research, Mr Turner. Like yourself, you see. It is nice to think that you and Harting have common interests. As a matter of fact that is why I asked whether you would replace him. My colleagues understand from Mr Allerton that you and Harting have *many* things in common.'

Hazel Bradfield looked up anxiously as they entered, and the glance she exchanged with Bradfield was eloquent of the emergency. Her four women guests sat on a single sofa. Mrs Vandelung was working at a sampler; Frau Siebkron in church black had laid her hands on her lap and was staring in private fascination at the open fire. The Gräfin, consoling herself for the untitled company she was obliged to keep, sipped morosely at a large brandy. Her parsimonious face was lit with small red flowers like poppies on a battlefield. Only little Frau Saab, her bosom freshly powdered, smiled to see them enter.

They were settled, resigned to boredom.

'Bernhard,' said Hazel Bradfield, patting the cushion beside her, 'Come and sit by me. I find you *specially* cosy this evening.' With a foxy smile the old man took his place obediently beside her. 'Now you're to tell me *all* the horrors I am to expect on Friday.' She was playing the spoilt beauty, and playing it well, but there was an undercurrent of anxiety in her voice which not even Bradfield's tuition had taught her wholly to suppress.

At a separate table, Siebkron sat alone like a man who travelled by a better class. Bradfield talked to his wife. No, she conceded, she had not been to Brussels; she did not go often with her husband. 'But you must insist!' he declared and launched at once upon a description of a favourite Brussels hotel. The Amigo; one should stay at the Amigo; it had the best service he had ever encountered. Frau Siebkron did not care for large hotels; she took her holidays in the Black Forest; that was what the children liked best. Yes; Bradfield loved the Black Forest himself; he had close friends At Dornstetten.

Turner listened in grudging admiration to Bradfield's inexhaustible flow of small-talk. He expected no help from anyone. His eyes were dark with fatigue, but his dialogue was as fresh, as considerate and as aimless as if he were on holiday.

'Come along, Bernhard; you're just a wise old owl and nobody ever tells me anything. I'm just the Hausfrau. I'm supposed to look at *Vogue* and make canapés all day.'

'You know the saying,' Vandelung replied. 'What else must

happen in Bonn before something happens? They can do nothing we have not seen before.'

'They can trample all over my roses,' Hazel remarked, lighting herself a cigarette. 'They can steal my husband away at all hours of the night. Day trips to Brussels indeed! It's quite absurd. And look what they did in Hanover. Can you imagine what would happen if they broke *these* windows? Dealing with that wretched Works Department? We'd all be sitting here in overcoats while they worked out who pays. It's *too* bad, it really is. Thank goodness we have Mr Turner to protect us.' As she said this her gaze rested upon him, and it seemed to him both anxious and enquiring. 'Frau Saab, does *your* husband travel all over the place these days? I am sure journalists make *far* better husbands than diplomats.'

'He is very true.' The little doll blushed unhappily.

'She means *loyal*.' Saab kissed her hand with love.

Opening her tiny handbag, she took out a powder compact and parted its gold petals one by one. 'We have been married one year tomorrow. It is so beautiful.'

'*Du bist noch schöner*,' Saab cried and the conversation disintegrated into an exchange of domestic and financial intelligence on the Saabs' newly-formed household. Yes, they had bought a plot of land up by Oberwinter. Karl-Heinz had bought it last year for the engagement and already the value had risen four marks per *quadratmeter*.

'Karl-Heinz, how do you say *quadratmeter?*'

'The same,' Saab asserted, 'Quadrate meter,' and glowered at Turner in case he should dare to contradict him.

Suddenly Frau Saab was talking and no one could stop her any more. Her whole little life was spread before them in an oriental tinkle of hopes and disappointments; the colour which had mounted so prettily to her cheeks stayed there like the warm flush of sexual success.

They had hoped that Karl-Heinz would get the Bonn *Büro* of his newspaper. Bonn editor: that had been their expectation. His salary would go up another thousand and he would have a real *position*. What had happened instead? The paper had appointed *den Flitzdorf* and the Flitzdorf was just a boy, with no experience and nothing and *completely* homosexual and Karl-Heinz, who had worked now eighteen years for the paper and had so many contacts, was still only second man and was having to make extra by writing for all the cheese-papers.

'Yellow press,' said her husband, but for once she quite ignored him.

Well, when that had happened they had had a long discussion and decided they would go ahead with their building plans although the *Hypothek* was appalling; and no sooner had they paid over the money to the *Makler* than a really terrible thing happened: the Africans had come to Oberwinter. It was quite awful. Karl-Heinz was always very sharp against Africans, but now they had actually taken the next door plot and were building a *Residenz* for one of their Ambassadors, and twice a week they came up and climbed like monkeys over the bricks and shouted they wanted it different; and in no time they would have a whole colony up there, with Cadillacs and children and music all night, and as for herself, she would be all alone when Karl-Heinz was working late, and they were already putting special bolts on the doors so that she would not be—

'They talk fantastic!' Saab shouted, loudly enough for Siebkron and Bradfield to look round at him sharply; for the two men had drawn away to the window and were murmuring quietly into the night. 'But we don't get nothing to drink!'

'Karl-Heinz, my poor chap, we are completely neglecting you.' With a final word to Siebkron, Bradfield walked down the room to where the decanters stood on their bright-cut silver tray. 'Who else would like a nightcap?'

Vandelung would have joined him, but his wife forbade it.

'And take *great* care,' she warned the young Frau Saab in a dreadfully audible aside, 'Or he will have a heart attack. So much eating and drinking and shouting: it affects the heart. And with a young wife not easily satisfied,' she added contentedly, 'he could die easy.' Taking her little grey husband firmly by the wrist, Frau Vandelung led him into the hall. In the same instant Hazel Bradfield leaned purposefully across the abandoned chair. 'Mr Turner,' she said quietly, 'there is a matter in which you can help me. May I take you away a moment?'

They stood in the sun room. Potted plants and tennis rackets lay on the window sills; a child's tractor, a pogo stick and a bundle of garden canes were strewn over the tiled floor. There was a mysterious smell of honey.

'I understand you're making enquiries about Harting,' she said. Her voice was crisp and commanding; she was very much Bradfield's wife.

'Am I?'

'Rawley's worrying himself to death. I'm convinced that Leo Harting's at the back of it.'

'I see.'

'He doesn't sleep and he won't even discuss it. For the last three days he's hardly spoken to me. He even sends messages by way of other people. He's cut himself off entirely from everything except his work. He's near breaking point.'

'He didn't give me that impression.'

'He happens to be my husband.'

'He's very lucky.'

'What's Harting taken?' Her eyes were bright with anger or determination. 'What's he stolen?'

'What makes you think he's stolen anything?'

'Listen. I, not you, am responsible for my husband's welfare. I have a *right* to know if Rawley is in trouble; tell me what Harting has done. Tell me where he is. They're all whispering about it; everyone. This ridiculous story about Cologne; Siebkron's curiosity: why can't *I* know what's going on?'

'That's what I was wondering myself,' Turner said.

He thought she might hit him, and he knew that if she did, he would hit her back. She was beautiful, but the arch corners of her mouth were drawn down in the frustrated fury of a rich child, and there were things about voice and manner which were dreadfully familiar.

'Get out. Leave me alone.'

'I don't care who you are. If you want to know official secrets you can bloody well get them at source,' Turner said, and waited for her to rise to him again.

Instead, she swept past him into the hall and ran upstairs. For a moment he remained where he was, staring confusedly at the muddle of children's and adult toys, the fishing rods, the croquet set and all the casual, wasteful equipment of a world he had never known. Still lost in thought, he made his way slowly back to the drawing-room. As he entered, Bradfield and Siebkron, side by side at the French window, turned as one man to stare at him, the object of their shared contempt.

It was midnight. The Gräfin, drunk and quite speechless, had been loaded into a taxi. Siebkron had gone; his farewell had been confined to the Bradfields. His wife must have gone with him, though Turner had not noticed her departure; the cushion where she had sat was barely depressed. The Vandelungs had also gone. Now the five of them sat round the fire in a state of post-festive depression, the Saabs on the sofa holding hands and staring at the dying coals, Bradfield quite silent sipping his thin whisky; while Hazel herself, in her long skirt of green tweed, curled like a mermaid into an armchair, played with the Blue Russian cat in self-conscious imitation of an eighteenth-century dream. Though she rarely looked at Turner, she did not trouble to ignore him; occasionally she even addressed a remark to him. A tradesman had been impertinent, but Hazel Bradfield would not do him the compliment of taking away her custom.

'Hanover was fantastic,' Saab muttered.

'Oh, not again, Karl-Heinz,' Hazel pleaded, 'I think I've heard enough of that to last forever.'

'*Why* did they run?' he asked himself. 'Siebkron was also there. They *ran*. From the front. They ran like crazy for that library. Why did they do that? All at once: *alles auf einmal.*'

'Siebkron keeps asking me the same question,' Bradfield said, in an exhausted moment of frankness. 'Why did they run? *He* should know if anyone does: he was at Eich's bedside; I wasn't. He heard what she had to say, I suppose; I didn't. What the hell's got into him? On and on: "What happened at Hanover mustn't happen in Bonn." Of course it mustn't, but he seems to think it's my fault it happened in the first place. I've never known him like that.'

'You?' Hazel Bradfield said with undisguised contempt. 'Why on earth should he ask *you*? You weren't even there.'

'He asks me all the same,' said Bradfield, standing up, in a moment so utterly passive and tender that Turner was moved suddenly to speculate on their relationship. 'He asks me all the same.' He put his empty glass on the sideboard. 'Whether you like it or not. He asks me repeatedly: "Why did they run?" Just as Karl-Heinz was asking now. "What made them run? What was it about the library that attracted them?" All I could say was that is was British, and we all know what Karfeld thinks about the British. Come on, Karl-Heinz: we must put you young people to bed.'

'And the grey buses,' Saab muttered. 'You read what they found about the buses for the bodyguard? They were *grey*, Bradfield, *grey*!'

'Is that significant?'

'It *was*, Bradfield. About a thousand years ago, it was damn significant, my dear.'

'I'm afraid I'm missing the point,' Bradfield observed with a weary smile.

'As usual,' his wife said; no one took it as a joke.

They stood in the hall. Of the two Hungarians, only the girl remained.

'You have been damn good to me, Bradfield,' Saab said sadly as they took their leave. 'Maybe I talk too much. *Nicht wahr, Marlene*: I talk too much. But I don't trust that fellow Siebkron. I am an old pig, see? But Siebkron is a young pig. Pay attention!'

'Why shouldn't I trust him, Karl-Heinz?'

'Because he don't never ask a question unless he knows the answer.' With this enigmatic reply, Karl-Heinz Saab fervently kissed the hand of his hostess and stepped into the dark, steadied by the young arm of his adoring wife.

Turner sat in the back while Saab drove very slowly on the left hand side of the road. His wife was asleep on his shoulder, one little hand still scratching fondly at the black fur which decorated the nape of her husband's neck.

'Why did they run at Hanover?' Saab repeated, weaving happily between the oncoming cars, 'Why those damn fools run?'

At the Adler, Turner asked for morning coffee at half past four, and the porter noted it with an understanding smile, as if that were the sort of time he expected an Englishman to rise. As he went to bed, his mind detached itself from the distasteful and mystifying interrogations of Herr Ludwig Siebkron in order to dwell on the more agreeable person of Hazel Bradfield. It was just as mysterious, he decided as he fell asleep, that a woman so beautiful, desirable and evidently intelligent, could tolerate the measureless tedium of diplomatic life in Bonn. If darling upper-class Anthony Willoughby ever took a shine at her, he thought, what on earth would Bradfield do then? And why—the chorus that sang him to sleep was the same chorus which had kept him awake through the long, tense, meaningless evening—why the hell was he invited in the first place?

And who had asked him? 'I am to invite you to dinner on Tuesday,' Bradfield had said: don't blame *me* for what happens.

And Bradfield, I *heard*! I heard you submit to pressure; I felt the softness of you for the first time; I took a step in your direction, I saw the knife in your back and I heard you speak with my own voice. Hazel you bitch; Siebkron you swine; Harting you thief: if *that's* what you think about life, queer de Lisle simpered in his ear, why don't you defect yourself.' God is dead. You can't have it both ways, that would be too medieval. . . .

He had set his alarm for four o'clock, and it seemed to be ringing already.

Chapter Eleven

Königswinter

It was still dark when de Lisle collected him and Turner had to ask the night porter to unlock the hotel door. The street was cold, friendless and deserted; the mist came at them in sudden patches.

'We'll have to go the long way over the bridge. The ferry's not running at this hour.' His manner was short to the point of abruptness.

They had entered the carriageway. To either side of them, new blocks, built of tile and armoured glass, sprang like night weeds out of the untilled fields, crested by the lamps of small cranes. They passed the Embassy. The dark hung upon the wet concrete like the smoke of a spent battle. The Union Jack swung limply from its standard, a single flower on a soldier's grave. Under the weary light of the front porch, the lion and the unicorn, their profiles blurred with repeated coats of red and gold, fought bravely on. In the waste land, the two rickety goalposts leaned drunkenly in the twilight.

'Things are warming up in Brussels,' de Lisle remarked in a tone which promised little elaboration. A dozen cars were parked in the forecourt, Bradfield's white Jaguar stood in its private bay.

'For us or against us?'

'What do you think?' He continued: 'We have asked for private talks with the Germans; the French have done the same. Not that they want them; it's the tug-of-war they enjoy.'

'Who wins?'

De Lisle did not reply.

The deserted town hung in the pink unearthly glow which cradles every city in the hour before dawn. The streets were wet and empty, the houses soiled like old uniforms. At the University arch, three policemen had made a lane of barricades and they flagged them down as they approached. Sullenly they walked round the small car, recording the licence number, testing the suspension by standing on the rear bumper, peering through the misted windscreen at the huddled occupants within.

'What was that they shouted?' Turner asked as they drove on.

'Look out for the one-way signs.' He turned left, following the blue arrow. 'Where the hell are they taking us?'

An electric van was scrubbing the gutter; two more policemen in greatcoats of green leather, their peak caps bent, suspiciously surveyed its progress. In a shop window a young girl was fitting beach clothes to a model, holding one plastic arm and feeding the sleeve along it. She wore boots of heavy felt and shuffled like a prisoner. They were in the station square. Black banners stretched across the road and along the awning of the station. 'Welcome to Klaus Karfeld!' 'A hunter's greeting, Klaus!' 'Karfeld! You stand for our self-respect!' A photograph, larger than any which Turner had so far seen, was raised on a massive new hoarding. '*Freitag!*' said the legend: Friday. The floodlights shone upon the word and left the face in darkness.

'They're arriving today. Tilsit, Meyer-Lothringen; Karfeld. They're coming down from Hanover to prepare the ground.'

'With Ludwig Siebkron playing host.'

They were running along some tramlines, still following the diversion signs. The route took them left and right again. They had passed under a small bridge, doubled back, entered another square, halted at some improvised traffic lights and suddenly they were both sitting forward in their cramped seats, staring ahead of them in astonishment, up the gentle slope of the market place towards the Town Hall.

Immediately before them, the empty stalls stood in lines like beds in a barrack hut. Beyond the stalls, the gingerbread houses offered their jagged gables to the lightening sky. But de Lisle and Turner were looking up the hill at the single pink and grey building which dominated the whole square. Ladders had been laid against it; the balcony was festooned in swathes of black; a flock of Mercedes was parked before it on the cobble. To its left, in front of a chemist's shop, floodlit from a dozen places, rose a white scaffolding like the outline of a medieval storming tower. The pinnacle reached as high as the dormer windows of the adjacent building; the giant legs, naked as roots grown in the dark, splayed obscenely over their own black shadows. Workmen were already swarming at its base. Turner could hear the piping echo of hammers and the whine of powered saws. A stack of timber struggled upwards on a silent pulley.

'Why are the flags at half mast?'

'Mourning. It's a gimmick. They're in mourning for national honour.'

They crossed the long bridge. 'That's better,' said de Lisle with a small grunt of satisfaction, and pushed down his collar as if he had entered a warmer world.

He was driving very fast. They passed a village and another. Soon they had entered the country and were following a new road along the eastern bank. To their right the tor of Godesberg, divided by tiers of mist, stood grimly over the sleeping town. They skirted the vineyard. The furrows, picked out by the mysterious darkness, were like seams stitched to the zig-zag patterns of the staves. Above the vineyard, the forests of the Seven Hills; above the forests, broken castles and Gothic follies black against the skyline. Abandoning the main road, they entered a short avenue which led directly to an esplanade bordered by unlit lamps and pollarded trees. Beyond it lay the Rhine, smouldering and undefined.

'Next on the left,' de Lisle said tersely. 'Tell me if there's anyone on guard.'

A large white house loomed before them. The lower windows were shuttered, the front gates open. Turner left the car and walked a short way along the pavement. Picking up a stone, he flung it hard and accurately against the side of the house. The sound echoed crookedly across the water, and upwards towards the black slopes of the Petersberg. Scanning the mist, they waited for a cry or a footstep. There was none.

'Park up the road and come back,' said Turner.

'I think I'll just park up the road. How long will you need?'

'You know the house. Come and help me.'

'Not my form. Sorry. I don't mind bringing you but I'm not coming in.'

'Then why bring me?'

De Lisle did not reply.

'Don't dirty your fingers, will you.'

Keeping to the grass verge, Turner followed the drive towards the house. Even by that light, he was conscious of the same sense of order which had characterized Harting's room. The long lawn was very tidy, the rose beds trimmed and weeded, the roses ringed with grass-cuttings and separately labelled with metal tags. At the kitchen door, three dustbins, numbered and licensed according to the local regulation, stood in a concrete bay. About to insert the key, he heard a footstep.

It was unmistakeably a footstep. It had the double imprint, slurred yet infallibly human, of a heel falling on gravel and the toe immediately following. A cautious footstep perhaps; a gesture half made and then withheld, a message sent and revoked; but beyond all argument a footstep.

'Peter?' He's changed his mind again, he thought. He's being soft hearted. 'Peter!'

There was still no answer.

'Peter, is that you?' He stooped, quickly picked up an empty bottle from the wooden crate beside him and waited, his ears tuned to the lightest sound. He heard the crowing of a cock in the Seven Hills. He heard the prickling of the sodden earth, like the tingling of pine needles in a wood; he heard the rustling of tiny waves along the river's shore; he heard the distant throbbing of the Rhine itself, like the turning of an unearthly machine, one tone made of many, breaking and joining like the unseen water; he heard the mutter of hidden barges, the shoot of anchor chains suddenly released; he heard a cry, like the lowing of lost cattle on a moor, as a lonely siren echoed on the cliff face. But he did not hear another footstep, nor the comfortable tones of de Lisle's courteous voice. Turning the key he pushed open the door hard; then stood still and listened again, the bottle rigid in his hand, while the faint aroma of stale cigar rose lovingly to his nostrils.

He waited, letting the room come to him out of the cold gloom. Gradually, the new sounds began. First from the direction of the serving hatch came the chink of glass; from the hall, the creak of wood; in the cellar, a hollow box was dragged over a concrete floor; a gong rang, one tone, imperious and distinctive; and from everywhere now, all about him there rose a vibrant, organic hum, obscure yet very close, pressing upon him, louder with every minute, as if the whole building had been struck with a flat hand and were trembling from the blow. Running to the hall, he charged into the dining-room put on the lights with a single sweeping movement of his palm and glared savagely round him, shoulders hunched, bottle clenched in his considerable fist.

'Harting!' he shouted now, 'Harting?' He heard the shuffle of scattering feet, and thrust back the partition door.

'Harting!' he called again, but his only answer was the soot slipping in the open hearth, and the banging of an errant shutter on the poor stucco outside. He went to the window and looked across the lawn towards the river. On the far bank, the American Embassy, brilliant as a power house, drove yellow shafts through the mist deep into the elusive water. Then at last he recognized the nature of his tormentor: a chain of six barges, flags flying, radar-lights glittering above them into the fog. As the last vessel vanished, so the strange domestic orchestra put aside its instruments. The glass ceased to chime, the stairs to creak, the soot to fall, the walls to tremble. The house settled again, ruminative but not yet reassured, waiting for the next assault.

Putting the bottle on the windowsill, Turner straightened himself and walked slowly from room to room. It was a wasteful, thinly built barrack of a place, built for a colonel out of reparation costs, at a time when the High Commission was stationed on the Petersberg; one of a colony, de Lisle had said, but the colony was never completed, for by then the Occupation had ended and the project was abandoned. A left-over house for a left-over man. It had a light side and a dark side according to whether the rooms looked on to the river or the Petersberg; the plaster was rough and belonged out of doors. The furniture was equivocal, as if no one had ever decided how much prestige Harting was entitled to. If there was emphasis, it fell upon the gramophone. Flexes ran from it in all directions and speakers to either side of the chimney had been set upon pivots to assist directional adjustment.

The dining table was laid for two.

At the centre, four porcelain cherubs danced in a circle. Spring pursued Summer, Summer recoiled from Autumn, Winter drew them all forward. To either side, two places were set for dinner. Fresh candles, matches, a bottle of burgundy, unopened, in the wine basket; a cluster of roses withering in a silver bowl. Over it all lay a thin layer of dust.

He wrote quickly in his notebook, then continued to the kitchen. It might have been confected for a woman's magazine. He had never seen so many gadgets. Mixers, cutters, toasters, openers. A plastic tray lay on the counter, the remnants of a single breakfast. He lifted the lid of the teapot. It was a herbal tea, bright red. Dregs of it remained in the teacup, staining the spoon. A second cup lay upside down in the plate rack. A transistor radio, similar to the one he had seen in the Embassy, stood on top of the refrigerator. Having once again noted the wavelengths, Turner went to the door, listened, then began pulling open cupboards, extracting tins and bottles, peering inside. Occasionally he recorded what he found. In the refrigerator half-litre cartons of Naafi milk stood in neat order along the inside shelf. Taking out a bowl of pâté he gently sniffed it, testing its age. On a white plate, two steaks were set side by side. Strips of garlic had been threaded into the flesh. He prepared it on the Thursday night, he thought suddenly. On Thursday night he *still* didn't know he was going to defect on Friday.

The upstairs corridor was carpeted with thin runners of coconut matting. The pine furniture was very rickety. He pulled out the suits one by one, thrusting his hands into the pockets, then throwing them aside as if they were spent. Their cut, like that of the house, was military; the jackets were waisted, with a small pocket midway on the right side; the trousers were tapered and had no turn-ups. Occasionally, as he continued his search, he drew out a handkerchief, a scrap of paper or a bit of pencil, and these he would examine, and perhaps record, before tossing the suit aside and seizing another from the rickety wardrobe. The house was trembling again. From somewhere—it seemed this time to be from the very depths of the building—came the sound of clanking metal like a goods train braking, one place calling and another answering, ascending from floor to floor. Barely had it died before he heard another footfall. Dropping the suit he sprang to the window. He heard it again. Twice. Twice he had heard the solid tread of feet. Pushing back the shutter he leaned into the twilight and stared down at the driveway.

'Peter?'

Was it the dark that moved, or a man? He had left the lights on in the hall and they cast a patchwork of shadows on the drive. There was no wind to set the beech trees nodding. A man then? A man hurrying past the window on the inside? A man whose shape had flickered on the gravel?

'Peter?'

Nothing. No car, no guard. The neighbouring houses still lay in darkness. Above him, Chamberlain's mountain woke slowly to the dawn. He closed the window.

He worked faster now. In the second wardrobe another half dozen suits confronted him. Recklessly he dragged them from their hangers, struck at the pockets and cast them away; and then that extra sense warned him: go slowly. He had come upon a suit of dark blue gabardine, a summer suit but very much for formal wear, more creased than the others and set aside from them as if it were awaiting the cleaner, or tomorrow. He weighed it cautiously in his hand. Laying it on the bed, he felt in the pockets and drew out a brown envelope carefully folded upon itself. A brown OHMS envelope, the kind of thing they use for income tax. There was no writing on the outside and the flap had been sealed and ripped open. It was a key: a

Yale key of dull, leaden colour, not newly cut but worn with age or use, a long, old-fashioned, complicated key for a deep and complicated lock, quite unlike the standard keys which comprised the Duty Officer's bunch. A despatch box key? Returning it to the envelope, he put it between the pages of his notebook and carefully examined the remaining pockets. Three cocktail sticks, one with grime at the point as if he had used it for cleaning his nails. Olive stones. Some loose change, four marks eighty, made up in small denominations. And a bill for drinks, undated, from a hotel in Remagen.

He left the study till last. It was a mean room, filled with cartons of whisky and tinned food. An ironing board stood beside the shuttered window. On an old card table, piles of catalogues, trade brochures and diplomatic price lists lay in uncharacteristic confusion. A small notebook recorded the commodities which Harting was evidently pledged to obtain. Turner glanced through it, then put it in his pocket. The tins of Dutch cigars were in a wooden box; there must have been a gross of them or more.

The glass-fronted bookcase was locked. Crouching, Turner studied the titles, rose, listened again, then fetched a screwdriver from the kitchen and with a single powerful wrench ripped the wood so that the brass came through suddenly like a bone through flesh, and the door swung uselessly open. The first half dozen volumes were German bound and pre-war, heavily ribbed and gilded. He could not read all the titles precisely, but some he guessed; Stundinger's *Leipziger Kommentar zum Strafgesetzbuch*; *Verwaltungsrecht*; and someone else on the Statute of Limitations. In each was written the name, Harting Leo, like the name on the coathanger; and once he came upon the printed emblem of a Berlin bear overwritten in a spiky German hand, very faint on the curves and very bold on the downstrokes *'Fur meinen geliebten Sohn Leo'*. The lower shelf was a medley: a Code of Conduct for British Officers in Germany, a German paperback on the flags of the Rhine, and an English-German phrase book published in Berlin before the war, annotated and very fingered. Reaching right to the back, he drew out a handful of slim, cloth-bound monthly newsletters of the Control Commission of Germany for the years forty-nine to fifty-one; some volumes were missing. As he opened the first volume the spine creaked and the dust rose swiftly to his nostrils. 'No. 18 Field Investigation Unit Hanover,' the inscription read, written out, every word, in a good clerical hand, very bold on the downstrokes and refined at the curves, in a black, powdery ink which only governments can buy. A thin line cancelled the title and a second title replaced it: 'No. 6 General Enquiry Unit, Bremen.' Beneath it again (for Bremen too had been crossed out) he read the words: 'Property of the Judge Advocate

General's Department, Moenchengladbach,' and beneath that again, 'Amnesty Commission, Hanover. Not to be taken away.' Selecting a page at random, he found himself suddenly arrested by a retrospective account of the operation of the Berlin airlift. Salt should be slung under the wings of the aircraft and on no account carried inside the fuselage . . . the transportation of petrol presented high risks on landing and taking off . . . it was found preferable, in the interests of morale if not of economy, to fly-in coal and corn rather than to make the bread in advance and deliver it ready-baked . . . by using dehydrated instead of fresh potatoes, seven hundred and twenty tons could be saved on a daily ration of nine hundred tons for the civilian population. Fascinated, he slowly turned the yellow pages, his eye halting at phrases of unexpected familiarity. '*The first meeting of the Allied High Commision was held on 21st September at the Petersberg, near Bonn . . .*' A German Tourist Office was to be opened in New York. . . . The festivals of Bayreuth and Oberammergau were to be resuscitated as swiftly as time allowed. . . . He glanced at the summary of minutes of the High Commission meetings: '*Methods of broadening opportunities and responsibilities of the Federal Republic of Germany in the field of foreign and economic activity were considered. . . . The wider powers for the German Federal Republic in the field of foreign trade, decided upon under the Occupation statute, were defined. . . . Direct German participation in two more international organizations was authorized. . . .*'

The next volume opened naturally at a page dealing with the release of German prisoners detained under certain arrest categories. Once again, he found himself compelled to read on: Three million Germans presently in captivity . . . those detained were faring better than those at liberty . . . the Allies faced with the impossibility of separating the wheat from the chaff. . . . Operation Coalscuttle would send them down the mines, Operation Barleycorn would send them to the harvest. . . . One passage was sharply sidelined in blue ballpoint: *On 31st May, 1948, therefore, as an act of clemency, an amnesty was granted from proceedings under Ordinance 69 to all members of the SS not in automatic arrest categories, except for those who had been active as concentration camp guards.* The words 'act of clemency' had been underscored, and the ink looked uncommonly fresh.

Having examined each, he grasped hold of the covers and with a savage twist wrenched them from the binding as if he were breaking the wings of a bird; then turned over what remained and shook it, searching for hidden matter; then rose and went to the door.

The clanking had begun again and it was far louder than before. He remained motionless, his head to one side, his colourless eyes vainly searching the gloom: and he heard a low whistle, a long monotone, resonant and mournful, patiently summoning, softly coaxing, eerily lamenting. A wind had risen; it was the wind for sure. He could hear the shutter again, slamming against the wall: yet surely he had closed the shutter? It was the wind: a dawn wind which had come up the river valley. A strong wind, though, for the creaking of the stairs was taut, and mounted its own scale like the creaking of a ship's ropes as the sails fill; and the glass, the dining-room glass, it was jingling absurdly; far louder than before.

'Hurry,' Turner whispered. He was talking to himself.

He pulled open the drawers of the desk. They were not locked. Some were empty. Light bulbs, fuse wire, sewing materials; socks, spare cuffs for shirts; an unframed print of a galleon in full sail. He turned it over and read: 'To darling Leo from Margaret, Hanover 1949. With fondest affection.' The script was clearly continental. Folding it roughly, he put it in his pocket. Under the print was a box. It was a square, hard box by the feel of it, bound in a black silk handkerchief, wrapped like a parcel and pinned upon itself. Unfastening the pins he cautiously drew out a tin of dull silvery metal; it must have been painted once, for the metal had the matt uneven texture of a surface scratched clean with a fine instrument. Loosening the lid, he looked inside, then gently, almost reverently, emptied the contents on to the handkerchief. Five buttons lay before him. They were each about one inch in diameter, wooden and hand-made to the same pattern, crudely but with the greatest care, as if the maker wanted for instruments but not for application, and they were pierced twice, generously, to admit a very broad thread. Under the tin was a German textbook, the property of a Bonn library, stamped and annotated by the librarian. He could not understand it very well, but it seemed to be a technical treatise on the use of military gases. The last borrower had taken it out in February of that year. Certain passages were sidelined and there were small notes in the margin: 'Toxic effect immediate . . . symptoms delayed by cold weather.' Training the light full upon them, Turner sat at the desk, his head cupped in his hand and studied them with the greatest concentration; so that only instinct made him swing round and face the tall figure in the doorway.

He was quite an elderly man. He wore a tunic and a peaked cap of the kind that German students used to wear, or merchant sailors in the First World War. His face was dark with coaldust; he held a rusted riddling iron like a trident across his body, and it trembled dreadfully in his old hands; but his red, stupid eyes were turned downwards to the pile of desecrated books, and he looked very angry indeed. Very slowly, Turner stood up. The old man did not move, but the riddling-iron shook wildly, and the white of his knuckles shone white through the soot. Turner ventured a pace forward.

'Good morning,' he said.

One black hand detached itself from the shaft and rose mechanically to the peak of his hat. Turner strode to the corner where the cartons of whisky were stacked. He ripped open the top carton, pulled out a bottle, tore off the lid. The old man was mumbling, shaking his head, still staring at the books.

'Here,' said Turner softly, 'Have a drink,' and held the bottle forward into the old man's line of sight.

Listlessly he let the iron fall, took the bottle and held it to his thin lips while Turner charged past him to the kitchen. Opening the door, he shouted at the top of his voice.

'De Lisle!'

The echo carried wildly into the deserted street and outwards to the river.

'De Lisle!'

Even before he had returned to the study, the lights were going on in the windows of neighbouring houses.

Turner had pulled open the wooden shutters to let in the new daylight, and now the three of them stood in a baffled group, the old man blinking at the broken books and clutching the whisky in his shaking hand.

'Who is he?'

'The boilerman. We all have them.'

'Ask him when he last saw Harting.'

The old man did not immediately reply, but instead, waking again to the whisky, drank a little more, then passed it to de Lisle, whom he appeared instinctively to trust. De Lisle set it on the desk beside the silk handkerchief and quietly repeated his question, while the old man stared from one to the other, and then at the books.

'Ask him when he last saw Harting.'

At last he spoke. His voice was timeless: a slow peasant drawl, the murmur of the confessional, querulous yet subjugate, the voice of an underdog in the hopeless quest for consideration. Once he reached out his black fingers to touch the smashed beading of the bookcase; once he nodded towards the river, as if the river was where he lived; but the murmur continued through his gestures as if it came from someone else.

'He sells tickets for a pleasure cruise,' de Lisle whispered. 'He comes at five in the evening on the way home, and first thing in the morning on the way to work. He stokes the boilers, does the dustbins and the empties. In summer he cleans the boats before the charabancs arrive.'

'Ask him again. When did he last see Harting? Here'—he produced a fifty mark note—'Show him this—say I'll give it him if he tells me what I want to know.'

Seeing the money, the old man examined Turner carefully with his dry, red eyes. His face was lined and hollow, starved at some time and held up by the long cords of his shrivelled skin, and the soot was worked into it like pigment into canvas. Folding the banknote carefully down the centre he added it to the wad from his hip pocket.

'When?' Turner demanded. '*Wann?*'

Cautiously the old man began putting his words together, picking them one by one, articles in the bargain. He had taken off his hat; a sooty stubble covered his brown skull.

'Friday,' de Lisle quietly interpreted. His eye was on the window and he seemed distracted. 'Leo paid him on Friday afternoon. He went round to his house and paid him on the doorstep. He said he was going on a long journey.'

'Where to?'

'He didn't say where.'

'When will he come back? Ask him that.'

Once more, de Lisle translated and Turner caught the half familiar words: *kommen . . . zurück.*

'Leo gave him two months' pay. He says he has something to show us. Something that is worth another fifty marks.'

The old man was glancing quickly from one to the other of them, fearful but expectant, while his long hands nervously explored the canvas tunic. It was a sailor's tunic, shapeless and bleached, and it hung without relation to his narrow frame. Finding what he was looking for, he cautiously rolled back the lower hem, reached upward and detached something from his neck. As he did so he began murmuring again, but faster than before, nervous and voluble.

'He found it on Saturday morning in the rubbish.'

It was a holster made of green webbing, army issue, suitable for a three-eight pistol. It had 'Harting Leo' stencilled on the inside and it was empty.

'In the dustbin, right on top; the first thing he saw when he lifted the lid. He didn't show it to the others. The others shouted at him and threatened to kick his face in. The others reminded him of what they'd done to him in the war and they said they'd do it again.'

'What others? Who?'

'Wait.'

Going to the window, de Lisle peered casually out. The old man was still talking.

'He says he distributed anti-Nazi pamphlets in the war,' he called, still watching. 'By mistake. He thought they were ordinary news-papers and the others caught him and hung him upside down. That's who the others seem to be. He says he likes the English best. He says Harting was a real gentleman. He says he wants to keep the whisky too. Leo always gave him Scotch. And cigars. Little Dutch cigars, a kind you can't get in the shops. Leo had them sent specially. And last Christmas he gave his wife a hair-dryer. He would also like fifty marks for the holster,' he added, but by then the cars had entered the drive, and the little room was filled with the double wail of a police horn and the double flash of a blue light. They heard the shout and the stamp of feet as the green figures gathered at the windows, pointing their guns into the room. The door was open and a young man in a leather coat held a pistol in his hand. The boilerman was crying, wailing, waiting to be hit and the blue light was rolling like a light for dancing. 'Do nothing,' de Lisle had said. 'Obey no orders.'

He was talking to the boy in the leather coat, offering his red diplomatic card for examination. His voice was quiet but very firm, a negotiator's voice, neither flippant nor concessive, stiffened with authority and hinting at injured privilege. The young detective's face was as blank as Siebkron's. Gradually de Lisle appeared to be gaining the ascendancy. His tone changed to one of indignation. He began asking questions, and the boy became conciliatory, even evasive. Gradually Turner gathered the trend of de Lisle's complaint. He was pointing at Turner's notebook and then at the old man. A list, he was saying, they were making a list. Was it forbidden for diplomats to make a list? To assess dilapidation, to check the inventory of Embassy furniture? It was surely a natural enough thing to do at a time when British property was in danger of destruction. Mr Harting had gone on extended leave of absence; it was expedient to make certain dispositions, to pay the boilerman his fifty marks. . . . And since when, de Lisle wished to know, were British diplomats forbidden entry to British Embassy livings? By what right, de Lisle wished to know, had this great concourse of militia burst upon the privacy of extra-territorial persons?

More cards were exchanged, more documents mutually examined; names and numbers mutually recorded. The detective was sorry, he said; these were troubled times, and he stared at Turner for a long time as if he recognized a colleague. Troubled times or not, de Lisle appeared to reply, the rights of diplomats must be respected. The greater the danger, the more necessary the immunity. They shook hands. Somebody saluted. Gradually they all withdrew. The green uniforms dispersed, the blue lights vanished, the vans drove away. De Lisle had found three glasses and was pouring a little whisky into each. The old man was whimpering. Turner had returned the buttons to their tin and put the tin in his pocket together with the little book on military cases.

'Was that them?' he demanded. 'Were those the ones who questioned him?'

'He says: *like* the detective, but a little older. Whiter, he says: a richer kind of man. I think we both know who he's talking about. Here, you'd better look after this yourself.'

Tugging the holster from the folds of his brown overcoat, de Lisle thrust it without pride into Turner's waiting hand.

The ferry was hung with the flags of the German Federation. The crest of Königswinter was nailed to the bridge. Militia packed the bow. Their steel helmets were square, their faces pale and sad. They were very quiet for such young men and their rubber boots made no sound on the steel deck, and they stared at the river as if they had been told to remember it. Turner stood apart from them, watching the crew cast away, and he perceived everything very clearly because he was tired and frightened and because it was still early morning: the heavy vibration of the iron deck as the cars thumped over the ramp and pressed forward to the best berth; the howl of the engines and the clatter of chains as the men shouted and cast away, the strident bell that put out the fading chimes of the town's churches, the uniform hostility of the drivers as they rose from their cars and picked the change from their pigskin purses as if men were a secret society and could not acknowledge each other in public; and the pedestrians, the bronzed and the poor, coveting the cars from which they were kept apart. The river bank receded; the little town drew its spires back into the hills like scenery at the opera. Gradually they described their awkward course, steering a long arc with the current to avoid the sister ferry from the opposite bank. Now they slowed almost to a halt, drifting down river as the *John F. Kennedy*, loaded with equal pyramids of fine coal, bore swiftly down upon them, the children's washing sloping in the wet air. Then they were rocking in its wake and the women passengers were calling in amusement.

'He told you something else. About a woman. I heard him say *Frau* and *Auto*. Something about a woman and a car.'

'Sorry old boy,' de Lisle said coolly, 'It's the Rhineland accent. Sometimes it simply defeats me.'

Turner stared back at the Königswinter bank, shielding his eyes with his gloved hand because even in that miserable spring the light came sharply off the water. At last he saw what he was looking for: to each side, like mailed hands pointing to the Seven Hills of Siegfried, turreted brown villas built with the wealth of the Ruhr; between them a splash of white against the trees of the esplanade. It was Harting's house receding in the mist.

'I'm chasing a ghost,' he muttered. 'A bloody shadow.'

'Your own,' de Lisle retorted, his voice rich with disgust.

'Oh, sure, sure.'

'I shall drive you back to the Embassy,' de Lisle continued. 'From then on, you find your own transport.'

'Why the hell did you bring me if you're so squeamish?' And suddenly he laughed. 'Of course,' he said. 'What a bloody fool I am! I'm going to sleep! You were frightened I might find the Green File and you thought you'd wait in the wings. Unsuitable for temporaries. Christ!'

Cork had just heard the eight o'clock news. The German delegation had withdrawn from Brussels during the night. Officially the Federal Government wished to 'reconsider certain technical problems which had arisen in the course of discussions'. Unofficially, as Cork put it, they had run away from school. Blankly he watched the coloured paper stutter out of the rollers and fall into the wire basket. It was about ten minutes before the summons came. There was a knock on the door and Miss Peate's stupid head appeared at the little trap. Mr Bradfield would see him at once. Her mean eyes were alive with pleasure. Once and for all, she meant. As he followed her into the corridor, he caught sight of Cork's brochure on plots of land in the Bahamas and he thought: that's going to be useful by the time he's done with me.

Chapter Twelve

'And there was Leo. In the second class'

'I have already spoken to Lumley. You go home tonight. Travel section will attend to your tickets.' Bradfield's desk was piled high with telegrams. 'And I have apologized in your name to Siebkron.'

'Apologized?'

Bradfield dropped the latch on the door. 'Shall I spell it out for you? Like Harting, you are evidently something of a political primitive. You are here on a temporary diplomatic footing; if you were not, you would undoubtedly be in prison.' He was pale with anger. 'God alone knows what de Lisle thought he was up to. I shall speak to him separately. You have deliberately disobeyed my instruction; well, you people have your own code, I suppose, and I am as suspect as the next man.'

'You flatter yourself.'

'In this case, however, you were placed specifically under my authority, by Lumley, by the Ambassador and by the necessities of the situation here, and specifically ordered to make no move which could have repercussions outside the Embassy. Be quiet and listen to me! Instead of showing the minimal consideration that was asked of you, however, you go round to Harting's house at five in the morning, frighten the wits out of his servant, wake the neighbours, bellow for de Lisle, and finally attract a full-scale police raid which, in a matter of hours, will no doubt be the talking point of the community. Not content with that, you are party to a stupid lie to the police about

conducting an inventory; I imagine that will bring a smile even to
Siebkron's lips, after the description you offered him of your work
last night.'

'Any more?'

'A great deal thank you. Whatever Siebkron suspected that
Harting had done, you have by now delivered the proof. You saw his
attitude for yourself. Heaven knows what he does not think we are up
to.'

'Then tell him,' Turner suggested. 'Why not? Ease his mind.
Christ, he knows more than we do. Why do we make a secret of
something they all know? They're in full cry. The worst we can do is
spoil their kill.'

'I will not have it *said*! Anything is better, any doubts, any
suspicions on their part, than our admission at this moment in time
that for twenty years a member of our diplomatic staff has been in
Soviet employment. Is there nothing you will understand of this? I
will not have it *said*? Let them think and do what they like, without
our cooperation they can *only* surmise.'

It was a statement of personal faith. He sat as still and as upright as
a sentry guarding a national shrine.

'Is that the lot?'

'You people are supposed to work in secret. One calls upon you
expecting a standard of discretion. I could tell you a little about your
behaviour here, had you not made it abundantly clear that manners
mean nothing to you whatever. It will take a long time to sweep up
the mess you have left behind you in this Embassy. You seem to
think that nothing reaches me. I have already warded off Gaunt and
Meadowes; no doubt there are others I shall have to soothe.'

'I'd better go this afternoon,' Turner suggested. He had not taken
his eyes from Bradfield's face. 'I've ballsed it up, haven't I? Sorry
about that. Sorry you're not satisfied with the service. I'll write and
apologize; that's what Lumley likes me to do. A bread and butter
letter. So I'll do that. I'll write.' He sighed, 'I seem to be a bit of a
Jonah. Best thing to do really, chuck me out. Be a bit of a wrench for
you, that will. You don't like getting rid of people do you? Rather
give them a contract?'

'What are you suggesting?'

'That you've a damn good reason for insisting on discretion! I said
to Lumley—Christ that was a joke—I asked him, see: does he want the
files or the man? What the hell *are* you up to? Wait! One minute you
give him a job, the next you don't want to know him. If they brought
his body in now you couldn't care bloody less: you'd pat the pockets
for papers and wish him luck!'

He noticed, quite inconsequentially, Bradfield's shoes. They were
hand-made and polished that dark mahogany which is only captured
by servants, or by those who have been brought up with them.

'What the devil do you mean?'

'I don't know who's putting the finger on you: I don't care. Siebkron, I would guess, from the way you crawl to him. Why did you bring us together last night if you were so bloody worried about offending him? What was the point of that, for one? *Or did he order you to?* Don't answer yet, it's my turn. You're Harting's guardian angel, do you realize that? It sticks out a mile, and I'll write it six foot high when I get back to London. You renewed his contract, right? Just that, for a start. Although you despised him. But you didn't just *give* him work; you *made* work for him. You knew bloody well the Foreign Office didn't give a damn about the Destruction programme. Or for the Personalities Index either, I shouldn't wonder. But you pretended; you built it up for him. Don't tell me it was compassion for a man who didn't belong.'

'Whatever there was of *that* has worn pretty thin by now,' Bradfield remarked, with a hint of that dismay, or self-contempt, which Turner now occasionally discerned in him.

'Then what about the Thursday meeting?'

A look of sheer pain crossed Bradfield's face.

'My God, you are insufferable,' he said, more as a mental note, a privately recorded judgment, than an insult directly intended.

'The Thursday conference that never was! It was you who took Harting off that conference; you who gave the job to de Lisle. But Harting still went out Thursday afternoons all right. Did you stop him? Did you hell. I expect you even know where he went, don't you.' He held up the gunmetal key he had taken from Harting's suit. 'Because there's a special place, you see. A hideaway. Or maybe I'm telling you something you know already. Who did he meet out there? Do you know that too? I used to think it was Praschko, until I remembered *you* fed me that idea, you yourself. So I'm going bloody carefully with Praschko.'

Turner was leaning across the desk, shouting at Bradfield's bowed head. 'As to Siebkron, he's rolling up a whole bloody network, like as not. Dozens of agents, for all we know: Harting was just one link in a chain. You can't begin to control what Siebkron knows and doesn't know. We're dealing with reality you know, not diplomacy.' He pointed to the window and the blurred hills across the river. 'They sell horses over there! They screw around, talk to friends, make journeys; they've been beyond the edge of the forest, they know what the world looks like!'

'It requires very little, in an intelligent person, to know that,' said Bradfield.

'And that's what I'm going to tell Lumley when I get back to the smoke. Harting didn't work alone! He had a patron as well as a controller and for all I know, they were the same man! And for all I bloody well know, Leo Harting was Rawley Bradfield's fancy boy!'

Having a bit of public school vice on the side!'

Bradfield was standing up, his face contracted with anger. 'Tell Lumley what you like,' he whispered, 'but get out of here and don't ever come back,' and it was then that Mickie Crabbe put his red, bubbling face round Miss Peate's connecting door.

He was looking puzzled and slightly indignant, and he was chewing absurdly at his ginger moustache. 'Rawley, I say,' he said and began again, as if he had started in the wrong octave. 'Sorry to burst in, Rawley. I tried the door in the corridor but the latch was down. Sorry Rawley. It's about Leo,' he said. The rest came out with rather a rush, 'I've just seen him down at the railway station. Bloody well having a beer.'

'Be quick,' said Bradfield.

'Doing a favour for Peter de Lisle. That's all,' Crabbe began defensively. Turner caught the smell of drink on his breath, mingling with the smell of peppermint. 'Peter had to go down to the Bundestag. Debate on Emergency Legislation, big thing apparently, second day, so he asked me to cover the jamboree at the railway station. The Movement's leaders, coming in from Hanover. Watch the arrivals, see who turned up. I often do odd jobs for Peter,' he added apologetically. 'Turned out to a Lord Mayor's Show. Press, television lights, masses of cars lined up in the road'–he glanced nervously at Bradfield–'where the taxis stand, Rawley, *you* know. And crowds. All singing rah-rah and waving the old black flags. Bit of music.' He shook his head in private wonder. 'That square is *plastered* with slogans.'

'And you saw Leo,' Turner said, pressing. 'In the crowd?'

'Sort of.'

'What do you mean?'

'Well the back of his head. Head and shoulders. Just a glimpse. No time to grab him: gone.'

Turner seized him with his big, stone hands. 'You said you saw him having a beer!'

'Let him go,' said Bradfield.

'Hey steady!' For a moment Crabbe looked almost ferocious. 'Well I saw him later, you see. After the show was over. Face to face sort of thing.'

Turner released him.

'The train came in and everyone started cheering pretty loud, and shoving about and trying to get a glimpse of Karfeld. There was even a bit of fighting at the edges, I think, but that was mainly the journalists. *Sods,* he added with a spark of real hatred. 'That shit Sam Allerton was there, by the way. I should think *he* started it.'

'For Christ's sake!' Turner shouted, and Crabbe regarded him quite straightly, with an expression which spoke of bad form.

'First of all Meyer-Lothringen came out—the police had made a gangway for him out of cattle pens—then Tilsit, then Halbach, and everyone shouting like gyppos. Beatles,' he said, incomprehendingly. 'Kids mainly they were, long-haired student types, leaning over the railings trying to touch the chaps' shoulders. Karfeld didn't make it. Some fellow near me said he must have gone out the other side, gone down the passage to avoid the crowd. He doesn't like people coming too close, that's what they say; that's why he builds these damn great stands everywhere. So half the crowd charges off to see if they can find him. The rest hang around in case, and then there's this announcement over the blower: we can all go home because Karfeld's still in Hanover. Lucky for Bonn, that's what I thought.' He grinned. 'What?'

Neither spoke.

'The journalists were furious and I thought I'd just give Rawley a ring to let him know Karfeld hadn't turned up. London likes to keep track, you see. Of Karfeld.' This for Turner. 'They like to keep tabs on him, not have him talking to strange men.' He resumed: 'There's an all-night Post Office by the hall there, and I was just coming out when it occurred to me'—he made a feeble attempt to drag them into the conspiracy—'that maybe I ought to have a quick cup of coffee to collect my thoughts, and I happened to look through the glass door of the waiting-room. Doors are side by side you see. Restaurant one side, waiting-room the other. It's a sort of buffet in there with a few places to sit as well. I mean sit and not drink,' he explained, as if that were a particular type of eccentricity he had occasionally met with. 'There's the first class on the left and the second class on the right, both glass doors.'

'For pity's sake!' Turner breathed.

'And there was Leo. In the second class. At a table. Wearing a trench coat, a sort of army looking thing. Seemed in rather bad shape.'

'Drunk?'

'I don't know. Christ, that would be going it, wouldn't it: eight in the morning.' He looked very innocent. 'But tired out and well, not dapper, you know, not like he usually is. Gloss, bounce: all gone. Still,' he added stupidly, 'Comes to all of us I suppose.'

'You didn't speak to him?'

'No thanks. I know him in that mood. I gave him a wide berth and came back and told Rawley.'

'Was he carrying anything,' Bradfield said quickly. 'Did he have a briefcase with him? Anything that could hold papers?'

'Nothing *about*,' Crabbe muttered, 'Rawley old boy. Sorry.'

They stood in silence, all three, while Crabbe blinked from one face to the other.

'You did well,' Bradfield muttered at last. 'All right, Crabbe.'

'*Well?*' Turner shouted. 'He did bloody badly! Leo's not in quarantine. Why didn't he talk to him, drag him here by the neck, reason with him? God Almighty you're not bloody well alive, either of you! *Well?* He may be gone by now; that was our last chance! He was probably waiting for his final contact; they've dirtied him up for the journey out! Did he have anyone with him?' He pulled open the door. 'I said did he have anyone with him? Come on!'

'A kid,' said Crabbe. 'Little girl.'

'A *what?*'

'Six or seven years old. Someone's kid. He was talking to it.'

'Did he recognize you?'

'Doubt it. Seemed to look through me.'

Turner seized his raincoat from the stand.

'I'd rather not,' said Crabbe, answering the gesture rather than the exhortation. 'Sorry.'

'And you! What are *you* standing there for? *Come on!*'

Bradfield did not move.

'*For God's sake!*'

'I'm staying here. Crabbe has a car. Let him take you. It must be nearly an hour since he saw him, or thought he did, with all that traffic. He'll be gone by now. I don't propose to waste my own time.' Ignoring Turner's astonished gaze, he continued, 'The Ambassador has already asked me not to leave the building. We expect word from Brussels any minute; it is highly likely that he will wish to call upon the Chancellor.'

'Christ, what do you think this is? A tripartite conference. He may be sitting there with a caseful of secrets! No wonder he looks under the weather! What's got into you now? Do you *want* Siebkron to find him before we do? Do you want him to be caught red-handed?'

'I have already told you: secrets are not sacrosanct. We would prefer them kept, it is true. In relation to what I have to do here—'

'*Those* secrets are, aren't they? What about the bloody Green File?'

Bradfield hesitated.

'*I've* no authority over him,' Turner cried. 'I don't even know what he looks like! What am *I* supposed to do when I see him? Tell him you'd like a word with him? You're his boss, aren't you? Do you *want* Siebkron to find him first?' Tears had started absurdly to his eyes. His voice was one of utter supplication. 'Bradfield!'

'He was all alone,' Crabbe muttered, not looking at Bradfield, 'just him and himself, old boy. And the kid. I'm sure of that.'

Bradfield stared at Crabbe, and then at Turner, and once again his face seemed crowded by private pains scarcely held at bay.

'It's true,' he said at last, very reluctantly, 'I am his superior. I am responsible. I had better be there.' Carefully double-locking the outer door, he left word with Miss Peate that Gaveston should stand in for him, and led the way downstairs.

New fire extinguishers, just arrived from London, stood like red sentinels along the corridor. At the landing, a consignment of steel beds awaited assembly. A file-trolley was loaded with grey blankets. In the lobby two men, mounted on separate ladders, were erecting a steel screen. Dark Gaunt watched them in bewilderment as they swept through the glass doors into the car park, Crabbe leading. Bradfield drove with an arrogance which took Turner by surprise. They raced across the lights in amber, keeping to the left lane to make the turn into the station road. At the traffic check he barely halted; both he and Crabbe had their red cards ready at the window. They were on wet cobble, skidding on the tramlines and Bradfield held the wheel still, waiting patiently for the car to come to its senses. They approached an intersection where the sign said 'Yield', and ran straight over it under the wheels of an oncoming bus. The cars were fewer, the streets were packed with people.

Some carried banners, others wore the grey gabardine raincoats and black Homburg hats which were the uniform of the Movement's supporters. They yielded reluctantly, scowling at the number plates and the glittering foreign paintwork. Bradfield neither sounded his horn nor changed gear, but let them wake to him and avoid him as they might. Once he braked for an old man who was either deaf or drunk; once a boy slapped the roof of the car with his bare hand, and Bradfield became very still and pale. Confetti lay on the steps, the pillars were covered with slogans. A cab driver was yelling as if he had been hit. They had parked in the cab rank.

'Left,' Crabbe called as Turner ran ahead of him. A high doorway admitted them to the main hall.

'Keep left,' Turner heard Crabbe shout for the second time.

Three barriers led to the platform; three ticket collectors sat in their glass cages. Notices warned him in three languages not to ask them favours. A group of priests, whispering, turned to eye him disapprovingly: haste, they said, is not a Christian quality. A blonde girl, her face chestnut brown, swung dangerously past him with a rucksack and well-worn skis, and he saw the trembling of her pullover.

'He was sitting just there,' Crabbe whispered, but by then Turner had flung open the glazed swing door and was standing inside the restaurant, glaring through the cigarette smoke at each table in turn. A loudspeaker barked a message about changing at Cologne. 'Gone,' Crabbe was saying, 'Sod's flown.'

The smoke hung all around, lifting in the glow of the long tube lights, curling into the darker corners. The smell was of beer and smoked ham and municipal disinfectant; the far counter, white with

Dutch tiles, glinted like an ice wall in the fog. In a brown-wood cubicle sat a poor family on the move; the women were old and dressed in black, their suitcases were bound with rope; the men were reading Greek newspapers. At a separate table a little girl rolled beermats to a drunk, and that was the table Crabbe was pointing at.

'Where the kiddie is, you see. He was having a Pils.'

Ignoring the drunk and the child, Turner picked up the glasses and stared at them uselessly. Three small cigar ends lay in the ashtray. One was still slightly smouldering. The child watched him as he stooped and searched the floor and rose again empty handed; she watched him stride from one table to the next, glaring into the faces, seizing a shoulder, pushing down a newspaper, touching an arm.

'Is this him?' he yelled. A lonely priest was reading *Bildzeitung* in a corner; beside him, hiding in his shadow, a dark-faced gypsy ate roast chestnuts out of a bag.

'No.'

'This?'

'Sorry old boy,' said Crabbe, very nervous now, 'No luck. I say, go easy.'

By the stained-glass window two soldiers were playing chess. A bearded man was making the motions of eating, but there was no food before him. Outside on the platform a train was arriving, and the vibration shook the crockery. Crabbe was addressing the waitress. He was hanging over her, whispering and his hand was on the flesh of her upper arm. She shook her head.

'We'll try the other one,' he said, as Turner joined them. They walked across the room together, and this woman nodded, proud to have remembered, and made a long story, pointing at the child and talking about '*der kleine Herr*', the little gentleman, and sometimes just about '*der Kleine*', as if 'gentleman' were a tribute to her interrogators rather than to Harting.

'He was here till a few minutes ago,' Crabbe said in some bewilderment. 'Her version, anyway.'

'Did he leave alone?'

'Didn't see.'

'Did he make any impression on her?'

'Steady. She's not a big thinker, old boy. Don't want her to fly away.'

'What made him leave? Did he see someone? Did someone signal to him from the door?'

'You're stretching it old son. She didn't see him leave. She didn't worry about him, he paid with every order. As if he might leave in a hurry. Catch a train. He went out to watch the hoo-hah, when the boys arrived, then came back and had another cigar and a drink.'

'What's the matter then? Why are you looking like that?'

'It's bloody odd,' Crabbe muttered, frowning absurdly.

'What's bloody odd?'

'He's been here all night. Alone. Drinking but not drunk. Played with the kid part of the time. Greek kid. That was what he liked best: the kid.' He gave the woman a coin and she thanked him laboriously.

'Just as well we missed him,' Crabbe declared. 'Pugnacious little sod when he gets like this. Go for anyone when he's got his dander up.'

'How do you know?'

Crabbe grimaced in painful reminiscence: 'You should have seen him that night in Cologne,' he muttered, still staring after the waitress. 'Jesus.'

'In the fight? You were there?'

'I tell you,' Crabbe repeated. He spoke from the heart. 'When that lad's really going, he's best avoided altogether. Look.' He held out his hand. A wooden button lay in the palm and it was identical to the buttons in the scratched tin in Königswinter. 'She picked this up from the table,' he said. 'She thought it might be something he needed. She was hanging on to it in case he came back, you see.'

Bradfield came slowly through the doorway. His face was taut but without expression.

'I gather he's not here.'

No one spoke.

'You still say you saw him?'

'No mistake, old boy. Sorry.'

'Well, I suppose we must believe you. I suggest we go back to the Embassy.' He glanced at Turner. 'Unless you prefer to stay. If you have some further theory to test.' He looked round the buffet. Every face was turned towards them. Behind the bar, a chrome machine was steaming unattended. Not a hand moved. 'You seem to have made your mark here anyway.' As they walked slowly back to the car, Bradfield said, 'You can come into the Embassy to collect your possessions but you must be out by lunchtime. If you have any papers, leave them with Cork and we'll send them on by bag. There's a flight at seven. Take it. If you can't get a seat, take the train. But go.'

They waited while Bradfield spoke to the policemen and showed them his red card. His German sounded very English in tone but the grammar was faultless. The policeman nodded, saluted and they took their leave. Slowly they returned to the Embassy through the sullen faces of the aimless crowd.

'Extraordinary place for Leo to spend the night,' Crabbe muttered, but Turner was fingering the gunmetal key in the OHMS envelope in his pocket, and still wondering, for all his sense of failure, whose door it had unlocked.

Chapter Thirteen

The strain of being a pig

He sat at the cypher room desk, still in his raincoat, packing together the useless trophies of his investigation, the army holster, the folded print, the engraved paper knife from Margaret Aickman; the blue-bound diary for counsellors and above, the little notebook for diplomatic discounts, and the scratched tin of five wooden buttons cut to size; and now the sixth button and the three stubs of cigar.

'Never mind,' said Cork kindly. 'He'll turn up.'

'Oh sure. Like the investments and the Caribbean dream. Leo's everybody's darling. Everybody's lost son, Leo is. We all love Leo, although he cut our throats.'

'Mind you, he couldn't half tell the tale.' He was sitting on the trucked bed in his shirt sleeves, pulling on his outdoor shoes. He wore metal springs above the elbows and his shirt was like an advertisement on the underground. There was no sound from the corridor. 'That's what *got* you about him. Quiet, but a sod.'

A machine stammered and Cork frowned at it reprovingly.

'Blarney,' he continued. 'That's what he had. The magic. He could tell you *any* bloody tale and you believed it.'

He had put them into a paper waste-bag. The label on the outside said 'SECRET. Only to be disposed of in the presence of two authorized witnesses.'

'I want this sealed and sent to Lumley,' he said, and Cork wrote out a receipt and signed it.

'I remember the first time I met him,' Cork said, in the cheerful voice which Turner associated with funeral breakfasts. 'I was *green*. I was really *green*. I'd only been married six months. If I hadn't twigged him I'd have—'

'You'd have been taking his tips on investment. You'd have been lending him the code books for bedside reading.' He stapled the mouth of the bag, folding it against itself.

'Not the code books. Janet. He'd have been reading *her* in bed.' Cork smiled happily. 'Bloody neck! You wouldn't credit it. Come on then. Lunch.'

For the last time Turner savagely clamped together the two arms of the stapler. 'Is de Lisle in?'

'Doubt it. London's sent a brief the size of your arm. All hands on deck. The dips are out in force.' He laughed. 'They ought to have a go with the old black flags. Lobby the deputies. Strenuous representations at all levels. Leave no stone unturned. *And* they're going for another loan. I don't know where the Krauts get the stuff from sometimes. Know what Leo said to me once? "I tell you what, Bill, we'll score a big diplomatic victory. We'll go down to the Bundestag and offer them a million quid. Just you and me. I reckon they'd fall down in a faint." He was right, you know.'

Turner dialled de Lisle's number but there was no reply.

'Tell him I rang to say goodbye,' he said to Cork, and changed his mind. 'Don't worry.'

He called Travel Section and enquired about his ticket. It was all in order, they assured him; Mr Bradfield had sent down personally and the ticket was waiting for him at the desk. They seemed impressed. Cork picked up his coat.

'And you'd better cable Lumley and give him my time of arrival.'

'I'm afraid H. of C.'s done that already,' Cork said, with something quite near to a blush.

'Well. Thanks.' He was at the door, looking back into the room as if he would never see it again. 'I hope it goes all right with the baby. I hope your dreams come true. I hope everyone's dream comes true. I hope they all get what they're looking for.'

'Look: think of it this way,' Cork said sympathetically. 'There's things you just don't give up, isn't there?'

'That's right.'

'I mean you can't pack everything up neat and tidy. Not in life, you can't. That's for girls, that is. That's just romantic. You get like Leo otherwise: you can't leave a thing alone. Now what are you going to do with yourself this afternoon? There's a nice matinee at the American cinema. . . . No. Wouldn't be right for you: lot of screaming kids.'

'What do you mean, he can't leave a thing alone?'

Cork was drifting round the room, checking the machines, the desks and the secret waste.

'Vindictive. Vindictive wasn't in it. He had a feud with Fred Anger once; Fred was Admin. They say it ran five years till Fred was posted.'

'What about?'

'Nothing.' He had picked a scrap of paper from the floor and was reading it. 'Absolutely sweet Fanny Adams. Fred cut down a lime tree in Leo's garden, said it was endangering the fence. Which it was. Fred told me: "Bill," he said, "that tree would have *fallen* down in the autumn."'

'He had a thing about land,' Turner said. 'He wanted his own patch. He didn't like being in limbo.'

'Know what Leo did? He made a wreath out of leaves. Brought it into the Embassy and nailed it on to Fred's office door. With bloody great two-inch nails. Crucified it near enough. The German staff thought Fred had snuffed it. Leo didn't laugh though. He wasn't joking; he really meant it. He was *violent*, see. Now dips don't notice that. All oil and how-d'you-do, he was to them. And helpful, I'm not saying he wasn't helpful. I'm just saying that when Leo had a grudge, I wouldn't fancy being the other end of it. That's all I'm saying.'

'He went for your wife, did he?'

'I put a stop to that,' said Cork. 'Just as well. Seeing what happened elsewhere. The Welfare Dance, that was. A couple of years back. He started coming it. Nothing *nasty*, mind. Wanted to give her a hair-dryer and that. Meet me up on the hill, that lark. I said to him, "You find your own hair to dry," I said. "She's mine." You can't blame him though, can you? Know what they say about refugees: they lose everything except their accents. Dead right, you know. Trouble with Leo was, he wanted it all back. So I suppose that's it: take the pick of the files and run for it. Flog them to the highest bidder. It's no more than what we owe him, I don't suppose.' Satisfied with his security check, Cork stacked together his brochures and came towards the door where Turner stood. 'You're from the North, aren't you?' he asked. 'I can tell by your voice.'

'How well did you know him?'

'Leo? Oh, like all of us really. I'd buy this and that, give him a saucer of milk now and then; put an order in for the Dutchman.'

'Dutchman?'

'Firm of diplomatic exporters. From Amsterdam. Cheaper if you can be bothered; you know. Do you anything: butter, meat, radios, cars, the lot.'

'Hair-dryers?'

'Anything. There's a rep. calls every Monday. Fill in your form one week, chuck it into Leo and you get the order the next. I expect there was a bit in it for him: *you* know. Mind you, you could never catch him out. I mean you could check up till you were blue in the face: you'd never find out where he took his divi. Though I *think* it was those bloody cigars. They were really shocking, you know. I don't think he enjoyed them; he just smoked them because they were free. And because we pulled his leg about them.' He laughed simply. 'He conned the lot of us, that's the truth of it. You too, I suppose. Well, I'll be slipping on then. So long.'

'You were saying about that first time you met him.'

'Was I? Oh well, yes.' He laughed again. 'I mean you couldn't believe *anything*. My first day: Mickie Crabbe took me down there.

We done the round by then. "Here," says Mickie, "just one more port of call," and takes me downstairs to see Leo. "This is Cork," he says. "Just joined us in Cyphers." So then Leo moves in.' Cork sat down on the swivel chair beside the door and leaned back like the rich executive he longed to be. '"Glass of sherry," he says. We're supposed to be dry here, but that never bothered Leo; not that he drank himself, mind. "We must celebrate the new arrival. You don't *sing* by any chance, do you, Cork?" "Only in the bath," I says and we all have a nice laugh. Recruiting for the choir, see: that always impressed them. Very pious gentleman, Mr Harting, I thought. Not half. "Have a cigar, Cork?" No thanks. "A fag then?" Don't mind if I do, Mr Harting. So then we sit there like a lot of dips, sipping our sherry, and I'm thinking, "Well, I must say you're quite the little king round here." Furniture, maps, carpet . . . all the trappings. Fred Anger cleared a lot of it out, mind, before he left. Nicked, half of it was. *Liberated*, you know. Like in the old Occupation days. "So how are things in London, Cork?" he asks, "Everything much the same I suppose?" Putting me at my ease, cheeky sod. "That old porter at the main door: still saucy with the visiting Ambassador, is he, Cork?" He really came it. "And the coal fires: still lighting the coal fires every morning, are they, Cork?" "Well," I says, "They're not doing too bad, but it's like everything else, it takes its time." Some crap like that. "Oh, ah, really," he says, "because I had a letter from Ewan Waldebere only a few months back telling me they were putting in the central heating. And that old bloke who used to pray on the steps of Number Ten, still there is he, Cork, morning and night, saying his prayers? Doesn't seem to have done us much good, does he? I tell you: I was practically calling him sir. Ewan Waldebere was Head of Western Department by then, all set to be God. So then he comes on about the choir again and the Dutchman and a few other things besides, anything he can do to help, and when we get outside I look at Mickie Crabbe and Mickie's *pissing* himself. Doubled up, Mickie is. "Leo?" he says, "Leo? He's never been inside the Foreign Office in his life. He hasn't even been back to England since forty-five."' Cork broke off, shaking his head. 'Still,' he repeated, with an affectionate laugh, 'You can't blame him, can you?' He got up. 'And I mean, we all saw through him, but we still fell for it, didn't we? I mean Arthur and . . . I mean everybody. It's like my villa,' he added simply, 'I know I'll never get there, but I believe in it all the same. I mean you have to really . . . you couldn't live, not without illusions. Not here.'

Taking his hands out of his mackintosh pockets, Turner stared first at Cork and then at the gunmetal key in his big palm, and he seemed to be torn and undecided.

'What's Mickie Crabbe's number?'

Cork watched with apprehension as he lifted the receiver, dialled and began talking.

'They don't *expect* you to go on looking for him,' Cork said anxiously. 'I don't really think they do.'

'I'm not bloody well looking for him, I'm having lunch with Crabbe and I'm catching the evening flight and nothing on God's earth would keep me in this dream box for an hour longer than I need.' He slammed down the receiver and stalked out of the room.

De Lisle's door was wide open but his desk was empty. He wrote a note: 'Called in to say goodbye. Goodbye. Alan Turner,' and his hand was shaking with anger and humiliation. In the lobby, small groups were sauntering into the sunlight to eat their sandwiches or lunch in the canteen. The Ambassador's Rolls-Royce stood at the door; the escort of police outriders waited patiently. Gaunt was whispering to Meadowes at the front desk and he fell suddenly quiet as Turner approached.

'Here,' he said, handing him the envelope. 'Here's your ticket.' His expression said, 'Now go back to where you belong.'

'Ready when you are old son,' Crabbe whispered from his habitual patch of darkness. 'You see.'

The waiters were quiet and awfully discreet. Crabbe had asked for snails which he said were very good. The framed print in their little alcove showed shepherds dancing with nymphs, and there was just a suggestion of expensive sin.

'You were with him that night in Cologne. The night he got into the fight.'

'Extraordinary,' said Crabbe, 'Really. Do you like water?' he asked, and added a little to each of their glasses, but it was no more than a tear shed for the sober. 'Don't know what came over him.'

'Did you often go out with him?'

He grinned unsuccessfully and they drank.

'That was five years ago, you see. Mary's mother was ill; kept on flogging back to England. I was a grass widower, so to speak.'

'So you'd push off with Leo occasionally; have a drink and chase a few pussycats.'

'More or less.'

'In Cologne?'

'Steady, old boy,' said Crabbe. 'You're like a bloody lawyer.' He drank again and as the drink went into him he shook like a poor comedian reacting late. 'Christ,' he said. 'What a day. Christ.'

'Night clubs are best in Cologne, are they?'

'You can't do it *here*, old boy,' Crabbe said with a nervous start. 'Not unless you want to screw half the Government. You've got to be *bloody* careful in Bonn.' He added needlessly, '*Bloody* careful.' He jerked his head in wild confirmation. 'Cologne's the better bet.'

'Better girls?'

'Can't make it, old boy. Not for years.'

'But Leo went for them, did he?'

'He liked the girls,' said Crabbe.

'So you went to Cologne that night. Your wife was in England, and you went on the razzle with Leo.'

'We were just sitting at a table. Drinking, you see.' He suited the gesture to the word. 'Leo was talking about the Army: remember old so-and-so. That game. Loved the Army, Leo did, loved it. Should have stayed in, that's my feeling. Not that they'd have had him, not as a regular. He needed the discipline, in my opinion. Urchin really. Like me. It's all right when you're young, you don't mind. It's later. They knocked hell out of me at Sherborne. Hell. Used to hold the taps, head in the basin, while the bloody prefects hit me. I didn't care then. Thought it was life.' He put a hand on Turner's arm. 'Old boy,' he whispered. 'I *hate* them now. Didn't know I had it in me. It's all come to the surface. For two pins I'd go back there and shoot the buggers. Truth.'

'Did you know him in the Army?'

'No.'

'Then who were you remembering?'

'I ran across him in the CCG a bit. Moenchengladbach. Four Group.'

'When he was on Claims?'

Crabbe's reaction to harassment was unnerving. Like his name-sake he seemed in some mysterious way to draw the extremities of his presence under a protective shell, and to lie passive until the danger had passed. Ducking his head into his glass he kept it there, shoulders hunched, while he peered at Turner with pink, hooded eyes.

'So you were drinking and talking.'

'Just quietly. Waiting for the cabaret. I like a good cabaret.' He drifted away into a wholly incredible account of an attempt he had made upon a girl in Frankfurt on the occasion of the last Free Democrats' Conference: 'Fiasco,' he declared proudly. 'Climbing over me like a bloody monkey and I couldn't do a thing.'

'So the fight came after the cabaret?'

'Before. There was a bunch of Huns at the bar kicking up a din; singing. Leo took offence. Started glaring at them. Pawing the earth a bit. Suddenly he'd called for the bill. "*Zahlen!*" Just like that. Bloody loud too. I said "Hoi! old boy, what's up?" Ignored me. "I don't want to go," I said. "Want to see the tit show." Blind bit of notice. The waiter brings the bill, Leo tots it up, shoves his hand in his pocket and puts a button on the plate.'

'What kind of button?'

'Just a button. Like the one the dolly found down at the Bahnhof. Bloody wooden button with holes in it.' He was still indignant. 'You can't pay bloody bills with a *button*. Can you? Thought it was a joke at first. Had a bit of a laugh. "What happened to the rest of her?" I said. Thought he was joking, see. He wasn't.'

'Go on.'

'"Here you are," he said. "Keep the change," and gets up cool as anything. "Come on Mickie, this place stinks." Then they go for him. Jesus. Fantastic. Never thought he had it in him. Three down and one to go and then somebody cracks him with a bottle. All the blows; East End stuff. He could really mix it. Then they got him. They bent him over the bar backwards and just worked him over. Never seen anything like it. No one said a word. No how d'you do, nothing. System. Next thing we knew was, we were out in the street. Leo was on his hands and knees and they came out and gave him a few more for luck, and I was coughing my guts out on the pavement.'

'Pissed?'

'Sober as a bloody judge, old boy. They'd kicked me in the stomach, you see.'

'You?'

His head shook dreadfully as it sank to meet the glass: 'Tried to bail him out,' he muttered. 'Tried to mix it with the other chaps while he got away. Trouble is,' he explained, taking a deep draught of whisky. 'I'm not the fellow I used to be. Praschko had hoofed it by then.' He giggled. 'He was half-way out of the door by the time the button hit the plate. He seemed to know the form. Don't blame him.'

Turner might have been asking after an old friend. 'Praschko came often, did he? Back in those days?'

'First time I met him, old boy. And the last. Parted brass rags after that. Don't blame him. MP and all that. Bad for business.'

'What did *you* do?'

'Jesus. Trod gently, old boy.' He shuddered. 'Home posting loomed large. Bloody flea pit in Bushey or somewhere. With Mary. No thanks.'

'How did it end?'

'I reckon Praschko got on to Siebkron. Coppers dumped us at the Embassy. Guard got us a cab and we sloped off to my place and called a doctor. Then Ewan Waldebere turned up, he was Minister Political. Then Ludwig Siebkron in a dirty great Mercedes. Christ knows what didn't happen. Siebkron grilled him. Sat in my drawing-room and grilled him no end. Didn't care for it I must say. All the same, pretty serious when you think of it. Bloody diplomat tearing the arse off nightclubs, assaulting citizenry. Lot of fences to mend.'

The waiter brought some kidneys cooked in vinegar and wine.

'God,' said Crabbe. 'Look at that. Delicious. Lovely after snails.'

'What did Leo tell Siebkron?'

'Nix. Nothing. You don't know Leo. Close isn't the word. Waldebere, me, Siebkron: not a syllable to any of us. Mind you, they'd really gone for him. Waldebere faked him some leave; new teeth, stitches, Christ knows what. Told everybody he'd done it swimming in Yugoslavia. Diving into shallow water. Bashed his face in. Some water: Christ.'

'Why do you think it happened?'

'No idea, old boy. Wouldn't go out with him after that. Not safe.'

'No opinions?'

'Sorry,' said Crabbe. His face sank beneath the surface, misted with meaningless wrinkles.

'Ever seen this key?'

'Nope.' He grinned affectionately. 'One of Leo's, was it? Screw anything in the old days, Leo would. Steadier now.'

'Any names attached to that?'

He continued staring at the key.

'Try Myra Meadowes.'

'Why?'

'She's willing. She's had one baby already. In London. They say half the drivers go through her every week.'

'Did he ever mention a woman called Aickman? Someone he was going to marry?'

Crabbe assumed an expression of puzzled recollection.

'Aickman,' he said. 'Funny. That was one of the old lot. From Berlin. He did talk about her. When they worked with the Russkies. That's it. She was another of those inbetweeners. Berlin, Hamburg, all that game. Stitched those bloody cushions for him. Care and attention.'

'What was he *doing* with the Russians,' Turner asked after a pause. 'What work was it?'

'Quadrupartite, bi-partite . . . one of them. Berlin's on its own, see. Different world, specially in those days. Island. Different sort of island.' He shook his head. 'Not like him,' he added. 'All that Communist kick. Not his book at all. Too bloody hard-nosed for all that balls.'

'And this Aickman?'

'Miss Brandt, Miss Etling and Miss Aickman.'

'Who are they?'

'Three dollies. In Berlin. Came out with them from England. Pretty as pictures, Leo said. Never seen girls like it. Never seen girls at all if you ask me. Emigré types going back to Germany. Join the Occupation. Same as Leo. Croydon airport, sitting on a crate, waiting for a plane, and these three dollies come along in uniform, waggling their tails. Miss Aickman, Miss Brandt and Miss Etling. Posted to the same unit. From then on he never looked back. Him and Praschko and another fellow. All went out together from England in forty-five. With these dollies. They made up a song about it: Miss Aickman, Miss Etling and Miss *Brandt* . . . drinking song, saucy rhymes. They sang it that night as a matter of fact. Going along in the car, happy as sandboys. Jesus.'

He'd have sung it himself for two pins.

'Leo's girl was Aickman. His first girl. He'd always go back to her, that's what he said. "There'll never be another like the first one," that's what he said. "All the rest are imitations." His very words. You know the way Huns talk. Introspective beggars.'

'What became of her?'

'Dunno old boy. Fizzled away. What they all do, isn't it? Grow old. Shrivel up. Whoopsadaisy.' A piece of kidney fell from his fork and the gravy splashed on his tie.

'Why didn't he marry her?'

'She took the other road, old boy.'

'Which other road?'

'She didn't like him being English, he said. Wanted him to be a Hun again and face facts. Big on metaphysics.'

'Perhaps he's gone to find her.'

'He always said he would one day. "I've drunk at a good few pools, Mickie," he said. "But there'll never be another girl like Aickman." Still, that's what we all say, isn't it?' He dived into the Moselle as if it were a refuge.

'Is it?'

'You married, old boy, by the by? Keep away from it.' He shook his head. 'It would be all right if I could manage the bedroom. But I can't. It's like a bloody grease-pot for me. I can't make it.' He sniggered. 'Marry at fifty-five, my advice. Little sixteen-year-old dolly. Then they don't know what they're missing.'

'Praschko was up there, was he? In Berlin? With the Russians and Aickman?'

'Stable companions.'

'What else did he tell you about Praschko?'

'He was a Bolshie in those days. Nothing else.'

'Was Aickman?'

'Could be, old boy. Never said; didn't interest him that much.'

'Was Harting?'

'Not Leo, old boy. Didn't know his arse from his elbow where politics are concerned. Restful that was. Trout,' he whispered. 'I'd like trout next. Kidneys are just in between. If it's on the secret vote, I mean.'

The joke entertained him off and on for the remainder of the meal. Only once would he be drawn on the subject of Leo, and that was when Turner asked him whether he had had much to do with him in recent months.

'Not bloody likely,' Crabbe whispered.

'Why not?'

'He was getting broody, old boy. I could tell. Sizing up for another crack at someone. Pugnacious little beast,' he said, baring his teeth in a sudden grimace of alcoholic cramp. 'He'd started leaving those buttons about.'

He got back to the Adler at four; he was fairly drunk. The lift was occupied so he used the stairs. That's it, he thought. That is the sweet end. He would go on drinking through the afternoon and he would drink on the plane and with any luck by the time he saw Lumley he would be speechless. The Crabbe answer: snails, kidneys, trout and scotch and keep your head down while the big wheels roll over. As he reached his own floor he noticed vaguely that the lift had been wedged with a suitcase and he supposed the porter was collecting more luggage from someone's bedroom. We're the only lucky people in the place, he thought. We're leaving. He tried to open the door to his room but the lock was jammed; he wrestled with the key but it wouldn't give. He stepped back quite quickly when he heard the footsteps, but he didn't really have much chance. The door was pulled open from inside. He had a glimpse of a pale round face and fair hair carefully combed back, a bland brow furrowed with anxiety, he saw the stitching of the leather as it moved down on him in slow motion and he wondered whether the stitches cut the scalp the way they cut the face. He felt the nausea strike him and his stomach fold, and the wooden club buffet at the back of his knees; he heard the soft surgeon's voice calling from the darkness as the warm grass of the Yorkshire dales prickled against his child's face. He heard the taunting voice of Tony Willoughby, soft as velvet, clinging like a lover, saw his pianist's hands drift over her white hips, and heard Leo's music whining to God in every red timber tabernacle of his childhood. He smelt the smoke of the Dutch cigars, and there was Willoughby's voice again offering him a hair-dryer: I'm only a temporary, Alan old boy, but there's ten per cent off for friends of the family. He felt the pain again, the thudding as they began slapping him and he saw the wet black granite of the orphanage in Bournemouth and the telescope on Constitution Hill. 'If there's one thing I really hate,' Lumley observed, 'It's a cynic in search of God.' He had a moment's total agony as they hit him in the groin, and as it slowly subsided he saw the girl who had left him drifting in the black streets of his own defiant solitude. He heard the screaming of Myra Meadowes as he broke her down, lie for lie, the scream as they took her from her Polish lover, and the scream as she parted from her baby; and he thought he might be crying out himself until he recognized the towel they had shoved into his mouth. He felt something cold and iron hard hit the back of his head and stay there like a lump of ice, he heard the door slam and knew he was alone; he saw the whole damned trail of the deceived and the uncaring; heard

the fool voice of an English Bishop praising God and war; and fell
asleep. He was in a coffin, a smooth cold coffin. On a marble slab with
polished tiles and the glint of chrome at the far end of a tunnel. He
heard de Lisle muttering to him in kindly moderation and Jenny
Pargiter's sobbing like the moan of every woman he had left; he
heard the fatherly tones of Meadowes exhorting him to charity and
the cheerful whistling of unencumbered people. Then Meadowes
and Pargiter slipped away, lost to other funerals, and only de Lisle
remained, and only de Lisle's voice offered any comfort.

'My dear fellow,' he was saying, as he peered curiously downward,
'I dropped in to say goodbye, but if you're going to take a bath, you
might at least take off that dreadful suit.'

'Is it Thursday?'

De Lisle had taken a napkin from the rail and was soaking it under
the hot tap.

'Wednesday. Wednesday as ever was. Cocktail time.'

He bent over him and began gently dabbing the blood from his
face.

'That football field. Where you saw him. Where he took Pargiter.
Tell me how I get there.'

'Keep still. And don't talk or you'll wake the neighbours.'

With the gentlest possible movements he continued touching
away the caked blood. Freeing his right hand Turner cautiously felt
in the pocket of his jacket for the gunmetal key. It was still there.

'Have you ever seen this before?'

'No. No, I haven't. Nor was I in the greenhouse at 3 a.m. on the
morning of the second. But how *like* the Foreign Office,' he said,
standing back and critically surveying his handiwork, 'to send a bull
to catch a matador. You won't mind my reclaiming my dinner jacket,
will you?'

'Why did Bradfield ask me?'

'Ask you what?'

'To dinner. To meet Siebkron. Why did he invite me on Tuesday?'

'Brotherly love; what else?'

'What's in that despatch box that Bradfield's so frightened of?'

'Poisonous snakes.'

'That key wouldn't open it?'

'No.'

De Lisle sat down on the edge of the bath. 'You shouldn't be doing
this,' he said. 'I know what you'll tell me; somebody had to get their
hands dirty. Just don't expect me to be pleased it's you. You're not
just *somebody*: that's your trouble. Leave it to the people who were
born with blinkers.' His grey, tender eyes were shadowed with
concern. 'It is totally absurd,' he declared. 'People crack up every

day under the strain of being saints. You're cracking up under the strain of being a pig.'

'Why doesn't he go? Why does he hang around?'

'They'll be asking that about you tomorrow.'

Turner was stretched out on de Lisle's long sofa. He held a whisky in his hand and his face was covered in yellow antiseptic from de Lisle's extensive medicine chest. His canvas bag lay in a corner of the room. De Lisle sat at his harpsichord, not playing it but stroking the keys. It was an eighteenth-century piece, satinwood, and the top was bleached by tropical suns.

'Do you take that thing everywhere?'

'I had a violin once. It fell to pieces in Leopoldville. The glue melted. It's awfully hard,' he observed dryly, 'to pursue culture when the glue melts.'

'If Leo's so damn clever, why doesn't he go?'

'Perhaps he likes it here. He'd be the first, I must say.'

'And if *they're* so damned clever, why don't they take him away?'

'Perhaps they don't know he's on the loose.'

'What did you say?'

'I said perhaps they don't know he's run for it. I'm not a spy, I'm afraid, but I am human and I do know Leo. He's extremely perverse. I can't imagine for a moment he would do exactly what they told him. If there is a "they", which I doubt. He wasn't a *natural* servant.'

Turner said, 'I try all the time to force him into the mould. He won't fit.'

De Lisle struck a couple of notes with his finger.

'Tell me, what do you *want* him to be? A goodie or a baddie? Or do you just want the freedom of the search? You want *something*, don't you? Because anything's better than nothing. You're like those beastly students: you can't stand a vacuum.'

Turner had closed his eyes and was lost in thought.

'I expect he's dead. That would be very macabre.'

'He wasn't dead this morning, was he?' Turner said.

'And you don't like him to be in limbo. It annoys you. You want him to land or take off. There are no *shades* for you, are there? I suppose that's the fun of searching for extremists: you search for their convictions, is that it?'

'He's still on the run,' Turner continued. 'Who's he running *from*? Us or them?'

'He could be on his own.'

'With fifty stolen box files? Oh sure. Sure.'

De Lisle examined Turner over the top of the harpsichord.

'You complement one another. I look at you and I think of Leo. You're a Saxon. Big hands, big feet, big heart and that lovely reason that grapples with ideals. Leo's the other way round. He's a performer. He wears our clothes, uses our language but he's only half tamed. I suppose I'm on your side, really: you and I are the concert audience.' He closed the harpsichord. 'We're the ones who glimpse, and reach, and fall back. There's a Leo in all of us but he's usually dead by the time we're twenty.'

'What are you then?'

'Me? Oh, reluctantly, a conductor.' Standing up, he carefully locked the keyboard with a small brass key from his chain. 'I can't even play the thing,' he said, tapping the bleached lid with his elegant fingers. 'I tell myself I will one day; I'll take lessons or get a book. But I don't really care: I've learnt to live with being half-finished. Like most of us.'

'Tomorrow's Thursday,' Turner said. 'If they don't know he's defected, they'll be expecting him to turn up, won't they?'

'I suppose so,' de Lisle yawned. 'But then they know where to go, don't they, whoever they are? And you don't. That is something of a drawback.'

'It might not be.'

'Oh.'

'We know where *you* saw him, at least, that Thursday afternoon, don't we, when he was supposed to be at the Ministry? Same place as he took Pargiter. Seems quite a hunting-ground for him.'

De Lisle stood very still, the keychain still in his hand.

'It's no good telling you not to go, I suppose?'

'No.'

'Asking you? You're acting against Bradfield's instructions.'

'Even so.'

'And you're sick. All right. Go and look for your untamed half. And if you *do* find that file, we shall expect you to return it unopened.'

And that, quite suddenly, was an order.

Chapter Fourteen

Thursday's Child

The weather on the plateau was stolen from other seasons and other places. It was a sea wind from March which sang in the wire netting, bending the tufts of coarse grass and crashing into the forest behind him; and if some mad aunt had planted a monkey-puzzle in the sandy earth, Turner could have hopped straight down the path and caught the trolley-bus to Bournemouth Square. It was the frost of November whose icy pipes encased the bracken stems; for there the cold had hidden from the wind and it gripped like arctic water at his ankles; the frost of a stone crevice on a north face, when only fear will set your hands to work, and life is treasured because it is won. The last strips of an Oxford sun lay bravely dying on the empty playing-field; and the sky was a Yorkshire evening in autumn, black and billowing and fringed with grime. The trees were curved from childhood, bent by the blustering wind, Mickie Crabbe's boyhood bent at the taps in the washroom, and when the gusts had gone they waited still, backs arched for the next assault.

The cuts on his face were burning raw and his pale eyes were bright with sleepless pain. He waited, staring down the hill. Far below to his right lay the river, and for once the wind had silenced it, and the barges called in vain. A car was climbing slowly towards him; a black Mercedes, Cologne registration, woman driver; and did not slow down as it passed. On the other side of the wire, a new hut was shuttered and padlocked. A rook had settled on the roof and the wind tugged at its feathers. A Renault, French diplomatic registration, woman driver, one male passenger: Turner noted the number in his black book. His script was stiff and childish, and the letters came to him unnaturally. He must have hit back after all, for two knuckles on his right hand were badly cut, as if he had punched an open mouth and caught the front teeth. Harting's handwriting was neat, rounding the rough corners, but Turner's was big and downright, promising collision.

'You are both *movers*, you and Leo,' de Lisle had said some time last night, as they sat in their deep armchairs. 'Bonn is stationary but you are movers. . . . You are fighting one another, but it is you against us. . . . The opposite of love is not hate but apathy. . . . You must come to terms with apathy.'

'For Christ's sake,' Turner complained.

'This is your stop,' de Lisle had said, opening the car door for him. 'And if you're not back by tomorrow morning I shall tell the coastguards.'

He had bought a spanner in Bad Godesberg, a monkey wrench, heavy at the head, and it lay like a lead weight against his hip. A Volkswagen bus, dark grey, Registration SU, full of children, stopping at the changing hut. Their noise came at him suddenly, a flock of birds racing with the wind, a tattered jingle of laughter and complaint. Someone blew a whistle. The sun hit them low down, like torch beams shining along a corridor. The hut swallowed them. 'I have never known anyone,' de Lisle had cried in despair, 'make such a meal of his disadvantages.'

He drew back quickly behind the tree. One Opel Rekord; two men. Registration Bonn. The spanner nudged him as he wrote. The men were wearing hats and overcoats and were professionally without expression. The side windows were of smoked glass. The car continued, but at a walking pace. He saw their blank blond faces turned towards him, twin moons in the artificial dark. *Your* teeth? Turner wondered. Was it your teeth I knocked in? I can't tell you apart. Trust you to come to the ball. All the way up the hill, they could not have touched ten miles an hour. A van passed, followed by two lorries. Somewhere a clock chimed; or was it a school bell? Or Angelus, or Compline, or sooty sheep in the Dales, or the ring of the ferry from the river? He would never hear it again; yet there is no truth, as Mr Crail would say, that cannot be confirmed. No, my child; but the sins of others are a sacrifice to God. Your sacrifice. The rook had left the roof. The sun had gone. A little Citroën was wandering into sight. A *deux chevaux*, dirty as fog, with one bashed wing, one illegible number plate, one driver hidden in the shadow, and one headlight flashing on and off and one horn blaring for the hunt. The Opel had disappeared. Hurry moons or you will miss His coming. The wheels jerk like dislocated limbs as the little car turns off the road and bumps towards him over the frozen mud ruts of the timber track, the pert tail rocking on its axle. He hears the blare of dance music as the door opens, and his mouth is dry from the tablets, and the cuts on his face are a screen of twigs. One day, when the world is free, his fevered mind assured him, clouds will detonate as they collide and God's angels will fall down dazed for the whole world to look at. Silently he dropped the spanner back into his pocket.

She was standing not ten yards away, her back towards him, quite indifferent to the wind, or the children who now burst upon the playground.

She was staring down the hill. The engine was still running, shaking the car with inner pains. A wiper juddered uselessly over the grimy windscreen. For an hour she barely moved.

For an hour she waited with oriental stillness, heeding nothing but whoever would not come. She stood like a statue, growing taller as the light left her.

The wind dragged at her coat. Once her hand rose to gather in the errant strands of hair, and once she walked to the end of the timber-track to look down into the river valley, in the direction of Königs-winter; then slowly returned, lost in thought, and Turner dropped to his knees behind the trees, praying that the shadows protected him.

Her patience broke. Getting noisily back into the car she lit a cigarette and slapped the horn with her open hand. The children forgot their game and grinned at the hoarse burp of the exhausted battery. The silence returned.

The windscreen wiper had stopped but the engine was still

running and she was revving it to encourage the heater. The windows were misting up. She opened her handbag and took out a mirror and a lipstick.

She was leaning back in the seat, eyes closed, listening to dance music, one hand gently beating time on the steering wheel. Hearing a car, she opened the door and looked idly out, but it was only the black Rekord going slowly down the hill again and though the moons were turned towards her, she was quite indifferent to their interest.

The playing-field was empty. The shutters were closed on the changing hut. Turning on the overhead lamp, she read the time by her watch, but by then the first lights were coming up in the valley and the river was lost in the low mist of dusk. Turner stepped heavily on to the path and pulled open the passenger door.

'Waiting for someone?' he asked and sat down beside her, closing the door quickly so that the light went out again. He switched off the wireless.

'I thought you'd gone,' she said hotly, 'I thought my husband had got rid of you.' Fear, anger, humiliation seized hold of her. 'You've been spying on me all the time! Crouching in the bushes like a detective! How dare you? You vulgar, bloody little man!' She drew back her clenched fist and perhaps she hesitated when she saw the mess his face was in, but it wouldn't have made much difference because at the same moment Turner hit her very hard across the mouth so that her head jerked back against the pillar with a snap. Opening his door he walked round the car, pulled her out and hit her again with his open hand.

'We're going for a walk,' he said, 'And we'll talk about your vulgar bloody lover.'

He led her along the timber path to the crest of the hill. She walked quite willingly, holding his arm with both her hands, head down, crying silently.

They were looking down on to the Rhine. The wind had fallen. Already above them, the early stars drifted like sparks of phosphorus on a gently rocking sea. Along the river the lights kindled in series, faltering at the moment of their birth and then miraculously living, growing to small fires fanned by the black night breeze. Only the river's sounds reached them; the chugging of the barges and the nursery chime of the clocks telling off the quarters. They caught the mouldering smell of the Rhine itself, felt its cold breath upon their hands and cheeks.

'It began as a dare.'

She stood apart from him, gazing into the valley, her arms clutching round her body as if she were holding a towel.

'He won't come any more. I've had it. I know that.'

'Why won't he?'

'Leo never *said* things. He was far too much of a puritan.' She lit a cigarette. 'Because he'll never stop searching, that's why.'

'What for?'

'What do any of us look for? Parents, children, a woman.' She turned to face him. 'Go on,' she challenged. 'Ask the rest.'

Turner waited.

'When intimacy took place, isn't that what you want to know? I'd have slept with him that same night if he'd asked me, but he didn't get round to it because I'm Rawley's wife and he knew that good men were scarce. I mean he knew he *had* to survive. He was a creep, don't you realize? He'd have charmed the feathers off a goose.' She broke off. 'I'm a fool to tell you anything.'

'You'd be a bigger fool not to. You're in big trouble,' Turner said, 'in case you don't know.'

'I can't remember when I haven't been. How else do I beat the system? We were two old tarts and we fell in love.'

She was sitting on a bench, playing with her gloves.

'It was a buffet. A bloody Bonn buffet with lacquered duck and dreadful Germans. Someone's welcome to someone. Someone's farewell. Americans I should think. Mr and Mrs Somebody the Third. Some dynastic feast. It was appallingly provincial.' Her voice was her own, swift and falsely confident, but for all her efforts it still possessed that note of hard-worn dexterity which Turner had heard in British diplomatic wives all over the world: a voice to talk through silences, cover embarrassments, retrieve offences; a voice that was neither particularly cultured nor particularly sophisticated but, like a nanny in pursuit of lost standards, doggedly trod its course. 'We'd come straight from Aden and we'd been here exactly a year. Before that we were in Peking and now we were in Bonn. Late October: Karfeld's October. Things had just hotted up. In Aden we'd been bombed, in Peking we were mobbed and now we were going to be burned in the Market Place. Poor Rawley: he seems to attract humiliation. He was a prisoner of war as well, you know. There ought to be a name for him: the humiliated generation.'

'He'd love you for that,' said Turner.

'He loves me without it.' She paused. 'The funny thing is, I'd never noticed him before. I thought he was just a rather dull little . . . temporary. The prissy little man who played the organ in Chapel and smoked those filthy cigars at cocktail parties. . . . Nothing there. . . . Empty. And that night, the moment he came in, the moment he appeared at the doorway I felt him choose me and I thought: "Look out. Air raid." He came straight over to me. "Hullo, Hazel." He'd never called me Hazel in my life and I thought: "You cheeky devil, you'll have to work for this."'

'Good of you to take the risk,' said Turner.

'He began to talk. I don't know what about; I never much noticed *what* he said; any more than he did. Karfeld I suppose. Riots. All the stamping and shouting. But I noticed *him*. For the first time, I really did.' She fell silent. 'And I thought, "Hoi: where have you been all my life?" It was like looking in an old bank book and finding you've got a credit instead of an overdraft. He was *alive*.' She laughed. 'Not like you a bit. *You're* about the deadest thing I ever met.'

Turner might have hit her again, were it not for the awful familiarity of her mockery.

'It was the tension you noticed first. He was *patrolling* himself. His language, his manners . . . it was all a fake. He was on guard. He listened to his own voice the way he listened to yours, getting the cadence right, putting the adverbs in the right order. I tried to place him: who would I *think* you were if I didn't *know*? South American German? . . . Argentine trade delegate? One of those. Glossy latinized Hun.' Again she broke off, lost in recollection–'He had those velvety German end-bits of language and he used them to trim the balance of every sentence. I made him talk about himself, where he lived, who cooked for him, how he spent his weekends. The next thing I knew, he was giving me advice. Diplomatic advice: where to buy cheap meat. The Post Report. The Dutchman was best for this, the Naafi for that; butter from the Economat, nuts from the Commissary. Like a woman. He had a thing about herbal teas; Germans are mad about digestion. Then he offered to sell me a hair-dryer. Why are you laughing?' She asked in sudden fury.

'Was I?'

'He knew some way of getting a discount: twenty-five per cent, he said. He'd compared all the prices, he knew all the models.'

'He'd been looking at your hair too.'

She rounded on him: 'You keep your place,' she snapped.

'You're not within shouting distance of him.'

He hit her again, a long swinging blow deep into the flesh of the cheek and she said 'You bastard' and went very pale in the darkness, shivering with anger.

'Get on with it.'

At last she began again: 'So I said yes. I was fed up anyway. Rawley was buried with a French Counsellor in the corner; everyone else was fighting for food at the buffet. So I said yes, I *would* like a hair-dryer. At twenty-five per cent off. I was afraid I hadn't got the money on me; would he take a cheque? I might just as well have said, yes I'll go to bed with you. That was the first time I saw him smile; he didn't smile often as a rule. His whole face was lit up. I sent him to get some food, and I watched him all the way, wondering what it was going to be like. He had that egg walk . . . *Eiertanz* they call it here . . . just like in Chapel really, but *harder*. The Germans were crowding the bar, fighting for the asparagus, and he just darted between them and came out with two plates loaded with food and the knives and forks sticking out of his handkerchief pocket; grinning like mad. I've got a brother called Andrew who plays scrum-half at rugger. You could hardly have told the difference. From then on, I didn't worry. Some foul Canadian was trying to get me to listen to a lecture on agriculture and I bit his head off. They're about the only ones left who still believe in it all, the Canadians. They're like the British in India.'

Hearing some sound she turned her head sharply and stared back along the path. The tree trunks were black against the low horizon; the wind had dropped; a night dew had damped their clothes.

'He won't come. You said so yourself. Get on with it. Hurry.'

'We sat on a stair and he started talking about himself again. He didn't need any prompting. It just came out . . . it was fascinating. About Germany in the early days after the war. "Only the rivers were whole." I never knew whether he was translating German or using his imagination or just repeating what he'd picked up.' She hesitated, and again glanced down the path. 'How at night the women built by arclight . . . passing stones as if they were putting out a fire. . . . How he learnt to sleep in a fifteen hundredweight using a fire extinguisher as a pillow. He did a little act, putting his head on one side and twisting his mouth to show his stiff neck. Bedroom games.' She stood up abruptly. 'I'm going back. If he finds the car empty, he'll run away; he's as nervous as a kitten.'

He followed her to the timber track, but the plateau was deserted except for the Opel Rekord parked in the lay-by with its lights out.

'Sit in the car,' she said. 'Never mind them.' For the first time she really noticed the marks on his face by the interior light and she drew in her breath sharply.

'Who did that?'

'They'll do it to Leo if they find him first.'

She was leaning back in the seat, her eyes closed. Someone had torn the cloth on the roof and it hung down in beggar's shreds. There was a child's driving wheel on the floor with a plastic tube attached to it and Turner pushed it out of the way with his foot.

'Sometimes I thought: "You're empty. You're just imitating life." But you daren't think that of a lover. He was a negotiator, an actor, I suppose. He was caught between all those worlds: Germany and England, Königswinter and Bonn, Chapel and the discounts, the first floor and the ground floor. You can't expect anyone to fight all those battles and stay alive. Sometimes he just served us,' she explained simply. 'Or me. Like a headwaiter. We were all his customers; whatever he wanted. He didn't live, he survived. He's always survived. Till now.' She lit another cigarette. The car was very cold. She tried to start the engine and put the heater on, but the ignition failed.

'After that first evening it was all over bar bed. Rawley came and found me and we were the last to go. He'd been having a row with Lésère about something and he was pleased at having come off best. Leo and I were still sitting on the stairs, drinking coffee, and Rawley just came over and kissed me on the cheek. What was that?'

'Nothing.'

'I saw a light down the hill.'

'It was a bicycle crossing the road. It's gone now.'

'I hate him kissing me in public; he knows I can't stop him. He never does it in private. "Come on my dear, it's time to go." Leo stood up when he saw him coming, but Rawley didn't even notice him. He took me over to Lésère. "This is the person you should really apologize to," he said. "She's been sitting alone on the stairs all evening." We were going out of the door and Rawley stopped to collect his coat, and there was Leo, holding it for him.' She smiled, and it was the smile of real love, rejoicing at the memory. 'He didn't seem to notice me any more. Rawley turned his back on him and put his arms into the sleeves and I actually saw Leo's own arms stiffen and his fingers curl. Mind you, I was glad. I *wanted* Rawley to behave like that.' She shrugged. 'I was hooked,' she said. 'I'd been looking for a fly and now I'd got one, feathers and all. Next day I looked him up in the Red Book. You know what that is by now: nothing. I rang up Mary Crabbe and asked her about him. Just for fun. "I ran into an extraordinary little man last night," I said. Mary had a fit. "My dear, he's poison. Keep *right* away from him. He dragged Mickie to a night club once and got him into *awful* trouble. Mercifully," she said, "his contract's running out in December and he'll be gone." I tried Sally Askew, she's terrifically worthy. I could have died'—she broke out laughing, then drew her chin down into her chest to copy the sonorous tones of the Economic Minister's wife: '"A useful bachelor, if Huns are in short supply." They often are here, you know; there are more of us than them. Too many diplomats chasing too few Germans: that's Bonn. The trouble was, Sally said, the Germans were getting rather old school again about Leo's kind, so she and Aubrey had reluctantly given him up. "He's an unconscious irritant, my dear, if you know what I mean." I was absolutely thrilled. I put down the receiver and I shot into the drawing-room and I wrote him a great long letter about absolutely nothing.'

She tried the engine again but it didn't even cough. She gathered her coat more tightly round her.

'Cor,' she whispered. 'Come on, Leo. You don't half put a strain on friendship.'

In the black Opel a tiny light went on and off like a signal. Turner said nothing, but his thick fingertips lightly touched the spanner in his pocket.

'A schoolgirl letter. Thank you for being so attentive. Sorry for claiming all your time and please remember about the hair-dryer. Then a lovely long made-up story about how I went shopping in the *Spanischer Gerten* and an old lady dropped a two-Mark piece into an orange-crate and no one could find it and she said it was payment because she'd left it in the shop. I delivered the letter to the Embassy myself and he rang up that afternoon. There were two models, he said, the more expensive one had different speeds and you didn't need an adapter.'

'Transformer.'

'What about colour? I just listened. He said it would be very difficult to make a decision for me, what with the speeds and the colour. Couldn't we meet and discuss it? It was a Thursday and we met up here. He said he came up every Thursday to get some fresh air and watch the children. I didn't believe him, but I was very happy.'

'Is that all he said about coming up here?'

'He said once they owed him time.'

'Who did?'

'The Embassy. Something Rawley had taken away from him and given to someone else. A job. So he came up here instead.' She shook her head in real admiration. 'He's as stubborn as a mule,' she declared. '"They owe it me," he said, "so I take it. And that's the only way I live."'

'I thought you said he didn't say things?'

'Not the best things.'

He waited.

'We just walked and looked at the river and on the way back we held hands. As we were leaving he said, "I forgot to show you the hair-dryer," So I said, "What a pity. We'll have to meet here next Thursday too, won't we?" He was *enormously* shocked.' She had a special voice for him as well: it was both mocking and possessive and it seemed to exclude Turner rather than draw him in. '"My *dear* Mrs Bradfield—" I said, "If you come next week I'll let you call me Hazel." I'm a whore,' she explained. 'That's what you're thinking.'

'And after that?'

'Every Thursday. Here. He parked his car down the lane and I left mine in the road. We were lovers but we hadn't been to bed. It was very grown-up. Sometimes he talked; sometimes he didn't. He kept showing me his house across the river as if he wanted to sell it me. We'd go all along the path from one little hilltop to another so that we could see it. I teased him once. "You're the devil. You're showing me the whole kingdom." He didn't care for that. He never forgot anything, you see. That was the survivor in him. He didn't like me to talk about evil, or pain or anything. He knew all *that* inside out.'

'And the rest?'

He saw her face tilt and the smile break.

'Rawley's bed. A Friday. There's an avenger in Leo, not far down. He always knew when Rawley was going away: he used to check in the Travel Office, look at the Travel Clerk's bookings. He'd say to me: he's in Hanover next week . . . he's in Bremen.'

'What did Bradfield go there for?'

'Oh God. Visiting the Consulates. . . . Leo asked me the same question: how should *I* know? Rawley never tells *me* anything. Sometimes I thought he was following Karfeld round Germany . . . he always seemed to go where the rallies were.'

'And from then on?'

She shrugged. 'Yes. From then on. Whenever we could.'

'Did Bradfield know?'

'Oh God. Know? Don't know? You're worse than the Germans. It was in between. You want things spelt out for you, don't you? Some things can't be. Some things aren't true till they're said. Rawley knows that better than anyone.'

'Christ,' Turner whispered. 'You give yourself all the chances,' and he remembered he had said the same thing to Bradfield three days ago.

She stared ahead of her through the windscreen.

'What are people *worth*? Children, husbands, careers. You go under and they call it sacrifice. You survive and they call you a bitch. Chop yourself in bits. For what? I'm not God. I can't hold them all up on my shoulders. I live for them; they live for someone else. We're all saints. We're all fools. Why don't we live for ourselves and call *that* service for a change?'

'*Did he know?*'

He had seized her arm.

'Did he!'

The tears trickled sideways over the bridge of her nose. She wiped them away.

'Rawley's a diplomat,' she said at last. 'The art of the possible, that's Rawley. The limited aim, the trained mind. "Let's not get overheated. Let's not put a name to things. Let's not negotiate without knowing what we want to achieve." He can't . . . he can't go mad, it isn't in him. He can't live for anything. Except me.'

'But he knew.'

'I should think so,' she said wearily. 'I never asked him. Yes, he knew.'

'Because you made him renew that contract, didn't you. Last December. You worked on him.'

'Yes. That was awful. That was quite awful. But it had to be done,' she explained, as if she were referring to a higher cause of which they were both aware. 'Or he'd have sent Leo away.'

'And that was what Leo wanted. That's why he picked you up.'

'Leo married me for my money. For what he could get out of me,' she said. 'He stayed with me for love. Does that satisfy you?'

Turner did not reply.

'He never put it into words. I told you. He never said the big things. "One more year is all I need. Just one year, Hazel. One year to love you, one year to get what they owe me. One year from December and then I'll go. They don't realize how much they need me." So I invited him for drinks. When Rawley was there. It was early on, before the gossip started. We were just the three of us; I made Rawley come back early. "Rawley this is Leo Harting, he works for you and he plays the organ in Chapel" "Of course. We've met," he said. We talked about nothing. Nuts from the Commissary. Spring leave. What it was like in Königswinter in the summer. "Mr Harting has asked us to dinner," I said. "Isn't he kind?" Next week we went to Königswinter. He gave us all the bits and pieces: ratafia biscuits with the sweet, halva with the coffee. That was all.'

'What was all?'

'Oh Christ, can't you see? I'd shown him! I'd shown Rawley what I wanted him to buy me!'

It was quite still now. The rooks had perched like sentinels on slowly rocking branches, and there was no wind any more to stir their feathers.

'Are they like horses?' she asked. 'Do they sleep standing up?'

She turned her head to look at him but he did not reply.

'He hated silence,' she said dreamily. 'It frightened him. That's why he liked music; that's why he liked his house . . . it was full of noise. Not even the dead could have slept there. Let alone Leo.'

She smiled remembering.

'He didn't live in it, he manned it. Like a ship. All night he'd be hopping up and down fixing a window or a shutter or something. His whole life was like that. Secret fears, secret memories; things he would never tell but expected you to know about.' She yawned. 'He won't come now,' she said. 'He hated the dark too.'

'Where is he?' Turner said urgently. 'What's he doing?'

She said nothing.

'Listen: he whispered to you. In the night he boasted, told you how he made the world turn for him. How clever he was, the tricks he played, the people he deceived!'

'You've got him wrong. Utterly wrong.'

'Then tell me!'

'There's nothing to tell. We were pen friends, that's all. He was reporting from another world.'

'*What* world? Bloody Moscow and the fight for peace?'

'I was right. You are vulgar. You want all the lines joined up and all the colours flat. You haven't got the guts to face the half tones.'

'Has he?'

She seemed to have put him out of her mind. 'Let's go, for God's sake,' she said shortly, as if Turner had been keeping her waiting.

He had to push the car quite a distance along the track before it started. As they careered down the hill, he saw the Opel pull out from the lay-by and hurriedly take up its position thirty yards behind them. She drove to Remagen, to one of the big hotels along the waterfront run by an old lady who patted her arm as she sat down. Where was the little man? she asked, *der nette kleine Herr* who was always so jolly and smoked cigars and spoke such excellent German.

'He talked it with an accent,' she explained to Turner. 'A slight English accent. It was something he'd taught himself.'

The sun room was quite empty except for a young couple in the corner. The girl had long, blonde hair. They stared at him oddly because of the cuts on his face. From their window table Turner saw the Opel park in the esplanade below them. The number plate had changed but the moons were just the same. His head was aching terribly. He had not taken more than half his whisky before he wanted to vomit. He asked for water. The old lady brought a bottle of local health water and told him all about it. They had used it in both wars, she explained, when the hotel was a first-aid post for those who were wounded while trying to cross the river.

'He was going to meet me here last Friday,' she said. 'And take me home to dinner. Rawley was leaving for Hanover. Leo cried off at the last minute.'

'On the Thursday afternoon he was late. I didn't bother. Sometimes he didn't turn up at all. Sometimes he worked. It was different. Just the last month or so. He'd changed. I thought at first he'd got another woman. He was always slipping off to places—'

'What places?'

'Berlin once. Hamburg. Hanover. Stuttgart. Rather like Rawley. So he said anyway; I was never sure. He wasn't strong on truth. Not your kind.'

'He arrived late. Last Thursday. *Come on!*'

'He'd had lunch with Praschko.'

'At the Maternus,' Turner breathed.

'They'd had a *discussion*. That was another Leo-ism. It didn't commit you. Like the Passive Voice, that was another favourite. A *discussion* had taken place. He didn't say what about. He was preoccupied. Broody. I knew him better than to try and jerk him out of it so we just walked around. With *them* watching us. And I knew this was it.'

'This was what?'

'This was the year he'd wanted. He'd found it, whatever it was, and now he didn't know what to do with it.' She shrugged. 'And by then, I'd found it too. He never realized. If he'd lifted a finger I'd have packed and gone with him.' She was looking at the river. 'Not children, husbands or any bloody thing would have stopped me. Not that he would have wanted me.'

'*What's* he found?' Turner whispered.

'I don't know. He found it and he talked to Praschko and Praschko was no good. Leo knew he wouldn't be any good; but he had to go back and find out. He had to make sure he was on his own.'

'How do you know that? How much did he tell you?'

'Less than he thought, perhaps. He assumed I was part of him and that was that.' She shrugged. 'I was a friend and friends don't ask questions. Do they?'

'Go on.'

'Rawley was going to Hanover, he said; Friday night Rawley would go to Hanover. So Leo would give me dinner at Königswinter. A special dinner. I said "to celebrate?" "No. No, Hazel, not a *celebration.*" But everything was special now, he said, and there wasn't much time anymore. He wouldn't be getting another contract. No more years after December. So why not have a good dinner once in a while? And he looked at me in a frightfully shifty way and we plodded round the course again, him leading. We'd meet in Remagen, he said: we'd meet here. And then: "I say, Hazel, what the devil is Rawley *up to*, look here, in Hanover? I mean, two days before the rally?"'

She had a ready-made face for Leo as well, a frown, a heavy German frown of exaggerated sincerity with which she surely teased him when they were together.

'What *was* Rawley up to, then?' Turner demanded.

'Nothing as it turned out. He didn't go. And Leo must have got wind of that, because he cried off.'

'When?'

'He rang up on Friday morning.'

'What did he say? *Exactly* what did he say?'

'Exactly, he said he couldn't make it that night. He didn't give a reason. Not a real one. He was awfully sorry; there was something he had to do. It had become urgent. It was his boardroom voice: "Awfully sorry, Hazel."'

'That was all?'

'I said all right.' She was acting against tragedy. 'And good luck.' She shrugged. 'I haven't heard from him since. He disappeared and I was worried. I rang his house day and night. That's why you came to dinner. I thought you might know something. You didn't. Any fool could see that.'

The blonde girl was standing up. She wore a long suit of fitted suède and she had to pull tightly at the crotch to straighten the sharp creases. The old lady was writing a bill. Turner called to her and asked for more water and she left the room to get it.

'Ever seen this key?'

Clumsily he drew it from the official buff envelope and laid it on the tablecloth before her. She picked it up and held it cautiously in her palm.

'Where did you get this from?'

'Königswinter. It was in a blue suit.'

'The suit he wore on Thursday,' she said examining it.

'It's one you gave him, is it?' he asked with unconcealed distaste. 'Your house-key?'

'Perhaps it's the one I wouldn't give him,' she replied at last. 'That was the only thing I wouldn't do for him.'

'Go on.'

'I suppose that's what he wanted from Pargiter. That bitch Mary Crabbe told me he'd had a fling with *her*.' She stared down at the esplanade, at the waiting Opel parked in the shadow between the lights; then across the river to Leo's side.

'He said the Embassy had got something that belonged to him. Something from long ago. "They *owe* me, Hazel." He wouldn't say what it was. Memories, he said. It was to do with long ago, and I could get him the key so that he could take it back. I told him: "Talk to them. Tell Rawley, he's human." He said, No, Rawley was the last person on earth he could talk to. It wasn't anything valuable. It was locked away and they didn't even know they had it. You're going to interrupt. Don't. Just listen. I'm telling you more than you deserve.'

She drank some whisky.

'About the third time . . . in *our* house. He lay in bed and just went on about it: "Nothing *bad*," he said, "nothing *political*, but something owed." If he was Duty Officer it wouldn't matter, but he wasn't allowed to do Duty, being what he was. There was one key, they'd never miss it, no one knew how many there were anyway. One key he must have.' She broke off. 'Rawley fascinated him. He loved his dressing-room. All the trappings of a gent. He loved to *see*. Sometimes that's what I was to him: Rawley's wife. The cuff links, the Edward Lear. . . . He wanted to know all the backstairs things like who cleaned his shoes, where he had his suits made. That was when he played his card: while he was dressing. He pretended to remember what he'd been talking about all night. "I say Hazel, look here. *You* could get me the key. When Rawley's working late one night, couldn't you? I mean, call on him, say you'd left something in the Assembly Room. It would be *frightfully* simple. It's a different key," he said. "It's not like the others. Very easily recognized, Hazel." That key,' she remarked flatly handing it back to him. '"You're clever," I said, "You'll find a way."'

'That was before Christmas?'

'Yes.'

'What a bloody fool I am,' Turner whispered. 'Jesus Christ!'

'Why? What is it?'

'Nothing.' His eyes were bright with success. 'Just for a moment, I forgot he was a thief, that's all. I thought he'd copy that key, and he just stole it. Of course he would!'

'He's not a thief! He's a man. He's ten times the man you are.'

'Oh sure, sure. You were big scale you two. I've heard all that crap, believe me. You lived in the big unspoken part of life, didn't you? You were the artists, and Rawley was the poor bloody technician. You had souls, you two, you heard voices; Rawley just picked up the bits because he loved you. And all the time I thought they were sniggering about Jenny Pargiter. Christ Almighty! Poor sod,' he said, looking out of the window. 'Poor bastard. I'll never like Bradfield, that's for sure; but Christ, he has my full sympathy.'

Leaving some money on the table he followed her down the stone steps. She was frightened.

'He never mentioned Margaret Aickman to you, I suppose? He was going to marry her, you know. She was the only woman he loved.'

'He never loved anyone but me.'

'But he didn't mention her? He did to other people, you see. Everyone except you. She was his *big* love!'

'I don't believe it. I'll never believe it!'

He pulled open the car door and leaned in after her. 'You're all right, aren't you? You've touched the hem. He *loved* you. The whole bloody world can go to war as long as you have your little boy!'

'Yes. I've touched the hem. He was real with me. I made him real. He's real whatever he's doing now. That was our time, and I'm not going to let you destroy it; you or anyone else. He found me.'

'What else did he find?'

Miraculously, the car started.

'He found me, and whatever he found down there was the other part of coming alive.'

'*Down?* Down where? Where did he go? Tell me! You know! What was it he said to you?'

She drove away, not looking back, quite slowly, up the esplanade into the evening and small lights.

The Opel drew out preparing to follow her. Turner let it pass, then ran across the road and jumped into a taxi.

The Embassy car park was full, the guard was doubled at the gate. Once more, the Ambassador's Rolls Royce waited at the door like an ancient ship to bear him to the storm. As Turner ran up the steps, his raincoat flying behind him, he held the key ready in his hand.

Chapter Fifteen

The Glory Hole

Two Queen's Messengers stood at the desk, their black leather pouches hung like parachute harnesses over their regimental blazers.

'Who's Duty Officer?' Turner snapped.

'I thought you'd gone,' said Gaunt. 'Seven o'clock yesterday, that's what—'

There was a creak of leather as the messengers hastily made room for him.

'I want the keys.'

Gaunt saw the cuts on Turner's face and his eyes opened wide.

'Ring the Duty Officer.' Turner picked up the receiver and offered it to him across the desk. 'Tell him to come down with the keys. Now!'

Gaunt was protesting. The lobby swung a little and held still. Turner heard his silly Welsh bleat, half complaining, half flattering and he grasped him roughly by the arm and pulled him into the dark corridor.

'If you don't do as I say, I'll see they post the hell out of you for the rest of your natural life.'

'The keys aren't drawn, I tell you.'

'Where are they?'

'I've got them. In the safe. But you can't have them, not without a signature, you know that very well!'

'I don't want them. I want you to count them, that's all. Count the bloody keys!'

The messengers, ostentatiously discreet, were talking to one another in awkward undertones, but Turner's voice cut through them like an axe: 'How many should there be?'

'Forty-seven.'

Summoning the younger guard, Gaunt unlocked the safe that was built into the corner and drew out the familiar bunch of bright-cut brass keys. Overcome by curiosity, the two messengers watched while the square, miner's fingers told off each key like a bead on the abacus. He counted them once and he counted them a second time, and he handed them to the boy who counted them again.

'Well?'

'Forty-six,' said Gaunt grudgingly. 'No doubt.'

'Forty-six,' the boy echoed. 'One short.'

'When were they last counted?'

''Tisn't hardly possible to say,' Gaunt muttered, 'They've been going in and out for weeks.'

Turner pointed to the shining new grille that cut off the basement stairway.

'How do I get down there?'

'I told you. Bradfield has the key. It's a riot gate, see. Guards don't have the authority.'

'How do the cleaners get down there then? What about the boilermen?'

'The boiler-room's separate access, now, ever since Bremen see. They've put grilles down there as well. They can use the outside stairs but they can't go no further than the boiler on account of being prevented.' Gaunt was very scared.

'There's a fire escape . . . a service lift.'

'Only the back staircase, but that's locked too, see. Locked.'

'And the keys?'

'With Bradfield. Same as for the lift.'

'Where does it lead from?'

'Top floor.'

'Up by your place?'

'What of it then?'

'Up by your place or not?'

'Near.'

'Show me!'

Gaunt looked down, looked at the boy, looked at Turner and then back at the boy again. Reluctantly he dropped the keys into the boy's hand and without a word to the messengers led Turner quickly upstairs.

It might have been daytime. All the lights were on, doors open. Secretaries, clerks and diplomats, hastening down corridors, ignored them as they passed. The talk was of Brussels. The city's name was whispered like a password. It lay on every tongue and was stammered out by every typewriter; it was cut into the white wax of the stencils and rung on every telephone. They climbed another flight to a short corridor that smelt of a swimming-pool. A draught of fresh air struck them from their left. The door ahead of them said 'Chancery Guard Private' and the label underneath, 'Mr and Mrs J. Gaunt, British Embassy, Bonn.'

'We don't have to go in, do we?'

'This is where he came and saw you? Friday evening after choir? He came up here?'

Gaunt nodded.

'What happened when he left? Did you see him out?'

'He wouldn't let me. "You stay there my boy and watch your telly, I'll see myself off the premises."'

'And that's the door: the back staircase.'

He was pointing to his left where the draught came from.

'It's locked though, see. Hasn't been opened for years.'

'That's the only way in?'

'Straight down to the basement it goes. They were going to have a rubbish chute till the money ran out so they put stairs instead.'

The door was solid and unrelieved, with two stout locks that had not been disturbed for a long time. Shining a pencil torch on to the lintels, Turner gently fingered the wooden beading that ran down the two sides, then took a firm grip on the handle.

'Come here. You're his size. You try. Take the handle. Don't turn it. Push. Push hard.'

The door yielded without a sound.

The air was suddenly very cold and stale; American air when the conditioners fail. They stood on a half landing. The stairs under them were very steep. A small window gave on to the Red Cross field. Directly below, the cowl of the canteen chimney puffed floodlit smoke into the darkness. The plaster was peeling in large blisters. They heard the drip of water. On the reverse side of the door post, the wood had been neatly sawn away. By the thin light of the torch they began their descent. The steps were of stone; a narrow strip of coconut matting ran down the centre. 'Embassy Club this way,' a very old poster ran. 'All welcome.' They caught the sound of a kettle bobbing on a ring and heard a girl's voice reading back a passage of dictation: 'While the official statement of the Federal Government describes the reason for the withdrawal as merely technical, even the most sober commentators . . .' and instinctively they both stopped, heart in mouth, listening to the clear words precisely spoken in to the stairwell.

'It's the ventilation,' Gaunt whispered. 'It's coming through the shaft, see.'

'Shut up.'

They heard de Lisle's voice languidly correcting her. '*Moderate*,' he said. '*Moderate* would be *much* better. Change *sober* to *moderate*, will you, my dear? We don't want them to think we're drowning our sorrows in drink.'

The girl giggled.

They must have reached the ground floor, for a bricked doorway stood ahead of them, and fragments of wet plaster lay on the linoleum. A makeshift noticeboard advertised vanished entertainments: the Embassy Players would present a Christmas performance of Gogol's *Government Inspector*. A grand Commonwealth

Children's Party would be held in the Residence; names, together with details of any special dietary requirements should be submitted to the Private Office by 10th December. The year was 1954 and the signature was Harting's.

For a moment Turner fought with his sense of time and place, and almost lost. He heard the barges again and the chink of the glasses, the fall of soot and the creak of the rigging. The same throbbing, the same pulse beyond the register of sound.

'What did you say?' Gaunt asked.

'Nothing.'

Giddy and confused, he led the way blindly into the nearest passageway, his head wildly beating.

'You're not well,' said Gaunt. 'Who did that to you then?'

They were in a second chamber occupied by nothing but an old lathe, the filings rusted at its base. There was a door in the further wall. He pushed it open, and for a moment his composure left him as he drew back with a short cry of disgust, but it was only the iron bars of the new grille reaching from the ceiling to the floor, only the wet overalls hanging from the wire and the moisture pattering on the concrete. There was a stink of washday and half burnt fuel; the fire had set a red glow trembling on the brickwork; small lights danced on the new steel. Nothing apocalyptic, he told himself, as he moved cautiously along the gangway towards the next door, just a night train in the war; a crowded compartment and we're all asleep.

It was a steel door, flush against the plaster, a flood door deep below the water line, rusty at the frame and lintel with KEEP OUT done long ago in flaking Government paint. The wall on his left side was painted white at some time, and he could see the scratches where the trolley had passed. The light above him was shielded with a wire basket and it laid dark fingers on his face. He fought recklessly for consciousness. The lagged water pipes which ran along the ceiling chugged and gurgled in their housings, and the stove behind the iron grille spat white sparks which turned small shadows on and off. Christ, he thought: it's enough to power the *Queen Elizabeth*, it's enough to brand an army of prisoners; it's wasted on one lonely dream factory.

He had to fight with the key; he had to shake the lever handle hard before the lock would turn. Suddenly it had snapped like a stick and they heard the echo fly away and resound in distant rooms. Keep me here; Oh God keep me here, he thought. Don't change my nature or my life; don't change the place or move the path that I'm following . . . There must have been a piece of grit beneath the door for it shrieked, then stopped and Turner had to force it with his whole body, force it against the water, while Gaunt the Welshman stood back, watching and lusting but not daring to touch. At first, fumbling for the switch, he saw only the darkness; then a single window thick with cobwebs came gloomily forward and it frightened him because he hated prison. It was high in the wall and arched like a brick oven and barred for security. Through its topmost panes he glimpsed the wet gravel of the car park. While he stood there watching and swaying, the beam of a headlight groped slowly along the ceiling, a prison spotlight searching for escapers, and the whole catacomb filled with the roar of a departing engine. An Army blanket lay on the sill and he thought: you remembered to black out the window; you remembered the firewatching in London.

His hand found the light switch; it was domed like a woman's breast, and when he pressed it down it thumped like a punch against his own body and the dust rolled longingly towards him over the black concrete.

'They call it the Glory Hole,' Gaunt whispered.

The trolley was in an alcove beside the desk. Files on top, stationery below, all in varying sizes, nicely crested, with long and standard envelopes to match, all laid out ready to hand. At the centre of the desk, next to the reading light, square on its felt pad and neatly covered with a grey plastic cape, lay the missing typewriter with the long carriage and beside it three or four tins of Dutch cigars. On a separate table, a Thermos and a quantity of Naafi cups; the tea machine with the clock; on the floor a small electric fan in two tones of plastic, trained conveniently upon the desk to help dispel the unfortunate effects of damp; on the new chair with the rexine seat, a pink cushion partially embroidered, by Miss Aickman. All these he recognized at a glance, dully, greeting them curtly as we greet old friends, while he stared beyond them at the great archive which lined the walls from floor to ceiling; at the slim black files each with a rusted loop and a rounded thumb-hole, some grey with bloom, some wrinkled and bent with damp, column after column in their black uniforms, veterans trained and waiting to be called.

He must have asked what they were, for Gaunt was whispering. No, he couldn't suggest what they were. No. Not his place. No. They had been here longer than anyone could remember. Though some did say they were Jag files, the Judge Advocate General's Department he meant, that's what talkers said and the talkers said they came from Minden in lorries, just dumped here for living space they were, twenty years ago that must be now, all of twenty years, when the Occupation packed up. That's all he could say really, he was sure; that's all he'd happened to hear from the talkers, just overheard it by chance, for Gaunt was not a gossip, that was the one thing they *could* say about him. Oh *more* than twenty years . . . the lorries turned up one summer evening . . . Macmullen and someone else had spent half the night helping to unload them. . . . Of course in *those* days it was thought the Embassy might need them. . . . No, nobody had access, not these days, didn't want it really; who would? Long ago, the odd

Chancery officer would ask for the key and look something up but that was *long* ago, Gaunt couldn't remember that at all, and no one had been down here for years, though Gaunt couldn't say for sure, of course; he had to watch his words with Turner, he'd learnt that now, he was sure. . . . They must have kept the key separate for a while then added it to the Duty Officer's bunch. . . . But a while back now, Gaunt couldn't say when, he had heard them talking about it; Marcus one of the drivers, gone now; saying they weren't Jag files at all but *Group* files, it was a specialist British contingent. . . . His voice pattered on, urgent and conspiratorial, like an old woman in Church. Turner was no longer listening. He had seen the map.

A plain map, printed in Polish.

It was pinned above the desk, pinned quite freshly into the damp plaster, in the place where some might put the portraits of their children. No major towns were marked, no national borders, no scale, no pretty arrows showing the magnetic variation: just the places where the camps had been. Neuengamme and Belsen in the North, Dachau, Mauthausen to the South, to the East, Treblinka, Sobibor, Majdanek, Belzec and Auschwitz; in the centre Ravensbrück, Sachsenhausen, Kulmhof and Gross Rosen.

'They *owe* me,' he thought suddenly. 'They *owe* me.' God in Heaven what a fool, what a plain, blundering, clumsy fool I have been. Leo, you thief, you came here to forage in your own dreadful childhood.

'Go away. If I want you I'll call you.' Turner stared at Gaunt sightlessly, his right hand pressed against a shelf. 'Don't tell anyone. Bradfield, de Lisle, Crabbe . . . no one, do you understand.'

'I won't,' Gaunt said.

'I'm not here. I don't exist. I never came in tonight. Do you understand.'

'You ought to see a doctor,' said Gaunt.

'Fuck off.'

Pulling back the chair, he tipped the little cushion to the floor and sat down at the desk. Resting his chin in his hand, he waited for the room to steady. He was alone. He was alone like Harting, contraband smuggled in, living like Harting on borrowed time; hunting, like Harting, for a missing truth. There was a tap beside the window and he filled the tea machine and played with the knobs until it began to hiss. As he returned to the desk he nearly tripped over a green box. It was the size of a narrow briefcase, but stiff and rectangular, made of the kind of reinforced leather-cloth used for bridge-sets and shot-gun cases. It has the Queen's initials just beneath the handle and reinforced corners of thin steel; the locks had been ripped open and it was empty. *That's what we're all doing, isn't it? Looking for something that isn't there?*

He was alone, with only the files for company and the stink of warm damp from the electric fire; and the pale breeze of the plastic fan and the muttering of the tea machine. Slowly he began turning the pages. Some of the files were old, taken from the shelves, half in English and half in cruel Gothic script jagged as barbed wire. The names were set out like athletes, surname first and Christian name second, with only a couple of lines at the top and a hasty signature at the bottom to authorize their ultimate disposal. The files on the trolley were new, and the paper was rich and smooth, and the minutes signed with familiar names. And some were folders, records of mail despatched and mail received, with titles underlined and margins ruled.

He was alone, at the beginning of Harting's journey, with only his track for company, and the sullen grumbling of the water pipes in the corridor outside, like the shuffling of clogs upon a scaffold. *Are they like horses?* Hazel Bradfield's voice enquired. *Do they sleep standing up?* He was alone. *And whatever he found there was the other part of coming alive.*

Meadowes was asleep. He would not for a moment have admitted it; and Cork would not, in charity, for a moment have accused him of it; and it is true that technically, like Hazel Bradfield's horses, his eyes were open. He was reclining in his upholstered library chair in an attitude of well-deserved retirement, while the sounds of dawn floated through the open window.

'I'm handing over to Bill Sutcliffe,' Cork said, loud and deliberately careless. 'Nothing you want, is there, before I knock off? We're brewing a cup of tea if you fancy it.'

'It's all right,' Meadowes said indistinctly, sitting forward with a jerk. 'Be all right in a minute.' Cork, staring down through the open window into the car park, allowed him time to collect himself.

'We're brewing a cup of tea if you fancy it,' he repeated. 'Valerie's got the kettle on.' He was clutching a folder of telegrams. 'There hasn't been a night like that since Bremen. Talk, that's all it is. Words. By four this morning they'd forgotten about security altogether. H.E. and the Secretary of State were just chatting direct on the open line. Fantastic. Blown the lot I should think: codes, cyphers, the whole bloody orchestra.'

'They're blown already,' Meadowes replied, more for himself than for Cork; and came to join him at the window. 'By Leo.'

No dawn is ever wholly ominous. The earth is too much its own master; the cries, the colours and the scents too confident to sustain our grim foreboding. Even the guard at the front gate, doubled since evening, had a restful, domestic look. The morning light which glistened on their long leather coats was soft and strangely harmless; their pace as they slowly walked the perimeter was measured and wise. Cork was moved to optimism.

'I reckon today might be the day,' he said. 'A father by lunchtime: how's that, Arthur?'

'They're never that quick,' Meadowes said, 'Not the first ones,' and they fell to counting off the cars.

'Full house, near as nothing,' Cork declared; and it was true. Bradfield's white Jaguar, de Lisle's red sports car, Jenny Pargiter's little Wolseley, Gaveston's shooting brake with the baby chair mounted on the passenger seat, Jackson's rugged Two Thousand; even Crabbe's broken down Kapitän, twice personally banished from the car park by the Ambassador, had crept back in the crisis, its wings bent outward like crooked claws.

'Rover looks all right,' said Cork. In reverent silence they duly admired its distinguished outlines against the fencing on the other side of the canteen. Nearer at hand, the grey Rolls stood in its own bay, guarded by an army corporal.

'He saw him, did he?' Meadowes asked.

'Sure.' Cork licked his finger, selected the relevant telegram from the folder which he carried under his arm and began reading out loud, in a facetious, nursery-rhyme voice, the Ambassador's account of his dialogue with the Federal Chancellor . . . '"I replied that as Foreign Secretary you had implicit trust in the many undertakings already given to you personally by the Chancellor, and that you had every confidence that the Chancellor would not for a moment consider yielding to the pressure of vociferous minorities. I reminded him also of the French attitude to the question of German reunification, describing it not merely as unsound but as downright anti-American, anti-European and above all anti-German—"'

'Listen,' said Meadowes suddenly. 'Shut up and listen.'

'What the—'

'Be quiet.'

From the far end of the corridor they could hear a steady drone like the sound of a car climbing a hill.

'It can't be,' Cork said shortly. 'Bradfield's got the keys and he—' they heard the clank of the folding gate and the small sigh of a hydraulic brake.

'It's the beds! That's what it is. More beds. They've got it going for the beds; he's opened it up for them.' In confirmation of his theory, they heard the distinct clank of metal on metal, and the squeak of springs.

'This place will be a Noah's Ark by Sunday, I'll tell you. Kids, girls, even the bloody German staff: Babylon, that's what it'll be. Sodom and Gomorrah, that's better. Here, what happens if it comes on while they're demonstrating? Just my luck, that would be, wouldn't it? My first kid: baby Cork, born in captivity!'

'Go on. Let's hear the rest.'

'"The Federal Chancellor took note of the British anxiety which he thought misplaced; he assured me he would consult his Ministers and see what could be done to restore calm. I suggested to him that a statement of policy would be very useful; the Chancellor on the other hand thought repetition had a weakening effect. At this point he asked that his best wishes be conveyed to yourself as Secretary of State, and it became clear that he regarded the interview as closed. I asked him whether he would consider reserving fresh hotel accommodation in Brussels as a means of ending uninformed speculation, since you were personally distressed by reports that the German delegation had paid its bills and cancelled its bookings. The Chancellor replied that he was sure something of that sort should be done.'''

'Zero,' said Meadowes distractedly.

'''The Chancellor asked after the Queen's health. He had heard she had a touch of influenza. I said I thought she was over the worst but would make enquiries and let him know. The Chancellor said he hoped Her Majesty would take care of herself; it was a tricky time of year. I replied that all of us sincerely hoped that the climate would be more settled by Monday and he had the grace to laugh. We left on good terms.'' Ha ha ha. They also had a little chat about today's demonstration. The Chancellor said we weren't to sorry. London are copying to the Palace. ''The meeting,''' Cork added with a yawn, '''ended with the customary exchange of compliments at twenty-two twenty hours. A joint communiqué was issued to the press.'' Meanwhile, Econ are going up the wall and Commercial are totting up the cost of a run on the pound. Or gold or something. Or maybe it's a slump. Who cares?'

'You ought to sit the exam,' Meadowes said. 'You're too quick for in there.'

'I'll settle for twins,' said Cork, and Valerie brought in the tea.

Meadowes had actually raised the mug to his lips when he heard the sound of the trolley and the familiar trill of the squeaky wheel. Valerie put down the tray with a bang, and some tea slopped out of the pot into the sugar bowl. She was wearing a green pullover, and Cork, who liked to look at her, noticed as she turned to face the door that the polo neck had brought up a light rash at the side of her throat. Cork himself, quicker than the rest, handed Meadowes the folder, went to the door and looked down the corridor. It was their own trolley, loaded high with red and black files and Alan Turner was pushing it. He was in his shirt-sleeves and there were heavy bruises under both eyes. One lip was cut clean through and had been summarily stitched. He had not shaved. The Despatch Box was on the top of the pile. Cork said later that he looked as though he had pushed the trolley through enemy lines single-handed. As he came down the passage, doors opened one after another in his wake: Edna from the Typists' Pool, Crabbe, Pargiter, de Lisle, Gaveston: one by one their heads appeared, followed by their bodies, so that by the time he had arrived at Registry, slammed back the flap of the steel counter, and shoved the trolley carelessly into the centre of the room, the only door that remained closed was that of Rawley Bradfield, Head of Chancery.

'Leave it there. Don't touch it, any of it.'

Turner crossed the corridor and without knocking, went straight in to Bradfield.

Chapter Sixteen

'It's all a fake'

'I thought you'd gone.' His tone was weary rather than surprised.

'I missed the plane. Didn't she tell you?'

'What the devil have you done to your face?'

'Siebkron sent his boys to search my room. Looking for news of Harting. I interrupted them.' He sat down. 'They're anglophiles. Like Karfeld.'

'The matter of Harting is closed.' Very deliberately Bradfield laid aside some telegrams. 'I have sent his papers to London together with a letter assessing the damage to our security. The rest will be handled from there. I have no doubt that in due course a decision will be taken on whether or not to inform our Nato partners.'

'Then you can cancel your letter. And forget the assessment.'

'I have made allowances for you,' Bradfield snapped, with much of his former asperity. 'Every kind of allowance. For your unsavoury profession, your ignorance of diplomatic practice and your uncommon rudeness. Your stay here has brought us nothing but trouble; you seem determined to be unpopular. What the devil do you mean by remaining in Bonn when I have told you to leave? Bursting in here in a state of undress? Have you no idea what is going on here? It's Friday! The day of the demonstration, in case you have forgotten.'

Turner did not move, and Bradfield's anger at last got the better of fatigue. 'Lumley told me you were uncouth but effective: so far you have merely been uncouth. I am not in the least surprised you have met with violence: you attract it. I have warned you of the damage you can do; I have told you my reasons for abandoning the investigation at this end; and I have overlooked the needless brutality with which you have treated my staff. But now I have had enough. You are forbidden the Embassy. Get out.'

'I've found the files,' Turner said. 'I've found the lot. And the trolley. And the typewriter and the chair. And the two-bar electric fire, and de Lisle's fan.' His voice was disjointed and unconvincing, and his gaze seemed to be upon things that were not in the room. 'And the teacups and all the rest of the hardware he pinched at one time or another. And the letters he collected from the Bag Room and never handed to Meadowes. They were addressed to Leo, you see. They were answers to letters he'd sent. He ran quite a department down there: a separate section of Chancery. Only you never knew. He's discovered the truth about Karfeld and now they're after him.' His hand lightly touched his cheek. 'The people who did this to me: they're after Leo. He's on the run because he knew too much and asked too many questions. For all I know they've caught him already. Sorry to be a bore,' he added flatly. 'But that's the way it is. I'd like a cup of coffee if you don't mind.'

Bradfield did not move.

'What about the Green File?'

'It's not there. Just the empty box.'

'He's taken it?'

'I don't know. Praschko might. I don't.' He shook his head. 'I'm sorry.' He continued: 'You've to find him before they do. Because if you don't they'll kill him. That's what I'm talking about. Karfeld's a fraud and a murderer and Harting's got the proof of it.' He raised his voice at last. 'Do I make myself clear?'

Bradfield continued to watch him, intent but not alarmed.

'When did Harting wake to him?' Turner asked himself. 'He didn't want to notice at first. He turned his back. He'd been turning his back on a lot of things, trying not to remember. Trying not to notice. He held himself in like we all do, sticking to the discipline of not being involved and calling it sacrifice. Gardening, going to parties. Working his fiddles. Surviving. And not interfering. Keeping his head down and letting the world go over him. Until October, when Karfeld came to power. He knew Karfeld, you see. And Karfeld *owed* him. That mattered to Leo.'

'Owed him *what*?'

'Wait. Gradually, bit by bit he began to . . . open up. He allowed himself to feel. Karfeld was tantalizing him. We both know what that means, don't we: to be tantalized. Karfeld's face was everywhere, like it is now. Grinning, frowning, warning. . . . His name kept ringing in Leo's ears: Karfeld's a fraud; Karfeld's a murderer. Karfeld's a fake.'

'What are you talking about? Don't be so utterly ridiculous.'

'Leo didn't like that any more: he didn't like fakes any more; he wanted the truth. The male menopause: that is it. He was disgusted with himself . . . for what he'd failed to do, sins of omission . . . sins of commission. Sick of his own tricks and his own routine. We all know that feeling, don't we? Well Leo had it. In full measure. So he decided to get what he was owed: justice for Karfeld. He had a long memory, you see. That's not fashionable these days, I understand. So he plotted. First to get into Registry, then to renew his contract, then to get hold of the files: The Personalities Survey . . . the old files, the files that were due for destruction . . . the old case histories in the Glory Hole. He would put the case together again, reopen the investigation. . . .'

'I have no idea what you are referring to. You're sick; you are wandering and sick. I suggest you go and lie down.' His hand moved to the telephone.

'First of all he got the key, that was easy enough. Put that down! Leave that telephone alone!' Bradfield's hand hovered and fell back on to the blotter. 'Then he started work in the Glory Hole, set up his little office, made his own files, kept minutes, corresponded . . . he moved in. Anything he needed from Registry, he stole. He was a thief; you said that. You should know.' For a moment, Turner's voice was gentle and understanding. 'When was it you sealed off the basement? Bremen wasn't it? A weekend? That was when he panicked. The only time. That was when he stole the trolley. I'm talking about Karfeld. Listen! About his doctorate, his military service, the wound at Stalingrad, the chemical factory—'

'These rumours have been going the rounds for months. Ever since Karfeld became a serious political contestant, we have heard nothing but stories of his past and each time he has successfully refuted them. There's hardly a politician of any standing in Western Germany whom the Communists have not defamed at one time or another.'

'Leo's not a communist,' Turner said with profound weariness. 'You told me yourself: he's a primitive. For years he kept away from politics because he was afraid of what he might hear. I'm not talking rumours. I'm talking fact: home-grown British fact. Exclusive. It's all in our own British files, locked away in our own British basement. That's where he got them from and not even you can bury them any more.' There was neither triumph nor hostility to his tone. 'The information's in Registry now if you want to check. With the empty box. There's some things I didn't follow, my German's not that good. I've given instructions that no one's to touch the stuff.' He grinned in reminiscence, and it might have been his own predicament that he recalled. 'You bloody nearly marooned him if you did but know it. He got the trolley down there the weekend they put up the grilles and sealed off the lift. He was terrified of not being able to carry on; of being cut off from the Glory Hole. Until then, it was child's play. He only had to hop into the lift with his files–he could go anywhere, you see; the Personalities Survey gave him the right–and take them straight down to the basement. But you were putting an end to all that though you didn't know it; the riot grilles queered his pitch. So he shoved everything he might need on to the trolley and waited down there the whole weekend until the workmen had done. He had to break the locks on the back staircase to get out. After that, he relied on Gaunt to invite him up to the top floor. Innocently of course. Everyone's innocent in a manner of speaking. And I'm sorry,' he added, quite graciously, 'I'm sorry for what I said to you. I was wrong.'

'This is hardly the moment for apologies,' Bradfield retorted, and rang Miss Peate for some coffee.

'I'm going to tell you the way it is on the files,' Turner said. 'The case against Karfeld. You'd do me a favour not interrupting. We're both tired, and we've not much time.'

Bradfield had set a sheet of blue draft paper on the blotter before him; the fountain pen was poised above it. Miss Peate, having poured the coffee, took her leave. Her expression, her single disgusted glance at Turner, was more eloquent than any words she could have found.

'I'm going to tell you what he'd put together. Pick holes in it afterwards if you want.'

'I shall do my best,' Bradfield said with a momentary smile that was like the memory of a different man.

'There's a village near Dannenberg, on the Zonal border. Hapstorf it's called. It has three men and a dog and it lies in a wooded valley. Or used to. In thirty-eight, the Germans put a factory there. There was an old paper mill beside a fast-flowing river, with a country house attached to it, right up against the cliff. They converted the mill and built laboratories alongside the river, and turned the place into a small hush-hush research station for certain types of gas.'

He drank some coffee and took a bite of biscuit, and it seemed to hurt him to eat, for he held his head to one side and munched very cautiously.

'Poison Gas. The attractions were obvious. The place was difficult to bomb; the stream was fast-flowing, and they needed that for the effluent; the village was small and they could chuck out anyone they didn't like. All right?'

'All right.' Bradfield had taken out his pen and was writing down key points as Turner spoke. Turner could see the numbers down the left side and he thought: what difference does it make about the numbers? You can't destroy facts by giving them numbers.

'The local population claims it didn't know what was going on there, which is probably true. They knew the mill had been stripped and they knew that a lot of expensive plant had been installed. They knew the warehouses at the back were specially guarded, and they knew the staff weren't allowed to mix with the locals. The labour was foreign: French and Poles, who weren't allowed out at all, so there was no mixing at the lower level either. And everyone knew about the animals. Monkeys mainly, but sheep, goats and dogs as well. Animals that went in there and didn't come out. There's a record of the local *Gauleiter* receiving letters of complaint from animal lovers.'

He looked at Bradfield in wonder. 'He worked down there, night after night, putting it all together.'

'He had no business down there. The basement archive has been out of bounds for many years.'

'He had business there all right.'

Bradfield was writing on his pad.

'Two months before the end of the war, the factory was destroyed by the British. Pinpoint bombing. The explosion was enormous. The place was wiped out, and the village with it. The foreign labourers were killed. They say the sound of the blast carried miles, there was so much went up with it.'

Bradfield's pen sped across the paper.

'At the time of the bombing, Karfeld was at home in Essen; there's no doubt of that at all. He says he was burying his mother; she'd been killed in an air raid.'

'Well?'

'He was in Essen all right. But he wasn't burying his mother. She'd died two years earlier.'

'Nonsense!' Bradfield cried. 'The Press would long ago—'

'There's a photostat of the original death certificate on the file,' Turner said evenly. 'I'm not able to say what the new one looks like. Nor who faked it for him. Though I should think we could both guess without rupturing our imaginations.'

Bradfield glanced at him with appreciation.

'After the war, the British were in Hamburg and they sent a team to look at what was left of Hapstorf, collect souvenirs and take photographs. Just an ordinary Intelligence team, nothing special. They thought they might pick up the scientists who'd worked there ... get the benefit of their knowledge, see what I mean? They reported that nothing was left. They also reported some rumours. A French labourer, one of the few survivors, had a story about experiments on human guinea pigs. Not on the labourers themselves, he said, but on other people brought in. They'd used animals to begin with, he said, but later on they wanted the real thing so they had some specially delivered. He said he'd been on gate duty one night–he was a trusty by then–and the Germans told him to return to his hut, go to bed and not appear till morning. He was suspicious and hung around. He saw a strange thing; a grey bus, just a plain grey single-decker bus, went through one gate after another without being documented. It drove round the back, towards the warehouses, and he didn't hear any more. A couple of minutes later, it drove out again, much faster. Empty.' Again he broke off, and this time he took a handkerchief from his pocket and very gingerly dabbed his brow. 'The Frenchman also said a friend of his, a Belgian, had been offered inducements to work in the new laboratories under the cliff. He went for a couple of days and came back looking like a ghost. He said he wouldn't spend another night over there, not for all the privileges in the world. Next day he disappeared. Posted, they said. But before he left he had a talk to his pal, and he mentioned the name of Doctor Klaus. Doctor Klaus was the administrative supervisor, he said; he was the man who arranged the details and made things easy for the scientists. He was the man who offered him the job.'

'You call this evidence?'

'Wait. Just wait. The team reported their findings and a copy went to the local War Crimes Group. So they took it over. They interrogated the Frenchman, took a full statement but they failed to produce corroboration. An old woman who ran a flower shop had a story about hearing screams in the night, but she couldn't say which night and besides it might have been animals. It was all very flimsy.'

'Very, I should have thought.'

'Look,' Turner said. 'We're on the same side now aren't we? There are no more doors to open.'

'There may be some to close,' Bradfield said, writing again. 'However.'

'The Group was overworked and understaffed so they threw in the case. File and discontinue. They'd many bigger cases to worry about. They carded Doctor Klaus and forgot about him. The Frenchman went back to France, the old lady forgot the screams and that was it. Until a couple of years later.'

'Wait.'

Bradfield's pen did not hurry. He formed the letters as he always formed them: legibly, with consideration for his successors.

'Then an accident happened. The kind we've come to expect. A farmer near Hapstorf bought an old bit of waste land from the local council. It was rough ground, very stony and wooded, but he thought he could make something of it. By the time he'd dug it and ploughed it, he'd unearthed thirty-two bodies of grown men. The German police took a look and informed the Occupational authority. Crimes against Allied personnel were the responsibility of the Allied judiciary. The British mounted an investigation and decided that thirty-one of the men had been gassed. The thirty-second man was wearing the tunic of a foreign labourer and he'd been shot in the back of the neck. There was something else . . . something that really threw them. The bodies were all messed up.'

'Messed up?'

'Researched. Autopsied. Someone had got there first. So they reopened the case. Somebody in the town remembered that Doctor Klaus came from Essen.'

Bradfield was watching him now; he had put down his pen and folded his hands together.

'They went through all the chemists with the qualifications to conduct high-grade research who lived in Essen and whose first names were Klaus. It didn't take them long to unearth Karfeld. He'd no doctorate; that comes later. But then everyone assumed by then that the staff were working under pseudonyms, so why not give yourself a title too? Essen was also in the British zone, so they pulled him in. He denied the whole thing. Naturally. Mind you: apart from the bodies there was little enough to go by. Except for one incidental piece of information.'

Bradfield did not interrupt this time.

'You've heard of the Euthanasia scheme?'

'Hadamar.' With a nod of his head Bradfield indicated the window. 'Down the river, Hadamar,' he repeated.

'Hadamar, Weilmunster, Eichberg, Kalmenhof: clinics for the elimination of unwanted people: for whoever lived on the economy and made no contribution to it. You can read all about it in the Glory Hole, and quite a lot about it is Registry. Among the files for Destruction. At first they had categories for the type of people they'd killed off. You know: the deformed, the insane, severely handicapped children between the ages of eight and thirteen. Bed-wetters. With very few exceptions, the victims were German citizens.'

'They called them patients,' Bradfield said, with intense distaste.

'It seems that now and then certain selected patients were set aside and put to medical uses. Children as well as adults.'

Bradfield nodded, as if he knew that too.

'By the time the Hapstorf case broke, the Americans and Germans had done a fair bit of work on this Euthanasia programme. Among other things, they'd unearthed evidence of one busload of "hybrid workers" being set aside for "dangerous duties at the Chemical Research Station of Hapstorf". One busload was thirty-one people. They used grey buses by the way, if that reminds you of anything.'

'Hanover,' Bradfield said at once. 'The transport for the body-guard.'

'Karfeld's an administrator. Everyone admires him for it. Then as now. It's nice to know he hasn't lost the old touch, isn't it? He's got one of those minds that runs in grooves.'

'Stop stringing beads. I want the whole thing, quickly.'

'Grey buses then. Thirty-one seats and room left over for the guard. The windows were blackened from the inside. Where possible, they moved them at night.'

'You said there were thirty-two bodies not thirty-one—'

'There was the Belgian labourer, wasn't there? The one who worked under the cliff and talked to the French trusty? They knew what to do about him all right. He'd found out a bit too much, hadn't he? Like Leo, now.'

'Here,' said Bradfield, getting up and bringing the coffee over to him. 'You'd better have some more of this.' Turner held out his cup and his hand was fairly steady.

'So when they'd pulled him in they took Karfeld up to Hamburg and confronted him with the bodies and the evidence, such as they had, and he just laughed at them. Bloody nonsense, he said, the whole story. Never been to Hapstorf in his life. He was an engineer. A demolitions man. He gave a very detailed account of his work at the Russian front—they'd even given him campaign medals and Christ knows what. I suppose they did that for them in the SS and he made a great *spiel* about Stalingrad. There were discrepancies but not that many, and he just held out all the time against interrogation and denied ever having set foot in Hapstorf or possessing any knowledge of the plant. No, no, no all the way. For months on end. "Okay," he kept saying, "if you've got the proof, bring a case. Put it to the Tribunal. I'm not bothered; I'm a hero. I never administered anything in my life except our family factory in Essen, and the British have pulled that to pieces, haven't they? I've been to Russia, I haven't been poisoning hybrids; why should I? I'm a little friend of all the world. Find a live witness, find anybody." They couldn't. At Hapstorf, the chemists had lived in complete segregation, and presumably the desk-men had done the same. The records were destroyed by bombing, and everyone was known by his Christian name or an alias.' Turner shrugged. 'That seemed to be that. He even threw in a story about helping the anti-Nazi resistance in Russia, and since the units he mentioned were either taken prisoner *en masse* or shot to pieces, they couldn't get any further with that either. He doesn't seem to have come out with that since, the resistance bit.'

'It's no longer fashionable,' said Bradfield shortly. 'Particularly in his sphere.'

'So the case never reached the courts. There were plenty of reasons why not. The War Crimes investigation units themselves were near to disbandment; there was pressure from London and Washington to bury the hatchet and hand over all responsibility to the German courts. It was chaos. While the unit was trying to prepare charges, their Headquarters were preparing amnesties. And there were other reasons, technical reasons for not going ahead. The crime was against French, Belgians and Poles if anyone, but since there was no method of establishing the nationality of the victims, there were problems about jurisdiction. Not material problems, but incidental ones, and they contributed to the difficulty of deciding what to do. You know how it is when you *want* to find difficulties.'

'I know how it was then,' Bradfield said quietly. 'It was bedlam.'

'The French weren't keen; the Poles were *too* keen and Karfeld himself was quite a big wheel by then. He was handling some big Allied contracts. Even sub-contracting to competitors to keep up with demand. He was a good administrator, you see. Efficient.'

'You say that as if it were a crime.'

'His own factory had been dismantled a couple of times but now it was running a treat. Seemed a pity to disturb it really. There was even some rumour,' Turner added without changing the tone of his voice, 'that he'd had a head start on everyone else because he'd come by a special consignment of rare gases, and stored them underground in Essen at the end of the war. That's what he was up to while the RAF was bombing Hapstorf. While he was supposed to be burying his poor old mother. He'd been pinching the goods to feather his own nest.'

'As you have described the evidence so far,' Bradfield said quietly, 'there is nothing whatever which attaches Karfeld to Hapstorf, and nothing at all to associate him with the complicity in a murder plot. His own account of himself may very well be true. That he fought in Russia, that he was wounded—'

'That's right. That's the view they took at Headquarters.'

'It is even unproven that the bodies came from Hapstorf. The *gas* may have been theirs; it hardly proves that the chemists themselves administered it to the victims, let alone that Karfeld knew of it, or was in any way an accessory to—'

'The house at Hapstorf had a cellar. The cellar wasn't affected by the bombing. The windows had been bricked in and pipes had been run through the ceiling from the laboratories above. The brick walls of the cellar were torn.'

'What do you mean: "torn"?'

'By hands,' Turner said. 'Fingers, it could have been.'

'Anyway they took your view. Karfeld kept his mouth shut, there was no fresh evidence. They didn't prosecute. Quite rightly. The case was shelved. The unit was moved to Bremen, then to Hanover, then to Moenchengladbach and the files were sent here. Together with some odds and sods from the Judge Advocate General's Department. Pending a decision regarding their ultimate disposal.'

'And this is the story Harting has got on to?'

'He was always on to it. He was the sergeant investigating. Him and Praschko. The whole file, minutes, memoranda, correspondence, interrogation reports, summaries of evidence, the whole case from beginning to end–it has an end now–is recorded in Leo's handwriting. Leo arrested him, questioned him, attended the autopsies, looked for witnesses. The woman he nearly married, Margaret Aickman, she was in the unit as well. A clerical researcher. They called them headhunters: that was his life. . . . They were all very anxious that Karfeld be properly arraigned.'

Bradfield remained lost in thought. 'And this word *hybrid*—' he asked finally.

'It was a Nazi technical term for half Jewish.'

'I see. Yes, I see. So he would have a personal stake, wouldn't he? And that mattered to him. He took everything personally. He lived for himself; that was the only thing he understood.' The pen remained quite still. 'But hardly a case in law.' He repeated it to himself: 'But hardly a case in law. In fact hardly a case by any standards. Not on the merest, most partisan analysis. Not any kind of case. Interesting of course: it accounts for Karfeld's feelings about the British. It doesn't begin to make a criminal of him.'

'No,' Turner agreed, rather to Bradfield's surprise. 'No. It's not a case. But for Leo it rankled. He never forgot; but he pressed it down as far as it would go. But he couldn't keep away from it. He had to find out; he had to take another look and make sure, and in January this year he went down to the Glory Hole and re-read his own reports and his own arguments.'

Bradfield was sitting very still again.

'It may have been his age. Most of all, it was a sense of something left undone.' Turner said this as if it were a problem which applied to his own case, and to which he had no solution. 'A sense of history if you like.' He hesitated, 'Of time. The paradoxes caught up with him and he had to do something about it. He was also in love,' he added, staring out of the window. 'Though he might not have admitted it. He'd made use of somebody and picked up more than he bargained for. . . . He'd escaped from lethargy. That's the point, isn't it: the opposite of love isn't hate. It's lethargy. Nothingness. This place. And there were people about who let him think he was in the big league . . .' he added softly. 'So for whatever reasons, he reopened the case. He re-read the papers from beginning to end. He studied the background again, went through all the contemporary files, in Registry and in the Glory Hole. Checked all the facts from the beginning, and he began making his own enquiries.'

'What sort of enquiries?' Bradfield demanded. They were not looking at one another.

'He set up his own office. He wrote letters and received replies. All on Embassy paper. He headed off the Chancery mail as it came in and extracted anything addressed to him. He ran it like he ran his own life: secretly and efficiently. Trusting nobody, confiding in nobody; playing the different ends off against each other. . . . Sometimes he made little journeys, consulted records, Ministries, church registers, survivor groups . . . all on Embassy paper. He collected press cuttings, took copies, did his own typing and put on his own sealing wax. He even pinched an official seal. He headed his letters Claims and Consular, so most of them came to him in the first place anyway. He compared every detail: birth certificates, marriage, death of mother, hunting licences—he was looking for discrepancies all the time: anything to prove that Karfeld hadn't fought at the Russian front. He put together a bloody great dossier. It's hardly surprising Siebkron got on to him. There's scarcely a Government Agency he hasn't consulted under one pretext or another—'

'Oh my God,' Bradfield whispered, laying down his pen in a momentary gesture of defeat.

'By the end of January, he'd come to the only possible conclusion: that Karfeld had been lying in his teeth, and someone–it looked like someone high up, and it looked very much like Siebkron–someone had been covering up for him. They tell me Siebkron has ambitions of his own–hitch his wagon to any star as long as it was on the move.'

'That's true enough,' Bradfield conceded, lost in private thoughts.

'Like Praschko in the old days. . . . You see where we're getting, don't you? And of course before long, as he very well knew, Siebkron was going to notice that the Embassy was making some pretty way-out enquiries, even for Claims and Consular. And that somebody was going to be bloody angry, and perhaps a bit rough as well. Specially when Leo found the proof.'

'What proof? How can he possibly prove such a charge now, twenty or more years after the crime?'

'It's all in Registry,' Turner said, with sudden reluctance. 'You'd do better to see for yourself.'

'I've no time and I am used to hearing unsavoury facts.'

'And discounting them.'

'I insist that you tell me.' He made no drama of his insistence.

'Very well. Last year, Karfeld decided to take a doctorate. He was a big fellow by then; he was worth a fortune in the chemical industry–his administrative talent had paid off in a big way–and he was making fair headway in local politics in Essen, and he wanted to be Doctor. Maybe he was like Leo; he'd left a job undone and he wanted to get the record straight. Or maybe he thought a handle would be a useful asset: Vote for Doctor Karfeld. They like a doctorate here in a Chancellor. . . . So he went back to school and wrote a learned thesis. He didn't do much research and everyone was very impressed, specially his tutors. Wonderful, they said, the way he found the time.'

'And?'

'It's a study of the effects of certain toxic gases on the human body. They thought very hightly of it apparently; caused quite a little stir at the time.'

'That is hardly conclusive.'

'Oh yes it is. Karfeld based his whole analysis on the detailed examination of thirty-one fatal cases.'

Bradfield had closed his eyes.

'It is not proof,' Bradfield said at last; he was very pale but the pen in his hand was as firm as ever. 'You know it is not proof. It raises suppositions I agree. It suggests he was at Hapstorf. It is not even half-way to proof.'

'Pity we can't tell Leo.'

'The information came to him in the course of his industrial experience; that is what Karfeld would argue. He acquired it from a third party; that would be his fall-back position.'

'From the real bastards.'

'Even if it could be shown that the information came from Hapstorf, there are a dozen explanations as to how it came into Karfeld's hands. You said yourself, he was not even engaged in research—'

'No. He sat at a desk. It's been done before.'

'Precisely. And the very fact that he made use of the information at all would tend to exonerate him from the charge of acquiring it.'

'The trouble is, you see,' Turner said, 'Leo's only half a lawyer: a hybrid. We have to reckon with the other half as well. We have to reckon with the thief.'

'Yes.' Bradfield was distracted. 'And he has taken the Green File.'

'Still, as far as Siebkron and Karfeld are concerned, he seems to have got near enough to the truth to be a pretty serious risk, doesn't he?'

'A prima facie case,' Bradfield remarked, examining his notes once more. 'Grounds for reinvestigation, I grant you. At best, a public prosecutor might be persuaded to make an initial examination.' He glanced at his telephone directory. 'The Legal Attaché would know.'

'Don't bother,' Turner said comfortingly. 'Whatever he's done or hasn't done, Karfeld's in the clear. He's past the post.' Bradfield stared at him. 'No one can prosecute him now, even with a cast-iron confession, signed by Karfeld himself.'

'Of course,' Bradfield said quietly. 'I was forgetting.' He sounded relieved.

'He's protected by law. The Statute of Limitations takes care of that. Leo put a note on the file on Thursday evening. The case is dead. There's nothing anyone can do.'

'There's a procedure for reviving it—'

'There is,' Turner conceded. 'It doesn't apply. That's the fault of the British as it happens. The Hapstorf case was a British investigation. We never passed it to the Germans at all. There was no trial, no public report, and when the German judiciary took over sole responsibility for Nazi war crimes we gave them no note of it. Karfeld's whole case fell into the gap between the Germans and ourselves.' He paused. 'And now Leo's done the same.'

'What did Harting intend to do? What was the purpose of all this enquiring?'

'He had to know. He had to complete the case. It taunted him, like a messed-up childhood or a life you can't come to terms with. He had to get it straight. I think he was playing the rest by ear.'

'When did he get this so-called proof?'

'The thesis arrived on the Saturday before he left. He kept a date-stamp you see; everything was entered up in the files. On the Monday he arrived in Registry in a state of elation. He spent a couple of days wondering what to do next. Last Thursday he had lunch with Praschko—'

'What the devil for?'

'I don't know. I thought about it. I don't know. Probably to discuss what action they should take. Or to get a legal opinion. Maybe he thought there was still a way of prosecuting—'

'There is none?'

'No.'

'Thank God for that.'

Turner ignored him: 'Or perhaps to tell Praschko that the pace was getting too hot. To ask him for protection.'

Bradfield looked at Turner very carefully. 'And the Green File has gone,' he said, recovering his strength.

'The box was empty.'

'And Harting has run. Do you know the reason for *that* as well?' His eyes were still upon Turner. 'Is that also recorded in his dossier?'

'He kept writing in his memoranda: "I have very little time." Everyone who speaks of him describes him as being in a fight against time . . . the new urgency . . . I suppose he was thinking of the Statute.'

'But we know that, under the Statute, Karfeld was already a free man, unless of course some kind of stay of action could be obtained. So why has he left? And what was so pressing?'

Turner shrugged away the strangely searching, even taunting tone of Bradfield's questions.

'So you don't know *exactly* why? Why he has chosen this particular moment to run away? Or why he chose that one file to steal?'

'I assume Siebkron has been crowding him. Leo had the proof and Siebkron knew he had it. From then on, Leo was a marked man. He had a gun,' Turner added, 'an old Army pistol. He was frightened enough to take it with him. He must have panicked.'

'Quite,' Bradfield said, with the same note of relief. 'Quite. No doubt that is the explanation.' Turner stared at him in bewilderment.

For perhaps ten minutes Bradfield had not moved or said a word.

There was a lectern in a corner of the room made of an old Bible box and long, rather ugly metal legs which Bradfield had commissioned of a local blacksmith in Bad Godesberg. He was standing with his elbows upon it, staring out of the window at the river.

'No wonder Siebkron puts us under guard,' he said at last; he might have been talking about the mist. 'No wonder he treats us as if we were dangerous. There can hardly be a Ministry in Bonn, not even a journalist, who has not by now heard that the British Embassy is engaged in a blood-hunt for Karfeld's past. What do they expect us to do? Blackmail him in public? Reappear after twenty-five years in full-bottom wigs and indict him under the Allied Jurisdiction? Or do they simply think we are wantonly vindictive, and propose to have our revenge of the man who is spoiling our European dreams?'

'You'll find him, won't you? You'll go easy with him? He needs all the help he can get.'

'So do we all,' said Bradfield, still gazing at the river.

'He isn't a Communist. He isn't a traitor. He thinks Karfeld's a threat. To us. He's very simple. You can tell from the files—'

'I know his kind of simplicity.'

'He's our responsibility, after all. It was us who put it into his mind back in those days: the notion of absolute justice. We made him all those promises: Nuremberg, de-Nazification. We *made* him believe. We can't let him be a casualty just because we changed our minds. You haven't seen those files . . . you can't imagine how they thought about the Germans then. Leo hasn't changed. He's the stay-behind man. *That's* not a crime, is it?'

'I know very well how they thought. I was here myself. I saw what he saw; enough. He should have grown out of it; the rest of us did.'

'What I mean is, he's worthy of our protection. There's a kind of integrity about him. . . . I felt that down there. He's not put off by paradox. For you and me there are always a dozen good reasons for doing nothing. Leo's made the other way round. In Leo's book there's only one reason for doing something: because he must. Because he feels.'

'I trust you are not offering him as an example to be followed?'

'There's another thing that puzzled him.'

'Well?'

'In cases like this, there are always external documents. In the SS headquarters; with the clinic or the transport unit. Movements orders, letters of authority, *related* documents from somewhere else that would give the game away. Yet nothing's come to light. Leo kept on pencilling annotations: why no record in Koblenz? Why no this or that? As if he suspected that other evidence had been destroyed . . . by Siebkron for instance.'

'We can honour him, can't we?' Turner added, almost in supplication.

'There are no absolutes here.' His gaze had not left the distant scene. 'It is all doubt. All mist. The mist drains away the colours. There are no distinctions, the Socialists have seen to that. They are all everything. They are all nothing. No wonder Karfeld is in mourning.'

What was it that Bradfield studied on the river? The small boats struggling against the mist? The red cranes and the flat fields, or the far vineyards that have crept so far away from the south? Or Chamberlain's ghostly hill and the long concrete box where they had once kept him?

'The Glory Hole is out of bounds,' he said at last and again fell silent. 'Praschko. You said he lunched with Praschko on Thursday?'

'Bradfield—'

'Yes?' He was already moving to the door.

'We feel differently about him now, don't we?'

'Do we? Perhaps he is still a Communist after all.' There was a strain of irony in Bradfield's tone. 'You forget he has stolen a file. You seem to think all of a sudden you can look into his heart.'

'Why did he steal it? What was in that file?'

But Bradfield was already pushing his way between the beds and the clutter of the corridor. Notices had sprung up everywhere: First Aid Post this Way . . . Emergency Rest Room . . . No Children Allowed Beyond this Point. As they passed Chancery Registry, they heard a sudden cheer followed by a desultory handclap. Cork, white in the face, ran out to greet them.

'She's had it,' he whispered. 'The hospital just telephoned. She wouldn't let them send for me while I was on shift.' His pink eyes were wide with fear. 'She didn't even need me. She didn't even want me there.'

Chapter Seventeen

Praschko

There is a tarmac driveway at the back of the Embassy. It leads from the eastern part of the perimeter northwards through a settlement of new villas too costly for British habitation. Each has a small garden of great value in terms of real estate, each is distinguished from its neighbour by those cautious architectural deviations which are the mark of modern conformity. If one house has a brick-built barbecue and a patio of reconstituted stone, the next will match it with an external wall of blue slate, or quarried rock daringly exposed. In summer, young wives sun themselves beside minuscule swimming-pools. In winter black poodles burrow in the snow; and every midday from Monday to Friday, black Mercedes bring the masters home for meals. The air smells all the time, if distantly, of coffee.

It was a cold grey morning still, but the earth was lit with the clarity which follows rain. They drove very slowly, with the windows right down. Passing a hospital, they entered a more sombre road where the older suburb had survived; behind shaggy conifers and blue-black laurel bushes, leaden spires which once had painted donnish dreams of Weimar stood like lances in a mouldering forest. Ahead of them rose the Bundestag, naked, comfortless and uncomforted; a vast motel mourned by its own flags and painted in yellowing milk. At its back, straddled by Kennedy's Bridge and bordered by Beethoven's hall, the brown Rhine pursued its uncertain cultural course.

Police were everywhere: seldom could a seat of democracy have been so well protected from its democrats. At the main entrance, a line of school-children waited in a restless queue, and the police guarded them as if they were their own. A television team was setting up its arc-lights. In front of the camera a young man in a suit of mulberry corduroy thoughtlessly pirouetted, hand on hip, while a colleague measured his complexion; the police watched dangerously, bewildered by his freedom. Along the kerb, scrubbed as jurymen, their banners straight as Roman standards, the grey crowd obediently waited. The slogans had changed: *German Unity First European Unity Second: This is a Proud Nation Too: Give us Back our Country First!* The police faced them in line abreast, controlling them as they controlled the children.

'I'll park down by the river,' Bradfield said. 'God knows what it will be like by the time we come out.'

'What's going on?'

'A debate. Amendments to the Emergency Legislation.'

'I thought they'd finished with that long ago.'

'In this place, nothing is resolved.'

Along the embankment as far as they could see on either side, grey detachments waited passively like unarmed soldiers. Makeshift banners declared their provenance: Kaiserslautern, Hanover, Dortmund, Kassel. They stood in perfect silence, waiting for the order to protest. Someone had brought a transistor radio and it blared very loud. They craned their necks for a sight of the white Jaguar.

Side by side they walked slowly back, up the hill, away from the river. They passed a kiosk; it seemed to contain nothing but coloured photographs of Queen Soraya. Two columns of students made an avenue to the main entrance. Bradfield walked ahead, stiff backed. At the door the guard objected to Turner and Bradfield argued with him shortly. The lobby was dreadfully warm and smelt of cigar; it was filled with the ringside murmur of dispute. Journalists, some with cameras, looked at Bradfield curiously and he shook his head and looked away. In small groups, deputies talked quietly, vainly glancing all the time over one another's shoulders in search of someone more interesting. A familiar figure rose at them.

'The best piece! My very words. Bradfield you are the best piece! You have come to see the end of democracy? You have come for the debate? My God you are so damn *efficient* over there! And the Secret Service is still with you? Mr Turner, you are loyal, I hope? My God, what the devil's happened to your face?' Receiving no answer he continued in a lower voice, furtively. 'Bradfield, I must speak to you. Something damned urgent, look here. I tried to get you at the Embassy but for Saab you are always out.'

'We have an appointment.'

'How long? Tell me how long. Sam Allerton wishes also; we wish together to have a discussion.'

He had bent his black head to Bradfield's ear. His neck was still grimy; he had not shaved.

'It's impossible to say.'

'Listen, I will wait for you. A most *important matter*. I will tell Allerton: we will wait for Bradfield. Deadlines, our newspapers: small fish. We must talk with Bradfield.'

'There's no comment, you know that. We issued our statement last night. I thought you had a copy. We accept the Chancellor's explanation. We look forward to seeing the German team back in Brussels within a few days.'

They descended the steps to the restaurant.

'Here he is. I'll do the talking. You're to leave him entirely to me.'

'I'll try.'

'You'll do better than that. You'll keep your mouth shut. He's a very slippery customer.'

Before anything else, Turner saw the cigar. It was very small and lay in the corner of his mouth like a black thermometer; and he knew it was also Dutch, and that Leo had been providing them for nothing.

He looked as if he had been editing a newspaper half the night. He appeared from the door leading to the shopping arcade, and he walked with his hands in his pockets and his jacket pulled away from his shirt, bumping into the tables and apologizing to no one. He was a big dirty man with grizzly hair cut short and a wide chest that spread to a wider stomach. His spectacles were tipped back over his brow like goggles. A girl followed him, carrying a briefcase. She was an expressionless, listless girl, either very bored or very chaste; her hair was black and abundant.

'Soup,' he shouted across the room, as he shook their hands. 'Bring some soup. And something for her.' The waiter was listening to the news on the wireless, but when he saw Praschko he switched it low and sauntered over, prepared to oblige. Praschko's braces had brass teeth which held doggedly to the grimy waistband of his trousers.

'You been working too? She doesn't understand anything,' he explained to them. 'Not in any damn language. *Nicht wahr, Schatz?* You are as stupid as a sheep. What's the problem?' His English was fluent, and whatever accent he possessed was heavily camouflaged by the American intonation. 'You Ambassador these days?'

'I'm afraid not.'

'Who's this guy?'

'Visiting.'

Praschko looked at Turner very carefully and then at Bradfield, then at Turner again.

'Some girl get angry with you?'

Only his eyes moved. His shoulders had risen a little into his neck, and there was a tautening, an instinctive alertness in his manner. His left hand settled on Bradfield's forearm.

'That's *nice*,' he said. 'That's fine. I like a change. I like new people.' His voice was on a single plane; heavy but short; a conspirator's voice, held down by the experience of saying things which should not be overheard.

'What you guys come for? Praschko's personal opinion? The voice of the opposition?' He explained to Turner: 'When you got a coalition, the opposition's a damned exclusive club.' He laughed very loud, sharing the joke with Bradfield.

The waiter brought a goulash soup. Cautiously, with small, nervous movements of his butcher's hand, he began feeling for the meat.

'What you come for? Hey, maybe you want to send a telegram to the Queen?' He grinned. 'A message from her old subject? OK. So send her a telegram. What the hell does she care what Praschko says? What does anyone care? I'm an old whore'–this too for Turner–'They tell you that? I been English, I been German, I been damn nearly American. I been in this bordello longer than all the other whores. That's why no one wants me any more. I been had all ways. Did they tell you that? Left, Right and Centre.'

'Which way have they got you now?' Turner asked.

His eyes still upon Turner's battered face, Praschko lifted his hand and rubbed the tip of his finger against his thumb. 'Know what counts in politics? Cash. Selling. Everything else is a load of crap. Treaties, policies, alliances: crap. . . . Maybe I should have stayed a Marxist. So now they've walked out of Brussels. That's sad. Sure, that's very sad. You haven't got anyone to talk to any more.'

He broke a roll in two and dipped one half into the soup.

'You tell the Queen that Praschko says the English are lousy, lying hypocrites. Your wife okay?'

'Well, thank you.'

'It's a long time since I got to dinner up there. Still live in that ghetto, do you? Nice place. Never mind. Nobody likes me for too long. That's why I change parties,' he explained to Turner. 'I used to think I was a Romantic, always looking for the blue flower. Now I think I just get bored. Same with friends, same with women, same with God. They're all true. They all cheat you. They're all bastards. Jesus. Know another thing: I like new friends better than old ones. Hey, I got a new wife: what do you think of her?' He held up the girl's chin and adjusted her face a little to show her to the best advantage and the girl smiled and patted his hand. 'I'm amazing. There was a time,' he continued before either of them could make an appropriate comment, 'There was a time when I would have laid down on my fat belly to get the lousy English into Europe. Now you're crying on the doorstep and I don't care.' He shook his head. 'I'm truly amazing. Still, that's history I guess. Or maybe that's just me. Maybe I'm only interested in power: maybe I loved you because you were strong and now I hate you because you're nothing. They killed a boy last night, you hear? In Hagen. It's on the radio.'

He drank a Steinhäger from the tray. The mat stuck to the stem of the glass. He tore it off. 'One boy. One old man. One crazy woman librarian. Okay, so it's a football team: but it isn't Armageddon.'

Through the window, the long grey columns waited on the esplanade. Praschko waved a hand round the room. 'Look at this crap. Paper. Paper democracy, paper politicians, paper eagles, paper soldiers, paper deputies. Doll's house democracy; every time Karfeld sneezes, we wet our pants. Know why? Because he comes so damn near the truth.'

'Are you in favour of him then? Is that it?' Turner asked, ignoring Bradfield's angry glance.

Praschko finished his soup, his eyes on Turner all the time. 'The world gets younger every day,' he said. 'Okay, so Karfeld's a load of crap. Okay. We've got rich, see, boy? We've eaten and drunk, built houses, bought cars, paid taxes, gone to Church, made babies. Now we want something *real*. Know what that is, boy?'

His eyes had not left Turner's damaged face.

'Illusions. Kings and Queens. The Kennedys, de Gaulle, Napoleon. The Wittelsbachs, Potsdam. Not just a damn village anymore. Hey, so what's this about the students rioting in England? What does the Queen think about that? Don't you give them enough cash? Youth. Want to know something about youth? I'll tell you.' Turner was his only audience now. "German youth is blaming its parents for starting the war." That's what you hear. Every day some crazy clever guy writes it in another newspaper. Want to hear the true story? They're blaming their parents for *losing* the damn war, not for starting it! "Hey! Where the hell's our Empire?" Same as the English I guess. It's the same horseshit. The same kids. They want God back.' He leaned across the table until his face was quite close to Turner's. 'Here. Maybe we could do a deal: we give you cash, you give us illusions. Trouble is, we tried that. We done that deal and you gave us a load of shit. You didn't deliver the illusions. That's what we don't like about the English any more. They don't know how to do a deal. The Fatherland wanted to marry the Motherland but you never showed up for the wedding.' He broke out in another peal of false laughter.'

'Perhaps the time has now come to *make* the union,' Bradfield suggested, smiling like a tired statesman.

Out of the corner of his eye, Turner saw two men, blond faced, in dark suits and suède shoes, quietly take their places at an adjoining table. The waiter went to them quickly, sensing their profession. At the same moment a bevy of young journalists came in from the lobby. Some carried the day's newspapers; the headlines spoke of Brussels or Hagen. At their head Karl-Heinz Saab, father of them all, stared across at Bradfield in flatulent anxiety. Beyond the window, in a loveless patio, rows of empty plastic chairs were planted like artificial flowers into the breaking concrete.

'Those are the real Nazis, that scum.' His voice pitched high enough for anyone to hear, Praschko indicated the journalists with a contemptuous wave of his fat hand. 'They put out their tongues and fart and think they've invented democracy. Where's the damn waiter: dead?'

'We're looking for Harting,' Bradfield said.

'Sure!' Praschko was used to crisis. His hand, drawing the napkin across his cracked lips, moved at the same steady pace. The eyes, yellow in their parched sockets, barely flickered as he continued to survey the two men.

'I haven't seen him around,' he continued, carelessly. 'Maybe he's in the gallery. You guys have a special box up there.' He put down the napkin. 'Maybe you ought to go look.'

'He's been missing since last Friday morning. He's been missing for a week.'

'Listen: Leo? That guy will always come back.' The waiter appeared. 'He's indestructible.'

'You're his friend,' Bradfield continued. 'Perhaps his only friend. We thought he might have consulted you.'

'What about?'

'Ah, that's the problem,' Bradfield said with a little smile. 'We thought he might have told *you* that.'

'He never found an English friend?' Praschko was looking from one to the other. 'Poor Leo.' There was an edge to his voice now.

'You occupied a special position in his life. After all, you did a great many things together. You shared a number of experiences. We felt that if he had needed advice, or money, or whatever else one needs at certain crises in one's life, he would instinctively seek you out. We thought he might even have come to you for protection.'

Praschko looked again at the cuts on Turner's face.

'Protection?' His lips barely parted as he spoke; it was as if he would prefer not to have known that he had spoken at all. 'You might as well protect a—' The moisture had risen suddenly on his brow. It seemed to come from outside, and to settle on him like steam. 'Go away,' he said to the girl. Without a word she stood up, smiled distractedly at them all and sauntered out of the restaurant, while Turner, for a moment of irrelevant, light-headed joy, followed the provocative rotation of her departing hips; but Bradfield was already talking again.

'We haven't much time.' He was leaning forward and speaking very quickly. 'You were with him in Hamburg and Berlin. There are certain matters known perhaps only to the two of you. Do you follow me?'

Praschko waited.

'If you can help us to find him without fuss; if you know where he is and can reason with him; if there's anything you can do for the sake of an old friendship, I will undertake to be very gentle with him, and very discreet. I will keep your name out of it, and anyone else's as well.'

It was Turner's turn to wait now, as he stared from one to the other. Only the sweat betrayed Praschko; only the fountain pen betrayed Bradfield. He clenched it in his closed fist as he leaned across the table. Outside the window, Turner saw the grey columns waiting; in the corner, the moon men watched dully, eating rolls and butter.

'I'll send him to England; I'll get him out of Germany altogether if necessary. He has put himself in the wrong already; there is no question of re-employing him. He has done things—he has behaved in a way which puts him beyond our consideration; do you understand what I mean? Whatever knowledge he may have is the property of the Crown. . . .' He sat back. 'We must find him before they do,' he said, and still Praschko watched him with his small hard eyes, saying nothing.

'I also appreciate,' Bradfield continued, 'that you have special interests which must be served.'

Praschko stirred a little. 'Go careful,' he said.

'Nothing is further from my mind than to interfere in the internal affairs of the Federal Republic. Your political ambitions, the future of your own party in relation to the Movement, these are matters far outside our sphere of interest. I am here to protect the alliance, not to sit in judgment over an ally.'

Quite suddenly, Praschko smiled.

'That's fine,' he said.

'Your own involvement with Harting twenty years ago, your association with certain British Government agencies—'

'Nobody knows about that,' Praschko said quickly. 'You go damn carefully about that.'

'I was going to make the very same point,' said Bradfield with a reciprocal smile of relief. 'I would not for a moment wish to have it said of the Embassy that we harbour resentments, persecute prominent German politicians, rake up old matters long dead; that we side with countries unsympathetic to the German cause in order to smear the Federal Republic. I am quite certain that in your own sphere, you would not like to have the same things said about yourself. I am pointing to an identity of interest.'

'Sure,' said Praschko. 'Sure.' His harrowed face remained inscrutable.

'We all have our villains. We must not let them come between us.'

'Jesus,' said Praschko with a sideways glance at the marks on Turner's face. 'We got some damn funny friends as well. Did Leo do that to you?'

'They're sitting in the corner,' Turner said. 'They did it. They're waiting to do it to him if they get a chance.'

'Okay,' said Praschko at last. 'I'll go along with you. We had lunch together. I haven't seen him since. What does that ape want?'

'Bradfield,' Saab called across the room. 'How soon?'

'I told you, Karl-Heinz. We have no statement to make.'

'We just talked, that's all. I don't see him so often. He called me up: how about lunch some time? I said make it tomorrow.' He opened his palms to show there was nothing up his sleeve.

'What did you talk about?' Turner asked.

He shrugged to both of them. 'You know how it is with old friends. Leo's a nice guy, but–well, people change. Or maybe we don't like to be reminded that they don't change. We talked about old times. Had a drink. You know the kind of thing.'

'Which old times?' Turner persisted, and Praschko flared at him, very angry.

'Sure: England times. Shit times. You know why we went to England, me and Leo? We were kids. Know how we got there? His name began with an H, my name began with P. So I changed it to a B. Harting Leo, Braschko Harry. Those times. Lucky we weren't Weiss or Zachary, see: they were too low down. The English didn't like the second half of the alphabet. That's what we talked about: sent to Dover, free on board. Those damn times. The damn Farm School in Shepton Mallet, you know that shit place? Maybe they painted it by now. Maybe that old guy's dead who knocked the hell out of us for being German and said we got to thank the English we're alive. You know what we learnt in Shepton Mallet? Italian. From the prisoners of war. They were the only bastards we ever got to talk to!' He turned to Bradfield. 'Who is this Nazi anyway?' he demanded, and burst out laughing. 'Hey, am I crazy or something? I was having lunch with Leo.'

'And he talked about his difficulties, whatever they may be?' Bradfield asked.

'He wanted to know about the Statute,' Praschko replied, still smiling.

'The Statute of Limitations?'

'Sure. He wanted to know the law.'

'Applied to a particular case?'

'Should it have been?'

'I was asking you.'

'I thought maybe you had a particular case in mind.'

'As a general matter of legal principle?'

'Sure.'

'What policy would be served by *that*, I wonder? It is not in the interests of any of us that the past be resurrected.'

'That's true, huh?'

'It's common sense,' Bradfield said shortly, 'Which I imagine carries more weight with you than any assurances I could give. What did he want to know?'

Praschko went very slowly now: 'He wanted to know the *reason*. He wanted to know the philosophy. So I told him: "It's not a new law, it's an old one. It's to make an end of things. Every country has a final court, a point you can't go beyond, okay? In Germany there has to be a final day as well." I spoke to him like he was a child–he's so damned innocent, do you know that? A monk. I said, "Look, you ride a bicycle without lights, okay? If nobody's found out after four months, you're in the clear. If it's manslaughter, then it's not four months but fifteen years; if it's murder, twenty years. If it's Nazi murder, longer still, because they gave it extra time. They waited a few years before they began to count to twenty. If they don't open a case, the offence lapses." I said to him: "Listen, they've fooled around with this thing till it damn near died. They amended it to please the Queen and they amended it to please themselves; first they dated it from forty-five then from forty-nine and now already they've changed it again."' Praschko opened his hands–'So then he shouts at me, "What's so damn holy about twenty years?" "There's nothing holy about twenty years; there's nothing holy about any number of damn years. We grow old. We grow tired. We die." I told him that. I said to him: "I don't know what you've got in your fool head, but it's all crap. Everything's got to have an end. The moralists say it's a moral law, the apologists say it's expedient. Listen, I'm your friend and I'm telling you; Praschko says: it's a fact of life, so don't fool about with it." Then he got angry. You ever seen him angry?'

'No.'

'After lunch I brought him back here. We were still arguing, see.

All the way in the car. Then we sat at this table. Right here where we are now. "Maybe I'll find new information," he said. I told him: "If you find new information, forget it, because there won't be a darn thing you can do: don't waste your time. You're too late. That's the law."'

'He didn't suggest by any chance that he already *had* that information?'

'Has he?' Praschko asked, very quickly indeed.

'I cannot imagine it exists.'

Praschko nodded slowly, his eyes on Bradfield all the time.

'So then what happened?' said Turner.

'That's all. I said to him: "OK, so you prove manslaughter: you're too late by years already. So you prove murder: you're too late since last December. So get screwed." That's what I told him. So then he gets hold of my arm and he whispers to me, like a crazy priest: "No law will ever take account of what they did. You and I know that. They teach it in the Churches: Christ was born of a virgin and went to Heaven in a cloud of light. Millions believe it. Listen, I play the music every Sunday, I hear them." Is that true?'

'He played the organ in Chapel,' said Bradfield.

'Jesus,' said Praschko, lost in wonder. 'Leo did that?'

'He's done it for years.'

'So then he goes on: "But you and I, Praschko, in our own lifetimes, we have seen the living witness of evil." That's what he says. "Not on a mountain top, not at night, but there, in the field where we all stood. We're privileged people. *And now it's all happening again.*"'

Turner wanted to interrupt, but Bradfield restrained him.

'So then I got damned angry. I said to him, see: "Don't come playing God to me. Don't come screaming to me about the thousand year justice of Nuremberg that lasted four years. At least the Statute gave us twenty. And who imposed the Statute anyway? You British could have made us change it. When you handed over, you could have said to us: here, you bloody Germans, take over these cases, hear them in your own Courts, pass sentence according to your penal code but first abolish the Statute. You were party to it then; be party to it now. It's finished. It's damn well, damn well finished." That's what I said to him. And he just went on looking at me, saying my name. "Praschko, Praschko."'

Taking a handkerchief from his pocket, he dabbed his brow and wiped his mouth.

'Don't pay any attention to me,' he said. 'I get excited. You know what politicians are. I said to him, while he stared at me, I said, "This is my home: look. If I've got a heart left, it's here, in this bordello. I used to wonder why. Why not Buckingham Palace? Why not the Coca-Cola Culture? But this is my country. And that's what you should have found: a country. Not just a bloody Embassy." He went on looking at me; I tell you I was going crazy myself. I said to him: "So suppose you do find that proof, tell me what it's all about: to commit a crime at thirty, to be punished at sixty? What does that mean? We're old men," I said to him, "you and I. You know what Goethe told us: no man can watch a sunset for more than quarter of an hour." He said to me: "It's happening again. Look at the faces, Praschko, listen to the speeches. Somebody had to stop that bastard or you and me will be wearing the labels again."'

Bradfield spoke first. 'If he *had* found the proof, which we know he has not, what would he have done? If instead of still searching for it, he had already found it, what then?'

'Oh Jesus; I tell you: he'd have gone crazy.'

'Who's Aickman?' Turner said, ending the long silence.

'What's that, boy?'

'Aickman. Who is she? Miss Aickman, Miss Etling and Miss Brandt. . . . He was engaged to her once.'

'She was just a woman he had in Berlin. Or was it Hamburg? Both maybe. Jesus I forget everything. Thank God, eh?'

'What became of her?'

'I never heard,' Praschko said. His little eyes were roughly hacked in the old bark.

From their corner still, the clean faces watched without expression; four pale hands lay on the table like weapons put to rest. The loudspeaker was calling Praschko: the *Fraktion* was waiting for him to appear.

'You betrayed him,' Turner said. 'You put Siebkron on to him. You sold him down the river. He told you the lot and you warned Siebkron because you're climbing on the bandwagon too.'

'Be quiet,' said Bradfield. 'Be quiet.'

'You rotten bastard,' Turner hissed. 'You'll kill him. He told you he'd found the proof; he told you what it was and he asked you to help him, and you put Siebkron on to him for his trouble. You were his friend and you did that.'

'He's crazy,' Praschko whispered. 'Don't you realize he's crazy? You didn't see him back in those days. You never saw him back with Karfeld in the cellar. You think those boys worked you over? Karfeld couldn't even *speak*: "Talk! Talk!"' Praschko's eyes were screwed up very tight. 'After we saw those bodies in the field. . . . They were tied together. They'd been tied together before they were gassed. He went crazy. I said to him: "Listen it's not your *fault*. It's not your *fault* you survived!" Did he show you the buttons, maybe? The money from the camp? You never saw that either, did you? You never went out with him and a couple of girls to have a drink? You never saw him play with the wooden buttons to start a fight? He's crazy I tell you.' The recollection moved him to despair. 'I said to him, sitting here: "Come on, let's go. Who the hell ever built Jerusalem in Germany? Don't eat your heart out, come and screw some girls!" I said, "Listen! We got to get hold of our minds and press them in or we *all* go crazy." He's a monk. A crazy monk that won't forget. What do you think the world is? A damn playground for a lot of crazy moralists? Sure I told Siebkron. You're a clever boy. But you got to learn to forget as well. Christ if the British can't who can?'

There was shouting as they entered the lobby. Two students in leather coats had broken the cordon at the door and were standing on the stairs, fighting with the janitors. An elderly deputy was holding a handkerchief to his mouth and the blood was running over his wrist. 'Nazis!' someone was shouting, 'Nazis!' but he was pointing to a student on the balcony and the student was waving a red flag.

'Back to the restaurant,' Bradfield said. 'We can get out the other side.'

The restaurant was suddenly empty. Drawn or repelled by the fuss in the lobby, deputies and visitors had vanished in their chosen directions. Bradfield was not running, but striding at a long military pace. They were in the arcade. A leather shop offered black attaché cases in fine box calf. In the next window a barber was working up a lather on the face of an invisible customer.

'Bradfield, you must hear me: my God, can't I even warn you what they are saying?'

Saab was dreadfully out of breath. His portly body was heaving under his greasy jacket; tears of sweat lay in the pouches under his yellow eyes. Allerton, his face crimson under his black mane, peered over his shoulder. They drew back into a doorway. At the end of the corridor, calm had descended on the lobby.

'What who is saying?'

Allerton answered for him: 'All Bonn old boy. The whole bloody paper mill.'

'Listen. There are whispers. Listen. Fantastic what they are saying. You know what happened at Hanover? You know why they rioted? They are whispering it in all the cafés: the delegates; Karfeld's men are telling it. Already the rumours are all over Bonn. They have been instructed to say nothing; it is all a fantastic secret.'

He glanced quickly up and down the arcade.

'It's the best for years,' said Allerton. 'Even for this doorp.'

'Why they broke the line at the front and ran like mad dogs for the Library? Those boys who came in the grey buses? Somebody shot at Karfeld. In the middle of the music: shot at him from the window of the Library. Some friend of the woman, the librarian: Eich. She worked for the British in Berlin. She was an *émigrée*, she changed her name to Eich. She let him in to shoot from the window. Afterwards she told it all to Siebkron before she died. Eich. The bodyguard saw him fire, Karfeld's bodyguard. In the middle of the music! They saw the fellow shooting from the window and ran to catch him. The bodyguard, Bradfield, that came in the grey buses! Listen, Bradfield! Listen what they say! They found the bullet, a pistol bullet from an English pistol. You see now? The English are assassinating Karfeld: that is the fantastic rumour. You must stop them saying it; talk to Siebkron. Karfeld is terrified; he is a great coward. Listen: that is why he is so careful, that is why he is building everywhere such a damn *Schaffott*. How do I say *Schaffott*, for God's sake?'

'Scaffold,' said Turner.

The crowd from the lobby swept them outwards into the fresh air.

'Scaffold! An absolute secret, Bradfield! For your own information!' They heard him cry, 'You must not quote me, for God's sake. Siebkron would be fantastically angry!'

'Rest assured, Karl-Heinz,' the even voice replied, absurdly formal in the turmoil, 'your confidence will be respected.'

'Old boy,' Allerton put his head close to Turner's ear. He had not shaved, the black locks were tipped with sweat. 'What's happened to Leo these days? Seems to have faded all away. They say old Eich was quite a swinger in her day . . . used to work with the scalphunters up in Hamburg. What have they done to your face, old boy? Close her legs too soon did she?'

'There's no story,' Bradfield said.

'Not yet there isn't,' said Allerton, 'old boy.'

'There never will be.'

'They say he bloody nearly got him in Bonn the night before the Hanover rally. Just wasn't quite sure enough of his man. Karfeld was walking away from a secret conference; walking to the pick-up point and Leo damn nearly got him then. Siebkron's chicks turned up just in time.'

Along the embankment the motionless columns waited in patient echelons. Their black flags barely lifted in the poor breeze. Across the river, behind a line of blue trees, distant factory chimneys puffed their smoke lazily into the drab morning light. Small boats, dabs of brilliance, lay marooned on the grey grass bank. To Turner's left stood an old boathouse which no one had yet pulled down. A notice on it proclaimed it the property of the Institute of Physical Exercise of the University of Bonn.

They stood on the bank, side by side. The palest mist, like breath upon a glass, drew in the brown horizons and filled the near bridge. There were no sounds but the echoes of absent things, the cry of lost gulls and the moan of the lost barges, the inevitable whine of unseen drills. There were no people but the grey shadows along the waterfront and the unrelated tread of feet; it was not raining, but sometimes they felt the moisture in the mist, like the prickling of blood upon a heated skin. There were no ships, but funeral hulks drifting towards the Gods of the North; and there was no smell but the inland smell of coal and industries which were not present.

'Karfeld is hidden until tonight,' Bradfield said. 'Siebkron has seen to that. They'll expect him to try again this evening. And he will.' He went over it again, rehearsing it as if it were a formula.

'Until the demonstration, Karfeld is hidden. After the demonstration, Karfeld will again be hidden. Harting's own resources are severely limited; he cannot reckon to be at large much longer. He will try tonight.'

'Aickman's dead,' said Turner. 'They killed her.'

'Yes. He will want to try tonight.'

'Make Siebkron cancel the rally.'

'If it were in my power I would. If it were in Siebkron's power, he would.' He indicated the columns. 'It's too late.'

Turner stared at him.

'No, I cannot see Karfeld cancelling the rally, however frightened he is,' Bradfield continued, as if a moment's doubt had crossed his mind. 'The rally is the culmination of his campaign in the provinces. He has organized it to coincide with the most critical moment in Brussels. He is already half-way to success.'

He turned and walked slowly along the footpath towards the car park. The grey columns watched him silently.

'Go back to the Embassy. Take a taxi. From now on there's to be a total ban on movement. No one is to leave the Embassy perimeter on pain of dismissal. Tell de Lisle. And tell him what has happened and put aside the Karfeld papers for my return. Anything that incriminates him: the investigation report, the thesis . . . anything from the Glory Hole that tells the tale. I shall be back by early afternoon.'

He opened the car door.

'What's the bargain with Siebkron?' Turner said. 'What's the small print?'

'There is no bargain. Either they destroy Harting, or he will destroy Karfeld. In either case I have to disown him. That is the only thing that matters. Is there something you would prefer me to do? Do you see a way out? I shall inform Siebkron that order must be restored. I shall give him my oath that we had no part in Harting's work, and no knowledge of it. Can you suggest an alternative solution? I would be grateful.'

He started the engine. The grey columns stirred with interest, pleased by the white Jaguar.

'Bradfield!'

'Well.'

'I beg you. Five minutes. I've got a card to play as well. Something we've never mentioned. Bradfield!'

Without a word, Bradfield opened the door and got out.

'You say we have no part in it. We have. He's our product, you know that, we made him what he was, crushed him between all those worlds . . . we ground him down into himself, made him see things no one should ever see, hear things that . . . we sent him on that private journey . . . you don't know what it's like down there. I do! Bradfield, listen! We *owe* him. He knew that.'

'All of us are owed. Very few of us are paid.'

'You *want* to destroy him! You *want* to make him nothing! You *want* to disown him because he was her lover! Because—'

'My God,' Bradfield said softly, 'if that were the task I had set myself I would have to kill more than the thirty-two. Is that all you wanted to tell me?'

'Wait! Brussels . . . the Market . . . all this. Next week it's gold, the week after it's the Warsaw Pact. We'd join the bloody Salvation Army if it pleased the Americans. What does it matter about the names? . . . You see it clearer than any of us: the drift. Why do you go on with it like this? Why don't you say stop?'

'What am I to do about Harting? Tell me what else I can do but disown him? You know us here now. Crises are academic. Scandals are not. Haven't you realized that only appearances matter?'

Turner searched frantically about him. 'It's not true! You *can't* be so tied to the surface of things.'

'What else is there when the underneath is rotten? Break the surface and we sink. That's what Harting has done. I am a hypocrite,' he continued simply. 'I'm a great believer in hypocrisy. It's the nearest we ever get to virtue. It's a statement of what we ought to be. Like religion, like art, like the law, like marriage. I serve the appearance of things. It is the worst of systems; it is better than the others. That is my profession and that is my philosophy. And unlike yourself,' he added, 'I did not contract to serve a powerful nation, least of all a virtuous one. All power corrupts. The loss of power corrupts even more. We thank an American for that advice. It's quite true. We are a corrupt nation, and we need all the help we can get. That is lamentable and, I confess, occasionally humiliating. However, I would rather fail as a power than survive by impotence. I would rather be vanquished than neutral. I would rather be English than Swiss. And unlike you, I expect nothing. I expect no more from institutions than I expect from people. You have no suggestion then? I am disappointed.'

'Bradfield, I *know* her. I know you, and I know what you feel! You hate him! You hate him more than you dare admit. You hate him for *feeling*: for loving, even for hating. You hate him for deceiving and for being honest. For waking her. For putting you to shame. You hate him for the time she spent on him . . . for the thought, the dream she had of him!'

'But you have no suggestion. I imagine your five minutes are over. He *has* offended,' he added casually, as if passing the topic once more in review. 'Yes. He has. Not as much against myself as you might suppose. But against the order that results from chaos; against the built-in moderation of an aimless society. He had no business to hate Karfeld and none to . . . He had no business to remember. If you and I have a purpose at all any more, it is to save the world from such presumptions.'

'Of all of you—Listen!—Of all of you he's the only one who's real, the only one who believed, and acted! For you, it's a sterile, rotten game, a family word game, that's all; just play. But Leo's *involved*! He knows what he wants and he's gone to get it!'

'Yes. That alone should be enough to condemn him.' He had forgotten Turner now. 'There's no room for his kind any more. That's the one thing we *have* learnt, thank God.' He stared at the river. 'We've learnt that even *nothing* is a pretty tender flower. You speak as if there were those who contribute and those who do not. As if we were all working for the day when we are no longer needed; when the world could pack up and cultivate its allotment. There *is* no product. There *is* no final day. This *is* the life we work for. Now. At this moment. Every night, as I go to sleep, I say to myself: another day achieved. Another day added to the unnatural life of a world on its deathbed. And if I never relax; if I never lift my eye, we may run on for another hundred years. Yes.' He was talking to the river. 'Our policy is that tide, taken at its three-inch flood. Three inches of freedom up and down the bank. That's the limit of our action. Beyond it is anarchy, and all the romantic clap-trap of protest and conscience. We are all looking for the wider freedom, every one of us. It doesn't exist. As long as we accept that, we can dream at will. Harting should never have gone down there in the first place. And you should have returned to London when I told you. The Statute has made a law of forgetting. He broke it. Praschko is quite right: Harting has broken the law of moderation.'

'We're *not* automatons! We're born free, I believe that! We can't control the processes of our own minds!'

'Good Lord, whoever told you that?' He faced Turner now and the small tears showed. 'I have controlled the processes of my own mind for eighteen years of marriage and twenty years of diplomacy. I have spent half of my life learning not to look, and the other half learning not to feel. Do you think I cannot also learn to forget? God, sometimes I am bowed down by the things I do not know! So why the devil couldn't he forget as well? Do you think I take pleasure in what I have to do? Do you think he does not challenge me to do it? *He* set all this in motion, not I! His *damned* immodesty—'

'Bradfield! What about Karfeld? Hasn't Karfeld stepped over the line as well?'

'There are quite different ways of dealing with his case.' The shell had closed again around his voice.

'Leo found one.'

'The wrong one as it happens.'

'Why?'

'Never mind why.'

He began walking slowly back to the car, but Turner was calling to him.

'What made Leo run? Something he read. Something he stole. What *was* in that Green File? What were those Formal and Informal Conversations with German Politicians. Bradfield! Who was talking to who?'

'Lower your voice, they'll overhear.'

'Tell me! Have you been having conversations with Karfeld? Is that what sent Leo on his night walk? Is that what it was all about?'

Bradfield did not reply.

'Holy God,' Turner whispered. 'We're like the rest of them, after all. Like Siebkron and Praschko; we're trying to make our number with tomorrow's lucky winner!'

'Take care!' Bradfield warned.

'Allerton . . . what Allerton said—'

'Allerton? He knows nothing.'

'Karfeld came in from Hanover that Friday night. Secretly to Bonn. For a conference. He even arrived and left on foot, it was so secret. You didn't go to Hanover after all, did you, that Friday night? You changed your plans, cancelled your ticket. Leo found that out from the Travel Clerks—'

'You're talking utter nonsense.'

'You met Karfeld in Bonn. Siebkron laid it on, and Leo followed you because he knew what you were up to!'

'You're out of your mind.'

'No, I'm not. But Leo is, isn't he? Because Leo suspected. All the time, in the back of his mind, he knew that you were secretly reinsuring against the Brussels failure. Until he saw that file, until he actually saw and knew, he thought he might still act within the law. But when he saw the Green File he *knew*: it really *was* happening again. He knew. That's why he was in a hurry. He had to stop you, he had to stop Karfeld before it was too late!'

Bradfield said nothing.

'What was in the Green File, Bradfield? What's he taken with him as a keepsake? Why was *that* the only file he stole? Because it contained the minutes of *those* meetings, was it? And that's what's drawn your fire! You've got to get the Green File back! Did you sign them Bradfield? With that willing pen of yours?' His pale eyes were alight with anger. 'When did he steal the despatch box, let's just think: Friday . . . Friday morning he had his verification, didn't he? He saw it in black and white: *that* was the other proof he was looking for. He took it to Aickman. . . . "They're up to their old tricks, we've got to stop it before it's too late . . . we're the chosen ones." That's why he took the Green File! To show them! *Children look*, he wants to say, *history really is repeating itself, and it isn't comedy at all!*'

'It was a document of the highest secrecy. He could go to prison for years for that alone.'

'But he never will, because you want the file and not the man. That's another part of the three-inch freedom, is it?'

'Would you prefer me to be a fanatic?'

'What he'd suspected for months, picked up in the wind of Bonn gossip and the scraps he got from *her*; now he had the proof: that the British were hedging their bets. Taking out a with-profits policy on the Bonn-Moscow axis. What's the deal, Bradfield? What's the small print *now*? Christ, no wonder Siebkron thought you were playing a treble game! First you put all your chips on Brussels and very wise too. "Let nothing disturb the enterprise." Then you hedge the bet with Karfeld and you get Siebkron to hold your stake. "Bring me secretly to Karfeld," you say to him. "The British also are interested in a Moscow axis." Very informally interested, mind. Purely explanatory talks and no witnesses, mind. But an eventual trade alignment with the East is not at all out of the question, *Herr Doktor Karfeld*, if you should ever happen to become a credible alternative to a crumbling coalition! As a matter of fact we're quite anti-American ourselves these days, it's in the blood, you know, *Herr Doktor Karfeld . . .*'

'You missed your vocation.'

'And then what happens? No sooner has Siebkron brought Karfeld to your bed than he learns enough to make his blood run cold: the British Embassy is compiling a dossier on Karfeld's unsavoury past! The Embassy already has the records—the *only* records, Bradfield—and now they're sizing up to blackmail him on the side. And that's not all!'

'No.'

'Siebkron and Karfeld have hardly got used to that little shock before you provide a bigger one. One that really rocks them. Not even Albion, they thought, could be that perfidious: the British are actually trying to assassinate Karfeld. It makes no sense of course. Why kill the man you want to blackmail? They must have been puzzled to death. No wonder Siebkron looked so sick on Tuesday night!'

'Now you know it all. You share the secret: keep it.'

'Bradfield!'

'Well?'

'Who do you want to win? This afternoon, out there, who's your money on this time, Bradfield? On Leo; or the cut-price ally?'

Bradfield switched on the engine.

'Cut-price friends! They're the only kind we can afford! They're the only kind we've got the guts to make! We're a proud nation, Bradfield! You can get Karfeld for twenty-five per cent off now, can't you! Never mind if he hates us. He'll come round! People change! And he thinks about us all the time! That's an encouraging start! A little push now and he'll run for ever.'

'Either you're in or you're out. Either you're involved or you're not.' He hesitated. 'Or would you rather be Swiss?'

Without another word or glance, Bradfield drove up the hill, turned right and vanished in the direction of Bonn. Turner waited until he was out of sight before walking back along the river path towards the cab rank. As he went there rose suddenly behind him an unearthly rumble of feet and voices, the saddest, deepest sound he had ever heard in his life. The columns had begun to move; they were shuffling slowly forward, mediocre, ponderous and terrifying, a mindless grey monster that could no longer be held back, while beyond them, almost hidden in the mist stood the wooded outline of Chamberlain's hill.

Epilogue

Bradfield led the way; de Lisle and Turner followed. It was early evening and the streets were empty of traffic. In all Bonn, nothing stirred but the mute, grey-clad strangers who swarmed the alleys and hastened towards the market square. The black bunting, becalmed, drifted in idle swathes over the ebbing tide.

Bonn had never seen such faces. The old and the young, the lost and the found, the fed and the hungry, the clever, the dull, the governed and the ungoverned, all the children of the Republic, it seemed, had risen in a single legion to march upon her little bastions. Some were hillsmen, dark haired, straddle-legged and scrubbed for the outing; some were clerks, Bob Cratchits nipped by the quick air, some were Sunday men, the slow infantry of the German promenade, in grey gabardine and grey Homburg hats. Some carried their flags shamefully, as if they had outgrown them, some as banners borne to the battle, others as ravens strung for market. Birnam Wood had come to Dunsinane.

Bradfield waited for them to catch up.

'Siebkron reserved space for us. We should enter the square higher up. We shall have to force our way to the right.'

Turner nodded, barely hearing. He was looking everywhere, into every face and every window, every shop, corner and alley. Once he seized de Lisle's arm, but whoever it was had gone, lost again in the changing mass.

Not just the square itself: balconies, windows, shops, every foothold and crevice was filled with grey coats and white faces, and the green uniforms of soldiers and police. And still they came, more of them, cramming the mouths of the darkening alleys, craning their necks for a sight of the speaker's stand, searching for a leader, faceless men searching for one face; while Turner peered desperately among them for a face he had never seen. Overhead, in front of the floodlights, loudspeakers hung like warnings from their wires; beyond them, the sky was failing.

He'll never make it, Turner thought dully; he'll never penetrate a crowd like this. But Hazel Bradfield's voice came back to him: *I had a younger brother, he played scrum half, you could hardly tell them apart.* 'To the left,' Bradfield said. 'Make for the hotel.'

'You are English?' A woman's voice enquired, teatime in a friendly house, 'My daughter lives in Yarmouth.' But the tide carried her away. Furled banners barred their path, dropped like lances. The banners formed a ring, and the gypsy students stood inside it, gathered round their own small fire. 'Burn Axel Springer,' one boy shouted, not with much conviction, and another broke a book and threw it on the flames. The book burned badly, choking before it died. I shouldn't have done that to the books, Turner thought; I'll be doing it to people next. A group of girls lounged on mattresses and the fire made poems of their faces.

'If we're separated, meet on the steps of the Stern,' Bradfield ordered. A boy heard him and ran forward, encouraged by the others. Two girls were already shouting in French. 'You are English!' the boy cried, though his face was young and nervous. 'English swine!' Hearing the girls again, he swung his small fist wildly over the lances. Turner hastened forward, but the blow fell on Bradfield's shoulder and he paid it no attention. The crowd gave way, suddenly, its will mysteriously gone, and the Town Hall appeared before them at the far end of the square, and that was the night's first dream. A magic baroque of candy pink and merchant gold. A vision of style and elegance, of silk and filigree and sunlight. A vision of brilliance and Latin glory, Palaces where de Lisle's unplayed minuets pleased the plumper burgher's heart. To its left the scaffold, still in darkness, cut off by the screen of arc-lights trained upon the building, waited like an executioner upon the imperial presence.

'Herr Bradfield?' the pale detective asked. He had not changed his leather coat since that dawn in Königswinter, but there were two teeth missing from his black mouth. The moon faces of his colleagues stirred in recognition of the name.

'I'm Bradfield, yes.'

'We are ordered to free the steps for you.' His English was rehearsed: a small part for a newcomer. The radio in his leather pocket crackled in urgent command. He lifted it to his mouth. The diplomatic gentlemen had arrived, he said, and were safely in position. The gentleman from Research was also present.

Turner looked pointedly at the broken mouth and smiled.

'You sod,' he said with satisfaction. The lip was badly cut as well, though not as badly as Turner's.

'Please?'

'Sod,' Turner explained. 'Sodomite.'

'Shut up,' said Bradfield.

The steps commanded a view of the entire square. Already the afternoon had turned to twilight; the victorious arc-lights divided the numberless heads into white patches which floated like pale discs upon a black sea. Houses, shops, cinemas had fallen away. Only their gables remained, carved in fairytale silhouette against the dark sky, and that was the second dream, *Tales of Hoffman*, the woodcut world of German make-believe to prolong the German childhood. High on a roof a Coca-Cola sign, winking on and off, tinged the surrounding tiles with cosmetic pink; once an errant spotlight ran across the façades, peering with a lover's eye into the empty windows of the stores. On the lower step, the detectives waited, backs towards them, hands in pockets, black against the haze.

'Karfeld will come in from the side,' de Lisle said suddenly. 'The alley to the left.'

Following the direction of de Lisle's outstretched arm, Turner noticed for the first time directly beneath the feet of the scaffold a tiny passageway between the pharmacy and the Town Hall, not more than ten foot wide and made very deep by the high walls of the adjacent buildings.

'We remain here, is that clearly understood? On these steps. Whatever happens. We are here as observers; merely observers, nothing more.' Bradfield's strict features were strengthened by dilemma. 'If they find him they will deliver him to us. That is the understanding. We shall take him at once to the Embassy for safe custody.'

Music, Turner remembered. In Hanover he tried when the music was loudest. The music is supposed to drown the shot. He remembered the hair-dryers too and thought: he's not a man to vary the technique; if it worked before, it will work again, and that's the German in him; like Karfeld and the grey buses.

His thoughts were lost to the murmur of the crowd, the pleasurable growl of expectation which mounted like an angry prayer as the floodlights died. Only the Town Hall remained, a pure and radiant altar, tended by the little group which had appeared upon its balcony. The names rose in countless mouths as all around him, the slow liturgical commentary began:

Tilsit, Tilsit was there, Tilsit the old General, the third from the left, and look, he is wearing his medal, the only one they wanted to deny him, his special medal from the war, he wears it round his neck, Tilsit is a man of courage. Meyer-Lothringen, the economist! Yes, *der Grosse*, the tall one, how elegantly he waves, it is well known that he is of the best family; half a Wittelsbach, they say; blood will tell in the end; and a great academic; he understands everything. And priests! The Bishop! Look, the Bishop himself is blessing us! Count the movements of his holy hand! Now he is looking to his right! He has reached out his arm! And Halbach the young hothead: look, he is wearing a pullover! Fantastic his impertinence: a pullover on such an occasion? In Bonn? *Halbach! Du toller Hund!* But Halbach is from Berlin, and Berliners are famous for their arrogance; one day he will lead us all, so young and yet already so successful.

The murmur rose to a roar, a visceral, hungry, loving roar, deeper than any single throat, more pious than any single soul, more loving than any single heart; and died again, whispering down, as the first quiet chords of music struck. The Town Hall receded and the scaffolding stood before them. A preacher's pulpit, a captain's bridge, a conductor's rostrum? A child's cradle, a plain coffin of boldly simple wood, grandiose yet virtuous, a wooden grail, housing the German truth. Upon it, alone but valiant, the truth's one champion, a plain man known as Karfeld.

'Peter.' Turner gently pointed into the tiny alley. His hand was shaking but his eye was quite steady. A shadow? A guard taking up his post?

'I wouldn't point any more if I was you,' de Lisle whispered. 'They might misunderstand you.'

But in that moment, no one paid them any heed, for Karfeld was all they saw.

'Der Klaus!' the crowd was calling, 'der Klaus is here!' Wave to him, children; der Klaus, the magic man, has walked all the way to Bonn on stilts of German Pine.

'He is very English, der Klaus,' he heard de Lisle murmur, 'Although he hates our guts.'

He was such a little man up there. They said he was tall; and it would have been easy enough, with so much artifice, to raise him a foot or so, but he seemed to wish to be diminished, as if to emphasize that great truths are found in humble mouths; for Karfeld was a humble man, and English in his diffidence.

And Karfeld was a nervous man too, bothered by his spectacles, which he had not had time to clean, apparently, in these busy days, for now he took them off and polished them as if he did not know he was observed: it is the others who make the ceremony, he was telling them, before he had said a word; it is you and I who know why we are here.

Let us pray.

'The lights are too bright for him,' someone said. They should reduce the lights.'

He was one of them, this isolated Doctor; a good deal of brain power no doubt, a good deal above the ears, but still one of them at the end of it, ready to step down at any time from that high place if someone better came along. And not at all a politician. Quite without ambition, in fact, for he had only yesterday promised to stand down in favour of Halbach if that was the people's will. The crowd whispered its concern. Karfeld looks tired, he looks fresh; he looks well; Karfeld looks ill, older, younger, taller, shorter. . . . It is said he is retiring; no, he will give up his factory and work full time on politics. He cannot aford it; he is a millionaire.

Quietly he began speaking.

No one introduced him, he did not say his name. The note of music which announced his coming had no companions, for Klaus Karfeld is alone up there, quite alone, and no music can console him. Karfeld is not a Bonn windbag; he is one of us for all his intellect: Klaus Karfeld, doctor and citizen, a decent man decently concerned about the fate of Germany, is obliged, out of a sense of honour, to address a few friends.

It was so softly, so unobtrusively done, that to Turner it seemed the whole massive gathering actually inclined its ear in order to save Karfeld the pain of raising his voice.

Afterwards, Turner could not say how much he had understood, nor how he had understood so much. He had the impression, at first, that Karfeld's interest was purely historical. The talk was of the origin of war and Turner caught the old catchwords of the old religion, Versailles, chaos, depression and encirclement; the mistakes that had been made by statesmen on both sides, for Germans cannot shirk their own responsibilities. There followed a small tribute to the casualties of unreason: too many people died, Karfeld said, and too few knew the cause. It must never happen again, Karfeld knew: he had brought back more than wounds from Stalingrad: he had brought back memories, indelible memories, of human misery, mutilation and betrayal. . . .

He has indeed, they whispered, the poor Klaus. He has suffered for us all.

There was no rhetoric still. You and I, Karfeld was saying, have learned the lessons of history; you and I can look on these things with detachment: it must never happen again. There were those, it was true, who saw the battles of fourteen and thirty-nine as part of a continuing crusade against the enemies of a German heritage, but Karfeld–he wished it to be known to all his friends–Klaus Karfeld was not, altogether, of this school.

'Alan.' It was de Lisle's voice, steady as a Captain's. Turner followed his gaze.

A flutter, a movement of people, the passing of a message? Something was stirring on the balcony. He saw Tilsit, the General, incline his soldier's head and Halbach the student leader whisper in his ear, saw Meyer-Lothringen leaning forward over the filigree rail, listening to someone below him. A policeman? A plainclothes man? He saw the flint of spectacles and the patient surgeon's face as Siebkron rose and vanished; and all was still again except for Karfeld, academic and man of reason, who was talking about today.

Today, he said, as never before, Germany was the plaything of her allies. They had bought her, now they were selling her. This was a *fact*, Karfeld said, he would not deal in theory. There were too many theories in Bonn already, he explained, and he did not propose to add to the confusion. This was *fact*, and it was necessary, if painful, to debate among good and reasonable friends how Germany's allies had achieved this strange state of affairs. Germany was rich, after all: richer than France, and richer than Italy. Richer than England, he added casually, but we must not be rude to the English for the English won the war after all, and were a people of uncommon gifts. His voice remained wonderfully reasonable as he recited all the English gifts: their mini-skirts, their pop singers, their Rhine Army that sat in London, their Empire that was falling apart, their national deficit . . . without these English gifts, Europe would surely fail. Karfeld had always said so.

Here they laughed; it was a warming, angry laugh, and Karfeld, shocked and perhaps the tiniest fraction disappointed that these beloved sinners, whom God had appointed him in his humility to instruct, should fall to laughing in the temple; Karfeld waited patiently until it died.

How then, if Germany was so rich, if she possessed the largest standing army in Europe, and could dominate the so-called Common Market, how was it possible for her to be sold in public places like a whore?

Leaning back in the pulpit, he removed his spectacles and made a cautious, pacifying gesture of the hand, for there were noises now of protest and indignation, and Karfeld quite clearly did not care for this at all. We must try to resolve this question in a pious, reasonable and wholly *intellectual* manner, he warned, without emotion and without rancour, as befits good friends! It was a plump, round hand and it might have been webbed, for he never separated his fingers, but used the whole fist singly like a club.

In seeking, then, a rational explanation for this curious—and, for Germans at least, highly relevant—historical fact, objectivity was essential. In the first place—the fist shot upward again—we had had twelve years of Nazism and thirty-five years of anti-Nazism. Karfeld did not understand what was so *very* wrong about Nazism that it should be punished eternally with the whole world's hostility. The Nazis had persecuted the Jews: and that was wrong. He wished to go on record as saying it was wrong. Just as he condemned Oliver Cromwell for his treatment of the Irish, the United States for their treatment of the blacks and for their campaigns of genocide against the Red Indians and the yellow peril of South East Asai; just as he condemned the Church for its persecution of heretics, and the British for the bombing of Dresden, so he condemned Hitler for what he had done to the Jews; and for importing that British invention, so successful in the Boer War: the concentration camp.

Directly in front of him Turner saw the young detective's hand softly feel for the partition of his leather coat; he heard again the crackle of the radio. Once more he strained his eyes, scanning the crowd, the balcony, the alleys; once more he searched the doorways and the windows; and there was nothing. Nothing but the sentinels posted along the roof-tops and the militia waiting in their vans; nothing but a countless throng of silent men and women, motionless as God's anointed before the Presence of the Word.

Let us examine, Karfeld suggested–since it will help us to arrive at a logical and objective solution to the many questions which presently assail us–let us examine what happened after the war.

After the war, Karfeld explained, it was only just that the Germans should be treated as criminals; and, because the Germans had practised racism, that their sons and grandsons should be treated as criminals too. But, because the Allies were *kind* people, and *good* people, they would go some way towards rehabilitating the Germans: as a very special treat, they would admit them to Nato.

The Germans were shy at first; they did not *want* to rearm, many people had had enough of war. Karfeld himself belonged to that category: the lessons of Stalingrad were like acid in the young man's memory. But the Allies were determined as well as kind. The Germans should provide the army, and the British and the Americans and the French would command it. . . . And the Dutch. . . . And the Norwegians. . . . And the Portuguese; and any other foreign general who cared to command the vanquished:

'Why: we might even have had African generals commanding the Bundeswehr!'

A few–they belonged to the front, to that protective ring of leather-coated men beneath the scaffold–a few started laughing, but he quelled them at once.

'Listen!' he told them. 'My friends, you must listen! That is what we *deserved*! We lost the war! We persecuted the Jews! We were not *fit* to command! Only to pay!' Their anger gradually subsided. 'That,' he explained, 'is why we pay for the *British* Army as well. And *that* is why they let us into Nato.'

'Alan!'

'I have seen them.'

Two grey buses were parked beside the pharmacy. A floodlight touched their dull coachwork, and was moved away. The windows were quite black, sealed from inside.

And we were grateful, Karfeld continued. Grateful to be admitted to such an exclusive club. Of course we were. The club did not exist; its members did not like us; the fees were very high; and as the

Germans were still children they must not play with weapons which might damage their enemies; but we were grateful all the same, because we were Germans and had lost the war.

Once more the indignant murmur rose, but he scotched it again with a terse movement of his hand. 'We want no emotion here,' he reminded them. 'We are dealing with facts!'

High up, on a tiny ledge, a mother held her baby. 'Look down,' she was whispering. 'You will not see his like again.' In the whole square, nothing moved; the heads were still, staring with cavernous eyes.

To emphasize his great impartiality, Karfeld once more drew back in the pulpit and, taking all his time, tilted his spectacles a little and examined the pages before him. This done, he hesitated, peered doubtfully downwards at the faces nearest him and deliberated, unsure how far he could expect his flock to follow what he was about to say.

What then was the *function* of the Germans in this distinguished club? He would put it this way. He would state the formula first and afterwards he would give one or two simple examples of the method by which it could be applied. The function of the Germans in Nato was briefly this: to be *docile* towards the West and *hostile* towards the East; to recognize that even among the victorious Allies there were *good* victors and *bad* victors. . . .

Again the laughter rose and fell. *Der Klaus*, they whispered, *der Klaus* knows how to make a joke; what a club that Nato is. Nato, the Market, it's all a cheat, it's all the same; they are applying the same principles to the Market which they applied to Nato. Klaus has told us so and that is why the Germans must stay away from Brussels. It is just another trap, it is encirclement all over again. . . .

'That's Lésère,' de Lisle murmured.

A small, greying man who obscurely reminded Turner of a bus conductor had joined them on the steps and was writing contentedly in his notebook.

'The French counsellor. Big chum of Karfeld's.'

About to return his gaze to the scaffold, Turner happened to look into the side street; and thus he saw for the first time the mad, dark, tiny army that waited for the signal.

Directly across the square, assembled in the unlit side street, the silent concourse of men waited. They carried banners that were not quite black in the twilight and there stood before them, Turner was certain there stood before them, the remnants of a military band. The oblique arc-lights glinted on a trumpet, caught the laced panels of the drum. At its head stood a solitary figure; his arm, raised like a conductor's, held them motionless.

Again the radio crackled, but the words were drowned in laughter as Karfeld made another joke; a harsh joke, enough to raise their anger, a reference to the decay of England and the person of the monarch. The tone was new and hard: a light blow on their backs, brisker, a purposeful caress, promising the sting to come, tracing like a whip's end the little vertebrae of their political resentment. So England, with her allies, had re-educated the Germans. And who better qualified? After all, Churchill had let the savages into Berlin; Truman had dropped atom bombs on undefended cities; between them they had made a ruin of Europe: who better qualified, then, to teach the Germans the meaning of civilization?

In the alley, nothing had stirred. The leader's arm was still raised before the little band as he waited for the signal to begin the music.

'It's the Socialists,' de Lisle breathed. 'They're staging a counter-demonstration. Who the devil let them in?'

So the Allies set to work: the Germans must be taught how to behave. It was wrong to kill the Jews, they explained; kill the Communists instead. It was wrong to attack Russia, they explained; but we will protect you if the Russians attack you. It was wrong to fight for your borders, they explained; but we support your claims for the territories of the East.

'We all know that kind of support!' Karfeld held out his hands, palms upwards. 'Here you are my dear, here you are! You can borrow my umbrella as long as you like; until it rains!'

Was it Turner's imagination or did he detect, in this piece of theatre, a hint of that wheedling tone which once in German music-halls traditionally denoted the Jew? They began to laugh, but again he silenced them.

In the alley, the conductor's arm was still raised. Will he never tire, Turner wondered, of that gruesome salute?

'They'll be murdered,' de Lisle insisted. 'The crowd will murder them!'

And so, my friends, this is what happened. Our victors in all their purity, and all their wisdom, taught us the meaning of *democracy*. Hurray for democracy. Democracy is like Christ; there is nothing you cannot do in the name of democracy.

'Praschko,' Turner declared quietly, 'Praschko wrote that for him.'

'He writes a lot of his stuff,' de Lisle said.

'Democracy is shooting Negroes in America and giving them gold beds in Africa! Democracy is to run a colonial empire, to fight in Vietnam and to attack Cuba; democracy is to visit your conscience on the Germans! *Democracy is to know that whatever you do, you will never, never be as bad as the Germans!*'

He had raised his voice to give the sign, the sign the band expected. Once more Turner looked across the crowd into the alley, saw the white hand, white as a napkin, fall lazily in the lamplight, glimpsed the white face of Siebkron himself as he quickly relinquished his

place of command and withdrew into the shadow of the pavement,
saw the first head turn in front of him, then a second, as he himself
heard it also: the distant sound of music, of a percussion band, and
men's voices singing; saw Karfeld peer over the pulpit and call to
someone beneath him; saw him draw back into the furthest recess
while he continued speaking, and heard, as Karfeld assumed his
sudden tone of indignation, heard through all Karfeld's new anger
and his high-pitched exhortation, through all the conjuration, the
abuse and the encouragement, the unmistakable note of fear.

'The Sozis!' the young detective cried, far out across the crowd.
His heels were together and his leather shoulders drawn well back
and he bellowed through cupped hands. 'The Sozis are in the alley!
The Socialists are attacking us!'

'It's a diversion,' Turner said, quite matter of fact. 'Siebkron's
staging a diversion.' *To lure him out*, he thought; *to lure out Leo and
make him chance his hand. And here's the music to drown the shot*, he
added to himself, as the *Marseillaise* began. *It's all set up to make him
have a go.*

No one moved at first. The opening strains were barely audible;
little, irrelevant notes played by a child on a mouth organ. And the
singing which accompanied it was no more than the male chant from
a Yorkshire pub on a Saturday night, remote and unconfident,
proceeding from mouths unused to music; and to begin with the
crowd really ignored it, because of its interest in Karfeld.

But Karfeld had heard the music, and it quickened him remarkably.

'I am an old man!' he shouted. 'Soon I shall be an old man. What
will you say to yourselves, young men, when you wake in the
morning? What will you say when you look at the American whore
that is Bonn? You will say this: how long, young men, can we live
without honour? You will look at your Government and say; you will
look at the Sozis and say: must we follow even a dog because it is in
office?'

He quoted *Lear*, Turner thought absurdly, and the floodlights
were extinguished at one turn, at one black fall of the curtain: deep
darkness filled the square, and with it, the louder singing of the
Marseillaise. He detected the acrid smell of pitch carried on the night
air, as in countless places the sparks flickered and wheeled away; he
heard the whispered call and the whispered answer, he heard the
order passed from mouth to mouth in hasty conspiracy. The singing
and the music rose to a roar, picked up suddenly and quite
deliberately by the loudspeakers: a mad, monstrous, plebeian, un-
subtle roar, amplified and distorted almost beyond recognition,
deafening and maddening.

Yes, Turner repeated to himself with Saxon clarity, *that is what I
would do if I were Siebkron. I would create this diversion, rouse the*

crowd, and make enough noise to provoke him into shooting.

The music boomed still louder. He saw the policeman turn and face him and the young detective hold up a hand in warning. 'Stay here, please, Mister Bradfield! Mister Turner, stay here please!' The crowd was whispering excitedly; all round them they heard the sibilant, greedy hiss.

'Hands out of pockets, please!'

Torches were lit all round them; someone had given the signal. They rose like wild hopes gilding the sullen faces with belief, making mad dreams of their prosaic features, setting into their dull eyes the devotion of apostles. The little band was advancing into the square; it could not have been more than twenty strong, and the army that marched in its wake was ragged and undecided, but now their music was everywhere, a Socialist terror magnified by Siebkron's loudspeakers.

'The Sozis!' the crowd cried again. 'The Sozis are attacking us!'

The pulpit was empty, Karfeld had gone, but the Socialists were still marching for Marx, Jewry and War. 'Strike them, strike our enemies! Strike the Jews! Strike the Reds!' follow the dark, the voices whispered, follow the light, follow the spies and saboteurs; the Sozis are responsible for everything.

Still the music grew louder.

'Now,' de Lisle said evenly. 'They've drawn him.'

A busy, silent group had gathered round the raw, white legs of Karfeld's scaffold; leather coats were stooping, moon faces flitting and conferring.

'The Sozis! Kill the Sozis.' The crowd was in mounting ferment; the scaffold was forgotten. 'Kill them!' Whatever you resent, the voices whispered, kill it here: Jews, Negroes, moles, conspirators, rejectors, wreckers, parents, lovers; they are good, they are bad, foolish or clever.

'Kill the Socialist Jews!' Swimmers leaping, the voices whispered; march! march!

We've got to kill him, Praschko, Alan Turner told himself in his confusion, *or we shall be wearing the labels again. . . .*

'Kill who?' he said to de Lisle. 'What are they doing?'

'Chasing the dream.'

The music had risen to a single note, a raucous, crude, deafening roar, a call to battle and a call to anger, a call to kill ugliness, to destroy the sick and the unwieldy, the maimed, the loathsome and the incompetent. Suddenly by the light of the torches the black flags lifted and trembled like waking moths, the crowd seemed to drift and lean until the edges broke and the torches floated away into the alley, driving the band before them, acclaiming it their hero, smothering it with close kisses, dancing in upon it in playful fury, smashing the windows and the instruments, causing the red banners to flourish and dip like spurts of blood, then vanish under the mass which, cumbersome and murmuring, led by its own wanton torches, had reached into the alley and beyond. The radio crackled. Turner heard Siebkron's voice cool and perfectly clear, he heard the mordant command and the one word: *Schaffott*. And then he was running through the waves, making for the scaffold, his shoulder burning from the blow; he felt the survivors' hands holding him and he broke them like the hands of children. He was running. Hands held him and he shook them off like twigs. A face rose at him and he struck it away, riding the waves to reach the scaffold. Then he saw him.

'Leo!' he shouted.

He was crouched like a pavement artist between the motionless feet. They stood all round him but no one was touching him. They were packed in close, but they had left room for him to die. Turner saw him rise, and fall again, and once more he shouted, 'Leo.' He saw the dark eyes turn to him and heard his cry answered, to Turner, to the world, to God or pity, to the mercy of any man who would save him from the fact. He saw the scrum bow, and bury him, and run; he saw the Homburg hat roll away over the damp cobble and he ran forward, repeating the name.

'Leo!'

He had grasped a torch and smelt the singeing of cloth. He was wielding the torch, driving away the hands, and suddenly there was no resistance any more; he stood on the shore, beneath the scaffold, looking at his own life, his own face, at the lover's hands grasping the cobble, at the pamphlets which drifted across the little body like leaves in the gathering wind.

There was no weapon near him; nothing to show how he had died, only the crooked arrangement of the neck where the two pieces no longer fitted. He lay like a tiny doll who had been broken into pieces, and carefully put together, pressed down under the warm Bonn air. A man who had felt, and felt no more; an innocent, reaching beyond the square for a prize he would never find. Far away, Turner heard the cry of anger as the grey crowd followed the vanished music of the alleys; while from behind him came the rustle of the light, approaching footsteps.

'Search his pockets,' someone said, in a voice of Saxon calm.